THE CALL OF ANCIENT LIGHT

THE COMPLETE TRILOGY

BEN WOLF

SPL⚡CKETY
PUBLISHING GROUP

The Call of Ancient Light
The Complete Trilogy

Published by
Splickety Publishing Group, Inc.
www.splickety.com

Ebook ISBN: 978-1-942462-53-8
Print ISBN: 978-1-942462-54-5

Cover design by Hannah Sternjakob
https://www.hannah-sternjakob-design.com

Contact Ben Wolf directly at ben@benwolf.com for signed copies
and to schedule author appearances and speaking events.

To Justin Shreeves:

*Thank you for your boundless inspiration, encouragement,
and support, both as a reader and as a friend.*

It means more to me than you know.

Julius –

Answer the Call!

CONTENTS

ORIGINAL MAP OF KANARAH

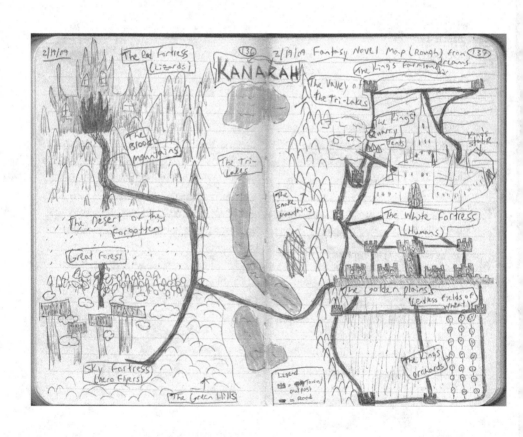

THE CALL OF ANCIENT LIGHT - BOOK ONE

THE CALL OF ANCIENT LIGHT

A LIGHT SHINES IN THE DARKNESS,
AND THE DARKNESS HAS NOT OVERCOME IT

BEN WOLF

PROLOGUE

L umen lay on a mound of ashes—all that remained of his once mighty army. After what seemed like millennia of fighting, he had lost the battle.

His sword, a silver-and-gold weapon of wondrous power, lay just beyond his reach. Close enough to tempt him, but not close enough to obtain.

Lumen's blurred vision focused on the tip of the spear that hovered over his chest. He traced its long bronze handle up to the stern face of its wielder.

The King.

"Your rebellion is finished, General of Light." The King stared at him with vibrant green eyes full of power. "And the people of Kanarah have paid the ultimate price for your betrayal."

Lumen returned the King's steely gaze. "I welcome death if it means freedom from you."

No discernible emotion crossed the King's face. "For your crimes, I banish you from Kanarah. You will descend to the deepest depths, to the Hidden Abyss itself. Your sentence shall last 1,000 years."

"You prove your foolishness yet again," Lumen said. "Spare me, and I *will* return to end this."

"Should you rekindle the fires of rebellion a second time, you will no longer face my mercy," the King's eyes narrowed, "but my judgment."

Lumen scoffed. "Mercy? A thousand years in the Hidden Abyss is *mercy* to you?"

"It is mercy for the people of Kanarah, not for you."

"The people of Kanarah are nothing but *slaves* to you," Lumen spat. "And when I return, I will free them from your oppression once and for all."

"*Enough.*" The King's jaw tightened with tension, and his green eyes narrowed. "Your sentence begins now."

The tip of the King's spear touched Lumen's breastplate, and fire spiraled through Lumen's veins. He screamed as his body disintegrated piece by piece, starting with his chest.

The sensation seared through his legs and arms to his fingers and toes, then crawled up his neck. Fiery grains of sand filled his vision before everything plunged into darkness and his

CHAPTER 1

999 Years Later
Western Kanarah

A twig snapped in the darkness to Lilly's left.

She jerked upright, her eyes wide, and snatched up her bow. She nocked an arrow and held two other arrows in her shooting hand, ready to fire them in quick succession as she scanned the woods around her.

Her campfire had reduced to smoldering coals, and she breathed relief for it. No need to attract any extra attention.

Except for the hiss of tree branches swaying in the wind around her, the ubiquitous chirping of crickets, and the occasional hoot of a nearby owl, the woods remained silent. She glanced at the opening in the canopy above her. The half-moon shone brightly in the star-studded sky, and despite the wind blowing through the trees, the air seemed warmer than last night.

She'd chosen this spot on purpose. If she needed to, she could launch straight up into the night sky and away from danger. Being a Windgale had its benefits.

Lilly waited another few moments to reclaim her sense of calm and to confirm she was, in fact, alone. Satisfied, she lowered her bow and arrows, but she didn't put the other arrows back in the quiver on her hip. She wanted them in hand, just in case.

She shifted her cape, still hooked to her armor at her shoulders, into a ball under her head again, and she lay down on the rock she'd adopted as her pillow. She sighed. Not as comfortable as home by any means, but it would have to do.

Exhaustion wracked her body. Sleep encroached on Lilly's eyelids once again, and they drooped shut. A yawn stretched her lips, and she reached up to cover her mouth with her hand. Always proper, even in the wilderness.

A nearby rustle cracked her eyes open. She jerked upright.

Something moved in the trees directly in front of her. She was sure of it this time.

Enough of this. With a powerful leap, she bolted to the sky, her bow and arrows primed to fell whatever or whoever had been hounding her for the last two days.

"Come out and let's settle this!" she yelled, now hovering twenty feet off the ground.

The forest responded with another long windy hiss, but no figures emerged from the darkness. Why would they? If someone *was* following her, they would've seen her skill with her bow by now. They would know that stepping out meant death—or at the very least, an arrow lodged somewhere important.

Minutes passed, but still Lilly hovered.

Had she imagined it? Dreamed it?

Whether or not anyone had actually been following her, exhaustion continued to wear on her senses. After a week away from the comforts of home, she longed for a good night's sleep, but that wouldn't happen out here in such an unfamiliar, ever-changing setting.

And she couldn't go back. Not until her parents came to their senses.

She exhaled another long sigh and relaxed the tension on her bowstring. Unless other Windgales were chasing her, she could just as easily fly a few miles over to a different location above all of these trees. But doing so without getting her pack, which still lay near the campfire below her, would complicate her time in the woods.

Maybe that's what they were waiting for—assuming "they" were even there to begin with. Paranoia was no way to live.

She remembered General Balena's words during her training: "Do not let fear rule you. Face it, overcome it, and become its master. Then you will be a true warrior."

A true warrior? Windgales under his charge remained soldiers for life. She wasn't one of them, and she never would be, but she took his meaning nonetheless: she wouldn't become a slave to fear.

Alright, Lilly. Enough stalling.

She'd need a free hand to grab her pack, so she tucked two of her arrows back into her hip quiver. She gripped her bow and the still-nocked arrow mid-shaft with her left hand, but with no tension on the bow's string. It freed her right hand to scoop up her pack. If needed, she could get her hand back in place in time to fire.

You're overthinking it, Lilly. Just go down, grab the pack, then fly away.

She exhaled another breath and swooped down with her right hand extended. Her fingers came within inches of the pack when a man's voice boomed from the woods.

"Now!"

Scratchy tendrils dropped over her and hauled her closer to the ground—a net, anchored by the strong arms of several men.

Lilly released the pack and shifted her right hand back to her arrow, then her right shoulder hit the ground. They had her pinned on her side, but if she could get one shot off, then maybe...

She drew the bowstring and pointed the arrow at one of the men holding the net, then released. The arrow knifed between the net's strands and plunged into his thigh. He screamed amid the other men's grunts and released his hold on the net to clutch his bleeding leg.

Good enough. Lilly clamped the arrows in her quiver to her leg so they wouldn't catch on the net and launched toward the new opening where the man had held it.

The man standing beside her victim cursed and shifted his hands over to close the gap in the net, but Lilly drove her shoulder into his chest. He fell back, and the net billowed open even wider. Lilly dug her boots into the ground and sprung out of the net's coverage, taking flight once again.

She'd ascended little more than a few feet when a pair of arms, strong and covered with dark armor, wrapped around her waist. The attacker's weight dropped them to the ground hard, stunning her. Dirt caked on Lilly's teeth, and pain from the impact sent shudders through her body.

"I've got her," a man's deep voice grunted next to her ear as his bear hug grasp adjusted to lock her arms against her sides. "Get her cape. Bring the shackles."

"No!" Lilly shrieked and tried to pull free. *Shackles?*

"Easy, Angel," the man whispered into her ear as if they were old friends. "I'm stronger than you'll ever be. No sense resisting."

Lilly strained all the more, but she might as well have been encased in steel. "Let me go!"

"Not gonna happen, Angel."

One of the other men, his eyes glistening with fiendish intent, reached for her neck. She snapped her teeth at his fingers, and he retracted his hand, then backhanded her cheek hard.

"*Hey!*" The armored man's arms released Lilly, but one of his hands still gripped her right wrist. His armored leg slammed into the chest of the man who'd slapped her and sent him skidding across the dirt until his body cracked against a tree. "No harm comes to her. *None.* Got it?"

Lilly sprang into the air again, but she couldn't free herself from the armored man's grip, and he pulled her back down. She whipped her boot at his jaw, but he yanked her to the side as if she weighed nothing before her kick could connect.

The abrupt motion wrenched her shoulder, and she yelped. The armored man pinned her to the ground facedown and held her there with his knee pressed into her back.

"Let me go!" she shouted to no avail.

"Any one of you so much as *touches* this girl and you'll deal with me, crystal?" The armored man unclasped her cape and her quiver and handed them to one of the others.

Lilly moaned. Without her cape, she couldn't fly away.

"This one's what we call a jackpot, boys. She'll fetch a pretty price, but only if she remains unspoiled."

The armored man flipped her onto her back and kept her pinned down with one hand on her sternum. He stared at her with devilish gray eyes. Spiky red hair jutted out from his head, and his square chin bobbed when he spoke.

"Oh, yes. I've got just the buyer in mind for you, Angel." To his men, he ordered, "Drug her, and remove her armor."

Lilly's stomach lurched. They were slave traders.

CHAPTER 2

Eastern Kanarah

A loud hiss stalled Calum's pickax mid-swing, and he jumped back. He scanned the patch of dried grass near his feet to find the serpent he'd just startled, but he didn't see anything.

The hiss sounded again, followed by deep grunts, this time behind him. Burtis, the quarry's fat foreman, led a group of armed men past him—the King's soldiers, by their black leather armor.

Among them walked a reptilian creature about seven feet tall with a long tail, a smooth green hide, and a dark-yellow underbelly. Thick steel chains and shackles bound its hands and feet, and a black leather muzzle encased its snout. As it walked past on its hind legs, it fixed its golden eyes on Calum.

He stepped back and bumped into something.

Hardink, a quarry worker in his mid-forties, shoved Calum away. "Watch where you're walkin', kid! Yous almost stepped on my bad foot."

"Sorry." Calum continued leaning on his pickax, grateful for the break, and kept staring at the creature. Its tail carved shallow streaks in the sandy dirt behind it as it walked. "What is *that?*"

Hardink scoffed. "What, never seens a Saurian?"

Calum shook his head in wonder. He'd never even heard the term before.

Hardink gingerly squatted to the ground and rocked back until he landed on his duff. There, he took to chiseling away at a stone loaded with shining gemstones embedded into it. With his bad foot, Hardink got relegated to do that kind of work rather than splitting rocks and hauling loads.

"He's a types of lizard," Hardink explained as he picked away at the stone. "But I isn't talkin' 'bout them little creepers that runs underfoot and clings to the outside of the tents at nights. I means an entire race of peoples, like that one. Walks on their hind legs. Skins get tougher the older they gets. Biggest ones gets to be eight or nine feets tall, so I hears."

"Never heard of such a thing." Through the morning sunlight, Calum squinted at the Saurian

"I seens 'em before. Not many 'round these parts. That's for sure." Hardink switched out his little chisel for a scrubbing cloth and wiped the dust from the stone in his hand. The gems caught even more morning sunlight, and they glinted with vibrant greens, blues, and reds.

The group of soldiers stopped, and their leader started talking to Burtis. Then they shook hands, and Burtis passed him a cloth bag that bulged to about the size of a child's head. In exchange, another soldier handed him a key.

Hardink squinted in the sunlight. "Looks like Burtis just boughts 'imself a new slave."

Calum frowned. "Slavery's illegal, isn't it?"

"*Ha.*" Hardink shook his head. "What do yous think *we* are?"

Calum's jaw tensed. "I'm *not* a slave."

"You're too young to knows the difference. Even so, not worth getting' upsets over it. We are what we are. Can't be helped, right?"

"No, I know the difference." Calum's eyes narrowed.

Hardink rolled his eyes and resumed his chiseling. "If yous say so."

The soldiers left the quarry behind with smiles on their faces, and Burtis approached the Saurian with one of his own. He reached to pat the Saurian on his shoulder, but the beast hissed at him.

Burtis grabbed the rope tied to the muzzle and jerked it down, and the Saurian's head went with it, finally breaking the beast's proud posture. Burtis leaned close and growled something at him, but Calum couldn't discern what it was.

"Probably shouldn't makes that Saurian mads, though." Hardink set the first gem, a ruby, in a rusted metal pan next to him. "Those things're 'bout ten times as strongs as any of us here in the quarry. He gets his hands free, he could kills Burtis or me or yous in no time. Probably could even *with* his hands bounds, for all I knows. Dangerous beasts, theys are."

Calum tilted his head. Out of all the other workers, he was both the youngest and the weakest. He'd always felt like the runt of the litter around the quarry, but the sight of the Saurian towering over everyone else made him feel even smaller, even more insignificant.

With creatures like the Saurian roaming Kanarah, what was Calum even worth?

"If they're so dangerous, why would Burtis bring one here?"

Hardink pushed himself up to his feet, leaning most of his weight on his good foot. He picked up the pan, and the gemstone rattled around in it. "Ten times as strongs means ten times the works, probably. Worth the risk. A boulder that takes seven or eight mens to moves? That Saurian can do that on his owns."

"If he's that strong, can't he break out of those shackles?"

"Now what're yous askin' me all these questions for?" Hardink shook his head and pointed at Calum's pile of rocks with the gem in his hand. "Get back to works. I gots this first gem near done, and you've made hardly any progress since thens. You wanna gets us all whipped?"

When Burtis looked over at them, Calum tightened his grip on his pickax. He raised it over his head and swung at a chunk of the boulder he'd already split once. It was a quick and careless swing that only glanced off the rock, but at least it would appear to Burtis that he'd been working the whole time.

After a few better-placed strikes, Calum stole a glance at the Saurian, whom Burtis had chained to a cart full of huge rocks.

As the Saurian pulled the cart behind him, a feat that even a trio of horses would struggle to accomplish, his golden eyes met Calum's again. Just as before, they contained nothing but disdain.

"Calum."

His head swiveled toward the call, and he almost dropped his pickax.

Burtis glared at him. One of his hands rested on his hip, and the other held a leather whip, all coiled up. For Calum and anyone else working in the quarry, that whip only meant one thing.

Pain.

He stood there, tan, hairy, and bare-chested with his belly lolling over the front of his belt. He wore his usual scowl and extended his pointer finger. "Get over here."

Calum swallowed the lump in his throat and glanced at Hardink, who didn't make eye contact with him. Hardink just kept chiseling and scrubbing the ruby in his pan.

"*Now.*"

When Calum got there, Burtis snatched the pickax from his hand and tossed it aside.

Calum braced himself for a blow, but it never came.

"You don't need that no more." Burtis held out his whip toward Calum, still coiled. "Take this. You're in charge of that thing over yonder."

Calum glanced over Burtis's shoulder at the Saurian. "You mean… *him?*"

"You deaf now? That's what I *just* said." Burtis grunted. "As it is, you're not good for much 'round here, so we're not losin' much by you not workin'."

Aside from his bald head and thick black beard, the only things that distinguished him from the other workers were a dirty purple foreman's sash he wore across his bare chest and the rusted sword hanging from his belt.

"Teach 'im all the jobs you've done here."

Calum couldn't believe his ears. Burtis wasn't known for his bright ideas, but this one was especially bad. "You trying to get me killed, boss? That thing's gonna eat me ali—"

The back of Burtis's hand stung Calum's cheek, and he staggered backward, woozy from the blow. He tasted the copper tang of blood in his mouth as he tried to regain his balance.

"What'd I say 'bout how you talk to me?" Burtis growled.

The wooziness faded, and Calum spat a red glob of saliva onto the ground. Then he clenched his teeth until Burtis grabbed him by the shoulders and shook him.

Burtis stood a few inches taller than Calum and was twice as wide, though aside from his gut, most of his bulk was muscle. And when he hit, he didn't hold back.

Before his promotion, Burtis had worked in the quarry along with the rest of the men, often doing the hardest work, including routine forays into the Gronyx's pit.

No wonder everyone feared him.

"I asked you a question, *boy*. You got an answer for me, or do I gotta beat one outta you again?"

Calum bit his lip. "You said I need to speak to you with the respect you deserve."

"Better start doin' it, then." Burtis shoved Calum to the ground and tossed the whip beside him. "You oughta count yourself lucky I picked you for this task. Make sure the Saurian learns every job, and I mean *every* job. I want 'im busy all daylight hours. He don't get no breaks. Doesn't need 'em. Crystal?"

Calum stared at the whip on the ground next to him. "If that's what you want."

"Don't be a'feared to use that thing. He's not movin' fast enough, you lash 'im once or twice. He's real sluggish, you give 'im a few more, just like I do with the men. You can't kill 'im with it, which means you can't use it too much."

"What do you mean?" Calum grabbed the whip and stood to his feet. It didn't happen often, but men in the quarry had died from excessive thrashing before, including a few by Burtis's hand.

"Saurians regenerate. They heal much faster 'an humans do. Least that's what the soldiers told me when I bought 'im." Burtis smirked, but Calum barely saw it through his thick beard. "So

8

flay 'im as much as you like. It'll hurt 'im enough to keep 'im workin', but it won't do any lastin' harm."

Calum had already decided he wouldn't whip the Saurian unless he had to. No sense in making an enemy out of a giant—and probably carnivorous—creature. And if Hardink had been right about Saurians being another race of people, then whipping the Saurian just because he was a Saurian and could handle it was unnecessarily cruel.

Calum might've been a lot of things, but cruel wasn't one of them. He'd endured enough cruelty in his life to never wish it on anyone or anything else.

"You're done with your old job 'til I tell you otherwise." Burtis glanced over at another group of workers, all big, burly men like him. "I'll send Jidon over to help you keep 'im in line. When he's learned everything else, Jidon can show 'im how to work the Gronyx's pit. I want 'im down there this afternoon."

Calum raised his eyebrows. The Saurian had just gotten there, and Burtis already wanted him down in the Gronyx's pit?

"Don't act surprised. Just 'cause Markham died down there last week don't mean anyone else will. Asides, if we lose that Saurian, I'm only out a few hundred in gems anyway. Better 'im than one of us."

Markham had tried to run off, and when Burtis and the others had caught him and brought him back, the Gronyx pit had been his "reward." He'd gone down into the pit and never come back up.

Calum shuddered. *No one deserves that kind of fate. No one.*

Aloud, he said, "If you say so."

"Look, kid..." Burtis clapped a meaty hand on Calum's shoulder and leaned down to look him in the eyes. "You're more or less a good worker, even if you can't do but a fraction of what the rest of the men can do. And I won't be here forever, y'know."

Calum kept his mouth clamped shut. *Hopefully not.*

"You do a good job with this, you might make foreman someday. Sounds pretty good, don't it?"

Calum raised an eyebrow. *Foreman? Why would I want to be foreman of this miserable place?*

But the more he considered it, the better it sounded. It would sure beat everything else he'd been doing here for the last eight years.

"It's not like you're goin' anywhere else. Might as well get the top job here." Burtis patted his shoulder. "So don't let me down, son."

Calum's blood instantly boiled. "I'm *not* your son."

Burtis glared at him and stood to his full height. "No, you're not. Then again, I didn't get myself killed by the King's soldiers eight years ago, neither."

Calum clenched his fists, wishing he could use the whip on Burtis for his unfair jab. Through gritted teeth, he said, "Those soldiers *murdered* my parents."

"You think I care?" Burtis scoffed. "Don't care what happened then, don't care what happens to you now. Long as I meet my quota at end-of-day, none of it matters. You don't want this job, I can find someone else."

Calum exhaled a sharp breath through his nose. Compared to hauling rocks and cracking stones open, Burtis's offer was practically a vacation. "No. I'll do it."

Burtis folded his arms across his chest. "You don't seem all that interested to me."

"Thought you said you didn't care," Calum muttered.

Burtis raised his hand for another swing, and Calum flinched, but the sting never came.

"Some day, Calum, I'm gonna lose my patience with you," Burtis warned. "Lots of ways a man can die in a quarry, and I've seen just about all of 'em. Keep it up with your disrespect, and you'll find out which one of 'em hurts the most."

Calum yearned to bite back, but he bit his tongue instead.

Burtis turned toward the Saurian, who had just stopped pulling the cart. Muscles rippled in the Saurian's powerful arms and legs as he turned around and lifted the cart up. In his wildest dreams, Calum could never have hoped to be that strong.

Boulders dropped out the back of the cart into a pile, and a group of pickax-wielding workers each quickly grabbed one and began to chip away at them, as if eager to get far away from the Saurian as fast as possible. In return, the Saurian only glared at them.

"Soon as he returns that cart to the lift, you start showin' 'im 'round."

Calum looked down at the coil of whip in his weathered hands. "He got a name?"

"You don't needa know his name," Burtis sneered. "Make one up for 'im, and not a good one, neither. Do *not* be nice to 'im. He's not your friend, and he's not like the rest of the men. He's a slave. *Scum.* Worse 'an that, if there is such a thing."

Calum nodded, though he didn't like any of what he was hearing.

Burtis pointed his finger at Calum's face. "Treat 'im like that for long enough, and he'll eventually *think* like that. And if you can get 'im *thinkin'* like that, he'll be your slave forever. Crystal?"

Just like you do with the rest of us. "Clear."

"Go on, now. I'll send Jidon over with the key to unlock 'im from the cart in a minute."

Calum approached the Saurian, who backed the cart up to the edge of the quarry where a rope-and-pulley system would deliver the next load of boulders within a few minutes.

When the Saurian finished positioning the cart, he noticed Calum. His black pupils—slits instead of round like a human's—darted between Calum's eyes and the leather whip in his hands.

Calum gulped down his rising nerves and stopped ten feet from the Saurian. He could do this. The beast was shackled and chained to the cart. As long as Calum kept his distance, he'd be fine.

"You're gonna come with me now, and I'm gonna show you what's what. Show you what else you're supposed to do around here."

The Saurian's embittered golden gaze persisted, and he exhaled a loud breath through his nostrils. He still wore the leather muzzle around his snout, and his large hands rested at his sides, still shackled and clenched into scale-covered fists. He was still chained to the cart by his neck, too.

Did he understand what Calum was saying? Could he talk? Did they even speak the same language? Calum had seen a keen spark of intelligence in the Saurian's eyes, but that didn't mean they could communicate.

"Jidon will be along soon to unlock you from the cart. Until then—" Calum let the business end of the whip drop from his hand, into the dirt, and he stepped forward.

The Saurian squared his body to face Calum, and a low growl rumbled from his throat.

Now only a few feet away from each other, Calum stared up at the Saurian and tried to hide his wonder—and his primal terror—at being so near to such a monstrous creature. Calum was neither short nor especially tall, but the Saurian towered over him all the same.

Calum squeezed the whip's leather grip tighter. Burtis's direction was clear. He didn't want to whip the Saurian, and he hadn't intended to do so, but he'd already angered Burtis enough for one day.

But would that whip even get the Saurian moving in the first place? Could Calum even swing it hard enough to get the beast moving?

Ultimately, this Saurian wasn't his friend, and Calum needed to establish who was in charge. He had the whip, and he supposed he had to try to make use of it. "Look, you and I—"

"You gonna talk 'im into submission?" A burly brown-haired man stepped forward from behind Calum and snatched the whip from his hand. Jidon. "You'll never get 'im workin' that way."

If Burtis hadn't made foreman, Jidon would have. As it was, Burtis relied on Jidon for extra muscle when he needed it, whether for work or keeping order. After all, who wouldn't want the biggest, strongest worker on his side?

But as big as Jidon was, the Saurian was bigger. Even so, that didn't stop Jidon from lashing the whip at him.

The Saurian recoiled from the blows with his eyes shut but didn't try to shield himself. He withstood eight of Jidon's lashes, each of which carved long red slits into his smooth reptilian skin, some along his chest, some along his arms, and one that stretched from just below his eye down his neck.

When the onslaught stopped, he opened his golden eyes, gave another low growl, and glowered at Jidon.

"*That's* how you do it." Jidon coiled the whip and smacked it against Calum's chest so hard that he had to take a step back to keep his balance. Then Jidon faced the Saurian again. "You stay still when I unlock you from that cart, or you'll get another eight. Crystal?"

The Saurian didn't move, but his gaze narrowed. When Jidon approached, the Saurian's muscles tensed.

Calum's heart seized. "Jidon, he—"

"He's not gonna do anythin'. Not 'less he wants to get lashed again." Jidon reached for the lock that connected the Saurian's shackles to the cart and twisted a key inside. The lock popped open and fell to the ground, and Jidon stepped back. "See? Nothin' to worry about. Now, go on. Take 'im to the pit like Burtis told you."

Calum nodded. He met the Saurian's eyes. "Come on."

ALONG THE NORTHWESTERN edge of the quarry wall, a gaping hole in the ground threatened to swallow anyone who stepped too close. As perilous as the hole appeared from the outside, its true terror resided within. The Gronyx lived inside that hole, though nowhere near the surface.

Of the seventeen or eighteen men who'd entered the Gronyx's pit for gems since Calum first came to the quarry, only three had ever made it out alive. Burtis and Jidon had not only survived several encounters with the Gronyx and lived to tell about it, but they had also recovered the most precious stones Calum had ever seen, and in the highest quantities.

The third survivor was Scrim, the oldest worker at the quarry, but he never said anything about his encounters with the Gronyx. He'd been down there more times than anyone else, but he'd made it abundantly clear that he was never going back again. Now he mostly just kept to himself and stayed quiet.

Hardink once told Calum that whatever had happened during Scrim's last time down there had scarred him permanently. What that was, Scrim didn't say. He *wouldn't* say.

Between Scrim's silence and Jidon and Burtis's stories, Calum hoped he'd never have to go down there.

The Saurian, on the other hand, didn't have a choice. Burtis had decided to send him down, so down he would go.

A few of the men strapped a leather harness to the Saurian's torso then fastened a rope through some iron rings attached to the harness's straps. The rope threaded into an overhead pulley system that hung from a tall wooden A-frame that stretched over the pit.

Prior to that day, Jidon had been the heaviest person strapped to that harness, but the Saurian weighed much more. Nonetheless, Burtis insisted it would hold.

Once they secured the Saurian, he glared at all of the men and let out the same low growl as before.

Burtis grabbed the harness and pulled the Saurian close. "I know you think you're bad news because you're a Saurian. Maybe you are. Here's your chance to prove it. Bring up as much glimmer as you can carry before that thing shows up. You see a green light, that means he's comin' for you. Hurry up and get out, or you're dead, and I'm out a few hundred in gems."

The Saurian's eyes narrowed at him, and a long hiss issued through his muzzle.

"Reminds me. Better take this thing off in case you gotta fight your way out. Same with the shackles." Burtis pulled a key from the ring on his belt. "I'm gonna unlock you, but if you try anythin', I won't just drop you down there. I'll *leave* you down there 'til it gets you. Crystal?"

The Saurian snorted.

"Good enough for me. Jidon, take off his muzzle. I'll get his shackles." Burtis eyed Calum while he worked on the Saurian's bonds. "You stand over there and spot 'im."

Calum glanced at the Saurian. "What do you mean?"

Burtis tossed the shackles aside and hooked the key back to the ring on his belt. "I mean stand there and watch what happens in that hole. You see green light, you holler so we can pull 'im out."

"Got it." Calum took his position about a quarter of the way around the pit from the men who held the rope. Last thing he needed was to get knocked into it by accident.

They began to lower the Saurian into the pit. In one hand he held a pickax, and in the other he held an empty burlap sack, which Burtis expected full of gems before the Saurian came back to the surface. He made eye contact with Calum one more time before he disappeared into the darkness below.

Nothing happened for the first few minutes. All Calum could hear was the intermittent chipping of the Saurian's pickax against the inside of the pit. The rope would occasionally tug twice in succession, which meant he needed more slack. Three tugs meant to pull him up.

By Calum's estimation, they had lowered the Saurian down at least fifty feet into the pit. At sixty feet, the rope tugged three times. Then three more. Then it just kept tugging rapidly, again and again.

"Pull 'im up," Burtis said.

The two men on the other end of the pulley yanked on the rope, but it didn't move.

Burtis blinked, then pointed to three more men nearby the pit. "Go help them."

Calum stepped closer to the hole and peered down, careful not to slip down the steep slopes around it. The pickax sounds had given way to growls and a guttural rumbling.

The rope still wouldn't move.

Burtis snapped his fingers and pointed to a group of six other men working nearby. They hurried over, grabbed the rope, and began to pull. It started to retract from the pit. One foot, two feet, three feet…

A roar ascended from the pit, followed by the sound of two voices in a dissonant shriek. At first, Calum recoiled at the sound, but then he stepped forward and peered into the pit again.

…seven feet, eight feet, nine… then back to eight feet again, then seven.

The men on the other end of the rope lurched forward, and half of them tripped. A chorus of grunts and groans emanated from their direction as the rope continued to pull them toward the pulley, toward the pit.

Burtis's eyes widened. He cursed and darted over to the men holding the rope, all the while yelling for more men. Jidon grabbed ahold of it next and started hauling with all of his might.

When Calum refocused on the pit, a faint green light glowed in the darkness below. Calum's heart stuttered at the sight.

"Burtis!" Calum shouted. "There's green light in the pit!"

"Pull 'im up!" Burtis shouted. The muscles in his big arms rippled with each yank. "More men —we need more men over here, now!"

Another half-dozen nearby men dropped their tools and ran over to the rope.

"Not good enough," Burtis yelled. "We need *more*. We need everyone!"

As more men came running, Calum looked down into the pit again. The green light had brightened, and the shrieking continued.

Something cracked to his right, then above him. Calum looked up.

The frame that held the pulley crashed toward him.

Calum dropped to the ground and rolled away from the pit with his arms shielding his head. When he looked up again, the entire framework capsized and dropped into the pit. The rope followed, and the twenty or so men who held the other end skidded toward the edge of the pit.

"Pull harder!" Burtis yelled. Easy for him to say—he was at the back of the group.

Petyr, the worker at the front of the rope, inched ever closer to the edge.

Let go. Calum's jaw hung down. *Let. Go.*

Petyr didn't let go. His foot slipped over the edge, and he tipped forward, still holding the rope, and his feet dangled over the pit.

Calum's eyes widened. *Don't let go!*

"Don't stop! Pull! Pull! Pull!" Burtis leaned back and pulled with all of his body weight. The other men did the same and synchronized with Burtis's pulls. They managed to pull the rope back far enough so Petyr could find his footing again.

Calum scrambled to his feet and ran over to help, but Burtis stopped him short.

"Get back, Calum!" Burtis hollered. "Back on the edge an' spot for us. *Now!*"

Several agonizing minutes later, the men had made significant headway with the rope, but the Saurian still wasn't out of the pit. All the while, the green light in the pit had intensified, as had the mixture of roars and wails from below. Yet even with the extra light, he still couldn't see anything down there.

The men pulled faster and harder, still keeping time with Burtis.

"That's it!" Sweat glistened on Burtis's bare shoulders. "*Pull. Don't stop.*"

All at once, the entire group jerked closer to the pit by two feet. Jidon's eyes widened, and so did those of several others. The pit was pulling back again.

More and more rope slid down into the pit, and the men skidded toward it.

Burtis cursed and swore. "Come on! Pull harder!"

The green light in the pit flared brighter, and the two-toned shriek screeched even louder from below. Men struggled and strained, but they couldn't help but be pulled closer, even though more than thirty of them strained at the rope.

Another wrench from the pit yanked the men forward. Their boots carved into the dirt, but it didn't help. Calum didn't know much about the Gronyx or the pit, but he knew *this* had never happened before.

On the next lurch, Petyr left his feet again, but this time he didn't hold onto the rope. He couldn't have, even if he'd wanted to. It happened too fast.

Instead, in a desperate attempt to survive, he leaped across the pit and grabbed an exposed tree root that protruded from the opposite edge. As he cried for help, the terror in his voice added to the swirl of sounds coming from the pit.

"Calum, help 'im!" Burtis yelled.

Calum rounded the pit and dropped to one knee in front of Petyr. He reached out with his right arm and kept his left behind him as a counterbalance.

Petyr glanced down at the pit, then he refocused on Calum with pure fear in his eyes. "Help me!"

Calum stretched toward him. "Grab my hand!"

Their fingertips touched, but Petyr couldn't get a grip. He latched on to the tree root again and shook his head. "You gotta get lower, or I can't reach!"

Would Calum even be able to pull him up anyway? Sure, he'd worked in the quarry for the last eight years, but Petyr was built of solid, heavy muscle.

It didn't matter. He had to try.

Calum dropped to his stomach and leaned forward as far as he could without falling in. "You gotta reach farther up. You can do it!"

Amid the screams and thundering from below, Petyr jerked upward and grasped Calum's wrist. He smiled. "Now pull me up."

Pull him up? Calum couldn't even get any leverage to get *himself* up.

He tried anyway, but he could barely hold Petyr in place, much less pull him up. "I—I can't—"

"Pull me up, kid!"

"You need to *help me*." Calum ground his teeth. "You're too heavy!"

Petyr's eyes filled with desperation again.

Calum slid toward the pit, and his bare chest scraped against the rough sand.

"Grab onto something!" he shouted to himself as much as to Petyr, but he didn't have an angle to get a good grip on anything.

Petyr groped for the tree root again, but his fingers scraped past it, and he sunk even lower than before. His body weight pulled Calum closer to the edge. Any more and Calum wouldn't have enough counterweight to stay out of the pit.

"Help me!" Petyr pleaded. *"Please."*

Calum shook his head. "I can't! I can't hold you."

Petyr's eyes ignited with fear and—*anger*. He wrenched Calum's arm down and reached with his other hand. He clamped onto Calum's forearm and tried to climb out of the pit using Calum's lean body as a rope.

"No—don't!" Calum's heart jumped as his body slipped forward and pitched over the edge toward a shrieking green hell.

CHAPTER 3

T he drop ended with a sudden impact. Calum's body hit something softer than rock, yet it still cracked upon impact. He rolled off whatever it was onto the pit's gravel floor. His back and arms protested with pain, but he was alive.

Green light blanketed the rocky cave walls around him. The rank odor of decay and stagnant soil hit his nose.

His head swam, and his vision blurred. Dazed, he tried to blink the sensations away, only to see a dark massive form reaching out for him. Something else wailed from behind him. The thing latched onto his wrist and pulled him close.

The next thing Calum knew, his feet left the gravel below, and his body began to ascend. Nausea from the abrupt lift seized his stomach, and he vomited. Some of his meager breakfast hit his boots, but the rest fell past down to the dirt, now a good ten feet below.

Something slithered beneath him, but it shrank away rapidly.

He craned his head and looked up. The blue-white opening of the pit came into focus above him and approached fast. Really fast.

Calum vomited again, this time missing his boots entirely.

The green light and the shrieks gave way to hot sunlight and grunts. Three pairs of hands hooked under his limbs and set him on the dirt. Fellow quarry workers.

What?

"Get 'em away from the edge." Burtis's bearded face appeared overhead. He reached down and took hold of Calum's left arm along with three other men and lifted him. "And don't let *him* escape."

Calum squinted in the sunlight. He turned his head to where Burtis was looking and blinked several times. The large form, the one that had grabbed him and pulled him to safety, stood to its full seven-foot height.

The Saurian.

Streaked with dirt and something like glowing green ooze, he strained against the men who pulled on his rope and harness while others surrounded him wielding pickaxes and shovels.

Now free of his restraints, he had an opportunity to try to escape, albeit not a great one, but he didn't engage the men.

Instead, he let them pin him to the ground, and he exhaled long breaths through his flared nostrils, all the while focused on Calum.

The Saurian had saved him…

But why?

Then Jidon's boot plowed into the Saurian's snout.

"No!" Calum shouted and twisted out of the other workers' grips. His boots hit the ground and he charged at Jidon, lowered his shoulder, and hit him from behind.

It wasn't much, but the impact sent Jidon forward just enough that he tripped over the Saurian's torso. He sprang to his feet in a hurry and stared steel at Calum.

Calum didn't back down. "Don't hurt him. He saved my life."

Jidon snarled and stepped toward Calum with his fist raised, but Burtis caught his wrist midswing.

"*Enough.*" Burtis shoved Jidon back with his other hand then turned to Calum. "Don't you *ever* side with that thing over your own kind again, crystal? A man's dead 'cause of him."

The men surrounding them muttered to each other.

Sickness tinged Calum's stomach. "But I'm *alive* because of him. Doesn't that—"

Burtis backhanded Calum hard enough to awaken every latent ache from his fall into the pit. He stumbled backward, stunned but not surprised, as the taste of copper tainted his mouth once again.

"What'd I just say to you?" Burtis snapped. "You don't side with 'im over us, over me. *Period.*"

Calum dabbed at his lip and found blood on his fingers. He scowled at Burtis.

"And if you don't get that sour look off your face, I'll smack it clear off you."

"Do you got any idea what a Gronyx does with its victims?" Jidon stepped toward Calum. "It rips its food apart before it feeds. I've seen it firsthand. That's what happened to Petyr. Shoulda been that Saurian, but instead, Petyr died. You expect us to feel good 'bout that? To let him off easy? No. He's gonna pay. A life for a life."

"Jidon, shut up." Burtis stared at him. "Petyr had bad luck, nothin' more. I paid good money for that Saurian, and he's gonna work here 'til the day he dies. You don't cut 'im off early 'less I say so."

Jidon grunted and folded his arms.

Burtis refocused on Calum. "Either case, I don't want you 'round the Saurian no more. I was wrong to let you try your hand at discipline when you obviously don't got any of your own. From now on, you're back on boulder duty."

Calum glared at Burtis, but he nodded. Burtis stepped away, toward the Saurian, and barked more orders to the surrounding men.

As Calum stood there, Jidon leaned in close. "Watch out, little man. You cross me again, and even Burtis won't be able to stop me from breakin' your neck."

Calum recoiled a step. Then Jidon spat a wad of saliva on the dirt at his feet, snarled, and plodded away.

As Calum watched Jidon go, he saw something small and metal disappear in the Saurian's scaly fist. Calum squinted at it and briefly considered telling Burtis, but after that rebuke, Calum didn't care to ever speak to him again.

Instead, he grabbed a pickax and headed toward the upper level of the quarry. He took one last glance back at the Saurian, just in time to see several workers surrounding him, many of them with whips in their hands. Burtis and Jidon stood among them.

Calum didn't look back again, even when the whips began to crack.

CHAPTER 4

Western Kanarah

Lilly woke up to find a hooded man crouched over her.

She gasped and pushed away from him, but her back hit metal bars. The ground under her bounced, and she stared at the hooded man, wide-eyed. She groped for something to use to defend herself, but her fingers found only straw.

"Easy, child." The man raised his hands and pulled the hood of his tattered cloak from his head. Long silver hair spilled out and draped over his shoulders. "I'm not going to hurt you. Quite the opposite, in fact. I was trying to make sure you were alright."

Unlikely. She'd been warned about the kind of indecent men who wandered Kanarah, men with no allegiance to anything or anyone but themselves and their own carnal desires. For all she knew, this old man was one of them.

"Do you know where you are?" the old man asked.

Her mind clouded with dark images and fright, but it finally started to focus. She remembered the spiky-haired slave trader ordering them to drug her and another man pressing a foul-smelling rag to her mouth and nose, but nothing after that.

The old man frowned. "Aliophos Nectar. They use it to drug their fresh captures and, on occasion, to subdue unruly slaves. You've been unconscious for about half a day."

Afternoon sunlight filtered through the trees and down into the cage in patches. She realized she was in a cage atop a wagon, moving along a road of some sort, but not a well-used one. The foliage around them was far too thick and the ride too bumpy for it to be a main road.

"What?" Lilly blinked, and her heart hammered. She'd been abducted by slave traders, but she didn't want to believe it. She couldn't.

"They removed your armor and put you in here with the rest of their haul from the past week." The old man motioned over his shoulder at the wagon's two other occupants: a middle-aged woman with brown hair who kept scratching at her scalp, and a man about the same age—scraggly, dirty, and sound asleep on a mound of hay. "Including me."

The ground rumbled beneath Lilly again, and she jumped.

"Relax." The old man extended his withered hand toward her. "They're taking us somewhere. Don't know where, yet."

Lilly noticed her legs, bare from mid-thigh down to her boots, no longer covered with her light-pink armor. She noted her bare arms and stomach as well, but her white armor-lining undergarments still covered her chest and her hips, tight against her skin.

Still, she might as well have been naked. She hugged herself and retracted her legs until she sat against the bars of her cage, her knees level with her face.

Worse yet, they'd taken her cape. Even if she could get out, without her cape, she couldn't fly away.

Lilly's eyes widened. *What if—?*

"No one has touched you, child." The old man offered a sad smile. "Roderick, for all his cruelty, lives for the next coin more than for momentary thrills. As such, you are wholly intact."

Lilly squinted at him over her kneecaps, but his blue eyes betrayed no aggression, no ill-will. "Who are you?"

"I'm no one of consequence. My name is Colm, but you may call me Grandfather if you wish. I have always wanted grandchildren, but I never settled down long enough to earn them." The old man smiled at her. "And you may regard me as such a person in your life, for I have no desire to harm you or take advantage of you whatsoever."

"I'll stick with Colm, thanks." *Grandfather? Weird.* "I'm Lilly."

"You should eat something, child." Colm reached for a thin leather satchel that hung from the inside of their cage-on-wheels and removed a crust of bread. "It's not much, I know, but the three of us have eaten our share for the morning, and I made sure to save this for you."

Lilly wanted to deny his offer, but her stomach accepted with a loud rumble before she could reply. She reached for the bread. "Thank you."

Colm grabbed her wrist and pulled her close in one quick motion. Warm breath hissed past her ear in a harsh whisper, and his stubble scratched her cheek.

"I meant what I said about not harming you, but don't expect such courtesy from anyone else. You're in a far different world than the one you left, judging by your armor and your beauty. The other slaves, the slave traders themselves, and even—*especially* the slave buyers are not to be trusted. Be on your guard at all moments."

Lilly pushed away from him, more shocked at his words than his actions, but he'd been honest about not harming her. If he'd wanted to hurt her, he could have done any number of things to her while she was sleeping, or just now when he grabbed her, but he hadn't.

When she looked down at her hand, she found the crust of bread in her palm. "How did you—?"

Colm put his index finger against his lips and gave a slight nod. "Remember what I said."

Lilly nodded. She put the bread crust to her mouth.

"If you'll pardon me saying so, it helps if you don't try very hard to chew it. Just let it sit in your mouth until it softens." Colm chuckled. "At least that's what I have to do. My teeth don't work as well as they used to."

Lilly crunched into the crust and leaned back against the bars. While she chewed, the wagon came to a halt. "What's happening?"

Colm shook his head. "Nothing you'll enjoy, I'm afraid."

Three men circled around the back of the wagon, and one unlocked the door with a large gray skeleton key. Two of the others held swords in their hands and began to climb up into the cart.

"Up against the bars, all of you." One of them grunted. Colm complied immediately, as did the woman, and Lilly mimicked their actions.

18

The man sleeping on the wagon floor didn't move until one of the slave traders kicked his ribs. He jerked awake, yelped, then scrambled toward Lilly. She recoiled as he lunged for her, but he got ahold of her long blonde hair and yanked her over to him.

"Let go!" she yelled and resisted him, but he held her between the approaching slave traders and himself. "Colm?"

Colm didn't so much as look over at her. He just faced the bars, his legs spread, and stayed still.

"Let her go, you sack of slime," one of the slave traders said. "Or we'll gut you right now."

"N-no." The man shook his head so wildly that his long brown hair smacked against Lilly's cheeks. He curled his arm around Lilly's throat, and she caught a foul whiff of body odor. "No, you're n-not gonna t-t-touch me. You let m-me leave, or she d-dies."

"Not gonna happen. Let her go, or you'll get twice the thrashing." The slave trader grinned a crooked yellow smile. "And I'm gonna enjoy it, too."

The man holding Lilly backed against the bars. "I—I'm serious. I'll k-kill her. I know she's w-worth a lot to you. I heard you s-s-say it. You want her alive, d-don't you?"

The slave trader and his buddy glanced to the man's left, to something just outside the cage, then they snickered at each other. "Fine, you win."

"That's right. I w-win. Now—you t-two s-s-step back out of the wagon and let me g-go. She and I are g-going to—"

The wagon shifted. A loud thump, like something hard banging against metal, resounded behind Lilly, and the man's grip around her went slack. He crumpled into a heap behind her, unconscious.

When she turned around, Lilly saw the man in the brown armor with the spiky red hair. He clutched the man's long hair in one hand and held onto one of the bars with his other. A dark splotch stained one of the bars red, and a wound oozed blood on the back of the man's head.

"Get to it, already," the spiky-haired man said. "Take him to the other wagon. No one touches her, crystal?"

"Clear, boss." The slave trader with the yellow teeth sheathed his sword, and together with his buddy, he hauled the man out of the wagon, then out of sight.

The spiky-haired man dropped down from the wagon and grinned up at Lilly with one eyebrow raised. Her stomach churned at the sight. He nodded to the third slave trader, the one who'd opened the cage to begin with. "Go on. Check them. Find it."

The slave trader at the door hopped inside the wagon and drew a dagger from his belt. He bypassed the woman and headed straight for Colm.

"Easy on me, Luggs. I'm just a bag of old bones."

Luggs shoved him against the bars. "You're a thief and a liar, you are."

"Come now, Luggs." Colm shot Lilly a look and a wink—why, she didn't know—and grumbled. "I don't call you names. Seems to me you ought to be nicer to your merchandise. Maybe we'd fetch higher prices if you took better care of us."

"No one would buy your old husk anyway." Luggs patted Colm's arms and legs at regular intervals. "Believe me, we've tried."

"If I'm really a thief and a liar, then surely you'd have found someone in need of those unique skills by now."

Luggs jolted him forward again, and Colm's head smacked against the bars. A line of blood trickled down Colm's pointy nose from a small cut on his forehead.

"Face forward," Luggs ordered.

After three solid minutes of searching Colm, Luggs still hadn't found anything.

The spiky-haired man rapped the bars, and Lilly jumped. "Well? We don't have all day. I want to make the pass sometime before the end of this season."

"He's clean, sorry to say." Luggs huffed and spun Colm around. He pointed a finger at Colm's face. "You sit down and don't move. Crystal?"

Colm nodded and sat, but a smirk curled his lips.

Luggs sheathed his dagger and rubbed his dirty hands together, his gaze fixed on Lilly. He licked his chapped lips. "Alright, missy. Your turn for friskin'."

The spiky-haired man clanged his gauntlet against the bars. "Luggs, don't you lay a grubby *finger* on her."

Luggs's grin melted into a frown. "But what if she's the one who—"

"She's not, Roderick," Colm said. "She just woke up ten minutes ago."

Shing. Luggs's dagger leaped into his hand and lurched toward Colm's neck. It stopped just under Colm's chin, but he didn't so much as flinch.

For a fat guy, Luggs moved well.

"I told you to sit down and *shut up*," Luggs repeated.

Colm cleared his throat and raised his chin. "You told me to sit down and not *move*. You never said anything about talking."

"Well, I'm tellin' you now." Luggs spat a dark glob of something into the hay near Colm's boot. "So *shut up*."

"The old buzzard's right." Roderick eyed Lilly slowly—too slowly—from head to toe. "Just look at her. She's barely wearing anything to begin with. She's not hiding anything. At least nothing I intend to let any of you idiots have a go at."

Lilly shrank away from the bars and huddled close to herself. Now, for the first time in her life, she understood what it meant to be exposed. She might as well be a roasted quail in the center of the Premier's table.

Luggs ogled her too, his gaze somehow even more suggestive and revolting than Roderick's. He pulled his dagger away from Colm's throat. "I'll check the other one, then."

"You do that." Roderick still hadn't removed his gaze from Lilly.

As Luggs approached the woman, she whirled around. Silver flashed in the sunlight—a knife. She stabbed at Luggs's throat, but he blocked her attack with his forearm and bashed the pommel of his dagger into her face. She dropped into the hay, stunned.

"Stupid harpy," Luggs scoffed. "They never learn, do they?"

The woman screeched and slashed at Luggs's leg, but she missed by a solid foot. She lunged for him again, but Luggs stomped on her wrist and she dropped the blade. She wailed and clutched her wrist, and Luggs grabbed her by her hair and wrenched her upright.

"You'll learn one of these days not to fuss." He raised his hand to strike her with the dagger's pommel again.

"Stop!" Lilly didn't realize she'd yelled it until Colm stared at her wide-eyed, his eyebrows up. Now Luggs, Roderick, and the woman all stared at her as well.

"What'd you just say?" Luggs released his grip on the woman, and she shrank into the nearest corner, her eyes aghast.

"I said—"

Luggs stormed toward her. Lilly backed up, but the bars kept her from escaping. He raised his free hand, but this time, she didn't recoil from his blow. She'd watched how he moved when he hit Colm and dealt with the woman. She was ready.

Roderick yelled at Luggs to stop again, but Luggs's arm was already in motion. Lilly ducked under his swat and rolled along the hay. On her way up, she snatched the woman's knife from the floor and darted for the wagon door, which still hung open. Cape or no cape, they'd given her a chance to get out of there, and she intended to take it.

Lilly flung herself through the open door and hit the ground running.

She didn't run often—why should she when she could fly?—but the sensation of her feet thudding along the bumpy road and her legs pumping against gravity's pull invigorated her almost as much as the thought that this nightmare would soon end. She'd escaped the wagon, and soon she would be—

She skidded to a halt in front of three armed men who'd emerged from the trees. She turned to her left, but two more men with bows and arrows emerged from the brush and took aim at her. A quick pivot and she faced the woods on the other side of the road, but two more archers stepped forward, their bows ready.

What she wouldn't give to have her bow in hand right then.

A slow rhythmic clapping sounded behind her. She spun back to find Roderick approaching. A smile split his square chin. "Well done, Angel. Well done."

She hissed a curse upon him and a prayer to the Overlord in the same breath—wrong on every level except for how honestly they both reflected her feelings. If only she had her cape.

"You didn't really think the wagon was the extent of the precautions we took to contain you, did you?" Roderick shook his head and wagged his forefinger, still coming closer.

He towered over her by almost two feet, and he had to be at least three times as wide. His armor made up some of his girth, sure, but the rest had to be muscle. She hadn't met many humans, but he certainly dwarfed any Windgale she'd ever seen, including General Balena.

"And even if you did escape, where would you go? You're barely clothed, without your cape, and with no weapons in this wilderness." Roderick eyed the knife in her hand. "Oh, *excuse* me. You have a knife. I take it all back. You'd be fine."

Lilly ground her teeth and squeezed her fists tighter.

"Look, Angel, you can either drop that knife and come back with us, and I'll let you off with a warning this time, or you can try to carve our eyes out with that toothpick while we take you back by force, and then you don't eat for two days." Roderick tilted his head and grinned at her. "Which will it be?"

Lilly clenched her eyes shut and exhaled a sharp breath. Carving his eyes out with the knife sounded pretty good, but she had to be realistic about her chances. Without her cape, her armor, and her bow, she didn't stand a chance.

Though she didn't want to do it, Lilly dropped the knife.

CHAPTER 5

Eastern Kanarah

A few minutes before sunset, Calum cracked open another rock and then bashed it into small enough pieces for Hardink to sift in his bowl tomorrow. Sixteen more and he'd be done.

He rolled a new rock into place, and this time he imagined it was Jidon's head when he swung the pickax. It was more or less the right size, but the rock was probably more intelligent.

Most of the other men had stopped by the shed to deposit their tools for the evening. Calum garnered more than one surly glare from the group, mostly from the men who'd been closest to Petyr, but he ignored them. It wasn't his fault Petyr had died, and he wasn't about to let anyone guilt him into believing otherwise.

About fifteen minutes later, Calum finished crushing the last of his pile and headed to the shed. He deposited his tools, but as he stepped outside, the plank leading up to the entrance shifted under his foot.

Calum stared at it for a moment, then he bent down to inspect it. Someone would need to repair that tomorrow if it had come loose. He pulled, and it separated from the parallel support rails underneath with little resistance. A glint of something crystalline stopped Calum's heart.

Gemstones shimmered under the moonlight.

Not many of them, but more than enough to bother Burtis. Well, *one* hidden gemstone would be enough to bother Burtis.

But these looked different. Brighter, somehow, and all with a greenish hue. They were stones from the Gronyx's Pit.

Burtis had once explained to him why the gemstones from the Gronyx's Pit were so much more valuable, so much more worth the risk, but Calum couldn't remember why. He'd been just a kid at the time, and he hadn't bothered to ask again.

Regardless, these were Gronyx stones, no doubt. But who had put them here?

Perhaps Calum should take them. Maybe he could use them to get himself out of this place.

But if Burtis found out—

"Heys."

Calum dropped the board in place and whirled around.

Hardink stood there with a shovel in his hand, leaning on it to give his bad foot a break. "What're yous doin' there?"

"This board's loose, and I—I found—" *Careful, Calum.* "—I found it like that when I stepped on it. Was gonna try to fix it real quick."

"What're yous gonna fix it withs?"

Calum tapped the board with the corner of his boot. "Maybe there's a hammer and some nails in the shed."

Hardink chuckled. "In all my years, I never seens neither of those things in the shed where just anyones can get at 'ems. Burtis keeps 'ems somewheres else, same as the last foremans, and the foremans before. Yous might as well let someone else find that spots and fix it in the mornin'. Go back to camp and eat somethin's before Burtis gives your rations aways."

Calum squinted at him. "Why are *you* out here?"

Hardink held up his shovel. "Found this on the ways back to camps. Decided I oughta bring it backs. You know how Burtis is in the mornin' when he finds out a tool's missin'. We *all* suffers."

Calum nodded. It made sense... but it didn't completely allay his suspicions.

A smirk cut into Hardink's left cheek. "Yous gonna move so I can put this backs?"

"Yeah." Calum stepped aside. "Sorry. Just watch your step. Don't want you to trip with that bad foot of yours."

"I'll be fines. Yous runs along, now. Don't want yous complainin' that you're hungry in the mornin'."

"Shouldn't I wait for you? If you fall on your way back to camp—"

"Then I'll gets up and keeps goin'." Hardink turned back to him. "My foot's messed up, but I can still walks. I'm not an old lady, yous know."

Calum feigned a laugh, then he regretted it. *Too obvious?*

Hardink shook his head. "Go ons. Gets outta here. I'll be fines."

Sweat trickled down Calum's back. He couldn't stay there. If he did, it would give something away, whether Hardink had stashed those gems or not. He nodded and started walking. He glanced over his shoulder once, but Hardink had already disappeared inside the shed.

Calum sighed and headed back to camp. He'd check the stones again tomorrow night after work. If they were still there, maybe he could make a run for it.

"THIS IS FOR YOU." Axel leaned forward and passed a small pouch no bigger than a man's fist across the table to Calum, then he scoured the tavern with his eyes. A few other quarry workers sat around some of the other tables, but no one seemed to be paying them any mind.

Calum squinted at it, then he met Axel's dark-blue eyes. He loosened the string, poked his fingers inside, and pulled out two small red peppers.

"These two ripened early, before the rest of the crop." Axel smiled. "Well, a few others, too, but these are the ones I managed to hide. Might be able to get you a few more over the next couple days."

"Thanks." Calum matched his smile.

Axel leaned back. "Don't mention it. Ever. Seriously. To anyone."

"Obviously."

"You're like a little brother to me. It's the least I can do. Actually, it's about the most I can do, too."

The men who worked at the quarry got the vast majority of their food from Axel's family farm. Ever since Calum had landed in that quarry camp, he'd gone along with the men every evening to collect their share of food.

When Calum first showed up, Axel was ten and already almost twice his size. Now, at sixteen, Calum had caught up a bit, but Axel, at nearly eighteen, still had three inches of height and a solid fifty pounds on him. Unlike Calum, he had dark-brown hair with a bit of curl to it, a stark contrast against Calum's short blond hair.

Axel had looked out for Calum ever since his first night with the workers, at least as much as he could. He worked on his farm all day while Calum worked the quarry, so they only got to see each other in evenings, and usually not for longer than an hour.

"What else did they ration out for you?" Axel asked.

Calum tucked the peppers back in the pouch and dropped it into his satchel along with the rest of his food. "Looks like a boiled potato, a roasted chicken leg, and a slice of barley bread."

Axel rested his fists on the table. "Heard something happened today. You alright?"

Calum nodded at the sobering reminder of the Gronyx's pit and what had almost become of him. "Yeah. I'm fine. A bit bruised up, but I'm alright."

"Heard a Saurian pulled you out. Big green brute. Might as well be a monster." Axel scratched at a rough patch on the table with his fingernail. "Lucky for you they're keeping him in line. He had plenty of lash marks all over him."

Calum's stomach soured. The last thing the Saurian deserved was that kind of treatment.

"Hey." Axel reached across the table and slapped Calum's bare shoulder. "After a day like that, you'll sleep real good tonight."

Calum smiled. "Burtis also told me I could be foreman someday."

Axel's grin melted.

Calum exhaled a sigh when he noticed it. What was Axel going to say now?

"He said you might make foreman, huh?"

"Yeah, he did." Calum read the frown on Axel's face. "Look, I know it's not much, but it's as good as it gets in this type of life."

Axel shrugged. "If you say so."

For all of his good brotherly qualities, Axel sure had some bad ones too.

"Not everyone gets to inherit a massive family farm when their parents are gone," Calum said. "Not all of us even have parents anymore."

"Come on, Calum. My parents work for the King, same as you do. Same as I do. This farm may be ours in ink, but we all know it belongs to the King and his soldiers, the same people responsible for what happened to your parents."

Calum shook his head. "Doesn't mean you should look down on me for wanting to accomplish something with my life."

"You think being the quarry's foreman is 'accomplishing something with your life?'" Axel scoffed. "It's the exact opposite of that. It's a waste. I want something better for you than that. I want something better for myself than inheriting a farm that doesn't really belong to me."

Calum rubbed his forehead with his fingers and closed his eyes. "Why? We'll both eat well for the rest of our lives. Does anything else really matter?"

"Absolutely." Axel smacked the table with his palm, and Calum's eyes opened. "I want to get out of here, find some adventure. I want to make some coin, learn to fight, and live life the way *I* want to live it. I want to find a beautiful woman and feel the warmth of her body close to mine. I want children of my own someday. Doesn't any of that matter to you?"

Calum thought back to the stash of gemstones he'd found under the walkway board. If he could get ahold of those and get a bit of a head start, maybe what Axel was proposing was possible.

Or maybe Axel's big dreams had infected them both long enough, and only a dose of reality would cure them.

"It *sounds* good, but I can't have any of it." Calum sighed. "I might as well stay here, do good work, and honor the King—with a full belly every night."

"You want to honor the man responsible for your parents' deaths?" Axel shook his head. "That's no way to live. Not all slaves wear chains. You're no different than that Saurian. You're a *slave*."

Calum exhaled a furious breath through his nose and clenched his teeth. If he weren't so sure Axel could pound his face in, Calum would have taken a swing at him.

Why did he have to be so weak? Why hadn't he been born stronger? Would he always be this way?

Calum's chest filled with frustration. In the end, all he'd ever be was a quarry worker.

Axel put his hands up. "Hey, don't get mad at me. I'm not the one who sent you to the quarry when your parents died. I just want something better for you. Better for us both."

Calum slung the satchel over his shoulder and stood up. "I need to get going. I gotta get up at sunrise, and I still have to eat. Good night."

"Come on, Calum. Don't be like that."

"No. You're right, Axel," Calum said, allowing his anger to underpin his words. "I'm a slave. I know I am. But I don't know how to be anything else, except maybe foreman someday. It's good enough for me, so maybe you should be happy for me instead of bringing me down."

Axel folded his arms, still sitting. "How can I be happy for you when being foreman is still being the King's slave? Just with more perks?"

Calum shook his head. "Fine. Then don't be happy for me. But don't talk to me about it either."

"Calum, I—"

"Enough. I'm leaving." Calum reached into his satchel and extracted the pouch of peppers. He tossed it on the table in front of Axel. "Here. A *slave* shouldn't get special treatment."

"Calum, those are for you," Axel hissed. "Take them."

"No. I don't want any favors from you."

Axel stood up and rounded the table with the pouch in his hand. He glanced around the room and uttered, "I don't care if you're mad at me. Don't make a scene. You're *going* to take these."

"No, I'm not." Calum ground his teeth.

"*Yes*, you are. Do you have any idea what my parents would do to me if they found out I took these for you?" He eyed the nearby workers, but as before, no one appeared to care. "Or what they'll do if I bring them back and they find them on me or in my room? You're taking them."

"I said I'm—"

"I will beat you *senseless* if you don't take them." Only a hint of humor lined Axel's threat. "I'll beat you senseless, stick them back in your satchel, and dump your unconscious body in your tent if I have to."

Calum glared at him and clenched his fists, powerless to do anything other than refuse.

"You know I will. Take them." Axel extended the pouch again.

Calum loosed an angry sigh. The only way he was getting out of there was with those peppers in his possession. Might as well get it over with.

He snatched the pouch from Axel's hand and dropped it into his satchel. He turned to leave, but Axel caught his wrist.

"Like I said before, you're like my little brother, my best friend." Axel clapped his hand on Calum's bare shoulder, just as Burtis had done earlier that day. It awakened the aches in Calum's body from his fall into the Gronyx's pit. "I only want what's best for you."

"Good night, Axel." Calum twisted out of Axel's grasp and headed out of the tavern.

BACK AT THE CAMP, Calum noticed the Saurian chained to a thick wooden post about twenty feet from the nearest tent. Even in the faint light of the dying campfire, Calum could see the red lines that streaked across his green hide. He hunched forward with his head leaned against the post.

Calum glanced at a few of the nearby tents then took a tentative step toward the Saurian. Then a few more. He got within ten feet before the Saurian looked up at him. When he did, the dismay in the Saurian's golden eyes sharpened to fury.

Calum stopped. The Saurian had his muzzle on again. Had Burtis and Jidon bothered to feed him anything after the whipping?

"Hey," he whispered.

The Saurian's gaze sank back down to the dirt, and he leaned his head against the post again.

After another quick scan of the camp, Calum took another step forward.

The Saurian's head swiveled toward him, and he gave the same low growl he'd given earlier that day.

Calum stopped. What was he even doing there in the first place? Maybe this was a bad idea.

But Calum *had* to continue forward. The Saurian had saved his life, after all. He swallowed the lump in his throat and stepped within five feet of the Saurian.

"Hey," he repeated, even quieter this time. "Did anyone feed you anything?"

The Saurian didn't move, didn't blink. He just projected golden-eyed anger at Calum.

Calum reached into his satchel and pulled out the potato. "Do you want this?"

Nothing.

Calum squinted at him. He dropped the potato back in the satchel and pulled out the slice of barley bread. "This?"

Still nothing.

What did Saurians eat anyway? Calum tried the peppers next.

Zero movement.

The only thing left was Calum's roasted chicken leg. It was a big piece too, for once. About half the thigh was still connected, plus the drumstick was a good size. He didn't really want to offer it, but... "How about this?"

The Saurian tilted his head, almost indiscernibly.

Shoot. That's what he wanted. Calum wished he hadn't offered it.

But after how things had gone that afternoon, the Saurian probably needed it more than Calum did. "Well... I guess you can have it."

Now the Saurian glanced around the camp just as Calum had a moment earlier.

"I'm serious. I'm not trying to fool you." Calum stepped closer. "I owe you at least this much."

The chain that connected the Saurian's shackles stretched around the post, but the silver talons on the tips of each of his scaly fingers gave Calum pause. Nonetheless, he took another step forward and extended the chicken leg.

His hand shook. Calum blinked and tried to calm his hammering heart. Hardink and Burtis had both warned him what the Saurian was capable of, and he'd seen it in action up close.

Calum stopped, and the Saurian huffed a sharp breath through his nostrils. Was a piece of chicken worth his *life*?

He was overthinking it. If the Saurian had wanted to harm him, he would've abandoned Calum at the bottom of the pit.

He was a slave. Just like Calum.

And even slaves needed to eat.

Now only three feet away, Calum took another step.

That's when the Saurian lunged forward.

Calum recoiled, but he was too slow. The Saurian grabbed his arm and pulled him forward. The chicken leg dropped to the dirt.

Something sinewy and strong pressed Calum's back and pinned him against the post, and the Saurian's other hand clamped over his mouth before he could cry out.

He'd made a mistake. A terrible mistake. And he was far too weak to pull free.

He should have listened to Burtis. To Hardink.

Too late now.

A long hiss overwhelmed Calum's hearing, and the Saurian's hot breath heated Calum's face. How would the Saurian do it? Would he snap Calum's neck? Would he jam his talons into Calum's gut and let him bleed to death on the ground next to him?

Nothing happened.

Calum just stood there, his heart racing, his breaths short and quick. Wide-eyed, he craned his neck to look up at the Saurian.

The beast nodded at him, then slowly pulled his hand away from Calum's mouth.

What was going on?

The pressure on his back subsided, and the Saurian released Calum's wrist. Calum staggered back and stared at the Saurian, who bent down and reached for the chicken leg, but it lay too far out of reach for him to get it with his hands.

His long green tail, which must've been what he'd used to pin Calum to the post, snaked through the dirt and pulled the chicken close enough that he could grab it. He held it up to his mouth, still covered by that muzzle, and tapped his snout with one of his fingers.

Calum didn't move. He still didn't understand what was happening.

The Saurian rotated his body around the post and tapped his snout with his other hand, the one not holding the chicken. He growled again, but it didn't sound as angry.

Now he wanted help? He'd just attacked Calum—kind of—and now he expected Calum to help him?

The Saurian turned again and tapped the back of his head.

Calum blinked again. "You want me to take off that muzzle?"

The Saurian nodded.

After what just happened, Calum didn't know whether he should trust the Saurian or not. Yes, he'd saved Calum's life, but why had he behaved so erratically when Calum had drawn near? And if Calum got that close again, what would happen?

"You're not gonna hurt me, right?"

The Saurian shook his head.

So it *did* understand Calum.

But if it understood Calum, that meant it could be lying, too.

Calum glanced at the chicken leg clutched in the Saurian's talons. He couldn't just leave the beast there with food in his hands but unable to eat it. It wasn't fair, wasn't humane.

Humane. Did that word even apply to Saurians?

27

Hardink had called Saurians a type of people, but Burtis's words resurfaced in Calum's head: *Do not be nice to him.*

Whatever, Burtis. He'd already gone this far. And Burtis was an idiot.

Calum swallowed and hesitated, then he closed the distance and started to unfasten the straps on the back of the Saurian's muzzle. A moment later, he pulled it off the Saurian's snout.

The Saurian opened his jaws wide, as if stretching them out, and Calum stumbled back at the sight of his long sharp teeth, his red tongue, and his gaping throat. Definitely a meat-eater.

The chicken leg and half-thigh disappeared in one large chomp, bones and all.

Calum realized how far down his jaw was hanging and shut his mouth. He looked at the muzzle in his hand, then back at the Saurian. "Do you have a name?"

The Saurian squinted at him.

"Do you speak?"

Nothing.

"Do *any* Saurians speak?"

Still nothing.

"Fine. But now I need to put this back on you."

A familiar low growl rumbled from the Saurian's thick throat.

Calum glanced around again. "Look, if they find you without this in the morning, you're gonna get whipped even worse, and then Burtis will start asking *us* questions. That means no more food for you, at least not from me. Is that what you want?"

The Saurian exhaled a long breath through his nose then motioned with his head for Calum to come back over. The Saurian stretched his jaws once, then he allowed Calum to secure the muzzle on his snout.

Calum stepped back and assessed his work. Good enough. "Well, I'm off."

As he turned away, a snort sounded, distinct against the crickets chirping somewhere in the moonlit woods beyond. Calum glanced back, and the Saurian gave him a slight nod.

Calum allowed himself a timid grin and nodded back, then he headed for his tent.

Inside, Calum set his satchel on his bedroll and sat next to it. Good thing he'd gotten a whole potato tonight, or he would've gone more hungry than usual. He unpacked the peppers Axel gave him plus the potato and the barley bread, then he tucked the satchel under his bedroll.

He picked one of the peppers up and studied it—red, with a tinge of yellow and some green close to the stem. He couldn't let them go to waste, no matter how much of a jerk Axel had been to him. Food was too precious a resource.

Still, he couldn't shake the idea that Axel was right. What if Calum just... left? What if he abandoned the quarry and tried to make his own way in the world?

Whenever other quarry workers—other *slaves*—had fled in the past, Burtis, Jidon, and some of the other men chased after them. They looked at it almost as if it were a sport, a welcome interruption to the everyday grind of quarry life.

Thus far, no one had ever escaped. Markham was the last one who'd tried, and it had gotten him sent down to the Gronyx's pit—and he never came back out.

Even if Calum had some of those hidden gemstones, he didn't stand a chance against Burtis and Jidon. So what was the point of even trying?

What he'd said to Axel back in the tavern was true enough: He'd be stuck in the quarry forever. That was the reality of his life, and no amount of dreaming would ever change it.

Calum lay on his side and took a bite out of his boiled potato, and within fifteen minutes of finishing his dinner, he fell asleep.

LIGHT PENETRATED the darkness until it washed out Calum's vision. He tried to shield his eyes with his hands, but nothing he did could block out the brilliance. It shined through him as if his body were made of glass.

From deep within the light, a figure emerged. White armor covered his strong limbs, and a silver-and-gold sword hung from his belt. A golden crown glistened atop the figure's head, and his eyes flickered like two balls of fire above a white half-mask that covered his nose and mouth.

Calum's jaw hung open. *What in the—*

The figure drew his sword and traced a circle made of white fire. In the center appeared an image of three lakes with a path that ran through the middle.

Calum could've been looking at a map, except the image moved as if he was seeing it while flying overhead. The view narrowed onto the path, followed it from one side of the lakes to another, then it centered on the base of some red mountains.

A black hole appeared in the rocks like a yawning mouth.

"Go, Calum. Find the Arcanum. Discover the way to set me free." A voice resonated around Calum. *Within* him. "Go, Calum."

CALUM BLINKED AWAKE, and the figure and the map vanished. What had he just—

"I said *wake up*, Calum." Someone shook him by his shoulders.

Calum blinked again. Rather than the ethereal face from his dreams, Burtis's ugly bearded mug hovered over him, and the sound of men chattering and shuffling around the camp reached his ears.

"What?" He tried to push Burtis's hands away.

"Get outside." Burtis straightened up, his head almost reaching the ceiling of Calum's tent. "The Saurian's escaped."

CHAPTER 6

Burtis stormed out of the tent, and Calum rubbed his eyes.

What a weird dream.

Calum pulled on his old wool shirt, then his trousers, then he stepped outside.

Sure enough, the camp buzzed with quarry workers, most of whom held torches and pointed in various directions amid a peculiar mix of yawns and frantic conversations. Some of them held ropes, and others held thick tree branches as makeshift clubs.

The weirdness of Calum's dream still lingered in his mind. The blinding light, the white figure who'd appeared, and the map—none of it made any sense.

And what was an "Arcanum?"

Maybe those peppers he'd eaten hadn't agreed with him. Whatever the case, he could sure use a few more hours of sleep.

A yawn stretched Calum's jaw, and he rubbed his eyes again. When Calum's vision refocused, Jidon stood in front of him. Then his fist plowed into Calum's gut.

Calum dropped to his knees and clutched his stomach, overwhelmed by pain and the sudden lack of breath in his lungs. He sucked for air, but his lungs felt like they'd shriveled to a fraction of their original size.

"*Where* is he?" Jidon spat on the ground only inches from Calum's head.

"I don't—" Calum wheezed and looked up at Jidon, wide-eyed. Why had Jidon singled him out? "—know."

Jidon grabbed Calum's wrist and yanked him to his feet. "You sure 'bout that?"

Calum glanced past Jidon at Burtis, who stood by the campfire talking to several other men, including old Scrim and Hardink. Burtis wouldn't be around to intervene this time.

That meant Calum would have to handle this himself… or he'd pay the price by himself.

"*Hey*." Jidon's stubbled, sour face filled Calum's view. "I asked you a question."

"I said I don't know." Calum tried to pry Jidon's hand free from his wrist, but Jidon wouldn't release him. "Let me go!"

"You spent more time with 'im today than anyone. He didn't say nothin' to you? Didn't drop

"Cut it out!" Calum dug his fingernails into Jidon's wrist. He doubted it would be enough to make him stop, but to his surprise, it worked.

Jidon retracted his arm and stared at the red marks Calum's fingernails had left. Given their size disparity, Calum only had one option now: he threw a kick square into Jidon's groin, and Jidon doubled over in pain.

"How do *you* like it?" Calum glowered at him.

Jidon roared. He flailed his arm at Calum, who was ready for some sort of wild attack and backed away, and Jidon missed.

But Calum hadn't expected to trip over something behind him. He fell and landed on his back, and the breath almost pushed of his lungs again.

Meanwhile, Jidon reached for the campfire and wrenched a burning log free by its unburnt end. Embers wafted into the night air, and Jidon started toward Calum.

Every alarm bell in Calum's head rang loud and clear as Jidon stormed closer. Calum scrambled to get back up to his feet, to run, to get away, but the well-worn soles of his boots kept slipping on the dewy grass.

Now looming over Calum, Jidon raised the flaming log high over his head.

Calum shielded himself with his arm.

Then two sets of strong arms wrapped around Jidon's arm and kept him from pulverizing Calum.

Burtis's voice split the night. *"Enough, Jidon."*

The log dropped, and Burtis kicked it back toward the fire.

Jidon twisted out of Burtis's grip and pointed an accusatory finger as Calum hurried to his feet. "He kicked me in my—"

"You got what you *deserved.*" Burtis stood neither as tall as Jidon nor as wide, but he had no trouble yelling louder. "Lay another finger on 'im again, and I'll crack your skull. Crystal?"

Jidon backed away from Burtis, but his steely-eyed focus remained on Calum.

Burtis shoved him and snarled, "I asked you a *question.*"

"Clear." Jidon spat on the ground at Calum's feet again.

"Take a quarter of the men north. I'll take a quarter east. Parkus will take another quarter west, and Scrim will head southeast to get the King's soldiers." Burtis spun around and surveyed the men in the camp. "First group to find 'im gets a double share tomorrow at breakfast. First man who spots 'im gets a whole day off. Now git!"

The men cheered and jogged in four different directions, including Jidon and Burtis. Calum pushed himself up to his feet and started after Parkus's group, but a glint caught the corner of his eye.

There, on the ground next to a set of shackles near the Saurian's post, something glimmered in the light of the campfire. Calum bent down and dug a small piece of metal from the dirt.

A bronze ring, bent straight. One of the rings used to secure the rope to the Saurian's harness before they lowered him into the Gronyx's Pit.

The Saurian had concealed it in his fist after the men hauled him back up to the surface. That's what Calum had seen. Then the Saurian must've somehow used it to pick the locks on his shackles.

A realization hit Calum's mind, stark and bright, just like the dream he'd had only minutes ago.

The plank at the shed. The hidden gemstones underneath. If Hardink hadn't hidden them…

Then perhaps the Saurian had.

The last place Burtis and the men would look would be back at the quarry. Why would the

Saurian go back there, of all places? He wouldn't have had a reason to—unless he'd hidden those gemstones on purpose and was using them to escape.

Calum didn't know when the Saurian would've had time to stash them away, but he hadn't been working around the giant lizard at all after the incident at the Gronyx's pit. Maybe he'd hidden the gems then.

Then another realization hit Calum. There would be no better time to flee the quarry than right now. With Burtis, Jidon, and the rest of the men distracted, Calum could just leave. But he would need those gemstones in order to get himself beyond Burtis's reach.

And if the Saurian was already going for them...

Calum made his choice. He ran back to his tent, grabbed his satchel, tied up his bedroll, and secured both to his back. If Calum could get to the gemstones before the Saurian, perhaps he could run and buy his way to freedom once and for all.

WITH ONLY THE moon and stars above, the quarry resembled a blue desert with a massive sinkhole in its center. Calum approached in silence, aware that the Saurian could be hiding somewhere nearby.

The shed looked undisturbed, at least from a distance, but that didn't mean anything. The Saurian could be inside or standing behind it. Or not there at all.

Did Saurians have better hearing than humans? Could they see better in the dark? They were stronger and could regenerate after being injured, but what else might Calum encounter that he didn't already know?

Calum snuck toward the shed, staying low. Nothing moved. What little grass rimmed the quarry's perimeter swayed in a slight breeze from the northwest.

When he made it to the shed, Calum headed straight for the loose plank. He lifted it up without a sound and reached his fingers into the space beneath.

Nothing.

He shifted so his body wouldn't block the moonlight, just to double-check.

Still nothing. The stones had been taken.

Calum's heart sank. Should he still try to run? How far could he get without the gemstones to help him along the way? Where would he even go? How would he find food?

Something rustled behind him.

Calum whirled around, and a thick tree branch slammed into his side. The blow sent him careening against the shed door.

Not a branch—the Saurian's tail.

Calum's ribs ached, and he crumpled to the ground, wheezing. Why did everyone keep knocking his breath away?

In one massive leap, the Saurian closed the distance to Calum and pinned him against the shed door with one massive hand against his chest.

"Wait!" Calum held his hands in front of his head and sank lower against the door, struggling to breathe.

"Do not presume to give me orders, *boy*." The words flowed from the Saurian's mouth like an angry flood.

Calum's eyes widened. "You—you can talk?"

The Saurian glowered at him.

"Just don't hurt me." Even as Calum said it, his gut and ribs flared with pain from the Sauri-an's tail strike. He added, "Anymore."

"I should *kill* you." The Saurian's deep voice rasped in his throat.

"Please don't!" Calum almost begged, holding his hands up.

"And why should I not?"

"You—" Calum shook his head, his heart thundering. The only response he could muster was the truth. "You saved me today. Why would you kill me now?"

The Saurian's golden eyes narrowed, but he pulled his hand away from Calum, who wheezed and rubbed his aching side. He stared up at the Saurian, who rose to his full height.

"Your life is just as worthless now as it was then," he growled.

In spite of his aching side, Calum pushed himself to his feet. He didn't know which hurt more—his ribs or the Saurian's remark. "Hey, I stood up for you today."

No response. With one arm, the Saurian shoved Calum aside, clearing his path to the shed. Calum tumbled into the prickly grass surrounding it, and the Saurian yanked on the old lock that secured the shed door. It ripped through the door latch and took a chunk of wood with it. The Saurian tossed them both away.

Though the sight amazed him, Calum refused to show it. He quickly stood back up, wincing. "I said I stood up for—"

"I heard you the first time."

"And?" Calum followed the Saurian inside the shed, which was now considerably darker inside at night than during the daytime.

"And what?"

"Doesn't that mean anything to you?"

The Saurian eyed the tools that hung from the walls rather than making eye contact with Calum. "You are alive. According to the laws of Kanarah, we are more than even."

Calum raised an eyebrow. "Why *did* you save me in the Gronyx's pit?"

"Why did you bring me food earlier tonight?"

"Because I didn't like how the others were treating you."

The Saurian reached for a large pickax, one that only the strongest men in the camp could wield. Calum could barely lift the thing, much less swing it, but the Saurian hefted it as if it weighed nothing.

"You didn't answer my question," Calum said.

The Saurian stopped and looked down at him. "What do you want, boy?"

Calum blinked. What *did* he want? "I—"

"If you intend to tell your friends where I am, you had better do it quickly. I will not tarry here much longer." The Saurian strapped the pickax to his back with a leather belt and fastened a coil of rope to another belt that he clasped around his waist.

"That's not what I—"

"Then *what?*" the Saurian snapped.

Calum's mouth hung open. *Maybe we could... but the gems aren't...*

Up until this point, fleeing the quarry had only been a foolish dream for Calum. The hidden gemstones, Axel's prodding, and the Saurian's escape had given Calum hope that maybe he'd actually be able to pull it off.

But now the Saurian had provided a way out, a means of escape—with or without the gemstones. Whether the Saurian had taken the gems or not, he was leaving the quarry. If he could do it, so could Calum.

"*Speak*," the Saurian grunted.

"I—" Calum's doubts got the better of him. "I don't know."

"Then get out of my way." The Saurian pushed past Calum, heading for the outside once again.

"I want to come with you," Calum blurted, but he wasn't sure he believed it.

The Saurian stopped in the shed's doorway. "You do not even know where I am going."

"I don't care," Calum said, his resolve growing. "I can't stay here. Anywhere is better than here."

"You are in training to become the foreman of this place someday. Is that not what you want?"

Calum frowned.

"Do not act surprised. I am not deaf."

Calum shook his head. Axel had been right all along. There was nothing for him here anymore. There never was.

"I want to go with you. I don't want to stay here. I can't be a—" Calum bit back the emotion rising in his chest. "I can't be a slave anymore. Please let me come with you?"

The Saurian stared at him for a long moment until he finally said, "No."

Calum's heart sank. He'd put himself out there, tried to grab at the freedom just barely within reach, and the Saurian had snatched it away with a single word.

Calum swallowed down his frustration. "Why not?"

"I do not want you around." The Saurian refocused on the wall of tools again.

The pit of Calum's stomach swelled with pain and emotion.

But he wasn't just going to give up.

"Why not?" he pressed, his voice hardening.

"Why do you humans ask so many questions?"

Calum glared at him. "I don't want to stay here anymore. I don't want to live this life."

The Saurian leaned close to Calum and stared into his eyes. "I do not care."

Calum exhaled a long breath through his nose. Was that it? Was the conversation over?

With one last look around the shed, the Saurian headed for the door and stepped outside.

No. Calum refused to accept this outcome. He chased after the Saurian and added some edge to his words. "You don't have to be so—"

"There he is!" a man's voice shouted, followed by a loud whoop.

The sound stalled Calum's words and his steps, and his heart jumped and jiggered in his chest.

The Saurian stopped short as a group of several men, all wielding torches or tree branches, emerged from the path through the trees. Men from the quarry.

Rather than running, the Saurian stood his ground with his fists clenched. Calum stopped just behind him.

When he saw Jidon standing at the front of the group with a smirk on his face, Calum's blood ran cold.

"So it was *you* who helped the beast escape." Jidon sauntered forward, and the other workers followed him. His eyes, lit only by torchlight, fixed on Calum. "You little traitor."

Calum's heart pounded in his chest. He shook his head. "Didn't have anything to do with it. I found him here only a few minutes ago."

"Shut your lyin' mouth, kid. You really expect me to believe that?"

Nothing he said to Jidon would change his mind. That much was clear. But the more Calum tried to justify himself to Jidon, the harder it would be to convince the Saurian to take him out of this place, so he decided to keep quiet.

"I'll deal with you later." Jidon shifted his focus on the Saurian. "First, we got us a slave to capture."

The Saurian stepped into a defensive stance and pulled the large pickax from his back.

"No." Calum darted forward and positioned himself between Jidon and the Saurian. "No one needs to get hurt."

"Get outta the way, Calum." Jidon motioned to the men behind him. They spread out and encircled the Saurian and Calum. "In fact, get in line with the other men, and help us bring 'im in. Maybe I'll forget 'bout how you kicked me back at the camp. Maybe I'll forget 'bout this betrayal, too."

"I didn't betray *anyone*."

The Saurian huffed behind him.

Calum bristled. He needed to fix this, needed to show the Saurian where he stood. To Jidon, he said, "But I'm not helping you."

Jidon shrugged and positioned the makeshift club in his hands and stepped forward. "Fine by me. Burtis isn't here to save you this time, you little rat."

For being such a big guy, Jidon moved quickly. He darted forward and swung the club at Calum so fast that he couldn't have possibly dodged the blow or shielded himself in time.

Were it not for the Saurian, who reached past and caught the end of Jidon's club in his huge hand only an inch from Calum's head, Calum would've met his end right then and there.

Calum blinked and staggered back, breathing frightened breaths.

Jidon wrenched the club from the Saurian's grasp and swung it again, but the Saurian absorbed the blow with his pickax.

"Get 'em!" Jidon yelled.

The Saurian swung his pickax at Jidon's head, but he ducked under it and drove the end of his club into the Saurian's gut.

A worker from the left charged into the fight and swung his torch, but the Saurian side-stepped the swing. Instead, the torch hit Jidon in his bare chest amid the sound of searing flesh.

Jidon hollered and leveled the worker with a wild thrash of his club, then he staggered back with his left hand pressed against the blackened spot on his chest. The Saurian's tail swiped Jidon's legs out from under him, and he landed on his back.

Another worker charged in, this time toward Calum, swinging his club. Surprised, Calum dove to the side, rolled, and quickly sprang back up to his feet.

Calum backed away from the next swipe and ducked under the one that followed.

"Catch!" the Saurian bellowed.

Calum turned in time to see a fiery torch soaring toward him. He shifted his stance and caught it, then he used it to block the worker's next blow. The impact rattled Calum's fingers, and embers spurted from the torch flames and dissipated into the night sky.

What am I doing? He'd never fought anyone before in his life. He was going to get himself killed if he didn't think of something fast.

The worker, a man in his forties with thinning black hair, glared at him and bared his crooked teeth. Calum had known his name once, but that didn't matter now. He wasn't as huge as Jidon, but he still outweighed Calum by at least thirty or forty pounds.

Calum swung his torch at the worker's head, but the worker blocked it with his club and threw a punch at Calum's face. His fist connected, and pain flared through Calum's cheek.

Calum staggered back. He'd been struck and whipped before, but this was a real fight. The stakes were completely different, and Calum couldn't just give in like he normally would.

This time, he was fighting for his life. And if he was going to survive, he had to do something drastic. A plan formed in his mind—a crazy plan. It probably wouldn't work.

But if he didn't try it, then it definitely wouldn't work.

So when the worker charged forward and swung his club again, Calum went for it. He dropped to his knees under the attack and jammed the burning end of the torch into the worker's shin, letting the fire do its job.

The worker dropped his club and went down with a yelp, clutching at his seared leg.

It had worked. Calum could scarcely believe it, but now wasn't the time for cheers and celebration. The fight wasn't over.

Calum tossed the torch at him, fiery end first, and snatched up the club instead. Now he had a better weapon, at least.

The worker batted the torch away and grabbed Calum's ankle.

Calum had to make a choice, and he made it quickly. With one heavy swing of the club, he whacked the back of the worker's head.

Crack.

The worker's grip went slack, and his entire body went limp. Blood oozed from a gash on the back of his head, and Calum stepped back, breathing haggard breaths.

Had he killed the man? Or was he simply unconscious?

Either way, Calum couldn't face the truth of it now. He was still in the middle of a fight, and any wrong move could be his last.

With his club at the ready, Calum turned back in time to see the Saurian deliver a stunning blow to the head of another worker with his tail. Yet another went down when the Saurian drove the bottom of the pickax handle into his chin. Several more workers lay unconscious or wounded around him.

The Saurian raised the pickax over his head to finish one of them for good.

Calum's eyes widened. "No!"

The Saurian stopped and glared at him. In that moment, Jidon plowed into the Saurian's chest, and they both went down. The huge pickax hit the dirt as the two of them struggled.

Somehow, Jidon managed to straddle the Saurian's waist, and he delivered three solid blows to the Saurian's reptilian jaw. The fourth punch stopped short in the Saurian's big hand, which clamped down around Jidon's fist.

Jidon yelled and gripped his wrist with his free hand, but the Saurian didn't let go, and the gut-twisting sound of crunching bones crackled. The Saurian shoved him off and stood to his feet while Jidon shrank down to his knees, all the while whimpering and screaming.

Calum tightened his grip on the club and started toward the Saurian with cautious steps.

Amid his struggling, Jidon lurched upward and drove his fist into the Saurian's gut. The Saurian released Jidon's hand and staggered back, doubled over. In one fluid motion, Jidon scooped the huge pickax into his good hand and hefted it over his head.

Out of instinct, Calum sprang forward and swung his club as hard as he could. Jidon's wild eyes flickered toward Calum just before a deadened crack split the night air.

Then Jidon dropped to the ground, and the pickax hit the dirt next to him. Blood oozed from a fresh gash on his forehead, and he stared up at the night sky with vacant eyes.

Calum dropped the club, shocked at what he'd just done. When he looked to the Saurian, the beast nodded to him.

Calum shook his head. Jidon had threatened to kill Calum, but... "I can't believe I just—"

"You did." The Saurian stepped toward him. "It is done."

"Is he...?"

The Saurian bent down next to Jidon and pressed two fingers against his neck. "He yet lives."

That gave Calum some comfort, albeit not much.

The three men who'd stayed out of the fight ran off, but they'd seen it all. They'd seen what Calum had done, both to Jidon and the other worker.

"They're gonna kill me anyway." Calum stared at Jidon's motionless body, his hands trembling. "They're gonna tell Burtis, and Burtis is gonna kill me tomorrow. Maybe even tonight."

"Then..." The Saurian exhaled a loud hiss. "...you must come with me."

CHAPTER 7

"I know someone who might help us." Calum led the Saurian through the forest adjacent to Axel's family farm, all while trying to forget what he'd done back at the quarry. "Maybe we can hide until this blows over."

"Hiding is not an option. We must keep moving." The Saurian adjusted his grip on the giant pickax and ducked under a low-hanging tree branch.

Calum exhaled a shaky breath. He was both afraid and relieved to hear the Saurian say that. "If we're actually leaving then we'll need food for traveling. Axel's farm is just a few minutes away from here. He'll help us."

They stopped at the tree line, and Calum squinted into the darkness. An expansive field of corn separated them from a small farmhouse drenched with silver moonlight.

Calum faced the Saurian. "Do you have a name?"

The Saurian nodded. "Magnus."

"Magnus," he repeated. "I'm Calum."

"I know."

"How well do you see in the dark?" Calum asked.

"Better than you, but not greatly so."

"Do you see anyone? Or do you hear anything?"

Magnus shook his head. "If we intend to see your friend, we should make haste."

"Follow me."

They cut across the field, keeping low so the corn stalks would provide them with some cover. When they reached the edge of the field, Calum looked Axel's house up and down. Two floors, a few windows. Nothing special, but a far cry from the tent Calum had slept in for the last eight years of his life.

"Well, we can't just knock on their front door."

Magnus stared at him.

"Can you lift me up to that second floor window?"

"I can, but to what end?"

"I'm pretty sure that's Axel's room. If I can knock on the window and get his attention, maybe his parents won't wake up."

"I see." Magnus nodded. "Very well. I will lift you, but do not fall."

"I won't."

Calum and Magnus cut across the moonlit gap between Axel's house and the cornfield. In the shadow of the house, Magnus hefted Calum up to his shoulders and then hoisted him up to the window.

Calum peered inside, careful not to lose his balance on Magnus's shoulders. There, in bed asleep, lay Axel. Calum looked around the room to see if anyone else was there, then he tapped on the window.

Axel rolled over in bed and faced the other way.

Calum sighed and tapped on the window again, this time louder.

Axel slowly sat up in bed and stared right at him, squinting and blinking. Then he reached next to his bed, pulled a long silver object into view, and flung the sheets off himself.

It was a sword.

When Axel started toward the window with a furious look on his face, Calum glanced down at Magnus.

"Uh… let me down," he said.

"Did you get his attention?"

"Yes—but you need to let me down *now*."

Magnus complied, and Calum's boots hit the dirt just as Axel pushed the window open and stuck his head out.

"Who are you? What do you think you're—" He laid eyes on Magnus. "What in the King's name is going on?"

"It's alright, Axel." Calum put up his hands. "It's me, Calum."

"Calum? What are you doing here?" Axel pointed his sword out the window at Magnus. "And what is that *thing* doing here with you?"

A long low hiss issued from Magnus's nostrils until Calum waved him down.

"It's a long story. The short version is, we're leaving the quarry. There are men after us, and we stopped here to ask if you could spare any food." Calum swallowed the lump in his throat. "I know you don't owe me anything, but I thought I'd ask. As a favor."

Axel shook his head. "Do you have any idea what they'd do to me if they found out I helped you?"

Calum hesitated. He hadn't thought of how he might be compromising Axel and his family just by showing up at his house. "Any chance you could come down here and talk to us?"

"*Us?*" Axel eyed Magnus again. "I'm not coming down there as long as that *thing* is with you."

"Come on," Magnus growled. "We cannot afford to waste any more time."

Calum held up his hands. "Please… let me try something."

Magnus exhaled a harsh breath through his flared nostrils.

"Axel, what if I send him into the cornfield? Then would you come down?" Calum asked. "Or can I come up there?"

Magnus shook his head, but Calum ignored him.

"Fine," Axel said. "Send the beast into the corn, and I'll meet you on the other side of the house at the front door. If I see him anywhere nearby, I'll kill you both."

Magnus huffed. "That is a delusion."

"Stop." Calum stepped in front of Magnus. "Just stop. There's been enough fighting for one night. Let me handle this."

"How long do you expect it will take our pursuers to realize we will seek out food and supplies?" Magnus growled. "This is the next place they will check. Every minute we stand idly by counts against us. We're wasting time."

"Well, we're gonna make time for this."

Magnus snarled at him.

"Are we doing this or not?" Axel asked.

"I'll meet you at the front door." Calum ushered Magnus toward the field and then circled around to the front of the house.

A moment later, the door opened. Axel stood in the doorframe and beckoned Calum forward with his left hand. Once Calum made it inside, Axel shut the door behind him without a sound.

"I'll try to be quiet," Calum whispered. "I'm sure your parents are—"

Axel's sword flashed to Calum's neck. "As bad as the punishment would be for helping you, the reward will be just as good for turning you in."

AXEL NARROWED his gaze at Calum, whose face betrayed his surprise. Calum had really ruined things this time. Now Axel didn't have any choice but to turn him in.

He'd looked after Calum, snuck him extra food, and even patched him up a time or two after a beating, but this was different. Axel couldn't save Calum from something like this.

"Axel?" Calum whispered, his voice strained. "What are you doing?"

Still, a part of Axel wanted to give Calum the benefit of the doubt. "Give me one good reason why I shouldn't hold you here until my father can go for help."

Calum grunted. "I can give you several."

"Then start talking. *Quietly.*"

"We're friends." Calum held up one finger, then another. "I haven't done anything wrong. I—"

"Not true." Axel shook his head. "You wouldn't be leaving if you hadn't done something wrong."

"I sided with the Sau—with Magnus. I didn't want—"

"So he's got a *name*, now?" Axel rolled his eyes. Leave it to Calum to befriend a beast instead of an actual person. "You two must be best buddies."

"You already know he saved my life today."

Axel clenched his jaw. He had to admit, that did count for something. "Why'd you have to leave?"

"He escaped after that, and I went to look for him. I found him at the quarry, and a group of the workers caught up to us there. I didn't want him to continue to get abused, so I sided with him, and they attacked us, and—"

"How many did you kill?"

Calum bristled. "I didn't kill anyone, but I—I—"

"Come on. Out with it." Axel leaned forward.

"I hit Jidon and one other man in the head with a club. They both went down," Calum explained. "When we left, they were still down, but Magnus said Jidon was still alive."

"Jidon? Big Jidon?" Axel snickered. "Yeah, right. He weighs more than you and me combined."

"He was gonna kill Magnus. One good swing to his forehead, and he dropped."

Axel huffed. "If you say so. Either way, you helped an escaping slave. That makes you a criminal, a fugitive. As such, if I turn you in, I get a reward."

Calum recoiled from the blade at his neck but couldn't back up thanks to Axel's front door. "What kind of reward do you think you'll get, Axel? At the end of the day, you'll still be stuck on this farm. Just maybe with some extra coin. I'm your *friend*. Doesn't that mean anything to you?"

"You're my friend, but you're also a criminal. The King's men are gonna hang you when they find out what you've done." Axel shook his head again. Calum had *really* messed up. "'Course, that's *if* they get to you in the first place. Burtis seems like he'd just as soon take care of you himself."

Calum's eyes narrowed. "So you would really hand me in for—"

"No. I wouldn't turn you over just for the reward." Axel motioned toward the staircase with his head. "But if I don't, then I'm responsible for not turning you in. That's gonna come back on me *and* my family."

"Then forget I was ever here. Just don't turn me in. Let me leave, and we're gone. Even if they catch us, I won't say a word about being here."

Axel shook his head again. "If I don't turn you in, I get whatever punishment you were supposed to get. You know that's how it goes."

"Come with us," Calum blurted.

"*Quiet.*" Axel pressed the sword against Calum's neck again and glanced over his shoulder. "You trying to wake my parents? You wake them up, and we're done talking. For good."

Calum smirked.

Axel furrowed his brow. "That doesn't mean I'm gonna let you go."

"Come on, Axel. Come with us. We both know you want to. You told me what kind of life you wanted back in the tavern. This is your chance to go live it."

Axel chuckled. "Are you kidding? That's a death sentence for sure."

"Only if they catch us."

"Even if they never did, it's still a death sentence. We don't know the first thing about how to survive in the wild."

"You work on a farm. You know plants and terrain and other stuff like that. Besides, I bet Magnus knows a lot, too."

Axel scoffed and rolled his eyes. "Yeah, 'cause I'm gonna trust that *thing* when we're all alone in the wilderness."

"He's not a *thing.*" Calum glowered at Axel. "He's a Saurian. A person. Someone with a name and a history and a life."

"Whatever." Axel shook his head. "I don't trust him. Not in the least."

"You don't know him, either," Calum countered. "My point is, said you wanted to get out of here and do something else with your life. You had big dreams and big plans. This is your chance to do all that. Maybe your best chance." Calum cleared his throat. "Maybe your only chance. Come with us."

Axel shifted his footing and pulled the tip of his sword away from Calum's neck, but he didn't lower it. He'd already made up his mind that he wouldn't—he *couldn't* kill Calum, even if he tried to escape. "I can leave whenever I want to."

"Then do it," Calum urged. "Axel, you were right. I don't want to work at the quarry for the rest of my life, and I don't want to be foreman. I'm done being a slave. I know you don't want to stay on this farm forever. It's like you said to me earlier tonight: I only want what's best for you. So come with us."

Axel bit his tongue. Everything in his heart longed to go along with Calum, but everything his mind resisted the idea. "No way."

"Do you really want to hand us over to Burtis? Or to the King's men? You *hate* them. They murdered my parents, Axel. They treat you and your family like slaves too, just like me. Just like Magnus."

"Don't you *dare* compare me to him."

Calum's voice hardened and his posture straightened. "It's true, and you know it. 'Not all slaves wear chains,' remember? Come on, Axel. We need your help. You need to get outta here. Either let me go or kill me now, because I'm leaving."

Axel scowled at Calum and sighed. Stupid Calum would get himself killed without help. He'd screwed everything up, and now Axel would have to bail him out.

And as a bonus, maybe Axel could finally find that adventure he'd been after.

He grumbled but lowered his sword. "Wait outside. I gotta pack a few things."

"FOLLOW ME IF YOU WANT FOOD." Axel stormed out of his front door dressed for an excursion into the wild. A small satchel and a bedroll clung to his back, and his sword hung from his belt in a sheath.

When Magnus emerged from the cornfield, Axel tossed one empty burlap bag to Magnus, then he cut away from the house into the corn.

"What did you say to him?" Magnus's gaze followed Axel as the cornfield devoured him.

Calum hesitated. Magnus wasn't going to like this. "He's coming with us."

"*What?*"

Calum shrugged. "It was either that or he was going to turn us in, and I barely convinced him to do this."

Magnus growled. "This is *not* part of our agreement."

"We don't have an agreement, Magnus."

"*Hey.*" Axel hissed from several yards into the corn. "You guys coming or not?"

Magnus growled again.

"Come on. We can talk about it later." Calum started after Axel. When he glanced over his shoulder and saw Magnus trailing behind, he smiled.

Within ten minutes, they made it to an old wooden storehouse on the far side of Axel's family property. A thick padlock hung from a latch that secured the double sliding doors on the front. Axel pulled out a key and inserted it into the lock while Calum and Magnus kept watch.

"What is taking so long?" Magnus hissed.

"Mind your own business," Axel shot back. He pulled the key out, blew a puff of air into the lock, and then reinserted it. "This lock was always finicky. Just give me a minute, here."

"We don't have a minute, Axel." Calum scanned the nearby woods. "We need to get going before someone—"

"Look, the more you yammer, the longer this is gonna take." Axel lowered the keys and glared at Calum. "So are you gonna keep talking or—"

Magnus grabbed the lock and yanked it clean off the door along with the latch, just as he had with the one at the quarry shed. As he pulled the sliding doors open, he said, "Let's go."

Axel stood in place, his jaw hanging open. He stepped toward Magnus and jabbed his yellow chest with his index finger. "This is my father's storehouse. You had no right to—"

"You presume to lecture me on breaking the door latch when we are already stealing food and trying to escape a band of angry quarry workers?"

"It wasn't your lock to break. Nor is it your food to steal."

Magnus shook his head and brushed Axel's hand away from his chest. "Next time you point a finger at me, I may just do to your hand what I did to that latch."

Axel gawked at him, then at Calum, who just shrugged and stepped inside the storehouse after Magnus.

Inside, mounds of food organized by type towered almost to the ten-foot ceiling amid bales of hay and a few farming tools. Calum had never seen so much food in one place before.

He scowled at Axel. "How is it that I barely got enough to eat every night at the quarry, but you have a storehouse full of food?"

"Actually, we have five storehouses. My family eats pretty well, but we gotta be careful with everything. The King's soldiers keep a close watch on what we produce and what we distribute."

Calum and Magnus frowned at Axel, who held up his hands.

"What I mean is that none of this belongs to my family, even though it came from 'our' land and it's on 'our' property in 'our' storehouse. Really, it all belongs to the King, or by extension, to his soldiers. We aren't supposed to touch it."

"Well, we're about to do more than touch it." Calum popped a strawberry in his mouth, which made it the fourth strawberry he'd ever tasted. He'd already decided to pack many more of them into his bag—and his stomach—before they left the storehouse that night. "Let's load up and get outta here."

It only took a few minutes for them to fill their sacks with a variety of grains, dried meats, fruits, and vegetables. By the time they finished, Calum actually had to strain to heft the loaded sack over his shoulder.

Axel elbowed him on the way toward the storehouse doors. "Think you guys got enough there?"

Calum chuckled. This running away thing might not be so bad after all. "Hey, I haven't eaten my fill for as long as I can remem—"

Something yanked him back, and a shovel clanged against the doorframe. Calum hit the wooden boards on the storehouse floor, and half the contents in his sack spilled out next to him. When he looked up, Magnus stood between him and the doorway.

A man, one of the quarry workers, stood in the doorframe and swung his shovel a second time, but Magnus caught the shovel by its shaft and leveled the worker with one vicious punch. He grabbed the worker by his legs and hurled him out of the storehouse, then he pulled the doors shut.

"C'mon out." A gruff voice ordered from the other side. "Surrender now, and I don't gotta kill you."

Calum knew that voice, and fear pulsed through his chest.

It was Burtis.

CHAPTER 8

"Calum, I know you're in there," Burtis called. "Saw you when Khoba almost took your head off with his spade."

Calum glanced at Axel and then looked at Magnus, who shook his head. He stood to his feet and backed away from the door. "We're not coming out, Burtis. You might as well just get out of here and let us pass."

Laughter bellowed from outside the storehouse. "You're funny, kid. Always good for a laugh. That's for sure."

"I'm serious, Burtis."

"You don't know the meanin' of the word, Calum." All the mirth dissipated from Burtis's voice, replaced by primal undertones. "Now get on out here, or I'll kill you my own self."

A part of Calum, the same part that had learned almost a decade ago to fear those in authority, whether the foreman like Burtis or the King's soldiers, wanted to step out and give up.

But another part held him back and loosed his tongue.

The part of Calum that refused to lie down anymore. The part that would no longer be bullied or abused.

The part that longed to be free.

"Burtis," Calum began, "if you kill me, then so be it, but I'm not your slave anymore, or anyone else's."

"You sure 'bout that?" Burtis called back.

Axel nodded and drew his sword. "I've already come this far. I'm not gonna let a bunch of quarry scum—no offense, Calum—keep me from my future."

Magnus growled and drew his pickax. "Nor will I be going back."

Calum smirked at them both, then picked up a wooden rake leaning against the inside of the storehouse. "We're not coming out, Burtis."

"Then we're gonna burn the storehouse down around you. How 'bout that?"

"You won't," Axel yelled. "The King's men will arrest you for treason."

"That the young farm boy I hear? So these fugitives recruited you to their lost cause as well?"

"*Recruited* me?" Axel winked at Calum. "Not a chance. I'm their *leader*."

Magnus huffed.

Burtis cackled. "You bein' in there won't stop us from burnin' it down, and neither will an empty threat 'bout the King's men. Just as easy to say you four burned it down when you were tryin' to escape. Since you'll be dead, you won't be 'round to argue your side."

Axel eyed Calum and Magnus then turned back toward the door. "Why don't you come in here, and we'll find out?"

"Oh-ho! Big words for a farm boy. Why don't you c'mon out here and make me?"

"Go ahead," Axel yelled back. "Burn it down. See if I care."

Magnus grabbed Axel's satchel and pulled him away from the door. "Easy."

"He can't talk to me like that." Axel pointed toward the door. "Without me he'd go hungry. Dumb brute."

Magnus started to say something, but one of the doors swung open. A torch zipped inside the storehouse and landed in a mound of hay. The fire quickly spread to the nearby wall, which caught fire.

Firelight flickered in Axel's wide eyes. "He's... actually burning the storehouse down."

Magnus grabbed Axel and Calum by their shoulders and pulled them close. "Listen to me. We have little time. We must fight our way out of this. Work together. Watch out for each other. Let them attack first. Wait for them to swing, then dodge and hit them with your weapons. They may be older and stronger, but you are younger and faster. Use that. Crystal?"

Calum nodded, but Axel brushed Magnus's hand off. "I know how to do this."

"Then make sure Calum does not get hurt. Keep him safe."

Axel nodded. "No problem."

"Follow me."

When Magnus stepped out of the storehouse, a barrage of clubs, pickaxes, and shovels swung at him. He avoided several and blocked the others with his own pickax.

Calum and Axel followed, ready for battle. One of the workers recovered from Magnus's deflection and hacked at Calum with a spade. He reacted and blocked the blow with his rake, but the impact sent a shock of pain into his hands, and he nearly dropped the rake. Now he understood why Magnus had told him to dodge the attacks instead of trying to block them.

The worker swung again. This time, Calum hopped back away from the swipe and then, while the worker was stuck in his follow-through, Calum whacked him in the side of his head with the blunt end of the rake, and he went down.

Calum stole a glance over his shoulder, and to his surprise, it actually *did* look like Axel knew what he was doing. He waited for the attacks to come, avoided them, and then lunged forward to deliver quick blows to his opponents with his sword, sometimes wounding them.

Magnus did most of the damage. The workers came at him in droves, but he batted them aside as if they weighed nothing.

Within minutes, the only workers still able to fight were Burtis and three of his men. Everyone else was either unconscious, wounded, or possibly dead, depending on the level of mercy Magnus had deigned to show them.

While Burtis and his three remaining men hesitated to come forward, they still blocked Calum and his friends' escape, and the storehouse fire still raged behind them.

"This is your last chance to give up, Calum." Burtis's eyes focused on him, then on Axel. "You too, farm boy."

"Do I look like a *boy* to you?" Axel started forward, but Magnus pulled him back.

"Yes." Burtis chuckled, and Axel scowled. "Either way, I figure you got 'bout ten minutes 'fore ol' Scrim gets back with the King's men. Then you'll really be in trouble."

Calum glanced at Magnus, but he didn't budge. Facing down Burtis and the idiots from the quarry was one thing, but dealing with trained soldiers...

"The King's men don't take kindly to thieves and murderers." Burtis tilted his head. "And neither do I."

Axel huffed. "I didn't steal anything from you."

"No, but them two did." Burtis extended his fingers one by one, listing his claims as he glowered at Calum and Magnus. "There's that pickax in the beast's hand and the belts strapped to 'im. Then there's the matter of the beast himself. I own 'im for no small sum, and now Calum's at fault for his escape."

Calum glowered at him. "He escaped on his own, and you know it."

"Did he?" Burtis asked. "Then why'd you whack poor Jidon in the head when he tried to stop the Saurian from escapin'? Nearly killed the man. As it is, neither he nor most of the men with 'im are gonna be back to work anytime soon. Or the ones with me, for that matter."

"He was gonna kill Magnus." Relief settled in Calum's chest. As awful as Jidon had been, he was glad he hadn't killed the brute. He threw in a smirk for good measure. "And he was a moron."

Burtis blinked and stared at Magnus. "It's got a *name* now?"

Calum's jaw tensed. He didn't have to defend Magnus, but he would nonetheless. "He's *always* had a name. He's a person too, just like you and me. And like I said before, we're not your slaves anymore."

"*My* slaves? You both belong to the King. I'm just one of his many stewards, here to keep you in line."

"You're doing a great job of that," Axel muttered.

"But you sided with the Saurian and ran away." Burtis shook his head. "Did you really think you'd get away with—"

"Enough talk." Magnus hefted his pickax higher. "We are leaving. Let us go, and we will not add you to the dead and wounded. Try to follow us, and you *will* perish this night."

"So he talks after all." Burtis huffed. "Not a word all day, but now you speak?"

Magnus glared at Burtis, then he refocused on Calum. "Let us go."

Burtis didn't move to stop them, but his gaze fixed on something behind Calum, and he smirked. A twig snapped from the side.

"Watch out!" Axel yelled.

Magnus swiveled his hips, pushed Calum to the ground, and swung his pickax. A man soared at him through the air and knocked Magnus to the dirt. When Magnus shoved the man off of him and onto his back, Calum recognized him.

Jidon lay before him with his head bandaged up—and the pick end of Magnus's pickax protruding from his chest. Burtis had lied about him being too wounded to work—but now it didn't matter. He was definitely dead now.

Burtis roared and lashed his sword, but Axel's blade caught the blow just before it could reach Calum. Axel threw two haphazard swings, then Burtis jammed his fist into Axel's gut so hard that it dropped him to the ground, gasping for air.

Already back on his feet, Calum swung his rake at Burtis's head, but Burtis batted it away with his forearm and sent Calum flying back with a wild kick to his chest. Then Burtis turned back to Axel and raised his sword as Calum scrambled to his feet again.

Calum had no hope of stopping Burtis's swing, but he could knock him off-kilter. He charged forward and drove his shoulder into Burtis's huge frame, just like he'd done to Jidon earlier. The impact barely knocked him off-balance, but it jarred Burtis enough that his swing thumped into the soft ground instead, missing Axel entirely.

Burtis retaliated with a ferocious backhand to Calum's cheek that sent him spiraling back down to the ground, his face ablaze with stinging pain.

Magnus leveled the three remaining workers in successive blows, then he charged at Burtis, who rolled out of the way. He slashed at Magnus's gut, and a red line split his yellow belly. A long grunt rumbled from Magnus's throat, and he pressed his hand against the bleeding wound.

His cheek still burning from Burtis's smack, Calum pushed himself to his feet for what felt like the millionth time that day. He started toward the fight, but Magnus caught him by his wrist and pulled him back.

Magnus's fingers left bloody red streaks on Calum's wrist. Magnus winced, pressed his free hand against his gut again, and said, "He is mine."

Calum glanced at the red line across his belly and the blood trickling from it. "But you're—"

"I am fine," Magnus insisted. "Help Axel."

Axel still lay on his side, gasping for air. He somehow hadn't ever released his sword, even after Burtis's punch. Calum darted over to Axel and helped him upright as Magnus started toward Burtis again.

"You may be bigger," Burtis growled at him. "But you ain't never gonna be *meaner*."

Magnus didn't move aside from breathing. His pickax still protruded from Jidon's chest, and Burtis now stood between Magnus and Jidon's body.

Why hadn't Magnus reached down to pick up any of the shovels or other tools that lay all around them? It didn't make sense to Calum.

Burtis waved his sword in front of him. "C'mon, Saurian. You talk like a human. Bleed like a human. Bet you can die like one, too."

When Magnus stepped forward, Burtis stepped back.

Magnus snorted. "Afraid?"

"I ain't afraid of *you*. Not in the least."

"I see torches in the distance." Axel pointed back toward his family's farmhouse, but Magnus didn't look. "Soldiers?"

"Still time for you to give up," Burtis sneered.

Magnus took another step toward him, and Burtis backed up again. This time, Magnus didn't stop, though. He took two more quick steps after the first, and Burtis swung his sword. At the last instant, Magnus hopped back, and the tip of the blade missed his gut by mere inches.

Burtis swung his sword again. Magnus spun away from the blow and whipped his tail at Burtis's head, but Burtis ducked under it. Magnus darted forward again, and Burtis's sword stabbed toward his gut.

From Calum's vantage, it looked as if Burtis had skewered Magnus and his sword now extended out of Magnus's back, but then a loud snap sounded, followed by a wail from Burtis.

Burtis's arm buckled at the elbow—the wrong way—in Magnus's huge hands.

Then the tip of Burtis's own rusty blade rotated toward him, disappeared in the center of his bare chest, and promptly reemerged from his back.

His eyes wide, Burtis dropped to his knees and rolled onto his side.

Magnus spat on the ground next to Burtis and wrenched his pickax out of Jidon's chest. Then, without so much as a word, he grabbed one of the bags of food from the fiery storehouse entrance and headed into the forest.

Calum looked at Axel, who nodded at him.

"Come on." Axel stood to his feet, finally breathing normally again. "I see torches at the edges of the cornfields. The soldiers are getting close. We'd better go."

Calum tossed his rake aside and grabbed the bag of food he'd dropped a few feet from the burning storehouse. After a final look back at Burtis and Jidon's bodies, he headed into the woods and left his old life—and Axel's burning storehouse—behind him forever.

CHAPTER 9

For Lilly's escape attempt, Roderick ordered that she go one day without food. That night, two of Luggs's goons, Gammel and Adgar, made sure she didn't eat. They were the same two men who'd carried out the male slave after Roderick knocked him unconscious.

Colm had tried to sneak her some food once, but they caught him. They stopped the entire procession, hauled him out of the wagon, and gave him five lashes for trying. Then they took his food as well.

That didn't stop silly old Colm, though. He'd managed to stash some extra bread crusts somewhere within his weathered cloak, and he waited until Gammel and Adgar thought he was asleep to slide one to her.

She thanked him with a sad smile. Part of her considered giving it back. After all, she was young and healthy, and he was just a poor old man.

He flashed her a glimpse at a gold coin he'd taken from Luggs after Lilly had tried to stand up for Sharion, the other slave woman in their wagon. Not just a poor old man—a poor old *thief*.

Under the moonlight, Lilly whispered, "How'd you manage to get that off him?"

"I may be old, but I still have nimble fingers, child."

"I'll say." She frowned. "Too bad it won't do us any good while we're in here."

Colm grinned. "I wouldn't say that. These slave traders love coin more than anything else, and they treasure it even more than loyalty to one another. I know of more than a few men in this bunch who'd trade me an apple, or a bowl of hot soup, or even a chicken leg for this."

Lilly's eyebrows rose.

"I'd share, of course."

A smile cracked her lips, then a chill ratcheted through her body. Without her armor, the night would be long and cold.

Colm scooted closer and spread his cloak over her shoulders. "Here, child. No need for you to shiver in the night."

Part of Lilly wanted to refuse him. It felt awkward and strange to sit so near a man not of her

47

family, someone she'd just met, even in spite of his age—and in nothing but her undergarments, no less—but it was cold. Colm had only helped her thus far, so she inched closer to him, and he curled his arm around her shoulders.

"You might think I'm trying to take advantage of you." He looked down at her. "Well, I am. I confess it."

She gawked at him, ready to pull away.

"Don't look so surprised. I'm old. The heat leaves my body faster than it used to." Colm grinned again. "Never fear. I still harbor no interest in you except that you fare well."

Lilly exhaled relief and leaned into him, and their shared warmth eased her tension. She rubbed the fabric of Colm's cloak between her fingers. "Your cloak wouldn't happen to have any aerosilk in it, would it?"

He shook his head. "Sadly, no. A luxury I could never afford, save for a few times in my life when the Overlord's generous blessings seemed to rain from on high. Why do you ask?"

"If it was aerosilk, I could use it as a replacement cape. Then I could fly out of here."

"Is that how it works?"

"Yes. Windgales need aerosilk in their capes, in significant quantities, in order to fly. The amount can vary from Windgale to Windgale, but in general, about fifty percent or more is necessary." Lilly watched Sharion dig down into the hay. "Sharion?"

Her head popped up and she glared at Lilly.

"Would you care to join us?" Lilly smiled. "There's room to keep warm over here."

"Leave me alone." Sharion dug back into the hay and disappeared beneath a mound of golden-brown straw.

"Well, if you change your mind—"

"I won't."

Lilly smirked, but her amusement faded far too soon. "Roderick mentioned the Pass. Does he mean...?"

"Trader's Pass?" Colm nodded. "That he does."

Lilly's breath caught in her throat. They meant to take her to Eastern Kanarah? So far from her family, from her home. And into what? Slavery? To whom?

"Colm." Her voice broke when she said his name. "What's going to happen to me?"

After a long pause, he squeezed her shoulders. "Easy, child. Best not to ponder a future that may never come. Survive the night, first."

Lilly closed her eyes and stifled her tears.

Eastern Kanarah

"STOP." Magnus held out his arms and halted his progress. He'd taken the lead position as they crept through the woods. Calum followed him, and Axel brought up the rear. They all stopped and turned back to Magnus.

"What?" Axel said more than asked.

"*Shhhhh,*" Magnus hissed. "We are not alone."

Calum scanned the surrounding trees, but thanks to the darkness he couldn't see much of anything. The moonlight barely broke through the thick tree cover, and where it did, it wasn't much help. "I don't see—"

Magnus grabbed his arm and yanked him down to the dirt behind a rotting log. His voice still a hiss, he said, "Quiet. Axel, get down."

Axel took cover behind a small bush, stared into the forest for a moment, and then refocused on Magnus, squinting.

Magnus tapped the side of his reptilian head. "Listen."

Sure enough, a faint rustle sounded several yards away, from the very direction they were heading. Through a hole in the rotted log, Calum saw a dark form materialize in the trees, then another, then another, and many more until a couple dozen men swarmed that portion of the forest.

Calum's heartbeat pounded like war drums in his ears, so hard that the men approaching had to hear it. How could they not?

Their footsteps grew louder, and as the men approached, they sharpened into focus. Black leather armor. Shining weapons in their gauntleted hands.

The King's soldiers.

From what Calum could tell, the first soldier who stepped past Axel's hiding spot didn't seem to notice them. Neither did the second, third, or fourth, but the fifth brushed his sword across the top of the bush in a slow, deliberate motion. The metal of his blade sang with tinkling notes as it scraped against the leaves and exposed branches.

"Billings."

The fifth soldier straightened his posture faster than a whiplash, and he turned to face the speaker.

"Focus."

A big man riding an armored horse came into view—or maybe he just looked big because he was on top of a horse. He held a long spear in his left hand and the horse's reins in his right.

A streak of silver ran across his black leather breastplate, something that none of the other soldiers had. It reminded Calum of Burtis's purple foreman's sash, and he wondered if it meant the man on horseback was their leader.

"Yes, sir." Billings turned back and rejoined the regiment, his sword in the ready position like all the other soldiers.

No one in the group said anything after that. They just continued to advance forward.

Soldiers disappeared from Calum's view as they climbed on top of his log and hopped over. The sound of their feet hitting the dirt shook Calum's chest.

Wood snapped next to Calum's ear, and he froze.

A metal-studded boot broke through the rotten log and crunched down only inches from Calum's face. Musty flakes and dust flecked across his cheeks, and curses rang out above him.

"Billings."

"Sorry, Commander Pordone. I didn't know the log was rotten, and I—"

"Billings." Commander Pordone pointed his spear forward. "Focus."

"Yes, sir."

Calum didn't dare reach to wipe off his face, not with Billings so close. Even so, the beginnings of a sneeze tingled in his nose. He had to do something soon. He didn't know if he could hold it back.

Billings pulled his foot out of the log, and more dust peppered Calum's face. After a few muttered curses, Billings stepped past Calum's position.

Calum reached for his nose without a sound and rubbed it, but that just made it worse. He had to hold back his sneeze. Their *lives* were at stake.

Commander Pordone's horse took the long way around the log and angled back behind the first five men. If Calum could just hold out for one more minute until the soldiers moved out of sight and out of hearing range, they'd be able to escape.

He could do it. He had to. He rubbed his nose again and tried to breathe through his mouth instead of—

Calum sneezed.

He muffled it as best as he could, but it was still too loud.

Commander Pordone twisted his torso and turned his head back. Calum was certain their eyes met, but the commander didn't move after that.

Calum's eyes watered. No, not aga—

A second sneeze.

"There!" Commander Pordone bellowed. He raised his left arm over his head and then thrust it forward in a vigorous point.

A gleaming spear embedded in the log next to Calum's shoulder.

"*Run!*" Magnus grabbed Calum's waistband and pulled him to his feet, then tossed him the bag of food he'd been carrying.

Calum tried to catch the sack, but it popped open, and half the food spilled out on the ground. He ground his teeth and reached for the nearest potato.

"*Leave it.*" Magnus shoved Calum forward, and three more fruits dropped from the sack. "Go!"

Commander Pordone drew his sword and kicked the sides of his horse, which charged forward.

Calum froze. He had exposed them all, and now they would die. Him first.

Magnus wrenched the spear from the log and hurled it toward the approaching commander. Instead, the spear struck the horse in the center of its head, and it pitched forward.

Commander Pordone toppled off the horse, and his body cracked against a nearby tree. Behind him, soldiers ran back toward Magnus, all of them yelling and shouting threats in the King's name.

"Nice throw!" Axel shouted.

"I was aiming for the rider." Magnus hissed at Calum, "Go!"

Enough. Calum resolved he wouldn't freeze again.

He broke free from the trance and ran alongside Magnus. Ahead of them, Axel beckoned them forward with his sword in his right hand and his sack of food in his other.

They ran through the woods with the soldiers close behind. Axel still led, and Magnus still followed Calum.

"They are gaining on us," Magnus yelled loud enough for both Calum and Axel to hear. "We are carrying too much. We each have to drop something."

"I thought you were supposed to be *strong*," Axel called over his shoulder. "Why don't you carry more?"

"I still tire from running." Magnus grunted from behind Calum. "We must drop the food."

"No," Axel shouted back. "Not the food."

"Either drop the food, drop your bedrolls, or drop the weapons. You are welcome to fight the King's men with tomatoes and melons if you wish, but I do not advise it."

Even amid the chase, Calum had to grin at Magnus's comment.

He dropped the half-bag of food he was carrying. Magnus was right—running was much easier without the extra weight, and they could find more food somewhere else along the way. They would have to.

Axel cursed as he ran, but he also dropped his bag of food. Calum, still following Axel, jumped over it so as not to trip.

Within a few minutes, when Calum looked back, he no longer saw the soldiers behind them. Even so, Magnus urged them on for another five minutes before he let them stop. Axel sheathed his sword, Calum wiped his brow with his wrist, and all three of them sucked in a trough's-worth of air.

Axel spoke first. "What now?"

"We make it through the rest of tonight." Magnus pointed to a ridge to the southwest. "We can take shelter among those trees."

Axel pointed east. "There's a cave right over there. Let's make use of it."

Magnus shook his head. "No."

"Why not?"

"It is not safe."

Axel scoffed. "It's a *cave*. One way in. Easy to defend."

Magnus squared himself with Axel. "You obviously know nothing of strategy or tactics. Given our situation, that cave is a terrible idea."

Axel stepped forward and looked up at Magnus. Calum had stood where Axel was, face-to-face with Magnus, and it was a terrifying place to be. He gained new admiration for Axel's courage.

Or was it stupidity?

"You know nothing about me, *Scales*." Axel practically spat the last word.

Courage or otherwise, Calum didn't want this devolving into an unnecessary conflict. He wedged himself between them with his hands and then his body. "That's enough. Both of you."

"He thinks he knows everything. No *Saurian* is gonna tell me what I can and can't do." Axel folded his arms.

Magnus's eyes narrowed. "If I must, I *will* put you in your place, child."

Axel huffed. "You don't scare me."

"It is your prerogative to say so, that you might appear brave in front of Calum, but your eyes betray the truth." A subtle grin curled up the ends of Magnus's mouth. "You are petrified."

Then Axel proved that it had been stupidity guiding his actions all along.

His jaw hardened, and he reached for the hilt of his sword, but Magnus was faster.

In one quick, jarring motion, Magnus pushed past Calum, knocking him to the side. He big reptilian hands clamped onto Axel, one on his right wrist, and another on his throat.

With a powerful heft, he shoved Axel against a tree, lifted him off his feet by his throat, and held him in place there. He leaned in close and exhaled a long hiss through his nostrils at Axel's face.

Though Axel struggled, he could neither draw his sword nor break free of Magnus's hold on him. He choked and sputtered, and even in the moonlight, Calum could tell his face was turning red from the strain.

"Magnus…" Calum said. "You're hurting him!"

"The next time you dare to pull your blade on me, I will grant you no mercy," Magnus warned. "Weapons are to be brandished only against enemies. If you choose to make one of me, I assure you we will not remain enemies for long. Do you comprehend what I am saying to you, *child*?"

Axel managed a desperate nod and some gurgling noises.

Calum just stood there, helpless to intervene. The more he considered it, though, the more he didn't really fault Magnus for his actions. Axel's brazen attitude had gotten him in this situation.

His response seemed to have satisfied Magnus, because he released his grip on Axel and let him drop to the ground. Axel coughed and rubbed at his throat, sucking in greedy breaths.

"So…" Calum began, "…the trees along the ridge, then?"

"If you think you're so smart," Axel rasped as he finally stood back up, "explain to me why that cave is a bad idea?"

"There are multiple reasons," Magnus said. "It is exposed, out in the open, which makes it visible to the soldiers looking for us. They will expect us to hide in a cave because it is a natural shelter—"

"Which is why we should stay in there," Axel insisted.

Magnus eyed him. "Are you finished?"

Axel motioned for Magnus to continue, then he folded his arms and leaned against the very tree Magnus had just pinned him to.

"It is a natural shelter, but it also presents a danger to us because we do not know what or who might already be in there. Nor do we know if that is the only entrance, and even if it is, if we cannot defend it or get caught off guard, we would have our backs up against a wall on the inside."

"Just like the storehouse…" Calum said as the realization clicked in his mind.

"Correct." Magnus nodded. "Hiding among the trees on that ridge is much safer."

"How do you know all of this?" Calum asked.

"Experience."

The way Magnus said it made Calum want to ask him more questions, because there was clearly a lot more Magnus wasn't letting on, but he held off. Something told Calum he ought to leave it alone… at least for now.

Axel sighed. "So are we going, or what?"

"Follow me." Magnus started toward the ridge.

———————

AFTER TWO FITFUL hours of sleep, Axel hugged his knees tighter, shivered, and half-glared at Calum, but so far he hadn't awakened.

Perhaps I shouldn't have gone along with this scheme after all. Where had it gotten him so far? Cold, lost in the woods, with his best friend and a monstrous Saurian bully. *I could be in my bed right now instead of… this.*

A mix of coniferous and broadleaf deciduous trees encircled their camp—if it could be called that. More like two guys and a Saurian laying on the ground in the woods. Calum stirred, and light from the small fire in the center of the camp flickered in his green eyes.

Either the air had cooled as the night deepened, or Axel's temperature had dropped now that he wasn't running around. Maybe he'd feel warmer if he had something in his stomach.

Too bad they'd abandoned all the food while running from the King's soldiers.

Axel scowled at Calum. "I wish you hadn't sneezed."

Calum broke his gaze at the fire and looked at him. "Me too."

"I could sure go for some of that food I helped steal." Axel eyed the Saurian. Scales. Magnus. Whatever. "Oh, wait. *Someone* told us to drop it all. Great plan, master strategist."

"You are welcome." Magnus didn't bother to make eye contact. He just lay on the ground and stared up at the stars.

Overhead, the sky had begun to yield to the first hint of daylight, so the stars didn't shine as brightly as they had against the solid black curtain of night.

"What do you mean, I'm 'welcome?'" Axel asked.

"You yet draw breath. I saved your life." Magnus leaned his head forward and squinted at Axel with golden eyes. "Twice."

Axel shook his head. "So starving us to death is your idea of 'saving my life?' And how long do you expect us to last out here without food?"

"You ate dinner before you went to sleep, right?" Calum asked. "You can't be *starving* yet.

Don't be so dramatic."

"All this fighting and running builds up an appetite. I'm not like you, Calum," Axel said. "I got to eat my fill every day. It's why I'm so much bigger than you."

"Your *head* is certainly bigger," Magnus mumbled.

Axel's focus whipped toward Magnus. "What'd you say to me?"

"You heard me." Now Magnus looked over at him. "What do you intend to do about it?"

A whole range of ideas cycled through Axel's head, but they all amounted to nothing but his imagination running wild. Though he'd never admit it aloud, he couldn't compete with Magnus.

And that frustrated him most of all. If Axel actually wanted to live the life of adventure he'd always wanted to live, he had to get stronger. He had to learn to fight. He had to learn to survive.

"That is what I thought," Magnus said.

Axel ignored him. Let the lizard have his hollow victory. One day, Axel would grow strong enough to take him on. Then it would be Magnus who'd have to shut up instead.

Calum asked, "What'd you do with those Gronyx stones you stole? We could sell those in a town somewhere and buy food."

Magnus stared at him. "What Gronyx stones?"

"You know what I mean," Calum said. "The gems with the greenish tint from the pit. You stashed a handful of them under one of the boards near the tool shed at the quarry. I found them at the end of my workday yesterday. Do you still have those?"

Magnus shook his head. "I never took any Gronyx stones."

Calum sighed. "Then it was Hardink after all."

Axel tilted his head. "Huh?"

"Nothing." Calum waved his hand. "Too late now."

More nonsense from Calum. Great. Axel said, "Whatever."

"Why don't we hunt?" Calum leaned forward. "Some of the quarry guys used to do it at night until Burtis found out and put a stop to it."

"Uh… look around, Calum. We have nothing to hunt with. No bows and arrows. No spears." Axel rolled his eyes. "Unless you can outrun a deer and cut its head off with my sword."

Calum looked at Magnus, but he just continued to stare up at the fading night sky. "The quarry guys didn't have bows and arrows either. Burtis never would've allowed that."

"Then how did they hunt? Throwing rocks?" Axel rubbed his arms to try to warm up.

"I think they used snares. I saw one of them carrying a rabbit by a rope attached to its foot once." Calum cringed. "That was the same night Burtis found out. The next morning, he strung the man up by his foot and lowered him into the Gronyx's pit."

"Burtis is no longer a concern of yours," Magnus said.

Calum grinned. "I know. Thanks."

"Snares," Axel said. "Do we have rope?"

Calum looked at Magnus again. "He grabbed some from the quarry, but I don't know if it will work for snares or not. It's pretty thick."

"So much for hunting, then." Axel scoffed and shook his head.

Magnus sat up, and Axel couldn't help but notice that the lash marks and even the slash across his yellow underbelly had already healed substantially. Apparently, Saurians healed a lot faster than humans.

"Though I am loath to admit it—" Magnus said. "—Axel is right."

Axel raised an eyebrow and waited for the inevitable snide comment.

"We cannot hunt. It will not work. And since we have no food, our options are limited."

No snide comment. Maybe it was forthcoming. Axel ventured, "What do you have in mind?"

Magnus glanced between Calum and Axel. "We need to raid the Rock Outpost."

CHAPTER 10

Axel would've laughed at Magnus's proposition, but he was too stunned to say anything at first.

Calum tilted his head. "Raid the what?"

"You've gotta be kidding me," Axel managed to say. Sure, he'd left his home on a whim to follow his own silly idea of getting away from the farm, but now things had gone too far. *Way too far.* "The Rock Outpost? You want to raid the *Rock Outpost?*"

"We do not yet possess adequate weapons. Calum does not have one at all." Magnus stared into the woods. "We have no armor. No supplies, no food. You said yourself that we will not last long out here if we are this ill-equipped."

"I'm clearly missing something here. What's the Rock Outpost?" Calum asked.

"When I said we wouldn't last long, I didn't mean that we should *attack* one of the King's fortresses as a solution," Axel said. "Are you crazy?"

"You want to do *what?*" Calum gawked at them both.

Axel held out his hand, palm up. Finally, they agreed on something. "Exactly my thoughts, Calum."

"I do not desire to attack the outpost," Magnus explained. "I want to *raid* it. An important distinction."

"Not enough of a difference to make it a good idea." Axel folded his arms and stared at the shrinking campfire. He might as well be one of the sticks he'd just thrown in. "Not even close."

"It will be easy. Sneak in. Seize what we require. Get out." Magnus nodded. "Simple."

Axel laughed. "You're nuts. You're living in a dream world."

"We will succeed," Magnus said. "I already have it planned out. Originally, I intended to do it myself, but it will be even easier with three of us."

"What do you mean, you already have it planned out?" Calum asked.

"I mean what I said." Magnus looked at him. "When you found me at the quarry, that was my intended destination."

Axel laughed again and stood up next to Calum. "You were gonna raid the Rock Outpost by yourself?"

"Absolutely."

"There have to be at least twenty or thirty soldiers stationed there." Axel hefted a log from the pile of sticks and wood they'd gathered for the fire. "You'd need an army."

Magnus shook his head. "Only if I wanted to *attack* the place. Like I said, I just want to raid it."

"Why even risk it?" Calum asked.

"They are in possession of some property that belongs to me. Some things that I hold very dear." Magnus's voice hardened. "And I want it back."

"*Pfft.* Good luck with that." Axel rolled his eyes and tossed the log into the center of the fire. Embers sprayed into the air toward the trees that hung over the camp and quickly cooled.

"Our only other option is to go back," Magnus said. "And we all know what that means."

Axel folded his arms. "I'm not risking my life just to help you get your stuff back."

Magnus shot a glare at him but returned to his spot around the fire. "Like I said, it will be simple, and it will equip us for the journey ahead. If we encounter any soldiers, I will deal with them."

"You're gonna take on twenty or thirty trained soldiers on your own?" Axel folded his arms again and leaned back against the log behind him. "You had a hard time keeping a bunch of quarry workers at bay. If it weren't for Calum and me watching your back, you would've—"

"There will not be twenty or thirty soldiers inside by the time we get there. The only hard part is actually getting inside without the rest realizing what we are doing," Magnus said. "Which is where you two will come in handy."

"Why would most of them be gone?" Calum asked.

Magnus grinned and eyed the pile of sticks next to the campfire. It was the first time Axel had ever seen a truly pleasant expression on his reptilian face.

He turned toward the forest. "Follow me. We have work to do before sunrise."

Western Kanarah

A CLANG JOLTED LILLY AWAKE, and someone snickered in the darkness behind her. She quickly shed Colm's cloak from her shoulders and tried to get away from the sudden sound, but she tripped over something in front of her.

"Watch yourself!" Sharion hissed. She swatted at Lilly's ankles and curled closer to Colm's legs—and farther under his cloak. So much for preferring to be alone all night.

Bony fingers clasped around Lilly's wrist. Colm gently pulled her close to him again, and she acquiesced. Back under his cloak, she found renewed warmth.

"Don't mind them," he told her. "They just want to bother you."

Lilly rubbed her eyes. "I'm bothered."

"We'll be on the move for some time, now. Get some more rest if you can."

"I don't think that's going to happen."

"No?"

"I have to… relieve myself." Lilly glanced around her jail-cell-on-wheels. "Am I supposed to do it here?"

Colm shook his head. "No. They don't like changing out the hay. Just rap the bars a few times and ask. They'll take you into the woods."

Lilly nodded and began to stand up, but Colm grabbed her hand again.

"Do not be unaware," he wheezed. "A bunch of men alone with a beautiful girl in the woods may forfeit their inhibitions."

"But Roderick said—"

"That doesn't mean his men won't try. Men's carnal desires often outweigh those of their purses." Colm fixed his gaze on Lilly, stern as ever. "Do not be deceived, and do not let your guard down, even for an instant."

Lilly swallowed the lump in her throat and nodded. She pounded on the bars.

Five minutes later, Luggs, Gammel, Adgar, and another slave trader shoved both Lilly and Sharion toward the woods. In the darkness, she stumbled over an exposed root—normally not an issue since she could just fly over entire forests when she'd had her cape—but she righted herself and continued forward.

"That's far enough," Gammel said. "Go on. Do it already."

Lilly stared at him, her eyes wide. "Here? In front of you?"

Adgar chuckled, and Luggs nudged the other slave trader. She recognized him, not by his face but by the bandage wrapped around his thigh. The one she'd hit with her last arrow.

"Of course, here," Luggs replied. "You don't think we'd just letcha wander off in the dark, do you?"

Next to Lilly, Sharion hiked up her tattered dress and squatted near a bush. Lilly looked back at Gammel, who licked his lips.

"At least let me go on the other side of that tree?" she pleaded.

Gammel, Adgar, and the bandaged slave trader all shook their heads "no," but Luggs nodded. "Let 'er go, boys. She won't get far even if she does run."

Lilly didn't waste time. She rounded the tree, relieved herself, and came back into view of the slave traders within less than a minute.

Except they weren't there anymore.

She looked right and panned left for a moment, then turned back.

Luggs and the slave trader with the bandage stood behind her. Luggs shoved her to the ground and grinned, and his eyebrows arched down.

Colm's warning ratcheted through Lilly's memory. This couldn't be happening.

But it was.

Lilly tried to stagger away, but Adgar and Gammel emerged from the brush behind her with Sharion, whom they thrust to the ground next to her.

"N-no—you can't do this!" Lilly more begged than said.

"Better if you don't resist 'em," Sharion muttered. "Just let 'em do what they do. It'll be over sooner."

Lilly turned to her, horrified. She couldn't be serious.

"Your friend has the right idea," Luggs said. "Except that on a sweet little thing like you, I know I'm gonna take my time. Ain't that right, boys?"

Their snickers chorused around her, and a deep sickness clenched in her gut. They'd ventured dozens of yards away from the wagons by now, and probably out of earshot, but she had to try. She wouldn't just let them take her.

She sucked in a deep breath and let out a piercing shriek—only to have it cut short by Lugg's hand to her mouth and his dagger to her throat.

"Not another peep, or your honor won't be the only thing we take from you." Luggs smelled like a trash heap up close, and brown spots dotted his yellowed teeth. "Besides, you shot poor Lorrence in his leg, here. Seems to me he oughta get somethin' for his troubles, don't you?"

Part of Lilly wanted to cry, and another part wanted to claw Luggs's eyes out. With his dagger to her throat, she didn't dare do either.

"You hold her," Adgar said. "Then I'll hold her for you."

Sharion moaned, but didn't resist.

By the Overlord—this *wasn't* happening. She never should have left home. Never should have disagreed with her parents. She should have just done what they'd asked.

Now it was too late.

Lorrence untied the cord that held his bloodstained trousers to his waist.

"Unless you wanna lose something dear to you, I suggest you cinch your pants back up, Lorrence."

All four slave traders and Lilly turned toward the source of the voice. A towering muscular form stepped out from behind a tree. Even in the waning moonlight, Lilly recognized the silhouette of his spiky hair.

Roderick.

"All of you, step back." When no one moved, Roderick added, "*Now.*"

Lorrence haphazardly retied his pants and limped toward Roderick. With indignation in his voice, he said, "She owes me for my leg, boss. It hurts, and I ain't got nothin' in return for my sufferin'."

Roderick's gaze shifted from Adgar to Gammel to Luggs, all within a matter of seconds. Each of them lowered his head, but Lorrence still approached.

"C'mon, boss," Lorrence's voice oozed. "I oughta at least get a taste for my trouble, don'tcha think?"

Roderick tilted his head, then he grabbed Lorrence by his throat and lifted him off of his feet with one hand. Lorrence gripped Roderick's wrist and sputtered until a loud crack echoed off of the trees.

The sound sent a jolt through Lilly, and she gasped.

Lorrence slumped from Roderick's grasp and tumbled to the ground in a heap. His right arm curled under his body at an awkward angle—but not nearly as awkward as the angle of his neck.

"Anyone else want to protest my decision?" Roderick glared at the other three men. "Anyone else want to try to have a 'taste?'"

No one said a thing. Lilly didn't know if she should breathe a sigh of relief or hold onto the air she'd sucked into her lungs. Roderick's strength exceeded even that of General Balena—by a considerable amount, it seemed. The way he so effortlessly lifted Lorrence from his feet and dispatched him... he might as well be part Saurian.

How could Lilly ever hope to escape from someone like that?

"Good. Next person I catch going after this girl gets worse—much worse." Roderick's eyes narrowed. "Get them back into their wagon."

Luggs pointed his dagger at Sharion. "What about her?"

Roderick stared steel at him. "What about her?"

"Can we at least... you know..."

Roderick's eyes narrowed. "Be quick about it. We have a schedule to keep."

Lilly's mouth hung open. Roderick had saved her but still intended to let them have Sharion? Not if she could do something about it.

She had no weapons, had no way to fight back against three grown men—*plus* Roderick—but she had to do something.

Was it futile? Yes, probably, but maybe all she had to do was buy Sharion time. Maybe Sharion would be lucky enough—and aware enough—to escape in the process.

Gammel and Adgar still stood near Sharion, the three of them bathed in moonlight. Luggs had maintained his position near her, and Roderick blocked off any hope of running back toward the wagons, but Lilly could run laterally with no problem. It wasn't much of a plan, but maybe it would be enough.

With a roar, she pushed up to her feet and charged Luggs.

Lilly drove her shoulder into his hip so hard that she almost knocked her arm out of its socket and barely managed to keep her footing. Luggs yelled and slashed at her with his dagger, but she'd already started running toward the trees—and toward Gammel and Sharion.

Gammel held onto Sharion's wrist, his eyes large and white like chicken eggs, as she jammed her left fist into his nose with a satisfying crack. Her hand smarted from the blow, but Gammel yelped and released Sharion.

Lilly had no time to help her up. Sharion was on her own now.

Lilly angled into the woods while Roderick barked orders to follow her.

She ran along the moonlit paths, this time more careful to watch her footing, even though it was even harder to see now in the dark. She leaped over fallen logs, ducked under low-hanging branches, and swerved through the trees. Her legs burned from the exertion, but a renewed chance at freedom tugged her heart forward.

A large, dark figure leaped at her from the forest to her right, and she skidded to a halt just in time to avoid his grasp. Adgar. She recognized his twiggish form and the stupid brown hat he always wore, the combination of which made him look like a scarecrow.

Her legs pumped against the hard ground, and she avoided his second grasp, but his jagged fingernails scraped her shoulder as she ran past.

Lilly had no idea how fast Adgar could run, but she had to assume he was faster than her. He stood even taller than Roderick, and his long legs meant long strides. She'd have to do something to lose him or he'd catch up.

Oh, to be able to fly again.

A low branch threatened to smack her as she ran. Perfect. Lilly charged straight for it, and Adgar's heavy footfalls plodded just steps behind hers. With her arms up, she grabbed the branch, pushed it forward and upward, and then ducked under it. A split-second later she heard a loud smack, a grunt, and a slew of curses.

Lilly snuck a look back and saw Adgar clutching his forehead under the moonlight. He'd fallen behind but still pursued her. He wouldn't fall for that again.

She'd slowed him down, but at the cost of some of her own speed. She caught a patch of flat ground and pounded against the dirt until she regained her full momentum.

Another slave trader, this one with a bow, jumped in front of her and took aim. Lilly skidded along the ground and dove to her left as he let the arrow fly.

He missed by several feet, and she tore through the woods away from him. Another arrow thudded into a tree to her right as she ran past. Had she been shooting instead, she wouldn't have missed.

Another man appeared on her right, swinging a gleaming sword at her legs. Lilly somehow managed to hop over his swing and rolled end-over-end until she wound up back on her feet, still running.

She knew what they were trying to do. The slave traders had more or less turned her back toward the direction from which she'd come.

She wouldn't let them divert her path. Lilly took a sharp right and cut deeper into the woods, bounding over rockier terrain. Her lungs strained, her feet hurt, and she was running out of tricks, but when she glanced behind her, no one followed.

Good. Maybe she'd escaped after all—an incredible bonus after only intending to distract the men from harming Sharion.

Brighter moonlight shone down on her, more than there should be in a forest. Lilly realized she'd reached a clearing. The night sky beckoned her forward and not much else—literally nothing else.

Lilly gasped and cut off her stride. She slid to a stop at the edge of a cliff that dropped several thousand feet and stretched in both directions as far as the moonlight allowed her to see. Her every impulse told her to leap into the void and take flight, but she forced her mind to remember that she didn't have her cape.

In the basin below the cliff, she saw the Valley of the Tri-Lakes—a flat, gray expanse, devoid of any vegetation. In the distance one of the Tri-Lakes sparkled under the moonlight.

"Nowhere to run now, Angel."

Lilly knew Roderick's voice without even having to turn around. The way he said "Angel" churned her stomach. She faced him nonetheless with her fists clenched.

"You either come with us, or you take the plunge." Roderick folded his arms at the head of the clearing while Luggs, Adgar, Gammel, and several other slave traders emerged from the dark woods behind him. All of them panted and wheezed, but Roderick showed no indication of strain except for a bit of perspiration that dotted his wide forehead. "What'll it be?"

Lilly stepped back and almost lost her footing on the edge, but she recovered before her instincts—to jump and fly away—kicked in.

She wished she could. She'd trade every moment from now until the end of time in obedience to her parents for her cape, even for five minutes.

But it was hopeless. No amount of wishing would secure aerosilk around her neck, and without it, she couldn't escape these ruffians.

Roderick extended his hand. "Come on, Angel. It's the only way."

Lilly stole a glance down at the chasm behind her—lined with jagged rocks and much, much too far for her to fall and hope to survive. The rebellion in her chest wanted her to jump, but that same rebellion had gotten her in this predicament in the first place.

She bit her lip, raised her hands, and walked toward Roderick.

Eastern Kanarah

After a few hours of executing Magnus's sprawling preparations for the raid still to come, Calum's exhaustion finally caught up with him. Along with Axel and Magnus, he stole another few hours of sleep.

When they awoke, Axel gave Calum a spare shirt he'd packed. It fit him poorly—more like a tent than a shirt—but Calum was grateful for it all the same.

Then the three of them headed southeast through the forest away from the Snake Mountains, which Magnus had pointed out to them earlier. Calum hadn't ever seen real mountains before, and the few glimpses he'd gotten of them through the forest canopy sent an exciting ripple of chills, wonder, and terror racing across his skin.

Perhaps one day—maybe even one day soon—he'd get to traverse those mountains. What kind of adventure awaited him along their rocky cliffs, among the people dwelling nearby? He couldn't know for sure, but his heart told him to anticipate marvels he'd never known before.

About ten miles south of the quarry, near the edge of the tree line, sat the Rock Outpost, silhouetted against the still-rising sun. From so far away, Calum couldn't distinguish it from one of Axel's family storehouses, except it might've been larger, and it looked spikier, somehow.

Calum wondered if the men who'd murdered his parents had ever been inside. Maybe some of them still occupied the fortress—or maybe not.

"Not what I was expecting," Calum said. "Then again, I didn't know it was there in the first place."

Axel eyed him. "Where did you think all those soldiers came from?"

Calum shrugged. "I figured they had to come from somewhere, but I don't remember much from the first eight years of my life, and for the last eight years, I've only ever been to the quarry, the camp, your farm, and now the forest. Burtis didn't exactly let us travel much."

"Well, you've got your chance now, don't you?"

"Quiet, both of you." Magnus handed each of them a thick stick with fabric wrapped around some twigs secured to one end. "Once these are lit, they will extinguish quickly. We cannot spare more fabric right now, and we have no pitch to keep them burning, so once they are lit, you must make haste. Crystal?"

Calum nodded. "Clear."

"I still don't think this is gonna work." Axel exhaled a long sigh. "But whatever."

"Just do not get yourself caught."

Magnus held out his own stick, the last smoldering survivor from last night's campfire. Calum and Axel held theirs against his, and fire spread between them all.

"Go quickly," Magnus urged. "Remember, light the bundles close to the ground so the flames have more time to climb up to the tree branches."

They dispersed throughout a pre-determined area with Magnus closest to the tree line and the outpost, Calum farther back in the woods, and Axel even farther back. With running between two forest fires and setting one of his own, Calum had the most dangerous job, but he was also the quickest on his feet. He had to light the fires and get out of there fast.

They'd spent most of the rest of last night gathering dry sticks and stacking them against certain trees Magnus thought would burn the easiest. Then they'd stuffed dried leaves inside those sticks as well to help everything catch fire sooner.

Magnus had planned it to create a big enough blaze to get the soldiers' attention—in theory, anyway. Even if the trees didn't catch, someone from the outpost was bound to see smoke rising from multiple spots within the forest and muster some sort of reaction.

Calum ignited the first bundle, then seven more, gradually working his way north. The fire shouldn't spread any faster than he could light it, so if he stayed ahead of it and at least even with Magnus and Axel, if not a bit ahead of them, he'd be fine.

Within ten minutes he'd ignited twenty bundles, and his section of the trees had begun to burn on their own. Thanks to Magnus's good planning, the fire continued to spread.

Calum caught up with Magnus, and Axel showed up not long afterward. They headed for the trees near the outpost's north gate and waited.

Twenty minutes later, ten armored soldiers filed out of the outpost, all with weapons in their hands, accompanied by one officer on horseback who carried a spear in his left hand. For all Calum knew, he could've been the same officer as last night in the woods, just riding a different horse.

"Not as many as I had hoped for." Magnus turned his head toward them. "We may have to do some serious fighting after all, boys."

"Wait." Calum pointed. "Look."

One of the soldiers headed toward the officer. They exchanged some words, the officer nodded, and the soldier headed back toward the outpost. A few minutes later, six more soldiers exited from the outpost and jogged toward the fire.

"Much better." Magnus grinned at Calum and Axel. "Follow me. We are going in."

CHAPTER 11

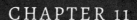

Up close, the outpost didn't impress Axel: a roof, twenty-foot stone walls, and a large wooden door on the north side, now shut tight. Then again, in such a remote area, perhaps the King didn't need to get fancy with his soldiers' accommodations.

Magnus led them straight to the main gate.

"Alright," Axel said. "We're here. How do we get in?"

Magnus smirked. "Sheathe your sword."

Axel tilted his head. "What? Why?"

"Trust me."

Axel glanced at Calum, who nodded, and he sheathed his sword.

Magnus grabbed Axel by his waistband and hooked his other hand under Axel's armpit. "Grab the edge of the wall."

"What the—" Before he could resist, Axel found himself soaring through the air. Calum and Magnus shrank underneath him as he flew higher, and his heart sank as he began to drop toward the ground, fast.

On his descent, his frantic fingers latched onto the edge of the outpost wall. His thighs slapped the flat stone and he banged his knees hard, but he held on nonetheless—falling would've been a lot worse. He hauled himself up, stood on the edge, and looked down with fire in his veins.

He shook his finger at Magnus. "If you *ever* do that again, I'll—"

"Just find a way inside and open the door for us," Magnus hissed up at him.

Axel scowled but nodded.

By design, the roof didn't connect to all the walls, and an open space about a third the size of the entire building served as a small courtyard. A pair of horses stood in the small stable in the northwest corner, alone in the otherwise empty courtyard.

Axel headed to one of the corners, jumped onto a wooden post that extended upward about three feet from the edge of the wall, and shimmied down. When his boots hit the ground, he

He scurried over to the door and pulled the bolt back to unlock the mechanism. As soon as it disengaged, the door opened, and Magnus and Calum strode inside the outpost.

"Good work." Magnus patted his shoulder. "Come. We have precious little time."

Axel and Calum followed Magnus's lead, and Calum picked up a sword in a rack leaning against one of the courtyard walls. Axel brandished his own, but Magnus held on to his pickax.

They headed into the interior of the outpost via a large door at the top of a wide staircase made of the same gray stone as the exterior walls. The door fed into a main hallway with wooden floors and stone walls.

As soon as they stepped into the hallway, Magnus held up his hand. They stopped and listened for a moment, and Axel heard at least two distinct voices from one of the rooms that lined the hallway.

His voice barely audible, Magnus said, "I will handle them. When I signal you, keep going. Search for the armory and the pantry."

Axel and Calum nodded.

Magnus crouched down low to the floor and hissed.

"What was that?" one of the voices said.

Magnus hissed again.

"Is… is that a snake in here?" another voice asked. "You know I'm terrified of snakes. This some kind of sick joke you're playing on me?"

"Calm yourself," said a third voice, gruffer than the first two. "Rovert probably just forgot to lock the main gate. You know how things just wander in here if you don't—"

"No, I locked the gate. When Brooks came back for more men, I locked it behind him. I remember it distinctly."

Three of them, not two. Axel bit his lip. Could Magnus handle all three?

Sure, he'd battled multiple quarry workers at once, but these weren't average idiots. They were trained soldiers, well-acquainted with violence and fighting.

"You left the gate open, so you take care of the snake, Rovert."

"No way," Rovert said. "What if it's venomous?"

"You're wearing leather boots. With steel studs," the gruff voice replied. "Haven't seen a snake yet that can bite through those."

"I—I don't do well with snakes, either," Rovert said.

A sharp sigh spilled into the hallway. "You have a sword, don't you? Just cut the thing's head off."

"I—I'm not—"

The gruff one cursed. "*Fine*. Come on, Rovert. I'll show you how it's done. Bring your sword, if it's not too *heavy* for you."

Axel's heart rate tripled. He gripped his sword tighter, ready to jump into the fray and help Magnus if he had to. Then he exhaled a calming breath. Better to not let the excitement of the moment get to him.

When the first soldier stepped into the hallway, Magnus clamped his hand around the soldier's ankle and yanked him off his feet. His sword clattered away. The second soldier got Magnus's pickax in his chest.

"Hold him down," Magnus ordered.

Calum and Axel jumped on the first soldier's chest, and Axel pressed his sword against the soldier's neck.

"Don't move. Don't make a sound," Axel said. "You do, and you'll end up like your friends over there."

To his credit, the soldier complied.

Magnus charged into the room and out of sight. A loud gasp followed, then came a dull thud on the wood floor.

The soldier Magnus had killed lay in the doorway with his lifeless brown eyes fixed on Axel and his chest oozing red blood onto the floor. Axel stared at him for a moment then looked away. The sight churned his stomach at first, but that soldier had deserved to die.

Anyone who serves in the King's army deserves death.

Even so, Axel didn't have to keep staring at him.

When Magnus returned, flecks of red blood dotted his neck and torso. He knelt down near the first soldier. "Where is your armory?"

The soldier stared at Magnus with wide eyes. "H-how did you—?"

"Escape?" Magnus leaned close. "Easily. You humans are predictable."

Axel shot Magnus a glare.

"This is one of the soldiers who bought me from the slave traders and sold me to the quarry," Magnus said. "Which also means you have my armor somewhere. So where is your armory?"

"Hopefully he didn't sell it like he sold you." Calum picked up one of the swords from the floor and looked it over as if considering whether to switch it out for the one he'd taken from the courtyard.

"If he did, he will die like his friends, here." Magnus glowered at the soldier, and iron filled his voice. "Must I ask you a third time?"

The soldier shook his head. His gruff voice quivered as he replied, "N-no, we didn't sell it. It's still here. It doesn't fit anyone we've ever run into. It's too big."

"That is because it was made for *me*, not for you or any other human." Magnus nodded to Axel, who pulled his sword back, and then Magnus jerked the soldier to his feet. "Show us. Now."

"What about food?" Calum asked.

"Armor first. It will ensure our safe departure from this place."

He led them to the end of the hall to two staircases, one that led up to the second floor and one that descended to a lower level. Axel glanced into each room they passed to make sure no one would sneak up behind them.

"The armory's downstairs with the cellar and the brig," the soldier said.

"What's upstairs?" Axel asked.

"Our sleeping quarters."

"Anyone up there?" Magnus asked.

"Everyone's out at the—" The soldier squinted at them. "*You* started the fire, didn't you?"

"Smart boy," Magnus said. "Where's your pantry?"

"Upstairs at the opposite end of the hall."

Magnus nodded to Calum and Axel. "Take him upstairs. Have him show you the pantry. Collect all the food and supplies you can carry, then find some rope and restrain him. Once I retrieve my armor, I will rejoin you there."

Calum nodded.

"Do *not* speak to him, and do *not* let him out of your sight. Crystal?"

"Clear." Axel poked the soldier with the tip of his sword, and he jumped. "Let's go."

Upstairs they passed several rooms with bunk beds, all neatly made. One room, smaller than the rest, had only one bed inside, with a large chest sitting at the foot of the bed.

"That's the commander's room," the soldier said.

"Keep quiet." Axel shoved him forward with his free hand. Calum scowled at him, but Axel ignored it.

Sure enough, at the far end of the hall on the right side, they found a room with a small iron stove in the corner and a long table lined with about two dozen chairs. Early morning sunlight filtered in through a window on the left side of the room.

The soldier pointed to a door in the corner opposite of the stove.

"Calum, go check it. I'll watch him."

Calum went over and pulled the door open. "Looks like this is it."

Axel gave the soldier another shove. "You. Help Calum load up a few bags."

While Axel watched, they filled three large sacks with a variety of tasty foods. Ultimately most of the food had come from his farm in the first place, so he figured he was just reclaiming what rightfully belonged to him. It wasn't stealing if it was his to begin with, right?

"You know we'll find you," the soldier threatened. "We'll hunt you down and exact the King's justice upon you for killing two of our own, for burning the King's timber, and for stealing from us. You've tied your own nooses."

"Be quiet," Axel said.

The soldier dropped a pair of apples into a sack. "You get marks for courage, though. I don't know of anyone who has ever dared to rob one of the King's outposts before. No one's ever done it and lived to tell about it, anyway."

"I said *be quiet*." Axel stepped torward him. "Or I'll make you be quiet."

Calum glanced at them but kept stuffing food into his bag.

"And you're doing all of this with a *Saurian*? How can you even stand to be in that thing's company?"

Axel backhanded the soldier's mouth, not out of any sort of love for Magnus, but because he'd warned the soldier twice.

It felt good to hit him. *Really* good.

"*Axel*." Calum glared at him.

"I warned him." Axel stared at the soldier, who held his jaw and glowered at him. "Say another word, and I'll kill you. Crystal?"

The soldier clamped his mouth shut. He wasn't a big guy—probably weighed somewhere between Calum and Axel. Short brown hair, a long scar across his left cheek. Black armor, but no helmet. Maybe in his forties.

What was taking Magnus so long? They'd been in the pantry for awhile now.

Axel glanced out the window. It didn't look like anyone was headed for the outpost, but the longer they tarried, the more likely they'd get caught inside.

"Hey!" Calum's voice snapped Axel back to attention.

The soldier and Calum grappled in the pantry. The sacks dropped and spilled food across the stone floor as the two fought for control. Somehow the soldier managed to wrench Calum's sword away and now held it instead.

He drew his elbow back, ready to impale Calum with the blade.

CHAPTER 12

Axel lurched forward, his sword extended. The blade knifed into the soldier's torso just under his armpit, one of the only openings in his leather armor.

The soldier dropped his sword and cried out, then toppled down to the floor, shuddering but still alive.

Axel adjusted his footing and jammed the sword farther in, and the soldier yelped again.

Calum staggered out of the pantry, almost tripping on one of the sacks as he stared at Axel with wide eyes.

Axel yanked his sword out of the soldier's body and stepped back. The soldier gurgled, and blood oozed down his cheeks.

"That'll shut you up." Axel moved close to the soldier again. Despite all of that, he was still alive.

Axel raised his sword over his head and rammed the tip of his blade through the soldier's leather breastplate and into his chest.

The soldier groaned a final breath and stopped moving. Axel jerked his sword free of the soldier's body and looked back at Calum, who'd clenched his eyes shut. Axel opened his mouth to speak, but a deep voice filled the room.

"What are you doing?"

Axel spun around to face whatever new threat had presented itself.

Instead, Magnus stood in the doorway, his hands full of gear. "What did you do?"

"He attacked Calum, so I killed him." Axel motioned toward the pantry with his head, even though Calum now stood to the side of it.

Magnus set the gear—a variety of weapons, supplies, and even some leather armor—on the table and headed toward them. He looked past Axel at the dead soldier and exhaled a long breath through his nostrils. "Now you know the cruelty of the world in which we live, and you have added to it."

Axel glanced at Calum. Why was Magnus on his case about this? "He was gonna run Calum through."

"You saved your friend's life at the expense of another's." Magnus glanced between him and

Calum. "This is what life on the run is like. Kill or be killed. Our foes will show us no mercy. From now on, every one of the King's soldiers is an enemy to be met only with the edge of your swords. We are all fugitives, all wanted men."

Axel nodded. A rush swelled within him. Traveling, living by the sword—it's what he'd wanted his whole life. "I have no problem with that."

Magnus turned to Calum. "And what about you?"

Calum swallowed. "I can do it too, if I have to."

"Only when necessary," Magnus said. "This man died because you two were careless. He saw an opportunity and overpowered you. Fortunately, Axel reacted first and saved you both."

If there was anything for Axel to feel bad about, it was that he'd let his guard down.

"It's partially my fault," Axel admitted. "I looked away for too long, and that's when he got the advantage."

"Your inattention almost cost Calum his life. I told you to watch the soldier at all times." Magnus shook his head.

"Did you find your armor?" Calum rummaged through the pile of supplies on the table, perhaps to distance himself from the bloody scene Axel had caused.

Magnus exhaled a sigh. "No."

"So where is it?" Axel asked.

Magnus stared at him. "Had you left that soldier alive, we could have asked him again."

Axel folded his arms. "Yeah, well, it was either him or Calum, like I said. I didn't exactly have time to think it through."

"Evidently."

Axel rolled his eyes. In the short time Axel had known him, Magnus had already killed like a dozen people. Why did he keep trying to make Axel feel bad about what he'd done?

Sure, some small part of Axel regretted that he'd had to do it, but the soldier had condemned himself by attacking Calum. Even before that, when he'd joined the King's army. Anyone clad in the black armor of the tyrannical King deserved the same fate, and Axel would happily disburse it to any who dared challenge him.

"The commander's room is next door," Calum said. "There's a big chest inside. Did you check there?"

"Not yet. First, I want each of you to select a couple of weapons from that table. Once we get out of here, I will teach you how to fight. Only take what you can carry along with a bag of food and a pack of supplies."

Axel walked over to the table and perused the assortment. "I think I did pretty well just now with my sword."

Magnus snorted. "I have no intention of arguing with you. If you do not wish to learn anything, I will not waste time teaching you."

Calum picked up a spear. "You know how to use all of these?"

Magnus nodded. "Yes, of course."

"What about this?" Grinning, Axel picked up an axe.

"You will be too slow with that. It is too heavy."

"Doesn't seem too bad." Axel hefted it up and down. It did have some good weight to it, but Axel hadn't worked on a farm all his life to be a weakling. "And you said I could pick whatever I wanted."

"You will both learn the sword either way, so pick a second weapon, and I will teach you that. If there is another spear, I would recommend that. Eventually, you can learn to throw it, and then our hunting problem is solved."

"Alright. Fine." Axel tossed the axe back onto the table, and it clattered to a stop. "Ruin all of my fun."

Calum peered out the window. "Whatever we do, we need to do it quickly. Looks like they're coming back."

Magnus growled and stormed toward the door. "Make your choices now. Find some armor that fits, and load up the bags with food."

Axel scooped up a padded shirt, leather armor, a pair of greaves, some steel-studded gauntlet-style gloves, and corresponding armor for his legs. He put it all on as quickly as he could then tucked a length of rope into the bag. Calum did the same, and then they gathered up what spilled food they could.

As they finished packing, Magnus returned to the kitchen, and despite his feelings toward the Saurian, Axel couldn't help but marvel at the sight.

Magnus wore bright blue armor from his legs up to his neck, plus a helmet clearly designed to fit a Saurian's head. Even his tail had armor, and it was tipped with a long blade. In his right hand he held a sword so large that a strong man would have to wield it with two hands. Its silver hilt gleamed, stark against its iridescent blue blade.

The closer Magnus drew to them, the more detail Axel could see in the armor. Up close, the metal, which matched that of Magnus's blade, had an opalescent sheen to it, and it gleamed with hues of pink and green, depending on how the light hit it. The effect was beautiful, but its application in the armor now covering Magnus's body sent chills through Axel.

"Whoa." Axel gawked at him. "Nice armor."

"It is made from Blood Ore, a rare metal found only in the mountains near my home. Much harder and lighter than steel, but supremely difficult to forge."

"Where'd you get it?" Calum asked.

Magnus clacked his talons on his breastplate and looked past Calum and Axel into the ether. "It was a gift."

Axel blinked. "A gift from...?"

"My father." A low growl rumbled from Magnus's throat. "But he is gone now."

Calum glanced between the two of them. "The breastplate is a work of art."

"And supremely necessary," Magnus said. "Saurians are somewhat naturally armored because of our scales. As we advance in age, they grow stronger and more durable, but even so, our underbellies are weak, hence the utilization of this specific piece of armor."

Axel asked, "If it's made from Blood Ore, then why is it blue?"

"We have little time. Walk with me, and I will explain." Magnus slid his broadsword into a long sheath that ran the length of his back and snatched two of the bags from the table.

He led them to the staircase, and they ventured downstairs again, with Magnus leading the way. Calum followed him, and Axel brought up the rear. It made sense to protect the weakest member of their party in such a way.

"Names can be deceiving," Magnus said to them. "The ore itself is a dark blue color, not red like its name suggests, but the rocks from which it is mined are a blood-red color. Once forged, Blood Ore brightens to the brilliant shade of blue you see here."

"Wow," Calum said as they entered the courtyard.

"We can discuss blacksmithing later," Magnus said. "We have already lingered here too long. We need to reach the cover of the forest before it is too late."

THAT NIGHT, Calum exhaled a long breath when they finally finished setting up the camp.

The three of them had made it back into the forest with their loot just in time to avoid the returning soldiers. Another substantial trek through the woods consumed almost the rest of the day, including a hike along the base of one of the Snake Mountains, which Calum could scarcely stop marveling up at.

Carrying all that extra weight had worked Calum's sore legs more than even the toughest day's work at the quarry. As Calum and Axel began unpacking food around the campfire, Magnus stood and started to walk into the woods, but he left his bag of food at the camp.

The sight surprised Calum, and he started to follow Magnus.

"Where are you going?" The thought that Magnus might leave them alone stirred worry in Calum's chest. "You're, uh… you're coming back, right?"

Magnus stopped, turned back, and looked down at him. "I need some time to myself. Time to meditate."

Calum blinked at him. "Meditate?"

"It means I will silence myself and listen. It is a relaxation technique and a means to connect to a deeper power than what any Saurian can achieve on his own."

"Well, you have fun with that." Axel's scoff sounded all the way from back at the campsite, and Calum inwardly cringed.

Ignoring Axel, Magnus gave Calum a slight nod, then he disappeared into the trees.

About fifteen minutes after Magnus left, Axel said, "He's so weird. He's huge and dangerous, but now he's going off to *meditate*?"

"He's not like us, Axel. He's a Saurian. I'm sure their ways are as different from ours as our appearances."

"I don't understand why he's sticking around with us. Why doesn't he just go?"

"Do you *want* him to go?" Calum countered.

"That's not what I mean." Axel leaned back against a tree and gnawed on an apple.

"Then what do you mean?"

"I don't like him, but from what I can tell, he doesn't like us much either. So why is he still here?"

Calum shrugged and reached for a piece of dried pork. He bit into it, and a tantalizing rush of smoky, meaty flavors teased his tongue. "I don't know. If he wanted to leave, we couldn't stop him."

"That's what I'm afraid of. He could do *whatever* he wanted, and we couldn't stop him."

Calum just shook his head at that, but Axel hadn't been there when Magnus saved him from the Gronyx's pit, or when Calum had given Magnus the chicken leg, or when they'd taken down Jidon and his men together. He wouldn't have the same perspective that Calum did.

Instead of trying to explain all of that to Axel, he asked, "Don't you think he'd have done it by now if he meant us harm?"

"No. He used us to help him get into the Rock Outpost, and now that we've done it, what reason does he have to keep us around? We're some of the only people who know he's on the loose. If he wanted to make sure we didn't talk, he could just kill us."

"But he won't."

Axel sat up. "You don't know that."

"I'm pretty sure, actually," Calum said. "I think we're safe. You have no idea how many times he could have killed me yesterday but didn't. Why would he suddenly want to do it now?"

"Believe whatever you want, but I'm not gonna let my guard down while he's around." Axel folded his arms and leaned back against the tree again. "Not for an instant."

A green foot emerged from behind Axel's tree and stomped the dirt next to him.

Axel jolted forward, groping for his sword, but he couldn't get it out of its sheath. When

Magnus stepped into full view, his blue armor glimmering in the light from the campfire, Axel gave up his struggle.

"I have no desire to harm either of you." Magnus eyed Axel. "Whether you are on your guard or not."

Axel glared at him, and Calum stifled a chuckle.

"Did you save me any food?"

Calum nodded and tossed Magnus the rest of the chunk of pork he'd been gnawing on. Magnus popped the entire piece into his gaping jaws, chomped on it a few times, then swallowed it while Axel recovered his position by the tree, still scowling.

"We have endured a long couple of days," Magnus said. "We will eat, then we will sleep. Tomorrow morning, we must continue our journey."

Calum nodded, though Magnus's words came as little consolation. That night, after the biggest dinner Calum had ever eaten, he fell asleep.

BLINDING LIGHT SHONE EVERYWHERE. Just like the night before, Calum's attempts to shield his eyes proved futile, and again, the light seemed to actually penetrate his body.

The same powerful figure emerged from the light. Same golden crown, same white armor, same silver sword, same gigantic white wings. As before, his eyes flickered like two balls of fire above the white armored mask that covered his nose and mouth.

Again, the sight left Calum dumbfounded.

The circular living map appeared again, first from a wide overhead view, and then much closer as it followed a path from one side of the lakes to the other. As before, it centered on the base of a range of red mountains.

A black hole opened among the red rocks.

"Go, Calum. Find the Arcanum. Set me free." The voice resonated around Calum. *Within* him. "Go, Calum."

Calum shook his head. He still held his hand up to shield his eyes from the light. It still didn't do any good. "I don't understand."

"You will," the voice said. "Go. I am with you. Always."

"Who are you?" Calum asked.

"I am Lumen, General of Light."

CALUM BLINKED and the vision disappeared, except for the bright light. He held up his hand again, but this time he actually blocked the light from reaching his eyes. That didn't make any sense.

He tilted his head and a shadow covered his face. It belonged to one of the many surrounding trees in the forest, and the light, he realized, came from the morning sun. A yawn escaped his throat as he sat up.

"Good morning," said a quiet, but deep voice behind him.

Calum spun around and saw Magnus seated on a tree stump, still clad in his armor except for his helmet. In the morning sunlight, his armor glimmered in glorious shades of light-blue with tinges of pink, green, and even some purple undertones.

Magnus held a finger up to his scaly lips. "Axel is still sleeping."

Calum nodded and rubbed his eyes.

"Sleep well?"

"Yes. No."

Magnus eyed him. "Well, which is it?"

Calum stretched a kink in his neck. Should he tell Magnus about his dream? Or would Magnus think he was crazy?

"It is a simple question, Calum."

"I—" Calum paused. He could tell Magnus. They'd saved each other's lives more than a few times each now. Calum owed him an honest answer, if not much more. "I had a strange dream last night."

"Do you dream often?"

Calum shook his head. "Never. Not since last night."

"Two dreams in as many nights?"

"Yes."

"Interesting."

"It gets even stranger," Calum said. "The dream was almost the same both nights."

Magnus leaned forward. "What did you dream?"

Calum glanced at Axel, who still lay flat on his back, his eyes closed. "A figure appeared to me out of the brightest light I've ever seen. He showed me a map and told me to find some place called the Arcanum to set him free. At first he didn't say who he was, but this time he said his name was Lumen, and he called himself the General of Light."

Magnus straightened his back. His mouth opened, revealing his pointed teeth, but no sound came out.

"What?" Now Calum leaned forward. "Does that mean something to you?"

Magnus blinked at him. "Do you know who Lumen is?"

"Um…" Calum stared at his boots, but they didn't give him an answer.

"Lumen, the General of Light. Do you not know your own race's history? The history of Kanarah itself?"

Calum shook his head. "My parents were killed when I was eight, and I spent the rest of my life in that quarry. There's not much outside of rocks, shovels, pickaxes, and hard work that I know."

Magnus exhaled a long breath. "Then there is much you must learn."

"About what?" Axel sat up and stretched his thick arms toward the sky.

"About the King and Lumen, and their battle a thousand years ago."

Axel tilted his head. "Maybe I should go back to sleep."

Calum could hardly comprehend what Magnus was claiming. "The King is… a thousand years old?"

"Some believe he uses a form of sorcery to prolong his life." Magnus sat back on his stump. "According to legend, a thousand years ago, Lumen rebelled against the King to set humans and the other races free from his tyrannical reign."

Calum looked at Axel, who shrugged.

"At the end of a long and arduous battle, Lumen was defeated. Instead of killing him, though, the King banished him to a secret place—the Arcanum—for a thousand years. Legend says he is still there, waiting to be set free.

"When he is released, he will lead an army to save the people once and for all. *All* people, not just humans." Magnus eyed Calum. "And now, almost a thousand years later, Lumen visited you in a dream not once, but twice."

Axel's head swiveled toward Calum. "What?"

Calum repeated the dream to Axel in more detail than he'd given Magnus, including the locations the living maps had shown. "And he showed me a spot at the base of some red mountains across a huge valley with some lakes—"

"Red mountains?" Magnus extended his hand as if to stall the conversation. "You saw red mountains?"

Calum nodded. "A black hole opened, like the mouth of a cave or something, at the base of some mountains, and they were red. Very red, like blood."

Magnus clacked his talons on his breastplate. "You are right to describe them as blood-red. That is their namesake. They are called the Blood Mountains for exactly that reason."

Calum straightened his spine. The places in his dreams actually existed?

"That is where the name for Blood Ore comes from—the mountains are red, even though the ore itself is blue. The path you referenced is also real, as are the lakes." Magnus waited a moment. When Calum didn't say anything, Magnus asked, "Surely you have heard of the Tri-Lakes?"

Calum shook his head.

"I've heard of them," Axel said. "Some of the King's soldiers were talking about them one night at the tavern. Said they're massive, and they're full of dangerous creatures, but the surrounding valley is dead. Nothing lives or grows there."

Magnus nodded. "That much is true."

"How do you know?" Calum asked.

"I have been there," Magnus said.

Silence hovered between them.

"The Valley of the Tri-Lakes connects the eastern half of Kanarah, where we are now, to the western half." Magnus stoked the campfire with a stick. "It is there you will find the Blood Mountains, home to my people. The city of Reptilius sits among the highest peaks in the mountain range. That is where the Saurians live."

Axel glanced at Calum. "So why aren't you there now?"

Magnus's eyes narrowed, then he exhaled a long breath and looked away.

After a long pause, Calum leaned forward. "Magnus?"

"I do not believe your dreams are coincidental or meaningless," Magnus said.

Axel rolled his eyes. "Or they're just dreams."

"Unlikely. The King himself foretold that Lumen would be released at the end of the thousand years." Magnus looked at Calum. "Though no one knows how. No one knows where Lumen is locked away. No one has had any idea—until now."

Calum's eyes widened. "You mean..."

"Yes." Magnus focused his gaze. "Calum, you may hold the key to setting Lumen free and saving all of Kanarah from the King's oppression."

CHAPTER 13

Western Kanarah

Lilly had succeeded in keeping Sharion from harm, but doing so had cost her. Roderick had personally assured her that the pair of rusty old shackles now clamped to her ankles would remain on not only while she rode in the wagon but also during trips to the woods to relieve herself. They would stay on her all the time, no exceptions.

What's more, Roderick informed Lilly that he would now personally oversee her trips to the woods—to protect his "investment." She didn't like how he smirked when he told her, but it was worlds better than enduring the threat of his men every time she had to answer nature's call.

As much as she hated to admit it, her life as a slave had settled into a miserable routine. The caravan drew nearer and nearer to Trader's Pass, carrying her farther and farther away from her home.

The night after she'd saved Sharion, she and Colm huddled close together, as always, to stay warm. Sharion had snuck closer to them as well, ever-willing to steal warmth yet never willing to ask for it or accept it when offered.

Then a chorus of loud whoops and hollers sounded from the forest around them, wresting Lilly from the relative safety and tranquility of the moment.

"What is that?" Lilly whispered, shuddering.

"None of your concern, child," Colm replied. "Try to rest. Tomorrow is another long day of travel. We should make Trader's Pass by midday."

The shouts eventually stopped, but about a half hour later, Roderick and several of his men appeared from the moonlit woods. They dragged a net behind them.

Inside, a black form thrashed and snapped at their hands, snarling and growling.

At first they headed toward Lilly's wagon with the thing, but instead of putting the creature into the wagon with Colm, Sharion, and Lilly, they tossed the thrashing pile of net and beast into a separate wagon far behind hers. Lilly caught sight of a pair of angry blue eyes before the beast disappeared out of sight.

She nudged Colm, who remained fixed on the pro ion, "What is that?"

"A Wolf, I suppose."

"They caught a Wolf?" Lilly gawked. "How? I've heard they can move like shadows through the darkness."

"Apparently you've never met one, then. Surely, there are many who can do as you say, but some are as incapable as the average human or Windgale." Colm coughed into the crook of his elbow. "Catching a Wolf for this bunch isn't that impressive. Not long before they seized you, they managed to capture a Saurian. Now *that's* a feat not easily accomplished."

Colm had seemingly only ever told Lilly the truth, but she had serious doubts about his claim. "These idiots managed to subdue a Saurian?"

"That they did," Colm replied plainly. "Now would you bless me with a few hours of sleep before the night ends? I don't sleep as well once the sun comes up."

"Sure. Sorry."

"No trouble. Just shift a bit closer, will you, child? This batch of night air chills me more than usual."

Lilly wrapped her arm around Colm's back and pulled closer. She leaned her head on his shoulder with her eyes closed and drifted off to sleep once more.

COLM HAD BEEN RIGHT. They reached Trader's Pass by midday, but before they headed into the pass, Roderick and Luggs let Lilly and Sharion relieve themselves in the ever-sparse woods.

"Enjoy the scenery while it lasts." Luggs chuckled. "From here on out, it's flat and gray."

Lilly ducked behind a bush so her lower half wouldn't be visible to the men. Sharion did the same right beside her. By now Lilly had adjusted to having to share space, but she still didn't like it.

Sharion remained an enigma. She seemed lucid about half the time, and the other half she scratched her scalp and mumbled nonsense. She'd made no mention of Lilly saving her from enduring Adgar, Gammel, and Luggs's abuse. Perhaps she didn't comprehend what Lilly had done or why she'd done it.

As they walked back toward Roderick and Luggs, Lilly said, "Sharion, I—"

"Don't speak to me. Don't you *dare* speak to me." Sharion hissed her words.

Lilly clamped her mouth shut. *Alright, then.*

While on her way back to the wagon, Lilly saw Gammel and Adgar escorting a lithe black animal toward the woods as well. The Wolf. She wore a muzzle over her snout, and each of the men guided her with ropes looped around her neck attached to the long poles they held. Her blue eyes locked on Lilly as they passed each other, and she issued a low growl.

Not a day for making friends, apparently.

Luggs escorted Lilly and Sharion back to the wagon while Roderick stayed in the woods to keep watch. As Luggs opened the door to the wagon, a howl and a series of snarls sounded from the woods.

"Look out! She's loose!" Gammel shouted.

As Luggs turned toward the commotion, Lilly seized her chance. She grabbed the cage door and yanked it open. Luggs turned back in time for the metal bars to smash into his forehead, and he dropped, stunned and bleeding from a nasty gash above his eyebrows.

Lilly wrenched the keys from the lock and fingered through them until she found one that she thought matched her shackles. Within seconds, she was free. Lucky guess.

"Here." She tossed the key ring to Colm and then bolted up the road, past the other wagons and away from Trader's Pass. By now she'd gotten good at this running thing, and she'd even begun to enjoy it. Arrows thudded into the dirt around her as she ran, but she didn't stop. She couldn't stop.

She'd run forever if she had to.

The men shouted behind her, but she didn't dare turn back. It would only slow her down.

A patch of trees beckoned her forward. Not much, but it beat heading into the barren gray surrounding Trader's Pass where they could easily see her.

She ran deep into the trees. They ended some fifty yards ahead and opened into a clearing of some sort. Based on what she'd seen while running to the trees, it didn't look like it was a drop-off like she'd encountered before. She hoped to find more trees and more woods farther beyond.

Lilly cleared the woods and stumbled into a small field of tall grass. The footsteps of the men behind her still thundered, but she'd put more distance between them. Without the cover of the trees to hide, though, they'd soon find her.

She breathed quick shallow breaths, and her heart drummed. She had to keep running, or she had to hide. The grass was tall, but not tall enough that she could hide. They'd see her if they came within ten feet of her position—maybe as little as five if she were lucky. But if she could make the tree line across the field, perhaps she could lose them.

Her legs burned and her stomach growled for food, but her resolve pushed her forward nonetheless. She bolted into the grass.

"There she is!" a voice shouted, followed by a chorus of rallying cries from even farther behind her.

Lilly kept running.

Halfway into the field, she tripped over something. A boulder. She skidded through the grass and it bit into her knees and her palms.

She chanced a look back. She couldn't see the men following her, but she could hear them. So much for her growing lead.

Lilly leaped up to her feet and kept running. The tree line drew ever nearer. She was going to make it. The wind whipped her face and cooled her perspiring forehead as she practically flew forward—even though running could never compare to the sheer exhilaration of flying.

Thirty yards from the trees, she heard the first metallic thunk, then the second soon after. Heavy, armored footsteps clanked behind her, growing closer, louder with each stride she took. She clenched her teeth and pushed forward even harder, but the sound persisted.

With fifteen yards to go, Roderick's massive form appeared in her peripheral vision as he ran alongside her. He even gave her a wave and a toothy smile. How was he so fast? It should've been impossible.

Lilly cursed and tried to dart to her right, away from him, but he clamped down on her wrist with his gloved hand and slowed them to a halt. She swung her fist at his face. He easily blocked the punch with his forearm and shoved her down onto her back in the grass.

"Why won't you let me go?" she screamed. Tears burned her eyes, and she kicked and punched at him, all to no avail. "I just want to go home!"

"Three escape attempts in what, three days' time?" Roderick whistled. "It all runs together out here in the wilds. I'm tempted just to cut you loose."

Roderick snatched her up, his arms wrapped around hers, restraining her while she thrashed and twisted and tried to break free until she couldn't anymore. Her fight gave way to miserable sobs as he started walking back toward the wagons with her in his restraining embrace.

"Then do it!" Her voice no louder than a pained whisper, she repeated, "I just want to go home."

"You already know that's not how this works, Angel." Roderick shook his spike-haired head.

"I'm selling you to an old friend of mine, a longtime client. You're gonna belong to him; but until then, you belong to me. Get used to it."

Lilly bowed her head and whimpered.

COLM HELD LILLY CLOSE, stroking her hair while she sobbed into his shoulder. "There, there, child. Breathe deeply. All will be well."

Lilly jerked upright, filled with rage. She glared at him.

"No, it *won't* all be well, Colm." She wiped the tears from her cheeks. "Roderick means to sell me to some pig friend of his, and every time I try to escape, somehow they catch me. Roderick is faster, stronger, and probably smarter than me, and he knows this area better than I do. I'm doomed to be a slave forever."

She buried her face in his shoulder again and heaved. The wagon jerked forward onto Trader's Pass.

"I'm afraid this new life is one to which you may need to adjust, child."

That was the last thing Lilly wanted to hear. A shudder racked her body, and the sickening twist of hopelessness infected her stomach once again. She released her grasp on Colm, sat up, and wiped the last of the tears from her eyes.

"While I greatly admire your tenacity, there does not seem to be any escape without them noticing or without them catching you again. Were I a younger man, I would fight for your honor and try to buy you time to escape, but these days I'm old, tired, and slow. I'd be a leaf attempting to dam a mighty river."

"If I had my armor and my cape, I could fly out of here. I would fly until they were out of sight, and I'd never look back." Lilly ground her teeth, focusing on calming her breathing next. "If I had my bow, I'd take a few of them down first, before I left. Luggs, Adgar, Gammel. Roderick too, if I had the shot."

"Easy, child. Vengeance is a path from which there is no return."

"It wouldn't be vengeance. It'd be justice. I'm not the only one they've hurt."

"The line between the two is often very thin and easy to cross." He smiled at her. "Forgive me for arguing, but I would hate to see such a beautiful soul blackened by thoughts of revenge."

"If I don't act, my soul will be blackened by something else." Lilly narrowed her eyes at him. "And why don't you want revenge for how they've treated you? You're locked in here, the same as me. You never get angry about anything."

Colm sighed. "Make no mistake, I do not want to be here. Nor do I know the reason why I'm here. But I know the Overlord watches me, and He has sustained me thus far, even in my current circumstance. I believe I am here, now, for a purpose. Perhaps to fulfill some greater good."

Lilly stared at him. *The Overlord wanted Colm here? Unlikely.* "You're locked in a cage. Wouldn't the Overlord rather see you set free to do more good?"

"I don't deny that a part of me wishes that were the case, but when freed I tend to make my way through Kanarah with little reservation about whom I harm in the process. I am a thief, child. Not the most honorable profession, nor the most charitable." He smiled. "But here, I have no choice but to behave and to do good things for my fellow slaves. And if I do steal, it's from people who deserve to be stolen from, and never solely for my benefit."

She frowned. "You have to be locked up to become a good person?"

"Isn't that the idea behind locking people up? To encourage them to become better people?" Colm winked at her.

Back at her home, criminals found within the Sky Realm were tried, convicted, stripped of their capes, and locked in cells under the Aeropolis. To her knowledge, once released, those same criminals almost always returned to their illicit behaviors, with or without their capes. She had no idea how they behaved while imprisoned, though.

"Either way, there's a good chance they still have your armor and your cape stashed somewhere. Probably in one of the smaller wagons without bars, the ones with two wheels and pulled by donkeys instead of horses.

"I've seen them loading and unloading other merchandise to sell, and your armor was quite nice. I imagine Roderick would keep it for its resale value, especially if your cape is aerosilk like you said it was. Plenty of Windgales in Eastern Kanarah would buy an extra cape if they could."

That gave Lilly hope. If she could get out, then perhaps she could get ahold of her cape, at least, if not her armor and her bow as well, and then get out of there. Now that she knew where she needed to look, maybe she could find a way.

She set her face once more and tightened her jaw. She *would* find a way.

"Luggs is pretty sour." Colm chuckled. "Big gash on his forehead. Not a pretty sight. 'Course, he wasn't particularly handsome to begin with."

Lilly smirked.

"Here." Colm glanced around, then under the draping of his cloak, he handed her a roasted drumstick from a chicken's leg.

"Your coin?" Lilly smiled at him.

Colm nodded. "I already ate the thigh. I hope you don't mind. I'm an old man and don't get such delicacies often."

Lilly wrapped her arms around his neck and squeezed him. "Thank you."

CHAPTER 14

Eastern Kanarah

A xel rubbed the bridge of his nose and clenched his eyes shut. He was still processing everything that Calum had shared and Magnus had explained, and he wasn't sure he believed or agreed with any of it.

"So your plan for us is to head toward the Valley of the Tri-Lakes, cross it, and find a secret cave at the base of the Blood Mountains so we can release a legendary warrior who's going to defeat the King and free us from his tyrannical reign once and for all?" Axel opened his eyes and folded his arms. "And you're getting all of this from a couple of dreams?"

Magnus glanced at them both and nodded. "Yes. That is precisely what I am saying."

"Right." Axel rolled his eyes. What had he gotten himself into? "I knew I should have turned you two in when I had the chance."

"Do you have something better in mind?" Magnus asked. "Or do you prefer to wander the wilderness aimlessly for the rest of our lives?"

"Well, I wasn't planning on wasting my life searching for something that isn't there." Axel nodded at Magnus. "And besides, what's in this for you? You got your armor and your sword back. Why do you even care?"

"Saurians view the return of Lumen not as a myth but as truth, a prophecy to be fulfilled. We have suffered at the hands of the King's soldiers as well, albeit not for several centuries now. Still, the King has done my people great harm over the years.

"We believe that Lumen's return and subsequent rise to the throne of Kanarah will bring about a time of peace and prosperity our land has never before seen, so we have been waiting, watching, and counting the years until his return. It appears our count was off by a few years, but his return is nonetheless imminent." Magnus clicked his claws against his breastplate. "Besides, my home is in the Blood Mountains. I wish to see it again."

"So what happens when we get there? Are you just gonna leave us in the mountains on our own?" Axel folded his arms again.

"I do not intend to."

"So you'll just walk us up to the gates of Reptile City and introduce us to all your scaly friends?"

"*Reptilius*." Magnus corrected him with a huff. "You need only concern yourself with finding Lumen."

"*If* he's even there."

"He's there." Calum leaned forward. "These dreams felt so real, Axel."

"I've had dreams that felt real, too, but that doesn't mean I went out and acted on them the next morning." Axel smirked and rubbed his hands together. "Although, if we're thinking about pursuing what happens in our dreams, the other night I dreamed about this gorgeous brunette I met in a town I visited with my father last year..."

"I see no other explanation for his dreams than the one I have provided," Magnus said. "It makes sense. Lumen's return is near, and with it, the salvation of Kanarah."

"Except you said no one was supposed to know how Lumen comes back or where he is."

"I have awaited Lumen's return for decades, and my people have awaited his return since the war itself. Many Saurians believe he will bring true freedom to Kanarah." Magnus pointed southwest. "The answers lie within that cave. Within the Arcanum."

Axel rolled his eyes. "Just two nights ago you said going into caves was a bad idea."

Magnus glared at him. "You know what I mean. All we have to do is visit it, and then we will know."

"Yeah, we'll know that there's nothing there worth finding." Axel scoffed. "And that's *if* we even make it there in the first place. We can't just waltz along the roads and stop at local towns and villages with Scales here out in the open. Won't be long before someone catches up with us, especially the farther south we go, toward more populated cities."

"We will stick to the mountains, to the woods. We can try to descend into the valley from the range if we can find a safe path down, though that may prove impossible." Magnus scanned the forest and scraped his talons across his breastplate. "Once I have trained you to properly use your weapons, the entire journey will get easier."

Calum nodded. "When do we start?"

Magnus refocused on him. "The training? Or the trip?"

"Both."

"Whoa, hold on." Axel held up his hands. This was moving pretty fast for a crazy idea. Then again, most crazy ideas he'd ever heard or come up with tended to move pretty fast as well—it's just that they usually died out fast, too. This one seemed to be gaining momentum. "I never agreed to go along with this. I don't think it's a good use of our time."

"I don't have anywhere else to be. Nothing else to do." Calum looked at him. "Axel, how long have you wanted to get out and see the world? If we free Lumen—if he's real—then you'll get your chance to do exactly that. Plus, we'll be on the move frequently, which means we'll be that much harder to catch."

"I have been absent from my home for too long." Magnus gazed toward the west. "And if we find Lumen, if we can set him free, then we can change Kanarah forever. We will no longer have to flee from the King's men."

Calum and Magnus stared at Axel.

He sighed and folded his arms again. This was a colossally stupid idea, but Calum was right about one thing: Axel didn't have any other plans, nor did he have somewhere else to be. This path would take him on an adventure, at least, and for now, that could be enough.

"Fine," he said. "You two want to go on your little quest? I guess I'll come along to make sure you're safe."

"Speaking of which," Magnus said. "Both of you, grab your swords. It's time for your first lesson. After that, we eat breakfast, then we get on the move."

"Can't we eat breakfast first?" Axel rubbed his stomach.

"Certainly. Calum and I will go through some basics while you prepare breakfast."

Axel frowned. "That's not what I had in mind."

"You are doubtless acclimated to awakening to breakfast on the table, thanks to your mother, but she is not here." Magnus smirked. "I would have packed her, but we were in such a rush…"

"Yeah, yeah. I get it." Axel glared at him. "Just so you know, I hate cooking, so eat at your own risk."

"In addition to combat training, reading, writing, and history, I will teach you both how to cook. The women in your futures—if any are magnanimous enough to tolerate you—will thank me for it." Magnus turned to Calum. "Come over here. Let us begin."

THE LESSON CAME AND WENT, as did breakfast, more lessons, and lunch. That afternoon, just when Calum was getting the hang of swordplay, Magnus announced it was time to head out. With Magnus in the lead, the trio traveled southwest toward the heart of the Snake Mountains.

Days passed, then weeks. Calum's dreams of Lumen persisted. Lumen kept reminding Calum that his time was near and that he'd soon return, but only with Calum's help. Despite the rough terrain, dwindling food supplies, and even less rest than he'd had at the quarry, Calum pressed onward, galvanized by Lumen's call.

The terrain at the edge of the Snake Mountain range proved as unforgiving as Magnus had suggested. Vegetation struggled to grow in the rocky ground, and they hadn't seen many animals, either. It reminded Calum of the desolate interior of the quarry.

Likewise, the Valley of the Tri-Lakes far below resembled a desert of grays with three massive pools of shimmering water spread across the land under the midday sun. Calum could only see two of the three lakes, but Magnus said there was a third much farther south.

After a fourth day of fruitlessly searching for a feasible route down into the valley, they set up camp about forty feet from the edge of the cliff separating them from the valley below.

Magnus shook his head and gulped down his last bite of smoked venison. "It is as I suspected; I do not believe we can find a way down after all."

Calum sighed. The journey thus far had exhausted him. Whenever they weren't hiking, they were training. And whenever they weren't training, they were hiking. And whenever they weren't hiking or training, Magnus made good on his promise to teach them to read and write, courtesy of sticks and symbols—letters—drawn into the dirt to form words.

As a result, Calum had no trouble falling asleep every night, but dreams of Lumen often woke him early. Whenever they did, he found it harder to fall back to sleep afterward.

"So what does that mean?" he asked.

"It means we must head to Kanarah City," Magnus replied. "That is the starting point for Trader's Pass, the only true path through the valley."

The idea of visiting a city, particularly one as big as Kanarah City, excited Calum, but it also worried him. If the King's soldiers were still searching for the three of them, a city might not be the best place to visit. "Where is that?"

"About a month's walk south. It would be less on a road, so I am factoring in the terrain."

"We'll never make it there in time. We'll run outta food long before then." Axel folded his arms. "Sure, we could hunt with the spears if there was anything around here worth hunting, but I haven't seen so much as a squirrel in the last four days. We gotta head east and either hunt in the woods or trade in a nearby village."

Calum raised an eyebrow. "Yesterday, you said you won't go into a village with Magnus."

"I *did* say that, and I meant it, too. But you and I can still try to come up with."

"Axel is right," Magnus said. "Someone will need to watch our supplies anyway. I am happy to oblige. Either way, you two are capable enough now that I can trust you on your own."

"Got that right." Axel smirked. "So we head east tomorrow?"

"Southeast," Magnus corrected. "Yes."

"Works for me," Calum replied.

They sat in silence for a few minutes and watched their pitiful campfire dwindle even smaller. Calum finally spoke up. "So I think I'm definitely better at throwing the spear than Axel, but I'm not as good at fighting with it as he is."

Axel rolled his eyes. "Whatever. I'm better at both, and you know it."

Magnus just stared into the darkness toward the east, away from the cliff. Calum expected he'd weigh in, but he hadn't. Perhaps he was just lost in thought, or reliving another dark memory from his past, none of which he'd ever discussed with them in meaningful detail.

Or perhaps it was something else entirely.

Calum leaned toward him. "Magnus?"

"*Quiet*," he hissed. "Something is out there."

A low growl sounded over the crackling of the dying campfire, and Calum's heart smacked against the inside of his chest. He still couldn't see anything, but the sound had come from the darkness only a few yards away from their position.

Axel slowly pulled his sword from its sheath, and Calum did the same with his own.

Another growl sounded, then another. Then three more.

"Sabertooths." Magnus latched his helmet onto his head and drew his huge broadsword.

"What?" Calum tried to make eye contact with him, but Magnus didn't divert his vision away from the darkness.

"Sabertooth tigers. Wild cats. Big ones. Carnivorous." Magnus exhaled a long breath through his nostrils. "On your feet, boys. Do not back away from them, no matter what. Stand your ground and fight."

Calum nodded. He could do this. He could defend himself. He'd survived a fall into the Gronyx's pit, after all. He'd battled quarry workers, and he'd raided the Rock Outpost. Remembering those things gave him courage, despite the hammering in his heart.

A set of large feline eyes flickered in the darkness. Then another. Then another. Then another. Then another…

Calum counted twelve sets of shining eyes before the first cat emerged.

An orange-and-black blur with large fangs leaped toward Magnus, who reacted with clean alacrity. He both sidestepped the cat and swung his broadsword at once, and the vicious blow knocked the cat off its trajectory. It skidded along the rocky dirt away from the campsite until it stopped against a boulder, motionless, with a devastating wound along its flank.

Eleven to go.

The other cats all charged at once. Wide-eyed, Calum sidestepped the first just like Magnus and the cat flew past. It clawed at the dirt as it slipped over the edge of the cliff and disappeared, roaring the whole way down.

But Calum couldn't have avoided the next cat no matter what he did. Its gigantic fangs just missed Calum's head as it tackled him to the ground with its front paws. The fangs had to be at least a foot long, if not more.

Up close, it smelled like rancid meat and the stink of nature gone sour. The cat was gaunt yet powerful, doubtless even more desperate than Calum and the others for a good meal. And if Calum didn't do something soon, he'd *become* the meal.

Calum tried to push the cat off him, but that proved impossible. He wasn't nearly strong enough, and the cat had dug its claws into Calum's leather chest armor, anchoring itself in place.

As the cat leaned its huge head toward his face, Calum plunged his sword into the side of the cat's neck. The cat stiffened and dropped on its side, off of Calum.

He'd done it. He'd actually killed one of them.

No time to celebrate. A third and a fourth cat charged at him, one right after another.

Instead of standing his ground like Magnus said, Calum stepped forward before the front cat could jump, timed his swing, and took it out with a vicious hack to its head. It was a trick he'd used on Axel a few times when they were sparring, and it was one of the only ways he'd managed to win so far.

Axel might've been stronger, but Calum was just a little bit faster.

But there was only ever *one* of Axel to spar with. Calum still had another cat to deal with.

He spun away to avoid the next cat, but by the time he repositioned, the cat reared up on its hind legs and swiped at his head. Calum wasn't fast enough to dodge the blow, but his reflexes brought his left forearm up in time to block the blow.

Sharp pain flared in his forearm as the cat's claws punctured through the thick leather armored gauntlet, and Calum winced. Better there than his unprotected head, but he'd paid the price all the same. The swipe also knocked him off-balance, but he quickly recovered his footing and held his sword at the ready.

The cat rose up on its hind haunches to swipe at him again, but this time Calum ducked low and jammed his blade up into the cat's chest. It toppled to Calum's left and lay still in the dirt.

Magnus's training had served him well. He hadn't hesitated, he hadn't been afraid. He'd just done what he had to do.

No more cats charged him, but two of them now circled Axel. Not good.

Calum hollered and ran toward the nearest one. It turned and pounced at him faster than he expected, but he managed to raise his sword and intercept its fangs with a loud clang.

Even so, the blow sent him reeling backward. His right foot caught on something and he landed on his back. His sword tumbled away, and as Calum groped for it, the cat mounted him with its fangs angled toward his head.

Calum shifted his torso hard to the left, and the fangs dug into the ground instead of his face. When Calum grabbed onto them with his hands, the cat roared and shook his head, shaking Calum along with it.

It swiped at Calum with both of its front paws and tried to pull him off, but he didn't let go, even when the cat's claws latched onto his right shoulder pad and wrenched him downward.

Calum yelled as the cat thrashed him about. He timed it just right and released his grip on one of the cat's more vigorous jerks, freeing him from the entirety of its weight for just a second.

He rolled toward his sword, scooped it into his right hand, twisted back toward the cat, and jammed it between the fangs, into the cat's gaping mouth. The cat stopped mid-lunge and dropped chin-first, but its upper half pinned Calum's legs to the ground.

Now another cat approached him, snarling. Its spotted face contorted as it spread its jaws wide and roared at him.

Calum yanked the sword from the dead cat's mouth and tried to push it off of him, but he couldn't. Was he really so weak that he couldn't even free himself from the carcass of a dead animal? Was that weakness going to be the death of him?

He managed to wrest one of his legs free, and he pushed with all his might to pull the other one loose, but he was already too late.

As the other cat shifted its weight against its back legs and sprang toward him, all Calum could do was raise his sword in a feeble attempt to fend it off.

CHAPTER 15

A green-and-blue blur rammed the cat from the side and sent it spiraling toward the cliff's edge.

Magnus.

Calum exhaled the breath he'd taken in.

The cat's claws stopped its momentum before it reached the drop-off. It righted itself, snarled, and charged Magnus, but he sidestepped again and grabbed one of its fangs with his free hand. He pulled the cat close, swiped its front legs out from under it with his tail, and raised his sword. In one hearty blow he severed the cat's head from its body and held it in his hand.

Axel skewered the last cat through its eye with his sword and a victorious yell. The cat slumped to the ground, and Axel looked around. "That's it? No more?"

"What, not enough for you?" Calum, with one leg still pinned under the dead cat, sucked in some quick breaths. He pushed against it with his other leg until he managed to pull his leg free.

Only when Calum stood to his feet and surveyed the aftermath of the battle did it truly hit him that they'd made it—that *he'd* made it. He'd used what Magnus had taught him, and he'd survived.

Sure, his left forearm was bleeding, and constantly getting knocked down had left his head aching, but he'd made it through.

Axel gave a mischievous grin. "I was having fun."

"Good work, you two." Magnus scanned the darkness around their campsite, then he tossed the sabertoothed cat's head near his spot by the fire.

"Thanks." Calum wiped the blood from his sword on the hide of the nearest dead cat. "So do we just leave these carcasses here, or what?"

"I wanna know if we can eat these things," Axel said. "I mean, it's not my first choice, but I'm pretty hungry."

"I have never tasted the flesh of this beast," Magnus started, "but drag this headless one over to the fire. Perhaps the smell of one of their own burning will serve to repel others, and perhaps we may find them to be edible. I am going to do a quick check of the surrounding area."

As HE WALKED into the main hall of the Rock Outpost, Commander Beynard Anigo could hear the men discussing Commander Pordone's death in hushed tones. It signaled a lack of respect, both for the situation and for the dead, and it represented one of many issues he would doubtless have to correct if he intended to complete his mission efficiently.

The moment Commander Anigo presented himself to the soldiers, all of whom had gathered before the stone fireplace in the common room, they went quiet.

Good, he mused. *They aren't completely lacking in discipline.*

"Greetings, fellow soldiers of the King," he addressed them. "I am Commander Beynard Anigo. In light of Commander Pordone's untimely demise and the business he left unfinished—namely the treason of two quarry workers and one farmhand—I have been sent here as a replacement to see that justice is served."

None of them said anything in response, nor did they dare to move. Perhaps Pordone hadn't been so lax in his standards for them after all.

Ever since their time together in the officers' academy in Solace, Commander Anigo had never liked Pordone, but he certainly hadn't wished injury upon him, either. However, more than mere injury had found him nonetheless.

The order he'd received a week earlier detailed the escape of two workers from the quarry and one from a family farm nearby. In the ensuing escape, worker casualties mounted, and Commander Pordone had sustained a fatal injury—a fall from his horse in the woods that broke his neck. The horse had died as well, courtesy of Pordone's own spear, as thrown by one of the escaping workers.

"The loss of one such as Commander Pordone is tragic, but it pales in comparison to the escape of the three fugitives responsible for this tragedy," he continued. "It has been made clear to me that our priority is the capture and return of these fugitives directly to Solace for trial and sentencing in the King's courts.

"As your new commander, I am authorized to modify the terms of these orders as they pertain to the situation at hand. Given the violent natures and actions of these fugitives, I hereby declare it also permissible that they be executed in the King's name should they refuse to comply with our orders."

He studied each of their faces. Some of them nodded, others remained still as statues, and still others stared at the floor.

Commander Anigo noted the bloodstained wooden slats both near the hearth and under his own boots—evidence of the escaped workers' incursion into this base—and frowned. The men who'd perished in those spots had died carelessly, and the men who'd tried to clean up the mess had been equally careless.

It disgusted him.

All of it.

The idea of leaving his cushy assignment in Solace, Kanarah's capital city, to serve as commander in this backwater province filled his veins with fury. He hadn't labored his whole career, serving at the pleasure of the King in hunting down the most egregious offenders and bringing them to justice, to be reduced to... *this.*

All that work, all of his successes wiped away by one order, one command relegating him to this rural nightmare. It was disgraceful. Demeaning. And he'd done *nothing* to warrant such treatment. Nothing whatsoever.

Yet here he was, all the same.

He clenched his fists and tensed his jaw.

But Commander Anigo had always prided himself on thriving based only on his needs, not his wants. He would make do here, in the middle of nowhere, and once he completed his mission, he would doubtless be welcomed back to Solace as a hero, a crusader who had righted the great wrongs inflicted upon this miserable place.

He let his hands and his jaw relax.

"That is all for now," he concluded. "See to it that these floors are cleaned of blood yet again, as they did not receive proper attention the first time. Our search begins tomorrow at dawn, and no later. Anyone who delays us will be whipped for the duration of time he makes me wait."

Commander Anigo strode up the stairs and found Pordone's room—now *his* room. Despite the relative chaos of the last weeks, the bed was made, the floors were clean, and afternoon sunshine streamed through the solitary window. It might've been that Pordone left it in this state before his demise.

The only thing off about the room was the chest at the foot of the bed, whose top stood open rather than being shut. A minor inconvenience, given the circumstances.

He walked forward and tipped the chest's lid forward. Its hinges squeaked as it fell into place and clomped shut, restoring the room to its otherwise acceptable state.

Acceptable, not comfortable.

Needs, not wants.

"Commander Anigo?" a soldier asked from behind him.

He turned around.

The soldier saluted, smiling. "I'm Corporal Bezarion. I dispatched the messenger to Solace as soon as we returned from our search."

"And?" Commander Anigo removed his gauntlets and handed them to the corporal.

"Sir?" Corporal Bezarion tilted his head as he received the gauntlets.

"Am I to commend you for doing your duty, soldier?"

"N-no, sir," Corporal Bezarion replied. "I just figured you'd—"

"Let me make one thing perfectly clear to you, Corporal." Commander Anigo approached Bezarion, who stood two inches shorter than him. When they stood face-to-face, Commander Anigo continued. "You are never to 'figure' anything as far as I am concerned. You will obey orders, and you will do so with haste.

"Assumptions and a lackadaisical attitude toward enforcing the King's law is what landed us in this dismal situation in the first place. Such blatant carelessness is reprehensible and a stain upon the reputation of the King's army. It ends today, with my arrival to this outpost. Crystal?"

Corporal Bezarion nodded. "Clear, sir. Perfectly."

"I will take my supper in my room this evening." The last leg of Commander Anigo's journey from Solace had worn both him and his horse out, though he had no inclination to explain that to Corporal Bezarion or the other soldiers. He added, "Immediately."

Corporal Bezarion glanced at the window and the afternoon sunlight aglow from it. "Apologies, sir, but it is still quite early. Dinner has not yet been—"

"I don't care to repeat myself, Corporal." Commander Anigo stared steel at him. "Ever."

Corporal Bezarion nodded again, this time more frantically. "My apologies again, sir. I'll have it prepared for you right away."

Commander Anigo shook his head and sat on the bed, again lamenting his appointment to this miserable place.

Needs, not wants, he reminded himself. *Needs, not wants.*

AT DAWN THE NEXT MORNING, Commander Anigo headed down to the courtyard. His horse, a white stallion he'd named Candlestick, munched on a bag of oats near a water trough with the other horses, already packed with provisions and weapons for their journey into the wild.

If nothing else, at least Commander Anigo had Candlestick with him, here in this backwoods province. Even if he couldn't trust anyone else, he knew Candlestick wouldn't let him down.

To their credit, the soldiers already awaited him with packs in tow and swords sheathed at their sides. Disheveled as they were, given the early hour, they snapped to attention upon his command.

"We will not return until our mission is complete. Mount up, if you have horses." He raised his fist and said, "For the King."

The soldiers shouted the second half of the mantra back at him, "May he forever reign!"

Commander Anigo turned toward the open gates of the Rock Outpost and stared into the wild forest beyond.

The fugitives' time was limited. He would soon find them, and he would bring them to justice.

THE NEXT MORNING, Calum woke up first and stretched his sore limbs. He sat up and checked the gouges in his forearm, which had crusted over in the night. He'd survive.

Axel moaned and pushed himself up to a sitting position. "It smells terrible around here. The cats must be starting to rot."

The remaining cat carcasses still lay around the camp where they'd been slain.

Calum wrinkled his nose at the stench and nodded. "At least we didn't get attacked again."

Axel grunted and muttered something, but Calum couldn't understand even a single word. "What do we have left for breakfast?"

"I think we had a bit of smoked venison left, and maybe a couple of potatoes." Calum scanned the campsite for the bag of food but didn't see it. Maybe it had been moved during the fight. "We definitely need to hunt today, unless you want to eat rotting sabertooth cat meat."

"No thanks." Axel stuck his tongue out. "Give me my spear any day, and I'll get us something. After breakfast, at least. Where's the food?"

Still sitting, Calum looked around again and shrugged. "I don't know. Maybe Magnus moved it."

"Well, get up and help me look for it."

After a few minutes of searching the campsite, they still hadn't found the bag.

"Alright. Enough of this nonsense." Axel walked over to Magnus, who lay in a shallow burrow in the dry dirt, still asleep, and kicked him in his hip. "Wake up, Scales."

"Axel, cut it out." Calum glared at him.

"What? He can regenerate. That cut Burtis gave him last month healed by the next morning." Axel kicked Magnus again. "I said wake up."

Magnus growled and latched onto Axel's ankle, then he yanked.

Axel landed on his rear-end as Magnus stood to his full height.

"What'd you do that for?" Axel glowered up at Magnus, who now towered over him.

"I do not enjoy being kicked."

Axel scrambled to his feet and stood well within Magnus's space. "And I don't enjoy getting knocked on my rear-end."

"Then perhaps you should alter your behavior."

"Enough, both of you." Calum held up his hands, and the two separated. "Magnus, where'd you put the bag of food?"

"I did not put it anywhere. I left it near the campfire where we always keep it."

"It's not there anymore."

Magnus tilted his head. "Then I do not know where it is."

"What do you mean, you don't know?" Axel extended his arms out to his sides. "You had it last. Where is it?"

"I said I do not know."

Axel pointed at him. "You ate the rest of the food after we went to sleep, didn't you?"

Magnus straightened up. "Why do you accuse me?"

"Why don't you answer the question?"

"I did not eat the rest of the food." This time, Magnus stepped into Axel's space. "And I categorically deny all assertions otherwise."

This time Calum physically stepped between the two of them. He had no doubt that Magnus was telling the truth. If anything, Axel's insistence made *him* look guiltier than Magnus.

But even so, Calum didn't believe Axel had eaten the rest of the food, either.

"Maybe we left the bag somewhere and forgot about it," he said, hoping his words would broker a more lasting peace between his friends. "Maybe it got kicked over the edge sometime during the fight with the sabertooths. Maybe something else happened to it."

Magnus's eyes narrowed, and he stepped away from Axel and Calum and examined the ground.

"That's right." Axel sneered. "Back up, Scales."

Magnus's tail whipped toward Axel and whacked his shoulder.

Axel staggered to one side, off-balance from the blow. "Hey!"

"Apologies," Magnus said flatly as he crouched low to the dirt. "I think Calum may be on to something."

Calum raised his eyebrows. "I am?"

"Perhaps. There appear to be some faint footprints here among ours and those of the sabertooths."

"Those cats trampled this whole area, and you think you're seeing footprints?" Axel rolled his eyes. "Sounds like another ploy to distract us from figuring out you ate the rest of the food."

Magnus pointed to a spot in the dirt. "Then how do you account for this?"

Axel and Calum leaned closer.

Axel shrugged. "What? I don't see anything."

"There. A perfect comparison. You can see a large paw print, and next to it, a smaller one." Magnus looked at Calum. "Do you see it?"

"I do, but what does that prove?" Calum asked.

"Proves you're gullible." Axel scoffed. "That's what it proves."

"Someone or something else was here last night," Magnus continued, ignoring Axel.

"So a smaller paw print proves something else was here?" Axel shook his head. "Maybe one of the cats had smaller feet."

"No. The shape of the paw is different. Entirely different." Magnus nodded. "It appears we had a unique visitor last night."

Axel nudged Calum's arm. "How are you falling for this? He's clearly making stuff up."

"I don't think so." Calum had ignored Axel for as long as he could. "Now that he pointed the prints out, I see more of them leading in the same direction, away from the camp. I think he's right."

"You can't be serious."

"The tracks enter the camp from the northeast and then exit due east." Magnus's eyes traced the route. "He was a quiet one, too."

Calum tilted his head. "He?"

Magnus turned to face him. "I'm assuming it is a 'he,' but I don't know for sure."

"It?" Axel squinted at him. "So what is this 'it' that supposedly stole our last bag of food?"

Magnus smirked. "A Wolf."

"Alright, now I *know* you're making this up." Axel scoffed again. "You're trying to tell us that a wild dog ran in here and stole our last bag of food in the night?"

"Exactly, except for the 'wild dog' part. He probably looks like a wild dog, but Wolves are sentient, intelligent beings just like you and me," Magnus said. "They differ greatly from the sabertooths we engaged last night. They are their own species, and they have souls just like we do."

Axel shook his head. "I still think you're making this up."

Magnus swept his hand toward the edge of the cliff. "Unlike me, you have never ventured to the other side of that valley. Humans rule this entire half of Kanarah, but across the valley, three races divide Western Kanarah. A member of one of them, the Wolves, robbed us last night while we slept."

Calum glanced at Axel. In all his sixteen years, he'd never learned about any other race except for humans. He hadn't even known what a Saurian was until the soldiers brought Magnus into the quarry all those weeks ago.

"There are more races than humans and Saurians?" Calum added, "And Wolves?"

Magnus nodded. "Yes. We Saurians live in the north, among the Blood Mountains and in Reptilius. The Windgales have the southern kingdom and the Aeropolis because they can fly. A rocky arid region known as the Desert of the Forgotten divides our two realms. It is controlled by the Wolves, most of whom live there."

"Then how come I've never seen any of these other races?" Axel challenged. "Aside from your ugly mug, of course?"

A hiss issued from Magnus's nostrils at Axel.

"C'mon, Axel," Calum said, again playing peacemaker. "It's not like you got out much before this."

"More than you," Axel countered.

"Yet clearly not enough," Magnus said. "If you had, perhaps you'd be less bigoted and insolent all the time."

Axel frowned and pointed an accusatory finger at Magnus. "I don't know what those words mean, but I don't have to take this kind of verbal abuse from a scaly freak of nature like you."

"The reason you do not see other races is because of the King's soldiers," Magnus explained despite Axel's anger.

"What do you mean?" Calum asked.

"The King claims dominion over all of Kanarah, but his soldiers clearly favor humans over the others to the point of mistreating or even abusing them. We have little reason to spend time on the eastern side of Kanarah in light of such persecution and favoritism." Magnus's gaze hardened and he glared at Axel. "That mentality has pervaded even the outermost fringes of the human race, I see."

Axel rolled his eyes and folded his arms. "Whatever."

"Nevertheless, I am certain our culprit is a Wolf."

"So…" Calum briefly considered what that could mean for them, but he came to very few conclusions. "What do we do now?"

"There is nothing else to do but follow the plan we set yesterday: head east and find some food, then return here and try to find a way down into the valley."

Trader's Pass/The Valley of the Tri-Lakes

THE FIRST TWO weeks of Lilly's journey across Trader's Pass had breezed by without incident.

She had precisely zero opportunities to escape as the slave traders watched her with even more diligence than ever. Two or more of them always escorted her to relieve herself—now only in broad daylight and usually without any hope of privacy whatsoever, as the Valley of the Tri-Lakes entirely lacked for foliage of any kind.

Sometimes she managed to find a large rock or a small hill behind which she could conceal herself when the time came, but rocks and hills didn't keep the men escorting her from indulging themselves in long, lascivious looks. Still, it had become so routine that she didn't even pay them any attention anymore.

Until one of them dropped to his knees in front of her with a spear lodged in his chest.

"Get over here, now!" the other slave trader shouted at her.

But behind him, at least a dozen dark forms leaped over a row of boulders that formed a hedge around the desolate area.

Bandits?

The slave trader whirled around and swung his sword at the first of them. He felled the bandit, but the second, third, and fourth rushed him, knocked him to the ground, and stabbed him repeatedly with twisted and tortured weapons while he screamed.

Lilly bolted back toward the wagons as fast as the shackles on her ankles allowed her to run. Colm had warned her about men like these—bandits who would just as soon kill her as free her. As much as she hated to admit it, she was safer with Roderick and his men.

"Roderick! Bandits!" she screamed as she hobble-ran. *Oh, to be able to fly again!* She rounded a large mound and shouted again. "Roderick!"

He stood near one of the short wagons, gnawing on an apple. Given the vacant terrain around them, he'd given up on personally escorting her anymore. After all, if she ran off, he'd be able to see her for miles in any direction.

As she approached, Lilly noticed the tan fabric that normally covered one of the wagons was pulled back. From inside, she caught a glimpse of shimmering blue fabric and light-pink plating —it had to be her cape and her armor.

She noted the brown color of the donkey pulling the cart compared to the gray donkey that hauled the other, and she committed the information to memory.

Roderick's gaze fixed on her then widened at the sight of the horde that followed her. He tossed his apple aside and drew his broadsword. "Formation!"

His slave traders formed around him with Luggs to his right and Gammel and Adgar to his left, each of them wielding swords. The archers among them took positions and drew their bows back.

Lilly clanked forward, but the huffs and unintelligible shouts of the bandits behind her drew ever closer. She chanced a look back.

The bandits would overtake her in seconds.

CHAPTER 16

When Lilly faced forward again, Roderick had already closed to within five feet of her position. He zoomed past her in a blur of brown armor and spiky red hair, and a series of heavy smacks and clangs sounded behind her.

"Archers!" Luggs shouted.

The archers let loose a flurry of arrows in rapid succession, and some of them barely missed Lilly. Gammel and Adgar met her partway and escorted her back to the wagon while the others charged forward and engaged the bandits.

In the center of the fracas, Roderick roared and swung his sword as if he were invincible. As Lilly watched him decimate half the bandits single-handedly, she wondered if maybe he was.

"Child, are you alright?" Colm reached for her with frail and tentative fingers

Behind him, Sharion dug into the hay and covered her head.

Lilly nodded and sucked in several deep breaths, more winded from fear than from running. In the distance, Roderick leveled three bandits in one swing of his huge sword.

Unbelievable.

Within minutes, the fight ended as the last of the bandits, a handful compared to the number they'd started with, fled back the way they'd came. Roderick wiped his sword on the tattered clothes of one of the dead bandits, sheathed it, and started back toward the caravan. Splotches of blood glistened on his armored chest and arms, and more dotted his smiling face.

Is he even human? Or is he something... else?

Eastern Kanarah

To Calum's relief, a few days and a few dead animals later, the trio reached the foothills at the eastern edge of the Snake Mountains and found a small village by the name of Pike's Garrison a few miles south, nestled among a forest full of towering evergreen and broadleaf trees.

As discussed, Magnus hid in an inconspicuous spot on the outskirts of the village while

Calum and Axel headed into its heart to see if they could trade for food.

"Is there even a market for sabertooths?" Axel pulled one of the fangs out of the sack he carried. "Er—saber*teeth?*"

Calum shook his head. "I don't know. Guess we'll find out."

Several villagers gave them tentative looks as they walked through the village. Whether it was from their scratched-up soldiers' armor or the foot-long sabertooth fang Axel constantly held in his hand, Calum didn't know.

Most of the homes in the village looked as if they'd been there for a hundred years. The stones that formed the houses' exteriors had long since smoothed from weathering, and the wooden doors and doorframes bore decades-old scars and gashes.

"Ever been in a village like this?" Axel muttered.

Calum shook his head. "Never."

A beautiful red-haired girl about their age walked past them. She wore a flowing orange dress, and a white flower adorned her hair. Her blue eyes lingered on Calum for a long moment, and he couldn't divert his gaze from her even after she walked past and looked away.

A whack to his chest jolted him back to the present.

"Eyes forward, Calum." Axel snickered. "You've probably never seen girls our age, have you?"

"Haven't seen women of any sort for eight years. None worth looking at, anyway." Calum smirked. "Aside from your mother, of course."

Before Axel hit him, Calum braced for the blow. A few traded punches later, their bodies hit the dirt, intertwined in a match of submission wrestling. Calum knew he wouldn't win, but the jibe alone was a victory.

Within seconds, Axel pinned Calum and twisted his arm the wrong way. "Submit."

Calum ground his teeth as pain surged through his shoulder. There was no getting out of this. Axel was too strong, and Calum wasn't any good at wrestling.

But his pride wouldn't let him give in—not yet.

Axel wrenched Calum's arm farther, and the pain brightened. "*Submit.*"

"Can I help you gentlemen?"

In spite of the pain, Calum raised his head. A black-haired man, his hair peppered with gray, stood over them. Brown dirt streaked his beige trousers, his green shirt, and his tanned face.

Axel released his grip on Calum, and relief flooded his sore arm. On his feet again, Axel replied, "No, sir. We're fine, thank you. Just some horseplay."

The man gave a slight nod. "You're making some of the townsfolk nervous, carrying on as such. Do you have reason to be here?"

Calum pushed himself up as well and rotated his arm to bring it further relief. "Yes, sir. We're hoping to trade for food and other supplies if anyone's willing."

"You're the King's soldiers, aren't you?"

Calum glanced at Axel. "No."

"That's standard-issue black leather armor." The man stepped toward them, and his left eye twitched. "Only the King's men wear that armor. If you're not them, then where did you—"

"We traded some deserters for their armor," Axel said before Calum had a chance to speak. "They fled the Rock Outpost north of here after a forest fire got too close. They were starving and hungry, so we traded them in exchange for half of what we had at the time. A few nights ago we ran out of our own supply, so now we're here to trade, if we can."

The man nodded but his left eye twitched again. "You're welcome to walk around freely with your wares, but we desire no trouble, so kindly do your business and kindly move on."

"Yes, sir," Calum said. "Thank you."

After the man walked away, Axel scooped up the sack of sabertooth fangs he'd dropped. "Old buzzard. He oughta mind his own business."

Calum shrugged. "It's his village."

"I don't even see why we need to trade these things. I doubt they're worth anything. We should just take what we want like we did at the outpost."

Calum stepped in front of Axel to keep him from walking. For him to even make such a suggestion flew in the face of everything Calum had fought against to earn his freedom.

"Absolutely not. These people are just like us," he asserted. "They're under the same oppression. We can't steal from people like this. It wouldn't be right."

Axel rolled his eyes. "If you say so. Come on. Let's visit that apothecary over there and see what we can get for these ivories."

In addition to the modest shops interspersed between the old houses, a few vendors lined the main thoroughfare that divided Pike's Garrison into two parts. Some of them offered food, others flowers, and a few dealt in weapons and traveling supplies, but they all seemed to lack both variety and quantity in their wares.

What few villagers occupied the streets seemed to do so with purpose—everyone darted from place to place. When they noticed Calum and Axel walking past, their paces quickened.

An hour later, having visited every shop and vendor in the marketplace, Calum and Axel still had eighteen of their original twenty fangs—plus a small bag of potatoes.

Axel tossed the bag of fangs on the ground behind a house. "This is ridiculous. No one wants these stupid things. We hauled them all this way, and we only got a measly bag of starch to show for it. You won't let us steal anything, so what do you propose we do now?"

Calum sighed. "I don't know."

"Well, one of us had better think of something, and soon, because..."

As Axel prattled on, Calum noticed a silver-haired lady seated in a rocking chair outside of a meager house. She'd sat there knitting ever since they arrived in the village, but now her hands covered her face, and her back heaved up and down, shuddering. Weeping.

Calum's heart went out to her. He'd wept like that before, with great shuddering sobs, when his parents were killed. When the soldiers dropped him off at the quarry. And many long nights for a few years after that, until he'd finally resigned himself to his fate.

He understood the kind of pain that brought a person to this point. He still felt a measure of it, even to this day.

"...back in the forest." Axel smacked Calum's shoulder. "Are you even listening to me?"

Calum looked at him. "Stay here. I'll be right back."

"Where do you think you're going?" Axel's voice trailed off in a flurry of muttering.

The old woman continued to cry even as Calum approached, but she hadn't seen him yet. Perhaps that was for the best.

"Excuse me, ma'am?"

The old woman raised her head. Tears streaked down her cheeks, and her dark-brown eyes were red and puffy. Upon seeing Calum, she pressed her hand against her chest and promptly resumed her knitting. "Oh, I'm sorry, sir. Didn't mean to pause for so long."

"No—I mean, I'm not a soldier," Calum explained. "You don't need to worry about that."

She studied him for a moment, hair roots to leather boots. "You're wearing a soldier's armor."

"Well, we traded some deserted soldiers—" Calum bit his lip. Even if he did remember all of Axel's story, he'd probably butcher it as it came out. "Look, I'm not a soldier. It's a long story. I just came over here because I noticed you crying. Is everything alright?"

She looked down at the yarn in her hands. "You're not from around here, are you?"

Calum shook his head. "No, ma'am."

"Then you don't know the oppression that regular folk suffer from men who wear armor like yours." The old woman resumed her knitting as if that concluded the conversation.

Calum bit his lip. "I have a pretty good idea of how cruel the King's soldiers can be."

"Then how do you justify wearing their attire?"

"The armor keeps me protected in battle and warm at night. It doesn't represent who I am or what I believe in any way."

The old woman chuckled and worked the yarn and needles in her hands. "I believe you, but the image suggests the contrary. Perhaps you ought to consider that when next you decide to—"

"Ma'am, my parents were killed by the King's soldiers when I was eight. I was forced to work in the King's quarry until just a few weeks ago. The only reason I'm standing before you right now is because I fought my way to freedom." Calum immediately regretted his tone, but he couldn't retract his words. He added, "...with some help from a friend."

"By the Overlord..." The old woman stopped knitting. She stood up, her mouth open and brown eyes forlorn, set her project on the chair, and pulled Calum into a hug. "You poor dear."

Calum didn't know what to do. This woman, who had just chastised him for wearing soldiers' armor, clung to him as if he were her own child.

"I'm sorry." The old woman squeezed him tighter. "I had no idea. Twenty years ago this winter, the King's soldiers killed my only son."

Calum exhaled a sigh. No wonder she'd been crying.

He wrapped his arms around her and returned the hug. In that moment, this woman became the closest thing he'd had to a mother in nearly a decade.

She pulled away from him but kept her hands on his gauntlets. She looked them over and then met his eyes again. "I'm sorry I spoke ill of your armor, though now you understand why it's such an affront to me. We share that horror in common. What's your name, child?"

"Calum." He couldn't hold her words against her. He gave her a half-smile.

"A strong, noble name. I'm Reginia. I can't express how sorry I am for your loss."

Calum nodded. "Your son—is he why you were crying?"

"I'm afraid not. I've cried rivers for him in my time, but not today." Reginia shook her head. She picked up her knitting and sat in her rocking chair again. "Forgive me if I sit down. My ancient legs wear out quickly, and I need to save my strength for making dinner this evening."

"Of course." Calum crouched next to her. He glanced back at Axel, who leaned against a nearby house and yawned. "But there is something going on."

"Our village's problems insidiously complement each other and compound our frustrations." Reginia sat back in her rocking chair and looked up at him. "A couple times a month, a group of bandits raids our village. They take most of our food, any gold or silver we earn from travelers passing through, and whatever else they want."

Apparently, the King's soldiers didn't have a monopoly on cruelty.

"I'm sorry." Calum turned back and motioned for Axel to come over, and Calum introduced him to Reginia. "Have the King's soldiers tried to help you?"

"Not in the least. They don't care about us any more than the bandits. It's gotten so bad that the bandits don't even bother to come at night anymore. They just walk into town and take what they want. They've been here so many times that we don't even bother to fight back now." Reginia sighed. "That's the other reason I'm not fond of your attire."

"But you *have* talked to the King's soldiers about this?" Axel asked.

"It didn't do any good." Reginia gave a sad laugh. "Three weeks ago, they came into town while the King's men were also here. We thought the day of reckoning had finally come, but we were wrong. Their leader nodded to the commander of the soldiers, and he nodded right back and stood by while they robbed us again. They did nothing to help us."

Axel growled and muttered a curse.

While Calum shared every ounce of Axel's rage, he wanted to express it in better terms for Reginia's sake. "What Axel means is that we want to help you if we can."

Reginia smiled. "You do?"

Axel's head turned toward Calum. "We do?"

"Of course. Since the King's men aren't doing what they're supposed to do, we'll do it instead." Calum raised an eyebrow. "For a price."

Reginia's smile faded. "Which is?"

"We get half of whatever we find. We'll clear out the bandits so they never bother you again."

Axel leaned close to him. "Bold plan, but I don't know if we can—"

"We most certainly can, and we will." He rubbed his hands together and grinned at Reginia. "What do you say, Reginia? Who do we need to talk to in order to make this official?"

The hopefulness in Reginia's eyes had returned at Calum's proposal. "What you suggest seems fair. My husband is the village's elder. If you'll excuse me, I'll go get him."

As she walked away, Axel twisted Calum toward him. "Are you crazy? We don't even know what we're walking into here."

"It's just a group of bandits. We can handle them. It'll be a quick easy payday."

"We've never done anything like this before. How do you know we—"

Calum elbowed him in the gut and turned to face Reginia, who led a white-haired man with a matching beard over to them. A long black chain hung from his neck over his gray-and-white robes. Two black earrings in each ear matched the metal of the chain.

Calum stepped forward and extended his hand. "I'm Calum. This is Axel. We'd like to help you solve your bandit problem."

The bearded man extended a gloved hand, also black, and his green eyes scoured them. "Stavian. Reginia told me of your proposal. I must tell you, she tends to be far more optimistic than me. I have my doubts about your ability to help us, especially if there are only two of you."

"We have another." Calum recalled how Magnus had severed the last sabertooth cat's head a few nights earlier and added, "He's a skilled fighter."

"And you're not?"

Calum's smile evaporated. "No—I mean, yes, we are too, but he's—"

"We're *all* skilled fighters." Axel pushed Calum aside and stepped forward. "Calum meant that our friend is the most experienced of all of us."

Calum glanced at him. *Sure, now he gets on board with the plan?*

"There are at least ten bandits. Possibly twelve or thirteen, but no more than that. They reside in a hideout somewhere west of here in the Snake Mountains. I can show you on a map where we think it is." Stavian cleared his throat. "But even if your friend is as capable as you describe, I doubt you could overcome such a large force."

"We can handle it, alright." Axel held up his hand. "Several weeks ago, we took control of a mighty fortress that housed more than twenty men."

Calum eyed him for the gross exaggeration, but Axel ignored him.

"And you also realize that if you fail, you'll be jeopardizing our village beyond even what we've suffered thus far?" Stavian's icy blue eyes fixed on Calum.

Calum glanced at Reginia. He hadn't considered that, but how could he back out now?

"Yes, of course," he said. "But we're not going to fail. We'll get your coin back, and—"

The yells of several men and women erupted from the other side of Reginia's house, followed by clashes of swordplay.

Axel and Calum looked at each other, then at Stavian and Reginia. They ran around Reginia's house to the village square, which had crowded with people formed into a loose ring.

There, in the center of it all, Magnus engaged several villagers in battle.

CHAPTER 17

C alum immediately knifed through the throngs of people toward Magnus. At least a dozen men surrounded him, all with pitchforks or hoes or other farming tools, aside from two of them who held actual swords.

Without drawing his own weapon, Calum pushed between two of the offending villagers and stood at Magnus's side. He raised his hands in the air. "Take it easy, people. Calm down."

Axel joined them, but he had his sword out. He waved it at the nearest villager with a weapon. "Back off, or this is going down your throat."

Calum grabbed his wrist. "Put it away. We're not fighting these people."

"Not gonna happen, Calum." Axel jerked free from Calum's grasp. "They're threatening us."

"Axel, trust me. If we want this job, we have to be on their side, not *against* them."

"Then maybe I don't want this job."

Since when had Axel decided to side with Magnus on anything? "You wanna eat, don't you?"

Axel glanced around them. "Not *this* bad."

Calum turned to Magnus. "Will you put your sword away?"

Magnus's eyes narrowed, but he complied. "You had better know what you are doing."

Axel glanced between them and the villagers. "Are you guys crazy? They're gonna kill us because *you* won't fight back."

"*Axel*." Calum's voice hardened. "Put it away."

Axel shook his head. "You can't be ser—"

"I am. Do it now."

Axel scowled at him for a moment, then he sheathed his sword.

"Put your hands up, like Magnus and me."

Axel complied with a sharp sigh.

"We're on your side," Calum said to the crowd. "This Saurian is with us. He won't hurt you unless you try to hurt him. And if you try to hurt him, I don't envy you in the least."

"Stand down, everyone." Stavian parted the crowd with his gloved hands and headed toward the center with Reginia not far behind. When he reached Calum and Axel, he stared at Magnus for a long moment. "You didn't tell me your friend was a Saurian."

Calum glanced at Magnus and Axel. "You didn't ask."

"Having seen him, I am more confident in your chances for success. I grant you permission to remove the bandits on our behalf." Stavian extended his gloved hand. "May the Overlord bless you with great success. If you will come with me, I can provide you with more details on your task."

Calum shook Stavian's hand. "Thank you."

Magnus leaned his head down next to Calum's. "What kind of foolery did you just commit us to?"

"The best kind." Calum gave him a wink.

INSIDE STAVIAN AND Reginia's house, Stavian unrolled a map and smoothed it across a wide oak table. Sunlight filtered in through a skylight in the ceiling above the table.

He pointed to a spot east of the Snake Mountains. "We're here." He pointed to another spot, almost exactly due west of Pike's Garrison. "The bandits' hideout is somewhere near here."

"This will not be a short venture," Magnus said. "We will need at least a day to get there, to get inside, dispatch the bandits, and recover your property, plus another day to return."

Stavian shrugged. "We're not going anywhere."

"We're low on food. Could we trouble you for a good meal before we set out?" Calum asked. "We can offer you some sabertooth cat fangs in exchange for—"

"Keep your cat fangs. We have no use for them here." Stavian waved his hand. "We're low on food as it is, but I'll find something to fill your bellies. And I'll even do one better: you can sleep in actual beds tonight and then set out in the morning. How about that?"

Calum's eyebrows rose. He hadn't slept in an actual bed since before his parents died.

"That would be incredible," Axel said.

Stavian nodded. "So it shall be tonight. In the meantime, while I gather you some food, please make yourselves comfortable. My home is your home. If you require anything, just inquire of Reginia or me."

THE NEXT DAY, Calum could scarcely control his excitement. It heightened when, after a day of traversing hills and weaving through thickets of trees, the trio found the hideout more or less where Stavian's map had placed it.

The structure amounted to little more than an old wood-and-stone house, albeit a large one, in the center of a gorge nestled at the intersection of three rocky hills. Natural rock barriers kept it hidden from the outside world and almost totally inaccessible—except for a solitary path that swerved between two of the hills adjacent to the gorge and led up to its front door.

Smoke rose from the stone chimney. The bandits were inside. Of that, Calum had no doubt. And that meant he'd be able to do some good for the people of Pike's Garrison.

"If we approach from that path, they will see us coming," Magnus said. "We need to find another way inside."

"What other choices do we have?" Axel asked. "Those rock walls look pretty steep. I doubt we can get down there without killing ourselves in the process."

"We have rope, right?" Calum pulled off his pack. "We don't have to scale the cliff without a safety system. Magnus could lower me down near the house with the rope. I can get in that way.

I'll cause a distraction, and then you two can come up the path, no problem. We'll take them out together, bring back the villagers' loot, and walk away with our reward."

Magnus glanced at Axel. "It sounds good in theory, but—"

"But if we don't get there in time, you could be fighting them alone." Axel challenged, "You sure you're up for that?"

The idea of battling up to thirteen bandits on his own exhilarated Calum—and it also scared the daylights out of him. But it was a moot point, since he'd be careful enough to not attract all the bandits to him at once. Obviously.

Even so, Axel had set him up, and Calum wasn't about to back down.

"I'm a better swordsman than you are, Axel." Calum grinned.

Axel scoffed. "We both know *that's* not true."

Calum shrugged "I don't know. I've been beating you pretty consistently when we spar."

Axel frowned. "I've been going easy on you. If we were fighting for real, you would've been dead a long, long time ago. I'm glad you feel so confident, though, even if it's a false confidence."

That stirred Calum's insides, and he smirked. "I'll prove it to you right now, if you like."

"Bad idea." Axel shook his head. "Getting inside that hideout will be a lot harder if you're dead. We need three people to pull this off."

"If you say so." Calum chuckled. "When you come in, bring me a bag for my share of the loot."

"Sounds like it could work." Axel shrugged. "Just don't get yourself killed."

Calum rolled his eyes. "I'll try to leave some of them alive for you."

———

THEY WAITED until nightfall to move into position. Both Magnus and Axel held the rope to which Calum clung, and they lowered him down into the gorge foot by foot.

For a moment, it reminded Calum of Magnus's descent into the Gronyx's pit and his own subsequent fall. He shuddered and shook the memory away.

When his feet touched the stony ground, he untied himself and tugged the rope three times to signal them. The rope zipped up the cliff and disappeared into the darkness.

Calum was on his own now.

He crouched down and surveyed the house. Maybe he could get in through a window on the first floor, or even on the second floor. Perhaps he'd find a rear entrance somewhere. No matter what he did, he'd do it in silence, and he'd avoid the pair of guards posted at the front door.

Calum darted toward the house and hid behind one of the few tall coniferous trees that stood watch in the gorge. A few more steps and he stood with his back to the house beside a window. He leaned his head over for a look inside.

Burning logs in the fireplace filled the room with yellow light. Gold, silver, and bronze treasures adorned the walls, but Calum didn't see anyone in the room. He tugged on the window, but it didn't budge. No sense breaking it. He'd have to find another way to get inside.

Around the back of the house, he found an unlocked door. He pulled it open, his sword in hand, and peered inside.

An iron stove sat in one corner next to a pile of wood, and a man with curly black hair stood at a counter with his back to Calum. He chopped some dark red meat with a big knife. Without hesitation, Calum stalked toward the man in silence with his sword ready.

The man kept chopping, oblivious to Calum's approach.

Calum closed the distance in less than three seconds. A small part of him wanted to run the man through right there, but he couldn't just stab the poor sap in his back, even if he was a treacherous bandit. Instead, he smacked the back of the man's head with his sword's pommel just like Magnus had shown him a few weeks earlier.

The man's knife clanked on the table, and he wilted to the floor, unconscious.

Perfect. Calum moved on.

He made his way through the halls without making a sound, and he didn't encounter any other bandits. Laughter sounded from upstairs on the second floor, along with the occasional stomp or creak or the scraping of wooden chairs across the floor.

Good. Better up there than down here. Hopefully they'd stay up there until he could get to the guards by the front door.

Now how could he cause some sort of distraction?

The next room he entered was the one he'd seen through the window—the one with the fireplace. Perhaps he could set something on fire again. It had worked in the woods outside the Rock Outpost.

Once inside the room, he dodged the chairs and tables and headed straight for the fireplace. All of the logs were too hot for him to grab, but if he could find something small—perhaps a book or some parchment or something—then he could easily spread the fire.

He found nothing of practical use in the fireplace room aside from the wooden furniture, but he couldn't just break it up; it would make too much noise.

The more he considered his plan, the less appealing it became. If he set the house on fire and it spread wildly enough to burn down, what would happen to the bandits' stash? It might get destroyed in the process.

No, fire wasn't a great idea after all. Instead, he headed to the next door.

When he opened it, he found himself staring up at a pair of confused hazel eyes above a big nose and a thick brown beard.

Instinct and shock thrust Calum's sword arm forward. The tip of the blade pierced the bandit's left shoulder, and he yelped.

His right fist plowed into Calum's left cheek, and Calum staggered back, reminded of Burtis's strikes.

The bandit clenched his injured shoulder with his hand and leaned against the doorframe as blood oozed between his fingertips. He opened his mouth to holler, but Calum threw a haphazard punch at his neck.

To his surprise, his fist connected, and the bandit's scream caught in his throat. Wide-eyed and straining to breathe, the bandit clutched at his throat with his hand, no longer concerned with his wounded shoulder.

Emboldened by his luck, Calum swung his sword in a lethal arc. The bandit backed away and then quickly lurched at him with both hands outstretched, still wheezing and still bleeding. When Calum tried to return with a backswing, the bandit caught his arm in both hands and wrenched it the wrong way.

Instead of yelling, Calum ground his teeth and tried to twist out of the bandit's grip, but the bandit readjusted. He tripped Calum and shoved him to the floor, and his sword clattered away. The struggle didn't last long—the bandit had a size advantage over Calum by at least a hundred pounds.

Now on top of Calum, the bandit drew his hand back for a punch. At the last instant Calum contorted his body and avoided the blow, and the bandit punched the stone floor instead. A pitiful yelp rasped out of his throat, and he clutched his fist.

Calum threw the best punch he could manage from such an awkward position, but he only managed to hit the bandit's stomach bulge. It didn't have any effect.

The bandit leaned forward, clamped his fingers around Calum's throat, and began to squeeze. Calum grabbed the bandit's wrists and tried to pry his hands from his throat, but the bandit was too strong, and he weighed too much.

Out of the corner of his eye, Calum saw the glint of the fire dancing across his sword blade. Could he reach it?

He stretched his right arm out, but the handle lay just beyond his fingertips.

"You're gonna die, kid." The bandit's voice scraped out of his throat, and then he displayed a twisted yellow smile.

Calum's vision darkened. He threw a left hook at the bandit's face and connected with his cheekbone. The bandit took the blow, but his grip didn't loosen. Instead, he laughed.

"Hit me as many times as you want. I'm not lettin' go 'til you're dead."

Calum groped for his sword again. His fingertips touched the end of the pommel, but he couldn't quite get a grip. He tried pulling at the bandit's hands again, but they didn't yield, either.

The bandit snickered. "Keep reachin', kid."

Calum noticed the hilt of something protruding from a sheath on the bandit's belt—a blade of some sort. Maybe a knife or a dagger. Instead of continuing to reach for his own sword, Calum grabbed the hilt and yanked it from its sheath.

He was going out fast. He forced his weakening hand to solidify its grip, angled the blade toward the bandit, and stabbed with everything he had left.

Shick.

The bandit twitched, and the smirk on his face evaporated. His grip loosened, and he rolled off Calum onto the floor with the dagger plunged halfway in his side.

Calum coughed and gasped and strained for air, but he knew the fight wasn't over. He couldn't rest yet. He scrambled over to the bandit on the floor and jammed the dagger deeper until it refused to go any farther. For good measure, he gave the hilt a sharp twist.

With a gasp, the bandit twitched, then he went limp. His wide eyes narrowed and glazed over, and he stared at the ceiling with a vacant expression.

Calum released the dagger and rolled onto his back again. He gulped in haggard breaths, and sweet air filled his lungs. His throat burned, but he was alive.

He lay there, sucking in breath after glorious breath until he finally felt well enough to stand. He headed over to his sword and picked it up, but he left the dagger in the bandit's body.

After all, it had been his in the first place. He deserved to keep it.

Calum realized he'd had no choice that time. It was either the bandit or him. He'd done what he had to do, just as Axel had done back at the Rock Outpost. Just as Magnus had said Calum would someday have to do.

He wasn't sure how he felt about it just yet, but he knew he didn't love the feeling. Still, he was alive. That counted for a lot.

The floor creaked behind him. Calum whirled around, his sword ready, abandoning any lingering concerns he might've had over his first kill.

Ten angry men, all with weapons in their hands, stood at the bottom of the staircase, glaring at him.

CHAPTER 18

O ne of the bandits, a lanky man with blond hair and a matching beard, pointed at Calum. "He just killed Norm!"

The group started toward him. He had to do something, and fast.

"Who's in charge here?" Calum's voice rasped against his sore throat. He put his left hand up, and to his surprise, they stopped their advance. Maybe he could stall them long enough for Axel and Magnus to get inside. "I want to talk to whoever's in charge."

The lanky blond bandit tilted his head and glanced at a couple of his comrades. "Norm was in charge."

Calum bit his lip. *Shoot.* "Guess that means I'm in charge now."

"What?" A dark-skinned bandit with long fire-red dreadlocks stepped forward. He carried an axe, and when he spoke, an unusual accent tinged his words. "Not a chance. You kill Norm. Now we gonna kill you."

The group took another collective step toward him.

Where were Axel and Magnus?

"No, that means you're gonna shut up and do what I say." Calum stepped back and put up his hands again, this time including his sword, and the bandits halted again. "I earned it. I killed your leader, so now I'm your new boss. Don't you know anything? That's how it works."

Several of the bandits eyed each other, and then him. A shorter, fatter bandit shook his head with vigor. He held a sword that resembled a large meat cleaver. "No, that *ain't* how it works. You don't belong here. You killed Norm, so now you gosta die."

They started toward him again.

Calum couldn't stretch this much further. Axel and Magnus needed to hurry.

He took several more steps back, but he was running out of room. "If Norm was in charge before, then I wanna talk to the man who's in charge now."

The bandits stopped their advance and exchanged glances.

More uncertainty. *Perfect.*

"You mean you don't know who's in charge now?" Calum smirked. "Then I'm in charge."

The lanky blond one pointed his finger at Calum again. "You're tryin' to confuse us. You killed Norm, so we're killin' you."

"Oh, so you're in charge, then?" Calum pointed back at him.

"He ain't in charge." The short fat one stepped forward and eyed the lanky blonde bandit.

Calum raised an eyebrow. These guys were almost as dumb as he'd hoped. "Then you are?"

The short fat one cracked a smile. "Well, I s'pose—"

"Not a chance. No way are you in charge, Goo." The dark one with the red hair yanked him backward. "Not a chance."

Goo swatted his hand away. "Get yer hands off me, Kumba. I could lead this outfit, no probbum."

"Where?" Kumba chortled. "Into a bakery?"

"*Shaddap*. You know I look like this 'cause I have a condition."

"Yeah." The lanky blond one snickered. "Your condition is that you're *fat*."

Goo turned toward him while the other bandits chuckled. "What'd you say to me?"

"Must be deaf, too." The lanky blond one leaned forward and repeated the words slowly. "I said you're—"

Goo jammed his sword into the lanky blond bandit's gut before he could finish, and he dropped to the floor face-first. "Yeah? Well, this fat guy just *killed* you."

"*Goo!*" Kumba yanked him away from the lanky blond bandit. "What are you doing?"

Goo spun around and slashed at Kumba next, but Kumba dodged the blow and cut him down with one powerful swing of his axe.

Three down. Calum nodded toward Kumba. "Looks like you're in charge."

Kumba's eyes hardened. "You got dat right, boy. Now *three* of us are dead because of you. And now you gonna pay for it."

Calum opened his mouth to speak, but Kumba didn't stop this time. He swung his axe at Calum's head, and Calum ducked under the blow and rolled away. As soon as he recovered his footing, Calum parried a hack from a black-haired bandit.

A roar sounded behind him. He dropped to the floor in time to dodge Kumba's next attack, which crashed into the black-haired bandit instead. The blow nearly split the bandit's head in two, and it definitely killed him.

Four down, including Norm.

Calum lunged at Kumba and struck his armored greave with his sword.

Kumba grunted and pulled his leg back. Then he swung his axe straight down at Calum, who blocked the blow with his sword. The force of the strike knocked Calum backward, but it didn't stop him from attempting a counterattack. He slashed at Kumba's torso.

The handle of Kumba's axe absorbed the swing, and he responded with a powerful kick to Calum's chest. Calum's back slammed into the wall, and again the axe sliced toward Calum's head, and again he ducked. The axe head stuck in the wall, and Calum found his opening. He drew his elbow back to run Kumba through.

Five dow—

He tried to stab, but something held his arm back. A bandit with vibrant green eyes and matted brown hair anchored his arm in place.

Still only four down.

Kumba cocked his arm, but Calum wrenched his body to the side and moved the green-eyed bandit's head to where his had just been. Kumba's punch thudded into the bandit's face, and he released his grip on Calum amid a colorful cascade of profanity.

Calum tried to swing his sword at the green-eyed bandit, but Kumba's boot hit his shoulder and knocked him off-balance. Before Calum could recover, Kumba delivered a stunning punch to his cheek, and he dropped his sword.

Another bandit kicked him in the gut, and Calum curled forward. The following blow to his back laid him out flat.

The beating escalated with Calum on the floor as the bandits kicked his ribs and punched his arms and face. Every blow hurt; every blow further shriveled Calum's body. It continued until Calum almost couldn't feel it anymore, and then, all at once, it stopped.

His eyes barely opened through the swelling, but Calum still saw what happened next. Kumba yanked his axe from the wall, strode over to him, and raised it above his head.

This was it. Calum had been doing so well, too. Though images of Lumen trickled into his mind here at the end, the prevailing sense in his mind was disappointment, not failure.

Then a spearhead pierced out of Kumba's chest, and he cried out, his face crumpled with pain. His axe clattered to the floor behind him, and he dropped to his knees and face-planted onto the floor next to Calum.

Twenty feet behind Kumba, Axel drew his sword from its sheath and charged the rest of the bandits. Magnus followed him into the room and skewered one of the bandits with his own spear then cut down another with his broadsword.

The bandits spread out and engaged them in battle, leaving Calum behind on the floor. Axel and Magnus each took on two of them at once. Clashing swords and hollers filled the house as bandit bodies fell, one by one.

Axel must've been telling the truth when he'd told Calum he was holding back in their sparring sessions, because he looked like he'd morphed into a seasoned fighter overnight. He ducked under a careless swipe from one of the bandits then ran him through the next instant, and then he proceeded to move on to his next foe without missing a beat.

Just behind Axel, Magnus parried an attack with the blade attached to his tail armor then whirled around with his broadsword extended. The hack leveled the bandit, nearly cleaving him in half.

The remaining two bandits regrouped and stood together, their weapons at the ready but trembling in their hands. Axel feigned an advance, then Magnus barreled forward and felled the one on the right with his sword.

The remaining bandit brought his sword down on Magnus's forearm, but the blade glanced off his Blood Ore armor. Magnus turned toward him as Axel closed in for the kill.

His eyes wide and desperate, the final bandit swung at Axel, who parried the blow, dodged the next one, then drove the tip of his sword deep into the bottom of the bandit's chin. The bandit slumped to the floor, unmoving.

After a quick scan of the room, Magnus and Axel darted over to Calum.

"Are you alright?" Axel dropped to his knees next to Calum and set his sword on the floor.

Magnus joined him. "He needs help. I'll carry him, you gather up those..."

The sound of Magnus's and Axel's voices slowed to garbled nonsense. Darkness encroached on Calum's vision until it was all he could see.

CHAPTER 19

The scout arrived only two hours after Commander Anigo and his men finished setting up their campsite in the forest. Commander Anigo read the report in the light of the campfire and, at first glance, he frowned. A group of bandits had been killed near a small town called Pike's Garrison.

Nothing in the report definitively indicated the involvement of the fugitives he'd been searching for, but when he reread the words scrawled on the dry parchment, something about them aroused his suspicions.

Pike's Garrison was south of their current location. If the Saurian with them was trying to make his way back to Western Kanarah, then it would follow that he, at least, would be heading south to Trader's Pass, the only known route across the Valley of the Tri-Lakes. If the others had stayed with him, then perhaps the three of them might've been responsible for this event after all.

Strictly speaking, Pike's Garrison was out of Commander Anigo's jurisdiction due to his appointment to Commander Pordone's old post, but Commander Anigo's superiors had tasked him with the unconditional capture of the missing fugitives.

That meant he had the King's authority—at least by extension, via his commanding officers—to do what needed to be done, regardless of where his search led him.

It wasn't much to go on, but it might be just enough.

"Corporal?" he called.

Corporal Bezarion approached. "Yes, Commander?"

"Rouse the men and ready my horse. We're heading south."

Corporal Bezarion's mouth opened, and he glanced back at the campsite. "Commander, we've only been at rest for two hours. I think it would be wise to—"

The stern scowl Commander Anigo leveled at Corporal Bezarion shut him up.

"Right, Commander. You don't care to repeat yourself. Apologies. I will go fulfill your order now, sir."

Within fifteen minutes, everything was repacked. Under the moonlight, Commander Anigo mounted Candlestick and led his men even deeper into the wilderness, heading south.

As with every other time he'd appeared to Calum, Lumen crafted the living map with his irradiated sword.

"Calum." Lumen's eyes flickered with white fire. "Release me."

But this time, something about the dream changed. Lumen did something completely new: he extended his sword and touched Calum's chest with its tip.

A warm sensation spread throughout Calum's body, and he sucked in a deep breath. Starting in his chest, strength returned to his exhausted muscles. The sensation extended into his limbs and ended in his fingertips and toes.

By the time it had saturated his entire body, Calum felt totally renewed—almost reborn, in a sense—and infinitely powerful.

"Rise." Lumen's unmistakable voice reverberated throughout the space around him and within him. "You must set me free."

Calum's eyes opened, and he promptly squinted and sat up in bed. Morning sunlight streamed into the room through the solitary window set into one of the walls to his left.

Bed? Windows? Walls? Where am I?

Definitely inside someone's house. A brown wooden chest with six drawers sat in the corner next to the window. Also to his left, beside the bed, a small round table held an unlit oil lamp and a wooden cup of water.

Calum patted the poofy pillows and the heavy quilt that covered him up to his stomach. Where was he? How did he get here? The last thing he remembered was—

"You have awakened."

Calum swiveled his head.

Magnus sat in a wooden chair nestled in the corner of the room to Calum's right. He held a thick leather-bound book in his large hands. He still wore his blue armor, minus his helmet, and his tail tapped the floor at random intervals. His broadsword leaned against the wall next to him, still in its sheath.

He shut the book, sending a plume of dust into the air, and grinned at Calum.

"How's the book?"

"Engaging. A fantastical tale about a ghost haunting a mine on some distant world. Truly fascinating." Without standing, Magnus replaced the book in an open slot between two other books on a floor-to-ceiling bookshelf behind him. "How do you feel?"

Calum stretched his limbs and twisted his back, and a litany of aches and pains awakened throughout his body, followed by a pervading sense of weakness and exhaustion. So much for Lumen's sword restoring his strength. Then again, it was only a dream.

"Sore," he replied. "My ribs hurt, and my face does too. Actually, pretty much everything hurts."

"You took quite a beating from those bandits. Do you feel like you can move around?"

"I'm not sure. My limbs feel stiff, and so does my back. I feel like I could stay in bed for a few days."

Magnus nodded. "You have already been in that bed for nearly three days, in and out of consciousness. We managed to get you to take a little water and some food a few times, but we endured long stretches where we feared you might not wake up."

Calum rubbed his neck. His head throbbed as if someone had dropped a boulder on it.

Multiple times. He closed his eyes to try to ward off the pain, but it did little good. "Where are we?"

"We are back in Pike's Garrison, inside Stavian and Reginia's house," Magnus said. "I carried you back while Axel carried as much of the treasure as he could, in addition to his supplies and yours."

"You really carried me all the way down the mountain?"

"Yes."

Calum's mouth hung open. "Why?"

Magnus tilted his head and blinked at him with scaly green eyelids. "Because you are my friend. My only friend."

Satisfaction swelled in Calum's chest, and he smiled. More than once, he'd wondered if Magnus was merely tolerating his presence in the group. After all, their initial partnership had been founded on little more than begging and convenience.

And once Magnus got free of the quarry and got his armor back, he had little reason to stick around Calum and Axel, at least from what Calum could tell. Why he'd bothered to stick around was a mystery to them both, but now more than ever, Calum was grateful that he'd done so.

"Thank you," Calum finally said.

"You would have done the same for me."

Calum chuckled at the thought of him carrying Magnus down an entire mountain. Maybe in Calum's dreams, but not in reality.

"Are you hungry?"

Calum nodded. "Yes. Very."

Magnus stood up, but he had to hunch to fit under the ceiling. "I will return with some food imminently. The good news is that we will not go hungry for awhile. Even with handing over the loot we recovered for the villagers, there is plenty left over for us."

"That much?"

"Yes. Stavian sent a group of villagers to bring their share of the spoils back. Even after they claim their share, there is much, much more to be collected from the bandits' hideout. When you are well, we will venture there together and retrieve more."

"What about Axel? Where is he now?"

"As soon as we arrived here, I sent him back to the hideout to recover more loot with the villagers. He should be back with the others sometime within the next day."

Calum lay back against the pillows again. Aside from nearly being pummeled to death, everything else seemed to have worked out. "Good."

"Rest. I will find you something to eat."

WHEN AXEL REACHED Pike's Garrison with the villagers that afternoon, Magnus met him at the edge of town, grinning.

"Calum is awake."

Axel dropped the huge sack of loot that hung over his shoulder and charged past Magnus toward Stavian and Reginia's house. He didn't stop until he made it inside Calum's room and stood at the foot of the bed, his heart pounding as he stared at Calum's bruised and battered face.

But his eyes were open, and he was sitting up in the bed.

"You're... alright?" He couldn't help but smile.

Calum nodded. "Yeah. I'm alright."

Axel pointed at Calum as he came around the side of the bed. "You had me really worried. After you killed that last bandit, I didn't know what was gonna happen to you."

Calum sat up and scooted back against the bed's headboard. "That makes two of us. Thanks for helping Magnus get me back here. I can't ever repay you for this and everything else you've—"

"Don't start that with me." Axel held up his hand. "We're best friends. Brothers. That's what we do for each other."

"Well, I owe you." Calum smiled.

"I'll be sure to cash in later on." Axel whacked his shoulder, and Calum winced. "Oh, sorry. Still sore?"

Calum nodded and rubbed the spot. "Might be for awhile."

"I know what you mean. After that last fight, everything hurt." Axel sighed. "Of course, since I actually know how to fight, I didn't get the sap kicked out of me like you."

"Keep it up, and I might die of laughter," Calum said, his voice flat. "Anyway, I had another dream about Lumen."

Axel glanced back at the door. "Did you talk to Magnus about it yet?"

"No. It was just before I woke up this morning. I forgot to mention it, and he's been outside helping people with odd jobs around the village."

"And?"

Calum shrugged. "And I think that's a nice thing for him to do. I'd be doing the same if I were able to get out of bed."

"No." Axel rubbed his forehead with his fingers. "The dream, Calum."

"Oh. Whoops." He gave a quick chuckle. "It, uh… it was basically the same as last time, except that this time he touched my chest with the tip of his sword. It felt like fire was spreading through my veins, strengthening me, and then I woke up."

Axel raised an eyebrow at him. "That's…interesting."

"Anyway, he said we—he said *I* am supposed to go release him."

"So you're still on that, huh?" Axel folded his arms. A part of him had secretly hoped one of those bandits had knocked some sense into Calum during that beating. Then maybe he wouldn't have to waste time on what would ultimately be a fruitless quest with a disappointing end.

"Definitely. I feel it inside of me. It's something I *need* to do," Calum insisted. "And if Magnus was right about the thousand-year legend, then we'll be doing Kanarah a favor, too."

Oh, Calum. You and your delusions of grandeur. "If he's even real."

"You're still skeptical?"

Axel shrugged. "In nineteen years I've never even heard of him, and neither had you."

Calum chuckled again. "Yeah, but we didn't exactly get out much."

"Hm." Axel had to concede that one. "True."

"Think about it—it's been a thousand years since Lumen was locked away. Plus, the King doesn't want him released because Lumen's gonna overthrow him and free us from his oppression. So there's the issue of a lot of time passing coupled with the idea that the King is probably stifling any murmurs about Lumen's return."

Axel supposed that made sense, but it still all sounded too farfetched for him to believe. If this ancient warrior was supposed to be so powerful, and if he was going to awaken in a thousand years anyway, what did he need the help of someone like Calum for?

Calum leaned forward. "It all sounds like a good way to hide someone as important as Lumen, if you ask me."

Axel cleared his throat and put his hand on Calum's shoulder, much gentler this time. "Look,

Calum. I know you want all of this Lumen stuff to be true, but it's pretty unbelievable. I don't want you to get your hopes up and then find out that you just imagined the whole thing."

"I know you don't," Calum said. "But I'd rather take the chance and see if we can change Kanarah for good rather than keep scraping by every day. I mean, if Lumen is real, and he really will save Kanarah from the King, can you even imagine what'll happen to us if we're the ones who set him *free?*"

The only thing Axel knew for sure was that he was growing weary of this conversation. He shrugged. "I have no idea."

Calum glanced at the window. "We'll be *heroes*. If we set him free, we'll be heroes. We could become generals, or princes, or nobility. We could rule Kanarah with him."

Axel held up his hands. "Alright, even if he is real, we don't *know* that any of that would actually happen."

"So we just shouldn't try?" Calum's blue eyes locked onto Axel. "You have to admit that just making the journey, seeing the Tri-Lakes up close, and visiting the Blood Mountains is gonna be the adventure of a lifetime. That alone is worth the effort."

Axel narrowed his eyes. Though they didn't agree about the whole freeing Lumen escapade, Axel had to admit Calum was right about the adventure part. Traveling and exploring Kanarah was exactly what he'd always wanted to do.

But Calum's irrational desire to go even farther, to venture across the valley to an unfamiliar land in hopes of finding something that may not even exist had less appeal for Axel. What did Western Kanarah even have to offer someone like him?

Wolves, Windgales, and more Saurians. The one he had to travel with was enough of a burden already, thank you very much.

"You don't have to believe it's true to come," Calum said. "I just want you there if we do find him. I want to free Lumen with my best friend at my side."

"Tone down the sappiness, will you?"

"Sorry." Calum chuckled. "It's true, though."

Axel sighed. How could he refuse? At least it was a plan of some sort. He could follow it... for now. At least until something better crested his horizon.

"Then you'd better get healthy soon," Axel said. "I'm not getting any younger, and neither is Scales."

Calum beamed. "Give me a day or two, and we can get out of here."

Axel pointed to him. "You got it. Two days. If you're not up by then, I'm gonna haul you outta that bed and drag you across the valley myself. Crystal?"

Calum nodded. "Clear."

WITHIN A DAY AND A HALF, Calum made it to his feet again, walking and even jogging a bit. The swelling on his face had gone down, and his bruised ribs didn't hurt as much. His limbs still ached, but far less so. By the next morning, he was ready to go on his way with Magnus and Axel.

They said their goodbyes to Stavian and Reginia, their newest and only other friends in Kanarah. Calum shook Stavian's gloved hand, and when he hugged Reginia, he couldn't help but think of her as his mother again.

She'd taken care of him while he recovered, let him sleep in one of her beds, and showed him kindness and compassion unlike anything he'd ever experienced. As they embraced, he realized he would miss her the most.

The journey back to the bandits' hideout took longer since Calum had to walk slower than normal and needed to stop more often. As dusk settled around them after their first day, Magnus began working on the campfire, and Calum unsheathed his sword and challenged Axel to spar.

"Take it easy, Calum." Magnus stacked chunks of wood over a small pit he'd dug out. "It is senseless to risk re-injuring yourself."

"I know, Magnus. I just want to gauge where I'm at in my recovery. You never know when we might run into trouble."

Calum squared his body with Axel's, and the sparring began. He circled Axel and threw a few quick jabs—though not as quick as before he'd taken his beating. His body just refused to cooperate exactly as it had before.

He wondered if he'd sustained any permanent damage. Hardink's bad foot came to mind, but that was an injury. Calum was just sore and needed to loosen up and reeducate his body in the ways of fighting.

To his credit, Axel took it easier than normal too—mostly.

A few strokes into the match, Calum overreached with his sword. Axel sidestepped the swing and drove his shoulder into Calum's, sending a bone-rattling shock throughout Calum's whole body.

Off-balance, Calum tottered to one side, but by the time he recovered, Axel had already moved behind him. The next thing Calum knew, he'd fallen to his rear-end, and fresh pain ignited throughout his body.

"That is more than sufficient for now," Magnus said. "We still have at least a half-day of travel until we reach the bandits' hideout. Save your strength."

Axel extended his hand down toward Calum, who grasped it and allowed Axel to help pull him up to his feet.

"At the end, there, what did you do?" Calum asked.

Axel smirked. "I grabbed the back collar of your armor and pulled you down. Once I had you, I could've done anything. Stabbed you. Cut off your head. Drove my knee into your spine. If you let your enemy get behind you, you're in for a world of hurt."

Calum glanced at Magnus, who nodded. *I'll remember that.*

DESPITE HIS LINGERING ACHES, around noon the next day, Calum was the first to crest the edge of the gorge that concealed the bandits' hideout. When they closed to within three hundred yards, Magnus yanked them both behind a row of pine trees and told them to be quiet.

"What's wrong?" Calum stretched his back after the harsh jerk on his armor.

"The King's soldiers." Magnus snarled. "Have a look, quietly."

Calum and Axel parted some of the conifer branches with their arms and peered down at the house. Even from far away they could see men with black armor patrolling the grounds, including one man on a white horse.

Magnus huffed. "They found the hideout."

CHAPTER 20

Axel cursed, and Calum couldn't blame him for doing it. He thought they'd struck a vein of good fortune—at least up until now. The King's soldiers had complicated everything, as usual.

"What're we gonna do now?" Calum asked.

"We cannot go down there," Magnus said. "So put any such thoughts out of your mind."

"That's exactly what I'm thinking." Axel rubbed his hands together and smirked. "Let's take them out."

"Are you serious?" Calum shook his head. Sometimes Axel came up with the worst possible ideas. "There are at least two dozen men down there, and maybe more inside. We can't handle them, even with Magnus."

"We just brought down eleven bandits without any problems."

Calum eyed Axel.

"Alright, *you* got beat up, but you're fine now."

Calum kept eyeing him.

"Mostly fine." Emphatic, Axel said, "*Come on*. We can take them."

"Keep your voices down, both of you." Magnus glanced over his shoulder. "Royal soldiers typically deploy a minimum of one scout for every five to ten men in a given area, so there is likely one nearby. If he finds us, we will quickly encounter a surplus of trouble. If you wish to discuss our options, we must find somewhere safer to talk."

Axel frowned, but nodded, and Calum nodded too.

After a ten-minute walk to the southeast, all three of them hunched behind a boulder about half the size of Stavian and Reginia's house.

Axel pointed toward the bandits' hideout. "That's our coin in there. *Ours*. We earned it. We can't just let them take it."

As much as Calum wished otherwise, he couldn't deny the truth. "I don't think we have a choice anymore."

"We can take them by surprise, just like we did the bandits."

Calum's voice flattened. "Yeah, we know how *that* turned out."

108

Axel shrugged. "Hey, *you* wanted to go in alone."

"I went in alone to make it easier for you guys to get inside."

"Yeah." Axel looked him up and down. "And we know how *that* turned out."

Calum scowled at him. "Maybe if you'd gotten inside *faster*, I wouldn't be in this sorry state."

"Not my fault you can't fight worth a—"

"Leave him alone, Axel," Magnus said. "He defeated four of them on his own before they overpowered him. I doubt you would have done as well."

"I would've done *better*." Axel folded his arms.

In fairness, based on how well he'd fought the other bandits once they finally *did* get inside, Axel probably would've done better, but Calum wasn't about to admit that.

"The point is, we cannot engage twenty-five of the King's soldiers at once. With only three blades, it is folly to think otherwise," Magnus said.

"Come on. You're as strong as ten of them, plus you can regenerate if you get injured, plus you have that incredible armor. What are you worried about?" Axel scoffed. "This should be *easy*. If there are twenty-five men inside, then twenty-five swings is all you'd need to end this, *plus* you'll have Calum and me to watch your back."

"I'm in no condition to fight." That, Calum could admit. Even the thought of doing battle again sent fresh aches throughout his body. "Our sparring today proved that. I can walk or even run, but I'd rather wait a bit longer to heal up before I jump back into fighting."

Axel raised his hands and smacked them on his thighs. "Then we wait a couple of days and then go in."

"I warned you to keep your voice down." Magnus hissed. He clicked his talons on his breast-plate. "If we wait that long, the soldiers may be gone, but so will our spoils."

"Then you and I can go." Axel nudged Magnus with his elbow. "We'll stash Calum somewhere safe and go in ourselves and—"

"Evidently, you have no understanding of what is transpiring down there." Magnus squared his body and stared down at Axel. "Those soldiers are not there by accident. They have almost certainly been pursuing us since we hit the Rock Outpost. Before that, even— since we left your family farm. They are *hunting* us, Axel, which means they are on to our trail."

A shock of terror filled Calum's chest. "They're tracking us?"

What did that mean? Were the soldiers going to catch up? If they got caught, would they send Calum back to the quarry, or would they just kill him outright?

Magnus nodded. "I have been tracked by the King's soldiers before. They will probably stop at Pike's Garrison next, and then they will head back into the forest to look for us again. As such, we need to disappear *now*. That means no more spoils."

Axel's jaw hardened. "That's unacceptable."

"It is *reality*," Magnus countered. "If they find us, I expect they will surround and kill us. The best I could hope for in such a dire situation would be escaping with my own life, not protecting yours as well."

Calum shuddered at the thought of fighting to the death, only to be the one dying at the end of the fight.

Magnus exhaled a long sigh. "It is not as easy as twenty-five swings of my sword. If it were, everyone would be a warrior. After all of our training, I thought you would have learned that."

Axel glared at him. "I learned enough to take out *half* of the remaining bandits in that house on my own, without your help. I could've taken all of them had *you* not been there."

"Your delusions know no limits," Magnus muttered.

"Alright. That's enough." Calum held up his hands. Why did Calum always have to get between these two? "I'm sick of this pointless arguing. It's not getting us any closer to a solution."

"He needs to realize he is not as capable a fighter as he believes," Magnus said, "or he may soon find himself wandering the afterlife with his ego in tow."

"I said *enough*, Magnus."

To Calum's surprise, Magnus didn't say anything else after that.

Calum refocused on Axel. "We're not going down there, Axel, so forget it. We'd just get ourselves killed. There's no scenario in which we'd win against those odds without serious help."

Axel shook his head. "You don't know that."

"I'm telling you," Calum firmed up his voice, "we're *not* going down there. Crystal?"

Axel stepped in front of him, his brow furrowed. "No, it's not *crystal*, Calum. You want me to go with you to find some fairytale warrior that probably doesn't even exist, but you won't back me when it's our lives and our livelihood on the line?"

Calum stood his ground, something he probably wouldn't have done had they been back at the quarry or on Axel's farm. "I'm not asking you to walk into an instant death-trap. That's what you're asking here. It's just a bad idea."

"And your little quest *isn't*?" Axel spat.

"Why are you attacking me?" Calum held his hands out to his sides.

"Because you think you're in charge, but you're not."

"No one is in charge," Magnus said.

"Easy for you to say." Axel scoffed. "You two always side with each other."

Calum sighed. Why was this so hard? "We're not trying to team up against you, Axel."

"Well, it sure seems like it."

Magnus snorted.

Axel held up his hand and started to walk away. "Whatever. You said we're not going down there, so there's no point in wasting time here. Gotta find Calum's mystery warrior and save the world before the thousand years is up, right?"

As Axel disappeared behind some trees, Calum sighed again and looked up at Magnus. "What am I supposed to do?"

Magnus patted him on his back. "He will come around. Come on. The last thing we need is to lose him in the forest when he is upset."

AXEL EXHALED a long sigh and tossed a piece of gristle from dinner into the campfire. The only reason he hadn't left these two jokers behind was because he had literally no idea where he was. Without Magnus to guide him, he'd get lost in the woods.

Frankly, he was already lost in the woods, just with other people who weren't. It frustrated him all the more to realize he was essentially trapped with Scales and Calum. He resolved to learn how to navigate using the stars so he'd never find himself in such a miserable position ever again.

"Do you intend to be sour all night?" Magnus asked.

Axel rolled his eyes. Didn't the Saurian realize that asking questions like *that* just made him angrier? "Yes."

Magnus shook his head and sat down next to Calum on the opposite side of the camp. "I suggest we set watches tonight."

Back in Pike's Garrison, before they'd tried to collect the rest of their plunder from the bandits' hideout, they'd traded their meager amount of loot for the King's royal currency—gold coins with his insignia stamped on them. Much easier to carry around a skull-sized leather pouch stuffed with gold pieces than a sack bulging with various trinkets and valuables.

"We cannot afford to get robbed again," Magnus continued. "If we each sleep four hours at a time and leave one man up, we can all get a good night's rest. I will gladly take the middle shift so you can both sleep without interruption."

Calum nodded. "Sounds good. You want the first shift or the last shift, Axel?"

"Whatever." If it mattered, Axel would've given a better response.

Magnus turned and stared into the dark forest. "Tomorrow we can head west toward the edge of the range again. We can continue our search for a way down."

"According to Stavian's map, we should be almost to Trader's Pass by now." Calum leaned toward the fire, extended his hands, and rubbed them together. "Why not just head straight to Kanarah City and use the pass?"

"Given our recent escapades, it is likely the soldiers there will be looking for us. If not, they will at least be aware of who we are. If they recognize us, it will complicate our journey, to say the least." Magnus smacked a beetle that had landed on his leg, then he licked it off his hand with his long, red tongue.

Axel wrinkled his nose and frowned.

"Excuse me." Magnus added, "Granted, I'm not certain they will come after us, but I'd rather not risk it unless we have no other choice."

"I understand." Calum looked at Axel. "What do you think?"

Axel rolled his eyes. "We all know that neither of you actually care what I think, so you don't have to keep asking my opinion."

"Axel—"

"Just drop it," Axel snapped. "From now on, I'm just gonna cooperate and do whatever you guys want me to do, alright? Like a dutiful soldier. An obedient slave."

And we'll see how everything turns out then.

Calum sighed. "Fine, then. You take the first watch. I'll take the last watch. I'm beat."

Axel nodded. "Sure thing, boss."

Now Calum rolled his eyes.

SOMETHING SHOOK CALUM AWAKE. When he opened his eyes, he saw a big green hand on his chest, connected to a matching arm. An imposing reptilian face startled him at first, until he recognized Magnus.

"Your turn for the watch, Calum." Magnus extended his hand and pulled Calum up.

"Thanks." Calum yawned and stretched his sore arms, grateful that they felt better now than when he'd gone to sleep.

"It will be sunrise soon, but I intend to sleep my allotted four hours. If Axel wakes up early, please ask him to keep quiet."

Calum nodded and yawned again, then he sat down on a boulder near the campfire. Despite the chilly night air, the fire warmed him up. The boulder, which had absorbed some of the fire's heat also warmed his bottom.

"The bag of gold is right here next to you. Guard this especially. It is paramount. Wake me if you need help. I seriously doubt anyone or anything will come after it with the fire burning and with you awake, but those sabertooths came for us under these same conditions, so be on your guard anyway."

"Yeah, yeah. I got it, Magnus." Calum waved him away and rubbed his eyes. "Go to sleep. I'll be fine."

Magnus nodded. "Good night, then."

An hour passed. Calum stoked the fire, added a few more logs from the pile they'd gathered, and considered all that had transpired since he left the quarry.

He'd traveled the Snake Mountains. He'd fought and killed sabertooth cats. He'd run away from soldiers and raided one of their outposts, and he'd gotten clobbered by a group of bandits almost to the point of death.

And he'd killed people—at least two for sure. Granted, everyone he'd fought had meant him harm or wanted to kill him instead.

Magnus had warned Calum it would happen, that he'd have to make those kinds of choices, and he'd made them. Now those men would never draw breath again because of his blade. Still, he took comfort in knowing that he'd spared lives when he could.

On top of all of that, he'd had multiple dreams of Lumen. Perhaps when Calum finally found and freed him, all of this strife and violence would end. Maybe peace—true peace, not the kind manufactured by the King's tyranny—would reign in Kanarah, and everyone would just—

A shadow moved beyond the campfire.

Was it a shadow? Or was he imagining things?

Calum stared at the spot, and his eyes traced around the camp in the direction he thought he saw it move.

Nothing.

Yeah, right.

Something was out there. Or at least that's the stance he intended to take. He wouldn't convey it, though. Better to give the thief confidence and let him try something.

Still, if this was a Wolf like Magnus had thought, how would Calum fare if he had to face off against it? Were Wolves vicious? Intelligent versions of the sabertooth cats they'd faced? Or did they prefer to remain in the darkness and avoid confrontation? Calum would soon find out.

If he'd actually seen a shadow move.

Calum patted the bag of gold with his fingers then leaned back and stared up at the stars for a moment. They shimmered against the night sky like glistening drops of water stuck in place, unable to fall.

Something rustled behind him.

Calum swiveled his head and peered beyond the darkness, but it was only Axel, shifting in his sleep. Calum turned back and stared at the flickering campfire for a moment. Again, he wondered if he'd actually seen a shadow move in the first place or if his mind and the flickering campfire were playing tricks on him.

It didn't matter. He needed to behave as if he hadn't seen it. Then he could get the drop on whoever was—

A twig snapped to his left. The thief—or whatever it was—wasn't very quiet, and now Calum knew for sure that he wasn't alone.

Calum turned his head and stared in that direction for a moment, then he thought better of it. Perhaps he was feeding into the thief's plan. Well, as long as he kept his hand on the—

His fingers grasped only air where the pouch should have been.

When he looked down, it was gone.

CHAPTER 21

"Magnus! Axel!" Calum's voice split the quiet night.

Magnus sprung to his feet and his sword sang into his hand. "What is it? Are we being attacked?"

"Someone took the bag."

Axel stirred from his sleep as well, but much slower.

"*What?*" Magnus stepped toward him. "Did you fall asleep? Were you not guarding it?"

Calum shook his head. "I was awake the whole time. It was sitting here next to me. I heard a sound over there, so I looked. I didn't see anything, and when I turned back, the bag was gone."

"Wait, what?" Axel stood. "What happened?"

Magnus glared at Calum, then he turned to Axel. "The bag is gone. Someone took it."

Axel's eyes widened. He stomped toward Calum. "You let someone take our coin? *All* of it?"

"He stole it when I wasn't looking," Calum explained. "I didn't hear any footsteps. I didn't hear the coins clinking when the pouch got stolen. I didn't hear or see anything. I couldn't have known—"

Axel grabbed Calum by the sides of his leather breastplate and shook him. "I'm gonna *kill* you."

Magnus pulled them apart and eyed Axel. "Channel your anger into finding the thief. He is already on the run, so he has a head start on us. Do you remember what the Wolf paw prints look like?"

Calum nodded, but Axel just kept glaring at him.

"Axel." Magnus jerked him. "Do you remember what the—"

"*Yes.*" Axel's jaw tensed. "What does that have to do with anything?"

"I think, perhaps, that we may have fallen victim to another Wolf. Let us see what we can find. Grab a stick from the fire and use it to light your way. Look around."

Within a minute, they found the footprints and started to follow them.

"Shouldn't someone stay with the rest of the supplies at the camp?" Calum asked. "That bag

"Stop it. Calum is only as accountable as either you or me, Axel. We could have divided the coins or taken further precautions to prevent something like this, but we did not." Magnus turned to Calum. "You are right that you should stay at the camp. Axel and I will search for the thief."

Axel shook his head. "He just let our gold get stolen, and now you want him guarding everything else?"

"He is still recovering from his injuries, so he is not as mobile as you are. Quit arguing, bring your torch and your sword, and follow me," Magnus said. "Calum, stay at the camp until we get back."

To CALUM'S DISMAY, Magnus and Axel returned an hour after sunrise with nothing to show for their search.

Axel slammed his sword down on the ground and glared at Calum. "I hope you at least had the good sense to start breakfast."

"Come get some stew." Calum tossed him a pewter bowl. It would take much more than a bowl of stew to appease Axel, but it was a start. "You didn't find him, I take it?"

"He must have realized we were following him. The trail circled back over itself and branched into four different directions. I could not tell where it began and where it ended." Magnus reached for a bowl of his own and sat down next to Calum. "I knew we had to get back, so I called it off."

Even now, after traveling with him for so long, Calum still marveled at Magnus's size.

"I'm really sorry," he said.

Magnus shook his head and filled his bowl from the small pot Calum had perched over the fire. "Wolves are skilled thieves. They are quick, and they can all but disappear in darkness. I doubt I would have done any better than you."

Calum knew Magnus was just trying to make him feel better. "If you say so. Recently I've felt like the weak link in this group."

Axel walked over and ladled some stew into his bowl. "That's because you *are* the weak link."

Magnus sprung to his feet and knocked the bowl from Axel's hand in one quick motion, splattering stew on the ground.

Axel, wide-eyed, dropped the ladle.

Then Magnus grabbed Axel by the throat and lifted him clear off his feet, all while still holding his own bowl of stew in his other hand, even as Axel thrashed and struggled to get free.

Calum gawked at the sight. "Magnus, what are you—"

"Do not *ever* say anything like that again. Calum is the *soul* of this group. Without him, I would have gone my own way a long time ago and left you to fend for yourself."

Axel squirmed against Magnus's grip and clenched his arm with both hands.

"Calum is our leader, without question. I may have said otherwise, but I was wrong. Either you will begin to treat him with the respect he deserves, or you will leave the group. Crystal?"

Axel sputtered and managed to reply, "Clear."

Calum stifled a smile. He didn't like being at odds with Axel, but Magnus standing up for him felt good. Great, even.

Magnus dropped him, and Axel's boots hit the dirt. Once he sat back down, Magnus resumed eating his breakfast.

Axel rubbed his throat, coughed, picked up his bowl, then slumped against a tree several feet from the others with his arms folded.

"You didn't have to do that, Magnus," Calum said.

Magnus swallowed a large gulp of stew and turned his focus to Calum. "Did you hear what I just said to Axel?"

Calum glanced at Axel, who didn't make eye contact with him. "Yes."

"Everything I said was true. You *are* this group's leader and its soul, regardless of what I have said in the past. Without you, both Axel and I would be dead by now. You alone have seen visions of Lumen, and you alone have been called to free him. We are following *you*. We need you here, mistakes or otherwise."

Calum stared at the fire, digesting Magnus's words. Even if it was all true, the thief had left them in a tight spot. "But what are we going to do about the coin?"

"We can find another village. There are plenty of bandits in these mountains. Maybe they have wronged others whom we can help." Magnus gazed into the woods. "Or we could try to pick up the thief's trail and follow him until we catch up, but that may never happen."

"We could probably chase him forever, but we need to keep heading toward the valley," Calum said. "These dreams of Lumen aren't going away. Each time I dream of him, I sense more and more urgency for us to free him."

"Perhaps if we stop at one of the villages south of Pike's Garrison before Kanarah City we could hire out for some manual labor. We could—"

"No." Axel looked up. "I'm not going back to that life."

"I do not recall asking your opinion." Magnus turned his reptilian gaze toward him.

"Easy, Magnus," Calum said.

Magnus hissed a sigh. "It would only be for a few days at the mo—"

"I said *no*." Axel's voice hardened.

"I'm with Axel on this one," Calum said. "I don't want to go back to manual labor unless I have no other choice. Eight years in a quarry was long enough."

Magnus hissed again but nodded. "Then what do you suggest we do?"

Calum glanced between them and stood to his feet. "After you guys finish eating, we'll pack up and head west toward the edge of the range. We'll keep trying to find a way down, farther south along the range. If we can't find anything, we go to Kanarah City and cross over Trader's Pass."

Magnus glanced at Axel, then downed the rest of his stew. "I will start packing, then."

BRILLIANT LIGHT FILLED Calum's vision, and Lumen appeared once again.

Another night, another dream.

"Go to the Arcanum," Lumen said in his all-pervading voice. "Time is short. Set me free, and I will bring justice to those who have done you and your friends harm."

Lumen had been watching them? Was he referring to what had happened to Calum's parents, or something else entirely?

"How do you know all of this?" Calum asked.

"I see many things," Lumen replied. "My power is burgeoning. Free me, and I will defeat the King, claim my rightful throne, and grant you the desires of your heart."

The living map snapped into view, and a grand city came into view. Towering gray walls surrounded it, and within its walls people bustled throughout its streets and buildings.

"What is this place?" Calum asked. "Is it Solace?"

"No," Lumen replied. "Solace is a far greater city. This is Kanarah City. Here you will find the entrance to Trader's Pass."

Calum nodded.

"Time is short, Calum." Lumen repeated. "You must reach Trader's Pass soon. I have chosen you to free me, and when you do, I will glorify you above all others." The living map swirled and evaporated into the light that outlined Lumen's powerful form. "Go forth. Find the Arcanum, and learn the secret to releasing me."

Lumen and his light spiraled into the blackness of Calum's dreams once again.

"I DON'T THINK we have a choice." Calum rubbed his sore neck and straightened his back. "It's been a week. Lumen told me we were supposed to go down to Kanarah City. We've already searched almost the entire edge of the range, and we still haven't found a way down. Kanarah City is the easiest way get to Trader's Pass, and then we can cross over to find the Arcanum."

Magnus shook his head. "We are certain to encounter trouble. I know it."

Axel rolled his eyes. "Look, if you ever wanna get across the valley, that's the way we need to go."

"Since when are you so willing to make the trip?" Magnus asked. "Or provide a useful opinion about… well, anything?"

"Didn't say I was, but I'm sick of wandering the woods without a reason to be here. I'm sick of rationing our food. I'd rather get to Kanarah City and try our luck there."

Calum smirked. Since Magnus's confrontation with Axel, they seemed to have reconciled their differences and meshed into more of a team, and Axel had grown much more cooperative. Hopefully, he'd stay that way.

"Besides, if Calum's having dreams about Kanarah City, then maybe we *are* supposed to go there," Axel said.

Calum's smirk widened into a smile. "Axel is right, Magnus. We need to get out of here and make better progress in reaching the Arcanum. There just isn't a safe way down to the valley from here or anywhere along the range."

Magnus huffed. "Then lead the way."

"Regret that you made me the leader yet?" Calum elbowed Magnus's armored ribs. He didn't even flinch.

"Moderately, yes."

Calum led them east through the woods for the next few hours until they reached a small clearing. Sunlight emblazoned the tall green-and-gold grass from above, and the entire color range of autumn leaves swirled in the wind.

About ten steps into the clearing, Magnus grabbed Calum's shoulder. "Stop."

Calum knew what that meant, and his blood tingled in anticipation. "What do you hear?"

"We are not alone. Axel, get over here."

Axel plodded over and scanned the tree line. "I don't see anything."

"They are not in the trees." Then, cryptically, Magnus added, "We have walked into a trap."

Dark forms rose from the tall grass all around them. First five, then ten. By the time all of them stood up, Calum counted twenty men surrounding them, all brandishing gleaming weapons.

Calum, Axel, and Magnus drew their swords.

This was bad.

Calum was still learning about strategy and tactics from Magnus, but he didn't have to be an expert to know that three fighters, surrounded by twenty in an open field with no cover and no chance of escape, had little chance of surviving, much less winning.

Yep. Definitely bad.

One of the men, clad in dark-red armor, sauntered toward them. He stroked his curly black beard with his left hand, and in his right, he gripped a shining sword with a slight curve at the end of its red blade. A long burgundy cape with a black lining hung from his shoulders.

Definitely not one of the King's soldiers.

He pointed a finger at Calum. "You killed my cousin."

Calum held his sword at the ready but glanced at Magnus and Axel. "Who are you?"

"My name is Tyburon, leader of the Southern Snake Brotherhood. You killed my cousin."

"Bandits and assassins," Magnus hissed.

Calum swallowed the lump in his throat. "Who was your cousin?"

"His name was Norm. He led the Northern Snake Brotherhood." Tyburon's gaze hardened, and Calum immediately recognized a resemblance to Norm.

Tyburon could have passed for a taller, thinner version of his cousin, but the way he carried himself suggested he was far more dangerous.

"You broke into his hideout and killed him along with most of his men."

Most of his men? Calum's eyes widened.

Tyburon tilted his head. "Thought you killed everyone, didn't you?"

Magnus and Calum glanced at each other.

"Nicolai, come here." Without shifting his gaze from Calum, Tyburon motioned with his left hand.

One of the men walked over. He wore dark-green armor and held what appeared to be an oversized meat cleaver in his left hand. The man removed his helmet, revealing curly black hair and dark eyes.

Calum had knocked him out in the kitchen at the bandits' hideout.

"You see," Tyburon patted Nicolai's armored shoulder, "Nicolai escaped through the back door before you three could finish him off, although it came at the cost of a nasty bump on his head. He came straight to me and told me what had happened, and we've been tracking the three of you ever since."

"What do you intend to do?" Magnus stood between Tyburon and Calum.

Tyburon smiled. "I'm here with twenty armed men, and you're asking what I intend to do?"

Calum pushed past Magnus. "Your cousin and his bandits preyed on innocent villagers, people who barely had enough to get by without suffering extra loss from your cousin's men."

"Hence the term 'bandits,' mmm?" Tyburon shrugged. "It's a living. Not a noble one, but a living nonetheless. In this age, everyone has to look out for themselves and their families. Now I'm looking out for mine."

"Killing us won't bring your cousin back," Calum said, now well within striking range of Tyburon.

"No, it won't," Tyburon said as Nicolai put his helmet back on. "But it will make me happy, and it will serve as a warning that anyone who dares to oppose the Brotherhood will meet the same fate."

Tyburon lashed his red-bladed sword at Calum, but Magnus jerked Calum back just in time. Magnus counterattacked with his own blade. Tyburon blocked the blow, but it forced him back a step.

They stood at odds, opposing each other but not approaching.

All Calum could think of was how fast Tyburon's blow had come at him. If Magnus hadn't yanked him out of the way...

Calum concluded that unlike Norm, Tyburon was a skilled and ruthless fighter. He probably had to be in order to maintain his authority over a bunch of murderous, thieving bandits. And he was fast—deadly so.

When Nicolai started forward, Tyburon put his hand against Nicolai's chest to keep him from advancing. "Not yet, Nicolai. You'll get your chance soon enough. Fall back in line with the others… and close the noose."

As the bandits backed away, Magnus said, "Let me handle Tyburon."

Calum nodded. "What are we gonna do?"

Magnus pulled Axel closer to them. "Put your backs against mine. Stay nearby. We are going to fight."

Axel nodded. "You'd better believe we're gonna fight."

"Let them come to you. Let them do the work," Magnus muttered so only they could hear him. "When they get close enough to strike, then strike, but not before then. Do not let them get any of us from behind. And most importantly, when I yell 'switch,' rotate one quarter turn to your left and take down whoever ends up in front of you."

"Will that even work?" Disbelief lined Axel's voice.

"It is worth a try. It will catch them off guard, but it will only work once."

"Alright," Axel said. "Let's do this."

As the bandits closed in around them, Tyburon yelled, "Save the little one for me. He killed Norm. He's mine."

Great. So much for avoiding Tyburon.

Six of the bandits, not including Tyburon or Nicolai, drew in closer, almost within the range that Magnus had referenced. Some of them wore mismatched armor, mostly on their chests and arms, and some of them wore robes or animal skins instead. Each of them wore a confident snarl.

Calum wanted to peek over his shoulder at Axel and Magnus, but he didn't. He kept his eyes focused on the two bandits in front of him.

One of them stepped within range.

Calum lunged forward and swung his sword in a broad swipe at the bandit's exposed left ankle, but the bandit jumped back just in time to avoid getting hit.

"You telegraphed your swing, Calum," Magnus hissed at him from behind. "I cannot even see you, and I knew what you intended to do. Conceal your intentions before you move. Let him do the work for you."

The first bandit stepped within range again. This time Calum waited.

The second bandit sprang forward and jabbed at him with a spear. Calum parried, then he ducked under the first bandit's sword. The clanging of weapons sounded behind him as Magnus and Axel engaged their foes, too.

Another spear jab just missed Calum's arm. He batted the spear toward the first bandit, and it stalled his next attack. Calum rolled under his next swipe and cut him down at his knees. The first bandit dropped, screaming.

The second bandit thrust his spear at Calum's face. Reflex jerked Calum's sword upward, deflecting the attack, but he'd wandered away from his friends.

He stumbled back closer to Magnus and Axel and waited for the next attack to come. He traded several swings and swipes with the spear bandit, but he couldn't get close enough to do any damage. The spear had the length advantage, and no matter what Calum did, he couldn't get past it.

"Switch!" Magnus roared.

Calum took three quick steps to his left and intercepted a haphazard axe meant for Axel. The bandit's axe skidded off Calum's incoming sword, but Calum's return swing caught the bandit just under his ribs.

If the bandit had been wearing armor, it would've saved him, but instead he wore only animal skins and fabric. He sputtered then dropped to the ground.

Calum stole a glance back in time to see Magnus wrench the spear away from the spear bandit he'd been fighting. Weaponless, the bandit turned and tried to flee, but Magnus hurled the spear at him. It skewered through the bandit's back, and he went down.

"Fall back," Tyburon hollered. "Fall back *now*."

Only two of the original six bandits had survived. They retreated back into their circle, now four men thinner than before.

"No more child's play. This time we *all* go in at the same time." Tyburon pointed his sword at Calum. "But the boy is still mine."

"Then come and get me." It sounded fierce and confident when Calum said it. Whether he actually felt either of those things was a different matter.

The noose tightened so that all sixteen of the remaining bandits plus Tyburon stood almost shoulder-to-shoulder around Calum, Magnus, and Axel.

Definitely, definitely bad.

"What do we do now?" Calum muttered.

"We kill them all," Axel said.

Magnus exhaled a long sigh. "No matter what happens, it has been an honor to know you both."

Calum tightened his grip on the handle of his sword.

A horse whinnied in the distance. Calum glanced in that direction, but he didn't see anything. He refocused on Tyburon and his advancing men, except now Tyburon had locked his eyes on something far away.

"By the Overlord." Tyburon's eyebrows arched lower.

"What is it?" Calum asked.

"Soldiers." Axel shielded the sun from his eyes with his left hand but didn't lower his sword. "A lot of 'em."

Calum grumbled, "As if things couldn't have been worse."

"They're coming this direction," Axel said. "What do we do?"

"Stay put, and stay on your guard," Magnus said. "Things are about to get very interesting, very quickly."

CHAPTER 22

"**B**rothers, regroup to me," Tyburon said. To Calum's surprise, the bandits abandoned their circle and formed two orderly lines with Tyburon in the center. He hadn't expected them to demonstrate that level of discipline.

"We should make a break for it," Axel said. "We're not surrounded anymore."

Magnus eyed him. "First you want to fight, now you wish to flee?"

"There are at least two-dozen soldiers approaching, plus seventeen bandits. Forty-one is too many to risk fighting on our own."

Calum chuckled. "So forty-one is your cut-off for too many enemies to fight at once?"

Axel scowled at him and quipped, "No, it's actually more like thirty-seven. Maybe thirty-eight if I'm feeling especially spunky."

Calum rolled his eyes. "Axel raises a good point. Why don't we just run for it?"

"If we flee, both sides will pursue us, and we will be killed," Magnus said. "If we stand our ground, perhaps it will end differently. Besides, the soldiers are too close now. It is too late to flee."

Calum wanted to say something else, but a yell stayed his words.

"By order of the King and with his full authority, I, Commander Beynard Anigo, command all of you to lay down your arms and surrender for crimes against the Crown."

Calum turned back. A commander on a white horse extended his spear as he and two-dozen soldiers approached.

"Do it," Magnus said.

"*What?*" Axel's tone could have shattered a boulder.

"Just *do it*, but keep them within reach. Trust me."

Calum and Magnus dropped their swords to the ground, but Axel hesitated.

"*Axel.*" Calum nudged him.

Axel grunted but dropped his sword at his feet, then he unslung his spear from his back and tossed that to the ground as well.

"Raise your hands, too." Magnus raised his hands into the air, and Calum and Axel mimicked

Commander Anigo reined in his horse about ten feet from their position, and the soldiers stopped just behind him. He looked them over and smirked, and Calum took in his handsome face and dark eyes. He exuded confidence, much as Tyburon or Magnus did, only in a more polished, official sense.

Commander Anigo eyed the bandits behind them next. "You men, drop your weapons as well. I order you in the name of the King."

As if on cue, Calum, Axel, and Magnus rotated so they could see both the soldiers and the bandits.

Tyburon stepped forward. "We will not relinquish our weapons. Our quarrel is not with you, but with these three villains."

Commander Anigo's voice hardened. "I said to drop your weapons."

"We will do no such thing."

"A violation of an order given by the King's representatives is equivalent to disobeying the King himself," Commander Anigo said. "You are hereby under arrest. Drop your weapons and surrender."

Calum glanced at Magnus who gave both Axel and him a wink. Whatever Commander Anigo wanted to achieve, he wasn't going to succeed at it.

Tyburon smiled and shook his head. "Commander, do you have any idea who I am?"

"Your identity doesn't factor into this matter." Commander Anigo narrowed his gaze. "Only the King's does."

Unfazed, Tyburon continued, "I am Tyburon, leader of the Southern Snake Brotherhood."

Now it was Commander Anigo's turn to look unimpressed. "So?"

Tyburon chuckled. "You really have no idea who I am, do you?"

"Like I said—" Commander Anigo pointed his spear at Tyburon. "—it doesn't matter who you are. You're still under arrest."

"Alright." Still holding his sword, Tyburon raised his hands in the air as if to dismiss Commander Anigo's words. "You obviously don't know what you're saying, so I'll grant you a pass for your ignorance... just this once. If you run along, you and your men don't have to die today."

Commander Anigo went stone-still, and his face warped into a mask of rage mixed with disbelief. "Did you just *threaten* me?"

"Threaten you?" Tyburon scoffed. "No, Commander. I'm trying to show you mercy."

The ranks of soldiers stirred behind Commander Anigo. He held up his right hand, the one that didn't hold the spear, and they fell silent. "No, sir. You threatened me. To threaten one of the King's representatives is to—"

"To threaten you is to threaten the King himself," Tyburon interrupted. "Yes, I get it. If you want to take it as a threat, fine. But I assure you that not a single one of your men will escape this field alive should you try to disarm and arrest us."

"Soldiers, prepare for battle." Commander Anigo raised his spear, and every soldier behind him drew their weapons and stepped into a balanced fighting posture.

"Last chance, commander. These three belong to me. They killed my cousin and his friends, and I'm here to do right by my kin." Tyburon extended his hands out to his sides. "I have no desire to spill your blood on this field as well."

"These three are wanted for the deaths of multiple quarry workers, the ransacking of one of the King's outposts, and for the murder of at least three of the King's soldiers. We have been pursuing them for weeks." Commander Anigo's jaw hardened. "Their penalty is death."

Calum's stomach twisted. He'd considered that the consequences of his escape and his actions since might end his life, but hearing Commander Anigo proclaim it aloud somehow made it more real, more ominous.

But the fear quickly yielded to obstinance. Why should he pay for the sins of others? He hadn't enslaved himself at the quarry. He hadn't subjugated people and forced them to work in order to better his own life. He hadn't ordered the death of anyone's parents.

The sheer gall of the King to rule his subjects in such a way kindled a righteous anger within Calum that he hadn't known was there before. Those four words passing sentence on him and his friends made him realize, for the first time, exactly why Lumen needed to save Kanarah.

Calum would do everything he possibly could to ensure that it happened.

"But it shall not be at your hands," Commander Anigo concluded.

Tyburon readied his red-bladed sword. "Then we have a serious problem."

"Soldiers, take the three outlaws into custody immediately."

About half the soldiers marched forward, still battle-ready, toward Calum, Axel, and Magnus. Tyburon waved his left arm in a big arc. "Brothers, forward."

"Great. Now they're closing in on both sides," Axel muttered. "We're in worse shape than before."

"That is precisely why I instructed you to keep your weapons close." Magnus's golden-eyed gaze darted between the two forces. "When I say the word, grab your weapons and back away from the main fight. Let them thin each other out, and we will clean up the rest. Only fight those who come directly for you. I will handle Tyburon."

"Good. That leaves the big-talking commander for me," Axel said.

Calum nodded. It sounded like a good plan, at least. "I hope this works…"

"If not, we will perish anyway," Magnus said. "At least I bought us a few more minutes to watch a good show on our way out."

Axel huffed.

Tyburon and his men charged forward. In response, Commander Anigo and his men also charged forward, including the twelve soldiers who'd already started marching in.

"Now!"

At Magnus's shout, Calum and Axel snatched their swords from the ground, and Axel grabbed his spear as well. All three of them retreated straight back.

About a quarter of the closest soldiers followed them, as did a quarter of the bandits, but the rest plowed straight into each other, their weapons flashing in the midday sun.

Axel fended off two of the bandits while Magnus handled two of the soldiers, and Calum had one of each. They stood in an awkward triangle, each of them glancing between the other two, but none of them moved.

The bandit swung his axe at Calum's head, but Calum dodged the attack. The soldier jabbed at the bandit with his spear, but the bandit parried the attack and returned with one of his own, and they continued to fight each other. Perfect.

Calum ducked away from the fight and snuck up behind Axel's opponents. Two swings of his sword from behind them dropped them to their knees, and Axel finished them off from the front. He and Calum exchanged nods and repositioned themselves to look for new enemies.

Magnus felled one of the soldiers with his sword, grabbed the other by his throat, and hurled the soldier toward three approaching bandits.

They all hit the dirt hard upon impact, and when the bandits made it back to their feet, they ganged up on the soldier. He didn't last long, but another soldier joined the fray and quickly cut down two of the bandits. He faced off with the one that remained.

Axel and Calum partnered against the next batch of soldiers and bandits. They had a good system: they waited until one of the soldiers attacked one of the bandits, or vice-versa, and then they threw a quick barrage at the attacker. Each time it happened, the initial attacker got himself wounded or killed.

In the distance, Calum saw Tyburon at work. He took down opponents with broad, sweeping swings, and otherwise walked through the battle as if strolling through a vacant field admiring the flowers and butterflies.

But when their eyes met, Tyburon's entire countenance changed to one of limitless fury. He started toward Calum, now walking much faster than his previous casual pace.

"I'm gonna take on the commander, alright?" Axel said.

Before Calum could respond, Axel stormed into the battle toward Commander Anigo, who deftly battled the bandits from atop his white horse.

Meanwhile, Tyburon drew even nearer.

"Magnus!" Calum cried.

Magnus carved through his opponents like a gigantic green-and-blue blur, but he'd ventured too far away from Calum. Instead, he engaged what appeared to be a mixed force of seven or eight men from both sides combined. He showed no indication of having heard Calum's call, so Calum started toward him.

A soldier whirled around and swung at Calum with a sword. He dodged the stab, clamped his left hand on the soldier's opposite wrist, and ran him through.

A second soldier came at him with an axe. Calum yanked his sword free and raised it to block the blow, but a red blade with a curve at its end intercepted it. One swift motion later, the soldier dropped to the ground, dead from a savage hack.

Tyburon stood in the soldier's place and glared at Calum with bloodlust in his hazel eyes.

CHAPTER 23

"I would kill every man on this battlefield to get to you," Tyburon said.

Calum glanced past Tyburon. Both Magnus and Axel still fought others, too occupied to even notice him, much less help.

He was on his own.

"Your friends can't save you now, *boy*."

Tyburon's first attack came so fast that Calum barely had time to avoid it, but somehow he managed to back away just in time. The second was predictable—a hard chop down at his head. Calum blocked it easily, but he couldn't do anything when Tyburon's boot slammed into his chest.

Calum skidded through the tall grass on his back. He pushed himself upright in time to bat away a series of quick strikes from Tyburon's sword.

A brick hit his face and pain flared in his right cheek. No, not a brick—Tyburon's fist.

Calum staggered back and shook his cognition back into place. Tyburon would maintain his advantage unless Calum could do something to interrupt it.

He knew one thing for sure—if Tyburon expected to kill him easily, Calum intended to disappoint him. Magnus hadn't trained him over the last few months for nothing, and Lumen hadn't called him for no reason, either.

Calum had been chosen, and he'd resolved not to fail, no matter what.

Tyburon laughed. "How does that feel, boy?"

"Not as good as killing your cousin." Calum cracked his neck and leveled his sword.

A solemn wave washed Tyburon's glee away. "First, you kill my cousin. Then you make me track you through the woods, away from my home and my bed. Now you're joking about it? By the time I'm done, no one will even be able to *recognize* you."

"You talk too much."

Tyburon slashed at Calum's head, but Calum rolled under the blow and swung at his legs. Tyburon blocked the attack and kicked Calum again. Calum's breastplate absorbed most of the kick, but the impact knocked him off balance. He fell to the ground, totally vulnerable.

Tyburon's red blade chopped at Calum's left leg, but Calum jerked it away. When Tyburon followed up with a chop at Calum's right leg, Calum shifted, dodged the blow, and planted the sole of his left boot on Tyburon's knee. He pushed off, and Tyburon's knee buckled as Calum rolled backward onto his feet.

Grimacing, Tyburon came at him right away with another swing, and sharp pain knifed across Calum's chest. Had Calum's sword not been there, and had his leather armor not absorbed some of the hack, the slash would've killed him.

As it was, Tyburon's red blade remained where it was, partway digging into the flesh of Calum's chest. Only Calum's sword and his strength kept it from delving any deeper.

With gritted teeth, Calum shoved his sword against Tyburon's, and the blade barely dislodged from Calum's leather breastplate. He staggered back a few desperate steps and dabbed at his chest. Blood tainted his fingertips.

"I hope it hurts," Tyburon said. "It's only the beginning."

Calum glanced at Magnus and Axel again. Magnus had whittled the number of his opponents down to three—all of them the King's soldiers.

Axel no longer held his spear, but he had somehow managed to get Commander Anigo off of his horse, which then bolted for the tree line. They now fought face-to-face in a flurry of clashing metal that made Calum glad he wasn't fighting Commander Anigo.

Then again, he still had Tyburon to deal with.

Tyburon smirked. "Truth be told, I'm impressed you even made it this far."

"That makes two of us." Calum swallowed the lump in his throat and sucked in several quick breaths.

"Not so confident anymore, are you?" Tyburon angled his sword so the tip pointed at Calum's face.

"It's just a cut."

"It's a harbinger of your demise," Tyburon said. "A promise of things to come."

To Calum's surprise, he defended Tyburon's next several attacks without incident, and he even managed to throw in a few of his own. He actually struck Tiburon's left thigh once, but the blow didn't pierce his armor.

Tyburon staggered back and shook his leg, all while calling down every curse and hurling every profane name under the sky at Calum. "You're gonna pay for that."

"Add it to your list of grievances." Calum sucked in quick breaths, trying to ignore the pain in his chest.

"Funny thing is..." Tyburon huffed and waved his sword through the tall grass, for now keeping his distance. "I didn't even like Norm."

Calum's jaw tensed, and anger briefly overpowered the pain in his chest. "Then why are you taking this so personally?"

Tyburon shrugged and began to circle Calum, still teasing the grass with his red blade. "He was my family, and part of the Brotherhood."

Calum wanted to sling a curse or two at him, but Tyburon didn't grant him the time. A hailstorm of attacks rained down on Calum. He parried some and dodged the others, straining to meet each blow.

"Just give up, already," Tyburon said between thrusts. "I'll make it quick and painless for you. Mostly."

"Why don't *you* give up?" If Calum could survive just a bit longer, then perhaps Magnus could come and assist him. "You're old. I'm only sixteen. I have a long life ahead of me. You're basically worthless now."

Tyburon glared at him and scoffed. "Kid, I'm only thirty-eight. That's not old."

As they'd fought, one thing in particular stood out to Calum—Tyburon was aware of everything happening around him in the battle. At one point, he even backed away from the fight to grab a soldier from behind and run him through, thus saving Nicolai, then he reengaged Calum the instant he released his grip on the soldier.

Perhaps Calum could use that to his advantage... but how?

Tyburon lashed at Calum's head, and he leaned back and out of the way. The red metal of the blade missed his nose by inches, and Tyburon continued to spin around for another hack.

As Magnus had taught him, Calum stepped into Tyburon's swing and met his sword with his own instead of falling back. The blades met, and Calum earned a slight advantage by catching Tyburon off guard.

The advantage didn't last long. Though Calum's blade blocked Tyburon's sword from harming him, Tyburon's other elbow freely slammed into Calum's right cheek. The blow stunned Calum, and Tyburon freed his sword with another hard shove to Calum's chest.

In that moment, he realized he'd never beat Tyburon outright. Despite Calum's words to the contrary, the effects of the fight fatigued his body. Even though Tyburon wasn't much stronger than Calum, he was just as fast, if not faster, and he had another twenty-plus years of experience reinforcing his every decision.

No matter how hard he fought, no matter how fast he tried to be, Calum couldn't win—at least not that way. But if he could use the surrounding battle to his advantage, perhaps he'd have a chance.

"Magnus!" he called. "Magnus, help me!"

He knew Magnus wouldn't hear him. The distance between them and Magnus had actually increased since he first called for help.

Sure enough, Tyburon turned his head toward where Calum was looking, although only very slightly. His gaze flitted away for just a moment then refocused back on Calum's.

"The Saurian can't help you now." Tyburon showed him a twisted smile. "You're going to die just as you are now: all alone."

"That's what you think." Calum diverted his gaze from Tyburon's for just a moment, looking over his shoulder, then looked at him again. When he did it a second time, Calum cracked a faint smile.

It worked.

Tyburon's head swiveled that direction for an instant, and his eyes followed, but that was all Calum needed. He sprang forward.

Calum anticipated the kind of reaction he'd receive. Tyburon's head and eyes jerked forward again, and he swung his sword at Calum on a downward angle from his right shoulder down to his left hip.

While still in motion, Calum ducked low and twisted his body away from the slash but toward Tyburon's right side. As Tyburon's blade streaked just over Calum's head and back and started his follow-up swing, Calum drove his shoulder into Tyburon's midsection.

As simple as it was, the move had worked before to knock both Burtis and Jidon off balance. It worked this time against Tyburon, too.

Tyburon pitched off-balance, and as the bandit tried to right himself, Calum found his opening. Just like Axel had done to him, he quickly rotated around Tyburon, grabbed him by the back collar of his armor, and yanked. Tyburon lost his footing and landed on his rear-end, just as Calum had in the woods.

As Tyburon struggled to regain his footing, Calum jammed his sword through Tyburon's burgundy cape and into his back. The blade punctured deep into Tyburon's body, out his chest, and through his breastplate.

Tyburon's struggle stopped, and he sat there, stunned as he stared down at the steel protruding from his chest. When Calum wrenched his sword from Tyburon's body, Tyburon rolled onto his back.

His blood-tinged mouth hung open, and his eyes widened as he wheezed, "I don't believe it."

Calum looked down at him. "If it's any consolation, neither do I."

With one mighty swing, Calum severed Tyburon's head from his body.

ASIDE FROM MAGNUS, Axel had never fought anyone so skilled before. Commander Anigo had proven to be more than a worthy opponent—he was dangerous and even downright scary at times. The guy was just intense... and really vicious and determined to win.

That didn't mean he was going to, though. Not if Axel had anything to say about it.

Axel threw a haphazard slice at him, but Commander Anigo ducked under the attack and jabbed his spear at Axel's chest. Axel parried it away with his sword, but as he did, he stepped back, and something rolled under his heel.

He staggered to stay upright and find his footing again, all while defending two subsequent jabs from Commander Anigo. Then he backed up to get a glance at what he'd stepped on.

His spear. He'd dropped it earlier and lost track of it, but now it lay at his feet.

Axel refocused on Commander Anigo, but positioned his feet on either side of the weapon. He'd practiced the move before and managed to fool Calum a few times, but he'd never tried it in a real battle.

Only one way to find out if it'll work.

Axel tossed his sword, blade-first, at Commander Anigo, not as an attack, but as a distraction. Sure enough, Commander Anigo's eyes followed the sword, not Axel's movements. While Commander Anigo dodged the weapon, Axel kicked his spear up into his hands.

By the time Commander Anigo refocused, Axel's spear was already headed for his chest. The spearhead pierced the commander's breastplate and dug even deeper still, and his eyes widened. He dropped his spear, clamped his hands around the spear shaft, and slumped to the ground.

Axel retrieved his sword, then once Commander Anigo stopped moving and went limp, he bent down and pulled the commander's sword from its sheath on his belt. He couldn't have counted the number of dents and chips in the edges of his old blade, but Commander Anigo's sword looked as if it had been sharpened that morning, so Axel swapped them.

He also took Commander Anigo's spear and left his behind, still lodged in the commander's chest.

Axel grinned and exhaled a long, relieved breath. "Thanks for the steel. Feel free to keep mine right where I left it."

Magnus had just finished off the last of the men battling him, so Axel scanned the field for Calum. It didn't take him long to find him since everyone else was dead.

Apparently, that included Tyburon.

Unbelievable. I really didn't think he had it in him.

Axel waved to Magnus and they both jogged over to Calum. When they arrived, Axel gawked at the sight of Tyburon's bearded head lying next to his body. "You beat him all on your own?"

Calum nodded. Between haggard breaths, he said, "Yeah. I still can't believe it. I used that move Axel showed me the other day. The one where he got behind me and pulled the back of my armor? It worked."

Axel glanced and Magnus and smirked. "Our baby is growing up."

Magnus frowned at him. "Even if Saurians and humans could procreate, you are the last person I would ever care to raise a child with."

"Ew. Not at all what I meant." Axel shook his head. "It was supposed to be a joke."

"Interesting. Are human jokes not designed to include humor?" Magnus asked.

"No, they are, but—" Axel caught Magnus smirking this time. "You're a big jerk. You know that?"

"I think I'll take his sword as a memento of today." Calum picked up Tyburon's sword and examined it. Its red blade glistened stark against its black handle, hilt, and the garnet set into the pommel. Definitely the most impressive sword Axel had ever seen.

Axel and Magnus glanced at each other. Still in disbelief, Axel asked, "You sure you didn't have help?"

Calum's brow furrowed. "You don't believe me? I swear it's true."

"That's... incredible," Axel said.

"Come on. Give me some credit here. I know what I'm doing." Calum bent down and unfastened Tyburon's belt, removed the sword's sheath, and slung it to his waist. He nodded to Magnus. "After all, I had a great teacher."

Axel cleared his throat.

"Oh, yeah. And an amateur sparring dummy to beat up on."

"One good kill, and his ego's as big as a house," Axel said.

"Reminds me of someone else I know," Magnus said.

Axel glared at him, then he shifted his glare to Calum. "We both know I could kick your brains out if I wanted to."

"Just be happy we survived this in the first place." Magnus's gaze fixed on something in the distance, and he threaded his broadsword between the two of them. "Gentlemen, it appears we have a straggler."

Axel and Calum followed Magnus's line of sight.

About fifty yards away, a man in dark-green armor with curly black hair hobbled toward the tree line.

Nicolai.

"Should I go after him?" Axel asked.

"We all will," Magnus said. "Come on."

RUNNING across a field wasn't exactly how Calum would've chosen to celebrate his victory over Tyburon, but Nicolai had left him with little choice. He followed Axel through the tall grass, and they caught up to him in just a few minutes, right before he made it into the woods.

Axel kicked the back of Nicolai's knee, and Nicolai fell to the ground. Calum reached them not long after. By then, Axel had his knee on Nicolai's gut, one hand pinning his chest down, and the other holding his sword to Nicolai's throat.

"Oh, please—" Nicolai shielded his face with his hands. He didn't have a weapon on him as far as Calum could see. "Please don't kill me!"

Axel glanced at Calum, who crouched down next to Nicolai with Tyburon's—now *his* red sword in his hand. He couldn't have been much older than Axel—maybe three or four years, tops. Calum couldn't help but wonder what had led someone so young to join up with a bunch of thieving bandits.

"*Please.*" Nicolai clasped his hands together, and tears streamed down his face. "Please— please don't—"

"Quiet." Calum glared at him. "From this point on, you don't say another word unless I give you permission. Crystal?"

Nicolai nodded at least six more times than necessary.

Axel stood up now that Calum had the situation under control.

"You brought this on yourself." Calum tapped Nicolai's chest with the tip of his new sword, and a bit of blood dotted Nicolai's dark-green breastplate. "I let you live, and you ran off to tell your friends about us?"

Magnus approached them from behind, and he, too watched the scene unfold.

"I'm sorry. I'm so, so sor—"

Calum pressed his sword against Nicolai's lips. "I don't recall giving you permission to talk."

Again, Nicolai nodded a bunch of times. When Calum pulled his sword away, someone else's blood tainted Nicolai's lips red. It made him look even more foolish than he already did, but he made no effort to wipe the blood away.

"Now," Calum continued. "I'm gonna let you go."

"What?" Axel stepped forward. "You can't let him go. He's just gonna run back to some other group of bandits, and they'll come after us next. We need to kill him."

Calum understood Axel's reservations, but he wasn't going to kill an unarmed man in cold blood. Even the thought of it sickened his stomach.

"If he convinces more bandits to come after us, we'll just handle them like we did these guys. He knows that." Calum stared daggers at him to emphasize his point. "Don't you?"

Nicolai nodded again.

"So instead, Nicolai is gonna find the nearest village, get help for his injured leg, and find a profession that keeps him out of trouble from now on. Right?"

Nicolai didn't move.

Calum rolled his eyes. "You can talk, Nicolai."

"Yes," Nicolai blurted. "I'll never do anything bad again. I swear. Plus I'll make up for all the wrong I've done by giving to the poor, by helping people, by—"

"We get it." Calum held up his hand. "Now listen, because I'm only gonna say this once. If I ever see you again, or if I hear you've joined another group of bandits, or if I find out you're oppressing common people or *anyone* less fortunate than you, I will drop whatever I'm doing, I'll find you, and I'll end your miserable life."

Nicolai swallowed, and his bulging Adam's apple jumped up to his chin.

Calum's voice hardened. "Crystal?"

Nicolai nodded for the hundredth time. "Clear."

"Then get out of my sight."

Nicolai struggled to his feet. "Thank you. Oh, thank you, thank you, thank—"

Calum pointed to the trees. "*Now.*"

Nicolai gave a slight bow, then he stumbled into the woods, heading southwest.

Axel shook his head. "You should've killed him. You didn't last time, and look what that got us into."

"I disagree," Magnus said. "The mark of a true warrior, as my father always told me, is not evidenced through his displays of strength and prowess, but through his acts of kindness, charity, and mercy."

Axel folded his arms. "Yeah, maybe if 'kindness,' 'charity,' and 'mercy' are the names of my sword, spear, and axe."

"I might actually name this sword 'Kindness,'" Calum said. "Because then I can kill people with Kindness."

Axel smirked and pointed at him. "That's actually pretty good."

Magnus just shook his head. "Come. Let us return to the battlefield to collect what we can.

Perhaps these brigands have some coin on them or something we can trade when we reach Kanarah City."

Axel grinned and rubbed his hands together. "Maybe both, if we're lucky."

ABOUT FIVE MINUTES after he heard the last of the survivors' voices fade into the distance, Commander Anigo wrenched the spear from his breastplate and let it fall to the ground next to him. He pressed his left hand against his wounded chest, and blood oozed between his fingers.

He chanced a look down. The spear had pierced through his armor and into his flesh, slowed only by the chain maille he wore underneath. The spear may have plunged deeper still, but he couldn't be sure. However bad it was, he needed to get help, and fast.

With his right hand, he pushed himself to a sitting position. His chest ignited with fresh, sharp pain as if he'd been stabbed all over again. He inhaled several quick breaths, then he raised his right hand to his lips and whistled.

The clop-clop-clop of approaching hooves sounded behind him, and soon a horse—Candlestick—sidled up next to him.

Even if he couldn't count on anyone else, he could count on Candlestick.

Commander Anigo grabbed one of Candlestick's stirrups and pulled himself up, then he gripped the saddle and sprang atop Candlestick's back. Everything hurt, but he'd mounted his horse.

As he prepared to ride off, he caught sight of Corporal Bezarion laying face-up in the field, staring at the blue sky with one vacant eye. An axe head protruded from the left side of his face, literally dividing it from the other side.

It appeared Commander Anigo wasn't the only one who'd underestimated the ferocity of the bandits and the fighting and strategic acumen of the fugitives. Even so, Commander Anigo had no sympathy for him. He couldn't afford to.

He urged Candlestick south toward the main road by which they'd initially found this field. From there, he could head to Kanarah City and get proper medical aid. Every bump and jolt of Candlestick's gallops sent fresh pain into Commander Anigo's chest, but he refused to let this wound kill him.

More importantly, he would remember every jolt of pain when he finally caught up to the three fugitives.

CHAPTER 24

Trader's Pass/The Valley of the Tri-Lakes

A week and a half had passed since the bandits' attack. As they drew nearer to the end of eastern Trader's Pass and Kanarah City, Roderick's men camped for the night.

Then, early in the morning while it was still dark, they blindfolded Lilly, Sharion, and Colm and shackled them, hand-and-foot. But instead of riding in the wagon, this time they walked.

"Do not be alarmed," Colm whispered while the slave traders locked the wagon door. "When we last traveled this way, they did this. It is to conceal the path we will take from now on."

"Why conceal it?" Lilly asked, now unable to see him.

"It isn't supposed to exist." Colm huffed. "Slave-trading isn't exactly a noble vocation, and it is generally frowned upon by the public."

"What about the wagons?" Lilly leaned close to him. "My cape and armor are still in one of them. They're my only hope for getting out of here."

"Your optimism never ceases to amaze me, child."

Lilly didn't know whether it was truly optimism or not, but she knew with certainty the alternative wasn't something she wanted to endure.

"I wish I held as much faith in myself as you do in yourself," Colm continued. "The wagons will advance as they always do: a small group of men will lead them through the western gate of Kanarah City while the rest accompany us through the tunnels below the city. Once we exit the tunnels, we will rendezvous with the rest of the group."

So she *would* still have the chance to be reunited with her cape and armor. Good.

Colm nudged her hip. "Above all else, child, hold the end of my cloak. Try to step where I step. These tunnels make for perilous passage, but we have no choice but to comply."

Roderick and his men marched them through the darkness of the tunnels for several hours, stopping only to rest when one of them couldn't walk any farther. Usually it was Colm who'd worn himself out, but after so much time sitting in a cart and being transported everywhere, Lilly found that even she grew fatigued faster than usual.

Or perhaps she just wasn't used to walking so much in general. Why walk when she could fly?

Their shackles clanked and the sound echoed around them as they walked. Fatigue aside, the repeated *step-clank, step-clank* of their footsteps and shackles nearly drove Lilly to scream. Just when she thought she couldn't take the repetition anymore, Roderick ordered them to stop, and Luggs distributed a few crusts of bread.

As she ate, she noticed a nauseating odor permeating the tunnel.

"What's that smell?" Lilly asked.

"Nothing good," Sharion replied from Lilly's left. "Nothing good at all."

Lilly turned toward her, but she still couldn't see anything thanks to her blindfold.

Colm piped in, "I imagine she's right, but I can't say for sure."

"It smells like something died."

"Perhaps something did," Colm said.

"It would have to be a very big *something*." Lilly wrinkled her nose. "Or lots of things. I suppose with so little airflow in here, a dead thing might smell bad forever."

"We're not far from Kanarah City's sewers," Colm said. "That's a stink you won't soon forget."

"Quiet, all of you," Luggs hissed. His voice had an edge to it when he spoke. "Not another word, hear? Next one who talks gets a thrashin'."

"Come on," Roderick said from ahead of them. "We're halfway there."

Within a few more hours, Colm's prediction came true. Lilly's boots squelched in the muck under her feet, and the stench around them changed from death to that of bile, feces, and urine. They'd reached the sewers. Lilly wished she could reach her nose to pinch out the smell, but while walking upright, her chains and shackles didn't allow it.

The clanking of their shackles gave way to the ever-present dripping of something in the distance, splashes and squelches through puddles, and the skittering of something—probably rats—all around them. Lilly shuddered at the thought, but she pressed on. She had no other choice.

A couple hours later, something heavy and metal groaned, and Luggs guided them up a short staircase and over a hump of some sort. A breeze of fresh air relieved Lilly's nostrils, and she sucked in the clean air in big gulps.

"Where are we supposed to meet 'em?" Luggs asked.

Roderick replied, "Follow me."

Another fifteen minutes of walking, and they ordered the slaves to halt. Someone yanked Lilly's blindfold from her head so hard that it tweaked her neck.

Luggs. She glared at him, but he didn't even bother to look her in her eyes. He just moved on to Sharion and tore off her blindfold next.

At least he wasn't leering at her anymore. Perhaps Roderick's numerous warnings that she wasn't to be touched had finally gotten through his thick skull.

They stood inside a large room big enough to house a fleet of wagons but empty except for a few bales of hay, a small platform topped with some wooden posts, and several torches, only two of which burned. Brown planks of wood formed the large room's walls, and the ceiling reached at least thirty feet at its highest point. A warehouse of some sort.

"Child, are you alright?" Colm whispered from her right.

Lilly nodded.

Half the warehouse away, Roderick spoke to a white-haired man in a red robe. Silver rings adorned his fingers, and a large silver medallion with what appeared to be a large ruby in the center hung around his neck. He laughed a raspy laugh and shook Roderick's hand, then Roderick placed a bulging pouch into his hand.

"Who's that man Roderick is talking to?" Lilly asked.

"If memory serves me correctly, his name is Wandell Thirry. I've not dealt with him personally, but his reputation is known in what you'd call Kanarah's underworld. He's sort of a go-between. He helps slavers get from Trader's Pass to auction houses. Arranges other things too, like auctions for stolen goods."

And slaves, Lilly realized. "So that's where we are? An auction house?"

"Yes. A secret place for the purpose of selling questionable merchandise."

"Us," Sharion grumbled. "They're gonna sell us."

Lilly's heart drummed in her chest. "Now?"

"Not until later. It's too early in the evening, yet. These types of deals are arranged in the latest of hours just before dawn." Colm sighed as he looked around. "I have only bad memories of this place."

"Don't get too excited, Angel." Roderick's velvety voice slithered down Lilly's spine as he approached. "No one's getting their hands on you until tomorrow night. We have to notify our usual clients that there's an auction happening first. Colm forgets these little details in his old age."

As much as Lilly wished she could punch Roderick in his throat, she just exhaled a quiet breath through her nostrils and reminded herself that she still had an entire day to find a way to escape. The slave traders may have managed to corral her while on the road, but this was a new environment, and that meant new opportunities for escape.

On his way out the door, Wandell Thirry gave Lilly a lingering look, and he raised his eyebrows. Though Lilly actually found him quite handsome for an older man, his occupation and the lascivious kiss he blew her soured her stomach.

"Come on," Roderick said to Luggs and the other men. "Let's get these darlings to their cells, and then we've got interviews to conduct."

Lilly turned to Colm and eyed him.

"New recruits," he said. "Replacing the ones they lost on our way here."

"Enough chatter." Luggs pushed between Colm and Lilly. He nodded to three other men, two of whom were Adgar and Gammel, and they took hold of Lilly, Colm, and Sharion. He gave Lilly a crooked yellow smile that made her cringe. "Time for bed."

The slave traders shoved the three of them into an adjoining hallway, down some stairs, and into a dark corridor lined with barred cells. The place reeked almost as bad as the sewers, and several moans sounded from the cells as they passed.

Forlorn faces of either Windgales or humans—Lilly couldn't be sure since none of them wore capes—Wolves, and even a Saurian pressed up against the bars as the slave traders escorted the three of them past. A few dying torches mounted to the stone walls between the cells provided mediocre light for the space.

Luggs unlocked a cell in the middle and shoved Lilly, Colm, and Sharion inside. He removed their shackles while Adgar and Gammel watched.

"Do we get anything for dinner?" Colm asked.

"What makes you think we'd give you dinner?" Luggs spat on the floor. "Feel free to lick that up if you're hungry."

"The last time I was here, we had a feast. Roasted duck, boiled potatoes with butter and bits of ham, fresh vegetables and fruit, and the dessert was—"

"Last time you was here, things was different, wasn't they, Colm?" Luggs huffed. "But you're where you belong now, you thieving derelict."

"That I am, Luggs. That I am." Colm's smile wilted into a frown and he bowed his head.

Luggs left the cell and locked it behind him, sealing them inside.

"Come on, boys." Gammel nudged Luggs's belly. "We've got ale to drink."

Luggs shoved him. "I'll come when I'm good and ready."

Adgar grinned and clapped his hand on Lugg's shoulder. "And wenches to woo."

"Good luck with that one." Luggs chuckled. "You couldn't pay a woman enough coin to spend the night with your ugly face."

Luggs had a point, Lilly decided. Just having to listen to them prattle on was miserable enough.

Adgar's jaw tightened. "Look who's talkin'. Your face looks like a bear mauled you."

"That's *her* fault." Luggs pointed at Lilly. "And you all know it."

Adgar grinned and raised his eyebrows. "I wasn't talkin' 'bout the gash on your forehead. I was talkin' 'bout your face in general."

Luggs swung for Adgar's head, but Adgar sidestepped the blow and darted up the corridor. Luggs gave chase amid a slew of profanity, and Gammel followed.

"At least it's not cold in here." Lilly squinted at the cell's contents: a few tattered rags that could double as blankets, plenty of hay, and not much else between the stone walls and the bars.

Sharion snatched one of the rags and dug under a mound of hay like she always did. With another furious scratch of her head, she curled up and started to snooze.

"For now, anyway," Colm said. "At least we're not here in the winter."

Lilly eyed him. He'd made an awful lot of comments about having been here in the past. But if that were the case… "Colm, when you were here last time, were you a slave?"

Colm's lips curled into a sad half-smile. "No, Lilly. I regret to say that I was one of the slave traders."

Lilly's hands balled into fists, and rage erupted in her chest. She had come to trust Colm, even to admire him, only to find out now that he'd been a slave trader himself.

The revelation shouldn't have come as such a shock to her, given how he'd managed to convince some of the slave traders to share extra food with him in exchange for whatever trinkets or coin he managed to pilfer from the guards. And he'd known a surprising amount about what to expect at various points along the way.

Still, Lilly became an inferno at the thought that she'd ever been close to him. She physically took a step back to separate herself from him.

"This whole time," she began, her voice low but furious, "you've been helping me, but you used to be one of *them?* You used to capture people and *sell* them? And the women—"

"I never touched any of the women, child." Colm held up his hand. "That flame inside of me extinguished a long time ago."

"But everything else… you did those things too?" Lilly glared at him.

Part of her refused to believe it was true, but he'd admitted to it openly. Her stomach churned with bitterness and anger. She'd been betrayed by the only person she'd come to even remotely care about since her capture.

Colm exhaled a shaky sigh. "Yes, child. And I regret my decisions every day."

"You told me you were better off being in here, that the Overlord *wanted* you here so you could do good." Tears burned the corners of her eyes. "Was that all a lie?"

"No. Not a single word. If I'm in here, I'm unable to hurt people out there. People like you and Sharion and others caught in this life." Colm stared into her eyes, pleading with his own.

She gave him no quarter in her heart. Lilly would listen to his miserable tale, but it wouldn't make her forgive him. As far as she was concerned, he was just as guilty as Roderick and the others, and he always would be.

"I know what I did was wrong," he continued. "I tried to expose Roderick's entire band to

Captain Fulton, one of the local officers in the King's army, but when I did, he betrayed me and handed me back to Roderick, who locked me up.

"That was almost a year ago. Roderick has tried to sell me as a slave twice since then, but no one wants an old man like me, much less one only trained as a thief." He gave a mirthless chuckle. "Apparently, the slave market in Eastern Kanarah is already saturated with enough old thieves."

Lilly narrowed her gaze at him. Her anger had begun to give way to a deep profound sadness instead. "I trusted you, Colm, but I shouldn't have. You're a thief and a liar. For all I know, you're lying to me now."

Colm shook his head. "I wish I could convince you otherwise, but you're exactly right. I'm a thief and a liar, and that's all you can be certain of."

She'd sat next him, shared her warmth with him while he shared his cloak with her. They'd shared food, shared long conversations on boring wagon rides, shared dreams of freedom in the evenings. He'd even asked her to call him "grandfather."

No way that would happen now.

Colm reached for her. "Lilly, I—"

"No." She pulled away. "I have nothing more to say to you."

"I understand." Colm's hand sank to his side and he nodded. "I'll leave you alone, then."

Lilly hugged her knees and leaned against the far wall, as far away from Colm as she could get.

From now on, all they would share was a cell.

LATER THAT NIGHT, a commotion sounded down at the end of the corridor. Lilly opened her eyes, having only flirted with the idea of sleep, but she didn't move. She recognized three familiar voices: Luggs, Gammel, and Adgar, all of them drawing nearer to her cell.

Why would they have come back? And so late? Lilly bristled at the possibilities, but only one of them mattered. She knew what these three were capable of.

Luggs led Gammel and Adgar into the corridor, each of them swaying to the rhythm of inebriation. They guffawed and laughed, oblivious that some of the slaves might be trying to sleep. Luggs stopped in front of Lilly's cell and stared inside, his eyes scanning for her, and he grinned when he noticed her.

"There she is, boys. Roderick's sack-o'-gold." Even from several feet away Lilly could smell the stink of alcohol on Lugg's breath.

Gammel and Adgar chuckled. Lilly tried to recede deeper into the hay, but she didn't dare take her eyes off them.

"Drunk again, Luggs?" Colm stirred from his spot across the cell and sat upright. "The drink has never once served you well since I've known you."

Luggs slurred, "No one's talkin' to you, old man. So shut up."

"I will as soon as you let me get back to sleep."

"Then you'd better learn to sleep through noise." Luggs pulled his key ring from his belt, wobbling on unsteady legs.

Gammel clamped his hand on Luggs's arm. "Roderick will kill you if you touch 'er. The auction's *tomorrow.*"

Luggs yanked free from Gammel in overdramatic fashion. "Don't touch me. I know the auction's tomorrow. Why else you think we're here tonight?"

"I—I don't want to face any more wrath from Roderick." Gammel rubbed his bald head. "He's still mad 'bout that she-Wolf breakin' free before we reached the pass."

"He's not mad at you." Adgar leaned against the bars and folded his long arms across his chest. "He's just not all that personable to begin with."

"You ladies really ought to take your conversation elsewhere," Colm said. "I'm sure it's fascinating to you dimwits, but we're not all that interested."

Luggs pointed a stubby finger at him through the bars. "What'd I say? You need to *shut up*."

"Doing my best, Luggs." Colm leaned back against the cell wall. "But you make it so easy to sling stones that it's hard to resist."

"You'll do better, or I'll smack you. No one's gonna buy you anyway, so it doesn't matter if you're beat-up and bruised."

"I still don't think we should go in there." Gammel shook his head. "Plenty of wenches back at that tavern lookin' to share a night with you or anyone else."

"That's exactly why we're *here*." Luggs smiled his wretched yellow smile through the bars at Lilly as his stupored fingers continued working the key into the lock. "Because she ain't like those wenches. She's cleaner. Prettier, too."

Lilly's heart thudded faster. Trying to escape tomorrow wouldn't matter if they came at her tonight.

They were drunk, though, so perhaps she could outmaneuver them and run away once the cell opened? Or maybe she could get ahold of the dagger hanging from Lugg's belt and use that to fend them off?

Across the cell, Sharion peeked out from under her mound of hay, then she promptly disappeared back under it.

"And that's exactly why we're here," Luggs repeated as he finally inserted the key into the lock and twisted it. The lock clunked, and the door inched open. Luggs turned to Gammel. "You don't like it, then get outta here. Crystal?"

Lilly stood up, her fists balled. Her muscles tensed. She would bite, kick, scream, scratch, shout, and thrash to get away from them. And if they gave her the chance, she would run.

Luggs stepped inside the cell with a twisted grin on his face and his hands on his belt. "Hey, cutie."

Colm stepped between him and Lilly. "Luggs, don't—"

Luggs lurched forward and grabbed Colm by his shoulder.

Shick.

Red spattered on the stone floor between them. Colm staggered backward, his mouth hanging open, his hands clamped over his stomach.

Luggs stood in place, his dagger in hand instead of in its sheath at his belt.

Its tip dripped with blood.

CHAPTER 25

C olm slumped to the floor, his eyes wide, his stomach wet with blood.

Emotion overwhelmed Lilly, and she shrieked and rushed to him and clutched him in her arms. "Colm? *Colm!*"

Luggs huffed and wiped the blood from his dagger with the corner of Colm's cloak. "I warned you not to touch me." He spat on the floor near Colm's face but didn't put his dagger away.

"You *stabbed* him!" Lilly shouted. She cradled Colm and helped him to lean up against her, and he moaned. His blood stained her undergarments, her skin, her hands. She tried to put pressure on the wound, but it continued to bleed. "Get some help—please!"

Gammel took three steps.

"*Stay* where you are," Luggs snapped, and Gammel stopped. "We're not done here."

"Yes, we are." Gammel scowled at him. "I'm getting Roderick. You just *killed* some of the merchandise."

"I didn't kill nobody. Just pricked 'im a bit," Luggs slurred. He wobbled even more, but he caught himself on the cell's bars and stabilized his footing.

"That's no prick, Luggs. Look at all that blood, you idiot." Gammel shook his head. "He won't survive that, old as he is."

Lilly's heart plummeted into her churning stomach. *Colm—not going to survive?*

Luggs grabbed Gammel by his shirt and threatened him with the dagger. "You tell Roderick, I'll run you through like I done to him."

"You really think Roderick won't notice anyway?" Gammel shot back. "You kill me, it's *two* deaths on your head. He'll skin you alive."

"*Fine*. Go tell Roderick. See if I care." Luggs shoved Gammel against one of the cell walls.

"Tell Roderick what?" A deep voice filled the cellblock.

Luggs whirled around, his reddened eyes wide.

Roderick stood outside the cell, his gray eyes fixed on Luggs. His gaze shifted down to Lilly and Colm, and he frowned. His deep voice flattened. "Come out of the cell. All three of you."

Luggs sheathed his dagger and followed Gammel and Adgar out, staggering. "It ain't what it looks—"

Roderick backhanded Luggs. "Did I say you could speak?"

Luggs rubbed his reddened cheek. His head slumped forward. "No."

"Gammel, what happened?"

"Well, uh…" Gammel hesitated. "We came in here after a few ales at the tavern and—"

"Give me the short version."

"Short version?" Gammel glanced at Luggs. "Well… Luggs stabbed Colm."

"He attacked me," Luggs said. "I had to—"

Roderick raised his hand again, and Luggs shrank away.

"He didn't attack Luggs," Lilly blurted. "Not at all. He was trying to protect me."

Roderick turned his attention to Lilly. For a long moment, he seemed to study her, then he squared his body with Luggs. "Why were you after her?"

Luggs swallowed and gave a nervous chuckle. "Come on, Roderick. You know why."

"I specifically said she was off-limits. Why do you insist on provoking me?"

Luggs backed up a step so Lilly could no longer see him from her vantage inside the cell. In her arms, Colm wheezed. She didn't know what else to do for him.

Luggs stammered, "It—it's just such a waste to not—"

"Come here."

"But—"

"*Now.*"

Luggs stepped back into view. Roderick raised his hand, and Luggs flinched.

Finally, justice for Colm, justice for everything Luggs had done to Sharion and Lilly since they'd captured her. With his power, Roderick could kill Luggs in one solid strike. Lilly had seen him do far more impressive things than that, and now Luggs's reckoning had come.

Instead, Roderick only swatted the back of Luggs's head.

"Don't do anything like that again. Stay away from her and the rest of the merchandise until after the auction," Roderick scolded. "And next time, lay off the drink the night before an auction. Crystal?"

Luggs nodded and rubbed his head. "Yeah, boss. Clear."

"Now, get out of here. All of you." Roderick pointed toward the exit.

As the men shuffled out, Lilly gawked at Roderick. Colm had just been stabbed, and all Roderick did was smack Luggs on the back of his head and chew him out?

"As for you—" Roderick pointed his finger at her. "—I don't want to hear another peep from you, ever. You've been more of a problem than any slave I've ever transported. If you weren't so valuable, I'd have let those dogs gnaw the meat from your bones weeks ago."

Lilly tensed her jaw and glared at him.

"I still might. Try something else, and find out."

Colm moaned in Lilly's arms.

Frantic, she asked, "What are you going to do about Colm?"

Roderick stared at him then shrugged. "I'll send someone to collect the body later."

Lilly's eyes widened. "That's it? You're just going to let him *die?*"

"Nothing to be done for him now, Angel." Roderick smirked. "But knowing him, I'm sure he's already weaseled his way into a far better afterlife than any other criminal ever could hope for."

Part of Lilly wanted to lash out and claw his face to shreds with her fingernails, but the other part knew she'd never be able to. She might cut Colm's life even shorter by trying it. Instead, she scowled at him and swore she'd exact justice for Colm.

Roderick winked at her and shut the cell door, then he locked it with his own set of keys.

"Sleep well, Angel."

The door to the cellblock latched shut, and Lilly looked down at Colm. Even in the miserable light of the cellblock, she could tell he'd gone noticeably more pale.

Regret filled her chest. Before Luggs had stabbed him, Colm had yet again tried to protect her, and that was after she'd chastised him for his past. Now he was dying, and it was her fault.

"Lilly…" Colm motioned for her to lean closer. She bent over him. "Inside the inner lining of my cloak."

She hurriedly reached into it, expecting to find something she could use to help him. Instead, she pulled out a small knife and a familiar ring of skeleton keys. She couldn't help but gawk at them. "Where did you get these?"

"Took them off… Luggs when he stabbed me. Almost got his coin purse too, but given the circumstances…" Colm managed a weak smile. "Keep them… Use them to escape."

Lilly's heart shattered. Even after he'd been stabbed, Colm's only thoughts were of protecting her and ensuring her safety. He'd risked his life to protect her, and he'd paid the ransom for her escape with his life.

"Oh, Colm." Lilly's voice cracked when she said it. Sorrow flooded her core, and she didn't restrain her tears. "You can't die. I'll be all alone here."

"Nothing to be done… about it now." Colm grunted, then coughed. Blood tinged the corners of his mouth. "Besides… you'll still have Sharion."

Lilly glanced at Sharion, who still crouched in the corner of the cell farthest from them and clenched handfuls of hair while she rocked back and forth. "Not helpful, Colm."

"It's better than… nothing." Colm wheezed again, and his body shuddered in Lilly's arms. Somehow he seemed even older and frailer than before. "My time… is near, child."

"No." Lilly sobbed. "You can't go. I—I—"

"I can… and I must, child." Colm closed his eyes. "When you escape… avoid Roderick at all costs. He… will sell you separately from… the auction. Do not flee… now. Too many… night guards posted. You must… use the distraction… of the auction… to escape."

"Enough about that. I—I owe you an apology." Lilly bit her lip.

Colm shook his head. "Don't want the last words… I hear in this life… to be an apology— from either my lips… or yours."

Lilly sniffed. She knew what he wanted. At first, the idea had struck her as strange, but now it seemed wrong not to say it. Given everything he had done for her, some simple words to carry him into the afterlife was a small price to pay, and she would pay it gladly.

"I love you, Grandfather."

Colm's blue eyes cracked open and welled with tears. He smiled at her, closed his eyes again, and one long exhale later, he was gone.

Lilly pressed her forehead into Colm's neck and sobbed.

"Quick," Sharion hissed from behind her. "Hide that stuff before someone comes back."

As much as Lilly wanted to continue to mourn Colm, Sharion was right. She reached for the keys and the knife and tucked them inside her boots.

"What are you doing? We need to get outta here!" Sharion scratched her head.

"You just told me to hide them."

"Forget what I said." Sharion glowered at her. "Aren't you going to break us out? It's the middle of the night. Everyone's asleep. Let's go."

"Now's not the time. Colm said to wait for—"

"I don't care what Colm said. You've got keys and a knife. We're getting outta here now."

"Keep your voice down." Lilly held her hands out. "If you keep talking so loud, they'll find out. Then we'll never escape."

"Gimme the keys." Sharion held her dirty hand.

Lilly shook her head. "No. Colm said—"

Sharion flung herself at Lilly, and they tumbled into the hay near Colm's body.

"Get off of me!" Lilly tried to push Sharion off, but she couldn't. Sharion thrashed and snarled at her, clawing at Lilly's face. "Sharion, stop!"

"Give 'em to me!"

Enough defending. Lilly couldn't afford this kind of problem on top of everything else. She balled her fingers into a fist and drove it into Sharion's chin.

Sharion's teeth clacked, and she rolled off of Lilly with her hands on her face. She whimpered, and Lilly pushed herself up to her feet.

"I'm sorry, Sharion, but you gave me no choice." Lilly backed away from her and leaned against the wall of bars opposite of where Sharion had curled into a ball. "When the time is right, I'll help you escape, but not before then."

Sharion muttered what Lilly assumed were curses, but she couldn't make out anything discernible. Lilly just shook her head.

She stared down at Colm. Once she worked up the courage, she stepped over to him, bent down, and covered his face and body with his cloak so only the soles of his boots showed.

Given his status as a slave and previously as a thief, he likely wouldn't get a proper burial according to human customs. Had they been back at Aeropolis, they would've burned his body, as was the Windgale way.

He'd been a scoundrel and a liar, but he'd done right by her and deserved better than what Roderick and his men would afford him, even if Lilly couldn't give it to him.

Lilly stole a glance at Sharion. She now sat huddled against the wall, her gaze vacant but not focused on Lilly. Regardless of what Sharion said or did from then on, Lilly would not sleep for the rest of the night.

She tried not to pay attention to Colm's sticky blood all over her hands, arms, legs, and torso. Even if she didn't sleep, she could still rest, so she leaned against the back wall of the cell and exhaled a ragged sigh.

"WHAT'D you say your name was?" Roderick's voice stirred Lilly from her rest.

So much for not sleeping.

She jerked back to cognition and stared at Sharion, wide-eyed, but the woman hadn't moved from her spot against the wall.

A second voice started to answer Roderick. "It's—"

"Never mind. I don't care," Roderick interrupted. "You wanna work for me, you gotta prove yourself before I give two fruits what your name is."

They were definitely in the cellblock.

Lilly patted her boots. The rough metal of the keys pressed against her left ankle, and she felt the smooth knife blade against her right.

"There. That one." Roderick's hulking form moved into view beyond the bars. "The cute one, not the ugly one. She's the one I was telling you about."

A young man about Lilly's age with curly black hair stepped into view. Next to Roderick and his brown armor, the young man's dark-green armor made the two of them look like the beginnings of a metal forest.

"Yeah, I see her."

"I'm assigning you to watch her from now until the auction. You'll deliver her to the buyer personally, and watch out, because she's a tricky one. She's tried to escape several times since we caught her."

Lilly sat up and glared at them both.

"Alright."

"Don't 'alright' me. This is serious. The most serious thing you've ever done."

"Yes, sir," the other man replied, his voice shaky.

Roderick positioned himself right in front of the new guy and towered over him. "Your references are good—if they're true—but since I can't verify anything you've told me, you're gonna have to prove yourself. You make sure she gets to the buyer and that he's satisfied, and then I'll learn your name. Crystal?"

The new guy swallowed, and his Adam's apple bobbed. "Clear. Who's that under the blanket?"

Roderick craned his head. "Oh, him. He's dead. I'll have someone pull him outta there before he starts to stink."

"I can do it, if you want."

Roderick grinned at him and folded his arms. "It's about time someone started to show some initiative around here. I'll send one of the others to help you. You ever lugged a dead body around before? They're heavier than they look."

"I did some butchering back at my last—"

"It was a rhetorical question."

"Oh," the new guy said. "Sorry."

"Anyway, the buyer will be here an hour before the auction starts," Roderick said. "Meet him where we discussed. Don't cut corners, and don't touch her except to get her to him. She needs to be as pristine as possible, or he'll want a refund, and that's *not* gonna happen."

Roderick turned and winked at Lilly, then he whacked the new guy's chest. "In the meantime, she's not going anywhere. Come with me, and I'll introduce you to the rest of the idiots. You can come back for the body later."

Roderick walked out with heavy steps. The new guy gave Lilly a sullen half-smile, then he followed Roderick out of the cell.

Sharion groaned, then she glared at Lilly.

"What's wrong with you?"

"You know what's wrong with me. You *know*." Sharion rubbed her chin.

Lilly met her eyes, unfazed. "Maybe you shouldn't have attacked me."

Sharion grunted.

A half-hour later, the new guy in the green armor returned with Gammel, and they entered the cell. Sharion shrank into the corner away from them, but Lilly stood her ground. Gammel wouldn't try anything after his hesitance last night, and the new guy seemed to want to please Roderick. Together, they wrapped Colm in his cloak and picked him up.

"Are you going to bury him?" she asked.

The new guy stared at her with dark eyes and his mouth hung open a bit. "Uh…"

"I don't know what Roderick's gonna do with him." Gammel glanced at the floor where Colm's blood, now dried and darkening to brown, had pooled. "But *I'm* not digging a grave for an old thief."

The new guy glanced between them and shrugged.

"Please bury him. It's the right thing to do." Lilly fixed her gaze on the new guy. "Every man deserves at least that, no matter what he did in life."

"I—I'll see what I can do." The new guy looked away.

"Come on. Let's get 'im outta here," Gammel said.

CHAPTER 26

Eastern Kanarah

To Calum's surprise, Kanarah City's population did not resemble that of the northern region in either numbers or diversity. Then again, with Kanarah City being the only viable access point for crossing the Valley of the Tri-Lakes into Western Kanarah, Calum should've expected that more races populated the city.

Saurians roamed freely among the humans. While the humans had the clear majority, the two races frequently walked past each other in the street without so much as a foul look or an extra glance. Quite the contrast to Pike's Garrison, where Magnus had still gleaned some glares even after they restored the villagers' wealth.

In addition, Calum saw his first Windgale. He'd swooped down from above, cape and all, and landed in front of their trio in the street. He offered Calum a head of lettuce and a tomato. For sale, of course. *Good price. Low price. Cheap price.*

All Calum could say was, "You can fly?"

"Tourists," the Windgale muttered and zoomed away.

Magnus had been right—they really did look just like humans. Humans who could somehow fly, thanks to their capes.

Tall towers and spike-topped walls formed the city's imposing perimeter, and rows of buildings lined its numerous streets. Soldiers stood guard at regular intervals inside the city walls, while merchants and shops beckoned travelers with offers of pleasure, luxury, or necessity.

But contrary to Magnus's fears, no one so much as blinked at them, much less tried to attack or arrest them. Apparently, the sight of two armed men walking through the city with a seven-foot Saurian in gleaming blue armor wasn't all that unusual.

Calum and Axel had also upgraded their armor by piecing together some of what the Southern Snake Brotherhood had worn, so they no longer looked like they had robbed one of the King's outposts. Instead, they looked like they couldn't match armor or colors to save their lives, but Calum liked to think it aided in keeping them anonymous.

"We need to unload as much of our spoils as possible," Magnus shifted a large sack from one shoulder to the other. "The trip across Trader's Pass is very long, and there are no animals to hunt or vegetation in the valley, so it is imperative that we plan accordingly."

"Shouldn't be too hard. There are dozens of vendors and merchants lining the streets who want to trade." Axel pointed to a small wooden shop with a weathered sign overhead that read *Garon's Fine Goods, Armory, and Exotic Antiquities* in what appeared to be a lousy attempt at a cursive script. "We could try in there."

Calum nodded. "Looks as good as any of the others."

"When we get inside, let me do the talking," Magnus said. "I have done this before. He will proffer a low price, and we will have to negotiate it up from there. You two hold onto your bags since they contain the soldiers' weapons and armor. I would rather not risk trying to sell those until we know for sure he is amenable to dealing in that kind of merchandise."

Inside, an older man with black-and-gray hair hunched over a counter. He wore fine white linens and a purple robe. Golden necklaces, rings, and a hoop hanging from his left earlobe added some shine to his look. At the sound of the bell jingling over the shop door, he looked up.

"Welcome, welcome. Name's Garon. What can I do for you gentlemen?" His raspy voice filled the small shop as he gestured to the walls lined with shelves of trinkets, weapons, and a variety of other things. "If you need something, I probably have three of it."

Magnus set his bag on the floor. "Do you purchase goods?"

Garon smiled at him. "I purchase, I trade, I sell, I deal, I beg, I barter. I even give, on occasion, but you fellows don't meet the criteria for that one."

Calum glanced at Magnus. "What criteria?"

"I give to the poor and needy, and, on occasion, to very, *very* beautiful women." Garon laughed, but it sounded more like he was wheezing. He waved his hand at them. "I'm just joking around. I don't give to the poor and needy. They're a bunch of gutter leeches. Alright. Let's see what you've got. Put it on my counter here."

Magnus dumped the contents of the sack onto the counter.

Garon sorted through it with his fingers, then shrugged. "Ehhh. Nothing special."

Axel gripped the edge of the counter with his hands. "What do you mean, 'nothing special?' That's high-quality steel and—"

Magnus held up his hand, and Axel went quiet. "What is it worth to you?"

Garon stared at the ceiling and counted his fingertips. "Seventeen gold coins for all of it."

"You've gotta be kidding me." Axel folded his arms and exhaled a sharp sigh.

"Axel," Magnus said. "Let me handle this."

Calum didn't show it, but he agreed with Axel. Seventeen gold coins was a pittance for all they'd brought in with them.

"That set of armor alone is worth twenty coins," Magnus said.

"Maybe if it was *new*." Garon shook his head. "Look, you seem like nice young men..." He looked up at Magnus. "...and a nice large lizard-person. I'll make it eighteen."

"No." Magnus folded his burly arms. "I want fifty."

Garon grabbed his chest. "By the Overlord—my heart stopped for a moment there. At my age, my hearing's not so good. Could you repeat that number?"

"Fifty."

Garon grabbed his chest again, feigning agony. "Yep. That's what I thought you said. In what world is this junk worth *fifty* gold coins?"

"In this one."

"Yeah, this one," Axel echoed.

Magnus shot him a glare, then he refocused on Garon. He pointed to each item. "Twenty for the set of armor, including the helmet, a coin for the two lengths of rope, five apiece for the two swords, nine for the axe, and ten for all that leather, including the four pairs of boots and belts."

Garon counted his fingers again.

"It adds up to fifty," Magnus asserted.

Garon stopped and narrowed his gaze. "Yes, thanks. I can add. If I couldn't, I wouldn't have lasted forty years as a merchant and another eight as a shopkeeper."

"So do we have a deal?"

"The only reasonable price you just quoted me was for the two lengths of rope—" Garon grabbed the ropes, dropped them behind his counter, then pulled a gold coin from his pocket. He slid it across the counter. "—for one coin. You're too high on everything else."

Magnus took the gold coin and handed it to Axel, who dropped it into a small coin pouch. "Then we will pack up our things and go."

"Where do you expect to get forty-nine coins for the rest of that?"

"We will visit one of the bigger shops. I expect they have more capital to trade with." Magnus reached for the suit of armor while Calum held open the sack.

Faster than Calum would've expected, Garon rounded the counter and held up his hand. "They'll rip you off. They're bigger, so they spend more on bigger items, but they always rip off the little guys. Always. Bunch of scoundrels and predators. You can't trust them. Not at all."

"Better than arguing with you," Axel muttered.

"Do you have another offer?" Magnus asked.

"Twenty even. Best deal you'll get for this stuff."

Magnus motioned to Calum. "Pack it all up."

Garon's hand clamped down on Magnus's wrist as he reached for the helmet, but he let go just as fast. "Wait. You don't have to leave yet. Let's try a new number. How about twenty-five?"

Magnus leaned toward him. "How about forty-nine?"

"King's *mercy.*" Garon clenched his eyes shut and clutched his chest a third time. "Your expectations are unrealistic. No one with half a brain will give you forty-nine gold for... *this.*"

"How about forty-eight?"

Garon glared at Magnus and pointed at the door. "Get out."

Magnus nodded. He reached for the helmet again, and again, Garon grabbed his wrist then quickly let go.

"I'll give you five coins for both swords."

"Five each?"

"Five total."

"I said five each."

"And I said five *total.*" Garon held one of them up, and sunlight from one of the windows glinted off the blade. "They've been used. I'll have to sharpen them, shine them, and oil them up before I can resell them."

Magnus folded his arms. "Fine. Eight."

"Six."

"Seven, plus a bigger coin pouch than the one we've got, and you have a deal."

"And you have a deal if I get to keep the smaller coin pouch." Garon smirked.

Magnus smirked as well. "Deal."

They exchanged the goods and the coins, and Axel double-checked to make sure he'd removed all of their own coins from the small pouch before he traded it for the new one.

"Now about that axe," Garon said. "It's not worth nine coins. Not a chance. I mean, if the handle were bejeweled with priceless diamonds, then maybe. So I'll give you three."

"*Three?*" Magnus recoiled. "I can get more by selling it to a blacksmith for the metal."

"Look, we can haggle all day, but I'm an old man and would rather sit outside my store and watch beautiful young ladies walk on by." Garon laughed his wheezy laugh again and smacked the counter with his palms. "I'll give you six, which is more than it's worth, just to shut you up."

"Deal."

"The leather's not worth ten, either. How about six for that as well?"

Magnus huffed. "Would you do seven?"

Garon shook his head. "No."

"Then I accept your six."

"Now about that armor—"

"You will not get it for ten. It would sell for triple that, new or otherwise. It is in good shape."

"I'll give you twelve."

Magnus clacked his talons on his breastplate. "Eighteen."

Garon sighed. "Look, son. I'm going to put a price tag of thirty coins on it. I'll tell customers it's on sale for twenty-five, and I'll probably settle for a sale price in the low twenties. So you asking eighteen for it is excessive, offensive, and just plain ridiculous. I'll give you thirteen."

"How about you give me sixteen, price it at thirty-five, and sell it for twenty-seven?"

Garon waved his hand. "If I price it at thirty-five, it'll sit there 'til I'm dead and gone and for the next three generations that follow me. Unless there's a war that engulfs all of Kanarah, no one would pay that much for a used set of armor. At least not that one. Thirteen's my limit."

"Fifteen, then, but I keep the helmet." Magnus picked it up and held it in his hand.

"*Fifteen?*" Garon groaned. "What are you going to do with a random helmet, anyway? Toss rocks into it when you're bored? Look, to shut you up, I'll do fifteen for the helmet *with* the armor, and then you can get out of my store. My heart can't handle more of your badgering."

"Deal."

After their final exchange of goods for coins, Magnus nodded to Calum, who brought over one of the other sacks.

"We have some… other goods," Magnus said. "But I do not know if you would deal in them."

Garon squinted at him. "Just now pulling out the good stuff, eh? After I've spent all my money on your boring junk?"

Magnus raised an eyebrow. "Like I said, I do not know if you are willing to risk dealing in what we have to sell. Is there anything you refuse to buy?"

Garon smiled and raised an eyebrow. "I can't think of anything in particular."

Magnus reached into the bag and removed a soldier's helmet. "How about this?"

The smile on Garon's face flipped, and his other eyebrow rose. All the mirth left his voice. "Get out of my store. Now. And don't ever come back here again. Never. Ever. Never ever."

Calum glanced at Axel. Garon's reaction was exactly what they'd feared, and Calum couldn't help but wonder if they'd made a critical mistake.

Magnus dropped the helmet back into the bag and handed it to Calum. "One last question. Do you know of anyone who might deal in this type of merchandise?"

Garon rounded the counter again, this time with his hands up. He shooed them toward the door. "I don't know anything about anyone. I don't know who you are, and I don't know what you've got in that sack. I've never seen you before, and we've never done business. Crystal? Now get out of my shop, and don't ever come back."

"Thank you for your time." Magnus nodded to him and stepped out the door behind Calum and Axel. Once they made it outside, Magnus grabbed them both by their shoulders. "We need to get out of here. Now."

"What?" Axel held his hands out, palms up. "Why?"

"Because Garon is about to find the nearest soldier and tell him what he has just seen."

CHAPTER 27

"Are we bringing the soldiers' gear with us?" Calum hefted the bag over his shoulder. He hoped they wouldn't have to keep lugging it around.

"No. It will slow us down, and if they catch us with it, it will only incriminate us. Better to leave it behind and gain some ambiguity in the process. Nor do we need it anymore anyway. We have enough coin to purchase supplies for the journey across Trader's Pass and then some."

"This is totally unnecessary," Axel said. "We can just go back in there and make sure he doesn't say anything."

Magnus eyed him. "We have no time to argue about this. We do not know this city like the King's soldiers do, and I have only been here once before. As far as I know, we are about as close to the center as we could possibly get, which means that no matter what direction we go, it will be hard to get out of here."

"Like I said, we won't have to worry about this hassle if I go back into the shop and—"

"And what?" Magnus stepped in front of him. "Kill him?"

Axel didn't back up. "If it came to that, sure."

"You cannot just kill your way out of every problem, Axel."

"Beats running from them, don't you think?" Axel smirked. "But that's what works for you, isn't it, Scales? You still never told us why you left your homeland. Are you *running* from something?"

Calum gawked at Axel's audacity. He'd been curious about Magnus, too, but he hadn't dared ask him about it. And he certainly wouldn't have challenged him about it like this, either.

Magnus glared at him. "That is not a conversation we have time for, nor is it any of your concern."

"Oh, so you *are* running from something." Axel tapped his chin with his fingers. "Let's see... you have special armor, a special sword... From what I've seen here in the city, no other Saurians have anything like it, do they? You must've been someone important, or rich, or both. I wonder what—"

"*Enough*, Axel," Magnus hissed. "I have nothing to say to you. Nothing. We must go. Now. Every minute you waste talking is another minute we could use to make our escape."

"Both of you, stop," Calum said.

Axel nudged Calum. "Got you kind of curious now, doesn't he?"

"Calum, please." Magnus turned to him. "This is not helpful. We must flee."

"And now he's being defensive. Must've been something pretty juicy if he's getting all worked up about it, huh?" Axel laughed.

Magnus grabbed Axel by his breastplate and lifted him off of his feet. "You know nothing about me. *Nothing.* So do not pretend you do."

"Put him down, Magnus." Leader or not, Calum was getting tired of mediating Axel and Magnus's tiffs. More importantly, if they had to run, carrying Axel wasn't ideal.

Magnus let him drop but turned away from Axel, who managed to land on his feet. "We need to go. Now. There is no time."

Calum nodded. "We're going. Axel, you're not killing anyone. We'll dump the bags in a trash heap behind one of these buildings, and then we'll head north back to the Snake Mountains for a few days until everything calms down here. Let's go."

"Whatever you say, oh great leader," Axel gave a mock bow that grated on Calum's sense of calm, but he forced himself to ignore it and started to move.

Everything went as Calum had intended, including dropping the sacks of gear on one of the trash piles, until they reached the city's north gate, the same one through which they had entered. A dozen soldiers who weren't there before now stood at the gate, huddled around their commander.

"Back. Back. Now." Calum swiveled on his heels and headed the opposite way.

"Oh, come on. We can get through them, Calum." Axel stopped him mid-stride. "We just handled more than double that number a week ago."

"There are other soldiers nearby. This is home to the third largest contingent of the King's soldiers in Kanarah, after Solace itself and the Border Fortress farther east," Magnus warned. "We cannot instigate any more trouble than we already have."

Axel exhaled a long sigh. "Whatever. I'm not gonna argue. I know it won't make a difference. Never does."

Calum sighed. *Not this whiny "woe-is-me" garbage again.*

"Whatever we decide to do, let's not discuss it in the street, in plain sight," Calum said. He glanced at the group of soldiers again.

One of them was watching the trio. He leaned to his side and said something to the soldier next to him. The soldier's head rotated, and he looked at Calum as well.

Definitely time to go.

They scampered behind a nearby building. Calum looked up at Magnus as they walked down an alley. "Is there an east gate?"

"There is, but I have never been there." Magnus glanced over Calum's shoulder. "They are pursuing us. Do not turn around."

Axel swore. "How many?"

Magnus growled. "All of them."

Calum eyed him. "What do you mean, *all* of them?"

"Too many to fight. More than were standing around at the gate. It is time to run."

"You ready?" Calum nodded at Axel.

"If you're not willing to fight, then I guess I don't have another choice."

"East gate it is. If we get separated, meet up there." Calum nodded to Magnus. "We're ready. Say when, Magnus."

Magnus paused for a moment, still watching over Calum's shoulder. "Now."

All three of them bolted from their spot behind the building and into the street.

From behind them, the cries and yells of several soldiers filled Calum's ears. He stole a glance back. Magnus hadn't exaggerated—the entire dozen soldiers who'd been standing at the gate now chased after them, plus many, many more. Too many to count with only a quick look.

Definitely too many to fight.

Calum faced forward in time to see a pretty young lady carrying a basket full of flowers step in front of him. She squeaked, and he barely skidded to a stop in time. Then he sidestepped her and kept running.

"Pardon me!" he called back to her.

With Axel in the lead, Calum chased Magnus's green tail through the streets.

A soldier emerged from an alleyway to his right. Calum reacted by slamming his gauntleted fist into the soldier's nose. The impact stung his hand, but the soldier got it way worse.

And it meant one fewer soldier chasing them.

Magnus took a hard left down an alley, and Calum followed. On his way in, Calum drew his sword and severed the leg of a cart full of apples, oranges, and walnuts. It tipped over, and its contents spilled in front of the alley. Calum hoped it would slow the soldiers down, though he didn't love hearing the angry shouts of the cart's owner behind him.

The alley drained into another street, one far more crowded than the one they just left. Calum had wanted to sheathe his sword, but he opted to keep it out in case he ran into any more soldiers while on the run.

Due to the thick traffic on the street, Magnus got in front of Axel and roared, and a path cleared through the crowd as people scattered away from the admittedly frightening sound. The trio continued to run.

Ahead of them, three soldiers emerged from the base of a watchtower in front of Magnus, but he couldn't stop in time. Instead, he whipped his tail around and sent all three of them crashing through the wall of a nearby shop. The surrounding civilians screamed and recoiled from Magnus, and Calum couldn't blame them for it.

They passed about ten more streets and came up to the east gate, but Magnus stopped short. Then he cut south, right past Calum and Axel.

"More soldiers. South gate," was all he said as he barreled past them.

Sure enough, a contingent of soldiers about the same size as the one at the north gate now ran toward them.

Calum's burning legs propelled him after Axel and Magnus. If they couldn't get out through the south gate, what would they do then?

Just run, Calum, he told himself. *Worry about the rest later.*

The three of them rounded a corner and stopped short. A platoon of soldiers four rows deep blocked the street. Had the soldiers in pursuit cut them off, or were these totally different soldiers?

Magnus faced Calum and Axel. "Rooftops. Now."

Before Calum could ask what that meant, Magnus grabbed him by his collar and his belt and hurled him into the air. Blue sky filled his vision, then his body smacked against something hard, and everything snapped to white, then black. His eyes reset in time to see Axel flying through the air down at him.

As if Calum's body didn't already hurt enough from running through the city and landing on the rooftop, all two-hundred-plus pounds of Axel landed right on top of him. The impact pushed the air out of Calum's lungs and sent fresh pain through his torso.

They both let out a loud "oof," and then Axel jumped up.

"Thanks for breaking my fall. Always knew you were a big windbag." He grabbed Calum by his wrist and yanked him up to his feet. "Come on. We gotta keep moving."

Wheezing, Calum headed for the edge of the roof. "Is Magnus coming after us?"

A gigantic green head popped up over the side of the building, followed by two big green hands. Magnus's talons dug into the wooden edge, and he shouted, "Go! Do not tarry on my account!"

Calum nodded, sheathed his sword, and spun around. He chased Axel, who deftly bounded from rooftop to rooftop. They ducked under clotheslines, sidestepped small chimneys, and even jumped over a pipe-smoking roof-dweller reclining in a low chair.

"Southwest, Axel!" Magnus yelled from behind them. "Calum, tell him!"

Calum repeated the words.

"I heard him the first time!" Axel corrected his course and cleared a wide gap between two roofs.

Calum jumped as well, but he didn't make it quite as far. He managed to grab onto the edge of the building, but his chest, knees, and thighs smacked the side. It would have hurt a lot worse had he not been wearing armor, but it still left him stunned and weakened.

Overhead, Magnus cleared the jump with no problem. Just when Calum thought his grip would falter, Magnus reached down, grabbed his wrist, and hauled him up onto the roof.

"Thanks," Calum said.

Magnus's eyes focused on something behind him, down at street-level.

Calum turned back. Down below, the masses of soldiers nocked arrows and drew them back in their bows.

"Get down!" Magnus yelled.

Both he and Calum dropped, and a flurry of arrows zipped through the sky.

Axel.

Calum hollered his name. "Take cover! Arrows!"

Axel spun around for a look, then he rolled behind a brick chimney just in time to avoid at least a dozen arrows that dug into the rooftop where he'd just been standing.

"Draw!" The cry came from below, in the street.

Magnus pulled Calum to his feet and shoved him forward. He shouted, "Axel, move!"

Axel burst from his cover and bolted for the next roof, and Calum and Magnus made the jump as another barrage of arrows plunged into the rooftop behind them.

A pair of soldiers kicked open a rooftop door in front of Axel and swung their weapons at him. He ducked under both attacks and kept going. The soldiers turned to follow him, but by then, Calum and Magnus came up behind them.

Calum bashed one in the back of his helmeted head with his elbow, dropping him immediately. Magnus leveled the other one with a punch that could've felled a horse.

The soldier's head jerked to the side with a sharp crack, and he slumped to the rooftop, but instead of continuing to run, Magnus stopped and scooped the soldier into his arms.

Calum eyed him and started to ask what he was doing, but Magnus yelled, "Keep going!"

Calum caught up to Axel at the edge of one of the rooftops. Below them, the south gate, set into the tall city walls between two watchtowers just like the north and east gates, was shut. A small army of soldiers stood guard down below.

Calum turned back to Magnus, who had just made it onto their roof with the motionless soldier still in his arms. "They're waiting for us at the south gate, too."

"Have they realized we are on the roof?"

"No," Axel replied. "They're focused on the street."

"Good. Then we need to—"

An arrow plunged into the base of Magnus's neck, just above his armor, and he went down.

CHAPTER 28

"**N**o!" Calum yelled. A few more arrows smacked the rooftop around him, all from the two watchtowers on either side of the gate, but Calum didn't care. He ran to Magnus and dropped to his knees, ignoring the arrows thudding into the roof around him. "Magnus?"

"I'm fine," he growled. "Just pull it out."

"Are you su—"

"*Pull it out.*"

Calum wrapped his fingers around the arrow and yanked it from Magnus's neck.

Magnus roared, then hissed, and blood burbled out of the wound and trickled down toward Magnus's breastplate.

Calum recoiled and stared at the bloody arrowhead for a moment, thankful it wasn't barbed, then he tossed it aside. "Can you move?"

Magnus grunted but stood to his feet. "Hurry—to the edge."

Calum headed back to the roof's edge, all the while shielding his head from the sporadic arrows that the soldiers in the watchtower now launched at them. Magnus came up behind him and stood there with the soldier in his arms again.

"You alright?" Axel asked.

"It was not deep. My skin is getting thicker, I think. It will heal quickly," Magnus said.

Calum wanted to ask about how Magnus could heal so much faster, but now wasn't the time. Instead, he asked, "What do we do now?"

"We jump."

"Where? Down to the street?"

Magnus shook his head, and more burgundy blood bubbled out of his arrow wound. "No. Over the gate."

From their position on the roof, the jump was manageable, at least from a distance standpoint. They had already cleared wider jumps between rooftops—the problem was the long metal spikes that lined the top of the walls and the gate. Calum had noticed them atop the walls when

Axel grabbed his shoulder. "Wait—you'll skewer yourself if you hit those spikes."

Magnus smirked. "That is what our friend here is for."

It made sense to Calum right before Magnus jumped.

Magnus flew through the air with the soldier in his arms, and as he approached the wall, he positioned the soldier's body under his own. As they landed, the spikes knifed into the soldier's body, and thanks to the weight of the soldier's body combined with Magnus's momentum, the spikes bent away from Calum and Axel.

Magnus rolled off and dropped out of sight behind the wall, seemingly unscathed.

Calum smacked Axel's breastplate with the back of his hand and backed up to get a running start. He charged full speed, planted his right boot on the edge, and leaped toward the wall. When his feet hit the soldier's armor, he tucked into a roll and dropped down outside the city walls.

The fall ended with no pain and no jarring impact. When Calum opened his eyes, he lay in Magnus's arms.

Calum blinked.

"It was a long drop. I figured you would not mind some assistance."

"Not at all. Thanks." Calum grinned. It had worked. Now they were just waiting for—

A raucous yell sounded above.

"Excuse me." Magnus set Calum on his feet and shifted his footing, then Axel tumbled from the wall down into Magnus's arms.

Axel rubbed his eyes. "What in the—"

"You are welcome." Magnus set Axel on his feet.

"I'm never doing that again," Axel said.

"No time to dally now," Magnus said. "Before long, they will deduce what happened, especially with you screaming like a little girl when you jumped."

Axel glared at him. "No time to fool around, but you're making jokes?"

"I could not help myself. In all seriousness, as soon as they get that gate open, we will yet again find ourselves in peril." Magnus pointed west. "We will head to the southern end of the Snake Mountains and take cover until this trouble subsides."

"What about Lumen and the Arcanum?" Calum asked.

"This is a temporary precaution. We need to allow this tension to cool down, and then we will head for Trader's Pass again."

"How long?" Calum asked. "My dreams are getting more and more urgent."

"A few days, at most. These things have an ebb and flow to them. They will lose interest soon enough."

"Alright. Three days, tops." Calum started west, and the others ran alongside him.

"Any chance they can cut us off from the west gate?" Axel asked.

Magnus shook his head. "No. The only way in or out of the west gate is via Trader's Pass. Everything around it is mountainous and lined with the same steep cliffs we found along the western edge of the range to the north. They can only chase us if they open the south gate or come at us over the Snake Mountains from the north, which they will not do."

"Good," Calum said.

Within minutes, they disappeared into the woods southwest of Kanarah City.

———

COMMANDER ANIGO RUBBED his sore chest, now bandaged and on the mend, but by no means restored to full health. A new leather breastplate covered his torso, and a local blacksmith had mended the chain maille shirt underneath as well.

When a soldier by the name of Corporal Jopheth reported a sighting of three fugitives—two young men and a Saurian in bright blue armor—Commander Anigo had to restrain every impulse to go after them, even in his weakened state. Now the corporal had returned with yet another update.

"Captain, we've lost sight of them." Corporal Jopheth pointed to the south gate. "We think they went over the wall. Should we open the gate to pursue them?"

"No." Captain Leonid Fulton, the commanding officer of the entirety of the King's forces in Kanarah City, yawned and waved his hand. "They're rabble-rousers. Nothing more."

Commander Anigo resisted the urge to correct him and remind him of the very specific orders he'd received prior to leaving Solace. Instead, he turned to the corporal. "Aren't the walls lined with spikes?"

Corporal Jopheth nodded. "Yes, they are."

"How did they manage to get over without getting impaled?"

"What does it matter?" Captain Fulton adjusted his breastplate, made of polished silver instead of black leather, for the umpteenth time.

Ever since the other day when Commander Anigo met him after leaving the infirmary, Captain Fulton continued to shift the breastplate every so often. It just didn't fit him the way it should.

Probably because he was a fat lush who refused to do his job properly.

But Commander Anigo couldn't say that to him, either.

"They're gone," Captain Fulton said. "They're of little consequence."

Commander Anigo narrowed his eyes. "Captain, they have killed or been party to the killings of dozens of men, including at least ten of the King's soldiers. They assaulted and robbed one of our outposts in the north, and they—"

"Yes, yes. I'm aware of their crimes." Captain Fulton yawned again.

Commander Anigo clenched his teeth. "My point is that they've ascended far beyond the level of a mere nuisance. I recommend we pursue them."

"Montrose?"

Corporal Jopheth stepped aside, and a slender lieutenant gave Captain Fulton a slight bow.

"Yes, Captain?" When Montrose looked up, his emotionless gaze met Commander Anigo's for a moment, then they fixed on Captain Fulton again.

"Are our dinner preparations ready for this evening?"

"Nearly, sir," Montrose replied.

Preparations? Commander Anigo fumed. He was trying to catch a trio of wanted fugitives known for their violence and cunning, and Captain Fulton was more concerned about his dinner plans for that night.

"Captain, I—"

"That will be all, Commander." Captain Fulton didn't even look at him. Instead, he was trying to adjust his breastplate again. "Head back to the barracks and rest your injured chest. Your vagrants are gone, and if they are foolish enough to return, we will swiftly bring them to justice then."

"With respect, Captain, I'd like to request a contingent of men to accompany me while I search for them outside the city walls."

"Your request is denied, Commander. Unlike you, I did not manage to get the men assigned to me killed."

Commander Anigo bristled at that remark. He could hardly be held responsible for the deaths of those men, especially in light of their rampant incompetence. If they'd fought harder and smarter, perhaps they would've survived. And perhaps he wouldn't have to be here now, either.

No, their failure and deaths reinforced what he'd believed about them upon his arrival to the Rock Outpost: Commander Pordone had been a pitiful excuse for a commanding officer. If anyone could be blamed for the demise of those men, it was Commander Pordone and his lax attitude toward enforcing the King's law.

"Besides, I require my men to remain here in Kanarah City to continue to ensure the safety of our citizens. These brigands you're pursuing have left the city, and therefore they are no longer our problem."

Commander Anigo gritted his teeth. "I respectfully disagree. If they were to—"

"You may disagree all you want, as long as you do so in silence," Captain Fulton said, his voice hard. He struggled to rise to his feet from his chair until Montrose took hold of his arm and pulled him up. "Now I take my leave. Rest and recover, Commander, and when you are well enough to travel, you may return to the north for more men. You surely shall not take any of mine."

With that, Captain Fulton waddled away. Both Lieutenant Montrose and Corporal Jopheth followed, leaving Commander Anigo standing there, snarling. Captain Fulton's lack of regard for his own office sickened Commander Anigo. Worse still, the pain in his gut persisted.

EVENING CAME SOONER than Lilly expected.

When the new guy showed up with a small sack tied with twine and slipped it through the bars, Lilly eyed him, but she didn't move.

"Roderick's orders," he said. "Your garments are old and soiled. These are new ones."

It was true. Lilly's skintight top and bottoms, once pristine and white, bore a myriad of dirt, sludge stains from the sewers, and now, Colm's blood.

Hardly appealing to a prospective buyer. She shook her head at her own distorted humor.

Lilly's stomach churned, but she snatched the sack from the new guy's hand and recoiled into the cell. She untied the twine and spread the sack open on the floor. Sure enough, a clean set of undergarments very much like the ones she wore lay before her.

"There's more." The new guy stepped aside and returned with a bucket and a cream-colored bar of soap. "He wants both of you to wash up before the auction tonight, and he said *you're* supposed to wash first." He pointed at Lilly.

The new guy unlocked the cell and slid the bucket and the soap inside, then he locked it again.

Lilly eyed the bucket and the soap then glared at him. "Do you really expect us to just strip down and wash in front of you?"

The new guy's eyes widened. "Uh—no?"

"Then could you please give us some privacy?"

He nodded. "Yeah. Sure. Sorry."

As the new guy headed toward the cellblock door, Lilly stared at her reflection in the bucket. Yes, she wanted more than anything to scrape the grime off her skin, but the idea that doing so would fetch a higher price sickened her.

Still, she needed to do it. Once the new guy shut the cellblock door behind him, she peeled her soiled undergarments off and started to wash. She couldn't do anything about the other prisoners in the cells, but at least she'd managed to keep Roderick's new puppy from staring at her while she did it.

An hour after Lilly finished scrubbing the blood and grime from her body and re-clothed herself in the new undergarments, the new guy returned and peered at her and Sharion through the bars. "You ready yet?"

What did he expect her to say? Lilly wanted to bash his head in. Instead, she just sighed.

The new guy swallowed. "I mean—are you dressed?"

"You've got eyes, don't you?"

"Well, yes, but—"

"I'm ready."

"Alright." The new guy stepped into full view and inserted his key into the lock.

Lilly eyed Sharion, but she didn't give any indication that she intended to reveal Colm's parting gifts. Perhaps she'd realized that Lilly was her only hope of escaping this place.

The new guy produced a burgundy gown and held it out for Lilly to take. "Here. This is for you. Roderick's orders."

She took it and rubbed the burgundy fabric between her fingers, then cursed to herself. Not aerosilk. Roderick knew better than to give a Windgale something made of aerosilk, or even an aerosilk blend.

And to top it off, burgundy really wasn't her color.

"Why?" she asked.

"He said he wants you to look your best for tonight."

"I couldn't care less what Roderick wants."

The new guy gawked at her. "What? But—"

"Where's *my* fancy dress?" Sharion folded her arms and glared at the new guy.

"I—I don't—"

Sharion spat on the floor in front of him.

His brow furrowed and he pointed at Lilly. "Just put it on, alright? We've got a schedule to keep."

As the new guy left the cellblock, Lilly traced her finger along the dress's black lace neckline. She'd never wear anything like it if she had the choice, but it beat staying in just her undergarments. She pulled it over her head and adjusted it on her body.

It fit well, but she hated it just the same, mostly because of what it represented.

Something tugged at her back. She turned and—

"Hold still," Sharion grunted.

Lilly went rigid. "What are you doing?"

"The back of this dress won't tie itself." Sharion pushed Lilly's cheek and faced her forward. "I said to hold still."

Lilly smirked, and she relaxed as Sharion did her work.

BY THAT NIGHT, Magnus's accelerated healing had already sealed and begun to repair the arrow wound in his neck. Calum marveled at the sight and wished he had that same ability. In the kind of life he and Axel were now living, quick healing like that would change everything for them.

In the end, it only amounted to wishful thinking. That healing remained exclusive to Saurians, so Calum would just have to be cautious.

And speaking of cautious, when they made camp deep in the wilderness that night, they tied the moneybag shut and kept it near whoever was designated to stand watch. They'd cleared a decent amount of coin from Garon's shop, but they still only had limited supplies and no food to speak of. With little else to do, they went to sleep early.

Calum took the last shift again, and again, about two hours before sunrise he heard noises and thought he saw movement in the shadows.

This time, he was ready, though.

He gripped his sword in his right hand and listened, always with his left hand on the bag.

Something snapped to his left, just like the last time he'd let the bag get stolen. But he wouldn't get fooled twice. Instead of looking toward the sound, he stared right at the bag of gold coins. It couldn't get stolen if he kept his eyes on it, right?

A low growl sounded from the opposite side of the campfire. Calum glanced in that direction, but he didn't remove his hand from the pouch.

Perhaps he should rouse Magnus or Axel? Or both of them?

No. He needed to stick to the plan.

The growl stopped. Calum tightened his grip on his sword and stared over the campfire. If the Wolf attacked, he'd kill it, no question, and then that would solve the thief problem for good.

The pouch zipped out of his grasp and into the darkness.

"Now!" Calum yelled.

Magnus jumped to his feet and yanked a cord he held in his hands. Axel had attached it to the string that tied the bag shut through a small hole he'd cut into the bottom of the pouch. It functioned like a fishing line without a proper hook—they were counting on the Wolf refusing to let go of the bag once he got his jaws on it.

It worked.

The cord tightened, and a mass of brown-gray fur soared toward them from the darkness. It landed hard and skidded along the grass until it stopped about three feet away from Magnus. Gold coins flickered in the night sky and pinged along on the rocky ground, but they were of secondary concern compared to the thief now among them.

The Wolf released the bag, hopped up to its feet, and tried to dart away, but Magnus already had it by its tail. It pulled against his grip at first, then whipped its head around and chomped on Magnus's fingers.

Magnus hissed and winced, but he didn't let go. He pulled the Wolf closer and drew his sword. As Magnus raised the blade, fright flickered in the Wolf's eyes.

CHAPTER 29

"No!" Calum stepped between Magnus and the Wolf, and Magnus stayed his hand.

The Wolf twisted free and darted into the woods.

"What are you doing?" Axel yelled. "We had him!"

"I—I don't know. I just couldn't let Magnus do it. He's a thief. He didn't try to kill us. It just didn't seem right to kill him for it." Calum shook his head. "I don't know."

"Well, now he's gonna come back, and he's gonna find a way to steal from us again." Axel glared at him. "Sometimes I just want to punch you, Calum. Hard."

"I'm sorry. I don't know what came over me." He glanced at Magnus. "Maybe I should've let you do it. I'm sorry."

"You should be." Axel threw his sword on the ground and dropped back into his spot. "I'm going back to sleep. You can pick up the coins without me."

Calum sighed. He deserved that. He'd botched the whole plan, and it had been working. He looked at Magnus again. "I'm sorry."

Magnus nodded. "Everything happens for a reason, Calum. Your compassion is something you should not lose if you can help it. It is the reason we are friends."

"If you say so."

"Indeed I do." Magnus patted him on his shoulder. "Come. Grab a stick from the fire. I will help you gather the coins."

A FEW MORE HOURS PASSED. Lilly assumed that night had fallen, but she didn't know for sure because the cellblock had no windows.

The new guy stepped into the cellblock and unlocked Lilly's cell. "It's time."

Lilly sat on the floor, wearing the burgundy dress. She stared at the patch of Colm's dried blood on the stone in front of her and shifted her foot in her boot. The knife blade pressed against her ankle as it had the last dozen times she'd checked for it. Good.

She could shift her leg under the hem of the dress and remove the knife, conceal it along the back of her wrist, and then jam it into his throat when he didn't expect it. From there, she could unlock the other cells and free the other slaves, and together maybe they could find a way to escape.

"*Come here.*" The new guy's dark eyebrows arched down. It was the first time he'd been stern with her so far.

Lilly lingered on the floor and moved her hand closer to her boot.

"What's the holdup?" Roderick's voice sent tremors into Lilly's stomach. He stepped into view behind the new guy and grinned at Lilly. "The show's about to begin."

Lilly froze, but she managed to scowl at him. The meager dinner of soup and stale bread they'd given her churned in her stomach at the sound of Roderick's voice.

She ignored the knife and instead pushed up to her feet. No chance of escaping now, not with Roderick around. She'd have to find another moment.

"Come on." Roderick motioned with his head. "We don't want to keep your buyer waiting."

Roderick shackled her wrists—but not her ankles this time. Then he shut the cell door behind her, and escorted her and the new guy to the auction house.

A row of thick black curtains prevented her from seeing the bustle on the other side. Through the occasional crack in the curtains she caught glimpses of a smattering of people in fine clothes. They held drinks and mingled like old friends at a wedding.

Didn't they realize what was about to happen? That people's lives were about to be changed forever? They had made the slaves' suffering into a social event, something to be celebrated. It sickened her.

Through the next opening in the curtains, she saw a fat, bearded man pat a thick pouch that hung from his belt, and the ugly woman talking with him laughed so hard that she almost spilled her drink.

Pigs. No—worse than that. Vermin. No better than the rats that had nipped at her ankles and squeaked around her as she traversed the city's sewers.

"That's not for you, Angel. Your buyer's better than any of them." Roderick stepped between her and the curtains. "At least he will be, until he resells you after tonight. If I were you, I'd try to make him really happy. Then he might just keep you around instead of tossing you to someone else when he's done with you."

Lilly's stomach lurched, and she vomited bile on Roderick's hip and down the side of his right leg. She hated the feeling, but at least she'd doused him in the process.

Roderick hopped back at first, then grabbed her by the back of her neck. His gray eyes burned and he raised his hand to strike her.

"Careful, Roderick." She glowered at him, then smirked. "You wouldn't want to forgo a higher price over a little vomit on your armor, would you?"

His jaw tightened and his eyes narrowed, but he let her go. He eyed the new guy. "You two keep going. He's waiting outside in a wagon. You'll know it when you see it. I have to get cleaned up before the auction."

The new guy nodded and yanked Lilly forward. "Come on."

"And wash her mouth out before you get to him. Can't have her smelling like—whatever it is she ate tonight."

"What do I do about the coin?"

"Don't worry about that. We already agreed on a price. He'll hand you a sack of gold once he sees her. Bring it straight to me once you get it." Roderick started toward them again and pointed his finger at the new guy. "And it's a lot of money. If you run off with it, I'll make you sorry you were ever born. And you know I can find you, too."

"Got it." The new guy nodded. He tugged on Lilly's arm. "Let's go."

They rounded a corner and stopped at a table behind the curtains. The new guy poured her a goblet full of cool water from a bronze pitcher. Lilly swished it around her mouth then spat it all back into the pitcher instead of on the floor.

The new guy pulled her away from it. "You wench! Don't you know there are people out there who were going to drink that?"

Lilly stared into his dark eyes and grinned. "Yes."

The new guy glared at her and shook his head. "Enough. We're going."

He led her back the way they had come and then out of the building. Sure enough, a large wagon adorned with purple awnings and gold trim awaited them under the moonlight.

Lilly's heart hammered in her chest. *When do I go for my knife? Do I feign being sick again and hunch over for it? What do I do?*

A thin man dismounted from the front of the carriage and started toward them. He wore black armor—the same armor the King's men wore—but no helmet, and he held a bulging leather pouch in his hands. A sword, sheathed, hung from his belt. He stared at her with vacant brown eyes, as if he was more dead than alive.

"This is her?" he asked, his voice monotone.

"Yep." The new guy urged Lilly forward.

She couldn't reach for her knife now. Not while there were two of them.

The soldier tossed the new guy the pouch. "That's all of it. The captain will be *very* pleased."

"Oh," the new guy said. "So you're not—"

"Run along, boy." The soldier grabbed the chain between Lilly's shackles and pulled her away from the new guy. "The transaction's done."

The new guy eyed them both, nodded, then turned back toward the auction house.

The urge to call him back swelled in Lilly's stomach, but he couldn't help her now even if he wanted to. And he wouldn't help her anyway.

What was she about to get herself into?

"Come on, wench." The soldier shoved her toward the back of the wagon, pulled back a fold of purple fabric, and opened the wooden door. He ushered her inside.

The wagon compared in size to one of Roderick's caged wagons, but the similarities ended there. Soft light glowed from the candelabras mounted on the interior walls of the carriage, illuminating the space. Plush purple fabric lined the walls and ceiling, and a layer of blankets and furs covered the floor.

In the center reclined a rotund, balding man clad in a fine white robe. What little hair adorned his head took on a reddish hue in the candlelight, but Lilly noted several gray hairs mixed in as well. A small gray mustache hung under his arched nose, and he clutched a golden goblet in his left hand.

He grinned at her with lust in his dark eyes.

She'd decided the people attending the auction were rats instead of pigs, but this man was truly the latter. Even the sight of him churned her stomach.

The soldier removed Lilly's shackles and shoved her toward the hairless ogre on the furs.

"That will be all, Montrose. You know the routine. Take a walk. Be back in an hour." The captain took a gulp of wine from the goblet, then licked his plump lips. "On second thought, make it a half-hour."

"Yes, Captain Fulton."

Fulton? Lilly remembered that name. *The officer who betrayed Colm to Roderick?*

Montrose shut and latched the carriage door, and his footsteps faded into the distance.

Captain Fulton pushed himself up to his feet and started toward Lilly. She tried to retreat, but the back of the carriage stopped her. There was no escape.

"Roderick wasn't lying." Captain Fulton reached for her. Lilly recoiled, eyes shut, but she still felt his thick fingers stroking her cheek. "You're the most beautiful creature I've ever seen."

Lilly almost reached for the knife then, but she stopped herself. *Not yet.*

Then again, she didn't know how much time she had left.

"Did Roderick tell you about me?" He took another greedy slurp from his goblet, and Lilly noticed two thick golden rings, one on his little finger and one on his ring finger of that hand. "Hm? He must've said *something.* Roderick is a loquacious sort if I ever met one."

Lilly had no desire to respond to anything he said. He reeked of wine and a pungent floral fragrance that overwhelmed Lilly's nostrils.

"I'm sure you're frightened, child, but I mean you no harm." He tangled his fingers in her blonde hair. "By the moon, you are *radiant.*"

Disgust swirled in Lilly's stomach. She thought she might vomit again, but she managed to hold her composure.

"I can assure you, I'm very experienced. You could enjoy this if you wanted to." He tossed his empty wine goblet behind him and it clunked against the wall, empty, then cupped her shoulders in his hands. "I know I will."

That's it. Enough. Lilly drove her knee into Captain Fulton's groin and shoved him back.

Red-faced, he dropped onto his hands and knees on the blankets with his teeth bared.

Lilly spun around and grabbed for the carriage door, but it didn't have a handle, only a keyhole. How would she—

Something jerked her head back. Captain Fulton had her hair.

He yanked her away from the door and thrust her onto the carriage floor. The lust in his eyes had given way to rage.

"You had your chance, pretty one." He towered over her, fists clenched. Perspiration dotted his forehead and rolled down his cheeks. "I don't mind a little fight, but that was too far."

Captain Fulton untied the front of his white robe and exposed his hairless chest—and a silver skeleton key that hung from a thin chain around his neck. The carriage door key?

Now or never. Lilly skinned the knife from her boot and scooted away from him until her back rested against the carriage wall opposite of the door.

"My, what a twist. You think one small knife will keep you safe from me?" Captain Fulton scoffed. "You obviously don't know who you're dealing with."

"Stay away." Lilly held up the knife, which kept Captain Fulton well beyond arm's length.

"Ah, so she does speak." Captain Fulton stalked closer, one cautious step at a time. "A lovely voice to match her lovely exterior. I wonder how she'll sound when she *screams?*"

"I said to stay back!" Lilly drew the knife back slightly, but her elbow hit the wall. She turned her head—a mistake. General Balena would have chastised her for it.

Captain Fulton sprang forward faster than she expected, given his girth, and clamped his hand around her wrist. She couldn't move her hand with the knife because of his grip, so she drove her fist into his round belly. It rippled, and he grunted, but he didn't stop his advance.

He grabbed her other wrist, wrenched her around, and pulled her close to him.

The stench of sweaty flowers almost suffocated her, and he squeezed her tight. She screamed, but he didn't release his grip.

"Roderick was right about you being wily." He chuckled. "I may have gained a few pounds since my prime, but I'm still a trained soldier. I know how to disarm a child with a knife."

He jerked her right hand downward at an awkward angle, and she dropped the knife with a yelp. He kicked it away and it plunked against the carriage wall, well out of reach.

A snort sounded over her shoulder, then another behind her neck. Was he—*smelling* her?

Lilly cringed and twisted in his grasp, but she stood no hope of breaking free. She shrieked.

"The less you fight, the easier this will be for both of us." He spun her around and pushed her down onto her back.

Every curse and insult she'd ever learned teased her tongue, but they all dissipated in dread when he crouched down over her. He clasped his thick hand around her throat and leaned in so close that his gut pressed against her abdomen, pinning her down.

His dark eyes narrowed and his nostrils flared. "I could just snap your neck, you know."

Lilly craned her neck in spite of his grasp until she got a view of the knife, and she stretched her arm toward it, but it lay a solid foot out of her reach.

"Still resisting? Very well. I don't like to do this, but I suppose I'll have to this time." Captain Fulton pinned her under his full weight and pulled a small vial of violet liquid from his waistband. "Aliophos Nectar won't kill you. It won't put you to sleep either, unless I give you half the vial, but a drop should make you more cooperative."

Aliophos Nectar—the same stuff Roderick had used to knock her out when he'd first caught her. Not again. Lilly strained for the knife, but no matter how she writhed against him, she couldn't reach. "I don't care what you do. I won't cooperate with *this*."

Captain Fulton grinned. "We'll see about that."

He released his grip on her throat to uncork the vial and she lashed her arm toward the knife, but his gut kept her pinned in place. She screamed and clawed at the floor for it, all to no avail. She couldn't reach the knife.

"Easy, little one. Soon you'll see things my way." Captain Fulton grinned.

Lilly summoned all the rage in her body into her mouth, and she spat in Captain Fulton's left eye. He recoiled with a snarl, and it freed Lilly to move.

She snatched the knife handle with her right hand.

Captain Fulton wiped the saliva from his face and groped for her throat. As he leaned down, Lilly plunged the knife into the left side of his thick neck.

He screamed, and as he clutched at the wound, blood oozed from between his fingers.

Lilly shoved against his chest with all her might and he rolled off of her onto his back. She jumped to her feet, yanked the key from the chain around his neck, and dashed to the carriage door. She jammed the key into the lock and began to—

Captain Fulton's hand clamped around her ankle, and he jerked her back. Her footing dropped out from under her, and she hit the floor chest-first. Lilly's breath pushed out of her lungs, and she gasped as Captain Fulton reeled her back toward him.

She twisted so she lay on her back. Even though the knife was still lodged in his neck, he still tried to press the fingers of his other hand against his wound. With her free leg Lilly kicked at his arm and his stomach and his chest, but he didn't relent. He kept pulling her, his wide eyes rabid with rage as red gurgles sputtered through his clenched teeth.

The sight gave Lilly a new target: his teeth.

She adjusted her footing and slammed the heel of her boot into Captain Fulton's mouth, then again into his nose. He lost his grip for a moment, and she recoiled, but he lunged forward and grabbed her other ankle instead.

Would he *never* give up? Why wouldn't he just die already?

Now that he had her other ankle, it meant her right leg was free. The knife still protruded from his neck, just where she'd left it.

It was her way out of this horror.

In one savage motion, Lilly shifted her body hard to the right and drove the heel of her boot into the end of the knife handle. Captain Fulton gasped, released her, and clutched his throat with both hands, his bloody mouth wide open.

Lilly drew her leg back again for another kick and let it fly, but Captain Fulton blocked her leg with his forearm and latched onto it. She wrenched her body to the side and hurled another kick with her left leg at his face, and it connected. He let her go again.

One more shift, one more brutal kick to that knife would finish it.

She glared at him as he slumped to the floor again, a look of pained desperation in his eyes. "This is for Colm."

She delivered a blow so hard to the knife hilt that her foot hurt afterward.

The knife hilt all but disappeared into Captain Fulton's thick neck, and his mouth widened even farther. He coughed and hacked up specks of blood onto her torso and face, then he slumped onto his side. His eyes rolled back, and he stopped moving entirely.

Either he was dead or he wasn't—Lilly had no desire to find out—but either way, he wouldn't be chasing her anymore. She whirled around and twisted the key in the lock, and the carriage door swung open. A gust of cool night air washed away the combined scent of sweat, flowers, and blood, and it renewed Lilly's spirit.

Freedom.

Part of her wanted to retrieve the knife from Captain Fulton's neck, but another part of her, a part she knew was totally irrational, worried he might come back from the dead if she pulled the knife out. She left the knife, but snatched up the vial of Aliophos Nectar that lay next to his motionless body.

She never would've expected it, but she found herself thanking the Overlord for the color of her burgundy dress. It disguised the spattered blood that coated her upper half, and she used the fabric near the hem to wipe off her face, neck, and hands.

Enough. It doesn't have to be perfect.

Lilly let the hem drop down and peered into the night. From what she could tell, Montrose hadn't finished his walk and wasn't yet nearby. Maybe she could make a clean escape.

No. Not yet. She still had to find and recover her armor and her cape, or she'd have no chance of getting home safely.

She crept back toward the auction house, but instead of going inside, she rounded the side of the building. If her armor was still in Roderick's wagon, the one pulled by the brown donkey, then perhaps she wouldn't have to go back inside at all.

Sure enough, she found a row of familiar wagons, some of them big barred boxes like the one the slave traders had confined her to during her trip across Trader's Pass, and some of them small and loaded with crates and barrels and other supplies.

The only problem was that all the donkeys and horses pulling the carts had been unhitched and now lingered in a small stable adjacent to where the wagons were parked.

Lilly cursed under her breath. A man emerged from the stables with a shovel in-hand. Lilly ducked behind the nearest wagon and crouched by the wheel.

The man shut the door and set the shovel next to it, then he walked in her direction. He stopped at the wagon just ahead of hers and leaned against the bars.

How would she get to the wagons with a guard posted there? The Aliophos Nectar wouldn't work unless he breathed its fumes or drank it, and the only thing around that could've served as a weapon was the shovel, but she couldn't get to that without him seeing her either.

Lilly cursed silently again.

"Hey," the man hissed. He craned his head and bent down, his eyes fixed on her location. "Who's there?"

She ducked behind the wagon wheel again and bit her lip. Apparently, she hadn't cursed silently enough.

Hurried footsteps approached her position.

CHAPTER 30

L illy had no time—she just reacted.

"Who are y—"

Lilly uncorked the vial, sprang at him, and tossed the full payload of the Aliophos Nectar at his head. The violet liquid splashed on his face, and he recoiled a step, sputtering.

"What is… what did you…?"

It was the new guy, the one who had escorted her to Montrose and Captain Fulton. The one with the dark eyes, green armor, and curly black hair.

He blinked at her and pointed an accusing finger. "You're… not supposed to…"

His legs wobbled, gave out, and he slumped to the ground, unconscious and snoring.

No time to enjoy the sight. Montrose would find Captain Fulton any minute now, and who knew how long the Aliophos Nectar would keep the new guy unconscious? She shuffled over to the wagons and began to rummage through their contents.

Three wagons in, she found her armor, her bow and arrows, and her cape. Joy and relief and excitement cascaded through her veins at the sight.

She sliced her dress down the center of the bodice with one of her arrowheads and shed it from her body, then strapped her armor on, piece by piece. She hooked her cape onto her back, and slung her bow across her chest.

Time to fly.

For the first time in nearly two months, her feet left the ground, and she ascended into the night air as effortlessly as taking a breath. She hovered ten feet off the ground, then twenty, then she matched the height of the building. Exhilaration swelled in her chest the higher she climbed. Now she could zoom away and leave all of this behind as nothing more than a bad memory.

But what about Sharion? What about the other slaves?

No. She didn't have time. Montrose had to be close to the carriage by now. More importantly, she had responsibilities to her family and her parents back home. She couldn't linger here.

But was she truly willing to condemn all of the other people in those cages to fates like the

It wasn't condemnation, she rationalized. She'd escaped. They could do the same if they wanted.

Could they? She pulled the keys from her boot and jingled them in her gauntleted hand.

"When the time is right, I'll help you escape, but not before then."

Lilly had said that to Sharion after Colm died, after she'd clocked Sharion in the chin for trying to use the keys and the knife to escape then and there.

Was it a lie?

Or was it a promise?

Lilly's jaw hardened, and she exhaled a sigh through her nose.

Then she drew an arrow from her quiver, nocked it in her bow, and headed back toward the auction house door.

LILLY PUSHED the cellblock door open. Thanks to the black curtains and the commotion on the other side, Lilly had made it through the auction house all but undetected, and the one guy she did encounter went down with an arrow to his throat, unable to call for help. At least she hadn't lost her accuracy.

She trotted down the cellblock, her head swiveling.

The cells were empty. Every single one.

She was too late.

She stopped at her cell and peered inside. Maybe Sharion had huddled in the corner and they had missed her?

No such luck. She was gone.

Well, she'd tried. Nothing left to do now but escape herself, once and for all. She turned toward the cellblock door and—

"Hey!" a voice, hushed, hissed from behind her.

She whirled around and drew her arrow back, ready to skewer whoever had found her, but found no one. The corridor was empty.

"Down here." The voice sounded from the end of the cellblock, in the last cell. Almost no light entered that cell from the torches in the cellblock. No wonder Lilly hadn't seen anyone in there.

Still, Lilly didn't move. She squinted and kept her arrow trained on the source of the sound—at least as best as she could tell. "Who's there?"

"Come closer."

"Why?"

"Your friend isn't here. They already took her." The voice had a feminine quality, but not like that of a human or a Windgale. "But if you free me, I can help you find her."

"Who are you?"

"My name is Windsor. Hurry—there's little time."

Lilly glanced over her shoulder, then she started toward the end of the cellblock. She relaxed the tension in her bowstring and pulled the keys from her belt. *"What* are you?"

"Unlock the cell, and I can show you."

Lilly pushed the key into the lock but didn't turn it. "How do I know you won't hurt me?"

"You don't. But if you want to see your friend again, you'll let me out."

Did she want to see Sharion again? They weren't exactly *friends*, after all...

"Open. The. Cell," the voice growled.

Lilly's eyes narrowed. She'd do it, but she'd be ready if the prisoner came at her. She turned the key, nocked her arrow, and—

The cell door burst open, and a black blur knocked her onto her back. Teeth flashed under a set of vivid blue eyes and a furry snout.

The Wolf. The one that had almost escaped Roderick's men and given Lilly one of her failed opportunities to escape.

She snarled at Lilly, and her forepaws gripped the top of Lilly's armor. "You shouldn't have tried to shoot me."

Lilly glared up at her and tried to shift, but Windsor was heavier than she looked. Bigger than Lilly had expected, too. "You shouldn't have been so brusque. Now tell me where my friend is."

Windsor growled. "You're in no position to make demands."

"I let you out. I held up my end. Now tell me where she is." Lilly raised an eyebrow. "Or does the word of a Wolf mean nothing?"

"I should kill you for saying that." Windsor leaned in close, and Lilly smelled rancid meat on her breath. "I could tear out your throat right now and I'd be none the worse for it. You'd be the first fresh meat I've had in a month."

"I don't have time for this." Lilly's voice sharpened. "If you're going to kill me, then either do it, or let me up so I can get out of here. If your word means nothing to you and you're not going to help me, then I'll find her myself."

"You're brave—for a Windgale." Windsor growled again, then she stepped off of Lilly's chest. "I'll help you find her, but then I'm out of here."

Lilly pushed herself up to her feet and recovered her bow and arrow. "Lead the way."

Windsor headed to Lilly's old cell first to pick up Sharion's scent from a scrap of the rags she'd worn, then she led Lilly out the cellblock and back into the auction house. Lilly noted a patch of white fur on the tip of her tail, the only part of her coat that wasn't black. It didn't seem to affect her ability to hide in darkness in the least.

Windsor melted into the shadows while Lilly slunk along the wall in the main room. The commotion on the other side had subsided, now replaced with Roderick's voice.

"...you can see this isn't our finest crop ever, but at least the opening prices are competitive." The crowd laughed, and Roderick continued, "As usual, we start at the low end and save the good stuff for later. We've got a gorgeous black she-Wolf locked up, but she's a handful, so she'll be the last prize for you to bid on. For now, let's start with this guy, here. He's got bad teeth, but he's cooperative. Who'll make me an offer?"

"One gold coin," a man from the audience called.

"Jethro bids one gold coin, but he always was cheap." The crowd laughed again. Roderick said, "Any other takers?"

The auction had begun, and patrons perpetuated it with shouts of various amounts of coin.

"Your friend," Windsor motioned toward the curtains with her head, "is already out there."

Lilly's jaw tightened. "How do I get her away from them?"

Windsor shook her head. "Not my problem. I'm out of here."

"But you—"

"I said I'd help you *find* her, and I did," Windsor snapped. "I'm not sticking around any longer than I have to. Neither should you. It's too late for her. You should get out while you still have the chance, before they find you again."

Windsor trotted toward the auction house's door, but Lilly took to the air and beat her there —how good it felt to fly again, even for a short amount of time. "Don't you want to take revenge on these guys for what they did to you? They locked you up. Abused you."

"And now I'm free, and I'm out of here." Windsor growled. "Move, or *I'll* move you."

"I need your help, Windsor. I have to free them. Not just Sharion, but all of them. This is wrong, and you know it."

"What I know is that it's none of my business," Winsdor snarled, "so get out of my way."

Lilly scowled at her but stepped aside.

"Have a nice life." Windsor nudged the door open with her nose and disappeared into the night.

You should get out while you still have the chance, Windsor had said. Perhaps she was right.

No. Lilly had made a promise to Sharion. She had to find a way to free her.

She rounded the corner of the curtains and spotted the table where the new guy had gotten her water after she'd retched all over Roderick. A big man stood there, his arms folded, but he wasn't looking her direction. A half-dozen slaves, all of them human, stood near him, shackled and chained to each other.

Sharion wasn't one of them.

Lilly drew her bow back and launched an arrow at him. It embedded in the side of his head and he slumped to the floor, dead. She swooped over and landed next to him, careful not to ascend above the curtains. The slaves gawked and gasped at her, but she shushed them.

"Easy, easy." She held her hands up to quiet them. True to Roderick's words, they looked healthier and more capable than some of the other slaves she'd seen. He really was saving the "good stuff" for later on. "I'm here to help you, but I need your help as well."

They ogled her with wide eyes and mouths agape.

"I'm going to unchain you. When I do, I need you to rush through the curtains to create a distraction so I can free the other slaves."

"Why in the Overlord's name would we do that?" one man hissed. "You're setting us free. We're leaving."

The others murmured in agreement.

Lilly shook her head. "How far do you think you'll get without coin or food? The crowd will have bags full of coin in their possession. These slave traders took your freedom from you so they could sell you to those pigs out there. You might as well get something in return, right?"

"B-but the s-slave traders have w-weapons," another slave stammered.

Lilly removed the dead slave trader's sword from his belt and tossed it to the slave. "Now you do, too."

"That's great, but what about the rest of us?" The first slave jammed his fists into his hips.

"You'll have to make do."

The slaves looked at each other, then at her. The first slave shook his head. "Sorry, miss, but we'd rather just be on our way."

First Windsor, now these people, too? "I need your help. What about the other slaves?"

"Beggin' your pardon, but if you had a chance at freedom, wouldn't you take it?"

"This *is* my chance at freedom. I was caged up with the rest of you not an hour ago, but I'm still here, trying to help all of you and those who are out on that platform right now."

A brief pause lingered between her and the slaves.

"Look, you're a good shot with that bow and all, but six of us against almost double the number of slave traders and dozens of other people? It's lunacy. Just unlock us and we'll leave."

"You're not goin' anywhere," a voice behind them said.

Lilly whirled around. She knew that voice.

Montrose stood there, sword in-hand, with Luggs, Gammel, and Adgar, each wielding weapons of their own. Two other slave traders also stood with them, bows nocked and ready.

They were trapped.

CHAPTER 31

The slaves huddled together behind Lilly, and the one to whom she'd handed the sword dropped it.

"Drop the bow, pretty one." Montrose pointed his sword at Lilly.

"And if I don't?"

"*Sold*," Roderick crooned on the other side of the curtains. "This one with the bad teeth goes to Jethro for five gold coins. As usual, you can claim your prize after the auction has concluded."

Montrose glanced at Luggs, who raised his arm. The archers drew back their arrows.

"If you come quietly," Montrose said, "I assure you that all of them will live, and so will you, though you must answer for Captain Fulton."

Lilly hesitated. She could bolt into the air and evade their arrows if she had to, but she couldn't let the other slaves die because of her.

Windsor had been right. She should've left when she had the chance.

She dropped her bow at her side.

Montrose nodded toward her. "Take her."

The archers relaxed their bowstrings, and Gammel and Adgar started forward.

A black blur launched out of the shadows and collided with Montrose. His sword clattered toward Lilly. The two forms tumbled to the floor, but the shadow mounted him and lunged for his throat as he screamed. Its tail waved with delight as Montrose thrashed, and Lilly noticed a patch of white fur on its tip.

Windsor. She'd come back.

Pandemonium seized the room. Lilly tossed the key ring to the first slave, and he began to unlock his shackles, then she snatched up her bow and skinned an arrow from her quiver.

In the chaos of the moment, the archers alternated surprised glances between Windsor tearing at Montrose's throat and face and at the slaves. One of them took aim at Lilly again, but her arrow hit him in his face before he could get a shot off. Thanks to Lilly's second arrow, the other went down right after noticing the first archer's fate.

Meanwhile, Luggs swung his dagger down at Windsor, but she darted away from Montrose, and Luggs's dagger lodged in Montrose's chest instead. Luggs staggered back, horrified, until

Lilly's arrow hit his shoulder. He yelped and went down, and Lilly regretted not hitting him as squarely as she'd hit the archers.

The curtains spread wide, and Roderick's towering form filled the open space. "What in the Overlord's name is—"

Lilly aimed her next arrow at him right as he noticed her. He glared at her, and she let the arrow fly.

Roderick sidestepped the arrow and charged at her, but she burst into the air, well out of his reach. By now the freed slaves had scattered, and Roderick yelled for more slave traders.

The set of keys Colm had given her lay on the floor near a pile of shackles. Lilly angled down and scooped them into her hands, bolted toward the ceiling again, and then she dropped down onto the platform in front of the slaves.

She landed in front of Sharion.

Sharion's eyes widened, and she recoiled a step.

Lilly smiled at her. "Told you I'd get you out."

Movement rushed behind Sharion.

"Get down!" Lilly yanked Sharion to the floor and a sword lashed where her head had just been. Adgar.

He swung at them again, but Lilly and Sharion rolled opposite directions, and his blade clanged against the platform instead.

Lilly sprang off her feet and drove her shoulder into his side, and Adgar lost his footing and fell. Still on her side, Sharion bashed him in the face with her elbow then got to her feet.

Adgar lay there, clutching at what appeared to be a broken nose. The stupid hat he always wore had tumbled off his head and lay next to him on the platform.

Lilly crushed it under her boot as she handed Sharion the keys. "Can you take it from here?"

Sharion nodded and smiled. "Thank you."

Lilly gave Adgar a kick to his ribs for good measure, then she turned toward the crowd—or rather, what remained of it. Windsor and some of the other slaves, including the Saurian she'd seen locked up in the cells below, had overrun them and caused a ruckus.

Lilly grinned. It was exactly what those pigs deserved.

A primal roar erupted behind her.

She spun around in time to see Roderick barreling toward her.

Lilly zipped away, but Roderick pursued her nonetheless. She wove through the crowd and arched toward the row of curtains, then angled up and over them.

Roderick's sword severed the rod that suspended the curtains in place, and he tore after her. He moved faster than she remembered.

She flew down the corridor toward the auction house door. Another archer stepped into view at the opposite end of the hall and took aim at her, but she dropped her flight path low and the arrow knifed past her. Roderick grunted behind her, but when she looked back, the arrow hadn't hit him.

Lilly just had to get outside, and then she could get away. The archer nocked another arrow and let it fly as she zoomed toward the door, but on instinct, she stopped short.

The arrow thudded into the doorframe just inches from her face.

She pushed through the door and pulled her bow from her shoulders as she took to the night sky.

The city dropped out from beneath her, but an arrow whizzed past her, then another. She looped and twisted and whirled, but they kept coming. She drew an arrow of her own, turned back and took aim.

Pain stabbed her left shoulder and her arrow loosed, but it hit nowhere near her intended target. Instead, someone else's arrow protruded from her shoulder, right between her breast-plate and her shoulder plate. She looked down.

Far below, Roderick fired more arrows at her in quick succession. Despite the pain, Lilly spun away from the next barrage and ascended above the cloud line.

She'd made it. She'd escaped, and she'd freed the other slaves, too, but not without cost. Blood trickled down her armor.

Lilly wanted nothing more than to rip it from her flesh, but she recalled General Balena's instructions about arrow wounds: she had to leave it in until she could get proper care, or she'd risk bleeding out.

It burned like no pain she'd ever felt before, but she could still fly, and she'd flown well clear of the auction house and Roderick and his men by now. All she had to do was find her way home.

Easier said than done. She'd never been to this half of Kanarah before, and she had no idea where she was. And it was nighttime, and she'd never really learned how to navigate using the stars.

Her head swam with disillusionment. Something wasn't right. Her vision wavered, and her body quivered as she flew. Not normal.

She looked at her bleeding shoulder and at the arrow sticking out of it. She hadn't lost enough blood to grow faint, so why would she—

Aliophos Nectar. It had to be. Roderick must've coated the arrowheads with it. Whether he had or not, she couldn't risk flying while only half-awake.

She descended below the cloud line and saw a small forest below her, and beyond that a sprawling field of gold drenched in silver moonlight. Wheat, maybe?

Her head throbbed, and her vision blackened. She couldn't see.

She blinked hard as she continued to drop lower and lower, and her vision returned in intermittent glimpses of what lay before her. She wanted to slow down—she needed to. Most of all, she needed to land face-up so the arrow wouldn't lodge any deeper in her shoulder.

The land rose up to meet her as her feet touched the ground, but her legs melted underneath her. Lilly managed to twist as she fell, and she landed on her back among the wheat.

Then everything faded to darkness.

CHAPTER 32

The sun hadn't yet risen when Corporal Jopheth burst into Commander Anigo's room.

He jerked upright in his bed, and a jolt of pain stabbed his chest—a reminder that while he was still alive, he was also still mortal. "What is the meaning of this, Cor—"

"I'm sorry for the interruption, Commander," Corporal Jopheth blurted. "Captain Fulton and Montrose have been killed."

Commander Anigo's rage iced over. "What happened?"

"It reeks of scandal, sir. It appears Montrose brought Captain Fulton to a slave auction and helped him procure a Windgale girl to... to..."

"I'm familiar with the concept of prostitution, Corporal."

"Anyway, it appears she brandished a knife and killed him, then she loosed the other slaves and escaped with most of them. The warehouse where it all happened has been vacated, but a man named Wandell Thirry alerted us to several dead bodies inside. Fresh bodies."

Commander Anigo's eyes narrowed. "At an auction? Were they purchasers?"

"Some, yes. Also some slaves and some slave traders, we presume."

"What about the other slave traders?"

"After the pandemonium of the auction, they cleared out. I have men watching the west gate to Trader's Pass right now in search of anything suspicious."

"Well done." Commander Anigo didn't care for Corporal Jopheth, but at least he'd proven somewhat competent.

"I'm afraid Captain Fulton's death means you're now the ranking officer in Kanarah City, Commander. I have dispatched a messenger to Solace requesting instructions on how we are to proceed," Corporal Jopheth said. "In the meantime, what are your orders?"

The ranking officer in Kanarah City? He'd lamented having to deal with Captain Fulton's insolence and disregard for the effective rule of law just yesterday.

Perhaps this was providence—the means and manpower to catch the three fugitives he'd been chasing for the last few months. He grinned.

"Sir?" Corporal Jopheth leaned forward.

Commander Anigo threw the sheets off his legs and stood. "Bring me breakfast. We have much work to do."

AXEL'S STOMACH grumbled for what had to be the third or fourth time that morning. They'd gone yet another day of camping in the woods with no food, so when Magnus suggested they head southeast toward the Golden Plains rather than staying in the mountains, the idea immediately appealed to Axel—at least at first.

"We can harvest some grain from the King's fields," Magnus said. "And if we travel far enough east, we can collect some fruit from his orchards. Along with our weapons and armor, we should be able to make the trip across the valley if we pack enough food. From there, we can begin our search for the Arcanum."

"I said I didn't want to go back to manual labor." Axel folded his arms and frowned. He'd done everything he could to get away from that life, and now Magnus was suggesting he go right back to it. Even if it was only temporary, the idea still grated on him. "I'm done with that life."

"We are enacting this plan precisely because of your farming background. You get to lead this expedition. You know the soil, the plants, the trees. You know the fruits and vegetables better than either Calum or me," Magnus said. "You know what will keep and what will spoil."

Axel's eyebrow rose. Everything Magnus had said was true, but the only thing that had any appeal to it was his suggestion that Axel lead this part of the journey.

"And besides, at this point, we cannot afford to spend any extra time in Kanarah City. I want to get us to Trader's Pass as fast as possible, so having food already packed is essential to our progress. This way, we do not need to linger in a populated area any longer than necessary."

Axel huffed, but he couldn't really argue with Magnus's logic. "I still don't like it, but I'll do it."

Magnus smiled. "We leave at your command."

EVEN AS A FARMER, Axel had never seen anything like it.

Expansive fields of gold shimmered under the afternoon sun. Wind rippled the grain like waves in a lake, a lake that never ended, for all he knew.

In a way, the fields made him long for home, but in another way, they reminded him that he could never go back to the life of a farmer.

"Do you think we're far enough away from Kanarah City?" Calum asked.

Magnus nodded. "Even though we can see it in the distance, we're too far for them to muster any actual response, even if they could see us. We just need to watch out for patrolling soldiers or workers who might be in the area."

Early that morning, they'd taken a circuitous southern road mostly devoid of travelers to the King's Orchards. There, they filled two sacks with various fruits, based on Axel's instructions on what would stay fresh the longest.

Then they'd headed northwest along the edge of the fields, back toward Kanarah City. Once they harvested a couple bags full of grain, they'd be ready to head for Trader's Pass.

"Stay near the edge, at least at first," Axel said. "If we venture too far into the heart of the crops, it'll be that much harder to find our way out if someone finds us."

"I don't know how the King's men could safeguard such vast fields, anyway." Calum scanned the fields. "But we can stick to the edges. The grain should be just as good, right?"

Axel nodded. He plucked a head of grain and held it up for them to see. "This is the part we need. Anything else is just plant fiber, and while we can eat it, it has no nutritional value, so try not to drop them in the bag."

Magnus nodded, and Calum said, "Got it."

They harvested for about a half hour and almost filled the first bag halfway.

"Hey," Calum said. "I'll be right back. Gotta pee."

"Don't stray too far," Axel said. "It's easy to hide or get lost in fields like these. All you have to do is crouch or lay down, and the grain does the rest. Watch yourself."

Calum nodded and stepped a few feet deeper into the sea of gold.

Axel elbowed Magnus in his ribs. "Remind me not to harvest over there, right, Scales?"

Magnus smirked. "No question."

"Uh… guys?" Calum said.

"What's wrong? Can't get it out on your own?" Axel chuckled and dropped another head of grain into his bag.

"No. I found something."

Axel glanced at Magnus, then they both walked over to where Calum stood.

There, among the golden grain, lay a beautiful young woman with blonde hair and an arrow sticking out of her upper chest between her left shoulder and her collarbone.

She wasn't moving.

THE GIRL WAS BEAUTIFUL—*REALLY* beautiful.

Definitely the most beautiful girl Calum had ever seen.

While he hadn't known many women throughout his life, he'd certainly seen a fair number in the last month or so of traveling with Magnus and Axel through the few villages they'd visited. But none of the others even came close to this girl.

Calum bent down next to her. Detailed white engravings of eagles and hawks adorned the pale pink armor that covered her legs, arms, and torso. Blood oozed from around the arrow in her shoulder, but her chest moved up and down slightly.

"She's breathing," Calum said.

"How did she get here? It looks like someone dragged her through the grain and left her here." Axel picked up the ornate bow and a pristine quiver of arrows that lay next to her and looked them over. "And who is she?"

"That does not matter right now." Magnus brushed her long blonde hair away from the wound. "Find me something I can use for a bandage."

"From where?" Calum asked.

"Anywhere. Just find me something." Magnus clasped his fingers around the arrow.

Axel knelt down, set the bow and quiver down, and pointed to the shimmering blue fabric spread out under her body. "What about this?"

Magnus grabbed his wrist. "Do *not* touch her cape."

"Cape?" Axel's eyes widened with the same realization Calum was having. "You mean she's—"

"She's a Windgale." Calum looked at Axel. "She needs it to fly."

"Bandage. Now," Magnus grunted. "Keep looking."

When Magnus pulled the arrow out of the girl's shoulder, she jerked awake and screamed. Her blue eyes darted between Calum and Axel, focused on Magnus, and then she screamed again. She clawed at the dirt and grain around her and tried to get away from them.

Magnus clamped his hand around her ankle and pulled her back, but when Calum and Axel reached down to try to help, he warned them to stay back. Though she kicked and hollered, he held her in place by her shoulders. He leaned in close and stared right at her.

"*Be silent.*"

Her mouth clamped shut, but her blue eyes opened wider.

"I will not hurt you," he said, slowly and pointedly. "Do you understand?"

She glanced at Axel and Calum.

"Neither will they hurt you," he continued. "You have taken an arrow to your shoulder. I removed it, but you are still bleeding. I need to stop it. But first, I need to clean the wound so you do not get an infection. In order to do that, I need you to stay as still and as calm as you can."

She nodded.

"Press your hand against your wound to help stop the bleeding." When the girl complied, Magnus dug his fingers under the armor along his wrist and pulled out a small vial of orange liquid.

Calum eyed the vial. "What is that?"

"It's veromine."

"Vero-what?" Axel asked.

Magnus eyed him. "Veromine. It fights against infection and speeds up the body's natural healing process. We Saurians have it in our blood. It is the reason we can regenerate from wounds so quickly. Did you find me something to use as a bandage?"

"Uhhh…" Calum and Axel eyed each other.

"Both of you remove your gauntlets and shoulder armor. Rip off your shirtsleeves and give them to me." While they complied, Magnus looked down at the girl. "What is your name?"

She glanced at Calum again, and her voice barely registered above a whisper. "Lilly."

"*Calum.*" Magnus's voice broke Calum's stare.

"Huh?" Calum blinked.

"Sleeves."

"Oh. Sorry." He hadn't realized he'd stopped moving. He tore off his sleeves and handed them to Magnus, who was already at work on Lilly's wound with Axel's sleeves.

Lilly winced when Magnus dabbed at the wound. Once he cleared most of her blood, Magnus opened the vial and poured in a few drops.

"Calum, Axel?" Magnus eyed them both. "Turn away, please."

They exchanged glances with each other then looked at Magnus again.

"I must tear away some of her undershirt to secure the bandage, so for her sake, please divert your eyes."

Calum nodded, and he and Axel turned around. As he slid his armor back onto his arms, Calum leaned over to Axel and whispered, "She's beautiful."

"Yeah, but she's beyond you," he whispered back.

Calum tilted his head. "What do you mean?"

Axel shook his head and secured his gauntlet to his left forearm. "A girl like that? You don't have a chance, brother."

On one level, Calum had never had a relationship with a girl before, and Axel knew more about life in general. He was older and wasn't confined to just his farm like Calum was to the quarry, so Calum felt inclined to believe what Axel said.

Yet a part of him wanted to believe that Axel was lying, or just plain wrong.

"Why not?"

"Someone that beautiful? Are you kidding me?" Axel scoffed. "By the look of her armor, her bow, and her quiver, she's probably rich, too. You're more likely to get struck by a bolt of lightning than to end up with her."

Calum's jaw hardened. He didn't want to believe it, but Axel was probably right. Even though he'd earned his freedom, he was still just a poor nobody.

But if he managed to free Lumen, then...

Axel put a gloved hand on Calum's shoulder. "I'm not trying to be harsh. I'm just trying to keep you from getting your hopes up."

"What's wrong with hoping?"

"I don't want you to get hurt. It's not a good feeling." Axel frowned. "Just trying to look out for you."

"There. Finished," Magnus said.

Axel rotated his head. "Can we turn around?"

"Just a second—there. Now you may turn around."

Lilly still lay there, now with one of Calum's and one of Axel's sleeves tied around her shoulder to cover the wound. Her undershirt was tied together over her shoulder where Magnus had ripped it, its white fabric now stained red.

"Are you alright?" Axel asked before Calum had a chance to open his mouth.

Lilly nodded. Her blue eyes still exuded distrust.

"What happened to you?"

Lilly stared at them but didn't say anything. The thought that she might be a mute crossed Calum's mind, but she'd told them her name. And as far as he knew, Windgales spoke the same language as everyone else in Kanarah.

Calum looked at Magnus then refocused on her. "Look, we're not going to hurt you. We'll even let you go, if you want. But if you need help, maybe we can help you."

After another pause, Lilly stood to her feet with Magnus's help. "I was captured outside my home by slave traders."

Magnus growled, and Lilly recoiled from him. He held his hand up to her. "Forgive my reaction. It is out of disdain for them and for your plight. Please continue."

She nodded. "They brought me across the valley and tried to sell me, but I escaped. I remember getting hit by an arrow as I was flying away, but I kept flying. Then my vision began to darken. As I coasted toward the ground to take a rest, I blacked out."

"You're from across the valley?" Calum asked.

"Yes," she replied. "My home is Aeropolis, in the Sky Realm."

"Calum." Magnus stared to the west. "Someone is coming."

All of their heads swiveled at once.

From the northwest, ten men approached them from deeper within the Golden Plains.

"Soldiers?" Calum reached for his sword, and so did Axel.

"No." Lilly shook her head. "They're the slave traders who abducted me."

"Do we run?" Calum asked.

"No, but back out of the field and into the clearing. If we run, they will continue following us. They want Lilly." Magnus turned to her as the four of them backed out of the grain. "Do not worry. I will not allow them to take you again."

"Me neither," Axel added with an overconfident smile.

Calum wanted to chime in as well, but it felt awkward to try to follow up Magnus's sincere promise and Axel's goofy addition. Instead, he gripped the handle of his sword tighter, but he didn't remove it from its sheath.

As the slave traders approached, Magnus squinted. "I do not believe it."

"What?" Axel looked at him.

"They are the same slave traders who captured me."

CHAPTER 33

Calum studied the group of slave traders. He noticed four archers among them, which would make the forthcoming conflict more difficult if it came to blows.

"I recognize their leader," Magnus said. "His name is Roderick."

Axel shifted his stance. "You're so strong, though. How'd they even manage to capture you in the first place?"

"I was foolish. They had been pursuing me for days, and I had grown weary. I thought to steal a few hours of rest one night, so I headed into a cave where I expected I'd be safe. I was wrong."

"So *that's* why you don't like caves." Axel folded his arms.

Magnus glared at him. "In part, yes. While I was asleep, a dozen of them pinned me down with a large net, and Roderick held his sword to my neck. We Saurians can heal from a lot of wounds, but we cannot reliably recover from mortal wounds without true medical aid."

"That's how they caught me, too," Lilly said. "They tried to get me with a net. I almost escaped, but Roderick grabbed me."

"They are brutal, treacherous people." Magnus drew his sword and turned to Lilly. "Today marks their final day of oppressing you or anyone else. That, I promise."

The slave traders stopped at the edge of the grain, about twenty feet from where Calum and his friends stood in the clearing. One of them, a man almost as tall and as broad as Magnus, stepped forward. He had spiky red hair and brown armor.

"Well, well. I don't believe my eyes." He displayed a big white smile. "Never thought I'd see you again, Magnus."

Calum glanced at Magnus, who didn't move. The man must be Roderick.

"It *is* you, isn't it?" Roderick said. "I mean, all you Saurians look the same to me, but no one has blue armor quite like yours."

Magnus exhaled a long breath through his nostrils.

"Ah, and there's our prize. How's your shoulder, Angel?" Roderick winked at Lilly, and she withdrew behind Axel and Calum. "Oh, don't be afraid. We aren't gonna hurt you—anymore."

"Yeah, you just wanna sell her to the highest bidder," Axel said.

"You're absolutely correct," Roderick leveled his gaze at Axel. "She's my property, and I'll do with her what I please."

Calum glared at him. "She's *not* your property."

"I beg to differ." Roderick tilted his head. "When I found her, she was all alone. Cold and hungry. I rescued her, fed her, gave her shelter. I even—"

"You held her against her will." Calum's grip on his sword tightened again.

Roderick raised an eyebrow, then he shrugged. "What's the difference?"

Axel drew his sword and started toward him, but Magnus caught him by his collar.

"O-ho! Did I say something you didn't like?" Roderick held his hands out to his sides. "I'm not such a bad guy. I could've done anything I wanted to that girl after we found her. *Anything.*"

Axel strained against Magnus's grip, but he couldn't get free. Calum didn't blame him. He wanted to rip Roderick apart, too.

Roderick put his left palm out toward them. "Easy, easy. Like I said, I *could have* done anything I wanted to her, but I didn't. You know why?"

Calum's stomach churned. He didn't want to guess at the answer.

"Because I can get more gold for her if she's unspoiled."

Now Calum brandished his sword and took a step forward.

"*Calum.*"

Calum stopped, but he didn't take his eyes off Roderick.

"He is *mine*," Magnus rumbled.

Roderick squinted at him. "Is that right, Magnus? Because last I checked, *you* belonged to *me*, and I sold you to a group of the King's soldiers several leagues north of here."

Magnus just stared at him.

"But I'm willing to let you and your friends go if you hand over the girl."

"No," Calum and Axel said in unison.

Roderick frowned, then smirked. "The alternative, of course, is that I take her back after killing you and your two human friends."

"Try it," Axel said.

Magnus didn't move except to narrow his eyes and hiss through his flared nostrils.

"You know, I may not kill you three after all. Magnus still has plenty of value, and you boys have some flavor in an otherwise bland world. It's usually more of the King's purview to enslave humans, but in your cases, I think I'll stake my own claim."

Roderick motioned to his men. The four archers raised their bows and nocked arrows.

"Last chance." Roderick drew his sword.

One of the archers yelped and dropped to the ground. An arrow protruded from his neck.

Everyone looked at Lilly, who stepped forward with a bow in her left hand and rubbing her injured shoulder with her right. "I'm *not* going back."

Roderick pointed his sword at her. "Go get her. Leave the lizard to me."

The three remaining archers launched their arrows, but Calum and Axel evaded them.

Calum turned back to Lilly. "Stay back and cover us. We'll protect you."

She nodded and pulled another arrow from her quiver, wincing but undeterred.

The slave traders with swords charged past Magnus toward Axel and Calum. Axel parried the first blow that came at him then ducked under the second.

A slave trader swung his ax at Calum's head. He sidestepped the blow and cut the slave trader down with one vicious slice.

Another slave trader jabbed at him with a spear, and Calum parried the blow. The slave trader's second lunge seemed like an over-lunge at first, but at the last second, the slave trader drew a dagger from his belt with his left hand and jammed it at Calum's throat.

Calum blocked the stab with his sword and gripped the shaft of the slave trader's spear with his left. They locked in a grapple, but neither could overpower the other.

Something moved to Calum's right—one of the archers taking aim at him.

Calum shifted his weight and forced the slave trader to the right as the archer let loose another arrow. Instead of hitting Calum, it zipped through the air and plunged into the slave trader's lower back. He dropped his dagger and released his grip, and Calum ran him through.

As the archer drew another arrow from his quiver, Calum switched his sword to his left hand and snatched the spear from the dead slave trader's hands with his right. The archer let the arrow loose, and it whistled by Calum's ear.

The archer jerked another arrow from his quiver and nocked it as Calum drew his right arm back. He'd been practicing his throwing technique ever since the fight with Tyburon, and he'd gotten pretty good at it. Now he'd find out if he could do it in the heat of battle.

The archer fired at Calum, who dove to the right. The arrow skipped off of Calum's left shoulder-plate as he hurled the spear. Calum hit the ground on his side, but the spear plunged into the archer's right thigh, and he also fell.

Calum jumped to his feet, charged over to the archer, and finished him off with his sword.

"Calum, behind you!" Axel's voice split the air.

Calum whirled around, but the incoming slave trader dropped face-first to the ground before Calum could react. An arrow protruded from the center of his back.

Twenty feet beyond the downed slave trader, Lilly lowered her bow and rubbed her injured shoulder again.

Pretty handy to have an archer on their side—especially one so pretty.

Calum smiled at her, perhaps a bit longer than he should have while in battle, then he engaged the next slave trader.

LILLY WATCHED A NOW-HATLESS Adgar and Gammel fall under Calum's and Axel's swords along with the three remaining archers, but Luggs had managed to get past them. Now he approached Lilly with his dagger in hand—the same dagger he'd used to kill Colm.

A bandage around his shoulder bore a dark red stain from where her arrow had hit him last night. Luggs bared his revolting yellow smile as he stalked closer. "You're comin' back with me, and this time, you're mine. Now that Roderick's got his money, he's got no reason to stop me."

Lilly nocked an arrow and aimed for the center of his chest. This time, she would hit him with a killshot. "Not a chance."

She let it loose, but Luggs shifted his considerable weight out of the way, and the arrow disappeared into the sea of grain behind him. Lilly nocked another arrow, but Luggs had closed too much distance. She leaped into the air, pulled back her bowstring—

Luggs caught ahold of her ankle and jerked her downward.

Terror seized her chest, but she didn't let go of her arrow this time. She wouldn't go back. She couldn't. Luggs wouldn't get his filthy hands on her ever again.

As Luggs pulled her toward the ground, she adjusted her aim and stared him right in his wretched eyes.

"This is for Colm." Lilly let her arrow fly, little more than two feet from his face.

Luggs's eyes widened, and her arrow plunged into his left eye. His mouth hung open, he released his grip, and he toppled onto his back, dead.

Lilly shot three more arrows into his chest just to make sure.

EVER SINCE HE'D been captured, Magnus had yet to face a truly worthy opponent. Now, as he stalked toward Roderick, Magnus realized he might, in fact, be outmatched due to Roderick's hidden advantage—unless Roderick had rid himself of it.

"Do you really want to do this?" Roderick sashayed toward Magnus with his broadsword scraping the dirt behind him. "You know I'm at least as strong as you are. Maybe stronger."

"Are you?" Magnus challenged.

"I still have it. I haven't sold it like I told you I would." Roderick grinned and raised his sword, ready. "So you know I can kill you."

Magnus squinted at him. Regardless of Roderick's strength, Magnus couldn't let him continue to operate as a slave trader any longer. And more importantly, for the sake of all Saurians, he had to recover what was rightfully his. "If you have it, I will take it back from you."

"You're welcome to try." Roderick swung his sword.

Magnus blocked the attack, but the force of the blow shook his arms all the way up to his shoulders. *Unbelievable.*

Roderick swung again, and Magnus parried. They exchanged blows until Magnus ducked under a slash and whipped his tail at Roderick. It smacked against Roderick's shoulder and knocked him to the ground, but he recovered before Magnus could take the advantage.

"You always were a tricky one with that tail." Roderick clanked the pommel of his broadsword against his chest and smirked. "Strength or otherwise, I guess you still have that advantage, small as it may be."

He jabbed at Magnus, then moved in close. Magnus deflected Roderick's left fist with his elbow and halted Roderick's next slash by catching his wrist in his left hand. Roderick locked his left hand around Magnus's right wrist, and they grappled for control.

At first, Magnus controlled the struggle, but Roderick pushed back until Magnus's knees buckled. He growled and tried to wrench Roderick's arms to the left, but he couldn't.

Roderick smirked and delivered a kick to Magnus's chest that sent him skidding twenty feet back into the wheat field. Magnus jumped to his feet quickly, but found he didn't need to.

Roderick sauntered toward him with his broadsword down again, smiling.

Magnus glowered at him. Roderick had always been arrogant, but that would end today. Strength wasn't the only way to win a battle, especially against a stronger opponent. He would find a way to defeat Roderick.

Magnus leaped forward and swung his sword, but Roderick blocked the blow with his sword and delivered a stunning left hook that almost dislocated Magnus's jaw.

Roderick's sword knifed toward Magnus's gut. Had Magnus not shifted his body in time, it would have skewered him. Instead, the blade glanced off his abdominal armor.

Roderick pitched forward, and Magnus grabbed his throat. One jerk of his wrist, and—

A gauntleted fist smacked Magnus in the side of his head, and he lost his grip on Roderick. Then a kick under Magnus's chin blacked out his vision.

He swung his sword in a wild arc to put some distance between Roderick and himself, but his sword clanged against something hard.

When his vision reset, Magnus saw Roderick's broadsword flashing toward him. He ducked, but the blade smacked into his helmet.

The force of the blow alone would've killed Magnus if he hadn't been wearing his helmet, let alone the blade cleaving through his skull. As it was, he dropped his sword and toppled onto his side in the grain, stunned.

By the time Magnus regained his cognition, Roderick stood over him.

"Told you I was stronger." Roderick raised his sword over his head for a final slash.

CHAPTER 34

Magnus lurched upward and caught Roderick by his forearms, stalling his mighty overhead swing, but no matter how hard he pushed, Roderick's blade still sank toward his neck.

Magnus's tail swept Roderick's legs out from under him, but he landed on top of Magnus and mounted him, pinning him to the ground. All the while, the edge of Roderick's sword inched ever closer.

"I meant what I said, Magnus. I don't like to waste money." Beads of perspiration dotted Roderick's forehead. "Surrender. I'll let you live, and I'll sell you to someone nicer this time. You don't have to die."

"*Never.*" Magnus strained, but no matter how hard he pushed, no matter how considerable his Saurian strength was, he couldn't stop Roderick's pressure. The quivering sword continued to descend toward his throat.

No. He would *not* die here, not at the hands of a slave trader. Not before he reckoned with his past and with those who had harmed him. His vengeance would not stall today; Roderick would fall first, soon to be followed by the rest of Magnus's enemies.

"Strength cannot be the only asset you rely on in a fight." Magnus clenched his teeth and pushed back.

"Funny thing for you to say now, with my sword at your neck." Roderick laughed. "Looks like I'll always own you, one way or another."

"Remember…" Magnus strained to get the words out in time. "…how you said my tail was my only advantage?"

Roderick's gray eyes darted to Magnus's tail, which he'd already pinned down under his left knee. "Yeah?"

Magnus smirked. "You were wrong."

Roderick scowled. He jerked his sword down even harder, but at the same time, Magnus yanked Roderick's arms down toward his chest. Instead of it cleaving into his neck, the edge of the sword skidded off of Magnus's breastplate, and Roderick's torso pitched forward, toward

His teeth fastened on Roderick's exposed neck, and he bit down hard. Metallic blood splashed across Magnus's tongue, but he didn't release his vice grip on Roderick's throat.

Roderick gurgled, convulsed, and let go of his sword to try to tear Magnus's teeth from his neck, but it was already too late. Within seconds, he stopped moving altogether.

Magnus pushed him off and stood up. He spat out the blood in his mouth and stared down at his vanquished foe. "So much for you owning me."

He spat a glob of Roderick's blood in the dirt next to his head, then he reached down toward a pouch that hung from Roderick's belt.

Calum breathed quick breaths as he and Axel finished off the rest of the slave traders. They made made eye contact, then turned back to Lilly. She nodded and slung her bow over her shoulder.

All in all, they'd made a pretty great team. Calum hoped she'd consider sticking around now that her pursuers were all dead. They could use her in spats like this.

Though, if he were honest, he would've wanted her around anyway.

"Come on." Calum had definitely grown accustomed to fighting—he'd overcome the slave traders without much difficulty, especially compared to his fight with Tyburon. "Let's regroup with Magnus."

When they made it over to Magnus, he held an emerald the size of a grapefruit in his hands.

Even though Calum had spent the majority of his life harvesting precious stones from rocks, he couldn't help but gawk at it. The emerald was the biggest gemstone he'd ever seen. It was a rich dark-green color, so deep that the sunlight couldn't even reach its center.

"Where did you find *that?*" Axel's eyes widened.

"Roderick had it," Magnus replied.

"That'll fetch a small fortune. I could retire. We all could." Axel rubbed his hands together.

Magnus shook his head. "No chance."

Axel's brow furrowed. "Hey, the agreement is that we split whatever we find."

"Except this was mine to begin with," Magnus said.

Axel scoffed. "Yeah, right. How do I know you're not just saying that?"

Magnus glared at him.

"Fair enough." Axel nodded.

"What is it?" Lilly asked.

All three of them looked at her, and Magnus held it up. "This is one of the last Dragon Emeralds known to Kanarah."

"A Dragon Emerald?" Calum raised an eyebrow.

"Yes." Magnus stared at it. *Into* it.

Lilly leaned forward. "What does that mean?"

Magnus smiled. "Dragon Emeralds have three phases. This one is in its first phase. When in a human's possession, it amplifies their strength to that of a Saurian's, or even greater. That is why Roderick put up so much trouble when I was fighting him."

"Yeah, I saw that." Axel chuckled. "Looked like he was beating you senseless, Scales."

Magnus ignored him. "Once a Saurian reaches a certain point in development, he or she can use a Dragon Emerald to transform into a Sobek."

Calum and Axel stared at him, but Lilly nodded.

"That's the second phase of Saurian development," she said. "I've seen a few in Aeropolis before. Kahn sent them as emissaries to Avian, the Premier of the Windgales."

"Who's Kahn?" Calum asked.

Magnus's eyebrows arched down, and he exhaled a long hiss through his nostrils. "He rules Reptilius."

"And he's the only dragon in Kanarah, at least since Praetorius died about a year ago," Lilly said.

Silence hovered among them as they stared at the Dragon Emerald. As before, Calum knew there had to be more to the story, but he didn't want to ask. Magnus didn't seem to want to talk about it.

Calum glanced at Magnus. "So... can you use it?"

Magnus lifted his golden eyes to Calum's. "Perhaps."

"Perhaps?" Axel tilted his head. "You don't know?"

"My skin has hardened some, which means I am showing the necessary signs of growth—" Magnus shook his head. "—but I cannot be sure."

"So why don't you just try it?" Axel asked.

"I am not sure I'm ready."

"What happens if you try it and you're not ready?" Axel pressed.

Magnus shook his head. "I do not know. For all I've learned in my two hundred and three years, I never learned how to tell when I would be ready to use this. It is a carefully guarded secret."

"Wait. Stop." Axel shook his head. "You're two *hundred* years old?"

The news had come as a surprise to Calum, too, so much that he couldn't speak.

Magnus blinked at Axel. "Two hundred and three."

"*What?*" Axel almost screeched the word.

"Saurians live a long time," Lilly said. "Ten times longer than humans or Windgales. Before he died, Praetorius was over five hundred years old."

"Older," Magnus muttered.

Lilly glanced at him. "Really? I learned about him in—well, growing up. I was taught he was just over five-hundred. How old was he?"

"I never had occasion to ask him."

Silence reigned anew as Calum and Axel processed the news about Magnus's age.

"I thought you were forty," Axel finally said. "Maybe forty-five. But two *hundred?*"

"And three," Magnus added. "If it helps, just pretend I am forty. It makes no difference to me."

Axel raised his hands. "I don't know what to think anymore."

Calum had to agree with him, but even more so, he found new admiration for Magnus. It was pretty incredible that he'd lived so long, and Calum could only imagine the things he'd seen in his lifetime—things that Calum would only ever know as a part of history.

"What do you have to do to try it?" Lilly asked. "The emerald, I mean."

Magnus's tone lightened up, as if he were glad for the change of subject. "I hold it in my hands and press it against my bare chest."

Axel nudged him. "Do it. See what happens."

"No." Instead, Magnus dropped the Dragon Emerald in a leather pouch and tied it to his belt. "It does not feel right."

Axel rolled his eyes. "Whatever. I still think we should sell it."

Magnus turned to Lilly. "How does your shoulder feel?"

She gave him a half-smile, rotated her left shoulder, and winced, though not as dramatically as before. "Better. Thank you for your help. And thank you all for stopping Roderick and his men."

"Our pleasure." Calum couldn't help but smile at her.

Axel stepped in front of him. "*Anything* for you."

Calum's jaw tensed, but Lilly's smile quelled the frustration rising in his chest.

"You're welcome to come with us, if you like. We're heading across the Valley within the next week or so," Axel said. "We can make sure you get there safely."

Lilly nodded. "I'd like that."

"Great." Axel smiled.

Calum thought he looked like an idiot, but he was also glad Axel had asked her to join them. He wasn't sure he would've found the courage if it had fallen to him.

"Let us collect our bags of food, loot the slave traders for weapons and supplies, and get out of here." Magnus's head swiveled. "I do not care to linger here any longer than we must. If any soldiers show up, count on a multitude of trouble."

They spread out and began to gather what supplies they could. With a sack in his hand, Calum approached one of the downed slave traders but stopped short when he moaned.

Calum brandished his sword, but the slave trader just lay on the ground with his hand on his forehead. Calum set down his pack and walked over to him. Better to put him out of his misery than to let him suffer.

Calum stopped short when he noticed a sword that resembled a large meat cleaver on the ground next to the slave trader. Now that he'd stepped closer, Calum recognized the slave trader's dark-green armor, his curly black hair, and his dark eyes.

Sure enough, there, staring up at him, was none other than Nicolai, the bandit he'd allowed to go free after defeating Tyburon.

"Axel?" Calum called. "Come over here. You're not gonna believe this."

When Axel saw Nicolai's face, his eyes widened. "You've gotta be kidding me."

Upon seeing them, Nicolai exhaled a breath and closed his eyes. "Oh, no."

"So much for promising to stay out of trouble," Axel said. "He stops being a bandit and ends up a slave trader. He couldn't have done much worse with his second chance."

Nicolai opened his eyes and rubbed his forehead with another moan.

"Well, I guess this time we have to finish him off." Axel unsheathed his sword, and Nicolai let out a yelp.

"Wait." Calum's hand kept Axel from swinging. "He's unarmed, and he's mostly harmless. We can't just kill him."

"His weapon's right there." Axel huffed and didn't lower his sword. "Calum, you need to move. This lurch had his chance. *Two* of them. He wasted them both. His time has come."

"You're not killing him, Axel." Calum's firm voice sounded more convincing to him each time he employed it, and he'd employed it a lot recently.

"Who's gonna stop me?" Axel scoffed. "You?"

Calum had no desire to measure sword lengths with Axel. Instead, he said, "Maybe the reason he keeps falling in with a bad crowd is because he doesn't know any good people."

Axel eyed him. "What are you suggesting?"

"I'm not saying we're the purest souls around, but we're certainly not slave traders or bandits." Calum tilted his head and stared down at Nicolai, who moaned again. "Maybe if we bring him with us, we'll rub off on him. Maybe there's hope for Nicolai yet."

Axel had started shaking his head even before Calum finished talking. "No way. He's not coming with us."

Calum waved Lilly over, then he refocused on Axel. "You need to start looking for the good in people, Axel. When we started out, you didn't want to travel with Magnus just because he was a Saurian."

"Yeah, and now we get along *so well*."

181

Lilly walked over and stood near them, her eyes locked on Nicolai. She seemed ready to bolt into the sky if he so much as looked at her wrong.

"My point is that Magnus, even though *you* may not like him, is valuable to the group. He's saved both of our lives on countless occasions." Calum stared down at Nicolai. "Who knows what Nicolai might become if we spare him?"

"If we finish him off, I know for a fact he won't be a bandit or a slave trader anymore."

Calum sighed. Magnus started toward them from a couple dozen yards away, where he'd been sifting through a slave trader's pack.

"Am I allowed to say something?" Nicolai raised his hand from his forehead a few inches, revealing a nasty red bump.

"*No.*" Axel pointed his blade at Nicolai.

"Yes," Calum countered.

Nicolai gave him a slight nod. "Please don't kill me. I know I made a mistake by joining this bunch of—"

"Got that right," Axel muttered. He folded his arms but still held onto his sword.

"—of slave traders, but this is the only type of life I know." Nicolai swallowed and sat up, his dark eyes fixed on Calum. "I'd be honored to join your group, if that's what you're offering."

Axel rolled his eyes. "You've gotta be kidding me."

Calum glanced at Lilly, then he focused on Magnus, who stopped short when he noticed Nicolai on the ground.

"Is that who I think it is?" Magnus squinted at him.

"Yeah. We were just discussing how we should kill him," Axel said.

"Actually, we were discussing how he might join our group." Calum cleared his throat and looked at Lilly. "If that's alright with you, Lilly."

She glanced between Magnus, Calum, and Nicolai. "He was new to Roderick's outfit. He didn't mistreat me, but I'm not inclined to trust him. I put him out with Aliophos Nectar when I was escaping. I could've killed him then, but I didn't." She exhaled a sharp sigh. "I hate to say it, but maybe there's a reason for that."

"Right, but he's still one of them, and he was a bandit before that." Axel raised an eyebrow at her. "Surely you don't want him traveling with us after all of that."

Lilly stared at Nicolai. "Like I said, I don't trust him—"

"Me neither." Axel raised his sword again, and Nicolai recoiled.

Lilly stepped between them. "—but we can't just execute him. We all make mistakes. If he wants to change, he will. Everyone deserves a second chance. "

"Last time *was* his second chance," Axel muttered.

"I want to change." Nicolai nodded. "Believe me, I *want* to change."

"Really?" Axel huffed and lowered his sword. "Come on, guys. You don't actually believe him, do you?"

"Here's how I see it," Calum said. "Either he changes, or he's on his own again. It's only a matter of time before he meets a foul end with the way he's been living."

"Yeah, like right now," Axel grumbled.

"Please give me a chance. I'll show you I can be different." Nicolai tentatively stood to his feet and stepped toward Calum, then he turned to Lilly. "I was just following orders. I'm so sorry. I won't do wrong by you anymore."

Lilly rubbed her wounded shoulder. "We'll see."

"You mess up, we toss you out on your own." Calum glanced at Magnus, who nodded, then he looked back at Nicolai. "Crystal?"

"Clear," Nicolai replied.

Calum extended his hand. "Welcome to the group, Nicolai."

THAT NIGHT, Commander Anigo tugged on the reins, and Candlestick slowed to a halt. Sure enough, as the message had read, he found the moonlit bodies of nine slain men near the western edge of the Golden Plains.

He'd only taken five soldiers to investigate the claims of the farmhand who'd deserted his post to deliver the news. He left the rest under Corporal Jopheth with orders to watch all of Kanarah City's gates at all times should they return. They were to be killed on sight if necessary, or captured if possible.

Under almost any other circumstances, he would've had the farmhand thrashed, but instead, Commander Anigo wrote him a decree that granted him the remainder of the day off. The catch, of course, was that he had to show Commander Anigo the location of the bodies.

"You said you saw the fight?" Commander Anigo asked.

The farmhand—Commander Anigo hadn't bothered to learn his name—stood at the edge of the fields and rubbed his arms. The night wind carried a harsher chill with it than previous nights, and the farmhand had neglected to don a shirt before running to Kanarah City.

"Yes, sir." He shivered. "Heard metal clashing. Knew somethin' was up. Ran over to see what was happenin' and caught the end of it."

Commander Anigo's eyes narrowed. "What did you see?"

The farmhand rubbed his shoulders. "Looked like a bunch of men swingin' weapons around. I didn't care to get too close. Hid in the grain. Safer there."

"The winners—did you see them?"

"Yeah. There was a girl with them. I think she was a Windgale. Saw her flyin' around at one point. Either that or she can jump higher than anyone I ever seen."

Captain Fulton's killer? The slave girl?

If so, then these slain men might've been the slave traders responsible for the debacle at the auction. Had they chased her and run into some other force? Surely she hadn't slain nine strong men on her own. "What else?"

"I saw two armored men and a Saurian."

Commander Anigo's eyes widened. "Which way did they go?"

The farmhand's teeth clicked. "They headed west, toward the road."

Commander Anigo urged Candlestick to face west. Had his three outlaws come to the aid of the Windgale girl? If they had left together, he'd be hunting four fugitives instead—convenient, given Captain Fulton's untimely death.

If Commander Anigo could bring all four of them to justice in one fell swoop, he was assured a glorious return to Solace, indeed. Perhaps even a promotion; after all, he'd been eligible for promotion to captain for nearly a year now.

"That's all I saw, sir. Do you—can I go home now?"

"You are released." Commander Anigo glanced back and saw the farmhand disappear into the grain. He turned to two of the soldiers accompanying him. "You two, go with him. Make sure he returns to his assigned post. I don't intend to chase another escaped worker."

The soldiers nodded and rode their horses after the farmhand.

Commander Anigo looked at the two other soldiers accompanying him. He pointed at one of them. "You, ride back to Kanarah City and have Corporal Jopheth ready a platoon of soldiers for a long-term search." He pointed to the other one. "You, come with me."

As the other soldier rode north, the remaining soldier asked, "Where are we going, sir?"

Commander Anigo faced the mountains to the west. "We're going after them."

AT THEIR CAMPSITE for the night, Calum sat on Lilly's left, constantly battling his emotions and feelings. Part of him was thrilled to be sitting next to her, another part was terrified of saying something stupid to her, and another part was enraged that Axel was sitting closer to her than he was—much too close to her for Calum's comfort.

Across from Calum sat Magnus, and Nicolai sat next to him, dabbing at the bump on his head with ginger fingers.

"So, unfortunately, we cannot just walk into Kanarah City and head straight to Trader's Pass," Magnus concluded the story of their journey from the quarry all the way through their rooftop escape from Kanarah City. He clacked his talons against his breastplate. "We cannot risk the soldiers recognizing us."

"But now that you're here—and Nicolai, too, I guess—we can get across." Axel winked at Lilly.

Calum noticed it and wanted to knock the smug expression off his face.

"I would not go that far, Axel," Magnus said. "Even if we divided up and entered the Pass using Lilly and Nicolai as extra people to throw off the soldiers, and even if I removed my armor, it is still a considerable risk. I would rather not put Lilly in any more danger, especially considering what she has just endured."

Lilly smiled at him. "Thank you, but I'm capable of handling myself."

"Forgive me. I did not mean to suggest otherwise." Magnus turned to Nicolai and sighed. "And Nicolai... well, I fear we cannot fully trust you yet."

Nicolai shrugged. "I'm not offended. I know I'm good at ruining things."

"So what are we gonna do?" Calum asked. "Try to go individually?"

Axel leaned forward. "We could try to—"

"Shh," Magnus hissed, his golden eyes wide. "I hear something."

Calum and Axel froze.

A low growl emanated from the darkness on the north side of the camp.

All five of them jumped to their feet and drew their weapons.

Out of the darkness emerged a mass of gray-and-brown fur with four legs, two light-blue eyes, a black canine nose, and sharp white teeth.

The Wolf had returned.

CHAPTER 35

When the Wolf emerged from the shadows, Calum had expected Lilly to cling to his arm or take cover behind him—or worst case, she'd cling to or hide behind Axel instead of him.

But instead of doing either of those things, she snatched her bow into her hand, nocked an arrow, and took aim at the Wolf.

At first, Calum didn't know how to react. He glanced at her, looked at the Wolf, then repeated the motion until Axel took Lilly by her arm and pulled her away. She glanced at him, confused, then relaxed the tension in her draw.

"Get behind me, Lilly." Axel ushered her back, then stepped between her and the Wolf with his sword in hand.

Calum shot a glare at Axel, but he didn't seem to notice.

"There's no need to be alarmed."

Calum blinked. Had the Wolf actually just *spoken?*

Magnus stepped forward. "You are not welcome here, *thief.*"

The Wolf growled at him, low but more annoyed than threatening. "Believe me. If I could be anywhere else, I'd be there. But you know the Law as well as I do."

Axel shifted his stance. "Law?"

A sharp sigh exhaled from the Wolf's mouth. "You humans created the Law—or at least your King did—and you don't even know it?"

Axel eyed Calum, but he could only shrug. He was still trying to figure out how the Wolf could talk. Magnus had called them intelligent beings, but he hadn't mentioned they could *talk* too.

"He means the Law of Debt." Magnus lowered his sword but didn't sheathe it. "If anyone saves the life of another, the one rescued is indebted to the rescuer for the remainder of his life. Not as a servant, but as a comrade."

Calum smirked. He'd saved the lives of both Axel and Magnus multiple times, and they'd saved him as well. Apparently that meant they were indebted to each other forever.

Magnus focused on Calum and smiled. "And as a friend. The bond is only broken upon mutual release, death, or betrayal—and betrayal is only acceptable if one party becomes an agent of evil. As children, Saurians are taught this Law above all others. I suspect it is the same for the Wolf tribes.

"Even so, not everyone subscribes to or follows the Law strictly, which is perhaps why you have never heard of it," Magnus continued. "And your upbringing in such a remote area of Kanarah was doubtless a hindrance as well. In any case, the Law is upheld by those who choose to do so, and it is incumbent on the one who was saved to accept the terms or not."

The Wolf nodded. His voice flattened, and he stared at Calum. "So… I'm here to fulfill my duty."

Calum raised an eyebrow, but he also lowered his sword. "And since I saved you from Magnus's sword, your duty is to me?"

The Wolf nodded again, somehow managing to frown—another thing Calum didn't know Wolves could do. "Yeah."

"Do you still have any of the property you took from us?" Calum asked.

"Um… no?" The Wolf squinted at him. "Why would I?"

"So you spent *all* the coin and ate *all* the food?" Axel glared at him.

The Wolf tilted his head. "A dog's gotta eat."

Calum sighed, sheathed his sword, and stared into the Wolf's sky-blue eyes. He motioned toward the rest of the group. "We've all saved each other more than once, but no formal obligation binds us. So I release you from your debt, if you so desire."

"I… uh…" The Wolf glanced between them. His eyes lingered the longest on Axel, who still held his sword in his hands as if he meant to cleave the Wolf in two. "I guess I'll be going, then."

Magnus followed suit with Calum and also sheathed his sword, and so did Axel. Lilly replaced her arrow in her quiver, and Nicolai sat back down near the fire. His new sword, one he'd taken from a dead slave trader to replace his old meat cleaver, hadn't even made it out of its sheath.

After a few steps, the Wolf turned back. "You know, I could be of use to you guys. I'm fast. I can hide in the dark. I'm good at stealing stuff."

"Yeah, we figured all of that out already," Axel said, his voice edged with sarcasm.

"You said you would rather be anywhere else but here, yet now you do not wish to leave?" Magnus asked. "Which is it?"

The Wolf's mouth hung open. "Well, I mean… I don't have much else going on."

"So you figure you'll just stay here with us?" Axel folded his arms.

The Wolf growled at him then sat his rear down like any normal dog would. He was definitely larger than any normal dog Calum had ever seen, but he didn't strike Calum as being especially large for a Wolf. In fact, he seemed somewhat on the small side from what Calum would've expected.

"Seems you could use someone like me in your group, especially if you actually wanna get to Trader's Pass."

Calum glanced at Magnus. "What makes you think we need to get to Trader's Pass?"

With another sigh, the Wolf rolled his eyes. "I just overheard you talking about it. Plus, I heard you talking about it the night the Saurian almost killed me. And the night you let me steal your first bag of money. And the night you killed the sabertooth cats. It's pretty much all you guys talk about."

Calum held up his hand. "Alright, we get it. You've been following us for awhile now."

"And robbed you twice, successfully."

Axel huffed. "And you failed once, spectacularly."

The Wolf growled at him.

"Let's get back on topic," Calum said. "You're right that we have to get to Trader's Pass. If you've been listening to us, then you know what we're up against. So how can you help us get past the King's soldiers and to the pass?"

"Simple," the Wolf said. "There's a secret path to get there."

Axel tilted his head. "There is?"

"No," Magnus said. "If there were another way to access the pass, I would have known about it."

The Wolf scoffed. "I don't think I'd be calling it a 'secret' path if a lot of normal people knew about it."

Magnus folded his arms. "What makes you presume I am normal?"

"Alright," the Wolf said, "what makes you different from any other Saurian?"

Magnus didn't say anything.

The Wolf raised one of his front paws, just like a dog begging for a treat. "It's like I said: the path is secret."

"Then how do *you* know about it?" Axel asked.

"It's how I got here from across the valley without drawing a lot of attention to myself. Also, some of my tribe helped dig the tunnels long, long ago."

"Tunnels?" Calum looked at Magnus. "There are tunnels?"

The Wolf growled. "Shouldn't have told you that. Look, even if you find them, there's only one path that actually connects from Kanarah City to Trader's Pass. The rest? Well, you'd probably rather not find out where they lead."

"Wait, wait." Axel held up his hand. "You said the secret path leads to Trader's Pass. Now you're saying it's in Kanarah City? I thought we were gonna bypass Kanarah City."

"Then you thought wrong." The Wolf shook his head. "I never said I could help you avoid Kanarah City. I said I could help you get to Trader's Pass via a secret path that very few people know about. You access it through the city's sewers."

"He's right," Lilly said.

Everyone turned toward her.

"Roderick and his men brought me over the valley on Trader's Pass along with some other slaves. At one point, they blindfolded us and took us on a secret path. I knew we'd gone underground by the horrible smell and the lack of wind, and we eventually wound up in the city's sewers before they brought us out. He's telling the truth."

"Nicolai?" Calum asked. "Have you ever been in those tunnels?"

Nicolai shook his head. "No, but Roderick and some of the other slave traders mentioned them a few times. I joined after they'd already made it over to this side of Kanarah, literally only a few days ago. My opinion? I think he's telling the truth."

"Well, no one asked *you*," Axel sneered.

"Cut it out, Axel." Calum shot a glare at him. "Nicolai made mistakes, but you need to start treating him like a member of the group nonetheless."

Axel scowled back at him. "Whatever."

Nicolai gave Calum a grateful nod.

"I'm… not touching that one." The Wolf gave Lilly a nod. "She's right that some slave traders have been known to use the secret path."

"Helps them avoid the King's soldiers, right?" Calum said.

"It would be awful hard to bring slaves through Kanarah City's west gate." The Wolf scratched behind his left ear with his left hind paw. "It's not unheard of, though. Certain guards will accept bribes, for example."

The five of them stared at the Wolf.

"But... that's not really pertinent right now, I guess."

"How far does the tunnel go?" Magnus asked. "Where in the sewers does it start, and where does it end?"

"Depends on which direction you're going."

Magnus glared at him. "You know what I am asking."

The Wolf exhaled another sharp sigh. "You access it through the sewers on the western side of Kanarah City, and it ends about five miles along the pass."

Magnus turned to Lilly. "Does that sound about right?"

"I can't say for sure on the distance, but the stench down there started out like death and gradually changed to more of a sewer-type stink before they brought us above ground," she replied. "And it took several hours from the time we entered the tunnels to the time we got out."

"Like I said, though, you need a guide to make sure you don't go the wrong way." The Wolf stood on all fours and walked past the campfire toward one of the bags of food. He pawed at the opening with his front right paw until an apple fell out onto the ground.

Axel snatched it away before the Wolf could get a bite and then he cinched the bag shut. "That's not for you."

The Wolf growled at him. "Don't you think that all the information I just gave you is worth one little apple?"

"Sure, puppy." Axel held the apple out in his hand, but yanked it away when the Wolf tried to take it with his teeth. "Ah, ah. Do you know how to play fetch?"

The Wolf half-barked, half-snarled at Axel, who startled, dropped the apple, and jumped back. The Wolf bit into it, reclined back on his haunches to lie on his stomach, and dropped it between his front forelegs.

While Axel swore and cursed, the others chuckled. Axel's glare landed on each of them before it stalled on Nicolai.

"No, I don't play fetch." The Wolf licked his chops. "Just be glad I'm not insisting on *meat* instead."

"Don't *ever* do that again. You hear me?" Axel pointed his finger at him, but the Wolf just rolled his eyes and started gnawing on his apple.

"What else is in those tunnels?" Magnus asked. "The ones that don't lead to the exits?"

The Wolf raised his head between bites. "Whatever it is, it's not something nice. Better if we don't run into it. I've heard of men going in and never coming back out, and the ones who survived to tell about it weren't in great shape, either."

After a long pause, Calum looked at Magnus. "Well, what do you think? Can we trust him?"

Magnus released a long sigh through his nose. "I do not like him, and I do not trust him. I think he is a treacherous cheat and a thieving fleabag who—"

"You do realize I'm sitting here in front of you, right?" The Wolf eyed Magnus. "Even if I didn't have exceptional hearing, which I do, I could still hear everything you're saying about me because you're standing like five feet away from me."

"—but I think he may be the only chance we have for getting to the pass without causing a ruckus that could get us killed," Magnus continued, unfazed. "Right now, I cannot conceive of a better option. I say we do it."

Calum nodded. He faced Axel.

"Don't look at me." Axel held up his hands. "My response is going to be the same as usual: whatever."

"What about you, Lilly?" Calum asked.

She shrugged. "I don't want to mess up your plans or anything, but I want to get home. If you're telling me that going through the west gate won't work—well, I'm not thrilled about going back into those tunnels, but I'd rather do it with all of you.

"Besides that, the trip across the valley is too long and too dangerous for me to make alone, and since you're already planning to head across, it makes sense for us to stay together. After my escape, the King's soldiers might be looking for me, too, so a few more blades on my side wouldn't hurt, either." Lilly concluded, "So I'm in."

"Any thoughts, Nicolai?" Calum asked.

"Uh…" Nicolai stared at him, and Axel scoffed. Nicolai glanced at him for a moment then refocused on Calum. "I'm just along for the ride. No one wants to hear what I think anyway."

"That's not true," Calum said, specifically to spite Axel. "It's like I just told Axel—you're a part of this group now. It means you have a say."

"I agree. Tell us your opinion." Magnus's reptilian gaze fixed on Nicolai.

Nicolai swallowed and ran his fingers through his curly black hair. "Based on what you already told me about your run-ins with the soldiers in Kanarah City and before that, I don't think you—we oughta risk running into them again."

"So you'd rather take your chances with whatever's killing people in those tunnels?" Axel folded his arms then nodded at the Wolf. "And with this Wolf, who robbed us twice?"

Nicolai shrugged. "He didn't rob me."

"No, I guess he didn't." Axel scowled at him. "It'd be too ironic for a thief to rob a bandit."

"I think it's clear what we've decided." Time to change the subject before Axel got any more riled up. Calum looked at the Wolf. "What's your name?"

"Riley."

Calum moved next to him and extended his right hand. "Welcome to the group, Riley."

Riley stared at Calum for a moment, then he sat up, reached out his right front paw, and placed it in Calum's open palm. "Glad to be here."

"How soon can we leave?" Calum asked.

"How soon will you be ready to go?" Riley lay back down and chomped into his apple again.

THE NEXT MORNING, Commander Anigo and the soldier with him crouched on the edge of a rock face. Far below them, six figures moved through the sunlit trees. He couldn't quite make them out, though he thought he glimpsed a Wolf traveling with the group, three men, and a distinctly feminine shape with blonde hair and pink armor.

When he noticed a set of vivid blue armor covering a green torso and tail, he knew he'd found them. They were heading north, toward Kanarah City.

But Commander Anigo and the soldiers in Kanarah City would be ready for them.

He got up and led the soldier to their horses. They mounted them and galloped down the mountain with abandon.

Soon he'd bring them all to justice. Soon he'd be restored to his former glory in Solace.

THE TREK from the mountains back to Kanarah City took a couple of days, and the group waited until nightfall again before they tried to re-enter the city. Riley knew a secret way into the city through an old drainage tunnel, so they avoided both the gates and the soldiers who stood guard there altogether.

They half-walked, half-jogged through the city under the moonlight. A few people moved about in the streets, but far fewer than in the daytime. Those who did were mostly drunks, vagrants, and beggars. Thanks to Riley's knowledge of the city's standard patrol routes and times, they managed to avoid running into any soldiers as well.

Riley led them on a complex but covert path to the city's west side through secluded back alleys and in the shadows of buildings. He finally stopped at a rusty iron grate at the bottom of a hill with a large pit just beyond. The opening behind the grate was barely wide enough for two large men to walk through if they stood side-by-side.

Calum's nose threatened rebellion at the stench. "This is the way into the sewers, I take it?"

Lilly's nose wrinkled. "I recognize the smell."

Riley let out a short, sharp sigh, something Calum had grown accustomed to but still didn't appreciate. "Yes, Calum."

"This is an overflow outlet," Magnus said. "Reptilius has a similar setup. If the area ever floods and the sewage rises, it flows out here and wherever else it gets too high, and it fills that pit. The stench is perpetually foul, but it keeps the sewage from ever rising to street level."

Axel tugged on the grate, and it barely moved. "You'd need at least two strong men to get this thing open. How did you get in and out?"

"I only came out of there once, and I haven't gone back in since. When I did come out, I waited for someone else to come along, and I just snuck out behind them before it could close. I think they were slave traders."

"It does not behoove us to waste any time. I would rather the soldiers—or anyone else—not realize what we are doing." Magnus reached for the grate. "I will open it, and you five can go inside. Then I will ensure it shuts behind us."

What would've been a challenge for Calum and Axel looked easy when Magnus did it. While Nicolai gawked at him, Magnus pulled the heavy grate open, hefting it over his head with ease and holding until all of them made it inside, and then he shut it in perfect silence.

Calum extended his hand toward Riley. "Lead the way."

COMMANDER ANIGO DROPPED a small pouch into Wandell Thirry's hand. "Your cooperation is much appreciated, Mr. Thirry."

"It's my pleasure, Commander." Thirry stirred the silver coins inside the pouch with his index finger adorned with a silver ring that shone under the moonlight. "And we agree that you'll make an introduction to your replacement when he arrives from Solace?"

"Gladly." Commander Anigo forced a smile.

Dealing with underworld scum wasn't something he was accustomed to anymore, and he'd forgotten how greasy it made him feel. In Solace, he'd already forced the disbanding of every major criminal enterprise, but here in Kanarah City, dealing with undesirable people seemed necessary to accomplish anything of significance.

In any case, Corporal Jopheth had recommended Thirry—which certainly said something about Corporal Jopheth—and Thirry had shown him the entrance to the tunnels under the city, originating almost five miles beyond the city's west gate along Trader's Pass.

It was a hunch, and nothing more, but if the fugitives he'd been chasing meant to use the tunnels to bypass his soldiers, they'd certainly be in for a surprise.

But in his exceptional career, his hunches had more often than not proven to be the deciding factor between success and failure. He wasn't about to abandon his instincts now, after they'd served him so well so many times in the past.

"Two of my men will escort you back into the city along the pass." Commander Anigo would've just as soon had his men kill Thirry and leave him along the pass as a message to other underworld slime seeking to avoid dealing with the King's men, but for now, he elected to let Thirry go.

Until his mission was complete, Commander Anigo couldn't be sure he was done dealing with Thirry. The thought of having to engage the man in the future brewed like soured stew in Commander Anigo's stomach, but he would no sooner discard a useful tool because it was covered in grime.

Needs, not wants.

"Many thanks, Commander. I hope your excursion is as profitable for you as it has been for me." Thirry smiled, and his white teeth almost glowed in the moonlight. His white hair certainly did.

Two of the soldiers mounted horses, Thirry mounted another, and they rode off toward the city.

Given the narrow opening and the steep decline into the tunnels, Commander Anigo had left Candlestick back in the army barracks stable for safekeeping. It meant that on this mission, he could only rely on himself. The pain in his chest from his last encounter with these fugitives no longer ached as it did, but it still ached enough to reinforce his caution this time around.

Commander Anigo looked at the twenty remaining men he'd brought with him, half of whom held burning torches, and said, "One lit torch for every four men, plus one near me. We'll find a place to hide, then we'll ambush them."

The soldiers nodded, and half of them snuffed their torches.

"Let's go." Commander Anigo led them down the dark stone stairs into the tunnels.

CHAPTER 36

Calum and the others followed Riley through the labyrinth of the Kanarah City sewers, all while wielding makeshift torches. Even though they walked along a rocky slab next to the slow-flowing river of waste in the center, muck and waste still clung to their boots. At times the stench grew so pungent that Calum almost vomited.

At one point, Axel stumbled and planted his hand against a brick wall to brace himself, but the ancient brick wall crumbled under the pressure, and his hand went through it instead. A few dozen rats poured out over his shoulders and skittered away in the sludge.

Axel yelped and whooped and danced away from them, and he lost his torch in the river of sewage in the process.

"There you go, screaming like a girl again." Magnus glanced at Lilly. "No offense, Lilly."

She laughed and shook her head. "None taken."

Axel called down a curse on the rats, then he glared at Magnus. "Yeah? Let's see how you react when a thousand rats jump out at *you* in a dark sewer."

"I will do one better." Magnus walked over to the hole Axel had just inadvertently made in the wall, stuck his hand inside, and pulled out a thick rat almost the length of Calum's forearm. "Lilly, you may wish to turn away for this part."

She pursed her lips and then complied.

As soon as Lilly's back was turned, Magnus dropped the rat into his mouth and crunched down on it with his pointed teeth. He swallowed it in two gulps.

Nicolai covered his mouth with his hand. "Did I really just see that?"

Axel closed his eyes and moaned. "I think I'm gonna throw up."

"Me too," Calum said.

"I dunno what the problem is," Riley said. "It's just meat. Not good meat, but meat nonetheless."

"Can I turn around now?" Lilly asked.

"Yes, it's over." Magnus licked his lips with his long red tongue.

She wrinkled her nose at him.

Magnus smirked. "Saurians are inherently carnivorous, but we can function on an omnivorous diet if we need to. Rodents make for a pretty standard meal on the streets in Reptilius."

"That's disgusting." Axel shook his head and covered his mouth with his hand. "I gotta keep moving. Come on."

Magnus just grinned.

A half-dozen turns later, Riley stopped in front of a large opening.

Calum and Magnus came up beside him and held their torches ahead to get a better look while Axel stood behind them with Lilly and Nicolai. Calum would've preferred to stand by Lilly, but with only two torches left, he had to stay near the front so they could see where they were going.

Even so, he preferred to have Axel with Lilly when around Nicolai, just in case. Nicolai had proven trustworthy so far, but it had only been a few days.

The torches revealed an opening about twenty feet high and twice as wide that narrowed to a tunnel about fifteen feet high and thirty feet wide farther inside.

"This is it." Riley sat down and scratched behind his left ear with his corresponding hind foot.

"This is a huge opening. How do more people not know about this?" Axel asked.

Riley exhaled another one of those short sharp sighs. "It's really not that complicated. We're in the sewer. Not many people come down here for evening promenades. It's also in a specific place inside the sewer.

"Sure, you might stumble upon it after a long search, but again, who just walks around a sewer for fun? Plus, it's dark down here. You could walk right past it and never know it. And on top of all that—"

"Alright, alright." Axel held up his hand. "I gotta be honest. You lost me at 'promenades.'"

"It means 'taking a walk,'" Riley explained, aggravated.

"The path is massive," Nicolai said.

"Scared?" Axel asked.

Nicolai turned to him, wearing the beginning of a scowl. "A little bit, yeah."

Axel rolled his eyes.

Riley nodded toward the opening. "Once we get inside, we go for about ten miles in pitch-black tunnels. Then we climb some makeshift stairs carved into the rocks before we finally pop out a little less than five miles west of Kanarah City along Trader's Pass."

Calum nodded. "Let's go."

"Remember," Riley said. "Stay close, and follow me. If you go the wrong way or step somewhere you shouldn't, you might as well be dead, so pay attention, and walk where I'm walking. Crystal?"

Everyone else nodded and followed Riley inside the enormous tunnel.

Nicolai hung back next to Calum while they walked. "Calum, I just wanted to tell you again how grateful I am that you spared my life. I really—I don't want to live my life that way anymore, so this second-second chance means a lot to me."

Calum smiled. He found it interesting how someone only a few years older than him had already found so much trouble this early in his life. "I'm happy you feel that way, Nicolai."

"Look, as far as I'm concerned, I'm indebted to you forever, just like what that Wolf was saying back at the camp." Nicolai unsheathed his sword.

The action set Calum on his guard at first, but Nicolai didn't threaten him with the weapon, though he did wave it around a bit.

"And I'm glad Magnus made me leave that old meat cleaver behind," he said. "This sword hardly weighs anything by comparison."

"I held that cleaver of yours after Magnus made you drop it, just to see how heavy it was,"

Calum said. "Honestly, I can't imagine how you or anyone not as strong as a Saurian could wield something like that. The blade was dull too."

Nicolai chuckled. "No wonder I was never any good in a fight."

"Have you had any training of any sort?"

"Not really." Nicolai shook his head. "I'm pretty observant though. Picked up a few moves from Tyburon and Norm, but they mostly kept me on menial tasks. I'm not what you'd call athletic by any means."

"Don't worry. With our luck, you'll get some experience in no time."

"Yeah, or I'll be dead in no time."

"Don't think like that." Calum patted Nicolai's shoulder, still a bit wary of his unsheathed sword. If Nicolai tired anything, at least Calum had his torch in hand. He could probably fend Nicolai off until the others came to help if it came to it. "We're a team. We watch out for each other. Sometimes we even bleed for each other. Just remember, we're here to help you."

Nicolai pursed his lips and sheathed his sword. His voice lowered, he said, "I don't think Axel feels the same way you do. Frankly, if a venomous spider was crawling on my nose, I don't think he'd walk three steps to punch me in the face."

Calum grinned. "He might surprise you with that one. He really hates spiders."

"You know what I mean. He doesn't like me."

"Yeah, I know." He stared at Axel's back as he walked next to Lilly. Together, they followed Magnus and Riley, while Calum and Nicolai brought up the rear.

When Axel's hand brushed against Lilly's arm, Calum wanted to charge forward and step between them, but he resisted the urge. He still didn't exactly know how he should behave around Lilly, but he knew enough to realize that kind of reaction wouldn't do him any good.

"So…" Nicolai started. "Any suggestions on how I can get on his good side?"

Calum refocused on Nicolai. He'd been happy to bring Nicolai along, but he hadn't expected so much conversation.

"Just give him time," Calum said. "He was grumpy when we started out on this journey, and he's still grumpy now. It's kind of just how he is. He didn't like Magnus, he doesn't like Riley, and most of the time I'm not sure he even likes me, even though I'm supposed to be his best friend. So far Lilly's the only one he's really taken an interest in."

Nicolai smirked and nudged Calum's armored ribs. "Can't blame him there."

Had Nicolai injected sleaze into his comment, Calum would've decked him with the burning end of the torch, but he'd said it so it didn't convey anything threatening or ominous at all. He'd said it very matter-of-fact, as if he had agreed to Calum's assessment of the weather or something equally mundane.

Nicolai stammered, "N-not that I'm thinking of—"

"I know what you meant, Nicolai." Calum exhaled a quiet breath and glared at Axel from behind again. "She is beautiful. That's for sure."

As they walked, every so often they had to adjust their path to avoid the occasional hole in the floor. Where they'd come from or how they got there, Calum had no idea, but he didn't want to get too close to any of them to investigate, either. With a burning torch in his hand, he had more than enough light to avoid them, and that was good enough for now.

"Do you think you could teach me some fighting basics some time?"

Calum blinked at him. "You want *me* to teach you?"

Nicolai shrugged. "I trust you more than anyone else in the group. I think you'd be less likely to 'accidentally' kill me while we were sparring."

Calum chuckled. "I know what you mean."

"…well?" Nicolai pressed.

Calum sighed. He'd come a long way since Magnus had started training him, but was he really ready to pass along that knowledge to someone else? What if he taught Nicolai something wrong, and it got him hurt... or killed?

Then again, what if he refused, and not teaching him got him killed instead?

"I'm flattered, Nicolai. I really am," Calum said. "But Magnus is the expert. He taught Axel and me. It's really him you should be asking."

Nicolai shook his head. "I don't want to learn from him. I'd be too embarrassed at how bad I am to work with Magnus."

"*Ha.*" Calum could certainly relate to that. "You should've seen me when I first started. I got lucky my first few fights, or I'd be dead too."

"Look, I want to learn from you." Nicolai stepped in front of him so Calum couldn't walk any farther. "Just get me through the basics that Magnus taught you, and then I'll learn the rest from him. That way I won't be squeamish or awkward when he's teaching me."

Calum stared at his dark eyes. "Alright. As soon as we stop for a break, I'll show you a few things. Probably a good idea anyway in case we run into whatever's lurking down here."

Nicolai beamed, then stepped aside. "Thanks, Calum. I won't let you down."

Let's hope not. Calum showed him a half-smile and kept walking.

Two LEFTS and one right turn later they stopped for a meal break, probably about six miles into the tunnels. Just like Lilly had said, the tunnel smelled just as foul as the sewers, but in a different way, as if something had died in there awhile back and had just been left there to rot.

Stench or no stench, they still had to eat. Calum handed Lilly his torch so he could unpack some food, and after their meal, Calum showed Nicolai some basic attacks as promised. To Calum's surprise, Nicolai caught on quickly; then again, he had mentioned he was observant.

About fifteen minutes into their training, Magnus pulled Nicolai away so the two of them and Riley could scout another area a bit. Riley hadn't been completely sure which path was the right one, so he wanted to investigate with someone to back him up.

For whatever reason, Axel had decided to go with them, possibly to keep an extra eye on Nicolai, or possibly because if something did attack them, he couldn't trust Nicolai to have Magnus's back in a fight.

Whatever any case, it meant Calum finally had some time to talk to Lilly without anyone else listening, without anyone else around. The idea of it sent shudders through his chest, but he couldn't deny his glee at having the opportunity.

"How's your shoulder?" he asked.

She still carried the torch he'd given her in her right arm, and she smiled and rotated her left shoulder. "A lot better. I think it's almost totally healed. Whatever Magnus gave me—that veromine, or whatever he called it—it worked fast."

"That's good. Great. I'm glad to hear it." He mentally kicked himself. Why was he jabbering so much?

"Yeah." Lilly nodded and her smile widened. "I guess you are."

"You able to fly again, yet?"

"I never lost that ability. I just haven't because I haven't needed to, and until we got into the tunnels the ceiling's been too low to make flying of any real use." She tugged on her shimmering blue cape. "As long as I have this, I can fly."

"Oh. Good to know."

Lilly leaned over, across Calum's chest, and peered into the food pouch. "Can I have one of those oranges?"

Her proximity to him sent chills rippling down his back and arms. His breathing quickened, and he struggled to find words.

He blinked and self-chastised his way out of the sensation. She was asking for an orange, not requesting his hand in marriage.

Still, he found his mouth refused to form words right away. Instead, Calum reached into the pouch and traded her an orange for his torch.

As she started to peel it, he found his voice again. "So you're from the Sky Realm?"

Lilly nodded. "Yep."

"How long have you lived there?"

"All my life." She pulled a big chunk of orange skin off and dropped it on the ground. "Seventeen years, at least until the slave traders got me. It's been almost two months since they first captured me."

"Your parents must be terribly worried by now."

Lilly sighed and leaned against the tunnel wall as she pulled the first segment of orange from the cluster. "I know. If he could, my father would conscript the entire Sky Realm's population to look for me."

"Maybe they're already looking for you."

"I have no doubt that they are. There was a chance they'd find me right after I left, but when Roderick and his slave traders took me across Trader's Pass, that chance all but disappeared."

"Why'd you leave in the first place?"

Lilly stared at him with her mouth open, then she shut it and looked away.

Idiot. Calum had thought he'd been doing well. The conversation was flowing, natural, easy. Then, with one question, he'd ruined it all.

"I'm sorry," he said. "It's none of my business."

She shook her head, but she still didn't look at him. "It's not your fault. It's a fair question."

"Yeah, but I didn't have to ask it. And you don't have to answer, either."

She looked at him with no lack of self-confidence in her eyes. "I know."

"I'm really, really sorry."

"Don't be." She gave him a small but kind smile. "I have my reasons. I made the choice to leave, and now I just want to get back. That's all I can say."

Calum nodded and leaned his shoulder against the tunnel wall, facing her. "Don't worry. We'll get you home soon."

"Thanks." She smiled and handed him half of the now-peeled orange. "Want some?"

"Sure, thanks." He leaned the torch against the tunnel wall, popped a segment into his mouth, and savored the burst of sweet citrus flavor. It almost negated the wretched smell of the place.

"So what about you?" Firelight from the torch flickered in her keen blue eyes.

He swallowed the orange pulp and licked his lips clean. "What about me?"

She chuckled. "How'd you end up working in that quarry?"

Memories of his parents flooded Calum's mind. "Actually, I—"

"We should keep moving," Riley's voice split the darkness. He trotted back toward Calum and Lilly with Axel close behind. "Something's not right. I think we should go."

"Did you find the right path?" Calum asked.

"I'm pretty sure," Riley replied, "but either way, we shouldn't linger here."

"Yeah," Axel said. "Puppy's got a bad feeling about this part, so we're moving along."

Riley growled at him. "Call me 'Puppy' one more time, and I'll rip your throat out in your sleep. Crystal?"

Axel rolled his eyes, unconcerned. "Whatever. Nicolai and Magnus are waiting for us up ahead. Are we going or not?"

Calum cinched up his food pack and tossed it to Axel. "Hey, do you mind carrying this for a bit? My shoulder's getting sore."

"Like I said: whatever."

"Thanks." He turned to Lilly, but before he could say anything, Axel called to her.

"Lilly, got a question for you," he said. "Care to walk with me for a minute?"

"Sure." She walked next to Axel as if Calum had never existed in the first place.

Calum sighed and started walking at the rear of the group. He let them get some distance between them so Axel wouldn't hear the things Calum muttered about him.

Three steps later, the ground under his feet gave way.

Calum's left hand caught the edge on the way down, but his torch kept falling. It dropped farther and farther down until it finally struck a large gray boulder and bounced off onto the dirt floor below. It had to be at least a fifty- or sixty-foot drop.

If he let go, it was over.

"Help!" he yelled. "Come back! Help me!"

Though higher quality, his upgraded metal armor weighed more than the old leather armor he'd worn before the fight with the Southern Snake Brotherhood. He strained to reach up to grab hold of the edge with his other hand, but his fingers had already begun to slip.

"Help!" he called again.

No one came.

The rock under his left hand shifted as if it were giving way, but he managed to hold on.

Calum glanced down at the torch again. If he fell, he'd follow its trajectory. His body would smash against that big gray boulder, then he'd bounce off and probably land facedown.

If the impact didn't kill him, broken ribs, punctured lungs, and internal bleeding eventually would. And even if he didn't sustain any major injuries, he'd never find his way back up.

He would land ten feet away from the boulder where the torch still burned, now surrounded by dozens of small sparkles. They reminded him of the gems he'd mined at the quarry not so long ago.

Great. He'd die among rocks, boulders, and gemstones, just as if he'd never stopped working at the quarry.

Calum's fingers slipped a bit more.

"Help!" he called again, his voice weaker. "Axel, Magnus—help me!"

The edge crumbled under his fingertips, and he fell.

CHAPTER 37

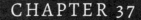

A dark hand clamped onto Calum's wrist.

He looked up and saw Nicolai's face, illuminated by the torch in his left hand.

"I've got you," Nicolai said. He clarified, "I—I think I've got you."

Good thing Calum had decided to spare Nicolai's life after all, despite Axel's objections.

Magnus appeared behind Nicolai. He reached down, clamped onto Calum's bicep, and pulled him out of the sinkhole in one fluid motion. He set Calum down against the tunnel wall. "What happened?"

Lilly landed next to him and touched his shoulder. "Are you alright?"

Calum nodded and sucked in several deep, quick breaths to calm his racing heart. "I'm fine. I was just walking, and the ground gave way. I grabbed onto the edge on my way down, but I dropped my torch. Thank the Overlord that Nicolai was there or I'd be dead."

"It's like you said—we're a team. We look out for each other." Nicolai smiled.

Axel huffed, but he nodded at Nicolai. "I guess you are good for something after all."

Nicolai's smile shrank to a smirk. "Thanks, Axel."

"Guess that explains the holes we saw in the ground," Calum quipped. "Now I know where they lead, and trust me—we don't want to end up down there."

Riley growled. "Well, we're down to one torch now. I can see in the dark just fine, but you all can't. You'd better not lose the other one."

Axel stepped near the sinkhole and peered into it. "I can still see it down there. You weren't kidding, Calum. That's a *long* way down."

Calum patted Lilly's hand, which was still on his shoulder, and nodded to her, then he stood up and walked over next to Axel. "No kidding. Plus that huge boulder down there would've broken my fall."

"Where?" Axel tilted his head. "I don't see any boulder."

Calum leaned over the hole for a look.

"Do not fall back in, Calum," Magnus said. "Nicolai may not be able to grab you in time if it happens again."

"Yeah, I'm only good for saving one life per day," Nicolai laughed. "I've reached my quota."

"I'll be alright," Calum assured them. He wouldn't have fallen in there in the first place had it not caught him by surprise.

Far below, the torch still flickered along with some of the shining flecks, but he couldn't see the gray boulder anymore. *Weird.*

"Well, when I fell in, the torch smacked a boulder on the way down. Maybe the torch has faded too much to see it now."

"Come on. Enough dawdling." Riley nodded into the darkness of the tunnel. "We need to move."

"He's right," Calum said. "Let's go."

As Calum and the others followed Riley, the ground shuddered beneath Calum's feet. He jumped to the side for fear that he'd drop down again, but he didn't fall, nor did another hole open underneath him.

"Did you guys feel that?" Calum asked.

Nicolai glanced back at him and nodded, as did Axel and Lilly.

"Tremors are normal in here," Riley said from the lead, his voice flat but firm. "Just keep moving."

As Riley said the word "moving," the ground shook again, this time with more force.

Nicolai glanced at Calum. "I sure felt that one."

"Just keep moving," Riley repeated. "We'll be fine."

After another mile or so of tremor-free progress through the tunnel, Riley stopped and sniffed the air. Within seconds, he began to growl.

"What is it?" Magnus stopped too, and the rest of the group stopped behind him.

Riley stepped back and snarled. "We're not alone."

"Now!" Commander Anigo yelled.

His twenty men poured out of shallow crevices in the tunnel walls not more than fifty feet from the Wolf's position with their weapons drawn.

Commander Anigo came out last, holding a torch. One of his men approached and sparked it to life with a flint and a knife, then the soldier took the torch and passed the fire to a few of his comrades.

The added light allowed Commander Anigo to see his catch with significant clarity. He couldn't help but grin. His plan had worked perfectly.

"We meet again," he said.

One of the men with the group, the one whom he'd fought and lost to, stepped forward. "You —I *stabbed* you with my spear. You should be dead."

Commander Anigo shook his head and took a few steps forward, into the torchlight. The high ceiling of the tunnel seemed to yawn open around them, trying to drain the additional torchlight away as if to preserve the inherent darkness of the space.

"I'm sorry to disappoint you," Commander Anigo said. "I've been pursuing you three for some time, as I said when we first met. But now I'm after the girl, too. She's wanted for the murder of my superior officer, Captain Fulton."

"Fulton was a backstabbing liar and a rapist pig," the girl spat. She'd drawn her bow and nocked an arrow. From what he'd read of the carnage that had ensued during her escape from Thirry's warehouse, she was quite an impressive shot with it.

"I am well aware of Captain Fulton's dealings, but you stand accused nonetheless. Lay down your arms, all of you."

None of them moved.

Commander Anigo pointed to the Saurian, two of the men, and the Windgale girl. "You four are under arrest for crimes against the King." He pointed to the other man in the green armor. "If you do not interfere, we will allow you to pass."

The Wolf growled.

"And you, Wolf—" Commander Anigo pulled his spear from where he'd secured it to his back. "—if you so much as twitch in my direction, I'll skewer you like the stray dog you are."

"We won't comply," the blond young man said.

Commander Anigo's eyes narrowed. "We have you outnumbered, and we *will* kill you if necessary. This is your last chance. Lay down your weapons and surrender, or face the King's justice—right here, right now."

CALUM GLANCED AT MAGNUS. Of course they would try to fight their way through the soldiers, but they were in for a difficult battle. This time there weren't any bandits to help them thin out the soldiers' ranks, and they only had scattered torchlight to help them see their enemies.

"We can take 'em," Axel whispered.

"I'm not so sure about that," Nicolai whispered back.

"No one asked you," Axel hissed.

As Riley backed toward them, Magnus addressed the soldiers. "We have not come this far to give in now. You may try to take us if you wish, but you will do so at your own peril. I will *never* surrender."

Magnus drew his sword, followed by Calum, Axel, and Nicolai. Lilly already had her bow out with an arrow nocked, and Riley crouched low as if ready to pounce.

Commander Anigo huffed. He pointed his spear at them. "Bring me their heads."

All twenty of the soldiers stepped toward them slowly with their weapons raised for battle.

As the soldiers approached, the ground shook with even more vigor than it had before, only this time it didn't stop.

Lilly toppled over into Calum, who caught her but struggled to keep his own footing. Together with Axel, they staggered over to one of the tunnel walls and braced themselves as the tunnel continued to shake.

Dust trickled down from the ceiling overhead, and a few small rocks clacked onto the ground. More rocks trickled down the cavern walls, knocked loose by the quaking.

Some of the soldiers fell over, and others moved nearer to the tunnel walls as well. Calum caught sight of Commander Anigo clinging to a rock protrusion, but it broke loose and crumbled at his feet, and he fell along with it.

Sinkholes opened up in the ground in the center of the tunnel. Calum saw at least three soldiers fall in, and he watched another get crushed under a cow-sized boulder that dropped onto him from the ceiling.

But he heard far more screams than that.

Riley, Nicolai, and Magnus made it to the opposite wall and leaned against it for support.

Amid the ruckus, Riley shouted, "This isn't normal. It didn't happen like this the last time I was here."

The shaking continued for another minute, then it stopped altogether.

Magnus stepped away from the wall first with his sword and his torch raised. He walked into the center of the tunnel, faced the direction they had come from, and held his torch out in front of him. The others filed in behind him, and Riley and Lilly kept watch on the soldiers who'd started to recover from the quake.

About thirty paces away, a large gray boulder, one that looked very similar to the one Calum had seen in the sinkhole, blocked most of the tunnel.

"How did that get here?" Nicolai asked.

"Heck of an earthquake, huh?" Axel shook his head, then turned back to face the soldiers, as did Calum. "We can't go back that way."

Calum nodded and raised his sword. "Now we have to fight."

"*Shh*," Magnus hissed, still facing the boulder. "Listen."

A faint sound permeated the tunnel, almost like the rats' squeals when they'd poured out of the wall and all over Axel. It intensified in volume and focused into two distinct voices, both of them wailing like old women in pain.

Axel, Lilly, and Riley turned back first, and at the sight of the horrified looks on the soldiers' faces, Commander Anigo included, Calum did as well.

When he did, he understood why no one was moving.

As the wails escalated to shrieks, the boulder began to change. It split down the center and slowly folded over until it touched the ground. Then the two halves split, and four rocky points touched the ground. From the center of the segmented boulder arose two tall forms, one on the right, one on the left.

They lacked definition at first, but they sharpened into forms that looked like human heads and torsos without legs, but the resemblance ended there. Instead of arms, the two forms sprouted a pair of narrow serpentine tentacles on each side of their torsos, and a gaping mouth full of jagged teeth opened in the centers of their abdomens, near the base of their bodies.

Two red eyes opened in each head.

Their high-pitched shrieks shook Calum to his core. Everything above the thing's boulder-like shell began to glow with an eerie green light that illuminated the tunnel.

Axel staggered back, his wide eyes reflecting the green light. "What in the Overlord's name is that?"

Calum's heart pounded. Although he'd never seen one, he'd heard those shrieks and seen that green light before.

"It's a Gronyx."

CHAPTER 38

"**R**un!" Riley yelled. He wove through the stunned soldiers, some of whom reached for him to no avail, and he disappeared into the darkness down the tunnel.

"Riley, wait!" Calum shouted.

Too late. The Gronyx lashed its tentacles at Magnus and grabbed his ankle before he could swing his sword. He dropped both his torch and his sword as he slid toward the Gronyx, all the while snarling and clawing at the dirt.

"We have to do something!" Calum pointed his sword at it. "Attack!"

Together with Axel and Nicolai, he charged the Gronyx. Tentacles whipped at them, but the trio cut them away as if they were low-hanging branches in the forest. Glowing green liquid oozed from the ends of the severed tentacles, and with each slice the Gronyx shrieked louder.

With a roar, Magnus reached forward, grabbed the tentacle that had coiled around his leg, and severed it with the blade attached to the end of his tail. He got to his feet and darted back to the rest of the group, where he collected his sword again.

The Gronyx recoiled on all four of its stony legs and writhed, screeching all the while.

WIDE-EYED, Commander Anigo stared at the monster.

"Sir, the Wolf got past us. We've already lost at least five men. Possibly six or seven. Do we engage the rest of them?" one of his soldiers asked.

Commander Anigo shook his head. He'd learned his lesson the last time regarding third parties. "No. Order the men to fall back and form a defensive perimeter. Let them fight it. We'll clean up whatever's left."

"THAT WILL NOT STOP it for long." Magnus gripped his sword with two hands. "And I do not know how to kill it."

Before Calum's eyes, each of the Gronyx's eight original tentacles flared with green light and then split into two tentacles each. By the time the process ended, the Gronyx had sixteen new tentacles, and it started to reach toward them again.

"Is that gonna happen any time we cut one off?" Nicolai asked.

Magnus nodded and glanced at Calum. "When I went into the Gronyx's pit at the quarry, I took out several tentacles with the pickax Burtis gave me, but they kept splitting and growing back in pairs. They don't traverse the ground quickly, but their tentacles are more than fast enough.

"I only got out of there alive because it went after the man who fell into the hole before you did. I even whacked one of its heads once, but that just made it mad." Magnus's voice deepened. "And that one was half the size of this one."

Along with the rest of the group, Axel stepped back as the Gronyx approached. "Then what do we do? And what about the soldiers?"

Magnus stole a look back. "They are not moving. Let's focus on this. If we can get past it, then perhaps we can go back the way we came."

"It's filling almost the entire tunnel. I don't think we're gonna get past it," Nicolai said.

"Lilly, try to shoot an arrow at it," Calum said.

She drew back her bow. "Where do you want me to aim?"

"Try to hit one of the heads if you can."

An arrow zipped past Calum's ear and lodged in the left head where the mouth should have been, and more green goo spurted out. The Gronyx's left torso reeled back, shuddered, and then dropped forward, and its eight tentacles draped over the front of its legs.

The right torso lurched around, and its boulder legs adjusted so the left torso was in the back. The right torso lashed its tentacles toward the group.

"Shoot it again!" Calum ducked under one tentacle and jumped over another, but he had to slice one away so it wouldn't hook his ankle. Irradiated green ooze splattered on the dirt next to his foot, and the tentacle retracted.

Lilly released another arrow, but the Gronyx raised its tentacles. The arrow skewered one of them, but the Gronyx kept coming toward them.

"Keep shooting at it!" Calum yelled.

She fired three quick arrows at the Gronyx's other head, but its tentacles intercepted them all. "I can't hit it if those tentacles are in the way."

"Then we have to risk cutting off the tentacles to kill it." Axel whacked Magnus's shoulder with the back of his hand. "You go right, I'll go left. Lilly, stay in the middle and wait for your shot. Calum and Nicolai, don't let it get Lilly. Divide its attention. Whoever has a chance to hit it, do it."

Magnus, Nicolai, and Calum nodded, and they took their positions. Tentacles zipped toward them and smacked Calum's armor, but he fended them off without having to cut any more of them. Axel's plan was working.

"Do you have the shot?" Axel called.

"Not yet," Lilly replied. She took to the air and shifted her position to try to get a better angle, but shook her head. "No shot."

The tentacle Calum had cut a moment earlier glowed bright green and split, just like the original eight had. One of them launched back toward Calum, but the other snaked around behind the Gronyx's right torso. Calum batted the tentacle away with his left forearm and craned his head to see where the other one went.

It curled around the arrow lodged in the left head and ripped it out. Green goo splattered on the dirt, and bright green light flared from the head. Then it began to move—

Toward Axel.

"Axel!" Calum yelled "Watch out!"

Too late.

The Gronyx's body swiveled and the left torso rose up, its tentacles flailing. Six of them latched onto Axel's limbs, torso, and neck, and reeled him toward the left torso's mouth at the base of its body. He screamed and strained against the tentacles.

Do you got any idea what a Gronyx does with its victims? Jidon had asked Calum after the incident at the Gronyx's pit. *It rips its food apart before it feeds.*

No. Calum couldn't let that happen. Not to Axel.

His legs pumped harder than they ever had. He yelled to Nicolai, "Take the right side!"

Axel's sword dropped from his hand, and despite his strong body, the tentacles stretched his limbs to their extremes. His cries reverberated off the tunnel walls, mixing with the Gronyx's wails in a cacophony of horror.

Calum leaped toward the tunnel wall, sprang off of it with his left foot, and soared toward the Gronyx's left torso with his sword cocked over his shoulder. Two tentacles caught Calum by his waist and his leg in midair, but they couldn't stop his momentum.

He swung his red-bladed sword with all of his might and severed the tentacles from Axel's body. Green fluid spurted all over Calum's face, arms, and chest, temporarily blinding him.

Something heavy batted him away from the left torso. His feet hit the ground first, then his body smacked against the tunnel wall. He dropped to the dirt, stunned, but somehow still gripping his sword.

A set of hands yanked him to his feet.

Axel smiled at him. "Wake up, brother. We're not done yet."

Calum wiped green goo from his face and blinked, and his vision sharpened back to normal. He spat more of it out of his mouth, disgusted by its bitter, putrid taste, then he re-gripped his sword and followed Axel to rejoin Magnus, Nicolai, and Lilly, who dodged and smacked tentacles away from themselves.

"We must find a way to kill it," Magnus urged. "We will not last much longer down here."

"It's your turn to try something stupid." Calum sucked in several deep breaths and wiped more green stuff off his face. "I'm taking a break."

"I'm on it." Nicolai raised his sword and started forward.

The tunnel shook with violence again, and the Gronyx stopped its attack. Calum's eyes fixed on the Gronyx, but the rumbling seemed to originate from behind him. Then a chorus of yells sounded from the soldiers.

Calum whirled around. A large gray boulder broke through the ground beneath some of the soldiers, and those who didn't drop into the sinkholes around it scrambled to get away from it.

Commander Anigo dropped halfway into one of the sinkholes, but he clawed his way out and rolled away from the boulder before it opened and began to separate as the first boulder had.

Familiar green light now emanated from both sides of the tunnel.

Shrieks flooded the cavern, not just from the first Gronyx, but also from the second one that now prevented them, Commander Anigo, and his ten remaining soldiers from escaping in either direction.

They were all trapped.

CHAPTER 39

Terror threatened to overwhelm Commander Anigo as he realized the futility of his situation. With the arrival of the second Gronyx, there was no hope of escape for either him or his soldiers.

Only about a hundred yards separated the two behemoths from each other, with Commander Anigo, his remaining soldiers, and the fugitives in the middle. Worse yet, the Gronyxes had begun to edge forward, gradually tightening the noose around their collective necks.

He shouldn't have even been here in the first place. It wasn't his job to battle grotesque, wretched monsters underground. He'd been trained to do so much more, to usher in a brighter future for all of Kanarah, but especially Solace.

It wasn't *fair*. He'd done nothing to deserve such a horrific fate. He should've been enjoying brunch with his superior officers in the capitol, but instead he was entombed in a dark hellscape aglow with pale green light.

"Commander?" someone called.

Commander Anigo whirled around with his spear raised and glared at the young blond man who had called his name.

"We need to work together on this." He pointed. "Have your men take that one, and we'll fight this one."

Commander Anigo clenched his teeth. He didn't need some fugitive kid telling him how to fight this battle, even if his strategy was sound.

"Commander, look out!" one of his soldiers yelled.

He turned back in time to see a tentacle lash at his head. Commander Anigo ducked and swung his spear at the tentacle, careful to knock it off its trajectory with the spear's shaft rather than risk severing it. He'd seen enough of the fugitives' fight with the first Gronyx to know what not to do.

But apparently, his soldiers hadn't been paying attention. Nearby, one of them hacked a

"Don't cut the tentacles!" Commander Anigo shouted. *Idiots.* "Aim for its bodies! For the torsos!"

Four of the Gronyx's tentacles ensnared one of the soldiers, one tentacle on each of his limbs, and raised him in the air. Commander Anigo watched as he struggled at first to cut at one of the tentacles to free himself, but the tentacles pulled his limbs taut.

Then they tightened.

The soldier screamed for help and dropped his sword. Another tentacle coiled around the soldier's neck and ceased his screams, and the Gronyx raised him above Commander Anigo's head.

A sickening crack sounded, and red liquid showered down on Commander Anigo. He recoiled with his spear primed to strike, but the Gronyx remained focused on the soldier who now lacked a left arm, which dangled freely in the Gronyx's tentacle.

Another crack. A leg this time, but it belonged to another of his soldiers.

It was ripping them apart.

He stood there, mouth agape. *King's mercy...*

"Attack its torsos and its heads!" Commander Anigo repeated. It was all he could think to do.

By the time he'd rallied them, he realized it was a lost cause. The Gronyx had already killed four of his ten remaining soldiers and mortally injured two others.

Instead of joining the last of his men in the fray, Commander Anigo backed away from the Gronyx with his spear at the ready. He'd come in here to capture or kill the fugitives who'd eluded him for the last few months, but now these tunnels threatened to devour him—literally.

Captain Fulton's death—providence? Certainly not anymore.

Within moments, the Gronyx killed the last of his men, tore his limbs off, and devoured his body in pieces. Commander Anigo's heart pounded as the Gronyx began to advance toward him.

Now he was alone.

Then he bumped into someone, and he whirled around.

CALUM SPUN around to find Commander Anigo facing him with desperate eyes and dread written on his bloodstained face. Behind him, the Gronyx advanced, and no soldiers remained to fight it.

"Don't give up," Calum told him. It was a peculiar thing to say to a commander in the King's army, but what else was Calum supposed to say? The situation was hopeless, but just giving in only meant they'd die quicker.

He shoved Commander Anigo to face the advancing Gronyx, and he stole a look back at the one his group had engaged, but they hadn't killed or even significantly wounded it. Calum had meant for his words to inspire Commander Anigo, but they withered away to nothing in the face of the terrible truth.

They were doomed.

Unless... One idea pierced Calum's mind like Lumen's light shining clear through his body in his dreams. He didn't even know if it would work, but it was truly their last chance.

"Magnus!" Calum shouted as he batted another tentacle away. "You need to use your Dragon Emerald!"

"What?" Magnus stole a furtive glance back at him.

"You need to become a Sobek *now*, or we're all dead!"

"Yeah, do it!" Axel sucked under an errant tentacle swipe. "We need you!"

Magnus dug his hand into the pouch attached to his belt and removed the Dragon Emerald, now appearing as little more than a black lump of stone in the green light blanketing them.

He held it in his left hand and knocked a trio of tentacles away with the sword in his right. "What if it fails to work?"

"Look." Calum pointed to Commander Anigo, who stood alone facing the Gronyx behind them as it eased toward them. "The soldiers are all but dead, and so are we if you don't try it. If it doesn't work, we're dead anyway!"

Magnus nodded. "Stand back. I do not know what's going to happen."

He sheathed his sword and hurriedly pulled off his breastplate and helmet. Then he loosened the straps of his arm, leg, and tail armor and let them fall from his body as well, leaving only the blade strapped to the tip of his tail.

Within a minute, the Gronyxes would converge on the group's position.

"You guys?" Nicolai held his sword higher. "They're getting *closer*."

"Is one of the requirements that you gotta be totally *naked*, Scales?" Axel shouted more out of frustration than joking. "We're running out of time here!"

Magnus paid him no mind as he worked to shed the rest of his armor from his body.

"Come over here." Calum pulled Axel and Lilly along with him toward the Gronyx that killed the King's soldiers, and Nicolai joined them. They lined up next to Commander Anigo, who eyed them with incredulity. "We'll hold this one off until Magnus can transform."

"That's *if* he can transform," Axel grumbled.

Nicolai turned toward him. "Are you ever *not* skeptical?"

Commander Anigo's gaze jumped between the two of them and then refocused on the Gronyx. He never lowered his spear, and he never said a word.

"*Guys*," Calum said. "Let's try to take this one down quickly in case this doesn't work. Maybe we can find a way to kill it before we have to fight the other one."

"How? The only time we even managed to hurt the thing was when Lilly put an arrow in one of its heads." Axel dodged an approaching tentacle.

Nicolai nodded. "Then that's what we do. We go for the heads and torsos and avoid cutting the tentacles if we can."

"So it's the same dumb plan as before?" Axel almost shouted, his eyes wild.

"It was working until it didn't," Calum countered. "Look, we have to do something!"

"Watch out for its mouths." Lilly drew back her arrow.

Calum looked at Axel. "Are you in?"

"Of course I'm in!" he shouted. "Even if the plan is stupid, do you really think I'd let you die alone? No. We're all gonna die together, because then it's *fair*."

Calum wasn't about to argue Axel's logic—or lack thereof—so instead, he nudged Commander Anigo, who sharply recoiled and stared at him with shock in his eyes.

"Easy." Calum held up his hand and nodded toward Commander Anigo's spear. "You any good with that thing?"

Commander Anigo's eyes narrowed, and his eyebrows arched down. Something had broken him out of his stupor. "Of course I am."

"I mean can you throw it and hit what you're aiming at?"

Commander Anigo scowled at him. "Yes."

"So aim for one of the heads and throw it. Then draw your sword and help us finish it off."

Commander Anigo's jaw tightened, but he turned toward the Gronyx and cocked his spear over his shoulder. "Fine."

The first Gronyx shrieked at them and charged, but a brilliant golden light flared from behind them and stopped it short. The light washed away most of the eerie green radiated by the Gronyxes, and Calum and the others all whirled around.

With both hands, Magnus pressed the Dragon Emerald against his bare chest. Golden light emanated from its center and streamed in every direction, including at Magnus—*into* Magnus.

The Dragon Emerald's light transferred to him, and his entire body began to glow the same golden color. Then the Dragon Emerald darkened to an even deeper green color than before he'd used it. There, before Calum's eyes, Magnus began to change.

His fingers and arms lengthened, and so did his legs, his torso, and his tail. His arm and leg muscles swelled to nearly twice their previous size.

Black spikes pierced through his scales along his spine. They extended down his tail, which had thickened as well. More spikes pierced through the skin on the top of his head, including a small one on the tip of his reptilian snout.

By the time the golden light faded, Magnus stood six inches taller than his previous seven-foot height and must've added fifty pounds to his already muscular form—maybe more. When Magnus opened his eyes and faced them, Calum wasn't sure he was the same Saurian he'd befriended back at the quarry.

"You take that one. I will handle this one." Magnus crouched down and tucked the Dragon Emerald back into the pouch on his belt, drew his broadsword from its sheath, which now lay on the ground, and started toward the Gronyx on his side.

Calum turned on his heels and pointed his sword at the Gronyx coming from the other direction. "Kill it."

Commander Anigo cocked his spear for a throw and launched it toward the Gronyx. It lodged in the center of one of the beast's heads, accompanied by a spurt of green blood, and Commander Anigo brandished his sword.

Calum grinned. "Nice wor—"

The tunnel swirled before Calum's eyes. The ground whacked his shoulder, then his head, and his body skidded along the tunnel floor toward the Gronyx. He swung his sword to sever the Gronyx's tentacle from his ankle, but he no longer held it. Calum glanced back and saw it lying on the stone floor three feet behind him. Then four feet. Then five.

Lilly shouted his name first, then Nicolai, then Axel. Four more tentacles curled around his wrists, his other ankle, and his waist, and they lifted him into the air. A fifth reached toward his neck, but an arrow pinned it to the ceiling.

"I've got you, Calum!" Nicolai charged toward him, hopped a tentacle that lashed at his ankles, and flung himself between the two torsos. He somehow found his footing at the base of the torsos and raised his sword.

Pressure swelled in Calum's shoulders and hips and quickly spread to his elbows, wrists, knees, and ankles. He pulled back, trying to resist, but the tentacle in his midsection pulled against his spine and arched his back, stealing the strength from his limbs. He fought them nonetheless, pouring every last bit of himself into the effort, but the tentacles were too strong.

And as usual, he was too weak.

The Gronyx was going to rip him apart.

Then Nicolai's sword cut the tentacles gripping two of Calum's limbs and his waist. A wave of relief spread through Calum's body, and his joints reset as he dangled upside down, suspended by his left leg and his right arm by two other tentacles.

They continued to pull, but Calum quickly grabbed his own wrist with his free hand and pulled back. With two limbs against one tentacle, he managed a stalemate—at least for the time being.

Below him, the Gronyx curled two tentacles around Commander Anigo's spear. Just as

Calum shouted for someone to stop it from pulling the spear out, the Gronyx ripped it from its head and dropped it. The spear clanged against the ground, and the torso straightened up.

Then the rejuvenated torso turned toward Nicolai.

Horror seized Calum's chest, and he yelled, "Get off of there, Nicolai!"

Nicolai spun around and hacked at the torso with his sword, but a wall of tentacles stopped his swing. Another tentacle swept behind his legs, and he dropped to his back.

"Axel, help him!" Calum strained and thrashed against the tentacles, but without a weapon, he couldn't get free.

"I'm trying!" Axel shouted back. He carved his way toward the Gronyx, hindered by its tentacles.

Arrows from Lilly's bow peppered the Gronyx but did nothing to stop it from attacking Nicolai.

Commander Anigo wove through and rolled under tentacles, but he couldn't reach Nicolai either.

None of them could.

"Help!" Nicolai cried as the Gronyx's tentacles pulled him toward the right torso's gaping jaws, all while preventing him from swinging his sword.

It pushed Nicolai into its mouth, and its jagged teeth clamped down on his legs.

Nicolai screamed.

All Calum could do was holler. "*Nicolai!*"

One of Lilly's arrows struck the Gronyx's right torso, and it convulsed. Axel ducked under a flailing tentacle and grabbed Nicolai by his arm, and Commander Anigo met him there. Together, they yanked Nicolai free from the Gronyx's mouth, onto the tunnel floor, and then dragged him away.

The lower halves of his legs were gone, and he wasn't moving.

An arrow knifed through the tentacle holding Calum's leg, and he fell upside down toward the hard ground. Before he could hit, the tentacle around his wrist went taught, and his legs swung down underneath him, righting him again. His blood rushed out of his head and back into the rest of his body, leaving him woozy for a second.

But this was his best chance to get free. He dug his gauntleted fingers into the tentacle around his wrist and pried it off, and it finally released him—until a flurry of new tentacles zipped toward him and latched onto his limbs again.

They pulled on his joints as they had before, and he again cried out for help. By now, his strength was all but gone. Nicolai was out of the fight, unable to save him, and Magnus had the other Gronyx to handle on his own.

Axel charged back into the fray but couldn't reach Calum.

Lilly shot more arrows, but they didn't stop the Gronyx from pulling on his limbs.

Commander Anigo ran forward as well, but a barrage of tentacles leveled him.

The tentacles pulled even harder, and though Calum's joints begged for relief, they found none.

Another tentacle coiled around Calum's neck.

He would die soon.

And he would die horribly.

CHAPTER 40

A mass of gray-and-brown fur filled Calum's field of vision and landed on the Gronyx's left torso.

Riley.

He chomped down on the torso's neck and thrashed his head back and forth. Glowing green blood and chunks of flesh splattered on the walls around them.

The Gronyx wailed and writhed, but Riley didn't let go.

The tentacles' grip went slack, and Calum hit the ground. They lashed to grab Riley, but Axel's sword severed them from its torso.

Commander Anigo recovered, darted forward, and together with Axel, he hacked at the torso's base. It disconnected altogether and dropped to the tunnel floor with Riley's jaws still locked onto its throat.

The other torso whipped its tentacles wildly—almost frantically. Commander Anigo ducked under them, but they batted Axel clear over Calum's head. He smacked into the tunnel wall with a clank.

"Get up!" Lilly shouted, perhaps to Axel, perhaps to Calum—probably to both of them. She sent another arrow at the Gronyx then zoomed toward Calum and Axel.

Riley darted over to them as well and nudged Axel with his nose until he clamped onto Riley's fur and pulled himself up.

While Commander Anigo bravely distracted the Gronyx, Calum recovered his sword. Axel recovered his, too, all while moaning about his left arm. It hung at a strange angle, and it looked like the impact with the wall had dislocated it, but Calum couldn't tell for sure.

Commander Anigo pulled back, breathing heavily, and regrouped with the rest of them. He glanced between all of them, his bloody face now streaked with glowing green slime as well. "We need a better plan."

"Riley, you're the fastest one," Calum said. "I need you to distract it. Get it to chase you, and try to get behind it if possible. If we can divide its attention, it'll be easier to fight."

Riley rolled his eyes. "Great. I get to be bait."

"Commander," Calum asked, "are you on board with this plan?"

"I am. We killed one of its torsos. Now we just need to kill the other."

Calum turned to Axel, but didn't take his eyes off of the shrieking, flailing beast before them. "Axel, are you alright?"

"My left arm is out, but thank the Overlord I'm right-handed. I can still fight," Axel grimaced, and his left arm hung limp at his side. "For your sakes, I'll have to if we're gonna get out of this."

Calum smirked. Even injured, Axel's confidence never ran dry. "Keep its attention focused on us. Try to distract it from reaching Nicolai again."

Lilly nodded. "Let's finish this."

Riley growled, and they started toward the Gronyx again.

A POWER unlike anything Magnus had ever felt permeated his body. It flowed through his veins, teased his taloned fingertips, and pulsed through his muscles, begging for release. Pleading to be used.

The Gronyx in front of Magnus lashed the full multitude of its tentacles at him. With his sword still in his right hand, Magnus allowed the tentacles to ensnare his limbs, waist, tail, and neck. The Gronyx lifted him off the ground and began to wrench his limbs in opposite directions.

Magnus glared at it and pulled back, using a portion of that newfound strength. The tentacles strained against his resistance but couldn't do him any harm.

Let us see what more I am capable of. Magnus concentrated his strength and jerked his arms and legs. The Gronyx's two torsos lurched forward and smacked into each other.

Amid the Gronyx's pained screeches, the tentacles released their grip, and Magnus landed on his feet. He lunged forward, grabbed all four of the right torso's tentacles in his left hand, and yanked on them so hard that the right torso not only tottered toward him, but the Gronyx actually had to take a rocky step forward in an attempt to right itself.

As the right torso lowered toward him, Magnus released his grip on the tentacles and leaped forward. The right torso's red eyes flickered at him until Magnus's broadsword cleaved clear through its head.

He wrenched the blade out, flinging green blood against the cavern walls, and swung it at the bottom of the torso. It severed from its base in one blow, and a geyser of glowing green blood erupted in its place.

The Gronyx wailed and shrieked again. The left torso's tentacles pummeled him into the tunnel wall, but he rebounded, unfazed, and reengaged the fight.

LILLY'S SCREAM stole every ounce of Calum's focus away from the fight. A tentacle had latched onto her ankle and now pulled her down toward its chomping ravenous mouth, unwilling to stop even though she rained arrows down on it like a thunderstorm.

Calum rushed toward her, but Commander Anigo got there first.

"Cut her free!" Calum shouted.

Axel dodged a pair of stray tentacles and severed the one that had hooked around Lilly's ankle. Commander Anigo caught her when she fell out of the air, and Calum exhaled relief.

"Thanks," she said.

As soon as Commander Anigo set her down, she drew another arrow and shot it at the left torso, then she took to the air again. The arrow embedded just above the fang-ridden mouth in its gut, but it didn't seem to faze the Gronyx.

"I can't get behind it!" Riley called between snarls.

"Axel, let's do a jump," Calum hollered. "Commander, come at it from the left."

Axel shuffled back over to Calum.

Riley darted behind him, barking, trying to steal the Gronyx's attention.

Together, Axel and Calum rolled under the first two tentacles and sliced through two more that came at them, then Axel dropped to the dirt in front of the right torso on his hands and knees.

Calum ran up behind him, planted his right foot on Axel's back, and leaped toward the Gronyx. He sliced his sword down at the left torso's head.

Before Calum's sword could make contact, a wall of tentacles smacked him away as if he weighed nothing, and he skidded to a halt on the tunnel floor. Dirt mixed with glowing ooze in a clump in his mouth, and he spat out the foul taste.

A tentacle coiled around his ankle and lurched him back toward the Gronyx. One swing from Commander Anigo's sword freed Calum, and he jumped to his feet and reentered the fracas.

MAGNUS BATTED four tentacles away in one swing with his left arm. The left torso shrieked and whipped its tentacles at him again. They latched onto his arms and legs, but they couldn't stop him from advancing.

Then, to Magnus's surprise, the monster actually started retreating.

No. Magnus smirked. *You started this. We are going to finish it.*

He plunged his sword into the hard-packed ground, grabbed the Gronyx's front left leg—originally a quarter section of its original boulder shape—and started to twist.

The Gronyx reeled back on its hind legs and released its tentacles' grip on Magnus. It used its tentacles to brace itself against the wall to keep from tipping over, but that was exactly what Magnus wanted.

With one jerk to his left, Magnus ripped off the Gronyx's boulder leg. Glowing green blood sprayed him from the wound, and the Gronyx pitched forward, shrieking like it never had before.

Magnus wrenched his sword from the ground, drew it back, and slammed it down on the monster's left torso. It cleaved all the way through the torso and into the base in another eruption of green blood.

The Gronyx let out a final pitiful wail, then it dropped, dead.

As LILLY DREW her last arrow from her quiver, every regret she'd ever had about leaving home sharpened in her mind.

She'd gotten into so much trouble in just a few months' time, all because she'd made one emotional decision. If there had ever been any doubt in her mind about whether or not she'd been right to leave, it was long gone, now.

She never should have left her home. It was an inescapable truth, and Kanarah, or the Overlord, or life itself had insisted on proving it to her time and time again ever since she'd left.

As Lilly moved to nock her final arrow, a tentacle lashed at her left arm. It caught her by surprise and batted her bow to the ground far below, but she still held that last arrow in her right hand.

She swooped down to retrieve her bow, but another tentacle wrapped around her waist and stopped her momentum. She gritted her teeth and resisted.

She'd already learned that no matter how hard she pulled, whether flying or not, she couldn't escape its grasp. But there were other ways to fight back, especially with an arrow in her possession.

"Lilly!" Calum yelled from somewhere beneath her. She caught sight of him trying to rush to her aid, but a tentacle tripped him. "Axel, Riley, help Lilly!"

A valiant attempt, and one Lilly felt grateful for, but she'd had enough of this mayhem. She had a plan, and she was going to see it through to the end.

Below her, the others moved to try to come to her aid. Axel ducked under one tentacle, but another leveled him with a blow to his face.

Riley leaped toward the tentacle that held Lilly but two others walloped him into the tunnel wall. He let out a miserable whimper and slowly forced himself back up to his feet.

Commander Anigo dueled with a trio of tentacles that kept trying to grab him, but he couldn't get away.

Lilly was on her own. Again.

The Gronyx pulled her toward its gaping mouth. This time, she didn't scream, didn't yell. She just drew her arm back and waited for the right moment.

She couldn't pull away from the Gronyx—it was too strong.

But she *could* push toward it.

She timed her move, pushed against the putrid air in the tunnel, and plunged her last arrow into one of the Gronyx's bitter red eyes.

Green fluid squelched out of its wounded head, and it wailed and slammed Lilly to the ground. The impact hurt—a lot, actually—but her armor kept her from sustaining any serious injuries. At least, she hoped that was the case.

Regardless of her own fate, she inhaled a breath of foul air into her lungs and shouted, "Kill it now!"

Dozens of tentacles flailed in every direction, lashing like glowing green whips as Calum, Axel, and Commander Anigo rushed forward. In a moment of perfect synchronization, they swung their swords with the timed dexterity of lumberjacks felling a mighty tree from three angles. They hacked and hacked at its base, relentless and furious.

The tentacles plowed into all three of them, pulling them in opposite directions up and away from its torso, which teetered forward and backward like a drunkard. They couldn't finish it.

A stone-shattering roar filled the tunnel.

Lilly grinned.

They couldn't finish it, but Magnus could.

The newly minted Sobek soared through the air, his brilliant blue sword clutched in both hands, and felled the right torso in one stunning slash.

The Gronyx released its grip on the other three, and they hit the ground in quick succession. Luminous green ooze splattered everywhere.

After a final moan, the Gronyx lay there, silent as its green light faded away.

Lilly lay on her back and exhaled a relieved breath. She couldn't help but laugh to herself—*at* herself. She definitely should never have left her home.

But if I'd never left, she reasoned, *I never would've gotten to experience all of... this.*

She lay there, staring at the green ooze coating every surface and everyone around her, and she continued to laugh.

As CALUM MADE it to his feet, so did Axel and Commander Anigo. Riley soon joined them, and the sight of the Wolf turned Calum's head toward Lilly.

To Calum's dismay, Axel was already helping her to her feet. He cursed himself for not reacting faster.

The five of them gathered together, their eyes fixed on Magnus and his new massive form.

Calum marveled at the sight. It felt like the first time Magnus had walked into the quarry, escorted by the King's soldiers, all over again. The effect of seeing him was the same: utter shock laced with a hefty dose of fear.

"Is it still you?" he asked.

Magnus's hard gaze softened into a grin, and his deep voice vibrated through Calum's chest. "Of course it is me."

Calum lurched forward and threw his arms around Magnus's midsection, now armored with darker yellow scales that felt rough and angry against Calum's face. But it didn't matter. His friend was alive, and he'd grown stronger—far stronger. Strong enough to save them all.

Soon after, Axel joined them, much to Calum's surprise.

Then, of course, he ruined it.

"Just when I thought you couldn't get any uglier," Axel said, still hugging them both, "you go and do somethin' like this, Scales."

Calum laughed, and even Magnus gave a chuckle. Whether it was out of pity or not, Calum didn't know.

He glanced at Lilly, Riley, and Commander Anigo. Dirt mired with glowing Gronyx blood covered all three of them. He grinned and motioned them over. "You belong with us, over here."

Commander Anigo declined, but Riley and Lilly looked at each other, then they joined their friends.

All except for Nicolai.

CHAPTER 41

Nicolai.

Calum tore free from the group embrace and ran past Commander Anigo to Nicolai.

He still lay on the ground, almost perfectly centered between the two dead Gronyxes. The Gronyx had clipped off his legs beneath his knees, but the wounds, instead of bleeding, had crystallized into a variety of brilliant, shining colors still visible in the Gronyxes' fading light.

Additional crystals had formed in the corners of Nicolai's eyes and mouth, and his breathing rasped against his lungs. Now Calum understood why Gronyx stones were so valuable—and what it cost to create them.

Calum knelt to the ground next to him, sighed, and hung his head. "I'm so sorry, Nicolai."

Nicolai looked up at him with those dark eyes, now glassy. He rasped, "Don't be."

"What's happening to him?" Lilly asked from behind Calum.

"Some kind of poisoning, I guess. When the Gronyx bit off his legs, it must've spread throughout his body." Calum clenched his teeth. "I don't know for sure, but it looks like his entire body will crystallize in time."

"Is there a cure?" Axel bent down next to Nicolai and touched one of the crystals that had formed on his severed legs. It broke off onto the dirt, still shimmering in the waning light, and Axel recoiled.

Calum smacked his hand away. "Don't touch him."

His eyes wide, Axel backed off. "Sorry."

"It's alright." Nicolai's voice scraped against his throat. "It doesn't hurt… much."

Lilly turned to Magnus. "Will your veromine help him?"

Magnus shook his head. "I regret that all the veromine in the world could not save him now."

"Calum." Nicolai's gritty voice pulled his attention back. "I know I don't have long, but I wanted to thank you again for sparing me back in the fields—both times. You believed in me when no one else did. You're—honestly—you're the best friend I've ever had."

Calum managed a half-smile. He felt horrible admitting it, but he owed Nicolai the truth, at least. "I barely know you."

215

Nicolai smiled, and tiny crystals rolled down his cheeks to the tunnel floor. "But I know *you*. You see the best in people, even when there isn't much worth seeing. Don't lose that."

Calum granted himself a sad chuckle, and Lilly touched his shoulder again. He turned back to glance up at her, and her warm smile eased the pain in his heart.

She gasped, and Calum turned back to find that Nicolai's chest no longer heaved up and down. His eyes had turned to glass—literally—and he'd stopped moving entirely.

You see the best in people, even when there isn't much worth seeing. Don't lose that.

Calum would remember those words as he continued his journey. They would drive him forward just as much as his dreams of Lumen did.

"Your debt to me is more than paid, my friend." Calum leaned over Nicolai and shut his eyelids with his fingers. "You have fulfilled the Law. Be at peace."

Lilly touched Calum's shoulder again, and he stood up and faced her. "He was right, you know."

"About what?"

She smiled. "About you. You truly are amazing, Calum. I don't know you that well either, but you have a genuine heart. That much is apparent."

"Thank you." He gave her hand a squeeze, though he longed for much more.

Maybe in time, he considered. After all, their journey was far from over. Who knew what the future held? *Maybe in time.*

Even in the growing darkness, Calum could see Axel glaring at him. "Are we just gonna hang around here all night and let another one of those things find us, or are we getting outta this death trap?"

"I'm afraid I can't let you do that," a firm voice said. A sword-wielding silhouette stood before the dead Gronyx's body, between them and the path to Trader's Pass, the way out of the tunnel.

Commander Anigo.

He must've been crazy to challenge five opponents in the near-darkness of the tunnel, one of whom could fly, and one of whom was the largest, strongest Saurian he'd ever seen, but Commander Anigo had a duty to perform.

He would bring as many of them to justice for their crimes as possible, even if it cost him his life in the process. He would die in the service of his King, as he'd intended for as long as he could remember, and he would receive his due reward from the Overlord in whatever afterlife awaited them.

"Come on, Commander," Calum said, exasperated. "We don't have to do this."

"On the contrary," Commander Anigo said, "we absolutely must."

"You really expect to stop all five of us?" Axel stepped forward. His left arm still hung at his side at an awkward angle.

Commander Anigo shook his head. "I don't. In fact, I expect to die in these tunnels with the rest of my men who perished if I face you in combat."

"I beat you once. I can do it again." Axel raised his sword. "Even with a dislocated arm."

Not likely. Commander Anigo smirked. "Then I'll be happy to kill you first."

"There's no need for this," Calum stepped between them, but he was smart enough to keep his sword up as well. "Commander, you'd be dead if it weren't for us."

"And I may yet die *because* of you."

The Wolf snarled at him, and the Saurian—Magnus—started forward.

216

"No." Calum shook his head, and Magnus stopped his advance. "You of all people should know the Law of Debt, that when one person saves another—"

"Don't presume to lecture me on the laws of this land, boy." Commander Anigo pointed his sword at Calum. "I've been studying the law since before you were born."

"Then you know you're indebted to us for saving you from death in these tunnels, just as we're indebted to you for your help in defeating these monsters," Calum said.

"That's—" Commander Anigo clenched his teeth and shifted his grip on his sword. The Gronyx's green blood had made his hilt slick in his hands. "That's not how it works."

Calum glanced at Magnus, then he looked back at Commander Anigo. "If that's not how it works, then explain where I've gone wrong?"

Commander Anigo's eyes narrowed. If he capitulated to Calum, he'd live, but he'd have to allow them to go free.

They had violated the King's laws, but the Law of Debt, which the Overlord had personally established millennia ago, superseded the King's laws.

If he refused to uphold the Law of Debt, he'd be violating the oldest and most sacred law there was—the Law he was bound to uphold first and foremost, according to the oath of service he'd sworn upon entering the King's service.

He couldn't win either way. He either forfeited his life and his obedience to the Law of Debt, or he could live and uphold the most sacred of all laws, but they would go free.

"Choose life," Lilly said from behind the others.

It was a compelling recommendation, not just because it came from someone of such beauty, but more so because she had an arrow trained on his face.

Needs, not wants, he reminded himself. He wanted to uphold the King's laws, but he *needed* to uphold the most important Law. *Needs, not wants.*

Commander Anigo exhaled an angry sigh, and he lowered his sword. "Very well."

Magnus huffed. "Wise decision."

Lilly let the tension in her bow slacken, Calum lowered his sword, and the Wolf stopped snarling, but Axel continued to glare at Commander Anigo.

"But I must make two requests of you," Commander Anigo said.

"Name them," Calum said.

"First, I request that you allow me to accompany you to the surface, and then we can part ways."

"Agreed. And the other?" Calum asked.

"I request that once we part ways, and I return to Kanarah City, that you consider me released from this debt, and I shall offer you the same courtesy," Commander Anigo said. "I have sworn an oath to the King, and I must see his mandate through to completion."

Calum glanced at Magnus, who nodded, then Calum turned back to Commander Anigo. "We would rather not have you as an enemy, but if we must agree, then we agree."

"Thank you."

"You should know, we plan to cross Trader's Pass over to Western Kanarah," Magnus said. "The King's soldiers are not a welcome sight west of the Valley of the Tri-Lakes."

"Then you should have little trouble avoiding coming into contact with me," Commander Anigo replied. "Unless you return to Eastern Kanarah, that is. Then I will be forced to continue my pursuit of you."

"Fair enough," Magnus said.

Calum motioned toward the ground. "If someone can find a torch while there's still a little light from the Gronyxes left, see if you can get it lit. Let's grab our belongings and start walking. I don't want to risk running into any more Gronyxes if we can help it."

The Wolf, Riley, nudged his leg, and Calum looked down and took the torch he held in his mouth. Commander Anigo sheathed his sword and pulled a flint from his belt. Like the other soldiers, he'd brought one of his own along.

He approached Calum, but stopped just beyond the tip of Axel's sword. He extended the flint in his hand. "Here. Use this."

"Easy, Axel." Calum pushed Axel's sword aside and took the flint from Commander Anigo. "Thank you."

With the torch lit, Lilly darted around in search of spent arrows to refill her empty quiver, and Riley roamed the tunnel looking for more torches and to identify any leftover sinkholes they might not be able to see in the darkness.

Commander Anigo stood by and watched them all. Despite his orders, he couldn't help but admit that the only reason he was still alive was because of the very people he'd been tasked to capture and bring to justice.

He rightfully had to let them go this time, but if they should happen to return to Eastern Kanarah, he would be there.

And he would be ready for them.

When they finished rounding up what supplies they could, Commander Anigo led them out of the tunnel with Riley and Axel close behind.

FINALLY FREE OF the tunnel's darkness, Calum stretched his sore limbs and sucked in his first breath of fresh air in hours.

On the horizon, the morning sun dawned over the Valley of the Tri-Lakes. In the distance, the waters of two of the lakes glistened with golden sunlight, one to the north of Trader's Pass and one to the south.

Axel moaned and rubbed his arm. "I think it's dislocated."

Magnus beckoned him over with a wave of his hand and set down the armful of Blood Ore armor he'd carried out of the tunnels. "Let me see it."

A loud pop sounded, followed by a scream almost reminiscent of the Gronyxes' shrieks, and then a slew of curses.

"Another scream like a weak, whiny girl." Magnus shook his head. "And I thought you were supposed to be the strong one."

Axel rubbed his left shoulder and scowled up at Magnus. "A little *warning* would have been nice, *Scales*."

Magnus shrugged. "You asked me to help you, so I helped you."

Riley just snickered.

"This is where I leave you." Commander Anigo stood facing the five of them with his back to Kanarah City, which amounted to little more than a dark blot against the horizon. "I do not wish you ill will, but I hope that you will remain far away from the scope of my influence."

"I understand." Calum nodded. He gave Commander Anigo a slight nod, then he faced his companions. "Are we ready to go?"

They nodded and turned west.

"Calum?"

He turned back to Commander Anigo.

"Thank you, all of you, for your help in the tunnels," Commander Anigo said. "What you said is true: I'd be dead without you. Regardless of our differences, I am grateful to be alive."

Calum smirked. "You know, if you want, you could come with us."

A long sigh sounded behind him. Axel asked, "Why do you insist on inviting every straggler we find to join us?"

Calum shrugged. "Look, I just figured he needed somewhere to—"

"No, thank you." Commander Anigo held up his hand. "My place is in the King's service. There is much I have left unfinished back in Solace. It is my life's work to see it done."

Calum felt exactly the same way about finding and freeing Lumen. "I understand."

As Commander Anigo turned and walked away, an invisible burden lifted from Calum's shoulders. He couldn't believe his eyes. He was actually here, on Trader's Pass, on his way to the Blood Mountains to uncover the secret to setting Lumen free.

He didn't know what would happen next, but whatever challenge rose to meet them, whatever threatened their lives, he knew they would overcome it together, glowing green blood or otherwise.

Together, Calum, Axel, Magnus, Lilly, and Riley took their first steps along Trader's Pass, their first steps toward their own bright futures and for all of Kanarah.

EPILOGUE

Lumen's eyes opened in the darkness.
He could see them, feel them. Especially the boy.
Especially Calum.
There was something special about him.
A determination, a drive, a hunger.
Those qualities had brought him and his friends much closer now.
Much closer to Lumen, to release.
As the King had proclaimed nearly a thousand years earlier, Lumen would soon be set free.
And when he was set free, he would save Kanarah.

<hr>

THIS BOOK IS OVER, BUT THE ADVENTURE DOESN'T STOP HERE!

The story continues in *THE WAY OF ANCIENT POWER*
Book Two of THE CALL OF ANCIENT LIGHT SERIES

If you enjoyed this book, please leave a review on Amazon.com!

THE WAY OF ANCIENT POWER

*THE LIGHT WILL AWAKEN THE DAWN,
AND THE DARKNESS FLEES BEFORE IT*

BEN WOLF

PROLOGUE

L umen's eyes opened in the darkness.

He could see them, feel them.

They were much closer now.

Three travelers had set out to discover the secret to release him, and two more had joined them. Two humans, a Saurian, a Windgale, and a Wolf.

As the King had proclaimed nearly a thousand years earlier, Lumen would soon be set free.

And when he was set free, he would save Kanarah.

CHAPTER 1

Calum ducked under a blade and drove his fist into the bandit's gut. A follow-up swipe with his red-bladed sword felled the bandit, then he whirled around to block an axe from cleaving him in half.

The tip of Axel's sword burst through the axe-wielding bandit's chest from behind, and the bandit slumped to the ground atop his dead comrade.

Beyond Axel, Magnus engaged ten—literally *ten*—bandits on his own, and he was winning, too. Now a seven-and-a-half-foot Sobek, his dark-green scales had hardened to the point where steel just glanced off them, and he only wore his Blood Ore armor over his chest and stomach.

Magnus swung his matching Blood Ore sword in massive arcs at the men who encircled him. Though they timed their blocks and parries well, they simply couldn't withstand his strength. Every blow sent shudders throughout their bodies, and in a matter of minutes, all ten of them lay the ground, slain.

As he marveled at the sight, an arrow zipped by Calum's ear, followed by a sound like a knife piercing an apple's skin. A bandit face-planted next to him, his sword tumbling across the arid dirt that spread out for miles north and south of Trader's Pass.

"Watch your back." Lilly swooped into view, still afloat on the air with an empty bow in her left hand. Her blonde hair shone under the afternoon sun, and her blue cape shimmered and billowed with the wind. A hint of teasing colored her words, and her half-smile and mischievous blue eyes added to the effect.

Marveling at Magnus was great, but the big lizard had nothing on Lilly.

"That's what I have you for." Calum drank her in. Beautiful didn't even begin to describe her. Had they not been in a battle, Calum could have stared at her all—

A brown and gray blur knocked him to the ground. Calum repositioned his sword to run the thing through, but it had already leaped off him.

Its furry tail wagged as it pounced on an approaching bandit. A few ferocious tears and bites later, it turned back to Calum with lupine ears and keen blue eyes.

"She *just* told you to watch it. Where's your head?" Riley gave him a low growl. "You're gonna get yourself killed."

"Sorry." Calum pivoted and absorbed a hack from another bandit's sword with his own. Before Calum could counterattack, an arrow lodged in the bandit's neck, and he dropped. Calum glared at Lilly, who still hovered above him. "Hey! I had that one under control."

She just shrugged and winked at him, then she nocked another arrow.

He smiled back until he noticed Axel's steely dark-blue eyes and his sour expression. As quickly as their eyes met, Axel refocused on the battle and downed the next bandit in one vicious swing. Calum was glad he'd never be on the receiving end of one of Axel's blows.

Magnus roared and whirled around. His sword took out three more bandits in one swing, and his whiplash tail flattened another two.

Riley knifed past another bandit, skidded to a halt, then sprang toward the bandit's back. He caught the bandit's collar in his teeth and slammed him to the ground. Another salvo of furious bites and tears at the bandit's throat finished him off.

Barely half a week had passed since their encounter with the Gronyxes in the underground tunnel from Kanarah City to Trader's Pass, and already trouble had found them again. Sometimes Calum wondered if their troubles would ever end, if they'd never get a real rest.

The constant trials and stress weighed on them all, but Calum kept reassuring himself it would all be worthwhile in the end. Freeing Lumen would transform Kanarah and everyone in it, and then all would be made right. The thought of it renewed Calum's resolve, and he refocused on the battle—or what was left of it, anyway.

Of the two-dozen bandits who'd initially confronted them, only three remained. Instead of surrounding Calum and the others, they were surrounded.

Still, these men were rough grizzled types accustomed to the harsh life of scavenging for whatever they could find, steal, or scrounge, either from travelers along Trader's Pass or from the expansive wasteland that stretched out as far as they eye could see.

They brandished their weapons and charged in three separate directions instead of as a group. Calum was still learning strategy from Magnus, but even he knew that was a huge tactical error. They felled the bandits with ease then stood in place and looked at each other.

"Anyone hurt?" Magnus wiped the blood from his broadsword with one of the bandits' shirts, then he sheathed it.

"I'm good, thanks to Lilly and Riley." Calum shook his head and did the same. He'd taken his red-bladed sword from a bandit in Eastern Kanarah named Tyburon. It had been his toughest one-on-one fight ever, so he'd kept the sword as a memento.

It was also a lot better than his previous sword, which was nothing but a standard weapon issued to the King's soldiers. By contrast, the red blade in his hand had a curve right at the end, near its tip, that made it especially good for slashing.

And it looked awesome, too.

"I'm fine." Axel still wore the same frown as when Calum had last looked at him.

"You sure?" Calum nodded to him and sheathed his sword. "You look frustrated."

"I said I'm *fine*," Axel insisted, now scowling at Calum. "Just sick of the constant fighting."

Even as Axel said it, Calum knew it wasn't the truth. If anything, the fighting was probably the only part of their journey along Trader's Path that Axel *did* like.

"At least you get to wear Magnus's arm and leg guards." Calum held out his arms, each with a different color and style of armor on them. Black gauntlets with steel studs in the knuckles covered his hands. "I'm still stuck with this mixed armor from the Southern Snake Brotherhood and the King's soldiers."

"Yeah, but there's no way you'd ever fit his armor. It barely fits me." Axel tapped his blue forearms with his sword. "I'm just tall enough and big enough to make it work."

"Once you tightened the straps to their max." Lilly landed beside Calum.

"Armor's overrated," Riley said. "If you're fast enough, you can avoid anything."

"But if you don't see the blow coming, armor could save your life." Lilly re-tied her shoulder-length blonde ponytail behind her head then drummed her fingers along the pale pink armor covering her arms. "I'm fast too, but I'm keeping my armor on."

"This conversation is the very definition of frivolous." Magnus turned west. "We need to cover far more ground before we make camp, so if you intend to talk, walk at the same time."

"Shouldn't we search the bodies first?" Calum asked.

"Yes." Magnus's golden Saurian eyes narrowed at him. "But make haste."

Three bodies in, Calum found a small lightweight sword not much bigger than a dagger. He pulled it out of its sheath, waved it around a bit, and then slid it back in. Nothing fancy, but it was well balanced and seemed durable enough.

"Lilly?" he called.

She hopped into the air and glided over to him. "Yeah?"

He showed the sword to her. "Could you use this?"

"I've mostly trained to use a bow and arrow. I don't know as much about swordplay." Lilly hooked the sheath to her belt and drew the blade. She met his gaze with a glint of mischief in her blue eyes. "But I'm willing to learn."

Calum matched her smile. It had taken him awhile to get used to her being anywhere close to him. Before the Gronyx fight, and even a little bit after that, he'd get nervous, jumble his words, and start sweating whenever she got too close.

Now he could carry on a conversation with her—while still being nervous and sweating. Not much of an improvement, but an improvement all the same.

"Magnus taught me," he said. "I'm sure he'd be willing to teach you too."

Lilly tilted her head, sheathed the sword, then nodded. "I'll keep that in mind. Thanks."

Her tone had flattened a bit, but Calum didn't know why.

Over her shoulder, Axel rolled his eyes.

Did I miss something?

"I'll be more than happy to teach you to use it." Axel cast a quick glance at Calum, then he put his gloved hand on Lilly's armored shoulder. "I have a feeling you'll get the hang of it quickly."

As the revelation of Calum's ignorance dawned on him, he opened his mouth to protest, but Magnus spoke first.

"Time to move on." Magnus sniffed at the air and turned to Riley. "Do you smell that?"

He growled. "Of course I smell it."

"What?" Calum glanced between them. "What do you smell?"

"Dactyls." Riley growled again.

"What?" Axel asked.

"Flying devils. Beasts with bat wings, eagles' beaks, and bodies like humans." Magnus shook his head. "Not something we wish to run into."

"Your skin's as hard as stone, and you're worried about flying monkeys?" Axel asked.

Magnus leveled his gaze at Axel and clacked his claws on his breastplate. "Their beaks and talons can pierce Saurian skin and most armor. Only dragonscales and exceptionally rare types of metal can withstand their attacks. Unlike the sabertooth cats we faced before we found Lilly and Riley, Dactyls are intelligent, cunning hunters."

"We just took down two Gronyxes not even a week ago." Axel pointed his thumb over his shoulder. "Why should we be worried about these things?"

"First, we barely survived that. If you recall, we lost Nicolai as a result," Magnus said.

"Not much of a loss, if you ask me," Axel muttered.

Calum whacked his shoulder for the comment, and Axel promptly whacked him back, much harder. Instead of retaliating at the sting in his arm, Calum just clenched his teeth.

Magnus eyed them both. "Second, these things can fly, they are impressively fast, and instead of two or three large ones, we would have to face dozens, or perhaps even hundreds of them. They eat flesh but prefer bone marrow, and they will crack your bones open while you still live to get it. I have witnessed what they can do firsthand, so believe me that we must avoid them."

Riley scanned the path ahead. "I smelled 'em when I crossed to the human side six months ago, but I didn't see any."

"So did I," Magnus said. "They did not attack me, either. They are migratory, to some extent. With autumn setting in, they are likely heading south to roost."

"We didn't run into any on my trip over with the slave traders either," Lilly said.

"How come we can't smell them?" Calum asked.

Riley raised on eyebrow. "Wolves, and to a lesser extent, Saurians, have an excellent sense of smell. Once we get a little closer, you'll smell them too. It's a scent you'll never forget."

"Why would we go closer?" Lilly glanced between Magnus and Riley. "I mean, I know we have to head west to get back to the other side of Kanarah, but—"

"They are coming toward us. I did not smell them when we started fighting the bandits, but now I do. That suggests they are headed our direction." Magnus frowned.

"They eat meat, right? Bone marrow?" Calum said. "Why don't we fall back near where we came out of the underground passage? Maybe they'll eat the bandits, and we'll be free to pass when they aren't hungry anymore."

Riley eyed Magnus. "That plan's not half bad."

"Except we'd have to backtrack three—no, almost four—days and entirely erase our forward progress along the pass," Axel said.

"Oh. Yeah. Not such a great plan after all." Riley frowned up at Calum. "No offense."

Calum shrugged. "Takes a lot more than that to offend me."

"Well, I'll keep trying, then," Riley replied.

"Worse yet, we would likely run out of food in the process, and Commander Anigo made it clear we were not to return to Kanarah City, or to Eastern Kanarah at all. We do not know how long it will take them to get here, if they even show up at all, and we also do not know if the bandits will satisfy them. If it is a larger flock, then it might all be for naught."

"You mean the puppy's nose can't tell us *everything* we need to know?" Axel quipped. "You made it sound like your snout was all-knowing."

"I told you *not* to call me that anymore." Riley growled and bared his teeth.

Axel held up his hands in mock surrender. "Just contributing to the conversation. Not that anyone cares about my opinion anyway."

"Cut it out, Axel," Calum said. "He hasn't done anything to you."

"In any case," Magnus cut in, "we cannot afford to linger here or anywhere else. We barely have enough food to make it to the other side, even with rationing."

"But if we move forward, we risk having to face those things, and you said yourself that it's not something we want to do." Calum glanced between the four members of his group. "I say we fall back and hide, let them eat their fill, and then move forward once they're gone."

"I'm with Calum," Lilly said.

"Me too." Riley stepped forward. "I know it's not a sure thing, but I can stick around here and watch them. Then I'll report back to you guys when I know it's safe to move forward."

"That could be days. Weeks, even." Magnus shook his head. "We will not have enough food." Magnus's golden eyes widened, and he clacked his talons against his breastplate. "Unless…"

"Oh, *great*. Where is this going?" Axel raised an eyebrow and sighed. "Unless what?"

Magnus grinned. "Unless we go fishing."

CHAPTER 2

C alum blinked. "Huh?"

Magnus stared out over the Valley of the Tri-Lakes. "We can catch our food. The lakes are teeming with fish and other creatures fit for eating."

"I thought the lakes were off-limits." Calum's gaze followed Magnus's line of sight.

"I'm not sure about the lakes to the south and north of that one—" Magnus pointed to an expansive stretch of blue water set into the gray wasteland around it. "—but there is at least one small port town that borders the Central Lake not far from here."

"A 'port town?' You told us nothing can survive in the valley." Axel folded his arms.

"And I was not lying. You will find no vegetation or animal life in this wasteland, but the lakes can provide ample sustenance for anyone willing to brave their dangerous waters."

"It's true," Lilly said. "Some Windgales live out here as well, fishing and whatnot. There's a high demand for fresh fish back in Aeropolis."

Magnus motioned to the east with his head. "And Kanarah City has a flourishing fish market in the southwest quadrant of the city, near the entrance to Trader's Pass. They get their goods from fishermen who catch fish and transport it back to the city."

"So we can just cast a line out from the shore and catch something?" Axel asked.

"No. We will have to charter a vessel already equipped for a fishing excursion and venture into deeper waters if we mean to catch enough to sustain ourselves."

"Good thing I'm scouting." Riley glanced between Calum and Magnus. "I don't do boats."

"So you wanna go to that port town, get a boat, and spend time fishing to replenish our food reserves?" Calum asked. "Instead of heading back along the pass and taking shelter until the Dactyls pass?"

Magnus nodded. "I think it would be to our benefit. I noticed a well-trodden path a couple miles back that led toward the Central Lake. We can backtrack a little and camp there for the night."

"I saw that path, too. That should put you out of range for the Dactyls. They avoid cities, so I don't think they'd travel that far east without a good reason. And when they run across these dead bandits, they'll be occupied for awhile, anyway." Riley eyed Calum. "I say you do it. I'll meet you later on, once the Dactyls have gone away."

Calum glanced between Lilly and Axel. "You two alright with this?"

"I still think we can take 'em," Axel placed his hand on his stomach, "but I've never been fishing before, and I'm sick of not eating my fill at dinner time. I say we do it."

Lilly shrugged. "I just need to get home to my parents. If this is the way we do it safely, then I'll go along with it."

Calum grinned. If nothing else, it was a new sort of adventure, and they had to find more food if they were going to make it across the pass to free Lumen, anyway.

"Riley?" he said.

"Yeah?"

"Stay safe. Don't take any unnecessary risks. If anything happens, we'll meet up with you at the western end of Trader's Pass. Crystal?"

Riley nodded. "Clear."

"A large dead tree stands about fifty paces south from the western end of Trader's Pass," Magnus said. "You cannot miss it. If you fail to find us on the pass, meet us there."

"Yeah, I know it." Riley nodded again. "I'll be there, if I have to be."

Calum unslung a sack of food from his shoulder, only about a third full, and set it in front of Riley. "This should last you awhile if you're careful. We'll see you later."

Riley maneuvered his head through the strap and shifted it over his back. "Thanks. You be careful, too."

Magnus grinned again, the same as when he'd first proposed the idea of going fishing. "Let us go."

In Calum's dream that night, Lumen's form materialized with so much brightness that Calum had to squint and shield his eyes with his hands. As before, Lumen traced a large circle with the tip of his sword, and an image focused within.

Tall red mountains, some with snowy caps, sharpened under Kanarah's golden sun. The image panned down to the base of the mountains, swooped over several red snowcapped peaks, and lowered down into a valley set between two ridges. The picture ended at a wall of red rock. A concealed door set into the wall opened like the giant mouth of a crimson beast.

"Find the Arcanum." Lumen's golden eyes glistened with fresh fire from behind his emotionless white mask. "Discover the way to set me free."

Before Calum could respond, the vision disappeared in a quick spiral.

When Calum's eyes opened, Lilly was standing over him with her hands on his shoulders.

She tilted her head. "Are you alright?"

Even in the dim light of the campfire, she looked incredible—like an angelic being staring down at him, her hair aglow with golden light.

He nodded, immediately restored. "Yeah. I'm fine."

"Bad dream?" It was Lilly's shift to stand guard for a few hours, which meant Axel and Magnus were asleep.

"Yeah, I guess."

He still hadn't told Lilly about his commission from Lumen, delivered to him in a series of dreams since just after he'd met Magnus. In truth, he didn't know how to tell her why they were traveling to Western Kanarah.

So far, she'd been operating under the assumption they were fleeing Eastern Kanarah as fugitives for escaping the quarry and Axel's family farm, and for resisting the King's men after that. Calum hadn't corrected her, Axel wasn't about to say anything, and Magnus undoubtedly felt like it wasn't his place to speak up.

But Calum was fast reaching a point where he couldn't hide what they were doing anymore. He really liked Lilly and had come to view her as a friend—more than that, if he were honest about it—and he really wanted her to know what he was trying to do.

Another part of him was mortified at what she might say or think of him. The reality of his intentions landed just shy of outright madness—and that was how Calum viewed his mission. How would someone like Lilly view his quest? Would she believe him? Accept him?

"Tell me about it," she said with a soft grin.

Calum chuckled, sat up, and rubbed the back of his neck. *Only one way to find out.*

"You're... you're gonna think I'm crazy," he said.

She smiled and sat down next to him, closer than he'd expected. "Try me."

"Alright." Calum swallowed the lump in his throat, ignored his nerves and the sweat trickling down the middle of his back, and explained his series of dreams to her, starting with his first dream while still at the King's quarry.

Lumen had appeared to him in several successive dreams since then, each of them almost identical up until this point. A path across the Valley of the Tri-Lakes formed in the center of Lumen's circle and then stopped at the base of the Blood Mountains, where a black hole opened like a gaping mouth.

Then, of course, this last dream seemed to get more specific as to the way to reach that opening. Lumen had called it the Arcanum, which somehow apparently held the secret to releasing him.

"So that's why we're out here in the first place." Calum let his gaze linger on her a little too long, and she turned her head away. *Stupid.*

"That's—" She bit her lip. "—different."

"Different?" Yep. She thought he was crazy. "That's all you have to say?"

She refocused on him, totally serious. "I believe you."

Calum blinked. He hadn't expected that. "You do?"

Lilly nodded. "Yeah. Why wouldn't I?"

"Because it's ridiculous. Because we're risking our lives for something we aren't even sure is real."

"No. You're risking your lives to make Kanarah a better place for everyone. That's a worthy cause, even if you fail, even if it's not real." Lilly broke eye contact with him and stared up at the stars. "Besides, I believe Lumen *is* real. I believe he can set Kanarah free."

"What makes you say that?" Calum stoked the fire with a stick, and a plume of orange and yellow embers spilled into the sky.

"When I was young, my parents taught me that he was real. It's not something I've really even questioned because I believe my parents. He's a part of Kanarah's history, and if you believe the prophecies, he's part of our future, too."

"The only things I know about Kanarah's history are what Magnus has taught me since we left the quarry." Calum tossed the stick on top of the flames and shifted a bit closer to the fire. "I didn't get much of a formal education working in a place like that."

"I bet you know more about rocks than I'll ever know," Lilly offered.

"Whoopee." Calum's voice flattened.

Lilly touched his shoulder. "Hey, I wasn't trying to make fun of you."

Calum nodded. "I know. It's just that I lost eight years of my life when the King's men killed my parents and sent me to the quarry. I don't have many pleasant memories from that place. My favorite one was the day I left with Magnus."

"I'm sure it was." Lilly positioned herself so she could look directly into his eyes again. "I can't imagine what you've gone through. When Roderick and his men captured me, I didn't know what to do. I thought my life was over. I hope you take comfort knowing you saved someone from a fate just as bad as what you endured during those eight years at the quarry."

Calum managed a half-smile. "It does make me feel better when you put it that way."

Lilly beamed. "Good."

"You know, if you want to start sleeping a bit early, feel free. I'm wide awake now, so I might as well start my shift early."

"I think I might." Lilly tried to stifle a yawn but failed. "Yeah, I will. Thanks, Calum."

Calum nodded. He watched her curl up and drape her cape over herself near the fire. After a moment, he whispered her name. "Lilly?"

"Hm?" She looked up at him.

"We will get you back to your parents. I promise."

Lilly smiled again. "I know you will. And I know you'll make it to Lumen."

Calum wasn't so sure of that, but he nodded nonetheless.

A SCREECH JARRED Axel from his sleep. He drew his sword and sprang to his feet.

Morning sunlight blinded him until a dark, winged form blotted out the sun. It grew larger and larger until he couldn't see the sun at all.

The screech ripped through the air again, this time aimed right at Axel.

The winged monster was headed straight for him.

He raised his sword.

CHAPTER 3

Red metal flashed, and the flying beast smacked into the rocks next to him in two halves leaking glowing purple blood.

Axel turned his head and saw Calum standing next to him, sword in hand, its red blade streaked with more of the same purple goo.

Axel scowled as he tried to calm his hammering heartbeat. "Guess I can't yell at you for not paying attention on your watch, can I?"

"Nope." Calum shook his head. "Next time, don't freeze up. I may not be there to save you."

Axel tried to say something back, but Magnus spoke first.

"We must flee. Now." Magnus motioned toward the path. "Dactyls can smell one of their own dead from miles away. They are doubtless headed for us right now. Calum, clean off your sword as best you can while we walk, and leave the rag behind. Their blood gives off a pheromone that attracts other Dactyls."

"Gives off a what?" Axel jammed his supplies into his bag, sheathed his sword, and then started to help Lilly pack, even though she really didn't need his help. But it was an excuse to get closer to her, and Axel didn't want to pass it up.

"Pheromone. It is like a scent, only much more potent. Only Dactyls can sense it."

"Watch out!" Lilly drew an arrow from her quiver and launched it into the sky. Another Dactyl screeched and plummeted to the ground right on top of their dwindling campfire.

Axel finished it off with one vicious swing at its neck, and it lay there, crackling and crisping atop the hot coals. The stench hit his nostrils then, and he almost retched all over the ground.

"Ugh. They really do stink." He buried his nose in the crook of his elbow and backed away from the dead beast.

The Dactyl had expansive wings, plus four additional limbs—two arms and two legs. Pale green skin covered its human-like body, but the resemblance stopped there.

It had a huge charcoal-gray beak in place of its mouth. Talons tipped each of its three toes, its three long fingers and one thumb on each hand, and on the tip of its tail, not unlike the spike on the end of Magnus's tail, except smaller.

The glow in its white eyes faded as more purple blood leaked from its severed head.

"Quit staring and clean off your sword, Axel," Magnus growled.

Axel unslung his pack and dug his hand into it. "Fragile birds, aren't they?"

"Make no mistake—if one of them gets ahold of you, you'll form quite the contrary opinion within a matter of seconds, if not less." Magnus started down the path. "Follow me toward the lake. Calum, bring up the rear, and make sure you watch our backs."

"Got it."

Lilly took to the sky. "I'll scout from here."

"No," Magnus waved her back down. "Stay low, with us. If they see you, it will only attract more of them."

She glided back and landed behind him. "Alright."

Axel wiped the edge of his sword with a piece of fabric he'd been saving in case someone needed a bandage, then he dropped it behind him as they ran. "I thought they attacked in groups. Dozens. *Hundreds*, you said."

Magnus didn't turn back, but Axel could hear him anyway. "We are fortunate there were not more. Just keep moving."

"There's one behind us," Calum called from the rear. "Two behind us."

Maybe they weren't so lucky after all.

"Keep moving," Magnus said. "We need to put distance between us and them. Lilly, can you shoot them down?"

"My pleasure." She nocked another arrow and took to the sky, but stayed low.

Axel refocused on following Magnus. The view wasn't nearly as good as when he'd trailed behind Lilly, but at least Magnus could get them somewhere safe.

Two bone-snapping crashes sounded behind them in quick succession. Lilly's voice followed. "We're clear."

Does she ever miss?

Lilly swooped down behind Magnus and followed him like before, and Axel's view improved once again.

He smiled.

To Calum's relief, Magnus's port town materialized on the horizon half a day later. After the first four Dactyls, they'd kept up their quickened pace for far longer than Calum thought he would last. Now, even at a walking pace, every step felt like a new and brutal punishment, both on his lungs and his aching feet.

"You don't think they got Riley, do you?" Calum walked side-by-side with Axel and Lilly while Magnus led.

Axel shrugged. "I don't know. Those things didn't seem all that dangerous to me, but I guess with a few dozen it could get pretty rough."

Calum rolled his eyes at Axel's posturing. "Yeah, but Riley's fast and stealthy, right? He probably made it past them, don't you think?"

"Like I said, I don't know," Axel repeated. "I can imagine plenty of scenarios where having a thief would be useful, so I hope he made it."

"I'm sure he's fine, Calum." Lilly put her hand on his armored shoulder, and he liked it. "He's a grown Wolf. He can take care of himself."

"Yeah. We just need to take care of ourselves now." Axel called ahead to Magnus, "You sure this is the right place?"

"Do you see any other signs of civilization around here?"

"No."

"Then I am sure."

A small wooden sign stuck in the arid ground in front of the town read "Sharkville" in scratchy letters marked with faded ink. Several months ago, Calum wouldn't have been able to read it, but Magnus had taught both Axel and him the alphabet and how to use it over the course of their journey.

Why they'd named it Sharkville, Calum couldn't say. Whatever a shark or a ville was, he didn't know, so it seemed like a nothing-word to him—just the name of the town.

Sharkville itself resembled the surrounding landscape: gray, unimpressive, and dull. A few of the buildings were large enough to constitute warehouses, but most of them barely rose above the ground on which they stood. Gray wood, occasionally patched with green mildew, made each structure in the town look like every other.

Beyond Sharkville itself lay the Central Lake, glistening and blue under the sunshine. It extended as far as the eye could see, and for some reason, the sheer breadth of it gave Calum chills.

Magnus motioned to them with his head. "Come. Let us find a vessel to charter."

A sprawling dock, also made of that same gray wood, lined the shore. Despite space for several dozen ships, only one—more of a large boat, really—floated in the waters adjacent to the dock.

"Doesn't look like we've got many options," Axel muttered.

Where Kanarah City's streets had seemed almost overcrowded to Calum, Sharkville's population either preferred to remain indoors or just didn't exist in the first place. No children played in the alleys. No merchants peddled goods from carts. No soldiers stood guard at the street corners. No one at all was outside, and none of the buildings had windows of any sort.

A weatherworn sign that hung from one of the buildings bore an image of a fish caught in a net with the word "Fishig" next to it.

"Wait here." Magnus clasped his hand on the wooden doorknob. "I will go inside and try to find out what I can."

Moments later, the door under the Fishig sign swung open again and smacked against the wooden wall.

Magnus stood in the doorway, beckoning them forward. "Come inside."

The inside of the building amounted to one room with a bookshelf, a bed, and a fat bearded man seated at a table. A big double-edged battle-axe leaned against the table leg on the man's right side, and he puffed on a pipe in his left hand.

The smoky-sweet smell of the tobacco reminded Calum of his father, who had also smoked a pipe long ago. How he'd remembered that so many years later, Calum did not know.

"Gill, here, is in charge of the docks," Magnus said. "He is willing to allow us to charter a vessel."

A man in a fishing town in charge of chartered vessels named Gill. What are the odds? Calum grinned.

Gill motioned to the chair on the opposite side of the table from where he sat.

Calum turned back to Magnus, who nodded. Behind him, Axel stood next to Lilly, closer than Calum would've liked, but in the small space, he supposed it was unavoidable.

Calum sat in the chair and faced Gill, who pulled a scrap of paper from his lap and flattened it out on the table.

He picked up a quill from the desk and dabbed it into the inkwell. "How long you gon' be fishin'?"

"Uh—" Calum looked back at Magnus, who held up three long fingers. "Three days?"

"Weeks," Magnus said. "Three weeks."

"That long?" Calum's eyebrows rose.

Gill chuckled and scribbled on his paper. "That's nothin'. Mos' our charters las' six months or longer."

"Oh." Calum faced him. "Well, three weeks, then."

"Heard you the firs' time, kid." Gill's voice flattened but he kept scribbling. "How many crew members you bringin' along?"

"Four, including me."

"Bait?"

Calum blinked. "What?"

"You bring yo' own bait, or you nee' some?"

"Uh—" Calum looked back at Magnus again.

"We need some," Magnus said. "Enough for a week. We'll make do after that."

Gill nodded then scribbled some more. "Got yo' own nets 'n lines?"

"No." Calum shook his head.

More scribbling, then Gill blew a puff of smoke from his pipe above Calum's head. "You all nev' done this befo', have you?"

"No."

"You wan' fishin' lessons too? Or a guide?"

Calum opened his mouth to speak, but Magnus beat him to it.

"No, but thank you."

Gill stared at him, then his quill danced some more. Then he set the quill down and spun the paper around to Calum. "What you think?"

There, before Calum, lay a drawing of some sort of bird—at least from what he could tell, anyway. He hadn't been sure what to expect, but a lousy piece of artwork wasn't on the list. "Very nice."

Gill laughed. It sounded like he'd *swallowed* a bird and its bones had lodged somewhere between his throat and his chest. "It's terrible, an' we bo' know it."

Calum raised his eyebrows, filled with uncertainty. "Alright…?"

"You got yo'seff a boat, kid, but I nee' somethin' to kee' fo' collateral 'n somethin' to pay fo' the charter isseff."

That might be a problem. "We don't have anyth—"

Magnus dropped a leather pouch on the table. "This should cover both."

Before Calum could respond, Gill snatched the pouch from the table and dumped out its contents. When shimmering gemstones in a variety of colors spilled across the table. Calum's jaw clenched. Magnus must've collected some of the stones from Nicolai's body after the Gronyx killed him back in the tunnel.

Gill extended his hand. "Deal."

Calum stared at the gems and sighed. He hadn't known Nicolai for long, but using his remains this way soured his stomach.

Calum exhaled a long breath and shook Gill's hand. "Deal."

Gill smiled, then he stood up and grabbed his battle-axe by the handle. "Follow me. I'll show you to yo' floater."

As Gill walked out the back door behind his desk, Calum stood and nudged Magnus. "Where'd you get those?"

"You know where I got them."

"You sure we should be using Nicolai's crystalized remains to pay for this?"

236

"He gave his life to save you in that tunnel. He would have wanted this, too." Magnus placed a hand on Calum's shoulder. "Besides, there is no other way."

Calum clenched his teeth, but nodded.

"Hey." Axel waved at them from the back door and pointed to the sign above his head. "Come on. I want to go 'fishig.'"

Lilly smacked his shoulder. "Don't be so obnoxious."

Outside, Gill's jovial persona reverted back to the solemn presence he'd displayed when Calum first sat down at his table. His eyes searched the skies and scanned the shoreline, and his knuckles whitened as he gripped his battle-axe.

Sure enough, Gill led them to the only ship—boat—docked there. The words *Baroness of Destiny* adorned the ship's hull. "She all yo's for three wee's. Bait's arready isside, same's the nets 'n lines 'n other s'pplies. Have fun."

Gill glanced over the lake again then started back toward the town with his sack of gems in one hand, his battle-axe in the other, and his pipe in his mouth.

"Dumbest name for a ship I've ever heard," Axel said once Gill was out of sight.

"And how many ships did you encounter in your years on your family farm?" Magnus asked.

Axel scowled at him. "It's still a dumb name."

The boat could certainly accommodate four people, but from its appearance, Calum didn't know how it managed to stay afloat. Black patches the size of human skulls dotted its gray hull, and a network of dark cracks worked from the ship's bow down to the water line. A mast, twenty feet tall with a patchwork sail, towered from the center of the boat.

Despite the boat's small size, the hull seemed thick enough that there could've been a small cabin inside. The main deck looked as if a whirlwind had tossed a bunch of barrels, ropes, and tools around.

Not that Calum knew anything about sailing or fishing or what most of that stuff was supposed to be used for, but still... Burtis never would've allowed the quarry's toolshed to get this messy. Not in a thousand years.

Calum knelt down for a closer look at the burgundy-brown marks that stretched across almost the entire deck. "What are these streaks?"

Magnus growled. "Blood."

CHAPTER 4

"What?" Calum straightened up. "Whose blood is it?"

"I have a bad feeling about this." Magnus shook his head. "Perhaps we should not take this boat out after all."

"Really?" Axel raised his hands and slapped the sides of his hips with a huff. "You dragged us all the way out here, and now you don't even want to go fishing?"

"I think you mean 'fishig,' Axel," Lilly interjected with a smirk. Then she winked at Calum, who matched her with a sly grin of his own.

"Funny," Axel said, still frowning. "But I'm serious. Are we doing this or not?"

"Where do you think all this blood came from, Axel?" Magnus asked. "Something attacked the ship and probably killed the crew. You saw the dire condition of the hull."

"Then how did Gill end up with the ship?" Axel jammed his fists into his hips.

"Perhaps some of them made it back, but some of them obviously did not." Magnus kicked a rope aside, revealing the largest dark red spot on the deck they'd found thus far. "This is a *lot* of blood."

"How do you know they didn't kill whatever attacked them? Maybe that's where the blood came from. Maybe they cleaned the fish they caught and that's where the blood came from."

"Then where are they?" Calum asked.

"I don't know." Axel shrugged. "Probably already left for Kanarah City, or they crossed to the other side to sell their catches."

"Or they are dead." Magnus stared at Axel, who set his jaw.

"Either way, we're low on food, and we're already here," Lilly said. "Many of the fish in this lake are considered delicacies in Aeropolis, and the fact that the ship made it back at all, regardless of whatever happened, is a good sign. I think we should go."

"I'm with Lilly." Axel folded his arms.

Magnus looked at Calum. "It is your decision to make."

Calum met each of their eyes. He didn't love that he had to make the call, but ever since Magnus had declared him leader of their group, it had fallen to him.

In any case, the reality of the situation was sobering: either they risked starvation while trying to cross the rest of the way to Western Kanarah, or they risked starvation while trying to catch fish out on the lake.

At least with the latter option, they would be doing something to try to change their fates.

"I don't think we have a choice at this point," Calum said. "We need to risk it. We're going fishing."

HIGH ABOVE THE SHIP, Lilly hovered on watch, her eyes scanning the endless waters both for schools of fish and any signs of trouble. Thus far, the waters and the skies had remained calm and clear except for a few patches of clouds. On the whole, it made for a sunny and pleasant autumn day.

Below her, Calum, Axel, and Magnus lowered the ship's nets over the side of the *Baroness of Destiny*, which now floated several miles out from the shore.

Within two hours, they managed to haul in a couple dozen fish, and Lilly dropped down for a landing. When Magnus showed them how to clean the fish with a knife, the foul stench of fish guts hit Lilly's nose.

"Now the only thing we gotta do is cook these before we eat 'em." Axel scanned the ship's deck. "But I don't know where we can safely set a fire aboard the ship."

Magnus smirked and stuffed a whole fish the size of a man's forearm into his mouth—scales, bones, head, and all. The sight of it shocked Lilly, but only for a moment. After all, he was just behaving like a Saurian.

Axel wrinkled his nose. "Unless you're a giant lizard, apparently."

"Let me see your knife," Lilly said.

"Huh?" Axel looked at her. "Why?"

"You don't have to cook the fish to eat it."

Calum glanced at Axel and then at Lilly. "How do you figure?"

"We eat it raw all the time in Aeropolis. You just have to prepare it the right way." Lilly reached toward Axel. "May I use your knife, please?"

Axel handed it to her, and she filleted one of the larger fish and delicately separated the scales from its flesh.

When she finished, she held the glistening orange filet in her bare hand. Not as good as a professional cook might've done, but not bad, either. "Who wants it?"

"How about *you* eat it first?" Axel motioned to her with his head.

Magnus chomped into another fish, this one still writhing in his hand. A second bite and it disappeared down his throat.

Lilly shrugged and bit off a sizable bite of the filet. It didn't taste quite as good as when the chefs prepared it for her back home, but it filled her belly all the same. "See? It's good. A little squishy and weird the first time you try it, but otherwise it's good."

Calum extended his hand. "I'll try it."

"Give me half, will you?" Axel held his hand out too, and Calum handed him his portion.

They both popped the fish into their mouths and chewed, then swallowed. Lilly grinned as their faces twisted with disgust, but they gradually softened to guarded curiosity.

She glanced between the two of them. "What do you think?"

"Not bad," Calum replied.

Axel swallowed his bite and stuck out his tongue. "I think I'm gonna figure out how to cook it before I eat any more."

239

Lilly chuckled and nodded. "It's not for everyone. Usually, you're supposed to eat it with some other ingredients too, and they can really improve the taste."

"*That* I believe," Axel said.

"I'm heading back up to scout some more," Lilly said. "Axel, if you figure out how to cook the fish on board, signal me."

He nodded. "Will do. Calum can keep cleaning the fish while I handle that."

"What?" Calum tilted his head. "That's not fair."

Magnus devoured another fish whole.

Axel shook his head. "And you can just keep eating them raw, I guess."

"Gladly." Magnus smiled and patted his armored belly.

Lilly gave Calum another look. Their eyes met, and drops of molten excitement dripped into her gut. She had to look away.

She sprang into the air, contemplating how and why Calum made her feel that way as the wind rippled through her cape.

They'd been friends ever since they'd helped her escape the slave traders. After that, as she'd gotten to know him, she'd formed a bond with him—closer than she'd have expected in such a short time, but nothing sky-shattering.

Still, she couldn't deny the feelings that soared through her body when their eyes met for too long. She'd come to love his blue eyes; they reminded her of the sky, a place where she felt totally free.

Perhaps that was the answer behind it all: when she was around Calum, she felt truly free.

Within seconds, she ascended fifty feet above the ship's mast. Down below, Axel and Calum continued arguing who would try to cook the fish and who would clean them. She shook her head at them with a smile.

In truth, they were both great guys. Axel was definitely the more outspoken and confident of the two, but Calum—well, there was just something about him. Something different. Something—

A dark form broke the golden horizon to the north of the ship. Lilly squinted at it, but it was too far away to see. Even so, she could tell it had to be large, given how big it seemed even from such a distance.

She swooped down in a wide arc and landed on the deck just behind Axel. He jumped and whirled around to face her.

"What'd you sneak up on me for?" He glowered at her.

Lilly didn't bother apologizing. "There's something on the horizon to the north."

Magnus, Calum, and Axel redirected their attention toward what she'd seen.

"I don't see anything," Calum said.

Axel shielded the sunlight from his eyes with his left hand and leaned over the edge of the boat. "I don't see anything."

"It's there," Lilly said. "I saw it from the air, but I couldn't make out what it was."

"I see it. It is quite far away," Magnus said. "But I have better vision than humans do."

Calum turned to her. "Can you get a closer look at it?"

"Of course." Lilly jumped up to the railing that lined the edge of the boat, leaped into the air, and zipped into the sky toward the form. Almost three minutes later, the form sharpened into the shape of a ship, a mammoth compared to the *Baroness of Destiny*.

It had black sails.

Lilly cursed under her breath, then she repeated it aloud.

She pivoted in midair and swooped back toward their boat faster than she'd left. By submitting to gravity's pull, she picked up incredible speed as she approached the water's surface. Just before she would have impacted the water, she pulled up and shot toward the boat like one of her arrows screaming through the air.

She made it back in less than a minute thanks to her fancy flying. The soles of her boots touched down on the boat's deck between Axel and Calum.

"What is it?" Magnus asked.

"Pirates. We need to get out of here now."

Axel and Calum looked at each other, then Calum squinted at her. "Pirates?"

Lilly tilted her head and her mouth hung open.

"They are identical to bandits, only they live on water and have ships," Magnus explained. "The difference is that they have an incredible advantage on the water. This is their home, and we are but strangers. Lilly is right. We need to get out of here."

"Hey, if they're bandits, I say we take 'em on. Sounds like fun. Fishing's kinda boring anyway." Axel glanced between the three of them, then centered on Magnus. "Plus, we've got you as a Sobek now. What have we got to lose?"

Lilly stared at him. Someday, Axel's confidence was going to get him in trouble. Part of Lilly hoped she'd be there to see it, and another part of her really hoped she wouldn't.

"Our lives." Magnus leveled his gaze at Axel. "You cannot go through this world fighting everyone you dislike."

"I guess we see things differently, Scales." Axel folded his arms.

"Furthermore, we lack the sailing ability and know-how to fend them off," Magnus continued. "My comprehension of water-based combat is nominal at best. If they sink this ship while we are still on it, we stand no chance of surviving, especially in these waters."

"We're also probably outnumbered, as usual," Calum added.

Axel shook his head. "I still say we should fight."

"And I say we leave. Head back to shore." Calum started toward the mast. "Which of these ropes does what again?"

Magnus's voice hardened. "Calum is right. We have enough trouble as it is without having to deal with pirates, too."

Axel sighed. "Fine. I'll get on the wheel."

Lilly heard their conversation, but her eyes had focused on the approaching ship. "Hurry. They're getting closer."

Magnus followed her line of sight. "They are approaching fast. Does this vessel have any oars?"

"Now you think you're gonna row us outta here?" Axel scoffed from behind the wheel.

"That must be how they are catching up to us," Magnus said. "The wind is too light to account for their speed."

Lilly shook her head. "What do you need me to do to help?"

Magnus pointed toward the top of the mast. "Fly up and unfurl the sails. You can get up there faster than we can, and even a little wind is better than none."

She zipped into the air and loosed the sails in seconds, and Calum continued to work beneath her. The modest wind caught the broad fabric, and within a minute, the boat began to carve through the water away from the pirates.

"Turn starboard," Magnus called to Axel. "Hard starboard. Away from their ship."

Axel tilted his head and held out one of his arms. "What?"

"To the *right*. Do it now."

"Why didn't you just say that?" Axel cranked the wheel.

Though the *Baroness of Destiny* began to pick up speed, the pirate ship still gained on them. Lilly landed next to Magnus and watched as the pirate ship loomed ever larger.

"We are not going to make it." Magnus shook his head. "They are too fast."

"What do we do?" Lilly asked.

Magnus stared down at her. "You should fly away. Get to safety. There is no reason you should have to endure the forthcoming bloodshed."

"Not a chance. You three saved my life. I'm fighting with you." Lilly slung her quiver and bow over her shoulder and unsheathed her new sword.

"I suspected you would say that." He turned to face Axel. "It looks like your wish is granted, Axel. Ready your weapons. You too, Calum."

Axel smirked and drew his sword. "Alright. Let's do this."

In minutes, the pirate ship closed within several hundred yards of their boat. That's when the attack began. Six Windgales with sabers flew ahead of the pirate ship and swooped toward the *Baroness of Destiny*.

Lilly shot straight up into the sky to try to draw them away, but only two of them followed her. The other four continued toward the *Baroness of Destiny*.

The two Windgales were quick and lithe, but she was quicker. She darted around the air and ducked under their saber slashes, all while wielding her own blade. Finally, she could properly test the bit of sword training she'd done since the fight with the bandits.

After awhile, the two Windgales stopped attacking and just circled her in the sky. Then, in a coordinated effort, they closed in on her and swung their swords. With a smirk she plunged toward the waters below, and the Windgales chased her.

As before, she pulled up at the last instant, only this time the tip of her left boot caressed the water in the process. Behind her a splash sounded. She stole a glance and saw a cape and some flailing limbs in the water. Impacting the water at that speed would be almost as bone-shattering as hitting solid ground.

A saber lashed at her from the right. Had she not already had her sword out to block the blow, it could have killed her or knocked her into the water, which was almost equally as dangerous.

She traded sloppy blows with the remaining Windgale, who seemed to have even less experience with a blade than she. Lilly adjusted her trajectory as she dueled with the Windgale, mostly dodging or avoiding his swings but parrying a few as best as she could manage for not knowing how to sword-fight.

The actual fight didn't matter, though. If she could keep his focus on her and not where they were headed—

The Windgale swiped at Lilly's head.

Perfect. She ducked under it then blasted upward in time to avoid colliding with the *Baroness of Destiny*'s hull. The Windgale didn't.

A sickening *thud* reached Lilly's ears from below, followed by a faint splash. He wouldn't recover from that.

TOGETHER WITH AXEL AND MAGNUS, Calum handled the other four Windgales, but not without difficulty.

The Windgales weren't more capable fighters—they were just quicker. A *lot* quicker, which made them hard to hit. Calum regretted not taking the opportunity to spar with Lilly more often.

Even so, he found success in baiting them to come after him, and once they did, he'd dodge the blow and Axel, positioned behind him, would take a swing at the Windgale. They downed two of them that way.

Magnus, on the other hand, didn't employ any such trickery. He simply waited for them to attack, and then he let them. Their puny swords deflected off his scales or off his breastplate, and on their follow-up swing, he would grab one of their limbs and slam them against the deck. Even though he didn't need to, Magnus followed each slam with a final blow from his sword.

Calum had to smile—until he realized what was coming next.

By the time the trio defeated the four Windgales, the pirate ship had pulled alongside the boat. Humans clad in dark clothing swung on ropes from the pirate ship's towering masts and landed on the *Baroness of Destiny*'s deck. More Windgales dropped aboard the boat from the sky, and even a handful of Saurians extended long wooden planks from the pirate ship to the side of the *Baroness of Destiny*.

Magnus, Calum, and Axel stood back-to-back, their swords ready, as the pirates swarmed aboard the boat. Within moments, the pirates had them totally surrounded.

"Give up yar weapons," a voice growled from behind the half-dozen Saurians who'd stepped across the planks.

From among them, a hulking, muscular form emerged, covered with dark-brown fur. A Wolf of some sort, but he walked upright and wore a burgundy wide-brimmed hat. A big white feather stuck out from the black ribbon that wrapped around the hat above its brim. He also wore a long black cape that billowed behind him in the wind.

"I said to give up yar weapons." The Wolf's vibrant amber eyes glistened under the brim of his hat. "Or we'll be takin' them from ye, along with yar lives."

Magnus stepped forward, his colossal broadsword still in-hand. "I do not fear you or any Werewolf. You may be faster than me, but neither you nor your crew can penetrate my skin or out-muscle me. Now get off our ship."

The Werewolf shook his head. "So's it may be, none of us can *individually* overpower ye or do ye much harm, but ye also be outnumbered three fives to one."

Something *thunked* above their heads.

The Werewolf jerked his hand upright and clamped his fist shut. A thin wooden shaft vibrated in his hand for an instant, then it stopped moving altogether, its arrowhead lingering about three inches from his head.

Calum chanced a look up. Lilly hovered above them, her mouth open and eyes wide. She still held her bow in front of her body as if taking aim again, but she hadn't nocked a new arrow.

The Werewolf tossed the arrow aside and shook his finger at her. "Ye be havin' to do better'an that to best the likes o' me, m'dear."

Magnus lunged forward and lashed his sword at the Werewolf, and the surrounding pirates converged on Calum and Axel while a few Windgales flew up to engage Lilly.

Calum swung his weapon with fervor and felled a few of the pirates, but it didn't take long for their numbers to overwhelm him. He took a few punches to his face and gut, then someone batted his sword from his hands.

Two burly human pirates wrapped up his arms and pinned him to the deck. Since leaving the quarry, Calum had gotten somewhat stronger, but not nearly enough to pull free of their grasp.

Axel fared a little better, but not by much. He broke free from the human pirates who initially held onto him and leveled one of them with a haymaker, but two of the Saurians grabbed him from behind. Though they'd anchored his arms in place, even they struggled to hang onto him.

Magnus's first three swings failed to connect with the Werewolf who, when moving to avoid

Magnus's attacks, resembled a dark blur to Calum. Three Saurians came at Magnus from behind and tried to restrain him, but he threw them off as if they weighed nothing.

When he turned back, Magnus caught a swipe to his face from the Werewolf's claws, which left four shallow cuts on the side of his snout. Magnus recoiled a half step then retaliated with a swat of his own, but the Werewolf easily ducked under it. One of the Saurians recovered and grabbed Magnus from behind again.

"I don't have to kill ye to beat ye," the Werewolf said. "I've other fine options to attain victory at me disposal."

Magnus reached over his shoulder, grabbed the Saurian's arm, and slammed him down in front of him. He raised his sword to finish the Saurian off, but the other two Saurians grabbed his arms again, stalling him just long enough.

Calum's heart seized in his chest as the Werewolf charged forward and drove his shoulder into Magnus's gut.

Magnus's footing faltered, and he tipped backward over the edge of the boat. Along with the two Saurians, he fell into the water below.

LAKE WATER SMOTHERED Magnus's senses. It filled his mouth, his nostrils, and his lungs. His eyes opened and he saw sunlight above him.

Sword in-hand, he kicked and clawed toward it, desperate for air. His armor weighed on him more than usual, and instead of being his ally, it continued to try to pull him down to the dark depths of the lake.

Had he taken a solid breath before he'd hit the water, he could have stayed under for at least ten minutes, and that was from when he'd tried it as a Saurian. As a Sobek, it probably would've been longer.

Despite his armor, his head finally surfaced, and he coughed out the excess water. Sweet air took its place and his ears opened.

"—agnus!" Calum's voice sounded from above. "Magnus! Look out!"

A hand grabbed his shoulder and pushed him underwater again. One of the Saurians.

Magnus flailed and broke free, then he resurfaced. A hard whip of his tail propelled him away from the Saurian, but also away from the boat. He glanced back.

The Saurian swam after him, but an arrow plunged into the top of his shoulder, and he stopped with a snarl.

Above Magnus, Lilly floated thirty feet above the water and twenty feet out from the boat. She nocked another arrow.

"After her!" The Werewolf pointed at Lilly, and three Windgale pirates darted into the sky.

Lilly twisted in the air and loosed her next arrow. It lodged in the forehead of one of the Windgale pirates, and he crashed down into the water about thirty feet from Magnus's position.

"Get away, Lilly!" Magnus hollered. "Fly away!"

She gave him a nod and shot into the clouds overhead.

The Saurian in the water ripped the arrow from his shoulder and started toward Magnus again. Blood pulsed from the wound, and along with the dead Windgale, the otherwise clear blue water around Magnus had accumulated a cloudy reddish tint.

Another set of hands latched onto Magnus's right arm and tried to wrest the sword from his iron grip. The second Saurian.

Magnus wrenched his arm away, launched himself up out of the water with a forceful thrust of his arms, legs, and tail, and he swung his sword down at the second Saurian.

The second Saurian dodged the blow and swam a few feet away from Magnus, and the Saurian behind Magnus grabbed his left arm. The second Saurian clamped onto Magnus's right arm as he raised his sword to finish off the first Saurian.

He sucked in a sharp but deep breath as they pulled him underwater. Combined with the weight of his armor, their combined strength managed to subdue him, even if only temporarily.

These pirates were no doubt accustomed to swimming in the deep waters of the Central Lake and had proven far more adept at it than Magnus was, but they wouldn't drown him. He refused to die here, in this way. He had too much unfinished business to resolve.

As Magnus strained against them, one of them released his arm, but not from anything Magnus did to twist free. When Magnus looked, the Saurian was gone, replaced by a large cloud of red.

Oh, no...

Magnus broke free from the other Saurian and surfaced again. As Magnus filled his lungs to capacity, Calum's shouts filled his ears again in another warning.

But Magnus already knew what had happened to the other Saurian, and he'd abandoned any thoughts of righting the wrongs inflicted upon him and his family in Reptilius. Instead, only one motivation drove him: survive.

But was it already too late? Not if he could get back aboard the *Baroness of Destiny* quickly enough to avoid the same fate.

The other Saurian grabbed and yanked on his right arm again, and Magnus's grip on his sword faltered. It dropped from his hand into the water. He jerked free and torpedoed down after it, his tail and all four limbs lashing at the cool water with full fury.

He had to get that sword before it disappeared forever.

The Saurian kept pace with him and grabbed Magnus's tail, but just as soon as grabbed on, he let go. A shadow passed over Magnus, and a bubbling roar bellowed through the water, then abruptly ceased.

Magnus didn't have to look back. He knew the Saurian was already dead.

The sword knifed down, down, down through the water, but Magnus chased it nonetheless, even as the waters grew murkier, darker. This time, the added weight of his armor was working *for* him as he descended into the depths.

Yet even as he chased his sword, the primal animalistic part of his brain crackled with warnings, threatening to override his calm and make him panic. Whatever had gotten the other two Saurians now chased him. He could sense it behind him, drawing closer and closer.

Magnus resisted the urge to flee, resisted the urge to abandon his sword to the depths. It was his only chance of defending himself. His only chance of staying alive.

His hardened scales and armor would do him little good against one of the fabled beasts that made its home in this lake, especially one big enough that it only left a cloud of blood in the water in the wake of its attack on the first Saurian.

Magnus kicked and whipped his tail with all his might until his fingers coiled around the sword's silver hilt. He tightened his grip, then he whirled around in the water to face the monster.

There was nothing there.

LILLY PLOWED through the nearest white cloud. Normally, she'd savor the puffs of water vapor that cooled her cheeks under the sun, but with two Windgale pirates not far behind, she didn't have time to idle. As quickly as she entered the cloud, she dropped out of it, then she curved up and into another one.

The Windgales chased her just as she figured they would: they followed the trail she carved through the clouds and didn't bother to try to cut her off or try anything else. Did they expect her to tire out? Or run out of ideas and give up?

Whatever they thought, they were wrong. She hadn't been kidnapped by slave traders, escaped, and survived an encounter with not one but *two* Gronyxes to be brought down by a pair of idiot Windgale pirates.

Again using gravity's pull to her advantage, she looped through the air with incredible speed and reentered the cloud from which she'd just exited. She drew her sword, waited a beat, then swung the instant she saw a dark form flicker toward her from inside the cloud.

Her blade connected just below a stunned face, and the Windgale pirate dropped out of the cloud, his arms and legs limp.

One down, one to go.

Magnus's head swiveled, but he couldn't see anything around him, partially due to the darker, deeper waters in which he floated. High above him, the sunlight amounted to little more than a pale orb, barely visible.

No reason to stay here any longer than he had to. Wherever the thing had gone didn't matter. The lake was home to dozens, hundreds—even *thousands* of other creatures both big and brutal enough to take him out.

The two vessels, now comparable in size to a big leaf next to a small leaf, floated on the surface. Magnus's tail swished back into action and he fought against his armor as he began to ascend again until his head broke through the surface.

"Magnus!" This time it was Axel's voice calling as Magnus inhaled a deep and wondrous breath.

Magnus wanted to respond, but his eyes locked on the Werewolf captain, who stared back at him.

"Like I said..." The Werewolf smirked. "*I* don't have to kill ye to beat ye."

Next to the Werewolf, Calum's eyes widened. He opened his mouth to scream, but his voice disappeared against the deafening thunder of water that surged at Magnus from his left.

His sword ready, Magnus braced himself for the blow as a dark finned form emerged from the swell. Dozens of spearhead-sized teeth lined its gaping mouth, all of them aimed at Magnus.

He swung his blade just as the beast hit him, and then everything went black.

CHAPTER 5

Calum's scream died in his throat.

Magnus was gone. Instead, a black dorsal fin and matching tail thrashed in the bloodied water, then it all disappeared beneath the lake's rippling surface.

"You brigand!" Axel strained against his Saurian captors and almost tore free until one of them punched him in his stomach. He doubled over and gasped in between curses.

Calum wanted to try to break free as well, but he knew there was no use. Even after taking down a few of the pirates before they got ahold of Axel and him, he knew they couldn't possibly overcome the rest of them, not without Magnus.

Magnus is... gone.

The image of the giant fish launching out of the water toward Magnus, its ferocious teeth bared, and pummeling his body below the water's surface twisted Calum's gut. All of his memories with Magnus, everything they'd endured and survived together—it all faded to darkness against the horror of Magnus's death.

When the Werewolf's dark-brown hind paws stepped into view, Calum realized he'd let his head droop. He raised his head with defiance on his mind.

The Werewolf smirked. "Ye've got a lot o' spirit. Ye contain it inside, unlike yar comrade here, who lets it lead 'im to shipwreck. Can't help but wonder what'll happen when ye finally loose your terrible fury. Will ye be able to control yarself?"

"I'm *not* your friend." Calum's jaw hardened. "You murdered Magnus."

The Werewolf waved his hand in front of his chest and shook his head. "I did no such thing. Ye saw what happened to 'im yarself. A shark got 'im."

Calum recalled the name of the meager town where they'd set sail: Sharkville. It had been a warning of sorts, but he hadn't known to heed it at the time.

Indignant, he said, "*You* knocked him overboard."

"Had he surrendered, he would surely still breathe this fragrant lake air. The Overlord has exacted justice upon 'im, and I shall not question it." The Werewolf leaned so close that Calum could smell the stink of fish on his breath. "Now what be yar name?"

"What do you care? Go on and kill us already. Get it over with."

The Werewolf straightened up and tilted his head. "Who said anything about killin' ye? Young 'n healthy, ye be. I'm making ye a part o' me crew."

"We don't want to be part of your crew." Axel stood up and kept straining against the Saurians who held him in place. "So let us go."

"Is he always so demandin'?" The Werewolf pointed at Axel with his thumb. Part of Calum wanted to say yes, but he bit his tongue. "Ye don't have a choice."

"You can't *make* us join your crew," Axel said.

"Aye, but I can, an' I will," the Werewolf countered. "I don't have to kill ye, and I don't have to let ye go. Like I said: ye don't have a choice."

Axel spat on the deck near the Werewolf's feet, which earned him a backhanded smack from the Werewolf's thick paw.

"What be yar name, boy?" the Werewolf asked.

Axel glared at him. "Axel. Remember it when you're laying at my feet, begging for mercy."

The Werewolf chuckled. "Yar sense of humor is palpable."

"I'm not joking."

"Nor am I, boy." The Werewolf stepped back to Calum. "And ye be called...?"

"Calum."

The Werewolf nodded. "I be Brink, cap'n o' the pirate ship *Malice*. Welcome to me crew."

BY NOW LILLY had to have lost the other Windgale pirate. He'd stopped following her, and she'd stopped popping in and out of clouds.

Still, if she'd learned anything from getting captured by Roderick and his men that first time, it was to never let her guard down in the vicinity of danger.

Perhaps the Windgale had given up and flown back to his ship, or perhaps he was hiding in one of the clouds, waiting for her to fly past and then ambush her. Either way, she'd behave like he was still out there, hunting her.

Hovering near the clouds had lost its advantages, so she dropped down to about ten feet above the water level and took a moment to regain her bearings. She'd flown northwest from the ships once Magnus told her to fly away, and she'd gone so far that now the ships were out of sight.

No matter—she'd find her way back to her friends, and she'd find a way to rescue them, just as they'd done for her.

Lilly maintained her ten-foot altitude as she headed back the direction she'd come, more or less. Every so often she'd glance down at the water and see her shadow tracing her route along the water. If another one showed up behind her or in front of her, she'd know she wasn't alone.

After a few minutes of constant flight, she stopped and scanned the waters. Still no ships in sight. Was she going the right way? Perhaps a higher altitude, while more dangerous, would give a better view of the surrounding waterscape.

As she climbed higher, something whistled on her right side.

She brandished her sword in time to fend off a savage attack from the Windgale pirate, but the force of his blow sent her careening down toward the water. She righted herself about twenty feet above the surf and dodged the pirate's next attack.

He blazed past her, but her body jerked down after him. His left hand had latched onto the corner of her cape, and he yanked her toward him.

Lilly reacted blade-first. Her weapon clanged against his, but this Windgale fought with more skill than the others. He deflected her next swing, clamped down on her right wrist with his left hand, then jabbed his sword at her gut.

She twisted her body out of the way just in time, then she caught the wrist of his sword hand with her left hand just as he'd done to her.

He glowered at her with bloodshot brown eyes and a snarl churning his scarred face. His cape billowed behind him, black like the sails of the pirate ship.

Lilly's hold didn't last long. He was stronger—much stronger. He wrenched free and lashed his chipped cutlass sword at her midsection.

She kicked both her feet up over her head, and his sword severed only the air. She rotated her wrist hard, breaking his grip. An errant slash at his hand only managed to carve a small cut into his palm.

He growled and charged. His arms wrapped around her waist, and from ten feet up, they slammed into the water—the one place she didn't want to be.

Everything blurred under the water, and her lungs begged for air. Panic threatened to overwhelm her. She'd swum before—certainly as a child and for fun—but she'd never engaged in water-based combat. Staying above the water had been her preference, but now she had no choice.

He still held onto her, and no matter how she thrashed, he refused to let go. Even when she dug the heel of her boot into his shin, he refused to release her. With no other options, she lurched forward, toward his scarred face, and sank her desperate teeth into his nose.

Blood erupted from the wound, and he released her to clench at the new scars she'd given him. Finally, she swam up to the surface.

Air expanded her lungs as she treaded water. Swimming wasn't like flying—it was so much harder. Her body felt as if it weighed five times as much as usual.

She pushed against the water to boost herself into the air so she could fly again, but as soon as she took flight, the pirate grabbed her cape again and hauled her back down into the water.

This time his hand clamped onto her hair and he held her underwater, facing away from him. She kicked and struggled and maneuvered, but she couldn't break free. Her body ached, and her lungs expelled the last of the air she'd sucked in before going under.

She shifted her grip so her sword pointed back at him, but he clamped onto her wrist and kept her from stabbing at him. Her left hand found his, and she dug her fingernails into his knuckles, drawing more blood, but he still didn't let go.

No matter what she did or tried, his grip continued to hold her in place.

The air in her lungs turned toxic. She needed to breathe.

But the pirate refused to budge.

This is it, she realized. She would die in the lake, at the hands of some common pirate. She'd never see her parents, her home, or her people again. *It's over.*

Lilly closed her eyes and prepared for the water to fill her anxious lungs.

Vertigo flipped her upside down and sent her spiraling through the water. The pirate had completely let go of her—both her hair and her wrist. She clambered for the surface and found it with a gasp and a lot of sputtering.

The pirate wasn't anywhere to be seen.

She jumped out of the water and ascended five feet into the air again, her sword ready, her eyes searching everywhere.

The pirate burst out of the water a second later, flying right at her with an expression of terror etched into his scarred bloody face, but before he could reach her, a massive black mouth full of huge pointed teeth chomped shut on his legs.

Lilly's eyes widened.

The pirate screamed.

The jaws opened again, and the rest of the pirate dropped inside the monster's gullet, but the monster didn't stop coming at her. Its lifeless black eyes rolled back into its wide head as its jaws opened even wider, greedy to taste her flesh next

Lilly recoiled and rolled to her left, and something solid smacked against her back. She hit the water again. She must've drifted too low, and now she was back in the waves, treading water.

And the monster was coming for her next.

A black dorsal fin pierced the surface, circled back, and raced toward her.

Lilly thrust herself out of the water and took to the sky as the monster leaped at her. Its angled nose smacked the sides of her boots and threw her off her trajectory, but she managed to stay in the air this time.

The creature smacked back down into the water as she flew higher and higher until she hovered a hundred feet above the waterline. Its dorsal fin circled a red spot in the water a few more times, then it finally submerged and didn't reappear.

Drenched, startled, and somehow still holding her sword, Lilly shut her eyes and logged a silent prayer of thanks to the Overlord. She sheathed her sword, gripped her cape in her hands, and twisted it until most of the water squeezed out, then she did the same thing to her hair. She could air dry the rest of herself with a few acrobatic spirals at higher altitudes later on.

Somehow, her bowstring hadn't snapped amid all the fighting and thrashing, so her bow was still slung over her shoulder. She still had all of her remaining arrows in her quiver, too—everything she hadn't already fired, anyway. It was designed specifically for Windgales so the arrows wouldn't fall out during loops and stunts. Apparently, it held up in water, too.

Good enough for now.

She had to get back to the boat to see what had happened to her friends. Lilly zipped upward, set her altitude to just below the clouds and plenty high above the water, and she headed southeast.

Fifteen minutes later, she found their boat, now empty and capsized. The bait and some of the equipment floated in crates in the water, and some of the fish still wriggled in the nets now strewn overboard while more of those huge black water monsters circled and occasionally nipped at the nets.

She counted at least three dorsal fins in close proximity to the boat—more than enough to keep her from descending too low, especially after her last close encounter with the beasts.

The pirate ship was gone, out of sight.

The last she'd seen of them, Magnus was in the water, and Calum and Axel were captured. She couldn't do anything about Magnus—either he'd made it or not—but if the pirates had taken Calum and Axel back to their ship, maybe there was still a chance to help them.

A voice inside her mind urged her to continue the journey back to Aeropolis alone, but her heart wouldn't abide it. If there was even a chance her friends were still alive, she had to do everything possible to save them.

Either way, she would know as soon as she found that pirate ship.

CHAPTER 6

Pain split Calum's back. Krogan, a scar-faced Saurian and first mate aboard the *Malice*, drew his hand back for another lash. The whip seared into Calum's flesh like a hot poker. He ground his teeth and dropped to his hands and knees.

"Hey, cut it out." From the tone of Axel's voice, Calum knew he was going to do something stupid. "You wanna whip someone, whip me."

Yep. Stupid.

The whip cracked again, and Axel landed on the deck next to Calum with a red laceration that stretched from just below his left eye down his cheek. Blood oozed from the fresh wound.

"I can take a beating, Axel," Calum whispered to him. "I had more than my share at the quarry."

"Doesn't mean you should have to take any more." Krogan's whip cracked again, and Axel winced.

"Doesn't mean you should take them for me, either."

"While you're down there, start scrubbin' the deck." Krogan grunted. "Wanna see my pretty green face in its reflection within the hour."

Krogan tossed two coarse scrub brushes in front of them, and a burly human pirate set down a sudsy bucket within their reach.

Right after Calum and Axel boarded the *Malice*, the pirates stripped them of their armor and confiscated their weapons. Another pirate took the remainder of their equipment and supplies away, and Krogan promptly put them to work.

Even in spite of their situation, Calum had to note the irony: Krogan, a Saurian, was whipping him in order to force him to perform manual labor, just as Calum had been ordered to whip Magnus back at the quarry. Funny how things turned out sometimes.

Fire flared along Calum's back again.

"I said *start scrubbin'*," Krogan roared.

Calum picked up the brush, dunked it into the bucket, and jammed it against the deck.

By NIGHTFALL, Lilly still hadn't found the pirate ship, and all her flying was beginning to wear on her. She'd begun to lose hope when she noticed an orange flicker down on the water, probably a couple miles away.

As she closed in on the sight, she recognized those familiar black sails under the moonlight and the deck of a pirate ship alive with multiple oil lamps.

If only Axel had found one of those aboard their now-sunken boat, perhaps he could've found a way to cook his fish with it, she mused, then she refocused on the task ahead.

"Got you," she muttered.

Yes, she'd found the ship, but what was she supposed to do now?

THE LOCK in the cell door clunked into place with a quarter-turn of the skeleton key, one of about a half-dozen lookalikes that hung from Krogan's belt on an iron key ring.

Axel had noted it the instant he saw Krogan. The Saurian always wore it on his right side, at least so far, and he knew it unhooked from Krogan's belt a certain way, or it wouldn't come off at all.

Important information to know and remember for later on. But at the moment, Axel faced more pressing concerns, like his own exhaustion, the lingering sting from Krogan's whiplashes, and the six disgruntled prisoners with whom he and Calum currently shared a ten-by-ten cell.

"Evening," he said with a nod.

None of them responded, but Calum nodded to them as well.

"I'm Calum," he said. "This is Axel. We're, uh—we're new."

"How do things usually go at night around here?" Axel's gaze flitted between the hardened faces in his cell to those of the prisoners in the adjacent cell.

No one said a word, but no one broke eye contact either.

Axel clapped his hands and waved. "Hello? Anyone? All your tongues get cut out or something?"

"Why don't you two just shut up?" came a voice from the back of the cell.

Axel squinted. Only one lantern burned under the deck, and it didn't give off a whole lot of light through its clouded glass panes. "Who said that?"

A massive human form arose from against the back wall of the ship and stepped into the light. Big guy, a good four inches taller than Axel, and broader, too. Short, scruffy hair crowned his head and stubble dotted his round chin. Bitterness oozed from in his brown eyes under a furrowed brow.

"I did," he said.

"You got a name?" Axel stepped toward him. Big or not, he'd stand toe-to-toe with the brute if it meant he and Calum would be safe among the prisoners. Maybe they could even organize an escape attempt and convince these losers to help.

"Yurgev."

"Well, *Yurgev*, I asked a question." Axel kept his hands at his sides in case Yurgev tried anything. Magnus—may the Overlord guide his soul to peace—had taught him to always be ready for a fight whether it looked likely or not. "When I ask questions, I expect answers. Crystal?"

Yurgev leaned forward. "And I told you to *shut up*. When I tell someone to shut up, I expect them to *shut up*. Crystal?"

Axel clenched his fists. If Yurgev wanted to play it this way, he would happily oblige. "I'll show you what's *crystal*."

Calum stepped between them. "Easy, guys. No need to—"

Yurgev shoved Calum against the bars adjacent to the other cell, rattled them.

It was all the excuse Axel needed to get to work.

He drove his left fist into Yurgev's gut, then his right cracked against Yurgev's chin.

Around them, the other prisoners whooped and hollered, both cheering Yurgev on and scrambling to get away from the fight itself.

Yurgev staggered back a half step, then he swung at Axel. Had it connected, the blow might've knocked Axel into another world, but he ducked under the punch, threw a sharp jab into Yurgev's stomach, then delivered a stunning uppercut to Yurgev's nose.

He dropped to the floor, stunned. Axel started to head toward him but Calum pulled him back when the other five prisoners, all with rage in their eyes and clenched fists, stepped between them and Yurgev.

"What did you just get us into?" Calum muttered.

"Nothin' we can't handle." Axel rubbed his sore right fist. Punching idiots hurt more without his armored gauntlets on.

The other five prisoners in the cell stalked toward them.

"*Hey*." A low growl split the tension. Krogan's taloned green feet descended below deck until he stood at the base of the stairs. "What's all the ruckus?"

Axel started to say something, but Krogan held up his hand.

"I'm puttin' you two in a different cell. You cause any more trouble, I'll get my whip back out." Krogan unlocked the cell and hauled them both out, then he thrust them into the adjacent cell. "Play nice. You'll be very, very sorry if I gotta come back down here tonight."

Axel watched him lock the cell with a different skeleton key than the previous cell—or at least he thought it was a different one—then he hooked his keys back onto his belt in the same way, same side as before. Consistency was good.

As Krogan clomped back up the stairs, Axel scanned the eyes of the eight men who'd already occupied the cell before he and Calum got here. Instead of anger, Axel found distress, dismay, and surprise. In some ways he preferred anger, as he could more easily channel it into action, but depression could work too.

He smiled at them. "So how are *you* guys doing tonight?"

"Thought I told you to *shut up*."

Axel turned back and stared at Yurgev, whose bloody face pressed against the shared bars of the cells. "By now you should've learned what happens when you try to order me around."

"This isn't over." Yurgev shook his head and spat on the floor. "Not even close."

Axel stared steel at him until he retracted back into the darkness of his cell. Part of him wanted to say something in response, but another part of him believed the rage in Yurgev's eyes.

As much as he'd won the fight—decisively—Axel couldn't help but wonder if he'd started something too big for him to finish.

LILLY SWOOPED in low and hovered only fifteen feet from the surface of the water, hopefully high enough that no other marine life would try to come after her but low enough that the pirates wouldn't see her approaching.

When she reached the back of the ship, she perched on a small ledge about seven feet below some windows, presumably belonging to the captain's quarters. If she could get on board and kill that Werewolf, then perhaps she could force the rest of the crew to release her friends.

She didn't know much about pirates, but perhaps they operated on a ruling structure like that of the Wolf tribes—whoever held the most power was in charge. Given the ship's Werewolf captain, that could be the case.

With her hands locked onto the windowsill, she pulled herself up for a look inside. Though the glass was foggy and dirty, she could still see clearly enough.

Four candles on a table in the center of the room cast an orange light on a bed, the table itself, the door, and two chairs, in one of which the Werewolf sat facing her. He still wore his hat and cape, but his head was down, and he was writing in a large book with a feather quill. Perfect.

Lilly lowered herself, stepped to the side, and then floated up toward the back of the ship so the Werewolf couldn't see her through the window. She peered between two rungs of a railing.

Two pirates stood at the wheel, both humans, both facing away from her. High above, in the crow's nest, two others gazed out across the moonlit waters with the aid of brass telescopes. Four pirates in total, two of them perched thirty feet higher in the air. Maybe she could ignore the crow's nest for now.

She dropped her altitude and curled around to the side of the ship, her eyes level again just below the railing so she could peek through with less chance of being seen.

A few more pirates milled about on the main deck, but apparently most of them had gone to sleep or at least had ventured below deck. Back toward the rear of the ship, Lilly noticed a door under the wheel. Probably the captain's quarters.

Now how do I get past two men at the wheel, a half dozen pirates on the deck, and two in the crow's nest? She headed back to the rear of the ship with the beginning of a plan in mind.

From just below the railing, she whistled loud enough for the two men at the wheel to hear her. They didn't move.

The second time she did it, they both glanced over their shoulders but stayed put. On Lilly's third whistle the one not steering the ship turned and headed toward the railing.

Lilly zipped around the side of the boat and flew up into the air. After a quick check on the pirate at the wheel, she landed in silence behind the pirate she'd lured to the edge.

As the pirate leaned over the railing, searching the churning waters below, Lilly made her move. She grabbed his ankles, and with all her strength she pulled up. The pirate pitched over the railing down into the frothy trail in the dark waters below.

He yelped on the way down.

Lilly mentally chastised herself. Too sloppy. Now she had to make up for it.

With no time to spare, Lilly darted toward the man on the wheel. When he'd fully turned around to investigate the sound, Lilly plunged her sword into his chest and clamped her left hand over his mouth.

His frightened eyes glazed over and he slumped to the deck. She twisted him around and hefted him up against the wheel. It didn't look great, and blood was practically raining out of his chest, but it should buy her a little extra time if she needed it.

Six pirates on deck, and two in the crow's nest. She could've tried to find a way to take the rest of them out, but even with her speed they'd probably notice her. Just wasn't worth the risk.

Instead of bothering with them, she landed near the captain's door and opened it in silence. She was inside.

There before her, not ten feet away, the Werewolf sat in his chair, head down, hat on, his cape draped over the back of the chair, just like she'd seen him five minutes earlier. Her sword still in hand, she left her feet and hovered toward him.

As Lilly approached, she noted that four candles still burned in front of him, and his book still lay sprawled open before him, but he wasn't moving. Must be deep in thought, or—

She gasped. *No!*

From her right, a dark blur launched toward her.

CHAPTER 7

The sword in her hand clattered across the floor, and so did she. Even though she wore armor, every inch of her body still hurt. Lilly reached for her weapon, but it wasn't there anymore.

A furry paw pulled her to her feet by her collar, and cool steel pressed against her neck. "Not bad, m'dear. Not bad at all—but not good enough, either."

Lilly struggled against his grip, but between his strength and her own sword at her throat, she stopped quickly.

"I really be impressed. Ye musta been trained to fight somewhere. An' yar armor—it be so pristine, so high-end. Ye must be a well-connected, *wealthy* Windgale."

Lilly didn't respond. She just glared at him.

"Not gonna tell me who ye be? Here, I'll start. Captain Brink. Ye're aboard the *Malice*, me pirate ship. Now go ahead. It be yar turn."

"Do you have my friends?" Lilly asked through gritted teeth.

Brink smiled at her. "As a matter o' fact, I do. Well, two o' them anyway. Yar Sobek friend—Magnus, wasn'it? He met an unfortunate end thanks to a fierce encounter with a lake shark. Overlord's sovereign justice, I reckon."

Lilly clenched her eyes shut. She would've been devastated had any of them died, but of the three, Magnus had truly saved her when she'd needed it most.

Though Calum and Axel had stumbled upon her in the wheat field, it was Magnus who had cared for her, bound her wounded shoulder, and set her at ease. It was Magnus who personally made sure that Roderick, the man who'd captured her for slavery, would never come for her again.

Lilly longed for her protector, and she fought to resist the tears stinging the corners of her eyes. They trickled down her cheeks anyway.

"For conversation's sake, ye only made one mistake in trying to get to me. That one mistake be why I've got a sword to yar throat instead o' lying on the floor with this same blade stuck in me back." Brink tilted his head. "Do ye care to know what your mistake was?"

Lilly shuddered, sniffled, and raised her eyes to meet Brink's. "Enlighten me."

"Yar mistake was comin' to get me. Ye shoulda waited for me to come to ye. I knew ye were comin' the instant ye twisted my doorknob. Everyone else aboard knocks. Only people who wish harm upon me come in without knockin'. Soon's I heard the door, I positioned my decoy and disappeared." Brink smiled at her. "Had ye been more patient, ye coulda killed me. Maybe."

"I'm done talking to you," Lilly asserted. "Just kill me already and be done with it."

Brink sighed. "Why does everyone think I'm gonna kill 'em? I'm not gonna kill ye. I'm makin' ye part o' me crew."

"And if I don't—"

"Trust me. You've no other choice, m'dear." Without breaking eye contact, Brink turned his head slightly and called out, "Krogan?"

Not long after, a knock sounded on the door.

Brink smiled at Lilly. "See? They know to knock."

Lilly rolled her eyes.

"Come in."

One of the biggest Saurians she'd ever seen stepped inside the cabin. He would've rivaled Magnus in size before Magnus became a Sobek, and his scaly face bore all sorts of scars. Lilly decided it must be a sort of rite of passage for a pirate.

"New catch, Krogan." Brink nodded to him, and he walked over. "Strip 'er down to 'er skivvies, an' make sure ye take off 'er cape so she can't fly away. Put it all with the rest o' the armor and weapons in me closet, then take 'er down to the brig and put 'er with the others."

"Aye, sir." Krogan nodded and unfastened Lilly's cape from her shoulder armor. Only then did Brink release his grip on her and lower the sword.

Brink stepped back and smirked at Lilly. "I hope ye enjoy yar stay aboard the *Malice*."

Lilly just glared at him.

CALUM STOPPED LISTENING to Axel talking with the prisoners in their cell when he noticed a shapely female form descending down the staircase.

She wore nothing but boots, skintight white armor lining that covered her from the waist down to her mid-thighs, and a matching upper lining, stained dark-brown near her left shoulder. The top defined her chest and shoulders but left her arms and stomach bare.

Long blonde hair hung down below her shoulders, and her blue eyes sparkled with relief when they met Calum's.

Overjoyed, he swatted Axel on his shoulder.

"What?" Axel snapped.

"Lilly." Calum pointed out of the cell.

Axel blinked, looked her up and down, then blinked again. "What's she doing here?"

Calum shrugged. Had she been captured? Given herself up?

Krogan started toward their cell and unlocked it, but instead of putting Lilly in with them, he ordered Calum and Axel out. Then he opened another cell across from theirs and swapped the four prisoners inside with Calum and Axel, and he shoved Lilly inside as well and locked both cells.

From their original cell, Yurgev and the other prisoners locked in with him leered at Lilly. One of them whistled at her, and Krogan whirled around and whacked the bars with his forearm. Everyone inside backed away.

Starting with their cell and ending at Calum's, Krogan panned his finger across all the cells. "The next prisoner I hear before sunrise gets keelhauled. Crystal?"

Calum had no idea what that meant, but they'd made enough fuss for one night. Now that Lilly was with them, Calum would rest easier.

Once Krogan disappeared back up the stairs, Calum turned toward Lilly and started to speak to her, but she flung herself at him and wrapped him in fierce hug. It startled him at first, but he quickly returned it.

He had to admit, he loved every second of it—the warmth of her lithe body against his, the faint scent of flowers on her skin... It was incredible. And she'd singled him out, specifically for—

Lilly abruptly let go and flung herself at Axel next, wrapping him in the exact same embrace she'd just shared with Calum.

The sequence left Calum confused and frustrated—but mostly confused.

When Lilly released Axel, she took hold of one of each of their hands in hers.

"Is it true?" she whispered, desperation and fear in her blue eyes. "About Magnus? Tell me it's not true."

Calum's heart tore in half all over again. Both he and Axel gave solemn nods.

Lilly's posture crumbled, and she stared down at the floor with empty eyes for a long moment.

Finally, she said, "I'm sorry."

Axel shook his head. "Why are you sorry? You didn't get him killed."

Though Calum wondered what Axel meant by that, the last thing he wanted was to start another argument, so he let it go. "He did everything he could to save us, but a shark—that's what those big black fish with all the teeth are called—a shark got him."

Lilly gave a solemn nod, and the three of them continued to stand there.

"We should get some rest," Calum said. "They worked us like dogs today. I have no doubt they're gonna do it again tomorrow."

The three of them sat down together, leaned up against the back wall of the cell, and stared at the bars until they couldn't anymore.

Not long after, the anchors tied to Calum's eyelids dropped, and blackness flooded his mind.

BLINDING light burned Calum's eyes, but this time he couldn't even lift his hands to block it. Lumen stood before him, his sword shimmering in his hand.

"Do not be discouraged. Your victory is at hand. You will find me, you will free me, and together we will reclaim Kanarah for its people." Lumen extended his open hand toward Calum. "Rise, Calum."

Calum hesitated at first, but gripped Lumen's hand with his. A jolt raised him to his feet and vibrated through his entire body, and then Lumen vanished.

WHEN CALUM AWAKENED from his dream, he found himself standing in the cell. Axel's body still lay sprawled across the cell floor, motionless, and Lilly lay with her head on Axel's shoulder, though it looked like Axel had no idea she was laying that way.

The sight sent pangs of hurt and jealousy through Calum's chest, but he realized that if she'd been laying on his shoulder instead, he probably would've scared her half to death with how quickly he'd just woken from his dream.

Lumen had visited Calum's dreams again, it seemed he had physically *pulled* Calum to his feet. And that jolt—had Lumen done something to him? Had Calum somehow been healed of the lashes he'd taken from Krogan?

Calum spread his arms out, and the dull sting of partially sealed wounds crackled across his back. He grunted.

Nope. Not healed.

Worse than that was Lumen's message: How could Lumen claim that Calum's victory was near while they were locked in a cage, trapped on this pirate ship indefinitely, now with six more enemies than they'd had before last night? In their current weakened condition, what chance did they have for escape?

"Someone else will have to let you out," Calum muttered. "We're not going anywhere."

He leaned against the bars and his gaze landed on Lilly again. Beautiful, but shaken by Magnus's death. Strong, yet fragile. Stuck or otherwise, being with her was worth every lash he took from Krogan.

She stirred, and her eyes opened. When she saw him she tensed at first, then, realizing she was on Axel's shoulder, sat up. "Calum?"

He nodded. "Yeah?"

"You look…" She studied him. "Are you alright?"

Calum shook his head and leaned against the bars. "No. And yes. I feel terrible about Magnus, but at least you're safe."

Lilly stood up and stepped toward him. She reached out and cupped his jaw with her hand. "Calum, I'm so sorry."

He closed his eyes and reveled in her touch, though he tried not to read into it. He wanted to take her hand in his, but his heart wouldn't let him. He couldn't trust himself to know how to behave at the moment. He didn't know what he wanted or what she wanted, and even if he did, they were still locked in a cell in the belly of a pirate ship.

"It's not your fault."

"I know," she said. "But I tried to save you, and I only made things worse."

While that was true, Calum didn't care. "You did what you thought was best. I can't fault you for that."

She shook her head.

"Besides, we're all together again," he said. "We can watch out for each other from now on."

"Except for Magnus. He's gone."

Calum sighed. His back ached, but the reminder of Magnus's demise shredded his heart all over again. First his parents, then Nicolai. Now Magnus. He slumped down against the bars and buried his head in his hands. He was running out of people to lose.

Lilly knelt down next to him and put her hand on his shoulder. "I'm sorry, Calum."

"I don't know what we're gonna do without him. He knew so much. He was so strong. He taught me everything I know about fighting. He taught me to read and write. He was my best friend."

Calum wished he could stop the tears from streaming down his face, wished he could keep his voice from shuddering.

He glanced at Lilly and gave a sad chuckle. "You must think I'm weak."

She shook her head. "Not at all. There's nothing wrong with crying when you're sad."

Calum scoffed. "Axel wouldn't cry."

"Maybe not, but Axel—" She turned and glanced back at him. He still lay there, arms and legs extended, taking long deep breaths with his eyes closed. "Axel is different than you. You've got a kind soul, Calum. It's what I love most about you."

Love? Calum blinked at her. "You… what?"

"I, uh—" Lilly looked away. "Nothing. Nevermind."

"No, I heard what you said." He *had* heard it... hadn't he? "What do you mean?"

"Nothing." She shook her head. "It's nothing."

Calum wanted to say something else, but Axel moaned and rolled over on his side.

"I feel terrible." He moaned again.

Lilly stood and put some distance between herself and Calum. The action filled Calum with even more confusion than before, especially since she'd said what she'd said. How was he supposed to make sense of any of this when everything kept changing?

"Everything hurts." Axel's words slurred. His eyes cracked open and he looked at Lilly. "You alright?"

She smiled and nodded. "I'm fine."

When Lilly glanced back at Calum and showed him that same smile, he managed to send one back at her. Forget Lumen in all his splendor—*she* was the most amazing being he'd ever seen.

Footsteps sounded behind Calum, and Lilly's countenance changed. She stood up and backed away from Axel, her eyes fixed on the newcomer.

Calum twisted his torso and craned his neck—both of which hurt—to get a look.

Captain Brink stood before their cell with Krogan and two other Saurians behind him.

"Mornin'," he said.

Calum scooted away from the bars and stood, as did Axel.

Brink approached the bars. His lupine snout twitched, and his nostrils flared. "I take it neither of ye gentlemen feel well this mornin'?"

Calum glanced at Axel, whose posture straightened, even though it must have racked every inch of his back to do so. Calum had nothing to prove, so he stayed hunched over.

"I regret that Krogan decided to put ye in with that bunch over there." Brink motioned toward the men in Yurgev's cell, all of whom now glared at them through the bars with bitter eyes alongside Yurgev's bruised face. "But what's done be done. Krogan has forced my hand, and so have you."

Lilly's hand touched Calum's shoulder. Any other day it would have felt good, but not after last night's events.

Brink nodded to Krogan, who stepped toward their cell with his keys out. "I'm afraid, in this case, it be in the ship's best interest to terminate yar stay with us."

"Over a little scrap?" Calum protested. "Are you serious?"

"We didn't even start that fight." Axel pointed at Yurgev's cell. "They did."

Brink held up his hand and shook his head. "I've made me decision. Can't tolerate fightin' amongst the crew. There be six o' them and three o' you. Simple math, really."

Calum's fists clenched. He wasn't just going to give in. Even though he had no hope of over-powering three Saurians and a Werewolf with just his fists, he'd already decided to fight every step of the way.

"What are you going to do to us?" Lilly asked.

Krogan inserted the skeleton key into the cell's lock and smirked at Calum.

"I be a merciful master." Brink brushed some hairs off his cape. "We're gonna toss ye over-board, an' ye can take yar chances in the lake. The Overlord will decide yar fates."

Axel stepped toward the cell door with his fists balled tight. "That's a death sentence, and you know it."

Krogan twisted the key and the lock disengaged. Calum wanted to charge the cell door and knock him on his back right then and there, but he knew that tactic wouldn't get him anywhere, so he waited.

Brink shrugged. "When ye're a pirate, that be as merciful as it gets, friend."

One glance at Axel's eyes told Calum he was considering an attack on Krogan, but his posture betrayed the reality of their shared situation. Resistance just meant they'd be more tired and more injured when it came time to swim for their lives.

Krogan hooked his keys on his belt, removed his whip from the opposite hip, and pulled the cell door open, his eyes fixed on Axel. "C'mon, now. Don't give me any trouble, and I won't give it back to you twicelike."

Axel set his jaw and didn't move.

A loud thud sounded from behind Brink. A contorted human body tumbled down the stairs, and both Brink and Krogan whirled around.

Something thudded on the deck over their heads. Men screamed, and metal clashed.

"Lock that cell, Krogan!" Brink growled and charged up the stairs, but his furry form promptly tumbled back down and crashed onto the floor. He cursed, hopped to his feet, and bared his jagged white teeth.

"Cap'n?" Krogan slammed the cell door shut and locked it. "You alright?"

Brink waved his arm and shifted the cape off his shoulders so it hung along his back. "Of course I be alright. Rally the men. We need to mount a resistance *immediately.*"

Calum glanced at Axel, who shrugged. Lilly did the same. Whatever it was, it was bad for the pirates, so hopefully it was good for them—if they could get out of this cell.

Another thud sounded, this time above their cell. Two more thuds in quick succession followed. Krogan charged up the stairs.

"What in the Overlord's name is going on?" Lilly asked.

Calum scanned the ceiling, but it gave him no answers. "More pirates?"

A roar sounded above them, then Krogan tumbled down the stairs just as Brink had. He landed face-up in front of his captain with a large broadsword protruding from his chest.

A familiar broadsword, one with a blue blade and a silver hilt, far too large for most humans to wield.

Calum's breath caught in his throat. *Impossible.*

Dark-green feet, legs, and a strong, scaled torso covered by a Blood Ore blue breastplate descended into the brig. A dark-green hand wrenched the broadsword from Krogan's chest.

Magnus stood at the base of the stairs, glaring at Brink with all the fury in the world.

CHAPTER 8

As soon as Magnus swung his sword, the Werewolf snarled, dodged the blow, and disappeared into the plentiful shadows below decks. All that remained of his presence were his black hat and cape.

Magnus growled. He should have drawn the Werewolf up to the ship's deck, where the sun now shined, instead.

"Magnus?" Calum called. "Is it really you?"

Magnus held up his hand. "Stay clear of the bars. This Werewolf and I have a score to settle."

"Brink," the Werewolf said. "Cap'n Brink. We be old friends now, *Magnus*."

A dark blur ratcheted out of the shadows and past Magnus. He whipped his sword at Brink but missed. The solitary lamp in the brig dropped to the floor and shattered, and its flame extinguished.

Even in the lack of light, Magnus could see well enough to locate the cell keys on the dead Saurian's belt. He snatched them into his left hand and clamped his fingers around them. If Brink got ahold of those keys, or if he had his own set, he might be able to get inside the cell and kill the others before Magnus had a chance to do anything about it.

He snapped the metal key ring with his fingers and tossed them up the stairs and out onto the main deck. It meant his friends would stay locked up, but against a foe as dangerous as Brink, they would be far safer that way.

"Your crew is dead, Brink." Magnus's head swiveled in the darkness. "All of them."

Behind him, the hatch at the top of the stairs smacked shut. He lashed his sword at the sound but failed to hit anything.

"We can stay down here for eternity if you wish, but we both know how this ends: you scratch me up, perhaps bite me a few times. It will hurt, but I will heal. Quickly.

"Then, at some point, I will catch you as you run past. Maybe clip you with my sword. I will eventually find you in the darkness, and I will kill you. You will pay for enslaving my friends and for hurling me into the lake."

A growl reverberated throughout the brig. Something chomped down on his shoulder, and pressure stung Magnus's nerves. He winced and jerked forward. Brink rolled over his head and disappeared into the darkness again with another growl.

"Go ahead. Get as frustrated as you wish." Magnus shook his head and dabbed at the blood that oozed from his shoulder. Nothing the veromine in his body couldn't repair in a matter of hours.

Still, knowing that Werewolf teeth and talons could penetrate his scales didn't set him any more at ease. He hadn't learned that back in Reptilius.

"You have nothing left, except your ship and your life, and I will not allow you to take anything else from my friends or me."

A half-howl, half-laugh echoed throughout the brig. "That's what ye think."

Wood snapped to Magnus's left.

"He's punching through the ship's hull!" Axel yelled. "Right here between the cells!"

Magnus charged toward the spot, but a blast of lake water sprayed his face.

More howling-laughter. "I hope ye be ready for another plunge in the brine, Magnus."

Magnus jabbed his sword into the gap between the cells but only struck solid wood. Brink had snuck past him again.

Water began to collect at Magnus's feet. "You really intend to sink your own ship out of spite?"

Brink laughed again from somewhere in the shadows. "If it means ye and yar friends go down with it, then aye. I can replace me ship. Can ye replace yar friends?"

Magnus glanced back at the trio, all of whom wore worried expressions.

"They will not go down with your ship," Magnus assured both them and Brink.

"A chance not, but they die the moment ye let 'em out. Or they drown. Yar choice."

Magnus scowled at the darkness. He needed to take action—extreme action—to reclaim control of this situation. And there was only one way to do that.

He sheathed his sword, raised his arms into the air, and intertwined his fingers. In one mighty blow, he smashed through the brig's wooden floor. Underneath, he recognized familiar gray wood—the hull. Another comparable blow gashed a hole into the ship's hull, and more lake water splashed up into his face.

"What are you doing?" Axel gripped the cell bars, frantic at the water swirling around his knees. "You're gonna drown us!"

Magnus faced him. "Trust me."

The water level rose to Magnus's thighs. Brink launched toward him from the shadows and knocked him to the floor, then vanished again.

The prisoners in the other cells rattled their bars and shouted as the water rose to their waistlines. So much for listening for Brink's next attack.

"You'd better do something quickly, Magnus—" The water had already reached to Calum's chest, yet his voice remained surprisingly calm. "—or we're gonna drown in here."

Magnus clenched his teeth until he noticed a splash in between the cells where Brink had punched the first hole in the hull. A furry brown tail disappeared under the water. The captain had abandoned his ship.

Amid the rising water and shouts of the prisoners, Calum, Axel, and Lilly gripped the cell bars and floated with just their heads above the water line, but they didn't have much space left to get air.

Magnus dove into the water as it rose almost to his neck. He zipped toward their cell, and instead of fiddling with the keys in the lock, he grabbed two of the bars. With one yank he ripped them out, creating a wide opening for them to escape.

Lilly swam out first, followed by Axel and then Calum. When Calum surfaced above the water again he said, "You have to get the other prisoners out."

Before Magnus could respond, Axel floated over. "No way. Half of them tried to fight us. We're not freeing them."

Calum shook his head, indignant. "They're all here against their wills. We need to let them out, and at least give them a chance at freedom. You wouldn't want to die in a cage in a sinking ship."

"They deserve whatever they get." Axel glared at him. "We let 'em out, and they'll come after us again. Lilly, too."

"Then we'll stop them again, like we did last time, only now we have Magnus back. With him around, she's safe, and so are we."

"And I can take care of myself," Lilly added, though of the three, her anxious water-treading and shuddering voice demonstrated the most anxiety about the possibility of drowning.

Calum refocused in Magnus. "We'll work on getting the hatch open. Get them out."

Magnus nodded and dove into the water again. Within moments he wrenched the cell doors from their hinges, and the prisoners spilled out after him. When he made it back to his friends, he realized they hadn't yet gotten the hatch at the top of the stairs open, and now the brig was totally submerged.

They were trapped with no air.

Magnus positioned himself under the hatch with his back against it and his feet on the stairs. He heaved against the wood above, and it snapped from the pressure. Sunlight streamed into the brig, and the prisoners began to scramble out.

Again, Lilly went first, and then Axel and Calum, followed by the rest of the prisoners, and Magnus brought up the rear.

WATER EQUALIZED EVERYTHING.

It had almost drowned all of them, including Lilly's friends and the other prisoners from below. Lilly kept an eye on the ones who'd come to blows with Calum and Axel especially, but the big guy, Yurgev, wasn't among them. Had he drowned before he could make it out in time?

"Everyone to the lifeboats," Magnus said. "Divide as evenly as you can."

Lilly grabbed Calum's wrist before he could leave. "I know where our armor and weapons are. If we hurry, we still have time to get to them."

Calum nodded, then told Axel their plan.

"Go on, then. Magnus and I will handle things here. And *hurry*." Axel began to work on one of the ropes that secured the nearest lifeboat to the ship.

Lilly led Calum up to Captain Brink's quarters. The curtains at the window were drawn shut, and none of the candles on the desk were lit.

The ship pitched to the right under them and Calum caught Lilly in his arms. He promptly set her back on her own two feet, saying, "Sorry."

The way he said it made her think he was apologizing for something else entirely.

"I'm the one who should be sorry." She hoped he would understand her meaning. "Come on. Our armor and weapons are in the captain's closet."

Calum pulled the door open. Sure enough, a pile of armor parts and weapons lay inside with Lilly's armor on top. Calum handed her a few pieces and then dug for his own.

"Good to get this stuff back again." Lilly stepped into her leg armor. "I felt exposed without it."

"You *were* exposed without it, almost entirely." Calum slid on his breastplate then picked up one of his greaves.

"You didn't seem to mind." While Lilly fastened her own breastplate over her undergarments, she stared at him to gauge his response.

He glanced at her then broke eye contact. "I—uh—"

Lilly stifled a smile and slung her cape over her shoulders. "You don't have to be embarrassed, Calum. You weren't dressed in much more than me."

Calum slipped on his gauntlets and brandished his red-bladed sword. "I think we'd better get going."

The cabin door shut and the room plunged into darkness. A man's heavy breathing sounded, and a large shadow advanced toward them, holding a gleaming blade.

"Stand back, Lilly." Calum extended his arm and physically pushed her back. "It's Yurgev."

He hadn't drowned after all.

Metal clanged against Calum's blade, then twice more in quick succession. How Calum had even seen to defend against them, Lilly didn't know. She backed away from the fracas toward the curtains.

"I'm gonna kill you first," Yurgev said to Calum. "And then I'm gonna move on to your little girlfriend."

Lilly's jaw hardened, and she drew her sword. Her bow was still in the captain's closet. She regretted not grabbing it first, but now it was too late. She'd had to make do with her sword.

As she pulled the curtain open to drench the space with more light, she noticed a stream of water trickling toward her from under the cabin door. They didn't have much time.

Calum blocked a savage blow from Yurgev and staggered back toward Lilly.

She stepped to his side and nudged him. "We're doing this together."

Calum nodded. He leveled his sword.

The ship pitched to the left, and all three of them lost their footing. Lilly recovered first because she took to the air, but Yurgev wasn't far behind her. He jabbed his sword at her and missed, then he swung it again. The blade should have connected with Lilly's sword, but it never made it that far.

From the shadows, a dark blur slashed at Yurgev. He dropped, his throat split open, facedown on the water-covered floor. His blood tinted the water red.

Now Captain Brink stood before them, his amber eyes burning with revenge.

CHAPTER 9

Lilly ran through the list of possibilities in her head, but in the end, the simplest explanation also made the most sense: Brink must've swum around to the side of the boat and somehow found a way back inside his quarters.

It didn't matter how—what mattered was that if they wanted to get off the ship alive, they'd have to get past Brink.

Lilly shot toward him.

"Lilly, no!" Calum reached for her, but she zipped past him.

With one swing of his arm, Brink sent her careening into the wall. Her body smacked against it, and she slumped down to the water-covered floor. The blow might've killed her if not for her armor.

She didn't move, except to grope for her sword, now hidden somewhere under the ever-rising water.

Then Brink charged Calum, who barely dodged his first attack but fell under his second. Calum slapped the water in search of his sword, but Brink kicked his ribs. He rolled over on his side, his teeth bared.

Brink turned back and started toward Lilly. "Ye, m'dear, be the reason me ship is goin' down. I should've killed ye last night when ye asked."

Lilly tried to back away, but the cabin wall kept her from moving anywhere. As she did, her hand brushed against something under the water.

Brink stalked nearer. "I think, for me next ship, I won't be takin' anymore slaves. I'll just kill 'em from the start. I guess in this age a pirate cap'n needs to be more ruthless to maintain order. I shall not repeat this mistake."

Lilly's fingers coiled around the hilt of her sword. She didn't dare glance at it for fear of giving it away.

As Brink raised his claws to strike, Lilly lifted her sword out of the water and sprang forward. The blade pierced deep into Brink's chest, and he dropped onto his back with his eyes wide and mouth open.

Lilly stood over him as water splashed over his astonished face. "I waited for you to come to me this time. Thanks for the advice. It worked."

Brink coughed, and then he lay back in the water. His amber eyes shut for good.

The cabin door burst open, and a cascade of water streamed inside. Lilly wrenched her sword from Brink's chest and pulled Calum to his feet. "Come on. We have to grab the rest and get out of here."

The ship pitched toward its stern, and they slid toward the cabin's windows, now submerged in lake water. Calum recovered his sword, sheathed it, and together with Lilly he darted over to the closet. They collected Axel's armor in a sack, she grabbed her bow and arrows, and they clawed their way back up to the door.

Lilly made it out first, and Calum followed with the sack slung over his shoulder. He found a grip on the outside of the doorframe and began to pull himself out of the captain's quarters, but the ship pitched again, this time so far that its bow pointed straight up into the sky.

The sack of armor slipped, but Calum snatched it before it could fall into the whirlpool below. Now he dangled over the watery chasm below with his right hand clamped onto the doorframe and the sack of armor hanging from his other hand.

He looked up at Lilly, who reached down to help him.

A loud crash sounded below Calum, and the entire ship shuddered. The cabin windows shattered, and the edge of Brink's table disappeared in the water rushing up to meet them.

"Take my hand, Calum!" she shouted over the ship's groans and the roiling, churning water below.

As she continued to reach toward him, a massive dark form materialized in the rising waters below. A black fin emerged from the water's furious surface and circled underneath Calum.

A shark.

"Drop the armor and grab my hand!" Lilly pressed her chest against the doorframe and reached even farther down toward him. She couldn't lose him.

Calum's face tightened with strain, and he hefted the bag up to her instead. Lilly grabbed it and slung it over her shoulder, then she reached down with her other hand. Just as Calum's grip slipped from the doorframe, Lilly caught him by his wrist.

He yelped, but he clasped his fingers around her wrist as well and anchored his free hand on the door frame again.

The shark spiraled closer, and the froth lapped at the bottoms of Calum's boots.

"Help me!" Lilly yelled at him. She yanked and pulled and used her flight to help with the strain, and Calum strained along with her.

Gaping jaws and spearhead teeth burst from the water below and chomped shut just beneath Calum's right foot as he made it above the doorframe. When Lilly looked down again the shark had clamped its jaws on Brink's body, and then it disappeared into the angry waters.

As Calum stood to his feet, Lilly glared at him. "Why didn't you just drop the armor?"

"Axel would've killed me if I didn't get it back for him." Calum shrugged.

Lilly rolled her eyes. "Come on. This ship is going down fast."

"I can't go into that water," Calum told her in calm tones. He hardly seemed worried about it. "My armor's too heavy, and I'm too exhausted and weak to keep my head above the water for long. I'll sink."

Calum grabbed the railing above his head, which, when the ship had been floating, lined the staircase that led up to the wheel and the captain's quarters. He pulled himself over it.

"Take the armor and get outta here," he continued, equally as placid. "I'll climb up higher to give the lifeboat a chance to circle near me."

Lilly took to the air, even though his plan baffled her. If he could fly like she could, then maybe it would work, but he couldn't. "How are you going to get to the lifeboat without getting into the water?"

"I'll swing over." He grabbed a rope and pulled himself off the rail toward the first of the masts. "If you hurry, you can drop that off and get back to help me."

Lilly nodded and sped off. She wouldn't let him die. It wasn't an option she'd even consider. She landed on Magnus's lifeboat and dropped the bag next to Axel. Both of them looked at her.

"We worried you were dead," Magnus said. "What happened? Where is Calum?"

"Long story." Lilly sprang back into the air. "Just get the boat as close to the ship as you can without letting it take you under. Hurry."

She darted back toward Calum.

WITH EACH TUG on the network of ropes that hung from the masts, Calum's body raged against him. Exhaustion and a lack of food plagued him. He felt weak, yet determined.

But if he let go, or if he slipped, he was as good as dead. So he kept going.

The ship's black sails tore loose and whipped past him as he climbed higher. Something above him snapped. A barrel from the ship's bow plummeted toward him.

He leaped clear, his arms outstretched, and he grabbed a rope with greedy fingers. It tightened, and he swung out of the barrel's path.

The ship seemed to be sinking faster. As soon as he swung back to the second mast, water licked his heels. Water meant sharks.

Maybe Magnus could survive one, but Calum didn't stand a chance. He had to get above the third mast, grab a rope, and then try to swing out over the water. Hopefully there'd be a lifeboat nearby, if not underneath him, by then.

Calum jumped up and clamped his fingers around an iron ring mounted to the third mast. His arms protested when he tried to pull himself up, but they did the job. He managed to grab one of the ropes just above the mast, and—

He dropped. Water smothered him. The rope was loose.

He surfaced and pulled on the rope still in his hand, silently praying it would catch on something, but the opposite end dropped into the water next to him. He had to get out of there.

Too late. A black fin cut through the surf toward him.

Calum scrambled and splashed, but couldn't get ahold of anything, and his armor kept trying to tug him ever downward toward a different kind of demise.

The shark zoomed closer, growing larger and larger as it approached. Its gigantic jaws broke through the water and spread wide to receive him.

Before the beast could reach Calum, the shark's jaws clamped shut, but it still collided with him. The impact spun him in the water as if he weighed nothing, and he sank down low, confused and trying to find the surface. Something red in the water blinded him, and his armor pulled him down fast. He flailed his arms.

It was blood. Was it his? He didn't feel wounded, but that didn't mean he was whole.

Something fastened on his wrist. Shark teeth, but much softer and more forgiving than he'd expected, dragged him toward the surface.

Not shark teeth—*fingers.*

The instant Calum's head broke through the water he gasped, and precious air flooded his lungs. His entire body left the water, and the sinking ship shrank beneath him. Then it rushed up to meet him once more. On the way down, he grabbed a rope on the third mast and held on to keep from plunging back into the water.

He looked down. All his limbs seemed to be intact, and he didn't see or feel any blood gushing out of his body.

When he looked up, he saw Lilly hovering just above him. She held her bow in one hand and beckoned him toward her with her other.

Had she *shot* the shark? That would explain the blood in the water.

"Wake up, Calum!" She motioned toward the lifeboat behind her, occupied by Magnus and Axel, who rowed furiously to stay out of the whirlpool created by the sinking pirate ship. "Swing over!"

Beneath him, the water continued to consume the *Malice*. The shark's head resurfaced, but something long and narrow was sticking out of its right eye.

An arrow.

Lilly *had* shot the shark. In its eye, no less.

Calum marveled at it. *Incredible.*

"Calum, now!" Magnus roared from the lifeboat.

Calum snapped back into the present. He kicked his feet back toward the mast and landed on one of the sail rods that extended from the mast itself.

He found a new rope to grab, and then he pushed off the sail rod with all his remaining strength and swung toward the lifeboat. But even with all his momentum, he'd never make it all the way to the lifeboat—it was too far.

When Calum released the rope, hoping for a well-timed release to get him as close as possible, Lilly grabbed onto his wrist with both hands and dropped toward the lifeboat right along with him. Her flying thrust helped him traverse the extra distance between the *Malice* and the lifeboat, and they fell into Axel and Magnus's open arms.

The lifeboat rocked so much that it almost tipped over, but it stayed upright.

Calum pushed himself up, amazed that he'd even made it into the lifeboat. Twenty yards away, the ship sank deeper and deeper until it disappeared under the water entirely.

"There she goes," Axel said, back to rowing along with Magnus. In all the commotion, he hadn't yet put his armor back on, so he once again resembled the farm boy Calum used to know back from his days in the quarry, rather than a budding warrior, strong and powerful.

Calum turned to Lilly, who also sat up. "Why didn't you just pull me to the lifeboat in the first place?"

"I can only fly with as much weight as I could carry on the ground." She smiled at him. "But I can redirect heavier things with my momentum, which is how I got us into the boat."

Axel whistled. "Can all Windgales do that?"

"Sure, they're capable, but not all of them know how. I've had special training."

"Thank the Overlord for that." Calum lay back down in the lifeboat, closed his eyes, and exhaled a long, painful breath. Everything hurt. *Everything.* He opened his eyes again and looked at Axel and Magnus. "How many prisoners survived?"

"Another three lifeboats, including one with the five men who tried to attack us, all big enough to hold about twenty men, but most of them are only half-full with limited supplies." Axel glowered at them over his shoulder then turned back.

"Speaking of which, we have seen no sign of either the man Axel called Yurgev or Captain Brink. Do you know what happened to them?" Magnus asked.

"Dead. Both of them." Even talking seemed to sap Calum of his energy. He wanted to closer his eyes again and rest, but he couldn't. Not yet.

"What happened?" Axel leaned forward and rubbed his lower back with his hand.

Calum motioned to Lilly so she could talk for the both of them. He couldn't make his mouth form words. He needed just a little more rest, so he lay back again and stared up at the blue sky above.

"Yurgev ambushed us while we were getting our armor back," she said. "Calum fought him off for awhile until Brink showed up. He killed Yurgev, then came for us. I put my sword through his chest when he wasn't expecting it, and he died. Last time I saw him, he was wedged between a shark's jaws."

With renewed energy, Calum sat up to look at Lilly, and his view greatly improved.

"Impressive. Brink was no ordinary foe." Magnus smiled. "Well done, Lilly."

"I never would've had a chance had Calum not held off Yurgev for so long." Lilly showed Calum a smile that totally eased his exhaustion for an instant, and then it returned full-force. "He was incredible."

"You wanna talk about incredible? Calum, did you see that *unbelievable* shot Lilly made to save you?" Axel whacked Calum's shoulder, probably on purpose. The blow disrupted most of the progress Calum had made through resting.

Calum ground his teeth and shook his head. "Only the result."

"She hit the shark right in its *eye*." Axel chuckled and turned to Lilly. "How does that even happen? How are you so accurate all the time?"

Lilly shrugged. "I've had a lot of practice. I started learning when I was four years old, and I've been shooting ever since."

"More 'special training?'" Axel asked.

She grinned at him. "Exactly."

Calum lay back in the boat again and exhaled a relived sigh. "So what do we do now?"

Magnus peered over the side of the lifeboat. "The sharks are circling the wreckage, probably picking at the dead bodies that were on board the ship. I expect they'll leave us alone for awhile, but all the same, I'd like to row toward shore immediately."

"Which way do we go?" Axel asked. "It all looks the same to me."

"South." The voice came from behind Magnus, but there was no one else on the boat.

Calum sat up too quickly, and this time his head throbbed as punishment. One of the lifeboats full of prisoners floated toward them. Calum recognized them as the mellow prisoners from the other cell while he and Axel—well, only Axel—fought off Yurgev.

"Head south from here." The man speaking had a long gray beard and matching hair, except for a bald spot on his head, and he wore gray rags about the same color as the *Baroness of Destiny* had been. His sharp, blue-green eyes resembled the color of the lake water on which they all floated. "Sharkville is south of here."

"He is right," Magnus said. "But with the sun overhead I cannot tell which direction is south. I got turned around after I boarded the ship, and now it is noon, or close to it."

The bearded man extended his hand and pointed to his left. "It's that-a-way."

"How do you know?" Magnus asked.

"When you've been sailin' these waters as many years as I have, you just know." The bearded man glanced at the young man next to him in the boat, who stared at Calum. "This here's my son, Jacobus, or Jake for short. I'm Puolo. Used to captain a fishin' vessel 'bout the size of that pirate ship before they found us and took most of us captive."

"Pleasure to meet you both." Calum marshaled enough strength to introduce his companions. "And thank you for not trying to kill us."

Puolo waved his hand. "You set us free. If anything, we should be thanking you, and we certainly do."

He bowed to Magnus, who returned the bow with one of his own.

Axel cleared his throat. "Anyway, how far do you think it is back to Sharkville?"

"A solid day, at least. Could be a day and a half." Puolo added, "Depends how fast you row."

"Hopefully we grabbed enough food to sustain us until then." Axel rummaged through a burlap bag in the boat with them. "There's not much in here."

"Pirates typically aren't fishermen. They survive by plunderin' and tradin'," Jake said. "We're lucky we found anythin' at all."

"We grabbed some basic fishin' equipment and some bait they took from your vessel yesterday, though." Puolo held up a harpoon. "We can do some fishing and see if we can supplement our supply. The only thing we got to worry about is rowing away from these sharks before they decide to…"

It all sounded great to Calum, but his body still weighed him down, and his eyelids drooped low. How Axel even could tolerate being awake, Calum didn't know, but now that they'd escaped harm, Calum couldn't fight his fatigue anymore.

As the others continued to talk, he lay back in the lifeboat and let the motion of the water slapping against the hull rock him to sleep.

A SMACK on the wood under Calum's head jarred him from his sleep. He jerked upright, and his body reverberated with dull pain. He sucked in a sharp breath.

"Are you alright?" Magnus asked from somewhere behind him.

The boat rocked against the waves under a starry moonlit sky. Calum stretched his limbs and his back but the tension only sharpened his misery. "Yeah. I'll be alright."

He turned to face Magnus, who sat in the center of the boat. He held an oar in each hand and rowed against the black surf in a steady rhythm. Farther behind him, the other three lifeboats chased his wake, two on the left and one on the right.

"How long have you been rowing?"

"All day," Magnus said. "Do not fret, though. I take pride that I am the only one rowing this lifeboat, yet we still lead all the others, each of which has at least six men rowing."

Calum smiled at him, fully contented. Magnus had survived, he'd saved them, and now they were all reunited, more or less unharmed. "I'm glad we didn't lose you, Magnus."

"Even if you had, I am certain someone else would have rowed in my stead."

Calum chuckled. "That's not what I meant, and you know it."

Now Magnus grinned. "Yes, I know."

"My body is—" Calum twisted his torso and a chorus of cracks and pops sounded. He didn't feel quite as exhausted as before, but the aches of all the strain he'd endured over the last few days still lingered. "—killing me. I just don't know how Axel does it sometimes."

"Even if he will not show it, Axel is just as beat as you are." Magnus must have noticed Calum's eyes scanning the back half of the lifeboat. "He is sleeping back there."

"Where's Lilly?"

"She's back there too, also sleeping."

Calum swallowed. "Together?"

Magnus smirked. "No. Near each other, but not together. It is not quite cold enough for Axel to use body heat as an excuse to draw close to her. Or at least not cold enough that she would agree to it."

Calum nodded, and Magnus chuckled.

"What are you laughing at?" Calum asked.

"I find humans much more entertaining now that I am not enslaved by them." His oars lifted out of the water and then dug back in almost parallel to where Calum was sitting. "Specifically, you and Axel."

"What do you mean?"

"Ever since the moment you discovered Lilly, neither of you have been able to restrain yourselves. You both posture like colorful birds displaying your finest plumage, you take risks you would not otherwise take, and you go at each others' throats whenever you think it will give you an advantage." Magnus snorted and carved another swath into the water with his oars. "I find it amusing."

Calum frowned at him. "I haven't done any of those things."

Have I? he wondered.

Magnus stopped rowing, tilted his head, and huffed through his nostrils.

"Alright." Calum bit his lip. "Maybe I've done *some* of those things."

"That is putting it mildly." Magnus started rowing again. "I could point out several instances where one or both of you went a bit overboard on her behalf."

"If I remember correctly, *you're* the one who went overboard," Calum countered with a smirk.

Magnus shook his head. "You jumped ship more recently than I did."

"That's because it was *sinking*." Calum pointed at him. "You fell off."

"I was *forced* off and nearly eaten by a shark, thank you very much." Magnus grunted. "Perhaps we should just drop the subject."

"I never did hear how you got away from that shark. What happened?"

"When it came at me, I stabbed it through the roof of its mouth and into its head. The blood in the water was the shark's, not mine." Magnus huffed again. "Believe it or not, that was the easy part of what I had to deal with."

Calum raised his eyebrows.

"The blood in the water must have attracted other sharks, because half a dozen others showed up within minutes of killing that one. I managed to escape while they fed on their kin, but by then the ship had already started to sail away. I swam after it until it slowed to a cruising speed, but by then it was already a day later."

"You swam after us for an *entire day*?"

Magnus let the oars go slack again and he shrugged. "You are my friends. I could not let you perish on that pirate ship."

A smile cracked Calum's lips. "If it wasn't for you, we would have. Brink was gonna kill us right when you showed up."

Magnus began to row again. "I heard as much from Axel and Lilly this afternoon."

Something smacked the wood under Calum's feet and the whole lifeboat pitched to one side. He looked at Magnus.

"Sharks again," he explained. "They bump against the bottoms or sides of the boat from time to time. I imagine they are testing for weaknesses."

"Can they break through the hull?" Calum did *not* want to deal with any more lake creatures if he didn't have to.

"The wood is stout, but I cannot say. They are imposing monsters. Easily the size of one of these boats. Maybe bigger. Even if they cannot break through, they could certainly tip the boats over with ease." Magnus sighed. "I would like to tell you with certainty that we will make it back to Sharkville, but I cannot."

Calum exhaled a long silent breath through his nostrils. The thought of ending up back in the water with one of those monstrosities again sent shudders from his spine down to his fingertips. For now, all he could do was put his trust in Magnus, the Overlord, and Lumen to see them through.

"I understand."

"Are you hungry?" Magnus motioned toward Calum with his head. "Search that bag next to you. You should be able to find something to satisfy your stomach for awhile."

As if on cue, a low rumble vibrated through Calum's gut. "Yeah. Have you eaten?"

Magnus didn't answer right away. "I will be alright."

Calum's shoulders drooped. "Magnus, you need to eat, too."

"The way I see it, I still owe you for that chicken quarter you brought me that night when I was chained to that post at the quarry camp." Magnus smiled. "I am happy to sacrifice so you may be satisfied. Besides, I think I swallowed a fish or two when I was swimming after the pirate ship. I should be good for awhile."

"If you say so." Calum sighed. "But you don't owe me anything. If anything, I owe you for saving me. Again."

Magnus shook his head. "As I have said before, we are friends, Calum. Friends owe each other nothing. Attempting to keep track is pointless because we will always owe each other, mutually. It is the Law of Debt in its purest, perfected form: we are indebted to each other forever."

"I know what you mean."

A dark sphere tumbled out of the bag and plunked on the wooden floor. Calum picked it up. An apple, bruised everywhere, but not rotten. Not long until it would begin to rot, though, either. He could eat that without feeling guilty.

Two pieces of stale bread, a small, dried-out piece of smoked fish, and that apple later, Calum lay back down and stared up at the stars. As he drifted back to sleep, he wished Lilly was sleeping "near" him instead of Axel.

He pushed the thought from his mind and closed his eyes once again.

———

"Calum, wake up!" Lilly's voice cut through the blackness that blanketed Calum's vision, and morning sunlight flooded his eyes.

He sat up abruptly again, and again his body reminded him to stop doing that. "What's going on?"

"Something's coming." Her voice rang hollow with fear.

Calum scanned the surrounding waters and saw nothing aside from the other lifeboats following theirs. "What? Where are they?"

"No, not more pirates." Lilly's eyes widened. "Something in the water."

Behind her, both Magnus and Axel, who now wore his armor again, rowed twice as fast as Magnus had last night. Determination—and hefty a dose of terror—etched into their expressions.

Whatever this was, it was bad.

Calum faced the lifeboat's stern and scanned the water. Three large black silhouettes followed them. "More sharks?"

Lilly shook her head. "Worse. Much worse."

"How do you know?"

"I was scouting around, and I saw it. A gigantic dark form under the water, headed toward us from behind." Lilly stared at him. "We're in trouble."

Calum glanced into the water behind the boat again. The three shark silhouettes weren't anywhere to be found. Definitely not a good sign.

"Do you know what it is?" Calum asked Magnus, who continued to row with purpose.

"Not for sure..." His oars carved into the water, and he spoke between rows. "...but it is probably... a Jyrak."

Calum blinked. "A what?"

"No." Lilly shook her head. "Jyraks don't exist. They're a myth."

"Then what do you think... you saw in the water?" Magnus pressed.

Lilly gave no answer.

"Huh?" Calum glanced between them.

"Jyraks." Magnus didn't stop his furious rowing. "Monstrous lake creatures... definitely not a myth."

Lilly shook her head. "No one has ever seen one and lived to tell about it."

"No one that *you* have heard of." Magnus dug his oars into the water three times before he continued. "My father saw one once... in this very lake."

Lilly started to say something, but a rumble sounded from behind her and Calum. They both turned.

From the water emerged a dark scaled monstrosity of gigantic proportions, seemingly at half-speed. A long neck lifted a colossal head from the water, complete with jagged bronze teeth and a dark red tongue.

Spikes adorned its head and two large horns jutted out from just behind its glowing, pupilless yellow eyes. The Jyrak's massive arms raised out of the water, also laden with spikes. Black talons tipped each of the four webbed fingers on its hands.

A droning roar split the air as the Jyrak slowly rose to its full height. It had to be the biggest creature in existence. Calum couldn't imagine how anything could be larger—and he was having difficulty even believing the Jyrak was real.

Then it started toward them.

Magnus stopped rowing. "We are in trouble."

CHAPTER 10

Calum pointed to the sky. "Lilly, get in the air now. Head south. Find out how far we are from land. And take the food with you. If our boat goes down, we can't risk losing that food."

Lilly nodded and took to the sky with the sack of food over her shoulder.

"Axel and Magnus," Calum said. "We need to row. We gotta try to get away from it."

"You direct us," Magnus ordered. "We will handle the rowing. We need your eyes and your focus."

Calum nodded, and the two of them began to row again in a furious rhythm.

The Jyrak droned another roar again and started after them.

Calum glanced back at the other lifeboats. He had to keep track of their progress forward and everything that was happening behind them.

In their boat, Puolo and Jake tried to keep pace, but even with several men rowing, they had a hard time keeping up with Magnus and Axel. A third lifeboat chased theirs, but the fourth, the one with Yurgev's friends, cut hard to the right.

Fine. If they wanted to split off from the group, so be it. Calum would use it to his advantage. He leaned back. "Magnus, Axel—hard left."

Their lifeboat angled left and sliced through the water away from the Jyrak. To Calum's relief, it glanced between its two options, then it turned toward the prisoners' boat.

"Row harder!" Calum yelled. Though the Jyrak had chosen to pursue the other boat, that didn't mean Calum's and the other boats were in the clear. But at least they could gain some distance from it in the meantime.

Their boat sped forward, more due to Magnus's efforts than Axel's. Each row on his part seemed to nearly lift the small boat out of the water, almost as if they were leaping forward instead of cruising along the water.

Calum glanced back again.

The Jyrak closed the distance to the prisoners' lifeboat in two colossal steps and reached for it. The men below screamed as its humongous hand grasped their lifeboat like a toy. Two of them squelched between its fingers and fell a hundred feet to the water below, but the others disappeared into the Jyrak's deadly mouth along with the fragmented boat.

The sight horrified Calum. Yes, those men had meant Axel and him harm, but seeing them eaten by this monster shook Calum to his core.

"Calum, get down!" Axel yelled from behind him.

Calum's head swiveled forward in time to see the Jyrak's gigantic tail swinging toward them. He ducked as low as he could, and the tail swept over their lifeboat with only a few feet to spare, then it smashed into the water in front of Puolo's lifeboat. The waves launched the lifeboats in opposite directions and capsized Puolo's lifeboat.

Calum pointed at them. "Circle back and pick them up!"

Axel shook his head and kept rowing. "We can't save them and still be able to escape."

"Axel is right," Magnus called over the noise. "We must continue forward. One of the other lifeboats is already heading toward the survivors to pick them up."

Calum didn't like the idea of leaving anyone behind, but the others seemed to have the situation handled, so he just nodded.

Behind them, the Jyrak slowly turned its attention toward the other lifeboats with another droning roar, and the lifeboat behind Puolo's helped some of the stragglers in the water into their boat, including Jake.

Puolo didn't climb in. Somehow, he managed to flip his lifeboat back over, and he clambered inside. He snatched a pair of oars floating nearby and rowed with fury toward the Jyrak.

Jake hollered and reached for him from the other lifeboat, but his comrades wouldn't let him dive back in to go after his father. Puolo waved and shouted something Calum couldn't make out, then he ground his oars into the surf.

Calum's lifeboat lurched forward again, and he dropped onto his side. When he made it back up, he saw Jake's lifeboat chasing after theirs and making decent time with the extra hands rowing.

All the while, Puolo's lifeboat raced toward the Jyrak. Once Puolo came within range, he waved his arms and yelled.

The Jyrak reared its head back with another droning roar and slammed his hand down on Puolo's lifeboat, smashing it to pieces. Puolo disappeared under the surf and never resurfaced.

Calum cringed. By stalling the Jyrak, Puolo might have just saved them all, but it had cost him his life.

Lilly swooped in close and kept pace with their lifeboat as Magnus and Axel continued to row. She shouted, "There's land in sight! You're almost there."

Calum shielded his eyes from the sunlight and gazed south. Sure enough, he saw dry land in the distance, and hope filled his chest.

"We can make it," he said to Magnus and Axel. To Lilly, he called, "Now get back to shore before that thing gets you."

She nodded and zipped away with the sack of food still on her back.

They cruised along the water at a good speed, but when Calum looked back, he realized they'd separated from the second lifeboat too much, which was also heading toward the shore, albeit at a different angle.

Worse yet, the Jyrak was coming after Calum's boat now.

In four enormous steps, it closed the distance to them and reached down for their boat. It would have grabbed them in its first grasp had the water swell from its steps not pushed them just out of range again.

If Calum hadn't totally believed in the Overlord before, it didn't matter now—he called out to Him just the same.

Real or not, the Overlord didn't stop the Jyrak's next swipe. Its taloned fingers knifed down toward them.

"Bail out!" Magnus shouted.

Calum, Axel, and Magnus dove into the water just before the Jyrak's hand pulverized the lifeboat. When Calum surfaced, he saw Axel clawing at the water toward Magnus, who had surfaced several yards ahead of his position.

Calum swam the same direction with every ounce of energy he had left. As before, his armor threatened to sink him, but he'd regained enough energy to keep his head above water for the time being. Even so, he couldn't keep it up forever, so he swam toward a long piece of curved wood, almost big enough to lie on, floating nearby.

As the Jyrak smashed the boat, its tail whipped around behind it again. The tail's velocity created a swell that pushed Jake's lifeboat back toward them. Calum saw the swell approaching and grabbed onto the large piece of his broken lifeboat.

As the swell hit, Calum kicked his legs to propel himself higher out of the water. He positioned the flattest part of the lifeboat against the water and let the cascade carry him toward the shore on his belly. A rush of excitement filled his chest, and he almost whooped as the waves ferried him along.

The same wave plowed into Axel and Magnus, and Calum zipped past where they had just been. He considered waving at them as he cruised by, but he decided it was more important to hang on instead.

The wave died slowly, and it deposited Calum in the water only about three quarters of the way back to shore. Jake's lifeboat actually ended up closer to shore than he did. He held onto his board and craned his head back for a look.

Axel's head popped up from the water about twenty yards behind him, and Magnus's did as well, but about five yards closer. Another man's head surfaced near Axel.

It was one of the two prisoners from Yurgev's cell who hadn't been eaten. He launched toward Axel and pushed him under the water, then swam toward the shoreline.

A hand emerged from the surf behind the prisoner's head and yanked him under the water, then Axel popped back up. He jerked backward and the prisoner surfaced again, only to get Axel's fist in his face.

Their struggle continued, and they traded off who went under the water and who got to breathe as the Jyrak reached down toward them.

"*Axel!*" Calum yelled.

Axel looked at him, and the prisoner dunked him under the water again. As the Jyrak's arm dropped down, the prisoner held a flailing Axel under the water. When the Jyrak's shadow passed over him, the prisoner's angry face went blank, and his eyes widened.

The Jyrak's hand pummeled the prisoner. When the Jyrak drew its hand out of the water, Calum could barely see the prisoner between its fingers, and Axel hung from the Jyrak's hand by his left arm.

Though he tried to pull free, he couldn't. He was stuck.

THE WATER below Axel dropped away, and his left shoulder socket burned with strain. He swore and cursed, but he couldn't get free. Above him, the prisoner's blood mingled with the lake water dripping from the Jyrak's massive hand, and his bare foot protruded just above the webbing between two of the Jyrak's fingers.

Axel twisted his body and tried to get out, but it didn't work. The Jyrak's sprawling chest passed by and gave way to its neck as Axel rose higher and higher. It wouldn't be long until its bronze teeth came into view.

The shouts of his friends sounded from below, now as distant as when his mother used to call to him from across their field to come home for dinner. He should never have left his farm.

At this point, even if he could get free from the Jyrak's grip, the fall to the water below would kill him, but Axel drew his sword from his belt nonetheless. If he were going to die, he'd cut off a chunk of the Jyrak's tongue on his way. Then he'd give it the worst stomachache in Jyrak history.

Before Axel's eyes, bronze teeth, each of them pointed and longer than he was tall, separated. A forked tongue emerged from behind them and licked the air. The Jyrak's jaws opened wide, ready to receive him, and a blast of hot air that reeked of death washed over him.

Terror gripped Axel's entire body, but he refused to succumb to it. Instead, he got angry. The mismatch of one little human with a sword against a beast of this size was enough to infuriate him. It wasn't fair, and he was going to make sure the Jyrak knew it.

Axel timed his swing as best as he could, but the Jyrak thrust him almost directly into its throat. Axel's sword clanged off its teeth, and he fell onto his side.

Next to Axel, the prisoner's mangled body crunched between the Jyrak's bronze teeth. The Jyrak's jaws closed, and darkness replaced the sunlight.

HORROR SATURATED CALUM'S CHEST. Axel was gone, devoured by the Jyrak along with the prisoner. He couldn't believe it had happened, even despite seeing it with his own eyes.

Something latched onto Calum's shoulder with so much force that his head almost submerged under the water. Magnus's hand.

"We must get to shore before it comes for us next." Magnus's voice rang with tones of sadness and anger, but mostly with urgency. "We can do nothing for him now. Come on."

Calum hated that Magnus was right, but he couldn't deny it. He clenched his teeth and dug into the surf with his tired arms.

THE PUTRID STENCH of decay and rotten flesh burned Axel's nostrils. The Jyrak's tongue slapped him against the roof of its mouth and toward its throat, but he dug the fingers of his left hand into its squishy flesh.

He maneuvered his sword and jammed the point into the Jyrak's gums at the base of the right side of its bronze teeth. Glowing orange blood spurted onto his face and armor. It tingled like warm liquid metal in his mouth, and he spat it out.

The Jyrak jerked, and its mouth opened wide in a deafening roar that knocked Axel onto his back. Still, this was his chance to get out. His only chance.

Axel recovered his footing and stumbled toward the spot where he'd stabbed the Jyrak's gums. He gripped the point of one of the shorter teeth with his free hand to steady himself and peered out across the vast expanse of water hundreds of feet below him, and the first hint of fresh air he'd inhaled in what felt like an eternity hit his lungs.

It was a surreal sight—towering more than a hundred feet over an expanse of perfectly blue water on a beautiful autumn day. The waters glistened under the sunlight, and a few clouds drifted lazily in the blue sky.

And all of it was framed by an enormous set of jagged bronze teeth.

The Jyrak's jaw began to shut.

Axel had no choice.

Still gripping his sword, he dashed forward and flung himself over the bottom row of teeth, just before the top row slammed down behind him.

Axel fell, and he screamed into the ether.

———

LILLY'S HEART had dropped into her churning stomach when Axel disappeared inside the Jyrak's mouth. She hovered well out of its reach and hung her head. Axel was gone.

A bloodcurdling cry for help snapped her attention back toward the Jyrak. A dark human form adorned with familiar blue armor on his arms and legs dropped from its mouth.

Axel... was *not* gone!

She abandoned the bag of food on the shore and exploded toward him at full speed. Based on her trajectory and his, Lilly aimed to reach him by the time he fell about halfway from the Jyrak's mouth to the water—provided the Jyrak didn't get him first. It had already locked its vision onto him and began to move its hand to catch him.

Not if I can do something about it.

Lilly swooped in to intercept Axel. He yelled until the moment her hand latched onto his left wrist, and then he stared up at her with astonished eyes.

Beyond him, the Jyrak's hand whipped toward them.

"Hold on!" Lilly yanked him to her left, and they dropped below the Jyrak's hand by inches.

"We're still falling!" Axel shouted as he managed to sheathe his sword.

Lilly pulled against the air, but they continued to fall. She couldn't lift him, but that wasn't the only way to get them both to safety. "You weigh... a *lot* more than Calum!"

Layers of dark scales passed them by as they plummeted toward the water below. Lilly focused all of her force into Axel, and their trajectory shifted, but not enough. She had to level them out or they'd both die upon impact.

Then the Jyrak's tail rose from the water and lashed toward them. Lilly couldn't lift him higher, above it, and if she tried to drop below it, Axel's weight might throw off any hope of her gliding them to safety.

"When you get close, let me go," Axel yelled amid the wind rushing past them. "I'll skid right off its tail, and you can pick me up again and redirect my momentum like you did to Calum."

"It won't—"

"If it doesn't, then I'm dead anyway!" Axel shouted. "I trust you."

When the tail got close enough, Lilly released Axel like he wanted. His body smacked hard against the tail, and his armor scraped the scales for a few seconds, then he dropped off the other side, no longer screaming.

Lilly spun under the tail and caught him by his ankle as he fell. She might as well have been trying to carry Magnus.

"Axel?" she called down to him, but she got no response. "*Axel!*"

He was either dead or unconscious. Either way, Lilly was on her own.

With all her strength and focus she pushed perpendicular to the shoreline, away from the Jyrak. The blue water jumped up to meet them. They were going to crash, and she couldn't prevent it. She couldn't pull Axel up.

When she let him go, Axel's body flew parallel to the water for just a moment before it crashed into the surf. She angled up as hard as she could, but it was too late.

She hit the water and skipped along the surface until she finally slowed down enough to sink. Water smothered her senses, and then it consumed her completely.

278

CHAPTER 11

W hen he saw Lilly hit the water, Calum knew she was in trouble. He'd seen Axel fall from the Jyrak's mouth—somehow—and then Lilly managed to get him away from it. Calum broke his swim back to shore and doubled back toward her.

She landed in the water about twenty feet to his left and then skidded another ten or so feet toward the shoreline. Thanks to his piece of the lifeboat, Calum made it to her within three seconds of her head disappearing under the water.

He reached down and flailed to find her, prepared to dive in if he couldn't, but his hand found hers before she sank too deep. He grabbed ahold of her wrist and hauled her up and onto the piece of the lifeboat.

A huge form knifed past him in the water, and Calum caught a gleam of iridescent blue under the sunlight—Magnus. He was heading for Axel.

Calum positioned Lilly on the piece of the lifeboat, got in front of it, and pulled it as he swam toward the surface. He had to get her to shore before he could check on her. It didn't take long for Magnus to catch up with him.

"Save yourself," Magnus said as he hefted Axel onto the curved piece of wood alongside Lilly. "I will get Axel and Lilly to shore."

Calum nodded and relinquished the makeshift life raft to him.

"Swim fast. It is still coming." Magnus cruised forward, hauling Axel and Lilly behind him.

Sure enough, the Jyrak plowed through the surf toward them, still upright, and, if possible, angrier-looking than before.

Calum didn't dawdle. He dove under the water and kicked his legs with fury until something propelled him up out of the water. The force of it sent him tumbling end-over-end in the surf.

When he finally resurfaced and cleared the water from his nostrils, Calum was facing the Jyrak, which towered over him. It pulled its hand out of the water no more than twenty yards from Calum and raised it to its chest.

Calum turned and dug his arms into the water. His legs launched him forward a few feet when he kicked, but he still wasn't making much progress. Terror powered every one of his desperate strokes, and he gritted his teeth.

279

He glanced over his shoulder and saw the Jyrak's hand plummeting toward him. He kicked harder and screamed.

The hand hit the water just behind Calum's feet and created a swell that carried Calum toward the shoreline. When the swell finally died down, Calum's boots scraped against the dirt at bottom of the lake. He sprang off the lake's floor and continued to claw toward the shore.

Magnus met him there and took hold of his wrist like a father escorting a child, but Calum didn't resist. Together they ran through the shallows.

Behind them the Jyrak roared, but it didn't pursue them any farther. Instead, it turned away and receded into the depths of the lake once again.

Calum exhaled a sigh of relief until he noticed Axel and Lilly lying on the shoreline, motionless, surrounded by Jake and his friends. He ignored his waterlogged boots and armor and ran over to them with Magnus close behind.

When he got closer, he noticed a man on top of Lilly. "Hey!"

Jake stepped into his path and stopped Calum before he could bash the guy's head in. "It's alright, Calum. He's helpin'."

It looked like the man was trying to take advantage of her—sort of. His left palm rested on the back of his right hand, and the heel of his right hand pressed into the center of Lilly's armored chest. He pumped on her chest five times, then leaned over and put his mouth on hers.

Calum sprang forward, but Jake reeled him back in.

"Let 'im work, Calum." For as wiry as he was, Jake managed to anchor Calum's arms in place. "He's gonna save her life."

"He'd better." Calum's tone surprised even him. It sounded like something Axel would say.

Lilly coughed and sputtered, and the man helped her onto her side. She hacked, and water trickled out of her mouth into the wet, gray sand below.

Calum's heart fluttered when her eyes met his. His relief at seeing the Jyrak descend back into the lake was nothing compared to this.

He twisted out of Jake's grip, ran to Lilly, and skidded to a halt on his knees next to her. He wrapped her in his arms and whispered into her ear. "I'm so glad you're alright."

She half-laughed, half-coughed, and returned his embrace for a moment, then she pulled away from him. Her head swiveled, and in a raspy voice, she asked, "Where's Axel?"

Calum blinked. He'd almost lost her, and she was asking about Axel?

Lilly's gaze fell on Axel, who lay next to her. The same man who'd helped her now leaned over Axel and pumped his chest the same as he had for her.

She covered her mouth. "Oh, no..."

It seemed like hours elapsed as the man worked on Axel. With every passing moment, Calum worried more and more for his friend, and Lilly clutched his hand in hers.

Then Axel's eyes finally opened. He coughed his lungs clear of lake water just as Lilly had, and he rolled onto his stomach with a moan.

Next to Calum, Lilly released her grip on his hand, sighed, and lay on her back. Just when Calum decided to get up, Lilly grabbed his hand again and smiled at him. "Thank you."

Calum couldn't restrain a smile of his own. He nodded and squeezed her hand in return.

Jake and Magnus stood over them. Magnus set the bag of food Lilly had rescued next to Calum and nodded toward the Jyrak, which had now fully disappeared into the Lake. "It does not appear the Jyrak means to follow us on land. After some rest, we should be safe to return to Sharkville."

Calum nodded.

Axel moaned again. Lilly gave a weak giggle, then she sighed. They had made it.

THEY REACHED Sharkville within a few hours of walking, and by that evening they made it back to Trader's Pass. It was there that Jake and his friends elected to part ways with Calum's group.

"We're headin' for Kanarah City," Jake had said. "My father had lots of friends in the fishin' industry there. They'll help me out with a new ship. We're gonna rebuild our crew and start fishin' again in the lake as soon as we can get the ship out there.

"Now that Brink is gone, the waters will be a lot safer, so thank you for that," he continued. "You ever need anythin', you let me know. We owe you our lives."

Calum nodded. "None of us would be here if it weren't for your father."

Jake gave a solemn nod. "I regret his death, but I understand why he did it. Your words honor 'im. Thank you."

Jake motioned toward one of the men standing behind him, and the man brought forward a sack bulging with food.

"I know it's not much, but our journey's far shorter than yours. Please take this." He offered the bag to Calum, who took it. "It's mostly dried or smoked fish. Nothin' fancy, but it should keep you goin'."

"Much appreciated," Calum said. "Thank you, and stay safe out there."

Calum extended his hand, and Jake shook it.

The two groups parted ways near where Calum and Lilly had killed the Dactyls and headed in opposite directions.

Several days and nights later, Calum, Axel, Lilly, and Magnus arrived at the western end of Trader's Pass hungry but alive. With the additional food given to them by Jake and his friends, they'd run out of rations only two days earlier. Thus far, the worst part about it had been Axel's complaining.

The moment they stepped into Western Kanarah, Lilly's smile widened. "It's good to be home."

Calum glanced at Magnus, whose face showed only quiet anger. Unlike Lilly, Magnus didn't seem happy to be back.

"So how do we find Riley?" Axel asked.

Calum turned to Magnus. "I've never been here before. Are we in the right place?"

"The dead tree is over there." Magnus pointed to a tall leafless tree to the south. Its body had turned a weatherworn charcoal gray. "We will wait for Riley there, as we discussed."

"If he doesn't show up within a few hours, then we should move on." Lilly scanned the skies. "We're near Raven's Brood territory."

Axel sighed and rubbed his forehead. "I take it that's a bad thing?"

Lilly nodded. "They're Windgale insurgents. They want to overthrow the Premier of the Sky Realm and establish their own alternate government. If they catch us in an open space like this, we're in trouble, so we shouldn't stay long."

They sat under the dead tree for an hour. In that time Calum took in the terrain around them. All in all, it didn't seem too different from the eastern half of Kanarah: both had trees and forests, dirt and rocks, and mountains in the distance.

Yet something about the western half set him at ease, even in spite of the potential threat of the Raven's Brood. Perhaps it was the lack of humans in this half—or more precisely, the lack of the King's influence and his soldiers. With no one in the King's employ chasing them, Calum felt free in an all-new way.

Lilly pointed along a road that headed southwest. "If you follow that road, you'll end up at the base of Aeropolis, where I live."

Calum nodded. "What about the one that heads north?"

"That leads to the Desert of the Forgotten, and then to the Blood Mountains and Reptilius, where Magnus is from." Lilly nodded toward Magnus.

Magnus's face hardened into a scowl.

"How far is it from here to Aeropolis?" Axel asked.

"I usually fly there, so I'm not sure how long it takes on foot. From the air it takes about a day at a steady pace, with a couple of stops for rest." Lilly leaned forward, shifted her quiver onto her lap, then leaned back against the tree again. She brushed her fingers through the fletching on her arrows.

Magnus squinted at the tree line. "Perhaps Riley ran into the Raven's Brood and had to take cover. That forest would be a good place to avoid them, and it is a type of terrain he is already familiar with."

"Makes sense," Axel said. "Maybe someone should go and—"

Lilly collided with him at nearly full speed and tackled him backward onto the ground.

Before Calum could question her action, a dark form slammed a sword into the earth where Axel had been sitting, then it zipped away just as fast.

Axel shoved Lilly away. "What in the—"

"Get down!" Magnus roared.

Calum dropped low and watched as three Windgales in dark armor flew at Magnus.

The first one lashed at Magnus with his sword, but the blow just bounced off Magnus's scaly shoulder. Magnus grabbed the attacker's ankle with his opposing hand and swung him at the second Windgale as if he weighed nothing. They smacked together and dropped to the dirt at Magnus's feet.

The third swung his sword at Magnus's head, but he ducked under the blow, latched onto the Windgale's cape with his hand, and slammed him against the dead tree face-first. He too fell to the ground, motionless.

Calum jumped to his feet and drew his sword, along with Axel. Lilly nocked an arrow in her bow and stepped up beside them.

At least fifty Windgales, all clad in dark armor, landed all around them. A black bird outlined in red emblazoned their breastplates, and each of them wore a black-and-red cape with the same image embroidered on the back.

The Raven's Brood.

CHAPTER 12

The last of the Raven's Brood landed in front of Lilly, and she immediately recognized him as their leader, Condor. He wore charcoal armor with the same raven on his chest, only it was all black. Instead of red accents on his armor like that of the rest of the Raven's Brood, they were black, and he wore no cape.

She remembered seeing him at the Sky Fortress several times before but hadn't remembered how handsome he was—tall and trim with black hair and sharp cheekbones. A pronounced scar ran from the outer edge of his left eyebrow to the top of his cheek. If anything, the scar intensified his cunning blue eyes and gave him an ominous appearance.

Too bad he chose the betrayer's path.

"Welcome to Western Kanarah. I am Condor, leader of the Raven's Brood." Condor focused on Lilly for a long moment, scrutinizing her and her armor. Then he placed his hands on his chest with his thumbs up, wrists crossed, and fingers extended over the wings of the raven on his breastplate, and he gave a slight nod.

"We're just passing through." Calum stepped forward without lowering his sword. "We don't want any trouble."

Condor smirked. His voice took on a casual tone. "Nor do we. But you've already harmed three of my men. And, unfortunately, that means there's a price to be paid."

"We just want to go our own way," Calum said. "We have nothing to give you anyway, even if we wanted to."

Condor nodded at Magnus. "That's quite a bulge in that pouch hanging from the side of your belt. You're certain you don't have anything of value?"

Magnus drew his hulking broadsword from its sheath. "Nothing I intend to hand over to you."

"Well then, it seems we're in a predicament, aren't we?" Condor eyed Lilly again, and another smirk formed on his lips. "I'll take her."

Axel pushed between Condor and Calum. "I'll die before that happens."

"What are you, a farm boy with a sword?" Condor chuckled and sighed. "Look, I'm happy to oblige you, but—"

Axel sprang forward and lashed his sword, but Condor took to the air the instant Axel began his advance.

Axel stared up at him, bewildered. "How is he flying without a cape?"

Magnus grabbed Axel's shoulder and yanked him back toward the group. "He's a Wisp. A promoted Windgale. He no longer needs a cape to fly."

Axel twisted free from Magnus's grip and glared at Condor, who hovered about ten feet off the ground with a grin on his face.

"He's also faster than any of us," Lilly said. "Significantly faster."

"We'll see about that." Axel shifted his sword and stepped forward.

"No." Magnus pulled him back again. "We must proceed with caution, not the reckless abandon you subscribe to. If you wish to get out of here, we must fight intelligently."

"The Sobek is right, Farm Boy." Condor's right hand rested on the pommel of his sword, which still hung from his belt in its sheath. "Except for the part about getting outta here. Like I said, we'll let you pass if you give up the girl."

Calum leaned close to Lilly. "Everyone seems to want you."

She huffed. Calum was more right than he even realized. She muttered, "Believe me, I wish that wasn't the case."

"Well?" Condor tapped his pommel with his fingers and descended to the ground well out of Axel's reach. As his feet touched the path, he asked, "What's your decision?"

In one fluid motion, one Lilly had practiced thousands of times, she raised her bow, drew back her arrow, took aim, and let it fly at Condor's chest. Armor or otherwise, the arrow would at least wound him and hopefully—

Condor sidestepped the arrow as if he'd seen it coming and had a full minute to avoid it.

Instead, the arrow struck the shoulder of a Windgale behind Condor, who yelped. The Windgales around him tensed up and raised their swords, but Condor gave a whoop, and they settled back into their positions.

Lilly's gaze narrowed and her mouth opened. She'd never seen anyone dodge an arrow like that before. Then again, Condor had been the youngest Captain of the Royal Guard before he rebelled and tried to assassinate the Premier. No doubt his speed and prowess had accelerated his rise to authority.

Condor extended his index finger at her and waved it. "Not very nice of you, my dear. Didn't your parents teach you any manners?"

Lilly's jaw hardened.

"Last chance." Condor's fingers curled around the hilt of his sword, but he still didn't draw it from its sheath. "What's your play?"

"We're not handing her over," Calum said.

Condor's sword flashed as he launched toward Calum, but Magnus pulled him back and absorbed the blow on his breastplate. The next two slashes skidded off his scaled arms before Magnus could even bring his sword up. Then Condor kicked his heel into the bottom of Magnus's chin, and he staggered back.

"Run for the trees!" Magnus yelled once he recovered. He swung his sword in a wide arc around him. Condor darted out of the way, but Magnus felled two approaching Windgales with his swing.

Lilly knew she couldn't help Axel and Calum from the ground, so she took to the air, even as they called after her. "Just run! I'll cover—"

A Windgale collided with her from the side and sent her careening through the air. She righted herself, drew another arrow, and shot him down. Another Windgale lashed his sword from above her. She reacted and blocked the attack with her bow, but the blade severed its string in the process.

Lilly whipped her right leg at the Windgale's face. Her shin slammed into the side of his head, knocking him from the sky. Lilly drew her sword with her right hand and wielded her unstrung bow in her left. She zipped higher into the sky and glanced behind her as she flew.

A dozen Windgales chased after her, two-dozen went after Axel and Calum, and the rest stayed with Condor to fight Magnus, who now ran after them toward the forest. So much for trying to cover them.

She angled down and spiraled toward the ground with the Windgales close behind.

AXEL COULD BARELY RUN for all the Windgales he had to kill along the way. They kept dropping in front of him, so he kept hacking them down or avoiding them as he and Calum raced toward the forest.

Something struck his back. He toppled forward in the tall grass and skidded to a halt on his chest. Axel whirled around in time to skewer a Windgale who dropped down at him with his sword raised high, primed to deliver a killing blow. Axel grinned until a second Windgale emerged from overhead.

He tried to pull his sword free of the first Windgale in time, but by the time he managed it, the second Wingale was already on top of him.

Had Calum not sprung from the tall grass and cut him down, the second Windgale would've killed Axel with his first swing. Calum reached down and pulled Axel to his feet. "What are you just laying around for?"

"Ha, ha," Axel said. "Not funny."

A dark blur materialized behind Calum. Axel yanked on Calum's arm, pulling him forward, and jabbed his sword at the next Wingdale. The blade lodged in the Windgale's throat, and he fell flat on his face.

Calum nodded to Axel, and they kept running.

MAGNUS BATTED Windgales away as he ran. On occasion, they managed to trip him up, but by far his biggest concern was Condor.

He was not only faster than the rest of the Raven's Brood but also stronger and an extremely skilled fighter. For every swing Magnus managed, Condor threw six or seven attacks back at him.

Worse still, Magnus hadn't landed a single blow on him. Every one of his hacks either missed Condor and hit a different Windgale, or missed everything entirely. At least their puny steel swords couldn't pierce his scales, and as long as he wore his breastplate, they couldn't cut into his soft underbelly.

Far ahead, Magnus saw Axel and Calum cross into the forest. They'd find some cover there, but the numbers still favored the Windgales. They had to work together to get out of this alive.

Then Condor abandoned his onslaught and instead shot into the sky, leaving about six Windgales to pester Magnus while he ran.

When Condor didn't return, Magnus realized he was going after Lilly.

And Magnus couldn't do anything to stop him.

LILLY KNEW she ought to slow down before she hit the top of the forest canopy, but she didn't. The Windgales pursuing her weren't going to slow down, and that meant she couldn't, either.

She hit what looked like an opening at about half of her top speed and wove down through a network of leafy branches. They clawed at her face and hair and smacked against her shoulders as she descended toward the forest floor.

By the time she cleared the canopy, she was no longer flying, but falling. A large prickly bush cushioned her body weight and dumped her onto the forest floor where she lay sprawled on her back for a moment, until a dozen dark forms crashed through the canopy and thudded against the ground around her.

Lilly sprang to her feet and gripped her sword and bow tighter. Half of the Windgales weren't moving, but the other six slowly stood to their feet. One darted toward her and swung his sword.

It clanged against her bow, and she ran him through with her blade. As he fell, two more Windgales shot forward. Lilly ducked under one swing and parried the second with her bow, then slashed the back of the first Windgale's knee. He tumbled to the ground, clutching at his wound.

The other Windgale chopped at her again, and she parried the attack with her sword. She whipped her bow at his head, but he blocked it with his armored forearm and smirked at her—until she drove her boot into his groin. He doubled over next to his friend, and she dispatched them both with two quick swings of her sword.

Though six of the Windgales still lay unconscious on the forest floor, covered in scrapes and scratches from the trees they'd crashed through trying to follow her, the three conscious Windgales launched into the fray, weapons brandished.

For Lilly, taking on one Windgale opponent at a time was reasonable, and two was pushing it. Three wasn't something she even wanted to attempt, at least not without her bow. If she meant to get away from the Raven's Brood, she had to use the forest to her advantage.

She leaped into the air and threaded through the thick trees with the Windgales close behind.

As AXEL and Calum reached the trees, the Windgales pursued them, still flying. He'd expected them to slow down some, but they flew into the forest with the kind of gusto he usually employed when he fought enemies.

"Take lots of sharp turns," Calum called to Axel. "Let the forest do the work for you."

"I know," Axel yelled back. *Obviously.*

Axel stole a quick glance over his shoulder as he ran. One of the Windgales was closing in on him with his sword extended, and fast. Ahead of Axel, a thick branch hung just above his reach. He leaped for it, grabbed ahold, and kicked his feet up.

The Windgale behind him couldn't alter his flight path in time and zoomed under Axel's legs, and as he looked back at Axel, he smacked into the next tree at almost full speed.

Axel smirked and dropped back down to his feet.

Another Windgale zipped toward him from his left side and almost took off Axel's head with his sword, but Axel noticed in time to duck under the swing. The Windgale swung again, but Axel blocked with his sword and drove his fist into the Windgale's gut.

With the Windgale doubled over, Axel grabbed a handful of his cape and whipped him against the nearest tree. The Windgale's body cracked against the trunk, and he fell to the ground, limp.

They were quick, but lightweight, too. Kind of fun to toss 'em around just like Magnus had before the rest of them showed up.

A third Windgale cut through the canopy at him. He hopped back, and when the Windgale tried to correct his trajectory, he crashed into the tree branch that Axel had just grabbed to avoid the first Windgale.

Quick, lightweight, and apparently not too bright. Either that, or they didn't have good combat training.

The third Windgale tumbled to the ground and struggled to get back to his feet, but the pommel of Axel's sword laid him out flat.

This wasn't just kind of fun, Axel decided. He was having a blast.

CALUM RECOGNIZED the smirk on Axel's face even from twenty yards away and while dodging a haphazard swing from one of the Windgales.

He drove the tip of his sword through the Windgale's armor and into his chest, and then he ripped it out to block another blow from another Windgale. Magnus had been right—the trees had negated the Raven's Brood's advantage from a combat perspective, though the Windgales still had the numbers in their favor.

A trio of Windgales hovered toward Calum with more caution this time, but the sound of wood snapping cracked from behind them. Magnus burst from the trees with a roar. He grabbed two of the Windgales by their capes and slammed them together, sandwiching the third Windgale in the middle. All three of them dropped.

Calum couldn't stifle a grin of his own. "Nice."

Magnus's face betrayed no such amusement. "Condor went after Lilly."

Calum's mirth fizzled, and his heart shuddered. "Which way?"

"Follow me."

LILLY HAD LOST two of the three Windgales in the forest, but the third managed to keep pace with her without colliding into any of the trees or branches. She'd taken more than a few close knocks herself, but she'd made it this far with only a few small cuts on her face and scrapes on her armored legs, arms, and torso.

She looped up toward the canopy and slowed her ascent enough to grab onto a branch. She pulled it up with her, and as soon as the Windgale came into view beneath her, she released her grip. Tension whipped the branch at the Windgale and it smacked him out of the air.

He dropped down to the forest floor, and Lilly followed him. She landed ten feet away and started toward him. As Lilly raised her sword to finish him off, the Windgale lashed his leg and swept her off her feet. Her back hit the forest floor and pushed the air out of her lungs, and her sword and bow tumbled out of her fingers.

Before she could recover, the Windgale stood over her, his wild eyes raging amid his bloodied face. He held his sword over his head. Just when Lilly thought it was all over, a dark streak flashed behind the Windgale's head, followed by a dull *thunk*. He dropped to the dirt face-first.

In his place stood Condor.

CHAPTER 13

"There's something oddly familiar about you." Condor stepped past the Windgale and slowly approached her with his sword down. "Have we met before?"

Lilly glanced at her sword. Still out of reach, but Condor might be far enough away for her to get it in time. Maybe.

"I asked you a question, love."

"I'm not your 'love.'" Lilly glared at him.

"But I *do* know you from somewhere, don't I?" Condor asked. "From back when I was still allowed in Aeropolis?"

Lilly clenched her jaw. The less Condor knew about her, the better off she was...

Unless he already knew too much.

"In fact, I believe I've seen you in the Sky Fortress itself." He rubbed his chin. "Perhaps you worked there as a servant to the Premier's family?"

"Yes." Lilly feigned frustration. He was close to the truth. Too close. "That's it."

Condor grinned and nodded. His tone remained casual and conversational, despite the sword in his hand. "Born into your caste, just like me. Just like all Windgales."

"That's how it is." Lilly eyed her sword again. Without it, she stood no chance of beating him. With it, her odds improved only marginally, but it was better than nothing.

"Go ahead. Take it up. I won't try to stop you." Condor motioned toward it with his own sword. "Wouldn't be a fair fight while you're unarmed."

Lilly didn't hesitate. She zipped over to the sword and gripped it in her right hand.

"Then again, your prowess *is* impressive." Condor squinted. "Especially for a servant girl."

A lump arose in Lilly's throat. Did he know?

"And your armor—far too fancy for any normal servant girl. Perhaps you found it." Condor chuckled. "No, no. You *stole* it. Even better, right?"

Lilly glared at him again. He was playing mind games, trying to throw her off.

"But we both know you're no servant girl, and you're certainly no thief. We both know the truth." Condor smiled and tilted his head to the side. "We both know who you *really* are."

Lilly's body moved before her mind caught up. She hurtled forward on wings of air and

288

lashed her sword at Condor's chest, but he sidestepped and somehow sent her spiraling to the ground, all without even raising his sword.

Condor waved his finger as he had when she'd shot the arrow at him. "Not very ladylike."

She should've known better than to attack him. Even with the sword in her hands, and even with the meager training she'd received from Magnus, Axel, and Calum over the last several weeks, what hope did she have of winning? Condor was too fast, too skilled as a fighter.

"Your skill with the bow is undeniable. Did General Balena train you himself?" Condor watched her stand up. "It was a suitable choice, given your station. Keeps you away from immediate danger. The drawback, of course, is that it limits your options in close combat."

Lilly bit her tongue. No need to affirm his questions. Every bit of information she gave him would work against her in the future, one way or another. She longed for a functioning bow.

"Would you care for a lesson?" Condor asked. "I'd be happy to teach you some techniques."

Lilly sprang into the air and dove toward him, blade first. This time, Condor batted her sword away with his blade and stepped aside. She skidded to a halt on her feet and zipped toward him again. Their blades played for a moment, and Lilly thought she was doing well—until Condor disarmed her.

He dropped the blade at his side and gave her a modest grin.

Lilly staggered back, surprised, furious, and empty-handed. She took to the air, but Condor grabbed her cape and yanked her down. Two hard strikes, one to her head and another to her leg knocked her to the ground.

She lay there stunned but aware enough to realize she'd landed within reach of her sword.

Condor stood over her. "I had hoped to use you as leverage against the Premier, but I'm not sure you'll cooperate, so I'm giving you a choice: come with me willingly, or die."

Through her haze, Lilly scooped her sword off the ground and jabbed it at Condor's ankle, but it didn't do any good. He simply stepped over her feeble attack and put his foot on her wrist until she released her grip, then he kicked her sword away.

"I take it that's your answer?"

Lilly gave him a glare before she lay back again and exhaled a long breath. "I'm not helping you with anything."

"Such a waste." Condor sighed and shook his head, then he raised his sword.

Lilly clenched her teeth, stared at Condor, and waited for the blow to come.

It never did.

Condor lowered his sword and smiled. "You didn't really think I was going to do it, did you?"

Before Lilly could answer, a dark blur burst from the woods to her left, collided with Condor, and knocked him to the ground. Condor's sword clanged against a nearby tree, and the two forms tumbled along the forest floor in a flurry of charcoal armor and gray-brown fur.

Riley.

He pinned Condor to the ground with his forepaws and clamped his jaws onto Condor's left wrist. Condor yelled, then he drove his right fist into the side of Riley's head.

Riley yelped, and he released his grip on Condor, who zipped through the air toward his sword. He grasped it in his hand and whirled around, but Riley had already closed the distance and leaped at him. Riley knocked Condor onto his back again, but this time his jaws gripped Condor's right hand—his sword hand.

Lilly rose to her feet, rubbed her head, and picked up her sword amid the growls and curses. As Lilly approached, Condor shifted his sword to his left hand and angled it toward Riley.

"No!" Lilly shouted. She couldn't stop it from happening in time.

The tip of the blade pierced Riley's fur just behind his right shoulder, and he yelped. Then Condor's sword knifed even deeper into Riley's torso.

CHAPTER 14

Riley jerked away from Condor and staggered back with a noticeable limp, both growling and whimpering.

"Bad Wolf." Condor pushed himself up to his feet and switched his sword to his right hand again, despite the blood dripping from it. He started toward Riley again. "Bad, bad Wolf."

Riley snarled and narrowed his blue eyes at Condor. Lilly didn't know how he was even still alive, but somehow Riley shifted his weight back on his hind legs, ready to spring forward.

A mass of green plowed into Condor from the right. The impact sent him tumbling through the air, and he smacked against a thick tree then landed facedown in the dirt. He started to get up but Magnus grabbed him by his throat and pinned him against the tree.

"Try to fly away now, bird." Magnus hissed at him and cocked his arm.

"Don't!" Lilly yelled.

Magnus swiveled his head toward her and glared, but held his arm in place.

"If we bring him to the Sky Fortress, we'll—"

"He stabbed Riley. He is too dangerous to be left alive," Magnus said. Condor clutched Magnus's wrist and squirmed in his grasp, but he couldn't escape.

"No, Magnus. Don't kill him." Lilly shook her head and started toward him, but her head still swam from Condor's blow. She stopped short and steadied herself. "He's extremely valuable to the Premier. We can use that to our advantage."

Magnus hesitated, then he lowered his other arm. "You had better be right."

Calum and Axel burst from the trees, their swords at the ready.

"There are more of them chasing us," Calum said between breaths. "We need to go deeper into the woods or they're gonna—"

Riley loosed a canine whimper and dropped onto his side. Blood trickled down the side of his right foreleg.

"Riley?" Calum ran over to him and skidded to a halt on his knees. "By the Overlord, what happened to you?"

A pair of Windgales shot out from the trees at Axel. He ducked under the first one's slash and batted the second Windgale to the ground with his sword. The first Windgale stopped short when he saw Condor in Magnus's hand.

"Tell your brood to stop the attack," Magnus said to the Windgale. "Or Condor dies."

The Windgale scowled at Magnus, then he shot up through the trees.

"They won't stop attacking unless I give the order." Condor twisted in Magnus's grip again. "They'll keep coming until they kill you and free me. We are united in our cause by blood, and we will not relent until—"

"Everyone in Aeropolis knows you're the only thing holding the Raven's Brood together," Lilly said.

She started toward them again, but her head rebelled with a spike of pain that left her dizzy. She exhaled a long breath with her eyes closed. When she regained her equilibrium again, she started toward Condor.

"You started an insurrection and tried to assassinate the Premier so you could succeed him, and when you failed, you took the survivors with you, but everyone in the Sky Fortress knows you're the only Wisp, the only real fighter out here."

Condor's dark eyebrows arched down. "You were only a child when it happened, and all you know is what you've been told. I suppose I can't fault you for not knowing the truth."

Riley whimpered again.

Calum shook his head as he pulled off his gauntlets. "Guys, Riley's in bad shape here. He needs help, and I don't even know where to start."

"Put pressure on his wound. Try to stop the bleeding," Magnus said. "Lilly, go over and help Calum, and Calum, come over here with Axel to hold Condor while I tend to Riley."

"Lilly, what happened to your face?" Axel stopped his advance toward Condor and instead walked closer to her, his sword still out. "Did he hit you?"

"Axel, don't—"

Axel's gaze locked on Condor, and his face crumpled with anger. "I'm gonna cut his feather-flyin' head off."

He stormed toward Condor with bloodlust in his eyes.

"You will *not*." Magnus pointed a thick, green finger at Axel. "Lilly wants him alive to present to the Premier."

"What do you mean, 'present him to the Premier?'" Axel shouted. "He stabbed Riley and tried to kill Lilly. Look at the mark he left on her face!"

Lilly touched her cheek where Condor had struck her. It felt tender and warm to her touch—definitely a nasty bruise. "It's not bad. It won't—"

"He's dead. I'm not negotiating this time." Axel didn't stop his advance toward Condor.

Magnus whirled around and pinned Condor to the ground in front of Axel, who stopped short. Magnus hissed, then growled, "You are *not* killing him."

"He hit Lilly. I'm gonna kill him, even if that means I gotta go through you to do it."

Axel advanced again and raised his sword. Condor looked up at him from the ground, almost grinning.

"*Stop.*" Magnus's voice reverberated off the trees, and Axel halted again. "You gain *nothing* by killing this man, either in Lilly's eyes or in anyone else's."

"Guys?" Calum's voice tanged with urgency. "There's a lot of blood, and his breathing is slowing down. I—I think we're losing Riley."

Magnus locked eyes with Axel. "You need to hold Condor down with Calum so I can tend to Riley before it's too late."

"You wanna save the Wolf? Then let me kill Condor." Axel's tone matched his steely expression. "Or they can both die, for all I care."

"Axel!" Calum shouted. Blood oozed between the fingers

Lilly couldn't believe Axel had just said that. How could he be so cold?

"Make your decision, Magnus."

"Axel, don't do this," Lilly said. "I don't want this! Please—we need to save Riley!"

Axel frowned at her. "Condor needs to die."

Magnus glanced at Calum, who shook his head. "Then you leave me no choice."

Axel's eyes widened as Magnus sprang forward with Condor still in-hand. Before Axel could so much as raise his sword, Magnus drove his fist into Axel's forehead. He withered to the ground, unconscious.

"Magnus!" Calum yelled. "What are you doing?"

Magnus held Condor up in front of him and delivered a comparable blow to his head, and he too passed out. When Magnus released his grip, Condor slumped to the ground.

Magnus pointed at Lilly. "Watch them. If either of them wake up, tell me right away."

Lilly nodded, still shocked at Magnus's blow to Axel, though she couldn't rightly say it was an overreaction—not when Riley's life was on the line.

When Magnus made it to Riley, Calum stepped aside.

"I can't believe you did that," Calum said, more shock than anger in his voice.

"What would you have done differently?" Magnus pressed his hand against Riley's wound.

"I—" Calum bit his lip. "I don't know."

"Get me something I can use to bandage this wound, and hurry," Magnus ordered. "His breathing is very labored, and he has lost consciousness."

Calum returned with one of the dead Windgale's capes.

Magnus frowned. "This fabric is not ideal, but it will have to do. Tear it into strips for me."

Axel and Condor lay next to each other at Lilly's feet, both out cold. She'd come to recognize Axel's attraction toward her, but he'd gone too far this time. Where Calum would elect to show mercy, Axel's responses always skewed toward payback or even outright revenge.

From the pouch on his belt Magnus pulled the vial of veromine he'd used on Lilly's shoulder when they'd found her unconscious in the Golden Plains.

With great care, he dripped three delicate orange drops into Riley's wound. Magnus paused, leaned closer, and then he dumped the rest of the vial into the wound. Afterward, he wrapped the strips of cape around Riley's torso several times to cover it.

"The veromine will protect his wound from infection and aid in healing it, but he is still in serious trouble." Magnus tied the ends of the strips together under Riley's belly. "He may have already lost too much blood, and if Condor's sword hit any of his vital organs, we may be too late. We have to get him help, and soon. We have to get him to Aeropolis."

"Before they attacked us, you said we were a day and a half away. Does he have that long?"

"No." Magnus shook his head. "But if we hurry, we will arrive sooner. He may have a chance."

Lilly pressed her fingers against the cut on her face. The whole area stung, but she couldn't focus on that now. "I know the way. Calum, can you help me round up as many of these Raven's Brood capes as we can? The Premier will want to know how many we defeated."

Calum looked at Magnus, who nodded. "Sure, I can help."

"I will stay with Riley and these two." Magnus squinted at Axel. "I expect Axel will awaken soon. I did not hit him that hard."

WHILE CALUM DIDN'T LIKE how Magnus's solution for traveling with a flight-capable prisoner had played out, he couldn't deny its effectiveness.

Magnus carried Riley, still unconscious, in his arms as they rushed toward Aeropolis, while Calum and a surly unarmed Axel walked on either side of Condor, to whom they were both tied. Lilly hovered behind them with her sword out, ready to cut Condor down if he tried anything.

Cords tied in tight knots restrained Condor's wrists behind his back, and a rope stretched between his ankles, both of which were tied so he could only jog at best. Another rope looped between his back and over the front of his elbows.

One end was tied to Calum's belt, and the other was tied to Axel's belt. That way, if he tried to fly away, he'd have to carry Calum and Axel with him.

They had stripped Condor's armor from him and left it in the forest along with his sword. Now the only thing that indicated he was a member of the Raven's Brood at all was a necklace made of delicate silver chain with a black-and-red raven pendant hanging from it.

They trudged ahead and pressed onward throughout the night, stopping for only minutes to eat and shift loads around. Calum bore both the extra burden of carrying Axel's sword and a sack stuffed full of the Raven's Brood capes that he and Lilly had collected.

Given their quickened speed and not stopping overnight, the day-and-a-half trip to Aeropolis only took a day. Even so, Calum worried they still might be too late. Riley was still alive, albeit only barely, but he hadn't woken up since he'd lost consciousness back in the woods.

Soon the Windgale city of Aeropolis towered overhead, but even from a distance Calum could only see glimpses of something sparkling from among the clouds. A network of thick gray pillars lofted the city far out of reach of anyone who lacked flight ability.

As a means of defense, it was ingenious in its simplicity. If the Windgales had enemies, they would have to learn to fly before they could mount a successful attack, or they'd have to possess a power capable of taking down the pillars that held the city up.

But Calum couldn't conceive of anything that powerful, except perhaps Lumen, and even then, Calum didn't know Lumen's capabilities. They'd only ever interacted in dreams.

"So... how are we supposed to get up there?" Axel asked, his voice more flat than furious.

"There's a lift that lowers three times a day for merchants and travelers," Lilly replied.

"When are the three times?" Calum asked.

"Once in the early morning, another around midday, and once more in the evening, but we already missed the morning lift."

"We do not have time to wait for the lift. Riley's condition is still deteriorating." Magnus glared at Condor, who rolled his eyes. "Is there something we can do about that?"

Lilly shook her head. "We can talk to the guard at the lift and ask him, but they rarely make exceptions. Premier's orders."

Condor huffed.

"You got somethin' to say?" Axel turned to him, his fury partially renewed.

"Not in the least, Farm Boy." Condor shook his head and stared up at the clouds shielding the bottom of Aeropolis from view.

Axel positioned himself in front of Condor and leaned forward. "Good. You don't speak unless we speak to you. And stop calling me 'Farm Boy.' I haven't worked on a farm for a long time now. Crystal?"

Condor met Axel's eyes. "You talk big for a Farm Boy whose hands are tied behind his back."

"Stop it, you two," Calum said.

Axel leaned even closer to Condor. "Just wait until my hands are untied. Then you'll see what this Farm Boy can—"

Condor bashed his forehead into Axel's nose, then he jumped into the air and kicked both of his feet at Axel's chest. Axel landed on his back in the dirt and before Calum could subdue him, Condor zipped into the sky with his limbs still bound.

CHAPTER 15

Calum yanked on the rope, but Condor was too strong. He pulled Calum off his feet, and the rope slipped through his fingers. Had the rope not been tied to Calum's and Axel's belts, Condor would've escaped.

From his vantage point on the ground, Calum saw Lilly take to the sky and lash her sword at Condor. He easily dodged the blow, and the tension in the rope jerked Calum onto his stomach. Two green, scaly feet planted just in front of Calum's face.

Calum rolled over, and Magnus grasped the rope and give it a sharp yank. Condor dropped from the sky, and his back smacked against the dirt. Calum drew his sword, scrambled over to Condor, and pressed the blade against his neck.

"Don't move."

"Wouldn't dream of it." Condor coughed and grunted, but didn't resist.

Lilly landed next to Riley, who lay on the ground, still unconscious but drawing shallow breaths.

"I'm gonna *kill* you," Axel growled. Blood oozed from his nose and down his chin as he stormed over to Condor.

Magnus clamped his hand on the front collar of Axel's breastplate and held him in place. "No, you will not."

"Get your hand off me." Axel twisted free from Magnus's grip, his arms still bound. "You knocked me out, took my sword, and tied me up like a prisoner to spare *his* life. You have no right to—"

"I did what was necessary at the time," Magnus growled. "If you expect an apology, prepare yourself for an eternity of waiting."

"Someday, Magnus," Axel warned. "Someday you won't be able to push me around."

Magnus grabbed Axel by his shoulders and pulled him close. In low, even tones, he said, "You were willing to sacrifice Riley's life to kill Condor. Would you sacrifice my life? Lilly's life? Calum's life? Your *own* life?"

Axel's jaw hardened, but to his credit, he didn't reply.

"You said I had no right to do to you what I did. I could have just killed you instead, and then you would not have had the *privilege* of enduring this conversation with me." Magnus's golden eyes blinked. "*You* have no right to wager others' lives for your own personal gain or to satisfy your own impulses. Someday someone might try to sacrifice *you* on a whim. We will see then how you react to it."

"Guys, we really need to get Riley help more than we need to argue," Lilly said.

Magnus released his grip on Axel and returned to retrieve Riley. He asked Lilly, "Can you get us up there?"

Lilly exhaled a long sigh and stared up at the Aeropolis. "I can try. Follow me."

Calum pulled Condor up to his feet and checked his bonds. He smacked Axel on the back of his left shoulder in a gesture of camaraderie, but Axel shrugged away from him. Calum decided to leave him alone for the time being.

Together, the bound trio hurried after Lilly and Magnus toward the base of the foremost pillar. As they approached, Calum noticed a long line of people.

"Lilly?" he called. "Are all those people trying to get up to Aeropolis?"

She nodded as she walked. "Most of them are poor, destitute Windgales who don't have capes and can't fly up to the city. This road is lined with beggars and the occasional thief, so watch yourselves."

The closer they got to the base of the pillar, the more people materialized ahead of them, though not all of them stood in line. Many just sat alongside the road, often wearing nothing but rags for clothing.

At one spot, four smiling children chased each other around a pair of adults sitting in front of a dark-green tent. Unlike the children, both of the parents wore sullen expressions. The female adult, probably fifteen years older than Calum, met his gaze with sad brown eyes and a frown.

Calum broke eye contact with her and trotted up next to Lilly. "Why don't any of them have capes?"

She shook her head. "If you break a law in Aeropolis, one of the punishments is defrocking —the removal of one's cape. Some Windgales are born into families who don't have capes. Others can't find work in Aeropolis or nearby, and they end up selling their capes to make ends meet."

"What does it matter if they sell their capes? Can't they just find a new piece of fabric and use that?" Axel asked. His nose seemed to have stopped bleeding by now.

Calum raised an eyebrow. At least Axel was saying something.

"Not all fabric can be used for capes," Lilly said. "It needs to be made of Aerosilk, like mine, or at the very least a blended fabric that is mostly Aerosilk. The Sky Realm has suffered an Aerosilk shortage over the last decade, so the number of capes produced has dwindled, and they certainly don't last forever."

Calum glanced back at the Windgale woman. She no longer looked at him, but instead hung her head and stared at the ground. "Why don't Wisps like Condor need capes?"

"That—" Lilly hesitated. "—is a mystery to me. Only Wisps know, and only the premier or one of his officers can promote a Windgale, and they only do that when the Windgale is deemed ready."

Condor scoffed. "It's all about control."

Calum and Lilly turned to look at him.

"What do you know of it?" Axel sneered. "You're a traitor."

Condor's blue eyes narrowed. "I happened to be the Captain of the Royal Guard, and one of fewer than a hundred Wisps throughout the entirety of Kanarah. I know the Sky Fortress's secrets. What do *you* know of it?"

Axel's jaw tensed.

295

"Like I was saying, it's all about control." Condor tilted his head and smirked at Lilly. As uncomfortable as it made Calum feel, it must've been ten times worse for Lilly.

She turned away from him and kept walking forward.

"The Premier is greedy. He's content to keep the poor in their caste and the wealthy in theirs," Condor continued. "Everyone in between works to satisfy the needs of the wealthy and the royal family. There's no room for advancement, no opportunity for anyone low-born to—"

"Then how do you account for yourself?" Lilly whirled around. "You have no right to make such accusations when you rose from nothing to the Captain of the Royal Guard as quickly as you did."

"I am an anomaly, to be sure." Condor showed off his white smile. "As are you."

Lilly extended her index finger toward his face. "Axel was right. You know nothing. You're as selfish as you claim the Premier to be."

"Am I? I could have revealed the Wisps' secrets to all of my men, but I didn't. And there are other secrets I could still reveal, but I haven't."

"That's because you wanted to have control over—" A realization widened Lilly's eyes, then she glared at Condor and turned back around and walked, her pace quicker than before.

Condor smirked again, and Calum wanted to backhand the expression right off his face.

As much as he'd been horrified at the cost Axel was willing to pay to kill Condor, Calum had to admit he understood Axel's rage. Every time he saw the bruise on Lilly's face, now somewhat faded, or a smug expression curling Condor's lips, he considered trying to teach the Wisp a lesson as well, but always he held back.

They continued to walk past multiple Windgales and their ramshackle homes. Some of them even looked semi-permanent.

Calum tilted his head. "Why don't we give the capes we confiscated from the Raven's Brood to some of these people?"

Lilly and Magnus stopped and turned back to face him.

"We have their leader," Calum said. "What do we need the capes for?"

Magnus nodded to Lilly. "It is an act of pure kindness. It will cost us nothing to do so, except time, but we may be waiting for awhile anyway. Perhaps you can proceed ahead and try to secure a way up?"

"I can do that. The Premier does really only care about Condor." Lilly's sullen expression melted into a guarded grin, which she directed at Calum. "You never cease to amaze me."

Calum returned her smile with one of his own. The compliment, especially coming from her, felt amazing. "I'm glad you, uh—you think so."

"Stay near Magnus and Condor. I'll fly up to the city and try to convince them to send the lift down." Lilly floated over to Condor and yanked the black-and-red raven pendant from his neck in one sharp jerk. "I suppose I'll need this to prove we actually have you, won't I?"

Condor chuckled at her. "It's a start, but I doubt you'll need it. I'm sure you can be very *persuasive* when you want to be."

Axel's boot lashed at Condor's shin from the side, and Condor toppled forward onto the ground. Axel followed the trip with a swift kick to Condor's ribs that left him gasping. "Do *not* talk to her like that."

"Axel—" Lilly started.

Just as Axel reeled his leg back for another blow, Calum stepped between them. "Enough, Axel. Enough."

Condor wheezed, then grunted. Calum tried to help him up to his feet, but Condor shook him away, hovered off the ground, and landed upright. He spat on the ground at Axel's feet.

"A day is coming when we will meet under different circumstances, Farm Boy," Condor said between ragged coughs. "And on that most glorious day, I will kill you."

Axel stepped forward, though not as close as he had last time. "I'm looking forward to it."

"I said that's *enough*." Calum pulled Axel away and started untying his bonds. He nodded to Lilly, who took off into the sky. "I'm untying you because I need your help handing these capes out. You and I will distribute them, and Magnus will watch Condor and Riley. If you try anything, Magnus will put you out again. Crystal?"

Axel's eyes narrowed at him. He didn't answer for a long moment as he searched Calum's gaze, then he finally replied, "Clear."

Calum let Axel's rope drop to the dirt, handed him the pack of capes, and tied Condor to Magnus before he untied himself. "Come on. Let's hand these out."

They left Magnus, Condor, and Riley behind and headed to the nearest capeless Windgale, a middle-aged man with a graying beard and brown rags for clothes.

Calum swallowed the lump in his throat and pulled a cape from the bag, which Axel held. Why did he feel embarrassed about this? He was about to do an awkward, somewhat foreign thing by giving these people a second chance at a life—at freedom.

In a lot of ways, it had been easier for Calum to agree to help Reginia, Stavian, and the people of Pike's Garrison by ridding them of the bandits plaguing their village than it was to step up to this haggard Windgale and offer him help. But Calum did it anyway.

"Excuse me, sir?" he said.

The Windgale man's weary eyes fixed on Calum. "Yeah?"

"I have something for you." Calum extended the cape to him.

The Windgale man glanced between Calum and the cape, then he looked back at Calum again. He scratched his scruffy neck. "This some sorta joke?"

Calum shook his head. "No joke. This belongs to you now. It's got Aerosilk in it."

After a moment of hesitation, the Windgale man snatched the cape from Calum's hand, slung it over his back, then fastened it to his ragged shirt.

"I don't know how long it's been since you last flew," Calum said. "But I imagine you may need some time to reacquaint yourself to—"

"Wahoooooo!" The Windgale man rocketed into the air in a wild spiral toward the sun. He curved his trajectory into three large loops, all the while hooting and hollering as if he'd never flown before in his life, but flying like he'd never stopped.

Axel huffed. "Well, at least someone's happy."

The Windgales around them on the ground level pointed up at the Windgale man and began to murmur. Some even cast guarded glances at Calum and Axel.

"Come on," Calum said to Axel. "We're gonna get rid of these things and help some people."

Calum knifed his way through the muttering crowd of Windgales that had formed to watch the spectacle in the sky, and he began handing capes out to anyone who made eye contact with him. Soon enough the crowd's focus shifted to Axel and Calum, and they all began begging and reaching toward them.

Calum distributed capes freely until he got down to his final two capes. Rather than giving them away at random, he headed back the way they'd come.

"Why are we backtracking?" Axel called from behind him.

"There's someone I need to give a cape to. Someone I saw earlier."

Calum emerged from the edge of the crowd and saw the Windgale woman who'd stared at him when he'd walked past. Her head still hung down.

Calum approached her and touched her shoulder with his hand. "Excuse me?"

She looked up at him with those sad brown eyes. The crowd behind Calum stopped behind them and fell silent.

Calum held a cape out for her. "This is for you."

She blinked at him, then she stared at the cape in his hands. The kids who'd been chasing each other around her tent stopped when they saw Calum. Their mouths hung open when they saw the cape in his hands.

"Go on. Take it. Fly again." Calum smiled at her.

The woman glanced at the ground, then at the cape, then she reached out and took it. Her brown eyes filled with tears, and she looked up at Calum again. In a voice so quiet that Calum could barely hear it at all, she said, "Thank you."

Calum's heart ached for her. Did all rulers treat their subjects this way? Was the Premier just the Windgale version of the King?

"You're welcome." He nodded to her, then he pulled the last remaining cape from the pouch in Axel's hands and extended it to the man who stood next to her. "Here. You can have this one."

The man shook his head and held up his hands. "I can't use it. I'm not a Windgale, but thank you anyway."

Calum tilted his head, and his gaze drifted between the kids and the woman, then back to the man. "Aren't you two—together?"

The man nodded. "Robynn is my wife, but I'm not a Windgale. I'm a human, like you two."

"And these are—your kids?" Axel asked.

The man smiled. "They are. Beautiful, aren't they?"

"Yes, very." Calum smiled. "So could one of them use the cape?"

"Children of Windgales and humans typically don't have flight ability," the man replied. "One is more than enough blessing for our family. You've given us our lives back. Give that last cape to another family and do the same for them. Thank you again."

Calum nodded and turned to face the crowd of Windgales waiting behind him and Axel.

"We've already given out almost thirty capes. There has to be at least a hundred more Windgales here, and we've only got one left." Axel tossed the bag aside and approached Calum. He lowered his voice. "You shoulda let me bring my sword. This could get ugly."

Calum smacked Axel's armored chest with the back of his hand. "Why do you always assume the worst about people? They're poor and hungry, just like I was. What if you had assumed the worst about me?"

Axel scoffed and folded his arms. "I'm beginning to think I should've."

Still, Axel had a point. With so great a need and only one cape left, how could Calum possibly choose just one person? He wanted to help them all.

Someday he would. Someday, after he freed Lumen, Calum would set things right. He didn't know how, but with Lumen on his side, there had to be a way.

He placed the cape in the hands of the Windgale nearest to him, then he backed up a step. Unlike what Axel had thought, the crowd did not rush forward and attack them, but unlike what Calum expected, they did not immediately disperse, either. Instead, they stood there, every set of eyes on Calum.

"What's your name, friend?" the man behind him asked.

Calum turned halfway back. "I'm Calum. This is Axel."

The man nodded. "Name's Bowman. You've already met Robynn, and these are our children, Rexane, Starrie, Luce, and Arquelle."

Calum smiled at them. "Pleasure. Now if you'll excuse me, I need to—"

"Let's hear it for Calum," Bowman called to the crowd. "Calum the Deliverer!"

The crowd crooned a loud whoop, all in unison, that reminded Calum of a type of bird he'd heard on warm mornings back at the quarry. He'd never learned that type of bird's name, but it had always reminded him that life wasn't always full of only bad things. Perhaps this was his chance to serve as such a reminder for many others.

When he looked at the crowd again, every single one of them had bowed their heads, but held their hands up against their chests. Their wrists crossed, their thumbs joined in the center and pointed up at their chins, and their fingers angled up and out toward their shoulders like the wings of a bird.

"I've seen that motion before," Calum said.

"Yeah." Axel folded his arms. "Condor did it when he introduced himself."

"It's a salute. Windgales salute those whom they owe respect, whether they be nobility, or royalty, or simply in a higher caste." Bowman smiled and motioned toward Calum and Axel with his hand. "Or emissaries of generosity, like yourselves. It is an act of submission."

Calum leaned closer to him. "Am I supposed to do it back?"

Bowman nodded. "Yes, but do not bow. Only bow if you initiate the salute."

Calum mimicked the salute with his hands on his chest but didn't bow, just as Bowman said. Axel just stood there, his arms still folded. Calum wanted to smack him for it.

Just when Calum wasn't sure if he should stop saluting or not, Magnus's voice parted the crowd with an obvious tone of urgency. "Calum, Axel. Come quickly."

"What is it?" Calum asked.

Even from far away Calum could see Magnus towering over the Windgale crowd as he worked his way toward them. He no longer carried Riley in his arms, but he pulled Condor behind him in tow.

"I fear we may be too late," Magnus said. "Riley stopped breathing."

CHAPTER 16

By the time Calum and Axel made it back to Riley, Lilly still hadn't returned. Just as Magnus had said, Riley no longer drew breath.

Calum caught his hands shaking. He still hadn't put his gauntlets back on after pressing his hands against Riley's bloody wound. Though he'd tried to wash them off at a stream along the way to Aeropolis, sticky bits of dried blood still clung to the creases on his knuckles, between his fingers, and under his fingernails.

"There's no time." Calum clasped his hands together to keep them from shaking and to calm himself enough to try to think rationally. Panicking on Riley's behalf wouldn't save him. "We need to get him to the lift."

"What if Lilly can't get it to lower?" Axel asked.

"We'll figure something out. We have to. Riley can't die."

"It may already be too late for that." Magnus's voice rang hollow.

"We have to try. Pick him up and follow me."

"Excuse me?" a voice behind Calum called.

Calum glanced back. It was Bowman.

"I'm sorry, Bowman. I don't have time to talk." Calum refocused on Magnus.

"Calum the Deliverer," Bowman said. "Let us help you."

Calum turned back around. "Help us how?"

Bowman pulled an older Windgale close, one to whom Calum had given a cape. "This is Kanton. He used to shepherd the royal flocks. He can help your friend."

Axel stepped forward, towering over both Bowman and Kanton. "How?"

Kanton tilted his graying head and rolled up his ragged sleeves. "In the thirty years I served the Premier, I saved the lives of countless livestock from wounds and illnesses of all kinds."

"Riley's a Wolf, not livestock." Axel folded his arms.

Calum wondered why Axel had decided to care about Riley now, all of a sudden. It grated on him, but to his credit, Axel was asking fair and helpful questions.

"Saved a few dozen of them too, if I recall. We're all more or less the same on the inside. It's knowing how to fix things that matters." His blue eyes centered on Calum. "You gave me a

300

second shot at life when you gave me this cape. Perhaps I can return the favor for your friend, here. What do you say?"

"Do it." Calum pulled Axel aside and led Kanton over to Riley. About half the crowd of Windgales swarmed around them.

"Please step back and give me some room to work." Kanton waved them away.

Magnus stepped close to Calum. "He seems capable."

Calum glanced at Kanton, who hunched over Riley with his fingers in the fur on Riley's chest. "I hope so, for Riley's sake."

Axel's cold stare focused on something over Calum's shoulder, and Calum traced his gaze back to Condor. Still bound and tethered to Magnus, he sat on the ground with his legs crossed, leaning forward.

"He's breathing again," Kanton said.

Calum whirled around. Sure enough, Riley drew short, faint breaths, but his eyes remained closed. "How did you do that?"

"His heart stopped," Kanton explained. "I pumped his chest a few times to get it going again."

"That's what the man from Jake's crew did to Lilly and you," Calum said to Axel.

He nodded. "Yeah."

Calum turned to Kanton again. "Can you heal him?"

Kanton shook his head. "Not without proper tools. And medicine. We don't have much to work with here outside Aeropolis. Even then, I don't know. He's hurt pretty bad."

A soft double-thump sounded next to Calum, and Lilly stepped into his line of sight.

"I couldn't convince them to lower the lift," she said. "They won't do it, even though we have Condor."

Calum's gut seized. "Then Riley's gonna die."

"He doesn't have to die," Kanton said. "You just gave us capes. We can take him up there, and you too."

"You'd do that?" Calum asked.

Kanton smiled and faced the crowd. "What do you say, Windgales?"

The Windgales with capes stepped forward from the crowd. They saluted Kanton as they had to Calum only a few minutes before and let out the same whoop.

"You're really gonna carry us up there?" Axel raised an eyebrow, then eyed Magnus. "*All* of us?"

"If we have to, we'll make a separate trip for the mighty Saurian, but I don't think we'll need to." Kanton raised his arms and motioned toward Calum and his friends.

The Windgales with capes approached. Two of them hooked their arms under Calum's, and a third grabbed him around his waist. They lifted him off the ground and did the same thing to Axel.

It took nine Windgales to even get Magnus off the ground plus six more of them to get him airborne, partially because he refused to release Condor from his grip. Six more Windgales, including Kanton, lifted Riley with obvious care and began their ascent toward Aeropolis.

"You'd better not drop me," Axel grunted at the Windgales who lifted him.

The ground dropped away from Calum's feet, and he almost left the contents of his stomach behind as well, but at least he was going up this time instead of falling with Lilly's help—over a shark-infested lake.

When the Windgales ascended above the clouds and Calum got his first glimpse of Aeropolis, his lungs failed him.

Dozens of crystalline blue spires jutted into the sky, each of them shimmering in the sunlight. Some towered above others, some clustered together, and all of them encircled a palatial structure that consisted of at least eight spires, each of them tipped with gold points. It had to be the Sky Fortress.

Whether one spire or many, each structure extended from gleaming silver platforms atop the thick gray pillars Calum had seen from the ground.

As they approached, Calum noticed that none of the platforms connected to each other. No bridges stretched between them, nor any walkways. Each platform stood free, on its own. Windgales flitted between the spires and platforms like hornets darting between sparkling nests.

Why walk between platforms when you can fly? Calum mused.

He found his breath again and exhaled a sigh of wonderment as the three Windgales landed with him on the nearest silver platform. A thick, but solitary spire pricked the sky before him. Lilly landed beside him.

"You're from *here?*" Calum sucked in another deep breath, but it didn't satisfy his lungs like it should have, so he sucked in another.

She smiled and nodded. "Yes. Beautiful, isn't it?"

Calum granted himself another long survey and cleared his throat. He rubbed his arms. Even with his armor on, he could tell the temperature had dropped substantially the higher they'd ascended, despite the clarity of the sky and the burning sun that seemed nearer than it ever had before.

"That's an understatement," he replied.

"Alright, put me down. Put me *down.*" Axel's feet touched the platform just ahead of where Calum and Lilly had landed, and he shrugged out of the Windgales' grips. He shivered and exhaled a vaporous breath. "Finally."

"It's—it's harder to breathe up here for some reason." Calum inhaled another long unsatisfying breath.

"The air is thinner this high up. A lot thinner. Until you get used to it, you'll tire much faster, you might get headaches or nauseated, and you may even pass out." Lilly patted Calum's shoulder. "Just don't get into any fights while you're up here, and you should be fine."

Calum huffed, and it came out as a cloud of vapor, just like Axel's words had. "I'll try not to."

"If you start feeling lightheaded, there's a trick we teach to visitors that might help you." Lilly held her hand up to her mouth, fingers together, and pressed the side of her index finger against her lips. "Position your hand under your nose, like this, and inhale a breath through your mouth. It doubles the air pressure of your breath as you take it in. Sometimes it helps, and other times it doesn't do anything."

Calum squinted at her, but he tried it. His lungs definitely filled up faster, but he couldn't tell if it did much to help his breathing. "Thanks. I'll keep that in mind."

"These towers are all made of the same blue crystal." Lilly motioned to the spire in front of them. "Several millennia past, it used to be common on both sides of Kanarah, but when my people built Aeropolis, we used almost all of it. Now it's as rare as gold, and almost as valuable."

"Why did they choose crystal?" Axel asked. "I can see through most of it. There's no privacy."

"It's a tradeoff," Lilly said. "With less air up here, it's also much cooler."

"No kidding." Axel huffed another plume of vapor.

"By using crystal, we've created a means to trap the sun's warmth inside without letting it out as quickly," Lilly continued. "If someone wants privacy they have but to enter a spire's inner room. Those are usually made of opaque building materials."

Nearby, the fifteen Windgales who carried Magnus deposited him on the platform, and he set Condor down on his feet.

"Good to be home," Condor muttered.

Axel grabbed his rope and gave it a tug. "Not for long, I suspect."

"I wouldn't hold onto that too tightly." Condor smirked. "If I take off again and you're holding on—well, it's a long way down, Farm Boy, and you look like the type who would splatter instead of bounce."

Axel released the rope and glared at Condor.

Magnus opened his arms to receive Riley from the six Windgales who'd brought him up, then he focused on Kanton, who waved the rest of the Windgales away. "Which way do we go now?"

Kanton motioned toward the nearest spire. "Follow me."

The spire didn't have a door—just a large hole at its base. As they walked inside, Calum caught himself marveling at the inside of the spire just as much as he had on the outside.

The blue crystal glistened all the way to the top of the spire, which had to reach a hundred feet tall, if not more. Several hallways snaked off in different directions inside, and half of them had translucent walls.

About ten paces inside the entrance, a Windgale sat at an oak table. She wore a white cape and a matching robe with red accents and scribbled on a piece of parchment with a quill. A pair of spectacles, blue like the crystal all around her, perched so close to the end of her pointed nose that Calum didn't know how they even stayed on her face at all.

As they approached, she scanned Kanton from head to toe with one eyebrow raised. "May I help you?"

"With respect, Madame." Kanton showed her the Windgale salute and bowed low. "I humbly request that you provide us with aid. My friends have a wounded companion in need of serious medical attention."

The woman's head recoiled a few inches, not unlike a bird's head would bob backward. Though she was thin, the action created a double-chin effect on her neck. "What seems to be the problem?"

Kanton motioned toward Riley, whom Magnus still held. "This Wolf was stabbed in his side and is dying. He needs attention immediately."

"We will gladly help him." If she had intended to express any enthusiasm, her tone failed to indicate it.

She picked up a small crystal bell on her table and gave it four distinct jingles. Four Windgale men, also clad in white robes with red accents, emerged from one of the hallways with a white board.

"Take the Wolf into chamber sixteen and notify Lord Elmond that he is needed immediately," the woman said.

The four men nodded and approached Magnus, who carefully set Riley on the board. As quickly as they had arrived, they vanished into one of the hallways. When Calum started after them, the Windgale woman held up her hand.

"Staff only, I'm afraid. No visitors are allowed beyond this point without authorization."

Calum wanted to say something, but Kanton gave him a reassuring nod. Instead, he approached the table. "How much do we owe you for your help?"

The Windgale woman recoiled her head again, and her double chin reappeared. "*Owe* us? Sir, we offer complimentary aid. Anyone in need may partake in our healing works."

Calum cracked a smile. He never would have guessed that based on her attitude. "Thank you."

"I'm happy to stay here and wait for word on your friend." Kanton nodded toward Condor. "I'm sure you have somewhere you need to take him in the meantime."

Calum extended his hand to Kanton. "Thank you, Kanton. We're indebted to you for this."

Kanton shook his hand then gave him the Windgale salute again. "No. It is I who am still indebted to you. Now and forever, Calum the Deliverer. Go, take your prisoner before the Premier. I imagine he'll have nearly as many praises for you as I do."

Calum returned the salute, and then turned to Lilly. "The platforms aren't connected. How do we get across to the Sky Fortress?"

She showed him a smirk. "I'll take care of that."

"That's what you said about the lift, too," Axel muttered.

"This time I mean it," she countered. "We didn't have enough time before."

"Whatever the case, we need to get you back to your parents soon." Magnus tugged Condor close. "I imagine they will be delighted to see you returned safely."

"*Thrilled*, I'm sure," Condor said.

Lilly shot him a glare, then she refocused on Calum. "Give me a minute, and I'll be back."

She zipped out the spire's entrance and disappeared into the sky, leaving the guys alone with Condor.

"You know, it's not too late to set me free." Condor smirked at Calum.

"You shouldn't have attacked us," Calum said. "If you had let us pass, the Raven's Brood would still be at full strength, and you'd still be a free man."

"We would have overcome you had it not been for the Sobek," Condor said. "I'll admit I made a tactical error in attacking you with your big green friend here. He's the only reason the rest of you aren't all dead."

Axel huffed. "You're giving him too much credit, if you ask me."

"Except I *didn't* ask you." Condor's vivid blue eyes centered on Axel, and he displayed a polite grin.

Axel steeled his voice. "We did just fine without Magnus. I took out ten of your men with barely so much as a scratch on my armor."

Condor rolled his eyes. "As I said before, I look forward to the day when you and I get to cross blades again."

Axel's eyes narrowed. "Likewise."

Magnus stepped between them. "We will see what the Premier says. Until then, no blades will cross."

"Speaking of which, when are you gonna give me my sword back?" Axel asked.

It was a fair question, but Calum looked at Magnus.

"Not until Condor is in the Premier's custody," Magnus said.

Lilly drifted back inside the spire. "Come on out. Ride's waiting."

Calum followed Axel and Lilly outside with Magnus and Condor in the rear. There on the platform sat two large boxes, each big enough to hold a half-dozen people, and each adorned with gold edging and embellishments. Eight rods, two on each of its four sides, extended out from the boxes. Two teams of eight large Windgale men in vibrant purple armor with white capes stood nearby.

"What is this?" Axel asked.

"They're Aeropolis's shuttle service. They get visitors from place to place in these chariots," Lilly replied.

Axel closed his eyes and rubbed his forehead. "This is the only way over?"

"I fear I must agree with Axel's query in this case," Magnus said. "It took sixteen Windgales to carry me up here, but now eight of them can supposedly carry me to the other platforms in a box?"

"They can, and they will." Lilly nodded. "Don't worry about it. This is what they do, all day, every day."

Magnus's brow furrowed, but he relented. "If you insist."

A long sigh escaped Axel's mouth. "Fine. Let's go."

Calum and Axel took one of the chariots, and Magnus and Condor boarded the other. The trip to the fortress lasted only a few minutes, but it gave Calum another chance to absorb Aeropolis's splendor. Even in his wildest imagination, he never could've conceived of a place like this.

The Sky Fortress towered above all the other spires by at least a few hundred feet, and its silver platform would have more than filled the King's quarry back in Eastern Kanarah. Its spires' golden tips glinted with yellow sunlight, making it look more like a crown than a building.

More Windgales in bright purple armor zipped around the exterior of the Sky Fortress. Wisps, who always wore armor a much darker shade of purple and with no capes, flew past less frequently, but they were still more common here than anywhere else Calum had ever been.

More interesting still, not all of the soldiers were men. Calum noticed several Windgales with long, flowing hair and rose-colored armor among the purple shades.

The chariots landed on the front of the Sky Fortress platform, and the Windgales stepped aside. Though also made of crystal, the fortress's walls lacked both the translucent quality and the easy access of the other spires. Two guards in vivid orange armor with purple accents and capes stood on each side of a large double-door made of polished brass. Each of them held a long spear.

"What now? Do we just walk in?" Axel stepped out of the chariot.

"Follow me." Lilly started toward the brass doors, and the guys followed her. As she approached, the guards moved to the doors and opened them without so much as a word.

Calum looked at Axel, who shrugged, then he glanced at Condor. That same familiar smirk formed on his lips, and he raised a dark eyebrow.

It bothered Calum. Why wasn't he more nervous? If what Lilly had said about him was true, he should've been terrified of coming back here. So why wasn't he?

The interior of the Sky Fortress resembled that of the medical spire they'd just left, except more opulent. Crystal chandeliers hung from the lobby's lofted ceiling, and brass torches, all unlit, adorned the walls along with matching flower pots, each of them stuffed with colorful flora.

White marble floors stretched throughout the space, and one central staircase spiraled upward in the center, no doubt a convenience for non-flying visitors. Grand hallways lined with blue crystal, gold, silver, and marble emptied out of the lobby to the left and to the right.

While the Windgales outside the fortress darted around as if in a constant state of hurry, those inside the fortress floated through its halls at their leisure. About half of them wore armor and carried weapons of one sort or another, and the other half wore fine robes similar to those of the Windgale woman who had received Riley in the first spire.

Many of them regarded Calum and his friends with raised eyebrows and wide eyes as they walked through the fortress, but almost every person they passed stared at Lilly in total wonder.

Calum noticed, but he didn't know what that meant.

"Come on," Lilly said. "It's this way."

Lilly led them around the staircase toward another set of doors, these made out of a deep brown wood and set into a wall made of opaque blue crystal. Two guards in familiar orange armor and wielding spears squinted at her, then they quickly moved to open the doors. Their eyes widened, though, when they noticed Condor walking between Magnus, Calum, and Axel.

Something definitely wasn't right.

At first Calum had attributed the looks they'd been given to Condor, but it wasn't by his authority—or infamy—that the doors continued to open for them as they headed deeper and deeper within the fortress.

They walked through a final set of doors made of black steel, and guarded by two Wisps in dark-purple armor, into the largest room of them all so far. Instead of crystal walls, dark metal formed the room's perimeter. Two rows of marble pillars, white and colossal, outlined the main walkway and reached up at least two hundred feet to the ceiling.

In the center of the walkway at the far end of the room, two Wisps in dark purple armor flanked both sides of a throne made of the same blue crystal and adorned with gold. Another Wisp with long blond hair stood just to the throne's right. He wore dark gray armor the shade that Condor's had been.

And there, on the throne, sat the Premier of the Sky Realm.

A network of angular yellow crystals connected by blue threads adorned the top of his white robe. A crown, also made of yellow crystal, reached up in multiple symmetric points from atop the Premier's head. His white hair and beard betrayed his youthful face and bright blue eyes.

As they approached, the Wisp in the charcoal-colored armor grinned at Lilly like a handsome idiot, but her only response to him was a curt nod.

Then the Premier stood and fixed his eyes on Lilly. "You're late."

Calum glanced at her, then at Axel, whose face mirrored Calum's own befuddlement.

"I'm sorry." Lilly performed the Windgale salute then knelt down with her head bowed. "It's good to be home, Father."

CHAPTER 17

"*What?*" Axel's question split the silence and echoed throughout the throne room, but he didn't care. "You're the Premier's daughter?"

Lilly stood upright and stared at him. "Yes, I—"

"So this whole time you've been with us," Axel interrupted, "you've been lying to us?"

"I never once lied to you," Lilly replied. "I said I left my home and my parents in the Sky Realm."

"But not that you were the Premier's *daughter*." Axel squeezed his fists tight.

Why had she lied to him? This changed everything. When she was just a normal Windgale, he thought he might've had a shot at being with her, at least once he got Calum out of the way. Now, though…

"Not telling you I was the Premier's daughter is not the same as lying." Lilly glanced at Calum, who squinted at her, then she refocused on Axel. "Mostly. I didn't know for sure if I could trust you guys until we made it here and I knew I was safe."

Axel's eyes widened. "After everything we did for you, after all the times we saved you from danger, you *still* didn't trust us?"

"A young woman in my daughter's situation can never be too careful." The Premier stepped forward. "Had you and your friends been less honorable, any number of calamities might have befallen her. What if you had learned her identity and decided to ransom her?"

"We would *not* have done that." Calum stepped forward. "Lilly is our friend—a part of our family, even."

The Premier grinned at him. "My daughter has exercised great wisdom. There are few people in this world who are unquestionably trustworthy, and she was wise to recognize that the first three beings to take an interest in her might not belong to their ranks."

Axel followed the Premier's line of sight to Condor, all while bristling at his words. Who was he to assume Axel wasn't trustworthy or honorable?

"I know what it's like to endure betrayal, and it is an experience from which I'd like to spare my daughter." The Premier's eyes narrowed on Condor. "Bring him forward."

Two of the Wisps zipped forward and clamped their gloved hands on Condor's arms. They wrested him from Magnus's grip and darted back to the Premier before Axel or anyone could do anything about it.

Axel motioned toward Condor with his hand. "Hey, he—"

"He is in our custody now, along with my daughter," the Premier said. "For which you will be greatly rewarded."

Rewarded? Axel raised an eyebrow. A reward was just the start as far as Axel was concerned, especially given all he'd lost. Now that Lilly was back—and she was a feather-flyin' *princess*—he'd probably never see her again once they left Aeropolis. At the very least, he needed to leave here a rich man.

"We don't want your gold," Calum said. "Or anything else, except one thing."

Axel's head snapped toward him. "Wait, what?"

Calum gave him a slight nod and continued to address the Premier. "We want your help in finding the Arcanum."

The Premier's eyes narrowed at Calum, and he scowled.

"Calum, that's—" Axel faced the Premier. "—that's *not* what we want. We're more than happy to take your—to *accept* your gold, and whatever else you have to offer."

The Premier's scowl persisted. "You desire to free Lumen, the ancient warrior, the General of Light, do you?"

"Yes." Calum showed the Premier the Windgale salute and bent down on one knee. "I will free him, and he will save Kanarah from the King."

"And why do you presume you are the one to accomplish this?"

Calum looked up. "I've had dreams, Premier."

Axel rolled his eyes. Not the dream talk again. If anything was going to ruin their chances of walking—or being lowered—out of here with more coin than they could imagine, it was Calum's wacky dream-talk.

"Lilly, bring him forward," the Premier gently ordered.

Lilly touched Calum on his shoulder and escorted him up the marble steps toward the throne.

The Premier's hard visage didn't change as he stared into Calum's eyes. "What kind of dreams?"

"Lumen has appeared to me several times. He has called me to free him, and he's showing me how to find him," Calum said. "It started with him telling me to cross Trader's Pass and head to the Blood Mountains, and in my last dream, he told me to find the Arcanum, which I believe is at a specific spot in the Blood Mountains."

"Lumen means to rule Kanarah, you know. *All* of Kanarah, both the East and West. When you set him free, that's his goal." The Premier raised his chin and looked down his nose at Calum. "What makes him any better than the King?"

Calum's jaw hardened. "I only know one thing for sure. The King's men murdered my parents when I was a child, and then they took me to a quarry where I worked as a slave for the next eight years. Any King who treats his subjects like that doesn't deserve to be King."

Axel raised an eyebrow. This was not the same Calum he'd grown up with.

In his place stood a strong man, both in will and in body, determined to follow the path laid before him, no matter how crazy it seemed to anyone else. While Axel didn't put much stock in Calum's dreams, he realized now that he'd begun to trust Calum's resolve more with every step they took toward the Blood Mountains.

No, Axel still didn't believe they'd find anything there, but he believed that Calum believed they would, and for now, that was good enough.

The Premier's stony visage cracked with a smirk. "You've obviously endured more than your share of hardships."

"Respectfully," Calum said, "you don't know the half of it."

"My court scholars will immediately search our royal archives for information on the Arcanum. You've granted me the deepest desires of my heart—my daughter's safe return—" The Premier eyed Condor again. "—and the life of my greatest enemy. It's the least I can do."

"Premier?" Magnus nodded to him and executed the Windgale salute across his chest. "If it pleases you, we would appreciate shelter, food, and a few days to rest while your scholars perform their search."

The Premier stared at Magnus for a long time, then nodded. "You are welcome in the Sky Fortress as our guests for as long as you wish to stay. We will provide for all of your needs."

"Don't do anything special for us," Calum said.

"*Calum.*" Axel wanted to smack him upside his head.

Calum shot a glare back at him. "We'd rather you take care of the Windgales who live at the ground level and can't fly because they don't have capes."

Axel rolled his eyes. They'd finally gotten in front of someone who was not only willing to help them but who actually *owed* them, big time. And here Calum was trying to redirect their reward to a bunch of nobodies down on the ground.

They'd already handed out free capes. What more did they have to give up to help those people? Why couldn't they enjoy something for themselves for once?

The Premier eyed him. "Their plight is an unfortunate reality of our age."

Condor scoffed, and the blond Wisp in the gray armor backhanded him in the face. Condor took the blow, straightened up, and grinned at him. "Oh, Falcroné. You're gonna regret that, old friend."

"We are no longer friends," Falcroné said. "And you have no authority here anymore, *traitor.*"

"And you never had any to begin with," Condor countered, still grinning.

Falcroné drew his hand back for another strike, but the Premier spoke before Falcroné could deliver the blow. "Hold, Falcroné. His time will come soon enough."

Falcroné used his raised hand to brush his long golden hair behind his shoulders instead, and he donned a smirk of his own.

The Premier turned back to Calum. "As I was saying, those poor souls are either victims of circumstance, or they are criminals. I regret that we cannot help all of our citizens meet their needs."

"After we defeated the Raven's Brood and captured Condor, we distributed what few spare capes we could to those in need on the ground level, but the need is still great." Calum motioned toward Condor. "He seems to think you can do more. He suggested that was part of why he rebelled."

Axel noticed a slight grin on Lilly's face while Calum spoke, and her gaze remained fixed on him.

The Premier's scowl returned and he extended a finger toward Condor. "That man is a liar and a murderer. You would do well to disregard every single word from his wretched mouth."

Axel stepped forward. "We don't believe him. He tried to kill us, and he tried to kill Lilly as well. He's the one who put that bruise on her face."

Lilly's eyes widened, and she shot a scowl at Axel. "Father, it's almost healed. It wasn't even a bad—

The Premier held up his hand and motioned Lilly close to him. He examined her cheek. Without looking at Condor, he said, "Falcroné, you may strike the prisoner again."

"With pleasure, Premier." Falcroné reeled his arm back and delivered a hefty blow to Condor's left cheek.

Now it was Axel's turn to grin. He already knew he liked Falcroné, even if the only thing they had in common was wanting to beat on Condor.

Condor glared at Falcroné again, but this time a drizzle of red blood seeped from the corner of his mouth. "You never could hit very hard. Why don't you summon General Balena? Perhaps he can show you how to throw an effective punch."

Falcroné drove his fist into Condor's gut, and he doubled over. A vicious uppercut from Falcroné jerked Condor's head back up, but the Wisps holding him didn't let go.

"Better?" Falcroné cracked his armored knuckles.

Condor spat a dollop of blood onto the floor at Falcroné's feet. "Easy to land a good blow when two men are holding your opponent in place. Untie me, and we'll see how things go then."

"I'd bring you down, just as I did when you rebelled."

Condor laughed. "You didn't bring me down. Not even close. I fled once I realized my men had turned against me. All you did was chase me for a few minutes until you gave up. You've never once defeated me in a fight, not in twenty years of sparring or otherwise.

"It's why, despite my caste, I made Captain of the Royal Guard and you didn't—at least not until I left the post vacant, anyway." Condor's condescending smile matched his tone. "I do worry for the Premier's safety now that I am gone, what with a lesser man filling the position. Tell me, Premier, how well do you sleep at night knowing you're protected by the second best?"

Falcroné raised his fist to strike Condor again.

"*Enough.* Falcroné, step back." Frustration lined the Premier's voice. "Condor will be dealt with according to our laws for treason, and not before then. Don't let him goad you into executing the law beyond your charge."

Falcroné bowed his head toward the Premier. "Yes, Premier. I apologize."

"You also can't think for yourself," Condor muttered. "Another reason why you didn't make Captain."

Falcroné whirled around and bashed Condor's face with his fist. "How's that for thinking for myself?"

Blood ran from Condor's nose onto his upper lip. He bared his teeth at first, but the corners of his lips turned up in a smile, and he laughed. "Barely felt that at all. Go ahead. Hit me again."

"*Falcroné.*" This time the Premier left his throne, actually grabbed him by the back collar of his armor, and jerked him away from Condor. "If you so much as lay another *finger* on him before his hearing, I'll try you for treason, too."

Falcroné's jaw tensed, but he nodded.

The Premier motioned toward the doors through which Axel and the group had entered. "Take him away. Lock him up until I have gathered the council."

The Wisps holding Condor yanked him down the main walkway. He protested the entire way to the doors, spouting off about the supposed injustices of the Sky Realm and the Premier's rule, but the sound of his voice ceased when the double doors shut.

The Premier refocused on Calum, his arms outstretched. "Forgive me for my rudeness. I have not properly introduced myself, and I do not know your names, either. I am Avian, Premier of the Sky Realm. Welcome to my fortress."

Axel frowned. Everyone always looked to Calum, always welcomed him as the group's leader.

At first it had been good for Calum. It had built his self-confidence, something which he'd been severely lacking.

Now it was just annoying. Axel had always been more decisive, more intelligent, more skilled, and thus more qualified to lead their little group, but he'd never gotten the chance to do it. Magnus had seen to that.

Someday that would change. Either he'd take control, probably when they reached the Blood Mountains and failed to find the mythological Lumen, or he'd leave. Then he'd truly be his own man, free to do whatever he wanted.

Avian waved his hand at another nearby Wisp, this one dressed in fine linen and adorned with silver jewelry instead of armed and wearing armor. "Ganosh will show you to your accommodations. Rest, relax, and recuperate in the safety of the skies."

Calum bowed again. "Thank you."

Let him make nice with the Premier. Why not? Axel needed to refocus on Lilly anyway. Even though Lilly hadn't so much as made eye contact with him for the past several minutes now, Axel was owed some answers, and he intended to get them.

Ganosh approached Axel and performed the Windgale salute. "Shall we?"

At least someone saw fit to acknowledge him. Axel cast another glance at Lilly and finally met her blue eyes. She showed him a half-smile then looked away.

Axel sighed and nodded to Ganosh. If nothing else, maybe he would get some rest. "Yeah. Let's go."

ALMOST A WEEK WENT by before Axel had an opportunity to talk with Lilly again. She had been busy re-acclimating herself to being home and to her role as princess, just as Axel, Calum, and Magnus had to adjust to life within the Sky Fortress and Aeropolis.

Tasks that Windgales would deem simple, such as moving from platform to platform, proved difficult, or at the very least inconvenient, and that made exploring the wondrous city challenging. For the most part, Axel had stuck with Calum and Magnus, though he'd also managed to get some light sparring in with some of the royal guards in a training facility.

Even so, the time to rest and recuperate had done Axel good. His aches from escaping the pirate ship and the Jyrak had all but deserted him by now, and the cut on his left cheek from Krogan's whip had healed into a scar he could be proud of for the rest of his life.

On top of that, he got to sleep in a bed again, the first time in months. It took a night to readjust to that level of comfort, but once he did, he slept as soundly as a freshly planted seed nestled in a soft bed of soil.

That day, Calum and Magnus had just left in one of the chariots to visit Riley, who had finally regained consciousness. Thanks to the combined efforts of Kanton and the elusive Lord Elmond, whom none of them had seen yet, Riley had started to recover from his wound.

Axel had elected to stay behind for this visit. He'd never been all that fond of Riley anyway, as he'd made more than evident after the battle with Condor and the Raven's Brood, so what was the point?

Still, some small part of him had to admit he'd acted irrationally, and he'd even considered offering Riley and the others an apology. Maybe he would, eventually. When he got around to it.

For now, he had just reclined in a feather-stuffed chair when a knock sounded on his door. Axel exhaled a loud breath, frustrated at the interruption and rubbed his eyes. "Come in."

At first, Axel didn't recognize the beautiful blonde woman who entered his room with Falcroné close behind, still clad in his charcoal armor. When he realized she was Lilly, he straightened then pushed himself up to his feet.

"Lilly, hi," he said, barely keeping himself from stammering.

Instead of her pink armor, Lilly wore a sky-blue robe with white accents. Her shimmering blue cape looked as if it had been replaced with a new version, this one a deep forest-green that matched the cuffs on her sleeves and the hem at the bottom of her robe. A silver tiara topped her blonde hair, which now coiled around her head in two braids instead of hanging down.

She looked incredible. Axel had appreciated the rough-hewn, armor clad warrior version, but the sight of her all cleaned up and wearing finer clothes than he'd ever seen on anyone, anywhere, set his heart quivering.

"Hello, Axel." She beamed at him then motioned toward her companion. "Have you met Falcroné yet?"

"I know who he is, but we haven't been introduced." Axel extended his hand.

Falcroné performed a casual Windgale salute and nodded but didn't reach to shake Axel's hand. "I owe you a debt of gratitude for saving my cousin."

Cousin? That explained their matching hair color. They could've been brother and sister, for all Axel knew.

"Does that surprise you?" The corner of Lilly's mouth curled upward.

Axel let his hand drop, clamped his mouth shut, and shrugged. "No, it makes sense."

"We're here to summon you and your friends to an audience with the Premier." Falcroné's sharp blue eyes flared wider for a moment, and then he grinned at Lilly, whose smile shrank slightly. "Now that Lilly has returned, we have some exciting news."

Axel squinted at him. "Which is...?"

"We'll save it for when we're in the Premier's presence," Lilly said before Falcroné could continue.

Axel looked to Falcroné for more, but the Wisp only showed off his pristine white smile, just like Lilly's. It made Axel self-conscious about his own teeth, and he made sure his lips stayed closed except when he had to talk.

"Well, Calum and Magnus just left to visit Riley," Axel said. "I don't know when they're coming back."

Lilly turned to Falcroné and put her hand on his armored chest. "Would you mind going over to fetch them? I'd like to speak with Axel alone, and we'll meet you in the throne room."

Axel's heart skipped at her suggestion. Finally, he had a chance to clear the air with her. Beautiful or not, she'd betrayed his trust, and he wanted—he *deserved* answers.

A spark of hope lit up his soul. Who knew where the conversation might go? Maybe once everything was sorted out, they could figure out what the future would look like. And maybe it might include the two of them—

"As you wish, Princess." Falcroné's voice yanked Axel out of his imagination. His pleasant demeanor faded and his eyes narrowed at Axel, but he nodded.

Once Falcroné floated out of the room, Axel raised an eyebrow and grinned at Lilly. "Thought I'd never get you alone."

Lilly showed him a half-smile. "I just wanted to thank you while I still have the chance."

Axel tilted his head. "What do you mean?"

"I—" Lilly bit her lip and stared at the floor. "I'm staying here. I'm not coming with you and Calum to free Lumen."

Axel raised his eyebrows. He'd expected as much, but her words implied he wasn't staying here, either. And that meant any hope of a future for the two of them was nonexistent.

Upon that realization, the spark in his soul fizzled to nothing.

When Axel didn't say anything, Lilly sighed and continued. "I'm home. I need to stay here now. I'm sorry, Axel."

He clenched his jaw to stifle the emotion rising in his chest. It felt foreign—and terrible—to him. He hated it, and he fought it with every ounce of his being. "It's not me you should apologize to. I have a feeling Calum is really gonna miss you."

Lilly took his hand in hers, and a shiver ratcheted through his bones. "You don't have to hide behind him. I know you're hurt, too."

Axel stared into her blue eyes, almost exactly the color of the crystal that formed the Sky Fortress's walls. The bitter emotion swelled in his chest, accompanied by an impulse—one he'd wanted to gratify ever since he first laid eyes on her in that golden field.

She was right there, in front of him, and they were alone.

That had to mean something, right? Something wonderful.

He pulled Lilly close to him, curled his arms around her, and pressed his lips against hers, but the kiss didn't last nearly as long as he had hoped it would. She planted her hands on his chest and pushed away.

"Axel, I—" Lilly's blue eyes focused on something over his shoulder, and her mouth hung open slightly.

Axel turned back.

There, in the doorway, stood Calum.

CHAPTER 18

Maybe *he didn't see us?* Axel's hope that Calum hadn't seen what he'd just done overwrote his dismay at Lilly's abrupt rejection. But the sight of Calum's rigid jaw and lowered eyebrows said otherwise.

"Hi, Calum." It was all Axel could think to say. He didn't even realize he was still holding Lilly until she twisted out of his grip and stepped back. Axel glanced at her then refocused on Calum. "Did you visit Riley already?"

"We have to meet with the Premier." Calum grabbed his sword from the inside of the door and hooked it to his belt. Unlike when they had arrived, neither Calum nor Axel wore any armor, but instead they had adopted the long robes customary for civilian life in Aeropolis. "Come on."

After Calum disappeared through the doorway, Lilly sighed and gave Axel a frown. "Are you coming?"

"Yeah." He found her eyes. "What just—"

"Don't, Axel." Lilly held up her hand. "Just don't."

He followed her shimmering green cape toward the door and grabbed his own sword on the way out. Calum had seen them kiss, and his reaction had confirmed Axel's long-held suspicion that Calum wanted Lilly for himself.

Well, too late, buddy.

Then again, it hadn't even lasted two seconds—glorious as they were.

But she had also seen Calum, so she understandably wouldn't want to engage Axel with him around.

But she was also staying here in the Sky Realm. Axel absorbed the sunlight that shone through the crystalline hallways and exhaled a pleasant breath.

He'd have to stay here, with her. He'd do it to make her life easier. He wasn't sure he was truly ready to give up the life of adventure he'd discovered over the last several months, but for a prize like Lilly, he'd give up anything.

Calum would just have to finish his quest alone—or at least without Axel.

He smiled. No more taking orders from Calum. No more bickering with and taking blows from Magnus. No more unending travel or sleeping on the hard ground only to wake up and have to fight off a bunch of bandits.

From now on, he'd live a life of luxury with Lilly at his side—or him at her side, anyway. *She* was the princess, after all.

"Hurry, will you?" Lilly's voice pulled him back to the present.

Axel smirked at her. "Anything for you."

She led him into the throne room again, a place to which he'd only been invited twice.

Premier Avian sat on his throne, still flanked by two Wisps on either side. He conversed with a female Wisp who wore attire similar to his, including a matching crown and a yellow crystal necklace that matched those draped over Avian's shoulders. Light-brown hair coiled around her head in a style similar to Lilly's. Axel figured she was Lilly's mother.

Calum stood before the throne already, his arms folded.

"So did you go to visit Riley, or not?" Axel whacked Calum's shoulder, probably too hard.

Calum shot him a glare. "I realized I'd forgotten my sword in the room. I ran into Falcroné on the way back, and he told me to go to the throne room."

"Oh, I see." Axel smirked and watched Lilly float over to Avian and the woman he was speaking to. Lilly gave the woman a hug and they both smiles. "I'm guessing you happened to—"

"If it's all the same to you, I'd rather not discuss it right now."

Axel bit his tongue. He wanted to flaunt his victory in front of Calum, but he restrained himself—mostly. "Alright. Whatever you say. We can always talk about Lilly and me later."

Calum exhaled a sharp breath through his nose but didn't say anything else.

Within moments, Magnus and Falcroné entered the throne room. They joined Axel and Calum, along with several dozen Windgales and Wisps. About half of them wore armor, and the rest wore regal robes in a variety of ethereal colors.

One Wisp stood out to Axel more than the others. Like Falcroné, his long hair hung down past his shoulders, but it was a mix of silver and black instead of blonde, and a thick beard of matching tones shrouded the lower half of his face.

His dark eyebrows perpetually arched down, and his hazel eyes constantly scanned the throne room. Black armor with golden accents covered his hulking body. He didn't look like he belonged with the rest of the Wisps and Windgales.

"Your attention, please." Avian raised his hands, and the assembled Windgales fell silent. "I have gathered you here today to make an announcement that will shape the future of the Sky Realm for generations to come."

Axel craned his head to get Lilly to make eye contact with him, but she didn't. Was she avoiding him on purpose?

"Lilly, come forward." Avian nodded, and she hovered over to him. "My wife Zephyrra and I are eternally grateful to the humans Calum and Axel, the Saurian Magnus, and their Wolf friend Riley, who is recovering from a critical wound, for returning our daughter to us.

"We feared the worst when Lilly disappeared, but she is back, and she is safe. The four of you are to be commended for your service to the Sky Realm." He extended his hand toward Axel and Calum. "Please come forward."

Axel glanced at Calum, but he didn't make eye contact, either. Instead, Calum stepped up to Avian and gave him the Windgale salute, complete with a deep bow.

Axel and Magnus mimicked Calum and stood behind him, almost shoulder-to-shoulder, and Axel couldn't help but think he might be on better terms with Magnus than Calum for once.

Then Axel remembered how Magnus had knocked him unconscious and tied him up like a prisoner while they traveled to Aeropolis. He scowled.

"I'm still mad at you," Axel muttered.

"I still do not care," Magnus muttered back.

Avian motioned toward the big Wisp in the black armor, whom Calum turned to face. The Wisp fastened a medallion made of blue crystal and gold to Calum's robe.

"Axel, come forward."

Axel approached Avian, whose gaze hardened until Axel performed the Windgale salute as Calum had. Better to do it properly now, seeing as though Avian might end up becoming a family member in upcoming years.

As with Calum, Avian directed him to the big Wisp, who pinned an identical medal onto Axel's robe. Avian called Magnus forward next, but since he hadn't taken off his breastplate to change into robes, the Wisp just handed it to him.

"These badges grant you the protection, authority, rights, and privileges afforded to all citizens of the Sky Realm, even though you are of different races," Avian said. "Whenever you visit our realm, you are always welcome guests, worthy of the highest consideration and treatment."

Axel looked at the medallion. A gold ring encircled two spread wings of stamped gold, set into a blue crystal background in the center—quite a display of craftsmanship and artistry, among the best Axel had ever seen.

"Behold your people." Avian stretched his arms toward the crowd, all of whom performed the Windgale salute and bowed to Axel, Calum, and Magnus, and then applauded. After a long moment, Avian said, "Please stand aside, friends. We have more to discuss."

Axel followed Calum and Magnus down off the throne platform and waited by the nearest steel pillar among several Windgales and Wisps in the crowd. Axel caught Lilly looking at him, and he winked at her. She gave him a small, polite smile, then turned her gaze back to Avian.

Axel smirked. *Truly a princess.*

"Now that Lilly has returned and we are reunited as a family, Zephyrra and I are pleased to make one final announcement on our daughter's behalf." Avian clasped Zephyrra's hand in his. "Falcroné, please step forward."

Falcroné grinned and floated over between Lilly and Avian.

"You all know that Falcroné is both Captain of the Royal Guard—the second youngest in our illustrious history—and that he is Lilly's cousin—" Avian motioned toward the big Wisp in the black armor. "—the son of General Balena and his late wife, my beloved sister, Evangeline."

Axel glanced at Lilly, then he elbowed Calum. "Did you know that?"

His face still stoic, Calum shook his head. "No."

Avian listed Falcroné's numerous accomplishments and feats in battle and described his fighting prowess, intelligence, and speed, emphasizing how Falcroné had all but singlehandedly stopped Condor's insurrection.

None of it mattered to Axel. He leaned in to Calum again. "Come on. Don't be so bitter. Just 'cause Lilly wants me doesn't mean we can't still be friends."

"Just drop it, alright?" Calum hissed. "I don't want to talk about it. Especially not here while we're listening to the Premier."

"Alright, easy. It's not a big deal." Axel folded his arms and rolled his eyes.

"It *is* a big deal to me, which is why I don't want to talk about it here." Calum glared at him.

"Fine." Axel had to get one more jab in. "Like I said, we can talk about Lilly and me later."

Calum's jaw tensed, but he didn't say anything else.

"In light of Falcroné's many successes, his integrity, and his quality of character, I am pleased to announce the continuation of our royal blood line—" Avian clasped Lilly's and Falcroné's hands together within his own. "—through a union of marriage between Lilly and Falcroné."

Axel sucked in a sharp breath and stared at Lilly with wide eyes.

CHAPTER 19

"The wedding will commence in three weeks, and we will host an engagement party for the happy couple in two days' time, in the evening." Avian patted Falcroné on his shoulder. "I couldn't have asked for a better son-in-law or a better match for my only daughter. Together, you will rule the skies when Zephyrra and I are gone."

Axel's stomach sloshed with grief, almost to the point of vomiting. How could Lilly have done this to him? And after their kiss only minutes ago?

Or had Calum's entry into the room not been the reason she pushed away from him?

Falcroné bowed and saluted Avian. "We will make you proud, Premier."

Unbelievable.

Axel glared at Lilly, but she did not—or would not—make eye contact with him. Instead, she smiled at Falcroné—at her *fiancé*—and her father as if that kiss had never happened.

"The very day that Lilly returned home, we sent envoys to Solace, Reptilius, and to the Desert of the Forgotten with word of the good news that their courtship could now continue." Avian's smile widened. "Perhaps you all didn't know this, but Falcroné has had his heart set on Lilly since they were children playing among the clouds."

A murmur of laughter swelled from the crowd around Axel. Falcroné had been after Lilly since they were children?

And they were *cousins?*

Creepy, to say the least—if not downright disgusting. The nausea in Axel's stomach returned, and he had to fight it from rising to his throat.

"Before Lilly's disappearance, Falcroné asked me for her hand in marriage. I hesitated to give him a response, and then she vanished from the safety of our realm." Avian shot a glance at Lilly. "But while she was gone, Falcroné organized dozens of search parties for her, and he stayed late into the night collecting information as to her whereabouts, all without neglecting his duties as Captain of my Royal Guard.

"It was then that I knew—though perhaps I've always known—that he was the perfect fit for my precious daughter. When she returned to us safe and sound, he asked me again, and I agreed immediately."

Axel couldn't believe what he was hearing. *Forming search parties? Collecting information?* *That* was the standard for what passed as "love" in this backward place?

He'd fought for Lilly. Bled for her. Killed for her. He'd saved her, and she'd saved him. They'd battled monsters together, fended off bandits, and escaped from a pirate ship.

And Avian thought that *forming search parties* and *collecting information* somehow trumped that? Axel's insides shifted from nausea to boiling fury.

Avian draped his arms around both Lilly's and Falcroné's shoulders, and he grinned at Lilly. "You know it took my direct orders and three strong men, including General Balena, to keep Falcroné from flying in search of you when you disappeared?"

Axel's mouth hung open. If Falcroné had truly loved her, he would've gone after her *regardless* of Avian's orders and the three men trying to hold him back. *Nothing* would've stopped him.

Lilly smiled at Falcroné again, and he smiled back.

Unbelievable. Axel grunted.

"What's your problem?" Calum asked, his demeanor noticeably improved.

"Did you really just ask me that?" Axel wanted to knock the smug look off Calum's face, but he'd draw too much attention in such a public setting. He pointed toward the throne. Despite his rage, he managed to keep his voice low. "Lilly and I, we were—she—"

Calum patted Axel's shoulder and smirked. "Don't worry. It's like you said before—we can talk about Lilly and you later."

Axel clenched his teeth and his fingers curled into fists.

LATE THAT NIGHT, Calum sat on the edge of a balcony near the top of the Sky Fortress.

Above and all around him, white stars sparkled in the cloudless sky, much brighter than he'd ever seen before, even on the clearest night from on the ground. The half-moon cast silver light on him and illuminated the rest of the Sky Fortress sprawled out before him with an ethereal blue glow.

Absolutely beautiful.

He looked down at his boots dangling over the chasm of clouds below. What a rush it must be to fly—twisting, turning, looping, spiraling. It had to be incredible to leap off such a platform, to free-fall through the layer of white fluff that swirled below, all the way down to the ground with a quick upturn near the end to keep from slamming into the dirt.

"Calum?"

He turned and found Lilly hovering behind him just a few feet off the platform. She still wore the same evergreen-and-blue robes she'd worn to Avian's assembly in the throne room several hours earlier. Her boots touched down on the platform and she started toward him.

"Oh. Hi, Lilly." Calum knew his tone was too sullen, but he didn't care. He'd had his heart broken twice in the same day. That hadn't happened since his parents' murders.

"Do you mind if I join you?"

Calum considered telling her he wanted to be alone, but a huge part of him still longed to be near her. Perhaps he shouldn't have given in, but he patted the cool flat crystal next to him, and she sat down.

"I need to talk to you about what happened earlier today," she began. Unlike other conversations they'd shared in the past, this time her tone was decisive—formal, even. Though it was her voice, it didn't sound like *her*.

Calum huffed. "Which one?"

"Both of them."

"I'm listening."

"Falcroné and I were courting long before I was taken from my home. Like my father said, he's my cousin, so we've known each other our whole lives. With royal families and bloodlines being what they are, and with Falcroné and me being close enough in age, it was only natural that my father and my uncle, General Balena, would make such a match."

Calum sighed. As much as he didn't want to know any of this, he knew he had to hear it, if for no other reason than to turn the page on this part of his life. "How old is he?"

"Falcroné is twenty-one," Lilly replied. "I'm seventeen, so we'll be married on my eighteenth birthday in three weeks."

A light breeze chilled Calum's face. "And this is what you want?"

Lilly stared out across Aeropolis and the cloudy night sky beyond. "I want what's best for my people. A marriage to Falcroné will ensure stability in the transition from my father's reign to ours, because Falcroné is my cousin. It couldn't have worked out any better."

Calum exhaled a long, vaporous breath through his nose and clenched his teeth. Even if that were true, it brought him no consolation. "If you say so."

She took his hand in hers. "Calum, look at me."

He didn't react at first, at least not outwardly. Her hand was warm and soft in his, and it sent familiar shudders down his arm and into his chest, quickening his heartbeat.

"You will always be important to me. You've saved my life more times than I can count. You're a great friend, but we aren't meant to be. I'm sorry."

"That's not the impression I got when we were traveling." Calum finally turned to look at her. "Call me crazy, but I was starting to think you liked me."

"I *do* like you."

"I guess you like Axel more." Calum looked out across the void again. Part of him wanted to scoot over the edge and be done with the pain of this conversation, the pain of this entire day, but he banished the thought as soon as it appeared in his head.

Lilly squeezed his hand. "Hey, are you going to let me explain that to you?"

"Didn't look like there was much to explain," he mumbled.

"He kissed me, and I pulled back."

"Because you saw me in the doorway."

"No. I pulled back because I didn't want him kissing me. I'm betrothed to Falcroné now, and I was then, too. He didn't know that, but I did." Lilly showed Calum a half-smile.

Calum met her eyes and studied them, searching for the truth. "I want to believe you."

She nodded. "Whether you believe me or not, I *am* betrothed to Falcroné. I'm accountable to him and no other."

"Have you told him about it?"

"Not yet, but I will. Falcroné isn't the forgiving type. I'd hate to think of what he might've done to Axel." Lilly chuckled. It might've been her way of trying to lighten the mood, but it wasn't working on Calum. "If I tell him after the fact, Axel has a better chance of surviving the—"

"Do you love him?" Calum blurted.

Lilly blinked at him. "Axel?"

"Falcroné."

She bit her lip. "Yes."

Calum shook his head. "You don't sound sure."

"Like I said, I've known him my entire life, and he's my cousin." Lilly sighed. "We grew up together. He's my best friend. Of course I love him."

Calum had to stop making eye contact again. It hurt too much to continue. "You don't seem happy about this arrangement."

"What gives you that impression?" Lilly leaned forward and tried to meet his eyes, but he wouldn't look at her. "Calum? Why won't you look at me?"

"It's your face," he blurted. "When you're around him, your face and your expressions don't match your words. And your body—" Calum searched for the right words. "—you're not affectionate with him at all."

Calum actually had observed those things about the two of them. He'd noticed even before Avian's announcement that night, but he hadn't thought anything of it at the time. Now, in hindsight, it made more sense.

"Hey." Lilly sat up straight again, took hold of Calum's chin and physically turned his head so he had to meet her eyes. "Let me make one thing perfectly clear. I *am* marrying Falcroné, and no one else. It is my duty to my parents, to him, and to my people."

Calum sighed. "Regardless of your feelings for him?"

Lilly pinched the bridge of her nose with her fingers. "I *just* told you that I love him."

"And I just told you I don't believe it." Perhaps Calum was saying too much, but at this point, what did he have to lose? "I believe you love him because you've known him all this time, but not romantically. And I believe you're only going through with this because you feel obligated to."

"Calum, this may come as a shock to you, but I don't *care* what you believe. If I say I love him, then I do." Lilly stood up. "I don't even know why I'm arguing this with you in the first place."

Calum dared to press it further. "Must be something to it if you're getting flustered."

Lilly stared down at him. "Can't you just be happy for me? What happened to the sweet, kind Calum I knew from not even a week ago? The Calum who gave thirty capes to my people in need at the base of the pillar? Where did he go?"

"You stabbed him in the chest when you let Axel kiss you." He stood up and matched her gaze, face-to-face. "And he died when your father announced your engagement."

Lilly shook her head. She looked as if she would burst into tears any moment, but instead she leaped into the sky. As she disappeared into the night air, Calum's chest exploded with grief, and he buried his head in his hands.

Had he imagined what he thought he'd seen? About her behavior with Falcroné? Or had he struck a nerve with her, and she just wasn't willing to admit it?

Either way, that was *not* how he'd intended that conversation to go, and now he couldn't shake the feeling that he'd made everything far worse for them both.

ON THE AFTERNOON of the engagement party, Ganosh swooped into Calum's room with a black robe in his hands. "Forgive the intrusion, sir. The Premier asked me to bring this to you at once."

"Another outfit?" Calum folded his arms and forced a smile that didn't match the ruins in his heart. "Don't you think you've given me enough already?"

"This is formal Windgale dress of the highest quality." Ganosh spread the garment on Calum's bed. "The Premier has spared no expense for you and your friends. Woven wool of the finest grain with a white Aerosilk undershirt."

Aerosilk? That fabric could've been used to make capes for the Windgales at the base of the pillars, yet the Premier had chosen to make a shirt for Calum instead, and presumably one for Axel as well. The fabric was soft and nice and shimmery and all that, but Calum couldn't fly, so it wouldn't have made a difference whether it was made of Aerosilk or burlap to him.

Ganosh leaned forward, and his long, brown ponytail slipped from behind his back and draped over his shoulder. "The Premier will be very disappointed if you don't wear this to the engagement party this evening. He specifically requested that I deliver this finery to you and that I ensure you wear it, according to our customs."

No sense fighting it. Calum held up his hand. "It's alright, Ganosh. I'll wear it."

Ganosh smiled and held out the Aerosilk shirt for Calum.

Almost fifteen minutes later Calum scratched his neck where the wool touched his skin. "Is it gonna itch like this all night?"

"If you are not used to this quality of dress, there will be a certain measure of adjustment required on your part." Ganosh folded his arms and examined Calum from head to toe. He hesitated then pointed at Calum's feet. "Don't you have anything other than those… *atrocities?*"

Calum stared at his boots, then looked up a Ganosh. "What's wrong with my boots?"

"First of all, they're brown and don't match the robe. Second, they're filthy and worn down. It's only a matter of time before your toes pop out the front of the leather." Ganosh rolled his eyes. "They simply will not do. Wait here. I'll be back with replacements for you."

"You really don't have to—" Calum stopped when Ganosh zipped out his door and disappeared. He sighed and scratched at his collar again.

Was all of this necessary? Especially in light of his conversation with Lilly? Had Riley been well enough to travel, he would've left the very night Avian announced Lilly's engagement to Falcroné. And maybe if he'd been lucky, he could've left Axel behind in the process.

Within another fifteen minutes, Ganosh returned with a pair of black boots shined so perfectly that Calum could see his face in them.

"These are much more appropriate." Ganosh set them at Calum's feet. Unlike his old boots, which would have flopped over on themselves, these stood upright like the Wisps who guarded Avian's throne room—and they looked about as unforgiving, too.

Calum sat on the bed and jammed his feet inside with Ganosh's help, then stood up.

Great. Itchy neck, and soon-to-be-sore feet. "I feel like I can't move."

Ganosh grinned at him. "But you *look* wonderful. I'm sure you don't yet understand how things work in our culture, but appearances are all that really matter at events like these."

"If you say so."

Ganosh scooped up Calum's old boots and started toward the door.

"Hey, where are you taking those?"

"I'm going to drop them off the edge of the platform."

Calum chuckled, but Ganosh's face showed no sign of amusement. "Wait, you're serious?"

"Of course I'm serious. That's what we do with unwanted items."

"I never said I didn't *want* them." Calum stepped forward—albeit awkwardly—and snatched the boots from Ganosh's hands. "Besides, it's probably not wise to just drop things from the sky. What if they had hit someone below?"

Ganosh shrugged. "The chances of that happening are infinitesimal."

Calum tilted his head. "They're what?"

Ganosh rolled his eyes again and sighed. "Small. Very, very small."

"Oh." Calum wondered why he hadn't just said that instead. "Even so, it can't be good for nature to just toss your trash over the edge."

"I have no time to debate civics with a foreigner." Ganosh jabbed his hips with his fists, elbows out. "*Especially* with a human. You have about a half-hour before the party starts. I suggest you walk around your room in those boots to break them in a bit before this evening, or your feet will rebel against you long before tomorrow morning."

No kidding. "Thanks, Ganosh."

Ganosh showed him the Windgale salute then darted out of the room.

Calum took Ganosh's advice and clomped around the floor for a half-hour, but by the time he finished, his feet felt far worse than when he'd started. If it persisted, he might have to sneak out of the party and change into his normal boots.

As a finishing touch, Calum pinned his Windgale medallion to the lapel of his robe.

Magnus ducked under the door arch and stepped into Calum's room. "Are you ready?"

Calum eyed him. "You're not wearing anything formal. How come you get to wear your breastplate and leather belt but I have to wear this stuff?"

"Have you ever seen a Saurian wearing clothes of any sort, aside from armor?"

"No, but I also haven't seen that many Saurians in the first place."

"We do not stand on ceremony for anyone with our attire. We wear what we wear, if anything at all, and the rest of Kanarah can deal with it."

"Alright, alright. I don't mean anything by it. I'm just making an observation." Calum scratched at his itchy neck again. "Where's Axel?"

"He was not in his room. I suspect he will meet us at the party when he is ready." Magnus clicked his talons on his breastplate. "He was displeased to hear the news of Lilly's engagement."

He wasn't the only one. "I guess we should go, then. No sense in being late."

LILLY PULLED ON HER BOOTS, stood, and looked at her image in the mirror. She pushed a stray lock of blonde hair behind her ear and admired her outfit again.

Gold embroidery accented her rose-colored gown in swirls and spirals that started at her strapless corset top and reached down to the hem. A gold Aerosilk cape hung from her neck.

She wished she didn't have to wear it, but she couldn't fly without it. She didn't yet know what it would take for her to become a Wisp, but she looked forward to the day when her father would honor her with that promotion.

A knock sounded on her door. "Come in."

The door swung open and Axel stepped inside. At first Lilly barely recognized him, clad in formal black Windgale robes with a burgundy Aerosilk shirt shimmering underneath.

Someone had even taken the time to comb his dark hair into something more presentable than the curled mess it usually was—probably Ganosh. The only thing that hadn't changed was his scruffy, unshaven neck and face, and the fact that he wore his sword at his belt.

Despite how she felt about him in light of what he'd tried earlier, Lilly had to admit he cleaned up really well. His dark blue eyes looked especially striking, and the scar on his left cheek added a sense of intrigue to his presence.

"We need to talk," he asserted in the way that only Axel could.

"You shouldn't be in here." Lilly faced him.

He wore his golden Windgale medallion on his robe, a reminder of what he'd done both for her and for the Sky Fortress. Even so, this conversation was *not* going to happen if she could help it, not after the one she'd had with Calum.

"And either way, we don't have time to talk," she continued. "The party has started by now, and I'm already late."

Axel's gaze started at her eyes, then he scanned her up and down. He shut the door, positioned himself in front of it, and folded his arms. "I'm not giving you a choice. We *need* to talk."

Lilly's vision darted to the marble vanity and the chair near her mirror, specifically in search of something—anything—she could use to defend herself from Axel if it came to that. Perhaps it was an irrational thought, but after what Roderick had put her through, she'd determined to never leave anything like this to chance again.

"I have nothing to say to you."

He stepped toward her with his hands still at his sides. "Why did you let me kiss you if you were courting Falcroné?"

Lilly bristled at his audacity, and she glanced at her vanity again. A hairbrush, a tin filled with crushed rose petals, a silver candle given to her by her late aunt Evangeline—all innocuous to the point that they wouldn't help her if Axel tried something.

"I didn't let you. I pushed you away as soon as you started kissing me."

"You could've pushed me away before that, when I got close to you, but you didn't."

"You're a big guy, Axel. Pushing you away isn't as easy as you make it sound."

The only other items within reach were two ivory hairpins that lay on her bed, both long with pointed ends. Lilly had elected not to use them in her hair tonight, but even so they wouldn't do much good against Axel's sword if he decided to use it.

Still, they were better than nothing.

"Had I known you would try to kiss me, I wouldn't have come at all," she countered. By the Overlord, she *really* didn't want to have this conversation.

"I don't believe that." Axel closed in on her. "I think you stopped because you saw Calum walk into the room."

What was with these boys not believing her? "Calum said the same thing, but I assured him that the reason I stopped kissing you wasn't because I saw him walk in. It's because I was about to announce my engagement to Falcroné."

"You don't love him."

"I don't need another person telling me what I do and don't feel. Calum already tried, and it didn't work then." Lilly glanced at the hairpins on the bed again, but this time Axel's dark-blue eyes followed. He'd noticed them, too.

"Really?" he scoffed and motioned toward them. "Is that what you think of me? That after everything I've done for you, I would try to hurt you?"

Perhaps she could dart around him and get to the door before he could try anything? Sure, she could get around him, but even if she did, she couldn't reach the door and get it open in time. And with so much extra fabric in her cape for him to grip as she tried to get past…

"Lilly." Axel's voice jarred her from her plotting. He stepped toward her again, this time with his arms outstretched to his sides. He must've known it would make it even harder for her to get past now. "I'm not gonna hurt you. I *love* you. I have since the moment I laid eyes on you."

"I know."

Axel huffed and took another step forward. "Of course you do. How could you not? It's not like I tried to hide it."

Lilly nodded and backed up a step, then she chastised herself for it mentally. She couldn't let him back her into a wall—it limited her options. One of General Balena's first lessons. "Yes, it has been obvious, alright."

"And that's how I know you didn't push away from me just because of your courtship with Falcroné. I've been so obvious, and you haven't tried to convince me otherwise, so—"

"*No.*" Lilly couldn't let that line of thinking continue. "You're wrong. I like you just fine, but I'm *not* in love with you. I love Falcroné. Not you, not Calum. Falcroné. Crystal?"

Axel's jaw hardened and his gaze transformed into a glare. "No. *Not* crystal."

Speaking of Falcroné, where was he? She sure could use his help right now. "Axel, I'm leaving for the party. This conversation is over."

Axel's face hardened with anger. "It's not over 'til I say it's over."

He started toward her.

CHAPTER 20

Lilly feigned a lunge for her hairpins, and Axel followed her trajectory toward the bed. Instead of going for them, Lilly reached back, grabbed her vanity chair, and slammed it against Axel's shoulder.

He let out a grunt, dropped onto the bed, then rolled onto the floor.

Lilly leaped over him and zipped toward the door. She flung it open, but fingers clamped around her ankle.

Axel looked up at her with rage in his eyes and gritted teeth. But amid those angry emotions, she also recognized deep, profound hurt.

Rage, hurt, love, or hate, Lilly was leaving. She spun around and whipped her other foot at Axel's face. Her boot connected hard with his jaw, and he let her go.

Now free, Lilly zipped out of her room. She rounded a corner and smacked into a broad purple chest embroidered with golden arcs. She pushed away, ready to fight him too, but she stopped when she realized it was Falcroné.

"Lilly?" He held up his hands, and the sleeves of his purple robe slid back on his muscular forearms. "Are you alright? Why are you breathing so heavily?"

Lilly stared into Falcroné's eyes and opened her mouth to speak, but hesitated.

"I wonder where Axel is." Calum craned his neck to peer at the small crowd of people not floating through the air around them. He figured Axel would be dressed more or less the same as him, but so were every other Windgale and Wisp in the room. "He should've been here by now."

Dozens of bronze lanterns hung from the throne room ceiling, each of them burning with flames that cast light through the multiple colors of glass that encased each one. The effect reminded Calum of a hundred tiny rainbows, captured and forced to enliven a dark space against their will.

Colorful ribbons stretched overhead between the pillars, each of them tied into bows on the pillars themselves. Servers clad in black robes with white sleeves darted through the air with trays in their hands, each of them loaded with drinks or food.

"Maybe he decided to stay in his room." Magnus waved down one of the Windgale servers and snagged a glass of bright-green liquid from the tray he carried. He downed the drink in one gulp and tried to place the glass back on the server's tray, but the server had already taken to the sky again. "Blasted Windgales. Too fast for their own good."

"That's not like Axel. He never passes up an opportunity for free food. Speaking of which..." Calum snatched a wooden skewer loaded with grilled vegetables, fruit, and meat from another server's tray as he hovered past. "...this looks delicious."

Just as Calum raised it to his mouth for a bite, a familiar voice stopped his motion. "What, not gonna share with your crippled friend?"

Calum turned his head and saw a gray-brown Wolf limp-walking toward him. White bandages covered the spot on his side where Condor had stabbed him, and Kanton walked alongside him.

Calum's mouth spread into a big smile. "Riley? I didn't think you were well enough to leave your room yet."

"He probably isn't." Kanton wore finery like Calum's, only he still wore the black-and-red Raven's Brood cape Calum had given him, just with the embroidered emblem plucked out. "But he insisted. And you're not crippled, just limping."

"Can't hide in my room. No shadows." Riley motioned over his right shoulder with his head. "It's nothing but clear blue crystal and sunlight streaming in from every angle. At night, they light a hundred lanterns to make sure I don't go anywhere. It's much darker in here, though. Feels better. Safer."

"He exaggerates." Kanton crouched down next to Riley and stroked the fur behind his ears. Riley snapped his jaws at Kanton's hand and he pulled back. "Was he this foul before the attack?"

"I'm not sure, to tell you the truth. I haven't known him for that long," Calum said. "But I know he's not a fan of people touching him or trying to pet him,"

"I'm not some common dog that you can stroke my fur like a pet." Riley growled, then he carefully sat down on his hind legs with a wince. "I was serious about sharing your meat, you know. The stuff they gave me over there barely counts as real food."

"Now *that's* a statement I'm inclined to agree with." Kanton stood up and pushed his black-and-red cape behind him again. "Trust me—he's right about that. I get all of his leftovers."

Riley tilted his head and whimpered at Calum, his blue canine eyes fixed on the skewer.

Calum sighed, but crouched down in front of him and held it out. "Here. I can always get another one."

"Keep the plants for yourself." Riley's pink tongue curled up and licked his nose. "I only want the meat."

As Calum plucked the first chunk of seared mutton from the skewer, Avian's voice filled the throne room.

"Friends and family, your attention please." Avian drifted high above the crowd with his hands raised, flanked by two armed Wisps on each side, as usual.

The crowd sank to the ground, followed by Avian and his men. Zephyrra stood at Avian's side, wearing an elegant silver dress that shimmered under the colored lights.

"Thank you for joining us on this most excellent occasion. Partake in the wine, drinks, food, and desserts at your leisure, but first allow me to introduce our guests of honor—my daughter, Princess Lilliana, and her new fiancé Falcroné, Captain of the Royal Guard." Avian motioned toward the rear doors with his right arm.

As if on cue, the crowd parted, and Calum went along with them. The grand doors at the rear of the throne room opened, and a procession of armed Wisps in orange and purple armor filed inside with General Balena at the head.

Calum leaned nearer to Magnus. "That's an awful lot of soldiers for an engagement party, don't you think?"

He nodded, and his golden eyes flickered with colored light. "I am not well-versed in Windgale customs, but it is unusual, to say the least."

About a dozen Windgale soldiers led the way inside, and Falcroné and Lilly followed them. Six more soldiers, three on each side, marched between them and the crowd as if forming a sort of barrier. Another eight Wisps marched behind them, four in the same deep vibrant orange color worn by the Royal Guard, and four more in dark-purple armor.

The procession ended at the throne and spread into a formation in front of the platform with Lilly, Falcroné, and General Balena standing near Avian and Zephyrra.

Despite their tense conversation the night her engagement was announced, and despite his breaking heart, Calum could scarcely take his eyes off her. Just when he'd thought she could never be more beautiful, she showed up looking even better than ever.

But the longer Calum stared, the more the longing he felt for her stabbed at his aching heart.

As the happy couple waved, General Balena leaned over to Avian and whispered something into his ear, and Avian nodded.

"Behold the future of the Sky Realm." Avian raised his hands, and the crowd performed the Windgale salute to Lilly and Falcroné.

Calum did it too, but without the fervor of the Windgales around him. He wasn't going to lie to himself about what he felt.

Something nudged his leg, and Calum looked down. Riley whimpered at him again until Calum tore another chunk of meat off his skewer and fed it to him.

"For not being a 'common dog,' you're sure acting like one," Calum muttered.

"I got stabbed," Riley reminded him. "I'm entitled to behave in a questionable manner for one night."

"More like a 'desperate manner,'" Calum countered.

"Yet however wondrous an occasion their engagement may be..." Avian continued. "...one among us has cast a dark shadow over this night. His jealousy of our ways, our rituals, our culture, and most importantly of Lilly and Falcroné's engagement is the reason you see such a demonstration of the might of the Sky Realm arrayed before you."

Calum eyed Magnus, who shook his head slightly.

"He visited my daughter before this party and accosted her in her room, but she fended him off with great skill, no doubt thanks to her training from General Balena." Avian nodded to him, and he bowed. "Now the assailant is in custody. Bring him forth, and we will make an example of him as a warning to anyone who dares to stand against this union or the Realm."

The doors opened again and two Wisps dragged a man with dark, curly hair and clad in black clothes toward the throne. They thrust him to the floor, where he landed on his hands and knees. Then he slowly lifted his head.

It was Axel.

CHAPTER 21

Would the surprises ever cease? Calum groaned and shook his head.

"The fool." Magnus exhaled a long hiss and clacked his talons on his breastplate. "His reckless behavior is going to get us all killed."

Blood trickled from the corner of Axel's mouth, but other than a few scuffs on his borrowed robes, he looked unharmed.

"This man, whom we honored a mere two days ago for his role in saving my daughter's life, saw fit to attack her this evening after she told him she did not love him. She escaped through her own cunning and told Falcroné, who apprehended him and notified General Balena of the situation."

The two Wisps grabbed Axel, spun him around, and then forced him back down to his hands and knees before Avian, Lilly, and Falcroné.

"Should we go up there?" Calum asked.

Magnus shook his head. "Be still for now."

Be still? If Axel *had* attacked Lilly, Calum wanted a shot at him first.

But even with Axel's legendary temper and bad attitude, Calum still couldn't believe that Axel would do such a thing—especially after all he'd sacrificed and risked for her right alongside Calum.

"You are fortunate to have been made a citizen of our realm, Axel," Avian said. "Were you an outsider, your punishment would have been death. But as an honorary citizen, your action will be treated as treason instead."

Condor was charged with treason as well, Calum considered.

"You will be locked away until our Council of Wisps convenes to determine your fate."

"*No.*" Calum dropped his skewer, pushed his way through the crowd, and stormed toward the throne with Magnus close behind.

Perhaps it was rash, but either way, Axel was his friend. His oldest friend. Even though they'd dueled and fought each other along the way, especially in the last two days, Calum couldn't just let these people lock him up.

"You can't do that to him," Calum said.

The Wisps who guarded the throne platform leveled their spears at him and he stopped short of becoming the next piece of meat to be skewered. Behind them, Axel craned his head and looked back at Calum with confusion in his eyes.

Now up close, Calum could see a large bruise on Axel's jaw, plus he hunched over, something he never did. Lilly must have given him quite the beating—or perhaps Falcroné had done the honors.

Magnus's hand clamped onto Calum's shoulder. "Calum, do not—"

Calum shrugged free. "Premier, suppose Axel made this mistake. If he did, it was *one* mistake. He made a bad decision and he paid for it."

Avian stared down at him for a long moment. "What is your point, Calum?"

"Look, I'm unfamiliar with your laws, so I don't really know what I'm saying..." *Great start, Calum.* "But don't throw him in your dungeon, or wherever. We were all shocked to learn of Lilly's relationship to you at first, and—"

"This has *nothing* to do with Lilly's relationship to the Premier." Falcroné pointed a long finger at Axel. "It has to do with his profession of love for her and the subsequent attack."

"In Axel's defense—" Calum started.

Should he finish the sentence? Doing so could risk invoking the wrath of Falcroné and Avian as Axel already had. And what if Axel was guilty? Calum would find himself defending his friend's stupidity.

He decided he couldn't remain silent. "—Lilly is not hard to love. She's sweet and charming and beautiful and intelligent—all of which are testaments to her upbringing under two wonderful parents—"

"Spare me your flattery, Calum." Avian held up his hand. "Make your point."

"My point is that—" Calum's eyes locked on Lilly's for a moment, but she pursed her lips tight and looked away. It was probably a mistake, but Calum continued anyway. "My point is that I love Lilly, too. And if you're gonna lock Axel up for that, then you'd better lock me up too."

Falcroné's jaw tensed, and he glared at Calum. "But you didn't *attack* her. Your friend did. That warrants time rotting in a cell, if anything ever did."

"I don't disagree with you," Calum said. "But I'm asking you to show him mercy nonetheless. We've already been through so much. Think about how we helped bring her back here and how we—"

"I've heard enough." Avian held up his hand again. "This is supposed to be a festive occasion, not a hearing. Axel will be locked up, and Calum and the rest of his friends will remain free. But if any of you breaks even the smallest of our laws, you will soon join your friend. Crystal?"

Calum clenched his teeth. It wasn't the result he'd hoped for, but he'd tried.

He nodded. "Clear."

"Then go, enjoy the food and drink, and you may plead your friend's case tomorrow when the Council of Wisps convenes to decide his fate." Avian waved toward Axel, who gave Calum a slight nod. "Take him away."

The Wisps took flight with Axel in tow. They exited through the doors from which they'd entered, and the Wisps guarding the platform raised their spears again. Calum caught Lilly staring at him, then she turned her attention back to Falcroné, who stroked her face with his fingers and touched his forehead to hers.

Calum turned away. He'd seen enough.

He looked up at Magnus. "What'll happen at the council meeting tomorrow?"

Magnus shook his head. "I do not know. We will fight to save Axel using words instead of weapons, I suppose."

"I'm better with my sword."

"I disagree, Calum," Magnus challenged. "You are gifted in many areas, and that is one of them. Do not underestimate yourself."

"If you say so." Calum figured he'd just butchered his attempt to get Axel released, but he appreciated Magnus's encouragement all the same. "We'd better get back to Riley and Kanton."

AXEL SANK DEEPER and deeper into the abyss, along with the two Wisps that gripped his arms. Far below, a single torch burned in the darkness. As they neared the light, Axel made out the crisscrossed bars of a cage mounted to the sides of the vertical tube in which they descended.

The Wisps slowed their descent, landed on the cage, and set Axel on the bars.

One of them, the one clad in orange armor, leaned over to him, his face barely visible in the light of the solitary torch. "If you try to run, you'll fall to your death. If you try to fight or resist, we'll *make* you fall to your death. Crystal?"

Axel bit his tongue and nodded instead of saying anything.

The other Wisp, in dark-purple armor, unlocked the cage's hatch. "Hop in."

Axel peered through the bars. "That's a twenty-foot drop. I'll break my legs if I just jump in."

"Then we'll lower you to ten feet and you'll have to manage from there."

"I don't—"

The orange Wisp shoved him forward. "Do it, or you'll fall a lot farther than twenty feet."

Axel sighed but stepped toward the hatch.

A sharp blow to his back pitched him forward. He plunged into the cage headfirst, but he managed to curl his body so he landed on his left shoulder instead of his face. The impact jarred his shoulder with a loud *pop*, and a shock of pain shot down to his fingertips like lightning.

He groaned as the Wisps locked the cage door. A flurry of curses poured from Axel's mouth, but when he looked up, the Wisps were already gone. He tried to push himself up, but his left arm hurt so bad that he couldn't move it.

"Here, let me help you," said a voice from the darkness around him.

Axel's heart flipped in his chest, and he gasped. Who else was in here?

A set of arms curled around his waist and started to pull.

"Get off me!" Axel flailed his right arm, also sore from when Lilly had hit him with her chair, but he only managed to flop back down onto his chest. His mind ratcheted through the possibilities of who could be in this cell with him—including someone like Yurgev. "Get away!"

"Easy."

The arms jerked Axel up in one quick motion, and he found his footing. He staggered across the cage and stood against the wall nearest the torch, which only illuminated about half the cage.

His left shoulder burned, and he couldn't move it. It was dislocated again, just like it had been after fighting the Gronyxes in the tunnel to Trader's Pass. How could he defend himself with only one functioning arm—"functioning," but also bruised and weakened?

"You don't have to be afraid. I'm not going to hurt you."

Axel squinted at the darkness. He'd stared at the torch for a moment too long on his way over to the cage wall, and the light had seared his vision, so he couldn't see properly. On top of that, the other man in his cell stood in the deep shadows on the far side of the cage.

"Who are you?" Axel demanded. "Step into the light so I can see you."

The man answered with laughter. There was something familiar about it, but Axel couldn't decipher what it was.

"After all the time we spent together on our way here, you have to ask who I am?" the man asked. "You know me so well already—*Farm Boy*."

CHAPTER 22

Axel's heartbeat multiplied, and he cursed again.

"I seem to remember you were looking forward to a day very much like this." Condor stepped out of the shadows with a cunning smile and sauntered toward him. The cuts on his face from Falcroné's beating had mostly healed, but that same old smirk remained.

"I remember agreeing with you at the time." Axel bit his lip and exhaled a sharp breath. Of all the people he could've gotten locked in a jail cell with, Condor might've been the worst. "You said you were gonna kill me. Looks like you finally get to try your luck."

Condor huffed and waved his hand, still bandaged with a blood-tinged cloth from when Riley had bitten him, in dismissal. "Please. You're in no condition to fight me. Or anyone else, for that matter."

Axel bristled at the comment, and he let his ego take over. "I could still take you down."

"Not with your shoulder dislocated, I imagine."

"Even with it dislocated, you wouldn't stand a chance."

Condor shook his head and smirked. "You don't need to keep up your tough-guy act down here, Farm Boy. The princess isn't here to admire your swelling ego, and you're not my type either."

Axel gritted his teeth and tried to rub his left shoulder, but it only felt worse. "You don't know what you're—"

"What did you do to earn yourself a holiday down here?" Condor leaned against the cage bars.

"That's none of your business."

"You don't have to tell me. I bet you made a move on the princess after you found out about Falcroné, didn't you? You probably couldn't help yourself." Condor chuckled. "And then he beat you like he beat me and had you tossed in here before your hearing."

"Falcroné barely laid a finger on me."

"Really? *That's* the only part of my guess you're denying?" Condor chuckled. "So you *did* make a pass at the princess. Was she the one who gave you that bruise?"

Axel touched his jaw with his right hand and winced at the pain in his arm.

"She *did*, didn't she? Oh, she always was a wily one. Unpredictable, even." Condor smiled, and his gaze wandered up into the tube's darkness. "Too bad you thought you had any chance with her in the first place."

"Whatever. Call me naïve, or stupid, or anything else you want. I don't care." Axel spat on the cage floor near Condor's boots. "And if you're gonna kill me, then get on with it already."

Condor stared at Axel's reddened spittle for a moment, then at him. "I'm not going to kill you when you have a dislocated shoulder and just got beat up by a girl half your size. Where's the fun in that? No, I'll wait until you're healed and feeling haughty before we settle our differences once and for all."

Axel rolled his eyes and sighed.

"Speaking of which, you should let me pop your shoulder back into place." Condor started toward him, but Axel shuffled away.

"Don't come near me, Condor. I mean it."

Condor held up his hands. "I'm going to help you. Be calm."

"I don't *want* your help."

"Whether you want it or not is irrelevant. You need it. Unless you can reset your shoulder on your own, you will endure profound pain for a long time. Unnecessarily so."

Reset his shoulder on his own? Axel didn't even know where to start. When Magnus had done it after the fight with the Gronyxes, Axel hadn't paid attention to how it had happened. He'd been too exhausted and beat-up from the battle.

Now he could barely see in the darkness of the cell, and the thought of even touching his shoulder made it hurt worse. But was the alternative of Condor fixing it for him any better?

In the end, he acquiesced. "Fine."

Condor nodded. He floated over and cupped Axel's left shoulder with one hand and his shoulder blade with the other. "This is going to hurt. A lot."

"Just do it, already."

"On the count of three. Ready?"

Axel nodded and clenched his teeth.

"One—"

Something popped, and a thousand arrowheads jammed into Axel's shoulder. He screamed and flailed at Condor with his right arm, but missed entirely. He had to fight to keep the tears pooling in his eyes from streaming down his cheeks.

Condor stood on the edge of the shadows with that same smirk on his face. "I told you it would hurt."

"It's been dislocated before. I knew it would hurt." Axel blinked away the remaining tears in his eyes and slowly rolled his left shoulder. "But you said you'd count to *three*."

"It's an old trick I learned from General Balena. He said that if you wait to count to three, the injured person will tense up and it's that much harder to pop the joint back into place. How does your shoulder feel?"

"Better," he admitted, though if it went anything like last time, the real soreness would come in a few hours.

"It appears you can move it now."

Axel rotated his arm slightly.

"In the meantime, at least you're right-handed." Condor chuckled again. "You screamed so loud, I bet they heard you all the way up in Aeropolis."

"Just stop, alright?" Axel rubbed his left shoulder. "I'm not in any mood."

"Nothing you can do about it anyway. I could cackle all night and all day, and you couldn't stop me." Condor leaned against the cage wall again and smiled. "Fortunately for you, I'm not the gloating type."

Axel growled, then slumped down onto his rear-end. "Is there any way outta here?"

"Don't even think about it. You can't fly, remember?" Condor waved his arm in a half-circle over his head. "In my three years as Captain of the Royal Guard, I dropped more thieves, brigands, derelicts, defectors, and villains in this cell then I can remember. There's no way through the bars, and even if there were, you'd never get back up to the fortress.

"There isn't a rope or a chain in this world long enough to reach down here." Condor's annoying grin returned, full-force. "Best to just accept that you're stuck in here. But at least you have me for company. And…" Condor squinted at him. "Yes, it seems we even have matching scars."

Axel touched the scar under his right eye. He couldn't see Condor as well in the dim light, but he remembered Condor had a similar scar in almost the exact same spot on his face, too. Axel chalked it up as nothing more than a coincidence.

He scanned what he could see of the tube. "Where are we, anyway?"

"We're deep within the pillar that holds the Sky Fortress in the air. It's the perfect prison to put anyone who can't fly: out of sight, inaccessible, and dark. The bars are too thick for almost anyone in Kanarah to cut through, break, or bend, including your Sobek friend." Condor smiled. "Welcome to the Sky Fortress's version of living death."

Axel frowned. "So…"

"So you're stuck in here until they feel like letting you out."

Axel sighed. "They said we'll have a hearing tomorrow when the council gathers."

Condor nodded and ran his fingers through his black hair. "Yes. The Premier doesn't decide the fates of prisoners on his own. A council of eight high-ranking Wisps, including Falcroné and General Balena, assist in passing judgment. Avian serves as the ninth vote."

"So I can count on at least those three of the nine ruling against me?"

"That's a safe assumption. Given that your advance was on Princess Lilly, I'd be surprised if even two of the council members sided with you. Aside from Premieress Zephyrra, she is the most beloved citizen in the realm. At times, perhaps even more beloved."

Axel clenched his teeth. "And if they rule against me?"

"A unanimous vote is required for the death penalty. If you lose their favor in the hearing, a lifetime of slavery or servitude is a common punishment doled out to the worst offenders."

"And my crime classifies me as one of the worst?"

Condor sat in front of Axel. The light from the torch flickered in his sharp blue eyes. "It's all contextual. What you did pales in comparison to my crimes, for example. You'd better pray that the council calls me first so I get the bulk of their wrath and that little remains for you."

Axel stared at him. "Why did you help me with my shoulder?"

"I already told you why. If we're going to settle our conflict someday, you need to be healthy and confident." Condor reached out and patted him on his left shoulder, and the thousand arrowheads tried to carve their way out of Axel's arm a second time.

"Ow!" Axel tried to kick him, but Condor moved away too fast. "I *hate* you."

"Good." Condor grinned his perfect smile. "Never change, alright?"

Through clenched teeth, Axel said, "I won't."

"So you and your friends are searching for Lumen?" Condor folded his arms.

"I'm not searching for anyone anymore," Axel grumbled.

"Stop being so overdramatic." Condor tilted his head and smirked. "Looking for the Arcanum, are you?"

"What do you care?" Axel glared at him.

"It's not an easy place to find. The Premier's scholars might be able to point it out to you on a map, but it's hard to reach."

Axel raised an eyebrow. "And how would you know that?"

Condor shook his head and receded into the shadows, out of Axel's sight. "That's my secret, Farm Boy."

"And you said *I* was being overdramatic."

"I prefer to think of it as theatrics." Condor stepped forward again, back into the light. "What time was it when they brought you down here?"

"It's a few hours after sundown, and I'd like to get some sleep." Axel grunted, then closed his eyes. "Try not to kill me while I'm sleeping if you can help it."

"Likewise. And if you happen to find yourself inclined to get me in the night, just remember that you don't need any of your man-parts to fight. Come at me while I'm asleep, and I promise you won't have them when we finally do cross blades. Crystal?"

Axel rolled his eyes. "Whatever."

THE NEXT DAY, Calum watched as the council assembled behind a long oak table set up just in front of the throne platform. Eight Wisps of superior stature and reputation within the Sky Realm sat at the table, four on each side of Avian, who sat on the ninth chair in the middle.

Falcroné sat immediately to Avian's left and General Balena sat to his right, both clad in their dark armor, but Calum didn't recognize any of the other Wisps.

"This council will convene immediately." Avian raised his hand, and the room fell silent. "We will first hear the case of the human, Axel, to whom we have granted all the rights of a citizen of the Sky Realm. Bring him forward."

Two Wisps ushered Axel over to the table from behind a pillar on Calum's right and positioned him directly in front of Falcroné. Thin white ropes bound his hands in front of him. He still wore his dress clothes from last night, but wrinkles and grime tainted the fabric.

"Axel, you have the right to face your accuser and defend yourself," Avian said. "Princess Lilliana, come forth and profess your accusation."

Lilly drifted into view from the opposite side and stood near the far end of the table. Her eyes met Calum's for an instant, then she focused on Axel.

Calum tried to meet Axel's eyes several times to reassure him, but he hadn't looked back.

Ganosh had explained the process: Lilly would accuse Axel of his crimes in detail as they happened from her point of view. Then Axel could refute the claims by telling his side. After that, witnesses from both sides would come forward and testify to both the character of the accuser and the accused, as well as to their personal experiences with the supposed crime.

Once both sides presented their cases, the council would confer and then convey a ruling over the incident. That ruling could land Axel back in the dungeon for several months, if not forever, since he'd been accused of attacking the Princess of the Sky Realm.

Calum still didn't want to believe that it had happened, but Axel's temperament had fractured more and more the longer they traveled together. What's more, he knew how Axel felt—used, betrayed, and then forgotten.

It's not that Lilly had deserved the attack—not in the least. Such a thing could never be justified, but Calum could at least appreciate the source of Axel's frustrations and the emotions that might have led him to behave so rashly.

Lilly stared at Axel for a long time, but he refused to look back at her.

Finally, she exhaled a long sigh. "I withdraw my claim."

CHAPTER 23

Falcroné pushed up and away from the table so fast that the back of his chair smacked against the marble floor. "*What?*"

Axel's eyebrows went up, and he turned toward Lilly. Why was she saying this? He had, in fact, been the aggressor, but now she wanted to withdraw her claim?

"You said he *attacked* you." Avian's blue eyes fixed on Lilly's. "Are you suggesting something to the contrary?"

"Axel came to my room and we had an argument," she began. "He told me he loved me, and I told him I loved Falcroné. I tried to leave, and he blocked my way because he wanted to keep talking, but I overreacted and hit him with my chair, then I kicked him while he was down." Lilly lowered her head. "Then I went out and told Falcroné that Axel had attacked me."

A subtle smirk formed on Axel's lips, and the heavy weight of the situation lifted from his shoulders. He couldn't believe it.

Maybe she *did* love him after all.

Falcroné hovered over the table and landed next to her. He took her hands in his and looked into her eyes. "The shock and fear you conveyed when you told me what had happened—those emotions are not easy to falsify."

"I was shocked and afraid of what *I* had done, and you heard my story with ears attuned to my well-being rather than the truth of the situation." Lilly shook her head and broke eye contact with him. "I lied to get myself out of trouble at Axel's expense. It is I who deserve punishment."

"You are aware that if you withdraw your accusation now, you may not ever bring the same accusation before the council again?" Falcroné said more than asked.

"Yes, I know. I choose to withdraw my claim, and I will face the consequences of my actions."

"You will not be charged with any crimes, Lilly," Avian said.

General Balena cleared his throat and stood. "I apologize for what I am about to say, but, Premier, the princess is bound to the laws of the realm just as you or I or anyone else would be. Her punishment is no longer a matter that you may excuse since it has been brought before this council."

Avian gave General Balena a glare that could have split a mountain in half. "I will *not* subject my daughter to a hearing."

"You will, or by law you must assume her place as the accused." General Balena's deep voice shook Axel's insides. "That is, if Axel chooses to make an accusation of the princess's guilt in this matter."

Avian's gaze whiplashed over to Axel.

Axel swallowed the lump in his throat and stared at Lilly, who met his gaze with eyes full of remorse. He could serve her up before this council's judgment with one sentence if he wanted to. He could make her pay for her lies, her duplicity. She had been right when she said she deserved punishment.

But he couldn't do it.

"No," he said. "I'm not gonna accuse her of anything."

"You do not need to fear repercussions for accusing the princess of wrongdoing." General Balena's dark eyes glanced between both Avian and Falcroné. "You are protected under our laws, the same as she or any other citizen of the realm."

Axel eyed Avian again then rotated his sore shoulders. "I'd rather just get outta here and never return, if that's alright with all of you."

General Balena motioned to the two Wisps who had escorted Axel into the throne room. "Free him at once."

One of the Wisps unsheathed a curved dagger from his belt and sliced through the ropes that bound Axel's hands.

"You may rejoin your friends." General Balena extended his open hand, palm up, toward Calum and Magnus.

Axel shook the bonds from his hands and nodded at General Balena, then he cast a lingering gaze at Lilly before he headed back to Calum and Magnus. She'd done the right thing in the end by following her heart, and he'd been right about her all along.

She gave him a solemn nod and then looked away.

Axel chuckled to himself. *Still playing aloof.*

The stares of dozens of Windgales who had gathered in the throne room for his hearing weighed on him, but he walked toward Calum and Magnus unashamed and confident.

"I don't believe it." Calum held his arms out at his sides. "You're free."

"I guess so." Axel admitted, "I wasn't expecting that."

"Why? Because you actually did accost her?" Magnus asked.

Axel frowned at him. "That's none of your business, Scales."

"I have my answer, nonetheless." Magnus folded his arms across his chest and scowled at him.

Axel started to say something, but Avian's voice filled the throne room again.

"The council's next and final hearing is that of Condor, the disgraced former Captain of the Royal Guard and leader of the rebel faction known as the Raven's Brood." Avian motioned toward the pillar to the right of the throne, and four Wisps, all of them clad in dark-purple armor and wielding swords, escorted Condor into view.

Where the Wisps had only secured Axel's hands with ropes, a thick chain bound Condor's wrists behind his back, and a matching strand stretched between his ankles. One of the Wisps gripped another chain attached to a steel collar around Condor's neck.

To top it all off, no one had bothered to change out the bandage on Condor's hand. The same ragged, frayed, and bloody cloth that they'd wrapped around his wounded hand after catching him still covered his hand.

Axel rubbed his sore left shoulder and recalled Condor's words from last night in the prison.

You'd better pray that the council calls me first so I get the bulk of their wrath and there isn't much leftover for you.

Too bad exactly the opposite of that had transpired. Axel and Condor might not get their day of battle after all.

"Good luck," Axel muttered. His shoulder had already started to feel better.

WHEN CONDOR'S piercing blue eyes met hers, Lilly's heart beat faster.

At first she disregarded the uneasiness in her stomach as the result of him trying to take her hostage, but the longer he stared, the more she realized the source of her anxiety wasn't their history—it came from him.

Just him.

Lilly had to look away.

"Since the accusations against you are innumerable, this council has elected to reduce the number of claims to the following list." Avian held up a scroll. "Insurrection, rebellion, treason, attempted extortion of the Premier for personal gain, theft, and the battery and murder of multiple Sky Realm citizens."

"I object." Condor's voice indicated very little, if any emotion whatsoever. He stood tall, stoic, and stared right at Lilly's father.

Avian shook his head. "You cannot object. These are the summations of the countless accusations we received from citizens regarding your—"

"I object because I do not recognize this council's authority."

"Regardless of your objection, this council stands in authority over you."

"You have me in chains, in shackles. You've kept me in a jail cell for the last week, or however long it has been. But you do not have any authority over me. Why are there only Wisps on this council and not mere Windgales as well?"

"Please do not play coy with us," Avian said. "You know full well that Windgales are not appointed to the council because—"

"Without representation from the lower caste, this council is a farce," Condor interrupted, shaking his head. "Everyone knows that *you* make the final decision on every issue. Everyone knows that the only man bold enough to side against you consistently is General Balena, and even he—"

"Condor, enough." General Balena held up his hand. "Your beliefs are not the subject of this hearing. Do you deny any of the Premier's accusations?"

"I deny all of them."

Grunts and murmurs swelled throughout the crowd. The Wisps who guarded Condor exchanged subtle glances, but Lilly noticed.

"So you deny that you instigated a rebellion?" General Balena leaned forward.

"No."

"You just said you denied all of the accusations."

"I deny that it was a rebellion. The people took a stand against corruption."

"It was a rebellion, regardless of what you call it." Avian rubbed his forehead. "And you admitted to leading it."

"It is the people's right to—"

"We're not talking about the people's rights. We're talking about your actions. Yours alone." Avian pointed at Condor. "More than one hundred people—*our* people—died as a result of your 'uprising.' How do you account for that?"

Condor scoffed. "*Your* soldiers killed them."

"What few members of the Royal Guard who followed you died at the hands of General Balena's soldiers, as well as some of the soldiers themselves, before you fled from the Realm," Avian said. "All of their deaths rest solely on *your* shoulders."

"And how many poor Windgales have died on the ground below Aeropolis because you refuse to provide them with aid? Because your excesses have diminished their resources, and thus their chances of survival? Because of your secrets?"

Condor stepped forward, but the Wisp who held his chain pulled him back. He winced, but otherwise it didn't prevent him from speaking.

"Those hundred fighters died because you refuse to divulge the truth, a truth that would make every Windgale free for the rest of their lives. If I bear the weight of a hundred deaths on my shoulders, you and your oligarchy bear the weight of *thousands* on yours."

Lilly glanced at her father, but he remained focused on the accused. *What is Condor talking about?*

"Your hypocrisy is boundless." Avian stood and smacked his palms flat on the table. "You could have revealed that secret to the dozens of Windgales in your brood, but you didn't. You maintained it for the same reasons that we do."

"Even if I had revealed it, it would've changed nothing for the Windgales who followed me, and you know exactly why that's the case." Condor's impassioned tone persisted. "You keep it secret solely because you need to maintain control."

"We need to maintain *order*."

Secrets? What are they talking about? What mysteries of Lilly's people had her father not yet revealed to her?

Condor shot back, "You're manipulating our people to enhance your luxurious lifestyle."

"When you were Captain of the Royal Guard, you partook in them as well, yet now you hang the blame on me? More hypocrisy," Avian countered.

"Except that unlike you, my excess ceased when I chose to try to level the terms. I gave up everything to reconcile our misdeeds to the people."

"*Enough*." Avian held up his hands. "My reign is not the subject of this hearing. *Your* decisions landed you before this council, and this council will now rule on your fate. Whether you recognize our authority or not, those chains that bind you belong to us, and thus, so do you."

General Balena leaned nearer to Avian. "Premier—"

Condor sneered. "You may own these chains, but you'll *never* own me."

"Premier?" General Balena touched Avian's forearm, but Avian brushed his hand away.

Avian shouted, "Your fate is all but sealed! I'll see you *executed* for your crimes."

"*Avian*." General Balena clamped his armored hand around Avian's wrist and pulled him away from the table so their backs faced Condor and the crowd. General Balena outweighed Lilly's father by at least fifty pounds, and he had no trouble physically moving Avian.

Lilly wished she could hear what General Balena whispered to her father. Instead, Condor's eyes met hers again, and her stomach leaped. Something about his eyes swirled her emotions.

She didn't feel this way when she looked at Falcroné, or Axel, or even Calum. His allure transcended any of theirs, but it was also accompanied by a sense of danger. Maybe that's why she found him so intriguing in the first place.

When Condor winked at her, Lilly had to look away again. *Dangerous, indeed.*

General Balena turned around first, then Avian, who said, "We will hear no more discussion on your crimes, Condor, as I have decreed."

Condor craned his neck to address the crowd. "Like I said, all the final decisions are made by one man instead of by the people."

General Balena pointed his index finger at Condor. "If he utters so much as another word without us asking him a direct question, cut out his tongue."

As far as Lilly knew, General Balena had never made a joke in his life, nor had he even laughed at one. His command regarding Condor was no exception.

The Wisp produced a small knife from his belt and held it near Condor's lips, but Condor's indignation persisted in the form of a rebellious smirk.

General Balena sat in his chair, but Avian remained standing.

"Condor, disgraced former Captain of the Royal Guard and leader of the defunct rebel faction called the Raven's Brood," Avian said, "on the charges brought against you for your crimes against the Sky Realm, we, the council will now rule on your case."

Down the line, from the Wisp closest to Lilly on the left side of the table down to the Wisp farthest from her on the opposite end, the council members repeated the word, "Guilty." As was their custom, the Premier's vote came last. Like all the rest, her father said, "Guilty."

"According to our laws, with a unanimous vote of guilt, we are obliged to call for a second vote to determine whether or not you deserve the death penalty." Avian motioned toward Lilly's end of the table. "By law, that vote—yea for the death penalty and nay to stay the sword of justice—must also be unanimous. Do you have anything to say in your defense before we decide your fate?"

The Wisp pulled the knife away from Condor's mouth, and Condor straightened his posture. "I'd rather die as a traitor than live as a servant of corruption."

"Very well." Avian's frown deepened, and he looked down the line. "Votes?"

"Yea," said the first council member.

Twice. Three times. Falcroné added a fourth without any hesitation, and then the vote fell to General Balena, who remained silent for a long moment. Finally, he looked at Condor with steel in his eyes and said, "Yea."

Condor bowed his head. He must have known, as Lilly did, that the three remaining council members would also vote for his death, and they did.

But neither of them expected Avian to say "Nay."

CHAPTER 24

ondor's head popped up and he stared at Avian with his mouth open slightly. Lilly, Falcroné, General Balena, and everyone else in the room did likewise.

"Death is too convenient for you, Condor. You expected an easy way out, a swift end to your miserable life in exchange for the harm you inflicted on your people." Avian shook his head. "I will not grant it.

"Executing you would make you a martyr to those in the Sky Realm who believe the lies you espouse, but martyrs cannot earn that title with the blood of others. No, you will live the remainder of your life as a slave. Not to me, nor to anyone in this Realm, but to harsher masters than any known to Kanarah."

Lilly covered her hand with her mouth. She already knew where her father meant to send Condor for his crimes.

"I sentence you to one hundred years of hard labor in the Blood Chasm."

The crowd rumbled with mutters and gasps until General Balena held up his hand. "Premier, decisions like these must be made by majority vote of the council. To send Condor to that place without—"

"Then we'll vote." Avian's gaze met those of each of the Wisps on the council. "What say you, Lord Elmond? Yea or nay to Condor's punishment?"

The Wisp nearest to Lilly shook his head. "Nay. That place ought to be shut down for good. No living creature deserves a fate like what you're suggesting."

"Very well. Lady Sandaria?"

"Yea."

Avian nodded to her, then focused on the next Wisp. "Lord Jansson?"

"Nay."

"Yea," Falcroné said before Avian could call his name. "He deserves the worst. I say we give it to him."

Having been captured by slave traders, the idea of anyone being enslaved grated against her judgment. Worse yet, having encountered two Gronyxes in the tunnels under Trader's Pass, she knew all too well what Condor might have to face in Western Kanarah's subterranean realm.

Lilly's eyes locked with Falcroné's, and she set her jaw. Falcroné had given his answer out of spite more than from a desire for justice. They'd once been friends while training to become officers, even as close as brothers, despite Condor's ascension from the lower caste.

Apparently, Condor's betrayal had destroyed whatever friendship they'd shared, but even so, Lilly couldn't help the disdain she felt for his behavior.

Avian smirked at Condor then turned to General Balena. "General?"

"I have seen the Blood Chasm and witnessed the evil that dwells there firsthand," he began. "I've watched the slaves fight for their lives against them, only to die slow, torturous deaths. I will not vote to subject even the worst offender to such a fate.

"Furthermore, the Blood Chasm should be abandoned indefinitely for the good of all Kanarah, not perpetuated by sending another soul to his demise there." General Balena folded his arms and stared at Avian. "I vote 'nay.'"

Avian's smirk dissipated while General Balena spoke, and it devolved into a scowl by the time he finished. He looked at the next council member. "Lady Katalina?"

"Nay. I agree with General Balena, Lord Jansson, and Lord Elmond. The punishment is too severe for one of our own."

Lilly raised her eyebrows. One more vote, and Condor would avoid the Blood Chasm.

Avian's scowl hardened. Through clenched teeth, he asked, "And what do you think, Lady Gremia?"

"Yea. Send him to the pit, and may he die the slow, miserable death General Balena described." Lady Gremia frowned and narrowed her dark eyes at Condor. "My eldest son is gone because of him. If I cannot ensure him the death penalty, I must do what I can to ease the pain and suffering he has caused my household and that of the other families whose sons died in his rebellion."

"Lord Namuel, the vote is yours."

For as hard as Lilly's heart pounded in her chest, she couldn't imagine what Condor's was doing in his. She knew nothing about Lord Namuel. Had he, too, lost someone in the rebellion? Did he tend toward mercy?

Lord Namuel rubbed his bare chin with thick fingers. "May he live to die a hundred deaths, one for each year of his sentence, one for each citizen who perished because of him. Yea."

The crowd erupted in a mix of cheers and droning boos. All but one of the Wisps who stood guard around Condor faced the crowd with their swords at the ready. The crowd did not advance toward the council, but their ruckus continued nonetheless.

Lilly watched as her father, General Balena, and Falcroné all ascended into the air from their seats. Avian extended his arms in front of him, palms down, and boomed over the crowd, "Condor, disgraced former Captain of the Royal Guard and leader of the Raven's Brood rebel faction, I hereby sentence you to one hundred years of slavery in the Blood Chasm."

Condor's stoic face did not crumble with emotion. He simply bowed his head again and closed his eyes.

Avian motioned toward the throne room doors. "Take him away."

The Wisps who guarded Condor shoved him toward the crowd, their swords still unsheathed and ready for action should it find them. The Wisp who held the chain connected to Condor's neck led the way, and the other three Wisps formed a diamond around Condor.

As they walked through the crowd, objects soared through the air at them. Shoes, rotten fruits and vegetables, and even stones whipped toward Condor from the crowd. The Wisps hurried him forward, but the crowd sealed off their exit before they could get out.

Lilly swiveled her head toward Falcroné, but he and General Balena had already darted toward the doors. They landed between Condor's guards and the crowd and barked orders in ferocious tones.

The crowd parted just long enough for Condor and the Wisps to get through, and General Balena followed them out. Falcroné took to the air and returned to Avian's side.

Lilly would never see Condor's piercing blue eyes again. Perhaps it was for the best.

"This hearing is dismissed," Falcroné bellowed. "Return to the day's labors at once. Stragglers will be considered a threat to the realm's safety and will be jailed immediately."

As the crowd dissipated, Lilly couldn't help but wonder if justice had been served in any capacity that day. She had lied to cover for Axel's transgression, and her father had damned Condor to a terrible fate, one arguably worse than death. And Condor had accused her father of multiple wrongdoings as well.

Secrets. Rebellions. Threats. Injustice. Death. Where was the truth in all of it? Why was the Sky Realm so broken, so confused? Or the rest of Kanarah, for that matter?

Lilly clenched her fists. *Someone ought to do something about it all.*

RILEY WHIMPERED, careful not to be loud enough to wake Calum. He lay still, taking short shallow breaths, concealed in the shadows to the left of Calum's bed.

He should've been safe there in the dark, but his brutal memories always managed to find him no matter where he went.

Silver flashed in his mind's eye, and pain flared in his side. Condor's blade pierced him again and again, every night in his memories and in his dreams. Nights like this one.

Hiding was about all he could do anymore. The wound may not have killed him, but he could no longer run, much less leap or jump or pounce.

He'd never amounted to much of a fighter anyway—he preferred to rely on his speed and his stealth to gain the advantage. When those failed, Riley could resort to the vicious, crazy part of him that he didn't let out except in the very worst of times.

But his speed was gone now, taken away with one vicious stab from Condor's blade, maybe permanently.

Perhaps he should have unleashed that vicious part of himself when he'd fought Condor. But even that vicious part had limits. Physical limits, more so now than ever.

Where Riley had always provided for himself, Condor's sword had reduced him to little more than a beggar who could *maybe* rob other beggars. He would have to depend on Calum and his friends for food since he couldn't hunt without pain.

Who was he kidding? He could barely *breathe* without pain.

Riley whimpered again and lay his head down on the floor. He was useless. A drag. He might as well stay here in the Sky Fortress as the Premier's hound, like the common dog he'd insisted he wasn't. He could eat scraps from the Premier's dinner table and gnaw the meat off the bones leftover in the kitchen.

In time, perhaps he would even learn some tricks. He could already roll over, already play dead. Condor had taught him that one.

A long sigh escaped his mouth until it hurt to exhale any more. He closed his eyes in the darkness and wondered what misery he'd have to endure tomorrow.

When Avian summoned Calum, Axel, Magnus, and Riley for a private audience, Calum knew what it had to mean. He'd dreamed of Lumen in all his glory again last night, and they'd stayed at the Sky Fortress for far longer than he'd intended already. Aside from Axel's sore arms and Riley's ongoing recovery from his wound, they were healthy and ready to go.

Lilly stood at her father's side in the throne room. Her golden hair seemed to sparkle under the sunlight that poured through the crystal-covered shafts in the throne room's ceiling.

Falcroné stood next to her, and his hair shimmered just as much, if not more.

Calum suppressed a disheartened chuckle as he approached them. Falcroné was almost as "pretty" as Lilly was.

Zephyrra sat next to the Premier in a chair smaller than the throne with a pleasant smile on her face.

"My friends, welcome." Avian lifted his arms, but did not stand. "Come forward."

Calum performed the Windgale salute first and snuck a peek back to make sure Magnus and Axel did as well. Riley just bowed slightly and licked his nose.

"We have news for you. In poring through our expansive archives, my court historians have discovered a map that may lead you to the Arcanum."

Calum glanced at Magnus, who nodded. "May we see it?"

"You may *have* it." Avian grinned. "No one in the Sky Realm desires to use it, so it is yours for the taking. Kanton?"

From behind the pillars on the right side of the throne room, Kanton floated into view. He held a rolled-up, yellow-brown piece of parchment in his left hand. He landed in front of them and extended the parchment to Calum.

"You're a court historian now?" Calum asked.

"No. Not in the least. I can't read a single word on this map, much less an entire book."

Calum glanced at Avian, then back at Kanton. "Then what are you doing here?"

Kanton smiled then turned back to the Premier. "Do you want to tell him, or can I?"

Avian grinned again and waved his hand toward them, palm up.

"I'm going with you." Kanton winked at Calum.

"What? Really?" Calum couldn't help but smile too. "Are you serious?"

"Serious as any man ever was." Kanton nodded toward Avian. "The Premier was kind enough to grant me this grand favor in light of my small role in helping Princess Lilly get home—that is, helping her rescuers up to Aeropolis in a time of need. When I asked to join your group, he gave me his blessing immediately. That is, if you'll have me."

Calum eyed Lilly over Kanton's shoulder, but she looked down at the floor instead of at him. She really wasn't coming along, just like she had said. Kanton was supposed to be her replacement, in a way. It was a nice gesture, but the thought of her not traveling with them ripped the hole in Calum's heart all over again.

"You already know I'm good with my hands—from a healing perspective, that is—but I'm also not too bad with a staff or a spear. Had plenty of years protecting the Premier's sheep on the ground level by fending off his kind—" Kanton nodded at Riley. "—and wild beasts of other sorts too.

"Even killed a sabertooth cat once. Got a nice pair of fangs from him, but had to sell them when my third cape wore out. Wish I'd kept them, though. Would've been worth a fortune in Aeropolis nowadays."

Calum and Axel eyed each other.

"Anyway, you don't mind if I come along, do you? I know I'll come in handy more than once." Kanton's blue eyes glistened with delightful expectation. "What so you say?"

Calum looked back at Magnus, who nodded and said, "We could use someone like him."

"Yeah, any time Calum gets himself injured, he'll have a healer to patch him up," Axel said.

"You're the one with sore arms and a bruise on your chin. I feel fine."

Axel glanced at Lilly, then he refocused on Calum. "Come over here, and we'll see how fine you feel after thirty seconds of me thrashing you."

Calum ignored Axel. "The answer is yes, Kanton. We'd love to have you join us."

Kanton let out a whoop, launched into the air, and executed a backward loop. He landed almost exactly where he'd been standing and nodded to Calum. "Sorry for the excitement, but I thought you'd say I was too old for an adventure."

"You think *you're* old?" Axel huffed. "Magnus here is two hundred sixty-something."

"Two hundred and *three* years old," Magnus said. "Not two hundred sixty-something."

Axel held up his hands. "My mistake. Didn't realize you were so sensitive about it."

"I am not sensitive about it. I just care that my age is represented accur—"

"Friends, friends," Avian interjected. "Let's not get sideswiped with meaningless chatter. You have your map. You have Kanton. You are free to go. The lift awaits your arrival for immediate descent. May the Overlord bless your journey."

Calum and Axel made eye contact again. They'd both taken the meaning of Avian's words.

Axel stepped forward and squinted at Avian. "What do you mean, 'immediate descent?' Are you throwing us out?"

Avian tilted his head and gave Axel a manufactured smile. "Of course not. You are welcome to stay as long as you please. I just wanted you to know you are free to go whenever you so desire."

Axel gave an incredulous nod. "Because it really sounded like—"

"We understand," Calum interrupted before Axel managed to get them tossed off one of the platforms. "Thank you for your generosity and hospitality so far. We'll head out this evening."

"It's too bad you'll have to miss the wedding." Falcroné's lips curled up in a sly grin, and he pulled Lilly close to him. "It will be an occasion like none in recent history."

Calum's jaw set, but he forced a smile and nodded. "We wish you all the best. Come on, guys. Let's go pack our things."

"Wait," Lilly said.

Calum's eyes found hers. What was it this time?

"Father." She looked at Avian. "I'm going with them."

CHAPTER 25

S ilence overtook the throne room, and part of Lilly couldn't even believe she'd said it.
  Avian raised his eyebrows at her.

"No, you're not." Somehow, Falcroné managed to say the words even before her father had the chance.

Lilly looked into his blue eyes and, her voice firm, said, "Yes, I am."

"No, you're *not*." That time her father said it. "Absolutely not. You just returned to us. If it were up to me, I'd never let you outside of the fortress walls again."

Of course he'd say something like that. Most fathers would, wouldn't they?

But he didn't understand what she'd experienced out there in the rest of Kanarah. He didn't comprehend the state of things with the King in power—the corruption, the suffering. He couldn't even acknowledge the struggles of his own people, so how could he possibly have any sense of what the land as a whole was dealing with?

Lilly renewed her resolve. "I'm going with them, Father. I want to help them free Lumen."

"No." Avian waved his hand laterally in front of him as if dividing the room in half. "Not in a millennium."

Mother stepped forward. "You have duties here. Obligations to fulfill."

"You're getting married in less than a month," Avian said. "That alone is reason enough for you not to go with them, and I have hundreds more besides."

"I don't care what I'm supposed to do or what your reasons are for wanting me to stay." Lilly's stern tone shocked even her, but she'd stated her plans and refused to back down now. "You tried to force me into a life I didn't want months ago, and look what happened: I got kidnapped by slave traders when I left here. You're not going to dictate my life to me anymore. I'm going with them, and that's final."

"Nothing is final until *I say* it is final, Lilliana!" Avian thundered. He leaned in close to her, his voice calmer as he said, "When you left, my heart broke. I will not allow it to happen again."

"Then *hear* me, Father," Lilly pleaded. "I left because you gave me no choice. I've agreed to your terms regarding my marriage, but with this delay. That's all. Can't you grant me leeway in this?"

Avian's eyes narrowed. "No. You are staying here, and you are marrying Falcroné on the eve of your eighteenth birthday. That is not negotiable."

"I'll marry him, but I'll do it when we return from freeing Lumen." Lilly glanced at Falcroné, whose sullen expression had softened at her most recent comment. She might have won him over, but how could she convince her father? "Kanarah is in a state of confusion and disarray. Lumen will—"

"You don't know what you're saying. Lumen will overthrow the King, and he intends to reign over all Kanarah. *All* of it. That includes *our* realm, Lilly." Avian's hot breath hit her face when he spoke. "Why would you free someone who intends to overthrow your own father?"

Lilly hadn't thought about it that way before. "He's... he's not going to overthrow anyone. Calum said he's going to bring order and peace to Kanarah by defeating the King."

"And you believe what *Calum* says? Why?" Falcroné asked.

"He's dreamt of Lumen multiple times. He's seen him, spoken to him, followed his instructions—and now I'm back home, safe because of what Calum has seen in his sleep." Lilly unclenched her fists. She didn't remember clenching them in the first place. "I *know* Calum is going to set Lumen free. I can feel it inside of me. I want to be there when it happens."

Falcroné huffed and folded his arms. "*If* it happens."

"Oh, it'll happen alright, Sunshine." Axel muttered.

"What did you just say?" Falcroné stepped off the platform toward Axel until they stood face-to-face.

"All that hair must make it hard to hear." Undeterred, Axel's eyes narrowed. "I said, 'oh, it'll happen, al—"

"Enough, both of you," Avian said. "Falcroné, come back up here."

Falcroné obeyed, but he snarled at Axel as he hovered back to the platform.

"Lilly, we don't know what Lumen is going to do if—or *when* he gets freed." Her mother frowned. "There's just no telling what's going to be affected by his return."

"Then who better to put right near the action than your own daughter? I can make sure we're in his good graces when the time comes to—"

"You are the *worst* person to have near the action," Avian said. "You are my only heir, who together with Falcroné must produce the next in our lineage to rule after you. What if you're stuck down or wounded, and are unable to have children? What will happen to our house then?"

Finally, a question Lilly had practiced answering in advance. "Falcroné can rule in my stead. He's my cousin, after all, and shares my ancestry."

"No, I can't." Falcroné reached for her hand and intertwined his fingers with hers. "Because if you go, I'm going with you."

"*What?*" Avian yelled. "No! She's not going, and neither are you."

"I think she may have a point, Premier," Falcroné said. "The prophecy regarding Lumen is clear—he will be freed 1,000 years from the day he was banished. Wouldn't it be better to help free him and side with him in his rebellion than to try to remain neutral in a conflict that will engulf the whole of Kanarah?"

"The prophecy says nothing about whether or not he will *defeat* the King, just that he will be released from his prison." Avian rubbed his forehead with his index finger and his thumb. "You want to go to your deaths, both of you. What did I do to make you wish to die far away from your home? Name your deepest desire and I will grant it, but not this. Anything but this."

"Father." Lilly let go of Falcroné's hand and took Avian's hands in hers. She stared into his eyes. "This is what I want. *This* is my deepest desire. I promise that when Kanarah sees justice, Falcroné and I will be wed, and in doing so, we will ensure the future of not only our line but also of the entire Sky Realm."

"I will see it done, Premier." Falcroné stepped forward, next to Lilly. "I will not allow any harm to come to her. I let her go once, and it is not a mistake I intend to repeat."

Falcroné really wanted to come along? Lilly hadn't figured on that. Not in a millennium.

Zephyrra touched Avian's arm and nodded, then Avian exhaled a long sigh. "Who will lead the Royal Guard in your place?"

"Promote Helion. He is a remarkable warrior of great strength and wisdom for his age," Falcroné said.

Avian's scowl deepened. "The boy is fifteen years old, Falcroné."

"All the same, he is as fit to succeed me as anyone. General Balena can provide him with extra insight as he did for me. Helion will excel if given more responsibility."

"He'll also beat Condor's record for youngest Captain of the Royal Guard by three years." Avian squinted at him. "Does that factor into your suggestion?"

Falcroné shrugged but donned a wry grin. "It couldn't hurt to wipe Condor from the realm's memory entirely."

"Please, Father?" Lilly employed her sad-eyes-pouty-lip face. It was a cheap ploy, but it almost always worked on him.

Avian frowned at her. "Lilly, I don't want anything to happen to you. I *just* got you back, and now you want to leave on a journey far more dangerous than the one which brought you home."

It *almost* always worked. "Father, Falcroné will protect me. Plus, I'll be traveling with Calum, Axel, Magnus, Riley, and Kanton, the former of which have already proven that they can keep me safe."

"None of them give me half as much comfort as knowing Falcroné would be with you. Even so, I would send a contingent of soldiers with you for extra protec—"

"No, Father," Lilly shook her head. "We'll draw too much attention that way. Better to keep a low profile."

"She's right, you know." A deep, almost melancholy voice sounded from behind Calum. He stepped aside, and Riley tilted his head.

"Excuse me—she's right, you know, *Premier*." Riley gave a modest bow. "I know a little something about stealth, and I can tell you it's much easier with fewer people to go unnoticed. The more men you send with us, the more of us won't make it back, in my opinion. Group's already too big for my taste *without* the happy couple."

Avian narrowed his eyes at Riley.

"That's—that's just what I think." Riley's voice quivered at the end of his sentence. Then he slunk behind Calum and murmured, "I'm gonna shut up now."

"Avian, let them go." Zephyrra touched his shoulder. "You can't protect her forever. She needs to discover the world and find her place in it. If you deny her this, you may lose her again for good, and our line will be lost with her."

Avian sighed and rubbed his forehead. "Even you are convinced now?"

Zephyrra nodded.

"I had hoped she would've 'found her place in our world' in the last few months she was gone, but now she wants to leave again." Avian shook his head and let out another sigh. He leveled his gaze at Lilly. "Promise me you'll come back unscathed."

Lilly didn't fight the smile that cracked her lips. "I promise."

Avian grabbed the sides of Falcroné's breastplate and yanked him close. "And *you*, boy. Promise me you'll bring her back unscathed, or so help me, your fate will be even worse than Condor's."

Falcroné nodded. "I swear on my mother's grave."

Avian released him. "Then you both may go."

CALUM WASN'T SURPRISED that Avian's attitude toward them didn't change all that much after he agreed to let Lilly go with them, but his approach certainly did. Specifically, he did everything possible to ensure they were well prepared and well stocked for their journey.

He ordered Ganosh to take Axel, Kanton, and Calum to the Royal Armory to update their armor and weaponry. By the time they left, Calum and Axel wore new lightweight armor—navy blue for Axel, in addition to Magnus's old light-blue Blood Ore leg and arm plating, deep forest-green for Kanton, and crimson red for Calum.

They'd tried to get Calum to replace his old boots for new ones, but he refused. Instead, they compromised at repairing and resoling his old ones. They also dyed the leather black at his request. He hadn't minded the brown, but Lilly had said black would look better with his new armor, so he'd gone for it.

The armorist even outfitted Riley's right foreleg with a steel cast of sorts that started just above his paw, covered his shoulder, and reached almost back to his hind leg along his torso. It more than covered the wound he'd take from Condor's blade, but the armorist warned that a blow to his right side would likely still hurt because of the original wound's severity.

Riley growled a bit and grumbled something about his stealth and speed abilities suffering as a result, but he kept the armor on nonetheless and nodded to the armorist in thanks.

Next, they visited the Sky Fortress's quartermaster, who took their old swords and exchanged them for lighter-weight blades.

Axel protested at first, saying that the lighter weight would mean less heft behind his swings, but the quartermaster assured him the blade's sharpness and speed would more than account for its lower weight. Both of them also received a curved dagger, which they strapped to their belts.

Calum gladly traded Tyburon's red blade for a new one. After so many battles, its once sharp edge had both dulled and sustained a variety of gashes and nicks that reduced its effectiveness in fights. A part of him regretted letting it go, but when he received his new weapon, he forgot all about it.

The quartermaster handed him a sword very similar in shape to the one Calum had given up, only it weighed two-thirds what Tyburon's did. Its blade gleamed silver with golden engravings of swirls and wispy designs befitting the Sky Realm.

Kanton received a short sword and a steel spear that had a hollow shaft. A broad-headed spearhead topped it off. The quartermaster pointed out a slight curve on the bottom of one of the spearhead's edges near the shaft and told Kanton he could use it to lock his opponents' weapons in place or even disarm them entirely.

The only one of their group who did not accept anything new was Magnus. He insisted that his Blood Ore breastplate and broadsword were more than sufficient, despite both the quarter-master and the armorist arguing otherwise.

He did, however, accept a new vial of veromine from the royal apothecary when Kanton requested a variety of medical supplies to bring along. Over time, he could've extracted some from his own blood, he'd explained, but the process was long and tedious, and not an ideal undertaking for a journey through the wilds.

By the time they made it back into the throne room, the sun had just begun to set. As before, Lilly stood next to her father, only this time she wore the same light pink armor she'd worn before they arrived.

Avian beckoned them forward, and as Calum approached, he noticed that Lilly's armor was indeed the same, only the various nicks and gashes had been repaired and retouched with pink lacquer the same color as the rest of the armor. When Calum got closer, he noticed the chips in the armor's faint white engravings of eagles and hawks had also been retouched.

Her new bow, a long white recurve with silver designs etched into its sides, hung with its string across her chest. A quiver full of arrows with silver shafts and white fletching hung from her hip.

The short sword she'd used before their arrival was gone, replaced by a curved blade with a white hilt that hung from her belt in its sheath. It looked like the same style as the daggers Calum and Axel had received.

She looked every bit as beautiful as she had the first time Calum saw her, only she now exuded a renewed sense of strength and confidence as well.

"What a transformation," Avian said. "Were you in orange or purple armor instead, you could have passed for General Balena's soldiers or Royal Guards."

Calum performed the Windgale salute and bowed low. "We appreciate your generosity, Premier. We're far better equipped than we've ever been."

"This is only the beginning, Calum." Avian smiled and leaned back in his throne. "You haven't seen the provisions I've had Ganosh and the kitchen prepare for your journey."

"We are very grateful."

Falcroné soared in from behind them and landed next to Lilly. He still wore his charcoal armor, only now he carried a spear like Kanton's in addition to the sword strapped to his belt. "Everything is ready. Are we heading out tonight or tomorrow morning?"

"Tonight," Axel said.

"Tomorrow morning." Avian's eyes narrowed at Axel. "Get a good night's rest here before you head out."

"Father." Lilly clasped Avian's hands in hers. "You have to let us go at some point."

"I definitely prefer to travel at night," Riley said. When Avian glared at him, Riley added, "But that's just me. We can leave whenever."

Avian cupped Lilly's cheek with his hand. "Are you so eager to leave me behind that you won't even stay one more night?"

Lilly chuckled. "It's not that. I just don't think you'll ever actually let us go."

"You can't fault me for wanting you around. You're my one and only daughter, and I love you."

"I love you too, Father." Lilly pulled away from him. "But we need to leave tonight."

Avian sighed, but nodded. "If that's what you desire, then so be it."

"Nice." Riley smirked. When Avian glowered at him again, he started to back into the shadow of one of the pillars. "You know what? Just ignore me. I'm not even here."

"Ganosh will provide you with the rest of your supplies," Avian said.

Lilly hugged Avian and smiled. "Thank you."

After their hug, Avian grabbed Falcroné by the sides of his breastplate as he had earlier that day. "Protect her. If she's not with you when you return, don't bother returning at all."

Falcroné nodded. "I understand."

"Go." Avian waved them away. "Before I change my decision, go. And don't forget to say goodbye to your mother, Lilly."

She smiled again. "I won't."

Calum saluted Avian again and bowed. "Thank you, Premier. We'll bring her back safely."

Axel, Magnus, Kanton, and Riley followed Calum toward the doors, and Lilly and Falcroné landed next to him and walked alongside him.

Then the throne room doors swung open before them, stopping the group in their tracks as a cluster of large dark-green figures stepped inside. Not Saurians—Sobeks, like Magnus. Six of them.

A pristine golden breastplate decorated the chest of the lead Sobek, who towered over the rest of the Sobeks by at least six inches. He had to be nearly eight feet tall—even larger than Magnus.

Four of the others wore black breastplates, and the last Sobek, shorter and stockier than the others yet still over seven feet tall, wore a scratched-up brown breastplate. His scarred face was stuck somewhere between a snarl and a perpetual sneer.

Calum couldn't help but stare as he passed them. They didn't give him a second look, but the lead Sobek eyed Magnus for a moment before refocusing on Avian.

"That's Vandorian in the lead," Falcroné whispered to Calum. "He's the nephew of Kahn, the Dragon King of Reptilius."

"He's *huge*. And I thought Magnus was big." Calum glanced over his shoulder. "Do you know him, Magnus?"

But Magnus wasn't walking behind them anymore.

Instead, he followed the group of Sobeks—and his hand was clamped around the hilt of his broadsword.

CHAPTER 26

The *shing* of Magnus's broadsword leaving its sheath sent shivers ratcheting through Riley's body. There wasn't supposed to be a fight here, now, but Magnus was starting one anyway.

One by one, the Sobeks turned back to face Magnus as he charged toward them with a room-rattling roar.

The first Sobek took the worst blow—a deadening shot to his scaled snout from Magnus's left fist. Magnus passed by the Sobek with the brown armor, who stepped well clear of Magnus's path and didn't even try to intervene. Then Magnus drove his shoulder into another of the Sobeks in black.

The final two Sobeks in black drew their own swords and positioned themselves between Magnus and the tall Sobek in gold, who finally turned back to assess the commotion behind him. Magnus ducked under the first Sobek's swing, parried the second Sobek's blow, and broke through to the lead Sobek with ease.

With another roar, he leaped at the Sobek in gold with his sword raised.

The lead Sobek showed no sign of fear, concern, or any emotion. Instead, he lunged forward as Magnus began to swing his blade and delivered a colossal blow to Magnus's breastplate with his fist.

The punch reversed Magnus's trajectory and knocked him back several feet. He skidded along the marble floor, and as his back smacked against one of the pillars, his broadsword clattered out of reach.

Three of the four Sobeks in black swarmed Magnus with their swords ready.

Riley had seen enough. Anyone who could hit Magnus hard enough to make him drop his sword was someone Riley had no intention of tangling with.

Amid the shouts of Calum, Falcroné, and Avian, Riley darted away from the group and took refuge in the shadow of one of the pillars. Fighting now was a terrible idea. Definitely not against six Sobeks.

Falcroné took to the air and zipped toward the Premier, whose four guards formed a barrier between him and the Sobeks' scuffle.

Calum drew his sword and hurried to join Magnus, and Lilly, Kanton, and Axel followed him, but the Sobek in brown, still upright, positioned himself between them and Magnus. He hissed at them and drew a ragged-looking curved sword.

"*Enough,*" a thunderous voice boomed, shaking Riley to his core.

The lead Sobek still hadn't drawn his sword, but the entire room ceased to move at his command. He stood in place, his face as calm as when he had leveled Magnus, and all eyes watched him.

"Get him up," he ordered. "Hold him."

The three Sobeks pulled Magnus to his feet. He strained against them, but they anchored him in place.

The lead Sobek tilted his head. "Bring him to me."

They dragged Magnus over to within ten feet of him, and Magnus roared, but he still couldn't get free.

"Be *silent.*" The lead Sobek narrowed his eyes. "I know you, do I not?"

Magnus hissed at him, long and low. Riley had scarcely ever heard a more threatening sound, and it sent chills spiraling through his body.

"Please, Magnus." The lead Sobek shook his head. "That is no way to treat your brother, is it?"

Riley's eyes widened.

THE TENSION in Calum's body went slack. Vandorian and Magnus were brothers? But that meant—

"Calum!" Axel shouted.

Calum barely got his sword into position in time to absorb the blow from the Sobek in brown, and Axel joined him. But the force of his swing sent both Calum and Axel sliding across the marble floor until they smacked into one of the pillars, just as Magnus had.

"Hold, Oren." Vandorian's voice filled the whole throne room once again.

"No one 'oo raises arms 'gainst my lord or me gets off wiffout *punishment.*" Oren almost spat the words.

"You have made your point. Hold."

"What is the meaning of this?" Avian asked from behind his Royal Guard.

"Patience, Premier." Vandorian gave a slight bow and held his right fist against his gilded chest. When he spoke, his voice carried an air of distinction and superiority to it. "All will be revealed soon."

Calum pushed himself up first, then helped Axel to his feet. Kanton and Lilly darted over to them, their weapons ready should Oren attack again, but instead he sheathed his weathered old curved sword and scowled at them.

"I hardly recognized you—until you chose to attack me." A smirk formed on Vandorian's lips. "But now you stand before me, wearing our father's old Blood Ore breastplate, and wielding his old broadsword. When last I saw you, you were a tiny lizard. Now you're a Sobek, just like me. You have certainly grown, brother."

Little? To Calum, Magnus had never been *little.*

"You ceased to be my brother the day our father died," Magnus uttered.

"That was a tragic day, indeed. I am surprised you survived, to tell you the truth." Vandorian clacked his talons on his breastplate, just like Magnus often did. "We thought you were dead."

Avian motioned for Falcroné to come near. He whispered something to him, and Falcroné darted through one of the throne room's side doors.

"It takes more than the likes of you and your seditious warriors to kill me."

With every word, Magnus's mysterious past further unraveled before Calum's eyes.

"Clearly." Vandorian stepped closer to Magnus. "Tell me, brother, where you came by a Dragon Emerald?"

"That is none of your concern," Magnus growled.

"It *is* my concern. There are no more Dragon Emeralds in Reptilius, or anywhere, that we know of." Vandorian eyed the leather pouch that hung from Magnus's belt.

"Take your query to our uncle instead."

Vandorian snorted. "Or I can take yours."

Magnus jerked and thrashed against the Sobeks who held him, but he couldn't get free.

Vandorian reached for the pouch.

"Stop this at once, Vandorian." Avian's voice split the commotion. He hovered behind his guards with steel in his eyes. "I did not receive you into my realm that you might steal from my guests."

Vandorian retracted his hand. He glanced at Calum and faced Avian. "No, Premier, but your 'guests' have attacked my warriors and me."

"Then we will deal with them under our laws. They are not subject to your command, nor is any of their property."

"This Saurian is a wanted fugitive, partially responsible for the death of our father, the mighty Dragon King Praetorius."

"That's a lie!" Magnus shouted.

Calum's mouth dropped open. It all made sense now.

"He fled the Crimson Keep five years ago, unbeknownst to us. We thought he was killed the same day of his rebellion." Vandorian's head swiveled and he stared at Magnus. "I am taking him back with me for judgment."

"No, you are not."

Vandorian turned back and he glared at Avian. His voice lowered and sharpened, losing most of its regal tone. "What did you just say to me?"

"I said you're not taking them with you." Avian returned Vandorian's glare with one of his own. "Magnus has attained citizenship here and is partly responsible for my daughter's safe return. He is now under my authority, and thus he is mine to protect."

"I am taking him, and that is final," Vandorian insisted. His voice low and threatening again, he added, "And you cannot stop me."

Avian floated toward him, beyond the safety of his men, until they were eye to eye. "If you remove him or any of his property from this fortress—even from this *room*—I will treat it as an act of war."

Calum glanced at Lilly, but she just gave him a slight shrug. An act of war? Over Magnus? What had gotten into Avian all of a sudden?

Vandorian's jaw hardened, and he exhaled a long hiss through his nose. "You would not dare. We would annihilate your people and destroy your fortress within less than one day. We have Kahn, a direct descendant of the original Saurians first created by the Overlord, the only dragon known to Kanarah. You tiny birds are no match for his might."

A loud slam sounded from the back of the room. All heads turned for a look as General Balena stormed into the throne room, followed by dozens of armored Wisps and Windgale soldiers who filled the air. They surrounded Vandorian and his Sobeks with weapons brandished and blocked the exits.

"Sheathe your weapons immediately," General Balena bellowed, "or we will view your noncompliance as a threat to the Premier's security, and we will be forced to attack."

At the word "attack," every Windgale soldier in the room pointed the tips of their weapons at the Sobeks. Calum froze in place until Axel and Kanton pointed their weapons at Oren, then Calum did as well. Like Avian had said—they were *not* taking Magnus.

Oren drew his old curved sword again and beckoned them forward with his long green fingers. "C'mere, li'l babies. Let's see 'ow you fare."

"Easy, Oren." Vandorian chuckled, at first, then he shook his head. "Premier, I came here as a gesture of goodwill to honor your daughter for her engagement, and you receive me with a third of your army?"

"The engagement party was several days ago, and this isn't even close to a third of our army." Avian's voice didn't waver. "Now do as General Balena commands, and tell your warriors to sheathe their swords, or we will take action against you. We may be 'tiny birds,' but with enough of us, we can yet peck you to death. There is no need for you to die today."

After a long pause, Vandorian nodded to his Sobeks. "Do as he says."

All of them except Oren complied. Instead, he leaned toward Calum, Axel, and Kanton and bared his jagged teeth in what almost passed for a smile. "I ain't afraid of any o' you bugs. Come at me, an' you'll learn the true meanin' of sufferin'. Make your move, li'l babies."

"*Oren.*" Vandorian's voice cut through the tension. "Sheathe your sword, or I'll use your hide to reupholster my throne."

Oren grunted but straightened his spine and sheathed his old sword. "Next time, babies. Next time."

"Release Magnus," Avian said.

Vandorian straightened to his full height. "By Saurian law, we are within our rights to—"

"Look around you, Vandorian," Avian cut in. "You're not in Reptilius. These walls are blue crystal, not red granite. The floors are white marble, not black obsidian. In the Sky Realm, you will obey Sky Realm laws. Those who do not will be punished."

"And what will happen to Magnus for his attack on me?" Vandorian tilted his head. "What justice will you dole out, great and powerful Premier?"

"The punishment will fit the crime, but it is no concern of yours. We will deal with him in our own way, as we would any citizen of our realm."

"How can I be assured—"

"You *can't,*" Avian snapped. "But as I said, it is not your concern. You will leave him to us for judgment, and then you will leave."

"We traveled a great distance to pay homage to your daughter and her fiancé. You would send us away?"

"My daughter is in this very room, hovering near your anxious friend in the brown breast-plate." Avian nodded toward Lilly. "You'll know her by her blonde hair, her pink armor, and her overly ambitious personality. You may honor her this very moment."

Vandorian's head turned, and he found Lilly. He started toward her with a cunning grin on his face that made Calum want to put himself between the two of them, but Avian's voice stopped Vandorian's progress first.

"That's far enough, Vandorian. You can wish her well from that distance."

"Had I wanted to do that, I would not have journeyed so far to do it in person."

"Even so, you'll do it now all the same."

Vandorian grunted, then he donned a malicious smile. "All the best, Princess, to both of you in your forthcoming nuptials. I had a gift for the both of you, but in light of all this chaos, I seemed to have—*misplaced* it. Do forgive my thoughtlessness. I'll just have to bring you something extra on your wedding day."

Lilly lowered her bow and arrow and faked a smile of her own. "Thank you for your kind words, Lord Vandorian. I trust our peoples can continue to live in peace, despite this small, isolated incident. You are always welcome in my court as an honored guest—any time after today, at least."

Vandorian clacked the talons of his right hand against his golden breastplate, then he closed his fingers into a fist and pressed it against his chest. "May the Overlord bless your union and give you peace, long life, and many children."

"Again, thank you." Lilly nodded.

"There. You've given your regards to my daughter," Avian said. "Now release Magnus and go in peace."

"In almost four hundred years of life, I have never experienced such rudeness and disregard from *anyone*, let alone the ruler of an entire realm." Vandorian shook his head and faced Avian. "Your hospitality has atrophied of late, Premier."

"Enough words, enough games. Release Magnus, or we will take him from you by force, whatever the cost." Avian's hands balled into fists. "*Now.*"

Vandorian stepped near Magnus and leaned his head close. He half-whispered, "It is too bad you failed to kill me, brother. Now I know you yet live. We will meet again, and I will finish what I started the day our father died."

Magnus didn't say a word. He just continued glowering at his older brother.

"*Now*, Vandorian," Avian nearly shouted.

Vandorian sighed and stepped back. "Release him."

The Sobeks shoved Magnus to the floor and backed away. He immediately pushed himself to his feet and stood face-to-face with Vandorian.

"I look forward to that day." Then Magnus left Vandorian behind, bent down and picked up his broadsword, sheathed it, and stood next to Avian with his huge arms folded.

Vandorian knocked his fist against his breastplate again and gave Avian a slight bow. "By your leave, then."

The Sobeks helped their injured friend—the first one Magnus hit—to his feet, and started toward the main throne room doors. All around them, the Windgale soldiers parted so as not to impede their progress, but neither did they lower their weapons.

They walked out the doors with Oren at the rear of the group. He turned back one last time, shot Calum a wink, gave a flourishing gesture with his hand, and then he disappeared around a corner.

Two Windgale soldiers shut the doors behind them, and immediately every weapon in the room reset to a relaxed position, including Calum's. He started toward Magnus.

"Thank you, Premier," Magnus said. "I owe you my life."

"You are Praetorius's heir. Why didn't you reveal this to me when first we met?" Avian asked.

"As you said the day we returned Lilly to you, 'there are few people in this world who are unquestionably trustworthy.' This is a secret I have kept from everyone, not just you." Magnus eyed Calum, who now stood next to him. "My companions did not even know the truth of my identity."

Axel scoffed and folded his arms. "You can say that again."

"Like my daughter, you are wise to have withheld this information." Avian nodded to General Balena, who motioned toward the doors. The soldiers began to form lines and file out of the throne room.

"But I am not my father's heir." Magnus hung his head. "Vandorian is."

"Vandorian is also a co-conspirator in your father's death."

Magnus looked up at him. "You know this? How?"

"The whole of Kanarah knows by now. It has been almost five years since Praetorius's untimely death. Everyone thought you perished along with the rest of his children. Besides, when Kahn and Vandorian arose from the ashes to take power, the rest wasn't hard to fill in."

Calum couldn't believe it. In less than two weeks, he'd learned that two of his traveling companions weren't just a Windgale and a Saurian, but the princess of the entire Sky Realm and the long-lost heir of Reptilius.

What next? That Axel was a distant relative of the King?

"Suffice it to say that Vandorian gave up his right to the throne when he helped Kahn rise to power. That makes you, the sole surviving child of Praetorius, his sole heir as far as the Sky Realm is concerned." Avian smiled and patted Magnus's forearm. "You have our support."

Magnus nodded. "Thank you."

"Frankly, dealing with you would be much more pleasant than dealing with either Vandorian or your uncle."

"I had hoped to remain anonymous for longer, but when I recognized Vandorian, I knew I would never get him alone with only five guards ever again. I beg your forgiveness, but I had to take the chance." Magnus sighed. "Now Vandorian will tell my uncle that I yet live, and they will both be on their guard. I have squandered whatever element of surprise I would have had."

"I understand what you mean. However," Avian stared at Magnus, "for the time being, I am beholden to Vandorian's demands concerning your attack."

Magnus's reptilian brow arched down. "What do you mean?"

Avian frowned. "I mean that since you're a citizen of our realm now, I still have to punish you for attacking him."

CHAPTER 27

"What kind of glass-backward place is this?" Axel stepped forward with his arms extended out to his sides. "He was totally justified in attacking. You can't punish him for that!"

Calum shook his head. Leave it to Axel to side with Magnus after all this time, after everything that had happened, just because he found out Magnus was royalty.

Magnus eyed him. "You do not even like me. I punched you in the head, humiliated you, and took your sword away. Why defend me now?"

"You're the same as I am, Scales. I didn't see it before, but I do now. You got handed a foul deal in life, just like Calum and me." Axel pointed at the throne room doors. "Plus, Vandorian and his friend Oren were a couple of arrogant harpies."

"That doesn't negate the fact that you broke our laws when you attacked Vandorian and his men. Typically, a crime of this caliber would be addressed through a hearing like those we held for Condor—" Avian shot a long glare at Axel. "—and your friend, here, but in this case, I believe I can make an exception since the other council members are indisposed."

Lilly hovered toward him. "Father, take into account Magnus's—"

Avian held up his hand. "I'll hear no testaments to his character, nor to his innocence or his guilt, Lilliana. He will be punished according to our laws, and my decision will be binding. Otherwise, I can summon Vandorian and his men back, if you prefer their brand of 'justice?'"

"No." Lilly bowed her head.

"Very well, then." Avian floated up to Magnus's eye level. "Magnus, I hereby banish you from the Sky Realm until you find and free Lumen, the General of Light. Not a moment longer, nor a moment shorter. You are banished for exactly as long as the journey is meant to last."

Calum grinned, and so did Axel, Magnus, and Lilly.

"Should you return for any reason before your quest is complete, you will be given three *full* days to vacate the realm once again, or you will face the penalty of death." Avian pulled Lilly close and positioned her between Magnus and himself. "And while you are banished, I implore you—I *command* you to safeguard that which is most important to me. Do you understand your punishment?"

Magnus smirked and gave a modest bow. "I do."

"Good. Then get out of my sight, and watch out for those Sobeks. I imagine there is an entire encampment of Saurians somewhere nearby, and they're headed in the same direction as you. Best to go now before they realize what I've done for you."

Calum performed the Windgale salute again. "Thank you again, Premier."

A yelp turned their heads.

From behind one of the pillars, a Windgale soldier in purple armor pulled a mass of brown-gray fur out of the shadows by the scruff of its neck. "I found this dog hiding. Don't know how it got in here, Premier. What should I do with it?"

"I'm not a dog, you moron." Riley snapped at the Windgale's hand and he let go, but then he leveled his spear. Riley hobble-darted back around the pillar into its shadow again, and the soldier followed.

"Oh, no you don't. Not getting away that easily, pup."

"He's with us, soldier," Falcroné said. "Leave him be."

Calum made it over to Riley first, then Lilly. She crouched next to him and asked, "Are you alright, Riley?"

"Fine. Why wouldn't I be?"

Axel came up behind them. "Were you hiding that whole time?"

Riley didn't answer him. He just growled from within the shadows.

"What happened to those razor sharp fangs of yours?" Axel scoffed and folded his arms. "Condor didn't stab you in the mouth, did he?"

"Cut it out, Axel," Calum warned.

"Yeah, leave him alone." Lilly scratched behind Riley's ears—she was still the only one he allowed to do that. "Come on. We need to get our supplies from Ganosh, and I need to say goodbye to my mother."

NIGHT FELL within a matter of hours after Axel and the team left the Sky Fortress. When he'd first left his farm behind to accompany Calum and Magnus, he'd never expected anyone else would travel with them, but now their number had grown to seven in total.

Axel didn't know whether to be impressed that they'd become so popular or annoyed because of all the extra people around to bother him. He supposed it would be better to have greater numbers when it came to fighting, especially since battles kept finding them wherever they went.

Speaking of battles, they located a large encampment near the base of the northernmost support pillar, just as Avian had suggested. Falcroné took to the sky to scout for patrols, then Magnus led them around the encampment where he supposed the Saurians would not be. Sure enough, they didn't encounter anyone.

Hardly anyone said much of anything for the first hour after they passed the Saurians' encampment, but that suited Axel just fine. It gave him time to think through everything that had happened at the Sky Fortress.

He still hadn't talked to Lilly about why she'd lied about the attack. She'd told him she loved Falcroné—another obvious lie. Her actions before the Council of Wisps suggested otherwise. They *strongly* suggested otherwise.

Yet even that didn't hold Axel's attention as much Magnus's revelation of his royal heritage. Despite their previous contentions, Magnus's plight had placed him securely in Axel's "He's alright" category. Still, Axel couldn't help but wonder who else might be hiding something from him.

He and Riley walked near the back of the group. The thought reoccurred to Axel that he should probably apologize to Riley for how everything that had transpired when Condor had stabbed him, but Riley hadn't brought it up, so Axel decided to keep ignoring the impulse.

Axel nudged Riley's left shoulder—the one on his uninjured side. "Hey, Riley."

"What?"

"*Shhh*," Axel hissed. "For someone who's supposed to be stealthy, you sure talk loud sometimes."

Riley sighed and rolled his eyes, but he lowered his voice. "What do you want, Axel?"

"You're not secret royalty too, are you?"

Riley barked a laugh. "Me? You gotta be kidding."

Calum turned his head back from the middle of the group about ten paces ahead of them. "Hey, don't lag behind, guys. Magnus and Falcroné said we've got another hour of walking before we camp for the night."

Axel gave him a slight wave, then he refocused on Riley once Calum faced forward again. "What's so funny about it?"

"Wolves don't operate like humans, Windgales, or even Saurians. Your hierarchies are all based on lineage and bloodlines, but we don't do things that way."

"How do Wolves do it, then?"

"Our structure is based on strength, not family lines. The strongest of us rules the tribe, the pack. If you think you can lead the tribe better, you challenge the Alpha. If you beat him, you become the new leader." Riley's ears lowered. "But if you lose, he kills you."

"Where's your tribe?" Axel asked.

Riley stifled another pitiful laugh. "Don't have one. Why else do you think you found me wandering the woods alone?"

"Why not?"

"Seriously? Look at me, Axel. For a Wolf, I'm tiny. Weak. Not a good fighter, and apparently not a very good thief either since you, Calum and Magnus managed to catch me in the act." Riley shook his head. "No one wants me in their tribe."

"Yeah, I can see that."

Riley shot him a glare.

"What? Would you rather I lie to you?"

"Forget it." Riley rolled his eyes again and trotted forward until he walked between Calum and Lilly.

Axel squinted at the two of them and rotated his sore shoulders. They weren't nearly as bad as they had been, and in only a few more days, he should be pain-free.

As far as Lilly was concerned, Axel had Falcroné to worry about, of course, but did Calum still think he had a chance with her, too?

She'd told Calum the same lie about loving Falcroné. If he also didn't believe her, then would he keep pursuing her as well? Or would he stand aside?

Time would tell, but no matter what happened, Axel had no intention of losing the contest. After all, he could beat Calum in pretty much every other category already. Adding one more to the list wouldn't be hard.

LILLY SAT ON A STONE, admiring the starry sky above while Calum and Magnus stacked wood next to the fledgling campfire Axel had just ignited.

Something nudged her shoulder, and she found Falcroné at her side. She scooted over to make room for him, grateful for his company on a cool night.

As he sat down next her, he asked, "So you didn't want to marry me?"

Lilly tensed. She'd known this conversation had to happen eventually, but she hadn't wanted to have it with him tonight. "Do you really want to talk about this here and now?"

"You said it aloud to your father in front of them. I assume you don't mind further discussing it in their midst."

Annoyed and frustrated, Lilly stood and pulled Falcroné to his feet. "Come with me."

They took to the sky together, and she led him deeper into the woods until several trees separated them from the group. She glanced around to make sure no one had followed them—Axel in particular.

She'd given a lot of thought to how this conversation needed to go, and it always circled back to one essential statement, so she led with that. "Fal, I'm sorry."

He shrugged—not the reaction she'd been expecting. "What for? You spoke your mind."

Nor were those the words she'd expected. She shook her head. "That doesn't mean it didn't hurt you."

"Lilly, I'm not worried. I know now why you left. I don't want to make a big issue of it. I just want to make sure this... *us*... is actually what you want."

At least he was making it easy on her. For that, she was very grateful.

She wrapped her arms around Falcroné's midsection, pressed her cheek against the cool armor covering his chest, and smiled. "It is."

I think.

He hugged her back. "Good. Me too."

She released him. "Come on. Let's get back to camp."

RILEY CROUCHED in the darkness beyond the perimeter of the camp they had set up, watching. Even from so far away, he could still hear every word they said, every piece of wood snapping, every footfall of every creature skittering through the trees around them.

Benefits of being a Wolf—even if he couldn't run and couldn't fight, he could still hide and hear and see better in the dark than any of the rest of them.

"If Vandorian and his Sobeks find us, we run." Magnus stoked the modest campfire with a long stick and ashes billowed into the air. "There is no way we could overcome even three of them, much less six. Taking on an entire encampment would be suicide. At best we could handle two of them, and that assumes one of them is not Vandorian."

"You took down four of them on your own," Axel said. "And you almost got Vandorian, too."

Magnus shook his head and reclined against a boulder he'd dragged into place near his spot. "I got lucky. Had those warriors been expecting trouble, I would not have made it past the first two before they surrounded me and struck me down."

Axel shrugged. "Looked like you were doing fine—up until the end, at least."

"My point is, if they come for us, we are in for a world of trouble," Magnus said. "If we can get away, fine, but if not, I will try to fend them off so the rest of you can escape. Vandorian likely wants me alive, anyway."

"We're not gonna leave you, Magnus." Calum extended his legs while seated and stretched out his hamstrings. "After all we've been through, we can't let them get you. We won't. We'll stay and fight."

"That cannot happen," Magnus said. "I wish it were that simple, but I cannot allow it.

Falcroné, Lilly, and Kanton could all escape if things escalated too quickly, but the rest of us would be stuck on the ground, outnumbered and overmatched. It is an impossible situation."

"I don't know." Axel eyed Falcroné and Lilly, who sat shoulder-to-shoulder near the flames. "I think we could take 'em. Especially with Sunshine over there on our side."

Riley smirked. Axel despised Falcroné. Riley could smell it in his sweat whenever Axel and Falcroné stood too near each other—and even more so when Falcroné got close to Lilly like he was now.

Of course, Riley didn't like Axel, either. How anyone did, he couldn't fathom. He was a top-tier idiot, rude, and cruel.

Riley had suspected as much when they first met, but when Axel tried to kill Condor instead of getting Riley help for his near-fatal wound, it sealed Riley's opinion of him forever.

"I'd appreciate if you didn't refer to me by any monikers other than my name. Or 'Captain.'" Falcroné's gaze hardened.

Axel squinted at him, but gave him a slight nod. "Whatever you say, 'Croné."

"It's *Falcroné*."

"Don't encourage him, Fal." Lilly patted Falcroné's knee with her hand. "He's just trying to jab you to get a reaction."

"If he jabs me again, I might have to *jab* him back." Falcroné tapped the pommel of his sword, which hung from his belt in its sheath.

The pheromones in Axel's sweat had intensified when Lilly patted Falcroné's knee, but the next swell hit Riley's nose like a flood.

Axel stood up. "You go right ahead, *Fal*. Skin that steel and find out what happens."

"Enough." Calum hopped up to his feet and stepped between Axel and Falcroné. His eyes locked on Axel. "You're not gonna do this again. Falcroné is on our side, and you won't alienate him from us."

"He's a pompous—"

"I said *enough*," Calum snapped. "If you keep causing division in our group, we'll leave you behind. I'm serious. There is no longer any place for that kind of talk here, so either fall in line, or we're done with you."

Axel scowled. Now both their pheromones wafted in Riley's direction—similar, but unique. Both very potent.

"I know how you feel, Axel," Calum said, his voice low so only he and Axel—and Riley—could hear. "Believe me, I do. But you're not gonna solve anything by fighting him."

"Is Axel always like this?" Falcroné leaned close to Lilly and asked, his whispered words overlapping the end of Calum's sentence.

"Somewhat, yes," she whispered back. "It takes some getting used to."

"I still don't understand why you covered for him at the council," Falcroné muttered. "We both know what really happened and what punishment he deserved."

Riley glanced at Axel.

"You don't know anything about what's going on between Lilly and me. We have a future together, and you don't, and it bothers you." Axel tapped his index finger on Calum's crimson breastplate. "You'd do anything to keep us apart so you can have her for yourself. She kissed *me*, not you."

Riley raised an eyebrow. Did Falcroné know about that? He turned back to their conversation.

Lilly shook her head. "After all we went through, I couldn't let the council jail him for something so trivial."

"*Trivial?*" Falcroné clamped his hand on Lilly's arm. "Lilly, he *attacked* you. That's not trivial."

Hmmm. Riley must have missed a few things while he was recovering.

"I'm done with this conversation, Axel." Calum turned away and sat down, his eyes fixed on the fire.

"Yeah, we're done alright." Axel sat down in his spot and folded his arms. He glared at Falcroné, but Falcroné didn't look at him.

"Just leave it alone, Falcroné," Lilly whispered and lay her head against his shoulder. "It's not worth getting worked up about."

Falcroné frowned at her. "Regardless, I don't trust him. I'm not letting you out of my sight if I can help it."

Lilly smiled and looked up at him. "I'll have to go to the bathroom at some point, you know."

"Then I'll watch *him* while you're gone."

Kanton floated over between Calum and Axel, and he glanced between them both. "So, who's taking the first watch shift tonight?"

Riley smirked. He preferred the night, the shadows. If he had things his way, he'd stay up all night and take the whole watch, but then someone would have to carry him during the daytime since he couldn't just sleep in the same spot, and *that* wasn't going to happen.

He lay his head down and listened to Kanton and Calum talk about the shifts, with Magnus interjecting every now and then, and his smirk stretched into a smile. Good to finally have friends, even if they didn't all like each other, and even if he didn't like Axel.

"Which route are we taking to the Blood Mountains?" Falcroné asked. "Do you intend to cross the Desert of the Forgotten?"

Riley's ears perked up at that. They weren't seriously considering going through that horrible place, were they?

"That is the most direct route." Magnus nodded to Calum. "Let me see the map."

Calum pulled it from his pack and handed it to Magnus, who studied it for a moment.

Falcroné hovered over to him and stared at it over Magnus's shoulder. "The only other route is through the Green Highlands to the east and then up the main road that connects farther south near Trader's Pass."

Magnus shook his head. "That path is circuitous and would take almost twice as long. We have enough supplies and water to take the desert path. That's what we'll do."

"*No,*" Riley barked from the darkness.

CHAPTER 28

All eyes looked toward Riley, but he knew they couldn't see him.

"Riley? Where are you?" Calum stood and looked out over the fire.

Riley sighed, and he reluctantly emerged from the shadows and stood next to Axel. Then he thought better of it and took a few steps farther away from him. "Here."

"Why don't you want us to go through the desert?" Magnus asked.

"It's—" Riley growled. He really didn't want to have to explain everything that had happened between him and Rhaza. "—not safe. That's where my kind live."

"What's a few Wolves?" Axel waved his hand in dismissal. "If they're all like you, we should be fine."

Riley leaped at Axel with his front paws extended and pushed him down onto his back. The impact sent pain shooting through his torso, but it was worth it to pin a wide-eyed, unarmed Axel to the ground and snarl in his face. "They're worse than me, Axel. They're faster, stronger, and a whole lot meaner than I am."

"Get off me!" Axel shoved him to the side, and Riley couldn't help but collapse. "What do you think you're doing?"

Riley stifled a whimper as he pushed himself back onto all fours and growled again. "Making a point."

Axel brushed himself off and stood up. "Well, don't make it anymore."

"Wolves are merciless. We hunt to kill. If we're gonna rob you, we'll tear you apart, too, if the numbers are in our favor." Riley eyed Axel. "And the numbers are *always* in our favor. We make sure of it. We're pack creatures, and our highest concentration is in that desert. No one passes through without us knowing."

"How do the Saurians get across, then?" Calum reached for the map, and Magnus handed it back to him.

"They travel in large groups, and Wolves typically don't attack Saurians to kill them anyway. Too difficult, usually, and not worth the effort." Riley sat down and nodded to Magnus. "Especially when they're Sobeks like Magnus. Our teeth can't usually penetrate their scales. Instead, we just rob them in the night while they sleep. They're slower, so it's not hard."

Magnus grunted and folded his arms.

Riley shrugged. "No offense. You actually move pretty well."

"For a Saurian?" Magnus asked.

"In general, actually. The only more adept Saurian I've seen is Vandorian."

Magnus grunted again.

"Anyway, we need to avoid the desert. With this group, we don't stand a chance against a pack of seventeen Wolves and nine Werewolves, or whatever assortment may come up against us out there."

"I'm inclined to agree with him," Falcroné said. "Windgales can fly, so we don't have to worry about the Wolves when we cross, but with more than half our party on foot, the risk of attack is heightened."

"No, no. Don't look at it as a risk. It's not." Riley stared at Falcroné. "It's a certainty. If we go to the Desert of the Forgotten, we'll be ambushed, attacked, scattered, and hunted down until we're all killed, with the possible exception of the Windgales who could fly away."

"What's more, based on what Riley is saying, Vandorian and his entourage will probably take that route as well," Lilly said. "If we go that way but can't make it through, and we need to go back, we could run into them. Then we'd be caught between Wolves and Saurians with no way to escape."

"Exactly," Riley said. "It's a losing scenario, and frankly, I don't want to die. Tried it once. Didn't take, but it wasn't any fun. So we need to take the long way."

Magnus turned to Calum, who looked back at him, then they both turned to Falcroné. Axel rolled his eyes, Lilly held Falcroné's hand in hers, and Kanton shrugged.

"Then we'll take the long way, starting tomorrow," Calum said.

THE GREEN HIGHLANDS were unlike any place Axel had ever seen, though it vaguely reminded him of the quarry, but with infinitely more grass and vegetation. He liked it for what it was, but he couldn't see how anyone would want to live there—not if they meant to do any farming, anyway.

They'd been traveling for three weeks, with Calum leading the group along one of the many paths that cut between the tall green hills and mounds that the Green Highlands were named for. Along the way, they'd encountered a mixture of rocky terrain, lush valleys, sparse forests, and the occasional jagged ravine with a shallow river flowing through.

Falcroné soared above the group in wide arcs and scouted ahead while Kanton hovered at the rear of the group to make sure no one crept up behind them.

Magnus, Riley, and Lilly filled in the center of the group, and Axel brought up the rear at Calum's order. Well, Calum had phrased it as a request, but it felt more like an order to Axel.

Either way, it meant Axel had no one to talk to except for Kanton, and half the time he just babbled on and on about how he used to shepherd the Premier's flocks, and how he'd saved the life of an albino sabertooth cat once, and how he'd lost his first cape. The other half of the time he had to ascend higher into the air to check their surroundings.

Axel preferred the half when Kanton wasn't around.

As he walked, he noticed a crystalline pebble on the path, and he scooped it into his hands. Not worth anything, but maybe...

He tossed it at Lilly and it plunked off the back of her left calf armor. She turned back and glared at him, then she faced forward again and resumed her conversation with Riley. Axel found and chucked another pebble at her, but this time she didn't even turn around.

"Lilly," he half-hissed, half-whispered.

She still didn't turn back.

"Lilly." This time he called for her with his regular voice, firmly. Maybe too firmly, in hindsight.

She looked back at him with the same glare.

"Mind if I talk to you for a moment?"

Lilly glanced at Riley, who nodded without looking at Axel, and then she stopped so he could catch up. "Yes?"

"Hi." Axel smiled at her.

Lilly rolled her eyes and accelerated her walk to catch up with Riley again, but Axel caught her by her arm. She gave him a look that could melt mountains, and he let go and held up his hands in surrender.

"Sorry." He'd learned his lesson the first time—no question there.

"Do you have something to say or not?"

"I wanted to apologize for what happened back at the Sky Fortress. I was out of line, I admit, and I acted foolishly. I'm sorry." Axel stared at her, but she continued to face forward as they walked. "And I wanted to thank you for doing what you did before the council. It's more than I deserved. Far more. So, thank you."

Lilly exhaled a sigh through her nose—her cute little nose. "I don't think I want to talk about this with you."

"Come on, Lilly," Axel said. "I'm trying to make amends here. Give me a chance."

"It's going to take more than an apology for you to make amends."

"What did you have in mind?" Axel leaned close her and whispered, "Another kiss?"

Her livid blue eyes locked on his. "You're hopeless."

That wasn't a no. "Lilly, I—"

She started to pull ahead again, so Axel grabbed the end of her cape and tugged her backward. Lilly whirled around and smacked his jaw with her fist, then kicked his chest. He dropped to the dirt on his back and glared up at her.

"Don't touch me anymore, Axel." She turned and kept walking.

Kanton dropped out of the sky and landed beside him with his hand extended. "You alright, son?"

"I'm fine." Axel scrambled to his feet without Kanton's help, only to find Magnus and Riley staring back at him. "What are you lookin' at?"

They, too, faced forward and began walking once Lilly had caught up.

"Saw what happened." Kanton patted Axel's shoulder. "Don't worry, son. Plenty of girls in this world will break both your heart and your bones. She's one of them. I remember one time there was this girl named Calraia. She—"

"Thanks." Axel shrugged Kanton's hand away. "Shouldn't you be scouting?"

Kanton pursed his lips and squinted at him. His voice flat, he said, "Yeah. Suppose I should."

Axel rubbed his jaw as Kanton took to the sky again. Somehow Lilly had managed to hit almost the exact spot where she'd kicked him about three weeks earlier. The original bruise had long since healed, but the familiar pain had returned with Lilly's punch.

He found another pebble as he walked, took aim, and lobbed it at Lilly's head. It bounced off the back of her head and skittered to a stop on the ground, and she turned back to face him again with rage on her face. "What?"

"I wasn't done talking to you," Axel said.

"Too bad. I'm done talking to you."

"I learned my lesson—again. Please, just two more minutes?" Axel didn't want to sound like he was begging, but he figured a little groveling might get her to come back. "Please?"

Lilly sighed, but she waited for him to catch up.

"Thanks." Axel grunted. "You didn't have to hit me, you know. You definitely didn't have to kick me, either."

"See, that's what you don't understand, Axel. I *did* have to do those things. Both of them, because you don't understand what I've been telling you." Lilly stared at him. "We're never going to happen, Axel. I'm marrying Falcroné, and that's the end of it. You don't have a chance."

Axel clenched his teeth, ignoring the arrows she'd just shot into his heart and his gut. "I don't believe that."

"Well, you'd better start."

"Lilly, I love you."

She faced him and opened her mouth to say something, but stopped. Her eyes fixed on something in the hills above them, and she stopped walking entirely.

Axel stopped too and followed her line of sight. "What is it?"

"I thought I saw something."

"Like what?"

"Movement." Lilly shielded the sun from her eyes with her hand. "I don't know."

"What kind of movement?"

"I said *I don't know.*" Lilly's tone hardened. "I'm going to go take a look."

Before Axel could say anything else, Lilly burst into the sky toward the hill. Convenient excuse to get out of the conversation. He'd mention that when she returned.

High above, Lilly looped around the hill with her bow in hand and an arrow nocked, but not drawn back. Good for show, but Axel wasn't fooled.

Until she pulled the drawstring back and launched an arrow downward. From behind the hill, a green form reared up and writhed, then it hurled a boulder at Lilly. She barrel-rolled out of its trajectory and nocked another arrow.

A roar reverberated through the valley, and the group stopped.

"Weapons!" Magnus called. "Form up!"

Calum fell back to the rest of the group, and Axel charged toward his spot in their formation, his eyes on Lilly the whole time. He drew his sword and watched her shoot another arrow at the thing. A thick tail lashed through the air and a loud hiss sounded.

It was a Saurian.

Falcroné and Kanton landed among the group, which formed a loose circle, until Falcroné noticed Lilly engaging the Saurian. He shot away from the ground and drew his sword.

"Falcroné!" Calum tried to call after him, but Falcroné kept flying.

He executed a loop and zoomed down toward the Saurian, who now faced Lilly. In one brutal blow Falcroné jammed his blade through the back of the Saurian's head, and it fell behind the hillcrest out of Axel's sight.

Falcroné and Lilly darted back down to the group and took their places in the formation as reptilian silhouettes materialized around them at the tops of the highlands and then started down toward them. Saurians, all of them armored, except for one Sobek who wore only a leather breastplate and gripped a large double-bladed battle-axe in his hands. Their leader.

Hissing and growling, they constricted around the group like a noose on a condemned man's neck. They likely weren't part of Vandorian's group; that much became clear as Axel noticed their mismatched and weatherworn armor. They were the Saurian version of bandits, apparently.

Then again, Vandorian still might have sent them or alerted them to the group's approach. Axel didn't know for sure.

Either way, this wouldn't make for an easy fight. Axel counted ten of them, including the Sobek.

The Sobek stepped to within fifteen feet of Magnus and displayed his jagged smile. "Well, well. If it ain't seven stragglers just waitin' to be snapped up. The lot of ya will make a nice haul for sure. Now lay down your weapons, an' we won't gotta cut nothin' off ya while we tie ya up."

The Sobek's odd manner of speech reminded Axel of the way Oren had talked. Perhaps they knew each other, or they'd come from the same town in the Blood Mountains.

"The only hauling you can expect to do if you refuse to let us pass is hauling your own carcasses out of this valley." Magnus straightened to his full height, at least six inches taller than the enemy Sobek. "Now stand aside."

"Can't do it, bub." The Sobek's tail swished back and forth in the gravel on the path. "Livelihood's at stake, an' all. You'll be slaves 'fore the week's out."

"Forget your livelihood, Saurian," Falcroné warned. "You forfeit your life if you so much as lay a hand on any of us. We've already killed one of your number, and we'll do it again if we must."

Axel raised an eyebrow. Regardless of what he thought of the pretty Wisp captain, Axel couldn't deny that Falcroné could back up his haughty talk—so far, anyway.

"Talk all ya want. We'll see 'oo's standin' an' 'oo ain't by the end o' this." The Sobek motioned toward them with his arm, and the Saurians advanced forward.

CHAPTER 29

Scaly green monsters surrounded Riley. Green monsters that he'd have to fight if he wanted to survive. Green monsters with swords, spears, and axes.

The wound he'd taken from Condor in his side had healed substantially in the three weeks since they'd left the Sky Fortress, but the damage remained nonetheless—both to his body and to his mind.

Ten against seven. Ten Saurians, all but impossible to kill with his teeth, much less his claws. Bigger than humans, far more difficult to knock down. And even if he could knock them down, he couldn't get to their throats easily thanks to their armor, makeshift though it may be.

They would catch him. Stop him from biting them. Then they'd take their swords and run him through, just as Condor had.

Only this time it wouldn't just happen once, but twice. Three times. Four. Five.

They might never stop.

Pain flared in Riley's side, then spread throughout his body. He knew most of it was artificial, contrived, imagined, but it still hurt anyway.

He had to run, had to escape. Had to find shadows and hide.

He wouldn't let them get him. He had to run.

PEBBLES SPRAYED into the air and clinked against the armor plates on the side of Calum's left leg. He stole a look and saw Riley bounding away from the fight, away from the Saurians and toward a gorge up ahead.

"Riley?" he called, but Riley kept running. "Where are you going?"

Two of the Saurians reached for him as he ran past, but he eluded them and darted down the path until he disappeared entirely behind some rocks in the gorge.

"Stay in formation," Magnus growled. "Tighten up and take his place. He can no longer help us."

"What do we do?" Calum asked, only loud enough for Magnus and Falcroné to hear.

"We fight." Falcroné nudged Calum with his elbow. "We kill as many of them as we have to until they leave us alone."

"You got that right," Axel said.

Well, at least they agreed on something.

"No. We run. Make for that gorge where Riley disappeared. Not everyone can fly away when they encounter trouble, so we need to adjust our strategy." Magnus nodded. "Falcroné, Kanton, and I will clear a path. Calum and Axel, run for the gorge. We will fight them there, where we can use the terrain to our advantage. Lilly, cover them with your bow. Ready?"

Calum nodded. "Ready."

The Sobek lunged forward and flailed his battle-ax at Magnus, who parried the attack with his sword then jammed his fist into the Sobek's armored gut. The blow stunned him for a second, and Magnus whirled around and whacked the Sobek's shoulder with his tail, sending the Sobek skidding along the gravel away from them.

"Go!" Magnus roared.

Falcroné, Kanton, and Lilly took to the sky, and Calum and Axel charged behind Magnus. Calum ran hard until one of the Saurians lurched toward him and lashed his sword. Calum ducked under the blow, but lost his footing and tripped. He slid to a stop in the gravel on his side, and when he looked up, the Saurian towered over him, sword raised.

An arrow plunged into the base of the Saurian's neck, and he twitched. He roared and ripped the arrow out of his neck, then he hissed up at Lilly, who stuck him with another one, this time in his throat just under his chin.

The Saurian dropped his sword and clutched his throat with wide reptilian eyes.

Calum pushed himself up and swung his sword at the Saurian, but he blocked the blow with his armored forearm. The Saurian spun around and battered Calum to the ground with his tail.

The impact might've snapped Calum in half were he still as scrawny as he'd been back at the quarry. Even so, he wondered if he'd ever be able to walk or even stand again. His lower half ached, and he cursed himself for his weakness again.

He'd grown enough to handle human bandits and pirates and soldiers, but trying to fight Saurians made him feel just as frail as the day he'd fled his life as a slave. He had to get stronger, fight better, or he wouldn't survive long enough to reach the Arcanum to free Lumen.

Despite the arrow in his throat, the Saurian just wouldn't go down. Worse yet, the other nine Saurians had closed in and started toward Calum.

Another arrow plunged into the Saurian, this time in the back of his neck. He roared again and reared back, alternating between groping at his throat and the nape of his neck with his free hand.

The next thing Calum knew, two sets of arms scooped him into the air and carried him away from the Saurians. Kanton and Falcroné.

"Thanks, guys," he said.

"Their skin is thick, and with all that armor on, it's hard to deliver a killing blow unless it's to their necks," Falcroné said. "If you don't kill them quickly, they heal."

Calum nodded. *Just like Magnus healed from the arrow he took back on the rooftops in Kanarah City.*

His feet touched down in the gorge about a hundred feet ahead of the nearest Saurian, and he met up with the rest of the group. Magnus had been right—the Saurians would be forced into a bottleneck here. That gave the six of them more of a level field.

The Sobek bellowed a command to halt that stopped the Saurians before they could enter the gorge. He tapped four of them on their shoulders and motioned toward the walls that formed the gorge. The Saurians nodded, split into two groups of two, and walked along the tops of the walls. Then he and the rest of the Saurians advanced into the gorge.

They were still trying to surround them.

"Deeper. We must venture deeper into the gorge," Magnus said. "We cannot let those four Saurians cut us off, or we will not make it."

"I can slow them down." Lilly nocked another arrow. "Kanton and I will take one side, and Falcroné can take the other side."

"Do it," Calum said.

Falcroné nodded, then he took to the sky toward one pair of Saurians, and Lilly and Kanton launched toward the other pair.

"Attack!" The Sobek yelled, and the Saurians lumbered forward, two at a time.

"Axel, Calum," Magnus said. "Retreat. I can handle two at a time."

Calum glanced at Axel, then looked at Magnus again, whose gaze remained fixed on the approaching Saurians. "Are you sure?"

Magnus shot him a glare. "*Go*."

Calum didn't hesitate. He and Axel ran deeper into the gorge. Above them, Lilly fired arrows at the two Saurians on her side of the gorge while Kanton executed quick diving attacks on them with his spear.

Across the gorge, the opposite wall became more of a steep hill. Falcroné zipped back and forth between the Saurians who ran across the top. Every time he passed them, a new spurt of dark blood flung down into the gorge.

The Saurians jerked with each of Falcroné's slices and tried to swing back at him, but he moved far too fast for them. Still, they kept moving forward, until Falcroné's next blow knocked one of them down into the gorge.

The Saurian smacked against a half-dozen boulders on his way down and rolled to a stop in front of Calum and Axel, who skidded to a halt. Behind the Saurian, his sword clanged down the wall's slope, accompanied by a miniature rockslide.

Before Calum and Axel could get around him, the Saurian pushed himself up to his feet and snatched up his sword. He snarled and stalked toward them, hunched over. Dark gray armor covered his chest and back, his arms, and his legs, but he'd lost his helmet on the way down into the gorge. Lacerations lined his face and neck.

Axel rapped his knuckles against Calum's arm and shifted to the right. Calum caught his intention and shifted left. If they could divide the Saurian's focus, they stood a better chance of bringing him down.

The Saurian slashed his blade at Calum but he leaped back in time to avoid the swipe. Axel darted forward and hacked at the Saurian's left arm, but its tail swept Axel's feet from under him before his blow could connect. He landed face-first in the dirt.

On his return swing, the Saurian brought his sword down at Axel, who rolled away just in time. Calum saw an opening and lunged, and his sword plunged into the Saurian's right thigh between two of his armor plates.

Before Calum could pull his sword back, the Saurian roared and backhanded him in the face. Calum's vision ceased in a white flash, then it reset to the blurry gray of the gorge around him as he hit the ground. Warmth trickled from his nose down to his lips, and the metallic tang of blood stung his tongue.

When Calum looked up, the blurred form of the Saurian blotted out the setting sun. He raised his sword.

A navy-blue mass slammed into the Saurian from the right and knocked him off-balance.

Axel.

The Saurian adjusted and swung his sword at Axel instead, but Axel ducked under the blow and sliced his blade straight up at the Saurian's wrist. The blade severed the Saurian's right hand from his arm, and it dropped to the ground next to Calum's shoulder, along with his sword.

The Saurian roared and clutched his bleeding wrist with his other hand. Calum's sword remained in the Saurian's thigh, so he rolled to the side, snatched up the Saurian's sword, and hacked at its leg. The dull blade lodged about halfway through its knee, and the Saurian crumpled to the ground.

Axel jammed his sword through its throat so far that it stuck into the ground. The Saurian convulsed once, then it stopped moving. Calum scrambled to his feet and wrested his sword from the Saurian's leg.

"Thanks," he said.

Axel planted his boot on the Saurian's snout and jerked his sword free of its throat. "No time to chatter now. We gotta keep running. Magnus was right. We can't fight all of them like that."

Calum nodded and looked up at the three Saurians who still ran across the top of the gorge. Far behind Axel and him, Magnus battled two Saurians at a time in the bottleneck, and another lay at his side, motionless and slicked with red. He'd already killed one of them?

A hiss sounded to Calum's left, but not from one of the Saurians. Small rocks and pebbles tumbled down the side of the gorge wall toward them. Far above, a network of gray boulders oozed rocks into the gorge. It looked like it could give way any—

That's it. Realization hit Calum harder than the Saurian's backhand. He knew how they could even the odds.

Axel's hand clamped onto Calum's wrist. *"Come on.* We gotta keep running."

"No, wait!" Calum shook free and pointed to the rocks above. "We can trap them in a rockslide."

"What?" Axel glanced at the boulders then back at Calum. "You're losing your mind. Let's go."

"No. Go help Magnus. He needs you." Calum motioned toward the sky. "Let them back you up, and Falcroné and I will loose the rocks. When you hear me yelling, run for it. The boulders will do the rest."

"But—"

"Just *do it*, Axel." Calum turned and bolted down the gorge. He couldn't waste time arguing—not if this was going to work. He called for Falcroné as he ran, and Falcroné met him in the gorge.

"What is it?" Dark blood streaked across Falcroné's face and charcoal armor, but Calum knew none of it was his own.

"Can you get me up to those boulders?" He nodded toward them.

Falcroné glanced at them. "Why?"

"I'm gonna create a rockslide to—"

"Say no more." Falcroné held up his hand. "I'm with you. How much do you weigh?"

"Uhh…"

"Stay here. I'll be back with Kanton." Falcroné burst into the air.

"Bring Lilly back with you," Calum shouted. He hoped Falcroné had heard him.

Behind him, Axel had joined Magnus in the fray. As they backed up, the Saurians approached. Soon they weren't fighting just two Saurians at once, they had to fight three. They would need help—Lilly and Kanton's help—if this was going to work.

Lilly, Kanton, and Falcroné landed next to Calum.

"Lilly, go shoot the Saurians who are fighting Axel and Magnus. Kanton and Falcroné—"

"We've got you, Calum." Kanton hooked his arm under Calum's, and Falcroné did the same. As Lilly sped toward Magnus and Axel, Calum ascended toward the boulders.

MAGNUS PARRIED two blows from two of the Saurians then slammed his sword down on one of them who'd left himself exposed. The hack cut through the Saurian's armor and severed his left arm at the shoulder. He roared. Magnus's follow-up lateral lopped off the Saurian's head, silencing him.

Two down. Four to go, including the Sobek.

As they backed deeper into the gorge, it widened, and the Saurians spread out. No way he and Axel could contend with four of them alone. Had they been humans, or even Windgales, Magnus could have taken them on his own, but not Saurians. They were too hard to kill.

The Sobek launched forward and battered Magnus's sword with his battle-ax. Magnus threw three quick counterattacks then absorbed another thunderous blow from the Sobek that vibrated through his arms.

The Sobek showed him an insidious grin, and his golden eyes flickered with malice.

Magnus readied another counterattack, but one of the Saurians whipped his blade at Magnus, so he had to parry instead.

Next to him, Axel dodged a blow from the second Saurian and blocked another from the third that almost knocked him off his feet in the process.

For being only a human, Axel was handling himself admirably against these Saurians, at least up until that moment. The second Saurian would've finished Axel off right then and there had it not been for the arrow that hit him in his neck. The Saurian recoiled a step, and Axel recovered his footing.

Lilly swooped into view behind them and shot two more arrows in succession, one that plunged into the shoulder of one of the Saurians, and another that skidded off the Sobek's head. The Sobek just shook his head and sneered at Magnus. He knew, as Magnus did, that arrows wouldn't do much beyond annoying and distracting these Saurians.

The Sobek started toward Magnus again, his battle-axe ready.

Whatever Calum had planned, he'd better do it quickly.

KANTON and Falcroné set Calum down near the top of the boulders.

"Kanton, go help the others in the gorge. When I yell to move, get outta the way."

He nodded then zipped away.

"Falcroné, I need you to hover on the other side of the rocks and tell me when they're gonna give out. And tell me when the Saurians are in place, too. Crystal?"

"Clear." Falcroné took his position and waited.

From Calum's vantage point, it seemed as if one of the boulders at the top could trigger the whole slide. He placed his foot on it and pushed, but it didn't budge.

It shouldn't have surprised him—the boulder looked about the size of a small cow and had to weigh over a thousand pounds. He stomped on the boulder again, but still no movement.

"Where are we at, Falcroné?"

"You've got about thirty seconds."

That was it? No time. He needed to loose these boulders *now*. He planted his right foot on the boulder and stepped onto it with his left. From so high up he could see into the gorge, and Falcroné had been right: Magnus, Axel, Lilly, and now Kanton were almost even with the stack of boulders.

Calum jumped, and landed hard on the boulder. It was a small jump, more of a test than anything. The boulder still didn't budge. Calum jumped again, this time higher, and he landed harder too. Still nothing.

He cursed. What if this didn't work? Had he just doomed his friends?

He jumped and stomped on the boulder a half dozen more times, but to no avail. Magnus and the others were even with the boulders now. If he didn't loose them soon, he'd miss his chance.

Why couldn't he just be stronger?

"Do you see any sign of them moving?" Calum called to Falcroné.

"No."

Calum grunted and jumped again. *Come on.*

The Saurians overlapped with the boulders' assumed trajectory.

"*Come on.*" Calum jumped again and stomped, then jump-stomped once more.

On the third jump-stomp, the boulder budged.

The next thing he knew, Calum was tumbling down into the gorge, surrounded by boulders the size of livestock.

He'd become part of the rockslide.

CHAPTER 30

A hand clamped onto Calum's wrist, and the rockslide dropped out from under him. Falcroné pulled him up and glided with him across the gorge down toward Magnus, Axel, Lilly, and Kanton.

Calum noticed right away that although Falcroné still couldn't fully fly with Calum's weight added on, they didn't drop nearly as fast as he had when Lilly had glided with him back over the lake water. Falcroné was definitely stronger.

As they coasted toward a landing about thirty feet behind the rest of their group, Calum yelled, "*Run!*"

WHEN MAGNUS HEARD Calum's voice, he parried a blow from the Sobek then drove his shoulder into the Sobek's chest. With the Sobek off-balance, Magnus turned back and charged away. As he ran, Magnus bent down and hooked Axel around his waist, hefted him over his shoulder, and carried him away from the incoming rocks.

Twenty long strides later, he watched as dozens of huge boulders tumbled into the gorge and smashed into the Saurians. At first, Magnus thought he'd pushed the Sobek back too far, but a boulder three or four times his size smacked into his chest, and he disappeared under the pile of rubble that consumed the other three Saurians.

"Hey!" Axel whacked Magnus's back. "Put me down, already."

Magnus obliged him, and Lilly and Kanton landed next to them. Together they watched as the final boulder settled on top of the pile. "I must admit, that worked a lot better than I expected it would."

"Yeah. No kidding," Axel said.

"Over here!" Calum called from behind them.

Magnus whirled around and saw the three remaining Saurians approaching Calum and Falcroné. He ran toward them along with Axel, and Lilly and Kanton zoomed overhead.

The six of them lined up together and faced the three Saurians, who stepped back. Several arrows protruded from the hides of two of the Saurians, and dark cuts streaked the other's face.

"Go now," Magnus hissed. "Or we will kill you, too."

The Saurians glanced at each other for a moment then refocused on Magnus.

"That way." Magnus pointed toward the pile of rubble. "And do not stop until you reach Trader's Pass. I do not want to so much as see you again."

The Saurians hissed at him through their noses but nodded. They passed by the group and kept going until they disappeared from the gorge entirely.

Magnus motioned to the others with his sword, and the rest of the group sheathed their weapons. He walked over to the pile with his sword still in hand and studied it until a faint hiss reached his ears.

He bent down and moved a couple of smaller rocks out of the way. There, pinned beneath a gigantic boulder, lay the Sobek, covered in gray dust.

He coughed and then hissed at Magnus.

"Next time Vandorian wants to capture me, he had better do it himself."

The Sobek chuckled, and dark blood trickled from the corners of his mouth. "Vandorian ain't sent us."

Magnus squinted at him and crouched down. He held his sword out for the Sobek to see. "Tell me who did, and I will accelerate your passing."

"'Oo else?" The Sobek coughed, and more blood oozed from his mouth. "There's only one slave lord in Western Kanarah. It's 'im 'oo sent us."

Magnus scowled at him. "Oren?"

The Sobek smiled. "Oren. My master. He'll bind you in chains an' send you to the Blood Chasm f'this."

"And why should he care about a mound of refuse like you?"

"My name's Troden. He's my brother. He'll make you suffa' *centuries* of agony for my death." The Sobek bared his reddened teeth.

Magnus raised his sword, tip down. "I will share your final remarks with him when next I see him."

Wide-eyed, Troden slung a string of curses, and Magnus drove the point of his sword through his head and into the gravel below. He retracted his sword, cleaned off its blade, and sheathed it as he stepped down off the mound of rubble toward the rest of the group.

"What did he say?" Calum asked.

"He was Oren's brother."

Axel shrugged. "So?"

Calum nudged him. "The Sobek in the brown from the Sky Fortress. Remember?"

Axel shrugged again. "So?"

"He is unlikely to forgive the death of his brother, even if his brother instigated the fight." Magnus exhaled a long hiss through his nose. "Plus, he heads of all of West Kanarah's slave trade."

LILLY'S EYES WIDENED. What was Magnus talking about? "What do you mean he's the head of West Kanarah's slave trade? Outside of the prisoners banished to the Blood Chasm, West Kanarah doesn't have any slave trade. It's the humans who deal in slaves."

Magnus shook his head. "I fear that is not the case, Lilly. The slave trade here has been in operation since even before my father was murdered. I had never encountered Oren before our meeting in your father's throne room, so I had no idea who he was. But apparently, Oren is the slave trade's prime operator, and perhaps its architect as well."

"This can't be true." Lilly stared at her boots. Had she been blind to this reality before she'd left the Sky Realm the first time? Had it taken her own capture and enslavement to reveal to her the bitter truth of it? Or had she been willfully ignorant all along? "How could anyone allow this to happen? Those slaves are *people.*"

"Oren reports directly to Vandorian. That much is evident. That explains why Oren accompanied him to the Sky Fortress." Magnus clacked his talons on his breastplate. "And it is not a stretch to assume that Vandorian receives a tribute every month to look the other way when it comes to Oren's dealings, even though slavery violates Saurian law."

Axel huffed. "It's against human law too, but that doesn't stop the King from enslaving whoever he wants—for entire lifetimes."

"Yes, but when we free Lumen, that will change," Calum said.

"Slavery violates Windgale law as well." Lilly focused her attention on Falcroné. Did he know anything about this? "You're the Captain of the Royal Guard. Why doesn't my father do something about this?"

Falcroné's mouth hung open for a moment, probably to Axel's delight. "Lilly, I merely follow orders and relay them to my men in order to protect the Premier. I'm not privy to—"

"Don't lie to me, Fal." Lilly pressed her index finger into his armored chest. "You're in the same room with him almost every waking hour of the day. I know you've heard things that normal Windgales don't hear."

"I—" Falcroné gulped. "I am not at liberty to divulge the content of the Premier's dealings with anyone unauth—"

"I'm his *daughter,* to whom you're engaged." Lilly hovered up higher so she could look him in the eye. "I'm going to *rule* the Sky Realm someday. If you think you can convince me that this isn't my business, you're wrong. Tell me what you know, Fal."

"Even if I could tell you what discussions he has, I wouldn't say anything with *them* around." Falcroné motioned toward their other companions.

Lilly didn't back down. She continued to stare into his blue eyes, unrelenting. He knew something, and she was going to drag it out of him.

"Either you tell me now, or this engagement ends immediately."

She could scarcely believe the words had just come out of her mouth, but they had. Lilly didn't dare look, but she imagined Axel was just short of all-out celebrating the potential death of her relationship with Falcroné, and Calum probably was, too, albeit less overtly.

But she didn't care. Right now, the issue at hand was far more important.

"That's unfair, Lilly." Falcroné glanced around. His voice had taken on a calm but firm tone. "And inappropriate, too, considering those around us."

"You don't have to worry about them," Lilly asserted. "You have to worry about me. When all of this is said and done, they'll go back to their homes, and you and I will go back to the Sky Realm. Whether you and I are still together when that happens is up to you, right here and right now. So tell me what I want to know, or we're done."

"*Please,* Lilly." Falcroné leaned in close to her with his voice lowered and tinged with desperation. "You are asking me to betray my oath to your father, and you're doing it in front of these people."

"Relationships are built on trust, Fal," she countered, not bothering to lower her voice as he had. "If I can't trust you, then there is no relationship. Do you understand?"

"If they could just grant us some privacy, or if we could go off somewhere to have this conversation instead, I—"

"Anything you tell me, they will hear from my lips afterward anyway, so you might as well spill it all, here and now." Lilly waited as the wheels in Falcroné's mind turned.

Finally, he sighed. "Your father is, more or less, unopposed to the slave trade."

Kanton shook his head, and Calum and Axel muttered between themselves.

Lilly ignored them all. Her voice hardened. "What do you mean by 'more or less?'"

"It means that he lacks the resources and manpower to fully shut the slave trade down—" Falcroné paused. "—but also that he participates in it from time to time."

Falcroné's admission hit Lilly like blow to her gut, and she felt physically sick upon hearing it.

"But it's not what you think," Falcroné quickly added. "He only sends criminals, derelicts— people like that—which you already know. That's exactly what they're going to do with Condor."

Falcroné was right. She'd been right there in the throne room when her father sentenced Condor to life at the Blood Chasm, but...

"Does he accept remuneration for the people he sends?" she asked.

Falcroné's jaw tensed, and he slowly nodded.

Lilly closed her eyes and shook her head. Her own father, a willing participant in Kanarah's slave trade? Even if it was only on occasion, it was still heinous. At the thought, Lilly wanted to vomit.

Roderick had captured her and sold her into slavery, and she'd barely escaped with her life. She would have never seen her home or her family again. Now she'd learned her father had supported people just like Roderick and his men.

It was wrong. All of it.

"In my opinion, there is only one thing for us to do now," Magnus said. "We must to venture to Oren's fortress near the Blood Chasm and put a stop to his enterprise once and for all."

Axel scoffed. "Talk about a waste of time."

Lilly redirected all of her anger at him with a single glare. "A waste of *time?*"

"Easy." Axel held up his hand. "I mean we're better off going to free Lumen. Won't he just take care of this sort of thing anyway?"

"And in doing so, do we forsake the people currently enslaved?" Calum asked. "I'm with Lilly and Magnus, here."

"I call that acceptable losses." Axel cracked his neck. "Think about how many we're gonna save once we free Lumen."

"Going to free Lumen instead of helping those people means we're giving up on them. Is that what Lumen would do?" Calum stepped toward Axel.

"Beats me." Axel shrugged and folded his arms. "You're the authority on ancient warriors. You tell me."

"He's coming back to liberate *all* of Kanarah," Calum replied. "He's made that perfectly clear."

"Then that's your answer," Axel concluded. "He'll take care of it."

"Practically speaking, it is wise for us to destroy Oren before he can rally a response to the death of his brother," Magnus said. "If we leave now, we can still catch him by surprise. If we cut off the head of the serpent, the body will wither and die."

Axel kept shaking his head. "If we just head straight to Lumen—"

"You still don't even believe Lumen exists," Calum cut in. "So why are you insisting on this now?"

"Consider me swayed toward believing," Axel replied. He still stood in the same position: legs spread apart with his arms folded across his chest.

"Why?" Calum pressed. "What swayed you?"

Axel began numbering his responses with his fingers. "The Premier certainly seemed to believe Lumen is real. Then he gave us a map that supposedly leads right to the Arcanarium, or whatever it's called. Lilly wanted to come along, so she obviously believes there's something to it.

"Lastly, you won't shut up about these dreams you keep having, so I'm starting to think he might be real." Axel held up four fingers. He considered telling them about how Condor had hinted at knowing something about the Arcanum as well, but he held that one back. "There. Four reasons. Good enough for you?"

"I'm glad you're finally on board with us," Calum said. "And now that you've caught up to that point, catch up to this next one: Lilly wants to free the slaves at Oren's fortress, so that's what we're doing."

Axel rolled his eyes again and folded his arms again. "Whatever."

When Calum looked at Lilly, she had to consciously stifle her smile.

"This is what you want, right?" he asked.

She nodded. "Yes. We have to help those people. Magnus and I know what it's like, and so do you, Calum. Better than anyone."

"Yeah. That's probably true." Calum rubbed the back of his neck. "Magnus, how far is it out of the way?"

"According to the map, once we reach the Blood Mountains, it is only a day's journey in the opposite direction from the Arcanum, near where the edge of the mountains meets a forest. We can reach it there in about a week."

"It's settled. We're going," Calum declared. "And we can raid the place for supplies while we're there, too. It makes sense to go. Right?"

Aside from Axel, who rolled his eyes again, everyone in the group nodded, some more enthusiastically than others. Falcroné's head barely moved.

Lilly frowned, and he frowned back at her.

"You alright with this, Falcroné?" Calum must've noticed it, too.

"I am charged with keeping Lilly safe above all else. If she goes, I'll go as well." He reached out and placed a gloved hand on her shoulders, but she shrunk away from him.

She wasn't ready to receive anything from him other than space and perhaps more answers, at least for the time being. Falcroné wouldn't like it, but he'd just have to deal with it.

"Good. Let's go." Calum faced north and took a few steps.

"What about Riley?" Kanton asked.

Calum stopped and turned back. "I don't know where he went. I hope he's alright. Where should we start looking for him?"

"Leave him. He ran away when we needed him." Axel waved his hand in dismissal. "If he doesn't need us, then we don't need him either."

Lilly wanted to smack Axel upside his head.

"Don't talk like that, Axel," Calum said.

Magnus started toward Axel. "What if someday we decided we did not need you?"

"Hey, *I* didn't run from the fight like a scared little puppy. *He* did." Axel met Magnus until they stood face-to-breastplate, with Magnus looking down at him. "Don't pick on me for it."

"Spread out in groups and start looking for him," Magnus said. "Call out his name. Wolves have excellent hearing. If he is nearby, he will hear us and will hopefully return. If we do not find him within the next hour, we will leave, and he can catch up to us later if he so wishes."

Calum gave Magnus a reluctant nod. Then he looked straight at Lilly and said, "Come on. Let's start looking."

Riley? Rileeeeeeeey? Where are you, Riley?

Friendly voices filled Riley's mind first, and then his ears. He hid under a rocky overhang in a space totally shielded from the sun.

Upon discovering the space, he'd chased a rock wallaby out of it and claimed it for his own. It was beautifully dark inside. The Saurians would never find him in there... if they even bothered looking.

"Riley?"

"Riley, helloooooo?"

The voices solidified, now more real than imagined. He recognized them, distantly, as friends, but his mind refused to identify specifically whom they belonged to.

In general, since the attack, his mind had refused to do a lot of things that it used to do just fine. Something in his head had severed along with Condor's stab, and he couldn't put it back the way it was.

Nor could Riley go back out to them—his friends. Not after he'd fled and left them to fend for themselves. How many of them had died because he wasn't there to help?

How many of them died anyway, regardless of whether or not you'd been there? His thoughts countered.

"Riley? Can you hear us?"

"The fight's over Riley. You're safe now."

Safe. But for how long? They'd fight again.

That's all that ever seemed to happen to this group—fights.

Fights with monsters in tunnels.

Fights with pirates—at least he'd missed those.

Fights with Windgale rebels that ended with him skewered like a stuck pig.

Fights, fights, fights.

He was better off hiding in here and waiting for them to pass him by. They were better off, too. If they couldn't count on him for help, he might as well not weigh their group down.

"Riley?"

"Are you in there?"

Calum and Kanton. His mind finally ascribed names to the voices—voices which were much closer now.

Aside from Lilly, those two were his favorites. Calum had spared his life back in Eastern Kanarah, and Kanton had saved it after Condor ran him through.

Still, he couldn't go out to them. Even if they welcomed him back, he couldn't face the shame of deserting his friends. His only friends.

His only friends *ever*.

"It's dark in there." Kanton's legs came into view as he landed near the opening of the overhang. He bent down and peered into the hole right at where Riley hid in the darkness. "I don't see too well these days. Maybe you'd better have a look?"

Calum's crimson armor showed up next, all scratched and chipped, probably from the fight. It certainly hadn't been beforehand. If he'd taken that kind of damage just to his armor, how bad had the rest of the group gotten it?

Calum got down on all fours and peered into the shadows. "It's definitely Riley's type of hiding spot. I can't make out what's in there, if anything. If he was in there, he'd have heard us by now, anyway."

"He would have heard us a long while ago," Kanton said. "If he's around, you don't think he'd be too timid to come out, do you?"

Calum shook his head and pushed himself back up to his feet. "He knows we're looking for him. He knows we don't want to leave him behind, but he's gotta make the call on whether or not he's coming with us, if he hasn't already."

Leaving? They were leaving? They were going to leave Riley behind?

How could they do such a thing? After all, they were friends… weren't they?

"Come on," Calum said. "We've got a lot more ground to cover and only ten minutes before we said we'd leave."

"Alright. I'll fly some more reconnaissance." Kanton's legs sprang into the air, and Calum's walked off to the side.

They'd left him.

They'd been right there, and they'd left him behind.

But it wasn't because they wanted to leave him. They'd made that clear.

It was because *he* hadn't spoken up. He hadn't made a sound. He'd hidden himself well—too well.

At least he was still good at something.

Riley raised his head. He was still good at *something*. And if they were still looking for him, even after he ran away, then they must still want him around.

And, he realized, he wanted to be around them, too, shame or otherwise.

Good enough.

He stood to his feet and padded his way out of the overhang.

CHAPTER 31

A week later, they reached Oren's fortress.

Lilly hadn't known what to expect before she saw the Blood Chasm. Its name conjured nightmarish images in her mind of a river of blood flowing through a fissure, but when she flew overhead for a look, the reality of what she saw dwarfed her imagination in both scale and terror.

Instead of a red river in a crevice, Lilly found a half-mile-wide bottomless pit in the crimson rock around it. Networks of rope bridges with wooden planks stretched between anchors mounted to the Blood Chasm's perimeter, and more rope bridges extended from those in every direction out over the chasm itself.

A ramshackle staircase, also made of wood and rope, spiraled deep into the chasm and ended in the first of many tunnels carved into its sides. Narrow walkways carved from the stone lined the outer edges of the chasm farther down.

Inside the chasm, slaves of every race milled about. Some of them pushed carts of red rocks to the edge of the chasm and dumped them into the abyss. Others hefted bulging bags of usable materials like iron and Blood Ore up the spiral steps or across the rope bridges.

How many of them had fallen into that Chasm while trying to carry their loads to the surface? How many had given their precious lives for a few pounds of raw metal?

Lilly's eyes narrowed. They would stop Oren tonight, and then they'd free these slaves. Every one of them.

At sundown, a pair of armored Saurians pulled about fifty or sixty slaves from the chasm. The third member of their group, a man in dark armor, tallied their number on a piece of parchment. One Saurian anchored the slaves to each other, and the other collected all of their various tools into a big cart.

Lilly couldn't make out what they were saying from so high in the air, but she caught enough to realize that the tally-man's hand signal—four fingers up—meant they had lost four slaves that day to the Blood Chasm.

She shook her head and scowled. Had they managed to get there only a few hours sooner, perhaps those four slaves would have lived. She was too late to help them now, but she took comfort in knowing that no more slaves would die after tonight.

As a unit, the Saurians marched the slaves toward the fortress, a two-story wooden structure made of vertical logs with their tops sharpened to points. The doors to the fortress swung open and swallowed the slaves, the Saurians, and the tool cart whole, then it shut again behind the tally-man, who entered last.

Night fell, and several torches within the fortress ignited. A few armored men stood watch on the fortress's flat roof, but mostly they gambled with dice for whatever small coins or trinkets they had with them. Probably property they'd taken from new slaves when they arrived.

Lilly completed her round of scouting then nodded to Falcroné, who had completed his own scouting flight, and together they flew back to the rest of the group hidden in the trees at the edge of the Blood Mountains.

"Well?" Calum asked.

"I saw two Saurians and one man, plus three more men on the roof," Lilly said. "And about fifty-five slaves."

Falcroné nodded. "I can confirm all of that, but I saw another Saurian inside in addition to the two that Lilly saw."

"That makes eight of them, including Oren." Magnus crouched down. "This is definitely doable, if we can be surreptitious. Those three Saurians and Oren himself concern me the most. Vandorian would never have granted him such a position of authority if he were not worthy of the job. He will not be an easy foe to defeat."

"What do you want to do?" Calum asked.

"I anticipate I will need help in defeating Oren. I want Axel and Falcroné with me on that. The rest of you must release the slaves and find a way to overcome the guards."

Lilly nodded. The plan was sound enough, and it left a little room for improvising if need be. Together with Kanton and Calum—and maybe Riley, if he could keep from running off again—Lilly believed they could get the job done.

"If we can reach the slaves, I imagine they'll help us fight," Kanton said. "I know I would."

"They pushed a cart of mining tools into the fortress behind the slaves." Lilly motioned toward the fortress with her head. "We can arm them with those."

"Perfect." Magnus smirked. "Even a simple pickax can be effective in the right hands."

Axel matched Magnus's smirk, and Calum nodded.

"The only question that remains is our approach. Riley, you are the stealth expert. What do you suggest?"

Before Riley could say anything, Axel held up his hand. "Whoa, wait a minute. He's not coming with, is he? He'll just run away again as soon as it gets too hot in there."

Riley growled, and Lilly considered joining him.

"We've been through this already, Axel," Calum said. "And we're not going through it again. Riley is still useful to this group, and if he wants to, he's coming along. Crystal?"

Axel scowled at him and sighed. "Yeah, clear. He's not gonna be in my group anyway, so he can't get me killed by not watching my back."

Calum ignored him and turned back to Riley. "How do you want to do this?"

"Thank you." Riley glared at Axel for a long moment, then faced the fortress. "It's exposed, right out in the open. That'll make the approach a pain. Did you see any other entrances besides the main door?"

"Entrances, no," Falcroné said. "Other than some windows and a hatch on the roof for the guards to get in and out, no."

"Alright. We've got enough manpower—and the right kinds of manpower—to get in there all but unnoticed, even though the place is exposed."

"What does that mean?" Axel asked.

Riley turned his head toward him. "It means *shut up*, and I'll tell you. Lilly and Falcroné need to take out the guards on the roof first. Once they're down, we can creep over to the fortress easily enough. You don't even have to be good at stealth to pull that off." He stared at Axel again. "And that's a huge advantage since some of us don't know the meaning of the word."

Lilly didn't bother to conceal her smirk. Riley's sarcasm was her favorite thing about him.

Axel folded his arms and leaned forward. "At least I don't run from fights."

"Stop it, both of you." Calum looked at Riley. "Continue, please."

"From there it's just a matter of sneaking inside without them hearing. The roof access seems like a natural place, but it'll be too hard to get all of us up there. I don't think the three Windgales combined could get Magnus up there, for example.

"Climbing isn't a quiet option, either, but if the three of you can get at least Calum and me onto the roof, then we can go in from the top. Then we'll meet you at the main entrance and let you inside."

"No problem." Falcroné grinned. "We'll get you up there, easy."

"From there, just try to take the guards by surprise if you can, and bring them down quietly. If even one of them hollers, we're all in trouble." Riley sat up straight and tilted his head. "Any questions?"

Calum smiled. "Let's go free some slaves."

CALUM WISHED he'd been close enough to see how they did it, but even from far away, he got the gist of what happened in the five seconds it took Lilly and Falcroné to deal with the guards on the roof. Two of Lilly's arrows had combined with two quick slashes from Falcroné's blade to silence the three of them for good.

Then Falcroné picked up one of the torches from the roof and darted through the air a few times to signal Calum and the others to head for the fortress.

Within minutes, Riley, Kanton, Lilly, and Calum all stood on the roof while Magnus, Axel, and Falcroné headed for the main doors.

A rope ladder lay on the roof next to the hatch door, and Calum pushed it away, but as he reached to open the hatch, he hesitated. When Lilly hovered directly over it with an arrow nocked in her bow, Calum subdued his nerves and quietly opened the hatch.

Riley poked his head down into the hatch for a moment, then he came back up. "Clear."

Calum nodded. "Can you get down there?"

Riley shook his head. "Not quietly. The drop is too far for me to land without making too much noise, especially with this shoulder armor on. Falling from this height wouldn't feel great, either. You'll have to use the rope ladder to get down there, and these two will have to lower me down since I don't have opposable thumbs."

"Let's do it," Calum said. "I'll go last."

Riley put his forepaws on Kanton's shoulders, and Lilly held him around his waist, and they squeezed together, making a Riley sandwich, and lowered down through the hatch. Once they gave Calum the all clear, he lowered the rope ladder and climbed down as quietly as he could.

From that platform they descended down to the floor. A pair of torches illuminated the room, empty aside from the rope ladder and two beds stacked on top of each other. The door on the south end of the room was shut.

"Walk softly, Calum," Riley whispered. "The Windgales can hover. You can't, and your boots are noisy. Watch your step."

"Got it," Calum replied.

The floor creaked on his very first step, and Riley glared at him. Calum shrugged and kept going. He couldn't know where the floor would and wouldn't creak.

They made it through the door and into an open walkway that led in two opposite directions. Two wooden staircases, one on each end of the walkway, led down to the first floor where the main entrance fed into the lobby.

Riley nodded to Lilly, who hovered over the rail that lined the edge of the walkway. She checked below to make sure no one was around and then dropped down. Calum and Kanton peered over the edge of the rail and watched her unbolt the doors. Magnus, Axel, and Falcroné filtered inside in total silence.

Riley trotted past each of the rooms to Calum's right, then nodded to him, and Calum followed, stealing a glance in each one. They were empty, too. He crept down the staircase behind Riley and met up with the others on the first floor.

"Maybe they're eating dinner or something?" Calum murmured.

"Makes sense. It *is* just after sundown." Kanton's hushed tone matched Calum's.

"Or there's a lower level," Riley whispered. "There isn't anywhere to hide the prisoners up on the second floor."

Something stirred behind them, and they whirled around. Lilly nocked an arrow in her bow, and Calum's hand went to the hilt of his sword.

Toward the back of the lobby, a large cage with black iron bars extended up to the ceiling, but Calum couldn't see anyone inside the deep shadows within. If anyone was in there, they'd get whoever it was out once they freed the slaves on the lower level.

"There is a staircase toward the back of this room." Magnus motioned to an opening in the floor next to the cage. "If you find Oren, stay down there, and we will confront him together. I suspect he is in the room to the right of that cage with several of his guards, though."

On the opposite side of the lobby, a wall of vertical logs partitioned almost a third of the first floor into a separate room. The tool cart, loaded full of mining equipment, sat in the corner immediately to the right of the main doors.

Though the setting differed from his life at the quarry, the heavy oppression of the place still felt all too familiar to Calum. But he could deal with his memories later.

First, he and his friends had to walk past that room to get downstairs. At least the door was closed; as long as they stayed quiet, it shouldn't be a problem.

"Go ahead," Falcroné urged. "We won't make our move until you get downstairs."

Riley started forward before Calum could respond, so Calum kept quiet and just followed. They descended down the stairs, Riley leading, into the dark basement under the fortress.

Several torches lined the walls of the lower level, which amounted to nothing more than a dungeon. Some of the original slaves had probably carved the lower level out of the red rock specifically for that reason.

A row of iron cages lined the basement's square perimeter. Even in the low light, Calum could see dozens of people inside—people of every race and type. Eager to get to work freeing them, he started toward the nearest cage.

"Calum, wait!" Riley hissed.

A dark figure emerged from the shadows and swung his blade at Calum's head.

CHAPTER 32

Axel bristled. Together with Falcroné and Magnus, he stood ready to kick open a door to a room that held three Saurians, one man, and one Sobek—at least according to Lilly and Falcroné's scouting report. Who knew what they would actually face once they made it inside?

Too late now.

Magnus held up two fingers, then three, and then he threw his entire weight against the door.

Wood snapped, and the meager door all but shattered. Falcroné darted inside first and slit the throat of one of the two Saurians in the room. Axel charged in behind Magnus and jammed his blade into the chest of a man who came at him with a sword.

Magnus parried the second Saurian's sword then lashed his blade straight down, cleaving into the Saurian's skull. He dropped to the floor, dead.

Axel smirked. They were doing better than he'd expected.

Then a green-and-brown mass slammed into Magnus.

The impact sent him careening into the wall next to the door, and his body snapped through it as if the logs were little more than dried sticks. He landed on the dirt floor about where Axel had stood before they broke through the door.

Oren stood in the center of the room and drew a curved sword, but it wasn't the ragged-looking one he'd drawn back at the Sky Fortress.

This one was bright blue, just like Magnus's armor.

Magnus pushed himself up to his feet and stepped back into the room through the hole in the wall. The pain in his chest from Oren's blow had already begun to fade.

"You're gonna pay for this, bugs." Oren hissed at Magnus, then eyed Falcroné and Axel. "All three o' ya."

Magnus noted Oren's blue blade. Even without a Blood Ore sword, Oren made a formidable foe, but with a weapon equal to Magnus's, Oren could very well win the fight.

384

Even so, Magnus remained undeterred. "Your slave trade ends tonight, Oren."

Oren tilted his head and gave an expression caught somewhere between a sneer and a snarl. It was hard to tell for all the scars on his face. "Ohhh, I recognize you now. You're Vandorian's kid brother. Speaking o' brothers, you done killed mine, ain't you?"

"Your brother and his Saurians attacked us. We gave him plenty of opportunities to let us pass, but he refused."

The Saurian whose throat Falcroné had cut crawled across the floor and groped at Oren's legs.

"Izzat right?" Oren shook his head and looked down at the Saurian. "That's not what I 'eard from Jerome, 'ere. But now you've cut 'is froat, so we can't ask him again, can we, my babies?"

Falcroné smirked. "You can blame that one on me."

"I saw you do it, an' I *do* blame you." Instead of helping Jerome, Oren kicked him down and ran him through. Once Jerome stopped convulsing and lay still, Oren pulled his sword out of his chest and glared at Magnus. "Now we really can't ask 'im. So I gets to believe whatever I wanna believe, an' we'll just 'ave to come to some sort of... *agreement.*"

Magnus growled at him.

"As for Vandorian, he'll pay me a hefty sum if I bring you to 'im—or if I lock you up 'ere 'til the next time he arrives."

Magnus stared at the dead Saurian at Oren's feet. He'd just finished off one of his own soldiers instead of trying to help him. What kind of sick person did that?

"What're you gawkin' at, li'l brother?" Oren smirked at Magnus. "I *know* you've seen a murder before, 'ey? Namely, your father?"

Magnus shifted his grip on his sword. Oren was trying to get inside his head. "Enough idle chatter. Will you fight, or will you continue to stall?"

Oren waved him away with his free hand, but he didn't lower his sword. Instead, he turned toward Axel.

"An' what're *you* lookin' at, ya bug?" Oren hissed.

"Nothing." Axel smirked just like Oren had a moment earlier. "I'm just really looking forward to making a new pair of boots outta your ugly hide after you're dead."

Oren's eyes narrowed, and instead of facing Magnus, he stormed toward Axel with a roar.

LILLY'S ARROW knocked the Saurian off-balance, but his sword still crashed down on Calum's left arm with incredible force. Had he not been wearing armor, the blow would've severed his arm. As it was, pain ratcheted through his bones from his shoulder down to his fingertips, and he hit the ground hard.

The Saurian's foot landed next to Calum's head. When he looked up, the Saurian had raised his blade for another swing. Despite his injured arm, Calum twisted around and held his own sword up in time to block. Even so, the strike sent jarring vibrations through his left arm, nearly as bad as the first hit.

The Saurian kept pushing his sword down, closer and closer to Calum's chest, and Calum couldn't push it away. As usual, he was too weak to do much of anything, and his weakened arm wasn't helping at all.

Kanton's spearhead zipped into view and hooked the Saurian's sword, which began to rise thanks to Kanton's help. Mostly thanks to his right arm, Calum gave the sword one last shove and then rolled away from the Saurian, and his sword clanged against the stone floor.

The Saurian flailed his free arm and sent Kanton flying across the room. Kanton smacked into the bars on one of the cages and dropped to the floor, either stunned or unconscious—Calum couldn't tell.

As soon as the Saurian turned around, he caught an arrow in his throat from Lilly, then another to his exposed chest. He roared, ripped the arrows out, and leaped toward her, but she darted away from his grasp. More enraged than ever, the Saurian returned his attention to Calum.

Calum recovered his footing and waited for the Saurian to come at him instead of pursuing him. Once the Saurian closed to within striking distance of Calum, he swung his sword in a wide arc. Unwilling to parry, given his left arm's condition, Calum backed away from the swipe and the one that followed.

The Saurian hefted his sword over his head again, and Lilly shot another arrow. It lodged in the left side of his stomach just above his belt, and the Saurian winced and abandoned his strike. When the Saurian reached for it, Calum lurched forward and drove his sword into the Saurian's gut.

The Saurian dropped his sword, but he also clamped his hand on Calum's wrist, anchoring him in place. Then he grabbed Calum's throat with his other hand and lifted him into the air.

The Saurian began to squeeze.

Calum tried to pull his sword free, and he tried to pry the Saurian's thick fingers away from his neck, but neither tactic worked. Calum felt as if his head was about to pop off his neck.

Kanton zoomed into view, spear-first. As its tip knifed into the Saurian's side, he released his grip on Calum. The Saurian swatted Kanton away again, but the spear remained lodged in his flank. Then Lilly drew her sword from its sheath and jammed it into the Saurian's flesh at the base of his neck.

He roared and convulsed wildly, but he didn't stop trying to fight them. No matter what they did, the Saurian wouldn't go down.

HAD Falcroné not tackled Axel out of the way, Oren would have crushed him. They landed on the floor in a tangled heap of armored limbs and exchanged quick glares, but Axel gave Falcroné a nod nonetheless.

They could have a stare-down some other time. Right now, they had a bigger problem to deal with.

As the two of them pushed to their feet, Magnus traded blows with Oren, who moved faster than Axel knew a Saurian could. He efficiently parried Magnus's blows then threw several counterattacks in quick succession. Magnus fielded most of them, but one of them clanged against the scales on his left arm, and he recoiled.

"In some trouble, are ya, Magnus?" Oren scoffed. "This blade's Blood Ore, jus' like yours. It's sharp enough to rend even your fine scales."

"You talk far too much." Magnus rubbed the spot where Oren had hit him, then he advanced again.

Falcroné swooped around the room and came up behind Oren with his blade out. Still flying fast, he jabbed it at the back of Oren's head, but Oren ducked and Falcroné crashed into Magnus instead. The impact all but leveled Falcroné, but it only knocked Magnus off-balance.

Oren took advantage of the situation and shoved Magnus back through the same hole in the wall which he'd broken through, and he kicked Falcroné to the side. That left Axel alone to face him.

Oren chuckled. "You babies make me laugh, thinkin' you can best me. You're all gonna die—if you're lucky. Otherwise, it's the chasm f'you. All o' you."

But despite Oren's words, he didn't advance. Either he was toying with them, or he was buying time. Given the way he'd fought so far, Axel worried it was the former. And if Oren was really that good, they might not make it out of this alive.

Falcroné got up next and shifted several long locks of blond hair from his face. He readied his sword again, glaring at Oren. Finally, Magnus stood to his feet, reentered the room, and raised his sword for battle.

"We attack him together, as a unit," Magnus said. "That is how we will bring him down."

"Ha!" Oren shook his head. "You fink you're in a dream world, but I'll bring you back to real life. Then I'll put you in a real cage, just to drive 'ome the point."

"Ready?" Magnus asked.

Axel nodded and raised his sword, and so did Falcroné.

AMID THE STRUGGLE FOR CONTROL, Calum managed to get ahold of his sword, which still protruded from the Saurian's gut, and he ripped it out.

The Saurian jerked to his left and wrenched Kanton's spear from his side. He feigned an attack that got Calum to raise his sword, then he kicked Calum square in his chest, launching him back into the bars. His head took the worst of it, and a white light flashed past his eyes upon impact.

He dropped to the ground, stunned. His vision fogged over and spiraled all at the same time, and he tried to stand but couldn't.

Lilly had her bow out again and shot another arrow, this time into the Saurian's head. It lodged just behind the Saurian's eye, and he whirled around and hurled the spear at her with a roar.

She ducked under it, but the spear pierced her cape and plunged into the wall. She yanked on it, but couldn't get it free.

Calum wanted to get up and help her, but his body refused to comply with what his brain tried to tell it. All he could do was stumble as he tried to get up. He couldn't even cry out to her to warn her.

All he could do was watch.

Oozing blood and rage, the Saurian picked up his sword and limped toward Lilly.

RILEY COWERED in the shadows as the Saurian thrashed his friends. The Saurian had taken multiple arrows, been stabbed three times in vital areas, and he *still* hadn't fallen. At this point, Riley didn't blame himself for not joining in the fray.

Except now that the Saurian had pinned Lilly to the wall, Riley knew he should intervene somehow. He should do *something*.

Everything in him yearned to emerge from his hiding spot and clamp his jaws down on that Saurian's ankle and shred his tendons, but his body refused to obey his commands.

But it was *Lilly* hanging there, all but helpless. Had it been Axel, he could have stayed hidden forever, but this was Lilly, his favorite of his friends. She'd always been the kindest to him.

He had to do something. He *wanted* to do something.

But he couldn't. The fear coursing through his muscles froze him in place.

Like Calum, still trying to stagger to his feet, all Riley could do was watch.

LILLY'S SCREAM snapped Axel's focus on Oren. He glanced back and almost caved to his urge to run to help her.

Falcroné's response nearly matched Axel's, except that his mouth hung open for a moment first. Then he turned and darted toward the door, but Magnus caught him by his arm.

"I need you *here*, Falcroné." Magnus's eyes narrowed. "I cannot defeat him without you."

"And I swore to protect Lilly above all else." Falcroné twisted out of Magnus's grasp and zipped out the door, even as Magnus called for him to come back.

Axel refocused on Oren. He wanted to go play the hero, too, especially for Lilly's sake, but someone had to make sure the ugly Sobek didn't try something in the interim.

Oren stretched his arms into the air and rotated his head on his neck in a cacophony of cracks. "Don't worry, li'l babies. I ain't goin' nowhere."

CALUM'S LEGS FOUND PURCHASE, and his hazy mind began to clear. He had to stop the Saurian, but a messy flow of thoughts interfered with his progress.

Where's Riley? Did he run off again? They sure could've used him right now.

Calum marshaled all his strength and focus, but he only managed a pitiful lunge. Without even turning around, the Saurian whacked him aside with his tail, and Calum skidded into a different set of bars, albeit not as hard.

He looked around. Maybe Kanton had recovered and could help.

Lilly yanked on the cape. The fabric tore, but not enough—she was still stuck.

But Calum couldn't see Kanton from where he lay. All he could see was the Saurian cocking his sword for a final swing. "*Lilly!*"

A gold-and-gray blur shot collided with the Saurian with such force that it knocked him into the nearby cages. It scrambled up to its feet immediately.

Falcroné tore the spear from the wall, freeing Lilly, and tossed it to Kanton, who was still on his hands and knees trying to get up. Lilly zipped behind Falcroné and drew an arrow from her quiver.

The Saurian roared and charged forward.

OREN'S TAIL crashed into Axel's breastplate and sent him flying out of the room through the hole Magnus had made. He skidded to a stop against the cage in the lobby and sucked in short, shallow breaths to steady his cognition.

Through that opening, as Axel tried to get back up to his feet, he watched as Magnus deftly engaged Oren on his own—at least at first.

They exchanged several blows with their swords, legs, and fists before Oren leveled Magnus with a stunning blow from his tail. He raised his curved blade and whipped it down at Magnus hard enough to split a boulder, but Magnus blocked it with his own sword and an unimaginable amount of strength and control.

Oren snickered, then he kicked Magnus in his left side twice. Magnus winced and grunted each time, but on Oren's third attempt, Magnus caught his foot with his left arm, jerked it forward, and swept his lower half at Oren's other leg. Oren dropped to the floor as well.

As Axel made it up to his knees, a voice hissed from the darkness behind him.

"*Hey.*"

Axel sprang the rest of the way up to his feet and recoiled from the voice with his sword ready. "Who said that?"

"In here." The whispered voice came from the cage, still drenched in shadows. "Let me out, and I'll help you kill Oren."

Metal clattered behind him, and Axel glanced back. Magnus's and Oren's swords tumbled across the floor toward Axel, and they grappled with each other in a myriad of roars, grunts, and hisses.

Axel eyed the lock that hung from the latch on the door. "I don't have a key."

The prisoner chuckled. "That wouldn't stop an industrious Farm Boy like yourself, now, would it?"

Axel's eyes widened.

CHAPTER 33

"C*ondor?*"

"We really must stop meeting like this."

Axel couldn't believe his ears... or his eyes.

The prisoner stepped out of the shadows so his face was visible. Even in the meager torch light Axel made out his piercing blue eyes, the pronounced scar that ran from the outer edge of his left eyebrow to the top of his cheek, and his black hair.

"Let me out, Farm Boy, and I'll help you." Condor nodded to Magnus's sword. "Your friend's blade could certainly cut through the lock, if you give it enough heft."

Magnus twisted Oren around onto his stomach and shoved his snout against the dirty floor with his left hand, then he wrenched Oren's right arm behind his back with the other.

But Oren jerked his body forward and Magnus toppled over his head, losing his hold. They scrambled, but this time Oren mounted Magnus. He drove his fist into Magnus's snout twice before Magnus managed to get a block up.

Axel shook his head. He couldn't justify releasing Condor.

Instead, he abandoned the cage and charged Oren with his sword raised, even as Condor called him to come back.

Axel lashed his blade down on Oren's right forearm, but it just clanged harmlessly off of Oren's scales. Oren's tail smacked into Axel's knees, and he dropped, but he rolled away in time to avoid Oren's fist, which slammed into the floor where Axel's head had just been.

The instant Axel made it back up to his feet, Oren's other fist hit him square in his chest, and he careened across the room until his back hit the wall of logs.

A torch dropped from its mount on and rolled toward the wall, and some of the pitch slathered between the logs at the base began to sizzle and burn.

Axel wheezed and sucked in more air to try to catch his breath. Oren's last blow not only knocked the wind out of him but also sent a bolt of pain ratcheting through his entire body. And it had left a sizable fist-shaped dent in his new breastplate.

"Farm Boy," Condor hissed again. "*Axel.* Free me, or Oren will kill you both."

Axel looked back at Magnus and Oren, who again rolled around on the floor, trading vicious punches and elbow strikes.

If Axel grabbed Magnus's sword and tried to use it on Oren, he might be able to end the fight. But if he failed, or if Oren saw him coming, there was no way could Axel take another blow like Oren's punch to his chest. No sense in getting himself killed while trying to help.

When Oren got back on top of Magnus again and fastened his hands around Magnus's throat, Axel knew what he had to do. He rushed over and picked up Magnus's sword, and instead of trying to hit Oren with it, he hauled it back to Condor's cage. As he hefted it over his head, he realized it wasn't as heavy as he'd expected.

A wretched gurgling noise sounded from Magnus's throat as he strained against Oren's grip.

Axel slammed Magnus's sword down on the lock, and it snapped off in one strike.

The door to Condor's cage swung open.

CALUM AND FALCRONÉ took turns swinging at the Saurian, Kanton jabbed at it with his spear, and Lilly circled him and pumped arrows into his hide.

Having Falcroné there to help more than made up their disadvantage, but Calum had no idea how Axel and Magnus were faring with Oren upstairs. He hoped Falcroné abandoning the plan hadn't ruined everything for them.

"Lilly, aim for his belt," Falcroné called.

Calum wondered why Falcroné wanted her to aim there, but Lilly nodded, nocked an arrow, and let it fly.

When the arrow hit his hip, the Saurian whirled around and swung his sword at Lilly, but she dropped out of the air under the blow and shot another one at him. This time it knifed through the leather strap around his waist and plunged into the side of his underbelly.

The belt dropped to the floor.

And so did the attached key ring.

Now it made sense to Calum. He called out, "Kanton, can you—"

"On it." Kanton's spearhead hooked the keys and slid them away as the Saurian bent down to reach for them.

While the Saurian was still bent over, Falcroné whipped his sword at the Saurian's face. The blade severed through the Saurian's lower jaw, and dark blood streamed out from the grotesque wound.

In blind rage, the Saurian roared and whipped his sword in a wide arc. Falcroné tried to block it, but the force hurled him into the bars behind them. Falcroné dropped to the ground, motionless.

"Fal!" Lilly hollered. She nocked another arrow and fired it into the Saurian's back.

"Unlock the cells, Kanton!" Calum yelled, and Kanton inserted a key into the nearest lock.

The Saurian charged Calum, who stood near one of the corners.

He didn't have anywhere to go. He couldn't get anywhere in time. He readied his sword, and braced himself for his one opportunity to run the Saurian through before it pulverized him.

A rush of bodies intercepted the Saurian as he approached and stopped his progress. Freed slaves sprang from the two cells that Kanton had unlocked and swarmed the Saurian, who thrashed at them but couldn't break free.

"Over here," called a gravelly voice from the cell behind Calum.

He turned back and saw another Saurian, one at least as big as the lizard they were fighting, gripping the bars of his cell.

The Saurian prisoner grunted at Calum. "Free me, and I'll finish him for you."

"Kanton, over here!" Calum shouted above the fracas. Kanton swooped over and eyed Calum for a moment, but he unlocked the cell and set the Saurian free.

With a roar, the Saurian slave launched into the fight. The other slaves parted, exposing the Saurian guard, and the Saurian slave took him down in one stunning punch.

The Saurian slave got on top of the Saurian guard and clamped his hands around his head. With one vicious jerk, a loud crack sounded, ending the fight.

DARKNESS ENCROACHED on the edges of Magnus's vision as Oren squeezed his throat tighter and tighter. Magnus pushed against Oren's wrists to try to pry his hands away and bucked with his hips to force Oren off of him, but Oren was stronger. Much stronger.

The tip of Magnus's snout tingled, as did his lips as less and less blood reached his brain. Just when Magnus lost feeling in his fingers, a loud metallic *pong* sounded above, and splinters of wood rained down on him. A shovelhead clanged on Magnus's shoulder then came to a stop on the ground next to him.

Oren's grip released, and fresh air flooded Magnus's lungs. The tingling in his extremities stopped, and his mind began to right itself.

Above him, Oren wobbled and clutched his head with his right hand. Magnus jerked up and decked Oren with a hardy blow under his chin, and Oren toppled onto his side on the ground.

Magnus wasted no time—he mounted Oren and threw punch after ferocious punch at Oren's scarred face. He only stopped when he realized Oren was no longer fighting back, even though he still drew breath.

When Magnus looked up, none other than Condor stood before him, clad in a white linen shirt streaked with red and holding a wooden staff in his hand.

One end of it was broken off.

AXEL GAWKED AT THE SITE. Condor had moved faster than anything he'd ever seen, including Falcroné. Now Oren lay underneath Magnus, unconscious, and the fight was over.

Behind Axel, the wall had caught fire from the torch, and dozens of people streamed from the basement staircase—mostly humans and Windgales—but also a gigantic Saurian. Axel wearily readied his sword, but Calum popped into view behind him and waved him off.

The slaves plodded through the main hall and out the main doors, to which the fire had not yet spread. Last of all, Lilly and Kanton helped Falcroné up the stairs. A moment later, Riley's perky Wolf ears and head peeked up from the basement as well, and then he bounded up the stairs last.

Axel clenched his jaw and glared at him. From the look of Riley, he hadn't fought again. What good was that special shoulder armor he wore if he refused to fight?

"Axel, bring me the chains from my cage." Condor tossed his broken shovel shaft aside.

Free for less than two minutes, and already Condor dared to give orders? Perhaps Axel had been too quick to free him after all. Even so, it was too late now, and he went ahead and retrieved the chains from the cell.

The fire on the wall spread up to the ceiling, eagerly lapping at timber that made up the second floor.

"Condor?" Lilly gawked at him.

Falcroné's head lifted, and whatever strength he'd lacked to make it up the stairs instantly returned to his body. "*You.*"

THE MOMENT RILEY heard Condor's name, his fur prickled, and he froze in place with wide eyes, only able to turn his head to look. Sure enough, Condor stood near Magnus and Oren, the latter of whom lay unconscious on the floor.

Condor had a sword in his hand before Falcroné could make a move, and he shook his head. "I advise that you don't come near me, Falcroné. I'd hate to have to cut you down so soon after we've been reunited."

"You have no authority to give me orders, *traitor.*" Falcroné drew his own sword and shrugged Lilly and Kanton away.

Instinct cranked Riley's bones into action. He darted to the nearest shadow, which happened to be inside the cage at the back of the room, and shrank into it.

This couldn't be happening. Condor was alive, and he was here, and someone had freed him.

Given the sentence Avian had passed over Condor at the council, it made sense that he'd be here, but Riley hadn't even given it a second thought. Even when the suggestion to find Oren and stop him at this exact place came up, Riley didn't put it together that Condor might be here.

Memories from that fateful day flashed through Riley's mind, and his side ached from phantom pain. Now that Condor was free, it was going to happen all over again.

Lilly grabbed Falcroné's arm. "Fal, you're in no condition to—"

"Let me go." Falcroné jerked his arm away. "I'm going to do what Avian and the Council of Wisps should have done on the day of your hearing."

Yes, kill him. A low growl rumbled from Riley's throat. If Condor died, then perhaps Riley would finally find some semblance of peace. *Kill. Him.*

"Hold, Falcroné." Magnus stepped between them, holding his Blood Ore sword once again. "Condor saved my life and helped me defeat Oren—in your absence, no less. You must not harm him."

What? Magnus was siding with Condor? He'd tried to murder Riley, and now Magnus was defending him?

"He's a convicted criminal," Falcroné said. "And he's dangerous to Lilly. He already attacked her once. I will *not* allow that to happen again."

Condor pointed to Axel, who dropped two pairs of heavy shackles at Condor's feet. "He attacked Lilly, too, but you don't seem all that worried about him."

Axel glared at Condor.

"No offense, Farm Boy. Just making a point."

"I *am* worried about him." Falcroné scowled at Condor, then at Axel.

Several flaming logs collapsed onto the floor between the others and Riley's hiding place, and Calum jumped. "Uh... do you guys think we can take this conversation outside? I don't think this fort is gonna last much longer."

Magnus eyed the ceiling. "Calum is right. We must go."

Condor zipped out the doors first, followed by Axel and Magnus, who carried Oren out with him. Kanton left next, then Lilly and Falcroné. Calum hung back and stared right at Riley's hiding spot.

"Are you coming?"

Riley growled again. Perhaps he should just die here, in the flames, rather than face the possibility of Condor stabbing him again. He would become a pile of ash, the same as everything around him, and then Condor could never hurt him again.

"Come on, Riley." Calum extended his hand. "I won't let him hurt you."

Another large chunk of the ceiling fell to Calum's right, and he jumped out of the way.

"Last chance. Come with me."

Riley closed his eyes and exhaled a long breath. When he inhaled, the smell of smoke and burning wood intensified. Did he want to stay put and add the putrid smell his own burning flesh next?

"Please, Riley?"

Above Calum's head, the ceiling crackled with flames, and he looked up.

Riley's heart clenched. *No.*

He bolted out of the cage as the ceiling collapsed and sprang at Calum with his forepaws extended. Riley's momentum knocked Calum away from the falling ceiling's wrath, and they tumbled against the wall adjacent to the doors. Both of them quickly jumped to their feet and rushed outside as the rest of fortress caved in on itself.

"I could've been in there." Riley stared at the dancing flames as the reality set in.

Calum crouched down next to him. "We *were* in there, but you saved us."

"I'm sorry I can't fight anymore, Calum. I just—" Riley bowed his head. He didn't want to admit it, but he had to. "I'm scared. I don't want to get stabbed again. And now that Condor's back, it's only gonna get worse."

"Maybe." Calum placed his hand on Riley's back and stroked his fur. Were Calum anyone other than himself or Lilly, Riley would have nipped at his hand. "But maybe this is a chance for you to face your fear once and for all, and in doing so, to overcome it."

Riley sighed, and the phantom pain in his side returned. "That almost sounds worse than getting stabbed again."

Calum patted Riley's shoulders. "It may be, but it's the only way to free yourself from your fear. The next time something like this happens, I may not be around to save you from a burning building. Either you face this, or it'll eventually get you killed, and that'll be the end of it. I really hope it doesn't come to that."

"Me neither." Even as Riley said it, he still wasn't convinced that he meant it.

"Hey." Kanton landed in front of them with his back to the flaming fortress. "Are you two alright?"

Calum smiled and stood. "We're a little singed and scraped up, but nothing too bad."

"Oh. Alright, then. I'm going to tend to some of the slaves. A few of them are in pretty bad shape, but I might be able to help them out." Kanton leaned close to Calum. "You'd better get back to the group. They're going to need a voice of reason right about now."

Kanton zipped away, and Calum looked down at Riley. "You coming?"

Riley steeled himself and nodded. "Yeah. I'm coming."

AXEL VOICED MORE than his fair share of arguments on both of the issues at hand: what should they do with Oren, and what should they do with Condor? Unfortunately, with so many extreme opinions and so much discord, his thoughts didn't seem to register with anyone.

Then Calum showed up, and everyone started listening to him.

Of course.

Within five minutes, everyone had their say: Magnus insisted they keep Oren alive so that a ruler like Lilly's father could pass judgment on him for his crimes, but Lilly pointed out that her father's involvement in the slave trade had compromised his integrity. Therefore, they should just throw Oren in the Blood Chasm where so many of his slaves had died over the years.

Falcroné agreed with her but didn't agree that they should dole out capital punishment. He thought they should send Oren back to Avian anyway and grant him the chance to bring Oren before the Council of Wisps. When Axel finally got his chance to speak, he shrugged.

"I didn't come all this way and risk my life to bring down Western Kanarah's slave trade only to allow for the chance that it might start back up again. If we let him live, that's a real risk." He pointed to Oren, who knelt before them with his wrists and ankles bound by the heavy shackles Axel had retrieved from Condor's cage. "I say we finish him off right now."

Axel glanced at Condor, who stood motionless at the fringe of their group, watching everything and being watched by Falcroné virtually nonstop.

"You couldn't even land a blow on me, baby boy, an' now you wanna kill me?" Oren chuckled amid the blood dripping from his snout. "You're a funny one, you are."

"He is our prisoner. We cannot just kill him. It is unjust," Magnus said.

"*Unjust?*" Lilly stared at Magnus. "He's responsible for hundreds if not thousands of deaths over the years. I could even argue that he's ultimately responsible for Roderick taking you and me into captivity."

"Oh, it's been more'an that, I'd wager." Oren's jagged smile oozed arrogance—and blood. "We 'ad a logbook in the ol' fortress. I could've given you an exact number if you 'adn't burned 'er down."

"Shut up." Axel glared at him. "Your life hangs in the balance. You wanna live? Start acting like it."

"You don't scare me. Not even a li'l." Oren sneered at Axel. "If you was gonna kill me, you'd 'ave done it by now."

Axel pointed at him. "I said—"

"I 'eard what you said. You say a lot o' things, baby boy, but you don't take no action. You're jus' a scared li'l bug, an' I'm gonna squash you." Oren bared his jagged smile again.

Axel started toward him, but Magnus held him back.

"He needs to face judgment from a ruler, not from people like us," Magnus insisted.

"You and I *are* rulers, Magnus," Lilly said. "Or at least we will be. A few years from now, we'll be making exactly this sort of decision for criminals like him."

Oren laughed. "No one's like me, ya bugs. Not a one. Nobody could 'ave run this enterprise like I done. Nobody could 'ave built it up from nuffin' into an empire that spanned Kanarah like I done. Nobody could 'ave—"

The metallic ring of steel leaving a sheath filled the air, and the next thing Axel knew, Oren knelt before them with the hilt of a dagger protruding from his left eye. He convulsed once, toppled onto his side and convulsed once more, and then he stopped moving entirely as blood oozed from the grisly wound.

Condor stood next to him and admired his handiwork, his face fixed in a contented smirk.

CHAPTER 34

"What have you done?" Falcroné roared. He sprang forward, his hand on the hilt of his sword, but Condor met him halfway and held another sword to Falcroné's throat before he could even draw his.

Axel gawked at the exchange. Condor had moved impossibly fast. And where was he getting all these weapons from?

"You always were too slow, Falcroné. It's why your own father promoted me to Captain of the Royal Guard instead of you." Condor locked his eyes on Falcroné's. "On your knees."

"Don't, Condor!" Lilly held up her hand. "Please, don't."

"I have no desire to kill Falcroné or any of you," Condor said.

He stared at Falcroné until he finally knelt down, then he turned his attention to Oren's body. His usually cheerful voice began to quiver.

"That *thing* beat me and abused me from the day I first arrived. Day after day, he and his soldiers chastised me until my back was raw from his whip, yet some of you wanted to grant him the mercy of bringing him before *Avian?* The very man who sent me to this abominable place?"

Axel glanced at Magnus, whose hand gripped the hilt of his broadsword, still in its sheath. No way he'd get the blade out in time. Condor could kill Falcroné and take to the sky before any of them could so much as think about intervening.

Condor's voice solidified again, and his optimistic timbre began to return. "Oren got what he deserved. That's my judgment. And anyway, it's done now, so if you're willing to move on, I say we ought to do just that."

Falcroné swallowed noticeably, but he didn't move otherwise.

"I'll even go one step further, if it puts you all at ease. Falcroné, my old brother-in-arms, if you want to kill me, then do it." Condor pulled his sword away from Falcroné's throat and tossed it aside. "I won't resist, and I can die with pleasure knowing that brigand is dead."

Falcroné's sword flashed in the moonlight, and he pinned Condor to the ground. Beyond them, the fortress continued to burn like a gigantic torch under the night sky.

"You attacked Lilly," Falcroné growled.

396

"*Enough*, Falcroné." The hard tone in Lilly's voice surprised Axel. "He just said he wouldn't hurt any of us."

"And you *believe* him?" Falcroné scoffed, still refusing to take his eyes off his prey. "Forgive me, Princess, but your youthful naivety is hardly enough to prop up this traitor's word."

"I know where the Arcanum is," Condor said.

No one made a sound until Calum asked, "How do you know where it is?"

Condor glanced at Axel, wearing that same cunning smirk as always. Condor had alluded to this piece of information when they were locked in the cell under the Sky Fortress together, but Axel couldn't convince him to elaborate.

"I've been there. A secret reconnaissance mission from before I earned my promotion to Captain." His piercing blue eyes showed no sign of deception. "I can take you there, too."

"He's lying," Falcroné said. "Everything he says is a lie. There's not an ounce of good in him anymore, if there ever was to begin with."

"How's your shoulder, Farm Boy?" Condor raised his chin and grinned at Axel.

"It feels fine." Axel rubbed it. "It came out of its socket again when the Wisps dropped me into the cell under the Sky Fortress. He popped it back in for me."

"He helped you?" Lilly asked. "And... you *let* him? You wanted to kill him after you learned he'd struck me."

Axel couldn't deny that. Even thinking about it now made him want to tear into Condor along with Falcroné, but he had to consider the rest of his experience with Condor as well.

"He was wrong to harm you. No question there," Axel said. "But when we were in that cell, he fixed my shoulder, didn't kill me even though he could've, and he also hinted that he knew about the Arcanum."

"You're sure?" Lilly eyed them both. "What did he say?"

"He said that your father's scholars might be able to point it out to you on a map, but it's hard to reach. When I asked him how he knew that, he just told me it was his secret and nothing more."

Lilly's eyes narrowed, and she turned to Falcroné. "Let him go."

"He's a murderer. He'll kill us in our sleep, starting with you," Falcroné said.

"I said *let him go*."

"Lilly, you don't understand how dangerous he—" Falcroné stopped talking when Lilly started toward him. "What are you doing?"

"If you won't let him go, I will free him from your grasp with my own hands. He knows exactly where to find the Arcanum, which means he is the key to freeing Lumen and liberating all of Kanarah," Lilly said. "If you think I'm going to let you kill our greatest hope for saving the entire realm, you're dead wrong."

Calum stepped toward her with his hands up. "Lilly, we still have the map. Are you sure you—"

"Stay out of it, Calum," Lilly snapped. "This is between Falcroné and me. A map is only good to a point. We need to free Lumen now, and Condor can to take us right to him." She faced Falcroné again. "Last chance. Let him go."

"I'm here to *protect* you," Falcroné said through clenched teeth. "Not to follow your every command, especially when you don't know what you're talking about."

"Nonetheless, you'd better follow this one." She reached toward Falcroné, but he swatted her hands away without removing his sword from Condor's throat.

To his credit, Condor didn't move a muscle.

Lilly reached for Falcroné again, and again he pushed her arms aside. "Lilly, *stop*. Your behavior is abhorrent. We're engaged to be married."

"I can find another husband," she countered, her voice cold as ice.

Condor smirked at that, and Axel's eyebrows rose. He glanced at Calum, whose mouth also hung open.

Falcroné glared at Lilly for a long moment, but he withdrew his sword from Condor's neck and stood.

Lilly didn't move. "Help him up."

"You can't be seri—"

"I said *help him up.*"

Falcroné grumbled something Axel couldn't understand and extended his hand to Condor, who took it and stood to his feet. He nodded to Lilly, who only then relaxed her posture.

She floated over to Condor and hovered off the ground a few inches so she looked him directly in his eyes. "Condor, I'm offering you a chance to join us. Do you pledge your life to the successful completion of our quest and to protect the Sky Realm and its rulers, including me?"

Condor grinned at her. "I'd be honored to serve you, Princess."

Falcroné fumed at Lilly with wide, angry eyes, but didn't say anything.

"Your first duty will be to lead us to the Arcanum."

"It would be my pleasure."

"Then kneel." Lilly drew her sword from its sheath and tapped Condor's shoulders with the flat of the blade. "I reinstate you as Captain of the Royal Guard, answerable only to me."

"You—you can't do that!" Falcroné pushed between her and Condor. "*I'm* the Captain of the Royal Guard, not *him.*"

"Easy, Fal." Lilly urged Falcroné back with the tip of her sword at his chest. "You will remain Captain alongside Condor. You are *both* my Captains of the Royal Guard, and you will *both* protect me with your lives. Crystal?"

Condor smirked and nodded. "Clear as the purest skies, Princess."

"No. Not clear. Not remotely." Falcroné waved his hand laterally in front of his chest as if cutting a person in half with it. "This man tried to kill you and your friends. He stabbed Riley, and he's responsible for a rebellion that almost resulted in your father's death and *did* result in the deaths of more than a hundred people... yet you're giving him his title back?"

"Yes, Fal. That's right." Lilly stared at Condor. "I'd rather earn him as a friend with my trust than have to kill him as my enemy."

Condor's eyebrow rose at that remark, but his smirk remained nonetheless.

"I don't believe this." Falcroné shook his head. "I don't agree with it. Your father will never approve."

"My father approved of Kanarah's slave trade by sending people like Condor into it for their crimes—the same slave trade that saw me captured and sold to the highest bidder. I'm not interested in his approval right now." Lilly stared into Falcroné eyes. "You will either accept this development or fly home and await my return. What's it going to be?"

Falcroné's jaw tensed.

As LILLY WATCHED the remains of Oren's fortress burning in the distance, she and the others made camp under the trees of the nearby forest.

The freed slaves had elected to move on as a group toward Aeropolis, led by Chorian, the big Saurian who had intervened to stop the Saurian guard in the fortress basement. They all wanted to get as far away from that place as possible, and many had families and loved ones to return to, so they left after Kanton finished tending to them.

When Condor pulled his shirt off for Kanton to tend to him next, Lilly's stomach dropped, partly at his physique, but also at the sight of the lattice of red slashes on his back. Some of them had scabbed over, but many looked fresh, as if Oren had whipped him only minutes before they'd arrived at the fortress.

Kanton applied some ointments and some salves and patched the worst of them. Condor put his shirt back on, and Lilly's racing heartbeat slowed.

The fortress continued to smolder late into the night. To no one's surprise, Falcroné offered to take the first watch, and he made it clear that it was because he didn't trust Condor.

What's more, Riley hadn't said a word or even made eye contact with Lilly since she'd welcomed Condor into their group. She didn't blame him for it, but she knew she had to do something to make it right.

After everyone else had fallen asleep, aside from Falcroné, of course, Lilly hovered across the camp to where Riley resided in the shadows. He lay there, perfectly still and totally awake.

The instant her feet touched the ground, Riley's ears perked up, and he raised his head. The waning light from the campfire reflected in the pair of blue eyes that stared at her from the darkness.

"Hey," she whispered and sat in front of him. "I wanted to talk about Condor."

Riley lowered his head.

"I know he stabbed you, and that it happened while you were trying to save me." Lilly held her breath. "I mean, you *did* save me."

Riley still didn't move.

"It sounds ridiculous now that I'm saying it out loud," she admitted. "I know I just recruited a man who attacked us both, but I did it because I see something in him that gives me courage and hope for the future."

Riley blinked slowly. He really wasn't giving Lilly much to work with. All she could do was press on.

"I don't expect you to understand, but I hope you do someday," she said. "I know Condor can help us, and I believe him when he says he knows where to find the Arcanum. More than that, I think he needs someone to believe in him so he can get his life back on track."

Still nothing from Riley. He just stared back at her with emotionless blue eyes.

"I also want you to know that I'm not doing this to attack you or anything like that. I really like you and don't want anything bad to happen to you, but at the same time, Condor needs our help." Lilly bit her lip. This wasn't going as well as she had hoped. "Aren't you going to say something?"

Riley broke eye contact with her for the first time since she'd come over and looked at the ground. "No."

Lilly exhaled a quiet sigh. "I understand. You know I'm still your friend, right?"

He muttered, "Yeah."

When she reached to scratch Riley's ears, she hesitated, but Riley still allowed her to do it. She smiled. "If there's anything I can do to help allay your concerns, will you let me know?"

"Yeah," he repeated, just as enthusiastically as the first time.

What more could Lilly do? Probably not much, if she were honest. She'd tried to make amends, and she wasn't going to change her mind. She just hoped she'd done enough to restore Riley's faith in her.

"Well, good night," she said.

"Night."

With another sigh, Lilly floated to her place near the campfire. Within minutes, exhaustion claimed her, and she drifted off to sleep.

Try as he might, Axel couldn't sleep that night. The crickets chirped too loudly. The campfire crackled too loudly. Even Axel's own breathing was too loud.

He wanted to blame it only on the ruckus of sounds all around him, but he couldn't. Not if he wanted to be honest with himself—honest about the conflict churning in his heart.

For once, it wasn't about Lilly. Rather, the fight with Oren had shown him something about himself. Something he hadn't wanted to face. He'd wanted to ignore it, to push it aside, to pretend it had never happened, but it had.

Axel couldn't do it any longer.

So he got up, careful not to wake anyone, and headed over to Riley's spot, where he lay crouched among the trees and underbrush, mostly hidden.

Even as Axel walked over there, the conflict raged within his chest. His pride reminded him that he'd been doing the right thing in trying to avenge Lilly after Condor had hit her. At the same time, his conscience reminded him that doing so had almost gotten Riley killed.

His pride fired back that Riley was weak and frail. He'd run away instead of joining his friends in battle. He'd abandoned them in their time of need.

Axel's conscience reminded him that he'd abandoned Riley in *his* time of need. He'd run away from fights and hid because of Axel's reaction to Condor. He was weak and frail because he didn't get the proper help soon enough, thanks to the frivolous delay that Axel had caused.

Axel groaned. It was all too much.

But despite the myriad of thoughts clunking back and forth in his mind, his legs continued to carry him toward Riley's position.

When he reached the edge of the trees, he stopped and searched for Riley's form amid the dark leaves and bushy branches, but he saw nothing.

A voice nearly scared him out of his armor. "If you're gonna urinate, do it somewhere else."

"What?" Axel squinted at the area where the voice had come from and spotted a vaguely wolflike shape among the plants. "No. I'm here to talk to you."

"I think I would've preferred the urine."

Axel bristled at the comment, not because he'd found it especially clever or biting, but because Riley had said it with absolute sincerity. He'd *meant* it.

"Well, say whatever stupid thing you came to say. Get it over with," Riley said.

His tone tempted Axel to lay into him like he usually did, but his conscience made him resist that urge. Instead, he forced himself to say the two words he'd been avoiding ever since the incident had happened.

"I'm sorry."

By the Overlord... Riley had been right. Axel had sounded stupid—exceptionally stupid—in saying that. Why had he even bothered to say it at all?

Riley didn't move. Didn't speak. Didn't respond in any noticeable way at all.

Then his Wolf ears perked up, and he raised his head. He sniffed the air several times and stood up, his body rigid.

At first, Axel wondered how any of that could possibly relate to his apology. He quickly realized it was a heightened wariness on Riley's part instead.

"What is it?" he asked, his voice low.

"Quiet," Riley whispered so softly that Axel almost couldn't make out what he'd said. His lupine head swiveled, and his light-blue eyes widened.

Axel tried to follow his line of sight, erratic as it was, into the trees around them, but he saw nothing.

A howl split the night, but it hadn't come from the woods around them. It came from Riley.

"What in the Overlord's name are you doing?" Axel hissed. "Everyone's asleep!"

"We need to wake them up. Now." He howled again, and Falcroné jerked upright, his sword in hand.

"What's going on?" he slurred.

Calum popped up next, then Magnus, Condor, and Kanton. Along with Lilly, they surrounded Riley and Axel in seconds, all with questions on their lips.

Riley shushed them. "Listen."

From the woods all around them, a cacophony of howls and yips sounded in varying tones and volumes.

"What is that?" Axel unsheathed his sword as he scanned the woods.

"Wolves," Riley replied. "Thirty of them or more, and at least one Werewolf. We're already surrounded."

CHAPTER 35

"What do we do?" Kanton asked.

Riley's fur bristled. Thirty-plus Wolves against the eight of them. At night. And they had a Werewolf as their Alpha. What *could* they do?

"If you try to run, they'll ambush you and kill you," he said. "Stay together. Make them come to you. The nearer you are to the campfire, the less effectively they can hide in the shadows."

Several weapons unsheathed around Riley, which only made his skin tingle more.

He glared at Condor. "And try not to kill me by accident. We all look similar in low light to the untrained eye."

"That won't be hard. You're wearing that shoulder armor," Axel said.

"No, I'm not." Riley craned his head back toward the armor and bit the leather strap that held it on his body. In one yank, the whole apparatus loosened, and he pawed it over his head and off.

Now more than ever, they needed his stealth and his speed. If he wore the armor, he could employ neither.

Axel cursed. "Then how will we know it's you?"

"I'll be the only Wolf not attacking you," Riley snapped. Axel reminded him of a walking brick sometimes. "Speaking of which, don't chase any of the Wolves back into the woods. Stay near the fire, like I said. They'll ambush you in the dark and rip you apart. Crystal?"

"Clear," Calum said.

"Stay near me," Magnus said. "Their teeth and claws won't penetrate my scales."

"The Werewolf's can. Even so, watch your throat, Magnus. All of you, watch your throats. We learn at a young age that if we can get our prey by the throat, we're all but guaranteed a kill." Riley nodded toward the fire. "Come on. Get near the flames."

A snarl sounded behind them as they took their first steps toward the fire. A blurred mass of fur and teeth launched at them out of the darkness, but Condor felled the Wolf from the air in one brutal swing of his sword. The Wolf landed next to a tree, dead.

Riley glared at him.

"What?" Condor shrugged. "At least it wasn't you this time."

"That's not funny," Lilly said.

402

"Look out!" Calum yelled.

A trio of Wolves dashed out of the woods and knocked Kanton off his feet. His spear clanged on the ground as the Wolves' teeth and claws scraped against his armor. One of the Wolves latched onto his gauntleted right hand, and he screamed.

Riley sprang forward and clamped his jaws around the ankle of one of the Wolves and yanked him away from Kanton, and Falcroné killed the one gnawing on Kanton's right hand while Magnus batted the other away.

The Wolf whirled its head around and snapped at Riley, but Riley kept pulling back so it couldn't reach him. Then a swift blow from Axel's sword downed the Wolf.

Riley's eyes met Axel's, and they exchanged nods. For now, given his abrupt apology only moments earlier, that was good enough.

"I'm going out there," Riley told the group. "I can run interference while they try to attack."

"Wait! Don't you think—" Calum's voice trailed off as Riley bounded into the woods, but it was too late.

Riley had committed to this, and he'd see it through.

LILLY GRIPPED her bow and drew back an arrow, but between the darkness and the Wolves' speed, she had yet to fire even a single shot. No sense in wasting the arrows if she couldn't hit anything. Thanks to the Wolves' hit-and-run tactics, she couldn't see her targets well enough.

Meanwhile, Condor helped Kanton to his feet. Blood dripped from his right hand—his dominant hand—and instead of holding his spear he wielded his short sword in his left hand.

"Are you alright?" Lilly floated down next to him.

Kanton shook his head. "I can't use my right hand. It's bad."

"Condor, stay with Kanton. Keep him safe."

The campfire's reflection flickered in Condor's piercing blue eyes, and he nodded. "I've got him."

"Lilly, watch out!" Falcroné's voice cut through Wolves' barking and howling.

She whirled around in time to see a mass of gray fur charging toward her with Falcroné chasing it through the air. Lilly drew her arrow back, but the Wolf had already leaped at her. No chance of bringing it down in time.

Instead, Condor's sword leveled the Wolf in one swift blow, and he darted back to Kanton's side before Lilly fully comprehended what had happened.

"Looks like I've got you, too." Condor gave her a wink then continued to scan the woods around them.

"I would've had him," Falcroné hissed as he drifted to a stop near them.

Enough of this. Lilly slung her bow over her back, dropped the arrow into her quiver, and drew her sword instead. If these Wolves wouldn't give her a decent shot, she'd bring the fight to them.

"Stay together, like Riley said." Calum shouted from the other side of Magnus, who occupied the spot just to Lilly's right. Falcroné covered her left side and stood next to Condor, who still guarded Kanton. Axel rounded out the circle between Kanton and Calum. "We'll wear them down, one by one."

The moment after he said it, at least a dozen sets of eyes appeared in the woods around them, illuminated by the campfire.

Lilly wished she'd kept her bow out after all.

THE FIRST WOLF padded right past Riley's hiding spot, then two more. Just hours earlier, he'd hid so as to avoid the fight, but now he was hiding with the hope of accelerating it to its end.

As the fourth Wolf trotted past, Riley lunged out of the underbrush at him and used his full body weight to slam the Wolf into a thick tree. The impact roused a dull pain in Riley's old wound, but a loud crack sounded from the Wolf's body and he yelped.

The Wolf slumped to the ground, and Riley latched onto his throat and finished him off in silence.

As Riley released his grasp on the Wolf's throat, a new scent reached his nose. It was similar to something he'd smelled before, but not since he'd been around Rhaza and the rest of the desert Wolves. He turned around in time to see a massive brown hand swinging at him.

The blow sent him careening through the underbrush where he'd just hidden, and he landed on his injured side, facing away from his assailant. The old wound throbbed with fresh pain. Riley pushed himself up to his feet and scanned the woods for his attacker, but he was nowhere in sight.

Another swipe hurled Riley across the ground, and his body smacked against a tree. The throbbing in his wound accelerated and intensified. He couldn't take much more of this.

This time, instead of just standing up and searching, he darted away from the tree and zigzagged through the woods, weaving around trees.

Even though he hadn't gotten a good look at his attacker, it had to be the Alpha. And if Riley could find a way to kill the Alpha before the rest of the Wolves closed in on his friends, then he could save them.

But killing an Alpha wasn't an easy thing. The more Riley thought about it, the more he regretted ever having run off to face the Alpha alone.

It was too late now, though. And no one else would ever be able to find it. Either Riley succeeded, or they'd all die. There were far too many Wolves in the pack to overcome.

Riley couldn't let that happen. He was their only chance. As long as he still drew breath, he wouldn't let any more harm come to his friends.

And that even included Axel.

As Riley ran, claws slashed his face, but Riley recoiled a step. When he opened his eyes, the Alpha Werewolf stood before him at its full height and snarled.

The next slash came before Riley could get out of the way, this time to the other side of his face. Pain streaked across his snout, and he couldn't stifle the whimper that squeezed out of his lungs as he staggered away from the Werewolf's hulking bipedal form.

The pain reminded him of the futility of what he'd set out to do. He couldn't outrun the Werewolf. Couldn't hide from it, either. As good as Riley's hearing, sight, and sense of smell were, even in the dark, the Werewolf's were better.

What options did he even have?

Only one, he realized.

And if he failed, it would absolutely cost him his life.

TEN WOLVES HIT the group in quick succession. Calum swung at the first of four Wolves who charged him, but it eluded his sword and nipped at his legs. Alone, their nips proved harmless, but as soon as Calum hacked at the Wolf at his legs, another leaped at his head.

The Wolf's claws scratched Calum's left cheek, and his arm absorbed most of the Wolf's mass, but the impact knocked him to his back nonetheless. The Wolf weighed close to a hundred pounds, and before Calum could try to push it away, the three other Wolves swarmed him. They chomped at his limbs as he covered his face and flailed his sword, but they didn't stop.

A sharp yip sounded above him, and one of the Wolves was gone, followed by the other three. He glanced up.

Magnus stepped over Calum and rumbled toward the four Wolves, who ran off. Magnus followed them a few strides away from the circle.

Calum started to call for him when a set of hands yanked him to his feet.

"Back at it, Calum." Axel smacked his armored shoulder.

"Thanks." He refocused on Magnus, who now stood separate from the circle and hissed at the woods around them. Calum cupped his hand on the side of his mouth. "Magnus, come back over here!"

"No." Magnus shook his head. "We must end this now. Let them come."

The howling intensified from among the trees, and the remaining Wolves who had engaged in the attack disappeared into the darkness again. Only ten of them had attacked the first time, and the group had managed to kill three of them.

Except for the campfire, silence reigned in and around the campsite

Then dozens of Wolves poured out of the shadows and flooded toward them.

Calum tightened his grip on his sword.

RILEY DODGED the next attack before it ever came. It was a risk, but a calculated one.

He'd endured enough blows from the Werewolf by now to figure out a pattern, and he knew that unless he dodged early and timed things just right, the Werewolf would hit him again.

When Riley dodged, the Werewolf's slash missed.

And when the Werewolf missed, it left him exposed.

Too fast for his own good.

Riley sprang at the Werewolf from the side and aimed his jaws for the Werewolf's neck. To his great surprise, they connected. He dug his teeth into the Werewolf's throat with what little strength remained in his body after the thrashing he'd suffered to learn the correct timing.

The Werewolf howled, but Riley clamped his teeth tighter around its neck and pushed against the Werewolf's chest with his paws. He was trying to use his body weight to tear the Werewolf's throat out of its neck or at least drag him to the ground, but the Werewolf refused to go down.

Instead, it grabbed Riley by his sides and dug his claws into Riley's fur, then into his skin.

Then through his skin.

Pain pierced into Riley's body, just like when Condor had stabbed him, only much, much worse.

Riley just bit down harder. Regardless of whatever happened to him, he had to hold on. He had to kill this thing, or the Wolves would overwhelm his friends.

THE WOLVES SWARMED THE GROUP. Everywhere Axel turned, he found another Wolf to fight, to kick, to slay. He'd cut down at least four of them so far—or maybe three—but they just kept coming.

Definitely more than thirty. Possibly even more than fifty.

Around him, Condor and Falcroné zipped through the air and dodged most of the Wolves' attacks, but their faces showed signs of strain with each new swing. Lilly hung just above the fracas and again launched arrows at the Wolves, but nothing stopped them from attacking.

Something heavy collided with the back of Axel's left knee. It hadn't hurt much, but he still went down.

Another Wolf barreled into him from the side and knocked him to the ground. Three sets of canine eyes darted toward him accompanied by three sets of teeth.

He lashed his sword at them and felled one, but the other two pounced on top of him. They started biting and scratching at his face, then at his arms when he tried to shield himself from them. Had it not been for his armor they would have shredded his forearms.

Axel should've figured something like this would happen. He'd just apologized to Riley, and now three of his distant relatives were trying to rip him apart.

"Magnus?" he yelled. "Calum—*anyone*, help!"

One of the Wolves toppled off him with a yip. An arrow lodged in its side. Axel grabbed the other by its left ear and wrenched it downward, then he bashed its head with the pommel of his sword. A quick follow-up stab killed the Wolf.

Axel tried to make eye contact with Lilly to thank her, but she had already nocked another arrow and focused her attention on the incoming Wolves.

With a half scowl, Axel did likewise.

ALMOST A DOZEN WOLVES converged on Magnus. Upon seeing them, Calum wondered how long it would take Magnus to fling them off.

But when Calum saw them take Magnus down instead, his jaw hung open. If they lost Magnus, they lost a third of their strength, if not more.

Axel went down next, overwhelmed by six wolves. When the Windgales zipped over to help Magnus and him, the Wolves pulled them out of the air, all except Condor, who looped around the fight and executed surgical strikes on the Wolves, but he could only do so much against so many—

A force knocked Calum to the ground, and a snarling mouth clamped down on his armored right wrist.

Calum gritted his teeth and swung his left fist at the Wolf, but the punch barely fazed it. Another Wolf went for his neck, but Calum jerked his body to the side and shoved its snout away with his free hand.

Two more Wolves replaced that one. One of them went for his ankle while the other aimed for his throat. He wouldn't last long with so many of them on him, and he wasn't strong enough to free himself. With his sword hand otherwise occupied, he couldn't even fight back.

Another Wolf latched onto his right wrist, and Calum's sword slipped from his fingers. Yet another mounted his chest and exhaled hot breath onto his face. It leaned in toward Calum's neck with its teeth bared.

RILEY COULD FEEL his life fading away, even as his jaws squeezed tighter around the Alpha's throat. Hot blood trickled down his sides, leaving him weak and dizzy.

The Werewolf's knees hit the ground, and Riley's back paws touched the earth. If he'd been stronger, he would've used the forest floor to help him jerk back and tear out the Werewolf's throat, but he barely had energy left to keep his jaws tight, so he just hung there, limp every-where except for his merciless jaws.

The Alpha had abandoned its attempts to gut him, and instead, its bloody hands now groped at Riley's throat. They latched onto his neck and began to tighten, and its talons threatened to pierce into him once again.

One of its hands released its grip on Riley and braced against the ground.

All Riley could do was hold on. He would die here, but in doing so, he would save his friends, just like they'd saved him time and time again.

He closed his eyes, and with the last of his strength, he bit down on the Werewolf's throat even harder.

CHAPTER 36

A howl split the night air and silenced the Wolves' snarls and growls. The Wolf chomping toward Calum's neck looked up, and the Wolves gnawing on his limbs released their grips and did the same. Between their legs, Calum saw a glowing form emerge from the woods.

Another Wolf, covered in blood.

A thin red light outlined the Wolf's lupine form as it approached. It walked on all fours at first, but three steps into the clearing it stopped, reared up on its hind legs, and started walking upright, just like Captain Brink had.

Its front paws elongated into clawed fingers, and its forelimbs shifted up and back with a loud snap, becoming arms. The muscles in the Wolf's forelimbs enlarged until they resembled shapes similar to those of a human's, only covered with fur.

The Wolf's leg muscles swelled like those in its arms. It hunched over at first, but it spread its hulking arms wide and straightened its back and neck in a chorus of loud pops and cracks.

A series of gouges and lacerations covered its torso and face. But as the creature stood there, the wounds sealed up as if the beast had never sustained them in the first place, leaving behind only the blood that streaked and matted its fur.

From its throat, another howl reverberated off the trees, this one deeper and more haunting. The glowing red outline around it faded. It was no longer a Wolf, but a Werewolf.

Its head rotated, and it looked at Calum and the others with a pair of familiar light-blue eyes.

Calum's voice rasped against his throat. "Riley?"

The Werewolf barked, and the Wolves rallied around him away from Calum and the rest of his group. He leveled his gaze at Calum and smirked. "Who else?"

Ten feet from Calum's spot on the ground, Axel sat up, gawking. "What in the name of the Overlord happened to you? Why aren't the Wolves attacking anymore?"

"I told you our hierarchies aren't based on bloodlines or lineages but on strength. Whoever's the strongest, whoever dominates the group, leads." Riley tilted his head and curled his new fingers. "I killed the Alpha Werewolf, so now *I'm* the Alpha Werewolf."

"But—how?" Axel asked.

"Wolves can transform by defeating a Werewolf in battle. I killed the Alpha who led this pack

—and managed not to die in the process—and now I lead them." Riley grinned. "In other words, they're with us now."

Calum and Axel stared at each other.

Lilly swooped over to him. "Are you hurt? You're covered in blood."

Riley shook his head. "The transformation process is like a rebirth. All my old wounds and injuries were healed, wiped out as if I had never sustained them in the first place.

"It was the same when I became a Sobek." Magnus stepped toward Riley and his Wolves, many of which growled at him. He nodded to Riley, who now stood only a foot and a half shorter than him, which meant Riley had surpassed both Calum and Axel in height as well.

Calum got up next and went over to him. A sense of pride filled his chest on behalf of his friend, who no longer had anything to fear from anyone. "You did it, Riley. You saved us all."

Riley's light-blue eyes fixed on Condor. "I know."

As the first ray of morning sunlight filtered through the forest, Axel stood near Magnus and Calum, watching as they tended to Kanton's wounds.

"I don't know what I'd do if I lost my right hand." Axel leaned over to stare at the bloody mess attached to Kanton's wrist, and he cringed. He'd seen worse—and done worse—to enemies, but for some reason, Kanton's wound unnerved him. "I'd be so unsure of myself in battle."

"He didn't lose it," Calum said. "A Wolf bit it."

"Chomped it, mangled it, more like." Kanton sucked in a sharp breath as Magnus fastened a bandage around his hand. He'd already applied a liberal portion of his new vial of Veromine to it, along with some other medicines from Kanton's pack. "In any case, for the time being, it's as good as lost."

"See?" Axel pointed at Kanton with his thumb.

Magnus snorted. "You are both overreacting. Your gauntlet sustained far more damage than your hand. These punctures are deep, but with the aid of the Veromine, you should regain full function of your hand in time."

Kanton sighed. "If you say so, Magnus. I've seen many a wound in my day, and I don't share your confidence."

Axel scoffed. "At least we felled the mangy beast that bit you."

A chorus of growls rose from the Wolves lounging behind Riley.

Axel turned and glared at them. "What? *You* attacked *us*."

Riley cleared his throat. "You're not helping, Axel."

"You're the one in charge." Axel gave him a dismissive wave. "So calm them down."

"Or I could sic them on you." As Riley said it, the thirty-plus Wolves that remained rose to their feet and snarled, primed to leap at Axel.

His eyes widened and his mouth hung open for a moment, then his expression hardened into a snarl of his own. This was the kind of treatment he got after apologizing? "That's not a good idea."

"That's what I thought." Riley barked, and the Wolves reverted back to their relaxed positions.

Axel sneered at him. "Whatever."

As much as he hated to admit it, the battle with the Wolves had shown him how ineffective he actually was when it came to fighting multiple quick opponents. But at least now that they were all on the same side, he'd have plenty of opportunities to practice fighting them.

"What happened to trying to keep a low profile when it came to traveling?" Axel muttered.

Riley must've heard him, because he replied, "The benefits of traveling with this pack far outweigh the drawbacks."

Of course Riley had heard him. It had been bad enough before, but now, as a Werewolf, Riley's senses had heightened even further. The only thing Riley couldn't hear was Axel's thoughts, and he wasn't even sure they were safe anymore.

"There." Magnus released Kanton's hand and stood to his full height. "Allow it time to rest and recover, and you will be healed in short order."

Kanton tried to grip his spear in his right hand. He winced and switched it to his left. "Guess that'll have to do for now. Afraid I may not be much good beyond what I can manage left-handed."

"We'll watch your back," Calum said, "and you can watch ours, too. And we can still rely on you if we get hurt."

Axel whacked Kanton's back. "Yeah. Like always."

Kanton grunted. "Thanks."

"I hate to interrupt," Condor said from behind them, "but the Arcanum is still weeks away. Now that Oren's dead, I suspect reinforcements aren't far behind. The lack of Blood Ore flowing from that Chasm won't be ignored for long."

"I agree. Condor's assessment does not even factor in the possibility of Vandorian following us. Now that day is upon us, we must go." Magnus picked up his pack and started walking.

THROUGHOUT THE COURSE of the next few weeks, Axel had never felt safer while traveling. With nearly three-dozen Wolves stalking their footsteps, plus a Werewolf, a Sobek, and two Wisps, he'd also never felt more obsolete.

Magnus had been all but invincible since he'd transformed into a Sobek, with the exceptions of when he'd fought other Sobeks. Falcroné and Condor were both trained soldiers—*leaders* of trained soldiers—which meant they ranked among the best the Sky Realm had to offer with regard to their fighting prowess and speed.

Even Riley, the scared "puppy" who had run away and hidden from the last handful of battles, had grown into a Werewolf bigger than Axel. Plus, he also led a pack of Wolves who would do anything he commanded them to do, including dying for him.

Besides being fast, Lilly could fly and shoot her arrows with phenomenal accuracy. Even Kanton, despite being an old man with an injured sword hand, still had the advantages of flight and speed over Axel, plus he knew some of the healing arts.

At this point, the only member of their party who didn't have anything amazing about him was Calum, yet somehow he still led the group and received dreams from Lumen, the ancient and mythical General of Light.

Axel exhaled a long sigh and unslung his pack as he walked at the back of the group. The morning sun shone above, and the forest had long since given way to rocky red terrain. Crimson peaks capped with snow loomed all around them, and according to Calum's map and Condor's direction, they should be reaching the Arcanum any time now.

He dug inside his pack and removed a piece of dried venison wrapped in a cloth, but before he could bite into it, a trio of Wolves rushed to his feet and whimpered.

"Noooo, no. Not a chance." He held it above his head so they couldn't reach it. "You all attacked me. This meat is mine."

"Come on, human," said a black Wolf with green eyes. "We're hungry, too."

"Yeah." A she-Wolf with yellow eyes and a silver coat pushed in front of the male that had just spoken. "You can spare a little bit for us, can't you?"

"I said *no*." Axel had thought Riley was annoying, but these three were pushing the very boundaries of the word. "Now get lost."

The Wolves who had spoken shot glares at him, then they bounded over a rocky crest, where they disappeared. Once Axel confirmed they had gone, he lowered the venison and took a bite.

A black blur darted in front of him and yanked the rest of the meat from his hands with its jaws.

"Hey!" Axel started to chase the Wolf, but another cut in front of him. He tumbled over its torso and hit the ground on his chest, but when he looked back, the Wolf who had tripped him was already gone. He slung a slew of curses at them and pushed himself up to his feet. "Bring that back!"

Lilly turned back with a grin on her face and shook her head. The sight of her pretty face both further frustrated Axel and brought him a much-needed distraction.

"What are you smiling at?" he grunted.

"Nothing. I'm just amused." She waited for him to catch up so she could walk next to him.

"They stole my snack."

Lilly shrugged. "They're natural thieves, Axel. It's what they do."

"That was my *last* piece of venison. Now it's gone."

"Is it really so life-altering?"

Axel rolled his eyes. He'd already resigned himself to knowing Lilly would never side with him again in anything less than a life-or-death situation, so he abandoned his complaint. "How far are we from the Arcanum?"

"Last I talked to Condor, he seemed to think we only had a few hours left of traveling, if not less. That was about an hour ago."

Ahead of them, Condor landed near Calum, and the whole party stopped once they caught up. Six of the Wolves formed a loose perimeter around Riley, and several more did the same thing around the group as a whole. Axel scoffed. Useful as they were, they were still dirty thieves, just like Riley had been before Calum spared his life back in Eastern Kanarah.

"It's just beyond that ridge," Condor said. "I didn't recognize it at first, but I'm almost certain that's the place. We're only five minutes away from the Arcanum, Calum."

A smile split Calum's lips, and he nodded. "Show me."

Axel raised an eyebrow and folded his arms. The moment of truth was near. Either they'd find out Calum had been right the whole time, or they'd realize it was all just a silly myth from Calum's loony brain and perpetuated by misinformation from everyone else who wanted to believe.

Whatever happened, Axel would be there to see it firsthand.

ANTICIPATION SWIRLED from Calum's stomach up into his chest as he approached the crest of the ridge. If Condor was right, then... well, he really didn't know what it meant, aside from being vindicated. It would prove his dreams really had come from Lumen and that he wasn't crazy after all.

When he reached the top of the ridge, all he saw was another ridge. Nothing struck him as out of the ordinary or unique about the landscape, and he didn't see anything that resembled the mouth of a cave anywhere ahead.

He turned to Condor. "Where is it?"

"I recognize that rock formation over there." He pointed to a weathered section of a rock that curved upward from its base. "One of my old mentors, General Regelle, showed it to me before he died. He swore me to secrecy and said I should never reveal its location except to the ruler of the Sky Realm. I figure Lilly's close enough."

Calum pulled the map from his pack and unfolded it. "I don't think this is where the map has it located."

"General Regelle said the maps were wrong," Condor explained. "Upon our return, he actually saw to it that they were never corrected so the Arcanum's true location would remain secret."

Calum frowned. He'd chosen to trust Condor, but this string of last-minute revelations unsettled him.

Condor held up his hands. "Hey, don't look at me. I'm just repeating what I was told. If it helps any, General Regelle was the most honorable person I've ever known. He wouldn't lie to me."

Lilly landed next to them, followed by Falcroné. "Is this the right spot?"

Calum shook his head and replaced the map in his pack. "I don't know."

"You said Lumen showed it to you in your dreams. What did it look like there?"

In his mind's eye, Calum recalled the image as Lumen had presented it in his dream.

Tall red mountains, some with snowy caps, sharpened under Kanarah's golden sun. The image panned down to the base of the mountains, swooped over several red snowcapped peaks, and lowered down into a valley set between two ridges. The picture ended at a wall of red rock. A concealed door set into the wall opened like the giant mouth of a crimson beast.

Calum opened his eyes and looked around. Despite the discrepancy between the map and General Regelle's account, he nodded. "This may be the place."

As he descended into the valley between the ridges, his heart rate quickened. After such a long journey, he may have finally reached the Arcanum. Now he just had to find out how to get inside.

The closer he got to it, the more the wall of red resembled the one in his dreams, and the more excitement flooded his veins. He took a few steps to his right, then he stopped. Backed up a step.

He pointed his hand toward the stone. It matched his memory perfectly. "There."

Condor, Falcroné, and Lilly landed next to him, and Magnus, Axel, Riley, Kanton, and the Wolves followed.

"Uh... you sure?" Axel asked from behind him. "I hate to break it to you, buddy, but that's a solid wall of rock."

It didn't matter what Axel said anymore. Calum had found the exact spot from in his dreams. Now he just had to prove it.

"This is it," he insisted. "I know it is."

"Mm. If you say so."

Axel's skeptical tone didn't deaden Calum's certainty.

"My only concern is how to open it," Calum said. "In my dream, it sort of just... did."

"And you are certain this is the exact spot?" Magnus stepped next to him.

"This is where General Regelle said it would be," Condor said. "The map was drawn to General Regelle's specifications, and only he and I knew the truth about it. Even Avian didn't know the map was wrong."

"Why wasn't he told?" Lilly asked, her eyebrows arched down.

Condor shrugged. "General Regelle trusted him about as much as I do."

Calum stepped toward the rock, his body centered in front of the spot from his dream. He waved his hand in front of it, but nothing happened.

"That's your plan? Just waving your hand in front of it?" Axel scoffed. "Good luck with that. I doubt it's gonna—"

CRACK.

A fissure split a section of the rock into two even sections. Red dust billowed from the rift, and hung in the air in front of the wall. The sound of heavy rocks scraping and grinding against each other echoed throughout the valley until the last of the red dust settled to the ground and the rocks fully separated.

A dark rectangle-shaped opening beckoned Calum to enter.

He turned back and stared at Axel with a grin and one eyebrow raised.

"Whatever." Axel folded his arms and rolled his eyes.

After almost an entire year of traveling, fighting, struggling, starving, and more fighting, they had made it.

They had found the Arcanum.

CHAPTER 37

Calum had always envisioned himself taking that first step into the Arcanum, regardless of who was with him at the time. This had been his quest, his journey. That monumental step was his to take before anyone else.

But even though Calum wanted to enter first, he yielded to Magnus's suggestion that Riley take the lead since he could see so well in the dark. That way, Magnus had reasoned, Riley could identify any booby traps or other perils potentially concealed within the cave's deep shadows. It made good sense, so Calum had agreed to it.

Magnus followed Riley in next, and then Calum went in third. Condor, Lilly, and Falcroné came next, and Axel brought up the rear while Kanton and the Wolves guarded the entrance. Riley had instructed them to obey to Kanton's orders should any trouble arise, and he also told them to behave themselves around the supplies the rest of the party had left behind.

The Arcanum plunged them into perfect darkness within a matter of a few sharp turns, so much so that Calum resorted to holding near the tip of Magnus's spiked tail as a guide while they walked. With each step they descended deeper into the mountain, farther into subterranean depths of unending dark.

The whole scenario reminded him of their time in the tunnels under Trader's Pass, of the Gronyxes they had defeated there, and of Nicolai, who had saved Calum once and then given his life to save them all.

Calum hadn't known Nicolai for long, and Nicolai had certainly done some terrible things before Calum added him to the group, but in the end he'd chosen a better path, one that ensured Calum and his friends could move on. With Lumen freed, his sacrifice—and those of everyone else in the group—would no longer be in vain.

"Stop." Riley's whisper bounced off the walls a half-dozen times.

Calum released his grip on Magnus's tail and felt his way up to Riley. "What is it?"

"The tunnel ends here," he replied. "We're about to walk into a cavern. I can't see how big it is, but it's huge and too dark, even for me to see. The darkness here is… different. Thicker, somehow. I can't explain why, but I won't be able to tell if there's danger ahead unless it's right in front of me."

"Strange that the 'General of Light' would have anything to do with a place this dark," Axel muttered from behind Calum.

"I'll go in first," Calum said, ignoring him. "I'm the one with the dreams that led us to this place. I'll go."

Magnus's heavy hand found Calum's shoulder before he could step forward. "Better not."

Calum turned to face Magnus, even though he couldn't see him. "We didn't come this far for me to get killed while on the cusp of learning how to set Lumen free. I have to do this."

Magnus sighed. "Do as you will. We're with you."

Calum exhaled a long breath and brushed his fingertips against the pommel of his sword as a reminder that it was there if he needed it. He calmed his bristling nerves and stepped past Riley into the darkness.

The sounds of his footsteps and his deep breathing accompanied his progress, but he neither heard nor saw anything else around him. His dreams with Lumen ended just after entering the Arcanum, so he had no idea what he was supposed to do now that he'd made it inside.

Nothing tugged at his chest, no instincts directed his movements, no ethereal light guided his steps. Instead, he wore a shroud of uncertainty.

Was he doing something wrong? Was he supposed to have brought something along with him? All Lumen had said was to go to the Arcanum. Did Calum need to sleep to have another dream?

Something twinkled above him, then it disappeared into the darkness. He stopped and stared up, but after a moment, he wasn't even sure he'd locked on to the right spot anymore. Maybe he'd imagined it in the first place.

Another light flickered, this time lower, and off to his left. He'd only caught it in the corner of his eye, but it looked as if a small tongue of fire had ignited then extinguished the next instant. Instead of the traditional yellow-orange color of fire, it had burned a vibrant blue. It returned a third time, off to his right, then it vanished again.

He stood there, motionless for a long time, just waiting to see what would happen, but nothing did. He still wasn't fully convinced that he'd actually seen the lights. Had any of the rest of his group seen them? He glanced back but saw only darkness.

With no better options, Calum took another step forward.

A column of blue fire burst from the floor in front of him and swirled upward. Calum staggered back and dropped to his rear-end as a dozen more fiery columns erupted all around him in a circle. Above him, the columns spiraled together into a single massive firestorm of blue flames.

Only then did Calum realize he was trapped in a cage made of blue fire.

The churning conflagration above him began to change shape. Parts of it separated, leaving black holes where the fire had once been. Other areas of the flames became shallower and more transparent, and the color of the fire paled to white, but the flames remained, nonetheless.

It didn't take Calum long to recognize the image of two eyes and a white armored mask that covered the face's mouth and nose.

It was an image of Lumen.

"Rise, Calum, son of Wilhelm," Lumen's voice boomed all around Calum, "you have proven yourself worthy, brave warrior. The location of my prison, the Hidden Abyss, is now made plain to you."

Calum pushed himself up to his feet and stared up at Lumen's face, his eyes wide and mouth open, but he didn't dare say a word. The blue fire around him continued to blaze, but it didn't cause him any harm.

"Behold the Tri-Lakes." The fire seemed to pulse with each syllable of Lumen's words. His face disappeared into the flames but gave way to an image of the Valley of the Tri-Lakes. The image closed in on the Central Lake then sharpened even more on the point where the lake bent at an angle and curved toward the north.

Calum knew that bend. He'd seen it on maps of the lake before.

"Deep within the waters you will find a submerged cavern."

The image plunged into the lake water adjacent to the bend. It dove down to an opening in the rocks that formed the lake's underwater perimeter, but the view did not venture inside the opening.

"The Hidden Abyss resides within that cavern. Access it and release me so that I may liberate Kanarah once and for all. One soul from each of Kanarah's four people groups must unite with that of yours; a Saurian, a Wolf, and a Windgale must accompany you in order to release me."

Lumen's face resurfaced in the flames.

"The portal ahead will take you to Trader's Pass, and then this place will close to the world forever. Time is short. Go, and know that I am with you, brave warrior."

Calum started to ask a question, but Lumen's face and the firestorm dissipated into nothing, and the columns of blue fire receded into the floor, all within a matter of seconds. The cavern plunged into darkness again as if it had never been illuminated in the first place, and silence enveloped the space.

A clawed hand gripped Calum's shoulder, and Riley's voice broke the quiet darkness. "You alright, Calum?"

"I—I'm fine." He turned back but still couldn't see Riley. "Did you see it?"

"I saw nothing except you falling backward. I came after you to make sure you were alright. What did you see?"

They hadn't seen it? They hadn't seen the towering blue flames or Lumen's face coming down and speaking to him? They hadn't heard Lumen's loud voice? How could they have missed it?

It didn't matter whether they'd seen it or not. Calum had, and he knew what they needed to do. "Not now. We need to—"

A shaft of golden light pierced through the shadows, and an opening across the cavern spread wide. The portal?

When Calum looked back, he saw Riley's lupine face aglow with golden light. "Tell me you see that, at least?"

Riley nodded. "That, I see."

"That's where we're going." Calum pointed at it. "Get your pack and everyone else. And hurry. We're going now."

PILLARS OF BLUE FLAMES? A firestorm that spoke and gave Calum instructions on how to free Lumen? A prison in a secret cave under one of the Tri-Lakes? A "portal?"

To Axel, it all sounded like vivid hallucinations. Had the Arcanum not opened on its own, and had that shaft of light at the far end of the cavern not started shining out of nowhere, Axel wouldn't have believed a single word out of Calum's mouth.

Even so, when the group reached the portal, Axel waved his hand. "There's no way I'm walking into that thing."

In place of an opening in the rocks, a glowing wall stretched ten feet high and half as wide. Shaped like a circle, it wavered as if wind rippled its surface, sort of like fire, but also like water.

Whatever it was, Axel wanted nothing to do with it.

Calum began, "Lumen said it would—"

"I don't care what Lumen said," Axel interrupted. "I said I'm not walking into that thing, and I meant it."

"Then get used to dark places with no food or water." Riley emerged from the shadows behind them, and Axel still had to marvel at his size increase since the fight with the Wolves. "After Kanton and the last of my Wolves entered the Arcanum, it shut on itself again. If this portal isn't the way out, we gotta find another one, because we can't get out that way."

"How many different ways do I have to say it?" Axel glared at Riley. "I'm. Not. Walking. Into. That. Thing."

"Good. Maybe we'll finally get rid of you." Riley folded his arms, but he didn't conceal the faint smirk curling the edge of his mouth.

Axel scoffed. "You're lucky to have me around, and you know it."

"Yes, Farm Boy," Condor said. "You're quite useful when it comes to obnoxious commentary."

"I'm going," Calum cut in before the conversation could devolve further. "Lumen said it will take us directly to Trader's Pass."

"How is that possible?" Lilly asked. "We're a month's travel away, at least."

"It is not possible," Magnus said. "But neither is solid rock supposed to open and close on its own, nor do shimmering portals appear out of nowhere. Calum has led us this far. I will not give up on him now."

"Maybe we should throw something into it. Test it out first?" Falcroné shrugged.

"Yeah," Axel said, "let's throw the Wolves who stole my last piece of venison in it. See what happens to them."

"No one's testing anything. Lumen said to go through it, so I'm going through it." Calum eyed Axel and Falcroné. "You don't want to go through it, then don't. Stay here if you like. Lumen said we need one Saurian, one Wolf, one Windgale, and one human to set him free. As long as we have who we need to free him, I'm satisfied."

Calum walked toward the wavering wall and stopped only inches away. He sucked in a deep breath, then he stepped into the golden light.

The portal warped as his body entered it, sending dramatic ripples throughout as if he were walking into a suspended pool of illuminated water. Calum's face and chest disappeared first, then his arms, shoulders, and finally the rest of his body.

Wherever he was, he wasn't inside the Arcanum anymore. The portal had at least succeeded in that, if nothing else. But Axel had no way of knowing that Calum wasn't dead, perhaps shredded into a million tiny pieces or segmented into seven big bloody chunks on the other end of that portal. It just wasn't worth the risk.

Without so much as another word, Magnus stepped into the portal after Calum. The last Axel saw of him was his tail, which snaked into the portal after him.

"I'm going too." Lilly started forward, but Falcroné grabbed her by her wrist.

"Princess—"

She pulled free from his grasp. "Don't you *dare* try to stop me, Fal. I thought I made it clear that—"

"*Lilly.*" Falcroné clamped his hands on her shoulders. "I was going to say you should let me go first. If I make it, I can ensure the area is safe for you in advance."

Lilly's frown and arched eyebrows relaxed, and a smile curled the corners of her mouth. She nodded. "By all means."

Falcroné stepped toward the portal, but Lilly clamped her hand on his wrist.

"Wait."

"Yes?"

She leaned forward and kissed his cheek. "I love you. Be safe."

The gesture twisted Axel's stomach, and he hoped all the more that Falcroné wouldn't make it on the other end.

Falcroné grinned at her. "I will. See you soon, one way or another."

He vanished into the portal, and Condor stepped up to Lilly next.

"Do I get a kiss, too?" He winked at her, then he darted into the portal before Lilly could respond, but she stood there with her mouth hanging open and a look of disdain on her face.

Axel grinned and started to say something, but she held up her hand.

"Don't even think about it." Lilly turned and entered the portal as well, followed by Kanton.

Only Axel, Riley, and the Wolves remained. "You wanna go first? It's gonna take awhile to get my whole pack through there."

Axel scowled at him and rolled his eyes.

Riley motioned toward the way they'd come in with a nod of his head. "I saw the entrance seal up with my own eyes, but if you want, I can leave a pair of Wolves with you to help you try to find a way out."

"No. Not interested." Axel waved his hand and shook his head.

Riley's generous offer had surprised him, but the idea of wandering around in the dark with two hungry Wolves didn't sit well with him. If, in fact, they were trapped inside, they'd soon be fighting each other over who would get eaten first.

"So you're going through, then?"

Axel sighed. He didn't want to, but... "Whatever."

He charged forward into the glowing waves.

Axel's body spiraled and rotated end-over-end in a tunnel made of rippling, waving water-fire, but the experience ended as quickly as it had begun. The next thing he knew he found himself skidding across a patch gray dirt on his chest. When he finally came to a stop, that same gray dirt caked the surface of his tongue and his teeth.

He dug a dollop of dirt out of his mouth and expelled the rest in half a dozen sputters, regretting that he'd kept his mouth open while jumping through.

Then his stomach lurched, and his sputtering became vomiting, and suddenly he no longer minded that the Wolves had stolen his last chomp of dried venison.

Two pairs of strong hands helped him to his feet once the last of his lunch cleared his stomach.

"Rough ride, Farm Boy?" Condor asked.

Axel moaned and wiped his mouth with the back of his left gauntlet. "I'm never doing that again."

Falcroné patted him on the back. "I doubt you'll have a chance. Look around."

The morning sun shone through the crystal blue skies above. In the distance, a large body of water shimmered against the dead gray terrain surrounding it.

Axel recognized his surroundings immediately—they were on Trader's Pass near where they had decided to head toward the lake to go fishing.

It was right where Calum had claimed the portal led. Axel couldn't deny it.

"Yeah. I guess you're right." Axel brushed the dirt from his chin and his breastplate and shot a glare at Calum. He'd been right, but so what? Axel had thrown up because of his stupid portal.

A howl sounded behind him, and Riley emerged out of nowhere—literally—followed by Wolf, after Wolf, after Wolf, until his entire pack appeared on Trader's Pack. They nipped at each other amid growls and snarls, but all of them fell silent with one sharp bark from Riley.

"See?" Axel pointed at the Wolves. "I'm not the only one who didn't like it."

"They're not reacting to the trip through the portal," Riley said. "They smell Dactyls. So do I. Probably only a few miles away, and getting closer."

"We need to get to Sharkville right away," Magnus said. "I do not care how many of us there are now. We still cannot risk running into them."

"Then let's go." Calum started north, toward the Central Lake.

To Calum's relief, they reached Sharkville in little more than half a day. The same dinky wooden sign, still stuck in the arid ground in front of the town, bore its name, and the dismal gray buildings still stood like weathered gravestones.

The Central Lake glimmered in the afternoon sun. The dock where they had boarded their chartered ship looked exactly the same, only this time each of its slots had a ship floating in it. Perhaps fishing season had hit the town, or perhaps it had recently come to an end. Either way, the lack of people in the empty streets indicated otherwise.

Calum smiled. People in the streets or not, they were there to free Lumen. Maybe even today, depending on how long it took them to reach the bend in the lake. All they had to do was find and charter a vessel to get them there.

A familiar weatherworn sign hanging from an equally familiar building caught Calum's eye. The sign bore the word "Fishig," which was scrawled next to an image of a fish caught in a net. Gill's place.

Calum started toward the door with Magnus and the others right behind him, but he stopped short when the door under the "Fishig" sign shattered. The body of a large man skidded to a halt about ten feet from Calum, followed by a double-sided battle-ax.

It was Gill.

Inside the door to Gill's place, a tall form materialized, and a pair of dark-green reptilian feet stepped out. As the form ducked under the doorframe and walked forward, its thick green fingers curled around the hilt of the sword that hung from a sheath on its belt, and sunlight glinted off its gold breastplate.

Vandorian.

CHAPTER 38

When Vandorian stepped out of Gill's place, Lilly's heart began to hammer in her chest. How had he found them? And how had he made it there before them?

Calum and Axel rushed over to Gill and helped him to his feet, battle-axe and all. He groaned, but they helped him get clear of Vandorian's path.

They leaned him up against the nearest building then dashed to Magnus's side with their swords drawn, and Kanton floated over to tend to the bloody gash in Gill's forehead.

"Magnusss." Vandorian elongated his pronunciation of Magnus's name with a long hiss. "Fancy meeting you here, of all places."

Magnus urged Calum aside and positioned himself between Vandorian and the rest of the group. "This is impossible. You should be at the Crimson Keep."

Vandorian tilted his head and smirked. "That would make sense, would it not? Unfortunately, your detour to murder Oren and burn down my fortress at the Blood Chasm cost you precious time—time that enabled me to get here first."

"You could not have known where we were headed," Magnus growled.

Vandorian dismissed Magnus's objection with a wave. "It was not difficult to ascertain your destination after a few short conversations with the Sky Realm's Premier. He hesitated to disclose much at first, but in the end he proved quite helpful after a bit of—" Vandorian's golden eyes fixed on Lilly. "—*persuasion*."

"What have you done?" Like lightning, Lilly drew an arrow, nocked it in her bow, and took aim at Vandorian's left eye, but she didn't release. If he had hurt her father, she would finish him off just like Condor had killed Oren, and she would regret it even less.

"You have nothing to fear, Princess. Your father still draws breath, and the Sky Fortress still stands—for now." Vandorian bared his pointed teeth at her. "Though I cannot guarantee their state of being will remain so for long."

She drew the arrow and her bowstring back and homed in on Vandorian's face. The shot was difficult enough because of the relatively small size of his eyes. Worse yet, if he moved his head even an inch, she could miss him entirely. Still, it was worth—

Magnus's big hand blocked her line of sight. "Do not attack him. He is my adversary, and you would only be wasting your arrows anyway."

Lilly fumed, but she nodded and relaxed the tension in her bowstring. She still kept the arrow nocked, though, just in case.

"That still does not explain how you knew to come *here* instead of the Arcanum," Magnus said.

"Right you are, brother." Vandorian sauntered toward him. "But consider the reason you went to the Arcanum in the first place. You needed to find the location of the Hidden Abyss. Do you really believe that in all of Kanarah, *no one* would know where it was without first finding the Arcanum?"

Magnus's mouth hung open as a revelation dawned in his golden eyes. "Father told you before he died."

"Aside from the King and his generals, he was the only other soul old enough to have witnessed Lumen's defeat and his descent into the Hidden Abyss. Father divulged that final secret just before Kahn crushed his head."

A violent yet brief shudder racked Magnus's huge body. Throughout all their time together, in spite of all the perils they'd encountered, Lilly had never seen him do anything of the sort. The sight made her want to shudder as well.

"The moment Avian told me of your plans, I headed straight here." Vandorian smiled again. "And now here I am, ready to finish what I began so many years ago."

Magnus drew his broadsword from its sheath. "Then come forward. My blade will taste your flesh this day, brother."

Vandorian grinned, then he cocked his head back and unleashed a roar that seemed to shake the ground itself.

Behind him, the wall that housed the doorframe to Gill's place burst into pieces, and four Sobeks in black armor stormed out. Across the street, the same thing happened from within another building, and then more Sobeks broke through the walls of a third not far from that one.

The Sobeks lined up around Vandorian, twelve in all, not including him. When they stalked forward, accompanied by an air of absolute confidence, Magnus backed up, and so did the rest of the group.

At the sight of Magnus's recoil, Vandorian laughed. "Do not tell me that the mighty Magnus is afraid? Surely you did not expect us to engage in this battle on equal footing?"

"If you had any honor, you would face me yourself in single combat," Magnus countered.

"It is not a question of honor, but of power. We have it all, and you have none," Vandorian replied. "Where power reigns, honor dies."

Vandorian and the Sobeks' approach continued, slow and methodical.

"We cannot withstand them," Magnus said aloud as he stepped back, his sword still ready. "Had it just been Vandorian and a few others, I would have said to fight, but against so many, we stand no chance."

"We're already here." Calum raised his sword higher. "We wouldn't have made it this far if we weren't supposed to free Lumen."

"No, Calum. Now is not the time. We need to flee." Magnus shot a glare at him.

"Though I hate to walk away from a battle, Magnus is right," Axel grumbled. "We'll all die if we fight these lizards. You weren't around when we had to fight Oren, and he was just *one* Sobek. Even with Riley's Wolves, thirteen is a death sentence."

"I know it seems like that," Calum said. "But there has to be a solution. We didn't come this far just to die on the verge of freeing Lumen."

A solution. Lilly's mind raced through the possibilities. There was a solution indeed—a risky one, but a solution nonetheless.

Lilly tucked her arrow back into her quiver, slung her bow over her back, and smacked the shoulders of Condor and Falcroné. "Come with me."

"What? Where are you going?" Axel's eyes widened.

"Just hold them off for a few minutes." She sprang into the sky amid protests from Axel and Calum, with even more coming from Falcroné as she soared in the opposite direction they had traveled, back south toward Trader's Pass.

Falcroné caught up to her in the air as she zipped along. "What are we doing? They need our help back there."

"You'll see. Just get ready to fly with all the speed you can muster when the time comes." Lilly pushed ahead of him, only to watch Condor cruise past her with a smirk and a wink.

Oh, how she loved to hate him.

Perhaps Lilly had a plan that could actually help them. Whether or not that was the case, Magnus resolved to give her as much time as he could.

"Riley, tell your Wolves to spread out and encircle the Sobeks." Magnus motioned to him with his free hand. "But urge them to use caution. These are the twelve members of Vandorian's personal guard, and all are formidable foes."

"Done." Riley howled, and the thirty Wolves darted away from the main group. They formed a perimeter around the Sobeks, who hissed at them and turned to face them.

"I see Father's tactical training still serves you well, brother." Vandorian smirked. "But thirty Wolves plus the few friends who have not yet deserted you cannot hope to overcome us."

Magnus squinted at him. Even if he had no other weaknesses, Vandorian was overconfident. Perhaps Magnus could somehow exploit that to his benefit.

"But I will offer you a bargain." Vandorian pointed his sword, its blade also blue Blood Ore like Magnus's, at Magnus's chest. "If you surrender now, I will spare your friends. I will not even deign to harm them. I will allow them to go free, and I will grant them a whole day to flee my presence."

Magnus glanced down at Calum. For the sake of his friends, he couldn't pass up that kind of deal. "You need to go, now. Take Axel and the others with you. This fate is mine, not yours."

Calum shook his head. "Not a chance. We're friends. If you die, I die, too. There's no way around that. And we need you to help us free Lumen anyway."

"Frankly, I'm sick of taking orders from both of you," Axel piped in. "At this point I'd rather die than continue to deal with your rudeness and constant disregard for my ideas. I'm not going anywhere."

Magnus snorted. Of course he wasn't.

Kanton left Gill leaning against the side of a building, retrieved his spear, and aimed its tip at the approaching Sobeks. His right hand had healed enough that he could use it again, just as Magnus had promised. "I'm with you, too."

Magnus looked at Riley, who shrugged.

"Hey, I *just* became a Werewolf," he said. "Supposedly my teeth and claws can penetrate Sobek scales. I'm dying to try them out, see what I can do. Well, hopefully *not* dying, but you know what I mean. Either way, I'm in, and my pack's in, too."

Magnus sighed. "Try not to fight them one-on-one, any of you, and especially avoid Vandorian. He is by far the most dangerous, and—"

"And you wanna kill him yourself." Axel rolled his eyes. "Yeah. We know, Scales."

Magnus couldn't help but smirk. "Exactly. Let's go."

This time, instead of backing up farther, they held their ground as the Sobeks approached.

AT FIRST, Lilly didn't know if she'd seen a bird flying through the air ahead of them or something else, but the nearer she drew to it, the more its image sharpened, and the fouler the air smelled around her. It noticed her and started toward them, along with two others just like it.

They each had expansive wings like a bird's, though they more resembled a bat's, plus four spindly limbs and bodies not unlike a Windgale's, all covered in pale-green skin. Huge charcoal-gray beaks protruded in place of their mouths, and talons tipped each of their three toes, their three long fingers, and thumbs on each hand, with one more on the tip of each of their tails.

Dactyls.

They screeched dissonance and swirled toward Lilly, Condor, and Falcroné.

Their beaks and talons can pierce Saurian skin and most armor. Only dragon scales and exceptionally rare types of metal can withstand their attacks, Magnus had said. *Their blood gives off a pheromone that attracts other Dactyls.*

Time to attract some Dactyls.

Lilly drew her sword. The lead Dactyl lurched toward her, and she severed its head from its body. Glowing purple blood sprayed into the sky from its neck, and the monster's wretched stench intensified.

Next to her, Condor jammed his sword into the second Dactyl's chest, and Falcroné cleaved the third clean in half with one vicious hack. Purple blood spattered all over his face, arms, and breastplate, and he sputtered.

"This is disgusting." Falcroné wiped the blood from his eyes. "You brought us out here to kill three of these things? How is that supposed to help the rest of the group?"

Lilly scanned the horizon to the south for a moment. "Dactyls can smell their dead from miles away. These three functioned like scouts. I figured that we could try to—"

She stopped at the sight of a solitary winged form rising from the horizon. It started toward them. Then another followed. Then another. Soon dozens of them ascended into the sky, until hundreds of dark forms swarmed toward them.

Falcroné's eyebrows raised. "Oh."

"Brilliant." Condor gave Lilly a smile that accelerated her heartbeat. Or perhaps it was the army of Dactyls she'd summoned instead.

The Dactyls were approaching fast. Really fast.

"We have to lead them back to Sharkville," Lilly said. "Fal, they'll come after you first since you're covered with their blood. Be careful."

Without another word, she zoomed north with her captains right behind her and the Dactyls right behind them.

CALUM ROLLED under the Sobek's swing and hacked at its leg, but his sword just clanged off its ankle. The Sobek's other foot slammed into Calum's chest, and he soared across the street into the wall near where Kanton had tended to Gill.

The impact almost knocked him senseless. When his vision finally righted itself, Calum refocused on the fight in front of him.

If his sword couldn't even penetrate the Sobeks' skin, how was he supposed to kill any of them? Had Lilly not taken Condor and Falcroné with her, perhaps they could've found a way to sever the straps that held the Sobeks' armor in place and thus expose their vulnerable underbellies, but she'd gone. What chance did they have now?

The Sobek who'd kicked Calum whirled around and felled one of the Wolves with his sword while another Wolf gnawed on the same ankle Calum had just struck.

Beyond them, Riley wove between several of the Sobeks and slashed them with his claws. He even managed to clamp his teeth onto one of the Sobeks' throats, but he caught a stunning punch to his ribs that dislodged him before he could finish the Sobek off.

Axel and Magnus worked in tandem, a far better team than either of them would ever admit, and Kanton darted over to Calum.

"Are you alright?" He extended his left hand.

Calum nodded. He had to find a way to win against these guys. And on top of that, Magnus had to survive the battle. Lumen's release depended on unifying one soul from each of the four races to set him free. Without Magnus, it wouldn't work.

Calum grabbed Kanton's hand and pulled himself up to his feet.

Kanton blinked at him, then stared over his shoulder. "Where's Gill?"

Calum stole a quick glance at the wall he'd just been leaning against. "I have no idea. Didn't you leave him right there?"

Kanton nodded. "He looked really out of it when I left him."

A loud slam sounded down the street, but no one still in the battle turned to look amid the cacophony of swordplay, roars, and barks. Calum craned his head in time to see Gill storm out of another gray building, his battle-axe in hand.

At his side, a wiry young man about Calum's age led a small army of humans and Windgales armed with spears, harpoons, and swords toward the fracas. Calum blinked.

It was Jake, the fisherman. Puolo's son.

So much for Sharkville being deserted.

Gill, Jake, and dozens of fishermen charged into the fight, and Calum did likewise. Maybe they had a chance after all.

LILLY FLEW AS FAST as she could, but somehow the Dactyls had caught up with her. It hardly seemed possible, even with Condor and Falcroné flying at her side, but they'd done it.

One of them clamped its long fingers around her ankle—its fourth attempt after three near-misses—and tried to pull her back, but a quick lash from her sword split its head wide open, and it dropped from the sky. Three more Dactyls took its place.

Lilly couldn't hope to fight them all, even with Condor and Falcroné's prowess at her disposal. Out-maneuvering them was her only hope.

She twisted and spun through the air, changing her altitude at unpredictable moments to throw the Dactyls off. Normally she enjoyed this kind of tense chase, but the pervading hunger and evil emanated by the Dactyls erased any semblance of joy from her evasions.

"This was not—" Falcroné looped underneath her then reappeared on her opposite side. "—a good idea."

Condor felled two Dactyls from the air and then joined them. "What are you complaining about? At least you still have armor to wear."

"You'd still have your armor if you hadn't—"

"Rebelled?" Condor finished for him. "Far too late for that now."

"I see Sharkville." Lilly pointed at a smattering of gray buildings in the distance. They looked more like tiny children's toys from so high up. "Come on."

They spiraled down toward it with the Dactyls still in close pursuit.

MAGNUS PARRIED Vandorian's first several blows with ease, but he could tell his brother wasn't engaging him with the full extent of his ability. He threw a ferocious counterattack that could have felled a Gronyx, but Vandorian deflected it as if Magnus were only a child swinging a stick.

"You never ranked among the stronger of our siblings." Vandorian shoved Magnus backward. "It baffles me that you survived when all of them perished that day."

Magnus ducked under the next swipe and lashed his broadsword at Vandorian's chest. His blade connected with Vandorian's breastplate and clanged off, but the impact forced Vandorian back a step to maintain his footing.

He smirked at Magnus. "Perhaps I was wrong. Even so, not even Blood Ore can penetrate this breastplate. If you wish to kill me, you will have to cut off my head."

From the side, one of the other Sobeks whipped his blade at Magnus's head as if Vandorian's taunt had commanded it.

In response, Magnus batted the blade away and slammed his tail into the Sobek's knees.

Vandorian raised his sword for another swing, capitalizing on Magnus's distraction and the newfound opening his Sobek guard had created.

But Magnus wasn't distracted.

As the Sobek pitched to the side, off-balance, Magnus adjusted his angle and drove his shoulder into the Sobek. He careened toward Vandorian, who had already initiated his attack. His sword cleaved deep into the Sobek's torso, and he fell under Vandorian's blade, dead.

Now it was Magnus's turn to smirk while Vandorian's countenance darkened.

WHEN AXEL SAW GILL, Jake, and almost a hundred men storm into the battle, he had to grin.

Gill might not have been able to draw or spell the word "fishing" on his sign, but he sure knew how to use his battle-axe. He plowed into the nearest Sobek with his full weight and swung his battle-axe with abandon, shouting something about the Saurians owing him coin for trashing the perfectly good wall of his shanty.

When Axel saw Lilly, Falcroné, and Condor dropping out of the sky at them with a few hundred Dactyls behind them, his grin evaporated, and his heart stuttered in his chest. *That* was her idea of helping?

May the Overlord have mercy on us all.

CHAPTER 39

Calum had just threaded through the skirmish to Jake when dozens of pale-green bodies pelted them from the sky. When Calum finally looked up, a dark gray beak set under a pair of glowing white eyes rushed toward his face.

He reacted and sliced at the thing with his sword, which clanged against its beak. A follow-up hack spilled the Dactyl's intestines from its belly, and it dropped to the ground, screeching and writhing.

What in the—

A man screamed next to him.

Jake.

In two slices, Calum cut down the two Dactyls on top of Jake and pulled him to his feet. Both of them were covered in glowing purple blood that reeked of death and refuse.

"Thanks." Jake shifted his harpoon in his hand. "Where in the depths did they come from?"

In the distance behind Jake, Lilly fired off arrow after arrow while Condor and Falcroné covered her. Calum exhaled a sharp breath. "I think I know where, but that's not important right now. What are you doing here?"

"Gill told us you guys were gettin' ambushed, so my men and I came to help."

"*Your* men?"

He nodded. "Like I said when we parted ways a few months ago, I headed to Kanarah City, met up with my dad's friends, and got a few ships out here. Turns out he had a lot of friends."

"Apparently." Calum smiled. "Jake, we need a favor."

Jake shoved Calum aside and skewered another Dactyl with his harpoon. Calum's sword severed its head from its body. Jake nodded. "Anythin'. Name it."

"We need you to take us to the bend in the Central Lake right away."

"You got it. I'll have my crew ready a ship for departure."

Calum chopped the wing off a Dactyl as it flew by them, and it spiraled into one of the Sobeks and smacked into the street. The Sobek turned back and stomped its head to goo.

"Thanks," Calum said. "We'll meet you over there soon."

A SURPRISE KICK from Vandorian knocked Magnus onto his back. Vandorian would have finished Magnus off were it not for the flurry of pale-green flesh that smacked into him and knocked him off-balance. Magnus looked up.

Dactyls. Hundreds of the winged monsters cascaded toward them.

If this was Lilly's idea of saving everyone—well, Magnus appreciated the thought, but she'd definitely underestimated the consequences of this decision.

A pair of Dactyls dropped down onto Magnus and dug their talons into the scales on his legs. Pain spiked through his thighs, and he cut both Dactyls in half with one furious swing of his sword.

He scrambled to his feet in time to see Vandorian's sword tear through another Dactyl, then it reset and crashed down toward Magnus next. He barely got his sword up in time to fend off the strike, which rattled his sword and stung his right hand. Vandorian's follow-up swing glanced off Magnus's breastplate and carved a long scratch in its wake.

Amid the chaos of hundreds of carnivorous monsters descending on Sharkville, Magnus righted his sword and stared into Vandorian's eyes, but something behind him stole Magnus's attention.

One of the Sobeks fell to the ground, covered with Dactyls. They jammed their gray beaks into his flesh and tore at him with their talons as he flailed, but he couldn't shake them. Eventually he just stopped moving, and the Dactyls craked his bones open to get at the marrow inside.

That would *not* happen to Magnus.

Vandorian flung himself forward and slashed at Magnus, and the brothers traded vicious blows once again.

IT DIDN'T TAKE LONG for the Dactyls to overwhelm the battle. Soon enough, Axel and his friends, the fishermen, and the Wolves no longer fought the Sobeks but instead focused on killing the invading Dactyls.

The Sobeks' focus also shifted. The remaining seven of Vandorian's original twelve guards rallied together in a tight circle and fended off Dactyls by the dozen, whereas the Wolves and Windgale fishermen darted throughout Sharkville's otherwise bland streets and airspace while engaging the rest.

Glowing purple blood streaked the buildings, the streets, and the town's occupants who'd taken up arms against their enemies, but Axel could hardly call it an improvement. The purple certainly added color to the gray town, but the horrible stink accompanying it threatened to overpower every other one of Axel's senses.

Axel and Kanton had joined up with Lilly, Condor, and Falcroné, all of whom fought as a team against the Dactyl swarm. Where Condor seemed to almost enjoy the back-and-forth with the Dactyls, Falcroné's face showed nothing but sheer determination and fury.

Lilly fired arrows when she could, relying on the rest of the group to protect her from stray Dactyls. Axel happily obliged, but he didn't enjoy having to fight next to Kanton. With his right hand healed but hardly fully restored, what little fighting prowess Kanton possessed had dwindled to almost nothing.

So far, by Axel's count, Kanton hadn't killed any Dactyls. He'd only managed to wound a few before another of the group finished them off. What's more, he'd been attacked and overwhelmed almost a half dozen times until Axel or Falcroné, who occupied the spot on the other side of Kanton, saved him.

Every time they came at him, Kanton ended up with more cuts on his face and more scratches on his armor. If they didn't find a way out of this mess soon, Axel had to assume Kanton wouldn't make it. And if Kanton went down, who would guard Axel's left side?

RILEY'S CLAWS dripped with a foul mixture of dark red and glowing purple blood.

His ears prickled with the sounds of battle—swords severing Dactyl limbs, shouts and screams, blood spattering on the ground, talons scraping against armor—but the smells were worse. Dactyl blood smelled even more wretched than their skin, and with so much of both scents so close nearby, Riley wanted to tear his own nose off.

The fishermen stank of fish, and the Wolves reeked of their own unique scents, but the Sobeks cast a very different scent, one surprisingly cleaner than he'd expected. In a brawl of this size, he could pick out the rare clean scents even easier amid the onslaught of grotesque smells.

Yet despite the mass assault on his nose, Riley couldn't deny how well the Dactyls' presence had worked in his favor. The Sobeks were so distracted by battling the Dactyls that they didn't see him coming. Then again, as a Werewolf now, he could move so fast that it didn't really matter anyway.

He leaped at the one farthest from the group and tackled him to the ground. He could have fastened his teeth around the Sobek's exposed neck or cut his scaled face into ribbons with his claws, but he didn't. Instead, he recovered his footing and darted away in time to avoid the half dozen Dactyls that landed on the Sobek and did the rest of the work for him.

He smiled, then he ducked between two low-swooping Dactyls. Ahead, a trio of human fishermen grappled with four Dactyls, and they weren't faring well. Not now, at least. He charged toward them and—

Something tripped him. Riley dropped to the ground face-first, and dirt caked on his snout and the fur under his chin. A dark green tail snaked out of his periphery, and he rolled over to find a Sobek towering over him. It bore teeth marks on his throat—Riley had tried to kill him at the beginning of the fight.

"Finally caught up to you, you filthy *dog*," the Sobek snarled.

He raised his sword to deliver the killing blow, but a blood-streaked blur zipped by, and a deep gash opened on the Sobek's neck, right between Riley's bite marks. Were Riley not a Werewolf now, his vision might not have been able to discern what had happened.

The Sobek convulsed once then dropped to the ground on his side, his eyes wide with shock and surprise. He clutched his bleeding throat and trembled.

Riley sprang to his feet and glared at Condor, his savior.

"Can we be friends now?" Condor asked.

Riley touched the spot on his side where Condor had stabbed him. The injury was long gone, totally erased during the process of becoming a Werewolf, but Riley remembered the pain all too well.

He wasn't ready to forgive Condor just yet. "Maybe next time."

"Fair enough." Condor raised an eyebrow at him then shot into the sky, leaving Riley alone with the dead Sobek.

Riley spun around and hurled himself at the Dactyls attacking the fishermen.

ABOARD HIS SHIP, Jake thrust his harpoon into the air and waved it around his head in a large arc.

Calum saw its blade glistening in the sunlight. He turned back toward the fracas, located Axel, Lilly, and the others, and then charged toward them with abandon. Jake was going to get them all out of there and get them to Lumen, but Calum had to round everyone up, first.

By now, more than half of the Dactyls littered the ground, most of them in pieces, but many still haunted the skies around Sharkville and dove down at their prey with their talons bared and beaks spread wide. If Calum and his companions didn't get out of there soon, there was no telling what might happen.

He whacked a Dactyl from the sky with the flat of his blade as he ran, then he ducked under another one but barely cleared it. Its talons scraped against the armor on his back, and Calum resolved to duck a little lower next time.

By the time he reached his companions, half of them had already noticed him.

"Come with me!" He pointed toward Jake's ship. "We can get away from here and free Lumen!"

No one hesitated. The Windgales all took to the sky and wove through the encroaching Dactyls with ease while Calum and Axel bounded over the corpses of Dactyls, Wolves, fishermen, and the occasional Sobek toward Jake's ship.

He still needed Magnus and Riley. Calum scanned the battle. To his right, a tall Wolf-shaped form thrashed four Dactyls that were attacking some humans.

To his left, in the distance, Magnus and Vandorian still clashed blades. Pulling Magnus away from that confrontation would be all but impossible.

MAGNUS PARRIED EVERY ATTACK, but Vandorian moved too quickly and was too strong. Every time Magnus thought he'd found a way to exploit one of Vandorian's mistakes, his efforts backfired, and Vandorian punished him for it.

Even so, he'd held his own against his older brother this long. Perhaps if he could endure a few minutes longer—

Vandorian's elbow smacked into the side of Magnus's snout, and the impact twisted Magnus's whole body. The blow itself hurt, but worse than that, Magnus knew he was exposed, and he couldn't do anything about it.

Fire seared through his right forearm from the surface, through his flesh and bone, and then out the other side again. The weight of his sword dropped away, and he staggered back a few steps.

When Magnus recovered his composure, he stared down at his sword. How would he retrieve it with Vandorian now standing over it?

A growing pool of red under the hilt seized his attention.

His hand still gripped the sword, but it was no longer attached to his arm.

CHAPTER 40

Calum saw it happen, but he didn't believe his eyes. In one horrifying instant, Vandorian had severed Magnus's hand from his forearm. The fight was over.

He whirled around and hollered for Riley, who sped toward him at an incredible rate then ran past with a howl when he noticed Calum's finger extended toward Magnus. Not far behind, the remaining ten or so Wolves who had survived thus far bounded after him.

"Get to the ship," Riley called back at him. "I'll get Magnus."

Calum wrenched his anchored feet from the ground and bolted toward the ship.

A ROAR SWELLED in Magnus's chest and erupted from his throat as he clutched the bleeding stump where his right hand had been.

"I have to *hand* it to you, Magnus," Vandorian said between disdainful chuckles. "You fought well—mostly."

Magnus stood there stunned until Vandorian leveled him with his tail.

"You were always a disgrace." Vandorian stood over him, sneering. "Always the weakest of my siblings, never an especially talented fighter. Intelligent, but ill-equipped to do anything with your breadth of knowledge. Twenty-first in line for our father's throne. It amuses me that you, of all my siblings, would survive so long, only to die here in the middle of nowhere."

Somehow Magnus mustered the clarity and fortitude to speak. "Kill me if you wish, Vandorian. If you do not, I will never stop coming for you. Ever."

Vandorian smirked, and his golden eyes fixed on the pouch that hung from Magnus's belt. "That reminds me. You have something very precious in your possession. Something I need if I am to succeed our uncle as ruler of Reptilius someday. I suppose I owe you for finding it and using it to become a Sobek. Had you not, it would have been useless to me."

All Magnus could do was watch as Vandorian reached for the pouch and pulled the Dragon Emerald from it. Pain ravaged his right arm.

"Such a small thing, but so powerful, so important." Vandorian rotated the dark-green stone in his hand and grinned. "And now it is all mine."

About a hundred feet above Vandorian's head, four Dactyls spiraled down toward them. Magnus diverted his gaze from them the instant Vandorian's focus returned to him.

"I will give your regards to our uncle." Vandorian bared his sharp teeth in a smile.

The Dactyls dropped toward them, and Magnus shifted his tail so it lay between Vandorian's feet.

Vandorian raised his sword in his right hand, still holding the Dragon Emerald in his left. "Goodbye, little brother."

The Dactyls smacked into Vandorian from above and clawed at him, and one clamped onto his left shoulder.

A howl split the air, then several more.

Magnus's tail hooked Vandorian's left ankle and yanked, and Vandorian toppled down onto his back.

A mass of dark fur appeared in Vandorian's place. It reached down and grabbed Magnus by his good arm and hauled him to his feet.

Riley.

Vandorian roared and thrashed at the Dactyls, but their attacks persisted. Amid the confusion, one of the Wolves leaped and clamped his jaws around the Dragon Emerald, then the Wolf wrenched it from Vandorian's hand.

"Come on," Riley said. "We've got a ship. We're going to Lumen."

"Until next time, brother. Do not forget to give my regards to Uncle Kahn." Magnus bent down, scooped up his broadsword with his left hand, and followed Riley away from Vandorian.

"That's everyone," Calum said to Jake as the last of the surviving Wolves scampered aboard the ship. Somehow the core of their group had all made it. Good. "Cast off before the Dactyls realize we're abandoning the fight."

Jake gave the order, and the ship eased away from the dock thanks to the two-dozen men diligently rowing from the lower deck.

Magnus moaned and growled and slumped down against a large barrel on the ship's deck. Calum had never seen Magnus in such a state, and he wished he could do more for his friend, but Magnus hardly wanted anyone near him.

When Kanton hovered over to him with a clean white cloth in his hands, Magnus held up his left hand. "Do not bind it with anything. Whatever you do, never bind this sort of wound on a Saurian."

Kanton blinked. "You'll bleed out. He's severed major arteries in your arm, and—"

"Do *not* bind it, Kanton. Do not even touch it." Magnus stared steel at him, and Kanton backed away.

Calum started toward him. "Magnus, you're gonna—"

"I will be fine. Just leave me in peace." He clutched his bleeding stump of an arm with his fingers and growled again. "Where is my Dragon Emerald? One of the Wolves picked it up."

"Dallahan, turn it over," Riley said.

A light-gray Wolf with white accents in his fur and blue eyes a shade darker than Riley's trotted forward and dropped the Dragon Emerald on Magnus's lap with a whimper.

"Thank you." Magnus exhaled a contented breath and tucked the Dragon Emerald back into the pouch at his belt. "I am indebted to you, friend."

Dallahan squinted at him and growled. "You're not kidding. That thing's gotta be worth a fortune."

Axel huffed. "That's what *I* said."

"How long until we reach the bend in the lake?" Lilly asked. Streaks of purple blood on her face and armor gave off a light glow, but sitting next to Falcroné, she looked clean by comparison.

"We're a day away, at least, and that's if the men row the whole time. I'd count on a day and a half before we make it there." Jake, also streaked with Dactyl blood, grinned at them. "Take a rest, why don't you? Heal up. There's plenty of room aboard the ship for you to stretch your legs, get a little shut-eye, perhaps. We'll let you know when we're getting' close."

Calum stretched his sore limbs. Enough fighting, already. At this point, he just wanted to free Lumen and be done with it. He stared back at Sharkville, over which a few dozen Dactyls still swarmed, then he closed his eyes.

They were almost there.

VANDORIAN BATTED three of the Dactyls away with his sword. The fourth gnawed on his shoulder until he dropped his sword, took hold of the monster, ripped it in half with his bare hands, and hurled it to the ground. Even then, its beak still stuck in Vandorian's flesh, so he yanked that off too and tossed it aside.

He retrieved his sword and felled six more of them, then he reunited with the five Sobeks who's survived the fracas. The rest of the fishermen had scattered. The Windgales among them had taken to the sky, and the others had boarded the rest of the ships and set off onto the lake after the lead ship, the one his brother had boarded, free from Vandorian's grasp.

Free for now, anyway.

With only a few dozen Dactyls left, most of them had either found carcasses to feed on or still circled high above the town. They likely wouldn't attack anymore, not with so few of them left and so much meat on the ground just waiting to be consumed.

"You." Vandorian tapped the shoulder of one of the remaining Sobeks, the one with the fewest number of scratches and claw marks on his head. "Swim after the nearest ship. Kill all who are on board and bring the ship back to shore."

The Sobek blinked, then he glanced at the other Sobeks. "But... Prince Vandorian... I—"

Vandorian grabbed the Sobek by his throat and threw him to the ground. "Go, or I will kill you right here."

The Sobek scrambled to his feet, lumbered down to the docks, and jumped into the water with his black breastplate still secured to his chest.

"What do we do now, my prince?" another Sobek asked.

"We wait." Vandorian watched the Sobek swim after the ship. "If our comrade succeeds in bringing back that ship, we go after my brother and his friends."

A huge black mass broke the surface of the water and slammed down on the Sobek teeth-first. He thrashed for a moment then disappeared under a swell of red that tainted the water.

Vandorian hissed. It was as he'd suspected, but he couldn't have left this place behind until he was certain he had no other options.

"We will return to the Reptilius," he declared. "Kahn must know of what has transpired here. I suspect he will demand a reckoning for the wrongs committed against our people this day. Gather what supplies you can for the journey home. We leave in ten minutes."

"Yes, my prince." The Sobeks smacked their breastplates with their knuckles and dispersed.

Vandorian stared at the lead ship, now far in the distance. *You were right, Magnus. This is far from over.*

AFTER SEARCHING ALMOST the entire ship—twice—Lilly finally found Falcroné in the crow's nest, of all places. She landed and shifted a coil of thick rope aside so she could sit beside him.

Like him, she let her legs hang off the edge of the platform and stared out across the lake. Stars glimmered in the night sky, and their reflections danced along the water's surface.

"What are you doing up here?" she asked.

Falcroné shrugged and didn't make eye contact with her. Instead, he stared into the starry night sky. "Just watching. After you returned home and told me of the Jyrak, I've been uneasy about venturing out onto this lake."

"It was horrible. Axel and I both almost died. He would have for sure had I not—"

"I know, Lilly. You told me already."

She bit her lip. Was he actually upset with her about having saved Axel? "What's wrong, Fal?"

"Nothing."

"Then why won't you look at me?"

He turned his head and stared right into her eyes, but it wasn't out of love. Instead, he'd donned fearless eyes, the kind only hardened soldiers knew how to employ. "Better?"

She squinted at him and exhaled a silent sigh. "No. It's not."

Falcroné looked away again. "Then I don't know what you want from me."

Lilly cupped his jaw with her hand and turned his face back toward her. "I want *you.*"

His soldier's glare softened. "Sometimes I wonder."

"Fal, how could you ever doubt my feelings toward you?" Even as Lilly asked him, she asked herself the same question.

"You let Condor join us. You refused to accuse Axel of a crime that we both know he committed against you." Falcroné numbered her offenses with his fingers. "And it seems like every time you look at Calum, you're about to start drooling over him."

Lilly's eyebrows rose. His accusations stung straight to her heart, but his characterization of her reactions concerning Calum filled her with rage. "That is *absurd*. I do *not* look at him that way."

"You don't see what I see. You're attracted to him. I know you are. Every time he's near you, you change. Your mannerisms adjust, you phrase things differently, and your eyes..." Falcroné sighed.

A pang of guilt stabbed Lilly's heart. She'd denied Falcroné's allegation because he'd framed it so rudely, but a part of her knew what he said was true. Calum was so—refreshing compared to everyone else she knew. His passion, his faith, his resolve.

He had sacrificed so much for what he believed, and now it was finally paying off. How could Lilly not be attracted to that?

"That's the look. You're doing it right now." Falcroné pointed at her face. "Those longing eyes, that slight frown. You look like you want something you can't have."

"I want *you*, Falcroné, and that's all you need to be concerned about."

Falcroné shook his head and gazed up at the stars. "I don't believe you."

"You have no idea what Calum means to me, or even Axel for that matter. They both saved my life countless times. They rescued me from—"

"They rescued you from Roderick, the slave trader. You've told me."

"It's more than that. So much more." Lilly took her turn staring at the stars.

"Then tell me."

"Why?" Lilly frowned. She could see where this was going. "You'll just use it against me."

"No, I really want to understand." He clasped his hands around hers. "What do you mean?"

Lilly's jaw tightened, and she sucked in a sharp breath as she stared into his eyes. She wanted to tell him the truth. Really and truly, she did. "I—"

Falcroné raised an eyebrow.

But if she told him the truth, everything between them would crash to an end.

"I can't." She bowed her head. "I'm sorry."

A long pause lingered between them. Lilly tried to use the time to formulate some sort of acceptable response, but everything that came to mind sounded successively worse than the previous idea.

"I release you from our engagement." Falcroné said it so softly that Lilly wondered if she had imagined it.

She squeezed his hands, her heart pulsing with anxiety. "No, Fal. That's not what I want. I—"

"You don't know what you want." Falcroné stroked her face with his fingers. It felt soothing, even as it grated against her nerves. "Don't try to tell me you do. You're young, and you have lots of time to figure it out. If it's me, then I can wait. And if not, then—"

"I want *you*. I'm telling you I want you." She grabbed him by the collar of his breastplate, resisting the urge to shed tears at this loss. Why wasn't he listening? "Don't you hear me?"

"I hear what you're saying, but your actions tell me something altogether different." Falcroné shook his head. "I can't continue to live a lie, and neither should you. I certainly won't be a part of it."

She released her grip on his breastplate, then she leaned back against the mast and rubbed her forehead with the heels of her hands. Part of her wanted to cry, and part of her wanted to fly away, but another part wanted to inhale her first breath of the freedom Falcroné had just granted her.

"Like I said, I'll be around when you make your decision. If it's me, I promise I'll do everything I can to make you happy." Falcroné's tone faded as he stood up. "And if it's not me, I'll try my best to be happy for you."

He faced the stars and bent at his knees to spring into the air, but she caught him by the wrist. She had to try one last time. "Don't do this, Fal. I love you."

Falcroné pursed his lips and nodded. "I know. I love you too, but I have to do it."

He pulled free from her grasp and plunged over the edge of the crow's nest, then he looped up into the starry sky and out of sight, leaving Lilly alone.

The first of what would be many tears that night streamed down her face.

LONG AFTER THE others fell asleep, and several hours after Magnus had managed to stanch the bleeding from his arm, soothing warmth spread throughout his wound, and the pain began to dissipate.

The veromine in his blood had begun its work.

LUMEN'S bright form burned Calum's eyes as it had so many times before. "You are near. I can feel your presence."

Calum shielded his face with his hands, but Lumen's light penetrated Calum's very being, deep into his soul.

"You will succeed, Calum. You will free me, and together we will liberate Kanarah."

Lumen's image spiraled into darkness with a loud pop.

SHOUTS, screams, and the nearby snapping of wood jerked Calum from his sleep. Exhausted from the battle, he'd fallen asleep on the ship's main deck well before yesterday's sun had set.

He groped for his sword and found it lying next to him in its sheath. He stood and strapped it to his belt in a hurry.

"What's going—" The words caught in his throat as his eyes fixed on the ship's central mast, which snapped in half and toppled off the side of the ship into the water. Splintered wood burst into the air and rained down on the deck, including on him. Lake water washed onto the deck up to Calum's feet, then receded.

What in the world could have—

A loud roar droned behind him, one all too familiar to his ears. He whirled to face the other side of the ship and his eyes panned up the tall, dark form that towered above them.

A long neck suspended a monstrous reptilian head in the air. A dark red tongue snaked from between its bronze teeth. Spikes adorned its head, and two large horns jutted out from just behind its blank glowing yellow eyes. Black talons tipped each of the four webbed fingers on its hands.

The Jyrak.

CHAPTER 41

"What in the Overlord's name is *that*?" Condor's piercing blue eyes widened. It was the first time Lilly had ever seen actual fear register on his face.

"It's a Jyrak. Probably the same one we encountered last time we braved these waters." Jake motioned toward one of his crew. "We've got no sails left. Get the men rowin' immediately, or we're all dead."

"How far are we from the bend?" Calum asked.

"It's right there." Jake pointed at the Jyrak. "Behind *him*."

A chill bristled Lilly's skin. They had to get *around* the Jyrak to reach Lumen's prison?

The Jyrak loosed another droning roar and turned its attention to another of Jake's ships, which it capsized in one ferocious blow with its enormous hand. Lilly could hear the screams of a dozen or so men before their bodies crashed into the surf.

"What do we do?" she asked, her attention fixed solely on Calum.

It wasn't just her, though. Axel stood at her side and stared at Calum with a look of terror on his face. Magnus gripped his wounded arm, which seemed to have sealed over during the night, and set his eyes on Calum.

Condor, Falcroné, and Kanton landed near Lilly and gave Calum their attention as well, and Riley and the remainder of his Wolf pack rounded out the circle. Even Jake, who didn't even know Calum that well, wouldn't look away from him.

This was what Lilly couldn't explain to Falcroné. Moments like these, when everything was at stake, she would turn to Calum, and Calum would make a way.

It was an irresistible force. An inevitable attraction.

It made Calum unique compared to everyone else she'd ever met.

"We need to work together." Calum peered across the water and squinted. "Jake, I need your other ships to head in one direction around the Jyrak, and we'll head the other."

Jake nodded. "Got it."

"Riley, take your Wolves to the ship's stern. If there's trouble, they can jump off before the Jyrak destroys the ship. Maybe they can swim to safety." Calum held up his hand. "But you stay with me. I need you to help me free Lumen."

Riley nodded too, then he shooed the Wolves away.

"Axel and Kanton, help out on this ship. Work together. Secure sails, tie knots—whatever Jake tells you to do, do it. Then find something heavy that will help us sink nice and fast so we don't drown on our way down to the Hidden Abyss."

They nodded and darted after Jake.

Calum pointed to Magnus and his voice hardened. "And you—don't you dare leave my sight. You're the only Saurian for miles. If we lose you, we can't free Lumen."

Magnus nodded.

"Lilly, take Condor and Falcroné. You three have the most dangerous job, but only you three can do it. Do whatever you can to distract that thing. Buy us time to work around it so the other ships don't have to sacrifice themselves to get us to Lumen." Calum's eyes locked on hers, and a flood of emotion filled her chest and stomach. "Whatever you do, don't get yourself killed."

She gave him a half smile then took to the sky, leaving him behind. He had never let her down before, and she wasn't about to let him down now.

Falcroné and Condor soared alongside her toward the Jyrak, which thrashed at the remnants of the ship it had just destroyed. As they approached, Lilly unsheathed her sword. What she planned to do with it, she wasn't sure, but she would try nonetheless.

The ring of two more swords leaving their sheaths sounded behind her. At least she had two of the best fighters in all of the Sky Realm with her. Together they would find a way to give Calum the time he needed.

CALUM STOOD at the edge of the deck, his fingers clamped on the rail, and watched Lilly fly toward the Jyrak. She had better make it out of this. If she didn't, he'd never forgive himself.

"We're pickin' up speed." Jake cranked the ship's wheel to the right and the ship curled away from the Jyrak. "I gotta take 'er wide at first to make sure we clear its tail, or it could tip us without even tryin'."

"Do what you must, Jake," Calum said.

Magnus's left hand gripped the rail on Calum's right, and Riley's did the same on his left.

"Wish I could do more," Riley said, his voice much softer than what it could've been given the situation. "But I just don't do boats. Or swimming. Or gigantic monsters."

"You'll have your chance soon enough. You're coming with me to free Lumen."

"You heard me say I don't like swimming, right? Because I just said it like five seconds ago."

Calum eyed him and motioned toward the Jyrak with his head. "I bet you'll like it more than you'll like *dying*."

Riley raised a furry eyebrow, then he nodded. "Tried it twice already. Not my favorite. So I guess you're right."

"You know I will have to dive down and find the entrance to the Abyss, right?"

Calum clenched his teeth. He hadn't considered that, but Magnus *was* the only one with a large enough lung capacity to survey the area without drowning. Still, if they lost their only Sobek... "If you get caught by a shark or some other—"

"No one else can stay down long enough to verify its location. Besides, the sharks swam away when the Jyrak showed up last time. Either way, you must let me do this, Calum."

"I know. I know I do." Calum sighed and focused on Magnus's right arm, which had scabbed over. "You sure you're up to it?"

"I will be fine. My arm is regenerating. I have never lost a limb like this before, but I have seen what happens if the veromine in our blood is allowed to do its work. I expect to have a new hand in a matter of days."

So unfair. Calum had to wear armor and do everything he could to defend himself, whereas Magnus, whose scales were nearly invulnerable in the first place, could just regrow lost limbs if he happened to lose one in battle.

"I trust you, but take your sword in case you run into any lake creatures that want to eat you."

As if on cue, the Jyrak roared again. Three dark forms zipped around its head, each of them wielding a gleaming metal blade that flickered under the afternoon sunlight.

Calum raised an eyebrow. "Like that one."

THEY HIT the Jyrak's left eye first. Lilly whipped past the glowing yellow orb and chopped at it with her sword, and Falcroné and Condor did the same thing. The Jyrak released a roar that shook her to her bones and clenched its eye shut. A trickle of glowing orange blood oozed out onto its scaly cheek.

Lilly wanted to celebrate, but the Jyrak's hand swung at her before she could so much as smile. She managed to barrel roll out of its path in time, and when she looked back, both Condor and Falcroné had avoided it as well.

They exchanged furtive glances and nods then curled back toward the Jyrak's head, leaving Lilly alone in the sky above. At first, Lilly was angry that they'd decided to go in for another attack without her, but watching them fly in tandem filled her with awe.

They wove between the Jyrak's flailing limbs and arced up toward its open mouth. Their swords lashed orange streaks across its extended tongue several times before it could retract it into its mouth. When the Jyrak tried to chomp at them with its bronze teeth, they split apart, circled around both sides of the its head, and slashed at its eyes again.

It reared its head back and roared as it clutched its eye with its enormous hands, but that just opened it up to more attacks on its tongue and gums from Condor and Falcroné.

Even amid the mayhem, Lilly had to snicker. For as much as they despised each other, Condor and Falcroné made the perfect fighting duo. They anticipated each other's actions and synchronized their attacks to inflict maximum damage on the Jyrak without endangering themselves.

Enough watching. Lilly propelled herself down toward the Jyrak, ready to fling herself into the fray once again.

FOR ALL HIS concern for Lilly, Calum had to admit she and the two Wisps were handling themselves just fine. The longer he watched, the more at ease he began to feel.

"We're clear of the Jyrak's tail!" Jake shouted. He cranked the wheel hard to his left. "Gimme five minutes, and I'll have you right at the bend."

Axel and Kanton came up behind Calum, Magnus, and Riley, and Calum glanced back at them. "Everything set? Did you find something we can use to help us sink?"

Axel nodded. "We'll use the ship's anchors. They're the obvious choice."

"Are they on this side of the ship?" Calum asked.

Axel's brow furrowed. "Yeah, why?"

"We need them on the opposite side. When Jake turns the ship, the side opposite of the Jyrak is the one we're jumping off." Calum scanned the deck. "Where are they?"

"I'll show you." Kanton darted toward the ship's stern and pointed to a pair of gigantic black anchors with ropes fastened to their ends, and Calum and the others followed.

"Cut them loose, and then we gotta carry them across the ship." Calum glanced over his shoulder at the Jyrak, which had just begun to turn toward them. "Hurry. We don't have much time."

DESPITE THEIR COMBINED EFFORTS, Lilly, Condor, and Falcroné hadn't managed to keep the Jyrak from noticing Jake's ship sneaking around behind it. When it began to turn toward the ship, Lilly knew she had to do something.

She knifed under the Jyrak's chin, looped up to its open mouth, then jammed her sword into its gums right between its two center teeth. Orange goo spurted onto the front of her armor and on her face.

The droning roar that erupted from the Jyrak's throat deafened her until she clamped her hands over her ears. She didn't see its tongue lash out of its mouth until it was too late.

The Jyrak's tongue plowed into her with the full force of a charging Sobek and sent her spinning through the air. Her senses dulled, and she tried to right herself, but she couldn't find her bearings.

Her body smacked against something solid and her momentum stopped. She rolled over and her fingers brushed against the smooth stones paving the surface below her.

Paved? How could she have landed on a street?

When her vision regained some focus, she saw three tall thick forms rising toward her, and she gasped at her realization.

The stones paving the street weren't stones at all.

They were scales.

Lilly had landed in the center of the Jyrak's open hand.

CONDOR SAW the Jyrak's tongue ram into Lilly, and in the worst example of bad luck he'd ever encountered, she careened straight into its waiting hand.

He immediately hurtled down toward her. He had to save her, and he would.

Condor swooped at her as the Jyrak's fingers closed and extended—

A heavy blow knocked him off course, and he missed the Jyrak's hand entirely. His sword slipped from his grasp and fell toward the churning waters below. Condor realized he would never get it back in time as he realized what had happened.

The Jyrak's other hand had swept in from the side and batted him away in the second worst manifestation of bad luck he'd ever encountered.

Now too far away, he righted himself and watched, helpless, as the Jyrak's fingers closed on Lilly.

A blur of blond hair and charcoal armor zoomed in, jammed a sword into the underside of the Jyrak's middle finger, and braced himself against its palm.

Falcroné.

Condor zipped toward them again.

STILL DAZED, Lilly couldn't believe her eyes.

Somehow, Falcroné had wedged himself between her and the Jyrak's middle finger with his sword, and he'd kept it from crushing her. Then Condor appeared next to Falcroné and also pushed against the Jyrak's finger with his hands.

Though both Wisps strained against the monster's might, the finger continued to lower, threatening to crush them all. Lilly tried to move, tried to fly away, but she couldn't.

"Get her out of here!" Falcroné yelled at him.

"Not without you!" Condor shouted back.

"*Do it*, Condor," Falcroné almost pleaded. "Take care of her."

Condor's mouth opened slightly. His eyes fixed on Falcroné's wobbling legs for an instant, then he scooped Lilly into his arms and sprang away from the Jyrak's hand while Falcroné bellowed a war cry that Lilly would never forget. She reached back for him, helpless to do anything else.

The Jyrak's middle finger slammed down on Falcroné, and his sword plunged into the churning waters below.

CHAPTER 42

L illy tried to scream, but nothing came out. When it finally did, it sounded distant, faint. She inhaled a sharp breath and screamed again, and this time her lungs delivered their full payload.

She begged Condor to take her back, to help Falcroné—anything, but he just kept repeating, "It's over. He's gone."

The Jyrak raised its hand and thrust Falcroné's rag-doll form into its gaping mouth, and Lilly's heart shattered.

CALUM and the others had just managed to get the second anchor across the deck when Jake crowed from the captain's wheel.

"We're there!" He stomped on the deck three times, and the men who rowed from their spots on the inside of the ship's hull raised their oars.

His ship had lined up with a large gray rock formation that jutted about a hundred feet above the surface of the lake and formed part of its perimeter for about a half-mile. Because of the way the surf thrashed and the proximity of the rocks, Jake couldn't have docked the ship even if he'd wanted to.

"Without anchors, I can't keep us steady for long. Go, now!"

Magnus leaped off the side of the ship nearest to the bend and dove into the water while Calum watched. If he didn't survive, if something happened to him down there, they were all as good as dead.

The double-thump of a Windgale landing sounded behind him, and he turned around. Condor stood there with Lilly in his arms, both of them coated in glowing orange blood. Lilly clung to Condor's neck, her body heaving with sobs.

Calum's mouth hung open. He searched the skies and looked up at the Jyrak, but he saw no one else. There were only two of them.

He swallowed the lump in his throat and managed to choke out one word. "Falcroné?"

Condor stared at him with the same stoic look in his blue eyes as the day the Premier had banished him to the Blood Chasm, and he shook his head.

Sickness twisted Calum's gut. So many had died for this cause already, and danger still loomed above them and swirled all around them. Would freeing Lumen be worth it all?

"Uh, Calum?" Jake motioned toward the Jyrak. "Your friend had better hurry. We're in trouble."

The Jyrak had turned toward them again. One step and it would come within reach of the ship.

"Get the anchors as close to the edge as you can. We need to be ready to go the moment Magnus resurfaces." Calum turned his attention back to the waters below, and muttered, "Come on, Magnus. Come on."

"Lilly, it's over. We still need you here."

Condor's velvet voice coaxed her to open her eyes, but when she saw his face, all she could think of was Falcroné's horrible death, and she burst into tears again.

"Shhh, it's alright," he crooned.

It wouldn't be alright. She *had* loved Falcroné, even if her emotions had been mixed. He was her oldest and closest friend, and now he was gone. Dead. Killed by that abomination.

"Put me down," she whispered. "Please."

Condor complied, but he gripped her shoulders in his hands. "He loved you, Lilly. That's why he did what he did."

She nodded and wiped the tears from her eyes. It came as little consolation now that he was gone. "I know."

"We're not done yet. We have to go find Lumen now."

Lilly stared at him. Ever since he'd joined their group, she had barely heard so much as a peep from him about Lumen's existence aside from sharing the location of the Arcanum.

Behind Condor, the Jyrak stepped closer to the ship.

"I'll protect you, Lilly. I promise I will." Condor gave her a faint smile. "Even if it means doing for you what Fal did."

"He did it for you, too, you know," Lilly said.

Was she trying to console him from her own hurt?

No. Her words were truth—truth that needed to be spoken.

"He always admired you. Always respected you. Even after—"

"I know, Lilly." Condor closed his eyes and gave a sullen nod. "I know."

"I don't need anyone else dying for me, so you stay alive. Crystal?"

He raised his head and met her eyes. "Clear."

Something about the way he said it chilled her from the inside out. She didn't have time to investigate the sensation before Calum's voice snatched her back into the real world.

"Over here!" Calum yelled. "Magnus is back up!"

Lilly and Condor zipped over to the edge of the ship. Sure enough, Magnus's dark-green head bobbed at the water's surface.

"I found it. It is quite far down, but I think we can—"

"*Look out!*" Jake's voice split the air.

Lilly turned around in time to see the Jyrak's hand descending toward the ship.

THE JYRAK's hand hit so hard and so fast that Calum didn't even have time to jump off the ship. When he finally resurfaced, he realized that the Jyrak's blow had flung him and everyone else aboard the ship into the water, along with the anchors.

The anchors. Their only way of getting down.

If they were both lost—

"Calum!"

He turned his head in time to see Magnus's head disappear under the water along with the end of something black and curved.

One of the anchors.

"Quickly, over here!" Calum yelled.

Riley, Axel, Condor, and Lilly joined him while Kanton, the surviving Wolves, Jake, and what remained of his crew clung to shards of the ship's wood.

"Down, now!"

Calum sucked the deepest breath he'd ever taken into his lungs and let his armor weight pull him under.

Below him, Magnus was still in view, struggling to slow the anchor's descent, but Calum could see he wouldn't last much longer. If they didn't get ahold of that anchor in time, they would drown before they ever reached the cavern that led to the Hidden Abyss.

Calum kicked and clawed at the water with all his might. He had almost reached Magnus's outstretched arm when a current pushed him away. Magnus reacted and lashed his tail through the water at Calum, who grabbed ahold of it. As his descent accelerated, something clamped onto his ankle.

It was Riley. In turn, Axel held onto him, Condor held Axel, and Lilly held Condor. They descended to the lake's depths as a unit, together.

The air in Calum's lungs had already begun to stale, but the anchor sank them deeper and deeper into the lake.

He stole a glance up at the surface. They'd descended far enough now that there was no hope of turning back. Calum would either find the Hidden Abyss and free Lumen, or he would die in these waters. He hoped he hadn't been imagining everything Lumen had told him up until this point.

All at once, Magnus released his grip on the anchor and it dropped into the darker waters below. He motioned toward the wall then swam toward a large, black opening. Calum released his tail and followed him into the hole, and the rest of the group followed him as well.

With each stroke of his arms and legs, Calum exhaled more air until he had no more breath in his lungs to expel. His chest burned from deprivation, but he swam forward through the darkness nonetheless, flailing, kicking, scraping his way through the murky water without knowing where he was going.

No air. No salvation. No Lumen.

He realized he was going to die in that underwater tunnel. He'd die with his friends. With Magnus, with Axel, Riley, Condor—if he could consider Condor a friend, anyway—and with Lilly.

Lilly, with whom he'd shared so much, but not even half as much as he would've liked.

Calum's vision darkened. His mouth opened and water cascaded into his lungs, and everything went black.

———

THE NEXT THING HE KNEW, Calum lay on his side, coughing that very same water onto an uneven stone floor. He sucked in a deep breath of musty air. Ancient air.

He was alive.

And they had made it.

"Are you alright, Calum?" Magnus's deep voice reverberated off the jagged walls inside the small cavern.

Calum rolled onto his back and looked up. Instead of total darkness, a faint white light from somewhere illuminated Magnus's green face. Calum coughed again and nodded. "Yeah. I'm alright."

Two sets of hands pulled him to his feet—Condor and Riley. Lilly and Axel stood on either side of Magnus wearing relieved expressions.

Calum was just as glad to see them, but he didn't dare tarry any longer. He took a few tentative steps forward and surveyed the cavern.

The space didn't compare to that of the Arcanum by any measure. The ceiling hung no more than twenty feet above their heads at its highest point, and stalactites jutted down at random. Overall, the entire cavern couldn't have been larger than a forty-by-sixty-foot area, and a solid ten-by-ten pillar of solid rock occupied the middle of the cavern.

Yet it was that ten-by-ten section that gave off the faint light.

Upon closer inspection, Calum realized the pillar amounted to little more than several large stalactites that had stretched so low that they eventually melded with the cavern floor. Over time, the mineral deposits had spread and widened the stalactites into one massive pillar that looked as if it supported the entire cavern's ceiling.

But Calum realized exactly what it was.

Faint light glimmered through dozens of tiny crystals embedded within the stone, no doubt refracted from the prisoner trapped inside. A round platform made of four sections of white marble encircled the pillar, identical except for the worn carvings in the center of each one: a Wolf, a Saurian, a Windgale, and a human.

"What are we supposed to do now?" Axel asked.

Calum eyed him. "So do you believe me yet?"

"Don't get smart." He glowered at Calum. "I almost died like a hundred times today."

"Some of us did die." Lilly's voice barely registered above a whisper, but the cavern amplified her words.

Axel's jaw tensed, and he didn't say anything else.

"At this point, there's only one thing to do." Calum motioned toward the marble platform. "Magnus, take your place."

Magnus nodded, then he stepped onto the section of marble designated for a Saurian.

"Riley, you next." After Riley complied, Calum looked at Condor and Lilly. "Which of you wants to do it?"

"I will." This time Lilly's voice rang clear. She looked up at Condor, who stood by her. "As long as you don't mind."

Condor grinned. "Not in the least. Fal would have wanted it this way."

Lilly showed him a shallow smile and took her place on the platform.

Calum turned and faced Axel. He motioned toward the platform. "Go ahead."

"What?" Axel's mouth hung open. "You're joking, right?"

"No." Calum shook his head. "I want you to be the one who sets Lumen free."

"Not a chance. I'm still not convinced this'll even work." Axel folded his arms and winked at Calum. "Besides, this moment, if it ends up being real, is for you. I can't take it from you."

Calum smiled at him. Axel had proven more of a burden than Calum had ever imagined when they first left his farm, but even so, Calum never would've made it this far without him. His first friend. His best friend.

"Go on, already." Axel nodded toward the pillar. "It's too cold in here for us to keep standing around like a bunch of idiots."

Calum chuckled, and he started toward the platform. He stopped just in front of it, exhaled a long breath, and placed his right foot on the marble, then his left.

The instant his left foot touched the platform, it lowered into the rock by three inches. Unsure what to do, Calum backed off, as did Lilly, Riley, and Magnus.

The platform sections jerked toward the pillar one at a time and slammed into it, sending long fissures up its sides. Rocks and dust trickled from the fissures as the last platform struck the pillar, and then all fell silent.

The faint light from within the pillar intensified and pierced through the fissures into the cavern. Each fissure branched into a hundred smaller cracks that spread around the pillar until the stone began to crumble away altogether, leaving only blinding white light in its place.

Light. So pure that it penetrated Calum to his very soul.

He tried to shield his eyes with his hands, but it burned through him.

Now, at long last, his friends knew what he'd experienced in his dreams, and he was finally experiencing it in real life. It saturated him with sheer joy, and he wanted to whoop and shout in delight.

An ethereal voice groaned in the ancient air around them, and the light faded enough that Calum could look upon Kanarah's savior with his real eyes for the first time. He stepped free of his prison and his presence filled the entire cavern with radiance.

There before them stood Lumen, the General of Light.

EPILOGUE

Inside his throne room, the King turned his head to the west. The words of the nobleman addressing him faded to nothing as a new awareness engaged his mind.

"Summon Matthios."

The nobleman silenced, and he stared at the King with wide eyes. "Your Majesty?"

The King fixed his eyes on the nobleman. "Summon Matthios *now*."

With a low bow, the nobleman retreated to do the King's bidding.

Not two minutes later, a muscular man in bronze armor stood before the King. He, too, bowed low. "What is your bidding, Majesty?"

"Muster your army. Head to the Golden Plains outside of Kanarah City."

Matthios raised his head and stared at the King with eyes like molten bronze. "Has the time come, my King?"

"Yes, Matthios. Lumen has been released." The King stood from his throne and handed Matthios the bronze staff he'd used to banish Lumen a thousand years earlier. "You once forged this weapon that I might use it to battle our enemy. It is yours to wield from now on. May it keep you safe as you face our enemies."

Matthios accepted the weapon and bowed. Then he turned back and headed for the throne room door.

THIS BOOK IS OVER, BUT THE ADVENTURE DOESN'T STOP HERE!

The story continues in *THE RISE OF ANCIENT FURY*
Book Two of THE CALL OF ANCIENT LIGHT SERIES

If you enjoyed this book, please leave a review on Amazon.com!

446

THE RISE OF ANCIENT FURY

AS THE DARKNESS HOVERS OVER THE WATERS,
THE LIGHT REVEALS THE HIDDEN TRUTH

BEN WOLF

447

PROLOGUE

Steel scraped against ancient stone, and Lumen's eyes cracked open. Four slams, one after another, tore fissures from the floor of his prison to its ceiling. Pebbles trickled from the cracks and collected around Lumen's feet.

His luminescence flared, and the crystals that dotted the inside of his prison glimmered. He focused his power, pushing outward, and thousands of smaller cracks spread out from the fissures until the entire tube crumbled around him.

Lumen stepped over the mound of rock shards and into the surrounding cavern, finally free of his prison, his place of coerced solitude for the last 1,000 years.

At last, he was free. At last, he would bring freedom to Kanarah.

Inside his throne room, the King turned his head to the west. The words of the nobleman addressing him faded to nothing as a new awareness engaged his mind.

"Summon Matthios."

The nobleman silenced, and he stared at the King with wide eyes. "Your Majesty?"

The King fixed his eyes on the nobleman. "Summon Matthios *now*."

With a low bow, the nobleman retreated to do the King's bidding.

Not two minutes later, a muscular man in bronze armor stood before the King. He, too, bowed low. "What is your bidding, Majesty?"

"Muster your army. Head to the Golden Plains outside of Kanarah City."

Matthios raised his head and stared at the King with eyes like molten bronze. "Has the time come, my King?"

"Yes, Matthios. Lumen has been released." The King stood from his throne and handed Matthios the bronze staff he'd used to banish Lumen a thousand years earlier. "You once forged this weapon that I might use it to battle our enemy. It is yours to wield from now on. May it keep you safe as you face our enemies."

Matthios accepted the weapon, bowed, then turned and headed for the throne room door.

CHAPTER 1

Calum's heart threatened to beat through his breastplate. Lumen, the General of Light, fabled warrior and the prophesied savior of Kanarah, stood before him.

White armor covered his strong limbs, and a silver sword hung from his belt. A golden crown glistened atop the figure's head, and his eyes flickered like two balls of fire above a white half-mask that covered his nose and mouth.

Just like in Calum's dreams.

Calum had actually done it. He'd made it to the Hidden Abyss, and he'd freed Lumen.

"Calum." Even Lumen's deep voice exuded power like nothing Calum had ever experienced.

His throbbing heart stilled for a moment, and he stared at Lumen.

"Thank you for freeing me." Lumen started toward him. He towered over Calum by more than two feet. "I have been watching you."

The words sent tremors through Calum's bones, but he stood firm. "Then you know we need your help now. Our friends above—"

"Say no more." Lumen extended his arms and looked at both Lilly and Magnus. "Gather round, children."

Magnus cast a tentative glance at Calum, but Lilly stepped forward without reservation. Condor followed suit, and Riley and Axel stepped forward next. With hesitance, Magnus complied and then looked to Calum, who stepped forward last.

Lumen nodded. "Prepare yourselves."

Without further explanation, Lumen opened a sort of white glowing void beneath their feet, and they all dropped into it.

Calum's stomach flipped, but the next thing he knew, he saw blue skies with a few fluffy clouds hovering over a great expanse of blue water. Beneath his feet, the rugged gray rock ended in a drop-off only ten paces behind him. It left Calum dizzy and disoriented at first, but the awe of what Lumen had just done overwrote that sensation quickly enough.

Calum, his friends, and Lumen all stood atop the very rock formation near where they had found Lumen's prison. Then recognized the sight he'd left behind only minutes earlier.

Only a few hundred feet away, the Jyrak reared back its massive head and released a droning roar.

Calum looked to Lumen again, but he was gone. He scanned the skies until Axel pointed toward the Jyrak, and they all faced the monster.

Well within the Jyrak's reach, Lumen unsheathed his sword as the monster raised its hand to strike. In one swift motion, Lumen cut a long white arc across the Jyrak's torso from its left shoulder to its right hip, and it roared again, this time in pain.

Glowing orange blood spurted out from the Jyrak's torso along that line and tainted the blue water below, and the Jyrak toppled over into the surf. Its illuminated yellow eyes faded, then they disappeared with the rest of its body under the water.

Calum couldn't believe what he'd just seen. He stood there, mouth agape as the Jyrak sank beneath the churning waves.

"Impossible," Axel said from behind Calum.

"He is the General of Light." Even Magnus's voice carried an air of disbelief. "An ancient warrior more powerful than any of us can imagine."

If Lumen could slay a Jyrak only moments after reawakening, what else could he do? And what chance did the King have of defeating him a second time? Who could stand against such power?

But now wasn't the time for marveling, not when there were people nearby who still needed help.

"Condor. Lilly." Calum focused on them. "I need you to fly down to the water and search for survivors in the shipwreck. Save as many as you—"

"That will not be necessary." Lumen's voice split the air, and he hovered toward the edge of the rock near where Calum stood. "I will retrieve them."

Before Calum could say anything else, Lumen plummeted toward the water. In a matter of seconds, another white void opened above the rocks behind Calum and the others. From it fell Kanton, Jake, dozens of Jake's crew, and three Wolves, all of them dripping wet and looking around with wide eyes.

"What in the Overlord's name?" Jake rubbed his head. "How—?"

As Lumen emerged from another void in the center of all of them, Calum pointed at him. "Lumen saved you. All of you. And all of us."

One of Jake's crewmembers immediately lowered to one knee and bowed, but the gesture soon spread throughout the entire group. Soon after, Calum bent his knee as well. It felt strange, at first, to bow to Lumen, but when Calum considered what he'd just witnessed, how could he not?

"Rise, my friends." Lumen's blazing eyes fixed on Calum's. "We are no longer needed in this place. There is a battle to be won for the soul of Kanarah. Join with me."

This time, when Lumen opened the void, Calum readied himself for it. His stomach still flip-flopped, but Calum wasn't as disoriented this time as he found himself standing in an ocean of golden grain underneath a clear blue sky.

"How do you do that?" Axel rubbed his eyes and clamped his hand on Calum's shoulder to stabilize himself.

"It is an ancient magic, one far older than even me," Lumen replied.

In the distance, the outline of Kanarah City loomed on the horizon. Calum recognized the spot as not far from where they had found Lilly with an arrow in her shoulder. It seemed like a lifetime had passed since then.

"What are we doing here?" Lilly's eyebrows lowered, and she glanced around the vast fields. "I don't have fond memories of this place."

"No kidding." Axel pushed a lock of brown hair away from his forehead. It had grown long—much longer than he'd worn it in the past—and his once youthful stubble bordered on becoming a beard.

"Gather round." Lumen raised his hands, and the group surrounded him.

Calum grinned at the awed expressions on the faces of Jake and his crew as they set their gazes on Lumen, proud that he'd been the one Lumen had appeared to in dreams. He'd been the one chosen and charged to set him free. And somehow, against everything Kanarah had thrown at Calum, he'd actually done it.

Lilly's eyes met Calum's for an instant, then she looked away, a reminder that they hadn't made it here without suffering loss. Calum sighed.

Falcroné had died less than an hour earlier, and Calum knew the subtle grief on Lilly's face delved far deeper in her heart than she wanted known. The only comparison he could draw was when he'd lost his parents, or perhaps what he'd feel if something were to happen to her.

"The end draws near for the King," Lumen said, his voice smooth and deep. "It begins here. Now. Together we will work to free Kanarah from his grasp forever. Gone are the days when you toiled under his oppression, under the heavy burdens he placed upon all of you. From this day forward, you live as free men and women."

The three Wolves yipped and their ears perked up. Riley straightened his spine and peered across the plains toward Kanarah City.

"What is it?" Calum asked.

"The King's soldiers." Riley growled. "Hundreds of them."

"*Hundreds?*" Axel gawked.

"Too many for you to handle?" Magnus quipped. He still clutched the stump where Vandorian had cut off his hand, and Calum cringed a little at the sight of it.

Axel straightened up a little taller. "Not at all. I just expected there'd be more."

"This is merely an advance force," Lumen said. "They have come here for me. The King knows I have been released. He is determined to quash our uprising before it begins, but he will fail."

"Got that right." Axel cast a glance at Calum with a smirk.

Apparently, Axel actually believed Lumen after all. Then again, after what they'd seen Lumen do so far, who wouldn't?

"Come with me. We must meet them in the field." Lumen's hand came to rest on Calum's shoulder, and Calum could feel raw power crackling under the ancient warrior's touch. Lumen looked to the rest of them. "All of us."

"Whoa. Wait a minute." Axel held up his hand. So much for him not saying anything. "You want us to *fight* them? That's not happening."

"I hate to agree with Axel, but we are in no condition to fight after all we have just endured." Magnus held up his right arm, which now ended in a scabbed-over stump thanks to Vandorian's blade. Eventually, the hand would regenerate, he'd said, and Calum assumed he'd be able to wield his sword once it did.

What's more, the Dragon Emerald remained in the pouch on his belt. After all this time and all the opportunities he'd had to lose it, Magnus had maintained its possession—in part thanks to Dallahan, one of Riley's Wolves, who'd recovered it from Vandorian.

"Now is not the time to shed blood." Lumen's eyes panned from Axel to Riley, Lilly, and Magnus. "But if you are to be my generals, my imperators in the battles to come, then you must witness firsthand how to deal with the King's men."

Calum nodded. He could do this, and he would. For his parents, for Nicolai, and for everyone else who'd died to help him along the way. "Let's go."

Instead of taking Lumen's hands and transporting up to the army, this time they walked among the golden heads of wheat. Though Riley's Wolves stayed behind, Condor accompanied Lilly.

Condor hadn't been the disruptive force Calum had expected when Lilly asked him to join their group. Had Condor not intervened back at Oren's fortress and in multiple battles since then, Calum doubted they'd even be alive right now.

Even so, Calum didn't like how close to Lilly Condor had already gotten in Falcroné's absence. That was something he'd have to watch out for.

When they made it about halfway to the approaching soldiers, Lumen stopped and turned back to face them.

"These men are led by Matthios, the Brazen General," Lumen said. "He is one of the King's Imperators, a mighty warrior who wields powers not unlike mine. Like the King himself, he has the ability to bewitch you, to plant seeds of confusion in your minds. Do not speak to him, and guard your minds from his poisonous words."

Minutes later, Lumen stood with Calum and the others facing Matthios and the three hundred men in gleaming silver armor who accompanied him. Like Lumen, Matthios towered above the rest of his men and wore armor almost identical to Lumen's, but bronze instead of white. Atop his bald head sat a small circlet crown made of bronze.

He, too, wore an armored mask that covered his nose and mouth, also bronze. Instead of blazing white orbs for eyes, his eyes burned like molten bronze, a sight that sent chills through Calum's body. The guy just *looked* evil.

No sword hung from Matthios's belt, but he wielded a long bronze staff tipped with two bronze spearheads, one on each end. Its shaft was textured with what appeared to be scales like those of a snake. When he stopped walking, Matthios plunged one of the spearheads into the soft ground at his feet and stood next to it, still gripping it with his right hand.

"Lumen, General of Light." Matthios's deep voice rattled Calum's insides just as Lumen's had. "Your King bids you welcome."

"He is my King no longer, Matthios." Lumen folded his arms and straightened his back. He had Matthios by a few inches in height, but other than that, they appeared to be more or less equals in every way. "And he never will be."

"Your time in the Hidden Abyss has not changed your mind?"

"It has reinforced my resolve. Any King who would banish one of his subjects to a thousand years of quiet nothingness deserves to be usurped."

Matthios remained quiet for a long moment, studying Calum and the others with him with those burning molten eyes. "You chose your punishment when you rebelled against your King. It is only by his grace that you yet draw breath."

"I rebelled against him because he is an unjust ruler and a tyrant." Lumen's arms lowered, and his hands clenched into fists. "A tyrant who is served by mindless drones and fools."

"Your King is merciful and has granted you a second chance. That is the message I have been sent to convey to you." Matthios's molten eyes locked on Calum's, and a rush of uneasiness spread through Calum's gut. "This applies to your companions as well. Your King will wipe away your transgressions and give you the freedom to start over."

"And how will the King continue to oppress them afterward? Will he demand backbreaking labor from them? Will he take what is rightfully theirs as he has for millennia?" Lumen scoffed. "No, Matthios. The King has corrupted the throne for long enough. It is time we had a new ruler, one who will love the people as a father loves his own children."

Matthios shook his head, menacingly slow. His voice hardened. "You know he will never allow that to happen."

"He might if you would add your strength to ours," Lumen suggested. "A warrior of your power could—"

"I am *loyal* to my King," Matthios interrupted. "And that will never change."

When Matthios glanced at Calum again, the same pang crimped his stomach—was this the sorcery Lumen had referenced?

Calum wouldn't succumb, though. The King's men had slain his parents and thrown him into a life of slavery and misery with no purpose. He would never harbor anything but hatred for the King.

"Here are your King's terms," Matthios said. "You will appear before him at once and—"

"I will hear terms from neither the King nor his mindless followers, least of all from *you*," Lumen snapped. "Here are *my* terms, which you will take back to the King. He will appear before me here, on the field of battle. He will lay down his crown and his sword at my feet, and he will bend his knee to me.

"I will grant him his life in exchange for his kingdom, of which I will be the better steward. He will publicly declare me the King of Kanarah and all its peoples, and he will renounce his claim to the throne for all eternity.

"On these terms I will not compromise; I will not bend. Most importantly, I will not fail to achieve that which I desire." Lumen folded his arms again. "Be a loyal dog and tell your King what I have said. I will wait."

In Calum's periphery, Axel nodded with enthusiasm. Axel, who had questioned Lumen's existence less than two hours earlier.

"Your King will reject these terms," Matthios said. "He is not enthroned at the whims of his subjects but rather by divine right, which he cannot simply give up. You know this as well as I do, as does even the youngest child within Solace."

"Then the King will perish by my hand, and I will pry Kanarah from his lifeless fingers."

Matthios's molten eyes narrowed. "You are hereby ordered to leave Eastern Kanarah, or you will face immediate destruction."

When Lumen unsheathed his sword, Calum's skin bristled as the air crackled with electric energy. He'd said they wouldn't have to fight, but now… Calum's hand went to his own sword.

"Stay back, Calum. Do not engage, any of you." Lumen's fiery gaze flitted between Calum and his companions, then he faced Matthios again. "You do not possess the power to defeat me. Not alone, not with hundreds of soldiers. Not even with the King's own spear, which you now wield. Had you brought Gavridel with you, you might have stood a chance."

"Even after 1,000 years, your arrogance knows no limits. I need neither an army nor Gavridel to defeat you, General of Light." Matthios shifted his feet into a wider fighting stance, but he didn't pull his dual-tipped spear from the ground.

"You never have before, Brazen General. Today will be no different."

Then, in a blast of white light, Lumen raised his sword and streaked toward Matthios.

CHAPTER 2

Thunderclaps rocked Axel's ears with every strike exchanged by these two warriors, and the ground beneath his feet seemed to tremble with every impact. Bronze clashed against light in a flurry of blows so fast that he could barely register them all.

Lumen's sword flashed when it connected with Matthios's double-bladed spear, but Matthios stood his ground, defending every strike with absolute confidence.

The prowess of both of these warriors exceeded anything Axel could ever dream of accomplishing on his own. For once, he was glad he didn't have to fight—one blow from either of them would've reduced him to paste.

But they had somehow gotten to this level. And if they could do it, why not him, too? There had to be a way.

Lumen slashed straight down at Matthios's head, but the center of the spear's bronze shaft blocked the attack. Another flash of white light mingled with a burst of bronze sparks, and both dissipated into the air.

Matthios jerked his left arm forward and pushed Lumen's blade away. In one insane motion, the spear somehow swiveled in his left hand, around the back of his neck, and he caught its shaft with his right hand and lashed it at Lumen's face.

The tip of the bronze spearhead smacked into Lumen's armored mask with a flash of bronze, and he staggered back. Had Lumen been anyone else, Axel supposed, the blow would have destroyed any trace of Matthios's opponent.

"You are out of practice, General of Light." Matthios's eyebrow rose as he reset his grip on his spear.

"You are welcome to strike me as many times as you like, Matthios." Lumen raised his sword. "We both know you cannot kill me with your two-headed Serpent."

"Perhaps. But perhaps you believe that only because I have not yet done it."

Lumen bolted forward before Matthios even finished his sentence. His first swing clanged against the spear in a blow that would have cut Matthios's torso in half, then he whipped the blade in a lateral swipe at Matthios's head.

Matthios ducked under the sword, but Lumen's right boot jammed under his bronze-covered chin and sent him soaring backward. He landed on his feet and adjusted his mask, which Lumen's kick had knocked askew. "Impressive."

"Bear in mind, my last fight was against the King himself." Lumen's voice dripped with boastful confidence. It reminded Axel of himself at times.

"A fight in which you were defeated and your abhorrent army was reduced to ashes," Matthios countered.

Lumen grunted and darted at Matthios in another streak of light. They traded thunderous hacks and cuts with neither of them landing any more hits on the other for minutes. Then Matthios jabbed at Lumen with his spear.

Lumen dodged the blow but clamped his left hand on the spear's shaft and lashed his blade at Matthios. Light emanated from Lumen's sword, and its blade crashed against Matthios's armored left forearm, which he'd raised to block the attack.

The force of the blow sent Matthios careening through the air. He landed on his back and skidded along the ground toward his army. He sprang up to his feet almost immediately, but he no longer held his spear.

Lumen held both his sword and Matthios's spear, one in each hand. "Missing something?"

Matthios extended his right hand, and the spear wrenched itself from Lumen's grip. It spun through the air, pinwheeling end over end, and Matthios caught it. Upon impact, the spearheads began to burn like the molten bronze of Matthios's eyes. "Not anymore."

Axel's mouth hung open. *Impossible.*

Then again, he'd seen a lot of impossible things in the last hour. He decided he ought to get used to it.

Matthios charged forward, trailing a wave of bronze energy in his wake. Lumen met him in the field, and their weapons clashed in an explosion of sparks and light. Glowing bronze spearheads danced around Lumen's head and shoulders in rapid succession, tracing streaks of power, but Lumen fended off each threat with clean alacrity.

Another jab almost skewered Lumen's chest, but he arched his torso farther back than humanly possible, and the spearhead lashed just above his stomach. Matthios twisted the spear in his arms and brought the other spearhead down toward Lumen's exposed torso, but the glowing sword intercepted the blow.

Lumen straightened his body and batted the spear away, only to absorb a blow intended for his head with his left forearm. Unfazed, Lumen lunged forward, and the tip of his sword slammed into Matthios's breastplate.

Another blast of bright light and bronze sparks exploded between them, and Matthios launched backward again. His body carved a deep trench in the soft ground and flung large clods of dirt and stalks of wheat into the air, then he lay motionless before his army for a long while.

Axel smiled. *Awesome.*

"It is as I said, Matthios," Lumen sheathed his sword and folded his arms, "you stood no chance of defeating me."

In the distance, Matthios pushed himself up to his feet with apparent difficulty. Mud caked on his bronze armor, and a black star, its multiple points erratic in length, had seared onto the metal in the center of his breastplate.

Matthios looked down at the star for a moment, then he wiped it off his chest with one swipe of his left hand, revealing shining bronze once again. He raised his spear over his head with his right hand and extended it toward Lumen.

Behind him, King's the army started to advance.

457

Axel's eyes widened again, and he drew his sword. The instant he did, Lumen turned back toward him and the others.

"Do *not* engage them. Stay back. I will handle this."

For a moment, Lumen's blazing white eyes centered on Axel, and a rush of excitement swelled in his chest. He'd been a fool not to believe in Lumen sooner.

Lumen faced the approaching army and slowly raised his arms, fingers extended.

The army stormed forward, their steel weapons and armor clanking.

Axel stood there, debating whether or not to draw his sword anyway. He gripped the hilt just in case, but then something different began to happen.

Before Lumen, a white ball of energy materialized and hovered at his chest level. It grew larger and larger, and lightning swirled around it in wide arcs. The ball flickered with bursts of light until it grew to almost the same size as Lumen.

The army continued their advance nonetheless, trampling through the wheat.

When they came within twenty paces of Lumen, he lurched forward. The massive ball of energy launched toward them, and as it impacted the first of the soldiers, it shattered into hundreds of shards of electric light that ratcheted throughout the soldiers' ranks.

The men screamed in pain until the entire army exploded in a dome of white light.

All Axel could see was Lumen's hulking form silhouetted against the explosion which sheared deep into the ground and reached into the sky by at least twenty feet. It lingered for a solid five seconds before it disappeared entirely, and the light from the explosion left Axel's vision temporarily scarred.

In place of the army and the field of wheat lay a steaming crater at least an eighth of the size of Kanarah City—and nothing else.

The entire army was gone. No weapons, no armor, no teeth, no bones.

Only a layer of wispy black ash remained, drifting along the crater floor in the breeze.

Axel marveled at the sight. Was there anything Lumen couldn't do?

He got his answer when a lone form rose from among the ashes.

He wore bronze armor, now aglow with the same burning hue of his eyes, and he still held his spear. As he rose to his full height, the bronze armor gradually cooled back to its original shade, but his eyes remained just as molten as ever.

Matthios.

CHAPTER 3

When Lumen killed the Jyrak with a single brutal swing of his sword, it was the most incredible sight Calum had ever seen—until the total destruction of Matthios's army. Calum had always believed in Lumen's ability to liberate Kanarah, but now he'd seen it first-hand. What chance did the King have against such power?

"You were foolish to send them against me, Matthies." Lumen folded his arms again and looked down at Matthios, who stood in the center of the crater, completely unscathed by Lumen's blast. "Will you continue to fight me until your death, like your men, or will you deliver my message to the King?"

Matthios's burning eyes fixed on Lumen, but he remained silent. He just stood there, down in the front of the crater, and glared at Lumen. Finally, he cast a menacing glance at Calum, which stirred that familiar emotion of uneasiness in Calum's chest, then he turned, lifted off the ground, and flew back toward Kanarah City as if he were a Windgale.

They watched him fly away until he disappeared from sight, and then Lumen faced Calum and the others.

"You now know what kind of evil we face, the kind of heartless tyranny and self-preservation we must expel from Kanarah. Matthios knew full well that his soldiers could not withstand me, yet he sent them into battle nonetheless." Lumen uttered, "Now all of them are dead."

No kidding. Calum raised his eyebrows.

"This is merely the beginning. Matthios was right—the King will not accept my terms, nor did I expect him to. Instead, he will muster the full strength of his army to meet us in a final battle." Lumen turned and stared at Kanarah City for a moment, then he refocused his blazing eyes on Calum. "But we will be ready for him."

"Why can't you just level his army like you did with Matthios's?" Axel asked.

"The King is far more powerful than Matthios. His presence would negate my ability to obliterate swaths of his army like I did here." Lumen's eyes narrowed. "He is the only being in Kanarah capable of defeating me, and in turn, I am the only one who can defeat him. Amid the battle, I will face him in single combat, and I will kill him. That will free Kanarah."

Calum tilted his head. "But in order to do that, you need us to fight everyone else?"

"I need far more than that from you."

Axel nudged Calum. "Yeah. We get to be his generals, remember?"

"You cannot become generals until an army exists for you to lead," Lumen said. "*You* must raise this army. You must travel throughout all of Kanarah and recruit those of your respective races to join our cause."

Silence hovered between them.

Calum truly didn't know what to think of Lumen's commission. He'd already traveled across most of Kanarah once. The idea of doing it again excited him... but it also annoyed him. He'd nearly died several times trying to find free Lumen—more times than he could count.

"How, exactly, are we supposed to *raise an army?*" Axel asked. "We've never done anything like that before."

"You have everything you need to convince your people to join us in liberating Kanarah. Lilly is the Windgale Princess. Magnus is an heir to the throne of Reptilius. Riley is—"

"I'm an outcast from the Wolf tribes, the weakest in my family, and I can't return under penalty of death," Riley said, his voice flat.

Lumen focused on him. "That may once have been true, but you have grown in strength, speed, and cunning since then. You now command a tribe of your own, small as it may be, and you are capable of influencing many to our cause. That aside, speed and stealth are not foolproof means to win a battle, even for the greatest Shadow Wolf."

Riley muttered something indiscernible, folded his arms, and looked away.

Axel's eyebrows arched down. "Who's gonna listen to us? We're fugitives pretty much everywhere we go, including here. Captain Anigo warned us not to come back."

Lumen's focus shifted to Calum and Axel. "You are indeed fugitives, but you are not without friends, even on this side of Kanarah. Together, all of you *will* succeed in this task."

Magnus shook his head. "If I return to the Crimson Keep, they will kill me on sight."

"You underestimate your importance, Magnus. I do not ask you to enter Reptilius unprepared or underequipped." Lumen placed his hand on Magnus's shoulder, and Magnus jerked upright, his eyes wide open. Lumen retracted his hand. "Recover that artifact, and you will have little difficulty making your way to Kahn."

Dazed, Magnus faltered and toppled toward Calum.

"Magnus?" Calum wrapped his arms around Magnus's torso and tried to hold him up, but the Saurian's sheer size threatened to overwhelm him. Calum gawked at Lumen, betrayed. "What did you do to him?"

"The same thing I have done with you. I showed him a vision."

Calum's eyebrows rose. "Of what?"

"The Dragon's Breath." Magnus's strength and cognition returned. He straightened on his own and rubbed the spot between his golden eyes with his fingers.

"The what?" Axel asked.

"The Dragon's Breath sword," Condor said. "It's a mythical artifact that was lost after Lumen's first rebellion against the King. It supposedly wielded the power of dragonfire, and it is one of the only weapons in history known to penetrate Dragon scales."

Lilly eyed him. "And how do you know this?"

Condor shrugged. "State secrets. It's the same type of knowledge as the location of the Arcanum, but the Dragon's Breath is believed to be lost forever."

"It is no longer lost." Magnus stared at Condor, then at Lumen. "He showed me exactly where it is."

"Where?" Axel asked.

"In the Desert of the Forgotten," Lumen replied.

Another low growl rumbled from Riley's throat.

Axel folded his arms and smirked at Lumen. "Well, I suppose if we gotta do this, it'll be a lot easier with you around."

"I am not going with you," Lumen replied.

"*What?*" Axel let his arms slump to his sides as he gawked at Lumen.

"I am not going with you," Lumen repeated. "I must remain here. There is much work to do in preparation for our uprising. That is why I need you to gather the army on my behalf."

Calum had suspected that would be the case when Lumen had first proposed the idea, but it still left him feeling abandoned. He'd done so much already, yet Lumen insisted there was still more to accomplish before all could be made right.

It made sense to Calum, but a part of him had expected it to be easier once Lumen was freed. He'd hoped Lumen would shoulder most of the burden from then on, but that didn't seem to be the case. It left Calum wondering if he'd simply had the wrong expectations going into all of this.

Axel clenched his fists. "You mean to tell me that after all we went through to set you free, after all we suffered, after all those miles we walked through Kanarah, now we have to do it all over again *without* your help?"

Lumen just stared at Axel with those blazing white orbs, and his eyes narrowed.

"Perhaps you're forgetting that Lumen spent the last millennium in isolation, Farm Boy." Condor smirked at Axel. "Comparatively, we still have it pretty good."

Axel frowned at him. "I just don't see why he's not coming with us."

Without so much as a word, Lumen pointed to Kanarah City. In the distance, a crowd of hundreds of people had spilled out of the city and started toward the crater. Among them stood Jake and those of his crew who had survived, staring at Lumen in awe.

"Those people saw what I did. My displays of power. They now come forth to join me, to join us in bringing our rebellion to the King."

Calum squinted. Perhaps hundreds was too low an estimation. Far more people came out of Kanarah City than the number of soldiers Matthios had brought against them. Calum had never been good at sizing up large groups, but there had to be at least a thousand people streaming toward them.

"Some of those people will stay, and others will return to their daily lives. Many will side with the King. Those who remain with us must be trained, taught, and cared for. I cannot do those things if I must also raise an army from the other half of Kanarah."

Lumen's gaze fixed on Axel for a long moment, then he shifted it to Calum. "But you can help me, as you have helped me so much already. You can unite *all* of Kanarah in my name, and together we can free everyone from the King's grasp once and for all."

A swell of purpose rose in Calum's chest, banishing the doubt that had threatened to take root there. "I want to, but no one will believe me. I'm nobody. Why would anyone listen to me?"

Lumen extended his fingers toward Calum. "Give me your left hand."

Calum reached forward, and Lumen's long armored fingers curled around it, enveloping it as if Calum were nothing but a child. Compared to Lumen, he supposed he was.

A white light emanated from Lumen's palm. A subtle burning sensation spread through the tendons and nerves in Calum's fingers. The light shone through Calum's hand and remained there even when Lumen pulled his hand away.

"This will serve as a sign to all who would doubt your claims that I am free and that I intend to liberate Kanarah. To summon the light, you need only to command it with your mind, and it will shine from your hand," Lumen said. "May it light your way in dark places, should you need it.

"Then, once your task is complete, I will grant each of you power, *real* power to do miraculous and impossible things. You will be my generals, my imperators, but not until you return with an army to command."

"Good." Axel rubbed his hands together. "We're gonna need it."

The light in Calum's hand flared with every command, no matter how subtle, that he allowed to cross his mind. When he commanded it to fade to nothing, it extinguished altogether, but it came back just as quickly as he summoned it, bringing the subtle burning sensation with it. The burn annoyed him, but it didn't stop him from exploring his newfound power.

Regardless of what Axel said or thought, Lumen had already granted Calum real power, if only a small measure of it. It would be more than enough to rally the people of Western Kanarah. If they could see his hand, touch it, examine it, and know that the power came from Lumen, how could they resist Lumen's call?

"We accept." Calum scanned the eyes of his companions. Even if he had to go alone, he would find a way, but he remained optimistic that he wouldn't be going alone. "We'll get you your army, won't we?"

Lilly nodded. "Yes. We will."

Her agreement sent a happy shudder through Calum's chest.

Condor shrugged. "I go where she goes."

Magnus exhaled a long hiss through his nose. "I have been away from home for far too long. If nothing else, I will relish the surprise in my uncle's eyes before he kills us all."

"Let's try to avoid that last part, alright?" Calum hoped Magnus wasn't serious.

Magnus smirked at him. "If you insist."

Calum turned to Riley. "What about you?"

Riley growled again. "The last place I wanna go is that desert, but if you go without me, you'll get yourselves killed, or robbed, or lost, or all of those things. I can go with you, but I'm bringing the last of the Wolves with me."

"Fine with me. They'll be useful to have around." Calum looked to Axel next. "You coming, or not?"

Axel glared at him. "What do you expect me to say? I don't like how this is playing out, but you've been right about basically everything else since we left. If I keep saying 'no' all the time, I'm gonna start lookin' like a fool."

"You 'started' that a long time ago," Magnus muttered.

"At least I still have all my parts, *Scales*," Axel sneered.

Magnus snorted and rolled his golden eyes. "Even without my right hand, I am still more than a match for you, boy."

"So you're in?" Calum interjected before Axel could fire back.

Axel pursed his lips and huffed. "Yeah. I'm in."

"Excellent." Lumen nodded. "I can take you as far as the center of Trader's Pass, but from there you must go alone. For now, you must rest. In three hours, we will depart."

LILLY STRETCHED her legs and lay on the ground, her eyes fixed on the clear blue sky above. In her periphery, golden wheat waved around her.

When her eyes had opened nine months earlier, after Roderick had hit her with that arrow, she'd seen much the same view, except that back then, Calum's, Axel's, and Magnus's faces had come into view as well.

She had once laid claim to the sky. Owned it. It had been her playground as a child, her escape in her adolescence, and her battlefield as she entered womanhood. Through all of it, she had ruled the air. She had tamed the vast blue ether over Kanarah.

But now that confidence, that youthful impression of dominion, had died along with Falcroné. With the exception of Lilly's time in Roderick's captivity and her return trip home, Fal had flown at her side almost every day since she was born. And now he was gone, crushed and eaten by the Jyrak.

The memory, still fresh in her mind, churned her stomach. While she was dazed and vulnerable, he'd darted between the Jyrak's fingers, jammed his sword into its middle finger, and kept it from squashing her. He'd bought Condor a few precious seconds to grab Lilly and pull her free, but not enough time to save himself as well.

Lilly shut out the sky with her eyelids, and tears streamed down the sides of her head toward her ears. The last thing she'd really said to him was...

Well, she'd said she loved him. They had argued high up in the crow's nest on Jake's ship, and he'd accused her of loving Calum. Then Falcroné had released her from her engagement to him.

And though she had insisted that she loved Falcroné, they both knew it wasn't true—at least not in the way she loved Calum. He exhibited qualities unlike anything she'd ever seen in anyone else before.

Kindness, but not weakness. Mercy, but not without a sense of justice. Empathy, but not without action to back it up. She probably could list them forever. Calum embodied everything *she* wanted to be.

Though she couldn't bring herself to admit it to Falcroné then, or even to herself in that moment, she'd come to fully realize the truth of it: she *did* love Calum. With everything she was, she loved him.

"Hey."

Lilly opened her eyes and saw Axel standing over her. She wiped the remnants of her tears from her face and looked up at him. "Hey."

"Mind if I join you?"

Lilly raised her head a few inches off the ground and glanced around, but all she saw from her vantage point was wheat waving in the wind. Golden wheat, only a few shades darker than Falcroné's hair, but close enough that it still reminded her of him.

"Lilly?"

She refocused on Axel and hesitated. After their exchange in her chambers back in the Sky Fortress, being alone with him made her uneasy.

"Calum and Condor are talking with Lumen. Magnus is resting, and Riley is rounding up the rest of his pack." Axel cleared his throat. "So... do you mind if I join you?"

Lilly sighed and lay her head back down. Whether out of a baseless sense of obligation or a boundless hope for reconciliation—or perhaps both—she replied, "Sure."

Axel lay down next to her, but to his credit, he left a solid six inches between them. Even so, she wished it had been more, but she didn't dare scoot farther away. Perhaps if she lay there, still, he'd leave her alone.

In the quiet that followed, aside from the hypnotic hiss of the swaying wheat, Lilly didn't dare close her eyes, no matter how much she wanted to. Not with Axel right there.

He'd already made two moves, the kiss and his tantrum, and Lilly didn't know how she would tolerate a third. Frankly, she hadn't tolerated his second, and he wouldn't have gotten away with the first had Calum not walked into the room before she could do something about it.

Now, with Axel lying next to her, she wondered if she was sending the wrong signal to him— the signal that this was somehow alright.

Axel cleared his throat again, but it sounded more like a grunt this time. "I'm sorry about Fal."

"Only his friends called him Fal, Axel. You weren't one of them."

Too harsh? Maybe, but after Axel had attacked her, Falcroné wanted to tear him to shreds, so Lilly's statement was true. Plus, it would serve as a reminder that she held no interest in him nor ever would.

Axel's jaw hardened. "What's your problem?"

Yep. Too harsh. "I don't want to talk about it."

"I came over here to tell you I was here if you needed anything, and you snapped at me." Axel frowned at her. "Did I do something to offend you?"

Lilly sighed. "Recently?"

Axel cleared his throat. "Look, I know I was wrong before, but—"

"I said don't want to talk about it." Lilly stared steel into his dark-blue eyes. *"Any* of it."

"Do you mind if I stay here with you anyway, or would you rather be alone?"

In truth, she would've welcomed company from anyone in their group other than Axel. Processing Falcroné's death was hard enough, but Axel being there only made things harder. She regretted ever letting him take a spot next to her.

"You can go," she finally said.

Without hesitation, Axel pushed himself up and stood over Lilly. "Fine. If you decide you want someone to talk to, I'm around."

"Thanks." Lilly's voice flattened.

She watched him go, her muscles tense and ready to propel her into the air if she had to, but he melted into the golden grain and didn't return. She lay there, on edge, until she couldn't resist her body's calls for slumber any longer, and she fell asleep.

THE KING CROUCHED next to a bed of red roses that ran along the back wall of his garden. Though a myriad of flowery scents permeated the air, everything was not as it should be.

He touched the withering petal of one of the smaller roses and frowned. "Ursula?"

Within seconds, a short woman in brown work boots, grass-stained tan trousers, and a green tunic strode to his side and bowed low. As she stood upright, she wiped her exposed forehead with the back of her gloved hand and mussed up her close-cropped red hair. "Your Majesty?"

"These roses need attention."

"Right away, Sire."

As Ursula trotted away, a soldier in silver armor emerged from the archway that led back into the palace. The King recognized his face.

"What is it, Torreon?"

"Your majesty, Matthios is returning. He's—" Torreon choked on his words. "—alone."

The King stood to his full height and scowled at Torreon with his fists clenched. Rage seeped into his chest and spread like wildfire through his veins.

"See him to my throne room," the King ordered. "Immediately."

CHAPTER 4

Within seconds of stepping into Lumen's portal, the Golden Plains evaporated from Calum's view, replaced by the dull gray of Trader's Pass and the nearby Tri-Lakes.

Calum's stomach sloshed, and this time he almost threw up. He'd hoped he might get used to the sensation, but so far, no luck.

Together with Magnus, Axel, Lilly, Condor, Kanton, Riley, and three of his Wolves, Dallahan, Embry, and Janessa, Calum surveyed the familiar surroundings.

"We have arrived." Lumen also scanned the barren wasteland with those fiery eyes of his then looked toward the Central Lake and smirked. "I do not expect you will run into any Dactyls. They are likely feeding on the Jyrak's carcass and will be for quite some time."

"Good." Axel straightened his back and sucked in a deep breath. "I've encountered more than enough of them to last me a lifetime."

"Make haste. Build this army, and bring our forces back across Trader's Pass to the Golden Plains. From there, we will launch our assault on the King and put an end to his destructive reign." Lumen's gaze fixed on Calum. "You will succeed, with my blessing."

Before Calum could say anything else, Lumen entered another void of white light, which promptly twisted into a spiral of white light and disappeared.

Wind whistled over the valley, the only sound until Axel spoke up. "Are we just gonna stand here, or what? This army's not gonna build itself."

Calum nodded. "He's right. Let's go."

"Can't you humans speed things up? We would've been there already if you could fly." Condor winked at Axel.

But Axel didn't find anything about Condor's presence amusing.

Ever since Falcroné died, Condor had lingered closer to Lilly than usual, and it bothered Axel to no end. Granted, they'd only started their journey from the center of Trader's Pass a few days ago, and Lilly *had* named him her Captain of the Royal Guard alongside Falcroné.

But did Condor always have to walk so close to Lilly? He *really* didn't have to let his arm would brush hers sometimes, and he definitely didn't need to keep touching her shoulders when she seemed sad.

It all bothered Axel.

Though he'd never liked Falcroné, Axel had respected his prowess as a fighter. Of course, when Falcroné died, it had stunned Axel like the rest of the group, but his death also meant Axel had another shot with Lilly.

Perhaps it was callous to think about such things while Lilly still grieved her loss, but she had to move on with her life eventually. And when she finally did, he intended to be in the picture. But in order for that to work, he couldn't abide Condor behaving this way around her.

The last thing he needed was interference from *another* Windgale, especially from someone like Condor. Yes, Axel would have to do something about—

"Hey, Farm Boy." Condor's voice snapped Axel back into real life. "Taking my joke a bit hard over there?"

Axel furrowed his brow. "I'm fine."

"No need to get worked up over it." A wry grin curled Condor's lips. "We all know you can't help being slow."

Axel's scowl deepened. "Just remember who set you free from that cell in Oren's fortress."

"I most certainly will. And you'd best remember who saved you from Oren himself." Condor winked at him again.

Axel's stomach twisted. He shouldn't let Condor get to him so easily, but his words somehow always managed to penetrate Axel's armor and prick him from the inside out.

"You look as though you're chewing on sour meat all the time. Cheer up." Condor made it to Axel's side in an instant, and he hooked his arm around Axel's armored shoulders as they walked.

Axel grunted and ducked away from Condor's. "*Don't* do that."

Condor raised an incredulous eyebrow. "Really? You're upset that I put my arm around your shoulders in a gesture of friendship?"

"All I'm saying is you might not like what happens if you do it again." Axel stared steel into Condor's vivid blue eyes.

"As tempting as your offer is, I can't be bothered to gratify it with a response." Condor's expression hardened and his eyes communicated a dangerous promise of their own, but only for an instant. Then they reverted back to nothing but cheers and celebration. "Today is not our day, Farm Boy."

Before Axel could respond, Condor leaped into the air, landed next to Lilly's side, and walked with her again, too close for Axel's liking.

The three Wolves barked and yipped behind Axel amid chattering conversation. As if dealing with Condor wasn't bad enough, he also had to put up with the Wolves' near-constant snarling, periodic sniffs, and their zigzagging forms racing through the rest of the group.

The combination of his helplessness to separate Condor from Lilly and the Wolves' erratic behavior would drive him to madness before long.

To compound Axel's frustrations, the three surviving Wolves were the same trio who'd stolen his last piece of dried venison just before they'd reached the Arcanum. *Mangy thieves.*

He didn't trust them. Axel's only consolation about their presence was that he didn't have anything left for them to steal. But even that wouldn't keep them from annoying him.

At the head of their group, Calum and Magnus led the way, as usual, and Riley followed with Kanton by his side. The two pairs murmured to each other as they walked, and so did Condor and Lilly.

Axel scowled. As usual, no one wanted to talk to *him*.

Only a few days in, and already everyone had begun to grate against him. This was going to be a long journey if he had to make it alone.

He couldn't talk to the Wolves because they'd annoy him, he couldn't talk to Lilly because Condor was always around, and he didn't want to talk to Calum and Magnus because they were both smug and obnoxious now that they'd been proven right about Lumen.

That left only one option.

Axel grunted and quickened his pace to catch up with Riley and Kanton. "Hey, guys."

They both stared at him for a moment, and then nodded to him, but where Kanton gave Axel his attention, Riley refocused on the road ahead of them.

"What can I do for you, Axel? Are you injured?" Kanton asked.

Axel shook his head. "I'm fine. How 'bout you? How's your hand?"

Kanton held it up and wiggled his fingers. "Still hurts, and I can't really use it yet, but it's been healing a little bit every day since the Wolf chomped on it. Faster than usual, thanks to Magnus's veromine."

"We almost lost you a few times in that battle with the Dactyls and the Sobeks," Axel said.

Kanton chuckled. "Don't forget about when we faced the Jyrak, too. I was all but useless. See, I never learned how to fight left-handed, and I never had much formal training in fighting anyway. I guess it all just comes down to the fact that I..."

As Kanton rambled on, Axel studied Riley's Werewolf form. He'd transformed from a scrawny Wolf into this menacing muscular creature, complete with elongated claws, an extended snout, and jagged teeth that jutted out beyond his lips.

Thanks to his transformation, Riley stood taller than everyone else in their group except Magnus. He commanded both his small pack of Wolves and the respect of everyone in the party.

But who respected Axel? He shook his head and sighed. No one.

"You still listening, Axel?" Kanton nudged his shoulder.

"Huh?" Axel stared into Kanton's blue eyes then blinked himself back into the moment. "Sorry. I let my mind wander."

Kanton grinned. "Happens to the best of us, friend."

Riley stared down at Axel, then he faced forward again.

"You got a problem?" Axel asked.

Riley didn't look at him. "No."

"I think I'll go check Magnus's hand. See how it's regenerating." With that, Kanton left his feet and zipped up to the front of the group near Magnus and Calum.

Axel frowned at Riley. "You remember I apologized to you, right?"

Riley just kept walking, his eyes forward.

"It was in the woods before the Werewolf attacked. Don't you remember how I—"

"I remember." Riley still didn't look at Axel.

"So what are you upset about?"

"I'm not upset."

Axel grunted. "We're part of the same team, Riley. I need to know that you've got my back in battles, and you need to know that I've got—"

"I don't need you to watch my back," Riley interrupted. "No one sneaks up behind me—*I* sneak up behind them."

Riley had been quick and stealthy before his transformation into a Werewolf, but now he could move in almost complete silence and with incredible speed. Thus far, Axel had only seen Condor move faster.

"My point is that we need to trust each other," Axel said. "For the good of the group as a whole. You never told me if you accepted my apology or not."

Riley said nothing.

"Look, Riley—"

"I'm not having this conversation." With that, Riley darted forward and walked next to Condor and Lilly. He cleared several yards in the same amount of time Axel would've needed for a single step.

And once again, Axel was alone. His frown turned into a mask of anger that mirrored the fury rising in his chest.

The Wolves behind him yipped and barked. It sounded like laughter.

Laughter directed at him.

Axel whirled around and snapped at them, "Would you *shut up* already?"

The three of them went silent and stared at him for a few seconds. Then they continued yipping and barking and chattering as they walked, as if he'd never even yelled at them in the first place.

Axel wanted to draw his sword right then and there. Not to hurt them, necessarily, but to frighten them into being quiet. The only reason he didn't do it was because he knew it wouldn't work. More likely than not, they actually *would* start laughing at him, and that would only make everything worse.

Axel turned around to find Calum there. He'd walked back to Axel.

"You alright back here?" he asked.

"Fine." Axel couldn't tell him what he was really feeling—alone, abandoned, worthless. What was the point of him even being there in the first place? He should've stayed with Lumen and gotten some real power for himself instead of going on this fool's errand to recruit an army.

"Try not to let them bother you." Calum smiled and patted Axel's shoulder. "They're just excitable."

"Apparently."

"Why don't you come up and walk with us?" Calum offered. "It's easier to pass the time with a little conversation."

Easy for you to say. Everyone loves you. Axel stifled a frown. He wanted to do it, to go up there and be a part of the group again, but what was the point? He'd be pretending as much as everyone else. No one actually wanted him here, so why perpetuate the lie?

"I'm fine back here," he replied.

"Suit yourself." Calum shrugged. "It won't be long now before we reach Aeropolis."

The instant Calum turned away, Axel's frown manifested again.

Just when things couldn't get any worse...

Of all the places in Kanarah, the Sky Realm was the one place he did *not* want to go back to.

MAGNUS STRETCHED the fingers on his right hand—his new right hand. As he'd assured Calum, he'd regrown what Vandorian had taken from him within a matter of days. Now five scaled fingers tipped with small talons opened and closed into a fist.

He'd never lost anything as significant as a hand before. As a child, he'd lost a finger when training to properly wield a sword with Garondus, one of his many older brothers. It hurt terribly, but it had grown back within a matter of days.

Like that finger, his new hand bore a lighter coloring than the rest of his arm. Where dark-green scales covered the majority of his hide, his hand looked more grass-green, and his talons were a dark-gray color instead of matching the black talons on his left hand.

"Your hand is back." Calum sat down next to him. "I'm jealous. If someone cut off my hand, I just wouldn't have one anymore."

"Yes, but you are human. You are not expected to regrow lost appendages."

"That doesn't mean it wouldn't come in handy." Calum grinned. "Pun intended."

Magnus scowled at him. "Normally, I have such great respect for you."

Calum chuckled, still staring at Magnus's new hand. "How does it feel?"

"Tight. Uncomfortable. I suspect I will need a few more days before I can properly wield a sword with it. Probably a few days after that to retrain myself to fight as efficiently as I used to." Magnus flexed his fingers again, and pain thrummed from his fingers into his forearm. "But I will be ready for him when next we meet. That is for certain."

Calum nodded. "I have no doubt."

DUSK SETTLED across the gray landscape as the group approached the end of Trader's Pass, and Riley's nose wrinkled. The air had a foul stink to it.

He let out a guttural woof, and Janessa strode up beside him.

"Smell that?" Riley asked. "Something's burning."

Janessa nodded and stared at him with glistening yellow eyes. "Not just some*thing*. A *lot* of things. Things that shouldn't be burning."

"I smell it too," Dallahan said from behind.

"I wasn't talking to you," Riley said.

"Doesn't mean I didn't hear you." Dallahan's inflection brought a grin to Riley's face. He'd finally found a fellow Wolf as sarcastic as he was, if not more so.

"Do we tell them?" Embry muttered.

"Do you know what's burning?" Riley met Embry's green eyes.

"I can't tell from this distance."

"I can." Janessa tipped her snout upward and sniffed the air, then stared at Riley. "It's coming from the southwest. You know what that means."

Riley nodded. He'd come to the same conclusion, and he couldn't keep it to himself. He darted over to Lilly and Condor. "Lilly."

She blinked at his sudden appearance in front of her. "Hi, Riley."

"I have bad news."

Concern filled her blue eyes. "What is it?"

Riley exhaled a deep sigh and glanced at Condor. "Aeropolis is burning."

CHAPTER 5

Had Condor not restrained Lilly, she would've taken to the sky and flown clear through the night and most of the next day toward Aeropolis. Yet even if she had gotten a chance to fly, Condor would have caught her within seconds anyway.

If only she were a Wisp, too, she might be able to evade him. More importantly, she could get back to Aeropolis sooner to ascertain whether Riley's claim was accurate or not.

"If the city is burning, then there's a reason." Condor still restrained her. His warm breath hit her ear, his voice quiet. "Even if you made it there on your own, what would you do? If something *is* happening, you'd rush in and get yourself killed."

"Then come with me." Lilly tried to twist free from his grip. She couldn't. "You're sworn to protect me, so do it."

"Let her go, Condor." Axel's voice had taken on that hard, dangerous tone he employed when he meant to enforce his words with violence. He stepped toward Lilly and Condor.

Condor's grip didn't loosen, and aside from a casual glance at Axel, Condor ignored him. "I'm protecting you right now."

How could he keep his voice so calm? Especially in a situation like this?

Didn't he realize that everything she knew and loved could be burning to ash, and she wasn't there to help?

"You don't care anymore," she spat. "It's no longer your home. Why should *you* care if it burns? Why should *you* try to stop it?"

In one quick motion, Condor spun Lilly around, gripped her shoulders, and stared at her with those piercing blue eyes of his. "Insult me as often as you wish, Princess, but you know my allegiance lies both with you and with our people. Do not mistake my caution for apathy. If Aeropolis burns, then my heart burns with it, but I will *not* allow you to fly to your doom."

"I said *let her go.*" Axel's warning sounded behind her, followed by the *shing* of his sword leaving its sheath.

"This doesn't concern you, Farm Boy." Condor extended his index finger at Axel. "This is Windgale business."

"I'm an honorary citizen. The Premier made me one, but he banished you from the Sky

Realm indefinitely. So it's actually more *my* business than it is yours."

Condor sighed, and his hand migrated to the hilt of his own blade.

Lilly's fingers curled around his wrist. "Don't, Condor."

He stayed his hand and met her eyes once again.

Though unsure why, Lilly leaned into Condor rather than trying to pull away this time. In Falcroné's absence, Condor was the closest thing she had to home—a living reminder. Perhaps that was the reason.

But perhaps it was something else. Something about Condor himself.

Condor wrapped his arms around her. He still hadn't donned any armor since they'd freed him from Oren's fortress, so she felt every bit of his warmth as she pressed her face against his chest. Lilly heard his heartbeat through his shirt.

A long sigh escaped her lips, and though it felt wonderful to be close to him, she still sobbed.

"It's alright," Condor whispered. She felt his fingers running through her hair and brushing against her left cheek. "We'll learn the truth soon enough."

Another *shing*, this time followed by an abrupt click, sounded behind her. She imagined the furious expression on Axel's face, and it brought her some measure of relief.

But then Calum's face sprang to her mind.

Lost in Condor's arms, she hadn't even considered how her actions might've affected Calum. After what she'd told Falcroné before he died, perhaps she shouldn't cling so close to Condor.

But it felt so right, being held by someone so powerful, so intriguing, so unique. A rebel. A handsome one at that, with his raven-black hair, that scar that ran from the outer edge of his left eyebrow down to the top of his cheek, and those piercing blue eyes...

She released her grip on Condor and looked up at him, wiping the tears from her cheeks. Just behind him, Calum stared at her with soft blue eyes, tinged with a hint of distress but also with a measure of reassurance.

Always on her side, no matter what. She granted herself a half-smile.

Whether or not she enjoyed holding Condor, and regardless of Calum's feelings, she needed to get back home. She could sort out her emotions later.

"Come on," Lilly said to all of them. "We've got to get to the Sky Fortress."

WHILE CONDOR and Lilly led the way, Calum and the rest of the group followed close behind at a quickened pace.

They passed the dead tree near the western end of Trader's Pass and the same field toward the forest where they had battled Condor and his Raven's Brood months earlier. But this time they traveled at night, and the moonlight cast the jagged shadows of spidery tree limbs across the road.

Calum's legs burned from the nonstop trek. They hadn't stopped since the short break after Riley revealed what he'd smelled, and Lilly showed no signs of letting up. Calum had to hand it to her—when she set her mind to something, she didn't relent.

An hour later, despite Lilly's reluctance, they made camp for the night. Six hours after that, they were back on the road as the first hint of daylight crept over the horizon.

As they approached Aeropolis, the smell of smoke stung Calum's nostrils. In the morning light, black plumes rose from the southwest, far away.

Tears streaked Lilly's otherwise stoic face, but she moved forward. Calum wanted to reach out and comfort her, but with Condor always so close, he never got an opportunity.

Within hours of their departure from the forest, they encountered their first refugee: a flightless Windgale man whose cape had burned half off. Lilly pleaded with him for information, but the man simply walked forward, his blue eyes vacant, mumbling the words "Filnia, Lucius, Harvold, Milarette" again and again.

No matter what Lilly or the others said or did, they couldn't break through the man's malaise, and they had to let him continue on his way.

The closer they got to Aeropolis, the more strays they encountered—some of them more lucid than the first refugee, some of them far, far worse. Most of them begged Calum's group for help, but with limited supplies, they weren't equipped to help even the smallest fraction of the hundreds of souls who now trudged toward them.

When Aeropolis itself finally crested the horizon, Calum's attention shifted to a new batch of refugees who approached: a dozen soldiers clad in vibrant purple armor, streaked with blood, led by a Wisp in dark-violet battle gear.

"Stay behind me, Lilly. At least at first." Condor positioned himself between Lilly and the approaching Windgale soldiers.

Calum, Magnus, Axel, Riley, and the Wolves surrounded her in a protective formation.

Condor extended his hand. "Captain, by the authority of the Princess of the Sky Realm, I order you to stand down."

The Wisp captain drew his sword, his eyes fixed on Magnus, and the soldiers in his unit did likewise. "The princess is gone. She left months ago and hasn't been seen since."

"Captain, that's Condor." One of the soldiers pointed at him, and half the soldiers in the squad mumbled in the affirmative. "The disgraced Captain of the Royal Guard."

Calum uncurled his fingers, ready to draw his sword. He stole a glance at Magnus, whose hands remained at his sides.

The Captain narrowed his eyes at Condor, who still wore plain clothes, now stained and dirty, a stark image against the soldiers and their fine armor. "Are you Condor?"

Condor's jaw tightened. "Yes. What is your name, Captain?"

"I am Captain Perine, of the fourth battalion under General Bravenstorm," the Captain replied, his sword still in hand. "How is it that you've come here? You were banished months ago. Avian himself pronounced your sentence."

Maybe Captain Perine talking to them was a good sign, but Calum didn't let his guard down.

Condor motioned toward Calum, Lilly, and the rest of the group. "Princess Lilly and her companions freed me from the fortress at the Blood Chasm, and we released dozens of slaves—humans and Windgales alike. A Saurian named Chorian led some of them back here."

The same soldier who'd recognized Condor nudged Captain Perine. "A Saurian and a group about that size showed up a mere three days before the attack. I think he's telling the truth."

"Who was it that attacked you?" Calum asked.

Captain Perine's jaw hardened, and he frowned at Calum. "Reptilius. The Saurians."

"The *Saurians* attacked?" Lilly pushed past Condor. "There wasn't an insurrection?"

Captain Perine's eyes widened, and he dropped to his knee before her. The soldiers behind him followed suit and pressed their hands against their chests, fingers outstretched with their wrists crossed—the Windgale salute.

"Answer me, Captain," Lilly commanded.

"Forgive me, Your Highness." Captain Perine stood upright and sheathed his sword. The soldiers stood and relaxed their weapons. "I didn't recognize you at first, but your armor is unmistakable, and I remember your face. I shouldn't have—"

"I said *answer me*, Captain." Lilly's voice took on a firm tone. "Tell me what happened."

"Right away, Your Highness. Less than two days ago, the bulk of the Crimson Keep's army assaulted our Realm—" Captain Perine swallowed. "—led by Kahn, the Dragon King, himself."

CHAPTER 6

"K ahn *himself?*" Magnus repeated.

Calum gawked. Kahn—Magnus's uncle—had killed Praetorius, Magnus's father, and then succeeded him as the ruler of Reptilius. Together with Vandorian, Magnus's oldest brother, Kahn had murdered Magnus's siblings in an attempt to secure his claim to power.

He would have murdered Magnus, too, had he not escaped—somehow. That part was still hazy for Calum.

What's more, Kahn reigned as the only living Dragon in Kanarah, which meant he was all but invulnerable, at least as far as Calum knew. Beyond that, Calum only had a limited sense of Kahn's capabilities, though he feared he might soon witness the aftermath of Kahn's power firsthand.

"Vandorian commands their army under normal circumstances, but for whatever reason, Kahn spearheaded the attack," Captain Perine said. "Dozens of Saurian warriors rode on his back up to Aeropolis and spread throughout the city like a cancer. Once they controlled the lift, we stood little chance. They just kept coming, more and more of them—"

"What of—" Lilly's voice cracked with emotion. She steeled herself and continued. "What of my father and mother?"

Captain Perine shook his head. "I'm not sure of their fate. When we fled a few hours ago, the outside of the fortress was swarmed with Saurian scum, but as you know, it is the most fortified structure in the entire realm. Perhaps they—"

"I've heard enough." Lilly's voice quivered, then it hardened. "You and your men will accompany us to the Sky Fortress at once."

"Your Highness," Captain Perine began, "I don't think it is wise to venture back to the city until we know for sure that—"

"No, Captain," Lilly cut in, resolve etched onto her beautiful face. "There will be no discussion or dissension. Your men will carry my non-flying companions the rest of the way. If there

CALUM HADN'T DECIDED which method of travel he disliked more: transporting via Lumen's portals or flying via the assistance of Windgales and Wisps. Jumping dozens or even hundreds of miles left Calum feeling sick and woozy, but the prospect of his feet leaving the ground and entrusting his life to someone else while in midair had more or less the same effect.

As usual, it took the majority of the soldiers just to get Magnus off the ground. With Condor, Lilly, and Kanton's help, the soldiers managed to get the rest of their party airborne, and they ascended toward Aeropolis. They climbed higher into the air, leaving both the ground and hundreds of battered refugees beneath them.

When they broke through the clouds, plumes of thick black smoke, stark against the otherwise clear skies, caught Calum's attention, but he soon found he couldn't look away from the devastation before him. Where he had marveled at Aeropolis's grandeur and beauty on his first journey up to it, the destruction he now witnessed saturated his gut with grief.

Aeropolis's spires, once pristine spikes of blue crystal, now amounted to mounds of blackened stone suspended by towering gray pillars. Bodies of slain Windgales, some soldiers and many more civilians, lay strewn across the silver platforms that served as the spires' bases.

Some of them lay in pools of red, and others amounted to nothing more than charred corpses. Calum spied a few green reptilian carcasses, most of them clad in full armor, scattered among the dead Windgales, but not nearly as many.

Even from a distance, Calum could see that the Sky Fortress yet stood, but its multiple gold-tipped spires and towers lay in scorched ruins on the expansive silver platform underneath it. Kahn had reduced it to a basic cube-shaped structure of black metal, devoid of all its former opulence, but as yet impenetrable as far as Calum could tell.

That impression changed as they closed in on the Sky Fortress. The once-polished brass doors at the front of the Sky Fortress now existed as a pool of cooling metal, and instead of two Windgale guards, two Saurians clad in black armor watched their approach.

The Saurians pulled swords from their scabbards and hissed. Condor, who'd been assisting Calum upward, released his hold under Calum's left arm and shot toward them.

The soldier holding Calum's right arm glided them both to the platform where they watched Condor dispatch the two Saurians in quick succession.

When Condor turned back, dark blood streaked across his chest and face from the two Saurians. He approached Captain Perine. "They've breached the fortress. We need to hurry to the throne room."

Captain Perine hesitated. "Again, I must ask, is it wise to bring the Princess into—"

"I'm going with you," Lilly asserted.

Captain Perine bowed his head. "I mean no disrespect, Your Highness. I just wondered if perhaps we should clear the way so as to ensure your safety."

"I am capable of defending myself, but you and Condor may lead us inside." She focused her attention on Calum. "Calum, Axel, and Riley will also protect me, as will Magnus."

Calum nodded and drew his sword. He would guard Lilly until the very end, even at the cost of his own life, if it ever came to it.

The interior of the Sky Fortress no longer exuded the grandeur Calum had witnessed during his first visit. Now it looked more like a firestorm swirling with blades had destroyed everything and everyone within.

The crystal chandeliers that once hung from the lobby's lofted ceiling lay shattered on the marble, and the torches and matching flower pots that had adorned the walls now existed only as pools and streaks of melted brass across the white marble floors, along with blood. The grand staircase that had spiraled upward in the center was entirely gone.

What proved the starkest difference to Calum was the lack of Windgales and Wisps zipping about. The fortress had once been a vibrant, active area, but now it had crumbled into an open-air crypt for dozens of Windgales and about a third as many Saurians. Half the Windgale victims wore armor, but the other half wore fine clothing, now torn and saturated with crimson.

Condor led them between two enormous piles of blackened crystal rubble, toward the throne room.

Calum recalled the polished wooden doors that fed into the next chamber. He lost himself staring at one of the wrought-iron handles lying in a pile of smoldering gray ash on the floor until a sharp hiss broke his concentration.

A platoon of a eight Saurians, two of them Sobeks, stood outside the black steel throne room doors—doors that were now horribly bent and contorted. One of the Sobeks pointed a spear at them that looked too big for even three men to carry, let alone to wield in battle.

"Captain, order your men into the attack phalanx," Condor ordered. "Take out the Saurians first, then assist Magnus and me with the Sobeks if we haven't already killed them."

Captain Perine hesitated at first and fixed his eyes on Lilly.

She nodded to him and nocked an arrow in her bow. "Do as he commands."

"Attack phalanx," Captain Perine barked. The Windgale soldiers formed a hovering wall, three Windgales high and four wide. The formation almost resembled a massive purple eye with Captain Perine as its deep violet pupil. "*Advance.*"

Each of the Windgale soldiers raised their arms until their knuckles leveled with their chins. Their elbows cocked behind their heads, ready to strike with their weapons. While Condor and Magnus circled toward the two Sobeks, Calum and Axel stood next to Lilly, one on each side, ready in case any of the Saurians tried to make it to her.

Riley growled, and Janessa, Dallahan, and Embry began to orbit Lilly's position in wide circles, and Kanton hovered nearby as well. Meanwhile, Riley evaporated into the shadows of the nearest rubble pile. He blended so perfectly with the darkness that Calum didn't know if he was still there or if he'd moved on to another spot.

These Saurians didn't stand a chance.

Captain Perine yelled another order, and two Windgale soldiers, one from the top level and one from the middle level, darted forward, blades first. Their swords clanged off those of two of the Saurians in quick succession, and then the two Windgale soldiers retracted back into formation. The attacks continued, rapid-fire, in a coordinated but complicated pattern.

Magnus stormed toward the Sobeks as Condor arced behind them, and they engaged the enemies in a harmonic union. Magnus traded blows with the Sobeks while Condor zipped between them, his blade clanging against their thick hides.

Condor's sword clipped the neck of one of the Sobeks, the shorter of the two, and he recoiled. Then Magnus whirled around and lashed his broadsword at the Sobek, opening a deep gash in his throat. He dropped to the white marble floor, clutching at his neck.

Apparently, Magnus's new hand was working properly already.

In a surprisingly fast motion, the other Sobek raised his sword to strike Magnus, who was defenseless to repel the attack. Calum opened his mouth to shout, but a dark blur rammed into the Sobek before he could swing.

Riley. He hooked his right hand around the Sobek's massive leg and lifted up, toppling the Sobek onto the hard floor. Condor dropped out of the sky and landed on the Sobek's chest, then jammed his sword into the Sobek's open mouth. The Sobek writhed and convulsed for a moment, then he stopped moving.

Axel gave a mirthless chuckle, and Calum had to smirk at their efficiency.

In the time it took Magnus and Condor to take out the two Sobeks, the Windgale soldiers had winnowed the group of Saurians from six to only two. A thrum sounded next to Calum's ear, and one of Lilly's arrows lodged in the left eye of one of the remaining Saurians. He half-roared, half-wailed, and the Windgale soldiers finished him the next instant.

The final Saurian didn't last long after that. Captain Perine grunted another order, and instead of two Windgale soldiers attacking at once, six of them attacked the final Saurian and brought him down in a flurry of stabs and slashes.

"Hurry." Tension twisted Lilly's expression. "We need to get inside that throne room."

Condor nodded to her, then to Captain Perine. "Shield phalanx around the Princess. Calum, Axel, and the Wolves, follow Lilly inside. Magnus and I will lead."

With one vigorous ram, Magnus plowed through the mangled steel doors and into the throne room. Condor followed him inside, then Captain Perine and the Windgale soldiers, who surrounded Lilly in a protective half-sphere. Calum, Axel, Riley, Kanton, and the Wolves entered last.

To Calum's surprise, the interior of the throne room looked almost the same as it had before he'd left Aeropolis with Axel, Magnus, Lilly, Riley, and Kanton in search of the Arcanum. Overall, its structure remained intact, unlike much of the rest of the Sky Fortress.

Instead of crystal, dark metal formed the room's walls. Two rows of marble pillars, white and colossal, outlined the main walkway and reached up at least two hundred feet to the ceiling, mostly untouched, except for the occasional chip or gouge.

The main difference compared to before was that the corpses of dozens of bloodied Windgale soldiers and nobles now covered the once-pristine floors. Multiple Saurians and a few Sobeks lay amid some of the Windgale bodies, and gleaming weapons lay in pools of dark blood just inches away from the lifeless fingers of their owners.

One of those corpses lay propped against the blue crystal throne, clad in shimmering blue robes like Lilly's cape and adorned with yellow crystal. A crown, also made of yellow crystal, lay on the floor next to him.

Avian, the Premier.

CHAPTER 7

"No!" The word spilled from Lilly's mouth as horror clenched icy fingers around her heart. She darted out from behind the layers of soldiers and landed before her father.

"Lilly, wait!" Condor called after her, but she ignored him.

Dark splotches of blood soiled the fabric on his arms and legs, and a large red stain marred his stomach. His eyes were pinched shut, and his jaw tensed with strain, but he still drew breath.

Lilly tuned Condor out and crouched next to her father, cradling his head in her left arm. She cupped his jaw with her right hand. "Father? Open your eyes if you can hear me."

His eyelids cracked apart, revealing his cool blue irises, and he looked at her. The tension in his jaw slackened, and his lips curled into a faint smile. "Lilly."

"By the Overlord, he's alive! Condor, Kanton—someone help me!"

Both of them zipped over to her.

Upon seeing Condor, the Premier's eyes narrowed, and his relief reverted into a scowl. "What is *he* doing here?"

"He saved my life, Father. Multiple times. Now he serves me in—" Lilly stopped short of telling her father about Falcrone's death. It would only make things worse. "—in our time of greatest need. He is an ally once again, and that is all you need know for now."

Her father scoffed and waved Condor away with bloody fingers.

Footsteps approached from behind, to which Condor said, "Stay back. Give them space."

"Don't—don't waste your time," her father moaned more than said, "I'm dying."

When Kanton hesitated, Lilly glared at him. He began to unpack his healing supplies.

"Don't say such things, Father. Kanton is one of the finest healers I know. Besides, Captain Perine is going to send someone to find Lord Elmond at once. He can repair any wound, no matter how—"

Her father pulled his bloodied hand away from the wound in his stomach, stalling Lilly's words. Neither Kanton nor Lord Elmond could save him now.

"Oh, Daddy..." She resisted the emotion rising in her chest and forced herself not to cry.

A crash sounded from the opposite end of the throne room, near the door through which they had entered. A cacophony of hisses and guttural roars filled the throne room, cutting Lilly's grief short.

Her head swiveled, and she laid eyes on a dozen Saurians, all of them Sobeks wearing silver breastplates.

"The Supreme Guard," Magnus growled. "Aside from Vandorian's personal guard, they are the most formidable Sobeks in all of the Crimson Keep."

Condor left Lilly's side and positioned himself at the head of the group next to Magnus, Calum, and Axel. "We protect Lilly, no matter what."

Magnus shook his head. "We cannot defeat this force with our current strength. They will overcome us."

"Just buy me some time," Lilly called to them. "Let me say goodbye to my father. Just a few moments, and then we can flee."

"Done." Axel rolled his shoulders back and held up his sword. "You want a few minutes, you got 'em."

Magnus huffed. "Axel, we cannot—"

"We're gonna have to," Axel interrupted, "for a few minutes, at least. If you could've had a few more minutes with your father, wouldn't you want 'em?"

Magnus's eyes narrowed, and he exhaled a long breath through flared nostrils. "Form a defensive perimeter around Lilly. Condor and I will take point."

"Captain Perine, establish a perimeter around the throne. Protect Lilly and her father at all costs." Condor hovered above the rest of the group and floated toward the Sobeks. "I'm Condor, Captain of the Royal Guard. If you surrender now like the cowardly lizards you are, I'll ensure quick and merciful deaths for each of you."

The Sobeks chuckled and hissed and then started forward.

"Lilly," her father said, his voice weak. "I have no time left. Your mother is already dead, and that means that upon my passing, you will succeed me as the next ruler of the Sky Realm."

Lilly's heart shuddered at the mention of her mother's passing, but she remained focused on him. She would mourn them both later.

Swords clanged behind them, near the doors, followed by hisses, roars, shouts, and screams. The battle had begun, and that meant Lilly had precious few moments left with her dying father.

The Premier turned his head toward his yellow crystal crown, which lay near his left hand, the one not covering his wounded stomach, and he reached for it with bloody fingers. Strain tensed in his face until Lilly leaned over and nudged the crown within his grasp.

That simple act threatened to tear her heart asunder, but for her father's sake, she held her resolve.

Her father exhaled a long breath, then he clenched the crystal crown in his hand.

"Normally we would hold a coronation ceremony in the presence of the entire Sky Realm to commemorate this moment, but your friend Kanton will have to suffice as our official witness, given the circumstances."

Kanton nodded. "I'm happy to serve, Premier."

A weak and furtive smile formed on her father's lips. "Lilly, lean forward."

She complied, clenching her eyes shut to stymie her tears. Her father placed the crystalline crown on her head.

"Rise. Look at me." Her father's body quivered, and he winced, but his eyes remained fixed on hers. "There is one more thing I must pass to you. It is knowledge… our secret knowledge. It is the only means we have to rule our people. Without it, the Premier or Premieress need not exist."

Lilly's eyes widened. She knew of what her father spoke—the secret to becoming a Wisp.

"You alone hold the power to keep this knowledge secret. You alone command the forces necessary to enforce its secrecy. You alone are its protector and guardian... as was I, as was my father before me, as was his mother before him, and back through the ages."

Her father coughed, and blood tinged his teeth and tongue. He cleared his throat, winced, and then continued, his eyes focused on Kanton.

"In telling you this, Kanton will also know, so I must be assured—"

"I will keep it secret with my life." Kanton smiled. "You have my word, Premier."

Lilly's father stared deep into her eyes and extracted a yellow gemstone from within the folds of his robes, similar to the crystalline crown he'd just placed on her head but richer in color and glowing.

"Lilly," he extended the gemstone toward her, "this is the Aerostone. It holds the power to promote any Windgale into a Wisp. It is unique in this world; there is no other like it. As soon as you touch it, you will no longer need your cape to fly."

Lilly marveled at the gemstone with wide eyes, her mind plagued by confusion. Her father had possessed the power to transform any Windgale into a Wisp at any point, and he'd kept it hidden? What did that mean? Why had he withheld it from everyone else?

"Do not share this power freely. You cannot," her father continued. "In order to maintain control, you must leverage this resource to temper the will of the people. They must not know it exists."

He winced again, and he almost dropped the stone.

Lilly reached out to grab it, to help steady him, but her father pulled it back.

"Promise me, Lilly," he wheezed. "Promise me you'll steward this power as if it were your own life. Promise me you won't throw it away."

How could Lilly promise anything to him? He'd hidden the Sky Realm's most valuable—and most damning—secret not only from her but from every Windgale in all Kanarah.

Now he expected her to uphold that secrecy even after his death? Even after their city had been razed by enemy forces?

Yet as she looked into her dying father's eyes, pleading with her for this one final request, she found she couldn't refuse him.

Against everything she believed, and solely for her father's sake, she replied, "I promise."

AXEL's back hit one of the marble pillars, and he grunted. The impact pushed the air from his lungs, and he sucked in two short, shallow breaths to compensate, but he had to cut the second one even shorter to duck. A gigantic blade slashed toward him and lodged deep within the marble pillar where his head had just been.

Out of breath or not, this was his chance. Axel shifted to his right and angled the tip of his sword toward the Sobek's silver armor, then he jammed it forward with all his strength. The blade pierced through the Sobek's hide just beyond the edge of his armor, close enough to his belly that it dug deep into his torso.

The Sobek curled over with a roar and released his grip on his own sword. His left arm dropped low, then lashed up in a ferocious backhand that sent Axel spinning to the marble floor.

Blood from Axel's nose warmed his upper lip and tanged his tongue. *Could've been worse—a lot worse.*

Even so, these Sobeks didn't go down easily. What's more, now Axel didn't have his sword— it remained lodged in the Sobek's torso.

The Sobek roared again and clasped his long, green fingers around the sword's hilt and slowly pulled it out of his body until he held it before him, its blood-streaked blade extended toward Axel. He hissed again and took a step forward, and dark blood burbled out of his wound and snaked down his leg in several streams.

Great. What now?

A blur shot between Axel and the Sobek, and the Sobek's golden eyes widened. A deep gash split open on his throat. He dropped Axel's sword and clutched his throat with both hands. Then he crumpled to his knees, his mouth open, unable to hiss or roar or make anything but gurgling noises.

To the Sobek's left, Condor materialized. He picked up Axel's sword, tossed it to him, and then winked before he zipped away again.

Axel caught his sword and started toward the Sobek, whose eyes had already taken on a deathly glaze. He shifted his grip on his sword hilt and rammed the tip of his blade into the Sobek's eye.

The Sobek dropped to the floor in a growing pool of blood, and Axel huffed. Even if Condor hadn't intervened, Axel would've found a way to finish off the Sobek anyway. He always did.

A quick scan of the surrounding battle made him realize that so far, only three of the original twelve Sobeks had gone down, including this one. He stole a glance at the throne and at Lilly, who now wore Avian's yellow crown on her head as she hunched over him.

"Axel!" Calum's voice severed his concentration.

Axel dodged an attack from another Sobek and rolled away from the next one. He recovered his footing right way, his sword ready to defend the next attack.

It was then that he noticed that he now faced not one Sobek, but two.

He inhaled a long breath, cracked his neck, and readied his sword.

LILLY'S FATHER smiled at her. "There is one last secret I must impart, and it is this: Once you take hold of the Aerostone, you will indeed unlock your true nature, but you are far more than a mere Wisp. You are a Valkyrie, a royal Wisp.

"It means you are faster than any being in Kanarah, and all but uncatchable because of the royal blood that flows through your veins. In time, you will learn to move as a bolt of lightning, faster than a hummingbird beats its wings, faster than the blink of an eagle's eye. You are the pinnacle of Windgale perfection, blessed with unparalleled speed by the Overlord Himself."

Emotion flooded Lilly's chest, most of it anger. She had almost died countless times because of her stupid cape, and now her father had revealed that he could have promoted her at any time? And on top of that, she would've been faster than literally everyone else in the world?

This great secret, the secret that all Windgales could have accessed the freedom to fly uninhibited, if only the Premier had allowed it, really *was* just a system of control, just as Condor had claimed. And yet somehow, she was supposed to be able to transcend all of that, both in word and in deed?

She'd always flown faster than her friends, and she'd even outflown Falcroné until his promotion to Captain of the Royal Guard, but this whole time her father had kept the truth, the true power, and her true nature from her.

She could have done so much more. She could have helped her friends more, helped herself.

Maybe she could've even saved Falcroné.

"Lilly, safeguard this knowledge. Keep it secret until a Windgale is ready to demonstrate his commitment to the Sky Realm—to *you*. Do not allow the likes of Condor—" he shot a glance toward Condor's general direction, "—to interfere with your reign. This is the only way to prevent total anarchy and disorder."

Rather than pointing out the breadth of destruction around them, Lilly bit her tongue instead and nodded. "I understand."

Her father sucked in a long shuddering breath. He raised his left hand and touched her cheek with the back of his trembling fingers, and he smiled. "My darling girl. My princess. I'm so glad I could see you once more."

Before Lilly could say anything else, her father's eyes rolled back, and he exhaled a sharp sigh. His left hand slipped away from her face and smacked the marble floor at the base of the throne.

"Father?" she asked, her voice shaking. "Daddy?"

Her father didn't move, didn't open his eyes, even when she gently shook him.

She had no more cause to hold back her tears, so she allowed them to flow. Her father had engaged in questionable—if not outright immoral—practices, but he was still her father.

And now he was gone.

She buried her face in his chest and wept. First Falcroné, now her father and mother—all within a matter of days. Did the Overlord delight in her misery? In her suffering? Why else would He blanket her with so much grief in such a short time?

Metal clanked behind her, a reminder of the men who still fought for her to have enough time to hear her father's dying words. Condor. Calum. Magnus. Riley. If she lost anyone else— maybe even Axel—she didn't know what she'd do.

Lilly straightened her spine and stood up. She unfastened the cape from her shoulders and let it slide to the floor, then she tossed her father's crystal crown onto his lap. She'd flown countless times while wearing her cape, but now she no longer needed it. Her father had said she could fly faster without it.

He'd said the capes didn't matter—only the Aerostone did.

Now she would find out.

She bent down again, took the Aerostone from her father's grasp, and held it. It flared with golden light, just like Magnus's Dragon Emerald had back in the tunnels under Kanarah City, and a cool sensation filled her body like a soft summer breeze flowing through her veins.

As quickly as it began, it ended. The light from the stone reduced to its usual glow, and she released her hold on the Aerostone. It landed on her discarded cape with a dull *thunk*, and Kanton moved to pick it up next. She didn't pay him any mind.

Instead, she unsheathed her short sword and clamped her fingers around it. When she took to the air, the marble floor dropped out from beneath her faster than she anticipated.

After a quick course adjustment, Lilly arced toward the two Sobeks who approached Axel, and she joined him in the fray.

AXEL WONDERED how many more times he could parry the Sobeks' thunderous blows before one of them managed to knock the blade from his grasp.

He'd done well so far, especially on his own, but even he had to admit he was far over-matched. He wasn't strong enough, and though he was quicker than the Sobeks, he wasn't quick enough to avoid both of them for much longer.

Axel braced himself for another swing from the Sobek on his left, but it never came.

Instead, a pink blur collided with the Sobek, and dark blood spurted onto the floor.

Lilly. It had to be—but Axel had never seen her move that fast before.

The other Sobek's head swiveled in surprise, and Axel took advantage. He sprang forward and lashed his blade. Somehow the Sobek defended Axel's attack with his sword, and the next thing Axel knew, he lay flat on his back, staring up at the throne room's black ceiling as the Sobek's scaly mug leaned into his range of vision.

The Sobek's tail had gotten him. It snaked back behind the Sobek's body, and he raised his sword high above his head for a finishing blow.

An armored hand and a shining blade flickered around the Sobek's neck from behind, carving a long red slit in its throat. The hand and the blade vanished just as fast, and the Sobek froze in place, eyes wide. He clutched at his throat, began to convulse, and then fell forward. Had Axel not shifted to the side, the hulking lizard would've landed right on him.

In the Sobek's place hovered Lilly, still clad in her light pink armor, but no longer wearing her cape. Yet, somehow, she was flying.

And she also somehow looked more amazing than ever. Axel had to stifle a smirk.

She floated toward him and extended her free hand. "Come on. We're not done yet."

CALUM FOUGHT side-by-side with Magnus and Riley, both of whom proved far more effective against their opponents.

Already more than half the Windgales in Captain Perine's party had fallen to their Sobek foes. While the group had managed to take down six Sobeks, they couldn't hold off the other six for much longer, and they certainly wouldn't be able to defeat them.

Calum couldn't fault Lilly for taking so much time with her dying father; if he'd had the chance to spend a few minutes with his father or mother before they had to leave again forever, he would've savored every last second of it.

But that didn't make it any easier for the rest of them.

He ducked under a vicious slash and whipped his sword at the nearest Sobek's chest. He put every last bit of his might into it, delivering a blow that would've knocked a grown man to the ground, but his sword just clanged off the Sobek's silver breastplate as if he were made of steel.

Yet again, Calum just wasn't strong enough.

In retaliation, the Sobek drove his shoulder into Calum's chest and sent him skidding across the marble floor until the body of a dead Windgale stopped his momentum.

Behind his Sobek opponent, a group of green reptilian heads emerged in the throne room doorway and then filtered in, some of them Sobeks, some of them Saurians, more than doubling the number of enemies.

Magnus recoiled from the Sobek he'd been fighting, and so did Riley and his Wolves. Captain Perine and what few of his men remained also pulled back, and Axel and Lilly, who no longer wore a cape but could somehow still fly, joined them in a tight semi-circle.

Calum pushed up to his feet and scrambled to join his friends as Condor landed beside Lilly.

"Time to escape, Princess," Condor said as even more Saurians filtered inside.

A loud slam sounded on the doors to their left, but a large wooden beam anchored the door shut. They couldn't go that way.

Calum's head swiveled to the only other set of doors in the room, to his right, but a mound of rubble blocked the exit. He swallowed. "There's no way out."

Condor exhaled a bitter sigh. "Then we'll have to fight our way out. Carve a path to freedom."

Riley growled. "Easier said than done."

"We will die if we do not act," Magnus said. "Stand tall, and beat them back."

As Magnus finished his sentence, the wooden beam across the doors to Calum's left snapped, and the doors burst open.

CHAPTER 8

Relief flooded Lilly's entire being as another fifty soldiers, all of them Windgales and Wisps, streamed inside the throne room.

This group wore a mix of purple and orange armor, and they followed a Wisp in black armor with gold accents. His long salt-and-pepper hair matched his thick beard, and his hulking frame towered over the rest of the soldiers.

General Balena—her uncle.

Lilly grinned, and the hopeless desperation in her heart snuffed.

General Balena pointed his sword at the Saurians. "*Attack!*"

The Windgale soldiers swarmed the Saurians and rained blows down upon them in a thunderstorm of flashing steel. Even General Balena himself engaged in the battle, and Lilly and her friends joined them.

Within ten minutes, the last of the Saurians went down, and the three remaining Sobeks, all wearing silver breastplates, fled the throne room with a dozen Windgale soldiers in pursuit.

General Balena wrenched his sword out of one of the dead Sobeks and hovered over to Lilly, who sheathed her own blade and stared at him as he approached.

"Princess," he said, his voice much softer than the steely tone he usually employed. He glanced over her shoulder at the throne. "Your father?"

Lilly shook her head, and a flood of emotion swelled in her chest. Tears stung the corners of her eyes.

To Lilly's surprise, General Balena took hold of her arms, pulled her close, and wrapped her in a sturdy embrace. He'd never been the kind of man to show affection, especially after the passing of his wife, Lilly's aunt, but Lilly leaned into him nonetheless and wept.

When he finally released his grip on Lilly, General Balena scanned the room. When his gaze landed on Condor, his hazel eyes narrowed and his eyebrows arched down, then he refocused on Lilly. "Falcroné?"

She couldn't hold back her tears anymore, and they streamed down her face freely. She

General Balena's jaw tightened, and his posture straightened. He again glared at Condor. Through gritted teeth, he asked, "How?"

Lilly followed his gaze and wiped her cheeks dry. "Condor had nothing to do with it. Fal saved both our lives, but it cost him his own."

General Balena's rigid expression softened, but had Lilly not known him her entire life, she wouldn't have noticed it.

"Before we freed Lumen," she continued, "a Jyrak attacked us from the Central Lake. It had me in its hand and was going to crush me, but Fal swooped in and jammed his sword into its finger. That gave Condor enough time to get me to safety, but not enough time for Fal to save himself. He died a hero."

With a short sigh, General Balena closed his eyes, then he, too, sheathed his sword. Lilly expected he would say something more about Falcroné, his only son, but he didn't.

"You freed Lumen?" he asked.

The anguish in Lilly's stomach began to subside, and she nodded. "Yes. Condor got us to the Arcanum, and from there, Calum led us to Lumen, and we freed him. He sent us back to gather an army for him. He means to supplant the King and to unite all of Kanarah under his rule."

General Balena scrutinized her for a long moment. "You're not wearing your cape."

"My father crowned me Premieress before he died. Kanton witnessed it." Lilly clenched her teeth. "He also told me the secret."

"*Soldiers*," General Balena barked. "Behold your Premieress."

Every Windgale in the room faced Lilly with their hands up against their chests, their wrists crossed, their thumbs joined in the center and pointed up at their chins. Their fingers angled up and out toward their shoulders like the wings of a bird. The Windgale salute. General Balena and Condor also saluted her, and so did Calum, Magnus, Axel, and Riley.

It was surreal. She'd grown accustomed to Windgales saluting her from an early age, but now the weight of the meaning behind that salute weighed heavily on her shoulders, as if she bore the woes of the entire realm on her back. And now, she realized, she did.

It was a responsibility she'd been prepared for her entire life. Since she was old enough to first float among the clouds, she'd studied and trained and pushed herself to become the best leader she could possibly be. The day of her ascension to the throne had come earlier than expected, but she wouldn't shy away from her birthright. Her people needed her.

Lilly waved her hand. "Enough, please. I haven't done anything to deserve your allegiance."

"The blood in your veins commands our allegiance." General Balena stood to his full height, and the rest of the soldiers followed suit. "You are our leader now, Premieress. We exist to serve you, and by extension, the Sky Realm."

So much power, so much authority. So much responsibility. Now, along with the weight of Falcroné's and her parents' deaths, she shouldered the destiny of the entire Sky Realm and its inhabitants, what few had survived the Saurians' attack. And now she would lead them into battle again on Lumen's behalf to overthrow—

The people. *Her* people. She couldn't lead them to Lumen without first caring for them. How many hundreds—*thousands*—of refugees had she passed on her way back home? How many soldiers still wandered the skies, trying to decide whether to return to Aeropolis and fight or flee for their lives?

Too many for her to ignore them. Far, far too many.

The weight of her parents' deaths and the secret her father had shared with her before he perished threatened to upend her resolve. He'd only entrusted her with the truth at the very end, when he'd absolutely had to, and he'd begged her not to reveal that truth to anyone.

Now the Aerostone lay somewhere nearby her father's body, which was just one among numerous others, while even more of her people needed aid outside the four remaining walls of the Sky Fortress. But the way she yearned to help them was precisely the way her father had entreated her not to.

As if reading her thoughts, Kanton hovered toward her, no longer wearing his cape. Instead, he held it in his hands, wrapped around a lump of something. He'd covered the Aerostone, and now he extended it toward her, concealed within the shimmering Aerosilk fabric.

She accepted it from him, unsurprised when he continued hovering without his cape. Even by her father's narrow definition of who was "worthy" to become a Wisp, Kanton had exceeded every qualification, particularly in loyalty. He'd deserved to become a Wisp, and now he was.

"General Balena," she said. "Divide your men into groups. Send them out to gather our lost and wandering citizens. We cannot risk the Saurians finding them. Return them—*all* of them—to the Sky Fortress."

"With respect, Premieress, that will take days. Perhaps weeks." Captain Perine stepped forward. "It will diminish our chances to mount a successful counterattack on the—"

"We aren't going to mount a counterattack on the Saurians," Lilly interrupted. "At least not until we have ensured the well-being of our own people."

Captain Perine hesitated. "But—the longer we wait, the weaker we will appear to—"

"My decision is final, Captain." Lilly bristled. She didn't recall any of the soldiers ever questioning her father in such a manner.

Captain Perine turned to General Balena. "General, I implore you. If we don't—"

Steel flashed. Captain Perine froze in place with General Balena's sword at his throat.

"If you ever *dare* question the Premieress's commands again, I will personally cut out your tongue and force you to wear it as a necklace," General Balena growled. "She is your ruler, your supreme leader, and your commander. You will heed her every word as if they came from the Overlord Himself. Crystal?"

A bead of sweat on Captain Perine's forehead trickled down his jaw as he nodded. "Clear."

General Balena released his grip on Captain Perine's shoulder and sheathed his sword. He cast a long stare at Condor, who raised an eyebrow.

"Lilly." Condor grinned at her, his piercing blue eyes alive with mischief. "*Premieress.* Excuse me."

She narrowed her eyes at him, and even amid the destruction around them, she had to stifle a smile. "Yes?"

"Might I suggest we first send the soldiers throughout Aeropolis to clear out any remaining Saurian invaders and search for survivors here?"

Lilly nodded. He was right. "Yes. Make it so."

As General Balena directed his captains to divide their men into groups for the search, Lilly caught Calum staring at her from the side of the room. He wore a sad smile and leaned against one of the marble pillars. If there was anyone in Kanarah who could empathize with her at this moment, it was him.

Still, she had work to do. People to help. Calum would also understand that. She left her feet and landed beside him.

He performed the Windgale salute and bowed his head.

"Stop. You're embarrassing me." She started smiling even before he raised his head.

His own smile reverted back to its sadder version. "Lilly, I—"

She flung her arms around him and pulled him close. Her tears flowed again, and with each heaving sob, she squeezed him tighter.

She wasn't sure why she'd done it. Maybe it was that shared sense of heartache, or her connection to Calum, or that he couldn't fly, so he'd been one of the few left behind with her—and she wasn't going to embrace Axel under any circumstances ever again.

"I know, Lilly," Calum whispered into her ear. It was all he said, and it was all she needed to hear. "I know."

———

AXEL CLENCHED his teeth and exhaled hot air through his nostrils. If he could have incinerated Calum with fire from his eyes, he'd have done it by now.

Why was Lilly holding onto *him*? Axel had saved her life more times than Calum had. He'd been there for her more often, too.

Yes, Axel had screwed up the last time they were here, but that was in the past, and he'd apologized several *dozen* times since then. So what did she see in Calum that Axel didn't also have?

Axel was stronger. Bigger, taller. A better fighter. Better-looking, of course. A real man, especially compared to Calum's boyish appearance.

Axel knew he came off as gruff and even ornery at times, but he couldn't help it. Besides, it was part of what made him unique. He was colorful. Vibrant. Interesting. And he didn't take lip from anyone.

Calum? *Boring.* Aside from the whole seeing-Lumen-in-his-dreams thing, at least.

Really? They're still holding each other? Axel clenched his teeth again.

"I wish you'd stop doing that."

The voice jolted Axel out of his funk. Instinct whirled him around and moved his hand to the hilt of his sword, but he didn't remove it from its sheath. He relaxed his grip when he saw Riley's blue eyes, the only part of him still visible from the deep shadows in which he resided.

"Stop doing what?" Axel asked.

"Grinding your teeth. It's annoying."

Axel's jaw tensed again.

"Like that. Stop it."

"I'm just clenching my teeth."

"Every time you do it, your teeth grind, and I can hear it from across the room."

"Not my fault."

Riley stepped out of the shadows, and Axel marveled at his upright Werewolf form again. Lithe, but strong. Something about his fur, something almost mystical, enabled him to melt into the shadows as if he belonged there.

"There's no sense in getting frustrated about her."

Axel raised an eyebrow. "I don't—"

"Please." Riley cocked his head to the side. "You love her. I know you do. It pains you to see her embracing Calum."

He was right. Axel clenched his teeth again.

"*Stop. It.*"

"Sorry." Axel relaxed his jaw again. "So you can read minds now, too?"

Riley huffed. "Hardly. We Wolves are watchers. Observers. It's part of why we hide in the shadows—so we can stalk our prey. Get to know its tendencies, habits—"

"Prey?"

"Not you." Riley smirked. "Not anymore, anyway."

Axel eyed him.

"We watch everything, not just prey. But that's how it begins for us. We're strategic, calculating creatures. We don't just jump in without assessing." Riley nodded toward Calum and Lilly, who'd finally stopped hugging and now stood shoulder to shoulder against one of the marble pillars, talking. "Those two? They love each other, but neither of them will admit it."

That was *not* what Axel wanted to hear.

"Don't glare at me. They're not acting on it mostly because of you. They both know it would hurt you too deeply if they did." Riley folded his thick arms. "There's also the external pressure of Lilly's family and friends, and Calum's mission to raise Lumen's army. Neither of them believe they have the capacity to support a relationship amidst all of that."

"I wasn't asking about them."

Riley cocked his eyebrow up. "You're livid about it. I've seen the way you look at them, obviously, but you carry it into everything you do. You vent your discontent when you fight, when you speak. I've even seen it in the way you stand and walk. Your footfalls stop just short of stomping."

Axel swallowed. Riley had seen all of that? Perhaps Axel should've been nicer to him earlier on. An ally this observant could have helped him win Lilly over. Maybe he still could.

"Would you consider—"

"No chance. I'm not taking sides in this."

"You don't even know what—" Axel stopped himself. Yes, Riley *did* know what he was going to ask. Axel's body language or tone of voice must have given it away. He sighed and looked back at Calum and Lilly. "Never mind. You said you weren't my friend. Why are you telling me this?"

"I'm *not* your friend." Riley tilted his head. "I'm telling you because I know it bothers you. And so you'll stop grinding your teeth around me."

Axel glared at him. "So you get a thrill out of seeing me suffer?"

"Thrill? Hardly. You're not interesting enough to thrill me." Riley grinned. "Satisfaction, though? *That* I do get."

"Whatever."

Riley's left ear twitched and he growled. "You're grinding your teeth again."

Axel turned away. "Deal with it."

JUST WHEN LILLY had finally started to relax, General Balena descended from the air and landed before her and Calum.

"Premieress," he said, "the soldiers are dispersed with the exception of ten of the remaining Royal Guard. If you are willing, I would have a word with you."

Lilly nodded. "Of course, General."

"Alone, if you don't mind." General Balena's stern gaze shifted from her to Calum.

"It's alright. He can stay." Lilly didn't want Calum to go. As she'd expected, he understood her pain, and he'd comforted her, commiserated with her.

General Balena's hard expression didn't change as he exhaled a steady breath through his nose—except his left eye narrowed almost imperceptibly as he stared at Calum.

"It's fine, Lilly." Calum gave her hand a squeeze. "We can catch up again later. I know you've got a lot to do right now."

Lilly wanted to say something but hesitated, and Calum nodded to General Balena and started walking toward Magnus.

"Premieress?" General Balena asked.

She returned her attention to him. "Yes, General?"

"Please, come with me. There are too many hungry ears in this room." He cast a furtive glance at Condor, who stood before the ten members of the Royal Guard, giving them instructions. He still wore the same tattered garb he'd worn since they rescued him from Oren's fortress at the Blood Chasm.

So *that's* what General Balena wanted to talk about.

Lilly nodded. "Lead the way."

General Balena escorted her outside and to the top of what remained of the Sky Fortress, now a flat metal box tainted by several mounds of charred blue rubble. A few of the spires' golden tips lay amid the heaps, now pitiful reminders of the fortress's former glory and splendor. A few others were melted and had cooled into solid pools of gold.

It all reminded Lilly of her father. She bit her lip to fend off more tears.

When they landed among the wreckage, General Balena took Lilly's hands in his own and stared into her eyes. "Premieress—Lilly. Why is Condor here?"

"Axel found him and set him free from captivity at the Blood Chasm. Had he not done so, we all would have died. Condor evened the odds, then he tipped them in our favor just enough to overcome Oren and his Saurians."

General Balena shook his head. "He cannot be trusted."

"He has proven trustworthy thus far, and he has saved my life multiple times."

"And once at the cost of Falcroné's life."

"No." Lilly shook her head. "I was there, Uncle. Falcroné gave his life to save me, but had Condor not been there to pull me from the Jyrak's hand while Falcroné kept it from crushing me, you would have lost both your son and your niece."

"*Why* do you defend him?" General Balena's sharp tone startled Lilly so much that she recoiled a step. "*Why?*"

"I—I believe he wants what is best for our realm, as do I."

"He tried to *assassinate* your father, Lilly! Had Falcroné and I not intervened, he would have succeeded."

Lilly hesitated. "Uncle, I—"

"You have no idea what Condor is capable of." General Balena gripped her shoulders in his gigantic hands. "He is faster than any Wisp I've ever known, and he is as skilled a fighter as I. Even your father, whose blade could have felled nearly any opponent in all of Kanarah, was overcome during Condor's attack."

"And I *trust* him," Lilly finally asserted. "He has protected me with his life since we freed him from Oren's fortress. He is indebted to me by the Law of Debt—his life for mine. There is no one else with whom I would rather entrust my life."

Lilly swallowed the lump in her throat. What about Calum? Magnus? General Balena himself? Or even Axel? Her three friends had protected her since the day they rescued her from Roderick, and General Balena had been a part of her life from the very beginning, yet now she sought to assign the task of her protection solely to Condor?

General Balena released his grip on her. "Your father said the very same thing to me when we promoted him upon Sevilon's retirement. I had wanted Falcroné to serve as the new Captain of the Royal Guard, not because he was my son, but because he was better suited to the job. Falcroné was a gifted fighter as well, but he could never seriously compete with Condor.

"I wanted Condor with me, on the battlefield. Selfishly, I knew he would keep me alive in any circumstance. I was confident that he and I could get out of any scrape together, as long as we had our swords. He was my protégé, even more so than Falcroné."

Lilly listened intently. She'd never heard any of this, either from her father or Falcroné before, and certainly not from General Balena, who was notoriously a man of few words.

General Balena exhaled a long breath. "Condor belonged on the battlefield. He would have made general within five years had your father not granted him the Royal Guard. I protested the appointment with vehemence, but your father was the Premier. It was his choice."

He stared into the clear blue skies around them, his hazel eyes searching. "Condor was smarter than Falcroné. More perceptive. *Too* perceptive. My real concern was that he would learn too much, being so close to the seat of power. That he would use that knowledge against the realm. I should have voiced that concern to your father, but I didn't."

Lilly touched his shoulder, and he turned. "Uncle, why are you telling me all of this?"

He looked at her with tears forming in his eyes. "You are the only family I have left. My beloved wife is gone. Your parents are dead. And now my only son is dead. Condor was like a son to me as well. When he rebelled, his assassination attempt failed, but he still managed to kill a part of me. If something happens to you—"

"It won't, Uncle. It won't." She cupped his bearded jaw with her hand.

"Evangeline said the same thing when she got sick."

A pit opened in Lilly's stomach. "Uncle, please. I've had more than my fair share of grief for today."

"I'm sorry, but my brother-in-law lies in a pool of his own blood at the base of his throne, because I—" General Balena stopped and clenched his eyes shut.

"You what?" Lilly asked.

He opened his eyes and stared at her. For the first time in her life, Lilly witnessed the resolve in General Balena's gaze falter.

"I let him die."

CHAPTER 9

Lilly's mouth hung open. "What do you mean?"

General Balena's jaw tightened. "When the Saurians attacked, we held them off for quite awhile. Our races generally match up neutrally when it comes to fighting—that is, our advantages of flight and speed do not necessarily outweigh their advantages of resilient scales and strength."

Lilly nodded. "I remember you teaching me about that. Go on."

"Through aerial acrobatics and quick, precise attacks, we had begun to repel the Saurian forces. Under my command, the army recaptured and protected the lift so they couldn't bring any more soldiers up to the fortress, all while your father remained in the fortress under guard. Everything was going well, but then we heard a distant boom."

Lilly's heart fluttered in her chest. "Kahn."

General Balena nodded. "That boom was the first of many. With each beat of his wings, another thunderclap jarred our crystal walls."

Lilly shuddered at the thought.

"In the handful of times Praetorius visited our realm, I never heard any sort of sound from his wings, except for one time," General Balena continued. "He'd flown miles away by that point and appeared to my younger keener eyes as little more than a large speck on the northern horizon. When he flapped his wings to gain more elevation, the boom took almost a full minute to reverberate around us, but it rattled my teeth just the same.

"When Kahn attacked, he came at us with abandon, each boom signifying a flap of his wings that propelled him forward faster than the one preceding it." General Balena grimaced. "Our walls held strong against his wing beats, as powerful as they were, but with his near-impenetrable scales and dragonfire breath, we could do nothing to stop him. He was a flying war-engine, a destroyer of nations, billowing emerald fire and carving into our realm with his merciless talons."

Lilly bit her lip and envisioned the horrific scene as General Balena described it.

"What he didn't burn, he shattered. What he didn't shatter, he burned. He didn't even bother to swat our forces away as we attacked him. He followed his own agenda, his own plan of attack, and we were powerless against him—" General Balena exhaled a long sigh. "—until your father took to the sky."

Lilly's mouth hung open. "He did *what?*"

"Against my wishes, your father summoned the armorist and demanded the Calios, our realm's sacred blade, and then he left the safety of the fortress to face Kahn." General Balena shuddered. "I tried to reason with him, but he refused. He insisted that no one else stood a chance of stopping Kahn but him.

"I should have done more. I should have taken the Calios myself and faced Kahn in your father's stead, or even restrained him myself if it came to it, but he refused to comply with my pleas. Instead, he ordered me to lead the army against the Saurian forces while he faced Kahn."

When General Balena didn't continue, Lilly asked, "What happened?"

"I don't know for sure, but Kahn eventually ceased his attack and flew away. We fended off the remaining Saurians and returned to the fortress as soon as we could, and that's where we found you." General Balena shifted his gaze from her eyes to his feet. "And now your father is dead because of me."

"No, no." Lilly put her hand on her uncle's armored shoulder. The obsidian armor that covered his body still glistened in the sunlight, devoid of anything that even resembled a scratch. The Saurians hadn't even so much as grazed him despite all their attacks. "You couldn't have stopped him even if you wanted to."

"I am charged with the protection of this realm, chiefly of its lord and ruler, your father, the Premier, who now lays at the base of his throne, dead." General Balena stared at her with the same lack of resolve she'd seen upon his initial confession. "If that isn't failure, I don't know what is."

"We both knew my father. He went his own way, and he would only be persuaded otherwise if he *allowed* himself to be persuaded. It drove my mother crazy." Lilly granted herself a chuckle and a small smile. "Stopping him would've violated your charge as well, as you would have stopped the only person in the Sky Realm truly capable of taking action against Kahn. It is precisely because you didn't stop my father that you were able to repel this invasion."

"But your father is *dead*," General Balena emphasized. "He's gone, Lilly, and the Calios is missing, and it's all my fault."

That the Calios was missing stung Lilly as well, but she didn't focus on that at the moment. They could search for it later.

"It's Kahn's fault, not yours. You protected my father as far as he would allow you to do so. Would you have also saved him from old age? Or disease? Or happenstance? We're all destined to die at some point, in some way. His death saved our people, and it's because of you that he saved our realm."

General Balena's stoic face cracked, and a smile, almost imperceptible, curled the corners of his lips.

"You are wise beyond your years, Lilly, and well-suited to rule in your father's place." He sighed. "Yet my lingering concern rests with Condor. We banished him for his crimes, yet he has returned."

Back to this again? Very well. "Uncle, he swore an oath of fealty to me. Falcroné and the rest of our group witnessed it."

General Balena shook his head again. "Oaths and fealty mean nothing to Condor. He swore oaths to protect your father as well."

Lilly was getting sick of having to defend Condor.

"Uncle, I trust him. He cares for me. He is concerned for my wellbeing. He is my Captain of the Royal Guard and will remain so until I release him from service." Lilly's voice hardened more than she expected, but General Balena didn't indicate any surprise.

Instead, he just nodded. "If you trust him, then so must I—to a point. I would encourage you to avoid being alone with him if you can help it."

Lilly gave a mirthless chuckle. "I already learned my lesson with Axel on that one."

"Even so, Condor is infinitely more dangerous than your human friends will ever be." General Balena sighed. "But enough about him. You mentioned that your father told you the secret."

"He told me..." Lilly bit her lip. The Aerostone now hung safely in a pouch at her hip. "He told me that keeping the stone's existence and its power secret was the only way to prevent anarchy."

"And what do you think of that?"

Did Lilly dare tell him the truth? How she believed that if the impoverished Windgales who occupied the area at the base of the Sky Realm could be given the power to fly freely, without capes, that they wouldn't have to live in poverty? How this system of control was exactly what Condor had rebelled against because he found it unjust and detrimental to the very fabric of Windgale society?

Yes, she absolutely dared.

"I think it's a travesty, and it's one of the great deceptions of our time. Countless numbers of our people live in poverty because they believe a lie that we have told them. And some of them die because of it."

"It's not nearly as simple as you or Condor would believe," General Balena said. "Long ago, your forefathers sought to better control our population. The Premier at the time realized from the annual census that the Sky Realm was growing dangerously overpopulated.

"In order to stave off population growth, the Premier and his advisors created a plan to with-hold the power of the Aerostone from certain people who could not exhibit 'true loyalty' to the realm." General Balena raised an eyebrow at her. "I think you can see where this is going. Before long, the Premier and his advisors had completely reorganized our social system, and now we have castes, albeit unofficially so."

Lilly frowned. The story twisted her stomach, but she needed to know it all.

General Balena concluded, "One thing led to another, and the tradition has continued for ages."

Tradition. Lilly shook her head. *Disgusting.*

That Premier had handicapped an entire society just to keep the population at a manageable level.

"You may not like it, but now more than ever, it is the only true leverage we have over our people. Without the full force of our army, we have no way of controlling the masses." General Balena put his hand on her shoulder. "The power of the Aerostone is a secret that must be kept safe, at all costs.

"Even Condor knows this. Why else do you think he was the only Wisp, and therefore the leader, of the Raven's Brood? For all his noble talk, he used the very same method of control to gather forces to him and make them do his bidding."

Lilly frowned. "He didn't have access to the Aerostone, either."

General Balena ignored her comment. "What's more, your father, in spite of maintaining this 'system of control,' as Condor calls it, gave his life to save his people from total destruction. For all his faults, and for all our society's imperfections, your father only ever did what he believed was best for our people. I encourage you to follow in his example."

Lilly stared off into the great blue around them. She could see General Balena's point of view, but she still wasn't sure how much of it she agreed with.

Even so, to placate him, she nodded. "I intend to."

"We have been gone long enough," General Balena said. "We should head back inside. I suspect the soldiers assigned to searching the realm will return soon, and we must ascertain the location of the Calios. It is our greatest weapon, and it falls under your stewardship now."

He pivoted to fly away, but Lilly caught his wrist. "Uncle?"

General Balena turned back. "Yes?"

"About Fal..." she started, unsure of what to say next. "He—I—"

"Say no more, Lilly. I will mourn him in my own way with the knowledge that he died the hero I always knew him to be."

Lilly nodded. That much, at least, was true. "Yes. He was."

The full weight of General Balena's solemnity returned to his expression. "Let's get back inside."

SOMETHING GLINTED into Calum's eye from under Avian's body, and he approached it with curiosity leading his footsteps. Axel was already there, hunched over. Apparently he'd noticed it, too.

"Don't touch the Premier's body," Condor said from across the throne room.

Axel retracted his hand and eyed Condor, but Calum didn't move. He stood next to Axel, his eyes fixed on the shining metal protruding from underneath the Premier's lifeless form.

When Calum crouched down next to Axel, Condor's voice sounded again, this time much closer. "Calum."

"There's something underneath him," Calum said.

"Stand back." Condor pulled both Calum and Axel up to their feet then crouched down in their place. His eyes widened with recognition. "By the Overlord..."

Calum glanced at Axel. He shrugged and refocused on Condor.

Metal scraped against the marble floor as Condor pulled a long sword from under the Premier's body and held it before them.

Its curved blade reminded Calum of the sword he'd taken after defeating Tyburon, but the similarities ended there. The polished ivory hilt, wrapped in crisscrossed strips of golden leather, accounted for a third of the sword's overall length, and a golden guard—more of a thin collar than an actual quillion—separated the hilt from the blade.

At first Calum thought the blade might be made of the same translucent blue crystal as the buildings of the now-obliterated city around them, but when Condor adjusted his grip on the sword, its color changed to a deep purple hue, still translucent.

Calum blinked. Had he imagined the shift?

A smirk formed on Condor's lips. "Incredible, isn't it?"

The blade changed again, this time to a bold shade of yellow accompanied by a faint glow of the same color.

Calum raised his eyebrows. "What is that?"

"This is the Calios," Condor replied, his smirk now a full-on grin. "Our realm's sacred blade and most powerful weapon. I've never seen it before today, but it could be no other blade. It is said that the Overlord Himself breathed life into this blade and thus anointed it with profound power."

"Why's it changing colors like that?" Axel asked.

"Each color represents a different type of attack," a gruff voice said from behind them.

Calum spun around, and General Balena and Lilly landed before him and Axel. General Balena's right hand gripped the hilt of his sword, still sheathed in his belt, as he stepped forward. When Lilly followed him, General Balena halted her progress with his other hand and then leaned close to her, his eyes fixed on Condor, and whispered into her ear.

She nodded and stepped back with her fingers curled around the hilt of her own sword. It would certainly take Calum some time to adjust to seeing her without her cape, but she seemed to have taken to her newfound aerial freedom as easily as the transition between running and walking.

But he couldn't account for her behavior now. He didn't know General Balena at all, aside from the handful of times he'd observed the man in this very room, but their defensive stances now that Condor had the sword confused Calum.

"Condor." General Balena extended his left hand, still gripping the hilt of his sword in his belt. "Hand me the Calios."

Condor squinted at him, then he ran his fingers up the flat of the blade, now a vivid orange. "How does it work, General? Is it true that it only obeys the commands of those within the royal bloodline, like the rumors suggest?"

General Balena's jaw tightened. "Give it to me. Lilly is its steward now."

"Or can *anyone* wield it?" For a moment, Condor's eyes widened so large that the blade's orange reflection glinted across his blue irises. "Can *anyone* bend the Calios's will to his own?"

"Condor." General Balena stepped forward but stopped when Condor pointed the Calios at him.

"Or does the Calios bend its wielder to do *its* bidding, as other rumors suggest?"

"That—" General Balena nodded at the Calios. "—is not to be trifled with. As you said, it is our realm's greatest weapon. You cannot—"

"Don't tell me what I can or cannot do, General. My days of obeying your every command ended long ago." Condor's voice took on a menacing tone.

General Balena opened his mouth to speak, but Lilly spoke first. "Yet your days of obeying my every command have just begun."

Condor raised an eyebrow at her but did not lower the Calios, even as Lilly started toward him.

General Balena reached for her as she passed him. "Premieress—"

"Enough." Lilly brushed his hand away, then she refocused on Condor. "General Balena doesn't trust you, Condor."

"I don't blame him." Condor winked at her, and Calum's stomach twisted at the sight.

"This is your chance to prove your loyalty to me, once and for all." Lilly held out her hand. "Give me the Calios, and put my uncle's concerns to rest."

"I shouldn't have to prove anything. I've saved your life dozens of times."

"And I trust you completely." Lilly closed to within a few steps of the Calios's point. "Now prove to General Balena that you're not a threat to me."

Condor didn't move.

CHAPTER 10

After a long labored breath, Condor lowered the Calios. He shifted his grip so he held out the sword's ivory hilt for Lilly to take.

Even as the tension in Lilly's gut relaxed, she hesitated. All her life she'd heard stories about the Calios, mostly from Falcroné and other friends who had both asked her what she knew of the weapon and shared their own lore as well.

According to them, the Calios could fatally poison a full-grown Sobek with the tiniest scratch. It could flash a light that would both reveal foes hidden in shadows and blind them at the same time. It could lay waste to dozens of armed enemies in a matter of seconds with a cascade of water, an explosion of flames, a blast of ice, or a flurry of cold hard steel.

And now Condor held that power in his hand, willingly extending it to her as if it were any other lifeless piece of metal.

But this was the Calios, the realm's salvation, its greatest weapon. If Condor truly knew what he held, he might not have offered it to Lilly so freely.

Then again, she didn't truly know what it was he was offering her, either. Taking it was the only way to find out.

Lilly reached for the Calios.

Her fingers touched the end of the hilt, but no fire surged through her body, no lightning zapped her veins. She clamped her hand around the leather-wrapped ivory and slowly extracted the sword from Condor's grasp, as if easing a honeycomb from a nest of thousands of bees—or at least one big blue-eyed one.

Then it was hers. The ivory grip conformed to her hand as if it had always belonged there, as if the sword had awaited this moment and knew how she would hold it. The blade changed from the vibrant orange to a pale-pink hue without any glow, then it faded to a white crystal, then it changed perfectly clear.

Condor's piercing blue eyes met hers, and he smiled. "I think it likes you."

Lilly nodded. "I think so, too." She turned back to General Balena. "Do you trust him now?"

General Balena released his grip on his sword hilt and allowed his hands to rest at his sides.

"Good." Lilly stared down at her father, specifically at the bejeweled sheath hooked to his belt. She bent down and began to unfasten it. "General, you will maintain command of the army, and Condor will continue to lead the Royal Guard. As there is nothing left in the fortress to guard, they will accompany me as my personal bodyguards, along with my friends."

"And what do you wish your army to do, Premieress?" General Balena asked.

"The army serves one primary purpose, as I see it," Lilly said. "You are to protect the people of the Sky Realm. I charge you to find them a safe place where they can rest in the meantime and to protect and organize them."

"'In the meantime?'" General Balena eyed her. "What do you mean?"

Lilly locked eyes with Magnus, who tilted his head and clacked his talons on his blue breast-plate. "We're going to the Crimson Keep."

IT TOOK Lilly a solid half-hour to "convince" General Balena to allow her to accompany Calum and Magnus to the Crimson Keep, and even then she had to give him a direct order to get him to leave the fortress without her.

She conceded to meet with the rest of the people before General Balena took them to safety, which they had determined would be in the various caves that gouged into the Firjian Foothills several miles to the southwest of the Sky Realm. The lush valleys would provide them with multiple sources of food, and abundant rainfall would ensure they never lacked clean drinking water.

Having restocked their supplies from what remained of the fortress's resources, Lilly led Calum and the rest of the group back outside, where they found Condor, now clad in his old set of charcoal–colored armor, complete with the black insignia of the Raven's Brood on his chest.

When Lilly eyed him, Condor shrugged. "What did you expect? There's no time to make me a new set."

It was a drastic improvement over the ragged clothes he'd worn since they'd rescued him from Oren's fortress, at least.

Condor directed the Royal Guard to help lower the non-flying types to the ground, and within half a day's time, they arrived at the foothills just as the sun began to sink toward the horizon.

General Balena approached the group with several of his captains and with General Tolomus, the only other surviving general, in tow. Like General Balena, he wore black armor, but with silver accents instead of gold.

General Bravenstorm, whom Captain Perine had previously served under, was reported killed while battling the Saurian forces, along with many of his men.

Condor chuckled at General Balena's approach. "As you can see, the Premieress is still alive and well."

Lilly stifled a smirk, but General Balena scowled at Condor. "Your attempts at humor regarding her safety are not appreciated. The Premieress's wellbeing is not a laughing matter."

"It's alright, General. Condor understands the conditions of his service better than anyone—" Lilly eyed Condor, who smirked at her. "—for multiple reasons."

"That's what worries me," General Balena muttered. "But we've been over that."

"Indeed we have." Lilly turned to General Tolomus, who bowed with his spear in hand. "General, it sets my heart at ease knowing you survived the attack."

General Tolomus nodded his graying head. Though he held the same title as General Balena, he'd only served as a general for the last five years or so, compared to General Balena's twenty-year tenure as Avian's right hand. While he appeared small next to General Balena's broad form, Lilly knew no one in the Sky Realm could match his skill with a spear.

"After that onslaught, I consider every day a gift, as each new day is another I can dedicate my service to the realm, to you," General Tolomus bowed again and performed the Windgale salute, "and to the memory of your father's reign."

Part of Lilly wanted to grin at the drama of his display, but his sincerity and the recent loss of her father stanched that impulse. "Thank you, General. Your loyalty is an inspiration to us all."

General Tolomus straightened his spine and started to say something, but he stopped short when he noticed Condor. His green eyes widened even more when he saw Magnus. He gawked at them for a long moment, then he turned to General Balena, who nodded.

With a raised eyebrow, General Tolomus refocused his attention on Lilly. "If you and your... *escorts* would follow me, I will lead you to our people."

When they crested the foremost foothill, Lilly's heart thrummed with joy. There, in the shallow valley below her, bustled thousands of Windgales. A smile, one more genuine than any she'd shown in what felt like years, parted her lips.

"Incredible," Magnus said. "Kahn himself attacked your city, and this many of your people survived?"

General Tolomus huffed. "We Windgales aren't the fragile doves you Saurians believe us to be. We're resilient, capable warriors."

"I meant no offense, General," Magnus said.

"Hundreds—perhaps thousands of the realm's finest soldiers and protectors gave their lives to save many, many thousands more from *your* kind." General Tolomus glared at him. "Why are *you* even here in the first place?"

Lilly positioned herself between the two of them. "General, if you knew to whom you spoke, you would—"

"Forgive me, Premieress, but I must speak for myself." Magnus placed a heavy hand on her shoulder. "I maintain no allegiance to Kahn or Vandorian. I stand independent of their rule, and I desire to bring an end to it. Until then, I exist to serve the Premieress as one of her many protectors."

"I don't know whom to distrust more." General Tolomus scoffed. His gaze flitted between Magnus and Condor. "The Sobek or the traitor."

"You will distrust neither of them," Lilly said, her voice firm. "Both have saved my life on multiple occasions. Without the two of them and my other friends here, I'd be dead, and you would be leaderless."

General Tolomus's nostrils flared, but he nodded. "Forgive my skepticism in these dark times, Premieress. I am only interested in the wellbeing of our realm and of what few of my men remain."

"I understand." Enough of this. Lilly needed to see her people. She shifted her attention to the throng in the valley. "Have you taken a count of how many survived?"

"Not yet." General Balena folded his arms. "Dozens of survivors have joined the camp even since our arrival, but I estimate our current population at no more than 5,000."

A pang stabbed Lilly's stomach. "Less than 5,000? The Sky Realm was home to more than 30,000 Windgales, plus a few thousand more who lived around the pillar bases."

"The Saurians—" General Tolomus eyed Magnus. "—showed no mercy. They slaughtered our people indiscriminately, whether soldiers or not. At least half of our casualties came from Kahn himself."

Lilly bit her lip. "And how many of our army survived?"

497

General Tolomus glanced at General Balena. "By our best estimates, we have about five hundred soldiers of our original force of 3,000."

"Plus thirty-one surviving members of the Royal Guard," General Balena said.

"We're crippled." The voice came from behind Lilly. It was Condor, who shook his head.

He was right, but Lilly shot him a glare anyway.

"I wish I could provide you with an assessment other than the one Condor just gave—" General Tolomus frowned at him. "—but he's right. If we are attacked again, we cannot defend ourselves. Our only hope is to flee and regroup elsewhere."

"What about the Windgales who don't have capes?" Calum's voice rose from behind Magnus and Axel.

Lilly stifled a smile when she saw him. He'd been so quiet, so respectful of her need to reconcile what had happened since that morning, that she'd almost forgotten he was there. Axel, on the other hand, had been all but ever-present with offers of support and help in whatever way he could while they'd traveled to the Firjian Foothills.

"I beg your pardon?" General Tolomus asked.

"I asked what would happen to the Windgales who don't have capes and can't fly. If they get attacked again, what are they supposed to do if that happens?"

General Tolomus straightened his spine. "If we are attacked again, our first priority is ensuring the safety of the Premieress, then that of our people. Our warriors will fend off any attack for as long as possible, but I refuse to leave my men in harm's way if any stragglers can't get away fast enough."

"So you would leave them to die? The Windgales without capes?" Calum folded his arms.

General Tolomus turned to Lilly. "Who is this *human* who presumes to tell me how to command my own forces?"

"Easy." Calum held up his hands and donned a casual smile. "I'm just asking a question."

General Tolomus glared at him. "You're attempting to boil the intricacies of war down to a hypothetical scenario, and you suggested that I would leave my own people to die."

"I didn't hear you say anything to the contrary." Axel stepped forward and stood shoulder-to-shoulder with Calum, his arms also folded.

"You know nothing." General Tolomus's green eyes flared with anger, and his grip on his spear tightened. He drifted toward them, stopping with his face just inches away. "*Nothing.*"

Of course, Axel didn't back down. It was both the quality Lilly most admired and despised about him.

"What's the function of your army if not to protect your people?" Axel challenged. "*All* of your people?"

"Our army exists to protect the population as a whole," General Tolomus countered. "In war, not everyone can survive."

"You mean the people who don't matter to you won't survive," Axel pressed.

"Take it easy, Axel." Calum faced General Tolomus. "We're concerned for the non-flying Windgales. If we get attacked, the Saurians will easily overrun and kill them."

"And if Kahn returns, then *no one* is safe." General Tolomus huffed, then he turned to Lilly and General Balena. "This inquisition is pointless. We should be discussing plans for a counterattack instead."

"A *counterattack?*" Now Magnus stepped forward. "The only thing a counterattack would accomplish is getting the rest of your soldiers killed and leaving the entirety of your population indefinitely vulnerable. Reptilius is far away from here, and Kahn aside, the Saurians' army numbers nearly ten thousand. To attack them now would be a fool's errand unlike any in recorded history."

"You would know." General Tolomus stared up into Magnus's golden eyes.

"I'm still amazed that you'd leave your own people to die when your men are the only ones who can protect them," Axel muttered.

General Tolomus leaned close to Axel until their faces were only inches apart. "People who can't fend for themselves don't *deserve* to survive."

Axel's jaw set, and then he shoved General Tolomus away with such force that General Balena had to catch him to keep him from falling. Despite General Balena's protests, General Tolomus tossed his spear aside, shot forward, and drove his shoulder into Axel's chest. They tumbled to the ground, each of them jockeying for the upper hand in the scuffle.

"That's *enough*, General!" General Balena clamped his arms around General Tolomus's chest from behind and hauled him off of Axel, while Condor grabbed Axel under his arms to keep him from springing forward.

"Both of you, *stop*," Lilly ordered.

Was it her fault this had gotten so out of control? She could've ordered General Tolomus to stop arguing, or told Axel to back off, but she hadn't. For her part, she'd wanted to see how it would play out, to see where General Tolomus's allegiances truly lay.

His responses had disappointed Lilly.

"Get off me!" Axel growled and tried to twist free from Condor's grasp. "I can take him!"

"Magnus? A little help, here?" Condor's jaw tightened with strain, but his pleasant expression somehow didn't fully disappear in spite of it. For all of Condor's speed, Axel was stronger.

As Magnus approached, Axel made the mistake of kicking out at him. Magnus reacted by grabbing Axel by his ankle, yanking, and pulling him up.

"What the—hey!" Axel hung upside down in Magnus's grip, his head at least two feet off the ground, still squirming. "Put me down!"

"Not until you calm yourself." Magnus grunted at Axel's jerks. "And if you fail to do so, I will smack you."

"He's an ingrate," General Tolomus spat. "A rapscallion. A mindless, brainless brigand with no concept of the realities of war."

"And you're a soulless, cold-hearted wretch who's more concerned with his status than with the wellbeing of the people he's supposed to serve!" Axel hollered, but Lilly couldn't take him seriously while he still hung upside down.

"I said *stop*. Both of you. Right now." Lilly stepped between them. "We're meant to fight our enemies, not each other."

General Tolomus shook free from General Balena's grasp and pointed a finger at Axel. "Just keep him away from me, and the other human, too."

"No problem there. The last thing I want is to be anywhere near a horse's back-end like you." Axel pressed his fingers against his forehead and clenched his eyes shut. "Would you let me down, please? My head is swimming."

Magnus dropped him on his head.

"Ow!" Axel rolled onto his back then sat up. "What's your problem?"

"Nothing, anymore." Magnus smirked at him.

Axel muttered several curses, all while alternating glares between Magnus and General Tolomus.

"We can't afford to attack the Saurians, and we can't protect our own people. We don't have a home where we're safe," Condor said. "Rebuilding the fortress is necessary, but time-consuming, and not an immediate solution. I don't know what other options we have to protect everyone."

Lilly did. At this point, only one thing would enable her people to safely evade any additional attacks. "I must address the people. Find a way to gather them and get their attention."

General Balena eyed her. "What are you going to tell them?"

Lilly matched his gaze. "I'm going to give them hope where they otherwise have none."

Within moments, the remnant of her people had gathered before her. Lilly inhaled a large breath and hovered about ten feet above the sprawling crowd. At first, the Windgales hummed like a bustling bees' nest disturbed by a harsh wind, but a hush cascaded over them as she raised her hands in the air.

"My people," she began.

Lilly had reached the point of decision. Should she tell them the truth about the Aerostone? Or should she keep them subject to her every whim through the system of control and manipulation that all the Sky Realm's rulers before her had utilized, including her father?

"It is with great sorrow that I appear before you today as Premieress in place of my father, Avian, who died this very day in defense of our Realm."

Murmurs swelled in the crowd, but they subsided when Lilly raised her hands again.

"My father sacrificed himself so that you and some of your friends, family, and neighbors might live. His sudden death necessitated my ascension to Premieress this very afternoon."

More murmurs, this time shorter, and quieter.

Lilly glanced at General Balena, who nodded, then she refocused on the people. An image of Falcroné's pristine, regal smile formed in her mind's eye, and her heart panged with regret.

"It is not my intention to waste your time with a long, elaborate speech. Instead, I'll simply say this: Lumen, the ancient warrior of old, has awakened, and he moves to march on Valkendell, the King's fortress in Solace. The majority of our fighting forces and any who might volunteer to join his cause shall do so with my blessing."

Gasps and whispers hissed among the crowd, swelling to chattering conversation.

"I'd like to tell you that the Saurians who attacked us are in league with the King, who has long oppressed our human neighbors to the East of the valley, but I have no evidence that such an alliance has formed."

The crowd simmered to silence.

Lilly cast a glance at Calum and Axel, both of whom stared at her, rapt. "I'd like to tell you that Lumen's movement against the King will ensure our safety for years to come, but I have not spoken with Lumen about our plight, as I have only just arrived from releasing him from his prison under the Central Tri-Lake.

"However, I have met him. I have looked into his burning eyes. I have seen his power first-hand. I've witnessed him vanquish an *entire army* with one unspeakable surge of power. He has made it clear that his goal is to unite Kanarah under his banner and under his leadership, but there is still no guarantee that he will help us. Even if he does, that help could be months away."

Lilly scanned the multi-colored faces in the crowd, all of them worn from distrust, from war, and some of them from the travails of daily life on top of the horrors they had all just endured.

"But I believe in him," she continued. "I trust him. I believe that if we help him liberate Kanarah—*all* of Kanarah—then we will discover our place under his benevolent reign, a place of peace and comfort, where all of our needs are met and even surpassed."

The crowd began to rumble, and smiles formed on several of the people's faces.

"Even so, I know that the death of our Premier and the destruction of our realm is no cause for celebration. I'll wager we've all lost something, or someone, or both, as a result of this attack. I won't lie to you. Our army is—"

General Balena cleared his throat from behind her, but she didn't look back at him.

"—in bad shape. We have only a fraction of our original strength thanks to Kahn's involvement in the attack."

"Lilly," General Balena grunted.

"As such, I request that any of you, whether you be men, women, or youths at least sixteen or older, volunteer to join our army to help protect your friends and family. Your people." Lilly exhaled a long breath. "I'm barely of age myself, but I'm committed to serving and protecting our realm with my very life, just as my father did.

"My entire family is wiped out, except for General Balena, my uncle. *You* are my family now." She extended her right arm and swept it in an arc across the crowd. "And for that reason, I have decided to treat you as family deserves to be treated: as equals, with love and respect."

She turned back and stared at General Balena for a moment. He would disapprove of her choice, as would General Tolomus and many of the other Wisps, if not all of them.

Condor's piercing blue eyes met hers, and he smirked, like he always did. He must've known what she was about to say.

She found Calum's eyes next, blue and free like the sky, but with a certain softness born of suffering. He would agree with her choice, too.

So would Axel, but she didn't bother to make eye contact with him.

"Don't." General Balena shook his head and stared steel at her. "Don't do it."

What little reservation that remained within Lilly died in the same rebellious flames that had spurred her to leave the Sky Realm a year ago. Her people needed to know the truth, for their own safety and wellbeing. How many more may have survived the Saurians' attack had they been granted the ability to fly?

Promise me you'll steward this power as if it were your own life, her father had begged. *Promise me you won't throw it away.*

Lilly intended to uphold that promise, but in her own way. She refused to let any more of her people die because of her family's secrets.

She pulled the Aerostone from the pouch at her hip and held it overhead.

CHAPTER 11

When Lilly spoke, Condor could scarcely believe his ears. "With the power of this stone," she proclaimed, "all Windgales can fly whether they're wearing a cape or not."

No one in the crowd made a sound for almost a minute after Lilly's proclamation, and Condor was no exception. But where others wore expressions of confusion or shock, he stood behind her, grinning.

She'd done it. She had freed her people.

Condor had always hoped Avian would do it, but he'd been a stubborn old bird. Now it no longer mattered; Avian was dead, and with this revelation, injustice would have a much harder time when next it tried to take root in the Sky Realm.

"All you need to do is touch the stone, and it will remove your need for capes. You will be able to fly freely, uninhibited. The stone is powerful enough to transform every Windgale in existence. Come forward and claim your inherent power."

With that statement, Lilly tossed the Aerostone into the crowd. A haggard man without a cape caught it, and his eyes widened with surprise, then delight, as his feet left the ground on their own. His eyes fixed on the skies, and he passed the Aerostone to the next person without even looking. Then he shot into the air, whooping and hollering as he flew.

The woman who received the Aerostone next tore her cape from her shoulders, then she held out the Aerostone for her two children and her husband to touch. They did, and the four of them ascended together as a family.

On and on, the Aerostone worked its way through the crowd, birthing new Wisps in seconds, never losing its power, never letting anyone down. Lilly had given the Windgales a profound gift, one unlike anything her father could've even conceived of.

Condor reveled in the moment. Ever since he'd rebelled against the Premier, this exact moment, this revelation of the truth to all of his people, had been his end goal. In one mighty blow, Lilly had shattered the system of castes within the Sky Realm forever.

The best part of it was that though Condor's greatest dreams had been realized, he'd done virtually nothing to make it happen. Perhaps it was better that way—the Premiers of old had instituted this method of control, and now one of their descendants had done away with it.

Condor's grin widened into a smile.

Next to him, General Balena exhaled a long sigh. Why shouldn't he? For all his good qualities, General Balena was both a product of the Sky Realm's status quo and perhaps its most stalwart defender now that Avian was dead.

"We're doomed," General Tolomus muttered. He stood on Condor's right and covered his face with his palm.

"Hardly." Condor probably shouldn't have said it, but he'd never liked General Tolomus anyway.

"I wasn't talking to you," General Tolomus hissed.

"When has that ever stopped me before?"

General Tolomus just rolled his eyes and shook his head.

"She did the right thing. I'm sure it bothers you because making the right decision isn't something you're used to," Condor said. "But it needed to happen."

"You're a traitor to the realm. Your opinion carries as much weight with me as the Sobek's." General Tolomus glared at him and motioned at Magnus over his shoulder with his thumb.

"They called me a traitor because I wanted to do what our Premieress just did. Would you brand her a traitor as well?"

"You're a traitor because you tried to assassinate the Premier and succeed him as ruler of our realm," General Balena interjected. "And whether she knows it or not, Lilly has just changed our society forever. Our entire social structure was built upon that secret."

Condor stared out over the crowd, now bustling with Windgales shedding their capes and taking to the sky. "Then we will just have to lay a new foundation in its place."

CALUM GRINNED at the sight of a young Windgale mother near the front of the crowd and her two young children, a boy and a girl. Together, they each touched the Aerostone, then the mother passed it along.

She'd already taken off her torn and tattered cape—a black garment that Calum recognized as one they'd taken from the Raven's Brood and later distributed to the Windgales at the base of the fortress several weeks earlier. Now she gripped her children's hands and hovered with them into the air.

Their dirt-streaked faces contorted with fear at first, then they shifted to wonder, then pure elation once they realized they could control this newfound ability. Within moments they looped through the air like excited blue jays, giggling with gigantic smiles on their faces.

When Calum chuckled, Axel grunted, "What's so funny?"

Calum hesitated. He wanted to point to the family, but they had vanished among the ever-growing swarm of Windgales swooping through the sky above the valley. He exhaled a short breath and nodded toward the Windgales. "They're all so happy."

"I find it interesting that the Premier and his goons kept that knowledge from their people for so long." Axel folded his arms. "They're just as bad as the King and his soldiers."

"Can't argue with you there." Calum caught sight of Lilly's blue eyes, and he found he couldn't stifle his smile. "But she made the right call."

"No doubt. She set them all free. And she just earned their lifelong loyalty."

Calum noticed General Tolomus, his posture rigid as if his spine were the straightest tree in Kanarah, scowling at Lilly. "Most of them, anyway."

"General Tolomus? He's a steaming pile of horse manure, as far as I'm concerned. He would've left all these people to die just to preserve the Windgales' secret." Axel huffed. "I bet he'd feel differently if *he* didn't already know the truth."

"At this point, he commands almost half the remaining Windgale army," Calum said. "He's not someone you want to aggravate."

"But he reports to General Balena, and they both report to Lilly now." Axel smirked. "She's officially the most powerful person we know, aside from Lumen."

"Power doesn't mean what we used to think it means. Her father had power, but Condor rebelled and almost managed to assassinate him."

"*Almost.* But he didn't."

"Still," Calum rubbed his chin, "I don't trust General Tolomus."

Axel thwacked Calum on the back of his shoulder. "No sense worrying about it. Nothing you can do about it anyway."

Calum didn't know if he believed that or not, but arguing with Axel wouldn't accomplish anything. "If you say so."

"What's next?"

"What do you mean?"

"I mean, what happens next?" Axel asked. "Lilly's in charge. She has an army—even if it's only a small one. She knows we're supposed to bring forces to Lumen to fight against the King."

"We head north, next," Magnus's deep voice said from behind them. "These Windgales will want blood for their fallen comrades and family members, and so do I. We will head toward Reptilius, and I will have my chance to avenge my father's murder."

Calum smiled. "And then we'll have two rulers on our side. And two armies."

Axel huffed. "And two over-inflated egos."

"Spoken as someone who has never known true power or the yoke of responsibility that accompanies it." Magnus shook his head at Axel. "We must stop in the Desert of the Forgotten along the way. I require that sword."

RILEY'S EARS perked up when Magnus uttered the words "Desert of the Forgotten."

He'd hung near the back of the group with Janessa, Dallahan, and Embry, just watching and observing the Windgales flying after touching the Aerostone. He'd heard Condor argue with the generals, and he'd heard Calum and Axel talking through their concerns regarding General Tolomus.

He'd heard everything, as usual.

But Magnus's mention of that place, his former home, bristled the fur on his hide. All but the bravest—or stupidest—of travelers avoided that desert so the native Wolf tribes wouldn't attack them.

Lumen had told Magnus that the Dragon's Breath sword, supposedly the key to defeating Kahn, was hidden somewhere in the Desert of the Forgotten, but Riley had never even heard of such a thing, let alone seen it. Traveling back to that desert for a mythical sword, whether it existed or not, was *not* something Riley wanted to do.

The last time he was there, it had cost him far too much, and it had entirely rewritten the path of his life in the process. If he had to go back there…

Behind him, Embry and Dallahan nipped at each other while Janessa watched, unamused. He envied them and their rambunctious demeanor. None of them had been banished from their tribe under penalty of death like Riley had. They could afford to behave like carefree pups in a litter.

They had always belonged somewhere, always had each other, but Riley had gone for more than a year without a home or a family or friends. Now, with Calum, Lilly, Magnus, Kanton, and even Axel and Condor to call his friends, plus three remaining Wolves under his charge, Riley finally felt like he'd found true companionship.

He growled, low and long. Returning to the desert would end all of that.

Along with his life.

"GENERAL TOLOMUS." Lilly approached him, focused and poised, yet certain of the sour turn this conversation would soon take. "I require one third of our army to accompany me north to Reptilius. The other two thirds will remain here to protect and train all able-bodied citizens to fight, should the need arise."

General Tolomus blinked at her and tilted his head as if she were a child who'd proposed an outlandish idea. "Premieress, do you mean to attack the Crimson Keep, despite assertions that doing so would be a fool's errand? And with only one hundred and fifty men?"

Lilly bit back her impulse to match his attitude with one of her own. "I mean to give Magnus his chance to end Kahn's rule once and for all."

General Tolomus scoffed. "Even if you could reach the Crimson Keep with so few warriors, how is one Sobek going to defeat a Dragon? Avian himself couldn't do it, and he had the Calios."

"Lumen revealed the location of the Dragon's Breath sword to Magnus." Lilly recognized that if her father had given the order, he wouldn't have had to explain any of this. General Tolomus would've just obeyed. She continued, "It's a legendary blade capable of piercing Dragon scales. It lies somewhere in the Desert of the Forgotten."

General Tolomus's eyes narrowed. "You wish to head to Reptilius by way of that desert? Premieress, it is a barren, desolate wasteland littered with savage beasts and Wolf tribes who would just as soon eat you as rob you."

"It's also the most direct route to Reptilius. As for the bandits, that is why I require one third of our army." Lilly smiled at Condor, who stood within a few paces of General Tolomus. "And my Royal Guard, of course."

"And who will command this army?" General Tolomus stopped short of sneering at her, but she could tell he wanted to. "With *respect*, Premieress, someone with more tactical experience than yourself ought to accompany you to provide counsel."

"I fully agree." Lilly shifted her smile to General Tolomus, who'd unwittingly played right into her hands. "*You* will join us and command the soldiers who accompany us. General Balena will remain with the rest of the army to protect our people here."

General Tolomus's nostrils flared, and his jaw tightened. He stole a glance at General Balena, who nodded. "By your command, Premieress."

"Divide the army at your leisure, but ensure that those who accompany us have the resolve to complete the journey. Let the remaining forces rest here with our people."

"At once." General Tolomus grumbled and hovered over to General Balena.

"Lilly?"

She turned her head and found Riley towering next to her. She still wasn't used to having to look up at him since he'd changed into a Werewolf.

His voice flattened. "Er—Premieress?"

"Yes, Riley?" She smiled at him.

He held out the Aerostone, glowing yellow as it had before, for her to take.

Her smile widened. "Honestly, I hadn't expected to see this again."

"I couldn't let it disappear after every remaining Windgale in your realm got their chance to touch it," Riley said. "Besides, I figure you'll need it the next time a Windgale parent has a baby."

Lilly chuckled. "Well, maybe not too soon after they're born. I wouldn't want any Windgale babies to float away while their parents weren't looking."

Riley smirked, but the smile didn't reach his eyes. Instead, a somberness lingered there that Lilly didn't quite understand.

"Anyway, I also realized, accidentally, that it doesn't just make Windgales into Wisps," he said.

Lilly tilted her head. "What else does it do?"

He held his hand out, and she placed the Aerostone back in his hand. Then, without warning, he lifted off his feet and hovered a yard off the ground.

Lilly gawked at him. "You're kidding!"

Riley's smirk returned, but this time, it was more genuine. Apparently, flight had that effect on people—especially when they couldn't normally fly.

"Not unless you can see strings attached to me."

"How high can you go?"

Riley glanced around. "High enough. I tested it out a bit on my own, but I wanted to keep it quiet. After all, a flying Werewolf is pretty much everyone's worst nightmare come to life," he quipped. "In the end, I decided I don't like flying all that much. I prefer to have my feet on solid ground."

With those words, he landed again and handed the Aerostone back to her.

Lilly couldn't imagine living her life without the ability to fly, especially after having that power stripped from her during most of her time in Roderick's captivity, but everyone was created differently.

"Thank you," she said to him as she slipped the Aerostone back into the pouch on her hip. "I really appreciate it."

"I also wanted to warn you of something." That somber quality returned to Riley's eyes. "A third of the army won't be enough. The desert is home to more than just my canine brethren. There are other things there, other dangers. General Tolomus was right to express his concern."

Lilly studied him. In the whirlwind of everything else that had happened in the last few days, she hadn't even thought to get his insight on how they should plan for their venture into the desert. "What should we expect?"

"You should expect to die," Riley replied, his voice flat. "Or at least to lose half of your forces trying to cross to Reptilius. The bigger our party, the more unwanted attention we'll attract."

"So you're saying we should travel to the desert in a smaller group?"

"Yes. We can more easily conceal twenty of us than a hundred and fifty."

Lilly wondered at his suggestion. "But if we encounter danger, won't more soldiers stand a better chance against whatever is out there?"

Riley raised a lupine eyebrow. "Perhaps, but only because there will be more of us to kill."

"What do you mean? What's out there?"

Riley's eyes narrowed. "Surely you've heard the rumors."

Lilly shook her head. "Enlighten me."

"Over the past several decades, a new threat has infected the desert. Horrific creatures, bearing the shape of Wolves but lacking in anything resembling a soul, have claimed more and more of the desert. We call them Wargs," Riley said. "They're monsters. Overgrown, mangy, vicious and brutal beyond anything you'd see from even the most enraged Wolf."

"They're like the Dactyls we fought back at the Central Lake," Condor piped in.

Both Lilly and Riley turned toward him. Lilly asked, "Another piece of secret knowledge from your time as the Captain of the Guard?"

Condor shook his head, and his smirk faded. "No. I learned of them from my time enslaved in the Blood Chasm. They killed many of us there." Condor stared off into the distance. "Too many."

"They primarily emerge at sundown, but when I left the desert a year ago, they'd begun to venture out in the daylight. Even the strongest of the Wolves avoid them."

"Riley's right." Condor nodded, and his smirk returned. "Every nightfall in the Blood Chasm, the Wargs emerged from the various caves and crevices and pursued us. We only found safety— if you could call it that—within the walls of Oren's fortress, and that's only because they couldn't get in. No opposable thumbs to open doors, and all that."

"When we were there, none of them bothered us." Lilly turned to Riley. "Didn't you pick up their scent?"

"That's part of what makes them so dangerous. Unlike Dactyls, they give off almost no scent whatsoever." Riley shrugged. "I don't have the slightest idea why, but they just don't. Wolves rely on their sense of smell for everything, but even a Werewolf like me can't smell one of them until it's almost too late."

Lilly weighed Riley's warnings and Condor's experiences in her mind. "You're saying these Wargs now occupy the desert?"

"A lot of it." Riley nodded. "Not all of it, but the Wolves have been avoiding them for years. It got so bad that about four years ago, we had to start actively resisting them and fighting back. The numbers were in our favor then, but even so, all we succeeded in doing was holding them at bay."

A moment of quiet contemplation lingered between them.

"None of this changes what we must do," Lilly finally said. "General Tolomus was right—if my father couldn't defeat Kahn with the Calios, I can't possibly hope to defeat him either. But if Magnus can get the Dragon's Breath, we have a chance. And if we intend to join with Lumen in his quest to overthrow the King, we need Reptilius's strength."

Riley sighed. "I was afraid you'd say that."

"You don't have to come along, Riley," Lilly said. "I can't make you."

"I'm bound to you by the Law of Debt just as you're bound to me. We're in this together no matter what." A low growl emanated from Riley's throat. "So I'm coming. I just want you to be aware of what we'll be up against."

Lilly smiled. "I'm honored to have your support. The question still remains—do we take a large force or a small force with us?"

"Our numbers at the Blood Chasm didn't matter," Condor said. "The Wargs came every night either way. As was suggested, a small force may escape notice easier, but a large force would better defend against enemies should we encounter them.

"Additionally, a smaller force will look more like an envoy of peace to the Saurians rather than an approaching army as well. Either way, we're risking our lives for the very soul of Kanarah," Condor concluded. "It is for us to serve, Premieress, and for you to decide how."

Lilly nodded and gave her decision. "We will take the smaller force. General Balena and General Tolomus will throw a fit, but we'll need all the soldiers we can spare to join Lumen's forces once we've seen this through. We depart tomorrow morning at dawn."

CALUM STARED at the light emanating from his left hand, the only light in the darkness around him aside from the stars above and what shone from the sliver of moon hanging in the sky. The light still burned inside his hand whenever he used it, and it intensified the brighter he made the light.

Even so, he could control the brightness and tolerate the burn to a point. Perhaps, in time, he'd learn to maintain the light for longer periods in spite of the burn. Maybe the light would even become a weapon.

Lumen had promised him authority and power. Perhaps this was the beginning of that manifesting within Calum.

He closed his fist, and the light faded along with the burn.

A WEEK INTO THEIR JOURNEY, Axel and the rest of the group crossed into the Desert of the Forgotten. A troop of ten soldiers, all of them under General Tolomus's command, and as many members of the Royal Guard, led by Condor, accompanied them.

Admittedly, Axel didn't really know what kind of mayhem they might be walking into, between the desert and Reptilius beyond, but the idea of a few extra Windgale soldiers, all of them ultra-fast Wisps, set him at ease. He'd seen what Condor and Falcroné were capable of, and though he doubted each of the additional soldiers could compare, some of them at least came close to that level.

Probably.

Condor's soldiers wore dark-purple armor, and General Tolomus's elites wore vivid orange armor with deep purple accents. He'd almost spoken up about them changing their armor colors —especially the orange ones—but he decided to leave it alone.

If they wanted to be obvious targets, that was fine with Axel. And if nothing else, he'd be able to see them wherever they went.

"Are we going the right way?" Lilly asked Condor. She walked with him at her side while Calum and Magnus followed right behind them. Axel, as usual, trailed at the back of the group. He didn't hear Condor's reply, but he saw Condor nod.

While the additional soldiers had given Axel an improved sense of security, he had almost elected to stay behind once he found out that General Tolomus was coming along. To his surprise, thus far they hadn't exchanged so much as a single word during their jaunt into the desert. General Tolomus mostly kept to himself and to his elites, and that suited Axel just fine.

Something skittered across his boots on the dry ground. A black scorpion, no bigger than his index finger, disappeared under a gray rock.

Yeesh. Axel shuddered. For all his fearlessness, he couldn't bring himself to deal with anything creepy and crawly larger than the pommel of his sword. Bugs freaked him out—especially the kind he'd found here.

Back home at the farm and near the quarry, there'd been flies, moths, and spiders aplenty, but none of them had grown especially large—aside from the occasional corn spider, which Axel had mostly managed to avoid. They were harmless anyway.

By contrast, one look at the tails and pincers of these scorpions had told him everything he needed to know, and he gave them a wide berth.

So far the desert appeared as he'd expected: arid, sandy, scattered with rocks and canyons and mesas and sparse vegetation. Reminiscent of the bleak Valley of the Tri-Lakes, only tan and brown instead of gray. No trees, no water. Just endless wasteland, as far as he could see.

Not a place he'd want to visit, to say the least, and certainly not a place he'd want to live. But now, at least, he could say he'd been there.

Four lines of vivid-orange soldiers hovered high above Lilly's personal entourage, led by General Tolomus. Ahead of Lilly, the ten purple-clad members of the Royal Guard floated ten feet above Lilly's group in a loose circle.

Far ahead of them, Kanton, Riley, and his Wolves led the group. Upon entering the desert, Riley insisted that he take the lead. Having been a resident, he knew the territory and could better alert the group to any approaching dangers.

His Wolves stayed with him, of course, but Axel had no idea what Kanton was doing up there. He wasn't good for anything unless it came to medical tasks.

A sharp hiss sounded to Axel's left, and he jumped back with his sword in hand. "By the Overlord!"

Another scorpion skittered away, but this one exceeded the size of a housecat—black with prickly hairs, crablike pincers, and a long black tail tipped with a menacing teal barb.

Axel's heart rate tripled, and he scrambled ahead to get away from the thing. He took his eyes off it for just a second to make sure he wouldn't run into Calum from behind, but when he looked back, it was gone, replaced by a plume of yellow dust.

"What is wrong with you?" Magnus looked back at him, and so did Calum.

Axel hesitated. No sense in showing weakness to these two idiots. "Nothing. Almost tripped over something. I'm fine."

"Sure you did." Magnus snorted and faced forward again.

Whatever. Knowing Magnus, he'd probably just as soon eat one of those scorpions like he had with the rats in the sewers under Kanarah City. The opinion of a scaly guy who ate rats didn't matter to Axel.

A few minutes later, Axel had again allowed himself to fall back from the group by ten feet or so when another hiss sounded from behind a large rock.

Enough of this. Time to face his fears and put a stop to these critters' harassment at the same time. Sword in-hand, he steeled himself, rounded the rock, and raised his sword.

A black teal-tipped tail lashed at him. Axel yelped and swung his sword, severing the scorpion's barb from its tail. Dark goo squirted out of the wound, and the scorpion gave off a shrill screech.

Then it skittered toward him with its pincers raised.

"Whoa!" Axel slammed the edge of his blade down on the scorpion and split it into two halves, oozing more black goo into the dry dirt.

It looked like the same one from before, but Axel couldn't be sure. It was about the same size, and equally horrifying. It didn't matter now, though. It was dead, and that's what counted.

Something touched his shoulder.

He yelped again and whirled around with his sword raised to find Calum standing there. "What in the—Calum! Don't sneak up on me like that! I almost killed you just now."

"Easy." Calum held up his hands. "I was just checking to see if you were alright. I heard you scream, and I—"

"I did *not* scream." Axel lowered his sword and glared at him. "I had to take care of a scorpion. That's all."

Calum craned his neck but Axel moved in front of him to block his view. "Why won't you let me see it?"

"It's nothing. I killed it. We're fine."

A hulking dark form materialized over Axel's right shoulder, and he jumped.

Riley.

"By the Overlord!" Axel exhaled a ragged breath. Why was everyone sneaking up on him? They were as bad as the scorpions. "Riley, I *know* you just heard me tell—"

"What did you just do?" Riley growled.

Axel glanced at Calum. "I killed a scorpion. It's not a big deal."

Riley's blue eyes widened. "Where is it?"

"Why does it matter?"

"It matters." Riley pushed past him and started toward the scorpion's carcass.

"Why?"

"Hey," Condor called from his spot next to Lilly, "what's the holdup? We're not stopping now. We've got at least thirteen more miles to cover before—"

"*Quiet*," Riley snapped. "Listen."

"To what?" Axel eyed him.

"*Listen.*"

A low rumble sounded, and then the ground began to vibrate beneath their feet.

Axel stepped back, but the rumbling intensified to quaking. Fifteen feet away from him, a gigantic mound of sand swelled from the ground. Pieces of it broke open, and dozens of black scorpions the size of the one he'd just killed streamed out.

But it didn't end there. The mound itself fell apart, revealing a massive black beast—another scorpion, bigger than any horse Axel had ever seen. An enormous teal barb tipped its tail, matching the jagged teeth in its bulging pincers.

It started toward Axel.

"Run!" Riley shouted.

Axel took off toward Condor and Lilly. When he looked back, the gigantic scorpion not only followed, but its gazillion legs actually propelled it forward so fast that it gained on him. Dozens of cat-sized scorpions skittered after it.

He screamed. He didn't care how he sounded at this point. A giant scorpion and its babies were chasing him through the desert. If that didn't call for screaming, nothing did.

Ahead of him, Lilly and Condor took to the sky, and Calum and Magnus ran behind Riley and his Wolves. Curses swarmed through Axel's mind, but he didn't bother saying any of them out loud. He was too focused on running for his life.

He followed the others toward a gorge framed by two rock walls that gradually narrowed. Axel's legs pumped faster. A cacophony of screeches trilled behind him as he reached the gorge and ran between the walls.

Ahead of him, Riley slid through the narrowest part of the walls and into a small canyon, followed by his Wolves, then Magnus, then Calum. Axel glanced back.

One of the scorpion's pincers snapped at his head, but he ducked out of the way. A loud *crack* echoed off the walls.

Axel's legs and lungs burned as he bounded over rocks and sand, all the while closing in on that narrow outlet. He eked through the opening, and another *crack* reverberated behind him, followed by a horrendous screech.

The scorpion writhed in the crevice with its left pincer reaching through the opening and clomping for Axel, who stood a solid five feet out of its reach.

"Ha!" He pointed his sword at it, dripping with sweat and breathing heavily. "That'll show you. Now you know what happens when you mess with me."

"Axel—" Calum called from behind him.

Axel didn't turn around. A slow but steady stream of the cat-sized scorpions squeezed between the rock walls under their enraged mother and skittered toward Axel. His chest clenched, and he quickly hacked three of them to pieces, but they kept coming. He backed up slowly, carefully, so as not to trip and fall.

The mama scorpion screeched even louder, but her cracking pincers stopped, and she receded from the opening.

"That's what you get for trying to eat me." Axel spat and chopped another baby scorpion in half.

"*Axel!*"

"What?" He turned around.

In the center of the canyon, between Calum, Magnus, Axel, Riley, his Wolves, and the only other way out, two large mounds arose from the ground.

The big scorpion behind him screeched again. Axel turned back as it crested the top of the rock walls, then it started to crawl down into the canyon, all while its babies flowed toward him, unhindered, from the crevice, blocking any hope of escape.

Now Axel did curse, and he did so prolifically.

CHAPTER 12

Lilly's heart thundered in her chest as she stared down at the canyon and her friends trapped inside. "We have to help them!"

"Stay back, Premieress!" General Tolomus flew in front of her, blocking her from trying to intervene. "Those creatures are filled with lethal venom. A single sting, even from one of the smaller ones, could kill you."

"All the more reason to *help* them, General!" Lilly pushed past him but darted straight into a charcoal breastplate decorated with a black raven insignia.

Condor caught her by the shoulders and looked down at her with those piercing blue eyes. Even amid the mayhem below, Lilly still found herself hypnotized by them.

"Easy, Lilly. Let us handle this for you." Condor barked an order to the Royal Guard, and they zipped down into the fray. "General, give us the aid of your elites, and we can end this much sooner. We needn't fight at all if we can grab our land-dwelling friends and pull them to safety."

General Tolomus fixed his exasperated gaze on Lilly. She nodded at him, and he gave the order. Condor followed a mass of vivid orange blurs toward the canyon, and General Tolomus hovered next to Lilly.

"He's going to get himself—and you—killed if he keeps hurtling into battle like that. Now I'm the only one left to ensure your safety." He scowled at her. "He is as unfit as ever to protect you, Premieress."

"Then I'd better make it easy for him to keep track of me." She zoomed down into the canyon amid General Tolomus's calls for her to stop.

———————

AXEL DUCKED under the big scorpion's pincer snap, rolled away from a spree of lashes from a half-dozen smaller scorpion tails, then dove behind a boulder to avoid the big scorpion's venomous tail. Its teal barb jammed into the dirt where Axel had just stood, then its second

He jumped back with a yell and lashed his sword at the rat-sized scorpion at his feet. It splattered into black goo, but mama scorpion's tail whipped toward Axel again. He started to raise his sword to defend, but something rammed him from the side. The teal barb embedded in the dirt once more.

Axel regained his footing in time to see General Tolomus and two orange Wisps latch onto his limbs with their hands, and he quickly lifted away from the fracas below.

He shouted, but they dropped him to the ground a half-mile away from the canyon from about seven or eight feet in the air, then dashed away. The impact knocked the wind out of him, but as soon as he got his breath back, he started after them.

Axel hollered, but soon a mix of dark-purple and vivid orange blurs flew overhead. Pairs and trios of Wisps each carried one of his friends. Calum. Riley. Each of Riley's Wolves. Magnus came last, carried by fifteen Wisps, some of whom had raced back for a second trip.

Condor, Lilly, Kanton, and General Tolomus landed last, and while Condor took a quick inventory of the Windgales who remained, Lilly approached Axel. "Are you alright?"

The truth was, he'd never been more afraid for his life than in those few short minutes in the canyon. The skittering and clambering and tail-lashing had worn his nerves raw, and it was all he could do to keep from physically shaking now that he was safe again.

But Axel wasn't about to convey any of that to Lilly.

He brushed some dust off his breastplate. "I'm fine. Was just starting to have fun."

General Tolomus glared at him. "Have your fun at your own expense next time."

Axel ignored him with an eye roll.

"Is everyone accounted for?" Lilly asked.

"This time, yes, but we were fortunate. It could have easily gone the other way." Condor eyed Axel. "I suppose they don't have scorpions where you're from, do they, Farm Boy?"

Axel's jaw tightened. "I told you not to call me that."

"Those are Gargantuan Scorpions. They're one of the desert's many dangers, but one easily avoided if simply left alone. They usually only attack if provoked." Riley also glared at Axel. "*So stop provoking them.*"

"Hey, the first one came after *me*." Axel pointed at him. "You would've done the same thing."

"Whatever the case, if you see any more, stay away from them," Magnus said. "You ran away from the first one you saw. Just do that from now on, please."

Axel's eyes narrowed. "I did no such thing."

Magnus hissed at Axel through his nostrils.

"*Fine.* I'll avoid them. We all will. Right?" He looked around the group, but no one replied. He nodded for good measure anyway. "Right."

"Let's not tarry," Lilly said. "We should keep moving."

At her word, the group resumed its formation as if nothing had even happened, and Axel soon found himself trailing behind yet again.

THEY CAMPED several hours later atop a mesa large enough to hold them all but small enough to defend from any encroachments, if it came to it. Its steep edges would also make scaling it a difficult task for any foe, whether Warg, Wolf, scorpion, or anything incapable of flight. The group could rest easy that night.

Calum recognized a hidden benefit of having so many extra soldiers accompanying them: more time to sleep. With more soldiers, he only had to stand watch for an hour once every two nights, a far cry from his days in the woods with only Magnus and Axel to split time with.

Still, he found he couldn't sleep. Ever since they'd released Lumen, Calum hadn't had any more of his dreams. Rightfully so, he mused—with Lumen freed, he no longer needed to reach out to Calum with instructions.

But now whenever Calum lay down, he grew restless and never managed more than a couple hours of sleep at a time. What was happening?

"Can't sleep?"

Calum whirled around, but saw nothing. Then a figure materialized out of the darkness. Riley. Calum shook his head.

"Me neither."

"What's keeping you awake?" Calum rubbed his eyes.

"History." Riley sat down next to him near the fire.

Calum squinted at him, but Riley didn't elaborate.

"You?"

Calum shrugged. "Not sure. I'm plenty tired. Just can't seem to fall asleep."

Riley nodded. "A lot on your mind."

Calum glanced at Lilly, who lay surrounded by three layers of soldiers and guards, including Condor and General Tolomus.

"Or maybe not."

"What?" Calum asked.

Riley grinned. "Maybe you don't have a lot on your mind. Just one specific thing."

Calum's mouth hung open for a moment.

"It's alright. I won't tell her. But you should."

Calum's breath caught in his throat. He stammered, "I—I don't know what you're—"

"Sure you do. It's been several months since you met her. Now that Falcroné's out of the way..." Riley didn't finish his thought.

He didn't have to. Calum's heart beat faster. "Look, I—"

"I'm not here to judge. I don't think anyone *wanted* him to die, and certainly no one wanted him to go out the way he did, but the end result still benefits you."

Were they really having this macabre conversation? "Riley, I didn't—"

Riley held up his paw. "Like I said, I'm not here to judge. I'm just—"

"*Riley.*" Calum eyed him, and Riley finally stopped talking. "I understand what you're saying, but her parents just died, and a Dragon and a bunch of Saurians obliterated her home and wiped out a huge chunk of her people. I don't think now's really the right time."

Rather than replying, Riley simply stared up at the night sky, as if lost in thought. Given the nature of their conversation, Calum couldn't help but wonder if Riley had gone through something similar to what he was now experiencing with Lilly.

He started to ask Riley about it, but the Werewolf spoke first.

"You'll say 'it's not the right time' forever if you let yourself." Riley put his hand on Calum's shoulder and then stood to his full height.

"Where are you going?"

"To get some rest. We've got another long day tomorrow—assuming we don't all get killed first."

Calum stood up and grabbed Riley's wrist. "Wait. What did you mean about letting myself say that forever?"

Riley squared his body with Calum's and looked down at him with a hint of sadness in his blue eyes. "I mean that there will always be a reason *not* to do something like this. There will never be a perfect time, Calum. There also may never be a *better* time. Just..." He sighed. "...don't wait so long that it ends up being too late."

Calum noted the dismay and the sense of loss in Riley's voice. Maybe he had a point.

"See that charcoal-coated brigand laying next to her?" Riley nodded toward Condor.

Calum glanced at him, nervous. "Yeah?"

"I hate to say it, but he's Lilly's future if you don't do something first."

"You really think so?" Calum's heart unhinged.

Riley nodded again. "Yeah, I do. He's got everything a girl would want: looks, speed, prowess, cunning, a bad-boy streak. He's the slightly nefarious version of Falcroné, and if Lilly was prepared to marry her own cousin without really loving him, Condor is a big upgrade. And if you let her make that choice—"

"I can't hope to compete with Condor on any level," Calum finished Riley's thought.

Riley sighed again. "But what do I know? I'm just a Wolf."

Calum smiled in spite of his dismay. "A Werewolf, now."

Riley huffed. "Yeah. I keep forgetting that."

As Riley turned to walk away, Calum said, "Hey, can I ask you one other question?"

"Sure." Riley turned back.

"If it came down to Axel and me—"

"Oh, I'd save you, for sure," Riley answered quickly. "Axel wanted to leave me for dead. You've been nothing but a true friend and supportive and—"

"No, no." Calum chuckled. "That's nice to know, but I meant Lilly. Do you think Axel has any chance of—"

"None." Riley's voice flattened. "Zero."

Calum smiled, and he nodded. "Alright. Thanks, Riley."

"Get some sleep, Calum."

"I'll do my best."

"Try counting sheep."

Calum stared at him as headed into the shadows again. "You do realize you're a Wolf, right? A Wolf just told me to count sheep."

Riley shrugged, then he melted into the darkness. "Where do you think the saying came from? Sheep are tasty. It's why we count them."

Calum rolled his eyes and lay back down. This time, instead of seeing Lumen's blinding light when he closed his eyes, he saw fluffy white sheep floating across his mind's eye.

One... two... three...

THE NEXT MORNING when Calum awoke, he realized he'd slept for the rest of the night. Apparently he needed to count sheep more often. He sat up, stretched, and headed straight over to where Lilly stood with Condor and General Tolomus.

Riley had been right. There was no time like the present to talk to Lilly, so that's what Calum had determined to do.

As he approached, six sets of dark-purple armor dropped from the sky and formed a barrier between him and the others. He recoiled a step and eyed them. "Good morning to you, too."

"It's alright, guys," Lilly called. "Let him pass."

The Royal Guard parted, and Calum resumed his path toward Lilly. She smiled at him, and it sent his stomach into a flurry of excitement.

"That's new," he said.

"The guards? They're being overprotective, I know." Lilly looked him up and down. "You look well-rested."

"Yeah. I do." Calum blinked, and the words that came out of his mouth seemed to make less and less sense the more he spoke. "I mean—you do. You do, too. What I'm trying to say is—"

Condor and General Tolomus stared at him, their faces expressionless except for their scrunched eyebrows. Lilly kept smiling at him.

Calum bit his tongue, took a breath, and started again. "Did you sleep well?"

"Premieress, I'm going to prepare my soldiers for departure. Please ask your flightless friends to be ready to descend from this mesa within five minutes." General Tolomus shot Calum a scowl and hopped into the air.

Calum glared back, but only briefly. "So…"

Lilly grinned. "So…?"

Condor cleared his throat. "I hate to break up this highly intellectual conversation while it's still in its infancy, but we should also prepare to leave, Premieress."

Lilly nodded and looked at him. "You're right. We should probably—"

"Lilly?" Calum refused to miss his chance. "Do you mind if we—if I talk to you alone for a minute?"

Condor folded his arms and squinted at Calum, then he turned to Lilly.

She gave him a subtle nod. "I'll be ready in time."

"Alright." Condor clicked his tongue and floated away from them.

"What can I do for you, Calum?"

Finally. He had her all to himself.

He glanced around just to make sure this wasn't an illusion or that the others hadn't formed a line behind him. He caught Riley's eyes, and Riley winked at him.

Then he found Axel's eyes, and he got a glare. But it didn't matter. This was his moment, and he wasn't about to allow Axel to—

"Calum?"

His head snapped back to Lilly. "Huh?"

She chuckled. It sounded wonderful. "You said you wanted to talk to me."

"I do." Realization hit Calum like a fist full of joy to his forehead. "I do! Yes. How are you?"

Lilly smiled. "I'm fine. How are you?"

"I'm good." Calum hesitated. "I'm really good, thanks."

"That's good."

Silence hovered between them.

Calum opened his mouth, but Condor's words sounded.

"Premieress? Are you ready?"

She looked at Calum and raised her eyebrows.

He sighed, and his fingers quivered at his sides. "Just one more minute?"

"Almost, Condor," Lilly called. She refocused on Calum. "Whatever it is, you'd better say it. We're leaving any minute now."

Calum silently cursed his nerves. This was it. He leaned forward and whispered, "Lilly, I think I—"

"Stop," she said, her eyes widening with realization.

He did. His spine straightened, and he stared at her. "What?"

Her smile had faded to an expression halfway between a frown and a scowl. "I'm sorry, Calum. I can't."

Calum gulped down the lump in his throat, and it settled like a rock in his gut. He knew what she meant, but he didn't want to believe they were talking about the same thing. His voice shook as he whispered, "Why not?"

She shook her head, and tears formed in the corners of her eyes. Her voice broke. "I can't lose you too."

Calum's mouth hung open again. "Lilly, you're not going to—"

"Excuse me." She pushed past him and took to the sky, then she promptly landed next to Condor.

Calum stood there as her Royal Guard also surrounded her. He exhaled a long breath, wishing he could exhale the sense of emptiness in his gut as well. He'd tried. He'd actually succeeded, at least on some level. He'd managed to get his message across, but unlike what Riley had suggested, he'd failed to win her over.

"Alright. Everyone who's flightless, move to the edge of the mesa," General Tolomus said.

Calum complied, but he noted the scorn in General Tolomus's voice whenever he said "flightless." Two sets of Windgale arms hooked under his and descended with him to the base of the mesa.

At least by now he was used to Windgales letting him down.

AFTER TWO SCORPION-FREE, Warg-free, and Wolf-free days and nights, Magnus and Riley led the group to the place Magnus had seen in his vision from Lumen.

Now, after weeks of travel and years of biding his time, waiting for a means to avenge his father's murder, Magnus would soon hold that means in his hands.

"This is it?" Axel asked, his voice as flat as the desert ground where they stood. "There's nothing here."

"Remember how unimpressed you were when we reached the Arcanum?" Magnus countered.

"Yeah. What's your point?"

"Remember how wrong you were?"

Axel's jaw hardened. "Again, what's your point?"

"You are about to be wrong again."

Magnus took three steps forward and bent down next to a dark-brown rock that stuck out from the sand by a few inches. He touched its smooth surface and grinned.

In his vision from Lumen, he'd seen exactly what he needed to do. He gripped the sides of the rock and twisted it counter-clockwise.

Something clicked, and the rock began to ascend from the sand. It stopped once it reached a height of about four feet tall. Though heavily worn, the pillar still vaguely resembled its original form: a Dragon with its wings now missing and a small emerald embedded in its chest.

Magnus turned and raised narrowed his eyes at Axel, who folded his arms and glared back at him.

"Now what?" Calum asked.

Magnus looked around the statue for an opening on the ground, something that would lead him down into the chambers buried beneath the ground, but he found none. Lumen's vision had stopped short of providing him with the answer to this part of the riddle.

"Magnus?"

He glanced at Calum. "I am not sure what must happen next."

Axel scoffed, and Magnus glared at him.

"Maybe it has something to do with that statue?" Lilly landed next to it.

"Like what?" Axel kept his arms folded.

She shrugged. "I don't know. Push on it."

Magnus leaned against it at first, but despite his considerable strength, it didn't budge. He pushed harder, but still nothing happened. He shifted his position and pushed at it from another angle, then another, then another, but all to no avail.

Nothing. He pushed down on it next. Still nothing. He pressed his finger against the emerald, but it didn't move either.

Frustrated, he growled at the pillar and stepped back. He smacked it with the palm of his hand, then reared back and punched the Dragon's head. Fleeting pain rapped his knuckles, and a fissure split near the Dragon's neck, but nothing else happened.

"So..." Calum began. "What do we do now?"

Magnus growled again. "We wait. We cannot leave without that sword."

"For how long?" Lilly asked. "I can already tell you what General Tolomus is going to say."

In unison, Calum, Axel, and Magnus said, "We are too exposed."

Lilly nodded. "Yeah. Exactly."

Axel rolled his eyes. "This is a desert. We're *always* exposed."

"I do not think we have a choice either way," Magnus said. "If necessary, the group can go on ahead, and I will stay here and try to solve this conundrum."

Calum shook his head. "No. I'm staying with you. If something should happen and you need help, I want to be here for you. I'm sure Riley, his Wolves, and Kanton would do the same."

"Count me in as well," Lilly said. "And with me, you get an extra twenty-two companions, because General Tolomus and Condor won't leave my side."

Magnus nodded to them both. "I appreciate your support. Thank you."

Axel kicked a stone and it tumbled toward the pillar. "Guess I'll just go camp somewhere by myself."

Now Magnus rolled his eyes.

AFTER HOURS of everyone trying and failing to usher in some significant change to the statue or its surroundings, night fell on the desert. Amid the chilly night air, Calum helped set up their camp, grateful that the Wisps could fly off to collect firewood and other burnables.

Eventually Magnus gave up and lay on the ground, huffing and snorting until he finally fell asleep. Calum didn't envy him; he'd been just as flummoxed by some of Lumen's dreams and vague instructions over the last year.

With no elevation to protect them, General Tolomus ordered two-hour shifts of watches for the Wisps in both his troop and the Royal Guard. Five soldiers stood watch to start, followed by the other five soldiers, and then two sets of five Royal Guards after that.

Calum stayed up with the third watch for good measure. He'd managed to sleep—thanks to Riley's numbered sheep—for a few hours, but once he woke up that night, he couldn't fall back asleep no matter how many sheep he counted. Better to be an extra lookout than waste his focus on wooly figments of his imagination.

His talk with Lilly the other day still gnawed at him from the inside, mostly because she'd confirmed her feelings for him. At least it *seemed* like she had, and she didn't want to commit to anything and then lose him.

That's what she'd said—or so he thought. He wasn't sure. Maybe she was speaking in girl-code or something.

Whatever the case, it gave him all the more reason to focus on the task at hand. If he didn't end up dead by the end of this whole ordeal, then maybe—just maybe—they could have some semblance of a future together.

He held out his left hand and opened his fist. He concentrated, and Lumen's white light began to emanate from under his skin, accompanied by the familiar burn.

The light flared a bit too brightly, and one of the Wisps keeping watch gave him a glare. Calum quickly closed his fist. Some of the light glinted off the emerald mounted to the statue before the light faded entirely.

Then a new light shined—a revelation, this one in Calum's mind. He stood up and started toward the statue. He looked down at his left hand, then he looked at the emerald.

I wonder if...

He held his hand out with his palm facing the emerald and concentrated again. The light shone faintly at first, but when nothing happened with the statue, Calum intensified the burn.

Still nothing.

He pulled his hand away and allowed the light and the burning to fade again, but he'd been wrong—something *had* changed. The emerald cast a faint orange glow, but it quickly faded, and the emerald reverted back to normal.

Calum grinned. This time, he pressed his palm against the emerald and ignited the light in his palm. He pushed every bit of light he could muster, despite the burn which now crept up his wrist and seared the inside of his forearm. The pain finally heightened to the point where he couldn't handle it anymore, and he released his palm from the statue.

As the pain in his arm receded, the emerald glowed a vivid orange reminiscent of fire, and this time it didn't fade. Behind the statue, rock scraped against rock, and the ground opened into a staircase that descended underground.

Calum walked around the statue, now flanked by three of the Wisps who'd been keeping watch, and he stared into the black opening at his feet.

He turned to the nearest Wisp. "Go wake Magnus."

CHAPTER 13

Upon seeing the opening in the ground, Magnus's grogginess dissipated, replaced by excited energy. Calum had done it. He'd gotten the statue to reveal its secret.

Magnus descended into the opening with Calum lighting the way from behind him. The staircase stopped fifty steps underground and spilled into an expansive circular room carved into walls of brown rock like that of the Dragon statue. No light permeated the area except for what emanated from Calum's hand.

Aside from the stairway, Magnus couldn't identify any other way in or out. He directed Calum to shine his light around the room to get a better look at everything. Calum complied and confirmed Magnus's fears.

There was nothing in the room but a dirt floor.

"I don't understand," Calum said. "Where's the sword?"

Magnus grunted. His dreams of avenging his father's murder threatened to slip through his fingers yet again. "Perhaps someone beat us to it."

"That's pretty unlikely. It only opened to us after I used the light Lumen gave me on the emerald in the statue."

"That was a variation of a Dragon Emerald. I have only heard of them before today, but the ancients, including my father, used them as a type of key. Only certain types of energy could activate and release the lock. It was a means to prevent those who were too weak from accessing weapons and relics too powerful and dangerous for them to properly wield."

"Certain types?"

Magnus nodded. "Dragonfire, primarily, though other powers clearly suffice."

"I guess so." Calum waved his hand in a slow arc. "Unless this light didn't actually work, and we ended up in the wrong area somehow."

"I suppose it is possible, but unlikely. I see no reason to create two rooms, even if one was to serve as a decoy."

"To hide one of the most powerful weapons in Kanarah? Seems like as good a reason as any

Magnus glanced back at him, proud of how Calum's critical thinking skills had developed since they'd been traveling together. "Point taken."

Calum grinned. "We'd better at least look around while we're here. Maybe we'll find a clue or something."

"Indeed."

They circled the perimeter of the room in search of a nook or a crevice or something indicative of a hidden door or anything at all, but to no avail. After fifteen minutes of careful scrutiny, Magnus growled.

"Perhaps it is time we head back up." Magnus didn't want to stop, but continuing to search while frustrated wouldn't do him any good. "We can search again after sunrise."

Calum stared down at the floor.

"It is alright, Calum. I am confident we are in the right place," Magnus said. "Do not look so forlorn."

He shook his head and started for the middle of the floor. "It's not that."

Calum swept the sole of his boot across a patch of dirt. He repeated the motion a few more times and pointed his illuminated left hand down at the ground. A glint of green shone after his sixth swipe.

Magnus's eyes widened. He rushed over, gently urged Calum aside, and uncovered the spot with one swift swipe of his tail. Another emerald, this one several inches in diameter and embedded in the floor, glistened in Calum's light

"I think we found your other room, Calum."

"We found something, at least."

Calum bent down and pressed his left hand against the emerald, and the light flared brighter from his hand. The emerald ignited with green light, then turned yellow, then a vibrant orange.

Calum bared his teeth, and the tendons in his neck tightened.

The sight of him straining so much filled Magnus's chest with concern. "Calum, are you—"

Click.

The light from Calum's left hand fizzled away, but it didn't matter—the emerald glowed orange like fire, illuminating the entire room.

Click-click.

Calum dropped to his rear and clutched his wrist with his eyes clenched shut.

"What is wrong?"

He shook his head and began to rub his forearm. "Nothing. The light—it just burns sometimes."

Magnus eyed him. "I do not think that is—"

Rocks scraped and ground against each other, and the fiery emerald arose from the floor atop a pillar of translucent blue crystal like that of the Sky Realm.

Within that pillar stood a long ornate sword.

The Dragon's Breath.

Magnus and Calum stared at it—this weapon that could wield the power of dragonfire. Magnus's heart rate accelerated with the renewed promise of achieving his goal.

"How do we get it outta there?" Calum asked.

Magnus clenched his fingers together, drew his arm back, and slammed his fist into the side of the pillar. Cracks spiderwebbed out from the impact.

Magnus smirked at Calum. "This blue crystal is aesthetically pleasing, but it is structurally weak compared to most alternatives. The Windgales used it primarily for its appearance in Aeropolis, and I suspect those who hid this sword used it for that same reason."

With a roar, Magnus hauled back and hit the crystal again, and a section of it shattered, spilling long shards onto the floor. He reached into the pillar, grabbed the sword by its hilt, and pulled it free. It compared to Magnus's Blood Ore sword in size, but it absolutely dwarfed it in grandeur.

Pale-green metal formed its gleaming blade, and turquoise metal masterfully sculpted to resemble Dragon scales comprised its hilt. An emerald in the center of the guard matched the ones embedded in the statue outside and the floor of the room, and another served as the sword's pommel.

"That's incredible." Calum gawked at it. "How does it make dragonfire?"

Magnus smiled. "I have no idea. Nor do I wish to test it down here and find out accidentally. You could be hurt."

"But if you don't try it, how will you know what it can do?"

"I will test it, but I want you to head back to the surface in case I cannot control it. If I do not return in five minutes, come back down."

Calum eyed him. "What will it mean if you're not back up in five minutes?"

Deadpan, Magnus replied, "Probably that I am dead."

"Stop fooling around, Magnus."

Magnus grinned. "I apologize. It is just that, for the first time since my father's death, I truly feel equipped to do something about it."

Calum nodded. "I understand. I'll head up, but don't get yourself killed, alright?"

"I am confident I will be fine."

Calum started toward the stairs.

"Calum?" Magnus called after him.

He turned back.

"Thank you."

"My pleasure." Calum smiled and headed up the stairs.

A few seconds later, Magnus tightened his grip on the sword's hilt, faced the crystalline pillar, and swung the Dragon's Breath sword at it.

GREEN LIGHT FILTERED into the bottom of the staircase from behind Calum, and he heard a faint crackling reminiscent of a campfire burning. He stopped for a moment. The green light flared again, and the crackling intensified.

Calum grinned and resumed his climb.

A HOWL SPLIT THE NIGHT, and Riley jerked awake.

Distress.

A call for help.

Dallahan.

Riley sprang to his feet and scanned the camp. Dallahan stood at the northeast perimeter along with three of the Royal Guard Wisps set to guard that section of the camp. Riley rushed toward them.

When he arrived, he barked, and Dallahan turned around.

"What is it?" Riley asked, though he suspected he already knew the answer.

"Wolves," Dallahan replied. "Hundreds of them. Maybe thousands. Enough that I can't pinpoint a number. They're going to surround us. Do you think this is—"

"Quiet." Riley stared into the night. He could only make out a few dozen forms moving in the distant darkness around them, but his nose picked up countless distinct scents.

This was happening. He'd been dreading it, hoping they could pierce through the desert and reach Reptilius before the Wolves found them, but he'd known all along this was inevitable. He'd prepared himself for it as best as he could, and he had a plan, albeit simple, but against the likes of a Shadow Wolf, there was only so much that *anyone* could do.

Most of the camp had to be awake by now, but Riley still ordered Dallahan, "Go and wake everyone now. We're gonna need every pair of hands and every weapon."

Dallahan bounded away.

One of the Wisps turned to Riley. "Hundreds or *thousands* of Wolves? We can't possibly fend off that many. We have to flee."

"No," Riley asserted. "This needs to happen. Hold your position."

The Wisp glared at Riley. "You're not my commander."

"No, but I am," a voice said from behind them. Condor. He landed between them and stared at the Wisp. "We're all deferring to Riley's lead from now on. This is his domain. He knows it best. He will lead us."

A few months earlier, Riley would've torn Condor to shreds if he'd had the chance. Now they stood shoulder-to-shoulder, ready to fight the same foes together.

Lilly, General Tolomus, and the rest of the Windgales landed around them. Calum, Magnus, Axel, and Janessa, Dallahan, and Embry approached the group on foot as well.

"What are we dealing with, Riley?" Lilly asked.

"Nothing good."

General Tolomus stepped into his view. "I sense we don't have much time to determine a course of action. Should we retreat?"

Riley eyed him then turned to Lilly. "Lumen said he needed the Wolves to join his army. Wolves respect strength. If we don't stand our ground, we'll stand no chance of winning them over."

"We can't fight thousands of Wolves, if there are indeed thousands, as you claim," said General Tolomus. "Nor even hundreds."

"We may not need to." Riley stared out at the horizon. His keen eyes picked out several streams of shadows moving under the moonlight toward their position. "Stand your ground, all of you, but don't attack. They have the advantage of numbers, but they won't harm us if we don't resist them."

"You sure of that?" Condor asked.

"Mostly." Riley glanced at him. "But if not, I want you, especially, to stay out of the fight."

Condor raised an eyebrow. "Why?"

"You couldn't even kill me." Riley gave him a wry smile. "What chance do you have against *hundreds* of them? They'll rip you apart."

Condor scoffed, but he matched Riley's smile with one of his own. "Funny."

"Form a tight defensive perimeter around the Premieress and the non-flying types. Be prepared to lift as many of them to safety as possible."

"You just said we couldn't retreat. Which is it?" General Tolomus folded his arms.

Riley's eyes narrowed. "Your task is to protect the Premieress. If things go wrong, protect her. Otherwise, stand your ground. Crystal?"

Within minutes, throngs of snarling, growling Wolves surrounded the camp. Several Were-wolves stalked among them, and it seemed as if they all stared directly at Riley. A plethora of smells, many of them familiar, hit Riley's nostrils.

There's no place like home...

A wave of Wolves parted under the moonlight, as did the few Werewolves nearby. A dark form advanced toward Riley and the others.

Janessa, Dallahan, and Embry growled, but Riley gave a sharp bark and silenced them.

The form materialized into a Werewolf, only different. It stood a few inches taller than Riley, and its black fur didn't reflect any of the moonlight at all, making it nearly invisible in the darkness.

Silver fur tipped its ears and its tail, and silver irises distinguished its black pupils from the rest of its eyes, also black. Black talons extended from its fingers and toes, and black teeth lined its mouth.

A Shadow Wolf.

CHAPTER 14

The Shadow Wolf sniffed the air, then he snarled. "Riley."

Riley's chest tightened, but he stepped forward, out of the relative safety of the Windgales' protective shell. "Rhaza."

"You guys know each other?" Axel asked.

"He's my cousin," Riley replied.

"Of course he is." Axel rolled his eyes. "Everyone not human has to be related to royalty somehow."

"We're cousins, but that means little to Wolves," Riley explained. "Distant cousins. Half his tribe could probably make the same claim."

"That we are." Rhaza's voice was deeper than Riley remembered but still every bit as menacing. "But it's more than that, isn't it?"

Riley's jaw hardened. "He banished me from my home more than a year ago."

"You banished yourself. Had I found you, I would've just killed you."

"I know."

"And now you're back. With friends." Rhaza studied those around him. "But not nearly enough."

Dallahan growled, and Riley barked again. Dallahan shut up.

"I see you have a small tribe of your own now. You've grown, Cousin."

Riley's gaze narrowed. "Don't patronize me."

Rhaza tilted his head. "You know I'm going to kill you."

"I know you'll try."

Rhaza bared his black teeth in a toothy smile. "You have less than thirty with you. I have thousands. You cannot possibly hope to—"

"Rhaza?" Calum stepped forward and stood next to Riley.

Rhaza squinted at him. "Who is this human morsel who addresses me?"

"I'm no one of any importance, but I bear a charge from one who would reign over Kanarah."

Rhaza snickered. "The King hasn't visited our fair desert in centuries."

Calum shook his head. "I do *not* represent the King. I come bearing the authority of Lumen,

525

the General of Light, who calls you to join him in his sovereign quest to usurp the King and rule in his place."

Rhaza didn't move, except his black-and-silver eyes narrowed as they fixated on Calum.

Calum glanced at Riley. "As evidence of Lumen's return, he has blessed me with the ability to show you his power firsthand."

He raised his left hand, palm up, and Lumen's light began to glow from within him. It filled his palm and beamed outward, a star in the dark night sky. The Wolves and Werewolves around them bustled and growled.

Rhaza barked, and they fell silent.

"Your trick is nice, but I have no reason to join this 'Lumen,' whoever he is.'"

"He is the General of Light, and he's going to free Kanarah," Calum explained. "He's going to put an end to the suffering and oppression—"

"Suffering?" Rhaza snapped. "*Suffering?* You don't know the meaning of the word."

Calum's jaw tensed, and the light in his palm blazed even brighter. "Don't tell me what I do and don't know. You know nothing about me."

"And *you* know nothing about *me*." Rhaza stalked forward a few steps, and Riley positioned himself in front of Calum. "I could snuff your little light in an instant."

"I've been threatened before. You don't scare me," Calum said. "Will you join Lumen's cause, or not?"

"No, little human. I will not," Rhaza said. "But I will gladly tear you and each of your friends limb from—"

"I challenge you to single combat," Riley blurted.

Everyone turned toward him, but he'd already given this enough thought. Since Rhaza had rejected the call to Lumen's army, this was the only way to ensure the support of the Wolf tribes. Riley would have to *make* it happen.

"Under the laws of our kind, the winner rules the tribe," Riley continued. "I demand that my friends be allowed safe passage through to Reptilius either way. That is the price I require for my life, should I fail."

Rhaza squinted at him. "You're in no position to make demands."

"Well, I'm making them anyway," Riley asserted. "The majority of our group is made of Wisps. Among them are General Tolomus of the Windgale Army, the renowned Captain Condor of the Royal Guard, and—"

General Tolomus cleared his throat.

Riley shot him a glare. "—and one who wields the sacred blade of their people. The Sobek is Magnus, heir to the throne of Reptilius, and he wields the Dragon's Breath sword of ancient times. The rest are all capable fighters and seasoned warriors. You're welcome to attack, but engaging them will cost you hundreds of your tribe."

Rhaza inhaled a long breath. "Ancient weapons and mighty warriors do not frighten me, Cousin."

"So it's the prospect of single combat against *me* that scares you?" Riley's mouth curled into a grin. "I'm flattered, but you know, you can just yield instead."

Rhaza laughed and shook his head. "No. I will honor your challenge, if you can call it that. As to the wellbeing of your friends, that remains to be seen."

"I will engage you underground, alone. There's a subterranean room nearby where we can do battle." Riley had already examined the underground room after Magnus had come back up with his Dragon's Breath sword in hand. It gave him his best chance at winning this contest, especially when the only alternative was fighting out in the open air.

"Don't want to get killed in front of your friends?" Rhaza grinned. "I understand. I've already humiliated you enough for a lifetime."

Riley growled, and the tension in his chest heightened. Everything hinged on this fight. "Follow me."

He darted away from Rhaza toward the pit where Magnus had recovered the Dragon's Breath. Riley knew that leaving first would mean one of two things to those following Rhaza—either it reinforced their opinions of Riley as a coward, or it made him look like the more dominant of the two. He hoped it was the latter.

He awaited Rhaza's arrival at the top of the pit. His friends and their Wisp escorts made their way over first, and then Rhaza and his army quickly enveloped the entire area.

"We enter the pit one at a time. The duel will then commence, and he who emerges alive, wins," Riley met Rhaza's fearsome eyes. "Do you agree to these terms?"

"Of course I agree." Rhaza displayed a wicked grin. "It will be a pleasure to kill you."

Riley looked at Condor and Magnus. "Whatever happens to me, protect Lilly and Calum. They need both of you. If you don't, I swear I'll come back as a ghost and haunt you until you join me in the afterlife."

Condor laughed. "I believe it. Fight well, friend, if I may dare to call you that. I'm truly sorry for our past, and I'm honored to have known you regardless of your fate today."

Riley nodded. It was a nice sentiment that Condor had finally apologized, but it wouldn't help Riley much now.

"He may be quicker than you and more adept at hiding in shadows, but you are smarter. He only knows how Wolves fight." Magnus clapped his enormous scaly hand on Riley's shoulder. "You have been with us long enough to have learned many tactics. Wield the ones that will bring you victory, and I will see you ascend from that pit victorious."

"I'll do my best."

Calum approached him next. "You can do this, Riley. You've come so far. Reclaim your honor, once and for all."

Riley nodded again.

Lilly walked up to him, and all ten of her Royal Guard surrounded them both. She reached out and scratched behind his ears, which he not only allowed but enjoyed. It helped to relax him.

"My Riley," she said. "You've been more than a companion. You've been a true friend. You're wise, full of insight, and the kindest soul I've ever met."

Riley chuffed. "And you're a fabulous liar."

Lilly chuckled, but her face took on a solemn expression. "I mean it, Riley. I can't do this without you. I need you to survive."

"I'll try." Riley caught Axel staring at him. "Got something to say?"

Axel shook his head. "Don't get killed. I'm not adopting your pups if you die."

Riley smirked. "They wouldn't have you anyway."

"Done yet?" Rhaza snapped. "I long to sate my claws' thirst for your blood."

Riley rolled his eyes. "You always were melodramatic."

"And you always were a coward," Rhaza cut back.

The jab stung, but Riley ignored it. Without so much as another word, he descended into the pit.

At the bottom of the stairs, a large emerald glowed with a faint yellow light atop a pillar of blue crystal, partially shattered. When Riley had ventured down there before, he realized that Magnus must've extracted the sword from inside the pillar, and now shards of the brittle blue crystal lay scattered around the base of the pillar.

But Riley didn't have time to examine his surroundings again. He darted into one of the shadows and melded with it in perfect stillness. He fixed his eyes on the staircase, watching and waiting for Rhaza, even though he might not be able to see him enter the room.

Riley's vision in the darkness surpassed that of his traveling companions, but Rhaza was the only Shadow Wolf Riley knew to exist, and Shadow Wolves could haunt the darkness like specters, invisible even to the most trained eyes.

Including Riley's.

And as well as Riley's eyes saw in the darkness, Rhaza's saw better.

A familiar smell wafted into the room, a mix of desert sand, agave nectar, unique canine pheromones, and a tinge of feces. A precise combination of normal smells that indicated only one thing: Rhaza loomed nearby.

Riley's gaze darted around the room, but his eyes identified nothing.

The light from the emerald quickly faded to a dull green glow, a passive and incredibly useful effect of Rhaza's nature as a Shadow Wolf. He alone could dampen, dim, or even extinguish many sources of light simply by drawing nearer to them.

The fading light of the emerald reminded Riley of his group's encounter with the Gronyxes in the tunnels under Trader's Pass, but the foe he faced now was no Gronyx. Rhaza was far more dangerous—faster, stronger, quieter, and more vicious than Riley.

"You shouldn't have come back, Riley," Rhaza said from within the darkness.

Riley's head jerked to his left, toward the direction of Rhaza's voice, but he saw nothing.

"After what happened, I'm surprised you ventured back here."

The voice came from Riley's right that time. Again he looked, and again he saw nothing.

"*She* was obviously not worth sticking around for," Rhaza taunted. "Is this Lumen nonsense really so important that you decided to return, only to face your death?"

Rhaza's words came from beyond the pillar, straight ahead of Riley that time. Either he could move so fluidly in darkness that Riley couldn't see him, or he was throwing his voice. Riley didn't know the full extent of a Shadow Wolf's capabilities, but either seemed just as likely.

"Meliamora? That was her name, wasn't it?" Rhaza's voice came from one spot in the room then jumped to another. "But you called her 'Melly.' Yes, I remember her. Beautiful black fur, cunning blue eyes…"

Riley bristled at Rhaza's mention of Melly, and rage filled his gut. Of course Rhaza would bring her up—Riley had expected it, but hearing her name after so long still hit him hard.

Wolf society functioned as a hierarchy. Those near the top subjugated those at the bottom and took what they wanted. When a lower-ranking Wolf had something of worth, a higher-ranking Wolf could take it. The lower-ranking Wolf could fight back if he wanted, but if he failed to overcome the higher-ranking Wolf, it meant his death.

And when Riley had left the desert, he'd ranked the lowest in the tribe.

"You never should've left, Riley. She needed you, and you fled with your tail literally between your legs. You vanished into the night at the hour of her greatest need—" Rhaza paused for a long moment, and then hissed, "—and she *suffered* for it."

His words echoed throughout the room and reverberated in Riley's chest. He clenched his teeth and restrained the growl rising from his throat. This was exactly what Rhaza wanted; if he could unsettle Riley before the fight even began or stir his emotions to the point of blind rage, Rhaza would win even more easily.

But Riley couldn't let that happen. Too much was at stake. And if he could just stick to his plan—

"And then she *died* for it." Rhaza's voice came from near the stairs this time.

Grief cascaded into Riley's heart and drowned his anger. He'd never known for sure what had happened to Melly after he left, but now he did.

He'd failed her. It should've been him facing Rhaza's wrath, but he'd run away, like a coward, like he always did, and he'd left her alone.

But this time, Riley hadn't run. He wasn't a coward anymore. Now as a Werewolf, he'd risked his life countless times for his friends.

Riley resisted the urge to give in to his emotions. The best way to honor her memory was to do what needed to be done and defeat Rhaza.

"And you're next." Rhaza's voice sounded directly behind him.

Riley whirled and lashed his claws at the darkness, but something solid blocked his swipe. Pain lit up the left side of his snout then slashed across the right side of his chest.

He flailed his left arm at Rhaza but hit nothing. From behind, claws raked down the back of Riley's shoulder to the middle of his spine, and he yelped.

Instead of fighting back, he dove toward the pillar and rolled up to his feet. Atop it, the emerald now barely cast any light into the space. He scanned the room for any signs of movement but saw none.

His face, chest, and back tingled with pain, but he was alive. No thanks to himself, but alive nonetheless. Had Rhaza wanted to kill him, he could have. Instead, Rhaza meant to make Riley suffer as Melly had.

That was a mistake on Rhaza's part, and Riley intended to exploit every second Rhaza was foolish enough to let him keep breathing.

Seconds later, the waning light from the emerald extinguished altogether. Now the real fight would begin.

Riley could see inside the room just fine without the light, but he couldn't see Rhaza anywhere. Rhaza's black fur and its light-defying properties gave him the utmost advantage in total darkness.

However, Riley could see other things—specifically the emerald, the pillar, and the shards of blue crystal at his feet.

Magnus's words echoed in Riley's memory. *He may be quicker than you and even more adept at hiding in shadows, but you are smarter. He only knows how Wolves fight. You have been with us long enough to have learned many tactics. Wield the ones that will bring you victory, and I will see you ascend from that pit victorious.*

Riley could see the shattered crystals, some of them reduced to glittering blue dust. They were the whole reason he'd wanted to bring the fight down here in the first place. It might give him just the edge he needed to pull through.

He crouched down near the shards and the crystalline dust, placed his left hand on top of them, and waited.

Knives dug into his right shoulder. Riley howled and flung the crystal shards where he thought Rhaza would be, then another blow leveled him to the ground.

Frantic, Riley rolled away and scrambled up to all fours, his eyes searching for any sign of movement, any indication of Rhaza's whereabouts in the room.

Laughter echoed all around him.

"You're just as pitiful as always. Being a Werewolf now makes no difference. You're still a disgrace, a cancer to our kind." Rhaza's voice sounded in multiple places this time. "It would've been better if you'd never been born."

Something blue glimmered in the periphery of Riley's vision. He turned his head, but it vanished. It appeared again to his right, closer this time, then it moved again.

A third time it appeared right in front of him about twenty feet away, and he recognized a left shoulder, most of an arm, part of a chest, and the upper half of a thigh all outlined with blue dust and crystal fragments.

Rhaza.

Riley stifled a grin and waited.

Rhaza stalked toward him, and Riley pretended to swivel his head and to look around. In total silence, Rhaza drew nearer, then he launched forward.

Riley caught him by his wrists. "I can see you."

Rhaza's black-and-silver eyes widened.

Riley jerked the Shadow Wolf to his right and hurled him into what remained of the crystal pillar. It shattered under Rhaza's weight and coated him with even more of the crystal dust. Rhaza sprang to his feet and snarled.

He could snarl at Riley all he wanted. The crystals had neutralized Rhaza's primary advantage, and now even more of his body, including both arms and half of his face, showed up in Riley's vision.

Had they fought on the surface instead, the crystals wouldn't have been a factor. Rhaza could've rolled around in the dirt all he wanted, but it wouldn't have made him show up any more clearly in Riley's vision.

But those crystals—something about them popped out at Riley, even in total darkness. As soon as he'd realized it during his first visit to this room, he knew he had to make use of it somehow to battle Rhaza.

Even so, Rhaza was plenty formidable even if Riley could see him.

Rhaza charged forward and lashed out, but Riley dodged the attack and counter-swiped at Rhaza's midsection. His claws ripped into Rhaza's torso, and hot blood oozed onto Riley's fingers.

In a whirl of dark fury, Rhaza backhanded Riley's snout with a blow that sent him spinning to the ground, stunned. Then Rhaza straddled Riley and slashed him with his talons again and again.

Pain seared Riley's face and neck, then it spread to his forearms as he raised them to defend against Rhaza's vicious attacks. He writhed as Rhaza's jaws snapped at his neck, and he felt something jagged pressing against his back.

Riley waited for an opening in Rhaza's barrage, then he shoved Rhaza up, repositioned his feet, and kicked Rhaza's chest, sending him skidding across the floor. In that fleeting moment of reprieve, Riley twisted his arm to grab the object under him, and his hand found a long pointed shard of crystal.

Rhaza launched toward him again, and Riley raised the shard.

A PITIFUL HOWL bellowed from within the pit, and it sent tremors through Calum's bones. Riley and Rhaza had been down there for ten grueling minutes.

He glanced at Lilly. She stood in the center of her usual entourage, only the phalanx around her had tightened so much that Calum could only pick her out due to her blonde hair. She didn't look back at him. Instead, she focused on the opening of the pit.

Her eyes widened.

A hulking form, black, covered in fur, and with black talons, teeth, and eyes, stepped out of the pit.

Calum's heart hammered.

A Shadow Wolf.

CHAPTER 15

Calum blinked. The Shadow Wolf's black eyes had vivid blue irises, and a bit of brown-gray fur tipped its ears and its tail. Blood dripped from its hands, and red claw marks on its chest, arms, and face sealed up before Calum's eyes. It heaved heavy, labored breaths, but they grew calmer the longer it stood there.

Calum dared to ask, "Riley?"

The Shadow Wolf nodded, and in a darker version of his usual voice, Riley replied, "Yeah. It's me."

Lilly shot toward him and threw her arms around him in an embrace. "I'm so glad you're alright!"

Riley returned her hug, which made Calum a little jealous, if he were being honest.

Magnus approached next and gave Riley a nod. "Well done."

"Thank you," he said. "Now, if you'll excuse me..."

Riley howled, and the Wolves surrounding their camp, all of whom had been pacing back and forth and snarling, stopped. They sat on their hind legs, and the Werewolves straightened their posture. All of them stared at Riley in total silence and total submission.

"They'll follow me from here on out." Riley walked over to Calum, and the rest of the group encircled them. "Lumen's army has just increased by thousands of Wolves."

Calum beamed. He turned to Axel. "We have the Windgales and the Wolves. This is beginning to look like destiny, don't you think?"

Axel nodded, and a smirk played at the corners of his mouth. "I hate to admit it, but I think you're right. At this rate, we may even have a chance with the Saurians."

Magnus grinned. "We will have more than a chance once I avenge my father."

Lilly smiled. "Then what are we waiting for? Dawn will break soon. Let's head to Reptilius."

Almost a half hour after Riley and the humans accompanying him left, a dark, bloody form crawled out of the pit. With trembling limbs and a quaking body, Rhaza stood upright.

531

Wheezing, he pulled a long shard of blue crystal from his side and dropped it to the dirt, then he turned and shambled the opposite direction, deeper into the desert, wounded, losing blood, and weak.

But he was still alive.

───────

EARLY INTO THE journey to Reptilius, Axel got the surprise of his life when Magnus extended his Blood Ore broadsword toward him, pommel first, as they walked.

"Take this," he said. "Riley does not use weapons, and you are the only other person among us strong enough to wield it."

Axel marveled at the weapon. He'd seen Magnus fell monstrous foes with it, and now Magnus meant to pass it to him?

In all their time as traveling companions, Magnus and Axel had grated against each other more often than not. Though Axel respected Magnus, he still didn't like the Saurian much, and he was certain that Magnus felt the same toward him.

For Magnus to offer Axel the Blood Ore sword now meant a lot. It was one of Magnus's most treasured possessions, one of the few that he still retained from his escape from Reptilius.

Axel looked up at Magnus, dumbfounded. "I—I don't know if I can—"

"Of course you can." Magnus snorted. "You are far stronger than you were when you left your farm so long ago."

"It's not that," Axel said. "This sword—it's one of the only things you have left to remind you of your father. That and your armor."

"It is special to me, and that is what makes it such an exquisite gift." Magnus gave him a modest grin. "You would be hard-pressed to find a finer blade anywhere in Kanarah, especially for free."

Axel hesitated. "I can't take it."

"You can, and you will. We are heading to Reptilius. With this sword, you will have no trouble piercing even the toughest Sobek hides. I hope the only bloodshed will be between Vandorian, my uncle, and me, but if not, I need you equipped to properly defend yourself and anyone else who may need your help."

Axel exhaled a long breath, and a wave of acceptance flowed through his body. "I'm honored."

"Do not get the wrong idea, Axel." Magnus smirked. "I still do not like you."

Axel raised an eyebrow, and his spirit dampened.

"But I *respect* you enough to entrust this sword to you. Take it and use it in a way that will make me proud." Magnus shifted his grip on the blade and extended the hilt toward Axel even more. "Take it."

Axel clenched his teeth, but he took the sword in his hands and held it up as he walked. The light-blue blade reflected his stern bearded face, and he smirked. "I will. Thank you."

Magnus handed him the sword's sheath next. "You will need this too."

"Again, thank you. I won't let you down, whether in Reptilius or anywhere else."

"I know." Magnus patted Axel's shoulder and pointed ahead of them. "If you squint, you can just barely see the Blood Mountains. We are getting closer."

Axel did squint, but he couldn't make anything out on the horizon. "Your Saurian vision's better than mine. I'm gonna have to take your word for it."

Magnus grinned again, still staring into the distance. "I am *almost* home."

"Yeah. And we're *almost* about to get killed by a Dragon."

"I would not count on that." Magnus tapped the Dragon's Breath, which hung from his back by a repurposed leather strap. "We have an edge that they will not be expecting. I *will* avenge my father, and I *will* take the throne in Kahn's place."

Axel raised his eyebrow again. "I hope so."

LILLY HOVERED NEXT to Condor while surrounded by her Windgale escort. Below them, Riley led his Wolves, and Magnus led everyone else.

Thus far, she felt like she'd taken to commanding her people fairly well. Condor had proven loyal and quick to act, and to her surprise, so had General Tolomus—mostly. At first, he'd hesitated at some of her commands, but as of late he'd fallen in line.

She turned to Condor. "I'm surprised we haven't seen any Wargs yet. Riley made them sound as if they were everywhere."

Condor shrugged, his eyes still fixed on the horizon. "I'd count that a blessing."

"It probably doesn't hurt that we have a few thousand Wolves and a few dozen Werewolves following us now."

"There's a certain safety in numbers, to be sure, but from what I experienced in the Blood Chasm, the Wargs didn't seem to care all that much. Perhaps we've avoided them so far because of the route we're taking."

"If we do encounter them, we'll deal with them. Though I can't imagine we'll personally have to face many of them, if any at all, because of our canine buffer." Lilly glanced down at Riley, now far more fearsome than she'd ever seen him, but also far more confident and proud. She smiled. "I don't think even you could fell him now, Condor."

He chuckled. "Perhaps not, but now I have no reason to." His expression went solemn. "Frankly, I wish I could go back and change what happened."

"*How much* of what happened?" Lilly eyed him.

Condor squinted at her. "On second thought, perhaps it isn't wise to delve too deeply into history. I'm loyally serving you now, and that's what matters."

He gave her a cunning smirk, and her heart jumped. His strong jawline, the tinge of stubble on his cheeks, chin, and upper lip, and his piercing blue eyes sent her blood pumping faster.

Coupled with the intense yet somehow honorable intent he conveyed with each look—*every* look—and Lilly often didn't know how she managed to control her impulses. She just wanted to grab him and kiss him.

Even so, Calum haunted her mind. Had Calum not been around, Lilly and Condor might have started something by now. Then again, had Falcroné not been around, perhaps Lilly and Calum might have had something more than a friendship instead.

"Are you alright, Premieress?"

Even when Condor's blue eyes showed concern, Lilly found them alluring.

She nodded and refocused herself. "I'm fine, thank you. Just thinking about Reptilius, about Magnus and Kahn and Vandorian and what we're up against. We can't possibly hope to fight the Saurians with twenty of the Sky Realm's finest, a few thousand Wolves, and a handful of other elite fighters—"

"Plus Kanton."

Lilly whacked his breastplate. "Stop it. Kanton is—well, you know what I mean."

Condor bared his perfect white smile again. "I do."

"If Magnus fails, we'll have to get out of there quickly. If my father couldn't defeat Kahn with the Calios, and if Magnus can't defeat him with the Dragon's Breath, then I don't think there's anyone in Western Kanarah who can."

"I understand." Condor glanced over at General Tolomus, who hovered along the outer rim of his soldiers. "He's prepared to help you escape, I'm sure. And, of course, I'd give my life to protect you."

Lilly's heart sank at his comment, and she met his captivating eyes. "I've already had someone do that for me. Once was enough. Please stay alive."

He grinned, not seeming to have lost any of his usual exuberance. "I'll do my best."

WEEKS LATER, Magnus led them to the base of the Blood Mountains, and they left the Desert of the Forgotten behind them. The sight of those red peaks in their full glory sent a slew of emotions running through Magnus's chest and mind, but overall he felt more hopeful than worried or afraid.

After a few more weeks of trekking through the Blood Mountains, the Saurian city of Reptilius came into view, carved into the side of Firebrand Mountain, the tallest mountain in all of Kanarah.

Red stones of uniform size formed the fortified city's exterior walls and the trio of watchtowers that ascended from three of the walls' corners. A yellow-orange gravel path wound its way through a valley and up to the tallest of the three towers—the one on the right—and to the gate housed at its base. The gate served as the only known way in or out of Reptilius except for going over its walls.

A red palace loomed beyond the wall—the Crimson Keep. Magnus knew the building well; he'd grown up inside of it with the rest of his brothers and sisters. He would soon see its grand rooms and view the seat of his father's power once more.

Anticipation set Magnus's heart beating faster. He hadn't looked upon his home for more than a year, and when he'd left, he'd done so the night of his father's murder. Now Vandorian and Kahn ruled Reptilius and its inhabitants.

But not for much longer.

"What's our plan once we reach the fortress?" Calum's voice snapped Magnus back into real time.

Magnus didn't tear his eyes away from the Red Keep. "I fight Kahn, I kill him, and I take back my father's throne."

"That simple, is it?" Axel rolled his eyes. "Doesn't leave much room for creativity."

"I do not require any of you to accompany me." He met Axel's eyes, then those of Lilly, Riley, and Calum, too. "In fact, it is better if you do not. Fewer liabilities."

"Liabilities?" Axel scoffed. "You just gave me this great sword, and now I'm a liability?"

"I have to say, Magnus," Calum's voice had a hard edge to it as well, "I agree with Axel. We can help you. And we want to."

Magnus regretted his tone, but only marginally. Above all else, he was focused on what he must do, and the fewer impediments he encountered along the way, the better. "This is a task I must perform on my own. I do not want Kahn or Vandorian to attempt to gain any leverage over me should they take any of you captive."

"Don't worry about us, Scales." Axel whacked his shoulder.

"That is precisely my point." Magnus stared at him, and his regret burgeoned and began to swirl in his gut. "I would *not* worry about you. Even if it came at the cost of one of your lives, I would not stop in my quest to destroy both Kahn and Vandorian."

Calum glanced at Axel with raised eyebrows. "I don't think you'd actually do that, Magnus."

"With respect, Calum, though we have been friends for more than a year, you do not yet know what I would or would not do in order to achieve vengeance for my father. Now, here in this place, I would cross any line and make any sacrifice to restore honor to the throne of Reptilius and to destroy the evil my brother and uncle have brought upon my people."

Calum's eyebrows rose, and he hesitated.

Magus hoped Calum would recognize the cold sincerity in his voice for what it was and stay behind, but Calum had a cause of his own, a mission to complete, a charge to fulfill.

"Even if that is the case," Calum finally said, "Lumen told me that I'm supposed to show Kahn the sign. I need to do what he asked."

"It will be a waste of your time, and it will likely mean your death if you accompany me. Vandorian has certainly told Kahn of my survival by now. They will be on their guard, and they will likely try to kill me on sight."

"I guess you have a point," Axel said, his voice flat.

Magnus shrugged. "I would apologize, but it is a reality I cannot change."

"I'm going with you anyway," Calum said. "I can't let you go in there alone."

Magnus shook his head. "Had you not escaped from the quarry with me, I would have been going in alone anyway."

"But I *did* escape with you." Calum insisted, "I'm coming along, Magnus."

"Me too," Axel said. "Someone's gotta watch your back while you're in there."

Magnus narrowed his eyes and turned to Lilly and Riley. "Premieress, you and Riley should stay back, at least, as commanders of your respective armies. If my people kill either of you, the entire plan will fall apart."

Lilly frowned. "Magnus, you saved my life in that field of grain. You saved me from Roderick, from slavery, from the arrow in my shoulder, and countless times since then. I'm indebted to you by the Law of Debt. Whether they like it or not, General Tolomus and General Balena can lead the remainder of our people should something happen. I'm coming with."

Condor cleared his throat.

"And so is Condor."

"I'm coming as well." Riley, now more impressive than he'd ever been, nodded. "As the new leader of the Wolves, or at least most of them, I need to practice this diplomacy thing. Meeting with other leaders and all that stuff." Riley quirked one eyebrow up. "Worst-case, I can always hide."

Axel groaned and shook his head, but Magnus grinned. Riley's change into a Shadow Wolf made him even more impressive, but he was the same old Riley in the end.

"I cannot stop any of you from coming," Magnus said. "I can only advise you against it."

"Consider us advised." Calum smiled. "Let's camp for the night, and tomorrow we'll reach the fortress."

Magnus nodded. If he were being honest, he was grateful for the show of support, though he wished his desires weren't so divided. If it came down to the lives of his friends or the throne of Reptilius, would he truly allow them to perish?

He touched the pouch hanging from his belt that held the Dragon Emerald.

It was almost time.

There *was* a way to ensure their safety *and* take the throne. But in order to do so, he would have to risk everything, and he would only get one shot at this.

"Gather round," Magnus said. "We must plan our approach." He motioned toward General Tolomus. "You, in particular, General, will want to be involved in this conversation."

THE NEXT DAY, Magnus led his friends toward Reptilius. His scales prickled with raw anticipation, and he continued to visualize his victory in his head. Perhaps envisioning it would help make it so.

General Tolomus reluctantly remained behind to lead the Windgales, and Kanton stayed with them. Riley left Janessa in charge of the Wolves despite her not being a Werewolf, but he commanded the Wolves to obey her or else they'd suffer his wrath.

Within four hours, Magnus and the other five descended into the valley that led to Reptilius's gates. Sparse vegetation lined the yellow-orange path, but it was still more than they'd seen in their entire journey through the Desert of the Forgotten.

"They're already approaching us." Riley sniffed the air. "They're already in this valley. Not far, either."

Magnus didn't care. Though he hoped to avoid killing any of his own people, no number of Saurians would stop him from reaching Kahn now. "I do not fear them."

"At least two-dozen of them," Riley said, still sniffing. "Most of them are Sobeks."

"Lilly and I can haul either Calum or Axel out of here if we have to, but not both," Condor said. "If we're as outnumbered as Riley says, we can't fight that many."

Magnus shook his head. "We move forward. We surrender if we must, but we move forward."

"Hate to break it to you, but you see those holes in the walls of rock around us?" Riley pointed toward a network of dark holes and caves in the walls that framed the valley on both sides. "They've got a small army spread throughout those caves. Even if we did turn back, we wouldn't make it. We're already surrounded."

CHAPTER 16

Magnus stopped walking, and the others stopped their advance as well. This sort of thing was exactly why he'd wanted to face Kahn alone.

But as Riley said, it was too late now.

"Show yourselves," Magnus bellowed. He raised his arms out to his sides, perpendicular to his body. "I am Magnus, son of Praetorius. I am the one Vandorian seeks. Take me to him and be assured of the reward he has no doubt promised you."

A moment slithered by, then dozens of Saurians emerged from their hiding places with weapons bared. As Riley had assessed, most of them were Sobeks, and most of them wielded Blood Ore weapons—axes, swords, spears, and more.

"Let me do the talking," Magnus said loud enough for his friends to hear, but not loud enough for the approaching Saurians.

One of them, a Sobek with a steel-gray breastplate, carried a familiar ball-and-chain mace studded with blue Blood Ore spikes as he approached Magnus. His dark-green scales bore more than a hint of gray as well, a telltale sign that he'd long since passed his 600th year.

Magnus recognized the Sobek and gave a slight bow, but he didn't take his eyes off him. "General Hanza."

"Magnus. I would say it is good to see you, but it would be an untruth." His voice scraped out of his throat in raspy, gravelly tones as it always had. He stopped ten feet from Magnus, and they stared at each other.

"I understand, General." Magnus would have liked to share a feast with General Hanza and recount the last year, since he'd escaped the Crimson Keep, but now wasn't the time. "I am surprised that Vandorian entrusted this task to you."

"There is no one more fit to lead Reptilius's forward defenses." General Hanza's scaly lips curled into a wry grin. "Besides, you have killed almost everyone else he trusts. He had no other options."

"Allow us to enter the city in peace, and take us to the Crimson Keep, and we will comply

General Hanza tilted his head and scanned the Saurians all around them. "It does not look like you have much of a choice, Magnus."

Magnus touched the pouch on his belt and reassured himself that the Dragon Emerald still hung in its place. "Then lead the way."

"I must require that you surrender your weapons."

"I fear we have to decline your request," Magnus said.

"Then I regret that we will have to deliver your body to Vandorian devoid of its soul instead of intact. The same goes for your friends."

Magnus raised his chin. "We would rather die than give up our weapons."

"There is no need for such drama, Magnus." General Hanza wasn't going to budge, and Magnus knew it. "They will remain nearby in my personal care. Should you be granted permission to carry them after your audience with Vandorian, I will return them to you immediately."

Axel cleared his throat, and Magnus glanced back and shot him a glare.

General Hanza closed the distance between them and lowered his voice. "Please, Magnus. My instructions are to bring you to Vandorian alive. I would hate to let him down, and I am sure you would prefer to see him while you yet draw breath than the alternative."

Magnus exhaled a long hiss through his nostrils. Ultimately, General Hanza was right. Magnus had no other choice. He unstrapped his sword from his back, stared at it, then took five steps forward. He held it by its sheathed blade and extended it to General Hanza, hilt-first.

General Hanza's golden eyes narrowed to slits as he scrutinized the weapon. For a moment, Magnus considered yanking it back, drawing his sword, and cutting the general down, but he decided against it.

General Hanza had always treated him fairly, and Magnus doubted that had changed. Not even Vandorian or Kahn could corrupt someone as honorable as General Hanza.

The chain of General Hanza's mace clinked as he stepped forward and reached for the sword. He grasped the hilt and nodded.

Magnus released his grip on the sheath then turned back and said, "It is alright. Hand them over."

The remainder of the group complied, though reluctantly. Lilly stood behind Condor and gave him her bow and arrows, and he handed them, along with his sword, to the nearest Sobek. She'd wisely left the Calios behind, in General Tolomus's keeping, for exactly this reason. Calum and Axel relinquished their swords as well.

General Hanza motioned with his head toward the Crimson Keep. "Come."

The platoon of Saurians escorted them the remainder of the way through the valley and up the path to the fortress. Magnus marveled at the height of the red walls, now seemingly shorter than when he'd left. Then again, he'd grown taller when he'd transformed into a Sobek.

Saurian sentries stared down at him from atop the wall, their expressions a mix of disdain and confusion. He didn't blame them—even if they didn't recognize him, they recognized the Blood Ore breastplate strapped to his chest.

When they reached the gate, chains rattled, gears clanked, and the lattice of Blood Ore bars groaned as the door lifted. Magnus and his friends followed General Hanza into Reptilius, and the gate shut behind them.

Magnus huffed. It hadn't been his first choice, but submitting to General Hanza had gotten him inside the city, at least.

Then again, walking straight up to Vandorian in the courtyard beyond the city's walls wasn't exactly what he'd had in mind either. But there Vandorian stood, his arms folded and flanked by what remained of his personal guard, plus a few new recruits. General Hanza led Magnus and his friends directly to him.

"I am impressed by your audacity, Magnus," Vandorian said. "I never expected you would actually return to Reptilius, especially after our encounter in Sharkville."

Magnus clenched his right fist, which had long since fully regenerated. "I am again whole, and with my new hand I will strike you from this world."

"Subtle," Axel muttered from behind him. "Really subtle."

Vandorian shook his head. "Magnus, for all your learning and knowledge, you lack the simple sense to know when you are defeated. You stand at our mercy—*my* mercy."

"You have never known mercy," Magnus countered. "I hold no hope for mercy. Only for justice."

Vandorian grinned. He approached Magnus, reached for his waist, and jerked the pouch from Magnus's belt. "I see you have not given up on carrying this around. How naïve to think you would ever be able to use it. Only one being in all of Kanarah knows how to use it, and he rules this fortress."

"Then why has he not told *you*, Vandorian?" Magnus eyed him. "Does he fear you will use it against him and betray him, just as you both betrayed my father?"

"Kahn will reveal its secret in his timing. He will grant me the right to transform at his leisure, and in the meantime, I am pleased to serve at his command."

"Then you are nothing but a shortsighted slave." Magnus shook his head. "You always were foolish, Vandorian."

"No, *you* were foolish to resist me back at Sharkville, but you are even more foolish to have returned here." Vandorian scoffed, and his gaze shifted from Magnus. "Much less with the Windgale Princess and a Shadow Wolf, whom I can only assume is the leader of most of those desert dogs."

Riley didn't say a word.

"Kind of you to bring so many high-value officials with you, Magnus. You have all but secured our dominance in Western Kanarah in doing so. But before we decide what to do with them, you die first." Vandorian drew his sword, and Magnus tensed.

"Wait!" Calum started forward but Magnus held him back.

"Stand back, Calum. If this traitor wishes to kill me without a sword in my hand, let him. It will only reinforce my claim of his cowardice."

Vandorian snarled and raised his sword.

Calum slipped under Magnus's arm and held up his left hand. White light flared from his palm and stalled Vandorian's swing.

Vandorian's eyes narrowed, and his personal guard recoiled a step with their weapons raised. Vandorian also backed up, but he didn't lower his sword. "What is the meaning of this sorcery?"

Magnus bristled and tried to pull Calum back, but Calum shook free of his grasp. "Calum—"

"Lumen, the General of Light, is free. He requests your help in overthrowing the tyrannical ruler of Eastern Kanarah, the King. This light is his sign, the evidence of his release." Calum stood his ground, and the light flared even brighter. "I humbly request an audience with Kahn to show him this sign and petition him for his support."

Vandorian scoffed. "An impressive trick, to be sure, but nothing more."

Calum refused to be dissuaded. "You know full well that we meant to free Lumen. You met us at the Central Lake because you knew we'd be there. Now we've done it, and you refuse to believe us?"

"Even if Lumen has been freed, what concern is the Eastern Kingdom of ours?" Vandorian pointed his sword at Magnus. "This usurper will be judged either way. His crimes against Kahn and Reptilius will not go unpunished."

"*My* crimes?" Magnus hissed. "The co-conspirator in Praetorius's murder speaks of *my* crimes?"

"Whatever the case—" Calum cut in, "—you must take us before Kahn and allow him to make the decision. If he chooses not to join Lumen, then he can kill us at his leisure."

Vandorian's glare centered on Calum. "I serve at Kahn's pleasure to *prevent* unnecessary interruptions from disturbing him."

"With respect, if Lumen has been freed, this isn't your call to make." Calum stared back at Vandorian and lowered his hand, and the glow faded to nothing. "It's Kahn's."

Silence pervaded the courtyard. Magnus's muscles tensed again. If Vandorian moved to attack Calum, he'd be ready to intervene.

Instead, Vandorian sheathed his sword. "Very well. If you wish to see Kahn, then you shall see Kahn. And then you will all perish in a flood of emerald flames, and I will revel in the sight."

Calum didn't flinch. "I'll take my chances."

Vandorian's brow furrowed, and he leaned forward, sneering. "Or I could just kill you instead and never tell Kahn."

Calum folded his arms. "Like I said, I'll take my chances."

Vandorian grinned, and his golden eyes met Magnus's. "Your human friend is as audacious as you. I will give him that."

"So are we gonna see the Dragon or not?" Axel called from behind.

"Be careful what you wish for, little human." Vandorian scanned Magnus's group again. Then, louder, as if declaring it to those Saurians around him, he said, "I would be remiss if I did not take the Princess of the Sky Realm, the leader of the Wolves, my treacherous brother, and Lumen's glowy-handed ambassador before Kahn."

Then he turned and headed toward the Crimson Keep, and the group, escorted by General Hanza and his soldiers, followed.

Red stone buildings lined the road to the Crimson Keep. The Communal Hall, where the Sobek lords of old would come to meet with Magnus's father, now lay as a mound of rubble. It must've been destroyed in Kahn's takeover and never rebuilt.

At the time, Magnus had been too busy trying to escape to care what did and didn't survive. Yet more than a year had passed, and no one had done anything about it. Apparently, Kahn needed no wise counsel from the ranking Sobeks of Reptilius.

As they walked, Magnus noticed additional signs of neglect in his city. Countless other buildings had entirely crumbled as well, and almost every building had fallen into some state of disrepair.

Likewise, the city lacked the usual energy Magnus had known prior to fleeing Reptilius. Where Saurians and Sobeks had once roamed the streets engaging in commerce, they now appeared sporadically and quickly vanished indoors or down alleyways as Vandorian and his guards approached.

Magnus stole a glance at General Hanza, who walked parallel to him but several steps away. Three Sobeks walked between Magnus and General Hanza as a sort of buffer. Even so, when Magnus looked over, General Hanza met his gaze. In it, Magnus caught a tinge of regret, or perhaps even shame.

Before long, the Crimson Keep loomed overhead. As a hatchling, Magnus had marveled at its size and architecture. Three red spires, each one taller than the next, arose from its western side and helped to shape out the enclosed portion of the structure, but the eastern half of the Crimson Keep opened directly to the sky. It made entering and exiting easy for Dragons.

Magnus recalled the rush of energy he felt when seeing his father taking off or landing from the courtyard. The sheer power of his wings, the rippling muscles under his impenetrable scales, the emerald fire blazing from his mouth...

"This is ridiculous." Axel's voice tugged Magnus out of his stream of thoughts.

Magnus turned back. "What is?"

"The size of that place. It's even bigger than the Sky Fortress was. No one needs a house that big."

"You do when you are the size of a Dragon," General Hanza said.

By the look on his face, Magnus could tell Axel wasn't satisfied, but he didn't say anything else, either.

They headed toward the Crimson Keep's main doors, twin panels of intricately engraved Blood Ore that parted in the center and pulled into the palace.

Inside, the familiar obsidian floors gleamed under the torches mounted to the walls and hanging from the lofted ceilings above. Sunlight shone through the irregular slits of windows carved into the red walls, diminishing the Crimson Keep's otherwise imposing ambience.

After more than two hundred years of living within these walls, Magnus knew every inch, every nook and cranny, every flaw. He remembered the stench of the torch smoke, the aroma of butchered cattle and wild game back in the kitchen, the musty odor of the caverns and tunnels beneath the Crimson Keep. Every familiar smell resurrected old memories.

He clenched his fists and measured the strength pulsing through his right hand—the replacement for the one Vandorian had removed. Though the lighter green scales covering it didn't match those of the rest of his body, the strength and the vengeance locked within that hand would soon break free.

They turned a corner and entered the eastern courtyard. The sun blazed overhead in a cloudless sky, warming the red stones that formed the courtyard's sprawling floor. At the far end of the courtyard, shrouded in darkness, a gaping cave in the side of the mountain beckoned them forward.

Magnus knew what—*who* lay inside it.

"My lord Kahn, Dragon King of Reptilius," Vandorian called. The group stopped behind him as he spread his arms out to his sides, a gesture both submissive and somehow arrogant at the same time. "Uncle, I have brought you honored guests, including your long-lost nephew, Magnus. He wishes to have a word with you."

A deep, guttural rumble emanated from the cave, followed by a voice equally as deep and menacing. "Magnus." A peal of terrible laughter followed next.

"Yes, Uncle. He has returned to us, and he promises to exact vengeance upon you for Praetorius's death." Vandorian clacked his talons on his golden breastplate. "Surely you do not wish to disappoint him?"

More laughter. "No, Vandorian. I do not."

The ground beneath Magnus's feet shook with rhythmic thuds. Calum and Axel stumbled to maintain their footing, but Condor and Lilly started floating. Riley crouched down and balanced on all four of his limbs.

A dark-green snout, almost black, emerged from the shadows, followed by a reptilian face with gleaming golden eyes. Eyes that Magnus recognized immediately. Eyes that renewed the disdain and the rage within his chest.

Two black horns spiraled from the Dragon's head. Its thick neck spread into a pair of colossal shoulders, and its giant arms flexed as it pushed against the red stone to move forward. Charcoal-colored scales plated its broad chest, and it stood on its back legs and rose to its full height of at least twenty-five feet.

Kahn, the murderer of Magnus's father and the only Dragon now known to Kanarah, spread his mammoth wings and stared down at Magnus.

He laughed again. "Welcome home, Nephew."

CHAPTER 17

Vandorian knelt. General Hanza knelt. The Saurian soldiers around them knelt.
But Magnus did not kneel.

He would *never* kneel to Kahn.

"You dishonor me, Magnus," Kahn rumbled, and smoke billowed from his nostrils. It was meant as a threat, but Magnus refused to give fear any quarter in his heart.

Instead, Magnus stared steel at Kahn. "You dishonored yourself the day you crushed my father's head and murdered my siblings."

Vandorian arose and turned back to face him, sneering. "Kingdoms are overthrown, Magnus. It is a part of life. You yourselves mean to overthrow Eastern Kanarah, yet you rebuke us for seizing Reptilius?"

Kahn tilted his massive head. "What do you mean by that?"

Vandorian pointed at Calum. "This human claims to wield power given to him by the General of Light."

Kahn's golden eyes fixed on Calum. "Power? What power?"

Calum stepped forward quickly, but Magnus could see him trembling as he tried to keep his back rigid. He couldn't fault Calum for it. A Dragon, especially one as treacherous as Kahn, was a terrible sight to behold.

Calum raised his left hand, held his palm toward Kahn, and brilliant white light shone on Kahn's face.

"This is a gift from Lumen himself," Calum began. "He gave it to me as a means of convincing those who would be his allies to join him in his quest to overthr—" Calum stopped. "—to *liberate* Kanarah from the King's tyrannical reign. We are here to petition you for your support, Lord Kahn."

Calum glanced back at Magnus, who nodded. He understood that Calum had a task to perform and wouldn't hold it against him.

Calum faced Kahn again. "Will Reptilius join the General of Light and help him make Kanarah free for everyone?"

Kahn's eyes narrowed. "No."

542

Calum closed his hand, and the light faded. "Are—are you sure?"

"I do not wish to repeat myself, *boy*," Kahn hissed.

"Alright." Calum nodded. He lowered his hand and stepped back, more defeated than afraid.

Axel patted his shoulder. "Saw that one coming."

"My lord," Vandorian said. "I would have dispatched them already, but the Shadow Wolf commands the Wolves of the desert, and the Sky Realm Princess is among them as well."

Kahn's mouth parted in a jagged, toothy smile. "I care nothing for the Wolves—"

"Of course you don't," Riley muttered.

"—but I remember battling your father and bringing your realm to the brink of ruin, Princess." Kahn's eyes narrowed at Lilly, and his wicked smile persisted. "How is old Avian these days?"

Lilly started forward, but Condor tried to hold her back. She twisted out of his grasp and shot him a glare, then she drifted toward Kahn. "My father is dead, and you now speak to the Premieress of the Sky Realm. I demand justice for the wrong you've done to my people, not just to my family."

"*Demand justice?*" Kahn laughed. "*You* rejected an envoy of peace sent at *your family's* request to celebrate *your* engagement. Your father cast Vandorian and his guards out of your realm as if they were rubbish to be dumped over the edges of your silver platforms."

"And that necessitated the genocide of our people and an attack that obliterated our home?" Lilly shot back. "You overreacted on a grand scale!"

Kahn's malicious smile widened. "I do not tolerate disrespect from inferior beings."

Lilly reached for her sword, but it no longer hung from her belt, so instead she drove her fist into her hip. "You think of us as lesser than you?"

"Look at me." Kahn spread his wings again, and his massive form filled the entirety of Magnus's field of vision. "You *are* lesser than me. I am the pinnacle of creation. No being in Kanarah can subdue me. Not even your father and his magic sword could vanquish me. I reign supreme."

"I intend to challenge that assertion." Magnus clenched his fists and stepped forward. This conversation had gone awry, and he needed to bring it back to the topic at hand. "And if I win, I will reclaim the throne on behalf of my father, the mightiest Dragon of all, Praetorius. And I will do so also on behalf of the Windgales, against whom you've trespassed violently."

Kahn laughed again and shook his head. "Magnus, I could incinerate you with one burst of emerald flame. Are you so eager to perish in such a manner?"

"I will not perish." Magnus leveled a glare at Kahn. With absolute certainty in his voice, he said, "Instead, I will kill you."

Kahn huffed, and two more plumes of smoke billowed out of his nostrils. "Then I choose to forgo my right to battle and grant Vandorian permission to dispatch you. He tells me he already took your hand once. Perhaps this time he can finish the job."

"I can, and I will." Vandorian grinned and rubbed his hands together.

"Are you so afraid that you would send your lackey against me instead of facing me your-self?" Magnus chided. "After all that talk about being the pinnacle of creation?"

Kahn remained unfazed. "You know our laws as well as any. The one challenged may choose a champion to fight in his place."

"Vandorian is no champion." Magnus spat and glared at his traitorous brother. It ultimately didn't matter which of them Magnus killed first. He'd resolved that either they would both die today, or he would. He would not be denied the opportunity to claim vengeance for his father. "And when I dispatch him, you will relinquish control of Reptilius to me?"

"If you defeat him, then I will agree to face you in single combat, short as it may be."

"He cannot defeat me, Uncle." Vandorian sauntered toward Magnus with his hand resting on the pommel of his sword, which still hung from his belt. "He is too slow. Too sluggish. Too weak. He is but a fraction of the warrior I am. I will hand you his *head* this time instead of his hand."

Magnus glared at him. Vandorian's arrogance grated on him, but he didn't let it break his focus. He simply replied, "Your death cannot come soon enough."

"Very well," Kahn rumbled. "Clear the area, give them space, and let the contest begin."

Magnus turned back toward his friends. "Condor, give the signal to General Tolomus. Go now."

Condor nodded. He gave Lilly a long look, then he sprang into the air, leaving the five of them behind. None of the Sobeks could grab him in time, and Kahn regarded the escaping Wisp as little more than an annoying fly buzzing away.

"Are your friends already deserting you, Magnus?" Vandorian scoffed. "I cannot blame them. Kahn and I will discuss what to do with those who remain after I have ended your worthless life. I suspect dragonfire will be involved."

Magnus faced him again and eyed the pouch secured to Vandorian's belt. His Dragon Emerald resided inside. Once he killed Vandorian, he'd take the stone back, and then he'd kill Kahn next.

Whatever doubts burned in his chest, he snuffed them. In their place, vengeance flowed, spreading throughout his body to his head, hands, feet, and tail.

He had envisioned this moment ever since he'd escaped this place on the night of his father's murder. He had planned and prepared himself to face the rigors of battling not only Kahn but also Vandorian to the death. He had deconstructed his mind and reforged it into an intense focused weapon that would ensure his victory.

Magnus would *not* fail.

Vandorian drew his sword, its blade gleaming the telltale blue of Blood Ore, and he motioned to General Hanza. "Well? Give him his sword. I am eager to stain the stones with his blood."

Behind Magnus, Condor landed next to Lilly as General Hanza approached. As before, the Sobeks barely reacted to him, and neither did Kahn.

"It's done," Condor said.

Magnus nodded and accepted his sword—his old Blood Ore sword—from General Hanza. "Thank you, General."

General Hanza's eyebrow rose. "It has been nice knowing you, Magnus."

"If I am to die, then I will join my father in a better place." Magnus raised his sword, and General Hanza stepped back into the perimeter among his soldiers. "Come, Vandorian, and meet the razor edge of justice."

Vandorian started forward, dragging the tip of his Blood Ore sword across the stone floor. It scraped and scratched, but he didn't raise it until he stopped ten feet from Magnus's position. "Give our father, our brothers, and our sisters my regards."

Overhead, a small, dark form flew into view. Magnus noted it in his periphery, but he didn't take his focus off of Vandorian. "I have anticipated this day for years, Vandorian. No amount of rhetoric or intimidation will repel me."

The form flew over their heads and out of Magnus's range of sight.

Vandorian snorted. "Then perhaps my sword will do the—"

Green-tinted metal flashed down from the sky, and a new blade embedded in the stone floor between them with a loud thud.

The Dragon's Breath.

General Tolomus's aim had been true, albeit too centered between Magnus and Vandorian. Still, from so high above, he'd done well. Magnus's plan had more or less worked thus far.

Both of the Saurians stared at the sword for a moment, then Vandorian's eyes widened with recognition. He knew what the sword was, and that was exactly the reason why Magnus hadn't brought it along.

Vandorian lurched toward it with his hand extended.

Magnus hurled his Blood Ore sword at Vandorian, who recoiled and barely managed to bat Magnus's sword away in time with his own blade. In that instant of hesitation, Magnus launched toward the Dragon's Breath.

Vandorian recovered with a snarl, plowed forward, and swung his sword at Magnus in a brutal arc.

Magnus's fingers clasped around the hilt, and he wrenched the sword from the stone as his forward momentum carried him into a roll.

Vandorian's blade slashed over Magnus's head.

The Dragon's Breath blade ignited with brilliant emerald fire.

Now on his feet, Magnus turned to face Vandorian, who swung at him again, and Magnus raised his sword to block.

Vandorian's Blood Ore sword met the fiery Dragon's Breath, and its blade shattered like glass.

He gawked at his sword, now lying beneath him in pieces except for the hilt, which he still held in his hands, then he looked up at Magnus, shocked to silence, except for one word.

"Brother...?"

Justice. Revenge. Reckoning.

Whatever it was called, Magnus could now claim it.

He lashed his sword at a wide-eyed Vandorian with a roar and felled him in one vicious blow.

Vandorian dropped to the floor in two pieces, severed on a diagonal line from his left shoulder down to his right hip. His golden breastplate had melted at the edges where Magnus's blade cut through it, and the metal fused to his seared flesh and organs. No blood spilled from his body—the Dragon's Breath had cauterized everything.

Stunned silence permeated the air.

Magnus snatched the Dragon Emerald's pouch from Vandorian's belt, secured it to his own, then turned to face his father's killer.

He pointed the Dragon's Breath sword, still ablaze with emerald flames, at Kahn, who stared at him with wide-eyed fury. "You are next."

Kahn roared and slammed his gargantuan fists on the red stone floor, shaking the entire fortress, but Magnus didn't so much as flinch. Instead, he charged forward.

As Magnus approached, Kahn whirled around and whipped his enormous tail toward Magnus like a tree trunk-sized club. Magnus found his timing and leaped over Kahn's tail—and the spike attached to the end of it. He landed on his feet and raised his sword.

Far faster than Magnus had expected, Kahn's tail lashed back at him from the other direction, this time leading with his spike. With no time to evade the strike, Magnus swung his sword instead, and the Dragon's Breath cut through the tip of Kahn's tail it as if it were a piece of parchment. The spike and the end of Kahn's tail dropped to the floor.

Another roar shook the courtyard, and Kahn hauled his tail back.

"What sorcery is this?" Kahn bellowed.

"No sorcery. This is the Dragon's Breath, an ancient sword of terrible power that can penetrate Dragon scales and rend Dragon flesh." Magnus grinned. "But that is not the limit of its powers."

Still several yards away from Kahn, Magnus raised the Dragon's Breath over his head and swung it in a wide arc straight down. A scythe of emerald flames from the sword streaked through the air toward Kahn.

Kahn shielded his face from the flames with his arms, and the attack hit his forearms, shoulders, and side. The flames scorched along his scales but quickly subsided.

Kahn raised his head and hissed, "Your blade may have wounded me, but your artificial fire cannot harm me. You will have to come closer, Nephew."

Magnus had anticipated as much. "I am happy to oblige. I will plunge this blade into your throat, carve down into your chest, and sever your black heart from its arteries."

"Then come here and do it, *hatchling*."

Magnus started forward, but Kahn's nostrils began to issue smoke as they had before. That meant only one thing, and Magnus dove to the side and rolled behind a large red rock for cover.

Kahn inhaled a large breath and exhaled a blast of emerald fire at him. The rock provided enough shelter to keep Magnus from perishing, but the heat still seared his shoulders and arms. He growled and grunted at the burn, and he tried to crouch even lower behind the rock, but the burn only intensified.

Magnus clenched his jaw tightly as the scales along his arms, neck, and legs began to blacken and crisp. The leather straps holding his Blood Ore breastplate in place withered and hardened from the heat.

But no matter how the pain persisted, Magnus would continue to fight until one of them perished.

The heat quickly subsided, and Magnus stole a painful glance from behind his cover. Kahn's flames had melted the front half of Magnus's cover into molten rock. It wouldn't survive another of Kahn's blasts, and neither would Magnus.

And now Kahn was drawing another deep breath.

Magnus could make only one move.

And it was the very move he'd been waiting to make ever since he'd recovered his Dragon Emerald from Roderick.

He sprang from behind the melting rock, tore his breastplate off, and tossed both his armor and the Dragon's Breath sword away. He extended his arms out to his sides and taunted the mighty beast before him.

"Go ahead, Kahn. You murdered my father. This is your one chance to kill me as well, if you can."

Kahn finished his inhale and leaned forward with his mouth open. Smoke continued to pulse from his nostrils, and the instant Magnus saw a flicker of green flame emanate from Kahn's throat, he tore the Dragon Emerald pouch from his belt and held it out before him.

This had better work.

CALUM WATCHED in horror as green fire cascaded over Magnus's body, but his concern quickly subsided when he realized that Magnus somehow still stood there, intact, and seemingly unharmed.

The leather pouch that contained Magnus's Dragon Emerald had incinerated upon its first contact with Kahn's green fire, but the Dragon Emerald itself remained. What's more, it now glowed with vibrant yellow light.

Shafts of orange light shone from between Magnus's fingers, and amid the endless flames, he pressed the Dragon Emerald against his bare chest, just as he had in the tunnels under Kanarah City.

Orange light penetrated his chest amid Kahn's green fire, but Magnus remained unscathed. Instead, his entire body began to glow orange like the Dragon Emerald. As Kahn's blast of fire subsided, Magnus began to transform.

His fingers and arms thickened and lengthened, as did his legs, his torso, and his tail. The spikes of black bone protruding from his spine elongated and sharpened, and a curved black razor sprouted from the tip of his tail. The spikes on top of his head also widened and grew larger, and two long black horns grew out from the sides of his head.

His green scales darkened to an even deeper green—almost black—and black plates of armored scales formed on his broadening chest. His jaw widened, and his teeth lengthened and sharpened as his neck stretched longer. Magnus convulsed and lurched forward onto his hands and knees, and the Dragon Emerald hit the ground, now solid black like a lump of coal.

The talons on his fingers and toes lengthened and dug into the red stone. His shoulder blades protruded from his back at severe angles and sprouted into small wings that continued to grow until they spread nearly as wide as Kahn's had.

He reared back on his legs, now a titan nearly as large as Kahn, and loosed a roar that shook Calum to his core.

Now there were two dragons in Kanarah.

CHAPTER 18

New strength and power unlike anything Magnus had ever felt coursed through his body. The burns on his scales were gone, and the transformation had reinforced his whole body in every conceivable way. A furious burn sizzled somewhere inside his chest, compelling him to advance, to destroy, to conquer.

He looked down—really far down—at his friends. They were always small compared to him, but now they more resembled dolls than people. They stared up at him, marveling.

"Impossible!" Kahn bellowed. "All the Dragon Emeralds were lost!"

"Not all of them." Magnus's focus locked on Kahn. Now the fight was even. Now Magnus could finally claim his vengeance once and for all.

His eyes narrowed, and he lunged forward.

Kahn hissed and bashed Magnus's head with his open palm. His talons scraped against the scales armoring Magnus's face, but it didn't stop him.

Magnus's new wings propelled his full weight into Kahn's chest, shoulder-first, and they both fell to the ground amid a thunder of roars. The impact seemed to shake the entire mountain.

Magnus drove his gigantic fists into Kahn's chest and face, all while Kahn writhed, trying to escape. He finally managed to break free from Magnus's grasp, and with several powerful beats of his wings, he took to the sky.

Magnus stood upright and stared at Kahn, who hovered fifty feet or so above the keep, his wings flapping in large, even strokes to keep him more or less in the same spot. Kahn extended his hand and curled his forefinger toward himself.

"If you are so eager to claim your revenge, then meet me in the sky and duel like a true Dragon," he taunted.

It was a trap, certainly. Magnus had never flown before. He wasn't familiar with tactics regarding battling in the air, and he'd only just grown wings.

But Magnus refused to allow Kahn the chance to escape. He had achieved everything he'd set out to achieve thus far, with only one exception: Kahn still drew breath. And that was about to change for good.

With a snarl, Magnus spread his new wings and pumped at the air, and he ascended from the stone floor. The sensation of leaving his feet and climbing into the sky because of the two brand new limbs that had sprouted from his back was exhilarating.

His wings walloped the air, and he rose into the ether faster than he'd expected, given his incredible size and increased mass. More incredible was the sight of the Blood Mountains burning red below him under the sunshine.

But he wasn't taking to the sky to admire the view. He had a Dragon to strike down, his people to save, and a dead father to avenge.

"Magnus!" a shout sounded from behind him.

He glanced back, surprised at how easily his elongated neck allowed him to do so. Lilly and Condor hovered in the air on either side of his shoulders.

"Be careful how you engage him in the air," Lilly continued. "My father had the Calios and was the preeminent warrior in our realm, and not even he could defeat Kahn."

"Your father was not a Dragon." Magnus refocused on Kahn, who now hovered higher than before and still glared down at Magnus. "And I have not come this far to suffer defeat now."

"Don't forget to keep flapping your wings," Condor said. "I don't have the slightest idea of how much punishment you can take, but if you fall from too high up, it'll at least hurt you, if not kill you. And keep the acrobatics to a minimum. We tell that to Windgale children when they're first learning to fly."

As if on cue, Kahn executed a broad aerial loop, tucked his wings into his sides, and shot toward Magnus and his two Windgale allies.

"Get down!" Magnus roared.

He pushed forward, barely noting Condor's distant call of "You look great, by the way," and met Kahn in the air. They collided, but Magnus took Condor's advice to heart and kept his wings flapping amid the impact of Kahn's body against his. Roars and growls emanated from both of them as they clawed and snapped at each other.

Kahn grabbed Magnus's throat and leaned forward with his jaws open as they flew. At the first sight of green flames, Magnus stopped flapping his wings and wrenched free from Kahn's grasp. He tucked them against his sides, just as Kahn had, and plummeted downward while Kahn pursued him through a plume of emerald fire.

Magnus banked to his right and tried to use his wings to glide, but he couldn't figure out how to get them positioned the right way, so they only served to slow him down as he fell. He'd have to work on that later when he had more time.

The mountain range leaped at him, and Magnus furiously beat his wings against the air to correct his course. He looked back to locate Kahn, finding him in hot pursuit.

Magnus dove again, and the slopes of Firebrand Mountain rushed up to meet him. He curved to his left and pounded his wings at the air, just barely avoiding smashing into the mountain. The trees dotting the mountainside waved and hissed as the wind from his wings sent them rocking.

He glanced back as he arced around the mountain and saw Kahn following, though not as closely as before. But as soon as Magnus climbed, Kahn lurched forward and slammed into his back, and they both fell.

Magnus contorted his body to loose himself from Kahn's grasp, but pain dug into his sides— Kahn's talons. Apparently Dragon talons could pierce Dragon scales easily enough.

Even so, Magnus was far from defenseless.

Magnus swept his arms at Kahn's wrists and broke free. As they separated, Magnus drove his foot into the side of Kahn's head and put some distance between them. Then his wings caught the air, and he curled away from Kahn and ascended again.

He'd achieved very little in the battle thus far. Magnus had mostly been on the defensive.

Kahn had chased him through the sky, outmaneuvered him, and nearly sent him crashing into the mountainside several times. Transforming into a Dragon had changed everything for Magnus, and battling in the air was far more difficult than he'd expected.

If he meant to triumph, he had to reconsider his approach.

Kahn swooped down low and arced up toward him, his nostrils streaming tendrils of smoke yet again. It meant a blast of dragonfire was coming soon. Kahn's torso swelled as he inhaled a giant breath of air.

Rather than trying to flee, Magnus snarled and advanced to meet him in the sky. His wings launched him forward with his head lowered and his right shoulder exposed.

Kahn's golden eyes widened, and his mouth opened wide, exposing the emerald glow of dragonfire in his throat. But Magnus's shoulder slammed into Kahn's chest and jarred him from his trajectory, and the fiery breath that had gathered in Kahn's throat expelled in a wild burst of dragonfire that sizzled through the air above them.

Magnus curled his arms around Kahn's midsection, forcing Kahn to carry his weight. Together they plummeted toward the ground, and Kahn's wings spread wide to try to slow their descent. He tried to beat his wings to keep himself airborne, but with Magnus's weight pressing down on him, they continued to fall.

Kahn roared, but the impact of his heavy body slamming into the mountainside cut his voice off. The force sent shudders ratcheting through Magnus's body, but Kahn had taken the brunt of the impact.

And now Magnus had him out of the air.

Kahn flailed a wild, taloned hand at Magnus's face, but Magnus's forearm blocked the attack. Even at many times his original size, some aspects of fighting remained the same.

Magnus delivered a stunning headbutt to Kahn's snout, and Kahn recoiled, scraping and clawing at Magnus's shoulders and chest to try to escape, but Magnus refused to let him go. Instead, Magnus continued his onslaught. He would never get a better chance than this.

He slashed at Kahn's face with his talons, carving four parallel lacerations clean to the bones in Kahn's skull. A rageful roar billowed from Kahn's throat, and he squirmed to get his wings free from underneath him.

The heat in Magnus's chest continued to roil and burn, continued to drive him to attack. He realized it was his own dragonfire, eager to burst forth. Smoke puffed out of his nostrils.

As Kahn finally tore away and clambered up the mountainside, Magnus inhaled a deep breath. Kahn's wings spread, but as the false Dragon King prepared to leap into the sky again, Magnus opened his mouth wide. He would not let Kahn escape.

The burning sensation in his chest raced up his throat and blasted past his tongue and teeth in a burst of emerald flames. The sensation startled Magnus at first, but he quickly focused the stream of fire on Kahn's wings.

The dragonfire crashed into Kahn's back in a cascade of emerald waves, shearing through his right wing and his right shoulder. Magnus's breath expended, but the damage was done. Kahn writhed and thrashed as the emerald fire gnawing at his flesh finally dissipated.

Magnus drew in another deep breath for another blast of flame, but the burn in his chest hadn't yet replenished, so nothing came out except a fearsome hiss. But he didn't need more fire to finish this contest.

Kahn's right wing was totally gone, and the fire had burned sporadic holes in the membranes of his left wing. His right arm hung limp at his side, dangling from what remained of his right shoulder. With his left hand and his legs, Kahn tried to crawl along the mountainside, away from the fight.

Coward.

Magnus reached for Kahn with his right hand, took hold of the back of his neck, and hurled him back down toward the Crimson Keep's courtyard, where he landed with a ground-shaking thud. Magnus leaped after and landed on top of him, pinning him to the red stone floor.

By that point, the whole of Reptilius seemed to have turned out to witness the battle's conclusion. Saurians both young and old stood beyond General Hanza and his soldiers, who'd formed a protective barrier to keep the citizens from getting caught in the fray.

Under Magnus's weight, Kahn strained to get free, but now that Magnus had him, he refused to let him go. Instead, he pinned Kahn's head to the stone floor with one hand and held it there. Kahn's good hand clutched at Magnus's wrist.

"Magnusss..." Kahn rasped. "I yield! I beg of you... show me mercy. I am still your uncle. The last of your kin. What kind of example will you be setting for our people? That you are unwilling to show mercy to your own family?"

A memory resurfaced in Magnus's mind—the memory of watching Kahn crush Praetorius's head in his hands. The pain of that moment didn't even allow Magnus to consider changing his course of action. Instead, it galvanized his resolve even further.

"*My* people will know that I am true to my word," Magnus countered. "They will forever know that I always do what I have promised to do."

Magnus clamped his other hand on Kahn's head. With one powerful push, he compressed his hands—and Kahn's skull.

Kahn roared, but only for an instant.

The crack of Kahn's collapsing skull echoed off the Crimson Keep's stone walls and reverberated throughout the Blood Mountains, chased by the gasps of the Saurians who had gathered to watch.

Magnus rose to his full height and surveyed his people and his friends, victorious. The Saurians stared at him with awe in their golden eyes, and his friends wore a mixture of shocked expressions and knowing smiles.

He reached down and picked up Kahn's body by the scruff of its neck, then he hurled it over the Crimson Keep's walls. It tumbled into the valley and landed in a deep gorge far below. The buzzards and scavengers would feast on it that night, and Kahn's bones would forever remain there as a reminder of his treachery.

With that, Magnus faced his people once again. Pride swelled in his chest. He'd done it. He'd avenged his father and taken back the throne to Reptilius once and for all.

He spread his wings wide, so much so that he blotted out the sun shining on the faces of his people.

"Saurians, I am Magnus, the last surviving heir to the great Dragon Praetorius," he began. "This day marks a new beginning for our people. It has seen the end of the traitor Kahn's reign, the death of the traitor Vandorian, and it serves as the genesis for the renewal of our strength, wealth, and power. From this day forward, our people will no longer live in squalor or poverty.

"But before we may claim our prosperous future, a singular task stands before us. The General of Light, the ancient warrior Lumen, has been released. He means to forever liberate all of Kanarah from the oppression of the King, including Reptilius. Our nation will help him achieve this worthy goal.

"We will journey through the darkness by following his light, and we will join him in battle against the King's forces. I will personally lead our mighty army on the field of battle to destroy the King and his stranglehold over Kanarah forever. Once that campaign draws to a close, I will return to reign here in Reptilius as your new Dragon King.

"Effective immediately, I am appointing General Hanza as the head of the Council of Sobek Lords. He will oversee the reconstruction of the Communal Hall and then the rest of Reptilius, and he will steward the city in my absence," Magnus concluded. "Until my return, be diligent, and rebuild our city to its former glory. Your Dragon King is with you once again."

At first, the crowd gave little reaction to Magnus's words, but applause gradually filtered through the throngs of Saurians gathered in the Crimson Keep. Then the applause broke out in full, accompanied by cheers and roars of approval.

Magnus couldn't help but smile. He had vanquished all of his enemies, and his people had a true king once again. The burning in his chest had returned full force, and he craned his head upward, opened his mouth, and loosed an explosion of emerald dragonfire into the afternoon sky.

———

THAT NIGHT, rather than feasting and celebrating the new leadership of Reptilius, Calum was helping the Saurians clear away rubble from damaged and dilapidated buildings around the city. He found it ironic that he'd come all this way, traveled miles across Kanarah to a different land, only to do exactly what he'd been doing when he first met Magnus at the quarry.

Only everything else was totally different now. They'd set Lumen free, Magnus had become the Dragon King of Reptilius, and Calum had raised an army—with considerable help from his friends—to overthrow the King of Kanarah.

Halfway through the next swing of his pickax, Calum stopped. Magnus was heading toward him from the far end of the wide central street that divided Reptilius's east side from its west.

The moonlight and scattered torches burning throughout the city somehow made Magnus look even bigger than ever—which he was—but the interplay between the light and dark, the muted sheen on his scales, and his colossal wings folded behind his back added to the effect.

Magnus motioned him over, and Calum set his pickax down and met him in the street. Rather than forcing Calum to look up at him, Magnus lowered to all fours to look Calum in his eyes. He was, if Calum had to guess, about three quarters of the size of the Jyrak that had attacked them in the Central Lake.

"Everything's progressing well here," Calum said. "Between you taking the throne and whatever General Hanza has been telling people, they've really gotten to work. I think they really wanted a change like this."

"I am also pleased to see the tremendous progress we have made in only a few hours' time," Magnus began, "but as I told them, we are not staying. Tomorrow, we will head back across Trader's Pass, and we will join with Lumen to finish the good work he has begun with our world."

Calum grinned at the eagerness rising in his chest. "It's really happening, isn't it?"

"It is." Magnus's own grin faded. "But if you are to survive the coming battles, there is one final gift I must give you."

Calum was about to protest, but when Magnus produced the Dragon's Breath sword from beneath the folds of his wings and held it out, Calum went silent. It looked like a large green toothpick between Magnus's huge fingers, but to Calum it was a full-sized sword, one far more dangerous than the one he'd received from the armorist back at the Sky Fortress.

A gift, indeed. Calum met Magnus's golden eyes again. "Are you sure about this? I mean, I know you don't need it anymore, but what about Axel? Or Condor? Or even General Tolomus? Any of them would be more worthy of a treasure like this than me."

"No." Magnus slowly shook his massive head. "Aside from Lilly, who already possesses the Calios, you are the only person in Kanarah to whom I would entrust this sword. Axel has my

Blood Ore sword, Condor is... Condor, and General Tolomus is a stranger. But regardless of whatever happens next, you and I will always be friends."

Calum understood his logic. "Thank you."

"You will steward it well," Magnus said. "And now you will face foes with the power of dragonfire, just like me."

Calum chortled. "Well, not just like you. You have a distinct size advantage."

"Come." Magnus grinned. "We must rest before our journey. I will show you how to wield that weapon tomorrow."

As Magnus turned away, Calum stared at the sword in his hands, its green-tinted blade gleaming under the moonlight. How far he'd come, indeed.

AXEL HAD NEVER FELT MORE powerful or important in his life.

In the weeks it took their combined army of thousands of Saurians, Wolves, and Windgales—all of them now Wisps—to reach Trader's Pass, they didn't encounter so much as even a single threat or obstacle—not even Dactyls. Even if they had, the huge force would've rolled over any opposition like an avalanche.

They couldn't possibly fail to overcome the King's forces now. With an army of that size, made up of all the peoples of Western Kanarah, the war was practically over already. And that was without whatever manpower Lumen had managed to raise while they'd been gone—and it didn't include Lumen himself, either.

They couldn't lose. There was no way it was even possible.

At least, that's what Axel thought until about halfway along Trader's Pass.

As it turned out, the surviving Windgales didn't get along very well with the Saurians. That made sense, given that Kahn and Vandorian's army had tried to raze the entire city of Aeropolis.

The Saurians didn't much care for the Windgales, either. Though they'd initiated the attack, the Saurians had still lost soldiers as a result of the battle, and naturally, they held the Windgales responsible.

They'd almost come to blows several times, but thanks to Lilly's bold leadership and Magnus's fearsome new form and a lot of loud roaring, the opportunity for conflict had mostly subsided.

Someone had suggested the Wolves travel in between the two armies just to add further separation between them. Everyone loved the idea... at least until the Wolves started doing what Wolves tended to do when they got restless: they robbed and stole from both the Saurians and the Windgales indiscriminately. And they often got away with it, too.

Riley did his best to keep them in line, but even he had to admit that Wolves were Wolves, and a certain amount of misbehavior came with the territory. Axel thought that was a copout, but when he spoke up about it, Riley and the other ranking Wolves just laughed at him.

Naturally, he challenged each of them to a fight to the death, but Calum, as usual playing his role as the wet-blanket leader of the whole group, didn't let it happen.

The balance they'd struck between the three armies wobbled like a three-legged table, and Lilly, Magnus, and Riley spent most of their time mediating disagreements and conflicts along the way. It meant Axel hardly got to see Lilly—at least in a conversational sense. That grated on him, because it also meant she was spending more and more time with Condor.

Axel had resolved to put it out of his mind for the time being. With so many troubles—including managing rations and supplies efficiently enough to get them across Trader's Pass—

it's not like Lilly would've had the time or energy to talk to him about anything meaningful anyway.

Ultimately, Axel chose to put it out of his mind. He couldn't control it, so it made no sense to worry about it.

At least, he couldn't control it *yet*. When they presented the army to Lumen, he expected Lumen to make good on his promise to transform them into his generals—his Imperators. Then Axel would have *true* power, and he could remake the world around him as he saw fit.

He grinned, even as he continued to slog across Trader's Pass along with everyone else. When he was finally strong enough, he could just take what he wanted, and no one would stop him.

WEEKS LATER, the army approached the western gate of Kanarah City with Calum, Lilly, Condor, Magnus, and Axel in the lead. Riley had stayed back with his Wolves, and Generals Balena and Tolomus remained with the Windgales.

Their advance halted at the sight of an army, clad in silver armor, barring them from reaching the end of Trader's Pass. The King's soldiers, probably a contingent based in Kanarah City.

Axel scoffed at them. It wasn't because they were lacking for numbers—the force was a good size, albeit not as large as the one at Axel's back. No, he scoffed at them because of their sheer audacity.

Who were they to stand against the combined might of three nations, including a Dragon King, a Shadow Wolf, a Windgale Premieress, and their respective armies?

From what Axel could tell, the army had no one in its ranks who wielded any power greater than what human strength and stamina would afford them. Rather than an Imperator leading them, as Matthios had against Lumen, a man on a white stallion rode to meet them in the center of the pass, accompanied by a trio of other soldiers.

As the lead soldier approached, Axel squinted at him. He wore a silver helmet that shielded his face from the sun and matched the armor on the rest of his body. His horse, likewise, also wore silver armor on its head and across its front. He carried a silver lance that gleamed orange in the afternoon sunlight.

The approaching soldiers slowed to a halt before them, and Axel recognized the man in the lead as Beynard Anigo, the commander who'd doggedly pursued them after they'd raided the Rock Outpost. Axel scoffed again, and his lips curled up in a smirk.

He elbowed Calum in his ribs, and his elbow clanked against Calum's armor. Not quite the same effect as usual, but it got Calum's attention all the same. "Look who we've got here. Commander Anigo's come back around for another thrashing."

"Maybe," Calum replied.

"I beat him before. Won't be a problem to do it again."

"I'd rather we didn't have to fight them at all," Calum said. "We need to get back to Lumen as fast as possible, so if we can avoid an unnecessary confrontation, so much the better. Plus, when Lumen finally overthrows the King, all these soldiers will be our countrymen again."

Axel's brow furrowed. He hadn't thought of it that way.

"What? You didn't think we were just gonna execute everyone who sided with the King, did you?" Calum teased.

"Of course not."

Axel actually *had* expected something along those lines, but he hadn't considered how many people might favor the King's rule. It couldn't be that many, given how cruel he was and how oppressive his soldiers were, and it's not like Axel would've gone along with the execution of women and children who happened to side with the King, either.

Still, he couldn't see how showing men like Commander Anigo mercy would help anything. Forgiving the bad guys seemed like a quick way to catch a knife in the back later on.

Commander Anigo didn't dismount as he looked them over, and his eyes lingered on Magnus the longest. But despite Magnus's Dragon form, the man didn't show even a hint of fear on his face or in his posture.

"I told you what would happen if you ever tried to return to Eastern Kanarah," he said.

Axel rolled his eyes. Straight to the point, as usual.

"It's good to see you, Commander," Calum greeted him with genuine goodwill, just like Axel had expected he would.

"It's Captain, now," Anigo corrected. "In the aftermath and ensuing confusion following our confrontation in the tunnels, I was promoted to oversee the entirety of the King's forces in Kanarah City."

"You mean after I killed that pervert, Captain Fulton," Lilly countered, her eyes set with anger.

"That played a role in my promotion, yes," Captain Anigo replied, all business. "In any case, it falls to me, now more than ever, to remind you of the agreement we made near this very spot. I cannot allow you to reenter Eastern Kanarah."

"Circumstances have changed," Calum said. "Lumen has been released, and we're joining up with him to overthrow your King."

"I have heard the reports," Captain Anigo replied. "But regardless of whether or not they're true, my position remains unchanged. I still serve the King, and I will uphold his commands until my dying breath."

"We're happy to accelerate that timeline for you." Axel drew his weapon—Magnus's old Blood Ore sword—and stepped forward, but Calum caught him by his shoulder and held him back.

"Lumen will overthrow the King," Calum insisted. "Just as his return was prophesied by the King himself, Lumen has raised an army, and he will use his power to set Kanarah free. I know you're just doing your job, Captain, and I know you're a man of duty and honor, but surely you realize you're on the wrong side."

"I have no doubts as to the nature of my allegiance or of the greatness of the King. This rebellion will fail, just as the first one did a thousand years ago."

Calum shook his head and held up his left hand. He winced noticeably as Lumen's light began to glow from within his palm, and Axel wondered about that, but only briefly.

"No, Captain." Calum's hand glowed so brightly that it even competed with the afternoon sun for brightness. "You're wrong. But even if I can't convince you to join us, you at least have to let us pass. This isn't a fight you can win."

Captain Anigo studied the glow in Calum's hand, squinting against its brightness. "I was ordered to keep you out of Eastern Kanarah, and that is what I intend to do."

"Are you stupid?" Axel could barely keep from laughing at him. "We have a Dragon, and you think a few hundred men are gonna keep us out?"

"Axel," Calum warned.

"If you have a death wish, there are better ways to go than getting burned alive by dragonfire." Axel's voice hardened. "Come a little closer, and I'll drive my sword into the back of your neck and put you out of your misery."

"Axel." Calum's hand rested on Axel's shoulder, but Axel shrugged it off and stepped forward again.

"You bested me in combat once," Captain Anigo admitted, "but it will not happen again."

"Then let's go," Axel held out his arms, still holding his sword. "You and me. One on one, right now. I win, and we pass. You win, and we'll go back where we came from."

Now a chorus of voices called Axel's name, and instead of Calum pulling him back, it was Condor. Axel protested, but Condor didn't relent.

"That's quite enough out of you, Farm Boy," Condor said. "Best to keep your mouth shut and let the adults handle things from here."

It took every ounce of willpower Axel could muster to keep from cutting Condor's head off then and there.

While he'd gotten used to that annoying nickname, Axel would never get used to Condor's constant condescension and patronizing tone, nor his perpetual proximity to Lilly.

One well-timed stroke from Magnus's old Blood Ore sword would put all of that to an end. It would solve multiple problems all at once.

But he didn't do it. He clenched his teeth and his fists tighter, gripping his sword as if he were squeezing Condor's throat.

"Captain Anigo," Calum said, his voice stern, "we aren't turning back. We've come too far. We have a mission, and we have a purpose. We're going to meet up with Lumen whether you try to stop us or not. So either move aside and we'll spare your lives, or prepare to fight."

"I have said what I needed to say," Captain Anigo replied. "If you try to enter Eastern Kanarah, we will stop you."

"Then you leave us no choice." The light from Calum's hand faded away to nothing. "Prepare to attack."

Without another word, Captain Anigo and the soldiers accompanying him turned and rode back toward their army.

As they did, Axel watched them go. "He's mine."

"Now is not the time for vendettas born of wounded pride," Magnus said.

"You spent the last few years seeking vengeance for your father, and you're gonna try to tell *me* about vendettas?" Axel looked up at him.

"That was an entirely different scenario."

"Whatever, Scales." Axel shook his head and watched Captain Anigo ride away. Fury burned inside his chest. "I said he's mine, and he is. Nobody else touch 'im."

"You have nothing to prove, Axel," Lilly said.

But she was wrong. Axel had everything to prove.

And he was about to do just that.

As their army approached the King's soldiers, Axel allowed his rage to take over.

CHAPTER 19

Captain Beynard Anigo had scarcely believed his eyes upon realizing that it was Calum and his friends advancing toward Kanarah City with a vast army behind them, but sure enough, it was them. They'd grown and changed in appearance—especially Magnus, who was now inexplicably a massive Dragon—but it was doubtless them.

He'd been certain they would perish when he'd allowed them to leave—or rather, after he'd sworn not to further pursue them. Yet somehow they'd survived the desolation of the valley surrounding Trader's Pass and the perils of whatever lay beyond, and now they'd returned with a formidable army and new powers the likes of which he'd never seen.

After Captain Fulton was killed, his superiors back at Solace had sent Anigo a message promoting him to the rank of Captain and commissioning him to take Fulton's place in overseeing the soldiers based in Kanarah City.

While it was doubtless a promotion, and while he'd enjoyed the initial phase of reorganizing the fractured structure in the void Captain Fulton had left behind, Captain Anigo despised the position itself. It kept him tied down with administrative duties and prevented him from the work he loved, the work he'd become known for—going into the field and making things happen.

Now the position had maneuvered him into a confrontation with an invading force of Windgales, Saurians, and Wolves. Were it not for the King's provision of aid just prior to the army's arrival, Captain Anigo might've resigned his post then and there.

But deep down, he knew he could never do that. He'd signed up for a life of service in the King's military, and now only death could separate him from his duty.

As he surveyed the force approaching them from Trader's Pass, he couldn't help but wonder if that day had finally come. From atop his horse, Candlestick, he glanced back at the green pods they'd entrenched at even intervals behind the city walls and hoped the King's provision would be enough to turn the fight to their advantage.

Captain Anigo ordered Commander Jopheth—who'd also received a promotion at the same time—to have his soldiers fall back into the city and seal the gate. With the Windgales' ability to fly, the city's walls wouldn't keep them out, nor would they keep the Dragon out, but they had made preparations to deal with that—at least for the Windgales.

Now they would find out whether or not their plan would work. Captain Anigo gave the command, and his men lit their torches.

WHEN THE GATE SLAMMED SHUT, Axel's fury intensified. Though Calum and the others behind him shouted at him to stop, he continued to run forward, propelled by impotent rage.

Arrows thudded into the road around him by the dozen, but he paid them no mind. He hadn't come this far to get picked off by a random arrow from some faceless archer on the walls of Kanarah City. Nor would his Blood Ore armor, now a full set since Magnus no longer had need of it, yield to measly little arrows.

But despite Axel's best efforts, he couldn't reach the gate before a searing blast of emerald dragonfire struck the wrought-iron portcullis and the wall from overhead, reducing it all to molten slag. Then an enormous shadow blotted out the afternoon sun from behind Axel.

The frightened shouts of the soldiers posted on the walls filled Axel's ears, and he saw several men go flying as the gate collapsed into a slurry of burning liquid. They were the lucky ones, he realized. Magnus's blast had reduced several others to ash in the blink of an eye.

Still, he didn't stop running.

Overhead, the flicker of Wisps dashing over the city walls tried to steal Axel's attention away, but he didn't let his focus waver. Thanks to Magnus, the gate was open, but in order to get inside, he'd have to jump over a pool of molten metal and stone. With one last push, he increased his speed, timed his jump, and leaped just before he reached the edge of the slag.

Despite wearing Magnus's old armor, Axel soared well over the pool of superheated liquid and was primed to land squarely on his feet—until something reminiscent of a thick tree branch covered with leaves knocked him backward.

The blow cracked into his armored chest, stealing both his breath and his momentum, and forcing him back out of the city the way he'd come in. He landed on his back and skidded to a halt some forty feet away from the gate entrance. Whatever had struck him had done it with incredible power.

It hadn't hurt all that much, but Axel struggled to find his breath as he stood back up to his feet. Had he seen the hit coming, he would've reacted differently, but it had seemingly come out of nowhere. At least he hadn't dropped his Blood Ore sword in the process.

From very near behind Axel, the thunder of countless Saurian footsteps approached. Now back on his feet, he glanced back and saw them charging toward the city, toward him.

Overhead, Axel noticed the Wisp warriors who'd flown over the city walls being rebuffed by… more tree branches? Or vines of some sort? They dueled with thrashing whips of brown and green, some of which even had specks of white, or pinks and reds, almost like flowers.

Even Magnus himself had refrained from diving down toward the city, instead choosing to remain airborne as he surveyed the happenings below.

As the Saurians passed by Axel, he peered through the opening where the gate used to be. At first, he saw only soldiers, but once the Saurians reached the gateway and the pool of melted metal and stone, now cool enough to walk over, branches and vines from the sides of the opening lashed out and repelled them.

The Saurians fought back, swinging axes and swords to fell the aggressive plants, but to no avail. The flora formed a flexible network across the opening, gradually filling in more and more of the space until an impenetrable wall of thorny vines and branches separated the Saurians from the interior of Kanarah City.

Among them, Axel even noticed crimson buds beginning to bloom into roses. Their petals alone were the size of his fist, and some of the flowers had swelled to twice the size of his head.

Axel marveled at the sight. He'd never seen anything like it before.

Then he looked up again in time to see the same wall of branches twisting and curling upward, gradually forming a natural dome of browns and greens, accented with white, pink, and rose-red flowers, over the entire city.

Axel growled to himself. However they'd done it didn't matter.

What mattered was that Axel still lacked the power to do anything about it.

He cursed under his breath, lowered his sword, and regrouped with Calum and the others farther back along Trader's Pass, still enraged, but now equally frustrated and defeated.

CAPTAIN ANIGO BREATHED a sigh of relief. He hadn't quite known what to expect when the pods had arrived. Green and seemingly made of a cluster of leaves, the pods had literally taken root in the shallow ditches the soldiers had dug around the inner perimeter of the city walls.

Then, as if prompted by the approach of the enemy soldiers, the pods had sprouted into gigantic swirls of vines that autonomously defended the city from all manner of attacks. Now the canopy overhead completely shielded them from attack, but it also blocked out the vast majority of daylight. Only a few seams of sunshine filtered through, not nearly enough to light up the city.

But that's what the torches were for. With each soldier holding a weapon in one hand and a torch in the other, the inner perimeter of the city remained well lit.

The sight of the vines twisting and curling in the relative darkness, ever reinforcing the foliage above them, unnerved Captain Anigo. They reminded him of the Gronyxes' unending supply of writhing tentacles in the sewers and tunnels below their feet, and he had to look away to banish the memory from his mind.

As far as he knew, there were still more Gronyxes down there, haunting the tunnels, but he couldn't think about that now. They kept to the darkness below, out of sight. Despite their fearsome nature, they weren't a concern, especially now.

He blinked away the last vestiges of eerie green light from his mind's eye and refocused on the task at hand. He redoubled his resolve and nodded to himself. Even if a few stragglers managed to break through the city's thorny shell, his men would quickly dispatch them. The King's provision was working, and soon reinforcements would arrive to bolster their numbers.

But when a blast of emerald fire sheared through the canopy high above, Captain Anigo's resolve faltered.

EVEN THOUGH HE'D seen it before, Calum couldn't help but revel in the sight of Magnus loosing emerald fire from his gaping mouth. A concentrated stream of flames sheared through the city's thorn-studded exterior, searing a smoldering line down to the city walls, which melted under the immense heat of the fire.

The canopy immediately started trying to mend the egregious wound Magnus had dealt to it, but a few dozen Wisps still zipped through the opening and into the city below. To Calum's shock and awe, Magnus actually landed *on* the top of the dome, which somehow held his weight.

His nostrils still smoking, Magnus dug his powerful hands into the burning fissure he'd created. Then, with every ounce of his considerable strength, he began to pull the network of vines apart. More impressively, it was actually working.

Though the vines fought back, coiling around Magnus's limbs and raking their thorns across his scales, the Dragon didn't relent. He drew in another deep breath and exhaled another blast of green fire down into the city.

Seeing it sent a twist rippling through Calum's gut. He supposed the soldiers resisting them deserved whatever they got, but he couldn't help but feel bad for them. It's not like they stood any real chance against Magnus's flames; they would just die, incapable of defending themselves, and painfully so.

But Calum was more concerned for the actual citizens of Kanarah City. If Magnus's attacks hit any of the buildings, innocent people might be hurt or killed as well.

Still, Calum knew Magnus well enough to know he wasn't reckless with his power. Because of the dome, he couldn't see what Magnus had hit inside the city, but he had to trust that it wasn't a soft target.

As the flames from Magnus's mouth ceased, a portion of the dome shuddered, shriveled, and turned brown, all within a matter of seconds. Then they fell away from the rest of the dome's structure like chaff blowing away on the wind.

It happened so quickly that Magnus almost fell into the city with them, but he readjusted with three vigorous wing beats that helped to right him on what remained of the dome.

In the aftermath of his blast, Magnus had reduced a large section of the city wall to molten stone, and a corresponding wide section of the canopy was also gone.

They had a way into the city.

Wielding the Dragon's Breath sword in his hands, Calum charged toward the city with Lumen's army behind and all around him.

WIDE-EYED, Captain Anigo watched as Magnus's flames obliterated several nearby pods in a row. The green fire had shorn through them as if they were paper, and the vines that had sprouted from them perished in short order, falling lifelessly to the city streets and onto buildings.

Though the remaining vines already reached for each other to bridge the new gap, it wouldn't happen soon enough. Windgales were already cruising through the opening, and Saurians and Wolves streamed through the destroyed section of wall, which was no longer molten beneath their feet.

Still atop Candlestick, Captain Anigo shouted orders to his men to fill the gap themselves. Dutifully, they abandoned their torches and obeyed, flinging themselves at the encroaching forces in a cacophonous clash of steel, talons, and fangs.

Like the vines struggling against the Dragon overhead, the soldiers couldn't stem the tide. The Saurians were too strong and durable, the Wolves too cunning and quick, the Windgales too fast and flighty.

The opposing army pierced through Captain Anigo's soldiers like a spike plunging into flesh. He didn't have enough men to resist the incursion, and even if he did, what good could mere soldiers and steel do against the weapons and powers of foes such as these?

Captain Anigo turned to Commander Jopheth, who rode a brown horse. Despite his initial dislike for the man, Jopheth had proven resourceful and competent as a corporal. Though he'd received his promotion to commander more out of necessity than merit, he'd become someone Captain Anigo could truly trust, even in the most uncertain of times.

And now certainly qualified as such.

"This will be my final order to you, Commander," Captain Anigo said. "Take four men with you. Enter the sewers beneath the streets and flee the city. Go to the King. Tell him what transpired here today. He must know what kind of foe we are facing."

"Captain, I—" Commander Jopheth began, but Captain Anigo cut him off.

"There will be no argument," he asserted. "Go now."

With a curt nod, Commander Jopheth urged his horse forward, and they trotted away.

Captain Anigo watched him for a moment, then he refocused his attention on the flow of enemies cascading over his soldiers. He raised his lance, kicked Candlestick's sides, and raced toward the battle.

As he did so, another burst of emerald fire from above consumed another swath of pods, felling another section of the dome. This time, thick branches riddled with thorns fell all around Captain Anigo as Candlestick charged forward. The foliage thudded onto the streets, rooftops, and even some soldiers on both sides of the conflict.

Captain Anigo didn't let Candlestick slow down.

The tsunami of enemies soon fixed their attention on him, and they rushed to engage him in battle. Windgales darted toward him from above, Wolves dashed toward him from the sides, and Saurians lumbered toward him straight on.

Since he had failed to do so in life, Captain Anigo would fulfill his duty in death.

He loosed a war cry and pointed the tip of his lance at the nearest Saurian.

Thorny vines lashed into Captain Anigo's periphery and shielded him from the onslaught only yards away. Something like hands, but made of green branches, swatted the first wave of Saurians aside as if they weighed nothing. Thorny fingers knocked Windgales from the sky and belted pouncing Wolves away.

In seconds, the only foe that remained in Captain Anigo's path was the Saurian he'd targeted, now wearing a shocked expression as the vines cleared out everyone around him. By the time he looked back to Captain Anigo, a lance was already screaming toward his face. It pierced deep into the Saurian's golden eye and burst out the back of his head.

Captain Anigo yanked his lance free, disregarding the blood dripping from it thanks to the mortal wound he'd inflicted, and looked to the vines that had saved him—only they weren't just vines anymore. Nor did the vines cover any part of the city in the dome any longer.

Instead, dozens of hulking green golems thrashed the invading forces with thorny fingers and whips all around, fighting side-by-side with the smattering of soldiers who'd managed to survive this long.

At the center of their chests were the pods the soldiers had planted. They'd uprooted and now walked—if it could be called that—on those roots as if they were legs, and vines coiled and twisted outward from their torsos to form arms. At the top of each pod bloomed a breathtaking rose flower, each two or three times the size of Captain Anigo's head.

Perhaps there is still a chance for victory after all, Captain Anigo mused.

Either way, he was still alive, and that meant he could still fight. So he readied his lance and followed a pair of the golems into battle.

AXEL HAD JUST TAKEN out his first soldier inside the city when the rose golems blossomed all around the King's soldiers, bolstering their numbers, and he cursed under his breath. Of course, right when he'd finally gotten to work, something had to go horribly wrong.

Above him, the dome of plants withered and began to fall onto the city like a greenish-brown blanket draped over the buildings and streets. They'd given up on their defensive shell in favor of a more direct—and violent—solution.

Ahead, the rose golems thrashed at the Saurians in the lead, swatting many of them aside like toys. They lashed their thorny vines at both the Wisps flying at them from overhead and the Wolves circling them on the ground, occasionally hitting their targets, albeit not as consistently as with the Saurians.

As Axel considered whether or not he could tangle with these viny beasts, he caught sight of a soldier atop a familiar white stallion skewering the head of a Saurian with his silver lance.

Captain Anigo.

Whether or not Axel could take on the rose golems, he knew he could beat Captain Anigo in a fight. He'd already done it once.

He squared himself with the horse and its rider and bellowed the captain's name over the ruckus of the battle around them. At first, he doubted Captain Anigo could've possibly heard him over the roar of the warfare, but then he turned his head and looked straight at Axel.

Axel clanked his sword against his Blood Ore chest armor and beckoned Captain Anigo to come to him.

With the adeptness of a seasoned rider, Captain Anigo smoothly redirected his stallion toward Axel and pointed his lance as they galloped forward.

Excitement prickled up Axel's spine in anticipation of their rematch. He readied his Blood Ore sword, adjusting his grip. It would cleave through both horse and rider if he swung hard enough.

The thunder of hoof beats hammered in Axel's skull and rattled his ankles as Captain Anigo charged at him, but Axel was ready. With perfect timing, he drew his sword back and—

A thick vine slammed into Axel's chest, knocking him back a dozen feet. He landed hard on his back and skidded to a halt against the exterior of a building. Stunned, he looked up in time to see a rose golem lumbering toward him on root-legs, its multiple vines drawn back to finish him off in a barrage of brutal lashes.

Axel cursed again. If only Lumen had granted him some power, he wouldn't be in this mess.

But he still had his sword, and he raised it to protect himself, praying that it and his armor would be enough to save him from the thrashing he was about to take.

CHAPTER 20

I t was bad enough that he'd been caught unaware, but it was worse that Axel had to be saved from the rose golem by Condor, of all people.

The Wisp collided with the rose golem at an incredible speed and then, inexplicably, went *through* the viny beast and landed on the other side. He held two daggers in his hands, both of them streaked with dark-green ooze of some sort, shiny and sticky like sap.

The rose golem staggered for a moment, either confused or stunned—Axel couldn't tell because it didn't have a face—until a dozen more Wisps attacked it from the sky. They knocked it to the street and plunged weapons of their own into its core, flinging more green ooze everywhere.

Only then did Axel see the tremendous hole Condor had carved in the rose golem's chest.

"Apart from their vines and their roots, they're actually quite fragile abominations," Condor said from Axel's side. How and when he'd moved there, Axel didn't know. He hadn't seen it happen.

Axel didn't bother to reply. He forced himself up to his feet and frowned at Condor, then at the rose golem again, now lying motionless under the Wisps who'd taken it down. Several of them continued to stab it, even though it was clearly dead.

"Took some trial-and-error to figure it out, but we got there in the end," Condor continued.

As if to reinforce the point, one of the Wisps brought down an axe near the rose at the top of the golem's torso, chopping it off entirely. Then he donned it as if it were an oversized wide-brimmed hat, which got the other Wisps to stop their stabbing and start laughing and begging to try it on, too.

"Given how easy they are to take down, I'm rather surprised you couldn't manage it on your own," Condor continued, a wry smirk curling the corner of his mouth.

Axel bristled at the comment. Condor was trying to get under his skin… and it was working. He tightened his grip on his sword and faced Condor with it at the ready, a snarl on his face.

"I'm ready to fight you right now," Axel said, his voice level despite his fury.

Condor shook his head. "Not even close, Farm Boy. But when you are, I'll come to you."

With that, Condor left his feet and floated into the sky, leaving Axel on the ground, unable to follow, and just as angry as before. Perhaps angrier still.

But the battle still raged on around him, and now he knew how to kill the rose golems. Plus, Captain Anigo was still out there, riding around in the fray, wreaking havoc alongside his remaining soldiers and the rose golems.

Axel couldn't fight Condor, but he *could* fight everyone else. He refocused his ire on the enemies ahead of him and rejoined the fracas.

With the power of the Calios in her hands, Lilly had no trouble cleaving through the rose golems or their vines. She hadn't really gotten the chance to use it before this battle, but once the dome of vines collapsed onto the city, she'd started exploring the ancient sword's capabilities and found them to be almost identical to what she'd been told.

She'd come to understand that the sword's power wasn't tied merely to her thoughts but rather to her *emotions*. When she wanted fire, she had to summon fiery anger within her, and then the sword would glow bright-orange like molten metal. When she wanted ice, she had to chill that anger into a cold, hardened resolve, one almost entirely devoid of emotion.

And that was just the beginning. She'd only used a few forms of attacks thus far—fiery anger and cold resolve were among the easier emotions to conjure in an already intense battle—and the sword had performed admirably.

She'd tinkered with trying to poison some of her foes as well, but she'd found that amid all the fighting, she couldn't hold onto the surreptitious deceit needed to sustain the effect for very long, so it wasn't practical for this kind of combat.

Water-type strikes came relatively easily as well, once she realized she needed to allow her emotion to flow like a river, but the attacks themselves didn't do much against the rose golems or the enemy soldiers. A few times, she had to defend herself from attacks, and the reservation of pulling the sword back reinforced her defense with a literal wall of stone.

Amid all of her experimentation, though, the fire proved the most effective. Tapping into her anger was simple; after all she'd lost in recent months, channeling that fury into her fighting proved easy, and the Calios's fiery attacks cut through all manner of foes just as easily.

With the combined strength of Lilly's people, the Saurians, the Wolves, and Magnus's cleansing emerald fire, the battle for Kanarah City drew to a swift close. The last of the rose golems perished thanks to a vicious slash from Axel, whose Blood Ore sword cleaved the beast in half, and then only the King's soldiers remained.

Captain Anigo, somehow still atop his stallion, stood with his remaining men—a few dozen in total—encircled by hundreds from Lumen's army. Then again, as Lumen had yet to actually take control of the force, perhaps it was more accurate to call it "Calum's army" instead.

Lilly stole a look at him, but he remained focused on the task at hand—that being the negotiation of the surviving soldiers' surrender.

"Lay down your weapons, and we will allow you to live," he called from among the crowd of Saurians and Wolves surrounding the last remnant of the soldiers.

He approached them with his left hand up, glowing brightly even under the afternoon sun. Blood and dirt streaked across his armor and his face, but from the bounce in Calum's step, Lilly could tell he was unharmed.

"I swear it with the authority of Lumen himself," Calum added as he stepped into the clearing, standing before Captain Anigo and the last of his men.

"Lumen has no authority," Captain Anigo countered, indignant. "Nor does any other *ruler* in Kanarah. Only the King sits on the throne. Anyone else is just a pretender."

Lilly thought she saw Captain Anigo glance her direction, and he definitely looked at Magnus, whose huge form now filled a good chunk of the space where he'd melted the city wall, next. She understood better than anyone why he might've suggested she wasn't a real ruler, but the audacity he'd shown toward Magnus baffled her.

It was like an ant shouting at a boot that it had no power.

"This offer isn't indefinite," Calum continued, unfazed. "Either accept it now and throw down your weapons, or I will allow my allies to finish you off."

Several of the King's soldiers exchanged uncertain looks, but every single one of them eventually tossed down their weapons.

Every one of them except Captain Anigo.

"Captain," Calum said, "I don't want to see any harm come to you. Please."

The way he said it, it almost sounded like he was begging Captain Anigo to relinquish his weapons. It made little sense to Lilly; the King's soldiers had killed Calum's parents when he was just a child, yet now he was showing them mercy?

Extending that mercy to Captain Anigo, in particular, was even more confusing. The man had pursued Calum, Axel, and Magnus all the way from northern Kanarah down to Kanarah City. Then he'd followed them into the sewers and tunnels beneath the city, intending to capture them and bring them to whatever twisted form of "justice" the King would level upon them.

Lilly hadn't shown that kind of mercy to the slave traders who'd captured her. Magnus hadn't shown that kind of mercy to Kahn and Vandorian. So why was Calum being so generous now?

As much as it baffled Lilly, it also endeared Calum to her yet again. This was part of what made him unique, she knew, and it was part of what had attracted her to him from the moment they'd first met.

But she couldn't think about any of that now. Or perhaps ever. It couldn't happen, and so it wouldn't. She had to focus on leading, not on anything else. So did Calum, for that matter. Best not to confuse anything in the process.

Still, she couldn't leave things as they were after their last real conversation. She'd shut him down without really even hearing him out, and they'd scarcely spoken to each other since. The resulting chasm in her chest and stomach had left Lilly miserable. Perhaps once this battle was truly over, she could talk to him again and sort it out.

"I swore an oath to my King—the King of all Kanarah," Captain Anigo began. "I swore to defend his kingdom even at the cost of my life. And if it must cost me my life to stand for my King when no one else will, then I will do so knowing—"

A blur of familiar gray-and-brown fur appeared out of nowhere and knocked Captain Anigo from his horse. Benefits of being a Shadow Wolf, Lilly supposed. In the next motion, Riley tore Captain Anigo's lance from his grasp and tossed it aside, all while keeping him pinned to the street with one powerful arm.

Though Captain Anigo struggled and protested and threatened, Riley didn't let go. Instead, he looked up at Calum with indifference in his black eyes. It had been the easiest thing in the world for him to take Captain Anigo down, and it would be easier still to kill him then and there, but he wouldn't do it without Calum's order.

Instead of directing Riley to finish Captain Anigo off, Calum ordered two Sobeks to take hold of him and restrain him. They did, and Captain Anigo's shouts and threats about the King's coming judgment only stopped when they stuffed a wad of fabric in his mouth to shut him up.

"Find the soldiers' barracks, and lock them all inside," Calum ordered the Sobeks. "Post guards to make sure they don't escape, and see to it that they have food and water and are not abused or harmed in any way."

The Sobeks glanced at each other and then looked to Magnus, who gave a slow nod. They hauled Captain Anigo off, even though he still kicked and struggled, and the rest of the soldiers followed behind, escorted by dozens of Saurians and Sobeks.

Only once they were all out of sight did Calum turn to face Lilly and the others. For an instant, his eyes found hers, and her heart awakened with a flutter. She steeled herself and forced the emotion away, thankful her hand wasn't on the Calios. She didn't know what it might do when activated by that kind of emotion, and she didn't want to figure it out, either.

"We're not done here," Calum said to everyone who still remained.

To Lilly's surprise, it looked like most of the Wolves had stuck around. She'd expected them to spread throughout the city by now, eager to start looting whatever and robbing whoever they could find.

"Gather our dead and their dead and bury or burn them outside the city," Calum ordered. "Then gather what food and supplies you can find, but do *not* take from anyone who can't afford it. We're here to liberate Kanarah, not to further oppress her people."

Lilly admired his desire to preserve good relations with the people of Kanarah City. It would likely make the road to peace easier on the other side of this war.

She and the other leaders conveyed the orders to their respective groups, and they set out to fulfill Calum's mandate. As their combined army got to work, Lilly hoped she'd get her chance to talk to Calum again, but the trio of General Balena, General Tolomus, and Condor swarmed her before she could get away.

They inundated her with reports and questions, all of which she half-listened to as she tried not to focus on Calum. She caught Condor giving her one of his piercing-yet-alluring stares, so she forced herself to look at General Balena instead.

But she quickly found that even that didn't work. Her eyes sought out Calum again, just in time to watch him disappear into the city with Axel and Riley at his side.

The chasm in her gut widened.

CALUM RECOGNIZED a lot of Kanarah City from the last time he was there, but some of it only seemed vaguely familiar. The last time he'd been in the city itself—as opposed to below it—he'd narrowly escaped capture by the King's soldiers.

At that point, he'd been fleeing through the streets along with Axel and Magnus, not really taking in the sights, and they'd eventually ended up running along the rooftops instead.

It didn't help that dead brown vines now covered most of the city, but with a little help from Axel and Riley, Calum managed to find the city's south gate. It was sealed shut, just like the last time he'd seen it.

"Tomorrow, we'll head through that gate and meet up with Lumen and his army," Calum said aloud, but not to either Axel or Riley in particular.

"I've never seen it open before," Axel said with a huff. "I'm starting to think it *doesn't* open."

"It does." Riley's black eyes and blue irises flashed toward Axel. "I've been through it several times, back and forth."

Axel met the Shadow Wolf's frigid gaze with incredulity. "Why would you have been here?"

"Back when I was traveling alone, Kanarah City was the closest center of commerce in the area." Riley's mouth curled into a smirk. "I had to go *somewhere* to spend all the coin I stole from you."

Calum grinned, but Axel's face twisted into a scowl. He said, "You're gonna pay us back for all of it, too."

Here we go. Calum rolled his eyes.

Riley raised one eyebrow. "I think gathering the largest pack of Wolves ever assembled and joining them to this army more than covers the debt."

"I can't spend it, so it doesn't count," Axel countered.

"Then get used to disappointment."

"That's not acceptable."

Riley sighed and turned to Calum. "I've got lupine concerns to attend to." He motioned toward Axel. "Can you deal with this, like you always do?"

Calum took a turn sighing. The last thing he wanted was to have to broker peace between Axel and Riley—or anyone else in their group—yet again, but here he was, doing just that.

He nodded to Riley. "I've got it."

"Thanks." With that, Riley melted into the shadow of a building—literally, it looked like he dissipated into the darkness itself—and was gone.

For a blessed moment, both Calum and Axel were too stunned at seeing Riley vanish into thin air to talk to each other, but Axel quickly found his voice.

"So you're gonna 'deal with me,' are you?" he challenged.

Calum bristled at his friend's tone, even though he'd heard it a thousand times before. Or perhaps *endured* was a better word. But maybe there was a way to avoid the conversation. After all, a few gold coins didn't really matter anymore in the grand scheme of things.

"I'm content to let sleeping Wolves lie if you are," Calum said.

"He can sleep all he wants as soon as he give us back what he stole." Axel folded his arms.

"Why do you do this?" The words tumbled out of Calum's mouth like a rockslide. He felt like he should've regretted saying it, but the truth was he really didn't. He'd needed to push back on Axel for far too long now, so this was going to be that moment.

"Do what?"

"Push everyone away. Constantly."

Axel recoiled in confusion and shook his head. "What are you talking about?"

It took every last bit of Calum's resolve not to explode at Axel right then and there. He forced his voice to remain level. "Your attitude. Your behavior. Your personality. It all pushes people away. You make near-enemies out of friends for no reason. You pick fights with anyone who has the audacity to breathe the same air as you. You always have to win everything."

Axel blinked at him. "Yeah... and?"

Calum's eyes widened, and the words erupted from his very soul. "You're a *jerk*, Axel. That behavior is *not* normal. From the moment we teamed up with Magnus, you didn't trust him. You called him 'Scales.' You argued with him about everything, even though he has way more life experience than both us and our parents combined."

"He was a seven-foot tall lizard person who'd broken out of captivity at the quarry, and he'd swept you, my best friend, up in his little escape plot," Axel countered. "What, exactly, should my reaction have been?"

Calum ignored his words and continued. "Then when Riley joined up, you treated him no better than a common dog. You put your interests and yourself first to the extent that you would've rather seen Riley *die* in order to inflict just a little more punishment on Condor for attacking Lilly."

"That's not fair," Axel interjected again. "I apologized to Riley for that. We're square now, and it wasn't like I was—"

"Will you *shut up?*" Calum snapped.

Axel's eyes widened with a familiar type of anger—the kind of fury he demonstrated whenever Calum and Magnus sided with each other against him, but more actively angry than mopey.

But he'd shut up, so Calum kept talking.

"And then there's you and Lilly—"

"Watch yourself, Calum," Axel warned with a point of his finger.

"You had her trust, then you completely broke it because of some misguided belief that she was in love with you." Calum felt good saying it, even though he knew it was prickling Axel. Perhaps that was *why* he was enjoying it. "After all your overtures and demonstrations of affection toward her, you screwed it up in one afternoon. You betrayed her, and it almost got you killed, and you *still* didn't learn from it."

"I'm not gonna warn you again, Calum." Axel's voice took on a menacing tone, and he spoke through gritted teeth. "Tread carefully."

"But that's nothing compared to how you've treated me this whole time." Calum yielded to the burning in his chest, to the words streaming from his core out into the open. "Even before we left, you always made me feel like I was less than dirt. Like I was nothing. No good. You're supposed to be my friend, but all you do is pick on me."

"You're lying." Axel was shaking his head.

"You fight me at every turn. I can't make a decision without hearing your opinion on it. I can't do anything without your royal seal of approval. I can't fend for myself unless you're there to clean up after me," Calum almost shouted. "You claim to be my friend, but that's not friendship. That's abuse. That's enslavement. That's—"

Axel's fist slammed into Calum's mouth, and Calum went down with the taste of copper behind his tingling lips.

CHAPTER 21

Calum could hardly believe it. Axel had punched him. He'd outright punched him.

Now Axel stood over Calum, pointing an accusatory finger at him. "You wanna call me out? You're an ungrateful, miserable excuse for a friend. I spent *years* looking after you, watching over you, slipping you extra food. Then, when we went on the road, I saved your life more times than I can count, and I can count pretty high.

"I've bled for you and your cause. I've killed for you, too. I helped you find Lumen. I helped you survive every imaginable threat along the way. I kept you alive *because* you're my friend," Axel asserted. "And *this* is the thanks I get? You compare me to when you were *enslaved?*"

Calum shook his head and scoffed. He wiped the blood from his mouth and spat some of it onto the street. It spattered red on the cobblestones, and he stood to his feet.

"Once again, you're proving my point. You think it's all about you."

"You *said* it was all about me!" Axel almost shouted. "That was pretty much your leading statement."

"I said you were a jerk because of how you treat people," Calum corrected. "Do you really not see the pattern? How you're like this with everyone, including me?"

"Everything I do, I do to protect you and me." Axel clapped his hand on his breastplate. "I couldn't care less about anyone else. It's you and me."

Calum shook his head. "So you just punched me because you were protecting me?"

If Axel tried to justify that one, Calum was going to—

"Absolutely," Axel said. "If you get out of line, someone's gotta put you back into your place."

That was it. Calum raised his left hand and summoned Lumen's light. The familiar burn raked from his palm through his fingers and crept up his wrist into his forearm. Then a bright flash emitted from his hand, and Axel recoiled, clutching at his eyes.

Calum lunged forward, driving his shoulder into Axel's gut. He wrapped both arms around the back of Axel's knees, lifted up, and angled to the left, taking him off his feet and to the ground. His armor clanked against the cobblestone street.

A litany of curses spilled from Axel's mouth, but curses alone wouldn't stop Calum from repaying Axel for the punch and much more. Calum got on top of Axel's chest and rained punch after punch down at Axel's head.

Axel blocked most of them with his forearms and hands, still cursing up a storm, but a few landed. One in particular smashed clean into Axel's nose, eliciting a yelp and igniting the first of many desperate thrashes to unseat Calum from his position.

Try as he might, Calum couldn't hold on, and Axel actually did manage to force him off. The two of them ended up on their sides, scrambling for the dominant position in the street.

Axel must've been able to see again because he started throwing more punches of his own. He managed to gain the upper hand and got on top of Calum, primed to repay him for the onslaught he'd just received.

But before Axel could land even a single blow, Calum flared Lumen's light again. The old burn returned, and Calum gritted his teeth from the pain, but the flash worked a second time. Axel flinched, again clutching at his eyes and crying out, and Calum managed to get free.

Now Axel was on his hands and knees, rubbing his eyes with one hand and feeling around for Calum with the other.

Calum wasn't ever going to be stronger than Axel. That was a reality he'd accepted long ago. But since they'd started training together, Magnus had taught Calum enough hand-to-hand combat that Calum knew how to win without the disparity in their strength levels being as much of a factor.

It was devious, but it would work, so Calum went for it.

While Axel was still on his knees, Calum faced him, reached down, and wrapped his arms around Axel's neck, careful to keep his head pinned under his chest. If Axel managed to get his head to pop free, the move wouldn't work, so Calum sprawled out his legs and used his weight to keep Axel in place.

Then he began to lift his forearms up, gradually choking Axel, who sputtered and tried to protest, but to no avail. He clawed at Calum's armored forearms and tried to shake him off, but it was too late. The choke was already too deep and too far progressed.

Calum kept squeezing. The choke wouldn't kill Axel, but if Calum held on long enough, it would send Axel on a nice little trip through the stars, and he'd wake up not long afterward confused and uncertain. It wouldn't do any lasting harm unless Calum held it for way too long, and no matter how horrible Axel had been, he didn't deserve that kind of treatment.

In seconds, Axel's arms went limp, and the sputtering stopped. Calum held on for another second, just for good measure. When he finally let go, Axel slumped to the street on his belly, unconscious.

Two times during his training with Magnus, Calum had been put to sleep as well. When he'd awakened, he'd seen Magnus standing over him, holding his ankles up, and gently shaking his legs. Calum didn't know exactly how it worked, but apparently it helped the blood get back to his brain faster.

With great difficulty, Calum flipped Axel onto his back, grabbed his ankles, and began to shake his friend's legs. Sure enough, Axel's eyes opened, and he began to blink and stare at the sky as fresh air filled his lungs anew. He convulsed a few times, but even that was normal, Magnus had said.

Once Calum was sure Axel had crossed over from the land of dreams, he let his legs drop and leaned over his face. Thanks to Calum's one really good punch, blood trickled from Axel's nose and down to his lips.

Calum wanted to say a lot of things to Axel in that moment, but none of them felt right. This moment, triumphant as it was for Calum, was bittersweet at best. Yes, he'd finally beaten Axel in a fight, but at what cost to their friendship?

What friendship? Calum's inner voice challenged him.

With nothing better to say, Calum looked down at Axel and said, "When you're ready to stop being unconscious, come back and join us."

Axel blinked and tried to speak, but his words slurred.

Close enough, Calum decided. Then he turned and left Axel in the street.

CALUM HAD CHEATED.

In a fair fight, straight up, there was no way Axel would've lost. That flashing palm-thing gave Calum an unfair advantage. How was Axel supposed to fight if he couldn't see?

No, he and Calum had not been created equally. Axel was strong, had great reflexes, and a natural sense of aggression that helped make him a better fighter.

And he *was* the better fighter—there was no doubt in his mind about it. Take away that stupid light in Calum's palm, and the outcome would've been very different.

Axel wiped another drip of blood from his nose as he stood to his feet. He gingerly dabbed at his nose. At least it wasn't broken.

Calum had gotten off easy. He could hide a bloody mouth just by keeping his lips sealed.

Axel cursed him for that and so many other reasons. *What an ungrateful twit.*

For the last year—longer than that, now—Axel had done nothing but have Calum's back throughout all of the madness that had entered their lives. It had resulted in a sprawling adventure, and if he'd had the chance to do it over again, he would've. The alternative was staying back at his family farm, living out the boring life that had been planned for him.

But hearing Calum say those things grated on Axel's very core. It wasn't that Calum was right —it's that he was so far off base that he'd stopped making sense, and Axel had given up on listening.

More importantly, after that fight, Axel had given up on Calum, too.

Axel tilted his head back and pinched his nose shut, trying to get it to stop dripping blood. He felt the coppery tang of the warm liquid oozing down the back of his throat, but he didn't care. As long as it stopped bleeding, he'd be content with that.

Faces peered at him from within the surrounding buildings, most of which still had dead vines from the rose golems draped over their sides. Whether or not they'd seen the fight didn't matter. It was too late now, and these people weren't a threat to him.

Although he kind of wished someone would come out and try something. It would give him a chance to vent some excess fury at what had happened with Calum.

In the aftermath of this fight, though, Axel had to ask himself if he'd actually gotten weaker, or if Calum had finally gotten stronger than him.

Yes, Calum had cheated, but Axel still should've been able to pull through and beat him. Yet he hadn't.

Axel cursed, cleared his throat, and spat a dark-red glob of blood and mucus onto the street. He was too weak. Worse yet, Calum had been granted power he didn't deserve.

Why should the weakest person be granted some great power? Or even a boring one like Calum's? Shouldn't it have gone to Axel instead? Someone already strong and capable?

It wasn't *fair*. If Lumen had given him the power he'd promised, this all would've been different.

By that point, the bleeding seemed to have tapered off. Axel sniffed hard a few times, collected another wad in his throat, and hacked it out. Another few sniffs told him he'd gotten the blood under control, and he huffed as he started walking back toward the army.

But he'd already made a decision about his future.

If they reunited with Lumen and he didn't grant Axel some real power, Axel was done. He'd collect his few belongings and go. Where to, he didn't know. He couldn't go back to the farm, but he'd visited plenty of interesting places along the way. Any of them would do for him to start over, away from all of this needless drama.

For now, that was the only reason he was sticking around. Calum had made it clear how the others felt about him—Lilly included... that one stung, if he were honest—so he might as well get out of there if he couldn't gain anything by staying.

This was Calum's fight. It always had been.

Either Lumen would grant Axel the power he desired, or he would leave, and none of them would ever see him again.

When he reached the army again, he exhaled a ragged breath, cracked his neck, and quickly disappeared among their ranks.

THE NEXT MORNING, Calum awoke earlier than anyone else. It was still dark out, and aside from the few dozen guards posted around the army's haphazard campsite near the melted wall, he had the morning to himself.

He glanced over at Axel's bedroll, which lay a few dozen yards away, separated by a row of other bedrolls and the Saurians and Windgales sleeping in them. They hadn't talked to each other since the fight. He'd hardly even seen Axel in camp outside of the one time their eyes met around dinnertime, but even that was fleeting as neither of them saw fit to maintain eye contact.

Part of Calum wondered if he'd been too hard on Axel. He'd said some pretty awful things to the man he'd once called his best friend.

But they'd been true things as well.

Still... Calum had unloaded all of it on Axel out of anger. Even if he'd told the truth, he'd done it with the wrong motivation. That still made it wrong.

And that meant Calum needed to try to make it right.

As if on cue, Axel stirred in his bedroll and sat up, blinking in the low light of predawn. He distinctly looked over at Calum, and though it was mostly dark, Calum had no doubt that their eyes met, for only the second time in nearly half a day.

Then Axel looked away, laid back down, and went back to sleep.

Calum sighed. Why did Axel have to make everything so difficult?

Well, he wouldn't fall back asleep now. He might as well get up and start making preparations for the army's exit from Kanarah City.

But first, some breakfast. He'd think better with a full belly.

Calum packed up his bedroll, stood to his feet, and headed toward the building they'd commandeered as a mess hall.

LATER THAT DAY, Lilly flew overhead as Calum led their army through Kanarah City and toward the south gate. She couldn't help but think the journey would've gone faster if they'd led the army back through the destroyed wall and around the city instead. It certainly would've been simpler.

It took a concerted effort on behalf of the ranking officers among both the Wolves and the Saurians to keep their numbers in order. The Wolves wanted to loot the entire city, the Saurians wanted to raze it to the ground, and both groups had no qualms about attacking the citizens hiding within their homes while no doubt praying the invading army would pass them by.

Part of Lilly wished the Wolves and Saurians could be more disciplined like her fellow Windgales, but that type of thinking was akin to wishing the stars would rearrange themselves in the sky. Neither race could change their inherent natures, and hoping otherwise amounted to nothing but foolishness.

In the end, the army reached the city's south gate with only minimal pilfering and damage along the way. Once there, a pair of large Sobeks hefted the huge crossbeam out of the brackets mounted to the doors and tossed it aside. Then the massive metal doors yawned open, and the southern road beckoned the army forth.

Rather than leaving Captain Anigo and his surviving soldiers behind, Calum had decided to bring them along, so he had them shackled and chained and escorted along with the army. Given the overwhelming numbers surrounding them, Lilly doubted any of them would be foolish enough to try to escape.

If any of them might've been a problem, it would've been Captain Anigo himself, but Calum had wisely separated him from the rest of the group and placed him under the charge of two Sobeks and two Werewolves whose only task was to see to it that Captain Anigo didn't try to escape.

Half the day later, the Golden Plains gleamed at them, aglow with amber under the afternoon sunlight. But no matter how beautiful it looked, Lilly could only think of one thing as she flew toward it. Phantom pain jabbed at her shoulder from the arrow wound, now long since healed thanks to Magnus's veromine.

"It really is a marvelous sight to behold, don't you think?" Condor's voice broke into Lilly's memories but didn't cut them off entirely. "All that grain waving up at us like an endless rippling pool of golden light."

Lilly glanced at him. She didn't really want to explain her feelings or share the memories of her escape from Roderick with him, so she simply replied, "It certainly is."

Though Condor's eyes scrutinized her, his words didn't dig any deeper. For that, she was grateful.

Unlike the last time she'd visited these plains, a dark island of timber and stone and the colorful fabric of tents punctuated the expansive ocean of grain. It had to be at least half the size of Kanarah City, which alone gave Lilly pause.

She didn't know for sure what the population of Kanarah City was, but a rough guess at how many men occupied the camp set up in the center of the Golden Plains told her that Lumen's army dwarfed theirs. Evidently, he'd managed to recruit far more humans than Lilly had imagined.

Then again, he was Lumen, after all. Even the mere sight of him had ignited a new fire within her, the likes of which she'd never known. She'd believed in him from the moment she first laid eyes on him, and afterward, he'd proven himself every bit as powerful as the legends had claimed.

Now it made sense that he'd sent her, Calum, and the others to muster a force from Western Kanarah; he'd done exactly what he'd promised and raised an army of his own during that time.

At the sight of Magnus's approach and his enormous form blotting out the sun, the camp buzzed with a mixture of excitement and fear. Shouts went up from the men standing watch, and before long, every soldier, whether they be man or woman, took up arms as if to fend him off with mere steel.

Several of the archers nocked arrows, but before anyone could loose even a single shot, Lumen materialized in the sky between his camp and Magnus's incoming form.

Even from far away, Lilly could hear his voice booming across the plains.

"Stand down," he ordered his men. "This Dragon leads one third of my Western Army. He is on our side, and he is a valuable ally in our endeavor to liberate Kanarah."

As Magnus's wings flapped faster to slow his descent, kicking up dirt and loose stalks of grain, the soldiers lowered their weapons and instead shielded their faces. Magnus landed with a heavy thud that elicited more than several surprised yelps and gasps, but they all soon quieted when he rose to his full height.

Magnus lowered his head, and Calum slid off and stood next to him. Lilly, Condor, and General Balena landed nearby, and Riley appeared from within the shadow of one of Magnus's wings to join them.

The throngs of soldiers marveled at their presence with wide eyes and open mouths—or perhaps they were still marveling at Lumen's glory as he descended to meet his generals.

As before, Lumen's brilliant appearance struck something deep within Lilly, filling her with hope and comfort as she looked upon him. The sensations replaced the negative feelings she'd associated with this place, and she hoped they would disappear forever from that point on.

Lumen's boots touched the bare dirt on which the camp had been erected, and he extended his arms out to his sides. "Come forward, you who are faithful and true, so that we can celebrate the union of our two armies."

Lilly caught Calum glancing at her and the others, but then they all stepped forward, except for General Balena and Magnus, the latter of whom was so big that he didn't need to. As if taking General Balena's place, Axel stepped out from among the army behind them and approached.

Lilly's brow furrowed at the sight of him. Naturally, he'd shown up when it was time to take credit.

But even though she'd had her fair share of disagreements and spats with Axel, he *had* been with Calum from almost the very beginning. For that reason, she supposed he deserved to stand among them.

Lumen surveyed the army behind Lilly and the others with those burning white eyes of his, and he gave a slow nod. "With the combined strength of all four of Kanarah's peoples, we are all but assured victory. All that remains now is to seize the freedom that is rightfully ours."

Lilly caught herself nodding along. How could she not? After all that had happened, she had to believe Lumen would make this world a better place than it had been before. Better than the one that had seen her taken captive as a slave, her parents murdered, her realm nearly destroyed, her people nearly obliterated.

If Lumen could truly usher in the liberty and peace he claimed, maybe no one else would ever have to suffer the sort of trauma that Lilly had endured.

"*Liar!*"

The shout came from behind Lilly, somewhere amid the army behind her. She and the others turned back to look as the voice shouted the word a second time.

"*Liar!*"

Before them, Lumen's arms slowly lowered, and his white-hot gaze landed on the person shouting the accusation: Captain Anigo.

The Saurians guarding him quickly moved to muffle his cries, but Lumen extended his hand forward and spoke.

"Do not silence him," he commanded, and the Saurians halted their efforts to quiet Captain Anigo. "Bring him forward."

A moment later, Captain Anigo stood before Lumen, still flanked by two Saurians and two Werewolves, as if Lumen somehow needed them around to manage their prisoner.

"I will not hold it against you, but do you truly refuse to bow before the savior of your people?" Lumen asked.

Captain Anigo scowled at him. "You're no savior of mine. I serve the King."

"You serve the King," Lumen repeated. "The same King who let your fellow soldiers perish only yesterday in a pointless battle against the army which now stands behind you? Why would you serve such a man?"

"He's more of a man than you'll ever be." Captain Anigo spat on the ground near Lumen's feet, but the action didn't faze Lumen at all. "He is the one true descendant of the Overlord, and Kanarah is his to rule by divine right."

"Your King oppresses his people and sacrifices them for his own gain, yet this 'divine right' you speak of somehow absolves him of his sins?" Lumen challenged. "A 'divine right' which is a blatant falsehood that has been perpetuated by the King for centuries?"

"Say whatever you want." Captain Anigo sneered at Lumen. "I will not yield to you. I will remain faithful to the oath I swore to my King until my last breath."

Lumen's stare didn't waver. "I wonder if, perhaps, your fellow soldiers will feel the same way?"

With another order, the remaining soldiers in captivity from the battle at Kanarah City came forward, escorted by Wolves, Windgales, and Saurians from within the army. The formed a loose cluster to Captain Anigo's left, and Lumen regarded them in silence for a long moment just as they regarded him.

Finally, he said, "Soldiers of the King, the time has come for you to choose. Either you will continue to serve a King who does not care for your wellbeing, who eagerly sacrificed you knowing full well that the forces stationed at Kanarah City would fail in the face of such over-whelming odds, who betrayed you unto death itself...

"...or you are welcome to join me in usurping the evil King and removing him from this world once and for all," Lumen continued. "And in doing so, you will become my co-heirs to the throne, just as every living soul in Kanarah will be free to rule themselves. You may choose the path that leads to certain death, or you may choose the path of light. Which will it be?"

The soldiers glanced among each other, and several looked to Captain Anigo as if for guidance, but he met them only with a stern expression and a perpetually shaking head.

"Perhaps a demonstration of my power is in order?" Lumen suggested. "Is there one who would volunteer?"

None of the King's soldiers dared to move, and Lilly couldn't blame them. They doubtless understood that Lumen's power far surpassed their own, and they hadn't even seen what he'd done to the soldiers accompanying Matthios into battle.

When still no one replied, Lumen pointed toward one of the soldiers at random. Glowing white light outlined the man, and his chains and shackles fell away as the light lifted him up from the crowd, into the air, and toward Lumen.

"You will do nicely," he said.

The soldier squirmed and struggled against Lumen's power to no avail, despite being freed from his bonds. The sight sent a shudder through Lilly's chest, but she didn't show any emotion.

"No! Please!" the soldier pleaded. "I'll join you! I'll swear fealty right now—just—please don't—"

"*Enough!*" Captain Anigo shouted. He somehow twisted free of his Saurian captors and stormed toward Lumen with his hands still shackled. The Werewolves caught up to him in a flash of darkness and clamped onto his arms, but he'd already separated himself enough from everyone else to stand out—to stand alone before the General of Light.

Lilly waited and watched.

Captain Anigo's heart roared in his chest, oversaturated with all manner of negative emotions. One of his soldiers had already defected to Lumen's army just to spare his own life. Did the man have no honor? No self-respect?

Worse than that, though, was the brilliant and terrifying being who stood before him, a beacon of blazing white daylight burning even brighter than the afternoon sun.

Lumen's eyes raged like two diamonds ignited with the purest white flame. His golden crown gleamed almost as if it were translucent, and a white mask of metal covered the bottom half of his face, matching the rest of his pristine armor.

Light emanated from every inch of his body. He had no shadow, no darkness within him or even near him whatsoever. His form was the picture of perfection—broad and powerful, tall, commanding. Faultless. Flawless. Ideal in every way.

The longer Captain Anigo stared, the more he questioned his resolve. He'd sworn an oath— he'd sworn his very *life* to the King's service, but here before him stood a being so immaculate that it called everything Captain Anigo had ever believed into question.

Why was he so intent on serving the King? Why shouldn't he join this righteous warrior? Why should he die for a lost cause? Why shouldn't he instead fight for someone worthy of his prowess and capabilities as a soldier? As a leader?

With power like Lumen's, who could ever hope to stand against him?

When Captain Anigo blinked, a negative version of Lumen's being imprinted on the inside of his eyelids, scarring his vision as if he'd glanced at the sun or stared too long into a campfire at night. The light Lumen emitted seemed to flow everywhere Captain Anigo could see, whether his eyes were closed or not.

It even seemed to pierce *through* him. It burrowed deep inside of his body, filtering into his veins and arteries, into his blood and bones, saturating his flesh and organs, all the while heading for his heart and his mind.

No, he realized—the light was already *in* his mind. It was shifting his thoughts. Twisting and turning his allegiances. Manipulating and manhandling his memories. Threatening to take from him everything he'd ever held dear in this life. Hunting down, capturing, and slaughtering his purpose.

The light knocked on the door of his heart, but Captain Anigo refused to open it.

His lips unlocked—he hadn't realized they'd been sealed shut in the first place—and he spoke for the first time in what seemed like ages.

"I reject your offer, *traitor*." He spat the insult as if he'd thrown his lance clear into Lumen's heart. "I serve the one true King of Kanarah, and I will not be swayed by your sorcerous ways. Whether I live or die, the King will put a swift end to your rebellion, and he will destroy you once and for all. I swear it by the Overlord himself."

Lumen shook his head, and his light seemed to dim ever so slightly. "A wicked and corrupt generation rejects the truth, even when I have given them a sign. I had hoped you, in particular, would join our cause, honorable Captain Anigo, but your misplaced loyalty to the King has damaged your soul beyond repair."

Captain Anigo's heart continued to thrum in his chest, and his breathing quickened. His death was imminent, and he knew it.

"As such, you will serve as an example to all who would stand against me," Lumen continued. "For anyone who is not for me is against me, and I cannot tolerate the scourge of oppression in any form if we are to remake Kanarah in the image of peace.

"But do not fear, Captain Anigo, for you shall serve as a beacon on a hill, as a light shining in the darkness for all who will follow after you." Lumen's voice took on a darker tone. "And then everyone will finally know the truth."

Lumen's hand rose, and the Werewolves released their grasp on Captain Anigo's arms.

An unseen force seized Captain Anigo from the inside of his chest and began to squeeze.

He gasped, but the pressure stole his breath.

He looked down and saw white light glowing through his silver armor as if his breastplate, undershirt, and skin were made of glass. The trampled grain beneath his feet dropped away, and he found himself hovering in the air, unable to breathe and barely even able to think.

Then a voice entered his mind, speaking in impressions rather than words.

It told him that even though his heart could not be won…

…it could still be crushed.

Captain Anigo's eyes widened as the pressure in his chest sharpened.

CHAPTER 22

"Stop!" Calum found himself shouting as he hurried forward. "Wait!"

To his surprise, Lumen actually did stop his attack—or whatever it was.

With a furrowed brow, Lumen fixed his blazing white eyes on Calum. The sight sent a shock of dread rippling through Calum's body, but he'd grown so accustomed to seeing Lumen in his dreams that he didn't let it alter his course or his mindset.

He positioned himself between Lumen and Captain Anigo, who still hung in the air by an unseen power, even though the light in his chest had faded to nothing. As far as Calum could tell, Captain Anigo was still alive.

"What are you doing?" Lumen asked.

Calum wondered that himself. His mind stuttered, but words refused to tumble out of his mouth. He swallowed the lump in his throat, recalibrated his thoughts, and spoke.

"I don't think you should kill him," Calum said.

Silence hung in the air around him. It permeated the entirety of both armies and their commanders. The only sound Calum could hear was the faint hiss of wind caressing the ocean of grain around them.

It lasted forever and ended abruptly as Lumen asked, "Why?"

Calum's breath caught in his throat. The only response he could muster was, "He can't hurt us anymore. He doesn't need to die."

"He stands with the King. He represents everything we are fighting to change," Lumen countered. "I gave him a chance, and he declined my offer to—"

"But he hasn't seen a world like the one you're going to make out of Kanarah." Calum realized he'd just interrupted arguably the most powerful being in the world, but he continued anyway. "He doesn't know what he's missing, and demonstrating your power alone won't be enough to convince everyone. I know. I tried."

The more Calum thought about it, the more he realized that the power Lumen had gifted him had actually convinced no one. He couldn't point to a single person in Kanarah who'd joined because they'd seen Lumen's light glowing in his hand.

Sure, the light had inspired the army once they'd all banded together, but Lilly, Riley, and

Magnus had done the heavy lifting when it came to actually rallying their people to join the cause. With only the light alone, Calum still would've been trying to raise an army, probably fruitlessly, in Western Kanarah.

It struck Calum as odd that it hadn't worked, but when he considered that the blessing he'd received from Lumen amounted to almost nothing compared to the General of Light's true power, it made sense. Seeing Lumen wield the entirety of his might dwarfed the little bit of light glowing from Calum's hand.

"Anyone who refuses to believe in our cause must be cast into the outer darkness," Lumen asserted. "But even in their denial of my power, they can still serve our cause. They can draw others to us as shining beacons of hope in the darkness, lighting the way for any who wish to be free of the King's oppression."

Calum started to say, "He doesn't need to—"

"Allow me to demonstrate." It was Lumen's turn to interrupt. He quickly added, "I will not harm him in any way. Rather, I will ask a question of his fellow soldiers. They have seen enough at this point to choose for themselves which path they will follow."

Lumen faced the soldiers, who continued to stare at him with bewilderment and fear in their wide eyes.

"Which path do you choose?" Lumen asked them. "Do you choose light and life, or will you suffer darkness and death? Step forward and swear your oaths to me, and in doing so, you will attain true freedom for the rest of your lives."

Without hesitation, every single one of the soldiers scrambled forward, their chains clinking as they moved. In quick succession, they each dropped to their knees and swore oaths to Lumen, none of which Calum could make out due to their quiet voices.

He got the impression that they were almost... *ashamed* to be doing it, but they'd come over eagerly enough, so he disregarded the notion as a foolish wandering of his mind.

By the time they finished, Lumen had added a few dozen more soldiers to his ranks, and he'd proven his point as promised: *without* harming Captain Anigo.

The soldiers' shackles and chains fell off in unison, and light from Lumen shined from each of their chests, though not as brightly as it had from Captain Anigo's. They marveled at the sight of their liberated limbs and at the lights emanating from inside of them, and then they exchanged huge smiles and laughter as they rushed past Lumen to join the rest of his army.

When Calum looked back, Captain Anigo was just shaking his head and staring at the ground with a look of disgust etched into his face.

"Better to have died," he muttered. "Better to have died."

"Now do you see, my child?" Lumen asked Calum.

Calum had seen it, alright, but he still didn't want Captain Anigo to die—or whatever else Lumen was going to do to him.

He faced Lumen once again. "Keeping him alive and unharmed costs us virtually nothing. I'm asking you, as a personal favor to me, to let Captain Anigo live."

As before, silence enveloped both sides of the army. Calum could feel the heaviness of his friends' gazes weighing on his back, almost as potent as the energy emitting from Lumen's eyes.

None of it changed his resolve.

With a slight tilt of his head, Lumen spoke once more. "If, by the end of our campaign, Captain Anigo still fails to see the wonders we will bring about in this world, then he will perish the same as the rest of our foes. Until then, I will relent. He will not be harmed. You have my word."

Relief flooded Calum's chest, though he didn't totally know why. Captain Anigo had, almost without exception, only tried to capture or kill Calum and his friends. The one time they'd cooperated was to survive against the Gronyxes under Kanarah City, and even then, they'd almost turned on each other right afterward.

So why had Calum intervened at all?

The truth was, he didn't know. He supposed it was like when he'd stopped Magnus from killing Riley back at their camp in the mountains. He hadn't deserved to die, and Calum couldn't definitively say that Captain Anigo deserved it, either.

Above all else, now, with Lumen set free and two massive armies unified under his command, Calum had to believe that even someone as staunch in his dedication to the King would see the truth for what it was. And if there was hope for Captain Anigo, there was hope for everyone in Kanarah to be set free.

"Better to have died," Captain Anigo repeated. He met Calum's eyes, frowning. "You'll see. When the King displays his full power, you'll see."

Something about Captain Anigo's tone—perhaps it was his certainty—unnerved Calum, but before he could respond, Lumen ordered the Werewolves to take Captain Anigo away.

"Come," Lumen opened his arms wide, beckoning Calum and the others forward. "We have food aplenty and much to discuss. Tomorrow, we march for Solace to take back Kanarah for her people."

THOUGH AXEL HAD to admit the feast that night was the stuff of legends, straight out of the songs and musings of old men with bushy beards and too much time on their hands, he couldn't help but be furious that Lumen still hadn't bestowed any power on him yet.

In fairness, Lumen hadn't granted any new abilities to Calum or the others, either, but it still bothered Axel that he hadn't gotten so much as a congratulatory handshake from the General of Light yet, much less the power he'd promised them.

Together with Lumen, Axel and the others had taken seats of honor inside a sprawling patch-work tent haphazardly sown together by blind men, from the looks of it. Rough-hewn logs, sawn in half lengthwise and placed atop hollowed out trunks of trees, formed impromptu banquet tables. Similar logs had been thatched together outside to form a robust wooden fence around the camp.

Axel folded his arms and leaned back in his chair. Unlike everything else in the tent, at least it was a real chair. Someone must've brought it with them from Kanarah City, or wherever they'd come from, when they'd joined Lumen's army.

But for all the lack of opulence inside the tent, the light produced by Lumen inside made up for it.

Crystalline streaks of pure light, some long like icicles and others the size of gemstones, glittered and shimmered overhead. They floated independently of each other, unhindered by the laws of nature, casting beautiful and tranquil light into the space.

Axel had to admit the lights were pretty impressive. But they also reinforced his frustration at having to wait for Lumen to give him what he rightfully deserved—no, what he'd *earned*.

Lumen had intended to make them into Imperators—or at least that's what he'd said before they'd departed to raise his army from Western Kanarah. Now Axel wondered if Lumen could even do such a thing.

He'd seen Lumen do other amazing things, from slaying a Jyrak with one swing of his incredible sword to obliterating all of Matthios's soldiers in a single powerful blast, but those events stood in stark contrast with the meager power he'd granted to Calum. It was weak and mostly useless—much like Calum himself, Axel supposed, but that wasn't the point.

The point was that if Lumen could have done more, why hadn't he?

Maybe he can't, Axel decided. *Or maybe he just won't.*

As Axel continued brooding, Calum plopped into the seat next to him. The skin on the back of Axel's neck bristled, and he thought to straighten his posture, but he didn't. He remained slumped in his own chair, arms folded, still scowling.

Axel had nothing to fear from Calum. After all, Calum had cheated during their fight, and Axel could still knock him out cold any time he wanted. But if he reacted to Calum's approach, it would show weakness. Axel wasn't weak, so he didn't allow himself to react.

Plus, he intended to ignore Calum anyway.

"I still can't believe we made it," Calum said. "And the size of Lumen's army is beyond—"

"I have nothing to say to you," Axel interrupted. *So much for just ignoring him.* "So move along."

"C'mon, Axel." Calum gave a small laugh. "It was just a scrap. You lost one—finally."

"I said I'm *not* talking to you." Axel had made eye contact with Calum once already, but he refused to do it again. He continued to stare forward, eyebrows arched down.

Calum sighed. "Look, I know I owe you an apology."

Axel met Calum's eyes, even though he'd just sworn not to. "I'm not gonna say it again, Calum. Get out of my face, or I'll *make* you leave."

An instant of hesitation crossed Calum's face, but it didn't last nearly long enough. His expression hardened to match Axel's, and he quipped, "Just like you did in our fight, right?"

Axel had to hand it to Calum—he'd always had a spine. Sure, he'd been little more than a weak child when they'd first set out on this wild adventure, but he'd risen to meet every challenge along the way.

Apparently, that also included Axel.

Even so, the comment brought Axel *thisclose* to lurching out of his chair, grabbing Calum by his shoulder, and smashing a bitter elbow into his teeth.

But Axel had decided to keep his rage in check. He was only there for one reason anymore— to claim the power Lumen had promised him.

Not to fight Calum again.

Not to argue with Magnus or Riley.

Not to endure Condor's witticisms.

Not even to pursue Lilly.

Axel just wanted that power. And once he got it, he was gone.

Instead of bashing his elbow into Calum's face, Axel just shrugged, stood, and said, "Fine, then. If you're gonna be a pest, I'll go somewhere else."

As Axel turned to walk away, Calum tried to say something, but thanks to the noise of the soldiers carousing in the tent around them, Axel blocked it out of his mind and kept walking.

"I'm sorry, Axel," Calum called, but even as he said it, he realized it wouldn't be loud enough to reach his friend's ears. Had Calum wanted to shout it, he could've, but he hadn't. Having to shout an apology ruined the idea of apologizing, at least in his mind.

That, and he hadn't actually meant it like he should've.

Calum sighed, but he reminded himself that he knew Axel better than anyone. He'd eventually come back around when his pride had recovered.

Calum allowed his gaze to wander throughout the tent. It landed, of course, on Lilly. She was by far the most pleasant of anyone in either army to look at.

She was wedged between General Balena and Condor, the latter of whom sat facing away from her, talking to Riley, of all people. Evidently, somewhere in all the traveling, they'd reconciled and left their violent past behind.

On the other side, General Balena's imposing form shielded Lilly like an enormous black owl protecting one of its young, but he, too, was entrenched in a conversation, this time with General Tolomus.

That left Lilly sitting there alone, wearing a disinterested expression and poking at the remnants of her dinner on the plate in front of her. Even bored out of her mind, she still captivated every iota of Calum's attention.

Then she looked up and found his eyes.

Neither of them broke their stare.

Calum tried to convey everything he felt for her through his gaze and his face, but he worried the combination might be making him look like he was grimacing, or in pain, or that he had a stone in his boot. He supposed, in a way, all of those applied to some extent when it came to Lilly.

Toward the end of their visual lock, Lilly's eyes seemed to soften, but then she blinked and looked away.

Calum wanted to go over to her, but he didn't. Not with Condor right there. Not with General Balena "guarding" her without actually guarding her.

Instead, he turned and started to say something to Magnus, but he remembered Magnus wasn't in the tent. He couldn't have fit in there even if he'd wanted to, so he'd taken several of his Sobeks on a hunting excursion back in the mountains rather than sticking around camp all evening.

With so many hungry Saurians and Wolves, all of whom preferred meat instead of fruits, vegetables, and grains, someone had to provide for their growling bellies as well.

Many of the Wolves had also gone out on their own, but according to Riley, they'd be back by sunrise for sure. They valued independence when possible, and smaller packs had often diverged from the main group to hunt or steal food and resources as they'd traveled from Western Kanarah to the eastern half of the land.

Calum sighed again. He missed having Magnus around to talk to. But now, as the Dragon King, he had less and less time for such things. And with Lilly and Riley both holding similar positions over their own races, and with Axel still mad at him, Calum was alone again.

Just like he'd been back at the quarry.

Calum shook away the feelings that accompanied that dreary thought and stood to his feet. He would find someone to talk to, or, failing that, he'd get some extra rest that night.

He waded into the center of the tent, tried to make eye contact with Lilly once more, and when that failed, he turned his attention to a group of men standing around the center tent post with mugs of ale in their hands.

He greeted them, and they welcomed him over. Someone passed him a fresh mug of ale, and though he'd had his fair share already, Calum didn't refuse.

One of them toasted to Lumen's return and extended his mug forward, as did the other men. Calum mimicked the motion and clanked his mug against several of the others, sloshing ale onto the hard-packed dirt floor, and then he took a drink along with the rest of the men.

Perhaps he wasn't alone after all. Everyone here was on his side. Everyone here wanted the same thing.

And together, they would achieve it.

...at least they would after they finished their drinks.

ONCE OUTSIDE THE TENT, Axel didn't bother to look back. Instead, he sought out his bedroll and his pack among the countless others that now lay outside the tent's outer perimeter like decayed berries fallen from their bush. He found it, snatched it up, and started heading toward the edge of the camp.

Along with Magnus's old armor, which Axel still wore, and the Blood Ore sword sheathed along his back, Axel now carried everything he owned. He'd done it many times before, but this time, he was going off alone, with no one to look out for him—and no one for him to babysit.

These people had frustrated him while they'd traveled together, and they'd outright disappointed him at the end. But nothing was more of a letdown than Lumen and his empty promises.

Axel shook off the sense of loss—not for the people he was leaving behind but for the power that could've been his if only Lumen had been true to his word. If Axel could've gotten even a *taste* of that power, it might've been enough...

But it didn't matter. Well, it *did* matter, but Axel was determined not to let it ruin the rest of his life, or even the rest of that night. He still had a great set of armor, a killer sword, and a lot of fighting and tactics training. He'd easily find work as a mercenary, or he could make a life for himself by protecting a town or a village from bandits.

Really, anything would be better than this.

Axel passed through the camp's perimeter fence and left the tamped-down dirt of the campsite behind. As he stepped into the golden waves of grain stretching for miles beyond, he heard the telltale *shing* of steel being drawn from a scabbard.

His eyes widened, and he reached for his own sword, but it was too late. A silver blade flashed at his midsection.

Axel's left arm moved to intercept the blow, and the weapon pinged off his Blood Ore armor harmlessly, aside from the dull sting of the sword's solid impact on his arm. The next strike came for Axel's head, also faster than he'd expected, but he ducked, and the sword thumped into his pack, still slung from his shoulder, instead.

He let it go and finally managed to get his own weapon drawn. Only then did his attacker emerge from within the grain, clad in amber attire that seemed to shift colors to match its wearer's surroundings. The man also wore a scarf around his head that covered every part of him aside from his eyes, and it, too, also changed colors.

Axel considered crying out for help, but if he couldn't take down one wimpy soldier on his own, then he didn't deserve to live, plain and simple.

Three quick strikes from his opponent clashed against his Blood Ore blade, and then one devastating counterstrike from Axel cleaved deep into the attacker's side. The man gasped and went down in the dirt, and his clothes shifted colors to match, rendering him nearly invisible on the ground.

Axel did him the mercy of finishing him off quickly, then he scanned his surroundings for signs of anyone else. Seeing no one, he reached down to grab the man by his ankle to pull him back toward the camp. As he did, something zipped over his shoulder, right where his head had just been.

He glanced back. Some thirty paces behind him, an had arrow lodged in one of the logs forming the camp's perimeter fence, and he cursed. As soon as Axel looked up, another arrow pinged off his breastplate.

That's when he saw helmets moving through the stalks of grain, drawing ever closer to the camp. If it weren't for the moonlight above that glinted off their metal heads, he never would've seen them.

A third arrow plinked off his shoulder, and he knew it was only a matter of time until one of the archers hit him in his head, so he turned back toward the camp and ran. As he did, he looked out across the sea of grain on both sides.

He saw thousands of glints of moonlight rapidly approaching his camp.

His camp. Was it really his anymore?

Well, with thousands of troops surrounding them, he couldn't get out, so yeah, it was still his camp… at least for now.

Once he made it back inside the fence, he pushed the makeshift gate shut and hefted the heavy wooden beam into its brackets, even though he knew it wouldn't hold for long. Then he headed straight for the main tent, shouting a warning to anyone and everyone who could hear him, as more and more arrows plodded into the dirt all around him, fired blindly by the archers outside the camp.

Almost immediately, the fence gate tore open behind Axel, snapping the wooden beam like a twig. The King's army had come like a thief in the night, and Axel knew they were only there for one reason: to destroy Lumen and his rebellion.

But as Axel yelled, a blinding light appeared before him, in front of the tent.

Lumen held his gleaming sword in his hand, and as if by some silent order, every tent collapsed at once, revealing thousands of armed men, inexplicably ready to engage the King's forces.

With a primal roar, they rushed to meet their enemies in battle.

CHAPTER 23

At the sound of someone shouting that the King's soldiers had come, Captain Anigo's ears perked up. Now, as the lone prisoner who'd remained loyal to the King, he grinned.

His faith and obedience had paid off. He hadn't strayed from his true path, and now escape was potentially only moments away.

The problem was, he was chained around the center post of the second largest tent in the camp. The post was well-rooted in the ground, and he stood no chance of being able to tip it over or break it in order to get free.

But just when he'd resigned himself to wait for rescue, the tent fabric collapsed around him, allowing the men guarding him to rush out into the battle in some sort of half-baked surprise counterattack. Perhaps Lumen had known or anticipated the arrival of the King's men tonight, or perhaps he'd made sure his men stayed vigilant at all times.

Either way, the tent went down, the men guarding Captain Anigo left him behind, and he realized there was, in fact, one way he could escape on his own: up.

The tent post loomed overhead, about fifteen feet high. Now, without the heavy tent fabric at the top of the post, all Captain Anigo had to do was climb up the post, unsling his chains, and then climb back down to his freedom.

Though he was weak and exhausted and had only eaten a few scraps reserved for him by his guards, he marshaled what strength he had left, bolstered by the prospect of escape, and began to climb.

CALUM HAD PICKED the worst possible time to carouse with his new friends, but even so, the arrival of the King's army hadn't caught him fully unprepared. At least he was still wearing his armor and still had the Dragon's Breath sword strapped to his back.

The idea of fighting while slightly inebriated—or perhaps more than slightly—concerned him, but the first clashes of battle around him sobered him quickly. Flanked by his new friends, he rushed out to meet the enemy head-on with his fiery sword in hand.

War raged under the moonlight, yet the Dragon's Breath sword and the light from Lumen cast much more light across the campsite. Even so, deep shadows reached across the campsite, grasping at the soldiers like long claws scraping for purchase against the light.

Calum ran through the camp, occasionally clashing with whichever of the King's soldiers managed to break through the front lines. Were it not for the extreme power of the Dragon's Breath sword, Calum would've succumbed to their numbers many times over. Instead, he easily cut through the approaching soldiers, their armor, and their weapons.

That is, until Calum swung his sword at a man literally twice his size.

Rather than cleaving through the man's axe as if it were paper, the weapon actually stopped the Dragon's Breath sword entirely. The axe flared with bright amethyst light upon impact, and it glimmered with crystalline refractions both up and down its shaft and within the axe head itself.

The sight briefly reminded Calum of the Calios, but this was different. It was more like the entire weapon was meticulously carved out of a single massive gemstone rather than forged of metal.

In the light given off by the Dragon's Breath, Calum saw the glint of several other gemstone-like elements that made up the man's armor.

His broad breastplate appeared to be cut from a single ruby, his helmet from blue sapphire and its faceplate from a yellow one, and his arm and leg armor looked to be made from emeralds. In his other hand, rather than wielding a shield, he held another axe, this one glistening with the white of crystal or perhaps diamond.

How any of this was possible, Calum couldn't fathom. He'd only ever seen armor made from fabric, leather, or metal—never from gigantic gemstones.

And though Calum had seen large and powerful fighters before, this guy was a literal giant. Even Magnus in his Sobek form wasn't as tall or as broad as this warrior. Perhaps it was just his armor, but every part of the man's body seemed unreasonably oversized, including his hands, his feet, his head, and his torso. It didn't seem possible.

Calum considered that he still might be slightly drunk from all the ale he'd downed prior to the battle, but when that diamond axe swung at his sword, he realized he wasn't imagining things. Though he raised the Dragon's Breath sword to defend, the blow lifted Calum off his feet and sent him tumbling across the campsite in a wild blur.

When he righted himself, the massive man outfitted with gemstone armor was nowhere to be found, but the battle raged on nonetheless. Calum had managed to keep his grip on the Dragon's Breath sword, and for now, that was good enough.

Someone else could handle the gemstone guy. Calum headed back into the battle with the rest of the King's men.

GENERAL BALENA and General Tolomus had abandoned Lilly at her table the instant the alarm was raised, and Riley vanished into the nearest shadow, but Condor stayed at her side, as usual. She found comfort in knowing he'd stuck around when her generals had blasted away without warning, but it also bothered her that she wasn't with them, leading her people.

"Just as I was beginning to get used to the rest and relaxation…" Condor sighed and tugged on her arm. "Come, Premieress. We'd best get you to safety."

Lilly pulled back immediately. "My place is with my people, fighting alongside them."

"A noble and just idea, to be sure," Condor began, "but one that might ultimately get you killed."

"I've survived this long with that 'idea,'" Lilly countered.

"That was before you had an army of Wisps to fight on your behalf and two capable generals to command them."

"And I also have the Calios, which offers even greater protection than you or any number of soldiers can afford me," Lilly asserted.

"Lilly," Condor said, his voice unusually firm, "these are the King's men, attacking us at night. There's a chance the King himself, or at least his Imperators, are among their forces. We cannot risk your life under these conditions."

As if Condor had planned it for that exact moment, half a dozen Wisps in the telltale bright-orange armor of the Royal Guard descended to accompany them.

Lilly knew she should listen to Condor. He was doing his job, and he was doing it well.

But she longed to join her people in battle, to add her power and speed to their cause. That was the whole reason she'd brought them here in the first place. The more she fought, the fewer of them would die trying to bring her vision to fruition.

"You will escort me above the camp, but we will not flee," she declared. "If any of our people —including Lumen's army—need aid, we will assist them. You will all protect me should I choose to engage in the battle."

Lilly stared into Condor's piercing blue eyes, partially for confirmation of her compromise and also for his reassurance that he would, in fact, keep her safe no matter what.

He gave her a solemn nod, and together they ascended out of the tent with her Royal Guard close behind.

AXEL HADN'T STOPPED FIGHTING EVER since he'd returned to the camp.

Lumen hovered above everyone, occasionally lashing out against the King's soldiers with targeted spikes of blinding light, dive-bombing cuts with his sword that reduced his enemies to ash, and even the occasional bolt of lightning from his fingertips. Most importantly, it was Lumen's light that enabled Axel to see who he was fighting.

Thus far, not a single blow had even come close to penetrating Axel's Blood Ore armor. He'd gotten to test it out before, but now, in the most frantic battle he'd ever fought, with enemies coming at him from all angles, the armor really proved its true worth. No wonder Magnus had sworn by it before he'd transformed into a dragon.

For that matter, so did his Blood Ore sword. It was heavy enough to knock most of his enemies backward whenever it connected with their bodies, and it was sharp enough to cut clean through their armor—at least sometimes—when he put enough heft into the swing. He'd even snapped a few lances and spears and managed to break a few swords along the way as well.

Still, he longed for a measure of Lumen's power. If he could match even a fraction of Lumen's wrath on behalf of his people, this fight would end much faster.

Instead, the fracas continued to rage all around him. Lumen's army, now a combined force of humans, Windgales, and a handful of Saurians and Wolves who hadn't gone off to hunt battled side by side, fending off the King's soldiers with fervor and zeal.

They were literally fighting for their freedom—absolute and everlasting, just as Lumen had described it. But even though they fought hard, the King's men continued to advance, continued to progress deeper and deeper into the camp.

No matter how many of them Axel killed or bashed unconscious, more still came. No matter how many Lumen zapped with his lightning or cut down with his silver-and-gold blade, the enemy soldiers continued to invade the camp.

Magnus had sure picked a terrible time to go off hunting with the majority of his Saurians. If he'd been here, they'd have another powerful ally to help thwart the uncountable numbers of soldiers streaming into the camp from every direction, plus durable Saurian soldiers to bolster their ranks.

But this was nothing new. When Axel really needed help from his friends, none came. Calum, Lilly, Riley, and Magnus were all nowhere to be seen. Yet again, Axel was on his own.

That suited him just fine. He didn't need anyone else.

For the time being, all he could do was continue to fight. So that's what he did.

Captain Anigo's boots hit the dirt next to the tent post, but now his hands were no longer shackled around it. He sucked in labored breaths and gave silent thanks to the Overlord.

The shackles themselves still hung from his wrists, but removing them would be nothing to the blacksmiths in Solace. Now he just needed to find a weapon so he could carve a way out of this mess and return to his King's ranks.

Just outside the perimeter of the tent where he'd been held captive, he got his pick of dozens of weapons amid the bodies of slain men, those of Lumen's army and the King's forces alike. Since his hands remained shackled, he chose a sword instead of his preferred weapon, a spear. It would make for easier fighting.

Then Captain Anigo scampered into the campsite, looking for the quickest way to escape.

In a brief lull in the attack, Axel noticed an unusually dressed man running away from one of the downed tents. The man wore neither armor nor even thick clothing, but he carried a sword. His appearance gave away his identity, even more so than the shackles Axel noticed around his wrists.

Captain Anigo.

He thinks he's gonna escape.

Not if Axel could do something about it.

He abandoned his position in the battle and raced after their escaping captive.

Calum noticed Captain Anigo's escape by virtue of him running past in the middle of the battle. Calum blinked to confirm that it was in fact Captain Anigo, and sure enough, his eyes told him the truth.

Their prisoner, the one Calum had shown mercy to, was now fleeing toward enemy lines.

Calum couldn't let that happen. He shoved the man he was fighting aside and then rushed to follow Captain Anigo.

Near the northwestern edge of the camp, the fighting still raged, but less so than in other areas. Calum chased Captain Anigo's footsteps, dodging swords, axes, and spears. He made a mental note to shackle prisoners' ankles from now on.

Out of the corner of his eye, Calum caught a flash of bright blue metal glinting in Lumen's light. He turned his head to the left and saw Axel, clad in his Blood Ore armor, running parallel with Calum some twenty feet away, also pursuing Captain Anigo.

Calum pushed down his sour feelings about Axel. At least they were unified in their purpose once again. They could sort the rest out later.

As Captain Anigo left the majority of the battle behind and approached the outer border of the camp, he slowed to a halt and looked around, as if trying to find a way out. The wall of ten-foot vertical logs, their tops whittled down to sharp points, that fenced in the camp would keep him inside.

"Stop!" Calum shouted at him.

Rather than running again, Captain Anigo turned back to face him, still holding his sword, still wearing shackles.

A battle cry sounded from Calum's left, and Axel charged into view with his Blood Ore sword ready to strike.

As Axel closed the distance, a flood of emotion overtook Calum. Axel was doing what he always did—barreling in headfirst without thinking—and it infuriated Calum. But because of what happened next, he didn't have time to be angry.

Axel's sword lashed through the air, but instead of Captain Anigo blocking the blow, an enormous axe swung into view, catching Axel's strike. Upon impact, bright amethyst light crackled throughout the axe like lightning, and as it faded, the whole weapon glimmered with crystalline refractions.

Terror replaced Calum's irritation with Axel as the gemstone warrior's gigantic form materialized out of thin air. In his wake, a portal burning with violet flames and crackling with amber lightning promptly sealed up behind him.

It was a power similar to Lumen's. If Calum hadn't been convinced that this warrior was one of the King's Imperators before, he certainly was now.

Unsurprisingly, Axel didn't relent. He swung his sword repeatedly, issuing grunts and shouts with each strike as he battled the Imperator, whose gemstone armor glistened with color in the moonlight.

What did surprise Calum was how deftly the Imperator parried each of Axel's attacks. Despite his undoubtedly heavy armor and weapon, the Imperator moved with the alacrity of a dancer, nimble and quick. Twin axes, one amethyst and one diamond, spun and twirled in purple and white blurs, batting Axel's attacks well clear.

Even if any of Axel's blows had gotten through, Calum couldn't imagine his sword would pierce the Imperator's armor. Blood Ore was an incredible metal, but if even the Dragon's Breath sword couldn't damage the Imperator's axe, then Axel's sword stood no chance whatsoever.

Of course, there was no telling Axel that—especially not in the heat of battle. And that elicited another deep emotion within Calum: fear.

The Imperator could easily kill Axel at any moment, and Calum could do nothing to stop it. Despite their differences, Calum didn't want to lose Axel. They were best friends, and no amount of arguing or scuffling would ever change that.

But death very well could.

"Axel!" Calum shouted as he charged to engage the Imperator alongside his friend, but he was already too late.

One massive hack from the Imperator's axe blasted through Axel's attempt to parry the swing, and its blade slammed straight into his chest. The dull *thwack* of Axel's breastplate taking the brunt of the blow resonated like a thunderclap in the night.

Axel's body launched backward, and he smashed into the side of a large wooden wagon and continued clear through it, shattering the wood and collapsing it in the center. He skidded to a halt not far behind, unmoving.

"No!" Calum shouted. The Imperator had no doubt just killed or, best case, severely wounded Axel, and the sight of it made Calum sick.

Rage threatened to overtake him, to hurl him into combat with the Imperator to avenge his friend, but he didn't react to his emotions. Instead, he exhaled a shaky breath and positioned his sword between himself and Captain Anigo and the Imperator, both of whom now stalked toward him.

LILLY HOVERED over the battle with her complement of Windgale warriors. She imagined they must resemble a floating ball of flame, clustered together and clad in bright-orange armor. She'd never quite understood why her ancestors had chosen the vibrant purple and orange colors for the Wisp soldiers; such armor diminished the chances for stealth or surprise almost entirely.

But perhaps that was by design, especially given the Royal Guard's commission to protect the Sovereign of the Sky Realm. Perhaps they were obvious so as to dissuade attacks in the first place.

She glanced at Condor, who drifted next to her, his handsome face illuminated by Lumen's white light. The guards' orange armor certainly hadn't dissuaded him from attacking her father.

But, as her grandmother used to say, "once the bird's been plucked, you can't put the feathers back on."

Below them, Windgale soldiers clashed with the King's forces in the night. Thus far, despite Condor's assurances to the contrary, Lilly had done little to intervene on behalf of her people in the fight.

It wasn't because Condor and the Royal Guard were trying to prevent her from engaging per se; rather, it was more so because whenever she did intervene, her entire Royal Guard descended with her in an intrusion so dramatic that it forced friends and foes alike to flee, or at least to back away.

Lilly's relative ineffectiveness thus far grated on her, but any thoughts of supporting her people on the battlefield faded to the background of her mind as a new threat presented itself.

His molten eyes burning, the Imperator Matthios, the Brazen General, leaped toward them from within the camp with his bronze spear in hand.

In a burst of copper light, his double-bladed spear delivered an explosive blow that sent the majority of Lilly's Royal Guard spiraling away like bright-orange flower petals caught in a maelstrom. Now she was exposed, except for Condor and a few others who'd managed to withstand the attack.

Rather than landing on his feet again, Matthios stayed airborne, continually spinning his spear in brazen arcs as he relentlessly thrashed the remaining Royal Guard protecting Lilly. The sight sent pangs of terror coursing through her veins, but she pushed it away.

She was no ordinary soldier. She wielded the legendary Calios, and she was the Premieress of the Sky Realm. She could fight back.

The Calios burned red-hot in her hands, matching her fiery fury, and she darted toward the Imperator, even as Condor called for her to stay back. He, too, quickly joined the fight as the last of her Royal Guards succumbed to Matthios's brutal attacks and fell from the sky.

The two of them traded lightning-fast attacks with the Imperator, whose bronze spear twirled and clanged against their weapons, deflecting every attack with precision. Only a few months earlier, Lilly doubted she could've even tracked what was happening in this fight, much less actually engage in it. Matthios's speed matched—or perhaps even exceeded—their own.

His bald head glinted with light from the moon and from Lumen's ever-present glow, and the bronze circlet crown on his head inexplicably stayed in place despite his violent swings and parries. Lilly likened fighting him to dueling with a demon; his molten eyes and the bronze face-mask that covered the lower half of his face made him look even more menacing at night.

The Calios hardened to a blade of ice with Lilly's cold resolve, and she sent a frozen stream of it at Matthios. It struck his left arm and coated it with heavy frost, but his constant movement shed the ice as if brushing off a layer of snow.

He counterattacked with ferocity, and Lilly's reservation activated the Calios's rock-solid defenses, transforming her very limbs into movable stone, all but impervious to Matthios's attacks. Meanwhile, Condor assaulted Matthios from behind, trying to land fatal blows on the Imperator while also attempting to pull Matthios's attention away from Lilly.

It worked, but not in the way either Lilly or Condor had hoped.

In a blinding flash of copper, Matthios whirled around and slammed the shaft of his spear into Condor's chest, loud as a blacksmith's hammer. The impact knocked Condor from the sky.

As Lilly's Captain of her Royal Guard fell, she drew in a frantic breath, more out of concern for him than for herself. Every feeling, every sensation she'd come to associate with Condor swirled in her chest and sloshed in her gut, unsettling her. Was she going to lose him?

Matthios didn't give her long to suffer those thoughts. He immediately resumed his attack on her, now even faster than before since he only had one Windgale to contend with.

Lilly did her best to keep up, but even she couldn't match his speed, and neither could the Calios match his power. He disarmed her, and she watched as the Calios plummeted toward the battlefield below.

The next thing she saw was Matthios launching toward her, his molten eyes ablaze, and then nothing but darkness.

THE DRAGON'S Breath sword cut through Captain Anigo's blade with ease, but Calum soon realized his mistake: he'd left himself open to attack from the Imperator.

The first blow nearly knocked his teeth clean out of his head. The Imperator had struck him with the flat side of his amethyst axe rather than with the blade, and the attack left Calum sprawled out in the dirt.

His head swimming, Calum forced himself up to his feet and raised the Dragon's Breath sword. Now, instead of one Gemstone Imperator coming for him, there were two. They both wiggled in his vision like mammoth gemstone-covered worms.

Calum blinked hard to clear the confusion away, and the image of the Imperator sharpened into a solitary wiggling gemstone giant. Not perfect, but better.

He waited for the Imperator to make the first move and ducked under the amethyst axe's first strike. The Dragon's Breath clanged harmlessly against the Imperator's diamond axe, and the amethyst axe came in with a follow-up strike, this time to Calum's left shoulder.

Calum both felt and heard the pop, and then his left arm decided to go limp. He looked down to find it severely dislocated, but he saw no blood. The limb just hung there like a dead fish.

The pain came next, and Calum couldn't stop himself from shouting.

He knew then and there that he'd lost. That it was over.

The Imperator's diamond axe came for him next, and Calum sucked in a final breath before everything went black.

CHAPTER 24

By the time Magnus returned to camp, the battle had already concluded. The King's soldiers, despite having the advantage of surprise and numbers, had fled, leaving behind the ravages of their incursion.

As the first rays of sunlight crept over the horizon, Lumen hovered over the camp, touting the outcome as a victory. The survivors responded with wild and raucous cheers, but for Magnus, it was anything but. Along with Riley, his Wolves, and Magnus's Saurians, they frantically searched the dead for any sign of Calum, Axel, and Lilly.

They found nothing. All three of them were gone.

"What happened?" Magnus asked Condor as Riley helped him to his feet.

Around them, Saurians and Wolves helped those of the Premieress's Royal Guard who'd survived to their feet as well. From their traumatic appearance and the brutalized condition of those who had perished in the battle, Magnus understood that they hadn't faced a normal foe.

Condor's usual sense of confidence and bravado had vanished along with Calum, Axel, and Lilly. Now, at the break of dawn, his haggard appearance more resembled that of when they'd rescued him from Oren's clutches back at the Blood Chasm.

"Matthios," was all he said, followed by a long pause. "It was Matthios. I couldn't..."

Magnus stared down at him. Condor had battled an Imperator and lived?

Magnus had chosen to reserve judgment until he'd gathered enough information to comprehend what had transpired, but upon hearing that Condor had fought with Matthios himself, he immediately abandoned his search for his friends. Instead, he headed straight for Lumen.

"Magnus?" Riley followed him, easily keeping pace with Magnus's thunderous footsteps. "What are you doing?"

Magnus's eyes remained fixed on Lumen, who still hadn't stopped commending his soldiers. "We must act now."

"Act how?" Riley dodged Magnus's heavy footfalls. "Act *how*, Magnus?"

Magnus didn't bother to reply.

As Magnus closed in on Lumen's position, Lumen truncated his oration and turned to face

"Even without the aid of two of our mightiest warriors, we managed to overpower the King's forces," he declared. The soldiers around him raised their weapons and roared with approval. "And now that the mighty Dragon King has returned, we are at full strength yet again. Our victory is assured."

More cheers erupted from the soldiers.

Riley stared up at Lumen with his black eyes and muttered, "Figures I don't even get mentioned."

Magnus ignored Riley's comments. To Lumen, he said, "May I speak with you in private?"

"What could we possibly have to speak about?" Lumen stared at him with burning white eyes. "Our victory is nigh. We have but to claim it."

"We cannot attack Solace." Magnus said it loud enough to grab the attention of everyone in the vicinity, but more so to force Lumen to hear him out, whether privately or here, in the presence of the entire army.

Lumen didn't so much as flinch. "That is absurd."

It appeared they were doing this here, in front of everyone, so Magnus continued. "They have taken three of our number, including Lilly, the Premieress of the Sky Realm, Calum, the Unifier of Kanarah, and…" Magnus didn't have a title for Axel, so he didn't bother to make one up. "…Axel. We cannot fight without them."

Lumen's blazing eyes narrowed. "I am the *Unifier* of Kanarah. *I* am its liberator. Calum was an important contributor in assembling my army, and his loss is unfortunate, as is the loss of the other two, but they perished in the service of freeing all of Kanarah."

"They did not perish," Magnus asserted. "Their bodies are not among the dead. I have examined every corpse. They were taken by Matthios, the King's Imperator."

"And by Gavridel, the other Imperator," another voice chimed in.

Magnus glanced back in time to see General Balena hovering toward them with General Tolomus and Condor in tow. It was General Balena who'd spoken.

"I saw a large warrior clad in armor made of gemstones take both Calum and Axel," General Balena continued. "They were, as far as I could tell, still alive."

"Even if they yet live," Lumen said, "they will not remain alive for long. The King is widely known for his ruthlessness and appetite for suffering. They are among the first casualties of this war, and regrettably, they will not be the last." Lumen redirected his words toward the soldiers. "It is up to us to ensure their sacrifices were not in vain."

"I can't believe what I'm hearing," Riley muttered again.

Magnus echoed the Shadow Wolf's sentiment. "No."

"No?" Lumen turned to face Magnus yet again, and his head tilted to one side. "No… what?"

"*No*," Magnus rumbled. "I refuse to accept that outcome. We must send envoys to bargain for their release. Perhaps we can trade Captain Anigo in exchange for our friends."

"Captain Anigo escaped when Gavridel took Calum and Axel," General Balena said.

"Then we will trade other captive soldiers instead," Magnus said. "We must have captured several of them in the course of the battle here."

"Our forces relentlessly eradicated our enemies at my command," Lumen countered. "There is no one left to trade, and even if there were, I would not lower myself to make such a request of my mortal enemy."

Fury ignited within Magnus's chest, but when he felt the heat of emerald fire creeping up his throat, he pushed it back down. Even so, he couldn't keep his nostrils from smoking.

He'd already made up his mind, though, about this situation. Magnus would neither allow the King to imprison his friends, nor would he allow Lumen to keep him from intervening on their behalf.

"Mighty Dragon King," Lumen's voice took on a hint of warning, "what scheme are you mulling inside your head?"

Magnus had to admit—Lumen was perceptive. Yet he saw no reason to conceal his intentions. "If you will not negotiate on their behalf, then I will go to the King myself and personally see it done."

Lumen fully squared himself with Magnus, and his hands relaxed at his sides. The motion struck Magnus as simultaneously docile and threatening—almost menacing. His gleaming sword still hung at his belt, within easy reach of his hand.

"I cannot allow you to put yourself in such peril," Lumen said. "The fate of our campaign relies on your presence and that of your army. Who would lead them should something happen to you as well?"

Magnus weighed Lumen's words. Coupled with Lumen's stance and positioning, they heightened the threat Magnus had already perceived.

Yet Lumen needed Magnus's strength—both his actual physical ability and power, as well as his army of Saurians. If Lumen followed through on his threat, and if they came to blows, Magnus couldn't be sure he'd survive the encounter. Even if he did, what condition would he be in afterward?

He'd seen Lumen slay a Jyrak with a single strike. What would prevent him from doing the same to Magnus, even in spite of his size and the resilience of his scales?

Magnus's eyes narrowed. He was overthinking it. It was foolishness to imagine that Lumen, the *Unifier* of Kanarah, would kill an ally simply for disagreeing with him.

Or was it?

Magnus studied Lumen's burning eyes. The General of Light had only one objective: to rule Kanarah in place of the King. If he was willing to uproot the entirety of Kanarah's society and government in order to achieve that end, then it wasn't a stretch to believe he'd walk right through Magnus or anyone else who stood in his way.

With that solemn conclusion in mind, Magnus relented—at least openly.

"Very well," he finally said. "If we are not pursuing their return, what is our next step?"

Lumen folded his powerful arms, and the pervading sense of danger ringing in the back of Magnus's mind subsided.

"We will press our advantage, as I said," he asserted. "We will attack Solace, and we will take Valkendell as our own."

WHEN CALUM'S EYES OPENED, towers of glistening white stone loomed overhead. With the exception of the platforms that reached above the clouds in the Sky Realm, they were the tallest structures he'd ever seen—dwarfing even the enormity of the Crimson Keep.

Where am I?

The sound of wagon wheels rolling over a street registered in his ears, and he found himself lying atop a wagon filled with hay, with his head at the back end and his feet toward the front. He blinked against the brightness of the morning sun shining in the blue sky overhead, and he rubbed his eyes—or rather, he tried to but found he couldn't.

Short chains, no longer than a few inches, bound him to the top of the wagon, both at his wrists and ankles. He blinked hard to clear the haziness from his vision.

When he looked down, he no longer wore the red armor he'd received from the armory at the Sky Fortress but rather only his underclothes. Nor was his weapon—the Dragon's Breath sword—anywhere to be found.

Calum tried to sit up, or at least lean his head forward to get another look around, but the wagon passed under a bridge or something—no, it had carried him *inside* one of the tall towers of white.

It was a tunnel. Where it was going, Calum didn't know, but it couldn't be anywhere good. He tried to look back, but the wagon's short walls obscured his sight.

As the wagon descended deeper into the inky darkness within the bowels of the tower, The brief sense of confusion he'd experienced upon waking up faded, and his memory cycled back to the last thing he could remember: the battle with the Imperator.

Captain Anigo had escaped.

Axel had been knocked clear across the battlefield, and his body had slammed into a wooden cart, reducing it to splinters.

The Dragon's Breath sword had failed to damage the Imperator's amethyst and diamond-forged weapons.

And at the end, the Imperator had delivered a final blow to Calum. He'd presumed the blow would've ended his life, but now he registered only a dull pain in his head, and his arm had been dislocated as well. He looked down and tried to move his left shoulder. It ached with angry pain, but it was still functional.

The Imperator had let him live. But why?

The answer, Calum decided, wasn't all that complex. They'd captured him and taken him back to Solace—the King's city, and the capital of Kanarah—for execution. Maybe he'd get a trial, but even if he did, it wouldn't be a fair one, especially with Captain Anigo around to speak against him.

Now, there in the dark beneath the tower, Calum could recognize the truth: the Imperator's mercy—if it could be called that—would only delay the inevitable. Calum would still die at the hands of the King's men, just as his parents had so many years before.

Unless he could do something about it.

As the darkness of the tunnel further enveloped him, Calum maneuvered his wrist, took hold of the chain securing him to the wagon, and focused on his left hand. He'd never done this before, but based on the burning sensation that spread farther and farther up his arm with each use of Lumen's light, he knew there had to be some real power behind it.

He squeezed the thick chain tighter and summoned the light from within. His palm began to glow, muted by the cold metal of the chain, but still obvious against the profound dark of the tunnel. The power's familiar burn reached up to his elbow this time, then past it into his biceps and triceps, creeping steadily closer to his shoulder the more he used it.

"What's that light?" a voice called from somewhere ahead of the wagon.

Calum's heart rate multiplied. If only he'd awakened sooner, he could've tried this in the sunshine where it would've been less noticeable. But he hadn't, so this was his only choice—and possibly his only chance. He gritted his teeth and pushed the limits of his concentration, funneling every ounce of power he could feel into his left hand.

The chain glowed red hot, as if it had just come out of a blacksmith's fire. Then it shattered in Calum's hand.

It surprised him—shocked him, even—but it had worked. His left hand was free.

"Hey!" another voice, this one much closer shouted. "Stop!"

With his left hand still burning white-hot and his shoulder aching from being previously dislocated, Calum ripped the chains from his right hand and both ankles away. They broke even easier than the first one had.

He was free—from his shackles, anyway.

Now he had to deal with the King's soldiers around him, however many there were.

The light in his left hand faded to nothing, as did the burning in his left arm and lower shoulder, and the darkness quickly returned as Calum moved to jump off the wagon and start running. He found he couldn't see anything—the light had scarred his vision, and his eyes hadn't had time to readjust to the deep black of the tunnel.

More shouts, then the clamor of footsteps. Calum jumped off the wagon anyway. His boots—at least they hadn't taken those from him—hit the solid floor, and he turned to run, but a set of hands caught him before he could advance.

Calum's left hand shot up, and he summoned Lumen's power again, full force. This time, Calum kept his eyes shut as the light in his palm flared like a miniature sun.

The burn climbed into the middle of his shoulder, but the pained shout of the man who'd grabbed him stole Calum's focus. The light had done its job, and the man released his grip.

Calum shoved the man back and ran.

Ahead of him, the distant light at the end of the tunnel was nothing more than a shining pinprick against the expansive shadows of the tunnel. His own light had faded to a gentle glow, just enough for him to see in the dark without blinding himself.

But before he could run toward his escape, half a dozen soldiers clad in silver armor formed a barrier. They all held swords in one hand, and with the others, they shielded their eyes against another potential burst of light.

He couldn't get out that way. If he'd had the Dragon's Breath sword and his armor, then maybe, but not without them.

Calum whirled back toward the front of the wagon. The man he'd blinded groped for his legs, but Calum gave him a swift kick to his nose that stunned him anew. Then he grabbed the soldier's sword and hacked at the traces securing the horse to the wagon until they snapped.

The horse whinnied and rose up on its hind legs, but as it came down, Calum grabbed its saddle and leaped atop its back. With the horse's reins in his glowing hand and his stolen sword in the other, Calum sped deeper into the tunnel, away from the soldiers. If he couldn't escape the way he'd come in, he'd just have to find some other way out.

The soldiers shouted at him from behind, but he wasn't about to stop now. Amid the clopping of the horse's hooves, their footsteps gradually faded away.

Calum let the light in his left palm flare brighter, but not brightly enough that it would blind him or the horse, and not hot enough that it would sear through the reins. The burn in his arm now reached up to the middle of his shoulder, but it wasn't as severe as before.

He still didn't know why it hurt in the first place, and he hadn't thought to ask Lumen about it when he'd had the chance. Perhaps the power was gradually remaking him, forging him like a blacksmith's flames into a more dangerous version of himself. The awakening of the light's destructive power certainly seemed to suggest that was the case.

For now, Calum focused on the road ahead.

The tunnel gradually curved to the left, and ahead, the orange glow of firelight gradually banished more and more of the darkness. After a few more minutes, Calum reached a large gate made of black iron bars. No soldiers guarded it, so he figured it must be locked.

Sure enough, when Calum dismounted the horse and checked, the door in the center refused to budge. With his sword still in his right hand, he pressed his left palm against the locking mechanism and summoned Lumen's light. It flared, and like the chains, the metal glowed bright red and then shattered.

Flecks of fiery metal pelted Calum's arms and chest, singeing his clothes and threatening to burn his skin. He stepped back, let the light in his hand fade, and brushed off the debris. The burning had nearly reached the top of his shoulder now. If he kept using the power, it wouldn't be long until the burn reached his chest or his neck.

What would happen then? Would it transform him into a being of light like Lumen? Would his power increase?

He'd keep using the light when he needed to, and he'd let the power run its course. So far he could tolerate the burn, even at its worst, at least for a little while.

He'd tolerate it forever if it kept him from being weak.

Calum pulled the door open and ventured inside the gate. Wrought-iron torches punctuated the tan walls, and he couldn't help but wonder how much of the stone that made them up had come from the very quarry where he'd grown up.

No time to linger in the past, he decided. He couldn't afford distractions. He had to find a way out.

The hall leading from the gate had a much higher ceiling than the tunnel itself—perhaps twenty or thirty feet up, and vaulted. It gave the otherwise drab hall a hint of elegance.

Thanks to the height of the ceiling, for the first time since waking up, Calum thought of Lilly. What had happened to her? Had she survived the battle?

Flanked with her Royal Guard and Condor, not to mention General Tolomus and General Balena and their army of Wisps, she was probably fine. Even so, Calum couldn't know for sure, and that gnawed at him. He cast a silent prayer to the Overlord on her behalf. Whether or not it would do any good, he didn't know.

His thoughts continued to wander along with his footsteps. Thus far, the halls had remained empty, but he stayed vigilant while considering potential outcomes of the battle.

The relative calm also gave him time to consider his own position. By now, the soldiers who'd been escorting him into the guts of this tower had likely raised some sort of alarm as to his whereabouts. That realization quickened Calum's steps.

As he progressed, Calum encountered multiple branches where the hall split off in other directions or intersected with other halls. None of the paths were labeled or had any distinguishing features; the same high ceilings, tan walls, and wrought-iron torches repeated with each new path he encountered.

Calum suspected this was by design. He was being taken here as a prisoner, so one of these paths likely led to a dungeon or jail cells of some sort. Should anyone escape confinement, they would find themselves in a labyrinth of nearly identical halls, stretching out in every conceivable direction and crisscrossing in a seemingly random arrangement.

Then Calum spotted a small yet crucial difference. Occasionally, one branch would take a modest incline. The hall would steadily and subtly climb upward. A malnourished, confused, and desperate prisoner would almost certainly have missed it, and even Calum hadn't noticed it at first, but now that he had, it gave him a path to follow.

Whether or not it was the right one, only time would tell.

Soon after traversing a few of those inclining halls, Calum noticed changes to the walls around him. The tan stone walls went away, replaced by walls of white stones akin to the ones he'd seen on the outside of the towers when he'd first awakened.

Here in the torchlight, they still glistened, but not to the same degree as under the light of the sun. Even so, they signaled to Calum that he was, in fact, making progress.

Additionally, he encountered his first doorway. He slowed as he approached it and, upon finding a closed wooden door, he crept past.

The doorways became more and more frequent the farther he progressed through the halls, and before long, he heard the telltale sounds of people bustling within the rooms and occasionally walking through the halls.

With a sword in his hand and wearing only underclothes, he knew he stood out like a stone-crushed thumb. He needed some sort of disguise, or he'd perpetually be darting in and out of rooms, trying to hide.

The solution presented itself sooner than he'd expected, but only barely in time. As he advanced, he found another door, this time cracked open, that led to a large storage room of sorts.

Inside, Calum discovered a dozen sets of long-sleeved wool shirts and trousers hanging on hooks from the wall. Around them, a variety of familiar tools leaned against the walls and sat on shelves, including shovels, pickaxes, shears, and hatchets. He leaned his sword in the corner between a couple of the shovels, still within reach if he needed it.

He quickly tugged off his boots and snagged a set of clothes from the hooks. All of them were varying shades of green, and some looked to be more faded than others. All the clothes seemed well worn and had an abundance of scratches, tears, and holes up and down the fabric.

The green trousers went on first, and he hurried to slide his boots back on. He donned the thick shirt next and reached for his sword again, but as he did, the door latch clicked, and the door swung open.

CHAPTER 25

C alum had expected to find a batch of soldiers standing there, but upon seeing a cluster of unarmed men and women dressed in gray under-layers of clothing, he grabbed a shovel instead so as not to alarm them.

One of the women, short, middle-aged, and wearing tan trousers instead of green like everyone else's, stepped inside. She had close-cropped red hair and scrutinized him with tentative brown eyes. "Who're you?"

By that point, the others had entered and claimed their work attire, and Calum could see that one set of clothing remained apart from the one he'd requisitioned for himself. As such, everyone else was staring at him while they shed their boots and put on their own sets of clothes.

The red-haired woman cleared her throat and leaned her head forward.

"I'm—" Calum hesitated. "I'm new."

It was the best he could come up with on the spot—neutral and succinct enough that it hid his true identity in obscurity, yet hopefully still enough to satisfy the small woman's inquiry.

"Obviously," she intoned with a roll of her eyes. "You're Barkul's replacement. You got a name? Come on, then. Spit it out."

Calum gulped down his fear. "Cal—" He paused. "Cal. Just Cal."

The woman looked him up and down again, tsking and shaking her head. "Scrawny young thing like you probably never did a day of hard labor in his life. At least you're punctual."

If you only knew. Calum bit his tongue to keep from saying it aloud.

"Well, Cal," she said. "I'm Ursula, the Head Gardener. You work for me now."

Calum nodded and didn't say anything.

Ursula eyed him again. "You touched in the head or something?"

Calum shook his head. "No, Ma'am. Just ready to work."

If she was buying his disguise, maybe any soldiers they passed along the way would take him for one of the workers, too.

"Not without an apron, you're not." She nodded toward a rack from which all the other workers were now claiming brown leather aprons for themselves.

599

"Of course. Sorry." Calum gave her a slight bow and immediately felt stupid for it. As far as he knew, it wasn't customary or anything like that, so it probably seemed weird to her that he'd done it at all.

He pushed his reservations aside, set his shovel down, grabbed an apron for himself, and put it on. It had loops and pockets on the front, and he noticed some of the other workers stuffing the pockets with leather gloves, smaller tools like clippers, and fist-sized bags of seed. Calum mimicked their actions.

As Calum finished, the other workers each grabbed either a shovel or a pickax. He figured he was all set and reached for his shovel until Ursula singled him out yet again.

"You ever use a pickax before?" she asked. "Or are your twiggy arms too weak to heft one?"

Calum bit back the truth yet again. Instead, he replied, "I've used them a time or two."

"You're gonna use one again today. Put that shovel back," she ordered. "Grab a pickax and follow me. And don't wander off."

Calum obeyed. He hated to leave his stolen sword tucked away in the corner, but if this helped him blend in, then he stood a far better chance of escaping. He could just follow at the back of the line and slip away when he got a chance.

The other workers didn't say a word to him, and none of them followed Ursula out of the storage room. Instead, they waited for him to go first. So he followed her, and the others followed him, like a trail of brown-and-green ducklings waddling after their mother.

So much for lingering near the back and slipping away.

Ursula deftly maneuvered them through the network of halls. Wherever she was taking them, she knew her way there as if she'd walked there a thousand times, and she probably had.

With each step, Calum glanced around, trying to make sense of their path, looking for distinct points of reference. After awhile, they started to pass by narrow windows, and sunlight streamed into the halls in long vertical strips. Whenever Calum tried to look out, he only saw flashes of the city beyond.

Along the way, they passed dozens of people, each of them clad in different color combinations, but all of them essentially wore the same type of outfit as Calum and the other workers in green, and all of them wore aprons.

All of them except for the soldiers.

Soldiers clad in the same silver armor as they'd worn during the battle that morning appeared at the end of the hall and jogged toward the group of workers. The hall was reasonably wide, but Ursula flattened herself against the wall nonetheless, and she yanked Calum against the wall next to her.

He complied, and he debated whether or not he should keep his head up or put his chin down. If he dared to stare at the soldiers as they passed, would one of them recognize him? If he put his chin down, would that look suspicious?

In the end, his indecision meant his head was still up as the soldiers plodded past the group. Despite the urgency etched onto their faces, none of them so much as gave him a second glance, let alone stopped for a closer look at him. They just kept jogging, determined to find him, yet too oblivious to realize they'd already passed him by.

"C'mon," Ursula muttered. "Don't know what that's about, but it doesn't change our mandate. We still got a job to do."

Several halls and corridors later, Ursula led them through a large opening into what appeared to be an enormous courtyard overloaded with trees, bushes, and plants, most of which Calum had never even seen before. An array of vibrant colors punctuated the lush greenery in the form of flowers and fruit.

A solitary fountain carved from the same white stone glistened in the sunlight. In the center stood a single white spire surrounded by a short circular wall, and the water spouting from the top of the spire also fanned out in a circle and landed just short of the interior wall.

More impressive than the fountain, though, was the sprawling bed of red roses that lined the back wall of the garden. Immaculate red petals crowned the stems of countless hundreds of pristine flowers, vibrant and stark against the rocky gray cliff face that loomed high above the perimeter walls of white stone.

Wherever Calum was, there was no chance for escape that way. The natural wall created by the cliff face of the mountain had seen to that.

As Calum took in the beautiful foliage around him, he searched the garden for another way to escape, but he found none. A network of gray stone paths lined with well-manicured plants branched throughout the garden, truncating at the tall white walls that outlined the courtyard's perimeter. Thanks to the robust flora that filled the garden, he couldn't even see where they all went.

Above those walls, a layer of paneled glass or something like it covered the entire garden in a dome-like structure. The glass was mostly clear, although it seemed to have a bluish tint to it at certain points. In any case, it would keep Windgales from getting in or out just as easily as the white walls would do the same where Calum was concerned.

"Spread out. Tend to the plants," Ursula ordered. "Draw water from the fountain, and for the love of peonies, do *not* prune the plants back too far."

To Calum's surprise, a third of his fellow workers left their feet and drifted over to some of the taller bushes and trees and began pruning them without the aid of ladders. They were Windgales—Wisps, specifically, as they did not wear capes.

He found the sight confusing at first, as most Windgales lived in Western Kanarah, although he had indeed encountered a handful of them here on the eastern side as well. Upon further reflection, he supposed it wasn't that unusual after all.

More pressing for Calum was a question that had pervaded his mind ever since those soldiers had taken him into the tunnel below this building: what was this place?

Given all he'd encountered so far, he guessed it might've been some rich person's home, or perhaps a military barracks of some sort. But if it were the latter, why would they maintain such a verdant garden on the property? Sure, it was beautiful, but it seemed like an awful waste of space.

Perhaps it was some sort of public venue, like a place within Solace for visitors to come and enjoy. Perhaps they held private events here, like weddings or parties.

The more Calum thought about it, the more the possibilities seemed both endless and narrow at the same time. He imagined the views of the stars at night, under that glass dome, were probably phenomenal.

Part of him longed to share such an experience with Lilly. How wonderful would it be if—

"You." Ursula's voice snapped Calum back into real time. "Come with me. Time to start digging."

He considered turning and making a run for it instead. After all, what would she do? He doubted she'd bother to run after him.

But Calum didn't run. Maybe it was part of his old self reemerging, wanting to comply, put his head down, and work like he'd done for Burtis back at the quarry. Or maybe it was a misplaced sense of loyalty to Ursula, who had indirectly and unknowingly kept him alive and relatively safe for longer than he'd anticipated.

Whatever the case, he hefted the pickax over his shoulder and followed her down one of the main paths without putting up a fuss.

As he walked along, Calum noticed a tall, powerfully built man standing on a path running parallel to his. A variety of flowering bushes and long-leafed plants and the occasional tree separated the two paths in a strip of vegetation about ten feet wide.

The man wore a simple white tunic and trousers. He had a rich bronze skin tone, a dark beard, and he wore a white crown atop his head that reminded Calum of Lumen's, only not shiny. He strolled through the garden at a leisurely pace with his arms behind his back, as if he didn't have a care in the world.

When the man looked over, his vibrant green eyes locked onto Calum.

A flood of emotion threatened to overwhelm Calum. Elation, fear, rage, shock, sorrow, anticipation, loathing. All of them at once.

And in that moment, Calum realized the truth of his situation.

After the battle, he'd been taken directly to Valkendell—the King's fortress in Solace.

And this man was the King himself.

Calum didn't know how he knew it, except that he sensed a sort of power—a presence like when he'd first encountered Lumen, like when he'd first laid eyes on Matthios and later with the Gemstone Imperator.

Calum gulped down the bile rising in his throat and tried to quell his emotional response. Should he look away? Should he keep staring to show he wasn't afraid? Should he run?

Ursula still led him onward, and Calum still followed, but how could he continue to do so now, upon realizing his whereabouts and upon seeing the King?

The King looked away first, as if disinterested—or rather, simply more interested in the plants of the garden around him instead. Then he continued strolling down a perpendicular path, facing away from Calum entirely.

Calum glanced backward and up through the glass dome to see a spike of glistening white stone rising into the sky. He hadn't seen it when he'd first surveyed the garden because he'd been facing away from it, but now that he'd progressed along the path, he could see up its side clearly.

He was definitely at the fortress. And he'd definitely found the King in the garden.

And the King was both unarmed and unguarded.

Calum had a weapon. Calum had the advantage of surprise. Calum had a chance to end this war once and for all.

All he had to do was kill the King, here and now, in this garden.

Calum's grip tightened on the handle of his pickax, and his jaw clenched as he took his first step toward the King.

He headed straight through the green space separating the two paths with total disregard. His boots stomped colorful flowers and verdant leaves, crushing them with abandon.

By the time his feet hit the gray stone of the King's path, Calum had left a swath of modest destruction in his wake, but he didn't care. They were just plants.

And he had a King to kill.

Ursula shouted something behind him, a lament for the damage he'd just done to the garden and a call for him to come back and face her wrath, but he ignored her.

As he closed the distance between them, Calum glanced side-to-side to double-check that no guards or anyone else could possibly interfere. It didn't matter what they did to him after the King was dead. They could tear him apart for all he cared; as long as he ended this war and freed Kanarah forever, he would gladly suffer any fate.

With ten paces to go, Calum quickened his pace and raised the pickax over his head.

But at five paces, he tripped.

CHAPTER 26

C alum stumbled, and then he fell.

He landed within three feet of the King's boots with a huff. The impact jarred his aching left shoulder, but somehow, he'd managed to hold onto his pickax.

When Calum glanced back, a thick greenish-purple vine receded into the brush lining the path.

On its own.

No one else was around to lash the vine at him to trip him up. The vine seemed to have done it of its own free will.

What irked Calum is that he'd been so focused on his target that he hadn't seen it snake out to trip him in the first place. It was a foolish mistake Magnus would've used as a teachable moment during their training, and it was a blunder Axel would've constantly reminded Calum of for weeks afterward.

But here in the King's very own garden, it was more than either of those things.

It was a fatal mistake.

When Calum looked up, he found the King's vibrant green eyes staring down at him as they had before, when they'd seen each other across the green space. The same swell of emotions cascaded throughout his body, but this time the darker emotions—fear, rage, sorrow, and loathing—took the forefront.

He'd come within striking distance of ending the war and freeing Kanarah, and he'd still failed. He wasn't strong enough. Smart enough. Cunning enough.

He wasn't... *enough*.

Despite the obvious attempt on his life, the King did not regard Calum with anger or even surprise. Instead, he looked down upon Calum with pity.

Pity? *Pity?*

The thought of it incensed Calum. This man—this King of all of Kanarah, the vermin responsible for the suffering of countless people across the land, the man whose soldiers had *killed* Calum's parents—now looked down on him with pity?

An explosion of fury burst within Calum's chest, flinging him up to his feet as fast as light-

603

ning. He re-gripped the pickax and swung it at the King, who hadn't moved, even when Calum had risen to his feet.

A tree branch kept the strike from ever reaching the King. It swung at Calum from his right side and intercepted the blow with a loud clack. When the tree branch recoiled, it dropped a handful of leaves and a pair of bright-yellow lemons on the path.

The King's green-eyed gaze never moved away from Calum's.

Calum couldn't understand it. How was this possible?

He hauled the pickax back for another attack. This time, an orange pumpkin the size of a warrior's shield collided with his knees from the left, not only interrupting his swing but also knocking him down to the stone path once again. The pumpkin broke into chunks, and its sloppy seeds and membranes splattered across the path and Calum's lower half.

What is going on?

All the while, the King stared at him dispassionately, aside from the pity in his eyes.

Before Calum could even try to stand, the hiss of leaves dancing on the wind drew his attention to his right. He turned to find a grainy cloud billowing into his face from a trio of pale blue mushrooms. He tried to recoil, but he'd already breathed some of the dust into his lungs, and he couldn't help but cough.

No other plants tried to intervene, so Calum started to rise to his feet again. As he did, he realized his legs weren't cooperating. And then his arms stopped cooperating, too. They weren't lifting him.

He could still feel his limbs, so he knew he wasn't paralyzed, but he couldn't make them do what he wanted them to do. Next, his fingers refused to function, and he could no longer grip the pickax. It clanked to the stone path, as useless as Calum felt.

When Calum blinked, his eyes threatened to stay shut. No—they actively tried to, as if he hadn't slept in days. Fatigue swept throughout his body, making his limbs even heavier and harder to move. The malaise spread to his head, and he squinted to keep his eyes open.

He looked up at the King again, who still hadn't moved and still stared down at him.

Those vibrant green eyes still pitied Calum, and he couldn't stand it.

But neither could he do anything about it.

He'd failed again. That was the last thought that flowed through Calum's mind as he succumbed.

Then Calum fell asleep on the path at the King's feet.

AXEL WOKE up in an infirmary of some sort.

The room's white stone walls told him he wasn't still in the camp. The shackles on his wrists and ankles and the lack of Blood Ore armor on his body told him he wasn't in friendly hands. The pain in his limbs and back told him he'd survived the battle, but at a cost.

His body ached, but his head hurt even worse. He clenched his eyes shut to block out the sunlight shining off the shimmering white walls everywhere. It helped his head hurt less, but only for an instant. Then the pain returned full force, and he groaned.

"You are awake," a feminine voice said.

Despite his miserable condition, Axel decided he liked how she sounded, so he opened his eyes a crack and turned his head toward her voice.

Two beds over, in a chair near a window, sat a lovely woman with black hair. She wore a fine red gown trimmed with green accents and held an open book in her hands.

Around her neck hung a decadent necklace decorated with blue gemstones that encircled a large yellow jewel. All of them were set into a silver frame reminiscent of vines, and matching earrings dangled from her ears.

Aside from Lilly, she might've been the most beautiful woman he'd ever laid eyes on, though a certain maturity underpinned her appearance. He estimated she was perhaps five or six years older than him, well into her twenties.

He couldn't help but raise an eyebrow at the sight of her. She wasn't a nurse—not dressed like that.

"Who're you?" he mumbled.

She gave him a simple smile. "Valerie."

Axel had expected her to elaborate, so when she didn't, he asked another question. "Where am I?"

"You are in the private infirmary inside Valkendell," she replied as if he should've expected to end up there all along.

Valkendell? The King's fortress in Solace? Someone had brought him to receive medical aid *inside* the King's palace?

That's not good.

Axel's confusion didn't seem to faze Valerie. She stared at him with green eyes like the sky on a stormy evening, still wearing a pleasant grin.

Didn't she realize he wasn't on their side?

"What happened?" he asked.

"You were brought here after the battle at Captain Anigo's insistence. Apparently, he has been tracking you for quite some time," she explained with a casual wave of her hand. Her manner of speaking was more proper, like Magnus's. "Something about a farm, a quarry, and you being a murderous fugitive."

So she *did* know he was on the opposite side of this conflict.

"Yeah." Axel pushed himself up to a sitting position, which his shackles only barely allowed. "That's more or less accurate."

"And you admit to it freely?" She closed her book, and her smile darkened. "I am not sure that is a wise defense strategy for your upcoming trial."

"Trial?" He blinked at her. "What trial?"

"You are an enemy soldier. You have betrayed your King and your people. Of course you will be put on trial for your crimes."

"Of course," Axel parroted back to her. If his shackles had permitted, he would've rubbed his aching forehead with his hands. "And when is this trial supposedly taking place?"

"I cannot say for sure. But now that you are awake, it will not be much longer."

"Can't wait," he muttered.

Axel looked her over again, and he really liked what he saw. If he was going to trial, presumably to be sentenced to death—because the King wasn't exactly known to be the merciful type—at least he'd be able to enjoy the view while they removed his head.

"Who are you?" he asked again.

Her smile broadened. "I told you. I am Valerie."

"Yeah, but who *are* you?" Axel tried to clarify. "Why are you here? You some sort of royalty?"

Valerie tilted her head to the side and scoffed. "Not exactly."

"Then why are you here?"

"When Captain Anigo insisted you be brought in, I took it upon myself to ensure you received proper care."

"You wanna make sure I'm healthy for my trial?" Axel's voice flattened. "So they can kill me when I'm feeling better?"

"The King is merciful," she countered. "Do not presume your fate is set."

Now Axel scoffed. The King was *not* merciful. Everyone knew that. "Execution seems pretty inevitable from where I'm sitting."

Valerie raised an eyebrow, and the sight of it set Axel's heart fluttering. "If you truly believed your fate was inevitable, you never would have made it this far."

Her words stopped his tongue—and, for a second, his brain, too. She had a point. He'd survived all sorts of crazy happenings and defied death so many times that he'd lost count.

Still, as Axel looked around the room again, the small flame of confidence she'd managed to ignite in his chest snuffed right back out. He frowned.

"Do not be troubled," she said. "Take comfort in knowing that no harm will come to you in this place."

"Until my trial," he added.

"Until your trial is complete, yes," she agreed. "And only if you choose to reject the King's mercy."

Axel huffed again. He'd seen the King's idea of "mercy" all his life.

Even so, he wasn't any more likely to convince Valerie to see things his way than she could convince him of the King's merciful nature, so he dropped the idea.

"So... Captain Anigo," he started. "You his wife or something?"

Valerie let out a sharp laugh, one that seemed somewhat undignified, given her appearance and otherwise proper demeanor. "No. Perhaps he may wish it so, but I belong to no one but myself."

A whirlwind of thoughts rushed through Axel's mind. Thoughts of Lilly, who'd scorned him. Thoughts of Valerie, obviously, because she was gorgeous and sitting right there looking... well, gorgeous. Thoughts of never leaving this place alive. Thoughts of his time in the battle and how it had come to an end.

The last thing he remembered was defending a thunderous blow from the enormous gemstone warrior who'd appeared next to Captain Anigo. Or at least, Axel *thought* he'd defended the blow—he'd held up his Blood Ore sword to parry the attack, anyway.

The more he thought about it, the more he recalled that it hadn't exactly worked. Somewhere in his mind, he heard the metallic *thunk* of his breastplate crumpling inward when the warrior's axe hit it, and then Axel left his feet. He couldn't remember anything after that, though.

Were it not for that Blood Ore breastplate, he'd probably be dead right now. He doubted any other armor could've withstood that kind of blow. Apart from being alive, Axel knew it had done its job because his chest was the only part of his body that didn't hurt.

"Your friend should be arriving shortly." Valerie's comment tugged Axel out of his memories.

"What friend?" Axel's eyebrows rose. "Someone else got captured?"

Please don't let it be Riley, or Condor, or—

The wooden door to the infirmary swung open, and two silver-clad soldiers carried a stretcher inside with a body laying on it. It was a male form clad in green workers' attire that Axel had never seen before.

When the soldiers slid the man off the stretcher and onto the infirmary bed nearest to Valerie, Axel realized who it was, and his eyebrows arched back down.

Calum.

Whatever they'd done to him, he was sound asleep—or maybe dead. But no, he wouldn't be dead. Why bother bringing him to the infirmary? It would already be too late.

Still, Calum showed no signs of life as they clapped shackles on his wrists and ankles to secure him to his bed, just like they'd done to Axel. It wasn't until the soldiers stepped aside, replaced by two infirmary nurses in red workers garb with white aprons overtop, that Axel saw Calum drawing slow, shallow breaths in and out.

As much as he hated to admit it, the sight gave him a sense of relief. He and Calum had crossed each other recently, and Axel had even gone so far as to mentally disavow Calum as his friend forever because of their squabble, but now wasn't the time to be petty. They'd have to work together if they had any chance of getting out of this place alive.

"See?" Valerie rose and nodded toward Calum, who lay on the bed right in front of her.

"What are you gonna do?" Axel asked, ashamed of the trepidation in his voice.

"As I promised, no harm will come to you—either of you—while you are in this place," she reiterated. From a small white chest of drawers next to the bed, she removed a small glass vial of burnt-orange powder and uncorked it. Then she bent close to Calum.

"What are you giving him?" Axel asked, wary.

"The antithesis to the mushroom spores he inhaled. These orange-and-black spores will negate the sleeping effects." Valerie squeezed Calum's cheeks and tapped about half the vial's contents into his open mouth. "He should wake up any—"

Calum's eyes opened wide, and he coughed and sputtered. "Ugh. What is that taste in my mouth? It's like honey—if it was mixed into a bowl of dirt."

Rather than answering him, Valerie gave Axel another simple smile. "I will leave you two to catch up."

With that, she turned and left the room. Axel watched her the whole way out, wishing he could've said something to keep her around, but nothing came to mind.

Calum looked at Axel as if noticing for the first time who he was. "Axel? What are you doing here? I—I thought you were dead!"

Axel thought back to the blow his breastplate had taken. It had come closer to killing him than he cared to admit, but he wasn't about to convey that to Calum. He raised his chin. "Takes a lot more than a hulking jewel-guy with an axe to kill me."

"Two axes," Calum corrected him.

"He only hit me with one of them."

"Who was that woman?" Calum looked toward the door. "I barely got a look at her before she left."

"Said her name was Valerie. Still not entirely sure who she is," Axel replied. If he weren't shackled up, and if she weren't on the King's side, he would've loved to get to know her a *lot* better. "She said she made sure I was taken here, to the infirmary after the battle."

"I still can't believe you survived," Calum said.

"What's that supposed to mean?" Axel glowered at him. Some of his recent rage toward Calum was creeping back in.

"I don't mean anything by it, Axel. Calm down." Calum tugged at his shackles, but they didn't budge. He looked around the room, the same as Axel had done when he'd awakened. "We're in Valkendell."

"Obviously," Axel said. "And we're awaiting trial."

"Trial? What trial?"

"That's what *I* said." Axel exhaled a frustrated breath. "Apparently, Captain Anigo has made good on his promise to bring us to justice—whatever that's supposed to be—and so now we're going to have a trial. But Valerie told me not to worry because the King is *merciful.*"

Axel and Calum both scoffed at the same time. At least they still agreed on that.

"Any chance Lumen or Magnus comes to rescue us?" Axel asked.

"You? Probably not. Me, maybe."

"Funny," Axel said, his voice flat.

"I'm not sure they even know we're here," Calum said. "They might think we're dead."

"We're definitely not." Axel sighed. "At least not until our trial finishes."

"We obviously can't let the trial happen," Calum said. "We need to get outta here before then."

"Agreed." A strange but familiar scent wafted into Axel's nose, but it didn't make sense that he'd be smelling it here, in the infirmary in Valkendell. He sniffed the air and noticed some stains on Calum's trousers. "Is that... *pumpkin* on your legs?"

"Leave it to the farmer to sniff out what kind of plant I've got smashed all over my knees." Calum sighed. "Yes, it's pumpkin."

Axel gave him a blank stare, expecting a response.

"It's not important," Calum said. "What's important is finding a way outta here. I almost escaped once, but then—"

"Escaped?" Axel didn't believe him. He raised a skeptical eyebrow. "But then, what?"

"Then I found the King, tried to kill him, and ended up in here," Calum said.

Now Axel *really* didn't believe him. "You're a terrible liar."

"It's the truth. I swear it on my parents' souls," Calum said. "I got close, Axel. Really close."

The way Calum said it made Axel more inclined to believe him. "Then tell me what happened."

Calum recounted the ordeal to him, starting with waking up on the wagon and concluding with his attempt on the King's life in the garden and the spores from the blue mushrooms that had put him to sleep. It was almost too unbelievable to be real, but Axel and Calum had survived enough wild scrapes for Axel to buy the story.

Plus, Calum failing to finish the job was exactly what Axel would've expected. "So you got close but couldn't get it done, huh?"

"Don't rub it in," Calum said. "I feel bad enough as it is."

Axel shrugged. "Maybe you should've done things differently."

Calum's head snapped to face Axel. "You think you could've done any better?"

Axel had been expecting that question. "I *know* I could've done better."

"You couldn't even beat me in a fight the last time we tussled, but you think you could've killed the King of all Kanarah, even though I couldn't?" Calum challenged.

The mention of their fight bristled along Axel's skin, and he clenched his teeth to ward off his anger. "I guess we'll never know, will we?"

"What would you have done differently?" Calum pressed, now with an edge to his voice.

"I definitely wouldn't have tripped over a bunch of plants. That's for sure."

"It was one plant that tripped me. The others attacked me and actively defended the King," Calum insisted. "I've never seen anything like it. Well, except for at Kanarah City, when those rose pod-things fought alongside the King's soldiers."

Axel thought back to that skirmish. It ranked among the stranger battles he'd ever fought—if not *the* strangest. Did the King somehow have control over plants? Or nature itself? Or... some other magic?

Lumen and Matthios had crazy powers, and if the King was supposed to be Lumen's match—or *more* than his match—then he had to have abilities that Axel didn't know about.

If so, maybe Calum's failure was justified after all. If the King possessed that kind of power, then maybe Calum never even stood a chance. Maybe he only *thought* he had a shot at killing the King.

"Look, we need to get outta here," Calum reasserted. "We'll be convicted at trial, no question. With Captain Anigo to testify, and with me failing to kill the King, both our fates are sealed. We have to find a way to escape."

That was another thing they agreed on. But it wasn't like they could just tear free from their restraints and walk out.

"How do we do that?" Axel asked.

Calum shrugged. "I don't know. We'll have to think of something."

Silence lingered between them for a long moment. Then Axel said, "Well?"

"Well, what?" Calum eyed him. "It's not like I'm the only one who can come up with ideas."

"*You're* the leader. You've made that perfectly clear." Axel laced his words with anger. "Plus, according to you, you already escaped once using Lumen's light. Just do that again."

"Stop being so overdramatic."

The familiar frustration at this entire situation returned to Axel's chest, and he clenched his teeth. "Am I wrong? On either point?"

"We already talked about this before we fought. Whether you're right or not doesn't matter. How you come across is what does."

"Whether or not I'm right is the difference between us escaping certain death or your feelings getting hurt," Axel snapped. "So you can either deal with my attitude as it is and we'll escape, or you can whine about how mean I am, and we'll both die in this awful place."

More silence. Axel regretted his tone, but not much. He *had* to be firm, or even harsh with Calum. It's what had kept them both alive this long.

"I can't reach the shackle to use the light," Calum finally said. "It's a different kind than before. My wrist is pinned to the bedframe, and I can't get my fingers around to touch the metal. They must've realized I broke the shackles somehow."

"Then use it on the bedframe itself."

Calum stared at him for a moment. "That's… actually a good idea."

"Then do it."

Calum's face scrunched up as if he were straining or in pain. Then a light even brighter than the sunlight streaming through the windows flared from his left side, and a loud *crack* filled the room.

But instead of Calum's hand breaking free, the entire bed collapsed underneath him. Splinters and chunks of wood scattered across the floor, and the sheets billowed outward as the bed crashed down.

Part of Axel wanted to laugh at the sight, but the other part of him couldn't deny that Lumen had in fact bestowed some real power upon Calum after all. Sort of.

Shattering metal shackles and demolishing furniture with a touch was all well and good, but it paled in comparison to what Lumen himself could actually do. Still, it was more than Axel had, and for that reason alone, he wanted it.

At least now they could find a way out of there.

"Hurry up and free me," Axel hissed. The bed's collapse was plenty loud enough, so why bother keeping his voice down?

As Calum twisted and contorted to try to free himself from the tangle mess of fabric and wood, the door to the infirmary swung open again, and Valerie stepped inside with a complement of silver-clad soldiers.

"Ah, good. You are already out of bed." She clasped her hands together and displayed that same simple smile while both Calum and Axel stared at her, bewildered. "It is time for your trial."

CHAPTER 27

When Lilly saw the same beautiful black-haired woman in the red dress escorting a downcast Calum and a battered Axel into the King's throne room, her heart leaped with momentary relief.

She'd initially thought they'd come to negotiate for her release, but the shackles on their wrists and ankles suggested otherwise. They'd been captured, too, which meant they would be tried as criminals, just like her.

Upon seeing her, both Calum's and Axel's eyes widened with relief. Calum smiled at her and tried to wave, but a chunk of a wooden beam connected to the shackle on his left wrist made it an awkward motion. Rather than wave back, she kept her own shackled hands down near her midsection.

By contrast, Axel alternated glances at her and then at the brunette as if comparing them. Lilly realized it immediately, and the heat of jealousy threatened to rise in her chest. She banished the sensation, though, by reminding herself of Axel's behavior back at her home in the Sky Fortress. There was truly nothing to be jealous of.

The soldiers accompanying her friends ushered them to standing positions next to her, and Calum and Axel took in the enormous throne room just as she had when she'd first been brought inside. Altogether, she estimated it to be at least twice the size of the throne room back home in the Sky Palace.

The same shimmering white stone that made up the entirety of Valkendell also formed the interior walls of this room. Silver and gold trimmed the room, and a colorful array of tapestries hung from the walls.

High above them, the vaulted ceiling shone with light from countless small windows which allowed sunlight inside at varying angles throughout the day. It was a beautiful and simple effect, and along with additional windows cut into the walls, the light easily banished the shadows from the room.

The floor was a spiraling pattern of white and gray stone, and in the center of the space rose a platform three steps higher than the rest of the room. On it sat a solitary throne of opalescent stone.

Everything in the throne room was perfect. Clean, polished, undamaged. Immaculate.

But the crucial difference that stood out to Lilly about the King's throne room was the distinct lack of people inside it.

Back home, her father had welcomed dozens of court officials and nobles alike to occupy his throne room nearly every waking hour. It was a place of commerce and cooperation, of relationships, of discussion. And, when necessary, it was a place of judgment, too.

Apart from Lilly, Calum, and Axel, and the woman and the four soldiers who'd accompanied their captives, on one else was inside. And just as Lilly noticed the lack of people, the soldiers started to return toward the grand entrance.

Were they really going to leave the three of them alone with only one woman to watch over them? An unarmed woman in a dress, no less? Surely they weren't so foolish or thoughtless.

Calum's voice interrupted Lilly's thoughts, but she still didn't take her eyes off the woman.

"What happened to you?" he asked.

"Matthios," she replied. "The Imperator. He tore through my Royal Guard, defeated Condor, and took me hostage."

That got Axel's attention again. He'd been unashamedly focused on Valerie ever since the soldiers had left, but at Lilly's story, he turned toward her.

"Are you alright?" he asked, his voice both concerned and edged with rage. "Did that bronze monster hurt you?"

"I'm fine," she replied. *You can go back to staring at your new obsession.* She didn't say it, but she wanted to.

Perhaps she was still a little jealous after all, even though she shouldn't be.

Calum looked her up and down. "They took your armor as well?"

"And my crown, and I dropped the Calios before Matthios hit me the last time," she said with a sigh. Hopefully Condor had recovered in time to grab the sacred weapon so it wouldn't fall into the wrong hands. "When I woke up, I was in a room—almost like a guest room—lying in bed, clad in this."

She motioned to the simple blue dress that now covered her body. Then she held up her wrists and jingled her shackles.

"And these."

"For what it's worth," Calum gave a modest shrug, "I like the dress. Brings out the color in your eyes."

A familiar rush flowed through Lilly's chest, and she could feel her cheeks heating up. They'd already discussed this. "Calum..."

He held up his shackled hands, including the chunk of wood still attached to his left wrist. "I know. I'm sorry. I won't say anything else."

The truth was, Lilly *did* want him to say more. For the sake of her people, she just couldn't follow through on any of it. And then there was Condor to consider...

Another pulse of emotion hit her, and she spoke to help push it away. "What happened to you?"

"A lot more than what happened to you," Calum said.

As he shared his story with her, he didn't bother to keep his tone quiet, despite the dark-haired woman patiently standing ten paces behind them like a mother hen watching over her brood.

Lilly figured she must've already heard what he had to say, so there was no reason to conceal anything. Or perhaps Calum had come to the same conclusion Lilly had: their trial would be swift, and their judgment even swifter.

When Calum got to the part about shattering the bed, Lilly couldn't help but smile. It was a very Calum-like happenstance, and the thought of it brought her relief even amid their situation.

But as soon as Calum concluded his story, the woman cleared her throat from behind them. Lilly and Calum turned to look at her, and Axel had scarcely torn his eyes from her since they'd entered the throne room.

She gave them a pleasant smile and motioned toward the throne. When they turned back, a man clad in white robes and wearing a white crown was seated on it.

The King.

The sight of him sitting there startled Lilly. It shouldn't have been possible—had he just appeared out of nowhere?

She recalled that Lumen could traverse great distances through glowing white voids as well, and that partially answered her query, but it did nothing to make her feel any less unnerved at the King's sudden appearance.

Even more unnerving was the overwhelming sensation that accompanied his vibrant green-eyed gaze. At first, Lilly felt as though she was suffocating, and the tips of her fingers and toes felt as if they were buzzing like bees. She realized she was trembling, and she clenched her fists tightly to resist.

Over the past few months, she'd finally come to realize and consider herself a ruler. But in the presence of the King of all Kanarah, she felt like a small child again, looking up at her father seated on the throne. Did Calum and Axel feel the same way?

As the King scrutinized them, the sound of footsteps resonated behind them. Lilly and the others turned back for a look. She, in particular, was grateful for the excuse to break eye contact with the King.

Then she saw Matthios walking into the throne room. His bronze armor, bald head, and double-bladed spear were unmistakable, even from a distance. He casually walked toward the platform, past Lilly and the others, ignoring them as if they weren't even there, despite Lilly trying to burn through him with her eyes.

He joined the King on the platform, standing left of the throne. Lilly didn't quite understand why, but the woman continued to stand behind Lilly and her friends, still pleasantly smiling.

The room stayed silent for a long moment, and Lilly fought to control her emotions. No matter how she tried to rationalize it, she knew she could never live up to the stature of someone like the King. In terms of ruling her people, she just couldn't compare to him. It left her feeling inadequate, like a failure.

I am a failure, she admitted. *I couldn't lead my people well enough, and now I'm stuck here.*

The realization broke her heart. After everything she'd done, everything her people had already endured, she couldn't fully give them what they truly needed.

I'm not enough. I never was.

And soon it would all be over. Amid the silence, she did her best to steel herself for whatever was coming next.

Then she felt a hand take hold of hers.

She looked down and saw a chunk of wood dangling from the shackle on Calum's arm, and she saw his fingers curled around hers.

It almost broke her the rest of the way. Lilly fought to restrain her tears, and she refused to meet his eyes. She couldn't. Not now. She even considered pulling away.

Instead, she exhaled a shaky breath and squeezed his hand in return.

No matter what, they were still friends, and they would be until the end. They would stand together, even in the face of certain death, as they had so many times before.

She locked her eyes onto the King with renewed resolve.

And then the King spoke.

THE FIRST TIME he heard the King's voice, Calum's heart hammered in his chest, but not because of what he said, or his tone of voice, or the volume.

Rather, Calum's heart thrummed because of something else—something both deep yet lofty, ethereal yet arcane, powerful yet gentle. What that quality was, Calum couldn't say, but its presence was undeniable.

It was so strong that Calum lowered to one knee and bowed, more out of reflex than anything. To his surprise, so had Lilly, and even Axel did as well, albeit with huge drops of sweat dripping from his forehead.

Calum felt beads of sweat clinging to his own face from whatever pressure the King was somehow exerting, but he didn't dare look up or try to stand up. He doubted he could've done either of those things even if he'd wanted to.

The one thing he could do was keep holding onto Lilly's hand, so he did.

Truth be told, Calum hadn't even heard what the King had said. But the second time the King spoke, Calum understood the word as if he had spoken it himself.

"Rise."

In unison with Lilly and Axel, Calum stood and dared to look at the King again.

Those vibrant green eyes locked on his, and although Calum couldn't discern whether he was seeing empathy or apathy behind them, he knew they lacked even a hint of anger or rage or fury.

It didn't make sense. Calum had tried to assassinate the King, but the King didn't even seem mad about it.

Perhaps if Calum had actually gotten closer to succeeding, the King wouldn't be presenting such a neutral front. Or, more likely, Calum was out of his depth and couldn't begin to guess at the King's thoughts. That seemed the most likely scenario.

The three of them remained silent as the King surveyed them yet again. A minute later, he reached within his robe and pulled out a crown made of bright-yellow crystal. Calum recognized it immediately, and Lilly perked up at the sight of it.

The King extended it toward Matthios. "Return this to the Premieress."

Matthios accepted the crown and, still carrying his spear, stepped off the platform.

When the Imperator reached Lilly, she squeezed Calum's hand tighter, but to her credit, she didn't recoil. Matthios held out the crown for her to take, and she accepted it and let go of Calum's hand to place it on her head. It seemed to reinvigorate her, and she didn't take hold of his hand again, and he didn't try to make her.

"Remove their bonds," the King ordered while Matthios still stood before them.

Without using a key, Matthios touched each pair of shackles, and they clanked to the floor. Then he collected each set and proceeded back to stand in his spot next to the King, still holding the shackles, including Calum's set with the chunk of wood still attached.

Now freed from their chains, all three of them rubbed their wrists. For another long moment, nobody spoke. Then, for whatever reason, Axel broke the silence.

"This isn't the kind of trial I was expecting," he said.

Calum agreed with him. He'd expected Captain Anigo would be there, at minimum, to speak against them, but they were alone. Maybe the King had already decided their fates. It was pretty obvious whose side they were on, after all.

The King's attention fixed on him. "And what were you expecting?"

Axel gulped audibly, then he opened his mouth to reply, but nothing came out for a few seconds. He finally said, "Accusations. Some evidence or witnesses. Maybe the chance to say something before you have me executed."

"What is it you wish to say?" the King asked.

The question caught Calum as off-guard as it had Axel, who stood there with his mouth agape again. Only this time, Axel didn't speak again.

Instead, Lilly did.

"Your Majesty," she repeated the term Matthios had used to address the King, "evidently you already know who I am in relation to my people, the Windgales. Before you pass any judgment, I must ask you to consider our reasons for joining Lumen's cause."

"So you admit to siding with the sworn enemy of the King?" Matthios barked at her.

The King raised his hand as if to quiet Matthios, and it worked. Matthios didn't speak again. Then the King leaned forward and motioned for Lilly to continue.

Thus far, Calum had to agree with Axel—this was definitely a weird experience so far. Was the King disinterested in them? Was he here out of some forced obligation?

It all confused Calum, so he refocused on the one thing that he knew for certain. The one constant throughout nearly his entire life. The one truth that no one could ever take away.

The King's men had killed Calum's parents, and although Calum would likely never find the exact men who'd done it, the man ultimately responsible for those soldiers' actions sat on the throne before him, impassive. It infuriated Calum.

Before Lilly could continue, Calum blurted his accusation.

"Your soldiers *murdered* my parents," he almost yelled. "*That* is why I oppose you."

Matthios flinched at Calum's outburst, but the King's hand stayed him again.

Those vibrant green eyes locked onto Calum's, displaying the same pity as back in the garden, only somehow deeper this time.

Again, the sight enraged Calum. He didn't need this man's pity. He needed vengeance—no, *justice*—for his parents' deaths. It was only right that the King die as well.

Just when Calum thought he couldn't grow any angrier, the King said two words that stoked the flames in Calum's heart to unprecedented heights: "I know."

Calum lurched forward with a roar. He had no weapon, no plan, and no hope of succeeding. Matthios would strike him down well before he ever reached the King.

Sure enough, even before Calum completed his first leaping step forward, Matthios had already pointed his spearhead directly at him.

But the King's hand froze Matthios in place yet again. Instead, he himself rose from his throne as Calum's second step hit the stone floor. He stood before his throne with his arms down at his sides, his eyes still full of pity.

Calum reached him in three more steps and slammed his right fist into the King's gut.

The King took the blow as if he'd been struck by a small child while play-fighting. Calum's next punch to the King's ribs did even less damage, it seemed. He threw another devastating attack, this time at the King's face, but the King's head barely moved.

On and on Calum threw punches, shouting in rage and frustration and impotence. The King absorbed every swing. When Calum finally stopped, sucking in rapid breaths and pushing them right back out to calm his rattling heart rate, he looked up into the King's green eyes again.

They stared at each other for an eternity, with Calum panting like a beaten dog and the King standing in place like a timeless statue.

The two words the King had previously said to Calum had enraged him beyond belief, but the two words he now spoke changed Calum's life forever.

The King said, "I'm sorry."

CHAPTER 28

Calum's parents were dead. They had been for years. And the King's response was "I'm sorry?"

What was he supposed to do with that? An apology, even from the King himself, wouldn't resurrect his parents. It wouldn't erase the lifetime of harm his soldiers had inflicted upon Calum. It wouldn't stop any of the ongoing atrocities perpetuated by the King's men across Eastern Kanarah. It wouldn't change anything out in the real world.

Yet despite Calum's fury at hearing those words come from the King's mouth, he couldn't deny that he felt different inside. It wasn't as if those words had wiped away the years of heartache and suffering Calum had endured, nor had they served to usurp his beliefs regarding the King, but he did sense a spark within himself that wasn't there before.

He felt… better. A little bit, at least. He didn't know why or how, but he couldn't deny it was there. It was almost as if a part of him that had long since been broken was now beginning to heal.

Calum blinked. Did he actually believe that? And even if it were true, would he allow it? Would he really let the King off that easily?

Then again, did Calum have any other choice? As he'd rightfully assessed, the King couldn't bring back his parents or erase the travails of the last several years.

But it wasn't only Calum's life that mattered. Others were out there now, suffering at the hands of the King's soldiers. A war was being waged to remove the King from power so Kanarah could reconceive herself and be reborn as a country where no one would suffer oppression.

Calum couldn't change his past, but perhaps he could still change the future.

"That's not enough," he finally said to the King, still standing only inches away.

The King still towered over Calum, staring down at him with those vibrant green eyes. "What would you have me do?"

Even before Calum spoke, he knew he was asking the impossible, but he asked anyway. "I want you to give up your crown to Lumen. Let him rule Kanarah in your place. He will see to it that the suffering of your people—the people of this world—comes to an end."

The King's visage, which had been almost compassionate before, hardened to stone. "That, I cannot do."

Calum's scowl returned. "Then you might as well execute me now, because I refuse to live in a world where your people live in mass suffering, slavery, and abuse. And I will never stop fighting until that changes." Calum injected heat into his eyes and his voice. "Which means I will never stop fighting *you*."

Matthios bristled in his spot at the King's side, but the King only exhaled a slow, even breath, never taking his eyes off of Calum.

"Please return to your place next to your friends so the trial may continue," he said.

Calum's confidence bottomed out as reality set in once again. He'd expended every ounce of his rage and strength to try to harm the King, to no avail. He was truly powerless and weak, just as he'd been all his life. He'd sworn to fight until his final breath, but against someone like the King, his final breath might come far faster than he'd anticipated.

With no better options, Calum reluctantly returned to his place among his friends. As he did, he refrained from making eye contact with either of them, and he stood a bit farther away from Lilly this time. He'd caused a scene by letting his emotions rule his actions, and now the shame of it had found him.

Calum kept his head bowed as he took his place. Lilly tried to reach for his hand again, a gesture he appreciated, but he couldn't reciprocate. Not as embarrassed as he was now.

Instead, he turned his heart to ice and stared up at the King again, cold and ready for whatever fate would soon befall him.

THUS FAR, Axel wasn't overly impressed with the King, or even all that intimidated. Sure, he had an undeniable presence and power about him, and Calum had unleashed a barrage of crazy punches and kicks on him to no avail, but Axel had fought Calum before, and Calum didn't hit that hard.

In fact, Axel was sure he could defeat the King in a head-to-head battle if it came down to it —in a fair fight, anyway. Obviously it was stupid to think he could beat someone with powers on the level of Lumen or Matthios or the King without powers of his own, but strip all that away, give each man a blade and some armor, and Axel felt pretty good about his chances.

None of that changed his current predicament, though. Even if Matthios alone had been standing there, Axel, Calum, and Lilly had no chance of fighting their way out of this one.

He stole a glance back at Valerie, who still stood behind them. Her bejeweled necklace glimmered and shined in the sunlight, and she looked even more radiant than when he'd first laid eyes on her. She gave him another simple smile, and it irked him that he couldn't seem to affect her emotions beyond that.

The King's words drew his attention forward once again.

"There is no question that the three of you have openly rebelled against me," the King began. "You yourselves do not even dispute it. Therefore, the only question that remains is what shall be done with you."

The King met Axel's eyes, but this time, instead of allowing his emotions to overwhelm him, Axel stood firm, folded his arms across his chest, and frowned at the King. No matter what sentence the King passed, it wouldn't shake Axel's resolve. He'd die as he'd lived since leaving his farm: free.

The King paused for another long moment, scrutinizing them as he had so many times before. Then he sat upon his throne once more and finally said, "I forgive you, and I absolve you of your crimes."

Axel's eyes widened, and his jaw unhinged. He let this arms slump to his sides, and he stared at the King, uncertain he'd actually heard what he'd just heard.

"Come again?" he blurted before he realized he'd said it.

The King fixed his green-eyed gaze upon him again. "I said that I forgive you, and I absolve you of your crimes. All three of you."

It made no sense. What they'd done—everything from fighting and even killing the King's soldiers, to traveling across the continent to set the King's mortal enemy free, to literally raising an army to dethrone the King—went beyond the confines of any normal crime. What they'd done was punishable not by one death but a *thousand*.

And yet the King had just absolved them of their crimes?

Axel recalled how he'd reacted when Valerie had mentioned the King's mercy. He'd almost laughed out loud at the suggestion that the man who ruled all of Kanarah, whose soldiers did as they pleased regardless of whom they hurt in the process, would even know the definition of the word.

Yet he'd just granted them mercy, like Valerie had claimed. And neither Matthios nor Valerie —Axel had glanced back to check—gave any indication that they disagreed with the King's decision.

No. It's a trick, Axel reasoned. *He's toying with us. We have information, and he needs it to thwart Lumen. He's only keeping us alive for as long as it suits him.*

"I have only one condition," the King continued.

Here it is. Here's where the trap is sprung. Axel braced himself for the inevitable conclusion.

"I invite the three of you to remain here, as my guests, so that we may find a way to peace-fully resolve this conflict," the King said. "So we may together transform Kanarah into a place where suffering, sorrow, and pain are no more."

"Ha!" Axel couldn't stop the laugh from escaping his lips. He scoffed and shook his head.

The King, Matthios, Calum, and Lilly all fixed their attention on him.

Might as well lean into it now.

"Nothing's gonna change," he said, glancing between them.

"What makes you say that?" the King asked.

"If you really wanted to make changes, you've had the last thousand years to get to work." Axel folded his arms again.

The King's response came in measured tones. "You presume I have not done enough to alle-viate the struggles of my people?"

"I don't actually know what 'alleviate' means, but I'm gonna say no," Axel replied. "You haven't done enough."

"And what do you suggest I ought to do differently?" the King asked.

Axel scoffed again. "You're supposed to be immortal, or whatever. In all that time, you haven't figured this out?"

"Clearly I do not comprehend your perspective." The King lowered his chin slightly.

"It's really not that difficult." Axel raised his hands and gestured toward invisible images conjured from his mind. "Make sure people get enough to eat. Make sure they don't get sick. Make sure your soldiers don't abuse or mistreat them. Protect them from harm. This is all basic stuff."

The King nodded. "And if I am to do these things for the people, what are they to do for themselves?"

Axel squinted at him and furrowed his brow. "Are you asking how they should serve you? Because that's pretty arrogant."

Upon uttering the word, Axel could sense the room constrict around him, mostly coming from Calum and Lilly. He'd just insulted the King to his face.

Then again, Calum had tried to beat the King to death with his bare hands and crack his head open with a pickax, so one little insult wasn't the end of the world. Probably.

"I am asking what the people will do for themselves. If I am to provide food, shelter, comfort, and security, then how will the people occupy their time?"

Axel hadn't considered that. "Well... they can just go about their own business. Live freely. Enjoy life."

"To what end?" the King pressed.

"What do you mean?" Axel shook his head. "There isn't an end. They live their lives, enjoy life, and thrive."

"How so?"

Axel blinked at him. "How so, what? What are you asking me?"

"How will they thrive?"

"With nothing to worry about, how would they *not* thrive?" It wasn't really an answer, but Axel couldn't think of anything better either.

"And this food, shelter, comfort, and security you wish me to provide," the King continued, "where will it come from?"

"...from you. From the kingdom."

"Who will produce the food? Who will build the shelters?" the King asked.

Alright... that was a dumb question, Axel mused. "Your men, obviously."

"And who, exactly, do you consider to be my 'men?'"

"Your soldiers." Another obvious question. What was the King getting at, here?

"My soldiers account for less than five percent of Kanarah's total population," the King said. "So you anticipate that fewer than five percent of all of Kanarah's people will be able to adequately provide food, shelter, comfort, and security for the other ninety-five percent, not to mention themselves?"

"Then your workers, too." As soon as Axel said it, he realized his mistake, but it was already too late.

"And who, exactly, do you consider to be my 'workers?'" the King challenged.

Axel bit his tongue.

"From what I understand, both you and Calum were among my 'workers' before you set out to find and free Lumen. Is that correct?"

How the King knew that, Axel didn't know. Perhaps Captain Anigo had told him or passed along that information somehow, so it wasn't outside the realm of possibility that he could've found out.

"So if it is my 'workers' who are to provide food, shelter, comfort, and security to all the people of Kanarah, then who will be left to simply 'live freely' and 'enjoy life?'"

The King's conclusion hit Axel like a punch to his chest. It reminded him of when the gemstone warrior had batted him halfway across the camp with his gigantic axe.

Axel had no response to the King's inquiry—at least, no good ones.

"I do not mean to dampen your enthusiasm," the King said to Axel. "The answers to these questions and the solutions to these problems are not simple. That is why I have extended my invitation for you to remain here as my guests. Perhaps together we can find some way to achieve the vision you have put forth."

Even though the King had said it in earnest, and even though he hadn't openly called Axel an idiot, Axel still felt like one anyway. He supposed he should've paid more attention when Magnus was teaching Calum and him about culture, economics, and society.

More importantly, the interaction reinforced how much Axel hated the King. Axel could admit he didn't have all the answers, but someone like the King, someone dripping with wealth and power—that person had to do better.

He stole a glance over at Lilly and Calum, but neither of them would make eye contact with him. It embarrassed him to realize that he'd made a fool of himself not only in front of the King and Matthios but also in front of his so-called friends.

Then that embarrassment turned to anger. They could've jumped in at any point to help him make his argument. After all, they were all striving toward the same end, weren't they? They'd all joined up to free Lumen, and they'd all joined Lumen's army to fight to accomplish the kind of world Axel had described. So why hadn't they spoken up, too?

"The time has come for you to make your decision," Matthios said from the King's side. "Will you accept the King's generous offer of mercy and absolution, or will you reject his mercy and return to your false leader, whose name I will not utter in this sacred place?"

Axel's skepticism hadn't changed. This had to be some ploy to extract information from them about Lumen, or the combined army, or their plans to overthrow the King.

"Trust me," Valerie's voice said from behind them. Axel turned to regard her, and she smiled and continued, "Accept the King's mercy. Speak with him. Find a way to work with him to create a better world for everyone."

Axel exhaled a sharp breath, venting his frustration along with it. He wanted nothing more than to leave this place, return to Lumen, and continue to fight to rid the land of the King and his men once and for all. But if staying here a bit longer kept him alive, he had to consider it.

He refused to believe the King was truly offering forgiveness. After going up against the King's men, enduring their abuses back on his farm, and seeing how they took advantage of everyone they possibly could, Axel wouldn't be tricked into cooperating with the King on anything.

But he could still be useful right where he was, too. From inside Valkendell, in close proximity to the King and Matthios, perhaps Axel could find a weakness to exploit. Perhaps he could find a way to bring down the King's reign from within. And if he could do that, there was no end to the rewards Lumen would heap upon him.

Plus, it wouldn't kill him to be around Valerie a bit longer.

"I accept," Lilly said first. "As the Premieress of the Sky Realm, I would be honored to work with the King to try to resolve the issues that face both our peoples."

Axel spoke up next, feigning complicity. "I accept, too. If it's not already clear that I want to work through this, it oughta be by now."

The two of them turned to look at Calum, and Axel hated that his decision was partly dependent on whatever Calum said next—yet another reason why Axel should've been leading this stupid escapade all along.

Calum stood there in silent contemplation for far too long. The choice wasn't *that* hard, even with the potential for divided loyalties, so Axel wasn't sure why he was stalling.

Finally, Calum gave a slight nod. "I accept, under the condition that you release us to return to Lu—to the other side within three days' time if we fail to reach a compromise before then."

The King stood up and matched Calum's nod with one of his own. He even showed a faint grin. "I look forward to resolving all of Kanarah's problems within three days' time."

Axel wondered if he'd caught a hint of condescension or sarcasm in the King's words... or had he just imagined it?

Then the King nodded to Valerie, who approached the trio from behind with clacking footsteps.

The King turned to Matthios, and the two of them shared a quiet conversation atop the platform while Valerie wrangled Axel and the others.

"Please follow me, and I will show you to your chambers for the duration of your stay," she said. "You will meet with the King in his garden for lunch in one hour's time."

Axel cast one last glance at the King and Matthios, both of whom still spoke to each other in hushed tones. The sight of them alone confirmed his suspicions that this was all some sort of setup, and not even a convincing one. He could see right through it.

But so much the better. If he could see the danger coming, he could protect himself from it—and maybe Calum and Lilly, too.

For now, he was content to follow Valerie, as she'd requested. One thing was for certain—he didn't mind the view one bit.

When Valerie had shown them to their chambers, Calum had expected to be sharing one with Axel, but that wasn't the case.

Of the three doors in the hallway, Valerie assigned Axel his own chambers—actually more like a full suite than a single room—at one end. Calum had the middle chambers all to himself, and Lilly had the one on the opposite end of the hall from Axel's.

Despite Lilly being actual royalty, her chambers weren't any better or worse than Calum's or Axel's, but that hardly meant anything, given how nice all three suites were. They each contained multiple rooms, including a bedroom, a small kitchen area, and a bathroom with a bronze tub inside. Fine stone floors and bronze accouterments solidified the chambers' elegant feel.

The windows in the chambers overlooked the city of Solace, which Calum finally got his first good look at. Far below, an ancient city of white-and-gray stone sprawled out before him.

In the distance, to the southwest, he could see the city walls towering over the nearest buildings and houses, a stalwart and robust means of defense that, according to Magnus, had never been breached by any foe in history—including Lumen himself a thousand years ago.

People, no bigger than ants from this distance, milled about in the streets, which bustled with commerce and energy. High above, the sun burned in the azure sky, casting everything in pure light, and glinting off the stone that formed Valkendell, most of which Calum couldn't see due to his chambers' position within the tower.

Several minutes after exploring his chambers, Calum heard a knock at his door. He turned to find Lilly standing in the open doorway. The sight of her still wearing the beautiful blue dress given to her by the King and her yellow crystal crown atop her head sent Dactyl wings fluttering in Calum's stomach.

He gulped back his emotions and smiled at her. "Sure beats getting executed, doesn't it?"

Lilly gave a mirthless laugh. "It does, but I can't help but wonder what the King is playing at." She paused. "May I come in?"

"Yes, sorry." He gestured toward the overstuffed leather sofa across from the unlit fireplace in the chambers' common room.

Was Calum supposed to invite her inside without being prompted? He didn't know the etiquette for situations like this. He'd never really *been* in a situation like this, except back at the Sky Fortress, sort of, after they'd returned Lilly to her family there.

Come to think of it, that was the only time in his life he'd ever been higher up in the air than he was now. The chambers they'd granted him there had a similar degree of polish to them, but the ones in the Sky Fortress weren't as large as these, and the décor was different, too.

Calum stood across the room from her to give her the space she'd said she wanted. He displayed an awkward grin and wondered if he was supposed to say the next thing or if she was.

"You don't have to stand all the way over there. I don't want to feel like I'm shouting at you to have this conversation." She patted the seat on the sofa next to her. Well, not *right* next to her, but it was the same piece of furniture, at least.

Calum obliged her and tried to fend off the flutters in his stomach again. Fortunately, she spoke up again so he didn't have to think too much.

"I've been trained in the art of negotiation, in how to communicate with other leaders and royalty," Lilly said. "My father and mother saw to it that I lacked nothing when it came to education. After all, I was to rule when they were gone, someday."

She paused, and Calum could sense the sadness permeating her being, as if she were recalling her parents and their deaths at the hands of Kahn and Vandorian's army. Calum wanted to reach out and touch her shoulder to comfort her, but their recent interactions had left him wary of how she might interpret the action, so he refrained.

Lilly cleared her throat and continued, "Regardless of that training and education, I'm not sure I can contend with someone who's been alive for literally over a thousand years."

"You won't be alone," Calum said. Then, realizing his involvement probably wouldn't help all that much, he added, "I mean... I understand what you mean, I think. It's a big task. Impossible, even."

Lilly raised two skeptical eyebrows at him. "You're not helping me feel better."

"Think of it this way." Calum held up his hands. "It was pretty much impossible for us to free Lumen, but somehow we managed to pull it off, right?"

Lilly nodded. "That's true."

"So..." Calum got lost in her blue eyes for a moment, and then he lost the sequence of his thoughts. "...what was I saying?"

Lilly's grin widened. "You're blushing."

Calum blinked. "I was talking about blushing?"

"No, but you *are* blushing." Lilly gave a chuckle. "You were talking about how impossible it was to free Lumen."

"Right." Calum's cheeks felt like they were on fire from the embarrassment. Being near her was simultaneously calming and nerve-wracking at the same time. "We managed to do that, and... uh..."

"So if we survived that, we can figure this out, too?" Lilly offered.

Calum held up his forefinger. "Right. Exactly. And like I said before, we're still alive, despite me personally attacking and trying to kill the King. Twice."

Lilly nodded. "I know it didn't work, but I bet it helped you feel better. I know I felt that my parents finally got the justice they deserved when Magnus killed Vandorian and Kahn."

"It did," Calum admitted. "Sort of."

"Only 'sort of?'"

"It wasn't that I couldn't kill him," Calum confessed. "It was that he *apologized* to me, even after I tried to kill him. Twice."

Lilly didn't reply. She just nodded again and stared into the empty hearth.

"Anyway, we're gonna be here for three days," Calum said. "I doubt we'll come to any reasonable agreement, but at least he's gonna let us go when we're done."

"You do realize that he only *said* he's going to let us go, right?" Lilly asserted. "He doesn't actually have to do it."

"Why would he keep us alive, treat us like guests, and spend time talking with us if he's just going to execute us afterward?" Calum asked.

Then again, the more he considered it, this *was* the King they were talking about. Valerie had insisted he was merciful, but Calum had yet to really see that for himself. Sure, he'd absolved them, but for how long? Until it suited him to change his mind?

As King, he could do as he pleased, and it appeared no one could stop him—except for Lumen. So if Calum and Lilly couldn't figure out a way forward with the King, at least they had Lumen to fall back on for help.

"Would you have trusted Kahn or Vandorian to let us go if they had captured us? No matter what they told us?" Lilly asked.

"For all their faults, Kahn and especially Vandorian made no attempts to conceal what they were thinking," Calum said. "I always knew they intended us harm. Ever since the day I met Vandorian in your father's throne room, I knew he would be our enemy until one of us died."

"And do you regard the King in the same manner?" Lilly asked.

Calum considered it. As much as it confused him to admit it, the King's apology had gone a long way to changing Calum's mind about him, even in a short period of time. "I still don't trust him. But he decided to let us live, despite all we've done against him. That gives me hope that we can find some sort of solution."

"Even if we do, will Lumen accept it?" Lilly asked. "He means to rule, one way or another."

"I don't know," Calum said. "All we can do is try."

Speaking of trying, Calum found himself gazing into her eyes again. The flapping wings in his gut returned, and he felt sweat beginning to coat his palms. Though he tried to banish his feelings for her, they kept popping up anyway. What was he supposed to do about them?

She stared back into his eyes, and the two of them sat there as if frozen in time. If he could've stayed there with her forever, he would've.

Calum swallowed the lump in his throat and asked, "Lilly, we're here for three days. Three days without anything from the outside world trying to creep in. No obligations, no distractions."

He could already see the tension forming on Lilly's face, and even though they weren't touching, he sensed her body starting to go rigid.

Calum had gone too far to stop now, so he continued. "Do you think we could have a serious conversation about trying to—"

"Excuse me?" a feminine voice called from the doorway.

He and Lilly turned to find Valerie standing just outside Calum's chambers, wearing the same pleasant smile as usual, beckoning them toward her with her hand.

"It is time for your lunch with the King," she said. "Please follow me."

Axel poked his head in next, and upon seeing Calum and Lilly together, he scoffed and walked ahead of Valerie.

Before Calum could respond, Lilly stood up from her spot on the sofa and headed toward the door.

"Thank you," she said. "I'm famished."

"I imagine so," Valerie said with a smile. "I do not expect you have eaten much since Matthios brought you here."

As Lilly reached her, Valerie took hold of her arm and started to mention something about how delightful Lilly looked in her crown and in that blue dress, but the conversation faded from earshot as they exited Calum's chambers.

Though the fluttering in his belly had subsided, the regret had only just begun to filter in. Yet

622

even as he told himself he'd have another opportunity to talk to Lilly, he knew in his heart that this—these next three days—would be his last chance.

After that, either they would find some miraculous solution to save the people of Kanarah, and then they would all go their separate ways, with Lilly returning to the Sky Realm, or the war would continue and they'd fight until death or victory, and they would be separated yet again.

Calum rose to his feet and resolved not to leave this place without talking to Lilly one more time. If it didn't happen now, it never would.

He followed her and Valerie into the hallway and hurried to catch up, but instead, he promptly ran into Axel, who shoved him back.

"Easy there," Axel said, though he didn't seem as mad about the encounter as Calum would've anticipated. "There's no rush."

"There is, actually," Calum said. "I don't know my way around. If we lose sight of them, we'll never find that garden."

Axel shook his head. "They'll come looking for us. Nothin' to worry about. Besides, I wanted to talk to you first."

"We can walk and talk at the same time." Calum pushed past Axel, who let him go. When Calum realized his footsteps were the only ones clacking on the floor, he turned back.

Axel was still standing in place, looking at him with his arms folded.

Ahead of Calum, Valerie and Lilly disappeared around a corner.

Calum sighed and walked back halfway to Axel. "What?"

Axel sauntered forward. "We both know something about this whole situation stinks."

"I don't trust anyone here, either," Calum said. "Least of all, the King."

Axel shook his head. "I'm talking about you and me."

Calum scrunched his eyebrows down. "Our fight? Axel, now is really not the time to—"

"Forget the fight. It's the words I'm more concerned about."

"Two hours ago, you were more than happy to put all that aside so we could find a way out of here."

"That's because our lives were in danger," Axel conceded, now only a step away from Calum. "I didn't know if we'd get out or not, and my chances of surviving were better with you on my side. Now we've got three more days, at least, to live."

"Yes," Calum said, exasperated. "Three more days. Which means we can have this conversation any time when we're not due to meet with the King. Now let's go."

As Calum tried to turn to walk away, Axel caught him by his arm and hauled him back.

"I wasn't done talking to you," Axel said.

When Calum noticed Axel's hand curl into a fist, he, too, clenched his fists.

CHAPTER 29

Calum looked down at his own arm, then he met Axel's eyes again. His voice lined with steel, he said, "Last time you put your hands on me, it didn't end well for you."

"Because you *cheated*," Axel insisted. "Take away that little light in your hand, and you'd never beat me in a straight-up fight."

Calum yanked his arm free and rubbed his face with his hands. "I can't believe I'm having this conversation. What do you want, Axel?"

"I want to know that I can trust you." Axel relaxed his clenched hand and folded his arms instead. "Because right now, I don't know if I can."

"We're best friends," Calum said, still on his guard. "Of course you can trust me."

Axel gave a quiet laugh. In a low voice, he said, "Alright. What I'm saying is, at the end of this, I'm going back to Lumen no matter what you and the King come up with. He's gotta go, and Lumen is the only one who can make that happen. I need to know you're with me on that."

Calum glanced around to make sure no one else was nearby, but he saw no one else in their hall. He finally unclenched his fists as well.

He kept his voice low as well and replied, "I understand what you're saying. I have no illusions that we're out of our depth, here, and I don't trust the King to stay true to his word. If, at the end of this time, we don't have a solution, I'll of course go back with you. But in the meantime, I have to at least *try* to work something out with him."

"Play whatever song tickles your toes, and dance whatever jig moves your feet," Axel said. "I just need to be sure that when the three days passes, you're coming with me no matter what. Understand?"

Calum sighed again. "Isn't that what I just said?"

"Actually, no. You didn't."

"Fine," Calum conceded. "Yes, I at the end of the three days, I'll come with you."

"You promise?"

Calum rolled his eyes. "We're not kids anymore, Axel. If I say something, I mean it."

Axel nodded. "Good enough for me."

As if on cue, Valerie rounded the end of the hall and started toward them, smiling as usual. "We thought we had lost you."

"Sorry." Axel pushed past Calum this time and sidled up next to Valerie. "Had to have a quick chat with my old friend, here. We're ready now."

Axel jutted out his elbow for Valerie to take, and to Calum's surprise, she did.

"Lead the way, gorgeous."

Valerie leaned away from him slightly, her eyebrows raised. "It is awfully forward of you to speak to me that way."

"It's in my nature. You're just gonna have to get used to it," Axel said. "And if you don't like it, well, it's only for the next three days."

With that, they rounded the corner, leaving Calum behind.

With another sigh, he scampered after them.

———

MAGNUS HAD INDEED DEVELOPED a plan to rescue Calum, Axel, and Lilly from Valkendell in Solace. Furthermore, it was a *good* plan, and Riley could see how it would work, as long as everyone did their part and no major hiccups ruined everything.

However, that didn't mean Riley *liked* the plan.

Lumen still hadn't announced exactly when he meant to attack Solace, but according to Magnus, it as only a matter of time—literally. As soon as the army was rested, fed, and reorganized, Lumen would almost certainly march on Solace. And by the time the attack began, it would already be too late to save their friends.

Under the guise of yet another hunting trip to gather food for their respective armies, Riley and Magnus had ventured deep into the wilderness. In truth, they were meeting with Riley's top Werewolves and Magnus's most trusted Saurian warriors to go over the plan.

"Lumen's window of attack is narrow," Magnus concluded his explanation. "Therefore, we have but one chance to enact this plan: tomorrow night. Solace is two days' travel from the encampment's current location, and it will take time to transport everyone there.

"In order for this plan to succeed, we must be within striking distance of Valkendell, and we must be able to escape to a defensible rendezvous point upon completion of our objectives. In other words, by the time we are camped outside Solace's walls, we will be perfectly positioned to attempt this rescue."

Riley had expected as much, and it made sense to utilize his Werewolves' and his own stealth abilities as a Shadow Wolf at night for the best chance of success. If they could sneak in, grab their friends, and sneak back out, that would be the end of it.

They didn't really have another choice, anyway, short of Magnus personally waging an all-out assault on Valkendell himself. But that wouldn't work for about a million reasons, not the least of which was the incredible resilience of the white stone that made up Valkendell and nearly the entire city of Solace.

Riley didn't know all the details, but in a recent briefing of his generals, Lumen had made it clear that not even he could pierce Valkendell's shimmering exterior. Something about it being reinforced by ancient magic, or whatever. That, and Lumen wanted to live and rule from inside Valkendell when the war was over, so destroying it made no sense.

It was all beyond Riley's understanding, and therefore he found it disinteresting, so he'd mostly ignored the explanation and instead focused on the information he could use.

And as it pertained to rescuing his friends, invulnerable stone walls didn't mean a whole lot.

If they still had doors and windows, Riley and his Werewolves could find a way inside. That was good enough.

"If we are to succeed, we must be quick, precise, and ruthless. We must silence anyone whom we encounter. There can be no witnesses. No liabilities. Crystal?"

Riley, his Werewolves, and the Sobeks all nodded or replied, "Clear."

"You're not going without me," a familiar voice said from within the trees around them.

Riley's head turned toward the sound, as did everyone else's. Some of the Sobeks hissed, and the Werewolves growled. He recognized the voice immediately; he would live the rest of his life and never forget that voice.

"So figure out a way to work me into your plan," the voice said again, this time from a totally different spot in the trees, now behind everyone.

As before, they all turned to try to spot the source, but Riley was the only one who possibly could've caught sight of its source. He was the only one fast enough to track the Wisp's movement.

Sure enough, Riley followed the blur of charcoal-gray armor as a figure descended into the center of their meeting and spoke again.

"Otherwise, I might have to inform Lumen of your little scheme."

The Werewolves caught up first, all of them still growling, followed by the much slower Saurians, who reacted by starting to draw their weapons. Upon seeing who it was, they clapped their swords back in place, but many of them still hissed at him.

Condor's feet touched the forest floor between Riley and Magnus. It was arguably the most dangerous spot in all Kanarah at that moment, sandwiched between the Dragon King of Reptilius and the alpha Shadow Wolf of the western Wolf tribes, but Condor had landed there as if he didn't have a care in the world.

"So what's my role?" he asked. His handsome face still bore some bruises from his encounter with Matthios, but otherwise he looked strong and ready to fight once again.

Magnus grinned. "I had anticipated you would wish to join us. How much of the plan have you already heard?"

Condor gave Riley a wink and then grinned up at Magnus. "All of it, of course."

"Good. Then here is where you come in..."

Riley smirked. *This is gonna work. I can feel it.*

THE WAY CALUM had described the King's garden simply didn't do it justice. To Lilly, the space was far grander than he'd shared, far more colorful and intricate, and incredibly beautiful. It looked like something from an idyllic painting more so than a place that could actually exist in the real world, yet now she sat near the center of it, surrounded by green.

She couldn't fault him too much for not mentioning the details of the garden itself, given that his story mostly focused on his escape and subsequent assassination attempt of the King. Nor was he usually one to highlight such details whenever he told stories, anyway.

What she *could* fault him for was delaying his arrival for lunch with the King, who now sat across a long stone table from her, staring at her with eyes as bright green as the plants, trees, and bushes all around them. His expression, a brew of pleasant curiosity with one corner of his mouth upturned in a pseudo-smirk, hadn't changed yet.

She forced an awkward smile, took hold of the gnarled wooden mug on the table before her, and drew it to her lips. The water inside was refreshing and cool, and it tasted faintly of sweet flowers.

All the while, the King stared at her, still pleasantly interested and almost-smirking.

This was strange. She had to break free from the weirdness of the moment, so she opened her mouth to ask him a mindless question about the garden.

"What do you think of my flowers?" he asked first.

Her mind pivoted. "They're lovely. Which ones are your favorites?"

"The red roses," he replied without hesitation. "They are temperamental, but their beauty is unrivaled. They are an exquisite flower beloved by everyday people, and they symbolize love and romance to many, but few appreciate the precision required to foster their growth."

Having grown up in the Sky Realm, plants and flowers didn't rank too highly on Lilly's list of interests. No vegetation grew tall enough to reach their home among the clouds, and thus the majority of her exposure to plants came in the form of what she was served for meals.

Occasionally, Lilly's father would send away for colorful flowers to be delivered to her mother, in which case Lilly always received a small bouquet as well, but they always wilted far too quickly for her taste. As such, she'd never really given them much consideration.

Here in the King's garden, however, she couldn't deny the rampant beauty of everything. It all looked so lush and vivid, perhaps because these plants had continual access to proper care, nutrients, and soil, unlike the dead and quickly fading flowers routinely stuffed into her mother's finest vase.

She looked to her right, past the gaudy stone fountain and toward the bed of roses in the distance. "They look lovely."

Lilly cursed herself. She'd used that word already. She hoped the King wouldn't notice.

Luckily for Lilly, the King's eyes had wandered over to the roses as well, which meant he was no longer piercing her with his inquisitive stare. Lilly exhaled a relieved breath and reached for her mug of water again.

"The mugs are made from a strong oak tree that finally grew too large to withstand a terrible storm some years back, before the dome above you was in place," the King said without turning to look at her. "It had too many leaves, and they extended well over the tall walls of this garden. A wild wind caught it and virtually tore the tree asunder.

"As you can imagine, the damage to the rest of the garden was also considerable," he continued. "My gardeners were picking up broken branches for a week after the storm, but it took nearly a decade for the other trees and bushes to recover. Nearly every single flower had to be replanted, as well as some of the flowering bushes.

"The winds stripped the fruit trees bare, and what wasn't irreparably damaged was only suitable as feed for the horses and livestock. For several years afterward, the fruit trees yielded only a fraction of what they had before the storm.

"For this reason, we erected the protective dome you now see over the garden. The glass is not glass at all, but panels of diamond, painstakingly cut by my Imperator Gavridel and installed as a means of ultimate protection for this place. Nothing can get through it, and thus nothing will ever harm this garden again."

Lilly stared up at the dome and then through it at the gray cliff face that rose several thousand feet high above the perimeter walls of the garden. Whoever had designed Valkendell had done so with its defensive capabilities in mind.

The sheer cliff face kept enemies from approaching from behind the city, and it allowed the King's forces to focus on enemies approaching them head-on. It made for simpler and more effective defensive tactics, especially compared to freestanding cities like Kanarah City.

Yet as with all such strategies, even this structure had one crucial drawback: if the city walls were ever breached, and if Valkendell were ever invaded, there was nowhere for its inhabitants to flee. An effective invasion could reduce both the city and Valkendell to a frothing stew of death and blood.

Lilly didn't want to consider such things. If they could find common ground and work toward solutions with the King, perhaps such a scenario could be avoided entirely.

The King met Lilly's eyes again, and said, "I am glad things are finally back to they way they ought to be."

Lilly considered whether or not there was a double meaning in what he was saying to her. Was it some sort of allegory or an illustration? Or was he just being weird again?

"Forgive our tardiness, Your Majesty," Valerie's voice said from the entrance to the garden. She walked in with her arm hooked around Axel's elbow, and Calum followed the two of them inside. "It seems your other two guests lagged behind, but we are all here now."

Lilly's eyes narrowed at the sight of Axel and Valerie walking in, arm-in arm, but she decided just to be happy for him. If he wanted to fall for some enemy woman, that was his business. It wasn't like it would ever work out for him anyway. They could never be together.

But she was still happy for him—as happy as she could be, anyway.

Calum, by contrast, looked as alone as he'd ever looked. Lilly partly had herself to blame for that, but the other person to blame was definitely Calum himself.

He'd chosen the path he was walking in life, and it was a path that diverged much too far from hers for anything to happen between them. If she were totally honest with herself, their paths had never really aligned all that closely in the first place. They'd been instrumental in helping each other for a time, but that was the furthest extent their relationship could ever go.

Regardless of how she felt about him.

She banished such thoughts from her mind. Now wasn't the time to muse about what could've been. Now was the time to focus on ransoming Kanarah from the man seated across the table from her.

Once Calum and Axel took their seats, Valerie gave them another simple smile and entreated them to enjoy their meal. Axel tried to coax her to stay, but she politely excused herself and left the three of them alone with the King.

A flurry of servants drifted in and laid out a spread of meats, cheeses, bread, fruits, and vegetables fit for royalty. Other servants delivered wooden plates and utensils to them, and Lilly wondered if they had come from the same oak tree as the one that had been repurposed as mugs.

Another servant approached with a decanter of burgundy wine and offered to pour some into a crystalline glass for Lilly, but she declined. Better to keep her mind sharp for the conversation to come.

Calum also passed, but Axel accepted the offer. Lilly shot a glare at him, but he didn't notice. He was too busy filling his plate with the delectable food before them.

The King, however, hadn't moved. He simply watched them, his white clothes and crown gleaming in the sunlight like the stones of his palace, twirling his finger through his dark beard.

When Lilly had claimed a modest share of the bounty on the table, she looked to Calum. Axel had already started stuffing his face. They came to a silent agreement, and Calum spoke first.

"So…" he began, "…how are we supposed to talk about this with you?"

The King's head slowly turned toward Calum, but he didn't respond otherwise.

Calum glanced at Lilly again, then back to the King. "I mean, where do we start? Kanarah has so many issues."

"What is it you wish to see changed?" the King asked.

The question was similar to one of the early ones in the sequence of questions the King had asked Axel. Lilly considered speaking up, but she wanted to hear Calum's response first.

"I want Kanarah's people to be free," he replied.

"In what ways are they currently not free?" the King asked.

Calum cast another glance at Lilly again. "I can only share with you my experience."

The King neither moved nor said anything in response.

"You already know your men killed my parents." Calum hesitated, as if waiting to see if the King would react to that statement. He didn't. "Because that happened, I was forced into a life of slavery working in your quarry. Or one of them, anyway. I don't know how many you have.

"Anyway, I grew up there, doing progressively harder and harder work all my life." Calum hesitated again. "It's not the work that made me despise the place. It was the conditions. The treatment of the people. They were slave conditions. No one should have to live like that."

Another pause. The King still didn't respond.

"Later, after I escaped that place, my friends and I ran across Lilly. She'd just escaped from some slave traders who'd captured her and tried to sell her to one of your soldiers for evil purposes," Calum continued.

The mention of Lilly's entanglement with the slave traders sent a shudder down her spine, but she resisted it. She'd escaped, and she'd driven a knife deep into Captain Fulton's neck on her way out. All of that was as much a part of her past as anything else, so she felt no need to dwell on it.

"Another of our friends, Magnus, who is now the Dragon King of Reptilius, was caught by the same slave traders. They sold him as a Saurian to some of your soldiers, who in turn sold him to Burtis, the foreman at the quarry I worked at," Calum explained. "That's how I met Magnus, and it's how we got connected and eventually escaped."

The King remained silent yet again. At this point, Lilly couldn't tell if he was listening attentively or if he was actually indifferent to their respective plights.

"Your soldiers really mucked things up at my family farm, too," Axel said with a mouth half full of food. "They'd always come around and take what was rightfully ours. They'd steal it right in front of us. It's not like we could do anything about it, either. They had weapons, and if we would've tried to fight back, who knows what they would've done then?"

The King's attention fixed on Axel, who blinked at him, still chewing his food.

"Don't look at me. He's the one talking." Axel nodded toward Calum, but the King didn't look away from him.

"We also encountered slavery on the western side of Kanarah. I am ashamed to admit my own father's involvement in the trade," Lilly said. That piece of information had sullied much of her view of her father, but she'd decided to forgive him before he died, so she tried not to dwell on it beyond that.

The King's quiet focus shifted to her.

"We actually succeeded in breaking up a large operation in the north," she continued. "Kahn, the last Dragon King, and his nephew Vandorian were running a slave trade operation at the Blood Chasm, where much of Kanarah's Blood Ore is mined. I don't even know how many slaves died working there, but it wasn't a small number."

Still no response from the King. It was beginning to frustrate Lilly. How were they supposed to have a dialogue if he wasn't ever going to say anything?

"I think the first thing we can agree on is that slavery needs to come to an end," Calum summarized, and the King's attention shifted to him once more. "And the second thing is that your soldiers need to be reined in. They're responsible for a lot of the hurt people are experiencing in Kanarah."

The King steepled his fingers over his empty plate, but he didn't say anything.

"So..." Calum ventured, uncertain. "What do you think?"

"I agree," the King said. But that was it. Those two words, and nothing else.

It aggravated Lilly more than if he'd remained silent.

"That's it?" Axel washed down the food in his mouth with a swig of wine. "That's all you're gonna say? 'I agree?'"

"Would you prefer I say something else?" the King asked.

"Yeah." Axel snatched a slice of bread and some cheese from the platter in front of him. "How about you throw out some ideas on how to make things better instead of just asking us to figure it out for you? You're the one who has all the power, the coin, the *years* of being alive. We're just a bunch of kids compared to you, and we're doing all the work, here."

"If I could end slavery with the snap of my fingers, I would do so immediately," the King said. "But the Overlord has not seen fit to grant me that ability."

"We know you can't fix it like that—" Axel snapped his fingers. "—but that's not what we're asking. We want you to help us figure out how to get rid of slavery. Pass a law, or issue a decree or something to outlaw it."

"Slavery is already against the law of Kanarah. It has been since the beginning," the King said. "Much like the Law of Debt."

Axel raised his hands over his head. "Well, I don't know this stuff. I'm just a farmer-turned-adventurer. But I know what I saw, and that's a lot of slavery and a lot of terrible people wearing black leather armor and doing bad things in your name."

"We routinely cycle soldiers who patrol the outer lands of Eastern Kanarah back to Solace," the King explained. "They seem to do better the closer they are to home."

"I don't think we've met a single soldier outside of Solace who has been a good person..." Calum said, "...ever. And we've encountered a lot of them. In fairness, most of them were pursuing us when we were on the run as fugitives, but still. I've only ever had bad experiences."

Now they were getting somewhere. It amazed Lilly that, despite her initial skepticism, the King of all Kanarah was actually sitting there, listening to them. Better still, he'd finally started to engage them in return.

Calum and Axel sat there for another hour, discussing and debating with each other while Lilly interjected as needed to moderate or clarify or share her opinion or experiences across a variety of issues. The King responded when prompted, and very occasionally of his own volition, but they failed to come to any concrete solutions for anything.

Even so, when Valerie showed up to conclude the meeting, Lilly remained optimistic about the entire exchange. It felt as though the two sides had come to somewhat of an understanding, at least, even if they hadn't figured out how to solve anything yet.

Most importantly, if the King was being honest with them, it turned out that he agreed with the majority of their concerns and also wished to address them. The issue, and the main thrust of discussion going forward, it seemed, was how to do so.

The King remained in his garden, staring into the swaths of green and colors while the three of them arose to depart.

As Lilly headed out, she noticed the King staring at his bed of roses again, and Lilly remembered the story he'd told her.

It preoccupied her mind for the rest of the afternoon.

CHAPTER 30

"Tell me about your parents."

The voice startled Calum, but he was even more surprised that it came from the window in the common area of his chambers. He set down the book he'd been reading and looked around, thinking maybe he'd imagined it, but he didn't see anyone.

He tentatively tugged the sheer curtains away from the window, wondering if perhaps a Windgale servant might've said the words. Instead, he found none other than Matthios, the King's Imperator and the Brazen General, floating just outside.

Calum staggered back, startled a second time, and he actually tripped over a small table and landed partway on it. The table held, mercifully, and Calum scrambled back up to his feet.

"May I come in?" Matthios asked.

Calum wondered what might happen if he said "no." Would Matthios go away? Would he barge in anyway? Would Calum survive the next hour regardless of his answer?

If Matthios had wanted Calum dead, he could've reduced him to ash long ago. That much was certain. So he opted to be hospitable.

"Sure." He swept his hand toward the hearth as if to gesture Matthios inside.

The Imperator drifted through the window, past the curtains, and stood before Calum. As usual, he wore the bronze circlet on his bald head. The mask that covered the lower half of his face matched the rest of his polished bronze armor, and his eyes blazed like molten bronze. He also carried his two-sided bronze spear with him.

Calum supposed that an Imperator had to be ready for battle at any moment, so he didn't begrudge Matthios for wearing his armor and carrying a powerful weapon around, but the guy had to realize the kind of effect he had on normal people, right? The sight of him was nothing short of terrifying, even when it was clear that he meant no harm.

Calum motioned toward the sofa. "Would you... uh... would you like to sit down?"

"Thank you."

Matthios walked over to the sofa and sat down, but rather than reclining in it, his back remained rigid, and his upper body faced toward Calum at all times, as if he were locked in on

Calum like a marksman archer taking aim at a target. Wherever Calum went, Matthios's focus followed, unbroken, unblinking, and unshakeable.

"You asked me something about my… my parents?" Calum said.

Matthios nodded. "Yes. Tell me about them, please."

Calum wasn't quite sure why an Imperator wanted to know about his dead parents, but he pulled over a wooden chair from a writing desk near the hearth, sat down, and began to talk.

"It's been years, and I don't remember much, but…"

Matthios just stared at him with his molten eyes.

"…I remember that my mother was kind and generous. And beautiful. She had blonde hair like me, only lighter. Kind of like Lilly's—er, I mean, like the Premieress's—"

"I know who you mean," Matthios interjected.

"Alright…" Calum rubbed the back of his neck and continued, "My father had hair like mine, I think. He was tall, but I'm not sure how tall. He was a strong man. I don't remember what kind of work he did, but he was strong. Smart, too. But then again, I guess everyone is tall, strong, smart, and beautiful when you're only a kid."

Matthios gave a small nod. "How did they die?"

Calum hesitated. This was an awful question to ask someone, especially someone who was basically a perfect stranger. Doubly especially given Matthios's position over the King's soldiers. Calum really didn't want to talk about this, but was he just going to refuse to tell Matthios?

Well, why couldn't he? Why *shouldn't* he? This was none of Matthios's business anyway.

"Please," Matthios added. Perhaps he'd sensed Calum's trepidation, or perhaps he'd simply remembered his manners. He repeated the word, this time in a softer voice. "Please."

Nothing about the Imperator was normal, but even this seemed especially strange to Calum. Still, he'd asked in earnest, and Calum sensed there was a reason for his inquiry, strange as it may be.

"I was a child. I'm not sure how old I was. You tend to lose track after working in the quarry for so long," he began. "One day, my parents and I were out in the woods walking. I'm not sure where we were going or why we were out there. I think maybe my dad was taking some goods to a local town to sell them in the marketplace, but I don't know for sure.

"I was riding in the back of the wagon with my mother, and my father was up front driving the donkey pulling the wagon. At some point, a band of soldiers—the King's men—surrounded us. I don't even know where they came from. Maybe they'd been hiding behind the trees, acting like bandits."

For as much as Calum couldn't remember details about his parents, he remembered far too much of that day after that point in his story. He paused for a moment to gather himself and collect his thoughts. Then he cleared his throat and continued.

"They demanded my father give them coin, or hand over whatever was in the cart, or something. I don't know." Calum's emotions rose from his chest into his throat, and he gulped them back down, but he knew it was only a temporary fix. "My father said no, and…"

Calum glanced at Matthios, who continued to stare at him with those unnatural molten eyes. He looked like a monster.

His voice shuddering, Calum asked, "Why are you asking me this?"

"Please," Matthios repeated, calmly and quietly like before. "I must know. Please."

"But why?" Calum insisted.

Matthios bowed his head for a few seconds, then he looked back up at Calum again. "I am powerful, but I am incomplete. I have existed in this world for many years, and in that time I have learned much, but there is still much I do not comprehend.

"I struggle to understand and experience emotions like you, like any other sentient person in

Kanarah. This is an asset when it comes to my proficiency as a warrior and as a general, as I can fearlessly fight and lead others into battle. But in most other situations, I lack the ability to connect with others on anything but an intellectual level." He repeated, "I am... incomplete."

"And how do my words—" Calum asked, "—how does this story help you with that?"

"I am learning," Matthios said. "I am trying to comprehend how to perceive your emotions, how they affect who you are, and how I might also one day experience them for myself."

"These are not emotions you want to experience," Calum said. "Trust me on that one."

"That is why I am trying to learn," Matthios said. Another pause filled the space between them. "If you are willing, please continue."

Calum exhaled a shaky breath and nodded. "My father said no, he wouldn't give them what they wanted. Then they hit him. He fought back, and one of the soldiers drew his sword and... The next thing I knew, my father was lying on the road in a pool of his own blood.

"My mother shrieked and left me in the wagon so she could tend to him. I don't know if the soldiers thought she was going to attack them or what, but they cut her down, too," Calum said. "After that, I don't remember much. I screamed and cried, and not long after, I was in the quarry, living a new life that never should've belonged to me."

Matthios gave a slow nod. "Thank you. Please forgive the intrusion."

With that, he stood and headed toward the window.

At first, Calum was content just to let him go, but Matthios stopped at the window and turned back.

"You may place your trust in the King," he said. "He is the One True King of Kanarah. There will never be any other."

With that, Matthios stepped out of the window and floated away, leaving Calum alone once again in his room with nothing but dark thoughts and bad memories.

———

DINNER THAT NIGHT came and went, and though the discussion seemed to make some progress, the King was pulled away early to deal with "some matters of great importance."

Whatever. Axel wasn't too worried about it. It wasn't like anything they'd discussed here would happen in the real world, anyway.

He was still convinced that the King was just putting on a show for them as part of some devious scheme to undermine everything Lumen was trying to do. Even if that wasn't the case, it meant the King was either too incompetent or too naïve to properly run this country, and either way it meant he still had to go.

As the black curtain of night descended over Solace, Calum and Lilly had wandered off somewhere in Valkendell, leaving Axel alone. At this point, he didn't even bother trying to follow them. They clearly weren't interested in spending any time with him, so what was the point?

Besides, Axel had Valerie to think about. He didn't need Lilly anymore. He supposed he favored blondes more than brunettes purely for aesthetic reasons, but he'd also resigned himself that Lilly was a prize he could never win. Calum couldn't either, he was sure, which gave him some comfort, but more importantly, that knowledge freed him up to pursue other interests.

And his current interests included Valerie, first and foremost.

Except she wasn't anywhere to be found. He'd roamed the fortress for a solid hour, peering into every open door and even trying to open some of the closed and locked doors as well. He checked the enormous kitchen, the enormous throne room, the enormous banquet hall—most of the rooms in this place were enormous—yet he didn't see Valerie in any of them.

More than a handful of servants wearing uniforms of various colors stopped him and offered to help him find his way back to his chambers, but he waved them away and kept searching. When a soldier clad in silver armor strongly insisted that he reconsider his wanderings, Axel frowned at him and left that area of the fortress behind... for now.

Another half hour later, he wandered back into the garden. With the stars blinking and winking overhead and only torches for light, the massive green space took on a totally different feel than the placid warmth it exuded during the day. The huge gray cliff face loomed over the back of the garden like a black specter, blotting out every star in that direction.

Axel stopped short when he heard familiar voices nearby, and then he darted behind a tall bush to take cover. He wasn't quite sure why he'd chosen to hide instead of just continuing to walk out into the open, but he'd already made his choice, so he stayed concealed.

He recognized Valerie's voice first; he'd grown quite attuned to its tone and the way she spoke her words, and he found he couldn't get enough of it.

Seeing her there, standing with the King and Matthios, Axel concluded that she must be some sort of trusted advisor to the King. She certainly had routine access to the King, and the King seemed to listen and value her presence.

Axel briefly wondered if she was the King's wife—which would make her the Queen of Kanarah. But when Axel had asked her if she was royalty, she'd said she wasn't. She'd also said she belonged to no one but herself.

Was she the King's daughter, then? Based on her regal demeanor, it was possible, but Axel had never heard of the King having children or having a wife.

These were thoughts for another time, Axel decided. With these three figures gathered before him, he was bound to learn something useful.

The King's voice came through next, subdued though it was. It had bothered Axel this whole time that aside from very obviously trying to play them for fools, the King was nothing like he'd imagined. He'd expected a raging bloodthirsty tyrant, but what he'd gotten was a demure introvert.

Third, Axel made out Matthios's voice. Between the King and his Imperator, Axel couldn't decide which one of them was the more peculiar. They King seemed like he was living in another world most of the time, but it was a world only he could access through his mind.

Matthios wasn't any better—Axel had passed him a few times in the halls of the fortress, and each time, he'd been mumbling to himself and walking with his back perfectly straight, as if he were a puppet with someone's hand controlling him. Axel had only made out a few of the words he'd spoken, but it sounded like Matthios was just listing random emotions as he walked.

From his vantage point behind the bush, Axel couldn't make out what they were saying. They were too far away, standing as three points of a triangle, and as usual, the King was talking too quietly. Axel probably could've heard Matthios if he'd been facing toward the bush, but his broad bronze-plated back was the only part of him that Axel could see.

Although he couldn't pinpoint most of what Valerie was saying, he took pleasure in watching her from afar. He had a good view of her, and he enjoyed watching the way she formed words with those luscious lips of hers.

Then Axel remembered the promise he'd made to himself upon accepting the King's mercy: he was there to find some sort of weakness they could use against the King. After all, the forthcoming battle with Lumen's forces was inevitable, if for no other reason than Lumen would never give up on his quest to rule Kanarah and set the people free.

The memory prompted him to consider inching forward, but that would mean abandoning the relative safety and concealment of the bush. And by doing so, he'd risk getting caught by either the King himself or by Matthios, or both.

Then again, if Valerie caught him, maybe she'd *punish* him. That couldn't possibly be that bad…

Focus, Axel, he chastised himself. *You've got a job to do.*

Axel decided to chance it. He eased out from behind the bush and, unlike mindless Calum, he thought to watch his footsteps as he advanced. As he'd expected, he didn't trip over any errant vines or roots, and no trees lobbed fruit at him. He crept closer, across a stone path as silently as he could manage, until he reached the edge of another planting bed.

Axel flattened himself out and slithered through the foliage like a snake. It made a little bit of noise, but he figured he was still far enough away that the three of them talking wouldn't notice the sound.

He found a spot among some taller flowers and remained on his stomach, watching and listening. Even if they looked in this direction, they wouldn't see him. Another bush in the next planting bed perfectly obscured his position. Better still, he could hear every word they were saying.

Axel scoffed inwardly. Riley had made this stealth stuff sound like it was difficult, like Wolves were the only ones who could pull it off. Well, if Riley could see Axel now, he'd have to eat his words.

Axel fixed his gaze on Valerie—of course—and listened, even though it was Matthios speaking.

"—already have 5,000 soldiers stationed in Solace, ready to defend their capital and their King," the Imperator said. "But I believe we should muster the remaining 2,000 in reserve. We have not faced a threat of this magnitude for a thousand years. It is wise to quash Lumen's rebellion once and for all."

"I do not have the mind for warfare that your esteemed Imperator does," Valerie nodded toward Matthios with a grin, "but I tend to agree with his assessment. If you do not stop Lumen now, forever, he will return. He is stronger this time, and wiser, and more determined to put an end to your reign for good."

True to form, the King was listening intently, as he'd done whenever Axel or his friends had spoken. He simply curled his finger through his dark beard and stared at a distant flowerbed.

The prolonged silence nearly drove Axel crazy. If he'd actually been a part of the conversation, he would've said something else by now just for the sake of saying something. He appreciated that the King at least pretended to genuinely consider everything people said to him, but at some point, enough was enough.

Finally, the King nodded. "See to it immediately, Matthios."

Matthios bowed, yet his back remained rigid even as he did so. "May your will be done."

With that, Matthios turned back and faced Axel's position, and he stormed directly toward Axel on his way to exit the garden.

Axel froze solid, and his breath caught in his throat. His heart rate multiplied, and he swore it was loud enough to give away his position.

Matthios's determined footsteps hammered the stone path adjacent to Axel's position in the planting bed…

And then he walked right past.

A few seconds later, Matthios exited the garden, leaving Axel still concealed in his spot while the King and Valerie continued their conversation. Axel took a moment to revel in his perfect silence and the quality of the hiding spot he'd chosen for himself.

Chew on that, Riley, he mused, then he refocused on what the King was saying next.

"As you know, Matthios is a blunt instrument," the King said. "Relentless and effective, but lacking in nuance."

"It is what I most admire about him." Valerie displayed her customary pleasant smile.

"But as a blunt instrument, he does not fully comprehend what must be done," the King continued. "If I could have merely destroyed Lumen and had that be the end of it, I would have."

Valerie's smile waned. "I do not fully understand, either, but you have my unending trust."

Another long pause lingered between them, until the King asked, "You planted the seeds I requested?"

"Deep in Kanarah's most fertile soil," she replied. "They lie in wait for their King's command, though I confess, I do not fully understand their purpose, either."

Seeds? Axel thought back to the pods that had transformed into the rose golems inside the walls of Kanarah City. Was the King plotting some sort of ambush? And what part of Kanarah would be considered the place with the most fertile soil?

"You need not concern yourself with such details at this time," the King said. "You trust me, and you trust the Overlord, and that is enough. Three days hence, amid the coming storm, I promise you will understand everything."

Valerie curtsied. "Yes, Your Majesty."

Axel had been a farmer. He should be able to figure this out. There were the King's orchards and the endless fields of grain where they'd first found Lilly.

But were those places any more fertile than Axel's family farm up north? He supposed they had to be. Why else would the King's workers have planted so many crops there?

From a tactical standpoint, it made sense as well. Lumen's army was heading toward Solace, away from those fields and orchards. If the King had planted—literally *planted*—an army of sorts behind them, something like the rose golems from Kanarah City, they'd box in Lumen's army from behind.

Axel was no strategic mastermind—after all, who needs a plan when you can just run in and pound all your enemies into paste—but he'd been in enough scraps to know that was an awful spot to be in.

That's what had happened to him, Calum, and Magnus when Tyburon and the Southern Snake Brotherhood had confronted them, only for Captain Anigo and his soldiers to also show up. They'd managed to pit the two enemy sides against each other and survive, but it could've very easily gone another way.

This time, the two sets of enemy soldiers definitely wouldn't fight each other; they would serve their King unto death, and they would surround Lumen's army and force them to fight the battle on two fronts.

Now this was information Axel could use. A few more morsels like this, and Lumen would *have* to bestow real power on Axel.

"It is getting late," the King said. "I wish to stay here in the garden for a time, but perhaps you should retire for the evening. Neither Matthios nor I require sleep, but I cannot expect everyone to measure up to that standard."

"That is a wise decision on your part, and it would be prudent of me to accept your recommendation. I believe I will." Valerie's smile widened, and she curtsied. "Have a pleasant night, Your Majesty."

"You as well, Valerie."

As before, Axel stayed hunkered down among the flowers and waited. He figured that if he could successfully hide from both Matthios, who'd walked right past him, and the King, who apparently maintained some measure of control over plants or nature or whatever, then hiding from Valerie would be as easy as beating up Calum.

Though he hated to admit it, Axel realized he needed to find a better comparison to draw.

Calum wasn't as weak as he used to be—even if he had blatantly cheated by using Lumen's light in their last fight.

Even so, Valerie passed by Axel's position without issue, and she, too, exited the garden.

The King surveyed his garden in perfect silence. Thanks to the dome above, which glinted from the torchlight like distant facets of a gemstone, not even the wind could rustle through the numerous trees below.

After an eternity of waiting, in which Axel almost fell asleep twice, the King finally abandoned his position in the garden and began walking toward the exit. He, too, passed Axel by, and then Axel was alone again.

He waited an extra ten minutes just to be certain the King had actually left and wouldn't be coming back, then he rose from his position in the flower bed, brushed himself off, and stretched out his sore limbs.

Axel now had one very important piece of the puzzle. Perhaps tomorrow he'd discover another, but for the time being, one was enough.

With his newfound knowledge secure in his mind, Axel made his way back to his chambers.

CHAPTER 31

To Lilly's relief, Axel hadn't tried to join them when Calum had invited her to go on a tour of Valkendell. Now he was off somewhere "doing stealth," as he called it.

Lilly had considered warning him to be careful, but at this point, Axel was going to do what he was going to do, and there was no dissuading him. If he got himself caught or killed, that was his problem.

Now Lilly walked through the white halls with Calum, her arms folded across her chest. Though she'd elected to accompany him, she didn't trust his intentions. Not that he would hurt her or try to take advantage of her like Axel had—Calum wasn't the sort to do that—but she feared he would urge her into a conversation she didn't want to have.

The alternative, however, was either staying in her room for the duration of the evening or venturing out on her own to explore Valkendell. Given those choices, she decided spending time with Calum was the best of the options.

For the first several minutes, she guided the conversation and kept it focused on their talks with the King. Calum engaged her consistently, but they soon ran out of King- and war-related topics to discuss, in part because they'd both grown weary from going over the same points of interest as they had already done that entire day.

Lilly shifted the focus to their surroundings, and they remarked on everything they observed. That led to occasional exchanges of stories from their childhoods, with Lilly comparing the layout and décor of Valkendell to her home in the Sky Fortress and Calum wondering aloud if any of the stones that formed the walls of the castle had been excavated from the quarry where he used to work.

They shared a few laughs along the way, and Lilly had to admit she was truly enjoying herself. Despite their situation as pseudo-captives of the King, inside his palace, it was nice to not have to worry about being in charge, or leading her people, or discussing battle strategies with General Balena and General Tolomus and...

Condor.

He came to mind as Lilly stood next to Calum on a balcony overlooking the city of Solace. She hadn't invited him into her mind, but he'd shown up there nonetheless.

By extension, she thought of Falcroné, too. She remembered his sacrifice to save her. Their betrothal, their separation, the constant tension between them…

Ugh. Why does this have to be so difficult?

"You alright?" Calum asked.

His voice snapped her out of her thoughts and memories, and she turned toward him.

"Yes," she replied, trying to conceal the exasperation in her voice. "I'm fine."

To his credit, Calum didn't press the issue. He kept leaning on the polished wooden railing, staring out over the city. Far below them, the windows of white-and-gray buildings glowed with gentle light from within, creating a golden version of the stars in the night sky above.

With the King's decision to absolve her of all wrongdoing, she could've simply leaped from the balcony, taken flight, and flown southwest until she found Lumen's army yet again. After all, they were alone here. No one was guarding them. They had roamed Valkendell freely, unescorted, as if they truly were guests.

But to flee now meant abandoning not only their efforts to come to some sort of resolution with the King but also Axel and Calum themselves. Perhaps she could've left Axel behind, but the thought of leaving Calum to whatever fate would befall him at the end of the three days of negotiations left a sour sensation in her stomach.

As it was, they were all lucky to even be alive. Matthios or Gavridel, the gemstone warrior whom Calum and Axel had both faced, could've easily killed them in the battle at Lumen's encampment, but they hadn't.

"After this is all over," Calum said, "I don't think I'll ever see you again."

His words shocked Lilly, and she turned toward him, her heart pounding. "Why would you say such a thing? Of course you'll see me again."

Calum shook his head, still staring out across the city. "No. I won't."

Lilly stared at him, searching his face because he refused to meet her eyes. "Calum, why would you say such a thing?"

Finally, he turned to look at her. "If we survive this, both of us… I won't see you again. I'll stay here on the eastern side of Kanarah and help rebuild and change things. I'll make things right for those who can't do it themselves. And you'll be in Western Kanarah, running your own kingdom, trying to do the exact same thing for your people."

"Surely there will be some crossover." Lilly offered the only scrap of hope she could rustle from within. "Your people need help from mine, and my people need help from yours. We'll have the chance to meet again. Assuming you'll be one of Lumen's generals, you'll have a lot of responsibility. Perhaps he'd even assign you to be an envoy to Western Kanarah."

"Why would he do that?" Calum asked. The question was genuine but also laden with skepticism.

"You are responsible for uniting the East and the West," Lilly explained. "You brought my people, the Wolves, and the Saurians together under one banner, to fight for freedom from the King. And even if we all find some sort of resolution by working with the King, you're an invaluable voice in maintaining that unity. You are the Unifier of Kanarah."

Calum shook his head and scanned the city again. "I'm nobody. I had a dream, and I followed it, and now I'm here."

Lilly took hold of his hand. "I don't know if you're just being hard on yourself or if you mean what you're saying, but I wish you'd stop talking like that. And I know we'll see each other again, Calum, however this all ends. I know it."

Calum looked down at her hand, and then he met her eyes once again.

Lilly immediately recognized that look: profound sadness, emptiness, loneliness. She'd endured all those emotions before she'd abandoned her home and her parents after they'd betrothed her to Falcroné. She'd felt as though no one would listen to her, and no one would understand her.

She understood Calum's feelings more than he knew, and they both understood why he felt the way he did.

"Lilly, I—"

"Calum," she interrupted. She hated that she had to be firm with him, but it was for the good of her people that she did so. She let go of his hand. "I know. And I'm sorry, but I can't do this."

"You don't even know what I was going to say," he said.

Lilly bit her tongue. "I think we both have a pretty good idea."

"I know how you feel," Calum said. "I'm sorry you feel this way. I'm sorry I feel it, too."

"You don't have to be sorry for how you feel," she said.

"I do if it means coming between you and your people," Calum said. "So, yeah, I'm sorry. If I could change this, I would."

"I wouldn't want you to change it." Lilly wished she could've taken back the words, but she couldn't. She'd said them aloud, and now it was too late.

Calum proved gracious about it, though. All he said in reply was, "I know."

They stood there in silence. Ever since their brief meeting in his chambers, Lilly had known Calum would try to talk to her about all of this again. And, truth be told, when she'd agreed to go walking with him, she'd known he would bring it up at some point while they had time to be alone.

He'd made it clear to her that he understood her decision and why she'd made it, but it seemed like he refused to accept it. Or perhaps he *couldn't* accept it. He was *incapable* of accepting it.

"Calum," Lilly finally said again, "I want you to know that I will always love you."

Calum's sad eyes looked up at her, flickering with hope.

"We will always be friends—dear friends, even…" She felt her own heart breaking even as she said the words. She gave a sorrowful sigh. "Calum, there are two versions of me. There is the Lilly that you love and who loves you in return, but there is also the Lilly who loves her people and would do anything—*anything*—to keep them safe.

"The Lilly who loves her people is the true version of me. She has responsibilities, obligations, and a commission to rule over the Sky Realm for the rest of her life," Lilly continued. "She is the Lilly whose life I must live, whose path I must follow. The other Lilly… she will just have to go along with it."

Calum shook his head. "There aren't two Lillys. I see only one standing before me."

Lilly sighed again. "Calum…"

"Please, let me say this," he insisted, and Lilly held her tongue. She owed him that much, at least. "There is only *one* Lilly. Those obligations and those feelings all reside within her—within you. You are one in the same. There is no escaping that.

"Your commission and your heart don't have to be at odds with each other," Calum said. "They don't. I know you think they do, but… Lilly, you're the Premieress. You can do whatever you want to do. You get to make your own path, and you get to live your life how you want to live it. You're one of the few people in Kanarah who can actually say that with any certainty.

"So if there's something you want to do, do it. If there's something you want to say, you can say it." Calum gulped, and his next words came out shaky. "If there's someone you want to love, you can love them, and no one—*no one*—can tell you otherwise."

Lilly waited until she was sure he'd finished. His words gnawed at her, but so did nearly two decades of rules, responsibilities, obligations, and the training to fulfill each of them. Only she could rightly divide between the two of them.

"Calum," she began, "I wish it were that simple, but it's not."

"It is, though," Calum insisted. "All my life, I've only ever been told that I was meant to be a slave. I mean, Axel told me I should've aimed higher than being a foreman at the quarry, but he's the only one who ever believed in me since my parents died.

"Then I began to dream of Lumen," Calum continued. "Then I met Magnus, and I left that life behind. I stopped doubting, and I began to believe. I faced death a hundred times and walked away unscathed… or maybe with some cuts and bruises, but I'm still here.

"None of us are forced to walk any specific path in life. We always have a choice," he continued. "I chose to pursue something greater, and along the way, I met you. And then I… I fell in love with you." Calum paused and met Lilly's eyes. "I don't believe in fate—I can't possibly after surviving everything I've survived, but that—you and I—it can't only be a coincidence."

The way Calum looked at Lilly and the words he spoke pierced her like an arrow. He loved her, and she loved him—there was no denying that.

And as for everything else… was he wrong? Or could she forge whatever path she wanted? Who would stop her from doing so?

If she wanted to love Calum, why shouldn't she be able to?

"That's why I can't ever see you again," Calum said, resigned. "Once all of this is over and done with, I'll go my way and you can go y—"

Lilly grabbed Calum's face and kissed him.

CHAPTER 32

I t just… happened.

Lilly hadn't anticipated it.

The urge was there, and Calum's words about never seeing him again were shredding her heart from the inside out, and…

It just happened.

But Lilly didn't regret it. Not one bit.

That's why she didn't stop kissing him.

She flung her arms around him and pulled him close to her, drinking deeply of his love. It took Calum a few seconds to respond in kind, but when he did, he matched her passion. His strong arms enveloped her, and he pulled her even closer, kissing her in return.

They both needed this. They had for so long, yet so many things had gotten in the way. Axel, Falcroné, Condor… not to mention monstrous enemies and insurmountable odds and finding a way to free the General of Light from his thousand-year prison.

Calum had been right. Apart from all of those interruptions, those distractions, the truth could finally blossom. It could finally breathe.

Speaking of which, Lilly had to pull away to get a breath. She did, but then she went right back in for more, clutching even tighter at Calum's back. She would never let him go. No matter what happened, Calum was hers now, and she was his.

They stood on that balcony for minutes, kissing and laughing and crying while the city of Solace twinkled far below and the stars danced overhead.

When they finally stopped, their eyes were red from crying, and their lips were pink from kissing. Lilly looked up at Calum and smiled the widest smile she'd ever smiled in her entire life, and fresh tears streamed down her cheeks.

Calum matched her exactly, both in glee and in tears. But then his smile shrank and his eyebrows scrunched down with worry, or skepticism, or confusion—Lilly didn't know what the emotion was, but she refused to let it interfere with this moment.

She cupped Calum's cheeks with her hands. "What's wrong?"

"Is this…" Calum hesitated. "Is this real?"

The question skewered Lilly's gut, but she understood where it was coming from. Her smile returned full force, and she nodded. "It's real."

Calum's eyes lit up. Tentatively, he asked, "You're mine?"

Lilly nodded again. "Yes."

More of Calum's joy returned. "Forever?"

Lilly bounced on her toes from her ecstasy. "Forever. There will never be another."

Calum broke into tears again and embraced her. He squeezed her so hard that it almost hurt.

She hugged him back with every bit of desperation she'd endured since the day they'd met.

But now she had him. And she would never let him go.

IT WAS REALLY HAPPENING.

Calum couldn't believe it.

He squeezed Lilly tight, and as he smelled her flowery perfume, he absently wondered if she'd put it on herself or if one of the King's servants had done it for her.

It wasn't important. Not nearly as important as the reality of that moment.

Lilly was finally his, and he was finally hers. Nothing could stand in their way anymore.

Well, except the most devastating war the land had ever known, perhaps. Or maybe the invulnerable King who held them as captive guests. Or maybe the ancient warrior bent on overthrowing said King.

But other than that, nothing else even stood a chance.

Condor.

The name filtered into Calum's mind like a poison, and he released his grip on Lilly. He looked into her eyes again.

"Condor," was all he could bring himself to say.

Lilly shook her head. "There was never anything there. Never anything real, anyway. Attraction, sure, but... it's not like this. This is love."

Calum's smile returned. "It is."

They embraced again, just holding each other under the stars, never closer to paradise than there in each other's arms. Calum never wanted it to end.

After far too short of an eternity, Calum asked, "What do we do now?"

FAR TOO EARLY THE next morning, Calum swung his feet out of the bed and sat up. Very late that night, he'd escorted Lilly back to her room from the balcony, and when he went back to his, he found he couldn't sleep due to his excitement. Now he was up at some unholy hour, well before sunrise, unable to manage his swirling thoughts.

He'd tossed and turned all night, vacillating between mentally planning their future together, reliving their best and worst moments with each other, and trying to force it all from his mind so he could get some rest. Altogether, he figured he'd gotten maybe two hours of sleep.

It was all so fresh, so unbelievable, that Calum wondered if it would actually be the same the next morning. It had felt genuine last night on that balcony, but was that just the byproduct of wishful thinking on his and Lilly's parts? Their young and frivolous belief that they could find a way to work everything out? That their love could overcome anything, just like in storybooks?

No, don't go down that road, Calum warned himself.

It was real. It was genuine. It was true.

Even so, he wasn't going to get any more sleep. He stood up, pulled on a shirt and trousers from the fully stocked wardrobe in the corner of the bedroom, slipped on his boots, and headed for the door to his guest chambers.

Out in the hallway, he considered knocking softly on Lilly's door to see if she was awake, too. Perhaps they could go on another walk together, or pilfer some early breakfast from the sprawling kitchen they'd walked past last night.

In the end, he chose not to. At least one of them should get some decent rest before their next meeting with the King. Romance or otherwise, they still had work to do on behalf of Kanarah.

By reaching an agreement with the King, Calum hoped they could put a stop to the fighting for good. Then all of his imagined plans for his life with Lilly could truly come to fruition.

As he strolled through the empty hallways, Calum gave a contented sigh. He'd answered Lumen's call. He'd walked Lumen's path and set him free. He'd raised an army to save Kanarah.

None of it compared to finally winning Lilly's heart.

All of his other dreams were coming true, but this was the most precious of them all.

Calum had grown more familiar with the layout of the halls inside Valkendell, but he still didn't feel comfortable wandering around, especially so early in the morning. It might look suspicious, and he didn't want to transgress against the King's mercy and hospitality. Axel was doing enough of that for the both of them. Instead, he headed to the garden.

Through the protective dome covering the garden, the stars still twinkled above, but the first rays of morning sunlight now shone from the east, painting the heights of the cliff face along the back of the city with subtle pinks and golds.

The garden itself was dark. The torches no longer burned, and the only light of any substance came from the silvery glow of the moon. It was just enough for Calum to be able to see, just enough that he didn't have to use Lumen's light to get around.

As he walked into the garden, he retraced his steps from his first visit. Though he'd only been there a single day at this point, Calum noticed that the flowers he'd trampled on his way to try to assassinate the King had already been replaced. Ursula and her crew worked quickly.

When he found the place where the King had been standing, surveying his garden while Calum approached from behind, Calum stopped. He had to chuckle at himself and at his fruitless attempt to kill the King.

In hindsight, he should've known better. If he'd tried the same tactic with Lumen, what would've happened? Even if he'd managed to strike a blow, he doubted a simple pickax could've killed a being like Lumen. So why had he thought it would work on the King?

It had been a moment of opportunity. Calum's best chance to end the war and free Kanarah. How could he not take it?

But now, even after only a day, the more he spoke with the King, the more he realized that perhaps there was a way to fix Kanarah that didn't require thousands more to die in the process. War was still an option, and it still might even be their best option, but Calum couldn't be sure until he'd exhausted every possible chance to find solutions with the King.

Part of him wondered—and even feared—how Lumen would react if they actually did find solutions. He doubted Lumen would just give in to whatever new way of things they might manage to create here. And if that was the case, what would happen then? Would the war go on anyway? And whose side would Calum be on?

Lumen's, of course, he decided.

It wasn't even really a decision; he'd answered Lumen's call and set him free for exactly this purpose. And above all else, Calum was loyal. Everything he'd done by talking with the King was, ultimately, a labor undertaken for the people of Kanarah—people just like him who couldn't live in suffering any longer.

A sound behind him drew his attention, and he turned back. The garden was otherwise entirely quiet, devoid of the usual noises that accompanied nature. No crickets, no birds, no rustling of wind through the trees or hissing over the grass.

So the sound of stone lightly scraping against stone caught Calum's attention immediately. He looked toward the bed of roses that ran along the garden's back wall. There, under the waning moonlight, he could just barely discern a door-sized opening in the wall.

When the King walked through the opening and into the garden with a basket in one hand, Calum dropped to the ground and flattened himself on the stone path. He immediately realized he wasn't supposed to have seen what he'd just seen. His heart quickened its beating, and he inhaled and exhaled quick, quiet breaths.

From his position on the ground, he could no longer see the bed of roses or the opening. Bushes and plants and trees lining the path obscured his vision, but he didn't need to see any more. He just needed to hide.

The King would either walk right past Calum on his way out of the garden, or he would take the path along the far side instead—if he meant to leave the garden at all. If he chose the side nearest to Calum, even in the low light, the King would almost certainly see him.

The soft scrape of stone sounded again, and then the King's distant footsteps clacked across the stone path. Fortunately, the King chose the path on the far side, and it took him around the central fountain and toward the central path, which led out of the garden.

Calum watched him from a distance, still as a rock, and holding his breath. There was at least a chance the King could still realize Calum was in the garden, especially if he could sense the presence of someone else through the various plants nearby. That had certainly seemed to be the case when Calum tried to attack him.

To Calum's great relief, once the King reached the central path before the fountain, he headed toward Valkendell and left the garden behind.

Only then did Calum push himself up to his feet. He stared long and hard at the archway denoting the entrance to the fortress. The sun had begun to crest the cliff face, so the increasing amount of light clearly showed that the King had left.

Calum looked over to bed of roses again. The back wall was once again solid, as if there had never been a door there in the first place.

Questions filtered into Calum's mind. As far as he knew, the walls of the garden also formed the back wall of this part of the city, and all that lay beyond were the steep rock faces of the mountains into which Valkendell was built.

Was there some hidden path back there that ran along the wall of rock? And if so, where did it lead?

More importantly, how long would it be until the King returned? Would Calum have enough time to investigate?

Calum didn't know, but this was his best chance to take a look without getting caught, so he took it.

Even though he was alone in the garden, Calum crept toward the bed of roses and the back wall as quietly as possible. His boots made that difficult, but he reached the back of the garden quickly enough that he hoped it wouldn't matter.

Next, he tiptoed through the roses, careful not to crush any of them along the way. Their thorns scratched at the leather of his boots as if trying to hold him back or keep him from advancing.

When Calum reached the wall, he stopped. The light was too low for him to make out any distinct cracks or lines on it, so he held up his left hand and summoned Lumen's light. His palm shone with a soft glow, the modest burn in his arm and shoulder oozed into his collarbone, and he scanned the area for seams.

He found none. Had he just imagined seeing the door?

No. It was there. The King had even walked through it. This was the right area; Calum just couldn't find the door.

He searched for minutes, running his fingers over the smooth stone of the wall, trying to find the door by touch, but to no avail. Nor could he decipher any way to get it open, either. Perhaps the King had used his powers to open it. Or perhaps there wasn't even a door there at all, and the King had somehow made a temporary one and then sealed it back up again.

Calum also remembered that the King was carrying a basket when he'd come through the wall, but he wasn't carrying it when he left. Was the basket still in the garden, then?

He doubted a simple basket would hold the answers to his questions about the King's secret door, but at this point, it was his only lead, so he crept back through the bed of roses and began his search. Calum found it a moment later, tucked under a stone bench under an apple tree.

He pulled it out and held it up. It was a simple wicker basket, wider than it was deep, but sturdy and well-made. It looked like something a street vendor in a large city might've used to display bread or trinkets at a cart. Nothing fancy.

It gave him no answers, so he put it back where he'd found it.

By that point, the sun was visible in the sky. Axel and Lilly would be waking up soon, and Calum had already overstayed his time in the garden, so he abandoned his quest for the secret door and crept back to his chambers before anyone could catch him wandering the halls.

Back in bed, exhaustion took over, and even though his mind tried to hold him hostage with more thoughts of Lilly, of Lumen, of his friends, of the war, and of the King and the secret door in his garden, Calum finally drifted off to sleep.

AXEL HAD BEEN POUNDING on the door for solid three minutes before Calum finally opened up. Calum stood there looking like as pallid as a Dactyl, with dark circles under his eyes and squinting at Axel against the brightness of the hallway.

Axel looked him up and down, unimpressed. "What's wrong with you?"

Calum muttered something Axel couldn't understand and rubbed his face at the same time.

"Yeah, yeah. Whatever." Axel pushed past him into the darkness of Calum's chambers, headed straight for the window in the main chamber, and flung the curtains open wide. Morning sunlight blazed into the space, banishing all but the room's shadows.

"No, no..." Calum protested. He shut the chamber door behind him and walked toward Axel while shielding his face from the sunlight at the same time.

"What, are you some sort of vampire?" Axel scoffed.

"A what?"

"A vampire. I read about 'em in this novel called *Blood for Blood*—" Axel waved his hand. "Never mind. Doesn't matter."

Calum groaned and tried to get past Axel to close the curtains, but Axel redirected him to the leather sofa. Calum toppled easily and landed facedown on the cushions with another groan. And there he lay, looking half-dead.

Just like a vampire, Axel mused.

"What do you want?" Calum growled into the cushions.

"We need to talk." Axel folded his arms. "Besides, it's three hours 'til midday. You can't sleep forever."

Still flattened out on the sofa, Calum peered up at him with one angry eye. "I only fell asleep a few minutes ago. Or at least it feels that way."

"Quit whining, *Calum the Deliverer*. The *Unifier of Kanarah*," Axel taunted. He hated those monikers, mostly because they'd been applied to Calum rather than to him, but also because they were terrible and cheesy. "You already missed breakfast. Good thing the King wasn't there, or you might've kicked off the war early with your disrespect."

"The war is already going on," Calum grumbled as he buried his face in the cushion again and covered his arms with his head. "And you *want* the war to happen anyway."

"Can't deny that. Got me there." Axel smirked. When Calum heard what he was going to reveal about what he'd learned last night, it would change everything. "That's why I arranged for Lilly to meet us in here so we could talk about it."

Calum's single exposed eye shot open, then he craned his head up to look at Axel.

"She'll be here any minute," Axel added.

As Axel had expected, that got Calum up and moving lightning-fast. If he wasn't so predictable, it might've been funny. Instead, watching him scramble to find clothes and try to fix his lopsided, pillow-pressed hair was just sad. Embarrassing.

"I don't know what's wrong with the two of you, but she missed breakfast as well." Axel shook his head and peered out the window overlooking Solace. "These days if I miss a meal, I get too ornery."

"You're always ornery," Calum called from the next chamber.

"That's different," Axel retorted. "It's called personality. Maybe you should try getting one for yourself sometime."

"Ha, ha," Calum replied, deadpan.

A knock, far gentler than how Axel had knocked earlier, sounded on Calum's chamber door. A curse from Calum in the adjacent room followed.

"You want me to tell her to get lost for a few minutes?" Axel chuckled.

"No, let her in," Calum replied, then he cursed his hair and the hairbrush and the mirror all in quick succession.

Axel just shook his head. He could pull off the rugged just-woke-up look. After all, he was far more handsome than Calum and had scratchy facial hair, so it wasn't a bad thing if he looked like a gruff mountain man most of the time.

He opened the door, and the sight of Lilly tickled at his gut. She looked fantastic, wearing a dress that started burgundy on the bottom but progressed to red, and then to orange near the top. The fabric had a distinct sheen to it which added to the effect.

Her yellow crystalline crown and blonde hair made her look like a walking tongue of fire, which had to be an intentional choice on someone's part. Whether it was Lilly's doing, or perhaps Valerie's, or even the King's, Axel didn't know. But whoever had done it either really liked fire or they'd gone a bit too far with the ensemble.

But Axel had long since given up on Lilly. And with Valerie roaming these halls, he felt fine acknowledging that Lilly looked good without having to hold a candle for her—a pun which, he decided, had just sparked a new flame to life in his mind.

Oh, yes. He was going to have fun with this one.

He gave her a sly grin. "Aren't you a little warm in that?"

Lilly's eyes narrowed. She'd understood his comment well enough. "May I come in?"

"Sure. Calum's doing his makeup, but he'll be out soon."

"Makeup?" Lilly eyed Axel as she walked inside.

"Yeah, you know. Paint for the old barn? A bit of rouge for his cheeks, some powder, maybe some juice pressed from berries to color his lips." Axel shut the door and followed her to the sofa. "You know, typical girl stuff."

"Ignore him," Calum called from the other chamber.

"I always do," Lilly called back as she took a seat.

Axel's bright mood dampened, and he muttered, "Isn't *that* the truth..."

Lilly looked up at him. "Hmm?"

Axel shook his head. "Nothing, Your Fireness. Oops. Excuse me. I meant 'Highness.'"

Lilly rolled her eyes.

Calum emerged from the other chamber. He'd missed a section on the back of his head where his hair still stuck out.

Axel considered telling him, but when Lilly stood to greet Calum and did so with a long embrace—much longer than Axel had ever seen her embrace anyone—he decided to keep it to himself. He realized then that he'd missed something important, and a pang of jealousy stabbed at his heart.

When the two of them finally ceased their embrace, they turned back to Axel.

He spoke before they had a chance to. "I get the picture. You don't have to say anything else." He forced a smile and lied to their faces. "I am *truly* happy for you both."

They smiled in return, clearly *not* forced.

"Thanks, buddy. Means a lot to me," Calum said, then he looked to Lilly. "To us both."

Every reason in the world why Lilly should never have ended up with Calum cascaded through Axel's mind, but he clamped his mouth shut so as not to spew them all over the two of them right then and there.

Instead, he stepped away from the sofa and motioned toward it in what he considered to be the most charitable act he'd done in recent months. "Why don't the two of you sit together, and I'll stand?"

They obliged him, and as his back was turned to them, he mouthed a dozen or so curses to the heavens. Then he reminded himself that women like Valerie existed, including Valerie herself, of course, and he began to feel better.

Still, it gnawed at him that in the end, Calum seemed to have won something Axel had once believed he could win for himself. In other words, Calum had beaten him in something else, yet again.

What was happening to Axel's life? How was Calum succeeding in every area while Axel continued to falter, especially when it had been exactly the opposite before they'd started this adventure with Magnus?

"Axel?" Calum asked from behind him. "You alright?"

When Axel turned back, the smile he'd plastered on his face almost didn't hold up at the sight of Calum sitting on the sofa with his arm around Lilly's shoulders. Axel exhaled a silent furious breath and nodded, still smiling so he wouldn't start shouting at them.

Instead, he eked out one single syllable. "Fine."

Calum glanced at Lilly, but he didn't press Axel further. Good thing, too, or Axel might've tossed him clear out the window.

"What did you want to talk about?" Lilly asked.

Axel briefly considered throwing her out the window, too, but since she could fly, that really wouldn't accomplish anything, so he pushed the thought and the fury from his mind and refocused on the news he'd uncovered instead.

"I came across some useful information," he managed to say. "I figured I should share it, and if either of you learned anything that might be helpful in our upcoming battles, now is the time to speak up."

Calum and Lilly glanced at each other, and Calum took his arm off Lilly's shoulders and leaned forward. The action actually went a long way to reduce Axel's anger and frustration, but he refused to let either of them know that.

"What did you find out?" Calum asked.

Axel decided to forgo the entire story and instead revealed that he'd overheard the King, Matthios, and Valerie talking in the garden about future plans. He explained that Matthios was currently mustering every soldier in reserve to fight, and more importantly, Valerie had planted some sort of seeds in the most fertile soil in Kanarah.

He went on to explain how that was probably the ocean of grain where they'd first found and rescued Lilly from Roderick and his slave traders, or perhaps the royal orchards nearby. In any case, he asserted, both pieces of information indicated that the King's conversations with them thus far had been nothing but lip service.

"He's not ever gonna make any changes. That much is clear," Axel said. "Otherwise, why bother preparing the rest of his army and planting those seeds? Personally, I think it's gonna be something like the rose golems we faced in Kanarah City."

Calum and Lilly contemplated Axel's words in silence for a long moment, just like the King had a habit of doing, and he almost spoke again, but then Lilly started talking.

"He isn't necessarily making preparations because he desires to battle Lumen and our army," she said. "He may just be taking extra precautions in case our negotiations fail. Or if Lumen refuses to accept whatever terms we come up with. Or if any number of other happenings go wrong along the way and Kanarah plunges into full-scale war."

Axel didn't like the sound of that, but he also really *liked* the sound of that. Lumen had promised them a war since the beginning. War was Axel's chance to truly make a name for himself, to gain power as one of Lumen's generals, as one of his Imperators.

"Keep in mind who we're dealing with, here," Axel said. "This is the King. He's a tyrant, and he'll do anything to stay in power. It's who he is, just like Magnus's uncle. There's no negotiating with men like Kahn and the King.

"The sweet music of 'cooperation' he's singing into our ears is a bunch of lies, nothing more. But now we know his plans, and we can take that information to Lumen so he'll be prepared for it when it happens," Axel concluded.

Calum and Lilly hesitated, and Calum spoke first. "Considering what you heard, and considering what we've experienced so far, I'm still torn. If he's lying to us, he is genuinely good at it... or he's actually being genuine and honest with us. I don't know how to tell which one it is, but I do know that we should already be dead by now, and we're not."

Lilly nodded. "That, I agree with. He showed us mercy when he didn't have to. That has to count for something."

Axel was shaking his head even before she finished. "It's a ploy. It has been all along. How can you not see that? I figured you'd be better at spotting when someone is lying to you by now, Lilly, after what your own father concealed from you all those years."

Calum stood abruptly, and his face hardened to stone. "That's *enough*, Axel."

Lilly's hand clasped Calum's, and she stood with him, also glowering at Axel.

Axel held up his hands. He'd known it was a cheap shot, but he had to get his point across somehow. "I'm just saying, we can't trust the King. Look to your own pasts and tell me who in your lives has ever really told you the truth. The whole truth, unsullied, unfiltered, unashamedly. I guarantee you the King is *not* gonna be on that list."

Lilly kept staring daggers at him, but Axel didn't care. He'd said what he needed to say, and that was good enough for now.

"Go on." Axel motioned toward the two of them. "Sit down. The excitement's over. Now, either of you got anything to share?"

Reluctantly, Calum and Lilly did sit back down, still clutching each other's hands.

"I learned something," Lilly said. "That dome over the garden? It's made of diamond, not glass. The King told me it was impenetrable."

Axel frowned at her. "So?"

Lilly glared at him again. "Pardon me—I forgot that you're neither good with strategy nor flight-capable. I had considered launching an aerial attack and entering Valkendell's interior through the garden, but that's no longer an option since the dome isn't glass. I doubt even Magnus could break through it."

Axel ignored her slight and shrugged. "When the time comes, we'll get inside another way. That's all."

Axel had to admit—it felt pretty great to be in charge of something for once. He'd led this little gossip session from the beginning, and they'd actually made some progress.

Well, *he'd* shared something useful, anyway. Lilly's dome-construction information was pretty much worthless. Or at least it was until Calum spoke up.

"There's a secret door at the back of the garden," he said.

CHAPTER 33

"I t's hidden in the back wall, and I think there's a hidden path along the rock face that lines the back of the fortress and the city," Calum continued. "There must be. I saw the King returning through that door early this morning."

Axel's eyebrows rose. Now *that* was something worth mentioning. Perhaps Calum wasn't so worthless to the war effort after all.

Calum described what he'd seen in more detail, including how he'd been unable to get the door to open again or to even really find it, but he swore up and down it was there.

He didn't have a reason to make any of it up, so Axel was inclined to believe him. Even so, a door no one could find or access wouldn't do anyone any good.

Then again, just because weak little Calum couldn't figure it out didn't mean Lumen, the General of Light and arguably the most powerful being in Kanarah, couldn't. Either way, it was something they could share with Lumen, and perhaps it would help in some way. Axel stored the information in the back of his mind for safekeeping.

"That's good. Very good," Axel said. "Anyone got anything else?"

They both shook their heads.

"Then Lilly, you're gonna need to take this information to Lumen right away," Axel directed. "Hop out this window and fly out to meet him and his army, then tell him what you know. We can finish up here without you."

Lilly tilted her head at him. "I'm… not doing that."

"What?" Axel frowned at her again. "Of course you are. You wanna win, don't you?"

"I'm not doing it," she repeated. "I made an agreement with the King, the same as both of you, that we would stay and negotiate with him for three days. It's only been one full day so far. I'm not going to break my promise to him."

Axel couldn't believe what he was hearing. He scoffed at her. "You're joking, right? If you are, it's not very funny."

"I'm stone-serious, Axel," Lilly said. "I'm not leaving until we all leave."

Axel turned to Calum. "Why don't you get your girl on board, here, Calum? Maybe remind her what's at stake, not just for her people but for *all* of Kanarah?"

651

"I agree with her, Axel," Calum said. "And we know what's at stake. That's why we're here."

Axel's eyebrows rose again. "Clearly, you don't."

"We absolutely do," Lilly insisted. "What do you think will happen if we break our agreement with the King?"

"That's why you need to get out of here and go tell Lumen *now*," Axel said it slowly and quietly, as if trying to instruct a stupid child.

"Watch your tone when you talk to her," Calum growled.

"It's very cute and chivalrous of you to defend your lady, Calum, but you're not intimidating or impressing anyone here."

Calum stood again and started toward Axel, but Lilly caught him by the hand again and held him back.

"I said I'm *not* doing it, Axel," Lilly said. "So stop being a jerk about it."

"Like I told your boy before you came in," Axel said, "I'm not being a jerk. It's just that I have a personality, and he doesn't."

"I think this conversation is over." Calum turned to Lilly and helped her to her feet. "We're going for a walk. Feel free to stay in here as long as you like, though."

"Whatever. Bye." Axel folded his arms across his chest and shook his head at them as they departed Calum's chambers, leaving him behind.

He should've expected they'd be too dumb to realize what an opportunity they'd been given. This information was critical, and he'd find a way to get it to Lumen one way or another. Lumen would finally reward him the power he was owed, and together, they'd win the war and free Kanarah from the King once and for all.

Until then, though, Axel was still in Valkendell, so he might as well try to uncover anything else that might be useful. He left Calum's chambers behind and found Calum and Lilly standing in the hall before none other than Valerie.

"Wonderful," Valerie said, her smile as bright as the morning sun and as white as the walls around them. "You are all here. The King has recommended that I give you a brief tour of Solace, our fair capital city, prior to meeting with him for lunch. He believes it will be instructive and informative with regard to the conversations you continue to share with him."

Axel had been curious about Solace and what it was like since before they'd been captured, and now he'd finally get to see it up close. He'd expected his first encounter with the city to involve fighting and killing soldiers both outside and inside its walls, but a casual stroll with a beautiful woman—and two morons—would also be nice.

Maybe he could even sneak off and find a way to smuggle the information he'd gleaned from the King and from Lilly and Calum to Lumen. But even if he couldn't, at the very least he'd have the chance to learn the layout of the city for when Lumen's army finally attacked.

Axel grinned at Valerie and extended his arm for her to take, which she did. Then he cast a sneer back at Calum and Lilly and said, "We'd be *delighted* to."

THE CITY of Solace reminded Lilly of Kanarah City, but easily triple the size in just about every way. From the ground level, it seemed the city's streets would never end. Buildings made of white stone like those of Valkendell and capped with gray-shingled roofs rose anywhere from one to four stories tall, and some she could see in the distance looked to be even taller.

A mix of light- and dark-gray cobblestones, worn smooth over time, formed a nearly perfectly flat surface throughout most of the city streets. And all along those streets vendors hawked their wares, merchants sold goods from inside shops, and citizens made their lives inside their homes.

Behind them, the central spire of Valkendell loomed over everything except the distant mountains. Its four other towers extended much higher than any of the other buildings in Solace as well, but the spire itself was by far its most impressive feature.

The streets were not devoid of poverty, but from what Lilly saw, there wasn't much of it to be found, either. When she did happen upon the occasional beggar along the street, she found an ample selection of gold, silver, and bronze coins already in his satchel.

The people of Solace seemed to be the generous sort, and it made her regret her family's disregard for the Windgales who'd languished at the base of the Sky Fortress for so long. She could've done better for her people if she'd been told the truth—or perhaps if she'd been unwilling to take everything her parents told her at face value.

"You alright?" Calum squeezed her hand.

"Yes," she replied. "Just thinking about home."

"We'll be back there soon," Calum assured her. "Together."

The thought brought a smile to Lilly's face. "You'll have to learn to fly, then. Can't rely on everyone else to carry you around from place to place in Aeropolis."

Calum gave her a nervous grin. "I'll, uh… I'll do my best."

Lilly pulled him close and squeezed him tight. "I'm just teasing. I promise you won't be stranded on one single platform for the rest of your life."

"I appreciate that." Calum embraced her in return.

The other element of Solace that Lilly hadn't expected was the profound crossover between the various races of Kanarah. Where she'd seen a handful of Saurians, Wolves, and Windgales in Kanarah City, here, all three races intermingled with humans throughout the course of everyday life.

A Saurian worker hefted a huge stone up to another Saurian atop a home that was undergoing repairs, and together with a human worker, they positioned the stone in place.

A Werewolf merchant wearing fine amber-colored robes haggled with a pair of Windgales at his cart in the street as they tried to agree on a price for a trio of shining steel swords.

A human guided a cart pulled by a donkey through the streets while a black Wolf with gray paws lay in the back, napping atop some blankets.

The harmony of the four races working together to this degree surprised Lilly. She'd grown up solely with Windgales and only interacted with the other races when envoys from Reptilius visited the Sky Fortress to confer with her father, and that only happened once or twice a year, at most.

The Wolves had never sent an envoy, as they preferred to be left alone. By contrast, she'd seen the most humans of anyone while growing up. Though they primarily lived across the Valley of the Tri-Lakes, visits from human merchants with fine wares to sell were relatively common.

The only other time she'd encountered so many people of each race in one place was in Lumen's army, but even then, the individual races mainly stuck to their own kind, with the majority of the overlap happening at the highest levels.

Condor, Generals Balena and Tolomus, and Lilly represented the Windgales, Calum and Axel represented the humans, and Magnus and Riley represented the Saurians and Wolves, respectively.

She hadn't even really considered that the races might interact with each other as they now did here in Solace, mostly because the Saurians had done such lasting damage to her people's way of life, destroying their homes and killing so many.

The thought of her people co-mingling with Saurians seemed as impossible as dying and then coming back to life. Yet here in Solace, it was an everyday reality.

"How come the King didn't join us?" Axel asked.

"The King has a sort of... attraction to him, you could say," Valerie replied with her usual smile. "Whenever he graces the streets with his presence, the people tend to flock to him, hoping to hear his voice, or touch the hems of his clothes, or simply get a glimpse of his face. He is always quite flattered by the response.

"As such, he does not venture out as much as he used to," Valerie continued. "He prefers to do his work from within Valkendell, as he is able to do more good from his seat of power than down here on the streets of his fair city."

"Maybe he oughta come down here more often. Then he'd actually know what's going on with his people," Axel countered.

Valerie, who'd been walking with him arm-in-arm almost the entire time thus far, stopped, pulled her arm free, and faced Axel. Her smile remained, but her green eyes carried a sternness that Lilly hadn't seen from her before.

"I assure you, the King is well aware of the condition of *all* his subjects the world over," Valerie insisted. Then her countenance brightened again. "Which is why you are all here, of course. To help him realize your mutual goal of improving conditions for everyone in Kanarah."

Axel pursed his lips and gave a modest nod. "If you say so."

Valerie took his arm again, and they continued to walk down the street with Calum and Lilly in tow. "We, his servants, are tasked with aiding those less fortunate than we are. Here in Solace, we take care of each other, and the King's soldiers are his primary emissaries of goodwill throughout the city as they preserve order and provide care and resources for those in need."

Axel scoffed at that one. "That's definitely not how they behave where we're from. Right, Calum?"

To his credit, Calum kept quiet. Lilly appreciated that he had a strong sense of when to keep his mouth shut and when not to.

"It is difficult to leave your home behind, along with everyone there who loves and supports you, and then go to another place and try to do everything precisely right," Valerie said.

"So that's supposed to be some sort of excuse for their behavior?" Axel pressed.

"Of course not. The heinous actions of the King's soldiers that you have detailed are a travesty, a betrayal of the highest order." Valerie's smile still lingered when she glanced back at Lilly. "And such behavior *will* be met with the proper punishment, as should any sort of abuse, whether in the public square or in private chambers."

Then Valerie turned back to Axel and looked up at him. "We must all be held to account for our actions. Mistakes, whether serious or otherwise, yield consequences. Do you not agree, Axel?"

Even from behind, Lilly could see Axel's face turn red. Apparently, Valerie had somehow learned about Axel's attack on Lilly back at the Sky Fortress. Lilly had long since forgiven him for it, but she had to admit the pleasure she was deriving from watching Axel squirm under Valerie's scrutiny.

"Yes," he finally said. "I agree."

"I knew you would." Valerie's smile broadened, and she gave Lilly a wink. "It is time for us to return to Valkendell. The King has prepared a special lunch for the three of you."

LUNCH CAME AND WENT, and to Calum's pleasure, the conversation primarily focused on how the behavior of the King's soldiers needed to change outside of Solace's walls.

As Valerie had promised, the King actually had prepared a special lunch for them, with the vast majority of it coming directly from his garden, where they once again ate and conversed. Fresh fruits and vegetables, tomatoes and peppers, and thinly sliced roasted pork atop warm bread with gravy filled Calum almost until he was ready to burst.

He'd never had a meal so good in his life. But as he sat there, staring at a red pepper the size of his fist laying on a platter before him, he couldn't help but think back to the finger-sized red peppers Axel had pilfered for him back when Calum was still working in the quarry. He'd gone hungry so many nights, yet here, in Solace, there seemed to be more than enough.

Once lunch concluded, Matthios took Axel, Valerie took Lilly, and Calum stayed with the King. At first, the trio refused to be separated, but when Matthios told Axel he'd have the chance to spar with some of Solace's strongest warriors, he couldn't resist.

Lilly was all the more hesitant to leave Calum, and he didn't want her to leave, either, but Valerie insisted that she and Lilly had plenty to discuss as it pertained to the role of the Windgales and the Sky Realm in future relations with humans and Eastern Kanarah.

"If we cannot find a way to bridge the gap between East and West, I hardly think you boys will fare any better," Valerie had said with her perpetual smile. Then she'd whisked a wide-eyed Lilly away, leaving Calum alone with the King in his immaculate garden.

The two of them sat there for a long time, just staring at each other across the entire length of the stone table in the garden, neither of them saying a word. It wasn't because Calum had anything to prove; he just wasn't sure what he was supposed to say.

Meanwhile, the King teased at the curls in his dark beard, delving into Calum with those vibrant green eyes.

They still unnerved Calum, but he had to admit he'd grown more accustomed to them over the last day-and-a-half since he'd first seen them. They no longer stirred up every single emotion in Calum's body like they had back in the throne room, so that, at least, was progress.

At long last, the King stood and motioned with his hand for Calum to follow him. "Walk with me."

Under normal circumstances, Calum would've been terrified that the King had invited him to stroll through the garden, but he'd decided that for the time being, at least, they didn't have to be enemies. Perhaps the King thought he and Calum could make progress just chatting on their own.

Calum obliged him. They walked through the garden together, the King with his hands clasped behind his back and a little bit hunched over, and Calum walking normally. Well, he tried to walk normally. When walking next to royalty, the definition of "normal" tended to shift.

He tried to have good posture, tried to take steps that were both casual but also large enough to match the King's longer stride, and, most importantly, he tried not to trip over anything, whether errant plants or his own two feet.

It was positively exhausting and nerve-wracking.

They left the stone table behind and advanced toward the spot where Calum had tried to assassinate the King. He'd expected the King to make a comment about the attempt, but instead he stayed silent.

Calum glanced down at the pale-blue mushrooms near the edge of the path and decided to keep his distance. No need for a repeat of last time.

He walked with the King for close to ten minutes, and he soon found he was actually enjoying himself. Occasionally, the King stopped at a particular plant and gave it more consideration.

The first couple of times, Calum didn't mimic the King's action, but the third time, when they stopped to look at a robust leafy green plant with orbs of blue flowers atop, Calum leaned toward it as well.

"That is a hydrangea." The King nodded toward it. "It is technically considered to be a shrubbery, and it blooms in the spring and summer. Its flowers only rarely give off an aroma, and we have bred this one specifically to do so. If you care to smell it, you will find it quite fragrant."

The King of all Kanarah was asking Calum... to smell some flowers in his garden?

It was a weird juxtaposition against everything Calum had once believed about the King, and many more things he was still uncertain about, but most importantly, the offer stood stark against the impending war that would be waged between them.

But regardless of how all that turned out, Calum had to admit it was a pretty incredible offer. Who else in Kanarah could say the King had personally invited them for a walk in his private garden and allowed them to smell the flowers?

Calum leaned forward even more, but he hesitated. Last time he'd inhaled too near a plant in the King's garden, it had knocked him out cold. He glanced up at the King.

"It is harmless," he assured.

Calum had no choice but to trust him or not, and he decided to take the leap. He sniffed the flowers, and their sweet scent, unique compared to anything else he'd smelled before, filled his nostrils.

"I like it," he said.

"Thought you would." The King motioned with his head again, and they continued walking.

Several more times, the King stopped and pointed out various plants to Calum. He'd never been all that into plants, per se, but the King seemed to be enjoying himself, so Calum went along with it.

When they reached the bed of roses, the King stopped again. He crouched down and touched the crimson petals of one of them with his fingers.

"I assume you already know what these are," the King said.

Calum crouched down next to him and nodded. "Red roses. Really pretty flowers."

"If you wish, you may collect a bouquet to take to the Premieress once we have concluded our conversation," the King offered.

Calum didn't know how to respond to that. He would've loved to, and he'd briefly considered snagging one anyway for exactly that purpose, but the King would probably have noticed, so he hadn't done it. And now the King was offering them to him freely?

"Uh... thank you, Your Majesty," Calum managed to say. Then Calum realized something else. "How do you know about Lilly and me?"

The King tilted his head and studied Calum. "It is written all over your face, evident through your mannerisms, through every delighted glance you cast her way. And if that were not enough, I can see it etched into the very fabric of your being. Your love for her is as unmistakable as the sun burning in the sky, and I dare say it burns just as brightly."

Calum gulped back the lump in his throat, embarrassed. He rubbed the back of his head. "It's that obvious?"

For the first time since Calum had met him, a small grin curled the corners of the King's mouth. "That would be putting it mildly."

Calum knew he was blushing now, and it only embarrassed him all the more. Once again, words escaped him.

Finally, he realized something else. "You and Valerie and Matthios seem to know a lot about the three of us. How is that possible? I mean, I suppose Lilly's life has been unusual since she was the Premier's daughter, but Axel and I were nobodies. We still are. So how do you know so much about us?"

The King's attention remained fixed on his roses. He delicately stroked a small bud that had yet to bloom, and before Calum's eyes, it began to grow, expand, and blossom to match the size of several of the other roses all around it. Then it grew even larger.

"I share a connection with this world unlike anyone else. It is a gift from the Overlord Himself." The King's rose continued to swell and expand until it was twice as large as any flower in the vicinity. "I can feel every blade of grass in the wind, every stone in the ground, every rolling wave of the Tri-Lakes. Kanarah and I are one."

When the King finally stopped influencing the flower, Calum couldn't believe his eyes. The rose was almost as large as his head, to the point where its abnormal size actually unnerved him. He recalled the rose golems that had defended Kanarah City and now understood how they'd been so effective—at least for a time—in defending the city.

The King himself may have very well been defending the city *through* them.

In one quick motion, the King plucked the flower cleanly from the base of its stem and extended it toward Calum.

"Use this as the bouquet's centerpiece," he said. "And mind the thorns. Even a beautiful flower may well defend itself should the need arise. But I suspect you already know that."

Calum accepted the rose and carefully held it with two fingers between its thorns. Up close, it was even wilder to look at. Its petals were the traditional blood-red color, but it had opened so wide that it revealed its center. Calum had expected to see seeds inside, but instead, sunlight glinted off something silvery, almost like mercury, inside.

He couldn't explain it, but he'd never seen a rose like it in his life. It was truly a marvel, something natural yet supernatural at the same time.

"I don't believe it," Calum said. "This is—you really are connected to all of Kanarah..."

As the words left Calum's mouth, the complete understanding of their ramifications hit him, and his excitement sobered. He'd believed every word, and he realized he believed the truth behind what the King was saying.

But more than that, he could feel it was true. He could sense it—a shaky but present connection to the King himself. Calum didn't understand it, but he *had* to acknowledge it.

In that moment, the truth changed everything for Calum.

"If you're connected to all of Kanarah," Calum started, "then if you die..."

The King finished the thought for him. "So will Kanarah."

CHAPTER 34

An hour later, Calum sat in his chambers alone, struggling with what he'd just learned. When Axel and Lilly had finally returned from their respective excursions with Matthios and Valerie, they'd sought him out, eager to share their experiences with him—or in Axel's case, to brag about how he'd beaten almost everyone in sparring, and all in quick succession, too.

Instead, they found him seated on his sofa in a melancholy state, staring off into nothing, sitting next to the bouquet of roses wrapped in white linen the King had sent with him. He was still aware enough that they'd entered to glance up at them, but otherwise, he didn't acknowledge their entry into his chambers.

Lilly rushed to his side. "Calum? Are you alright?"

What a question. Calum started to nod at first, but then he stopped. "I don't know."

"Are you hurt?" Lilly asked. "Did the King do something to you?"

Calum blinked at her. Then he reached for the bouquet of roses and handed it to her. The single rose in the center still glistened with silver in its center. "These are for you."

Lilly's brow furrowed as she accepted them, and then she smiled. It helped Calum feel a bit better, knowing he'd made her happy.

"They're beautiful." Now Lilly was beaming.

Axel just scoffed and shook his head.

Lilly set the flowers aside. "But I'm concerned about you. What happened?"

Calum shook his head. How could he even possibly begin to explain what he'd experienced? What he'd come to understand about the King and all of Kanarah?

Yet he knew he had to. Everything was at stake.

"I don't think we can kill the King," Calum said.

"Of course we can." Axel shut the door to Calum's chambers, which was a good idea, given the nature of their conversation.

Then again, did it matter anyway? If the King was who he said he was, wouldn't he be able to hear them regardless?

"It won't be easy, and it'll probably have to be Lumen actually doing the job, but there's gotta be a way," Axel continued.

"No. That's not what I mean," Calum said.

The two of them looked at him.

"I mean… I don't think we should."

They met his words with silence and confused looks.

"The King is *part* of Kanarah. That's why he's the King," Calum explained. "He can sense and control nature itself, which we had already figured out. But then I saw what he could do first-hand, with my own eyes. I felt it. He's more than just a powerful figure. He's connected to Kanarah itself. He *is* Kanarah. So if we kill him—"

"That's a load of horse chips if I ever heard it," Axel interjected. "He's no more a 'part' of Kanarah or 'connected' to it than you or me."

Calum shook his head. "No, you don't understand. It's like…"

Calum hesitated. How could he possibly explain this revelation to anyone else? To someone who hadn't been there to experience it like he had? To feel what he'd felt?

Lilly took his hand. "Go on."

Reassured, Calum said, "It's like he's the soul of Kanarah. And if the soul dies, so does the body."

"If we kill the King, Kanarah dies," Lilly stated.

Calum nodded.

Axel scoffed. "He's got you wrapped up in some witchcraft or something. Fooled with your head. How could that even work, Calum? What would even happen? It's absurd."

"I don't know," Calum replied. "But I know what I saw. I know what I felt."

"So we're going based off of your *feelings*, now?"

"Axel," Lilly warned.

"Don't 'Axel' me," he countered, mocking her higher-pitched voice. "We came here to do a job, and we're gonna see it through to the end."

"We came here because we were captured, tried, and absolved of our wrongdoing," Lilly fired back. "They could've killed us, but—"

"Yeah, yeah. I get all that," Axel interrupted. "It just goes to show how naïve and incompetent the King and his goons are. They'll wish they'd killed us by the time we're done with 'em."

Calum stared at him in disbelief. "You're delusional. Absolutely delusional."

"What did you say to me?" Axel matched his stare with narrowed eyes.

"If you're starving and someone offers you bread, do you slap their hand away?" Calum asked. "If you're cold, and someone offers you a blanket or shelter, do you refuse them?"

"Obviously not."

"That's what you're doing here, Axel," Calum said.

Axel shook his head. "Accepting charity from my enemies is different. Totally different."

"Have you ever once considered that maybe these people *aren't* your enemies?" Lilly suggested.

Calum and Axel both turned toward her. Calum had just been ready to say the same thing, but he hadn't. Did Lilly understand what he was saying? Or had she had some revelation of her own somewhere along the way as well?

"You've gotta be kidding me." Axel scoffed again. "They've bewitched you, too?"

"I'm *not* bewitched," Lilly insisted. "I'm considering our options based on the information we've received since arriving here. Nothing is for certain anymore."

"Sounds like you're both pretty certain about this," Axel countered. "And you're *wrong*, by the way."

Axel's attitude grated on Calum, but he chose to ignore it. "I really don't think I am, Axel."

"That's the problem, Calum. You're not *thinking* at all." Axel tapped his own forehead. "The condition of an entire world doesn't rest on the wellbeing of one man. That's just stupid. The world won't die without the King. It's not possible. But you know what is? That he *lied* to you."

Calum had considered that. It had been his most pressing objection to this whole line of thinking. The King had every reason to lie to him, but… Calum just didn't feel that he had.

"He showed you some magic tricks with his plants, and that got you thinking he's more than he really is. That's what it boils down to." Axel started listing points on his fingers. "You gotta remember that this guy has been around for well over a thousand years, so he knows how to manipulate people better than you or I ever will…"

Calum didn't really have any desire to manipulate anyone or to get better at doing so, but that was beside the point.

"Second, he's trying to convince you of his worth beyond what it really is as a means of scaring you. Then you'll take that fear back with you to Lumen's army, and it'll spread like a disease, infecting everyone until they're all too divided to fight. Third, he's downright evil. You and I have experienced that firsthand multiple times."

Calum didn't agree with that last statement, but he had to consider that to Axel, "firsthand" didn't actually mean "firsthand." More likely, he meant that they'd suffered at the hands of the King's men rather than actually suffering harm from the King personally.

"Fourth, he's been on the throne for too long and done too little while he's been perched up there," Axel continued. "I could go on, but really, what's the point? He's got you fooled, Calum. And what about Lumen? He was prophesied to return after a thousand years of being locked away, and now he's free, ready to fulfill the rest of the prophecy."

Calum had considered that as well. Lumen's return had been prophesied long before he actually returned, but given what he'd learned about the King and Lumen since, Calum had to wonder if the term of Lumen's imprisonment was simply just that: a timed sentence, one that was only supposed to last a thousand years.

He kept circling back to his dreams. Lumen had called to him specifically, and because Calum had answered the call, they'd managed to set Lumen free. Calum was no expert in prophecies, but that part of how it had all played out felt very much like a prophecy being fulfilled. And if Calum had just ignored the dreams, would Lumen even be free right now?

But after his last interaction with the King, and believing what he now believed, how could Calum remain on Lumen's side? Especially if the King was telling the truth about Kanarah dying along with him?

"I saw what I saw," Calum finally said. "It doesn't mean I've made up my mind."

"Then what does it mean?" Axel pressed.

"It means we need to continue to be careful," Lilly said. "It means we need to keep working with the King to find solutions to make Kanarah better, to unify her people."

"Lumen is gonna handle all of that himself," Axel insisted. "That's why we set him free."

Calum sighed and rubbed his eyes. "I don't know what to think anymore."

"You need some rest." Lilly gave his arm a squeeze. She turned to Axel. "And you need a bath. You smell like sweat."

"Ladies love a man who works hard." Axel puffed out his chest and smirked at her.

"Not this one," she countered. "Go get cleaned up. It'll be dinner before long, and whether or not you care what the King thinks of your stench, I guarantee Valerie's opinion matters a whole lot more to you."

Axel's confident countenance dissipated. "Did she… did she say something to you? About me?"

"Trust me," Lilly said. "A woman like her won't be won by a man who reeks of sweat and grime."

Axel glanced between Calum and Lilly as if he'd just experienced a grand revelation of his own. "I agree with Lilly. You should get some rest, Calum. I'm gonna leave you to it. Stay strong, and we'll get through this."

Axel put up his fist in a show of solidarity, then he opened the chamber door and headed out, leaving Calum and Lilly alone.

Finally.

Calum released another sigh, this one more exasperated, and he flopped down with his head on Lilly's lap. To his great relief, she let him do it and even started running her fingers through his hair. He closed his eyes and reveled in her gentle touch.

"What are we gonna do, Lilly?" he asked.

"I don't know," she replied. "But we'll figure it out together."

Calum grinned. At least he had that as a comfort.

More importantly, he had her.

As Magnus had anticipated, Lumen's army came within view of the city of Solace just after nightfall. Had Magnus been leading the army, he would've taken a less overt approach than Lumen had. The General of Light had led the way, hovering before his army like a blazing star amid the night sky.

Perhaps his strategy was to strike fear in the hearts of the men who would be fighting on the King's side, but Magnus couldn't help but think that they might've found more success by approaching the city in secret, surrounding it, and then beginning their invasion before the sun even had a chance to rise.

Lumen had insisted they would attack Solace at dawn instead, so that's what they would do. He'd probably formulated this plan during his millennium of imprisonment, and Magnus doubted anything could dissuade him from pursuing it exactly as he'd envisioned it countless times. For now, at least, it was best to just go along with it.

Once the army finished setting up camp, Lumen's light finally faded, and sleep settled among the weary soldiers. In only a matter of hours, the attack would begin, and they would need to recover their strength from the journey in order to fight.

That night, as planned, Magnus, Riley, their warriors, and Condor would set out to Valkendell to rescue Calum, Lilly, and Axel from captivity.

An advance scout, a black Wolf with gray paws sent by Riley, had reported seeing the three of them roaming the city streets, accompanied by some dark-haired woman. As of that morning, at least, the three of them were still alive and, by all appearances, unharmed.

Magnus found it strange that the King's men had allowed his three friends to wander around the city more or less freely. He'd found it stranger still that Lilly hadn't taken the opportunity to flee and return to Lumen's camp when she'd had the obvious chance, but he also trusted Calum and Lilly implicitly. There must be a reason, or several, for what the Wolf had seen.

The Wolf had watched them return to Valkendell itself not long afterward, which seemed to confirm they were being held inside. It suggested the King and his men realized their importance as prisoners—or at least Lilly's, as the Premieress of the Sky Realm, and perhaps Calum's as the person who had ensured Lumen's release.

And if the King had recognized their value, he had likely kept them alive for a reason. Perhaps he, too, wanted to bargain for something, or he wanted to use them as leverage against Lumen.

The problem was that Lumen was content to do without them entirely, so they were, in effect, useless to the King. Disposable, even.

The King hadn't realized that, yet, but when he did, Magnus feared his friends' lives would come to an abrupt end, right along with their supposed usefulness.

That made tonight's rescue attempt all the more crucial.

Following a compulsory meeting with Lumen to discuss plans for their attack tomorrow morning, Magnus, Riley, and Condor went their separate ways and returned to their respective sections of the camp. Then they reunited in secret far outside the camp, shrouded in darkness, along with the small team of warriors accompanying them that night.

His voice as low and as quiet as he could make it, Magnus asked, "Is everyone ready?"

He received a wave of nods and a few whispered assents.

"Then climb on."

At his command, the Sobeks who'd accompanied them climbed atop Magnus's back and took seated positions between the black dorsal spines lining his back. Riley and his Werewolves had already rushed toward the city on foot, keeping low and melting into then fields of grain, tall grass, and trees along the way, while Condor disappeared into the night sky ahead of them.

Once the last of the Sobeks climbed into place, he patted Magnus's flank. With a nod of his own, Magnus took to the sky.

They only had one shot at this, and they couldn't fail. If they did, more than just Calum, Lilly, and Axel's lives would be on the line.

AT DINNER with the King that night, this time in a large banquet hall lit by candles and torches rather than in the garden, Calum could hardly focus on the conversations they were sharing or on the elegant spread of food on the polished wooden table.

Instead, his mind continued to thrum with questions he couldn't answer—questions that perhaps no one else could answer for him, either.

He studied the King the whole dinner long, mostly letting Lilly do the talking, while he tried to gauge whether or not the King was being disingenuous with his words or actions. True to form, the King was reserved and cautious with his words and responses, revealing nothing more than he'd already revealed to Calum back in the garden.

Just as Calum considered excusing himself to fend off the confusion stretching his mind from overwhelming him, Matthios entered the banquet hall with quick pronounced footsteps, severing the conversation with his presence.

"Your Majesty," he said, his voice as emotionless as Calum had ever heard it, "Lumen's army has made camp outside the city walls."

CHAPTER 35

Calum's heart rate increased, and the confusion that had threatened to overwhelm him before multiplied. He closed his eyes and breathed slow deep breaths to try to collect himself.

"Gavridel and I have already made preparations for the inevitability of an attack tomorrow morning," Matthios continued.

The King considered Matthios's words for a long silent moment.

When Calum dared to open his eyes again, he caught Axel smirking. He tried to get Axel to cut it out with only his facial expressions, but it didn't work. Axel just winked at him instead, and his smirk turned into an all-out grin.

Lilly, still clad in her fire-colored dress and seated next to Calum, clutched his hand under the table. They were running out of time. With Lumen's army primed to attack, they might not even reach the end of the three days they'd agree to with the King.

Worse yet, they weren't any closer to truly resolving the majority of the issues they'd presented to the King than they'd been since their first slate of conversations two days earlier. They'd shared ideas and made suggestions and hoped to develop a real plan of action, but truthfully, they had little to show for it.

Had that been intentional on the King's part? Perhaps a stalling tactic of some sort? Had he been unwilling to commit, or had he too readily met their suggestions with objections?

If Calum were honest with himself, he would've said no. The King had seemingly dealt with them in earnest, and even now, a flicker of hope that they might be able to resolve their differences still burned in Calum's heart.

"Very well," the King finally said. "Thank you, Matthios. Please send word if you require my direct intervention."

Matthios bowed low. "Yes, Your Majesty."

As Matthios moved to leave, Valerie entered the hall next. She curtsied to Matthios, who gave her a quick nod and then rushed out. The King's attention fixed on Valerie next, and she bowed to him, albeit not as low as Matthios had.

"Your Majesty," she said, smiling as usual, "if it pleases the King, I would like to request a private audience with you."

"It cannot wait?" the King asked.

"Regrettably, no." Valerie's smile shrank. "It is, in fact, quite urgent."

Rather than asking Calum and the others to give them the room, the King rose from his chair and apologized to them. "Forgive my rudeness in truncating our dinner and conversation, but I must attend to other matters."

Without waiting for their responses, the King followed Valerie out of the banquet hall.

"Should we go after them?" Lilly asked.

"With all this food still here? And Lumen's army at the city gates?" Axel reached for another chicken leg, bringing the total number on his plate to four. "Nah. This might be our last chance to have a good meal for a few days. Better to enjoy it. Let them panic while we feast."

He opened his mouth almost comically wide and bit into the chicken leg.

Calum chose to ignore Axel again. He turned to Lilly. "I'm not sure what else we can do."

"How long do you think it will take them to breach the city walls?" Lilly asked. "My Windgales will have no problem getting past their archers, ballistae, and catapults, but I can't say the same for the Saurians, Wolves, or humans."

"I'm not sure," Calum said. "I doubt Lumen will attack until sunrise at the earliest, though. If the army has only just arrived, they can't fight until they are rested and fed, and that'll take time. My bigger concern is what might happen to us when Lumen does attack."

Axel stopped chewing and let one the chicken leg drop to his plate. Grease still coated his lips and cheeks. He swallowed the mass of food stuffed in his cheeks and said, "I can't believe I didn't think of that. If Lumen attacks before our three days are up, does that mean the King is gonna…"

Axel's eyes widened, and he grabbed a cloth napkin from the table. Without another word, he snatched up his half-eaten chicken leg and placed it onto the napkin, followed by several rolls, chunks of meat, cheese, and fruits.

"What are you doing?" Lilly asked.

"Stocking up," he replied. "If we have to try to escape, we need to have food stores in case we have to hide until we can safely escape the city. You guys should do this, too."

By the time he finished, the cloth napkin was so overloaded with food that half of it fell out onto the table when Axel tried to tie the corners together. Then, without so much as another word, he took his bundle of food and rushed toward the door to the banquet hall, occasionally dropping bits of food behind him as he went.

"As much as I hate to admit it, he's got a point." Lilly clarified, "About how the King might react to us when Lumen attacks, I mean. Not about the food."

Calum nodded. He was still having trouble focusing with everything that was going on, but Lilly might've been right.

"The King said he wouldn't let any harm come to us, but I agree that might've been a tempo-rary promise." Even as Calum said it, the idea that the King would just kill them didn't sit right. He shook his head. "But I don't believe it was. I don't think he'll go back on his word."

"I hope not." Lilly's voice carried a guarded tone to it.

Calum squeezed her hand and stood. "I've lost my appetite. Let's go see if we can get a glimpse of the army from one of the windows overlooking the city. I know it's silly, but seeing Magnus lumbering around the camp would do a lot to calm my nerves right now."

Lilly stood and gave him a smile. "It's not silly. I understand."

The two of them left the banquet room behind, and servants filtered in after them to clean up the remnants of their dinner.

To Axel's relief, he'd not only managed to find his way back to the training grounds for sparring that afternoon, but he'd also located the small room where they had stored his Blood Ore armor and sword.

Better still, the area was totally unguarded thanks to the arrival of Lumen's army. Everyone was preoccupied with preparing for the beginning of the battle tomorrow.

Axel set down his makeshift satchel of food, confused as to why it felt so much lighter than when he'd first run off with it, but right now, getting his gear back was more important. He wiped his hands clean on his trousers—really, the King's trousers, since this current set of clothing had come from the King—and he prepared to kick open the armory door.

A thought hit him, and he stopped. Instead, he reached for the ring mounted to the front of the door and pulled. It swung open. They'd left it unlocked.

Stupid, trusting fools, he mused.

Axel grabbed a nearby torch from one of the walls and used it to light up the inside of the storage room. The distinct iridescent shine of light-blue metal caught his eye immediately.

His armor and his sword.

Axel planted the torch in an iron bracket mounted to the wall and stripped off his borrowed clothes down to his undergarments. He wouldn't need them any longer.

As soon as he'd realized the end of his time within Valkendell was fast approaching, he'd decided it would be on his own terms rather than on anyone else's. If he could escape, he'd just as soon do it now, in the confusion of the moment. And if they tried to kill him, he'd go down fighting.

He'd been surprised when they'd brought out his armor and sword for him to use while sparring with—or rather, beating the sunshine out of—the King's soldiers, but he hadn't complained. Someone had even fixed the huge dent that the gemstone warrior—the Imperator known as Gavridel, he'd learned—had left in there with his axe.

That had surprised Axel the most. Somehow, they possessed the capability to repair even Blood Ore armor if it had been damaged. He'd thought that skill was exclusive to Saurians, but apparently, he'd been wrong.

Within minutes, he'd strapped his armor back on and tightened his grip on his sword. It felt just as amazing and empowering as it had that afternoon. It felt *right*.

Amid the sea of silver- and black-clad soldiers throughout Solace, he'd pop out like a badger in a bakery, but he'd stand a better chance of fighting through his enemies with his armor and sword than without, so the choice was easy.

Plus, maybe he could cover himself up with a bed sheet or a blanket or something. He had to head back to his chambers to try to convince Calum and Lilly to come with him anyway—though he doubted they'd go for it—so finding something to cover himself with shouldn't be too hard.

He snatched up his satchel of food, and then he rushed for the hallway once again.

Lumen's eyes were always open. He lacked the ability to see everything at once, a power that, according to the oldest lore, only the King possessed, but he could still see just about everything that happened within a certain range of his presence. Wherever there was light and Lumen was nearby, he knew what was happening with relative certainty.

He'd discovered a few days before that the Dragon King and the Shadow Wolf were plotting something behind his back. Were it a coup, he needn't be worried; they couldn't have killed him even with the combined strength of both their armies put together, plus fighting him themselves.

Instead, he realized they were planning something equally as nefarious: they were planning to attempt a rescue of Calum, Axel, and the Premieress, Lilly.

The rescue itself wasn't the issue; it was their insubordination that infuriated Lumen. After the trio had gone missing, Lumen had closed the issue, despite Magnus and Riley's objections. Now they were moving forward with a rescue attempt anyway.

Insubordination could not be tolerated. If these so-called "leaders" of their races refused to adhere to Lumen's orders, then the solution was simple:

They would be replaced.

NORMAL PEOPLE in Solace might not have noticed an enormous black thing blotting out sections of the starry sky above, but Riley was anything but normal.

With his enhanced eyesight in the dark, he could see not only Magnus's outline but also some definition in his wings, his head, and even vague Sobek shapes riding atop his back. And that was all while running through the fields toward the city walls at an incredible speed.

Riley thought back to when he'd just been a Wolf—a scared one, at that. Condor had stabbed him, and Axel had wanted to leave him for dead. He'd been virtually worthless to their group for most of their first journey to Western Kanarah.

Things had changed. *He* had changed. He was unique among all the Wolves.

Powerful. Skilled. Strong. Fast. Silent.

Finally, he was no longer weak. He had reached the pinnacle of what his kind could become, and now that he'd killed Rhaza, Riley was the only Shadow Wolf in all of Kanarah, just like Magnus was the only Dragon.

He commanded the full strength of the Wolf tribe of the Desert of the Forgotten, and he had their undying loyalty. They would beg, bite, kill, and steal for him. Or, as was the case tonight, they would sneak into the world's most secure fortress and rescue three of Riley's friends.

Well, two of his friends, anyway, plus Axel.

The city's white walls reached some twenty feet high. Even in the moonlight, they glistened, smooth like alabaster but as hard as Magnus's scales—or perhaps even harder. As such, there was no climbing up these walls. Not without a rope or a ladder, anyway. But he and his Wolves had brought neither.

As he ran toward the walls, Riley felt as though he could've jumped clear over them. Were it not for the plan, he would've. But as he was the only Wolf capable of such a feat, he had to wait. His time would soon come.

Once he reached a spot about fifteen feet from the wall, he concealed himself in the tall grass and surveyed the walls. As they'd expected, the city gates were barred shut, and dozens of guards clad in black leather armor patrolled the tops of the walls. Even in the night, Riley's keen eyes could pick each of them out as if they were walking torches.

He glanced up at the night sky. High above, Condor waited to play his part in this plan.

Riley waited for the guards to pass each other on the wall. Whenever they did, there was a brief period of time where the guards' attention wasn't attuned to a small section of the wall. That was their chance to get inside.

As the two guards in question approached each other, Riley signaled the first of his Were-wolves to begin his approach. Though the Werewolf's footsteps barely registered any sound amid the tall grass, Riley heard them as if they were thundering drumbeats moving ever closer.

The two guards passed each other, and then the Werewolf reached Riley—perfect timing.

Riley crouched low and created a foothold with his hands. The Werewolf stepped onto Riley's palms, and he jumped as Riley flung him high into the air—almost high enough that he could've cleared the wall had they been closer, but any closer than they already were would put the entire operation at risk.

When the Werewolf reached the zenith of his leap, Condor shot in like a bolt of black lightning. He caught the Werewolf by his extended arm and carried him high over the guards' heads and into the city.

Wisps and Windgales could only fly with as much weight as they could carry on the ground, so it was more of a glide than actual flying, but it got the job done. Condor dropped the Werewolf into a bed of shadows behind some buildings and zoomed back over the wall as Riley adjusted his position in the grass.

A couple of the guards glanced around and up to the sky, but they saw nothing. Perhaps they'd heard something when Condor had rocketed past them, but they'd never be able to see him. Nor would they see the Werewolves gliding in, either—as long as Riley got the timing right.

Before long, Riley and Condor had launched half a dozen Werewolves into the city. Then Riley himself made the leap. He landed on the city street with a roll and disappeared into the nearest shadow as if he were part of it.

It was a silent, seamless transition, so much so that a young man walking the street and facing right toward him hadn't even noticed. Riley waited for the teenager to pass him by, then he left the security of the shadows and began to make his way through the city.

Compared to flinging his Werewolves over the city walls with perfect timing, reaching Valkendell was easy. At night, with only the moon providing light from above, the ample shadows of the buildings proved more than sufficient as a means to traverse the city.

As planned, Riley established a rendezvous point based on his scout's recommendation, and the other Werewolves came to him. Thanks to Condor, the supplies they needed for the next phase of the plan were already there, waiting for them in the shadow of a large building across the street from Valkendell.

From that point on, all they could do was watch and prepare as Magnus and his Sobeks completed the next phase of the plan. With the claw on his forefinger, Riley ripped open the first bag of flour and got to work.

THOUGH MAGNUS'S talons couldn't pierce the slick white surface of Valkendell's central spire, he'd flown high enough that he'd managed to secure a tight grip to its spiked point with one hand. Even so, without purchase from his feet or tail, he knew he couldn't hold on forever.

He tucked his wings tightly against his back, pulled his legs in close, and hung by one arm from the impressive structure. His Sobek warriors lowered themselves on ropes attached to the spikes and dorsal spines along Magnus's back toward the uppermost windows of the spire.

Though he was considerably stronger than he'd ever been as a Sobek, he also weighed much more. If Valkendell's exterior had any grip to it whatsoever, it wouldn't have been so bad. As it was, Magnus had to resist the impulse to claw at the stone with the talons on his feet in a vain attempt to pull himself up higher.

It didn't help that half a dozen Sobeks were crawling down his limbs and inadvertently tugging him lower and lower with each passing second. Before long, though, the tugging stopped, and then a three-tug sequence signaled to Magnus that the Sobeks had safely made it into the windows.

With that, Magnus pressed the soles of his feet against the spire and kicked off. His wings billowed open and caught the air, and with several mighty flaps, he'd ascended high above the city once again. Someone would've heard his wings thundering against the air, but given the absence of Dragons in the East, he hoped the people of Solace wouldn't know what to make of the sound.

He soared over to the mountains that formed a natural barrier along the eastern border of Solace and landed among the cliffs. From his vantage he could view the tower, remain concealed among the rocks in the darkness, and swoop back in to finish his role in the rescue operation when the time came.

For now, though, all he could do was wait.

IN THE DEAD OF NIGHT, Rhaza feasted on the mountain goat he'd captured and killed. Though wounded and permanently weakened thanks to the shard Riley had plunged into his side, Rhaza could still use enough of his powers to hunt. He wasn't dead yet, and that gave him hope.

Hope for vengeance.

When a brilliant white light flashed over the desert scrub and stopped before Rhaza, he staggered back, away from his kill, and tried to shield his face with his hands. It didn't work. The light was far too bright.

Rhaza thought perhaps he'd finally met his end. Something had gone wrong, and the wound in his side had finally given out, and now he was looking at the physical embodiment of his path to the afterlife.

Instead, a huge humanlike figure emerged from the light—or perhaps he was the light itself. Rhaza couldn't tell. His eyes were better attuned to manage darkness, not stare into blinding white light.

As if the light-man had heard Rhaza's thoughts, his light faded some. He hovered in the air, staring down with blazing eyes of pure white light.

"I bid you greetings, Rhaza of the Desert of the Forgotten," the light-man said through the mask that covered the lower part of his face. Matching white armor covered the rest of his body, a gold-hilted sword hung from his side, and a golden crown sat atop his head. "And truly, there was never a more apt name for your current state of being than 'forgotten.'"

Rhaza ignored the insult. It was, after all, true. His tribe had left him behind, now following Riley instead. He was supposed to be dead, and had Riley actually finished the job properly, Rhaza would've been.

But more importantly, recognition sparked in Rhaza's mind. Riley and his insufferable friends had mentioned allegiance to someone known as the General of Light—a being known as Lumen. Could this be him?

"Who are you?" Rhaza asked, still wary.

In his current condition, he stood no chance of fighting back against anyone. He was surprised that some errant Werewolf hadn't tracked him down and tried to kill him with the hope of transforming into a Shadow Wolf.

Then again, Rhaza had been careful. He'd avoided the usual routes the Wolves took through the desert, and he'd lingered nearer to the mountains than he would have otherwise had he been well.

"I am who you believe me to be," the light-man—Lumen—replied. "And I have come to make you an offer. Join me, serve within my army, and I shall restore to you everything you have lost."

Everything? Rhaza's eyes narrowed. His tribe, his standing... his health and his abilities... Could this Lumen fellow really give him all of that back?

"And much more," Lumen added. "I will grant you power unlike anything you've ever known. Will you join me?"

Rhaza was either incredibly lucky, or he was hallucinating as he died. Either way, he decided to answer Lumen's call.

"I only want one thing," he replied. "Revenge."

"You shall have that, too." Lumen extended his hand, massive and glowing. "Do you accept?"

Rhaza didn't hesitate. He took hold of Lumen's hand, and they both vanished in a flash of light.

THANKS TO THE FLOUR, Riley and his Werewolves looked like lupine ghosts, front and back. About the time they finished, the first of the ropes lowered by the Sobeks reached the bottom of Valkendell.

Riley signaled, and the Werewolves rushed out of the shadows and began their frantic climb up the ropes.

Riley stayed back at first to keep watch. The flour was supposed to help camouflage them against the white backdrop of the fortress's walls, and the ropes themselves were braided from lighter strands, but none of it would make the Werewolves invisible. Riley was prepared to silence anyone who noticed and tried to call out a warning.

No one did. Before long, the Werewolves had made good progress up the steep climb, despite their talons being unable to grip the surface of the spire, so Riley darted forward and began climbing himself.

It only took a few minutes for him to reach the window. Together, along with aid from the pair of enormous Sobeks who'd lowered the rope, Riley and the two Werewolves who'd entered through that window patted off the flour in a cloud of dust.

When they finished and were more or less back to their original colors, Riley led his two Werewolves and the two Sobeks deeper into the fortress.

WITH HIS ROLE in the first portion of the rescue complete, Condor spent the next several minutes flying around the spire of Valkendell, peering through its various windows. It was a whiplash sort of reconnaissance, but he was only looking for one thing: Lilly.

He spiraled up and down the tower as fast as he could fly and still process what he was seeing through each window. At one point, he caught a glimpse of something fiery red-and-orange and shimmery with some yellow-gold on top. It captured his attention, so he circled around again for a closer look.

There, through one of the windows, he could clearly see Lilly standing next to Calum. The two of them were speaking with someone Condor couldn't see from his vantage point in the sky, but the two of them, at least, looked unharmed.

As much as Condor liked Calum, Lilly was his true priority. And he could get her out of there himself in no time.

He lined himself up with the window and waited for his moment.

"WHAT DO we do if the King decides to imprison us," Lilly asked as they headed back to their chambers, "or worse yet, kill us?"

Calum had given that a fair bit of consideration already, but he wasn't so sure his plan was any good. Axel had doubtless already made plans of his own and was already enacting them, as evidence by his disappearance after dinner. He'd run off, and they hadn't seen him since.

"Your escape plan has been the same this whole time," Calum said. "You jump out one of those windows and fly away."

"I won't leave you alone." Lilly squeezed his hand and gave him a reassuring grin. "So get that thought out of your mind right now.

"Well..." he began, "I was thinking I'd jump out the window, too. Then you could glide with me like you did when we were escaping Captain Brink's sinking ship until it was safe to let me down."

Before Lilly could respond, a trio of soldiers rounded the corner ahead of them, so she and Calum moved to the side of the hall and let them pass. They both glanced back to be sure the soldiers were out of range before continuing their conversation.

"That was a lot different," Lilly muttered. "We were over the water, and we weren't that high up in the air. If you fell, or if I had dropped you, it wouldn't have killed you."

"No, but those lake sharks sure would've," Calum countered. Even thinking of them renewed his shudders. "Plus, you're faster now, and probably stronger. You're the Premieress, after all."

"Being the Premieress doesn't make me the strongest Windgale in all the land, though. That title probably belongs to General Balena, or perhaps to Condor," Lilly said. "But you're right that I'm faster. Meaning I could probably crash us into a building or the street much quicker than before."

If she could joke about the peril they were in, so could he. Calum looked her up and down with a grin as they reached the hall with their chambers. "I'm sure that dress of yours would create enough drag to slow our descent."

"Very funny." Her voice was deadpan, but she was smiling anyway.

They stood there before one of the windows in the hallway. A fresh warm breeze washed over them from outside, and the stars twinkled overhead. She leaned forward to kiss him, and he matched the motion.

"Guys!" Axel's frantic voice pulled them apart.

They both looked up in time to see Axel clanking through the hallway, clad in his blue Blood ore armor and wielding his Blood Ore sword. Calum noticed a thin line of discoloration where Gavridel's axe had struck Axel's chest, but otherwise his armor looked as good as it had when Magnus had first bequeathed it to him.

Lilly gawked at him. "What in the Overlord's name are you doing?"

Calum stared at him, too, but he forestalled his questions for the time being. Lilly's question had pretty much summed them all up anyway.

"I'm getting outta here before the King decides to drop us in the sewers along with yesterday's bathwater." Axel held up the makeshift satchel of food he'd harvested from the banquet hall. "Got supplies, got my armor and sword back, and I'm ready to go. I came back for you two, though. With everyone distracted by Lumen's army, this is our best shot."

Calum glanced at Lilly, and she returned it. With no additional hesitation, Calum said, "We're not going."

"Don't be stupid, Calum. This is our chance," Axel insisted. He even shifted the satchel of food to the same hand he was carrying his sword with and extended his hand as if he were some grand hero there to rescue them. "It's now or never."

Before Calum could answer, a dark form burst through the window and landed between them. The figure's sudden appearance nearly hammered Calum's heart clear from his chest, and he positioned himself in front of Lilly to shield her from whatever threat had just presented itself.

Then Calum recognized charcoal armor, black hair, and piercing blue eyes.

"Condor?" Lilly stepped out from behind Calum.

Condor crouched on the stone floor, looking up at Calum and Lilly, and then at Axel, who'd dropped his satchel of food and drawn his sword back to strike.

"Hello," Condor said, grinning at them.

Then he shot toward Lilly, grabbed her around her waist, and zipped back out the window, leaving Calum and Axel alone in the hall.

CHAPTER 36

"Let me go!" Lilly demanded.

Condor's entrance had nearly scared Lilly out of her skin, but once she'd realized it was him, a sense of comfort had replaced her surprise. When he'd grabbed her and hauled her out the window he'd just entered, that pushed everything back in the wrong direction.

"Easy, Your Highness," Condor said, his voice far too calm given what he'd just done. "You're safe now."

"I was safe before!" Lilly pushed against him to break free, but he refused to let her go. "I *order* you to release me, Condor!"

He complied, albeit with noticeable reluctance. By the time he let her go, they were nearly back to Lumen's camp, which was positioned about a half mile away from the city walls. Though Lilly couldn't pinpoint Lumen's exact location, she saw soft golden lights glowing from inside several of the tents down below them.

Instead of speaking to Condor, Lilly immediately faced Solace and launched back toward it, but he caught her by the hem of her dress.

"Your Highness," he said, "I don't think it is wise to return to—"

She swatted his hand away from her dress and stared daggers at him. "I'm going back, Condor. I promised Calum I wouldn't leave him, and I don't intend to do so."

She tried to take off again, but Condor's hand caught her wrist this time.

Lilly met his piercing blue eyes again, this time with every bit of fury she could muster.

"Premieress..." His voice took on a more sullen tone. "Lilly, I—"

"*Condor,*" she interrupted. She almost got lost in his eyes like she had so many times before, but this time, she managed to keep her head above the water.

She did it by thinking of Calum and what they now shared.

Condor was still handsome, cunning, and capable, but he wasn't Calum, and he never would be.

"Condor," she repeated, this time less abrasive. "I need to go back."

Condor gave a slow and reluctant nod. "If you intend to stay, then I will stay with you."

Lilly shook her head. "I don't think—"

"Regardless of whatever else may have changed," Condor said, "my duty to you has not. It never will. Please, Your Highness. I once gave up everything to be able to serve the Sky Realm. Please don't take this away from me as well."

Lilly hesitated, but she couldn't deny his words. He had endured much to be able to serve as her Captain of the Royal Guard, just as he had on behalf of her father for a time. Whether or not he'd be of any help should the King try to kill her, Lilly didn't know, but she had to admit she would feel safer if he were around.

"Very well, but we must go back now," she agreed.

Condor gave her that priceless smile. "Lead the way, Your Highness."

Together, they shot back toward Valkendell.

CALUM AND AXEL crowded the window as soon as Condor took Lilly away, but before either of them could say anything in response, a familiar voice called Calum's name.

"Calum?" Riley called.

"Riley?" Calum turned back and found Riley standing before him in all his Shadow Wolf glory, flanked by two Werewolves and two towering Sobeks. "How in the world did you get in here?"

It wasn't the only question on Calum's mind, but it was the one that came out first.

"And is that flour in your fur?" Axel pointed at a white patch on Riley's left hip.

Riley glanced down and patted it away. Sure enough, a plume of white dust poofed into the air. "No time for any of that. We're here to break you out. Magnus is gonna be waiting for us down on the street to fly us outta here."

"Let's go." Axel started toward them. "I'm ready now." He walked past Calum and glanced back. "You comin'?"

A huge part of Calum wanted to go. The familiarity of Riley, and soon, being reunited with Magnus, tugged him closer to just saying yes.

But everything he'd learned about the King so far kept his feet rooted to the floor.

"Calum?" Axel said. "Are you—"

Riley's head whirled around, and a fierce growl issued from his throat.

From behind them, two figures emerged from the adjacent hallway. Only then did the other Werewolves and the Sobeks turn back for a look as well.

The King and Matthios stood there, blocking one of their exits.

Behind Calum, heavy footsteps shook the floor. He looked back and watched as Gavridel, armored in his full gemstone regalia, filled almost the entirety of the hall in the opposite direction, both side-to-side and top-to-bottom. Gavridel again held both his amethyst and diamond axes at his sides.

They were trapped between three of the most powerful beings in all of Kanarah.

"Stand down." Matthios's eyes flared brighter than the usual amber hue of molten bronze. He pointed his double-sided spear at Riley, who was clearly the biggest threat of the group, but he was addressing all of them. "Or we will eradicate you."

Calum's eyes locked on the King's. They stared at each other for a long moment as Riley and the infiltrators backed away from the King and Matthios, clustering together with Calum and Axel to the right of the window.

As the group began to take a battle formation with Riley in the lead, the two Sobeks on either side of him, and the Werewolves flanking Axel and Calum, the King and Matthios began to advance.

Calum's heart pounded in his chest. He hadn't wanted any of this. He hadn't needed to be rescued. Riley and Magnus had done it anyway, and now it had gone all wrong.

Calum glanced back at Gavridel again. The Imperator still hadn't moved. He didn't need to. He was virtually a wall unto himself, glistening with every gemstone color in the torchlight.

They couldn't win. Even with Riley's speed, it wouldn't happen. And as much as Calum hated to admit it, the Sobeks and Werewolves wouldn't even register as threats to warriors at the level of these Imperators, and even less to the King.

"Don't fight them," Calum said, hoping Riley would quickly understand they were far outmatched, if he hadn't already. "We surrender!"

"No we don't!" Axel countered. He pointed his Blood Ore sword at Gavridel. "This is the rematch I've been waiting for. I thrashed a bunch of your soldiers today. Now I'm gonna do the same thing to you, big boy."

"Axel, stop!" Calum snapped at him and grabbed his shoulder to pull him back, but Axel shrugged Calum's grip off and stormed toward Gavridel. "Axel!"

Riley seemed uncertain of what to do. He'd continued backing up, and so had the Sobeks flanking him, but the King and Matthios had also continued to advance, tightening the noose.

"Your Majesty," Calum shouted quickly, "I'm prepared to honor the terms of our deal. These are my friends. Please don't harm them. I didn't call them here. They don't know what we've been—"

A charcoal blur launched into the hall from the window, just like before. Silver flashed, but somehow the King moved even faster. He caught Condor with both hands—one clamped down on the wrist of Condor's sword hand, and the other fastened around his throat—totally stopping him in midair.

The King wore the same indifferent expression as usual, but Calum knew that meant nothing.

Based on Condor's wide-eyed expression, the King was going to crush his throat.

Calum did the only thing he could do.

He shoved past the Sobeks and Riley, stretched out his left hand, and summoned the full power of Lumen's light.

As LUMEN APPEARED in the Blood Mountains near Reptilius, he registered the distant clap of power—*his* power—all the way from Solace. Calum had finally summoned the full power Lumen had given to him.

Perhaps Calum will return to my army after all, Lumen mused.

But that was no longer his focus. Whether Calum did or didn't make it out of Solace was of little concern. Lumen had more pressing concerns to attend to.

It didn't take him long to find the carcass of the mighty Dragon King, Kahn. Magnus had crushed his skull and hurled him down the mountainside, and his body had lain there ever since as a testament to Kahn's apathy and failure to secure his power.

Lumen harbored no sympathy for him. He'd wasted his power as the ruler of Reptilius, and a stronger force had sent him to his demise.

But a Dragon was still a Dragon, whether alive or dead. Lumen could not create such a creature—not yet, anyway... not until he had the throne of Kanarah—but that didn't mean Kahn's form was useless to him.

Although carrion birds and scavengers had long since devoured his tongue, eyes, wing membranes, and some of the flesh inside his mouth, Kahn's armored scales had kept most of his body intact. Though it had bloated and reeked of decay, the empty husk was still quite usable.

Lumen descended toward Kahn and, with a single touch of his hand, he initiated the process of resurrection. It wasn't truly a resurrection, as Kahn was dead and could not be brought back, but rather more of a reanimation.

Though Kahn had died, Lumen's power would flow throughout the Dragon's body, making him even more powerful than he'd ever been in life—and also totally under Lumen's control, unlike the current Dragon King.

It only took a moment for the first twitch to shudder throughout Kahn's body. The sight of it filled Lumen with eagerness. He had remembered the magic of reanimation, but he'd forgotten the profound power of the end result.

Once again, the world would see his true power, and they would tremble before it. The King himself would bow before Lumen, and then Lumen would put an end to him forever.

And then Kanarah would again be free.

PAIN IGNITED in Calum's fingers, and it screamed into his hand, his wrist, up his forearm and then all the way into his shoulder. It seared the inside of his veins, raced into his collarbone and up his neck, and it crept down into his chest, scorching his lungs. Tendrils of fire even reached for his heart.

The light stunned the King, and he dropped Condor, who hit the ground and clutched his eyes, as did everyone else who saw the flash, including Riley, the Sobeks, and Matthios. Only the King and Calum remained standing.

Steam rose from the King's white robe, half of which was now gone, exposing more of the bronze skin of his upper torso, now tinged red from the burn Calum had inflicted on him. Embers fizzled and smoked away to nothing on the ends of the King's beard.

But the King was still standing.

Calum, on the other hand, couldn't move.

After the blast, his left arm had betrayed him. It curled up like a dead withered branch, pressed tightly against his side, and his desperate fingers clutched at the burning spreading throughout his chest.

Though he was no longer summoning Lumen's light, the pain continued to delve deeper into his body, conquering his veins and arteries like a wildfire devouring dry brush. It wasn't just spreading, he realized—it was *consuming* him from the inside out.

Was he finally realizing the full potential of the power Lumen had bestowed upon him?

If he was, why did it hurt so much? Why did he feel like he was dying instead?

As the pain reached his hammering heart, Calum threw his head back and screamed.

Then he fell to the floor.

Lilly's face loomed over his. He heard her voice, perfect and pure and desperate and distant. He felt her touching his chest, his arm, and his face, but numbly, as if he were awakening from a dream—or perhaps she *was* the dream.

Riley's face appeared next, then Axel's, then Condor's, all of them frantic.

Then burning light began to sear at the edges of Calum's vision, threatening to wash everything white.

All he could do was scream again.

"Someone help him!" Lilly shouted.

Axel wanted to do just that, but he had no idea what was happening. He'd never seen anything like this before. Calum had used Lumen's power, and then he'd collapsed. His left hand, arm, neck, and chest all glowed with bright light from inside his veins. It was easily the most horrifying thing Axel had ever seen.

It got even worse when the veins in Calum's face began to glow white as well, followed by his eyes. When he opened his mouth to scream, light shone from within his throat as well.

Was this Lumen's power? Or was this something else?

More importantly, what could Axel do to help Calum? What could any of them do?

He'd abandoned his plans to duel Gavridel when Calum's flash had stunned everyone in the hallway, including the King himself. The attack had actually harmed the King, too, which was the most impressive part about it.

But the end result was catastrophic, and Axel could do nothing to help his friend.

When Axel looked at Lilly again, she was looking up at the King.

"Help him!" Tears streamed down her cheeks. "Please!"

For the first time since Axel had known him, the King moved quickly. He was at Calum's side in an instant, just as fast as Condor or Riley might've gotten there.

Up close, with the left upper quadrant of the King's robe obliterated by Calum's blast of light, Axel could clearly see the redness of the burn that had taken to the King's bronze skin. It canvassed his exposed chest up to his shoulder, and then it went back down his arm again.

Incredible. Axel marveled at the sight. Calum had hurt the King—the most powerful being in all of Kanarah, other than Lumen—with the power Lumen had given him.

"I can help him, but I cannot do so unless he consents," the King said to Lilly.

The King's words infuriated Axel. "Why can't you just help him anyway?"

The King's vibrant green eyes met Axel's. "He accepted this power freely. He must accept mine freely as well."

It made no sense to Axel, but he wasn't about to argue. The King was their only shot at saving Calum.

"Calum." The King cupped Calum's glowing cheeks and leaned his face in close. "Calum, will you accept my aid?"

Calum's mouth opened, but no sound came out.

Instead, he closed his glowing eyes and began convulsing.

"Calum!" Lilly cried.

"Calum!" Axel shouted, too, and he even went so far as to try to hold Calum's arms down. He felt stronger than ever.

The light had spread throughout almost his entire body now, and it shone so brightly that Axel thought it might sear through Calum's clothes.

"Calum, if you cannot respond, then just take my hand." The King pressed his hand against Calum's trembling right hand.

Lilly continued crying out to him, and Axel continued trying to keep Calum still. All the while, he begged the Overlord to let Calum live, to get him to respond.

Come on, Calum...

Calum could hear their shouts. He could see the King. He'd heard every word from all of them, albeit distantly, as if they'd shouted at him from across a huge field.

The pain in his body had jolted through every blood vessel, every nerve, every fiber of muscle, every organ. All he knew now was pain, and it had paralyzed him.

He was going to die, and though he wanted to accept the King's offer of help more than anything, he couldn't communicate it. He'd lost control of his body because of Lumen's power.

Whatever it was doing to him, it would kill him before it could possibly remake him. Why would Lumen have gifted him power like this? Or had he misused it somehow?

Or was he actually supposed to die before he would truly understand?

When the King's hand touched Calum's, he realized that was his last chance.

He couldn't speak, and he couldn't see the King's hand—everything had gone white in his vision, whether he kept his eyes open or closed them.

But he could still feel the King's hand. Its presence. Its warmth.

Its power.

And all Calum had to do was take hold of it.

But could he even do that?

His left hand seemed to be shaking more than any other part of his body. Perhaps it was because he'd accepted Lumen's power through his left hand, and it had spread up his left arm the more he used it.

But his right hand…

His right hand was shaking hardly at all. It still burned like the rest of his body, but Lumen's power hadn't fully corrupted it yet.

But Calum still couldn't move it. The power was overriding his will, molding it into something else—something arcane and furious. Something born of pain and agony. Something…

Something not human.

If Calum didn't try now, he would cease to exist forever.

With every last fragment of focus he could mash together, he gave his right hand one final command.

CHAPTER 37

A xel couldn't help but gasp when Calum's right hand latched onto the King like a newborn child grabbing at his father's fingers for the first time.

The King's huge palm swallowed Calum's right hand, and his fingers closed around it. Then a green energy similar in color to the King's eyes began to glow from the King's hand.

It transferred to Calum's hand and enveloped it, and then it crept up his right arm, dispersing the white-hot light in Calum's veins. Wherever the green glow traveled, and wherever the white light vanished, Calum's convulsing stopped.

Axel shifted his attention to the King and immediately noticed the incredible strain on his face. The act of saving Calum was taking a toll on him—perhaps it was even killing him instead.

They couldn't possibly be that lucky.

Unless... had Lumen planned this all along? Had Lumen set Calum up to expire right then and there, to somehow force the King to use his power to save Calum instead of reserving it for the upcoming battle?

Axel couldn't comprehend the amount of planning that would've gone into a scheme like that. But then again, Lumen had been locked away for a thousand years. That was a long time to plan revenge on a massive scale, to nail down even the finest details, like when the power inside Calum would reach the point where it overwhelmed him.

It seemed too good to be true, but so was Lumen, and he was as real as can be. For now, Axel just took note of the King's growing weakness. With Gavridel and Matthios so nearby, even if Axel wanted to kill the King, he knew he'd never get away with it.

But he didn't have to be the one to kill the King. Lumen wanted that honor, anyway. And when Axel got out of there, he would tell Lumen exactly what he'd seen.

Calum had stopped convulsing, and the white light no longer burned inside his veins. He looked normal again, except for a centralized glowing orb on the left side of his chest—his heart, Axel realized. It burned just as brightly as Calum's veins had, through Calum's tunic, but it wasn't moving anywhere. It was stable.

The King sat back against the wall with his elbows resting on his knees, looking truly exhausted. He drew in long, labored breaths, and sweat trickled down from his forehead and pooled on the floor between his legs.

It was an incredible sight. Axel had never imagined the King could get so tired. He never even slept, so seeing him worn out like this boggled Axel's mind.

"Is he going to be alright?" Lilly asked, her face still streaked with tears.

The King gave a haggard nod in response, but he said nothing.

Then Calum's eyes opened, and he inhaled a shaky breath.

"Calum!" Lilly reached down and embraced him. She pressed her face into his shoulder and sobbed, and as he realized what was happening, he wrapped her in an embrace as well.

"We need to get him outta here," Axel said, looking at Riley now.

Lilly's head snapped up, now wet with fresh tears. "What are you talking about? Didn't you just see what happened?"

"Our way out is waiting for us," Axel said. "And I'm taking it. Calum needs help now—*real* help from Lumen."

"It was Lumen's power that did this to him." Lilly almost snarled the words at him.

Axel shook his head. "You don't know that. We don't know what would've happened."

"If he goes back to Lumen now," the King interjected from his place against the wall, "Lumen's power will reawaken, and it will kill him. I have stabilized it, but Lumen can still alter it."

"And we're supposed to believe you?" Axel scoffed.

"Axel!" Lilly snapped. "He just saved Calum's life! Isn't that enough for you to start trusting him? Even a little?"

The more Axel saw of the King, the more it all threatened everything he'd ever believed about Kanarah, about the King, about life itself. Part of him wanted to trust the King, but a bigger part of him had already made up his mind.

The King was the ultimate villain, and every move he made was calculated. He would never deal with them earnestly. He would never fix Kanarah, because he couldn't. His soldiers would continue ravaging the men and women of this land, and no one would ever hold them accountable.

Not unless Lumen took over. It was their only chance.

"I will *never* trust him," Axel stated.

His eyes found the King's, and Axel noted how they'd lost most of the vibrancy he'd grown accustomed to over the last two days. He had really poured himself out to save Calum. Axel appreciated that, but in the end, the King still had to go.

Axel fixed his eyes on Calum, who still lay on the floor.

"Calum, it's time. You went out and found Lumen. You risked your life countless times to set him free," Axel said. "Don't just throw all of that away. Especially not for the King whose men killed your parents."

Axel extended his hand toward Calum, who slowly rose to his feet on his own. When Calum took hold of Axel's hand, everything fell back into place. They were best friends again, and they were going to tear this broken system down piece-by-piece, right alongside Lumen.

Calum pulled Axel close and embraced him. Axel wasn't the hugging type, but his best friend had just come back from death's door, so he leaned into the embrace and gave Calum a strong man-hug.

But then everything that had fallen into place kept falling. It all shattered on the floor when Calum said, "I'm staying."

Axel broke off their embrace immediately and glared at Calum. "No."

"I'm staying," Calum repeated. The white light—Lumen's light—still glowed within his chest.

Axel shook his head. "You promised me, Calum. You swore you would return with me. You promised me right here, in this very hallway."

"I'm sorry," Calum said, resolute, "but I'm staying. This is where I belong."

"He's bewitched you. *Corrupted* you."

"He saved my life, Axel. By the Law of Debt, I owe him mine in return."

"That's an ancient law that has no meaning anymore." Axel spat the words, furious at Calum. He *couldn't* make this choice. They'd been through everything together. They'd survived living nightmares together.

And now Calum wanted to tear their friendship apart for good.

"Stay here." Calum gave him a modest smile. "In time, you'll come to understand what I see. It's all so clear to me now..."

"You're losing it." Axel corrected himself, "You've *already* lost it. You can't do this. You promised me."

"I'm staying," Calum repeated.

Axel had one more card to play, and he played it. "If you do this, our friendship is over. We will be on opposite sides of the same war. We'll be enemies."

Calum didn't even hesitate. "I'm staying."

Axel clenched his fists and his teeth. "By the Overlord... you're so *stubborn*."

"I'm staying. You don't have to go."

Axel shook his head. Calum had made his choice, and Axel had made his.

Only days earlier, they had fought each other over something so asinine that Axel couldn't even remember what it was. Now, when he most needed to knock some sense into Calum, he couldn't.

It wasn't because the others would stop him—he didn't care if they tried or not.

Axel couldn't fight Calum again because he knew it wouldn't do any good. His mind was made up. It was done.

With every ounce of steel built up in his heart, Axel uttered, "Goodbye, Calum."

Then he turned and headed toward Gavridel.

When Axel reached the Gemstone Imperator, Gavridel didn't move.

"I don't care what powers you have," Axel said, "or what fancy armor you wear. If you don't move, I'm gonna go *through* you, one way or another."

Gavridel's armored head seemed to look down at him. His voice deep, heavy, and muffled by his helmet, Gavridel replied, "If you leave now, and we should happen to meet again on the battlefield, I will not grant you this mercy a third time."

"I'm looking forward to it," Axel said.

Gavridel didn't move right away, but he did ultimately step aside so Axel could pass.

Axel turned back one last time, but not to call for Calum. Instead, he focused on Riley.

"Any of you wanna come back with me, this is your only chance."

"I'm staying," Lilly insisted. "Condor is, too."

Condor could stay all he wanted, for all Axel cared. Maybe once the fighting started, they'd finally get to have that rematch they'd been talking about for so long.

Riley motioned with his head, and the Sobeks and Werewolves followed him toward Axel. Riley glanced back at Calum, who nodded at him, and that was that.

"Fine," Axel said.

Then he led them all down to the street, unhindered by any other soldiers along the way.

Magnus landed in the street before Valkendell's gates not long afterward, and his golden eyes searched their group plus the remaining Werewolves and Sobeks who'd also made it down.

Axel knew he was scanning for Calum and Lilly. "They're not here."

"What?" Magnus asked. "Where are they?"

"They decided to stay," Axel said. When Magnus eyed him, Axel insisted, "I'm serious, Scales. They wanna stay."

"It's true," Riley said, his voice sullen and devoid of it usual sarcasm. "We could've gotten them out but... they chose to stay there."

Magnus seemed stunned to silence as the Sobeks and then the Werewolves began to climb onto his back.

Axel patted Magnus on his scaly hide. He didn't like leaving them behind, either, but they'd made their choice. Now they'd have to live—or die—with it. "Let's go, Scales."

CALUM WAS ALIVE. The King had saved him.

He crouched down in front of the exhausted King, looked him in his eyes, and said, "Thank you. I'm in your debt."

The King didn't respond except to continue to stare into Calum's eyes. Finally, after a long moment, he said, "Then help me up."

Calum stood up, reached down, and hauled the King up to his feet. The King's legs wobbled, and he braced himself against the wall with one hand. Matthios moved in to help as well, but the King waved him away.

"That light in your heart," the King began, "is there permanently. I cannot remove it."

Calum looked down. The glow sent a shudder throughout his body, but it was his memory of what had happened before, when Lumen's light was trying to kill him, that sparked the sensation rather than the light doing it this time.

He glanced at Lilly, who immediately came to his side and clutched his right hand in hers. Condor followed, keeping a fair distance away, but Calum noted a bit of a frown on his face at the sight of Lilly holding Calum's hand.

"Will it kill me?" Calum asked the King.

"Only if Lumen gains access to it once again," the King replied. "Otherwise, it is a power that is now yours to wield."

Calum's eyebrows rose. "I can... still use it?"

"As I said earlier," the King inhaled a long slow breath, "the power is stabilized. It is also centralized. You are free to do with it what you wish. It cannot and will not harm you anymore. What Lumen had intended for harm, I have reclaimed for good."

Calum held up his left hand. With barely a thought, white light began to flare from his fingers and palm. It appeared just as it had before, but with one crucial difference: there was absolutely no pain and no burning sensation whatsoever. Instead, he felt a cooling sensation, as if the power had been rubbed in a poultice of mint leaves before leaving his heart.

"It doesn't hurt," he said aloud, mostly for Lilly's benefit.

She squeezed his right hand. "I'm glad, but I'm more glad you're alive."

"Takes a lot more than a shiny light to kill me." Calum puffed out his chest... his glowing chest. He wondered if he could do something about that, too. "I used to work in a quarry, after all. Hard manual labor, day-in and day-out."

"That is humorous," Matthios said from behind them.

He'd taken up a position next to Condor and stood there with his arms folded. His molten eyes still blazed, but he no longer gave off the same threatening air he'd displayed when everyone had been trying to escape only moments earlier.

"...correct?" Matthios asked. "Or am I wrong?"

"I thought it was very funny," Calum said.

Lilly shook her head. "Needs work."

"I agree with the Premieress," Condor added.

"Curses," Matthios muttered.

Calum concentrated on his glowing heart, and within seconds, the light vanished. *Interesting.*

"I didn't know you could do that," Lilly said.

"Me neither," Calum replied. "I wonder what else I can do."

"Perhaps it is best that we all get some rest." Gavridel's deep voice sounded from down the hall. The mammoth Imperator walked toward them at a slow pace with footsteps that shook the floor and the walls. "Matthios and I will see to it that the King gets some as well."

As Matthios and Gavridel met with the King to escort him out of the hall, Calum said to him again, "Thank you, Your Majesty."

"You are welcome," the King replied.

A moment later, Calum and Lilly were alone again...

And also, Condor was there.

"You can take Axel's chambers." Lilly pointed to the door down the hall.

"Not adjacent to yours?" Condor said. "I'd prefer to be physically closer to you..."

I bet you would, Calum thought.

"...so that I may better protect you should the need arise," Condor concluded.

"If anyone here meant me harm, I would've been dead a long time ago," Lilly said. "You will take Axel's chambers, and you *will* get some rest. We're safe here. So relax."

"Very well, Your Highness," Condor grumbled.

When he didn't move, Lilly shooed him away with her hand.

Condor grumbled some more and retired to his new chambers.

As soon as the door shut, Lilly flung her arms around Calum's neck, and she kissed him long and hard. When they stopped, she looked into Calum's eyes and said, "Don't ever scare me like that again."

Calum smiled at her. "I'll do my best not to."

"You'd better."

"I'll be fine." He tucked a blonde strand of hair behind her ear. "After all, I worked in a quarry, day-in and day—"

She stopped his mouth with another kiss.

IN THE EARLY hours of morning, as the first rays of sunlight crept over the eastern mountains, Magnus returned to Lumen's camp with his riders—two fewer than he'd hoped. They slid off his back, and as their feet hit the ground, Magnus called Riley aside. Axel stuck around, too, even though Magnus hadn't necessarily wanted him to.

"You are certain they did not wish to come with us?" Magnus asked Riley.

"Positive." Riley nodded. "They could've left, same as Axel, but they wanted to stay. Strangest part was that the King was willing to let 'em go. Wasn't expecting that."

"Nothing about the King is what you'd expect," Axel said. "He's weird instead of intimidating, quiet instead of demanding. He doesn't eat or sleep. He's basically invincible, although Calum hit him with a blast of Lumen's light and hurt him a little bit."

"He didn't seem like much of a tyrant to me." Riley folded his arms. "I mean, they could've stomped us out at any point, but they didn't."

"They?" Magnus asked.

"The King and his two Imperators," Riley said. "Matthios and... the other one."

"Gavridel," Axel said. "He's the big one covered in gemstone armor that we walked past on the way out."

"The King and his Imperators had you cornered," Magnus eyed Riley and Axel, "and then he just... let you go?"

"Pretty much," Axel replied.

"A lot more than that happened," Riley said.

"Such as?" Magnus asked.

Before Riley could respond, a blinding light shone within the camp and shot toward them like a blazing spear. Magnus recoiled and prepared himself to grab Riley and Axel to fly away if need be, but the light stopped before them and materialized into Lumen. As he spoke, his light faded so Magnus could make out his features without squinting.

"You have *betrayed* me," Lumen's voice boomed.

It was a poor way to initiate a conversation such as this, but Magnus took it in stride. "We did no such thing. We rescued one of our lost compatriots and returned with him."

"You disobeyed my command regarding this matter," Lumen asserted.

"No. We did the right thing," Riley spoke up. "They were alive. All three of them. We were right to go in and try to rescue them, and we even got one back." Riley shrugged. "Not the one I wanted. Not even my second choice, but still... it's better than nothing."

"Thanks," Axel said, his voice flat.

"I was explicit," Lumen continued. "I said I could not allow you to enact such a foolhardy plan, and you agreed."

"You refused to allow us to negotiate with the King on your behalf, to which I agreed," Magnus corrected. "There was no negotiation to be had. We extracted Axel from Valkendell by force, and we did not lose even a single soldier in the effort."

"Do not play coy with me, Dragon King," Lumen spat. His hands rested at his sides, too near the golden hilt of his sword for Magnus's liking. "You fully understood the meaning of my words, yet you disregarded them to fulfill your own ends."

"We did what was necessary," Magnus insisted.

Fury burned within Magnus's chest, and he felt the familiar heat of emerald fire creeping up his throat. Unlike the last time he'd stood his ground before Lumen, this time he did not push it back down. Rather, he kept it chambered in his neck, ready to release it should Lumen try anything.

"Axel," Lumen said, "return to the camp."

Axel glanced between Lumen and Magnus. "Sure, but I've got some information you may want to hear before we—"

"*Now*, Axel," Lumen ordered.

Axel stared at him, confused at first, but when Magnus turned his blazing eyes toward him, he immediately headed for the camp.

By that point, many of the soldiers had awakened from the sound of Lumen chastising Magnus and Riley for their actions. Thanks to Lumen's light and the break of dawn, Magnus could see men, Saurians, Wolves, and Windgales alike standing on the outskirts of the camp, watching it all unfold.

"I have sacrificed a millennium of my existence, and even more than that, to see to it that Kanarah could one day be free," Lumen declared, aware of the crowd that had gathered behind him. "Yet you do not seem to value my sacrifice. You certainly do not honor my authority. It is clear that your goals no longer align with ours."

Magnus tensed. This wasn't going in the direction he'd hoped it would go.

"Therefore, you must be punished for your insubordination," Lumen continued. "And if you wish to remain a part of this army, you will be reeducated before you will be allowed to lead your soldiers into battle."

Riley spoke before Magnus had the chance. "No."

"You would really refuse these generous terms?" Lumen asked. "I could simply have you executed, but I have elected to show mercy instead. Yet you *refuse?*"

Magnus and Riley had discussed this in private before they had even begun to gather soldiers willing to help them try to rescue Calum, Lilly, and Axel. They had already agreed that if Lumen tried to punish them or make an example of them, they would leave the army and take their respective soldiers with them.

Magnus had warned Riley in advance that Lumen might actually attack them if they tried to leave, but it didn't deter the Shadow Wolf's resolve. Neither of them had trusted Lumen since he'd so casually decided to give their friends over to the enemy. It had made them wonder if they had joined the right side of this war to begin with.

That, combined with what Riley had shared about Calum and Lilly choosing to stay behind and Lumen's tantrum playing out before them, had all but made up Magnus's mind. He didn't know for sure that the King was in the right, but after everything that had happened, he knew for certain that Lumen was in the wrong.

"We refuse," Magnus replied. "And we hereby withdraw from your army, along with our soldiers." Louder, to his Saurian warriors who'd gathered in the crowd behind Lumen, Magnus called, "Saurians, pack your belongings. We leave this place in one hour."

"Belay that order!" Lumen's voice registered like a thunderclap, but he never took his blazing eyes off Magnus and Riley. "You will remain where you are, and you will fight alongside me for Kanarah's salvation."

The Saurians remained in place, looking at each other in confusion.

"Saurians," Magnus called back. "*I* am your king. You will obey *my* commands."

"He is your king no more," Lumen shouted even louder. "And neither is this pitiful excuse for a Shadow Wolf the leader of the Wolf tribes."

"Hey!" Riley barked at him. "That's rude."

"Now you will answer to new leaders," Lumen declared.

The plurality of the word "leaders" caught Magnus's attention. Had Lumen already chosen replacements for them from within their own armies? Magnus had suspected it was a possibility, but if that were the case, then it meant Lumen had been planning to replace them for longer than they'd known.

"Saurians and Wolves," Lumen spread his arms wide and faced the soldiers, "I present to you your new lords."

Twin flashes of light blazed into being out of nowhere. They each formed a line of blazing white light, and then they expanded into circles. The one on Lumen's left stayed about the size of Lumen himself, but the other elongated until it was more than twice as tall as Magnus if he stood upright on his hind legs.

Then, from within the voids of light emerged two figures.

Magnus and Riley recognized them immediately.

The first was Rhaza. Apparently, he'd survived the encounter, only now, he was larger than before—more than twice the size of Riley—and white light shone from a sort of puncture wound on his side.

His eyes, previously black with silver irises, had changed as well, and now the irises glowed white instead. His claws were longer and also glowed with white light, as did his teeth. His hands and feet were bigger, and his body looked so pumped full of power that his muscles were threatening to burst through his mangy fur-covered skin.

But compared to the sight of Kahn emerging from the void, Rhaza looked tame.

The former Dragon King's foot touched the ground with a boom that shook the camp and everything nearby. It might've even rattled Solace's city gates.

When the rest of Khan's body stepped out of the light, Magnus glared at it in disgust. In truth, this wasn't Kahn anymore at all, but rather an abomination. Magnus had crushed Kahn's skull and hurled his body down the mountainside, but Lumen had transformed him into a beast that Magnus and Riley were all-too familiar with:

A Jyrak.

Kahn towered over everything for miles. He was easily as large as the Jyrak Lumen had slain back in the Central Lake.

His scales had turned black, and the spikes on his back had elongated to a freakish size, just like the rest of him. Bronze teeth lined his mouth when he opened it wide, but unlike the Jyrak they'd faced at the Central Lake, Kahn had no tongue.

He still had wings on his back, but they were shriveled and gray like dead tree branches that could snap off at any moment. Unless Lumen had bequeathed Kahn the ability to fly after this grotesque resurrection of sorts, Kahn would never be able to get off the ground. For that, at least, Magnus could be thankful.

But the most hideous part of Kahn's appearance was the shape of his head. It still looked like it had after Magnus had crushed Kahn's skull: caved in and horribly misshapen, more resembling a jellyfish than a dragon's head.

How he was even still functioning with his head in that condition, Magnus didn't know. Yet somehow, despite the lingering trauma to Kahn's head, his eyes still glowed with yellow light like the first Jyrak's had.

Kahn loosed a droning roar that matched the first Jyrak's voice almost exactly, and Rhaza joined in with a horrific howl. The two dissonant noises sent a wave of shudders throughout the army gathered at the outskirts of the camp.

To Magnus's great regret, he shuddered as well.

Lumen turned to face them once again, and so did Kahn and Rhaza. With his mask on, Lumen looked as cold and emotionless as ever, but Magnus knew that if Lumen could've smiled, it would've been now.

"Behold your replacements," he said. "Behold your demise."

Then Kahn and Rhaza lurched toward Magnus and Riley.

CHAPTER 38

Instead of facing down Lumen and the two monstrosities he'd crafted from Rhaza and Kahn's bodies, Magnus snatched Riley into his hand and leaped into the sky.

As Magnus ascended, smoke plumed from his nostrils, and the fire chambered in his throat blasted out toward Lumen, their true enemy. The General of Light let the flames wash over him as if it were a pleasant summer rain. It did no harm to him whatsoever.

Magnus knew they were abandoning their armies to Lumen's control—to those abominations below—but they'd had no other choice. It was either flee or be destroyed.

Together with Riley, he might've been able to kill Rhaza and perhaps even Kahn as well, but they couldn't have hoped to battle both monsters and Lumen at the same time.

To Magnus's relief, once they'd flown high above the camp, well out of reach of those beasts, Riley thanked him and shouted above the ruckus of the air rushing around them, "You made the right call. There's no way we were getting out of that alive."

"He set us up," Magnus growled. "He found them and altered them before we returned. He knew what he was going to do, and he was going to do it regardless of whether or not we accepted his punishment.'"

"They *were* the punishment," Riley said.

"Exactly." Magnus turned toward Solace and Valkendell.

"You sure this is wise?" Riley asked.

"Our other choice is to fade into oblivion, powerless to influence the outcome of the war," Magnus said. "We have friends in Valkendell. Friends who will be glad to see us, and who, according to your report, can get us an audience with the King. But first, you must tell me everything that happened when you were in there."

"Sure," Riley said. "But do you mind letting me climb onto your back instead? I don't want to look like I'm just a stuffed toy in your hand when we land in the middle of the city. Talk about embarrassing..."

AXEL COULDN'T BELIEVE his eyes. He'd half-expected Lumen would follow Magnus and Riley, but instead he'd stayed put, watching them go.

Then Lumen turned around to face the army, condemned Magnus and Riley for their betrayal and called them cowards for fleeing. He gave a grandiose speech about how they would still liberate Kanarah even without Magnus and Riley, but all Axel could focus on was the mammoth Jyrak and the overgrown Shadow Wolf standing at Lumen's sides.

How was such a thing even possible? He'd encountered a Jyrak before—he'd even been inside one's mouth—and he knew they weren't tame-able creatures.

Yet there stood Kahn, reborn as a massive corruption, like a castle-sized puppet waiting for Lumen to make him dance on strings, but with his head still smashed in.

Rhaza struck Axel as even more terrifying, but he had no plans to get anywhere near either of the two of them. And while Axel lamented—well, perhaps "lamented" was too strong a word —the loss of Magnus and Riley as fellow soldiers in Lumen's army, he couldn't deny that the two monsters flanking Lumen would undoubtedly be even more effective in the battle to come.

Even so, it struck Axel as strange, if not coincidental, that he'd lost his four closest friends to poor decisions and treachery all within less than an hour. He remained grateful to Magnus and Riley for freeing him from the King's clutches, but in the end, Lumen's mission came first. And Axel had already chosen his side.

"Axel."

Lumen's booming voice tore Axel from his thoughts. He looked up at the General of Light, the leader of their army, and awaited his next words.

"Come forth."

Axel obeyed, even though the thought of getting anywhere near either Kahn or Rhaza—or Lumen, for that matter, especially after what had just happened—terrified him.

As he did, he caught sullen scowls from General Balena and General Tolomus of the Windgales. Then he spotted Janessa, Dallahan, and Embry, the trio of Wolves who'd harassed him and stolen his rations throughout the journeys across Trader's Pass. They eyed him as well, and one of them—Axel couldn't tell which one—even growled at him.

What was their problem? Were they upset that Lumen had banished Magnus and Riley? Or were they just jealous that Lumen had called him forward and no one else?

Axel crossed the open field and stood twenty paces from Lumen, who still hovered in the air between Kahn and Rhaza.

"You mentioned you had valuable information to share," Lumen said. "Speak, and if you are true to your word, I shall grant you that which your heart has always desired."

Axel gulped, and his heart thundered in his chest. Was this it? Was this the moment he'd been waiting for? Tentatively, he asked, "Power?"

"All that I have promised you and more," Lumen said. "You will be my first and only Imperator, and I will grant you not only the portion of power I reserved for you, but also the portion I reserved for Calum, as he is now an apostate. You shall be my masterpiece."

Axel's mouth stretched into a giddy smile. *It's finally gonna happen.*

"But first, you must speak," Lumen concluded, folding his arms.

Axel opened his mouth, and without hesitation, he told Lumen everything. When he finished, he looked up at Lumen expectantly, glad he'd gotten it all out, but also relieved that neither Kahn nor Rhaza had moved from their places at Lumen's side.

Lumen lowered to the ground and walked the twenty paces from his position to Axel's in only eight strides. He stopped well within arm's reach of Axel and stared down at him with his blazing white eyes.

"You have done very well." Lumen extended his hands, palms up. "Take my hands."

Despite his glee, Axel hesitated. He'd seen what Lumen's power had done to Calum, and he'd seen how it had transformed Kahn and Rhaza. What would happen to him if he accepted this gift?

"Will I still be... me?" Axel asked.

"You will be more you than you could have ever been without me," Lumen replied. Then he waited for Axel to make his choice.

"I don't want to be me." Axel dared to meet Lumen's eyes. In them, he saw an eternity of white light, of raw power, of limitless potential. "I want to be *you*."

"Then you shall be," Lumen said. "Give me your hands, and I will make it so."

Axel ignored the conflict raging in his soul and placed his hands on top of Lumen's.

Lightning screamed up Axel's arms and into his body, seizing every inch of it in a second. His nerves frayed and burst. His arteries and veins caught fire. His mind catapulted over itself and distorted.

And his body was remade.

Lumen pulled his hands away, and Axel collapsed to his knees, but not from weakness—it was from the new power coursing through his body, reconstructing every part of him from the inside out. Forging him into a living weapon. Transforming him into a warrior of legend.

When Axel finally arose, steam hissed from his armor. *Everything* was different now.

Axel could sense things he'd only been vaguely aware of before. He could hear and see for miles. He could feel the ground pulsating with every vibration beneath his feet. He could taste the fear of his enemies in Solace.

"There is one more thing I must do to unleash your true power," Lumen said. "It will not be pleasant."

"Do it," Axel said. Even his voice sounded different. He'd always been confident, but now he sounded like he was on a whole new level... and he was.

Lumen leaned in close, positioning his face close to Axel's—so close that, even in spite of his new power, Axel couldn't help but feel awkward.

Then Lumen pulled off the mask that covered the lower half of his face.

Axel's eyes widened, and he screamed.

CHAPTER 39

"Calum, wake up!"

Calum's eyes flickered open, and he stared up at Lilly, who stood over him in his bedroom. He'd dropped her off at her chambers—under Condor's watchful eye, of course—and then retired to his own, so it confused him to see her here.

Rays of morning sunshine streamed through his window, but the heavy curtains blocked most of the light. It couldn't be very late. From the rose-gold color of the sunshine, he guessed it was just after dawn.

A thought hit Calum, and he jerked upright in the bed. Had Lumen's army already attacked? Was that why Lilly had awakened him?

"Relax," she said, rubbing his shoulder. "It's good news, for once."

He blinked at her. "What news?"

"Magnus and Riley are here."

Nothing could've gotten Calum out of that bed faster than those five words.

With total disregard for his appearance, Calum bolted past her into the hallway. He hadn't quite anticipated what he'd find out there, especially since there was no way Magnus could fit into most of the halls inside Valkendell.

Sure enough, nobody was out there except for Condor, who tried to stifle a yawn, but upon seeing Calum clad only in his undershorts shook his head and grinned.

"Now I see why the Premieress is so interested in you," he said.

Calum's cheeks caught on fire, and he looked down. Then he darted back into his chambers, only to turn around and hurry back out again. Lilly walked out a moment later, gave him a wink, and then Calum rushed back inside, threw on some clothes and his boots, and met the two of them in the hallway once again.

"Sorry," he said.

"Don't apologize," Lilly said with another wink. "I didn't mind."

"On the contrary, *do* apologize," Condor insisted. "If I wasn't awake before, the sight of you in your skivvies was more than enough to do the trick. At least warn us next time, will you?"

"Sorry," Calum repeated, and again, his cheeks ignited with heat.

Condor escorted Calum and Lilly down to the ground level and outside to the front of the fortress. As soon as the doors opened, Calum saw an unmistakable mass of dark-green scales, and he rushed toward Magnus with his arms outstretched.

He felt no shame upon flinging himself at Magnus and wrapping his right hind leg in a huge embrace. "You came back!"

Magnus returned the embrace by gently reaching down and wrapping his right arm around Calum's back. It enveloped the entire back side of Calum's body, except for his head, and then some.

"That we did," he replied. "But only barely."

Calum released his embrace, and so did Magnus. Riley appeared from behind Magnus's right wing, and he slid off the side of the Dragon King's flank and landed on the street next to Calum.

"What do you mean?" he asked as he shared an embrace with Riley, all the while remembering how he used to be so much bigger than the Wolf. But now Riley had him by several inches in height and a lot of muscle mass.

"We must speak to your King," Magnus said.

The phrasing of it—"your King"—struck Calum as odd, but he didn't bother to correct Magnus. After everything that had happened, Calum had no trouble admitting it was the truth.

"He's inside," Lilly said. "We can take you to him."

To Calum's surprise, Magnus somehow managed to squeeze through the narrow halls leading to the King's garden. The King had been there ever since saving Calum's life the night before, and now he sat on a wooden bench lining one of the many paths in the garden, resting.

He'd donned new clothes after the incident with Calum's light blast, and the redness on the side of his face and neck seemed to have reverted back to the usual bronze color of his skin. Valerie sat beside him on the bench, holding an oak mug filled with steaming liquid. Whether it was for her or the King, Calum didn't know.

Matthios and Gavridel were nowhere in sight, likely both tending to the forthcoming defense of the city and of Valkendell.

When Magnus approached, the King looked up at him with weariness in his green eyes rather than the usual vitality Calum was accustomed to. Then the King looked at Riley, and to both of them, he said, "Welcome to Valkendell, honored guests."

Magnus and Riley glanced at each other and then at Calum.

Magnus spoke first. "You would consider us guests, even though we were leading armies to overthrow you?"

The King's brow furrowed, and he craned his neck as if to look past Magnus's enormous form, which reached almost to the diamond dome overhead. "Forgive me, but I see no armies behind you."

"Ouch." Riley cleared his throat and rubbed the back of his head. "Uh... yeah. About that. We sort of... lost them."

"They were taken from us," Magnus corrected him.

Calum had yet to hear how it had all gone down. Maybe now he would get the chance.

"I do not mention it to further wound your pride," the King said, "but rather to demonstrate that you are here of your own accord, despite your past transgressions. Therefore, you are honored guests."

"Thanks, Your Majesty." Riley gave a slight bow. "That's, uh, really generous."

Magnus didn't seem as convinced. "I do not understand. We openly rebelled against you.

Were it not for Lumen's recent actions, we would still be leading our armies with the end goal of usurping you. How can you possibly trust us?"

Despite his haggard appearance and lax posture, the King gave Magnus the same devoted attention that he'd given Calum every time they'd spoken.

After a long pause, he replied, "I do not believe either of you are disloyal individuals. On the contrary, your loyalty to Calum is perhaps the most crucial element in bringing you to this place. Lumen's actions are what they are, but it is because of your loyalty to Calum and your shared friendship that you are here. Regardless of the minutiae of what happened and how it led you to this place, that loyalty is always constant. It is that loyalty within you that I trust."

Now it was Magnus's turn to digest the King's words. He did so with a bow of his own and said, "Thank you, Your Majesty. You are a man of great wisdom."

"Please, sit." The King motioned toward the path and the grassy section of the garden beyond. "Tell me what you know. Any advantage, no matter how small, will aid us in the battle to come. Make yourselves comfortable." He added, "Do take care to mind the foliage, though, Magnus."

Magnus and Riley explained what had happened on their end, and then Calum and Lilly had the chance to explain what had transpired here inside Valkendell. He skipped over the part about getting together with Lilly, but he figured they'd realize that development soon enough.

Not long after they finished updating each other, Matthios entered the garden, double-bladed spear in hand. He glanced up at Magnus a few times and then stood before the King.

"Your Majesty," he began, "Lumen awaits you at the city gates."

RATHER THAN GOING down to meet Lumen face-to-face, the King, Matthios, and Valerie escorted Calum and the others to a balcony overlooking the city. From their vantage point high above, Calum could see Lumen and his army pooled like liquid just outside the city gates.

But this time, a hulking monstrosity stood beside Lumen. It was unmistakably both a Jyrak and Kahn, the dead former Dragon King killed by Magnus. A smaller, yet still impressively large Shadow Wolf stood on Lumen's other side, and though they were far away, Calum could tell it was Rhaza, just as Magnus and Riley had said.

"Who is leading the Windgales?" Lilly asked.

Condor shook his head. "I can't see that far. But since General Balena hasn't tried to defect to our side, I fear…"

"He would never side with anyone over his own flesh and blood. He was relentlessly loyal to my father, and his behavior has not changed since I ascended," Lilly said. "If he still leads the Windgales, it is compulsory. He has seen what Lumen is capable of, and he is no fool. He must be biding his time until he can make whatever move he intends to make."

Condor nodded but gave no reply.

"Now you see why Lumen was expelled from Valkendell," the King said.

"Expelled?" Calum asked.

The King didn't say anything else, but Valerie spoke up in his place.

"Lumen, the General of Light, was once an Imperator like Matthios and Gavridel," she explained, but this time her smile didn't reach her eyes. "He was the strongest of the Imperators, capable of controlling light itself. When he rebelled, the King cast him out, but Lumen's power remained. He used it to create an army of abominations like the two you see before you."

Calum exchanged glances with Lilly. Valerie's explanation made total sense.

"The battle raged for days, and many of Kanarah's citizens perished," she continued. "The cost was high, but the King, in his generosity and mercy, sought to give Lumen a means to atone for his wrongdoing, so he banished him to his subterranean prison for a thousand years. He had hoped Lumen would see the error of his ways, but instead..."

Valerie motioned toward the city gates and the army that lay beyond it, and morning sunlight glinted off the jewels in her sapphire necklace.

The idea that Lumen had been one of the King's Imperators fascinated Calum for multiple reasons. It answered a question Calum had never bothered to ask: where had Lumen come from? And it also explained why Lumen despised the King so vehemently. The sour grapes between them dated back even farther than Calum had assumed.

"Lumen violated the Overlord's laws," the King added. "By reanimating the husks of dead beings, he has rejected the power of the Overlord's ability to create life and replaced it with a hideous facsimile.

"But he went even further than that. He stopped experimenting on the dead and began to infect the living with this scourge as well." The King nodded toward Lumen. "And here you see both crimes on full display. Kahn has been reanimated, and Rhaza has been transformed. Both are abominations, and both of them are slaves to Lumen's every whim."

Slaves.

For the longest time, Calum had known exactly what that word meant. Or at least, he thought he had.

Now, upon seeing Kahn and Rhaza standing there like a child's dolls, ready to be manipulated and moved to whatever end Lumen could conjure, he realized a new definition of the word.

Calum had almost become one of Lumen's victims. Were it not for the King's intervention...

"This is Lumen's vision for Kanarah," the King continued. "Several of his army have also received his touch, just as you have, Calum, only they lack the means to recover from their affliction. They cannot access true healing while also serving at Lumen's side."

"So they're destined to become puppets, just like Kahn and Rhaza?" Riley asked.

"By now, you are all too familiar with the fell beasts of Kanarah," the King said. "The Gronyxes roaming below the surface. The Dactyls roaming the skies. The Wargs haunting the desert. The Jyraks lurking beneath the waves." The King paused and met each of their eyes in turn. "All of them are Lumen's dark creations, twisted beyond recognition."

Calum couldn't believe what he was hearing. Could it really be true?

"The Gronyxes are men, driven by their lust for power, now corrupted and laid low," the King explained. "The Dactyls are Windgales, prideful of their ability to fly, now reduced to scavengers of carrion. The Wargs are Wolves, confident in their concealment within shadows, now banished to walk in darkness forever. The Jyraks are Saurian Dragons, overflowing with strength, now cursed to roam the seas where their strength means nothing."

Calum exchanged glances with Lilly, and he was sure the look of horror on his own face matched hers. Riley also reacted in kind, but Magnus continued staring out at Lumen, his golden eyes full of fury.

"Lumen destroyed the lives and souls of these wretched beasts. While he was gone, they served only themselves, but now that he has returned, they await the call of their dark master," the King continued.

Calum had to wonder why the King's army hadn't been hunting these beasts during all that time. Perhaps they could've eradicated some of them entirely.

Then again, maybe they already had been. Solace had come across as a pretty peaceful place so far.

"And when he calls, they will answer," the King concluded. "Mark my words."

Their *dark* master? But Lumen was the General of *Light*. Calum was about to ask about that when a flash of white light from below nearly blinded him.

Lumen appeared in front of the balcony about thirty feet away, blazing in all his glory, far brighter than Calum had ever seen, even in his dreams. The light radiating from Lumen actually caused Calum physical pain, primarily in his eyes, but also in his chest—in his heart.

Only the King and Matthios withstood Lumen's light at its brightest, and even then, Calum noticed the King's trembling arms and his white-knuckled grip on the wrought-iron railing at the edge of the balcony.

"At long last, we again meet face to face, Taleph," Lumen said, neither reducing his brightness nor acknowledging the King's sovereignty.

Taleph? Was that the King's name? Or was it a derogatory term of some sort? Calum couldn't tell just by hearing it, and Lumen's tone hadn't given anything away. The King didn't bother to respond, either.

"Nothing to say? A millennium ago, an ocean of words spilled out of your mouth as you banished me to the abyss." Lumen's voice had distorted ever so slightly, making it sound darker, more enraged, more furious.

More *evil.*

"A millennium ago, I said only what needed to be said, heretic," the King replied. "And in due time, I will speak to you once more, and then never again."

Lumen laughed, and it seemed to warp the very air around them with waves of power. "Yet another 'prophecy' from a failed tyrant. A weak one, at that."

The King's arms still quaked as he gripped the railing. Perspiration dotted his forehead once again, and he squinted against the incredible brightness of Lumen's light. Saving Calum must've really sapped a lot of his power.

Calum didn't know how it all worked, or how long it would take the King to recover his full strength, but he hoped it was soon. Against a foe like Lumen, Calum feared that only the King himself could vanquish him.

"If you really knew what strength was, or the true nature of power, you would not be so arrogant," the King retorted.

Lumen's blazing eyes narrowed, and he hovered closer to their position on the balcony. "When I first emerged from my prison, your dog Matthios met me in the field of battle. I gave him my terms for your surrender. Since he undoubtedly failed to communicate them to you, I will reiterate them here and now.

"You, King Taleph, will lay down your crown and your sword at my feet, and you will bend your knee to me. You will renounce your claim to the throne for all eternity, and you will publicly declare me the King of Kanarah and all its peoples, of which I will be the better steward.

"And once you have done so, I will execute you before the people so they will know your reign of tyranny has finally come to an end. On these terms I will not compromise; I will not bend. Most importantly, I will not fail to achieve that which I desire," Lumen declared.

His terms had changed from when he'd first leveled them at Matthios so many months before, particularly when it came to the King's fate.

Back then, Calum had believed Lumen capable of accomplishing everything he'd proclaimed. Now, as the King struggled to even remain upright against Lumen's overwhelming power, Calum wondered if they even had a chance of stopping him.

"I will *never* yield," the King uttered, his voice far stronger than his appearance. "And the throne of Kanarah will *never* be yours."

At long last, Lumen's light faded, and everyone managed to face him again. Why he'd let up, Calum didn't know.

Then Calum found out.

Lumen extended his hand toward Calum, and though he was several yards away, he somehow managed to take hold of Calum and lift him off his feet—from the inside.

It felt like fingers made of white-hot fire had taken hold of Calum's heart and proceeded to lift him into the air by it. His chest felt like it was about to burst into flames from the inside, and at the same time, it seemed like Lumen was about to rip his heart out.

Calum screamed and clawed at his chest, all to no avail. He heard his friends calling for him, and he heard Matthios ordering Lumen to release Calum.

The pain didn't stop, but not long after his feet left the balcony, Calum managed to glance down through the pain and saw the city far below. Lumen had suspended him in the air, and now Calum dangled over certain death. Despite the pain, he very much didn't want Lumen to let go of him, even though Matthios kept demanding it.

"It was foolish of you to think you could escape my light, Calum." Lumen squeezed tighter still, and Calum thought his heart would burst in his chest. "You are merely a human. How could one such as you stand against someone like me?"

Even if he'd had a good answer, Calum's chest hurt far too much for him to respond.

But then the burning tension loosened, and Lumen's fingers retreated from Calum's heart. Calum immediately looked down, expecting to plummet to his death, but he remained hovering in the air, still facing Lumen.

When he looked over his shoulder, Calum saw the King standing on the balcony with his hands outstretched, as if about to catch a baby. His green eyes had regained some of their vibrancy, and Calum felt the cool sense of relief wash over him.

The King had Calum in his hands, and he wasn't going to let go.

Lumen laughed again and shook his head. "You would sacrifice so much of your power to save one tarnished soul?"

"Yes," the King answered without even a hint of hesitation as Calum drifted back and landed safely on the balcony once again. "I would do it for any of them."

Lilly wrapped her arms around Calum, and Riley patted him on his shoulder, welcoming him back onto solid ground.

"Then you truly are a fool, and you do not deserve to be King," Lumen said. "And now I will show you."

Lumen disappeared in a flash and reappeared down at the city gates between Kahn and Rhaza once again. He bellowed a war cry that rattled the floor beneath Calum's feet, and the attack on Solace began.

Then the King collapsed to the floor.

CHAPTER 40

"Your Majesty!" Matthios cried. For someone who struggled with understanding emotions, Calum thought he'd nailed the tones of concern and worry in his voice.

"The soldiers need you more than the King does, Matthios." Valerie pressed her hand against the bronze plating of his breastplate, stopping him from reaching the King. "Go to them. Be their bronze beacon of hope. Remember—you are more than a match for Lumen. Do not believe otherwise."

Matthios nodded, turned, and leaped off the balcony without so much as another word. The exchange got Calum wondering about Valerie's role within the kingdom again, but the King's miserable state was even more pressing.

"The rest of you, retreat to the safety of the garden," Valerie ordered. "Magnus, you must carry the King there. He draws strength from it, and he will need to recover far more if he is to aid us in this battle."

"Understood." Magnus scooped the King into one hand as if he were a rag doll, and then he followed Valerie through the halls of Valkendell with Calum, Lilly, Riley, and Condor following close behind.

Axel had awakened in perfect darkness, without pain. He'd remembered everything up until the point when Lumen had removed his mask. After that, his memories went black.

That had been hours earlier. Now he was awake, ready, and brimming with new power.

He'd wanted to test the breadth of his new abilities on the front lines of the battle, but Lumen had tasked him with an even more crucial task. Were it not so integral to the success of their plan, Axel would've declined. After all, with his new power, he now rivaled Lumen in strength... probably.

So while the battle raged at the city gates, Axel was on his own, searching for that which was known but had never been found. Thanks to his newly augmented vision, Axel could now see through rocks and stone—an ability he'd never even dreamed to request but that had already become a crucial part of his skillset.

As he scanned the mountainside, he wondered what else he might be able to see through. The idea of trying it out—perhaps on Valerie—came to mind, but he banished the thought to the recesses of his mind. He had work to do, and only he could do it.

Though Axel's enhanced vision revealed much, he wouldn't use it all the time. He couldn't—not if he actually wanted to see what was right in front of him. And whenever he wasn't using it, his helmet and the mask on the lower portion of his face narrowed his field of vision more than he would've preferred.

He'd just have to get used to it, he decided. After all, with power like his, what enemy could even dare to challenge him in the first place?

After another few minutes of searching, Axel located what he'd been looking for: a tunnel, shallow and dug from just outside the city to a house that was positioned along the inside of the city's back wall.

He traced its path back aboveground outside the city walls and found a narrow path that threaded between the steep cliff face and the back wall of the city.

Axel ascended higher—he could fly now, too, just like Lumen or Condor or Lilly—and continued to follow the path from overhead.

As he'd suspected, it terminated outside the city walls when the cliff face narrowed so far that it actually touched the back wall of the city.

Based on his positioning near Valkendell's diamond dome, Axel realized he'd found what he was looking for—mostly.

Either way, now it was time for the second phase of Lumen's plan to begin.

RILEY HAD SENSED them when he'd first entered the garden less than an hour ago, but now they weren't even bothering to hide. He found the sight of them both incredibly reassuring but also destructive to his ego, as their presence proved his existence was not as important as he'd thought.

Five Shadow Wolves, just like him, awaited their arrival in the garden.

When Magnus hesitated to enter, Valerie smiled at him and said, "Do not fear them. They are the King's most trusted protectors. They also double as spies and, occasionally, as assassins if need be."

Assassins? Riley marveled at the sight of them. Not one, but *five* Shadow Wolf assassins?

Riley didn't know whom the King might've wanted dead or why, but sending five Shadow Wolves would more than get the job done every time—that was for sure.

The closer Riley studied them, the more he realized they outclassed him. He'd thought he was the pinnacle of lupine perfection now that he'd transformed into a Shadow Wolf, but these five... they were on a whole different level altogether.

As Magnus gently set the King onto a patch of soft grass, Lilly took notice of one of the Shadow Wolves in particular. The Shadow Wolf, her fur as black as a starless night sky, looked pretty much the same as the others, only she was slightly smaller and had a white patch right on the tip of her otherwise black tail.

Riley recognized the patch immediately, but could it be? It had been so long, and after Riley had fled the tribe, she had suffered and died in his absence... hadn't she?

When her blue-irises flashed toward him and lingered there for the briefest moment, Riley knew it was either the uncanniest coincidence of his life, or he was seeing a ghost.

Or it was really her.

"Windsor?" Lilly said, using a name Riley had never heard before.

He had always known her as Meliamora, or Melly for short.

Windsor's head turned toward Lilly, and her eyes narrowed. "I don't believe it. You clean up rather nice for a slave, Windgale girl."

Her voice—that was what sold it for Riley. This wasn't some Shadow Wolf named "Windsor." This was Melly, very much alive and somehow promoted to a Shadow Wolf.

Just like me, Riley mused. *Alright... now what? You know it's her, and she doesn't recognize you, so...*

"Will five Shadow Wolves be enough to protect the King?" Calum asked. He quickly added, "I don't mean to insult any of you. It's just that Lumen himself is here, and—"

"We are more than capable of defending the King from any threat," said Windsor—Melly—whatever she was calling herself now.

"Melly?" Riley said. It just spilled out of his mouth, uninhibited.

She turned to regard him with her eyes narrowed. Then recognition widened them again.

"Riley?" she asked, her voice low. "Is it really you?"

Riley grinned. He couldn't believe it—she was alive. "Yes. It's m—"

Windsor had him pinned to the ground before he could even finish his sentence. Though he'd followed her movement quickly enough, he'd allowed her to hit him because he'd expected a hug or a joyous embrace.

Instead, once she got on top of him, she snarled and slashed at his face with her claws.

Riley took the first attack, and lines of pain carved from his furry cheek down his snout. He blocked the rest of her blows, shoved her away, and leaped back up to his feet in time to see that the other four Shadow Wolves had joined up with her, all of them now regarding Riley as a threat.

"Enough!" Lilly darted between them with her arms outstretched, and Condor followed her into the middle of the fray, his hand on the hilt of his sword. "The King needs rest, and you're causing a ruckus. What is this all about? Clearly, you know each other."

"He left me for dead," Windsor growled, only barely restraining herself. The other Shadow Wolves looked just as ready to strike if Riley made even one wrong move.

"I was banished from our tribe." Riley dabbed at the claw marks she'd gouged onto the side of his snout, and his fingers came back bloody. The wound was superficial, but it stung.

"You *ran away* so you wouldn't have to fight." Windsor seethed at him. "You were a coward then, and you're still a coward now."

Her words hurt far worse than the scratches she'd inflicted. After all, they were true.

Riley wanted to lash out at her in return, to tell her he'd been right, in the end. Had he stayed, Rhaza would've killed him. By leaving, he'd found a way to grow stronger. He'd returned to his tribe as a Werewolf and even managed to defeat Rhaza, and now he was a Shadow Wolf. Everything had worked out.

But even though that was true for him, it didn't—it *couldn't* negate what she'd gone through in his absence.

Riley relaxed his stance and hunched over into a submissive posture. "I'm sorry, Melly."

"*Don't* call me that," Windsor snapped at him. "Melly is dead. She died the day you ran off."

"Then I'm sorry, Windsor. To you and Melly."

Windsor growled at him, but her aggressive stance relaxed some as well. "That doesn't change what happened."

"That's all I have to offer," Riley said.

Windsor chuffed. "Then there is nothing more to say."

"Thank you for working out your differences in a peaceful manner," Valerie interjected. She seemed to smile in virtually every situation, no matter how dire or grave. It was... off-putting to Riley, to say the least. "Dear Shadow Wolves, please take your positions within the garden. We must be prepared in case of an attack."

Riley couldn't conceive of how anyone or anything could possibly get into the fortress, short of maybe Lumen himself. And even then, if Lumen did get inside, Riley doubted that five Shadow Wolf assassins could even harm him, much less stop or defeat him.

But with the King weakened, what other option did they have?

Windsor met Riley's eyes with another cold stare, and then she spread out with the other Shadow Wolves, who melted into the various shadows of trees and large bushes throughout the spacious garden.

Riley had to admit—these Shadow Wolves were good. He'd seen where every single one of them had hidden themselves, but now it appeared as though they'd never even been there in the first place. They'd left no trace of themselves behind, and he couldn't see them in the shadows, even with his enhanced vision.

More compelling than their prowess was their very existence, and the idea that they'd chosen to serve the King of Kanarah rather than strike out on their own to form tribes.

And that there were five of them. *Five.*

Riley had thought he was the only Shadow Wolf in the world, just like Magnus was the only Dragon, but he'd been utterly wrong. It all made him wonder more about the King and what was really happening here in Solace. Maybe it was better than roaming the desert in search of food for the rest of his life. If it was, Riley might just have to stick around once this was all over.

If he survived, of course. Death was always a possibility, even for a Shadow Wolf.

For now, Riley fixed his attention back on the King, who lay on the grass with a serene expression on his face and his fingers clutching clumps of grass blades. If the King couldn't recover in time, would Lumen and his army break through to the city? Or into Valkendell?

Or would Matthios and Gavridel and the King's soldiers be able to hold them back?

Riley didn't know, but either way, he would be ready.

BY THE TIME Lilly realized Valerie had left the garden, she had already returned with a pair of silver-clad soldiers. Both of them toted large burlap sacks over their shoulders and set them down before Lilly and Calum. Within, Lilly found her pink armor, the pouch containing the Aerostone, and, most importantly, the Calios.

Up until that point, she hadn't dared to ask about the sword's whereabouts, but even just the sight of the Sky Realm's sacred blade gave her a sense of relief. She picked it up, and as she held it, the sensation of the sword's ivory hilt conforming to her hand inspired new confidence.

She separated herself from the group to don her armor in private, and when she returned, Calum also wore his armor and wielded the Dragon's Breath sword once again. She'd always thought him good-looking, but seeing him standing there, clad in the Windgale armor her father had given him, Lilly had to fight to contain her excitement.

Valerie stood at the entrance to the garden and addressed them, still smiling. "Your task is simple: Guard the King. Valkendell's defenses are stout, and her soldiers are valiant, but should they fail, you are the King's last line of defense."

"Where are you going?" Calum asked.

"I am responsible for overseeing a number of logistical concerns here in the fortress when there is not a battle raging on the city's doorstep," Valerie replied. "When we are at war, my list of duties constricts to only a few crucial tasks. It is those tasks that I must now attend to."

Lilly tried to imagine what those tasks might be, especially from the perspective of someone like Valerie, who'd seemed to function in a sort of administrative role at the King's side, but she came up empty. Lilly had assumed Valerie's primary role at the moment would involve personally taking care of the King, but apparently that wasn't the case.

Valerie gave them all another genuine smile, a gracious nod, and said, "May the power of the Overlord protect you."

Then she left the garden.

Lilly turned to Calum and kept her voice low. "Do you find it at all strange that less than three days ago, we were on the exact opposite side of this war?"

He nodded. "Yes, but a lot has happened since then."

Lilly considered that as she glanced back at the King, who still lay on the grass with his arms outstretched, tranquil and calm. "What confuses me is that we've been entrusted to guard the King of all Kanarah. Out of everyone in this kingdom, why choose us?"

Calum turned to face her. "Why not us?"

Lilly grinned at his naivety. "Because we were his sworn enemies until only last night."

"Sure, but you are the Premieress of the Sky Realm, Magnus is the Dragon King of Reptilius, Riley is the alpha Shadow Wolf of the desert Wolf tribes, and I'm Calum the Unifier." Calum gave her a wink. "Who else is better-suited to protect him?"

Lilly was about to rib him for his "Unifier" comment, but a familiar face entered the garden through its main entrance. Unlike the group of silver-clad soldiers following him, the man wore golden armor denoting him as a general, and he carried a daunting golden spear unlike any Lilly had ever seen before.

Lilly found the man's eyes first, and upon recognizing her, the man shifted his gaze to Calum and fixated on him.

"*You.*" Captain Anigo pointed straight at Calum.

Then he raised his golden spear and stormed forward.

BEYNARD ANIGO HADN'T SEEN the boy named Calum since they'd battled in Lumen's camp a few nights earlier.

Now another battle had begun, this time down at the city gates. Lumen's army had finally come, and it was up to the valorous soldiers in the King's employ to prove their mettle once and for all.

In the aftermath of Anigo's escape and subsequent return to the city of Solace, he'd been taken to meet with the King personally, the first time he'd received such an honor. After providing a detailed debrief, Anigo apologized for having failed to properly defend Kanarah City, and he had openly welcomed whatever punishment the King saw fit to levy against him.

To his profound surprise, the King had promoted him instead, and now he was *General* Anigo.

It made no sense to Anigo, and he'd expressed as much to the King, who'd listened intently to every objection Anigo presented. He'd explained every fault, every failure, and every mistake he'd made along the way. He'd revealed his deepest deficiencies to the supreme sovereign of this land, the man whom Anigo had sworn to protect and serve with his very life.

None of it had fazed the King.

Instead, when Anigo finally stopped describing his shortcomings, the King had praised him for his loyalty.

His *loyalty.*

Anigo had been rewarded, promoted, and preserved because of his *loyalty* above anything else. It was truly a transformative moment for him in terms of his service to the King.

He'd been effective as a commander in pursuit of local fugitives and deserters here in Solace, but upon leaving the city, he'd done nothing but flounder, flop, and lose. It had made no sense to do anything but demote him and relegate him to menial tasks for the rest of his career.

The King hadn't agreed, and so now he was General Anigo, charged first and foremost with leading the King's personal guard. After all, the King had reasoned, who better to oversee his personal protection than a soldier who'd proven his loyalty—even on the brink of death?

Like every charge he'd been tasked with before, General Anigo took his new commission seriously. So when he saw Calum standing in the King's garden, flanked by his usual cadre of misfits, holding the sword he'd used to cut through General Anigo's blade when he'd been trying to escape Lumen's camp, he reacted as his loyalty dictated.

He attacked.

CALUM DIDN'T WANT to fight Captain Anigo again. They were on the same side now, and though it probably looked like Calum and his friends had infiltrated the garden and overpowered the King, that wasn't what had happened.

But how could he convince Captain Anigo, a man who hated him and who was already charging toward him with a golden spear in his hands, of that truth?

Calum realized he couldn't, so he raised the Dragon's Breath sword and defended himself.

The impressive golden spear in Captain Anigo's hands clashed against the Dragon's Breath sword, hard and solid. Unlike conventional weapons, the spear didn't break due to the over-whelming power of the Dragon's Breath sword.

Instead, a flash of golden light rippled down the spear, and Captain Anigo immediately attacked again. It was some sort of magical weapon, just like the Dragon's Breath and the Calios, only Calum didn't know for sure what kind of powers it wielded.

Calum defended every one of Captain Anigo's strikes until the King himself intervened.

He appeared at their side and caught an elbow from each man, mid-swing, stalling their blows. Through his malaise, he simply said, "Stop."

Captain Anigo looked at him as if the King had just ordered him to jump off Valkendell's highest balcony.

"General Anigo," the King said, his voice as fatigued as he looked, "you already know Calum. He is now your ally."

With that, the King returned to his spot on the grass and lay back down.

Calum met Anigo's eyes, and they stared at each other for a long moment.

Finally, Calum said, "*General* Anigo, huh?"

"Yes," he replied, glancing around, still wary of the situation. Then he motioned to the group of soldiers positioned behind him. "I now lead the King's personal guard. It would appear my stubbornness has yielded unexpected and undeserved blessings."

Calum waited for a quip from Axel, but it never came. Then he remembered they'd parted ways, and heartache crept into his chest. He washed it away with the distraction of talking to General Anigo.

"I owe you my thanks," Calum said. "If you hadn't told Gavridel who I was, he probably would've killed me instead of capturing me."

"You owe me nothing," General Anigo said. Then, reluctantly, he added, "In fact, I suppose it is I who owe you my gratitude. Had you not convinced Lumen to spare me, I would be long dead by now, rather than alive and well and tasked with the King's protection. So... thank you."

Calum couldn't help but smile. At the time, he'd wondered if convincing Lumen to spare Anigo was the right call. "I'm glad it all worked out."

General Anigo scoffed, and it, too, reminded Calum of Axel. "I'd hardly say that. They're fighting a war down in the city."

"Do you have any news?" Lilly asked. "Updates from the battle below?"

Condor hovered right behind her, his hand on the hilt of his sword, just in case General Anigo tried anything.

"I'm afraid I do not," General Anigo replied. "We were cautioned to avoid the windows as much as possible, and I have heard no reports other than what was relevant to my charge of keeping the King safe."

Lilly's brow furrowed. "I see."

Calum put his hand on her shoulder. "I'm sure we'll learn your uncle's fate and the condition of your people soon enough."

She touched his hand with hers and gave it a squeeze. "Thank you."

"In the meantime, you needn't fear," General Anigo said. "We are surrounded by thousands of men, led by two Imperators, and we are shielded by layers of impenetrable white stone. We are perfectly safe in here."

A realization struck Calum like an arrow to his gut. He turned toward the back wall of the garden, his eyes wide.

The secret entrance.

He'd discovered it, and he'd told Axel about it, and then Axel had gone back to Lumen.

If Axel had told Lumen about the secret entrance, then—

Calum recognized the sound of stone lightly scraping against stone.

He'd heard it that night when he'd seen the King entering the garden from the secret entrance. He'd seen the section of the wall moving. He wasn't supposed to see it, but he had.

And now he was seeing it again.

Someone was coming through the secret entrance.

Panic gripped Calum's chest as he ran to face whoever it was, but he stopped short upon seeing a dark form emerging from the shadows within the tunnel behind the wall. Its black boots crushed several roses as it walked into the garden.

The hulking figure wore tortured black armor and a matching helmet, with its edges jagged and flared out, almost as if someone had ravaged the metal during the forging process. In between the armor, an aura of darkness shrouded the figure's joints as if it were a constant flow of some arcane energy from within the armor.

He wore a black metal mask on the lower half of his face just like Lumen and Matthios. Between the mask and his helmet and the angle he was holding his head as he entered, Calum couldn't see any of his face. He also carried a large sword, its black blade jagged and brutalized like the armor.

Was this some new terror conjured by Lumen? Some ancient evil that he had awakened to serve him?

At first, Calum didn't recognize anything about the figure, but then the sunlight hit the metal edges of the sword and the armor, revealing the telltale light-blue glint of Blood Ore. The figure raised its head, and Calum froze in place.

Calum stared into the figure's bloodshot dark-blue eyes, and his heart dropped into his churning stomach.

It was Axel.

CHAPTER 41

The horror in Calum's eyes was priceless. Axel almost laughed aloud, but he thought better of it. He wasn't there as Calum's best friend or as an ally. He was there for one reason, and now he'd achieved his goal.

"Axel..." Calum started to say. "What happened to you?"

Even though Calum couldn't see it, Axel smirked behind his mask. He replied with only one word: *"Power."*

Five dark forms darted at Axel from their hiding places across the garden—five Shadow Wolves. They'd tried to hide from him, but he'd seen them as plainly as he'd seen Riley standing out in the open, or Calum, or the King himself, lying on the grass, soaking in the sunlight from overhead.

With his sword, Axel swatted away the first Shadow Wolf as if she were nothing but a fly. The second Shadow Wolf raised its black claws to strike, but Axel shuddered to the side and jammed his elbow into the side of its head. The Shadow Wolf tumbled across the garden and came to a hard stop against a tree.

The third and fourth Shadow Wolves came at him from opposite sides. He caught them both by their throats, stopping them dead in their tracks, and then he slammed them together, head-to-head. They dropped at his feet.

The final Shadow Wolf launched at him from behind. Axel opened a black void in the air behind him, and it swallowed the Shadow Wolf whole. Another void opened in front of one of the garden's white walls, and the Shadow Wolf reemerged and slammed into the wall with a loud crack.

It all happened within less than a second's time, but Axel had perceived every attack coming as if in slow motion while he reacted twice as fast.

When he met Calum's eyes again, the horror in them had disappeared. Instead, Axel saw fear.

Calum looked at the two Shadow Wolves lying unconscious at his feet, then he looked over at the other three Shadow Wolves, each of them in various stages of consciousness or recovery.

Behind him, Riley darted over to the first Shadow Wolf, the one Axel had swatted away with his sword, as if to tend to her. She rose to her feet and growled, but she didn't attack a second time.

"What have you done?" Calum uttered.

"Only what was necessary." Axel loved how menacing the mask made his voice sound, even though it was somewhat muffled.

"What happened to you?" Calum repeated.

This time, Axel did laugh. He tapped his helmet. "You always were a slow one. What do you think happened? Lumen made me his Imperator, just like he promised."

Calum took an involuntary step back, which Axel appreciated. It wasn't as good as bowing, but it still demonstrated reverence. The best part was that Calum had done it out of reflex, so it was a genuine response.

Axel laughed again. "I told you to come with me."

Calum shook his head. "This... whatever *this* is... it's wrong, Axel."

"If you could feel what I feel, and if you could do what I can do, you wouldn't be saying that." Axel's feet lifted off the ground, and he hovered in the air five feet above the top of Calum's head. He smiled wide, even though Calum couldn't see it. "I can *fly*, Calum. Isn't that incredible?"

A charcoal blur hit him from the side and slammed him into one of the walls.

The impact jarred Axel, but it didn't hurt. He'd been distracted, so he hadn't seen it coming this time. But it didn't matter—he had power now. He could handle anyone or anything.

"Good to see you again, Farm Boy."

Axel's smile widened, and he pushed back on Condor as if he weighed nothing.

Condor, though, didn't just accept it. He'd seen what Axel had done to the Shadow Wolves, and as one of the only beings in the room capable of tracking what had happened, he'd prepared himself to have to deal with Axel accordingly.

Condor slipped under Axel's arms and drove the pommel of his sword hard under Axel's chin. The blow stunned Axel for an instant, but in that time, Condor managed to draw his sword and get behind him.

It was enough to spur Axel to stop being lazy. He spun around and batted Condor's blade away, only to find it slicing at his neck this time. Axel parried again and threw a powerful counterattack that knocked Condor halfway across the garden.

When Condor didn't immediately attack again, Axel called to him, "You said you would come to me when I was ready to fight you. Looks like that day has finally arrived."

"I do recall saying that. And I suppose you're right," Condor said. Then his voice darkened. "You *are* ready."

"Condor!" Lilly shouted. She dashed up to hover beside him, wielding the Calios.

"Stay back, Premieress," Condor said. "I have to put this Farm Boy out to pasture."

Before Axel could make another move, a thundering voice cut through the tension, followed by a blinding light.

"Axel," Lumen said as he emerged from within the secret passageway. "Enough. You have done well."

Axel lowered his sword, but he didn't sheathe it. It, along with his Blood Ore armor, had warped and adapted to his new dark powers, providing him with an exceptional level of protection, so much that when Condor had tried to run him through from behind, Axel had almost let it happen.

He doubted Condor's normal steel sword could've actually pierced his armor, but he hadn't wanted to find out that way, either. New power didn't mean he could become a stupid fighter. Better to repel the attacks instead.

As Lumen drifted farther into the garden, his light faded some, but everyone still recoiled from his presence—at least at first.

Calum, predictably, was the first to stand up to Lumen, followed by Magnus, Lilly, Condor, Riley, and the female Shadow Wolf. They all faced him in a miserable attempt to block him from reaching the King, all the while ignoring Axel completely.

It irked Axel, but at the same time, he understood his role. Lumen was to be the new king, not him, and that was fine with Axel. For now, he was content to lean against one of the walls and watch.

"Please," Lumen said, as if mildly annoyed, "you cannot seriously hope to defeat me, nor will you keep me from that which is rightfully mine."

"We won't let you kill him," Calum said.

"We will fight you to our last breath." Magnus's nostrils began to smoke, a telltale sign that he was preparing to loose his dragonfire.

Lilly and Condor readied their weapons, and Riley took up a position next to Calum. Behind them, some guy in a set of golden armor and wielding a matching golden spear directed a group of silver-clad soldiers to surround the King.

Now it was Lumen's turn to laugh. "You are all fools. Solace will fall within the hour. Valkendell is already mine. Only one thing remains: to kill the King and seize the throne."

Axel nodded. It was finally happening. They were exactly where they needed to be.

He wished Calum would've come back with him, but he'd made his choice, and it was the wrong one. Now he'd have to deal with the consequences.

"And you will all get to watch me do it." Lumen clapped his hands together, and then he began to pull them apart.

The white stones making up Valkendell had some sort of protective quality to them that prevented Axel and Lumen from simply opening portals and entering the fortress, but now that they were inside, they could both use them freely.

Beneath Calum's feet, a gleaming white void tore open. It widened rapidly, growing larger and larger until it had stretched wide enough to devour Calum, Magnus, Lilly, Condor, Riley, and the female Shadow Wolf.

It happened in an instant, and in the next instant, the void inhaled them all into it. Not even the Windgales managed to fly away in time, though Lilly got close.

They reappeared high above—on the outside of the garden's dome. They realized what had happened quickly enough, and they pounded frantically on the diamond panels. They struck it with their weapons, and Magnus even hit it with a blast of emerald dragonfire, all to no avail.

As the King had said, the dome was impenetrable. Unbreakable.

That's why Lumen had done it this way.

Now that the others had been cleared out, Axel saw the golden-armored man for who he was: Captain Anigo.

Before Lumen did anything else, Axel dashed over to Captain Anigo and appeared before him in a blink.

"Hello, Captain Anigo."

To his credit, Captain Anigo reacted by swinging his fancy new spear at Axel. But as with the Shadow Wolves, Axel saw it coming, and Captain Anigo's attack wasn't nearly as fast as any of theirs.

Axel caught the spear in his hand, anchoring it in place.

"It's General Anigo now," Anigo grunted.

"Great," Axel said, his voice flat.

"Let go of my spear."

"Sure." Axel released it, and General Anigo immediately thrust it straight at Axel's chest. He dodged it easily enough, and he avoided the next several attacks General Anigo threw at him as well. Finally, he caught the spear again. "Satisfied?"

"I will not let you harm the King."

Axel shrugged. "That's no longer your concern."

He yanked the spear, and General Anigo jerked forward with it. Then Axel opened a void of darkness behind General Anigo and shoved him inside. A second later, a dull clank sounded overhead, followed by more desperate pounding on the dome high above.

Axel ignored it. Instead, he focused on the soldiers surrounding the King. They stood there like lost puppies, confused and scared, but unwilling to abandon their guard duty.

Axel would put them out of their misery soon enough.

But before he could do anything, vines and branches latched onto each of the soldiers from every direction. The plants were doing their King's bidding, just as they had when Calum had tried to kill the King the first time.

The vines and branches flung the soldiers away, sending them tumbling toward the entrance to the garden, where other plants ferried them out entirely. Then those same plants formed a thick network of foliage that sealed off the entrance to the garden.

It all made for an erratic and humorous display, but ultimately, the King had only delayed their inevitable deaths by saving them.

Axel watched as the King struggled to rise to his feet. He resembled a toddler pushing himself up after having fallen over—and then wobbling some more once he got upright again.

It was pitiful.

Once he found steady footing, the King stared at each of them in turn with those verdant green eyes of his. But now, due to his weakened condition, his eyes were the only part of him that still held any vigor.

"All that effort," Lumen chastised, "just to save a few souls from a quick and merciful death. You bought them a few more days to live, at most, unless they are willing to bow to me as their new King."

"You will *never* be King," the King said. Even his voice sounded worn out and tired, as if he'd been shouting for hours on end.

"Your delusions are never-ending," Lumen said. "But your tyrannical reign, on the other hand, ends now."

"My power comes from the Overlord Himself, and He will never grant it to you," the King said.

"Then call out to Him, and let Him save you." Lumen drew his gleaming sword and drifted forward.

The King's eyes flashed bright green, and plants attacked Lumen and Axel from every angle. Axel grunted and peeled off vines left and right, but none of it even slowed Lumen down. He continued to float toward the King, and the vines tore free from their bases behind him, fell off his body, and then withered and died.

The King recoiled a step and summoned a faint green light into his palms, but Lumen was too quick. In a literal bolt of lightning, Lumen shot forward, leading with his sword.

When the flash subsided, Lumen's sword was buried in the King's chest.

CHAPTER 42

C alum screamed as he clawed at the diamond dome, unable to reach the King. Even if he could have, he knew he couldn't have stopped Lumen. At this point, he couldn't have even stopped Axel.

Axel's transformation was horrible enough, but Lumen's murder of the King was heart-rending. The King of Kanarah was dead, slain by Lumen.

He'd accomplished his goal, and now it was only a matter of time before he conquered the remainder of the King's forces and took over Valkendell—and with it, the city of Solace and all of Kanarah.

With tears streaming down his cheeks, Calum hammered on the dome with his fists until a gigantic green hand curled around from behind and lifted him up. Then, with one powerful flap of his wings, Magnus launched into the air.

The dome and the garden below dropped away as Magnus climbed higher and higher. When Calum got control of his emotions, he looked to his left, stunned to find that Magnus had also snatched up General Anigo into his other hand. Riley and Windsor had mounted Magnus's back and rode him as he flew, and Lilly and Condor flew alongside them as well.

To Calum's surprise, they weren't the only Windgales accompanying the Dragon. General Balena and hundreds of other Windgales quickly joined their flight. They hadn't sided with Lumen after all; they'd remained loyal to Lilly. The entire group turned south and flew away from the city.

From their vantage overhead, Calum saw the gates of Solace lying just inside the city's towering walls, now reduced to shards of wood and twisted iron. Throughout the city, Lumen's army battled with the King's soldiers. Even from high above, Calum couldn't tell who was winning, but he suspected it wouldn't be long before Lumen's forces overwhelmed the King's.

The whole situation had hollowed him out. Calum felt worthless, which confused him, as he'd been on the other side of this conflict only days before, but that somehow made it all worse. After all, this was all his fault.

He'd freed Lumen. He'd raised an army for Lumen to use to overthrow the King. He'd revealed Valkendell's secret entrance to Axel, who'd returned to Lumen and shared it with him.

And now the King was dead because of it.

How could Calum have been so wrong the whole time?

When Magnus finally landed, it was so far south of Solace that they couldn't even see it anymore. As soon as Magnus released Calum, he collapsed into the grass and dug his fingers into the earth, hoping he could somehow sense the King. It was a wild, random thought, one that made hardly any sense, but in his desperation, Calum didn't know what else he could do.

He felt nothing but the cool dirt on his fingers, now turning to mud from the wetness of his tears. He was truly helpless, and now he'd cost all of Kanarah everything.

Lilly landed at his side and placed her hand on his armored shoulder. It should've been all the comfort he needed, but it wasn't.

"Calum," she said.

He tried to ignore her, to continue to dwell in his pain instead, but her next words hijacked his attention.

"Someone is here."

He turned to look.

There, standing in the field between Magnus and Riley, stood Matthios and Gavridel. Behind them, the rest of the field was filled with silver- and black-armored soldiers, at the head of which stood General Anigo.

"THE KING'S soldiers have fled the city, and Matthios and Gavridel have retreated, my lord," reported the human messenger. "We've won!"

Lumen didn't react to the news aside from offering a slight nod. He was too focused on the corpse of the King still lying in front of him.

"Thank you," Axel said from somewhere nearby. "You may go."

Lumen had really done it. He'd killed the King. It had taken him more than a millennium to do it, but he'd found a way. His army had successfully taken the city. He'd proven he was worthy to reign over all Kanarah.

All that remained now was to take the throne.

Instead, Lumen continued to stare down at his nemesis.

Once Lumen had extracted his sword from the King's body, the King's blood had all but totally drained into the ground below. His once-vibrant green eyes, two beacons of vitality, were now dark and lifeless, staring far beyond this world.

Lumen couldn't help but wonder if the King was now freer than Kanarah would ever be, now that he'd returned to the Overlord.

"Lumen?" Axel said, again from somewhere behind Lumen. "I mean, Your Majesty? Your army is awaiting you."

"Let them wait," Lumen said, still scrutinizing the King's lifeless form. "There is one more thing I must do."

Lumen sheathed his sword, then he reached down, picked up the King's body, and hefted it over his shoulder. The grass beneath where the King had lain glowed with an even brighter green than the rest of the immaculate garden.

"Maintain order," Lumen told Axel. "I will not be long."

With the King's seal of protection no longer in effect, Lumen was again free to warp out of Valkendell, and he did so through a portal made of light.

He emerged in a place that was all too familiar to him, deep under the Central Lake: his prison.

For a thousand years, he'd been locked within this cavern of darkness, sealed away from the rest of the world—from *his* world—simply for trying to serve it the best way he possibly could. The King had confined him to this awful place, and Lumen could think of no better resting place for the King than a prison of his own making.

Lumen brushed aside the lingering chunks of stone and rubble that remained from when Calum and his friends had released him from the column of stone, and he laid the King on the platform.

Again, he pondered the King's death. Lumen had indeed killed him, but it had been far easier than he'd expected. The amount of resistance the King had put up was laughable, especially compared to the all-out war they'd fought during Lumen's first rebellion. This time, the King hadn't even bothered to use his spear.

From the look of him when Lumen had first appeared in the garden, the King probably couldn't have lifted it anyway. Something had weakened him, just as Axel had reported, and that same weakness had enabled Lumen to destroy the King quickly.

Regardless of how this rebellion had concluded, Lumen was decidedly the victor. Now he would claim his prize, and he would rule Kanarah in the King's place. Lumen was the king now, and he would reign forever.

With one last glance at Taleph's lifeless form, Lumen, the new King of Kanarah, vanished from his prison for the last time.

He reappeared in the garden, where he was alone. Axel or some of Lumen's other soldiers must've cleared out the dead and wounded Shadow Wolves, or perhaps they'd escaped instead.

Either way, it wouldn't matter. With the King dead, there was no question now that Lumen was the most powerful being in all of Kanarah. No one could challenge him now.

As he headed back into Valkendell, Lumen noticed a patch of brown grass on the spot where the King had died.

He chose to ignore it.

"WE MUST RECLAIM the city of Solace and Valkendell before Lumen can establish his power there," Valerie said, her smile stern and hopeful, but as ever-present as usual. She still wore a fine dress and her blue-and-yellow sapphire necklace with matching earrings. "There are still many who would fight to prevent him from…"

Calum listened to her words, but they did nothing to inspire or motivate him. Despite the incredible showing of soldiers who'd fled Solace after the battle, they couldn't hope to take back Solace or Valkendell. Not without the King. Lumen was too strong, and Axel…

Calum closed his eyes and pushed Axel from his mind. They'd each made their own choices, and despite the outcome, Axel had clearly made the wrong one.

Gavridel had gone back to the city in search of survivors. He'd never been any good at talking anyway—worse than Matthios, according to Valerie—so in his stead, Valerie and Matthios had gathered everyone around to discuss their futile plans of trying to continue to fight Lumen.

"It won't work," Calum interrupted.

Valerie stopped her speech, but her smile remained. "Why not, Calum?"

"The King is dead." Calum folded his arms. "Kanarah is going to die without him, no matter what we do."

"We can still fight," Valerie encouraged. "If we can defeat Lumen, perhaps there is a way to save Kanarah as well."

"But we can't defeat him." Calum shook his head.

"We can," Matthios asserted from Valerie's side. "Gavridel and I together are more than his match."

"Not anymore. Not with those abominations at his side. Not with Kahn and Rhaza. Not with…" Calum cringed at the thought. "Not with Axel."

Lilly took hold of Calum's hand. It felt warm and reassuring to have her skin against his, but he couldn't bring himself to enjoy it. Not when everything else was so bleak.

"And even if we could defeat him, we can't save Kanarah," Calum said. "I've seen what will happen. The King—"

Calum stopped. How could he convey what he'd come to understand about the King to everyone else? Perhaps Valerie and Matthios already understood, but he doubted the rest of their soldiers would.

"The King was Kanarah's core," Calum finally said. "Without him, the rest of Kanarah will die. Imagine if someone ripped out your heart. You wouldn't live very long. It's the same thing."

The imagery shocked everyone to silence, or perhaps it was the message itself. Either way, no one else spoke for a long time.

Then Valerie finally smiled and said, "Then we will just have to find Kanarah a new core."

Calum blinked at her. Apparently she didn't understand after all. "That's not how it works."

Her smile persisted. "I am certain you believe you understand the true extent of the King's power and influence across Kanarah, down to every blossoming flower, every germinating seed, every drop of rain, and every newborn baby's cry." Her eyebrows rose. "I can assure you that you do not."

Calum felt a bit like Axel probably had whenever he'd insisted on something, only to be proven entirely wrong—except that Valerie hadn't *proven* anything yet.

Still, he'd only known the King for fewer than three days. Valerie seemed to have had regular access to him for a long time, and Matthios would've been with the King for well over a thousand years. Perhaps they knew something Calum didn't.

"What do I not understand?" Calum asked it as earnestly as he could manage.

Valerie's smile widened. "Yourself."

Calum's eyes narrowed at her. Was this some sort of philosophical musing on Valerie's part? It sounded like something Magnus might've said to him while he'd been educating Calum and Axel as they traveled.

"I don't get it," Calum confessed. "Is this some sort of 'we're-all-connected' thing? If we all band together, we can save Kanarah?"

"Not really," Valerie replied.

"Then what are you talking about?"

"You, Calum," Valerie replied. "You will be the next King of Kanarah."

CHAPTER 43

I n the deepest depths of the Central Lake, the water began to stir. The fish scattered away from a particular spot on the lake's floor as something disturbed the mud.

It rippled with movement, and then something long and lean snaked from the soil at the bottom of the lake floor. It had no definition, no true shape yet, but it was strong and bore the determined resilience of new life.

The water around it continued to stir, to move, to dance.

The appendage continued to grow, reaching ever higher, climbing toward the surface far above.

As flattered as Calum was at the notion, he could think of a million reasons why it would never work. The first reason was the reality of the situation: they wouldn't be able to defeat Lumen. If they couldn't take back the throne, everything else was irrelevant.

Then there was the fact that Calum had never ruled anyone. He hadn't been born into royalty.

He supposed someone could make the case that he'd led a group to free Lumen in the first place and then helped to lead his army afterward—though both of those should count against him more than in his favor. More importantly, it didn't equate to ruling... well, *everything*.

"No." He shook his head, chuckling. "No, not me. No chance. I'm the worst choice. I'm no one."

"You are the *only* one," Matthios insisted. His molten eyes locked on Calum's.

Calum matched his stare with one of confusion. "Why would you even say that?"

"I was there when the King saved you," Matthios replied. "I saw him ransom you from the brink of death. In doing so, he chose you to receive a portion of his power."

Calum glanced down at his chest. Because he'd learned to control it, his light wasn't glowing through his armor, but it was still there. Was that the power Matthios was referring to?

"Not the light," Matthios said, as if reading Calum's thoughts. "There is another power. Once that goes even deeper. It is the very power that healed you, that restored you. The King gave you a piece of himself—so large a piece that it weakened him enough that Lumen could kill him."

"He saw this coming, Calum," Valerie insisted. "And he chose *you* as his successor."

Calum searched within himself, wanting to disbelieve their claims, to prove them wrong. Instead, he realized they were right.

It had taken their words to make him notice, but he had discovered something within himself that hadn't been there before—or at least, he hadn't noticed it.

As he gave it consideration, a cool sensation, like when the King had healed him, spread outward from his heart. It chilled his insides and eased down his limbs and into the tips of his fingers and toes.

It was the King's power—some of it, anyway—still residing within him.

It felt incredible, and he did feel stronger now that he'd tapped into it, but his mind reasoned with him, and he spoke his thoughts aloud.

"Even this," he began, "is not enough to justify making me the King of Kanarah."

"Tell that to your eyes." Valerie beamed at him.

Calum blinked, and he furrowed his brow. "What do you mean?"

"They are green, like the King's," Valerie replied.

Calum looked to Lilly, whose own eyes widened at the sight of him. He looked to Magnus next, and he nodded.

When Calum turned to Riley, the Shadow Wolf said, "Yep. They're green, alright."

Valerie produced a small hand mirror and held it up for Calum. In its reflection, he saw a familiar pair of green eyes, every bit as vibrant as the King's had been.

Calum blinked, but the effect didn't go away. His body still felt cool, and his eyes refused to revert back to their original blue color. It was a phenomenon, to be sure, but that was the extent of it.

He shook his head. "Eye color doesn't qualify me to be the king."

"No, not that alone," Valerie said. "But combined with everything else, it does."

"How can you say that?" Calum's heart shuddered at the thought. He could never measure up to the King himself. It would never work. "I'm not ready. I never will be. I'm not the one."

"You are the only one," Matthios repeated.

"He is right," Valerie said, still grinning. "Matthios and Gavridel can defeat Lumen, but only you can rule. They are powerful, but they are not touched by the King's power. Or, rather, by the Overlord's power. It is, in fact, His power which flows through you. It is His power which signifies His hand on you. It is His power which will make you king."

Calum wanted to refuse again, but when he saw Magnus nodding, his stance on the matter shifted. Magnus believed this. So did Riley.

Calum turned to Lilly, but she gave him nothing but a solid stare, one bordering on terror. Were his eyes frightening her?

He looked back to Magnus, hoping he'd say something, and Magnus obliged his silent pleading.

"You have been my leader from the day we first met in that quarry," Magnus said. "You will continue to lead us ever forward as king. Only you can, and you will not be alone."

Riley nodded along as Magnus spoke.

They believed it. They believed in *him*.

Calum exhaled a deep breath. Was this something he could actually do? Was he really the only choice?

His mind continued to bombard him with objections, but a small voice from his heart told him the truth. He listened to it long and hard, weighing whether it was something he'd conjured within himself or another voice, one that didn't belong to him.

The voice told him to heed their words.

Calum exhaled a long sigh. He still didn't feel like it should be him, but he'd chosen to listen to that voice.

"Alright," he finally said. "I'll do it."

Valerie smiled and clapped. Matthios gave him a somber nod. Magnus and Riley grinned at him.

But when he turned toward Lilly, she was gone. He caught sight of her flying away, with Condor accompanying her several feet behind.

In that moment, Calum realized what a fool he'd been.

AXEL WASN'T sure what might happen when Lumen physically sat on the King's throne. Given how steeped in magic the likes of the King and his Imperators had been, Axel had figured the throne might've been enchanted or something.

But when Lumen sat down on it, nothing happened. Nothing changed.

Lumen didn't glow any brighter. The chair didn't somehow extend his power throughout the entire fortress. The walls and floors didn't shake.

He just sat down, and that was it. Pretty underwhelming.

Lumen stood up a moment later and said, "A good king does not merely sit on his throne while his people languish in poverty and suffering. Come. I must meet with my subjects."

As Axel followed Lumen out of the fortress, he couldn't help but revel in their victory. The sun hadn't even set, and they'd already killed the King, ended the war, and taken control of Kanarah. High marks for efficiency.

When he reached the city streets, however, Axel's pleasant outlook darkened.

He'd seen the horrors of battle many times before, but the scale of the devastation and death in Solace made him shudder. Bloody bodies lay in the streets, most of them humans and probably some Windgales. Occasionally he spotted a dead Wolf or a Saurian, but they were by far in the minority.

The carnage extended to the homes and buildings in the city as well. Several of them still burned, even though the fighting had stopped nearly an hour earlier. Others were reduced to nothing but mounds of rubble. Blood had pooled in low spots on the streets all around them, intermingling with other kinds of filth and refuse.

Still, he told himself, *it had to be done.*

He'd known from the beginning that this would be a bloody fight, that people would die. They had sided with the King, and those who'd fought and died on Lumen's side had nobly done so. Through their sacrifices, they'd won the war.

Axel kept telling himself that, even when he noticed the bodies of several men, women, and even children clad in normal clothing lying in the streets as well. They'd tried to avoid killing citizens when they'd taken Kanarah City, but evidently, that "rule" hadn't also extended to Solace.

Lumen walked through it all, unfazed. He'd seen far more warfare in his long life than Axel ever would in his, so that probably explained why it wasn't bothering him as much.

At least, that's what Axel hoped it was.

"It appears your interpretation of the seeds was incorrect," Lumen said.

Axel looked up at him, confused. "Huh?"

"The seeds. You overheard the King and his dog discussing the planting of seeds in fertile soil prior to our arrival at Solace."

Axel recalled the conversation he'd overheard. It had been between the King and Valerie. He wouldn't have considered Valerie a "dog" by any stretch of the imagination.

Though he'd only known her a few short days, she'd definitely made an impression. His heart ached a bit at having to leave her behind, especially without saying goodbye, but it was too late now. He hoped she hadn't been killed or hurt during the attack. He hadn't seen her when they'd killed the King, so hopefully that meant she was safe.

"Yeah," Axel finally said. He'd anticipated that rose golems or some other weird plant-based thing would follow them toward Solace, but nothing had. "Guess I was wrong about that."

As they continued walking, Axel noticed Saurians, Wolves, and humans gathering weapons and supplies and ushering people into their homes. Those who no longer had homes were either paired with those who did, or they were relegated to manual labor among the soldiers in Lumen's army.

The sights confused Axel enough that he finally asked, "Why are we out here? I mean… what are we here to do?"

Lumen stopped walking and turned to face him. Though Axel had received powers, Lumen still towered more than two feet taller than him, so Axel had to look up to meet his blazing white eyes.

"We are preparing for the next battle," Lumen replied.

"The next battle?" Axel squinted at him from under his helmet. "What next battle? We won."

"They will return," Lumen said. "Even now, they are gathering their strength to try to retake the throne."

"But the King is dead," Axel said. "Who do they think is gonna take his place? Matthios? Gavridel?"

Lumen just stared down at Axel without replying.

That meant Axel was supposed to know the answer to the question he'd just asked. But if it wasn't Matthios or Gavridel, who would it be? Magnus, Lilly, and Riley were all rulers in their own regard, but they each had Kingdoms to lead already. So who was left to—

Axel realized the answer, and he cursed openly. "You've gotta be kidding me."

It was *Calum*. They meant to make him the king.

Lumen nodded. "Absurd, is it not? He is just a boy. He cannot possibly rule."

"Stupidest idea I've heard in a long time," Axel agreed.

More than being shocked or confused, Axel was angry. He'd finally received incredible powers of his own, and Calum had *still* found a way to outdo him.

Who in their right mind would want Calum to be king, anyway? It was a terrible idea for every possible reason, but mostly because Calum was far too weak to do justice to the position. Stack him next to Lumen, and he'd fall short every time—*way* short.

"When they arrive," Lumen said, "Calum is mine."

Axel squinted at him again. "What do you mean?"

Lumen just stared at him again.

And Axel realized what he meant.

Ice trickled through Axel's veins, but he'd sworn his unending loyalty to Lumen. Calum was the enemy now, and he'd abandoned their friendship, even though Axel had tried to keep it alive.

It had to be done.

"Axel," Lumen said.

"Alright," Axel responded quickly. "I won't get in your way."

It had to be done.

CHAPTER 44

G ill of Sharkville, the largest town in the Valley of the Tri-Lakes and the only remotely habitable place anywhere along the Central Lake, picked up his "Fishig" sign.

Together, with help from Jake and his fishing crew, they'd rebuilt Gill's shanty after those nasty Sobeks had wrecked it. Gill still bore a gnarly scar on his forehead from the gash he'd taken well before the real fighting had started. It had bled like a son-of-the-beach at the time, but now he figured it made him look intimidating, so he didn't mind so much.

With his hammer in one hand, he tucked the sign under his arm and plucked a nail from his mouth. Then he climbed the stepladder and positioned the sign above the door, all while holding the nail to it nice and tight.

He raised the hammer back for a swing, but he never did. Instead, he froze in place at the sight of something enormous rising from the lake beyond his little shanty.

Then Gill fell off his stepladder.

"Premieress!"

Condor's voice chased Lilly's flight path, but she'd refused to slow down until she'd climbed high above the clouds, far out of reach for anyone but other Windgales.

As the Premieress, blessed with her royal bloodline, she could fly faster than any other Windgale. Plus, the cool air dried her tears just as fast as she could cry them, so going fast was very much her prerogative.

Condor was plenty fast, but she was faster. He wouldn't catch her unless she allowed it. She considered that now, after everything, maybe she *wanted* him to catch her, though.

Calum's acceptance of his new role as king-elect had perfectly demonstrated that he didn't need her, that she wasn't a priority. After all, if he'd really believed that they could have a relationship, if that was something he'd really wanted, he wouldn't have agreed to become Kanarah's next king.

He'd promised her they would be together. He'd sworn they would make it work between them. This was the exact opposite of that. Calum was severing their relationship for good.

When Lilly finally broke through the cloud line, she eased to a hovering stop, inhaled a deep breath of thin air, and blew it out as icy vapor. Her tears chilled her cheeks, and though she wiped them away with her hands, more followed them.

"Premieress?" Condor's voice carried from nearby. He'd broken the cloud line, too, and he'd spot her soon, if he hadn't already. Now much closer, he said, "Premieress."

Lilly needed comfort. She wanted to turn around and throw her arms around Condor, but how could she? She'd already made it clear to him that she was with Calum now. If Lilly and Calum were done, as she expected, Condor wouldn't want to be her follow-up romance.

She'd made the wrong choice in choosing Calum, regardless of what her heart had told her.

"Lilly," Condor said as he drifted in front of her.

Lilly kept her head down. She didn't want him to see her in this state. She considered turning away from him as well, and another part of her told her to fly off again, to try to lose him in the clouds, to just run away from all of this.

But she'd done that before, and she'd paid the price for it. She couldn't do it again—her people needed her, and she refused to abandon them.

"Lilly," Condor repeated. He gently lifted her chin with his fingers, and through her tears, she met his piercing blue eyes.

It took every ounce of her willpower not to latch onto him right then and there. She almost did until Condor's next words froze her in place.

"He didn't know what he was saying."

Lilly blinked at him. "What did you just say?"

"Calum didn't know what he was saying."

"Are you... defending him?" Lilly didn't know whether to be outraged at Condor or confused. She thought he loved her, or at least had strong feelings for her, just as she'd harbored feelings for him.

So why would he defend Calum?

Condor shook his head. "He can defend himself, if he must."

"Then why did you say that?"

"Because it's true," Condor replied.

Lilly scoffed. Was he taking Calum's side? "What are you talking about?"

"He wasn't thinking. He didn't realize that what he'd said would hurt you," Condor explained, but every word that came out of his mouth only reinforced Lilly's anger.

"*Exactly*," she said. "He wasn't thinking. He didn't even consider me. Not once. I was standing right next to him the whole time, and he just..."

Lilly flung her arms around Condor. She couldn't help it. She needed a release, comfort, support—something. Condor held her close, and they hovered in the air for a long moment as she clung to his neck, heaving heavy sobs just as she had after Falcroné died.

When she finally pulled away, she glanced between his piercing yet compassionate eyes and his lips. His face was perfect, even with the scar that ran from the outer edge of his left eyebrow to the top of his cheek.

Lilly moved to kiss him.

Condor recoiled, and Lilly's heart plummeted from her chest down to the ground thousands of feet below.

"Premieress," Condor said quietly, holding her at arm's length from himself. "I can't."

"Why not?" she asked just as quietly, on the verge of crying again.

Condor shook his head. "You and Calum are meant for each other. Anyone can see that. And I refuse to insert myself where I don't belong."

Lilly stared at him, searching his eyes. "Do you really believe that?"

"How can I not? You did choose him over me, after all." Condor gave her a wink.

"I'm starting to regret it," Lilly muttered as another tear trickled down her cheek.

"Don't," Condor said.

"Why not?"

"He is young and impetuous. So are you," Condor explained. "He made a mistake. So will you. What the two of you share should be stronger than any mistake, whether great or small. Talk to him. Work it out. Forgive him, and move on."

Lilly sighed. Condor was right, of course. Calum hadn't been thinking when he'd accepted Valerie's charge to become king, but she'd been no better; she'd reacted, and she'd flown away instead of staying to talk with him about it.

"You're supposed to be my protector, not my counselor." Lilly managed a small grin.

"I serve to protect not only your body but also your mind and your heart," Condor countered. "Now, shall we return?"

Lilly sighed again. After running off like that, returning would be embarrassing. Seeing Calum again would be hard enough, but she'd also flown off in front of General Balena, her uncle. She'd let him down, too, in a way.

"Do we have to?"

"We do, Premieress," Condor replied.

Lilly wiped the last of her tears from her eyes, even though the wind would've just as easily done it for her on their descent. "Fine. Let's go."

Condor readied himself to zoom downward, but he was waiting for her.

"And Condor?" she said.

"Yes, Premieress?"

"Thank you."

Condor grinned at her. "Any time."

"Good luck catching me, though." Lilly winked at him and dashed downward. When she looked back, Condor was close behind, but not close enough.

She laughed, thankful to have him truly on her side.

"THIS ORANGE IS ALREADY ROTTEN, TOO!"

A human soldier, one of Lumen's recruits, tossed a shriveled brown ball aside. It hit the cobblestone street and splattered at Axel's feet.

The soldier looked up at him with terror in his eyes. "Imperator... I—I'm sorry. I didn't mean to—"

"Quiet," Axel ordered. He had no interest in the soldier's apologies. He had, however, taken an interest in the orange itself. "Pick it back up."

The soldier hopped up from his seat on a barrel and scurried over. He snatched up the orange—or some of it, anyway—and held it in his hands as he eyed Axel. He no doubt expected some sort of punishment, but Axel wasn't going to levy any consequences against him for haphazardly tossing a rotten orange.

But neither was Axel going to take a closer look at the orange by touching it himself, either.

"Show it to me," Axel said.

The soldier's eyebrows scrunched down in confusion, but he complied.

The orange had indeed gone rotten. Its rind had taken on a bitter brown color, and its insides had darkened as well. It stank of the hyper-sweet scent of fruity decay.

Axel nodded to him, and the soldier let the rotten fruit drop to the street again. "You said this wasn't the first of these you had seen this way?"

"No, Imperator," the soldier said. "Practically the whole bushel has gone bad. And it's not just the oranges. Other fruits are going rotten, too. The grain is drying out and turning black. Vegetables are turning brown too fast. Something is wrong. Perhaps a scourge of some sort?"

Axel frowned, though his mask concealed it. "What about the fields surrounding the city? Have you heard any reports of similar things happening there?"

The soldier shook his head. "No, but I've noticed the greenery throughout the city is doing the same thing. The leaves on the trees and bushes are brown already, but it's not yet autumn. The grass is turning yellow, too."

"Imperator?" called a gruff voice from behind him.

Axel turned back.

A Saurian approached him with a large empty bucket in his arms. "Imperator, there is a problem with the water."

Axel's eyes narrowed. What was it this time? "Which well?"

"All of them," the Saurian replied. "They seem to have dried up."

"Impossible." Even as he said it, Axel's gut churned. Perhaps it *was* possible. If Calum had been right about the King's connection to Kanarah... "Show me."

The Saurian led him to the nearest well, around which a large crowd of both civilians and Lumen's soldiers had gathered, all of them clamoring to get access to the water. Rather than trying to push his way through, Axel took flight and hovered over the well.

Using his enhanced vision, he stared through the stone and down into the earth itself, searching for the water. He found some, but much farther down than the well could reach. And the longer he watched, the more the water seemed to be receding from the surface.

Decaying fruits and vegetables. Dying trees and bushes. Diminishing water resources. It couldn't all be coincidental.

Axel had to know for sure. He had to know if anything could be done about it.

He abandoned the Saurian and the people at the well and flew over the city back toward Valkendell. Normally, flying would've thrilled him as it had when he'd first tried it, but instead, the trepidation in his chest threatened to overwhelm him entirely.

If the land really was dying, as Calum had suggested would happen, then how could they possibly fix it? They'd already killed the King, and if he truly was the heart and soul of Kanarah, had they doomed everyone to drought and famine in the process?

When Axel arrived, he entered and headed straight for the garden. They had long since cleared away the vines and branches the King had erected over the entrance to keep his soldiers safe, so Axel strode right inside, only to stop short as soon as he laid eyes on the interior.

It was exactly as he'd feared.

Everything was dead.

It had only been a few hours since they'd killed the King, but fully everything in the garden had already withered and died. The flowers had all shed their petals. The trees had dropped their leaves and their fruit. The branches had turned deathly gray, and the grass had gone brown.

Rather than a verdant paradise, the garden had deteriorated into a wasteland like the Valley of the Tri-Lakes, all in a matter of hours.

The sight twisted Axel's gut into knots. Had they made a mistake? Had they condemned all of Kanarah to death?

No, he reassured himself. *Lumen can fix this. He has to.*
Axel left the garden behind and rushed to find him.

CALUM EXCUSED himself from his conversation with Valerie and Matthios, grateful that he finally had the chance to do so. When Lilly had flown off, he'd hardly been able to concentrate on anything aside from her and how horribly he'd handled all of this king-talk.

Now that she'd returned, Calum would have his chance to try to make things right.

As he and Lilly approached each other, Calum noticed Condor landing a good distance away. Their eyes met for an instant, then Condor headed over to confer with General Balena.

Upon finding Lilly's eyes again, Calum began to issue her an apology, but she grabbed hold of him, wrapped her arms around her neck, and kissed him, long and deep.

It surprised him at first, but he leaned into it and kissed her in return, holding her close. Perhaps he hadn't ruined everything after all.

When Lilly finally released him, she spoke first. "I'm sorry."

Calum blinked at her. "Sorry for what? I should be apologizing to you."

"You should," she agreed, "but I'm the one who flew off instead of talking to you. I'm sorry for that. I should've stayed."

Calum touched her face with his hand. "I'm sorry, too. I should've considered you, and us, in all of this, and I didn't."

Lilly wrapped her arms around his waist and pressed her head against his breastplate. "Promise me we'll find a way to make this work."

Calum grinned, and his heart totally relaxed. "From the moment I first laid eyes on you, that's all I've ever wanted."

"I know," she said, "but now you're going to be the King of Kanarah. That'll complicate things for us."

Calum chuckled. "Yeah, *if* we can defeat Lumen. I still have my doubts about that."

"One thing at a time," Lilly said, still holding him. "Let's just get through today first."

"I love you, Lilly," Calum said.

Lilly let go of him and looked into his eyes again. "I love you, too, Calum."

He leaned in for another kiss, and she met him in the middle.

"Er-hemm." Riley cleared his throat from nearby, and they cut their passion short.

Calum hadn't heard or seen him approach, even though they were essentially in the middle of an open field. Then again, he'd closed his eyes while he was kissing Lilly.

"Yes?" Calum asked as he and Lilly let go of each other and faced Riley.

"Gavridel is back," Riley said. "Says it'll take a few days to get back to the city, based on how far away we are. So it's time to go, before things get any worse."

"Thank you," Lilly said. "How are things with Windsor?"

Riley's shoulders slouched. "Not great, but I'd rather not talk about that right now."

"I understand. If you like, I can talk to her?" Lilly offered.

"Thanks, but I think that'll do more harm than good. She no doubt can hear everything we're saying right now anyway," Riley sighed, "so I'll just continue to eat crow until she comes around. Or doesn't. Could go either way at this point."

Lilly nodded, and Calum empathized with him.

"Hang in there, bud," Calum said.

"Trying." Riley motioned toward the rest of their ramshackle army with his head. "I'd better get back over there. Don't be long. Can't retake Valkendell without a king to sit on the throne."

Calum huffed and shook his head. The idea of him possibly becoming King of Kanarah still baffled and amazed him, but he was doing his best to try to acclimate to the role anyway.

As Riley headed back to join the group, Lilly said, "We should join them."

Calum would've much preferred to stay with her instead, but he knew she was right. "Yeah. I guess so."

"Before we do, though, I have a gift for you. Might help in the coming battle," she said.

Calum had expected her to kiss him again, which would've been great, but he'd guessed wrong. Instead, she opened the pouch at her hip and removed a glowing yellow stone. It was similar to the crystalline crown on her head, but somehow more vibrant in color, almost as if lightning itself dwelled inside.

The Aerostone.

She extended it toward him. "Take it."

Calum stared down at the stone. It was a kind thought, but he couldn't possibly accept it. "I can't take this. It's sacred to your people. Without it, Windgales can't become Wisps."

"And it'll enable you to fly," Lilly said.

Calum blinked at her. "It'll what?"

Lilly grinned, and a hint of mischief glinted in her blue eyes. "Riley realized it. He recovered it after I threw it to the Windgales so they could become Wisps. He returned it to me and showed me. He said he didn't want to be able to fly, though. Can you believe that?"

Calum's eyebrows rose. The thought of a flying Werewolf was truly the stuff of nightmares. "Crazy."

"So take it." She took hold of his wrist and placed it in his hand.

A lightness unlike anything he'd ever felt washed over him and mingled with his body. He didn't understand it at first, but the more he concentrated on it, the more it made sense. With nothing but a thought, he lifted off the ground and continued to ascend higher and higher.

By the time he finally looked down, he was at least fifty feet up in the air. Lilly had accompanied him on his journey upward, and it was a good thing, too, because when Calum looked down, he freaked out and almost dropped the stone.

Then he began to fall.

She grabbed him and clamped her hand overtop of his, which still gripped the stone. Using her flight ability and strength, she slowed his descent, all the while instructing him, "Fly, Calum! Release your fears and embrace the wildness of the air."

As the two of them plummeted from the sky, Calum clenched his eyes shut and tried to do what she'd said. They eased to a stop only a few feet off the ground and hovered there.

When Calum opened his eyes, Lilly was beaming at him.

"You did it," she said. "Now try again. I'll go with you."

Calum exhaled a deep breath, focused on the Aerostone's power, and launched upward once again.

THANKS TO FALLING off his ladder, Gill now had a lump on the back of his head to go with the scar on the front of it. Jake had tended to him, good boy that he was, while they both watched the mammoth brown thing still rising out of the Central Lake.

It had started as a pillar-like structure that extended from the waters, far wider than any boat Gill had ever seen, and taller than any of their masts, too. As it rose, it not only got taller but widened further, which seemed necessary just to support its own mass. Before long, it would surpass even the height of the distant mountains.

Gill had figured the size of the thing would end up displacing a lot of the lake water, but instead, it appeared as if the water level had actually gone down. He'd spent most of his life staring at that lake, whether from the back porch of his shanty or, in his younger days, on a boat, fishing, so he could tell when something was amiss.

The water level definitely hadn't risen any, and the more he watched the phenomenon, the more certain he became that the water was draining from the lake. Why that was happening, he didn't know. After all, he'd been staring at the surface of the water for nearly fifty years, not at whatever was underneath, unless it was in a net or attached to the end of a fishing line.

As he watched, Jake pointed at the big brown column. "Look! Do you see that?"

Gill's eyes weren't so good anymore. "See what?"

"That… thing. There's something on the… whatever the big thing is. There's something on it, sticking out," Jake insisted, still pointing. "It wasn't there before."

"Whatchu sayin'?" Gill squinted, but he couldn't see a darned thing. "I don' see nothin'."

"Wait here." Jake ran off, only to return a couple minutes later with a brass spyglass. He extended it to its full length and looked through it. "It's there! It's there! Look!"

"What?" Gill accepted the spyglass from him and held it up to his eye. The glass was scratched and fuzzy around the edges, but it did magnify his view considerably. Even so, all he saw was the brown pillar itself. "Still don' see nothin'."

Jake adjusted the spyglass's angle for Gill, who slapped his hand away.

"I got it," he growled. He followed the column up until something flickered in his vision.

Something he recognized but hadn't seen for well over a decade.

He lowered the spyglass.

"Well, drown me, drag me out, an' dig me a grave," Gill said.

"Did you see it?"

"'Course I seen it," Gill said. "I ain't blind."

"How it is possibly there?" Jake asked. "It doesn't make any sense."

On that, Gill had to agree.

It made absolutely no sense for something so colossal to have grown out of a lake, so tall that it would soon tower over the distant mountain peaks.

Especially a tree.

CHAPTER 45

In the three days following the King's death, food in Solace had become frighteningly scarce, and finding water was no easier.

Thanks to the gift of Lumen's power, Axel no longer had to eat much, drink much water, or sleep, but those privileges didn't extend to the tens of thousands of people dwelling in Solace. While Lumen's army focused on rebuilding the city's main gate, Axel had taken to searching the city and an ever-widening area for food and water so he could send people to claim it.

The end result was all the more negative. Throngs of people had fled the city, unwilling to be trapped in a place with no food, water, or prospects of finding either anywhere nearby.

When Axel asked Lumen if he wanted the soldiers to keep them there, Lumen had waved off his concerns entirely. Apparently, whether they lived or died here in Solace or outside the city was of no consequence to Lumen.

Instead, the new King of Kanarah had focused on something entirely different—something secret and, Axel feared, terrible.

After they'd slain the king, Lumen's soldiers had captured hundreds of the King's men. As he'd done following the battle for Kanarah City, Lumen had offered them the choice to either join forces and swear fealty to him as the new King, or they would simply be killed.

To Axel's surprise, hardly any of them agreed to join Lumen. It had struck him as foolish at first, but the more he watched the King's men deny Lumen's offer, the more Axel realized they weren't fools at all.

Rather, they were loyal men—loyal to a fault. Even with their King dead, they refused to bend to the whims of another.

Lumen hadn't killed them right away, like Axel had expected he would. Instead, he touched each man's chest, shooting a spike of light into their hearts.

The men screamed every time, but they didn't die. They just collapsed, breathing hard, as something within Lumen's power spread throughout their bodies like a plague. Then their desperate eyes began to glow faintly red, and their skin took on a sickly greenish pallor.

Even now, those same men still languished in the dungeons below Valkendell—dungeons that, prior to Lumen's arrival had been empty. When Axel had first gone down to set potential prisoners free to join Lumen's side during the battle, he'd found no one inside.

What was the point of having dungeons if the King hadn't thrown anyone into them?

After that first day, when Lumen had driven spikes into the hundreds of prisoners now crammed into only a few dozen calls, Axel hadn't returned. He had no reason to. The soldiers were going to die, and someone else would clean up the mess.

Frankly, given the sorry state of the city, Lumen had done them a favor. Fewer mouths to feed. Fewer parched lips desperate for water.

It was hard enough to care for their own soldiers, many of whom had resorted to eating whatever rotten food they could find. Others had chosen to go without entirely, fasting rather than deigning to eat wretched food.

Axel had taken his concerns to Lumen multiple times, but always to no avail. Lumen, he'd decided, was either unwilling or incapable of fixing the problem. He'd only insisted that all would be put right in the end. He claimed that once they had truly defeated and destroyed the last remnant of the King's followers, Kanarah would be saved.

What could Axel do other than believe him?

He could search for food and water, like he'd been doing. Beyond that, all his newfound power and strength amounted to nothing—at least until the final battle began.

And now that he could see a mass of soldiers in silver armor gleaming in the distance, it wouldn't be much longer until this war finally and truly came to an end.

THROUGHOUT THE COURSE of three days, Gill and Jake had watched the enormous tree in the Central Lake sprout innumerable branches, all of them covered with vibrant green leaves.

It seemed to have finally stopped growing upward, and now it extended outward instead. A canopy of green leaves blanketed the top of the tree, so thick that no sunlight could penetrate it to reach the lake waters below.

On the second day, with the aid of Jake's spyglass, Gill had picked out tiny dots of various colors hanging from some of the branches. If he squinted, he could just barely make them out as flowers. Then again, he hadn't seen flowers in more than a decade, so he had Jake take a look to confirm, which he did.

By the third day, some of the flowers remained, but most of those from the day before now yielded fruit—all sorts of fruit. Gill recognized bananas first, because of their color and shape. Then he picked out oranges and apples, then he noticed some more exotic fruits that looked like pineapples and mangoes.

Vines curled around several of the branches, and clusters of red and green grapes hung from them alongside tomatoes, olives, and even some melons. Strawberries—at least, Jake thought they were strawberries—sprouted from other branches, intermingled with raspberries, blueberries, blackberries, and cherries.

It made no sense to Gill that one single tree, even despite its enormous size, could yield different types of fruit, but his eyes weren't deceiving him. Stranger still, the tree was also producing numerous different types of vegetables—peppers, heads of cauliflower, and even big orange pumpkins.

The whole time, Gill had paid close attention to the water level, but even if he hadn't, he would've easily noticed how far down it had gone. The tree must've been sucking all the water in through its roots, because the lake was virtually nonexistent at this point. It was more of a chasm with some water down in the bottom of it.

Gill guessed there was maybe fifty feet of water down there in terms of depth, which left several hundred feet to go before it had any chance of reaching the surface again. And that meant no boats or ships had any chance of doing any fishing any time soon.

Try as he might, Gill couldn't fathom what was going on. He had no idea where the tree had come from, no concept of why it was there, and he didn't even want to think about what this would mean for the fishing trade in Kanarah.

Probably less scurvy, he decided.

Apart from that, what would his life become? Would he start selling fruit-picking excursions instead of fishing excursions? And if he were going to do that, how would they even reach the tree without falling to their deaths in the chasm that had once been the Central Lake?

It was all too much. For now, all he could do was watch. Maybe the thing would die, and the lake would come back. He hoped so.

SOLACE LOOMED on the horizon like a cemetery of white gravestones. The sun still shone upon it, and its walls still glimmered in the light, but something about it churned Calum's stomach.

He approached it from the air now, accompanied by Magnus, Lilly, Condor, General Balena, General Tolomus, and the remaining Windgale soldiers. Matthios also flew alongside them, but Gavridel marched with the rest of their troops far below, along with Riley, Windsor, and General Anigo.

Their army still consisted of members of each of Kanarah's four races. A smattering of Wolves and Saurians had survived the first battle and managed to escape, many of them thanks to the aid of Matthios and Gavridel.

But, to Calum's dismay, there weren't many of them. For the most part, he anticipated that Magnus, Matthios, and Gavridel would do the majority of the fighting, especially when it came to Lumen, Kahn, and Rhaza.

That left Calum, Lilly, Condor, and perhaps Riley and Windsor to deal with Axel. With the King's power inside of him, and with the Aerostone secured inside his armor, Calum might even be able to face off against Axel alone if he had to, but he didn't know for sure.

It was nearly midday by the time they reached the city's gates, which had been repaired but now inexplicably hung open. Condor offered to fly reconnaissance around the city to assess their defenses, and when he returned, his report wasn't at all what Calum had expected.

"There's no one there," he shouted over the heavy flapping of Magnus's wings. "The streets are empty. There are no soldiers on the walls. Valkendell is silent. It is as if they have all just vanished."

"They're there," General Balena said. "Of that, I have no doubt."

Calum was inclined to agree with him. "What about the people?"

"The houses and buildings are deserted, just as our scouts reported yesterday," Condor said. "The people seem to have fled. I checked several homes myself just to confirm, and short of an army consisting solely of Werewolves and Shadow Wolves, there was no one hiding inside."

Prior to Gavridel's return, Valerie had arranged to send scouts out to investigate the condition of Solace in light of the King's death. Two days later, as Calum's army—if it could be called that—was making their final camp for the night, the scouts returned with news.

The city was broken. There was no food, no water, and no hope of either returning any time soon. The people were leaving in droves, hoping to find food and water somewhere else.

On the surface, Calum would never have believed it had he not shared his crucial encounters with the King. In the absence of the heart of Kanarah, the land was dying.

And it was happening far faster than Calum had imagined.

By contrast, wherever Calum and his army went, their food stayed fresh and edible, and their water supply never seemed to run out. Whatever power the King had bequeathed to Calum, it was sustaining them. It gave him hope that they could somehow save Kanarah.

But first, they had to get through Lumen.

"So what do we do?" Calum asked. "Do we draw Lumen out? Along with Axel, Kahn, and Rhaza? Or do we bring the fight to them?"

"They possess the strongest defensible position in all of Kanarah," Magnus said. "I do not believe anything could possibly draw them out."

"I agree with the Dragon King's assessment," Matthios said. "We cannot hope to win this fight unless we retake what was lost by force."

Calum looked to Lilly, who looked to General Balena.

"Their reasoning is sound. I agree as well," he said.

"So those of us who can attack from the sky will do so, and then our ground forces will enter the city through the main gate, led by Gavridel?" Calum proposed.

"We must be wary of traps," Magnus said. "Their army is there, somewhere, and so is Lumen. They know we are coming and have chosen to conceal themselves for a reason."

"Surprise," Matthios said. "They mean to ambush us."

Calum nodded. "We're already anticipating that, so we'll be ready when it happens."

He got nods all around.

"Alright, then," Calum said. "Let's take back the city and save Kanarah."

LUMEN COULD SEE THEM APPROACHING. He could feel them.

They were much closer now.

But he was ready. His plans were set. As soon as they all entered the city, the war would end.

He watched as Gavridel clomped through the open city gates first, holding that familiar amethyst axe in one hand and the diamond axe in the other. The Gemstone Imperator's heavily armored head swiveled back and forth, scanning for threats.

Noble of Gavridel to enter first, but one soldier—even an Imperator—wouldn't spring Lumen's trap so easily. Only Lumen could do that, and only when the time was right.

Hundreds of soldiers filed in after Gavridel, and they divided into robust groups to begin sweeping the streets of Solace. They checked houses and searched buildings, all to no avail.

Meanwhile, hundreds more Windgales accompanied the Brazen General Matthios, the Dragon King Magnus, the Premieress Lilly, and Calum the "Unifier" in the air. They, too, searched the city, again finding nothing at every turn.

But when all of them had actually entered inside the city's walls, Lumen knew the time had come.

First, he would eradicate these insects. Once he finished with them, he would kill Calum himself and summon the last remnant of the King's power from his corpse.

Then, and only then, could Lumen truly rule Kanarah.

Then, and only then, would it be done.

Lumen reached out with his mind and activated his trap.

CHAPTER 46

W hen the ground began to shake under Calum's feet, he knew something bad was about to happen. But he hadn't guessed exactly how bad it would be until the cobblestone streets tore open and spilled all manner of horrors into the city.

All around him, huge rocky spikes ripped through the streets, flinging dirt and stones in every direction. The rocky spikes, Calum quickly realized, were connected to a legion of Gronyxes carving their way up from the sewers below the city streets. Their glowing red eyes fixed on Calum's soldiers, and they lashed their green tentacles at their new targets.

Along with the Gronyxes emerged hundreds of Dactyls and even some Wargs, all of which also attacked anything and everything they saw. Calum launched into the air to avoid the first wave of attacks, and he hurled several flaming arcs from the Dragon's Breath sword to take out approaching monsters as he did so.

Calum and his army had prepared for an ambush, but not of this sort. Now his soldiers and friends battled abominations on the land and in the air, clashing their blades against talons, teeth, beaks, and tentacles.

A Dactyl screeched toward Calum, and he reduced it to nothing but ash with the help of the Dragon's Breath sword, all while maintaining his own flight. The familiar stink of these wretched creatures filled the air once again.

Even so, Calum lamented each Dactyl he killed. Knowing that Lumen had corrupted Windgales to create them was sobering, and the only comfort Calum took in killing them was the opportunity to end their suffering.

Lilly fought nearby, setting Dactyls ablaze with fire from the Calios or occasionally freezing them so they plummeted from the sky and shattered into messy chunks on the buildings and streets below. She zipped to and fro, untouchable in the storm of threats, deftly slaying the monsters that had once been her people.

Condor took the strategy of evading attacks and slashing at the Dactyls' wings as they screamed past him. They, too, careened down to the city below and crashed into the houses and streets. A few survived the impact but were hobbled from broken limbs and severed wings.

General Balena, General Tolomus, and their Windgales battled the Dactyls with such ferocity that Calum had to wonder if they weren't still venting their anger over the Saurians' invasion. Or perhaps it was just the sheer overwhelming desperation of the situation.

Thanks to Magnus's Dragon scales, Dactyls couldn't harm him, but that didn't stop them from harassing him anyway. While still airborne, he peeled them off his body, crushed them in his powerful hands, and flung them aside. A follow-up blast of dragonfire from his mouth destroyed a formation of them flying through the air.

Down below, Calum's soldiers battled alongside Matthios and Gavridel, each of whom deftly took out Gronyxes in a single blow. General Anigo also fought alongside them, admirably and effectively thanks to his powerful golden spear.

But with so many Gronyxes swarming the streets, now accompanied by Wargs who'd climbed atop nearby buildings only to leap off their roofs and pounce on unsuspecting soldiers, even the Imperators couldn't keep up.

"I'm going down there!" Calum shouted to Lilly over the ruckus. "The soldiers need help!"

"Be careful!" Lilly shouted back as Condor skewered a Dactyl next to her and held it in place so she could lop off its head.

"You too!" Calum zoomed toward the nearest cluster of soldiers fighting for their lives, surrounded in a small town square by four Gronyxes and half a dozen Wargs.

One of the Gronyxes lashed its tentacles at him, but Calum didn't resist. He barreled forward, still flying, as the tentacles coiled around his arms and legs. His momentum kept him racing toward the Gronyx's mouth, which yawned open and revealed its jagged teeth.

Calum had no fear this time. He'd done this before. He knew exactly what to do.

One powerful strike from the Dragon's Breath sword severed the left side of the Gronyx from its base. Rather than an eruption of glowing green blood, the flames from the sword cauterized the wound. The tentacles wrapped around Calum's body went slack, and in a follow-up swing, he severed the other half of the Gronyx's body from its base, stopping its shrieking.

The Gronyx's two humanlike forms smacked onto the cobblestones below, fully separated from its rocky base, which shuddered and collapsed.

A pair of Wargs launched at Calum next. He loosed an arc of emerald fire from the Dragon's Breath sword at one of them, charring it black and killing it, and the other went down with another swing of the sword, headless and smoking.

"Attack the Gronyxes' bases!" he shouted to the soldiers. "Cut off their bodies like I did, low near their mouths, but don't get bit!"

Even as he said it he noticed one soldier lying on the ground, clutching at his left leg and wailing. Everything below his knee was gone, and the rest was already turning to colorful gemstones and breaking off.

Calum winced and thought of Nicolai, who'd died saving him. If the King were here, he might've been able to save the soldier, but it was already too late.

Or was it? Calum darted over to the soldier, who gasped as more and more of his leg crystallized from the Gronyx's corruption pulsing through his body.

"Stay still!" Calum ordered. Then he placed his hands on the soldier's wounded leg and summoned the King's power.

Green light glowed from his hands and filtered into the soldier's body. Calum realized he could actually sense the corruption itself, but it was more than that—he could feel every vein and artery in the soldier's body, and he could feel the corruption attacking every single cell.

Calum put a stop to it immediately.

The corruption died and disappeared, and then Calum started to reverse the process. As he watched, the man's leg reverted from crystals back into flesh, and then it actually grew back until his entire leg and foot were restored.

It was simultaneously horrifying and incredible to watch, but when the man flexed his leg and moved his now-bare foot around, Calum had to grin.

The soldier looked up at him in total shock. He managed to say, "Th-thank you!"

"You're welcome," Calum replied. He hadn't known he was capable of doing such a thing, so he was nearly as surprised as the soldier was. Were it not for the King healing him first, he never would've even thought to try it. "Be safe."

Then Calum rose and rejoined the battle. He felt like he'd lost some power, but it was already recovering quickly. What did that mean? And what else could he do? Could he heal himself? Could he use the King's power to attack as well?

And what about the rest of Lumen's power lingering within him? He already knew how to use that to some extent, but was there more that he could do with it?

Another Warg bolted at him, its blue eyes aglow and its mouth hanging open. This time, Calum extended his hand and summoned the light. A spear of pure white energy skewered the beast in midair, and with a yelp, it crashed to the ground in a heap.

Glowing pink blood pooled beneath it, and Calum got a clear look at its mangy hide. It was larger than a normal Wolf, had larger yellow teeth that barely allowed its mouth to close, and glowing blue eyes. Unlike the Dactyls high above, these things didn't smell like anything, despite being just as ugly and warped.

Calum launched toward the next nearest foe—one of the other Gronyxes—and summoned the King's power this time. He pointed his hand at the Gronyx and loosed a blast of green energy that seized the corruption coursing through the monster's body. As he did with the soldier, he tried to heal the corruption.

It didn't work—not in the same way it had with the soldier, anyway. Instead, the Gronyx went rigid and loosed a shriek that split Calum's ears, but only at first. Then its entire body withered and dissolved into dust.

The soldiers who'd been fighting the Gronyx glanced back at him, stunned.

Calum was stunned too. The King really had blessed him with unbelievable power.

Now he had to decide how best to use it to save his people.

From high above the battle in Valkendell, Axel watched as the streets of Solace erupted with hundreds of monsters. The sight both thrilled and horrified him.

His gut twisted at the knowledge that the Gronyxes and the Dactyls were soldiers who'd refused to join Lumen's army—it explained the red glow he'd seen in the human soldiers' eyes and the green pallor of their skin after Lumen hit them with his light spike.

But even though the idea revolted him, Axel couldn't deny the tactic's effectiveness. These monsters, mindless as they were, just kept coming. They attacked relentlessly, carving through swaths of the King's soldiers and tearing them apart.

And if they were going to win this final battle, this was a surefire way to do it.

If nothing else, everyone would see Lumen's power on display, and no one would dare oppose him ever again.

Finally, Axel had chosen the winning side.

At least he'd thought so, until the tide of the battle started turning against them. The King's soldiers below had rallied and survived—and even thrived—against the monsters.

He'd hoped he wouldn't have to order the rest of Lumen's army, hungry and parched as they were, to attack, but the time had come. They couldn't lose this fight.

Axel opened a black void in front of himself and stepped into it.

Despite the horrors of everything happening around them, Riley felt good about being near Melly—Windsor—again. It had cost him everything when he'd left her behind, and it had cost her everything, too, but fate had seen fit to reunite them once again.

And this time, neither of them were helpless.

As Shadow Wolves, they evaded the Gronyxes, Dactyls, and Wargs with ease. They were infinitely faster, and their claws tore through the Gronyxes' and Dactyls' flesh and the Wargs' thick matted fur alike.

It had gone well, at least for the two of them, until someone lashed a sword at Riley.

The blow had come seemingly from nowhere, and he'd barely dodged it in time. When he turned to face his attacker, he saw a sword-wielding Sobek warrior stepping out of a black void just like the one Axel had conjured back in the King's garden.

Riley easily ducked under the next swing and drove his claws deep into the Sobek's armored chest, killing him, but one errant Sobek wasn't Riley's concern. The dozens of black portals opening all around him were.

Humans, Saurians, Wolves, and even a few Windgales emerged from them. Weapons drawn, they flooded the city with steel. Now Calum's army had to contend with not only the monsters bursting out of the streets but also Lumen's soldiers.

"We have to work together!" Windsor shouted at Riley through the raging battle.

"Thought you'd never ask," Riley called back as he took down another soldier, this time one of the Wolves who'd once been a part of his tribe. A pang of regret stabbed at his heart, but he pushed it aside. These Wolves had chosen to side with Lumen.

"I'm not *asking*." Windsor batted away a sword strike from a human attacker and returned the attack with a devastating slash of her own that dropped him.

"You never do," Riley countered, but he moved closer to her—close enough that he could hear her growling at him amid the battle.

He smirked. It had always been easy to aggravate her. It had been part of their dynamic before he'd fled the tribe. Apparently, some things never changed.

In tandem with Windsor, Riley attacked dozens of enemies in a flurry of vicious slashes, tearing through ranks of soldiers and monsters alike. It felt like old times, when they'd coordinated their hunting efforts to corner jackrabbits and deer in the desert.

It felt right.

Then an unearthly howl droned from behind them.

They turned back in time to see Rhaza emerging from one of the black voids. He rose to his full height, now twice as tall as Riley and swollen with corrupted power.

The puncture wound in his side from where Riley had stabbed him with the shard still glowed with white light, and the same light also glowed from his white irises, his claws, and his teeth. He was a hulking, horrifying mass of Shadow Wolf, bolstered by Lumen's corruptive power, and he'd fixed his attention on the two of them.

Rhaza said no words, but Riley could see the twinge of recognition in his eyes when he saw the two of them together. He knew who they were. Some part of him remembered their past, and it enraged him.

He hunched over as if to pounce and loosed another droning roar that rattled the buildings around them and reverberated through Riley's chest.

"We need to run, Riley." Windsor's bloody hand found Riley's, and it brought him some comfort—at least until she tried to tug him away from Rhaza.

"No." Riley resisted her pull and stood his ground. "I'm done running from him."

"He'll kill us! We can't possibly beat him!" Windsor protested. She tugged on him again, but he refused to move.

"*No*," Riley repeated.

He found Windsor's eyes, all black except for the blue irises, and he took hold of her other hand as well. Both of them were bloody messes from all the fighting, even though none of it was actually their blood, but Riley didn't care. He stared deep into Windsor's eyes and spoke the truth in his heart.

"I need you, Windsor. Together, we can do this, but I can't kill him alone," he said. "And if we don't kill him now, he'll always be out there. He'll always be a threat."

Windsor growled, but she didn't deny it.

"He ruined our lives. Separated us," Riley continued. "We need to do this. We need to put him behind us for good. Then, finally, we'll be free, one way or another."

Windsor growled again, but she nodded. "I'm with you."

Together, they face Rhaza, the source of their greatest fears and regrets. He issued another droning howl, as if beckoning them forward, and they leaped at him with their claws extended and teeth bared.

THE EMERGENCE of thousands of new soldiers had complicated the battle enough that Calum had to make a hard decision. Even with the King's new power, he couldn't do anything more to end this battle than he was already doing.

Unless they could reach Lumen. If they could get to him and defeat him, perhaps they could finally end this war.

Calum gathered the most powerful warriors he could find—Magnus, Lilly, Condor, Matthios, Gavridel, and General Anigo—and they carved a path toward Valkendell.

Gavridel led the way, barreling through literally every foe in his path and reducing them to paste. General Anigo followed close behind, and Magnus flew overhead, scorching enemies who tried to attack from the sides, while Matthios defended the rear. Calum, Lilly, and Condor filled in the center, mostly doing nothing thanks to the effectiveness of their team around them.

They reached the front of Valkendell in record time, only to find the fortress's front gates shut and guarded by a dozen Gronyxes and several dozen more soldiers. The group made quick work of the monsters and the guards, thrashing and hacking and burning their way through.

But as they approached the gate, a black void opened up before them.

Calum recognized it immediately as Axel's work. He also realized by its ever-increasing size what was about to come out of it.

Sure enough, the massive form of Kahn, the Dragon-King-turned-Jyrak, stepped through. His first footstep splattered the remains of one of the Gronyxes, shooting glowing green blood in every direction. Once he fully emerged, he towered nearly half as tall as Valkendell itself, even with his head partially caved in.

The group looked up at Kahn as he loosed a droning roar from his misshapen mouth.

"Stand aside, everyone," Magnus started forward. "I will handle this abomination."

"You really think you can take him alone?" Calum asked. "He's double your size."

"I killed Kahn once. I can and will gladly do it again." Magnus looked at Calum and winked. "Go save Kanarah. Leave this to me."

Then Magnus hurtled through the air at the Jyrak's head with a roar of his own.

CHAPTER 47

From high above, Axel had watched as Calum and his powerful friends crashed through the city, plowing over all manner of monsters and Lumen's soldiers in the process. It was all thanks to Gavridel, the Gemstone Imperator, who apparently couldn't be stopped—at least not by conventional means.

The moment Axel laid eyes on Gavridel, rage ignited in his chest. That muscle-bound/over-armored idiot had won their first contest because of the obvious power disparity between them. But this time, things would be different.

As Kahn stepped out of the void and blocked their path into Valkendell, Axel used the distraction to his advantage. He opened a new void and flew inside.

Traveling through the void was easy: A shadow dimension of nearly pure darkness opened up, and with his mind, Axel controlled where the next opening would be. He decided to open one right next to Gavridel.

From within the shadows, sunlight streamed through a crack. It widened to a circular opening, revealing Gavridel's huge form, his armor gleaming with the colors of every fine jewel known to Kanarah.

Axel launched forward and rammed into Gavridel at full speed. His shoulder struck solid armor, jarring him, but the mountain moved.

Axel wrapped his arms as far around Gavridel's immense form as he could, pinning the Imperator's left arm to his side, and they thundered forward until they hit the wall of a building and crashed through it.

They tumbled and skidded to a stop just inside the building, covered in dust and plaster and splintered wood.

"Gavridel!" Calum called from somewhere behind Axel, who was already on his feet, drawing his blackened Blood Ore sword.

He glanced back to see Calum hesitating about whether to come into the building to help. As usual, Calum couldn't make a decision when the time called for it. If it came to it, Axel would fight them both at once.

"Go! Defeat Lumen!" Gavridel shouted as he, too, rose to his feet, shook the dust from his armor, and brandished his axes. Then, with his voice lower and more menacing, he said, "This one is *mine*."

Axel scoffed. "I'm yours, alright. And this time, I've got the advantage."

"By what measurement?" Gavridel asked.

"You don't know how to fight. You're just big and strong and durable." Axel sneered at Gavridel, though neither of them could see the other's facial reactions because of their masks. "I'm faster, more skilled, and more powerful. You're gonna lose this time."

"If you truly believe that, then step forward and test your mettle," Gavridel taunted.

In a burst of speed, Axel's sword clashed with Gavridel's axes in a dazzling display of purple and white lights. It should've been quick enough for Axel to land several blows, but Gavridel had reacted far quicker than Axel had anticipated, even in the close quarters of the building they were in.

Axel hurled another attack, and Gavridel's axes clanged against his blade yet again. It happened a third time, then a fourth, and then Gavridel got in a counter-swing.

Axel barely managed to reposition his sword in time, and the power behind Gavridel's diamond axe slammed him into the inside wall of the building. The wall cracked, and when Axel ducked under Gavridel's amethyst axe, the wall shattered completely instead of his head.

Gavridel's flank should've been exposed, and Axel swung at his side to capitalize, but Gavridel's diamond axe intercepted the blow, rippling with light. Then the amethyst axe came at him again, this time from overhead.

Axel opened a void beneath his feet and dropped into it, and Gavridel's attack missed. When he reappeared behind Gavridel, the Imperator was ready for him and defended Axel's next three strikes, each one more vicious than the last.

But the under-curve of Gavridel's diamond axe hooked the inside of Axel's knee, and he slammed Axel to the floor with a loud *crack*.

Axel felt the floor cave in underneath him, and then the stone foundation beneath that fractured as well.

Gavridel stood over him, no longer attacking but instead watching Axel struggle to regain his footing. He uttered, "Care to rethink your assumptions about my fighting prowess?"

Axel snarled and launched forward for more.

HIGH ABOVE THE enormous tree in the Central Lake, a storm began to brew. Clouds of gray began to swirl, gathering moisture from the air.

Gill sat on his porch as the clouds expanded and darkened to a furious black tinged with green.

"Nev' seen a storm like this'n," he muttered. "All mah years, not a once."

Jake, still seated next to him, asked, "Should we take shelter? Looks like it could be really bad."

"Coul' be."

A bolt of lightning, tinged green, lashed across the blackening sky, accompanied by a peal of thunder that rattled every building in Sharkville.

"Coul' also be dat we ain't safe no mattah where we go," Gill said.

"Do you... do you see that?" Jake pointed to the left and to the right of the lake.

"What I done tol' you 'bout askin' me dat question?"

"You can't see it, so I should just give you the spyglass for a look?"

Gill held out his hand, and Jake placed the spyglass in it. Gill put it up to his eye and peered through it to the left of the lake. Far in the distance, he saw a column of water rising—not falling, but actually *ascending* toward the maelstrom in the sky. It could've only come from one of the other lakes.

Gill looked to the right and saw the exact same thing: a column of water flowing upward, feeding the storm overhead.

"By Bartholomew's beard..." he muttered. "What is goin' on?"

Lightning crackled through the sky again, and again the thunder rattled every building in Sharkville.

"HE'LL BE in the throne room," Matthios said as they set foot inside Valkendell. "I can already sense him there."

Though nothing had physically changed about the fortress, and though daylight still shone through all the windows, the place seemed far darker and more foreboding to Calum. A heaviness weighed down the air in the halls, and every footstep seemed like a day's labor.

They ascended higher and higher through the empty fortress, making their way toward the very throne room where the King had decided to show Calum and Lilly—and Axel—mercy. When they arrived, they found Lumen seated on the King's throne, hunched over with his elbows on his knees and his head in his hands.

His glowing body heaved up and down as if he were... weeping? It didn't make sense to Calum. The war wasn't over yet, and Lumen still seemed to have every advantage. Why would he be crying?

As they approached, Calum realized he'd been wrong. Lumen wasn't weeping.

He was laughing.

"Surrender, traitor," Matthios ordered, "or I will—"

"*Be silent*, Matthios," Lumen's voice clapped like thunder and echoed throughout the cavernous room, even though he still held his head in his hands. "You and I both know that you mean to destroy me whether I surrender or not." Lumen looked up at them with his eyes ablaze with white light. "And I will *never* surrender."

Matthios pointed his spear at Lumen. "Then you will die."

Lumen began to laugh again. It started as a low rumble but gradually built into a robust belly laugh, almost to the point of being uncontrollable. He put his head in his hands again and kept laughing louder and louder.

The sound of it sent chills coursing through Calum's body. What was happening?

"I thought I could control it," Lumen said as his laughter came to an end. "I thought I could take the King's place. I thought I could figure it out. I thought I could rule, that I could keep Kanarah alive. Instead, it has become a place of darkness and death."

Calum tensed at Lumen's words.

"But I like darkness and death." Lumen looked at them again. "I *am* darkness. I *am* death." Then he shouted, "I am your *end!*"

Lumen rose to his feet and stepped down from the platform slowly, methodically, scrutinizing them. Each of them recoiled slightly, except for Matthios.

"This is all of you?" Lumen said between chuckles. "The five of you mean to battle *me*? All of you combined do not even amount to a fraction of my power. Where is Gavridel?"

"Fighting your false imperator," Matthios said, "and then rejoining us soon."

"And you expect to hold me off in the meantime?" Lumen laughed again. "Matthios, you always were such a fool. Senseless, yet practical, and far too confident in your own abilities."

Lumen raised his hand, and a spike of white light shot toward Matthios. It struck him in his chest and knocked him backward, and he skidded to a stop against the inner wall of the throne room with a grunt.

He was back on his feet the next instant, but the attack had done its damage. Matthios's breastplate now had a dark hole in it, outlined with white-hot bronze.

His voice ragged and strained, Matthios said, "It will take... far more than that... to kill me, traitor."

"If you insist." Lumen raised his arm again, but this time Calum was ready.

He reached out with the King's power and grabbed hold of Lumen with it. He yanked hard, and Lumen's next spike fired wide. Matthios spun his spear and further deflected the spike, which struck the wall in an explosion of sparks and then dissipated into nothing.

Calum had marshaled all of his focus for that one pull, so small that he'd only managed to move Lumen's arm a few inches. It had been enough to save Matthios from further harm, but in the grand scheme of things, it had accomplished very little.

Calum exhaled a labored breath and quickly inhaled another. The effort had strained him a lot more than anything else he'd tried with the King's power. Even healing the soldier's leg had taken less energy from him than that one simple motion.

Was Lumen really that much stronger? Or was there some sort of dampening effect in here that made everything harder? That would explain the heaviness of the atmosphere in Valkendell.

Calum didn't know, but they only had one chance at this. Whatever it took to kill Lumen, they had to do it, no matter the cost.

Lumen fixed his blazing eyes on Calum—eyes Calum had seen in his dreams countless times. Eyes that now haunted him and peered deep into his soul.

"You again," Lumen said. "But this time with a measure of power that does not belong to you. It should belong to me instead."

"It'll never be yours," Calum said, holding the Dragon's Breath sword up as if to ward off Lumen.

Lumen tilted his head to the side. "Then why did you bring it to me?"

Calum's eyebrows rose as Lumen reached out his hand and, from twenty feet away, he seized Calum's heart just as he had on the balcony overlooking the city.

Calum screamed.

Riley and Windsor were getting thrashed. There was no other way to put it.

Claw marks raked up and down their bodies, across their faces, and along their arms and legs. Every wound hurt, and all of them dripped blood.

Rhaza, by comparison, still loomed in the distance, relatively unharmed, save for a few slashes across his midsection, legs, arms, and one lucky swipe along his neck. If Riley had only carved a little deeper, maybe that would've done the job.

Windsor looked up at Riley from a crouched position next to him, breathing hard. "This isn't working."

"I know," he rasped. What he wouldn't give for a mug of cool water right then. "But we can't stop."

"I'm not gonna stop," Windsor said. "We have to find a way to kill him."

"I'm open to ideas."

"That puncture on his side." Windsor nodded toward the old stab wound that glowed with bright light. "Looks vulnerable to me."

"You really think it's that obvious?" Riley panted when he wasn't talking.

"Worth a try."

"We'd need a weapon to jab in there."

"Look around," she motioned to the general area around them. "Plenty of debris. Take your pick."

Riley nodded. "We'll have to get in close."

"Obviously."

"It's gonna hurt."

"Obviously."

"We'll probably die." Riley stopped her. "And if you say 'obviously' again, I'm gonna kill you myself."

"You couldn't, even if you tried," she countered with a sneer. "And besides, I was gonna say 'probably.'"

"Appreciate your optimism." Riley looked up at Rhaza again. The hulking Shadow Wolf abomination stalked toward them, staring down at them with his glowing eyes. "Wasn't there some old lore about driving a wooden stake through a Werewolf's heart to kill it?"

"That's something else." Windsor shook her head, also panting. "But I'm pretty sure if you drive anything sharp through any living thing's chest, it'll kill it."

"But is he even still alive?"

"We killed the Dactyls, Gronyxes, and other Wargs easily enough," Windsor said. "Why should he be any different?"

"Look at him."

"I'm trying not to."

Riley sighed.

Rhaza had closed in close enough to lurch toward them in a flurry of glowing claws and teeth. The two of them evaded every attack and raced down a perpendicular street to buy more time, but Riley doubted their rest would last for long.

"Look, you killed him once, or you almost did, by jabbing something sharp into his side." Windsor reached down and grabbed the pointy half of a broken spear. "So let's do it again."

She handed it to him.

"Why me?" he asked.

"You've had more practice than I have."

"I don't know about that," Riley countered. "You're pretty adept at stabbing people in the back."

"But not in their sides," she said without missing a beat. She held it out for him. "So this one's on you. Of the two of us, I'm faster, anyway."

Riley took the broken spear in his hands. The spearhead on top looked plenty sharp, but he doubted it would pierce through all the layers of muscle on Rhaza's enhanced body on its own. Riley would have to perfectly drive it into the wound on Rhaza's side, at the correct angle, in order to reach Rhaza's heart.

Easy, he thought. *Just another day in the sunshine.*

"I'll distract him," Windsor said.

"Hopefully it's not with your looks," Riley quipped. "Unless you're trying to scare him to death with that dogface of yours."

"When this is over," Windsor warned, "I'm gonna throw you off a cliff."

"Better than having to look at you for the rest of my life."

"Then maybe that'll be the punishment instead," she fired back.

Riley grinned at her, even though the wounds on his face made it hurt to do so. "I can live with that."

"Not if you get your idiot self killed. Pay attention. Do this right," Windsor said.

"Waiting on you."

Windsor darted around to the right while Riley took the left.

As Rhaza turned the corner, his attention landed on Windsor, then he fixed his glowing eyes on Riley. He issued a low, menacing growl, and Riley's progress stalled.

There was no way to hide from Rhaza. The way the battle had gone so far, it was clear he could see them whenever they tried to hide in the shadows. As such, speed was their only real asset against him. Speed and viciousness, both of which Rhaza also possessed.

But as was the case with most Saurians Riley had faced, the bigger something got, the slower it moved. Rhaza was still plenty fast, but not as fast as Windsor, who proved it by streaking toward Rhaza's legs in a blur of black fur. Rhaza reacted just a hair too slow, and his swipe missed her.

She leaped onto his thigh and clawed her way up his back, avoiding his arms in the process. Rhaza roared his droning roar again, and he reached up to try to grab Windsor and pull her off. As he did, he exposed the glowing wound on his side.

Riley bolted forward, fixated on that spot. He bounded over debris and bodies, moving faster than ever before. He reached Rhaza in less than a second, and he drove the spear toward the wound.

Rhaza's hand caught the spear, stopping it in place. Then he tried to move it away.

Riley pushed back, fighting to keep it lined up with the wound, but even his two hands against Rhaza's one arm couldn't match the abomination's new strength.

But Riley didn't solely need strength. Not when he had teeth.

He clamped his jaws on Rhaza's wrist and bit down hard.

Rhaza flinched, but he didn't let go of the spear. Worse yet, he managed to grab hold of Windsor and peel her off his back. He held her in the air by her left leg, and she dangled in front of him, thrashing and scratching but only hitting air.

Riley had to do more. He matched Windsor's thrashing, whipping his head back and forth as his teeth dug deeper into Rhaza's wrist, shredding flesh and snapping tendons. Riley abandoned the spear and instead gripped Rhaza's hand and forearm. Then he yanked his head back, tearing through the abomination's wrist.

Rhaza's grip on the spear faltered, and he dropped it. Riley snatched it up, and as Rhaza raised Windsor higher to slam her into the ground, Riley jammed the spear into the glowing wound in his side.

Rhaza did more than flinch this time. He loosed a roar that sent shudders throughout the entire city, and he flailed his useless hand at Riley while also dropping Windsor.

Riley dodged the attack and drove the spear even deeper into Rhaza's body, so far that the light ceased to shine from the wound. Instead, glowing pink blood trickled out.

With his good hand free, Rhaza tried to grab the spear in his side, tried to get enough of a grip that he could yank it out, but he couldn't. It was already in too deep. He kept roaring, kept groping for it, unaware that Windsor had regained her footing and was leaping toward him again.

As Rhaza had hunched over to try to pull the spear free, it had exposed the opposite side of his throat. Windsor found it and latched onto it with her jaws immediately.

When Rhaza reacted to that new threat, it exposed the other side of his throat, which Riley then attacked, also clamping down hard on it with his teeth.

Rhaza flailed and tried to yank them off, but they refused to let go. Riley's eyes locked on Windsor's as they both bit down on Rhaza's throat, and he gave her a wink.

Then together, they tore his throat wide open.

Rhaza went down hard, clutching at his bleeding throat, but he bled out in seconds as Riley and Windsor watched.

The sight was beautiful—the perfect end to a perfect hunt. And now Rhaza was dead.

But most importantly, Riley was with Windsor again, and they were safe.

Well, safe-ish.

"Hate to break it to you," Riley said between ragged breaths, "but there are still way too many monsters around here for us to rest. We have to keep fighting."

"I thought you'd never ask." Windsor grinned at him, also breathing heavily.

"I... wasn't asking," Riley said. "It wasn't a question."

"I'm answering it anyway," she said. "Catch me if you can."

She bounded away and pounced at the nearest Gronyx battling a group of soldiers.

Riley smiled. He could chase that tail all day.

So he did.

THOUGH IT WASN'T the first time he'd seen Lumen do this to Calum, Matthios had finally come to understand the sensation of it. Thanks to Lumen's first spike, he'd been able to associate and identify his emotions and feelings with what Calum now endured.

It wasn't just the pain of being wounded. It was the fear of losing control over his body. The fear of the unknown. The fury and desperation of wanting to make it stop, and the hopelessness of helplessness.

Matthios had wanted it to stop when he'd experienced it, and now, upon seeing Calum experience it as well, he knew it had to stop, or else Calum would be overcome.

It made sense.

Matthios launched forward in a streak of bronze and swung his spear at Lumen, who blocked the shaft with his armored gauntlet, keeping the blade from reaching his head. The impact sounded like a blacksmith's hammer striking an anvil, only ten times louder.

Matthios attacked again, spinning his spear over his head and striking at the other side of Lumen's head. Lumen blocked it again and shrugged off a blast of ice from Lilly's Calios sword. Condor dashed in as well and attacked, and so did General Anigo, but neither of them managed to have any effect either.

All the while, Lumen did not stop pulling at the light in Calum's heart.

"The King may have told you that the light within you now belongs to you," Lumen said to Calum, even as he defended against Matthios's attacks, "but that was untrue. The light has always belonged to me... and it always will."

Matthios threw a new flurry of blows, each of them expertly blocked either by Lumen's single arm or by his leg, always on the spear's shaft, never on its blade. He knew as well as Matthios that the blade could actually pierce Lumen's armor if he struck it right. The spear, after all, had once belonged to the King himself.

Yet even though he tried and fought and strained, nothing Matthios did broke Lumen's hold on Calum. If he couldn't separate the two of them, Calum would die. Matthios had no doubt about that.

He had to get in closer to Lumen. He had to physically separate them.

But to do so was a massive risk.

Matthios glanced at Calum between attacks. This boy carried a measure of the King's power, and Lumen was killing him for it.

Above all else, Matthios existed to serve the King of Kanarah—the *true* King of Kanarah. With the King dead, this boy was as close as he'd ever get. The King had chosen Calum to reign in his place, which meant Matthios now served Calum with his very life.

Thus, when it came to the boy's life, there was no risk too large.

Matthios lowered his spear and his body and charged toward Lumen's midsection. The impact of the blow pushed Lumen back and doubled him over. His grip on Calum faltered, then broke.

Together, they crashed into the back wall of the throne room in a mass of shining bronze and glowing white light. Lumen recovered first and drew his sword, cursing Matthios, and he attacked.

They traded blows as Lilly, Condor, and General Anigo tried to tend to Calum.

Matthios's spear became a bronze blur, alternating between lashing at Lumen's sword and at his body and head. Lumen parried each attack and then threw several more of his own in response, so much that Matthios strained to keep up.

But he was an Imperator, commissioned by the King himself. He was strong enough to defeat Lumen—or at least he had been when the King was still alive. Now it seemed as though each successive blow left him more and more fatigued.

Then, to Matthios's great surprise, Lumen left him an opening. Perhaps it was a mistake, or perhaps he'd been too slow, but Lumen had exposed his flank. Matthios swung his spear to take advantage of it, hoping to even the odds in the fight.

Only after it was too late did Matthios realize it was a trap.

With his sword in one hand, Lumen parried Matthios's spear away, which left Matthios exposed instead, right in the center of his chest, where Lumen had already destroyed a portion of his armor. Then, with his other hand, Lumen pushed another spike of light through Matthios's heart.

And this time, it pierced clean through the other side and struck the wall behind him.

Pain unlike anything Matthios had ever experienced seized his body, and he staggered backward. His vision shuddered, and so did his limbs. The same fears he'd realized when Calum had been dying returned, as did the desperate fury to fix it, and the hopelessness.

But this time, he recognized a new emotion as well: sadness.

He'd failed. He could no longer protect Calum or defeat Lumen. He'd lost.

Would he carry that emotion, more so than all the others, into the afterlife with him?

As Lumen's sword flashed toward his head, Matthios heard Calum shouting his name for the last time.

CHAPTER 48

"I warned you when you left Valkendell that if we met again in battle, I would not grant you mercy a third time," Gavridel intoned.

"I don't need your mercy," Axel growled. "But I'll take your head."

Axel had finally managed to coax the Imperator out of the building where they'd been stuck battling, but their fracas had actually carried them even farther away from Valkendell in the process. Over the rooftops, he could still see Magnus and the Jyrak battling, but they seemed to have moved away from the fortress as well.

The Jyrak could handle itself, Axel reasoned. He'd done his part. He'd brought it back, and now it would fight Scales to the death. Whether it won or lost didn't even matter—Axel and Lumen would finish off whatever was left of Magnus after the fight ended.

But first, he had Gavridel to deal with.

Outside the confines of that house, Axel could fly around and warp through the void much easier. The added mobility helped him deal with Gavridel's attacks, as the big Imperator could maneuver his axes quickly, but he couldn't advance or retreat as fast, perhaps due to his bulky armor.

Still, Gavridel proved more than a match for Axel's fighting prowess. Even when Axel pulled out his most dastardly tricks, Gavridel always seemed to have an answer.

Whenever Axel disappeared into the void, Gavridel did so as well, vanishing into a portal burning with violet flames and crackling with amber lightning. When Axel finally emerged, Gavridel would be behind him, ready to strike, forcing Axel to evade the attack.

They traded blows, but no matter what Axel did, he couldn't get past Gavridel's axes. Outside of their first impact, when he'd caught Gavridel by surprise, Axel hadn't landed a single hit.

He tried to think of what Lumen might do in this situation. After all, Axel was essentially a dark copy of his new master. As he recalled Lumen's attacks, he conjured a spike of darkness in his left hand, and he hurled it at Gavridel from ten feet away.

The diamond axe batted it away, and the spike shattered into bits of darkness that fizzled away into nothing. Axel hurled another spike, then another, faster and faster. Gavridel deflected all of them and started to charge forward.

Rather than move away, Axel opened another void in front of himself to swallow Gavridel whole, but the Imperator vanished into a portal of his own before he reached Axel's void. Instead of waiting for Gavridel to reappear, Axel leaped into his own void and promptly rolled back out.

Gavridel was already there, swinging his axes down at Axel.

A desperate block with Axel's sword saved his life, but it also laid him flat on his back with Gavridel looming over him, pushing down, trying to crush him. Axel strained with all of his newfound strength, but Gavridel was stronger—and much heavier.

Axel opened a void beneath himself, and he and Gavridel both fell into the darkness.

Inside the shadow dimension, Axel thought he would have control, but Gavridel held onto him, and Axel couldn't break free. When he opened another portal, the two of them fell back into Kanarah from high above the city, entangled in a mass of color and darkness.

Axel tried to shake Gavridel off so he could fly away, but the Imperator managed to stay on top. Rather than be crushed upon impact by Gavridel's incredible mass, Axel opened another void halfway down. This time, once they fell through, Axel opened a portal back to Kanarah that repositioned him so he was on top instead. Then he flew down.

Gavridel still clung to him, now on the bottom, and they landed hard on the city streets, reducing several of the cobblestones beneath to powder. The impact shook the entire city, and Gavridel grunted. It wasn't much, but it signaled Axel that this was his chance to triumph.

He forged thick chains of darkness and clamped them around Gavridel's wrists, then he connected the chains behind Gavridel's back so he couldn't move his arms forward. Axel had realized early on in the fight that Gavridel would never let go of his axes, so restraining him, even if only temporarily, was the next best option.

Then Axel raised his tortured Blood Ore sword and swung it at the base of Gavridel's sapphire helmet, where the Imperator's neck should've been, and he flooded his sword with dark power.

Gavridel strained against the chains to try to defend himself, but Axel got there first. His sword cleaved through the gemstones that formed Gavridel's helmet and severed his head from his body.

Axel watched, partially in disbelief as Gavridel's head tumbled across the street and clacked against a pile of rubble. He'd done it. He'd won.

He couldn't believe it—but then he reconsidered. Axel was an Imperator now, too. He wielded incredible power, and he'd put it to the test against one of the strongest warriors in the world. And, of course, he'd won.

He supposed he *could* believe it after all.

Axel stood up, exhaled a relieved breath, and stared down at Gavridel's motionless armored body. Finally, he'd released his grip on his axes, which now lay at his sides, limp in his lifeless hands.

The shadow chains released, and Axel sheathed his sword and bent down to pick up the diamond axe. It had to be worth a fortune—not that he needed coin, now that he and Lumen would rule all of Kanarah—but it would still make a fine keepsake, a memento which would remind him of his excellent victory here.

But as Axel reached for the axe, Gavridel's armored hand lashed up and grabbed him by his throat.

Axel's eyes bulged, and he grabbed hold of Gavridel's wrist to try to pry it off, but Gavridel refused to budge. Axel glanced over at the Imperator's head lying near the debris and saw that he'd missed something—that being Gavridel's head—entirely. He'd only knocked off the Imperator's helmet, and nothing more.

Except that when Gavridel rose to his full height, he still had no head. There was no sign of any blood, either—just the scorched black line cutting across where his neck should've been, courtesy of Axel's sword.

Was Gavridel just a collection of armor inhabited by a spirit or a ghost? Was this more of the King's magic at work? Had he created a hulking automaton out of jewels, empowered it, and set it on its way to wreck whatever needed wrecking?

As Axel strained to breathe and fought against Gavridel's incredible grip, a head popped out from within the massive torso. Someone had been inside all along.

The head had long brown hair, green eyes, and a familiar face that stunned Axel to his core.

Valerie stared at him with anger in her eyes. And for the first time since Axel had met her in Valkendell's infirmary, she wasn't smiling.

MATTHIOS WAS DEAD. No final words, no drawn-out goodbyes. Lumen had driven a spike of light through his chest and then severed the top half of his head from the bottom half with his sword.

Calum had watched it all, helpless to intervene. Matthios had sacrificed himself to save Calum, but to what end? Calum, Lilly, Condor, and General Anigo together stood even less chance of defeating Lumen without Matthios.

If Gavridel were there, or Magnus, or Riley, or all of them, perhaps they could find a way, but they weren't. Calum and the others were on their own.

"I tire of these games," Lumen said, "of dealing with petulant children. If you surrender, I will make your deaths quick and painless, as I did for Matthios."

Calum scowled at Lumen, holding his sword at the ready. Matthios's death may have been quick, but the spike he'd taken through his chest had to have been excruciating.

"No matter what he says," Calum began, "or what he promises, we do not yield. This is bigger than any of us. We cannot give in."

"I will stand with you until the end," General Anigo said.

"As will I," Lilly said.

It broke Calum's heart to know he'd already let her down. They would die here, in this throne room, by Lumen's hand. More likely than not, she would have to watch Lumen rip Calum's soul apart to try to access the King's power for himself, and that would be even worse for her than dying.

"Thank you," he said.

Between the four of them, Condor was the only one whose weapon definitely couldn't harm Lumen, so when he darted past Lumen and retrieved Matthios's bronze double-bladed spear, Calum felt a renewed sense of hope.

"There," Condor said as he returned to Lilly's side. "At least now I'll die with some style."

Calum smirked, but it was short-lived.

Lumen stared down at them. "You refuse to surrender? Very well. Then we shall do this the hard way."

Then he streaked toward them in a blinding blur of light.

AXEL STILL COULDN'T BELIEVE his eyes.

Valerie? This whole time, that gemstone armor had been protecting *Valerie?*

Gavridel had never been a man. It had always been Valerie.

740

It explained why Axel had never seen the two of them together. It explained why she had granted him mercy when he left Valkendell. It explained what she'd said to him back in the infirmary about Captain Anigo insisting that Gavridel capture Axel and Calum instead of killing them. It even explained the decadent sapphire necklace she always wore.

But even though Axel understood everything, he still couldn't fathom how he'd been so thoroughly beaten by a woman—even one with powers.

Vexed? Sure. Women vexed him all the time. Practically every day.

But this was more than simple vexing. Valerie was just as powerful as him, if not more so. She'd demolished him in their first encounter but left him alive. She'd let him pass her by the second time, even when she could've squashed him like an insect. And this time, even when he'd had his full complement of new powers, he still couldn't defeat her.

Now she stared green-eyed daggers at him as she choked the life from his body.

"I told you I would not show you mercy a third time," she uttered, definitely still not smiling.

Axel wanted to respond, but he couldn't. The only sounds he could produce were sputtering and choking noises. He scraped at her huge armored fingers, trying to pull them free but failing. His vision had started to go black and hazy around the edges.

"I am sorry, Axel," Valerie said. "I had hoped you would know the truth, but it appears you cannot accept even that which is right before your eyes."

Axel had one chance to escape. It was a crazy idea, but it was his only option, so he took it.

He opened a void beneath Valerie's diamond axe, which still lay on the ground, and it fell in. By the time she realized what he'd done, the axe was already falling out of another portal above her, right toward her unprotected head.

It collided hard with her head, but not with the blade. Still, because of its weight, the impact knocked Valerie unconscious, and she released her grip on Axel as she toppled to the ground.

He landed on his hands and knees, coughing and wheezing. He yanked his mask off so he could breathe, and his lungs sucked in greedy breaths of air. A moment later, he rose to his feet again, gradually recovering from the ordeal. Then he fastened his mask to his helmet again, drew his sword, and approached Valerie's unconscious form.

He'd never even considered trying to use his enhanced vision on Gavridel before, but he used it now. Sure enough, under the intricate layers of gemstone armor, he could faintly make out the feminine outline of her body.

Axel had been such a fool. He'd fallen in love with the enemy—and one of the strongest ones—without even knowing it. Now he would have to tear her from his heart before the end.

He lined his blade up with her neck, finally exposed above her armor. But as he stared down at her beautiful face, and as he noticed a small bit of blood pooling under her head, he realized he couldn't do it. Nor could he leave her out here with dozens of Lumen's abominations still roaming the city.

Instead, he retrieved her helmet and tried to push it back onto her head. It sort of worked, but he guessed there was some trick or magic to it that would properly seal it in place.

Rather than leaving her there, vulnerable, Axel opened a void and deposited her inside one of the cells beneath Valkendell. If Lumen wanted to execute her later, he could, but Axel would have no part of it. Maybe after some time, he could even convince Valerie to join them instead.

Either way, it was out of his hands now. He left her inside the cell and locked it with actual chains, though he doubted anything would hold her for long. Hopefully it would give him enough time to aid Lumen in defeating Calum and his friends. Then they could finally put an end to all of this.

Axel opened a void and stepped inside. But as he opened a portal to the throne room, something crashed into him, knocking him back into the shadow dimension.

CHAPTER 49

Under General Balena's tutelage, Condor had trained with spears alongside Falcroné. He'd always preferred the sword, though, as it proved more versatile when fighting at fast speeds while airborne. The disparity between the reach of a blade and the reach of a spear didn't mean as much when he could fly incredibly fast.

Now, against Lumen, he wielded Matthios's double-edged spear as best he could. At least it had a spearhead on each end. And since it had been imbued with power beyond any other weapon Condor had ever brandished, with the possible exception of the Calios, it actually proved rather effective.

Or so he thought.

Condor landed a fair number of strikes on Lumen's body and limbs as he zoomed around the room. He employed the old hit-and-fly tactic of zipping in, wounding his opponent, and then darting away before the enemy could counterattack. Meanwhile, the others kept Lumen preoccupied from opposing angles, jabbing their own weapons at him.

It had worked well enough—until Condor realized that every time he tore into Lumen's white armor with the bronze spear, the metal plating sealed up almost immediately afterward. If he couldn't effectively penetrate the armor, how could they wound—much less kill—Lumen?

As Condor pondered this conundrum, he noticed a familiar black void opening near the entrance to the throne room. He knew what it meant, and he knew it would mean the death of everyone on his side of the conflict.

Condor had sworn to protect Lilly, and if Axel showed up, Condor had no hope of keeping her safe from both Lumen and Axel.

In the split second between noticing the portal beginning to open and calculating his options, Condor realized he truly had only one choice.

He pointed himself at the void and hurtled toward it.

Axel had just begun to emerge from the portal by the time Condor collided with him. The two of them fell back into the void and reemerged in Solace but on the street rather than in the air. They tumbled across the cobblestones until they came to a stop about five feet away from each other.

They both sprang to their feet and readied their weapons, but Axel didn't advance. His eyes flickered with recognition, and he shook his head slowly.

"Really?" he asked.

"Really," Condor said, his voice stern.

"After the thrashing I gave you back in the garden?" Axel chided. "You really want to go another round?"

"I'd love nothing more, Farm Boy."

The nickname visibly changed Axel's demeanor, his posture—everything. He'd just defeated Gavridel, or else he wouldn't have been returning to Valkendell at all, so he had to be feeling pretty good about himself.

At least he had been until Condor had reduced him to a moniker from his past, and nothing more.

"Then this is it," Axel finally said, his voice equally stern as Condor's. "You get your chance to try to kill me."

"You are finally ready." Condor shifted the spear in his hands, reminding himself of its feel, its weight distribution, its power. Without it, he doubted he would've stood any chance against Axel whatsoever. "So come and prove to me you're not just a big talker."

Axel launched forward, far faster than Condor had expected, but Condor reacted quickly enough to avoid the first attack. He shot straight up into the sky, his domain, where he had all the experience. Axel had only been flying for a few days at most, so there was no way he could outmaneuver Condor in the air.

They traded blows in the sky, with Matthios's spear valiantly defending against Axel's every strike when necessary. Condor had to admit the boy had grown much faster and stronger, but Condor had a whole array of tools at his disposal that Axel couldn't compete with.

Axel slashed at him, and Condor dropped low in the air and took hold of Axel's ankle with his free hand. Then he dove toward the city below, hauling Axel behind him. The idea was to slam Axel into the ground using their combined momentum, but a black void opened beneath them instead.

Condor adjusted his path just in time, and instead he flung Axel into the void and flew away. Instead of waiting around for Axel to reappear, Condor shot toward the spire of Valkendell. Another void opened up ahead, and Axel drifted out, seething.

"Not bad," he said. "Almost had me there."

"Next time," Condor replied.

They clashed again in a storm of black and bronze, high over Valkendell.

CONDOR'S DISAPPEARANCE had confused Lilly until she realized he'd left to keep Axel from joining the fight. Even so, of the four of them, Condor had been the only one even able to strike Lumen thus far. Losing him meant losing the majority of their offense.

Even without Condor, Lilly continued to fight. The Calios dueled on her behalf, hurling fire and ice and light and poison at Lumen, but none of it seemed to affect him. The fire, ice, and light dissipated upon touching his armor, and the poison had no noticeable effect.

The lack of effectiveness of her attacks led her to stick to defense, and the Calios's blade often turned brown and erected walls of rock for protection for her or the others against Lumen's powerful strikes. On occasion, the Calios turned pale-blue, and bursts of wind physically moved Calum, herself, or, most often, General Anigo out of the way.

Despite Lilly's defensive attempts, Calum proved the most capable of battling Lumen. His eyes had long since changed to vibrant green like the King's, and he either intercepted or deflected every attack Lumen threw at him.

For the most part, Lumen kept his focus on Calum. He occasionally swatted at Lilly and General Anigo as if they were flies buzzing around and annoying him, but otherwise he stalked closer to Calum, who defended himself with an array of powers that Lilly had never seen before.

He'd abandoned his Dragon's breath sword early in the fight. It was a powerful weapon, but neither its emerald fire nor its blade could harm Lumen. Now he focused solely on calling forth the power the King had bequeathed him.

It had worked so far in keeping Lumen at bay, but every attack Calum threw amounted to nothing in the end.

We have to get out of here. Lilly realized it before anyone else.

Apart from the open throne room door at their backs, they were essentially trapped in a large room with the most dangerous being in all of Kanarah. And he had some sort of advantage here in Valkendell that they couldn't comprehend. Their weapons were weaker here.

Even Matthios, the Imperator who'd withstood Lumen's immense power in the fields outside of Kanarah City, had only lasted a few minutes.

If they continued to try to fight Lumen in this place, he would eventually overpower and destroy them. It already seemed like he was toying with them most of the time.

But how could they get out of there and manage to get Lumen to come with?

MAGNUS HAD REALIZED that if he wanted to triumph over Kahn, contending with the Jyrak's freakish strength was a poor strategy. As a testament to that realization, Magnus now lay in the rubble of the building Kahn had just hurled him into.

The impact had hurt, but nothing had broken. Magnus gave silent thanks to the Overlord for creating Dragons with durable scales and even stronger bones.

He'd tried dragonfire as well, but Magnus's emerald flames only heated up the Jyrak's armored scales and then glanced off. Kahn would move just enough to keep the fire from burning through, and he shielded himself with his arms when possible.

And though Magnus's talons could pierce Kahn's armor, they were too small to inflict significant harm. It teased at Magnus's sensibilities to consider that his talons would be considered small in any other circumstance. Aside from this Jyrak, he doubtless wielded the largest talons of any creature, sentient or otherwise, in all of Kanarah.

Yet when it came to Kahn, they were all but worthless—except when it came to latching onto Kahn. Magnus's talons did that very well.

The first few times, Magnus had tried to pull Kahn down to the street. He'd hoped to pin the Jyrak to the ground and gradually pick him apart, but Kahn had proven far too strong. This last time, he'd hurled Magnus into a nearby building.

Magnus needed to change up his tactics. As he took to the air, leaving the dust and debris of the destroyed building in his wake, he blasted Kahn's head with dragonfire. Like before, it hardly affected the Jyrak, and he raised his arms to shield himself from it.

But this time Magnus took advantage of his opportunity and landed on Kahn's back, just above the shriveled gray wings still protruding from his shoulder blades. His jagged dorsal bones pressed against Magnus's body, but Magnus latched on with his talons anyway.

As expected, Kahn roared and bucked and reached for Magnus to try to pry him off, but neither his arms nor his thrashing tail could reach his back. Magnus held on tight, refusing to release his grip now that he had it.

Then Magnus inhaled a long breath, summoned his fire, and sent a blast of it into the back of Kahn's neck, where he couldn't reach to protect himself. The flames burned so hot that the scales on Kahn's neck began to glow red, then yellow, then almost white, stark against the dark green of the rest of his body.

Kahn continued to roar and rage against Magnus's grasp. It almost worked, but Magnus readjusted his grip, inhaled another deep breath, and loosed even more fire onto Kahn's neck. It wasn't pretty, and it took far longer than Magnus had hoped, but his fire eventually melted away Kahn's scaly armor.

One final blast tore through Kahn's flesh, his spine, and burst out the front of his throat, stopping his droning roar forever. Then Kahn did what Magnus had wanted him to do all along: he fell.

He landed face-first, crashing through several homes on his way down. Magnus held on and rode out the fall. Once Kahn settled, Magnus released his grasp on Kahn's back and climbed up to his misshapen head.

Somehow, Kahn was still alive and struggling to get back up, but Magnus was prepared to finish the job. He dug his talons, sharp as they were, under the sides of Kahn's huge jaws, and he began to pull.

The strain was incredible, and Magnus had to brace his legs against the ground to get enough leverage, but he soon heard what he'd been hoping for: the sickening sounds of tearing flesh, cracking bones, and blood splattering at his feet.

Then Kahn's enormous head fully separated from his neck, and Magnus stumbled backward with it in his arms.

Kahn was dead again, and this time, he would stay that way.

As the last of Kahn's glowing orange blood drained from its neck, Magnus tossed the head aside and said, "Good luck coming back from *that*."

THE COLOSSAL STORM over the Central Lake hurled a gigantic green lightning bolt straight down into the enormous tree, and it sheared clear through the center of the tree's trunk in a brilliant array of sparks and flames.

Gill blinked several times at the sight and tried to shield his eyes from the brightness of the display. The deafening boom of thunder that followed threatened to blow out his eardrums. The power of the blast created a shockwave that not only rattled the buildings in Sharkville but also knocked some of them over as if they were stacks of straw in a strong wind.

Gill's shack actually lifted off the ground, but only the back end, which faced the lake. When the shockwave passed, his shack settled back in place with a loud clatter, and he knew that every piece of glass and pottery he'd acquired over the years had crashed to the floor in the process.

He paid it no mind, though—not with everything else happening right before his eyes.

The tree tore apart at the top, its leaves and trunk ablaze with orange fire where the lightning had split it in half. Then a burst of green light, nearly the same color as the bolt of lightning, pulsed up from the center of the tree and extinguished all the flames in a whoosh.

It shot straight into the black clouds overhead and lodged in its center, a fiery green eye of the storm around which everything else began to swirl.

As the mighty tree slowly collapsed, the storm began to move east—fast—as if it had been summoned to do so. Gill, who had finally retrieved a spyglass of his own from inside his shack, watched it for a moment, but the sight of the tree falling apart stole his attention again.

The two halves of the tree toppled east and west, landing just short of the impassable mountain ranges lining each side of the valley. The rumble and the vibrations of the huge tree smacking the valley shuddered the ground under Gill's feet and rattled his teeth.

"What in the Overlord's name is going on?" Jake asked.

Gill shook his head and aimed his spyglass back toward the fleeing storm. "Beats me. But it ain't nothin' good."

VALERIE'S EYES POPPED OPEN, and her head throbbed with pain. She reached up to touch it but instead found her helmet back on her head.

That didn't make any sense.

She recalled fighting Axel in the street, recalled him dropping her own axe on her, and that was it. Now, as she considered her surroundings, she realized she was in the King's dungeons below Valkendell.

Axel must've taken her here instead of killing her. It was too bad he'd chosen the path of rebellion after all. He'd been a nice enough guy, if not a bit rough around the edges.

Alright—*very* rough around the edges. Jagged, even. But he'd showed promise in so many ways...

Valerie couldn't dwell on that now. The distant booms reverberating through Valkendell above told her that not much time had passed. The stones that made up the walls told her the story of what was transpiring both inside and outside the fortress.

She had little time to act. The battle still raged on, and she was missing it.

She fastened her helmet to the rest of her armor and rose to Gavridel's full height. Her head swam and throbbed even more when she did, but she exhaled a calming breath and focused herself. A little headache wasn't enough to stop her from doing her duty.

Her axes were nowhere to be found. It made sense that Axel wouldn't have brought those with her, but she could get back to them easily enough.

She ignored the chains and the lock on the door and instead entered her own dimension. Inside, rather than the abject darkness of Axel's shadow dimension, jewels and gems of every conceivable color and size sparkled all around her so brightly that it almost hurt her eyes to look upon them.

As she moved through the gemstone dimension, the ocean of colorful stones parted to allow her to move. She pinpointed her axes with ease and found them still lying in the street where Axel had left them. They appeared as opaque black objects, easy to spot against the rainbow of color everywhere else she looked.

Like her armor itself, she had painstakingly carved and shaped the axes from individual stones she'd found within this dimension. It had taken decades to complete the full set, but in the end, it had all been worth it.

Now was not the time to reminisce, however, so she opened the portal into the real world yet again. Amber lightning and purple flames tore through the gemstones, revealing the bleak streets of Solace, and she stepped out, leaving the gemstone dimension behind.

As she picked up her axes, she realized some sort of storm was rolling in from the west. The otherwise sunny day had darkened thanks to the angry black clouds overhead.

When Valerie saw the eye of the storm aglow with green light, she recognized the maelstrom for what it really was. Inside her mask, she smiled.

She had to get back to the fight with Lumen. There was still a chance they could win.

LUMEN'S POWER was overwhelming Calum. He'd tapped every last bit of the King's power just to defend himself, and it had left him exhausted and withered like a dying rose.

But even a dying rose still had thorns.

Emptied of the King's power, Calum summoned the light Lumen had given him. It was probably a terrible idea, but he'd run out of other options. If he didn't keep Lumen's focus on him, it might put Lilly at risk. And if something happened to her...

The light from Calum's chest filtered into his arms and down to his fingertips, no longer burning like before, but cool like a refreshing flow of water through his veins. As Calum's hands began to glow, Lumen regarded him with curiosity.

"You would use my own power against me?" Lumen laughed again.

"It's not your power anymore," Calum said. "The King made it mine forever."

"The King is a liar and a fool." Lumen added, "A dead fool. What I have given, I will also take away."

Calum forged a spike of pure light, just as Lumen had when he'd thrown them at Matthios. He held it in his hand as if it were real—he could feel it as if it were solid, yet somehow thrumming at the same time. Then he hurled it at Lumen.

The light zipped across the throne room, but before it could strike Lumen, it slowed to a stop. Then it turned back and launched at Calum instead.

With his jaw clenched, Calum tried to grab it with his mind and wrest control of it back from Lumen. Sure enough, the spike slowed yet again, but Calum couldn't get it to turn back or completely stop. It continued creeping ever closer to him, even as General Anigo and Lilly tried to batter Lumen with their own weapons.

Calum strained, pumping more and more of his concentration into the single spike. He sensed it fracturing the instant before it shattered, and instead of one large spike, dozens of smaller shards jabbed at his chest and arms. His armor stopped some of them, but a few of the larger shards broke through and punctured his skin.

He yelped and recoiled as warm blood oozed from the wounds. He hoped they were superficial, but he couldn't tell for sure.

"Calum!" Lilly shouted to him. "Are you—"

In that miniscule moment of distraction, Lumen struck.

His sword flashed through the air and slammed into the Calios. The force of the blow knocked Lilly across the throne room and into the wall with a sickening smack, and she dropped to the floor, motionless. The Calios tumbled from her limp hand and rattled to a stop next to her.

"Lilly!" Calum shouted.

He forgot his own wounds and darted over to her. He found her still alive, still breathing but definitely injured. He didn't know how badly.

Had Lilly been holding the Calios any differently, and had she not been wearing her armor, Calum was certain the blow would've killed her.

He wanted to stay with her, but they were still very much in danger. As he rose to his feet and turned back, Calum noticed a lone form separating him from Lumen.

General Anigo stood before Lumen with his golden spear at the ready.

CHAPTER 50

General Beynard Anigo had a nice ring to it, he'd decided.

Pity he'd only gotten to enjoy the new title for a few days.

But at least he'd die knowing he'd always stood for the truth. For what was right.

For the King.

He raised his golden spear, a gift from the King himself and forged by Matthios's own hands, and pointed it at Lumen. "I told you I would never yield."

Lumen looked down at him with those insidious blazing eyes. "And I told you what would happen if, in the end, you still failed to see the wonders I have brought to this world."

General Anigo recalled Lumen's words as clearly as the day he'd spoken them. "You told me I would perish the same as the rest of your foes."

"Precisely."

General Anigo had stared down this particular death before. Regardless of what happened to him, the truth was still the truth, and he was obliged—even *commissioned* to speak it.

"Whether I live or die," he repeated his own words, "I serve the one true King of Kanarah. And that will *never* be you."

Lumen remained silent for a long moment. Finally, he said, "You may not realize it, but I gave you the same gift I gave your valiant friend Calum. When I skewered you through your heart back in Kanarah City, I left a taste of my power inside of you as well."

General Anigo recalled the uncontrollable pain in his chest, the difficulty of breathing, the horrible sensation of dying while yet living.

Then Lumen raised his hand, and General Anigo experienced it all over again.

An unseen force seized General Anigo from the inside of his chest and began to squeeze.

The golden spear dropped from his hands and clanged on the floor.

He gasped, but the pressure stole his breath.

He looked down and saw white light glowing through his golden armor as if it were made of glass. The stone floor beneath his feet dropped away, and he found himself hovering in the air, unable to breathe and barely even able to think.

Then Lumen's voice entered his mind, just as it had before, speaking in impressions rather than words.

Even though your heart cannot be won...

...it can still be crushed.

Captain Anigo's eyes widened as the pressure in his chest sharpened, and then he saw nothing else but the brightness of pure white light as he exhaled his last breath.

TRY AS HE MIGHT, Condor couldn't keep up with Axel for much longer. The boy was relentless in his attacks, chasing Condor through the ever-darkening sky, thwarting his tricks, stymying his plans, and ruining his chances at landing any significant blows with Matthios's spear.

Axel's void-hopping didn't help things, and neither did Condor having to use a spear. The nasty storm brewing overhead made Axel harder to see, as he blended in with the angry storm clouds above. Condor felt fatigue digging deeper and deeper into his body, whereas Axel only seemed to be moving faster, hitting harder, and reacting quicker.

"Well done, Farm Boy," Condor said between haggard breaths as they traded blows and parries in the air. "You've certainly proven a worthy opponent."

"Don't quit on me yet, buzzard," Axel taunted. "I'm just getting warmed up."

Condor swatted Axel's sword aside, spun his spear overhead, and slammed it into Axel's shoulder. It was a superficial blow, but it knocked Axel askew for an instant. But when Condor threw a follow-up swing, Axel had already dodged it.

Condor didn't see Axel's boot coming toward him until it was too late. The kick didn't hurt, but it forced Condor back. He tried to come forward again, only to realize that Axel had opened a void behind him—a void that was now pulling Condor into it.

He strained against the void's pull, but he knew if he managed to break free, he'd be flying right into Axel's range of attack. After constantly fighting for what seemed like hours, he just didn't have the energy left to resist, and the void won.

It inhaled him into the darkness and promptly shut, and Condor readied his spear to attack the instant he saw the waning rays of daylight again.

A portal behind him opened, and Condor whirled to face Axel once again.

As he did, an intense pain plunged into his back.

When he looked down, the tip of Axel's sword was protruding from Condor's chest, right through the center of the Raven's Brood emblem emblazoned on his breastplate.

Blood streaked along the sword's bright-blue edges, tainting them reddish purple, and it trickled down the front of his charcoal-gray breastplate.

Condor tried to suck in a breath, but he couldn't. He drifted out of the void with Axel behind him. Axel must've opened two rifts at once—one to distract Condor, and another to attack him from behind.

It had worked.

Condor's grip on the bronze spear faltered, and it fell end-over-end toward the city streets below. He absently hoped it would cut a wandering monster in half as it landed, but in his next thoughts, the pain of his imminent death registered full force.

The taste of copper flooded Condor's mouth, and with the last of his strength, he twisted away, pulling Axel's sword out of his hand. With the blade still lodged in his back and sticking out of his chest, Condor stared at his foe.

He'd been wrong. All along, Condor had truly hoped Axel would find his way. Instead, he'd stumbled into darkness, lured there by the promise of power.

He'd received the power, alright, but it had come at an incredibly high cost. He'd abandoned all of his friendships, everyone and everything that he loved, and he'd become the very monster he'd sworn to destroy.

Condor wanted to say all of that and more to Axel, but he couldn't speak. He barely had energy to stay airborne.

He locked onto Axel's bitter blue eyes one final time and marshaled the last of his breath to utter four final words: "I forgive you, Axel."

Then Condor's eyes closed, and he dropped from the sky.

IT ALL HAPPENED before Calum could even get close.

Now General Anigo was dead, as was Matthios.

Lilly was unconscious and injured.

Calum was alone and powerless to fight back.

"Now do you finally understand?" Lumen faced Calum again and hurled General Anigo's corpse to the side like a child discarding an unwanted doll. "Nothing any of you do can stop me. I rule Kanarah, and I *will* remake her in my image."

"You're *killing* everything!" Calum shouted at him. "You're not the King! You have no control, no love for this place. You just want it for yourself, not for the people."

"It is mine by *right*," Lumen declared. "If something can be taken from you, then you do not deserve to have it."

Lumen hovered closer and closer to Calum. He didn't fear for himself—his death was as inevitable as Matthios's or General Anigo's at this point.

But he couldn't let Lumen hurt Lilly any more.

Inside his chest, Calum gathered what little of the King's power he had recovered. He only had one last attack before the end. It would either be enough, or it wouldn't.

As Calum called forth one last blast of power, he noticed a line of purple flames accompanied by the crackling of amber lightning opening wide behind Lumen.

That was his chance.

Calum loosed the blast, and a stream of green energy as wide as his chest collided with Lumen's breastplate, halting his progress and then forcing him back about six inches, but no more.

And that was it. Calum had given everything he had.

Lumen stared down at him, shaking his head. "Pitiful."

But behind him, the purple-and-amber void yawned open wider. Then a pair of familiar emerald-armored arms wrapped around Lumen's waist from behind and hauled him backward.

Lumen tried to react, but Gavridel pulled him into the void before he could resist. Then the void sealed shut, and Calum was left alone in the throne room with Lilly and the corpses of Matthios and General Anigo.

Calum regretted not saving some of the King's power to help heal Lilly. He'd been thinking of saving her from Lumen, but maybe he should've saved her life so she could flee instead. Had he made the wrong choice?

As he bent down to examine her again, she stirred and looked up at him. "Calum?"

"Yeah," he said. Tears stung the corners of his eyes. "It's me."

"Is it over?" she asked.

He shook his head. "No. Not yet."

Lilly blinked, then her eyes widened. "Calum... I can't feel my legs."

Her words sickened him to his core. He really had failed her.

"It'll be alright," Calum said to her, hoping it would be true. Then he lied to her a second time. "I used some of the King's power to numb you up. You're hurt, but it'll pass."

A look of relief filled her eyes, and she gave him a faint smile. "I love you."

Calum smiled back as tears streamed down his face. "I love you, too. I always will. Now I have to go."

"I know," she said. "Find a way to stop him, alright?"

Calum nodded. His voice shaking, he replied, "I'll try."

"Live or die," Lilly reached up and cupped his face, "this is not the end for us. I promise."

Calum just nodded again. If he didn't leave now, he'd stay with her until Lumen destroyed all of Kanarah around them, until he separated them forever.

Calum stood and wiped the tears from his eyes, and then he flew out of the throne room without looking back at her.

WHITE-HOT SPIKES of pain jammed through Gavridel's armor and dug into Valerie's flesh. Lumen had punctured her armor with dozens of light spikes as a means of defending himself.

She grunted, but she didn't release Lumen until they fully emerged from the portal in the sky over Valkendell. By then, the maelstrom had blanketed the entire city in darkness, except for the vibrant green glow in the center of the storm and the occasional arc of green lightning streaking through the clouds.

Valerie normally didn't try to stay airborne while wearing Gavridel's armor; it was a strenuous enough task to just move in it, let alone keep it flying, but she had to see the look in Lumen's blazing eyes once before she succumbed to her wounds and her ever-growing weakness.

He noticed her, and then he noticed the storm. His eyes fixed upon its green center, no doubt pondering its meaning just as Valerie had pondered it upon first seeing it.

Then he looked at her again.

She knew he could see her smiling at him, even from behind her helmet.

"The King told me I wouldn't understand," she called to him, her voice modulated to sound like Gavridel's thanks to her helmet. "And I didn't. Not until I saw this storm."

Lumen continued to stare at her.

"He said to me, 'Three days afterward, amid the coming storm, I promise you will understand everything,'" Valerie continued. Inside her helmet, tears streamed down her face, but she maintained her smile all the same. "I thought he meant *you* were the coming storm."

Lumen's grip tightened on his sword.

"I was wrong," Valerie said, her smile the widest and truest it had ever been.

Then Lumen flashed toward her and cut her out of the sky.

CHAPTER 51

Magnus had seen Condor fall to the streets below with Axel's sword—Magnus's old Blood Ore sword—protruding from his body.

After his duel with the Jyrak, he'd been too far away to intervene, and far too late to stop Axel. It all happened under the darkest storm Magnus had ever seen, casting the scene in bleak tones of black and gray.

The sight of Condor's death filled Magnus with rage. Every memory he had of Axel chastising him, or making snide comments, or complaining about any insignificant thing replayed rapid-fire through Magnus's mind. Then he recalled Axel's outright betrayal of his friends, his role in the King's murder, and his continued combat support of Lumen's reign.

It all burned at the back of Magnus's skull, and it propelled him into the air, straight toward him.

Axel had killed Condor, and now Magnus was going to make him pay for it.

Axel had been so preoccupied with watching Condor fall that at first, he hadn't noticed Gavridel—Valerie—and Lumen hovering in the air halfway across the city. When Lumen flashed toward Valerie and struck her from the sky, Axel turned in time to see her armored form dropping toward the barren city streets.

Horror seized his chest. He hadn't wanted Valerie to die—that's why he'd saved her in the first place. But he'd also known that Lumen would ultimately determine her fate.

And Lumen had clearly made his choice.

The storm overhead swirled and raged with a fury unlike any storm Axel had ever seen before. The thunder of the lighting ratcheting through the clouds was so constant that it sounded like hammers striking the air, or like the wing beats of a huge Dragon tearing through the sky.

Axel's eyes widened with realization, and he whirled around.

He tried to open a void to escape, but an enormous scaly hand snatched Axel's entire body into its grasp. A deafening roar ripped through Axel's ears, and he found himself staring at the enraged face of the Dragon King of Reptilius himself.

Magnus.

Axel squirmed to try to get free, but Magnus didn't loosen his grip in the slightest.

"Hello, Scales," Axel sneered at him.

A low growl issued from Magnus's throat, and then his nostrils began to smoke. But instead of unleashing dragonfire, Magnus began to squeeze.

Axel heard his bones popping and cracking before he felt the pain, and though he struggled to free himself, he couldn't. He gaped at Magnus with desperate eyes, and then he saw nothing anymore.

CALUM REACHED the sky in a state of heartache, but upon seeing the storm overhead, it shifted to confusion. Had he really been inside Valkendell so long that a maelstrom had time to gather without him realizing it?

Somehow, though, his reservoir of the King's power seemed to have fully replenished. He could feel it pooling inside his body yet again, ready to be used. He considered going back to use it to heal Lilly, but he stopped himself. He had to try to finish off Lumen, or it wouldn't matter what he did for her.

When he noticed a strange green glow from the eye of the storm, positioned perfectly over the center of the city, Calum felt something stir within him, but he couldn't make sense of it.

The impression immediately truncated as a terrible pain took its place. A familiar pain screaming through Calum's chest. Hot white light glowed from his heart, shining even through his armor.

He whirled around and saw Lumen soaring toward him with his hand extended. With his teeth clenched, Calum summoned the King's power and pried Lumen's grip from his heart.

It was surprisingly easy, especially compared to how he'd struggled against Lumen's pull inside the throne room.

Lumen tilted his head at Calum, and then his blazing eyes narrowed. "Even now, at the end, you still defy me?"

"Get used to it," Calum fired back.

Overhead, rain began to fall from the storm, but not just a smattering of drops. It swelled to a torrential downpour almost immediately, so thick that it even managed to dim Lumen's light.

Lumen reached out and grabbed Calum's heart again, and this time his grip multiplied in intensity. The pain almost made Calum pass out, but a burst of the King's power kept him coherent, and another burst began weaving its way between Lumen's grip and Calum's heart.

Lumen noticed, and his eyebrows scrunched down in fury.

Calum had expected Lumen would redouble his efforts to seize control of the light, but instead, he raised his sword and darted closer to him.

Weaponless, Calum raised his left arm and called the King's power yet again. A shield made of green energy deadened the blow, but the force of Lumen's attack still sent tremors shuddering up Calum's arm.

"You cannot resist me forever," Lumen said as he pulled even harder on Calum's heart. "I am too powerful for the likes of you."

Calum ground his teeth and pulled back. He pulled for his very life.

And as he pulled, he sensed something familiar in the air—no, in the rain. Familiar, yet different. New—renewed.

Power.

The rain itself had taken on the same radiant quality as the eye of the storm, and it now glowed green as well.

It was as if Calum's skin was drinking in the rain, and every drop of it filled him with a little more power.

With the King's power constantly renewing within him, Calum pried Lumen's grip from his heart once again. When Lumen swung his sword, Calum's energy shield blocked it with ease, and this time the blow hardly rippled through his arm at all.

Lumen spouted ancient curses at him and summoned half a dozen spikes of pure light. They materialized in the air, visible even through the downpour, but as he sent them flying toward Calum, they disintegrated in the rain, becoming nothing but steam.

Lumen roared and launched forward, swinging his sword in vicious world-destroying arcs. Calum kept his shield up and deflected every blow, even as they grew more and more powerful with each successive strike. He found himself gritting his teeth as the King's power struggled to keep up with Lumen's onslaught.

"You are nothing!" Lumen growled between strikes. "You always have been."

Though Lumen's sword hadn't breached Calum's defenses, his words had found their way into Calum's mind and heart all the same.

"That's not true," Calum fired back. He was saying it to himself as much as to Lumen.

"Oh, but it is." Lumen's blade crashed against Calum's shield. "Do you think you are important because I appeared to you in your dreams? Do you really think I chose *you* to set me free?"

Calum held his tongue. Lumen *had* chosen him. He *had* appeared in Calum's dreams.

"You are a fool if you believe that," Lumen jabbed, as if he could read Calum's thoughts. "I did not choose you. I sent dreams to *thousands* of halfwits just like you. You were the only one deluded enough to answer the call."

Calum's heart shuddered at Lumen's admission. Was that really true? Or was Lumen just waging mental warfare against him?

"You are *nothing*," Lumen repeated, his voice even more menacing than the first time. "You will always be nothing."

It couldn't be true. It would mean that everything Calum had done in his life, especially since he'd fled the quarry, had meant nothing. It meant that he was the only person in the whole world who'd been dumb enough to answer Lumen's call, to set him free, and to destroy Kanarah in the process.

"You know it is true." Lumen's sword pressed against Calum's shield, which began to crack under the pressure. "You are weak. You always have been. But with me, you can finally be strong. Join me, Calum, and together, we can save Kanarah—forever."

In that moment, Lumen pushed Calum too far. He'd overstepped, overplayed his advantage, and Calum knew it.

He *felt* it.

But more importantly, he felt that familiar impression again. Familiar, yet different. New, and renewed. Powerful beyond measure.

Calum began to reinforce his shield with more of the King's power.

Lumen shook his head. "Do not resist. You must know you will never be king. You are too weak to reign."

Those words were absolutely true. Hearing them from the Father of Lies made them all the more poignant.

They helped Calum realize the truth about what was really happening.

He looked up at the maelstrom overhead. Though the rain continued to pour down, the eye of the storm no longer glowed green.

That was because the storm wasn't just a storm. It wasn't a means to empower Calum to defeat Lumen. Even with all the power he could hold, he never could've done that.

No—the storm *was* the power.

"You're right, Lumen," Calum said through gritted teeth as he pushed back against Lumen's sword. "I'll never be king."

Lumen tilted his head and narrowed his eyes at Calum.

Behind him, a form began to materialize out of the rain. It was the size of Lumen, and it, too, wore all white armor and a crown of white atop its head.

Calum already knew who it was, but upon seeing the figure's vibrant green eyes ignite in the darkness, every last bit of his reservations vanished.

"And you're right— I'm too weak. I could never defeat you." Calum nodded over Lumen's shoulder. "But he can."

The form drifted forward, revealing itself in the entirety of its glory.

The King had returned.

CHAPTER 52

L umen whirled around and swung his sword in a vicious strike that would've obliterated an
entire army, but a bronze spear stopped his attack mid-swing.

Matthios's spear. But it wasn't Matthios holding it.

When Lumen saw who now wielded the weapon, his eyes widened. "*Impossible.*"

The King hovered in the air before him, clothed in white armor, wearing a crown of white,
and radiating more power than Lumen had ever known. His green eyes burned with righteous
fury, and they were fixed upon Lumen.

"I killed you. I buried you!" Lumen shouted as he drew his sword back for another strike.

This time, his arm didn't even make it all the way back. A bolt of green lightning screamed
down from the storm and struck his arm, shearing it off in one brutal strike.

Lumen recoiled and shouted as he watched his arm and his sword fall into the watery abyss
below. He looked up at the King again. "I *killed* you! I *buried* you! You were dead!"

"Not anymore," the King replied.

Desperation filled Lumen's chest. It was a sensation he hadn't felt for a thousand years—not
since the King had defeated him at the end of his last rebellion and cast him into his prison
beneath the Central Lake.

"How?" he asked.

"The Law of Debt," the King replied.

Lumen just shook his head.

"Kanarah was suffering. No matter what I did, no matter how I tried to intervene, your rebellion lingered among my people. They violated Kanarah's laws. They oppressed each other. Even
my own soldiers participated in harming their fellow man. There was only one way to fix it. The
Law of Debt was the answer.

"I allowed you to kill me," the King continued. "By sacrificing myself and dying at your hand,
I took on the burden of your rebellion, and thus, the rebellion of all Kanarah. I gave my life in
order to reclaim this land forever."

"Impossible," Lumen repeated. "You mean to indebt everyone in all Kanarah to you?"

"I already have," the King replied. "And not just its people, but also its plants, its animals, its waters, its atmosphere, its mountains, and its valleys. The land itself. All of it. Before, I was merely connected to Kanarah, feeding it with every beat of my heart. Now I truly *am* Kanarah."

A shudder pulsed through Lumen's body. This couldn't be happening. He'd done everything right. He'd succeeded in killing the King and taking the throne. He'd ruled the whole world— only to have it ripped away from him in just three days' time.

"Now only one task remains," the King concluded. He said nothing else. He just looked at Lumen intently, intensely, boring into him with those furious green eyes.

"No," Lumen held up his remaining hand. "You cannot. I will not let you!"

He began to summon the same ball of white-hot energy he'd used to obliterate Matthios's army right after he'd been released. If he could loose it on the King, it might be enough to—

A bronze streak clanged against Lumen's head, destroying the ball of energy, ripping the mask from his face, and exposing the true horror that lay beneath—a black void of darkness lined with the rotten brown teeth of a skeleton. The rest of Lumen's face followed suit, reverting back to its true form—that of death and darkness, decay and destruction.

With one final roar, Lumen flung himself at the King, starving for vengeance.

The King's spear skewered him through his chest, stopping his advance far short.

Lumen strained and wailed against the searing pain of the spear in his body, but to no avail. Then he looked up, toward the storm as another bolt of green lightning crashed down toward him, reducing him to ash.

Then the rain washed him away forever.

———

AXEL'S broken body lay on the city streets near Magnus and Riley, all of them staring up at the battle raging under the storm. The rain had somehow erased some of the profound damage that Magnus had done to Axel's body, slowly but painfully, and he'd reawakened not long after he'd gone out.

At first, he'd been eager to fight Magnus again, but the instant the green lightning bolt vaporized Lumen, Axel's powers vanished with him, leaving him weak, frail, and thoroughly human. As he lay there, he realized that the power had never truly been his at all. In the end, Lumen hadn't kept his promise.

Alone once again, Axel closed his eyes and let the rain continue to do its healing work. There was nothing else he could do, and nowhere he could go.

———

AS SOON AS the King destroyed Lumen, Calum abandoned the storm and dashed back into Valkendell. He darted up the long hallways until he finally reached the throne room again—until he finally reached Lilly again.

She wasn't moving. She wasn't even breathing.

Thanks to the storm, Calum was filled with the King's power, but was he already too late? Healing that soldier's leg had been one thing, but if Lilly was already dead…

He had to try. Calum placed his hands on her body, one on her stomach and one on her head, and he poured new life into her with the King's power. He saturated her body with so much energy that her entire body began to glow green.

Calum could feel the power fusing her bones back together, mending broken blood vessels, shrinking hemorrhages, eliminating bruises, knitting torn tendons and flesh. Her physical body was being repaired, but he couldn't tell if her soul was still in there or not—if *she* was still in there or not.

When he'd emptied the last of the King's power into her limp form, he waited.

Nothing changed.

"No." Panic set in. "No, no, no!"

He reached down for her, took her by the shoulders, and shook her.

"Lilly, come on." He said it quietly at first, as if he could just rouse her from sleep. With each attempt, his volume increased. "Lilly, wake up. Lilly. Lilly! Lilly, *wake up!* Please!"

Tears streamed down his cheeks and he tasted salt on his lips.

"Lilly!" He was shouting now. "Oh, please... Lilly, *please* wake up!"

She didn't move.

"*Lilly!*" he screamed into her face and shook her again. Then he couldn't restrain himself any longer. He pulled her into his arms and wailed, clutching her tightly against his body.

She was gone. Lumen had killed her after all, and Calum had been too late.

He'd helped to save Kanarah, but it had come at the cost of Lilly's life.

Amid his tears, Calum managed the strength to whisper, "I love you" one last time.

To his surprise, she whispered it back to him.

He jerked backward, staring at her with his mouth hanging open in shock—beautiful, horrible shock. She opened her blue eyes and gazed into his, smiling like she had that night when she'd kissed him.

His shock transformed into a smile, but the words he wanted to say never made it out of his mouth. He couldn't have said them even if he'd wanted to.

Instead, he leaned forward, and he kissed Lilly again.

And this time, he was never going to let her go.

EPILOGUE

B y the time the massive storm overhead had disappeared, it had saturated Solace nearly to the point of flooding. Were it not for the city's sewers, it probably would have.

The rain also served to cleanse the streets of the surviving abominations; wherever the rain touched them, it melted a little bit more of them away. And since the storm was a nonstop downpour, the monsters disintegrated almost immediately, whether alive or dead.

In the coming weeks, new life sprouted across all of Kanarah. The rivers flowed again. The wells refilled with clean water. The grass and trees and plants regrew and flourished, including the King's garden, which blossomed with more brilliant colors than ever before.

Even more incredibly, the Valley of the Tri-Lakes went from being a barren wasteland to a verdant paradise loaded with all kinds of fruit trees and bushes, vegetable plants, and more.

Even Gill had to admit he'd been wrong about the storm when he'd remarked that nothing good would come of it. For as long as he lived, he never again had to worry about what he was going to eat.

Perhaps more importantly, he never had to go on a boat ever again, either. Thanks to the storm and the tree, his "fishig" days were solidly behind him, and he spent the rest of his days honing his drawing skills.

He still cannot draw birds.

At Axel's trial, the people cheered when the King pronounced him guilty on all counts, including sedition, rebellion, and murder. Protests soon followed when the King chose not to execute him for his crimes.

Calum had mixed feelings about the verdict. Axel had been his best friend, once, but he'd strayed far from the path he should've been walking and instead dove headfirst into his pursuit for power. In doing so, he'd abandoned his friendships, turned on those who loved him, and killed Condor.

Calum wanted to forgive Axel for all of it, though he doubted Lilly ever could, especially for

Condor's murder. It was something that Calum would struggle with probably for the rest of his life. Perhaps they both would.

Axel didn't avoid all punishment, though. The destruction of Lumen stripped him of all his dark powers, reducing him to a mere human once again. Further, the King forbade him from entering one of Kanarah's cities ever again, including Solace.

He was not permitted to establish a permanent home anywhere in Kanarah for any length of time, but rather he was to live a nomadic life, perpetually traveling and living off whatever he could scrounge from the wilderness.

It was the kind of life Axel had once said he wanted to live. Now he would get his chance, whether he still wanted to or not.

The King also put a mark on Axel's forehead that changed based on who was looking at it. When Calum looked at it, he saw a teardrop shape. Lilly described it as a bloody sword. Magnus said it looked like a pair of fangs to him.

The storm had already repaired Axel's body, so the King sent Axel away with nothing but the clothes on his back, a rusted steel sword, and a sack full of fruits and vegetables—exactly what he'd brought with him when he'd first fled his family farm.

Many years later, Calum saw Axel traversing Trader's Pass from high above as he flew overhead. Axel looked as haggard as he'd ever looked, with a long beard now turning gray. He'd come up with some mismatched armor along the line, but he still carried that rusted old sword with him.

Calum considered stopping to speak with him, but he didn't. He had nothing to say to him.

He never saw Axel again after that day.

WITH THE HELP of the King's power, Valerie recovered from her wounds and soon returned to her nebulous role as the King's smiling advisor. It took Calum almost a week after the final battle to realize Valerie had actually been Gavridel the whole time.

Even then, he still didn't fully believe it until the King told him it was so. Apparently it was a longstanding safety precaution they'd instituted. If no one knew about Valerie's true role with regard to her proximity to the King, they wouldn't see her coming if she needed to intervene as Gavridel.

It seemed like a lot of unnecessary secrecy to Calum, but he'd already resigned himself to not understanding most of what the King had done or why he'd done it, so he just went with it.

RATHER THAN RETURNING to the Desert of the Forgotten—a place which Calum suspected was no longer a desert due to the sprawling environmental changes happening across the land—Riley and Windsor decided to accept the King's invitation to stay in Solace and rebuild his team of Shadow Wolf assassins.

The King didn't really need assassins, what with being all-powerful now, but both Riley and Windsor needed a place to belong, and they needed each other, so they all agreed it was a good idea.

Several months later, Windsor would give birth to her first litter of Wolf pups. Much later in life, one of them grew up to be every bit as sarcastic as Riley, which he, of course, found hilarious. Windsor did not agree, and Riley thought that was even funnier.

AFTER SOME TEARFUL GOODBYES, Magnus returned to Reptilius with the surviving Saurians from his original army. He ruled his people with the King's full and unconditional blessing for hundreds more years, and Calum was fortunate enough to be able to visit his best friend often, exchanging stories and reliving old adventures in their memories.

Under Magnus's rule, the Saurians thrived more so than under any previous ruler, Praetorius included. He successfully eradicated the last vestiges of the slave trade set up by Kahn, Vandorian, and Oren, and he also committed dozens of Saurians to help with the reconstruction of the city of Aeropolis.

WHEN IT CAME time for Lilly to return to her home in the Sky Realm, the King not only blessed her as the realm's rightful ruler but also pledged to send funds, resources, and workers to help the Windgales rebuild Aeropolis. She thanked the King for his generosity and support, as did General Balena and General Tolomus.

Calum was all set to accompany her when the King called him forward.

"Calum the Deliverer," the King said from his throne. "Calum the Unifier."

Calum knelt before him with his head bowed. "I'm not worthy of such titles, Your Majesty."

"But you are, truly," the King countered. "You came to know the truth, and ultimately, it was the truth that set you free."

Calum kept his head bowed. He didn't know what to say to that.

"That is why I have decided to make you an Imperator ," the King continued.

Now Calum looked up. He'd secretly hoped for an opportunity like this ever since he'd seen Matthios withstand Lumen's attacks during their first fight.

But he already knew he couldn't accept. Doing so would mean he'd be separated from Lilly. It just wouldn't work.

"Thank you for your generous offer, Your Majesty," Calum said. "But I have to decline."

"I was not asking," the King uttered.

Calum swallowed the lump in his throat. Even though he'd joined the King's side, he couldn't help but revere the man and respect his endless power. If Calum were honest with himself, it frightened him more than a little. How could he refuse an all-powerful King?

"Your Majesty," Calum began, "please understand... I've committed myself to the Premieress. We're due to be wed as soon as we return to the Sky Realm so we can spend our lives together. I can't serve as an Imperator and be a good husband to her. So, respectfully, I have to decline."

Valerie stood next to the King, smiling. Maybe it was because of Calum's boldness, or maybe it was because she was pleased that Calum and Lilly had committed to each other. Or maybe it was that she just liked to smile all the time.

The King twirled the hair in his dark beard and stared at Calum with his vibrant green eyes. His voice hardened a bit, and he leaned forward. "Perhaps I was not clear. You *will* serve as my Imperator."

Calum closed his eyes. He couldn't lose Lilly... not after everything they'd gone through. He wanted to serve the King, but... his heart would be torn either way.

The King sat back in his throne. "I need someone I can trust, after all. Someone loyal. Someone who can personally oversee the funds, resources, and manpower I am sending to the Sky Realm to help rebuild the fine city of Aeropolis."

Calum's eyes popped open, and he gawked at the King.

"I can think of no one more trustworthy, capable, or qualified than you," the King said. "After all, you have extensive experience in working with all sorts of stone, do you not?"

Calum beamed. "Yes, Your Majesty. As you know, I worked in a quarry for a long time."

"Then you will prove an invaluable asset as Aeropolis is rebuilt to its former grandeur." Now the King was smiling as well.

It wasn't the first time Calum had seen him smile since the war ended, but he could count the number of times it had happened on one hand.

"And once that project is complete, you will continue to serve as my Imperator and representative in Western Kanarah for a long as you shall live."

Calum bowed again. "Yes, Your Majesty. Of course. And thank you very much!"

"Step forward that I may grant you the full measure of an Imperator's power."

Calum obeyed, and the King rose from his throne and placed his huge hand on Calum's head. A rush of power cascaded throughout Calum's entire body, amplifying the power of the light inside his heart—the light left over from Lumen.

The whole process only took a few seconds, and then it was done. When Calum looked down, his hands radiated brilliant white light. He looked up at the King, confused.

"Calum, I hereby dub you Calum the Imperator, the General of Light," the King said. "There is no one more worthy to replace that which we have lost. May you truly shine as a beacon of light in the darkness, as hope for the hopeless, in our world."

Calum bowed again. It was a lot of bowing, but this was the King of all Kanarah, after all. And after everything that had happened, the King deserved that and much more.

"Thank you, Your Majesty. I will serve you well," Calum said.

The crowd around them applauded briefly, and then the King spoke again.

"Now, please do not let me hold you up. You have a wedding to plan, do you not?" The King gave both Calum and Lilly a wink.

Calum nodded and turned back to Lilly. He wrapped her up in a huge hug and kissed her again, just because he could.

They left Solace that afternoon, and so began the rest of their lives together.

THE END

Thanks for reading the CALL OF ANCIENT LIGHT series.
If you enjoyed this book, please leave a review on Amazon.com!

If you love fantasy, check out my BLOOD MERCENARIES books next!